Collected Works of F. Scott Fitzgerald

Collected Works of F. Scott Fitzgerald

WORDSWORTH EDITIONS

For my husband
ANTHONY JOHN RANSON
with love from your wife, the publisher.
Eternally grateful for your unconditional love,
not just for me but for our children,
Simon, Andrew and Nichola Trayler

Readers who are interested in other titles from
Wordsworth Editions are invited to visit our website at
www.wordsworth-editions.com

For our latest list and a full mail-order service, contact
Bibliophile Books, 5 Datapoint, South Crescent, London E16 4TL
TEL: +44 (0)20 7474 2474 FAX: +44 (0)20 7474 8589
ORDERS: orders@bibliophilebooks.com
WEBSITE: www.bibliophilebooks.com

First published in 2011 by Wordsworth Editions Limited
8B East Street, Ware, Hertfordshire SG12 9HJ

ISBN 978 1 84022 659 1

Typeset in Great Britain by Antony Gray
Printed and bound by Clays Ltd, St Ives plc

CONTENTS

THIS SIDE OF PARADISE

This Side of Paradise

A novel first published in 1920

TO SIGOURNEY FAY

CONTENTS

BOOK ONE
The Romantic Egotist

INTERLUDE

BOOK TWO
The Education of a Personage

. . . Well this side of Paradise!
There's little comfort in the wise.

RUPERT BROOKE

Experience is the name so many people give to their mistakes.

OSCAR WILDE

BOOK ONE
The Romantic Egotist

1

Amory, Son of Beatrice

Amory Blaine inherited from his mother every trait, except the stray inexpressible few, that made him worth while. His father, an ineffectual, inarticulate man with a taste for Byron and a habit of drowsing over the *Encyclopaedia Britannica*, grew wealthy at thirty through the death of two elder brothers, successful Chicago brokers, and in the first flush of feeling that the world was his, went to Bar Harbour and met Beatrice O'Hara. In consequence, Stephen Blaine handed down to posterity his height of just under six feet and his tendency to waver at crucial moments, these two abstractions appearing in his son Amory. For many years he hovered in the background of his family's life, an unassertive figure with a face half-obliterated by lifeless, silky hair, continually occupied in 'taking care' of his wife, continually harassed by the idea that he didn't and couldn't understand her.

But Beatrice Blaine! There was a woman! Early pictures taken on her father's estate at Lake Geneva, Wisconsin, or in Rome at the Sacred Heart Convent – an educational extravagance that in her youth was only for the daughters of the exceptionally wealthy – showed the exquisite delicacy of her features, the consummate art and simplicity of her clothes. A brilliant education she had – her youth passed in Renaissance glory, she was versed in the latest gossip of the Older Roman Families; known by name as a fabulously wealthy American girl to Cardinal Vitori and Queen Margherita and more subtle celebrities that one must have had some culture even to have heard of. She learned in England to prefer whisky-and-soda to wine, and her small talk was broadened in two senses during a winter in Vienna. All in all Beatrice O'Hara absorbed the sort of education that will be quite impossible ever again; a tutelage measured by the number of things and people one could be contemptuous of and charming about; a culture rich in all arts and traditions, barren of all ideas, in the last of those days when the great gardener clipped the inferior roses to produce one perfect bud.

In her less important moments she returned to America, met Stephen Blaine and married him – this almost entirely because she was a little bit weary, a little bit sad. Her only child was carried through a tiresome season and brought into the world on a spring day in ninety-six.

When Amory was five he was already a delightful companion for her. He was an auburn-haired boy, with great, handsome eyes which he would grow up to in time, a facile imaginative mind and a taste for fancy dress. From his fourth to his tenth year he *did* the country with his mother in her father's private car, from Coronado, where his mother became so bored that she had a nervous breakdown in a fashionable hotel, down to Mexico City, where she took a mild, almost epidemic consumption. This trouble pleased her, and later she made use of it as an intrinsic part of her atmosphere – especially after several astounding bracers.

So, while more or less fortunate little rich boys were defying governesses on the beach at Newport, or being spanked or tutored or read to from *Do and Dare* or *Frank on the Mississippi*, Amory was biting acquiescent bellboys in the Waldorf, outgrowing a natural repugnance to chamber music and symphonies, and deriving a highly specialised education from his mother.

'Amory.'

'Yes, Beatrice.' (Such a quaint name for his mother; she encouraged it.)

'Dear, don't *think* of getting out of bed yet. I've always suspected that early rising in early life makes one nervous. Clothilde is having your breakfast brought up.'

'All right.'

'I am feeling very old today, Amory,' she would sigh, her face a rare cameo of pathos, her voice exquisitely modulated, her hands as facile as Bernhardt's. 'My nerves are on edge – on edge. We must leave this terrifying place tomorrow and go searching for sunshine.'

Amory's penetrating green eyes would look out through tangled hair at his mother. Even at this age he had no illusions about her.

'Amory.'

'Oh, *yes*.'

'I want you to take a red-hot bath – as hot as you can bear it, and just relax your nerves. You can read in the tub if you wish.'

She fed him sections of the *Fêtes Galantes* before he was ten; at eleven he could talk glibly, if rather reminiscently, of Brahms and Mozart and Beethoven. One afternoon, when left alone in the hotel at Hot Springs, he sampled his mother's apricot cordial, and as the taste pleased him, he became quite tipsy. This was fun for a while, but he essayed a cigarette in his exaltation, and succumbed to a vulgar, plebeian reaction. Though this incident horrified Beatrice, it also secretly amused her and became part of what in a later generation would have been termed her 'line'.

'This son of mine,' he heard her tell a room full of awestruck, admiring women one day, 'is entirely sophisticated and quite charming – but delicate – we're all delicate; *here*, you know.' Her hand was radiantly outlined against her beautiful bosom; then sinking her voice to a whisper, she told them of the apricot cordial. They rejoiced, for she was a brave *raconteuse*, but many were the keys turned in sideboard locks that night against the possible defection of little Bobby or Barbara . . .

These domestic pilgrimages were invariably in state; two maids, the private car, or Mr Blaine when available, and very often a physician. When Amory had the whooping-cough four disgusted specialists glared at each other hunched around his bed; when he took scarlet fever the number of attendants, including physicians and nurses, totalled fourteen. However, blood being thicker than broth, he was pulled through.

The Blaines were attached to no city. They were the Blaines of Lake Geneva; they had quite enough relatives to serve in place of friends, and an enviable standing from Pasadena to Cape Cod. But Beatrice grew more and more prone to like only new acquaintances, as there were certain stories, such as the history of her constitution and its many amendments, memories of her years abroad, that it was necessary for her to repeat at regular intervals. Like Freudian dreams, they must be thrown off, else they would sweep in and lay siege to her nerves. But Beatrice was critical about American women, especially the floating population of ex-Westerners.

'They have accents, my dear,' she told Amory, 'not Southern accents or Boston accents, not an accent attached to any locality, just an accent' – she became dreamy. 'They pick up old, moth-eaten London accents that are down on their luck and have to be used by someone. They talk as an English butler might after several years in a Chicago grand-opera company.' She became almost incoherent – 'Suppose – time in every Western woman's life – she feels her husband is prosperous enough for her to have – accent – they try to impress *me*, my dear – '

Though she thought of her body as a mass of frailties, she considered her soul quite as ill, and therefore important in her life. She had once been a Catholic, but discovering that priests were infinitely more attentive when she was in process of losing or regaining faith in Mother Church, she maintained an enchantingly wavering attitude. Often she deplored the bourgeois quality of the American Catholic clergy, and was quite sure that had she lived in the shadow of the great Continental cathedrals her soul would still be a thin flame on the mighty altar of Rome. Still, next to doctors, priests were her favourite sport.

'Ah, Bishop Wiston,' she would declare, 'I do not *want* to talk of myself. I can imagine the stream of hysterical women fluttering at your doors, beseeching you to be *simpatico*' – then after an interlude filled by the clergyman – 'but my mood – is – oddly dissimilar.'

Only to bishops and above did she divulge her clerical romance. When she had first returned to her country there had been a pagan, Swinburnian young man in Asheville, for whose passionate kisses and unsentimental conversations she had taken a decided penchant – they had discussed the matter pro and con with an intellectual romancing quite devoid of sappiness. Eventually she had decided to marry for background, and the young pagan from Asheville had gone through a spiritual crisis, joined the Catholic Church, and was now – Monsignor Darcy.

'Indeed, Mrs Blaine, he is still delightful company – quite the cardinal's right-hand man.'

'Amory will go to him one day, I know,' breathed the beautiful lady, 'and Monsignor Darcy will understand him as he understood me.'

Amory became thirteen, rather tall and slender, and more than ever on to his Celtic mother. He had tutored occasionally – the idea being that he was to 'keep up', at each place 'taking up the work where he left off', yet as no tutor ever found the place he left off, his mind was still in very good shape. What a few more years of this life would have made of him is problematical. However, four hours out from land, Italy bound, with Beatrice, his appendix burst, probably from too many meals in bed, and after a series of frantic telegrams to Europe and America, to the amazement of the passengers the great ship slowly wheeled around and returned to New York to deposit Amory at the pier. You will admit that if it was not life it was magnificent.

After the operation Beatrice had a nervous breakdown that bore a suspicious resemblance to delirium tremens, and Amory was left in Minneapolis, destined to spend the ensuing two years with his aunt and uncle. There the crude, vulgar air of Western civilisation first catches him – in his underwear, so to speak.

A KISS FOR AMORY

His lip curled when he read it.

I am going to have a bobbing party [it said] on Thursday, December the seventeenth, at five o'clock, and I would like it very much if you could come.

Yours truly,

Myra St Claire

RSVP

He had been two months in Minneapolis, and his chief struggle had been the concealing from 'the other guys at school' how particularly superior he felt himself to be, yet this conviction was built upon shifting sands. He had shown off one day in French class (he was in senior French class) to the utter confusion of Mr Reardon, whose accent Amory damned contemptuously, and to the delight of the class. Mr Reardon, who had spent several weeks in Paris ten years before, took his revenge on the verbs, whenever he had his book open. But another time Amory showed off in history class with quite disastrous results, for the boys there were his own age, and they shrilled innuendoes at each other all the following week: 'Aw – I b'lieve, doncherknow, the Umuricun revolution was *lawgely* an affair of the middul *clawses*,' or 'Washington came of very good blood – aw, quite good – I b'lieve.'

Amory ingeniously tried to retrieve himself by blundering on purpose. Two years before he had commenced a history of the United States which, though it only got as far as the Colonial Wars, had been pronounced by his mother completely enchanting.

His chief disadvantage lay in athletics, but as soon as he discovered that it was the touchstone of power and popularity at school, he began to make furious, persistent efforts to excel in the winter sports, and with his ankles aching and bending in spite of his efforts, he skated valiantly around the Lorelie rink every afternoon, wondering how soon he would be able to carry a hockey-stick without getting it inexplicably tangled in his skates.

The invitation to Miss Myra St Claire's bobbing party spent the morning in his coat pocket, where it had an intense physical affair with a dusty piece of peanut brittle. During the afternoon he brought it to light with a sigh, and after some consideration and a preliminary draft in the back of Collar and Daniell's *First-Year Latin*, composed an answer:

My dear Miss St Claire – Your truly charming envitation for the evening of next Thursday evening was truly delightful to receive this morning. I will be charm and inchanted indeed to present my compliments on next Thursday evening.
Faithfully,

Amory Blaine

On Thursday, therefore, he walked pensively along the slippery, shovel-scraped sidewalks, and came in sight of Myra's house, on the half-hour after five, a lateness which he fancied his mother would have favoured. He waited on the doorstep with his eyes nonchalantly half-closed, and planned his entrance with precision. He would cross the floor, not too hastily, to Mrs St Claire, and say with exactly the correct modulation: 'My *dear* Mrs St Claire, I'm *frightfully* sorry to be late, but my maid' – he paused there and realised he would be quoting – 'but my uncle and I had to see a fella – Yes, I've met your enchanting daughter at dancing-school.' Then he would shake hands, using that slight, half-foreign bow, with all the starchy little females, and nod to the fellas who would be standing round, paralysed into rigid groups for mutual protection.

A butler (one of the three in Minneapolis) swung open the door. Amory stepped inside and divested himself of cap and coat. He was mildly surprised not to hear the shrill squawk of conversation from the next room, and he decided it must be quite formal. He approved of that – as he approved of the butler.

'Miss Myra,' he said.

To his surprise the butler grinned horribly. 'Oh, yeah,' he declared, 'she's here.'

He was unaware that his failure to be cockney was ruining his standing. Amory considered him coldly.

'But,' continued the butler, his voice rising unnecessarily, 'she's the only one what *is* here. The party's gone.'

Amory gasped in sudden horror. 'What?'

'She's been waitin' for Amory Blaine. That's you, ain't it? Her mother says that if you showed up by five-thirty you two was to go after 'em in the Packard.'

Amory's despair was crystallised by the appearance of Myra herself, bundled to the ears in a polo coat, her face plainly sulky, her voice pleasant only with difficulty.

' 'Lo, Amory.'

' 'Lo, Myra.' He had described the state of his vitality.

'Well – you *got* here, *any*ways.'

'Well – I'll tell you. I guess you don't know about the auto accident,' he romanced.

Myra's eyes opened wide.

'Who was it to?'

'Well,' he continued desperately, 'uncle 'n aunt 'n I.'

'Was anyone *killed*?'

Amory paused and then nodded.

'Your uncle?' – alarm.

'Oh, no – just a horse – a sorta grey horse.'

At this point the Erse butler snickered.

'Probably killed the engine,' he suggested. Amory would have put him on the rack without a scruple.

'We'll go now,' said Myra coolly. 'You see, Amory, the bobs were ordered for five and everybody was here, so we couldn't wait – '

'Well, I couldn't help it, could I?'

'So mama said for me to wait till ha'past five. We'll catch the bob before it gets to the Minnehaha Club, Amory.'

Amory's shredded poise dropped from him. He pictured the happy party jingling along snowy streets, the appearance of the limousine, the horrible public descent of him and Myra before sixty reproachful eyes, his apology – a real one this time. He sighed aloud.

'What?' enquired Myra.

'Nothing. I was just yawning. Are we *surely* going to catch up with 'em before they get there?' He was encouraging a faint hope that they might slip into the Minnehaha Club and meet the others there, be found in blasé seclusion before the fire and quite regain his lost attitude.

'Oh, sure Mike, we'll catch 'em all right – let's hurry.'

He became conscious of his stomach. As they stepped into the machine he hurriedly slapped the paint of diplomacy over a rather boxlike plan he had conceived. It was based upon some 'trade-lasts' gleaned at dancing-school, to the effect that he was 'awful good-looking and *English*, sort of'.

'Myra,' he said, lowering his voice and choosing his words carefully,

'I beg a thousand pardons. Can you ever forgive me?' She regarded him gravely, his intent green eyes, his mouth, that to her thirteen-year-old, Arrow-collar taste was the quintessence of romance. Yes, Myra could forgive him very easily.

'Why – yes – sure.'

He looked at her again, and then dropped his eyes. He had lashes.

'I'm awful,' he said sadly. 'I'm diff'runt. I don't know why I make *faux pas*. 'Cause I don't care, I s'pose.' Then, recklessly: 'I been smoking too much. I've got t'bacca heart.'

Myra pictured an all-night tobacco debauch, with Amory pale and reeling from the effect of nicotined lungs. She gave a little gasp.

'Oh, *Amory*, don't smoke. You'll stunt your *growth*!'

'I don't care,' he persisted gloomily. 'I gotta. I got the habit. I've done a lot of things that if my fambly knew' – he hesitated, giving her imagination time to picture dark horrors – 'I went to the burlesque show last week.'

Myra was quite overcome. He turned the green eyes on her again. 'You're the only girl in town I like much,' he exclaimed in a rush of sentiment. 'You're *simpatico*.'

Myra was not sure that she was, but it sounded stylish though vaguely improper.

Thick dusk had descended outside, and as the limousine made a sudden turn she was jolted against him; their hands touched.

'You shouldn't smoke, Amory,' she whispered. 'Don't you know that?'

He shook his head.

'Nobody cares.'

Myra hesitated.

'*I* care.'

Something stirred within Amory.

'Oh, yes, you do! You got a crush on Froggy Parker. I guess everybody knows that.'

'No, I haven't,' very slowly.

A silence, while Amory thrilled. There was something fascinating about Myra, shut away here cosily from the dim, chill air. Myra, a little bundle of clothes, with strands of yellow hair curling out from under her skating cap.

'Because I've got a crush, too – ' He paused, for he heard in the distance the sound of young laughter, and, peering through the frosted glass along the lamp-lit street, he made out the dark outline of the bobbing party. He must act quickly. He reached over with a violent, jerky effort, and clutched Myra's hand – her thumb, to be exact.

'Tell him to go to the Minnehaha straight,' he whispered. 'I wanta talk to you – I *got* to talk to you.'

Myra made out the party ahead, had an instant vision of her mother, and then – alas for convention – glanced into the eyes beside her. 'Turn down this side street, Richard, and drive straight to the Minnehaha Club!' she cried through the speaking tube. Amory sank back against the cushions with a sigh of relief.

'I can kiss her,' he thought. 'I'll bet I can. I'll *bet* I can!'

Overhead the sky was half crystalline, half misty, and the night around was chill and vibrant with rich tension. From the Country Club steps the roads stretched away, dark creases on the white blanket; huge heaps of snow lining the sides like the tracks of giant moles. They lingered for a moment on the steps, and watched the white holiday moon.

'Pale moons like that one' – Amory made a vague gesture – 'make people *mystérieuse*. You look like a young witch with her cap off and her hair sorta mussed' – her hands clutched at her hair – 'Oh, leave it, it looks *good*.'

They drifted up the stairs and Myra led the way into the little den of his dreams, where a cosy fire was burning before a big sink-down couch. A few years later this was to be a great stage for Amory, a cradle for many an emotional crisis. Now they talked for a moment about bobbing parties.

'There's always a bunch of shy fellas,' he commented, 'sitting at the tail of the bob, sorta lurkin' an' whisperin' an' pushin' each other off. Then there's always some crazy cross-eyed girl' – he gave a terrifying imitation – 'she's always talkin' *hard*, sorta, to the chaperone.'

'You're such a funny boy,' puzzled Myra.

'How d'y' mean?' Amory gave immediate attention, on his own ground at last.

'Oh – always talking about crazy things. Why don't you come skiing with Marylyn and me tomorrow?'

'I don't like girls in the daytime,' he said shortly, and then, thinking this a bit abrupt, he added: 'But I like you.' He cleared his throat. 'I like you first and second and third.'

Myra's eyes became dreamy. What a story this would make to tell Marylyn! Here on the couch with this *wonderful*-looking boy – the little fire – the sense that they were alone in the great building –

Myra capitulated. The atmosphere was too appropriate.

'I like you the first twenty-five,' she confessed, her voice trembling, 'and Froggy Parker twenty-sixth.'

Froggy had fallen twenty-five places in one hour. As yet he had not even noticed it.

But Amory, being on the spot, leaned over quickly and kissed Myra's cheek. He had never kissed a girl before, and he tasted his lips curiously, as if he had munched some new fruit. Then their lips brushed like young wild flowers in the wind.

'We're awful,' rejoiced Myra gently. She slipped her hand into his, her head drooped against his shoulder. Sudden revulsion seized Amory, disgust, loathing for the whole incident. He desired frantically to be away, never to see Myra again, never to kiss anyone; he became conscious of his face and hers, of their clinging hands, and he wanted to creep out of his body and hide somewhere safe out of sight, up in the corner of his mind.

'Kiss me again.' Her voice came out of a great void.

'I don't want to,' he heard himself saying. There was another pause.

'I don't want to!' he repeated passionately.

Myra sprang up, her cheeks pink with bruised vanity, the great bow on the back of her head trembling sympathetically.

'I hate you!' she cried. 'Don't you ever dare to speak to me again!'

'What?' stammered Amory.

'I'll tell mama you kissed me! I will too! I will too! I'll tell mama, and she won't let me play with you!'

Amory rose and stared at her helplessly, as though she were a new animal of whose presence on the earth he had not heretofore been aware.

The door opened suddenly, and Myra's mother appeared on the threshold, fumbling with her lorgnette.

'Well,' she began, adjusting it benignantly, 'the man at the desk told me you two children were up here – How do you do, Amory.'

Amory watched Myra and waited for the crash – but none came. The pout faded, the high pink subsided, and Myra's voice was placid as a summer lake when she answered her mother.

'Oh, we started so late, mama, that I thought we might as *well* – '

He heard from below the shrieks of laughter, and smelled the vapid odour of hot chocolate and teacakes as he silently followed mother and daughter downstairs. The sound of the graphophone mingled with the voices of many girls humming the air, and a faint glow was born and spread over him:

'Casey-Jones – mounted to the cab-un
Casey-Jones – 'th his orders in his hand.
Casey-Jones – mounted to the cab-un
Took his farewell journey to the prom-ised land.'

SNAPSHOTS OF THE YOUNG EGOTIST

Amory spent nearly two years in Minneapolis. The first winter he wore moccasins that were born yellow, but after many applications of oil and dirt assumed their mature colour, a dirty, greenish brown; he wore a grey plaid mackinaw coat, and a red toboggan cap. His dog, Count Del Monte, ate the red cap, so his uncle gave him a grey one that pulled down over his face. The trouble with this one was that you breathed into it and your breath froze; one day the darn thing froze his cheek. He rubbed snow on his cheek, but it turned bluish-black just the same.

The Count Del Monte ate a box of bluing once, but it didn't hurt him. Later, however, he lost his mind and ran madly up the street, bumping into fences, rolling in gutters, and pursuing his eccentric course out of Amory's life. Amory cried on his bed.

'Poor little Count,' he cried. 'Oh, *poor* little *Count*!'

After several months he suspected Count of a fine piece of emotional acting.

Amory and Frog Parker considered that the greatest line in literature occurred in Act III of *Arsène Lupin*.

They sat in the first row at the Wednesday and Saturday matinées. The line was: 'If one can't be a great artist or a great soldier, the next best thing is to be a great criminal.'

Amory fell in love again, and wrote a poem. This was it:

Marylyn and Sall*ee*,
Those are the girls for me.
Marylyn stands above
Sall*ee* in that sweet, deep love.

He was interested in whether McGovern of Minnesota would make the first or second All-American, how to do the card-pass, how to do the coin-pass, chameleon ties, how babies were born, and whether

Three-fingered Brown was really a better pitcher than Christy Mathewson.

Among other things he read: *For the Honour of the School*, *Little Women* (twice), *The Common Law*, *Sappho*, *Dangerous Dan McGrew*, *The Broad Highway* (three times), *The Fall of the House of Usher*, *Three Weeks*, *Mary Ware*, *The Little Colonel's Chum*, *Gunga Din*, the *Police Gazette* and *Jim-Jam Jems*.

He had all the Henty biases in history, and was particularly fond of the cheerful murder stories of Mary Roberts Rinehart.

School ruined his French and gave him a distaste for standard authors. His masters considered him idle, unreliable and superficially clever.

He collected locks of hair from many girls. He wore the rings of several. Finally he could borrow no more rings, owing to his nervous habit of chewing them out of shape. This, it seemed, usually aroused the jealous suspicions of the next borrower.

All through the summer months Amory and Frog Parker went each week to the Stock Company. Afterwards they would stroll home in the balmy air of August night, dreaming along Hennepin and Nicollet Avenues, through the gay crowd. Amory wondered how people could fail to notice that he was a boy marked for glory, and when faces of the throng turned towards him and ambiguous eyes stared into his, he assumed the most romantic of expressions and walked on the air cushions that lie on the asphalts of fourteen.

Always, after he was in bed, there were voices – indefinite, fading, enchanting – just outside his window, and before he fell asleep he would dream one of his favourite waking dreams, the one about becoming a great half-back, or the one about the Japanese invasion, when he was rewarded by being made the youngest general in the world. It was always the becoming he dreamed of, never the being. This, too, was quite characteristic of Amory.

CODE OF THE YOUNG EGOTIST

Before he was summoned back to Lake Geneva, he had appeared, shy but inwardly glowing, in his first long trousers, set off by a purple accordion tie and a 'Belmont' collar with the edges unassailably meeting, purple socks and handkerchief with a purple border peeping from his breast pocket. But more than that, he had formulated his first philosophy, a code to live by, which, as near as it can be named, was a sort of aristocratic egotism.

He had realised that his best interests were bound up with those of a certain variant, changing person, whose label, in order that his past might always be identified with him, was Amory Blaine. Amory marked himself a fortunate youth, capable of infinite expansion for good or evil. He did not consider himself a 'strong char'c'ter', but relied on his facility (learn things sorta quick) and his superior mentality (read a lotta deep books). He was proud of the fact that he could never become a mechanical or scientific genius. From no other heights was he debarred.

Physically: Amory thought that he was exceedingly handsome. He was. He fancied himself an athlete of possibilities and a supple dancer.

Socially: Here his condition was, perhaps, most dangerous. He granted himself personality, charm, magnetism, poise, the power of dominating all contemporary males, the gift of fascinating all women.

Mentally: Complete, unquestioned superiority.

Now a confession will have to be made. Amory had rather a Puritan conscience. Not that he yielded to it – later in life he almost completely slew it – but at fifteen it made him consider himself a great deal worse than other boys . . . unscrupulousness . . . the desire to influence people in almost every way, even for evil . . . a certain coldness and lack of affection, amounting sometimes to cruelty . . . a shifting sense of honour . . . an unholy selfishness . . . a puzzled, furtive interest in everything concerning sex.

There was, also, a curious strain of weakness running crosswise through his make-up . . . a harsh phrase from the lips of an older boy (older boys usually detested him) was liable to sweep him off his poise into surly sensitiveness or timid stupidity . . . he was a slave to his own moods and he felt that though he was capable of recklessness and audacity, he possessed neither courage, perseverance, nor self-respect.

Vanity, tempered with self-suspicion if not self-knowledge, a sense of people as automatons to his will, a desire to 'pass' as many boys as possible and get to a vague top of the world . . . with this background did Amory drift into adolescence.

The train slowed up with midsummer languor at Lake Geneva, and Amory caught sight of his mother waiting in her electric on the gravelled station drive. It was an ancient electric, one of the early types, and painted grey. The sight of her sitting there, slenderly erect, and of her face, where beauty and dignity combined, melting to a dreamy recollected smile, filled him with a sudden great pride of her. As they kissed coolly and he stepped into the electric, he felt a quick fear lest he had lost the requisite charm to measure up to her.

'Dear boy – you're *so* tall . . . look behind and see if there's anything coming . . .'

She looked left and right, she slipped cautiously into a speed of two miles an hour, beseeching Amory to act as sentinel; and at one busy crossing she made him get out and run ahead to signal her forward like a traffic policeman. Beatrice was what might be termed a careful driver.

'You *are* tall – but you're still very handsome – you've skipped the awkward age, or is that sixteen; perhaps it's fourteen or fifteen; I can never remember; but you've skipped it.'

'Don't embarrass me,' murmured Amory.

'But, my dear boy, what odd clothes! They look as if they were a *set* – don't they? Is your underwear purple, too?'

Amory grunted impolitely.

'You must go to Brooks and get some really nice suits. Oh, we'll have a talk tonight or perhaps tomorrow night. I want to tell you about your heart – you've probably been neglecting your heart – and you don't *know*.'

Amory thought how superficial was the recent overlay of his own generation. Aside from a minute shyness, he felt that the old cynical kinship with his mother had not been one bit broken. Yet for the first few days he wandered about the gardens and along the shore in a state of superloneliness, finding a lethargic content in smoking 'Bull' at the garage with one of the chauffeurs.

The sixty acres of the estate were dotted with old and new summer houses and many fountains and white benches that came suddenly into sight from foliage-hung hiding-places; there was a great and constantly increasing family of white cats that prowled the many flower-beds and were silhouetted suddenly at night against the darkening trees. It was on one of the shadowy paths that Beatrice at last captured Amory, after

Mr Blaine had, as usual, retired for the evening to his private library. After reproving him for avoiding her, she took him for a long tête-à-tête in the moonlight. He could not reconcile himself to her beauty, that was mother to his own, the exquisite neck and shoulders, the grace of a fortunate woman of thirty.

'Amory, dear,' she crooned softly, 'I had such a strange, weird time after I left you.'

'Did you, Beatrice?'

'When I had my last breakdown' – she spoke of it as a sturdy, gallant feat – 'the doctors told me' – her voice sang on a confidential note – 'that if any man alive had done the consistent drinking that I have, he would have been physically *shattered*, my dear, and in his *grave* – long in his grave.'

Amory winced, and wondered how this would have sounded to Froggy Parker.

'Yes,' continued Beatrice tragically, 'I had dreams – wonderful visions.' She pressed the palms of her hands into her eyes. 'I saw bronze rivers lapping marble shores, and great birds that soared through the air, parti-coloured birds with iridescent plumage. I heard strange music and the flare of barbaric trumpets – what?'

Amory had snickered.

'What, Amory?'

'I said go on, Beatrice.'

'That was all – it merely recurred and recurred – gardens that flaunted colouring against which this would be quite dull, moons that whirled and swayed, paler than winter moons, more golden than harvest moons – '

'Are you quite well now, Beatrice?'

'Quite well – as well as I will ever be. I am not understood, Amory. I know that can't express it to you, Amory, but – I am not understood.'

Amory was quite moved. He put his arm around his mother, rubbing his head gently against her shoulder.

'Poor Beatrice – poor Beatrice.'

'Tell me about *you*, Amory. Did you have two *horrible* years?'

Amory considered lying, and then decided against it.

'No, Beatrice. I enjoyed them. I adapted myself to the bourgeoisie. I became conventional.' He surprised himself by saying that, and he pictured how Froggy would have gaped.

'Beatrice,' he said suddenly, 'I want to go away to school. Everybody in Minneapolis is going to go away to school.'

Beatrice showed some alarm.

'But you're only fifteen.'

'Yes, but everybody goes away to school at fifteen, and I *want* to, Beatrice.'

On Beatrice's suggestion the subject was dropped for the rest of the walk, but a week later she delighted him by saying: 'Amory, I have decided to let you have your way. If you still want to, you can go to school.'

'Yes?'

'To St Regis's in Connecticut.'

Amory felt a quick excitement.

'It's being arranged,' continued Beatrice. 'It's better that you should go away. I'd have preferred you to have gone to Eton, and then to Christ Church, Oxford, but it seems impracticable now – and for the present we'll let the university question take care of itself.'

'What are you going to do, Beatrice?'

'Heaven knows. It seems my fate to fret away my years in this country. Not for a second do I regret being American – indeed, I think that a regret typical of very vulgar people, and I feel sure we are the great coming nation – yet' – and she sighed – 'I feel my life should have drowsed away close to an older, mellower civilisation, a land of greens and autumnal browns – '

Amory did not answer, so his mother continued: 'My regret is that you haven't been abroad, but still, as you are a man, it's better that you should grow up here under the snarling eagle – is that the right term?'

Amory agreed that it was. She would not have appreciated the Japanese invasion.

'When do I go to school?'

'Next month. You'll have to start East a little early to take your examinations. After that you'll have a free week, so I want you to go up the Hudson and pay a visit.'

'To who?'

'To Monsignor Darcy, Amory. He wants to see you. He went to Harrow and then to Yale – became a Catholic. I want him to talk to you – I feel he can be such a help – ' She stroked his auburn hair gently. 'Dear Amory, dear Amory – '

'Dear Beatrice – '

So early in September Amory, provided with 'six suits summer underwear, six suits winter underwear, one sweater or T-shirt, one jersey, one overcoat, winter, etc.', set out for New England, the land of schools.

There were Andover and Exeter with their memories of New England dead – large, college-like democracies; St Mark's, Groton, St Regis's – recruited from Boston and the Knickerbocker families of New York; St Paul's, with its great rinks; Pomfret and St George's, prosperous and well-dressed; Taft and Hotchkiss, which prepared the wealth of the Middle West for social success at Yale; Pawling, Westminster, Choate, Kent, and a hundred others; all milling out their well-set-up, conventional, impressive type, year after year; their mental stimulus the college entrance exams; their vague purpose set forth in a hundred circulars as 'To impart a Thorough Mental, Moral and Physical Training as a Christian Gentleman, to fit the boy *for meeting the problems of his day and generation*, and to give a solid foundation in the Arts and Sciences'.

At St Regis's Amory stayed three days and took his exams with a scoffing confidence, then doubled back to New York to pay his tutelary visit. The metropolis, barely glimpsed, made little impression on him, except for the sense of cleanliness he drew from the tall white buildings seen from a Hudson River steamboat in the early morning. Indeed, his mind was so crowded with dreams of athletic prowess at school that he considered this visit only as a rather tiresome prelude to the great adventure. This, however, it did not prove to be.

Monsignor Darcy's house was an ancient, rambling structure set on a hill overlooking the river, and there lived its owner, between his trips to all parts of the Roman-Catholic world, rather like an exiled Stuart king waiting to be called to the rule of his land. Monsignor was forty-four then, and bustling – a trifle too stout for symmetry, with hair the colour of spun gold, and a brilliant, enveloping personality. When he came into a room clad in his full purple regalia from thatch to toe, he resembled a Turner sunset, and attracted both admiration and attention. He had written two novels: one of them violently anti-Catholic, just before his conversion, and five years later another, in which he had attempted to turn all his clever jibes against Catholics into even cleverer innuendoes against Episcopalians. He was intensely ritualistic, startlingly dramatic, loved the idea of God enough to be a celibate, and rather liked his neighbour.

Children adored him because he was like a child; youth revelled in his company because he was still a youth, and couldn't be shocked. In the proper land and century he might have been a Richelieu – at present he was a very moral, very religious (if not particularly pious) clergyman, making a great mystery about pulling rusty wires, and appreciating life to the fullest, if not entirely enjoying it.

He and Amory took to each other at first sight – the jovial, impressive prelate who could dazzle an embassy ball, and the green-eyed, intent youth, in his first long trousers, accepted in their own minds a relation of father and son within a half-hour's conversation.

'My dear boy, I've been waiting to see you for years. Take a big chair and we'll have a chat.'

'I've just come from school – St Regis's, you know.'

'So your mother says – a remarkable woman; have a cigarette – I'm sure you smoke. Well, if you're like me, you loathe all science and mathematics – '

Amory nodded vehemently.

'Hate 'em all. Like English and history.'

'Of course. You'll hate school for a while, too, but I'm glad you're going to St Regis's.'

'Why?'

'Because it's a gentleman's school, and democracy won't hit you so early. You'll find plenty of that in college.'

'I want to go to Princeton,' said Amory. 'I don't know why, but I think of all Harvard men as sissies, like I used to be, and all Yale men as wearing big blue sweaters and smoking pipes.'

Monsignor chuckled. 'I'm one, you know.'

'Oh, you're different – I think of Princeton as being lazy and good-looking and aristocratic – you know, like a spring day. Harvard seems sort of indoors – '

'And Yale is November, crisp and energetic,' finished Monsignor.

'That's it.'

They slipped briskly into an intimacy from which they never recovered. 'I was for Bonnie Prince Charlie,' announced Amory.

'Of course you were – and for Hannibal – '

'Yes, and for the Southern Confederacy.' He was rather sceptical about being an Irish patriot – he suspected that being Irish was being somewhat common – but Monsignor assured him that Ireland was a romantic lost cause and Irish people quite charming, and that it should, by all means, be one of his principal biases.

After a crowded hour which included several more cigarettes, and during which Monsignor learned, to his surprise but not to his horror, that Amory had not been brought up a Catholic, he announced that he had another guest. This turned out to be the Honourable Thornton Hancock, of Boston, ex-minister to The Hague, author of an erudite history of the Middle Ages and the last of a distinguished, patriotic, and brilliant family.

'He comes here for a rest,' said Monsignor confidentially, treating Amory as a contemporary. 'I act as an escape from the weariness of agnosticism, and I think I'm the only man who knows how his staid old mind is really at sea and longs for a sturdy spar like the Church to cling to.'

Their first luncheon was one of the memorable events of Amory's early life. He was quite radiant and gave off a peculiar brightness and charm. Monsignor called out the best that he had thought by question and suggestion, and Amory talked with an ingenuous brilliance of a thousand impulses and desires and repulsions and faiths and fears. He and Monsignor held the floor, and the older man, with his less receptive, less accepting, yet certainly not colder mentality, seemed content to listen and bask in the mellow sunshine that played between these two. Monsignor gave the effect of sunlight to many people; Amory gave it in his youth and, to some extent, when he was very much older, but never again was it quite so mutually spontaneous.

'He's a radiant boy,' thought Thornton Hancock, who had seen the splendour of two continents and talked with Parnell and Gladstone and Bismarck – and afterwards he added to Monsignor: 'But his education ought not to be entrusted to a school or college.'

But for the next four years the best of Amory's intellect was concentrated on matters of popularity, the intricacies of a university social system and American Society as represented by Biltmore Teas and Hot Springs golf-links.

. . . In all, a wonderful week, that saw Amory's mind turned inside out, a hundred of his theories confirmed, and his joy of life crystallised to a thousand ambitions. Not that the conversation was scholastic – heaven forbid! Amory had only the vaguest idea as to what Bernard Shaw was – but Monsignor made quite as much out of *The Beloved Vagabond* and *Sir Nigel*, taking good care that Amory never once felt out of his depth.

But the trumpets were sounding for Amory's preliminary skirmish with his own generation.

'You're not sorry to go, of course. With people like us our home is where we are not,' said Monsignor.

'I *am* sorry – '

'No, you're not. No one person in the world is necessary to you or to me.'

'Well – '

'Goodbye.'

THE EGOTIST DOWN

Amory's two years at St Regis's, though in turn painful and triumphant, had as little real significance in his own life as the American 'prep' school, crushed as it is under the heel of the universities, has to American life in general. We have no Eton to create the self-consciousness of a governing class; we have, instead, clean, flaccid and innocuous preparatory schools.

He went all wrong at the start, was generally considered both conceited and arrogant, and universally detested. He played football intensely, alternating a reckless brilliancy with a tendency to keep himself as safe from hazard as decency would permit. In a wild panic he backed out of a fight with a boy his own size, to a chorus of scorn, and a week later, in desperation, picked a battle with another boy very much bigger, from which he emerged badly beaten, but rather proud of himself.

He was resentful against all those in authority over him, and this, combined with a lazy indifference towards his work, exasperated every master in school. He grew discouraged and imagined himself a pariah; took to sulking in corners and reading after lights. With a dread of being alone he attached a few friends, but since they were not among the élite of the school, he used them simply as mirrors of himself, audiences before which he might do that posing absolutely essential to him. He was unbearably lonely, desperately unhappy.

There were some few grains of comfort. Whenever Amory was submerged, his vanity was the last part to go below the surface, so he could still enjoy a comfortable glow when 'Wookey-wookey', the deaf old housekeeper, told him that he was the best-looking boy she had ever seen. It had pleased him to be the lightest and youngest man on the first football squad; it pleased him when Dr Dougall told him at the end of a heated conference that he could, if he wished, get the best marks in school. But Dr Dougall was wrong. It was temperamentally impossible for Amory to get the best marks in school.

Miserable, confined to bounds, unpopular with both faculty and students – that was Amory's first term. But at Christmas he had returned to Minneapolis, tight-lipped and strangely jubilant.

'Oh, I was sort of fresh at first,' he told Frog Parker patronisingly, 'but I got along fine – lightest man on the squad. You ought to go away to school, Froggy. It's great stuff.'

INCIDENT OF THE WELL-MEANING PROFESSOR

On the last night of his first term, Mr Margotson, the senior master, sent word to study hall that Amory was to come to his room at nine. Amory suspected that advice was forthcoming, but he determined to be courteous, because this Mr Margotson had been kindly disposed towards him.

His summoner received him gravely, and motioned him to a chair. He hemmed several times and looked consciously kind, as a man will when he knows he's on delicate ground.

'Amory,' he began. 'I've sent for you on a personal matter.'

'Yes, sir.'

'I've noticed you this year and I – I like you. I think you have in you the makings of a – a very good man.'

'Yes, sir,' Amory managed to articulate. He hated having people talk as if he were an admitted failure.

'But I've noticed,' continued the older man blindly, 'that you're not very popular with the boys.'

'No, sir.' Amory licked his lips.

'Ah – I thought you might not understand exactly what it was they – ah – objected to. I'm going to tell you, because I believe – ah – that when a boy knows his difficulties he's better able to cope with them – to conform to what others expect of him.' He a-hemmed again with delicate reticence, and continued: 'They seem to think that you're – ah – rather too fresh – '

Amory could stand no more. He rose from his chair, scarcely controlling his voice when he spoke.

'I know – oh, *don't* you s'pose I know.' His voice rose. 'I know what they think; do you s'pose you have to *tell* me!' He paused. 'I'm –

I've got to go back now – hope I'm not rude – '

He left the room hurriedly. In the cool air outside, as he walked to his house, he exulted in his refusal to be helped.

'That *damn* old fool!' he cried wildly. 'As if I didn't *know*!'

He decided, however, that this was a good excuse not to go back to study hall that night, so, comfortably couched up in his room, he munched Nabiscos and finished *The White Company*.

INCIDENT OF THE WONDERFUL GIRL

There was a bright star in February. New York burst upon him on Washington's Birthday with the brilliance of a long-anticipated event. His glimpse of it as a vivid whiteness against a deep-blue sky had left a picture of splendour that rivalled the dream cities in the *Arabian Nights*; but this time he saw it by electric light, and romance gleamed from the chariot-race sign on Broadway and from the women's eyes at the Astor, where he and young Paskert from St Regis's had dinner. When they walked down the aisle of the theatre, greeted by the nervous twanging and discord of untuned violins and the sensuous, heavy fragrance of paint and powder, he moved in a sphere of epicurean delight. Everything enchanted him. The play was *The Little Millionaire*, with George M. Cohan, and there was one stunning young brunette who made him sit with brimming eyes in the ecstasy of watching her dance.

'Oh – you – wonderful girl,
What a wonderful girl you are – '

sang the tenor, and Amory agreed silently, but passionately.

'All – your – wonderful words
Thrill me through – '

The violins swelled and quavered on the last notes, the girl sank to a crumpled butterfly on the stage, a great burst of clapping filled the house. Oh, to fall in love like that, to the languorous magic melody of such a tune!

The last scene was laid on a roof-garden, and the cellos sighed to the musical moon, while light adventure and facile froth-like comedy flitted back and forth in the calcium. Amory was on fire to be an *habitué* of roof-gardens, to meet a girl who should look like that – better, that very girl; whose hair would be drenched with golden moonlight, while at his elbow sparkling wine was poured by an unintelligible waiter.

When the curtain fell for the last time he gave such a long sigh that the people in front of him twisted around and stared and said loud enough for him to hear: 'What a *remarkable*-looking boy!'

This took his mind off the play, and he wondered if he really did seem handsome to the population of New York.

Paskert and he walked in silence towards their hotel. The former was the first to speak. His uncertain fifteen-year-old voice broke in in a melancholy strain on Amory's musings: 'I'd marry that girl tonight.'

There was no need to ask what girl he referred to.

'I'd be proud to take her home and introduce her to my people,' continued Paskert.

Amory was distinctly impressed. He wished he had said it instead of Paskert. It sounded so mature.

'I wonder about actresses; are they all pretty bad?'

'No, *sir*, not by a darn sight,' said the worldly youth with emphasis, 'and I know that girl's as good as gold. I can tell.'

They wandered on, mixing in the Broadway crowd, dreaming on the music that eddied out of the cafés. New faces flashed on and off like myriad lights, pale or rouged faces, tired, yet sustained by a weary excitement. Amory watched them in fascination. He was planning his life. He was going to live in New York, and be known at every restaurant and café, wearing a dress-suit from early evening to early morning, sleeping away the dull hours of the forenoon.

'Yes, *sir*, I'd marry that girl tonight!'

HEROIC IN GENERAL TONE

October of his second and last year at St Regis's was a high point in Amory's memory. The game with Groton was played from three of a snappy, exhilarating afternoon far into the crisp autumnal twilight, and Amory at quarter-back, exhorting in wild despair, making impossible tackles, calling signals in a voice that had diminished to a hoarse, furious whisper, yet found time to revel in the blood-stained bandage around his head, and the straining, glorious heroism of plunging, crashing bodies and aching limbs. For those minutes courage flowed like wine out of the November dusk, and he was the eternal hero, one with the sea-rover on the prow of a Norse galley, one with Roland and Horatius, Sir Nigel and Ted Coy, scraped and stripped into trim and then flung by his own will into the breach, beating back the tide, hearing from afar the thunder of cheers . . . finally bruised and weary, but still elusive, circling an end, twisting, changing pace, straight-arming . . . falling behind the Groton goal with two men on his legs, in the only touchdown of the game.

THE PHILOSOPHY OF THE SLICKER

From the scoffing superiority of sixth-form year and success Amory looked back with cynical wonder on his status of the year before. He was changed as completely as Amory Blaine could ever be changed. Amory plus Beatrice plus two years in Minneapolis – these had been his ingredients when he entered St Regis's. But the Minneapolis years were not a thick enough overlay to conceal the 'Amory plus Beatrice' from the ferreting eyes of a boarding-school, so St Regis's had very painfully drilled Beatrice out of him, and begun to lay down new and more conventional planking on the fundamental Amory. But both St Regis's and Amory were unconscious of the fact that this fundamental Amory had not in himself changed. Those qualities for which he had suffered, his moodiness, his tendency to pose, his laziness, and his love of playing the fool, were now taken as a matter of course, recognised eccentricities in a star quarter-back, a clever actor, and the editor of the *St Regis Tatler*: it puzzled him to see impressionable small boys imitating the very vanities that had not long ago been contemptible weaknesses.

After the football season he slumped into dreamy content. The night of the pre-holiday dance he slipped away and went early to bed for the pleasure of hearing the violin music cross the grass and come surging in at his window. Many nights he lay there dreaming awake of secret cafés in Montmartre, where ivory women delved in romantic mysteries with diplomats and soldiers of fortune, while orchestras played Hungarian waltzes and the air was thick and exotic with intrigue and moonlight and adventure. In the spring he read *L'Allegro*, by request, and was inspired to lyrical outpourings on the subject of Arcady and the pipes of Pan. He moved his bed so that the sun would wake him at dawn that he might dress and go out to the archaic swing that hung from an apple tree near the sixth-form house. Seating himself in this he would pump higher and higher until he got the effect of swinging into the wide air, into a fairyland of piping satyrs and nymphs with the faces of fair-haired girls he passed in the streets of Eastchester. As the swing reached its highest point, Arcady really lay just over the brow of a certain hill, where the brown road dwindled out of sight in a golden dot.

He read voluminously all spring, the beginning of his eighteenth year: *The Gentleman from Indiana*, *The New Arabian Nights*, *The Morals of Marcus Ordeyne*, *The Man Who Was Thursday*, which he liked without understanding; *Stover at Yale*, that became somewhat of a textbook; *Dombey and Son*, because he thought he really should read better stuff; Robert Chambers, David Graham Phillips and E. Phillips Oppenheim complete, and a scattering of Tennyson and Kipling. Of all his class work only *L'Allegro* and some quality of rigid clarity in solid geometry stirred his languid interest.

As June drew near, he felt the need of conversation to formulate his own ideas, and, to his surprise, found a co-philosopher in Rahill, the president of the sixth form. In many a talk, on the highroad or lying belly-down along the edge of the baseball diamond, or late at night with their cigarettes glowing in the dark, they threshed out the questions of school, and there was developed the term 'slicker'.

'Got tobacco?' whispered Rahill one night, putting his head inside the door five minutes after lights.

'Sure.'

'I'm coming in.'

'Take a couple of pillows and lie in the window-seat, why don't you.'

Amory sat up in bed and lit a cigarette while Rahill settled for a conversation. Rahill's favourite subject was the respective futures of the sixth form, and Amory never tired of outlining them for his benefit.

'Ted Converse? 'At's easy. He'll fail his exams, tutor all summer at Harstrum's, get into Sheff with about four conditions, and flunk out in the middle of the freshman year. Then he'll go back West and raise hell for a year or so; finally his father will make him go into the paint business. He'll marry and have four sons, all boneheads. He'll always think St Regis's spoiled him, so he'll send his sons to day school in Portland. He'll die of locomotor ataxia when he's forty-one, and his wife will give a baptising stand or whatever you call it to the Presbyterian Church, with his name on it – '

'Hold up, Amory. That's too darned gloomy. How about yourself?'

'I'm in a superior class. You are, too. We're philosophers.'

'I'm not.'

'Sure you are. You've got a darn good head on you.' But Amory knew that nothing in the abstract, no theory or generality, ever moved Rahill until he stubbed his toe upon the concrete minutiae of it.

'Haven't,' insisted Rahill. 'I let people impose on me here and don't get anything out of it. I'm the prey of my friends, damn it – do their lessons, get 'em out of trouble, pay 'em stupid summer visits, and always entertain their kid sisters; keep my temper when they get selfish and then they think they pay me back by voting for me and telling me I'm the "big man" of St Regis's. I want to get where everybody does their own work and I can tell people where to go. I'm tired of being nice to every poor fish in school.'

'You're not a slicker,' said Amory suddenly.

'A what?'

'A slicker.'

'What the devil's that?'

'Well, it's something that – that – there's a lot of them. You're not one, and neither am I, though I am more than you are.'

'Who is one? What makes you one?'

Amory considered.

'Why – why, I suppose that the *sign* of it is when a fellow slicks his hair back with water.'

'Like Carstairs?'

'Yes – sure. He's a slicker.'

They spent two evenings getting an exact definition. The slicker was good-looking or clean-looking; he had brains, social brains, that is, and he used all means on the broad path of honesty to get ahead, be popular, admired, and never in trouble. He dressed well, was particularly neat in appearance, and derived his name from the fact that his hair was inevitably worn short, soaked in water or tonic, parted in the middle, and slicked back as the current of fashion dictated. The slickers of that year had adopted tortoiseshell spectacles as badges of their slickerhood, and this made them so easy to recognise that Amory and Rahill never missed one. The slicker seemed distributed through school, always a little wiser and shrewder than his contemporaries, managing some team or other, and keeping his cleverness carefully concealed.

Amory found the slicker a most valuable classification until his junior year in college, when the outline became so blurred and indeterminate that it had to be subdivided many times, and became only a quality. Amory's secret ideal had all the slicker qualifications, but, in addition, courage and tremendous brains and talents – also Amory conceded him a bizarre streak that was quite irreconcilable to the slicker proper.

This was a first real break from the hypocrisy of school tradition. The slicker was a definite element of success, differing intrinsically from the prep-school 'big man'.

THE SLICKER	THE BIG MAN
1 Clever sense of social values.	1 Inclined to stupidity and unconscious of social values.
2 Dresses well. Pretends that dress is superficial – but knows that it isn't.	2 Thinks dress is superficial, and is inclined to be careless about it.
3 Goes into such activities as he can shine in.	3 Goes out for everything from a sense of duty.
4 Gets to college and is, in a worldly way, successful.	4 Gets to college and has a problematical future. Feels lost without his circle, and always says that schooldays were happiest, after all. Goes back to school and makes speeches about what St Regis's boys are doing.
5 Hair slicked.	5 Hair not slicked.

Amory had decided definitely on Princeton, even though he would be the only boy entering that year from St Regis's. Yale had a romance and glamour from the tales of Minneapolis, and St Regis's men who had been 'tapped for Skull and Bones', but Princeton drew him most, with its atmosphere of bright colours and its alluring reputation as the pleasantest country club in America. Dwarfed by the menacing college exams, Amory's schooldays drifted into the past. Years afterwards, when he went back to St Regis's, he seemed to have forgotten the successes of sixth-form year, and to be able to picture himself only as the unadjustable boy who had hurried down corridors, jeered at by his rabid contemporaries mad with common sense.

2

Spires and Gargoyles

At first Amory noticed only the wealth of sunshine creeping across the long, green swards, dancing on the leaded window-panes, and swimming around the tops of spires and towers and battlemented walls. Gradually he realised that he was really walking up University Place, self-conscious about his suitcase, developing a new tendency to glare straight ahead when he passed anyone. Several times he could have sworn that men turned to look at him critically. He wondered vaguely if there was something the matter with his clothes, and wished he had shaved that morning on the train. He felt unnecessarily stiff and awkward among these white-flannelled, bareheaded youths, who must be juniors and seniors, judging from the *savoir faire* with which they strolled.

He found that 12 University Place was a large, dilapidated mansion, at present apparently uninhabited, though he knew it housed usually a dozen freshmen. After a hurried skirmish with his landlady he sallied out on a tour of exploration, but he had gone scarcely a block when he became horribly conscious that he must be the only man in town who was wearing a hat. He returned hurriedly to 12 University, left his derby, and, emerging bareheaded, loitered down Nassau Street, stopping to investigate a display of athletic photographs in a store window, including a large one of Allenby, the football captain, and next attracted by the sign 'Jigger Shop' over a confectionary window. This sounded familiar, so he sauntered in and took a seat on a high stool.

'Chocolate sundae,' he told a coloured person.

'Double-chocolate jiggah? Anything else?'

'Why – yes.'

'Bacon bun?'

'Why – yes.'

He munched four of these, finding them of pleasing savour, and then consumed another double-chocolate jigger before ease descended upon him. After a cursory inspection of the pillowcases, leather pennants and Gibson Girls that lined the walls, he left, and continued along Nassau

Street with his hands in his pockets. Gradually he was learning to distinguish between upperclassmen and entering men, even though the freshman cap would not appear until the following Monday. Those who were too obviously, too nervously at home were freshmen, for as each train brought a new contingent it was immediately absorbed into the hatless, white-shod, book-laden throng, whose function seemed to be to drift endlessly up and down the street, emitting great clouds of smoke from brand-new pipes. By afternoon Amory realised that now the newest arrivals were taking him for an upperclassman, and he tried conscientiously to look both pleasantly blasé and casually critical, which was as near as he could analyse the prevalent facial expression.

At five o'clock he felt the need of hearing his own voice, so he retreated to his house to see if anyone else had arrived. Having climbed the rickety stairs he scrutinised his room resignedly, concluding that it was hopeless to attempt any more inspired decoration than class banners and tiger pictures. There was a tap at the door.

'Come in!'

A slim face with grey eyes and a humorous smile appeared in the doorway.

'Got a hammer?'

'No – sorry. Maybe Mrs Twelve, or whatever she goes by, has one.'

The stranger advanced into the room.

'You an inmate of this asylum?'

Amory nodded.

'Awful barn for the rent we pay.'

Amory had to agree that it was.

'I thought of the campus,' he said, 'but they say there's so few freshmen that they're lost. Have to sit around and study for something to do.'

The grey-eyed man decided to introduce himself.

'My name's Holiday.'

'Blaine's my name.'

They shook hands with the fashionable low swoop. Amory grinned.

'Where'd you prep?'

'Andover – where did you?'

'St Regis's.'

'Oh, did you? I had a cousin there.'

They discussed the cousin thoroughly, and then Holiday announced that he was to meet his brother for dinner at six.

'Come along and have a bite with us.'

'All right.'

At the Kenilworth, Amory met Burne Holiday – he of the grey eyes was Kerry – and during a limpid meal of thin soup and anaemic vegetables they stared at the other freshmen, who sat either in small groups looking very ill at ease, or in large groups seeming very much at home.

'I hear Commons is pretty bad,' said Amory.

'That's the rumour. But you've got to eat there – or pay anyways.'

'Crime!'

'Imposition!'

'Oh, at Princeton you've got to swallow everything the first year. It's like a damned prep school.'

Amory agreed.

'Lot of pep, though,' he insisted. 'I wouldn't have gone to Yale for a million.'

'Me either.'

'You going out for anything?' enquired Amory of the elder brother.

'Not me – Burne here is going out for the *Prince* – the *Daily Princetonian*, you know.'

'Yes, I know.'

'You going out for anything?'

'Why – yes. I'm going to take a whack at freshman football.'

'Play at St Regis's?'

'Some,' admitted Amory depreciatingly, 'but I'm getting so damned thin.'

'You're not thin.'

'Well, I used to be stocky last fall.'

'Oh!'

After supper they attended the movies, where Amory was fascinated by the glib comments of a man in front of him, as well as by the wild yelling and shouting.

'*Yoho!*'

'Oh, honey-*baby* – you're so big and strong, but oh, so *gentle*!'

'Clinch!'

'Oh, *clinch*!'

'Kiss her, kiss 'at lady, *quick*!'

'Oh-h-h – !'

A group began whistling 'By the Sea', and the audience took it up noisily. This was followed by an indistinguishable song that included much stamping and then by an endless, incoherent dirge.

'Oh-h-h-h-h
She works in a Jam Factoree
And – that-may-be-all-right
But you can't-fool-me
For I know – Damn – Well
That she Don't-make-jam-all-night!
Oh-h-h-h!'

As they pushed out, giving and receiving curious impersonal glances, Amory decided that he liked the movies, wanted to enjoy them as the row of upperclassmen in front had enjoyed them, with their arms along the backs of the seats, their comments Gaelic and caustic, their attitude a mixture of critical wit and tolerant amusement.

'Want a sundae – I mean a jigger?' asked Kerry.

'Sure.'

They suppered heavily and then, still sauntering, eased back to 12.

'Wonderful night.'

'It's a whiz.'

'You men going to unpack?'

'Guess so. Come on, Burne.'

Amory decided to sit for a while on the front steps, so he bade them good-night.

The great tapestries of trees had darkened to ghosts back at the last edge of twilight. The early moon had drenched the arches with pale blue, and, weaving over the night, in and out of the gossamer rifts of moon, swept a song, a song with more than a hint of sadness, infinitely transient, infinitely regretful.

He remembered that an alumnus of the nineties had told him of one of Booth Tarkington's amusements: standing in mid-campus in the small hours and singing tenor songs to the stars, arousing mingled emotions in the couched undergraduates according to the sentiment of their moods.

Now, far down the shadowy line of University Place a white-clad phalanx broke the gloom, and marching figures, white-shirted, white-trousered, swung rhythmically up the street, with linked arms and heads thrown back:

'Going back – going back,
Going – back – to – Nas-sau – Hall,
Going back – going back –

To the – Best – Old – Place – of – All.
Going back – going back,
From all – this – earth-ly – ball,
We'll – clear – the – track – as – we – go – back –
Going – back – to – Nas-sau – Hall!'

Amory closed his eyes as the ghostly procession drew near. The song soared so high that all dropped out except the tenors, who bore the melody triumphantly past the danger-point and relinquished it to the fantastic chorus. Then Amory opened his eyes, half afraid that sight would spoil the rich illusion of harmony.

He sighed eagerly. There at the head of the white platoon marched Allenby, the football captain, slim and defiant, as if aware that this year the hopes of the college rested on him, that his hundred-and-sixty pounds were expected to dodge to victory through the heavy blue and crimson lines.

Fascinated, Amory watched each rank of linked arms as it came abreast, the faces indistinct above the polo shirts, the voices blended in a paean of triumph – and then the procession passed through shadowy Campbell Arch, and the voices grew fainter as it wound eastward over the campus.

The minutes passed and Amory sat there very quietly. He regretted the rule that would forbid freshmen to be outdoors after curfew, for he wanted to ramble through the shadowy scented lanes, where Witherspoon brooded like a dark mother over Whig and Clio, her Attic children, where the black Gothic snake of Little curled down to Cuyler and Patton, these in turn flinging the mystery out over the placid slope rolling to the lake.

Princeton of the daytime filtered slowly into his consciousness – West and Reunion, redolent of the sixties, Seventy-nine Hall, brick-red and arrogant, Upper and Lower Pyne, aristocratic Elizabethan ladies not quite content to live among shopkeepers, and, topping all, climbing with clear blue aspiration, the great dreaming spires of Holder and Cleveland towers.

From the first he loved Princeton – its lazy beauty, its half-grasped significance, the wild moonlight revel of the rushes, the handsome, prosperous big-game crowds, and under it all the air of struggle that pervaded his class. From the day when, wild-eyed and exhausted, the jerseyed freshmen sat in the gymnasium and elected someone from

Hill School class president, a Lawrenceville celebrity vice-president, a hockey star from St Paul's secretary, up until the end of sophomore year it never ceased, that breathless social system, that worship, seldom named, never really admitted, of the bogey 'big man'.

First it was schools, and Amory, alone from St Regis's, watched the crowds form and widen and form again; St Paul's, Hill, Pomfret, eating at certain tacitly reserved tables in Commons, dressing in their own corners of the gymnasium, and drawing unconsciously about them a barrier of the slightly less important but socially ambitious to protect them from the friendly, rather puzzled high-school element. From the moment he realised this Amory resented social barriers as artificial distinctions made by the strong to bolster up their weak retainers and keep out the almost strong.

Having decided to be one of the gods of the class, he reported for freshman football practice, but in the second week, playing quarterback, already paragraphed in corners of the *Princetonian*, he wrenched his knee seriously enough to put him out for the rest of the season. This forced him to retire and consider the situation.

'12 Univee' housed a dozen miscellaneous question-marks. There were three or four inconspicuous and quite startled boys from Lawrenceville, two amateur wild men from a New York private school (Kerry Holiday christened them the 'plebeian drunks'), a Jewish youth, also from New York, and, as compensation for Amory, the two Holidays, to whom he took an instant fancy.

The Holidays were rumoured twins, but really the dark-haired one, Kerry, was a year older than his blond brother, Burne. Kerry was tall, with humorous grey eyes, and a sudden, attractive smile; he became at once the mentor of the house, reaper of ears that grew too high, censor of conceit, vendor of rare, satirical humour. Amory spread the table of their future friendship with all his ideas of what college should and did mean. Kerry, not inclined as yet to take things seriously, chided him gently for being curious at this inopportune time about the intricacies of the social system, but liked him and was both interested and amused.

Burne, fair-haired, silent and intent, appeared in the house only as a busy apparition, gliding in quietly at night and off again in the early morning to get up his work in the library – he was out for the *Princetonian*, competing furiously against forty others for the coveted first place. In December he came down with diphtheria, and someone else won the competition, but, returning to college in February, he dauntlessly went after the prize again. Necessarily, Amory's acquaintance with him was in the way of three-minute chats, walking to and from lectures, so he failed to penetrate Burne's one absorbing interest and find what lay beneath it.

Amory was far from contented. He missed the place he had won at St Regis's, the being known and admired, yet Princeton stimulated him, and there were many things ahead calculated to arouse the Machiavelli latent in him, could he but insert a wedge. The upper-class clubs, concerning which he had pumped a reluctant graduate during the previous summer, excited his curiosity: Ivy, detached and breathlessly aristocratic; Cottage, an impressive *mélange* of brilliant adventurers and well-dressed philanderers; Tiger Inn, broad-shouldered and athletic, vitalised by an honest elaboration of prep-school standards; Cap and Gown, anti-alcoholic, faintly religious and politically powerful; flamboyant Colonial; literary Quadrangle; and the dozen others, varying in age and position.

Anything which brought an under classman into too glaring a light was labelled with the damning brand of 'running it out'. The movies thrived on caustic comments, but the men who made them were generally running it out; talking of clubs was running it out; standing for anything very strongly, as, for instance, drinking parties or tee-totalling, was running it out; in short, being personally conspicuous was not tolerated, and the influential man was the non-committal man, until at club elections in sophomore year everyone should be sewed up in some bag for the rest of his college career.

Amory found that writing for the *Nassau Literary Magazine* would get him nothing, but that being on the board of the *Daily Princetonian* would get anyone a good deal. His vague desire to do immortal acting with the English Dramatic Association faded out when he found that the most ingenious brains and talents were concentrated upon the Triangle Club, a musical-comedy organisation that every year took a great Christmas trip. In the meanwhile, feeling strangely alone and restless in Commons, with new desires and ambitions stirring in his mind, he let the first term go by between an envy of the embryo successes and a puzzled fretting with Kerry as to why they were not accepted immediately among the élite of the class.

Many afternoons they lounged in the windows of 12 Univee and watched the class pass to and from Commons, noting satellites already attaching themselves to the more prominent, watching the lonely grind with his hurried step and downcast eye, envying the happy security of the big school groups.

'We're the damned middle class, that's what!' he complained to Kerry one day as he lay stretched out on the sofa, consuming a family of Fatimas with contemplative precision.

'Well, why not? We came to Princeton so we could feel that way towards the small colleges – have it on 'em, more self-confidence, dress better, cut a swathe – '

'Oh, it isn't that I mind the glittering caste system,' admitted Amory. 'I like having a bunch of hot cats on top, but gosh, Kerry, I've got to be one of them.'

'But just now, Amory, you're only a sweaty bourgeois.'

Amory lay for a moment without speaking.

'I won't be – long,' he said finally. 'But I hate to get anywhere by working for it. I'll show the marks, don't you know.'

'Honourable scars.' Kerry craned his neck suddenly at the street. 'There's Langueduc, if you want to see what he looks like – and Humbird just behind.'

Amory rose dynamically and sought the windows.

'Oh,' he said, scrutinising these worthies, 'Humbird looks like a knock-out, but this Langueduc – he's the rugged type, isn't he? I distrust that sort. All diamonds look big in the rough.'

'Well,' said Kerry, as the excitement subsided, 'you're a literary genius. It's up to you.'

'I wonder' – Amory paused – 'if I could be. I honestly think so sometimes. That sounds like the devil, and I wouldn't say it to anybody except you.'

'Well – go ahead. Let your hair grow and write poems like this guy D'Invilliers in the *Lit*.'

Amory reached lazily at a pile of magazines on the table.

'Read his latest effort?'

'Never miss 'em. They're rare.'

Amory glanced through the issue.

'Hello!' he said in surprise, 'he's a freshman, isn't he?'

'Yeah.'

'Listen to this! My God!

> "A serving lady speaks:
> Black velvet trails its folds over the day,
> White tapers, prisoned in their silver frames,
> Wave their thin flames like shadows in the wind,
> Pia, Pompia, come – come away – "

Now, what the devil does that mean?'

'It's a pantry scene.'

' "Her toes are stiffened like a stork's in flight;
She's laid upon her bed, on the white sheets,
Her hands pressed on her smooth bust like a saint,
Bella Cunizza, come into the light!"

My gosh, Kerry, what in hell is it all about? I swear I don't get him at all, and I'm a literary bird myself.'

'It's pretty tricky,' said Kerry, 'only you've got to think of hearses and stale milk when you read it. That isn't as pash as some of them.'

Amory tossed the magazine on the table.

'Well,' he sighed, 'I sure am up in the air. I know I'm not a regular fellow, yet I loathe anybody else that isn't. I can't decide whether to cultivate my mind and be a great dramatist, or to thumb my nose at the *Golden Treasury* and be a Princeton slicker.'

'Why decide?' suggested Kerry. 'Better drift, like me. I'm going to sail into prominence on Burne's coat-tails.'

'I can't drift – I want to be interested. I want to pull strings, even for somebody else, or be Princetonian chairman or Triangle president. I want to be admired, Kerry.'

'You're thinking too much about yourself.'

Amory sat up at this.

'No. I'm thinking about you, too. We've got to get out and mix around the class right now, when it's fun to be a snob. I'd like to bring a sardine to the prom in June, for instance, but I wouldn't do it unless I could be damn debonaire about it – introduce her to all the prize parlour-snakes, and the football captain, and all that simple stuff.'

'Amory,' said Kerry impatiently, 'you're just going around in a circle. If you want to be prominent, get out and try for something; if you don't, just take it easy.' He yawned. 'Come on, let's let the smoke drift off. We'll go down and watch football practice.'

Amory gradually accepted this point of view, decided that next fall would inaugurate his career, and relinquished himself to watching Kerry extract joy from 12 Univee.

They filled the Jewish youth's bed with lemon pie; they put out the gas all over the house every night by blowing into the jet in Amory's room, to the bewilderment of Mrs Twelve and the local plumber; they set up the effects of the plebeian drunks – pictures, books and furniture – in the bathroom, to the confusion of the pair, who hazily discovered the transposition on their return from a Trenton spree; they were disappointed beyond measure when the plebeian drunks decided to take it as a joke; they played red-dog and twenty-one and jackpot from dinner to dawn, and on the occasion of one man's birthday persuaded him to buy sufficient champagne for a hilarious celebration. The donor of the party having remained sober, Kerry and Amory accidentally dropped him down two flights of stairs and called, shamefaced and penitent, at the infirmary all the following week.

'Say, who are all these women?' demanded Kerry one day, protesting at the size of Amory's mail. 'I've been looking at the postmarks lately – Farmington and Dobbs and Westover and Dana Hall – what's the idea?'

Amory grinned.

'All from the Twin Cities.' He named them off. 'There's Marylyn De Witt – she's pretty, got a car of her own and that's damn convenient; there's Sally Weatherby – she's getting too fat; there's Myra St Claire, she's an old flame, easy to kiss if you like it – '

'What line do you throw 'em?' demanded Kerry. 'I've tried everything, and the mad wags aren't even afraid of me.'

'You're the "nice boy" type,' suggested Amory.

'That's just it. Mother always feels the girl is safe if she's with me. Honestly, it's annoying. If I start to hold somebody's hand, they laugh at me, and *let* me, just as if it wasn't part of them. As soon as I get hold of a hand they sort of disconnect it from the rest of them.'

'Sulk,' suggested Amory. 'Tell 'em you're wild and have 'em reform you – go home furious – come back in half an hour – startle 'em.'

Kerry shook his head.

'No chance. I wrote a St Timothy girl a really loving letter last year. In one place I got rattled and said: "My God, how I love you!" She took some nail scissors, clipped out the "My God" and showed the rest of the letter all over school. Doesn't work at all. I'm just "good old Kerry" and all that rot.'

Amory smiled and tried to picture himself as 'good old Amory'. He failed completely.

February dripped snow and rain, the cyclonic freshman mid-years passed, and life in 12 Univee continued interesting if not purposeful. Once a day Amory indulged in a club sandwich, cornflakes and Julienne potatoes at 'Joe's', accompanied usually by Kerry or Alec Connage. The latter was a quiet, rather aloof slicker from Hotchkiss, who lived next door and shared the same enforced singleness as Amory, due to the fact that his entire class had gone to Yale. 'Joe's' was unaesthetic and faintly unsanitary, but a limitless charge account could be opened there, a convenience that Amory appreciated. His father had been experimenting with mining stocks and, in consequence, his allowance, while liberal, was not at all what he had expected.

'Joe's' had the additional advantage of seclusion from curious upper-class eyes, so at four each afternoon Amory, accompanied by friend or book, went up to experiment with his digestion. One day in March, finding that all the tables were occupied, he slipped into a chair opposite a freshman who bent intently over a book at the last table. They nodded briefly. For twenty minutes Amory sat consuming bacon buns and reading *Mrs Warren's Profession* (he had discovered Shaw quite by accident while browsing in the library during mid-years); the other freshman, also intent on his volume, meanwhile did away with a trio of chocolate malted milks.

By and by Amory's eyes wandered curiously to his fellow-luncher's book. He spelled out the name and title upside down – *Marpessa* by Stephen Phillips. This meant nothing to him, his metrical education having been confined to such Sunday classics as 'Come into the Garden, Maude', and what morsels of Shakespeare and Milton had been recently forced upon him.

Moved to address his *vis-à-vis*, he simulated interest in his book for a moment, and then exclaimed aloud as if involuntarily: 'Ha! Great stuff!'

The other freshman looked up and Amory registered artificial embarrassment.

'Are you referring to your bacon buns?' His cracked, kindly voice went well with the large spectacles and the impression of a voluminous keenness that he gave.

'No,' Amory answered. 'I was referring to Bernard Shaw.' He turned the book around in explanation.

'I've never read any Shaw. I've always meant to.' The boy paused and then continued: 'Did you ever read Stephen Phillips, or do you like poetry?'

'Yes, indeed,' Amory affirmed eagerly. 'I've never read much of Phillips, though.' (He had never heard of any Phillips except the late David Graham Phillips.)

'It's pretty fair, I think. Of course he's a Victorian.' They sallied into a discussion of poetry, in the course of which they introduced themselves, and Amory's companion proved to be none other than 'that awful highbrow, Thomas Parke D'Invilliers', who signed the passionate love-poems in the *Lit*. He was, perhaps, nineteen, with stooped shoulders, pale blue eyes, and, as Amory could tell from his general appearance, without much conception of social competition and such phenomena of absorbing interest. Still, he liked books, and it seemed for ever since Amory had met anyone who did; if only that St Paul's crowd at the next table would not mistake *him* for a bird, too, he would enjoy the encounter tremendously. They didn't seem to be noticing, so he let himself go, discussed books by the dozens – books he had read, read about, books he had never heard of, rattling off lists of titles with the facility of a Brentano's clerk. D'Invilliers was partially taken in and wholly delighted. In a good-natured way he had almost decided that Princeton was one part deadly Philistines and one part deadly grinds, and to find a person who could mention Keats without stammering, yet evidently washed his hands, was rather a treat.

'Ever read any Oscar Wilde?' he asked.

'No. Who wrote it?'

'It's a man – don't you know?'

'Oh, surely.' A faint chord was struck in Amory's memory. 'Wasn't the comic opera, *Patience*, written about him?'

'Yes, that's the fella. I've just finished a book of his, *The Picture of Dorian Gray*, and I certainly wish you'd read it. You'd like it. You can borrow it if you want to.'

'Why, I'd like it a lot – thanks.'

'Don't you want to come up to the room? I've got a few other books.'

Amory hesitated, glanced at the St Paul's group – one of them was the magnificent, exquisite Humbird – and he considered how determinate the addition of this friend would be. He never got to the stage of making them and getting rid of them – he was not hard enough for that – so he measured Thomas Parke D'Invilliers' undoubted attractions and value against the menace of cold eyes behind tortoise-rimmed spectacles that he fancied glared from the next table.

'Yes, I'll go.'

So he found *Dorian Gray* and the 'Mystic and Sombre Dolores' and the 'Belle Dame sans Merci'; for a month was keen on naught else. The world became pale and interesting, and he tried hard to look at Princeton through the satiated eyes of Oscar Wilde and Swinburne – or 'Fingal O'Flahertie' and 'Algernon Charles', as he called them in *précieuse* jest. He read enormously every night – Shaw, Chesterton,

Barrie, Pinero, Yeats, Synge, Ernest Dowson, Arthur Symons, Keats, Sudermann, Robert Hugh Benson, the Savoy Operas – just a heterogeneous mixture, for he suddenly discovered that he had read nothing for years.

Tom D'Invilliers became at first an occasion rather than a friend. Amory saw him about once a week, and together they gilded the ceiling of Tom's room and decorated the walls with imitation tapestry, bought at an auction, tall candlesticks and figured curtains. Amory liked him for being clever and literary without effeminacy or affectation. In fact, Amory did most of the strutting and tried painfully to make every remark an epigram, than which, if one is content with ostensible epigrams, there are many feats harder. 12 Univee was amused. Kerry read *Dorian Gray* and simulated Lord Henry, following Amory about, addressing him as 'Dorian' and pretending to encourage in him wicked fancies and attenuated tendencies to ennui. When he carried it into Commons, to the amazement of the others at table, Amory became furiously embarrassed, and after that made epigrams only before D'Invilliers or a convenient mirror.

One day Tom and Amory tried reciting their own and Lord Dunsany's poems to the music of Kerry's graphophone.

'Chant!' cried Tom. 'Don't recite! *Chant!*'

Amory, who was performing, looked annoyed, and claimed that he needed a record with less piano in it. Kerry thereupon rolled on the floor in stifled laughter.

'Put on "Hearts and Flowers"!' he howled. 'Oh, my Lord, I'm going to cast a kitten.'

'Shut off the damn graphophone,' Amory cried, rather red in the face. 'I'm not giving an exhibition.'

In the meanwhile Amory delicately kept trying to awaken a sense of the social system in D'Invilliers, for he knew that this poet was really more conventional than he, and needed merely watered hair, a smaller range of conversation, and a darker brown hat to become quite regular. But the liturgy of Livingstone collars and dark ties fell on heedless ears; in fact D'Invilliers faintly resented his efforts; so Amory confined himself to calls once a week, and brought him occasionally to 12 Univee. This caused mild titters among the other freshmen, who called them 'Dr Johnson and Boswell'.

Alec Connage, another frequent visitor, liked him in a vague way, but was afraid of him as a highbrow. Kerry, who saw through his poetic patter to the solid, almost respectable depths within, was immensely amused and would have him recite poetry by the hour, while he lay with closed eyes on Amory's sofa and listened:

'Asleep or waking is it? for her neck
Kissed over close, wears yet a purple speck
Wherein the pained blood falters and goes out;
Soft and stung softly – fairer for a fleck . . . '

'That's good,' Kerry would say softly. 'It pleases the elder Holiday. That's a great poet, I guess.' Tom, delighted at an audience, would ramble through the *Poems and Ballads* until Kerry and Amory knew them almost as well as he.

Amory took to writing poetry on spring afternoons, in the gardens of the big estates near Princeton, while swans made effective atmosphere in the artificial pools, and slow clouds sailed harmoniously above the willows. May came too soon, and suddenly unable to bear walls, he wandered the campus at all hours through starlight and rain.

A DAMP SYMBOLIC INTERLUDE

The night mist fell. From the moon it rolled, clustered about the spires and towers, and then settled below them, so that the dreaming peaks were still in lofty aspiration towards the sky. Figures that dotted the day like ants now brushed along as shadowy ghosts, in and out of the foreground. The Gothic halls and cloisters were infinitely more mysterious as they loomed suddenly out of the darkness, outlined each by myriad faint squares of yellow light. Indefinitely from somewhere a bell boomed the quarter-hour, and Amory, pausing by the sun-dial, stretched himself out full length on the damp grass. The cool bathed his eyes and slowed the flight of time – time that had crept so insidiously through the lazy April afternoons, seemed so intangible in the long spring twilights. Evening after evening the senior singing had drifted over the campus in melancholy beauty, and through the shell of his undergraduate consciousness had broken a deep and reverent devotion to the grey walls and Gothic peaks and all they symbolised as warehouses of dead ages.

The tower that in view of his window sprang upward, grew into a spire, yearning higher until its uppermost tip was half invisible against the morning skies, gave him the first sense of the transiency and unimportance of the campus figures except as holders of the apostolic succession. He liked knowing that Gothic architecture, with its upward trend, was peculiarly appropriate to universities, and the idea became personal to him. The silent stretches of green, the quiet halls with an occasional late-burning scholastic light held his imagination in a strong grasp, and the chastity of the spire became a symbol of this perception.

'Damn it all,' he whispered aloud, wetting his hands in the damp and running them through his hair. 'Next year I work!' Yet he knew that where now the spirit of spires and towers made him dreamily acquiescent, it would then overawe him. Where now he realised only his own inconsequence, effort would make him aware of his own impotency and insufficiency.

The college dreamed on – awake. He felt a nervous excitement that might have been the very throb of its slow heart. It was a stream where he was to throw a stone whose faint ripple would be vanishing almost as it left his hand. As yet he had given nothing, he had taken nothing.

A belated freshman, his oilskin slicker rasping loudly, slushed along the soft path. A voice from somewhere called the inevitable formula, 'Stick out your head!' below an unseen window. A hundred little sounds of the current drifting on under the fog pressed in finally on his consciousness.

'Oh, God!' he cried suddenly, and started at the sound of his voice in the stillness. The rain dripped on. A minute longer he lay without moving, his hands clenched. Then he sprang to his feet and gave his clothes a tentative pat.

'I'm very damn wet!' he said aloud to the sundial.

HISTORICAL

The war began in the summer following his freshman year. Beyond a sporting interest in the German dash for Paris the whole affair failed either to thrill or interest him. With the attitude he might have held towards an amusing melodrama he hoped it would be long and bloody. If it had not continued he would have felt like an irate ticket-holder at a prizefight where the principals refused to mix it up.

That was his total reaction.

'HA-HA HORTENSE!'

'All right, *ponies*!'

'Shake it up!'

'Hey, ponies – how about easing up on that crap game and shaking a mean hip?'

'Hey, *ponies*!'

The coach fumed helplessly, the Triangle Club president, glowering with anxiety, varied between furious bursts of authority and fits of temperamental lassitude, when he sat spiritless and wondered how the devil the show was ever going on tour by Christmas.

'All right. We'll take the pirate song.'

The ponies took last drags at their cigarettes and slumped into place; the leading lady rushed into the foreground, setting his hands and feet in an atmospheric mince; and as the coach clapped and stamped and tumped and da-da'd, they hashed out a dance.

A great, seething ant-hill was the Triangle Club. It gave a musical comedy every year, travelling with cast, chorus, orchestra and scenery all through Christmas vacation. The play and music were the work of undergraduates, and the club itself was the most influential of institutions, over three hundred men competing for it every year.

Amory, after an easy victory in the first sophomore Princetonian competition, stepped into a vacancy of the cast as Boiling Oil, a Pirate Lieutenant. Every night for the last week they had rehearsed *Ha-Ha Hortense!* in the Casino, from two in the afternoon until eight in the morning, sustained by dark and powerful coffee, and sleeping in lectures through the interim. A rare scene, the Casino. A big, barnlike auditorium, dotted with boys as girls, boys as pirates, boys as babies; the scenery in course of being violently set up; the spotlight man rehearsing by throwing weird shafts into angry eyes; over all the constant tuning of the orchestra or the cheerful tumpty-tump of a Triangle tune. The boy who writes the lyrics stands in the corner, biting a pencil, with twenty minutes to think of an encore; the business manager argues with the secretary as to how much money can be spent on 'those damn milkmaid costumes'; the old graduate, president in ninety-eight, perches on a box and thinks how much simpler it was in his day.

How a Triangle show ever got off was a mystery, but it was a riotous mystery, anyway, whether or not one did enough service to wear a little gold Triangle on his watch-chain. *Ha-Ha Hortense!* was written over six times and had the names of nine collaborators on the programme. All Triangle shows started by being 'something different – not just a regular musical comedy', but when the several authors, the president, the coach and the faculty committee finished with it, there remained just the old reliable Triangle show with the old reliable jokes and the star comedian who got expelled or sick or something just before the trip, and the dark-whiskered man in the pony-ballet, who 'absolutely won't shave twice a day, doggone it!'

There was one brilliant place in *Ha-Ha Hortense!* It is a Princeton tradition that whenever a Yale man who is a member of the widely advertised 'Skull and Bones' hears the sacred name mentioned, he must leave the room. It is also a tradition that the members are invariably successful in later life, amassing fortunes or votes or coupons or whatever they choose to amass. Therefore, at each performance of *Ha-Ha Hortense!* half a dozen seats were kept from sale and occupied by six of the worst-looking vagabonds that could be hired from the streets, further touched up by the Triangle make-up man. At the moment in the show where Firebrand, the Pirate Chief, pointed at his black flag and said, 'I am a Yale graduate – note my Skull and Bones!' – at this very moment the six vagabonds were instructed to rise *conspicuously* and leave the theatre with looks of deep melancholy and an injured dignity. It was claimed though never proved that on one occasion the hired Elis were swelled by one of the real thing.

They played through vacation to the fashionable of eight cities. Amory liked Louisville and Memphis best: these knew how to meet strangers, furnished extraordinary punch, and flaunted an astonishing array of feminine beauty. Chicago he approved for a certain verve that transcended its loud accent – however, it was a Yale town, and as the Yale Glee Club was expected in a week, the Triangle received only divided homage. In Baltimore, Princeton was at home, and everyone fell in love. There was a proper consumption of strong waters all along the line; one man invariably went on the stage highly stimulated, claiming that his particular interpretation of the part required it. There were three private cars; however, no one slept except in the third car, which was called the 'animal car', and where were herded the spectacled wind-jammers of the orchestra. Everything was so hurried that there was no time to be bored, but when they arrived in Philadelphia, with vacation nearly over, there was rest in getting out of the heavy atmosphere of flowers and grease-paint, and the ponies took off their corsets with abdominal pains and sighs of relief.

When the disbanding came, Amory set out post haste for Minneapolis, for Sally Weatherby's cousin, Isabelle Borge, was coming to spend the winter in Minneapolis while her parents went abroad. He remembered Isabelle only as a little girl with whom he had played sometimes when he first went to Minneapolis. She had gone to Baltimore to live – but since then she had developed a past.

Amory was in full stride, confident, nervous and jubilant. Scurrying back to Minneapolis to see a girl he had known as a child seemed the interesting and romantic thing to do, so without compunction he wired his mother not to expect him . . . sat in the train, and thought about himself for thirty-six hours.

'PETTING'

On the Triangle trip Amory had come into constant contact with that great current American phenomenon, the 'petting party'.

None of the Victorian mothers – and most of the mothers were Victorian – had any idea how casually their daughters were accustomed to be kissed. '*Servant*-girls are that way,' says Mrs Huston-Carmelite to her popular daughter. 'They are kissed first and proposed to afterwards.'

But the Popular Daughter becomes engaged every six months between sixteen and twenty-two, when she arranges a match with young Hambell, of Cambell & Hambell, who fatuously considers himself her first love, and between engagements the PD (she is selected by the cut-in system at dances, which favours the survival of the fittest) has other sentimental last kisses in the moonlight, or the firelight, or the outer darkness.

Amory saw girls doing things that even in his memory would have been impossible: eating three-o'clock, after-dance suppers in impossible cafés, talking of every side of life with an air half of earnestness, half of mockery, yet with a furtive excitement that Amory considered stood for a real moral let-down. But he never realised how widespread it was until he saw the cities between New York and Chicago as one vast juvenile intrigue.

Afternoon at the Plaza, with winter twilight hovering outside and faint drums downstairs . . . they strut and fret in the lobby, taking another cocktail, scrupulously attired and waiting. Then the swinging doors revolve and three bundles of fur mince in. The theatre comes afterwards; then a table at the Midnight Frolic – of course, mother will be along there, but she will serve only to make things more secretive and brilliant as she sits in solitary state at the deserted table and thinks such entertainments as this are not half so bad as they are painted, only rather wearying. But the PD is in love again . . . it was odd, wasn't it? – that though there was so much room left in the taxi the PD and the boy from Williams were somehow crowded out and had to go in a separate car. Odd! Didn't you notice how flushed the PD was when she arrived just seven minutes late? But the PD 'gets away with it'.

The 'belle' had become the 'flirt', the 'flirt' had become the 'baby vamp'. The 'belle' had five or six callers every afternoon. If the PD, by some strange accident, has two, it is made pretty uncomfortable for the one who hasn't a date with her. The 'belle' was surrounded by a dozen men in the intermissions between dances. Try to find the PD between dances, just *try* to find her.

The same girl . . . deep in an atmosphere of jungle music and the questioning of moral codes. Amory found it rather fascinating to feel that any popular girl he met before eight he might quite possibly kiss before twelve.

'Why on earth are we here?' he asked the girl with the green combs one night as they sat in someone's limousine, outside the Country Club in Louisville.

'I don't know. I'm just full of the devil.'

'Let's be frank – we'll never see each other again. I wanted to come out here with you because I thought you were the best-looking girl in sight. You really don't care whether you ever see me again, do you?'

'No – but is this your line for every girl? What have I done to deserve it?'

'And you didn't feel tired dancing or want a cigarette or any of the things you said? You just wanted to be – '

'Oh, let's go in,' she interrupted, 'if you want to *analyse*. Let's not *talk* about it.'

When the hand-knit, sleeveless jerseys were stylish, Amory, in a burst of inspiration, named them 'petting shirts'. The name travelled from coast to coast on the lips of parlour-snakes and PDs.

DESCRIPTIVE

Amory was now eighteen years old, just under six feet tall and exceptionally, but not conventionally, handsome. He had rather a young face, the ingenuousness of which was marred by the penetrating green eyes, fringed with long dark eyelashes. He lacked somehow that intense animal magnetism that so often accompanies beauty in men or women; his personality seemed rather a mental thing, and it was not in his power to turn it on and off like a water-faucet. But people never forgot his face.

ISABELLE

She paused at the top of the staircase. The sensations attributed to divers on springboards, leading ladies on opening nights, and lumpy, husky young men on the day of the Big Game, crowded through her. She should have descended to a burst of drums or a discordant blend of themes from *Thaïs* and *Carmen*. She had never been so curious about her appearance, she had never been so satisfied with it. She had been sixteen years old for six months.

'Isabelle!' called her cousin Sally from the doorway of the dressing-room.

'I'm ready.' She caught a slight lump of nervousness in her throat.

'I had to send back to the house for another pair of slippers. It'll be just a minute.'

Isabelle started towards the dressing-room for a last peek in the mirror, but something decided her to stand there and gaze down the broad stairs of the Minnehaha Club. They curved tantalisingly, and she could catch just a glimpse of two pairs of masculine feet in the hall below. Pump-shod in uniform black, they gave no hint of identity, but she wondered eagerly if one pair were attached to Amory Blaine. This young man, not as yet encountered, had nevertheless taken up a considerable part of her day – the first day of her arrival.

Coming up in the machine from the station, Sally had volunteered, amid a rain of question, comment, revelation and exaggeration: 'You remember Amory Blaine, of *course*. Well, he's simply mad to see you again. He's stayed over a day from college, and he's coming tonight. He's heard so much about you – says he remembers your eyes.'

This had pleased Isabelle. It put them on equal terms, although she was quite capable of staging her own romances, with or without advance advertising. But following her happy tremble of anticipation, came a sinking sensation that made her ask: 'How do you mean he's heard about me? What sort of things?'

Sally smiled. She felt rather in the capacity of a showman with her more exotic cousin.

'He knows you're – you're considered beautiful and all that' – she paused – 'and I guess he knows you've been kissed.'

At this Isabelle's little fist had clenched suddenly under the fur robe. She was accustomed to be thus followed by her desperate past, and it never failed to rouse in her the same feeling of resentment; yet – in a strange town it was an advantageous reputation. She was a 'Speed', was she? Well – let them find out.

Out of the window Isabelle watched the snow glide by in the frosty morning. It was ever so much colder here than in Baltimore; she had not remembered; the glass of the side door was iced, the windows were shirred with snow in the corners. Her mind played still with one subject. Did *he* dress like that boy there, who walked calmly down a bustling business street, in moccasins and winter-carnival costume? How very *Western*! Of course he wasn't that way: he went to Princeton, was a sophomore or something. Really she had no distinct idea of him. An ancient snapshot she had preserved in an old Kodak book had impressed her by the big eyes (which he had probably grown up to by now). However, in the last month, when her winter visit to Sally had been decided on, he had assumed the proportions of a worthy adversary. Children, most astute of matchmakers, plot their campaigns quickly, and Sally had played a clever correspondence sonata to Isabelle's excitable temperament. Isabelle had been for some time capable of very strong, if very transient emotions . . .

They drew up at a spreading, white-stone building, set back from the snowy street. Mrs Weatherby greeted her warmly and her various younger cousins were produced from the corners where they skulked politely. Isabelle met them tactfully. At her best she allied all with whom she came in contact – except older girls and some women. All the impressions she made were conscious. The half-dozen girls she renewed acquaintance with that morning were all rather impressed and as much by her direct personality as by her reputation. Amory Blaine was an open subject. Evidently a bit light of love, neither popular nor unpopular – every girl there seemed to have had an affair with him at sometime or other, but no one volunteered any really useful information. He was going to fall for her . . . Sally had published that information to her young set and they were retailing it back to Sally as fast as they set eyes on Isabelle. Isabelle resolved secretly that she would, if necessary, *force* herself to like him – she owed it to Sally. Suppose she were terribly disappointed. Sally had painted him in such glowing colours – he was good-looking, 'sort of distinguished, when he wants to be', had a line, and was properly inconstant. In fact, he summed up all the romance that her age and environment led her to desire. She wondered if those were his dancing-shoes that fox-trotted tentatively around the soft rug below.

All impressions and, in fact, all ideas were extremely kaleidoscopic to Isabelle. She had that curious mixture of the social and the artistic temperaments found often in two classes, society women and actresses. Her education or, rather, her sophistication, had been absorbed from the boys who had dangled on her favour; her tact was instinctive, and her capacity for love-affairs was limited only by the number of the susceptible within telephone distance. Flirt smiled from her large black-brown eyes and shone through her intense physical magnetism.

So she waited at the head of the stairs that evening while slippers were fetched. Just as she was growing impatient, Sally came out of the dressing-room, beaming with her accustomed good nature and high spirits, and together they descended to the floor below, while the shifting searchlight of Isabelle's mind flashed on two ideas: she was glad she had high colour tonight, and she wondered if he danced well.

Downstairs, in the club's great room, she was surrounded for a moment by the girls she had met in the afternoon, then she heard Sally's voice repeating a cycle of names, and found herself bowing to a sextet of black and white, terribly stiff, vaguely familiar figures. The name Blaine figured somewhere, but at first she could not place him. A very confused, very juvenile moment of awkward backings and bumpings followed, and everyone found himself talking to the person he least desired to. Isabelle manoeuvred herself and Froggy Parker, freshman at Harvard, with whom she had once played hopscotch, to a seat on the stairs. A humorous reference to the past was all she needed. The things Isabelle could do socially with one idea were remarkable. First, she repeated it rapturously in an enthusiastic contralto with a soupçon of Southern accent; then she held it off at a distance and smiled at it – her wonderful smile; then she delivered it in variations and played a sort of mental catch with it, all this in the nominal form of dialogue. Froggy was fascinated and quite unconscious that this was being done, not for him, but for the green eyes that glistened under the shining carefully watered hair, a little to her left, for Isabelle had discovered Amory. As an actress even in the fullest flush of her own conscious magnetism gets a deep impression of most of the people in the front row, so Isabelle sized up her antagonist. First, he had auburn hair, and from her feeling of disappointment she knew that she had expected him to be dark and of garter-advertisement slenderness . . . For the rest, a faint flush and a straight, romantic profile; the effect set off by a close-fitting dress suit and a silk ruffled shirt of the kind that women still delight to see men wear, but men were just beginning to get tired of.

During this inspection Amory was quietly watching.

'Don't *you* think so?' she said suddenly, turning to him, innocent-eyed.

There was a stir, and Sally led the way over to their table. Amory struggled to Isabelle's side, and whispered: 'You're my dinner partner, you know. We're all coached for each other.'

Isabelle gasped – this was rather right in line. But really she felt as if a good speech had been taken from the star and given to a minor character . . . She mustn't lose the leadership a bit. The dinner-table glittered with laughter at the confusion of getting places and then curious eyes were turned on her, sitting near the head. She was enjoying this immensely, and Froggy Parker was so engrossed with the added sparkle of her rising colour that he forgot to pull out Sally's chair, and fell into a dim confusion. Amory was on the other side, full of confidence and vanity, gazing at her in open admiration. He began directly, and so did Froggy:

'I've heard a lot about you since you wore braids –'

'Wasn't it funny this afternoon –'

Both stopped. Isabelle turned to Amory shyly. Her face was always enough answer for anyone, but she decided to speak.

'How – from whom?'

'From everybody – for all the years since you've been away.' She blushed appropriately. On her right Froggy was *hors de combat* already, although he hadn't quite realised it.

'I'll tell you what I remembered about you all these years,' Amory continued. She leaned slightly towards him and looked modestly at the celery before her. Froggy sighed – he knew Amory, and the situations that Amory seemed born to handle. He turned to Sally and asked her if she was going away to school next year. Amory opened with grapeshot.

'I've got an adjective that just fits you.' This was one of his favourite starts – he seldom had a word in mind, but it was a curiosity provoker, and he could always produce something complimentary if he got in a tight corner.

'Oh – what?' Isabelle's face was a study in enraptured curiosity.

Amory shook his head.

'I don't know you very well yet.'

'Will you tell me – afterwards?' she half whispered.

He nodded.

'We'll sit out.'

Isabelle nodded.

'Did anyone ever tell you, you have keen eyes?' she said.

Amory attempted to make them look even keener. He fancied, but he was not sure, that her foot had just touched his under the table. But it might possibly have been only the table leg. It was so hard to tell. Still it thrilled him. He wondered quickly if there would be any difficulty in securing the little den upstairs.

BABES IN THE WOODS

Isabelle and Amory were distinctly not innocent, nor were they particularly brazen. Moreover, amateur standing had very little value in the game they were playing, a game that would presumably be her principal study for years to come. She had begun as he had, with good looks and an excitable temperament, and the rest was the result of accessible popular novels and dressing-room conversation culled from a slightly older set. Isabelle had walked with an artificial gait at nine and a half, and when her eyes, wide and starry, proclaimed the ingenue most. Amory was proportionately less deceived. He waited for the mask to drop off, but at the same time he did not question her right to wear it. She, on her part, was not impressed by his studied air of blasé sophistication. She had lived in a larger city and had slightly an advantage in range. But she accepted his pose – it was one of the dozen little conventions of this kind of affair. He was aware that he was getting this particular favour now because she had been coached; he knew that he stood for merely the best game in sight, and that he would have to improve his opportunity before he lost his advantage. So they proceeded with an infinite guile that would have horrified her parents.

After the dinner the dance began . . . smoothly. Smoothly? – boys cut in on Isabelle every few feet and then squabbled in the corners with: 'You might let me get more than an inch!' and, 'She didn't like it either – she told me so next time I cut in.' It was true – she told everyone so, and gave every hand a parting pressure that said: 'You know that your dances are *making* my evening.'

But time passed, two hours of it, and the less subtle beaux had better learned to focus their pseudo-passionate glances elsewhere, for eleven o'clock found Isabelle and Amory sitting on the couch in the little den off the reading-room upstairs. She was conscious that they were a handsome pair, and seemed to belong distinctively in this seclusion, while lesser lights fluttered and chattered downstairs.

Boys who passed the door looked in enviously – girls who passed only laughed and frowned and grew wise within themselves.

They had now reached a very definite stage. They had traded accounts of their progress since they had met last, and she had listened to much she had heard before. He was a sophomore, was on the *Princetonian* board, hoped to be chairman in senior year. He learned that some of the boys she went with in Baltimore were 'terrible speeds' and came to dances in states of artificial stimulation; most of them were twenty or so, and drove alluring red Stutzes. A good half seemed already to have flunked out of various schools and colleges, but some of them bore athletic names that made him look at her admiringly. As a matter of fact, Isabelle's closer acquaintance with the universities was just commencing. She had bowing acquaintance with a lot of young men who thought she was a 'pretty kid – worth keeping an eye on'. But Isabelle strung the names into a fabrication of gaiety that would have dazzled a Viennese nobleman. Such is the power of young contralto voices on sink-down sofas.

He asked her if she thought he was conceited. She said there was a difference between conceit and self-confidence. She adored self-confidence in men.

'Is Froggy a good friend of yours?' she asked.

'Rather – why?'

'He's a bum dancer.'

Amory laughed.

'He dances as if the girl were on his back instead of in his arms.'

She appreciated this.

'You're awfully good at sizing people up.'

Amory denied this painfully. However, he sized up several people for her. Then they talked about hands.

'You've got awfully nice hands,' she said. 'They look as if you played the piano. Do you?'

I have said they had reached a very definite stage – nay, more, a very critical stage. Amory had stayed over a day to see her, and his train left at twelve-eighteen that night. His trunk and suitcase awaited him at the station; his watch was beginning to hang heavy in his pocket.

'Isabelle,' he said suddenly, 'I want to tell you something.' They had been talking lightly about 'that funny look in her eyes', and Isabelle knew from the change in his manner what was coming – indeed, she had been wondering how soon it would come. Amory reached above their heads and turned out the electric light, so that they were in the dark, except for the red glow that fell through the door from the reading-room lamps.

Then he began: 'I don't know whether or not you know what you – what I'm going to say. Lordy, Isabelle – this *sounds* like a line, but it isn't.'

'I know,' said Isabelle softly.

'Maybe we'll never meet again like this – I have darned hard luck sometimes.' He was leaning away from her on the other arm of the lounge, but she could see his eyes plainly in the dark.

'You'll meet me again – silly.' There was just the slightest emphasis on the last word – so that it became almost a term of endearment. He continued a bit huskily: 'I've fallen for a lot of people – girls – and I guess you have, too – boys, I mean, but, honestly, you – ' he broke off suddenly and leaned forward, chin on his hands: 'Oh, what's the use – you'll go your way and I suppose I'll go mine.'

Silence for a moment. Isabelle was quite stirred; she wound her handkerchief into a tight ball, and by the faint light that streamed over her, dropped it deliberately on the floor. Their hands touched for an instant, but neither spoke. Silences were becoming more frequent and more delicious. Outside another stray couple had come up and were experimenting on the piano in the next room. After the usual preliminary of 'chopsticks', one of them started 'Babes in the Woods' and a light tenor carried the words into the den:

'Give me your hand –
I'll understand
We're off to slumberland.'

Isabelle hummed it softly and trembled as she felt Amory's hand close over hers.

'Isabelle,' he whispered. 'You know I'm mad about you. You *do* give a darn about me.'

'Yes.'

'How much do you care – do you like anyone better?'

'No.' He could scarcely hear her, although he bent so near that he felt her breath against his cheek.

'Isabelle, I'm going back to college for six long months, and why shouldn't we – if I could only just have one thing to remember you by – '

'Close the door . . . ' Her voice had just stirred so that he half wondered whether she had spoken at all. As he swung the door softly shut, the music seemed quivering just outside.

'Moonlight is bright,
Kiss me good-night.'

What a wonderful song, she thought – everything was wonderful tonight, most of all this romantic scene in the den, with their hands clinging and the inevitable looming charmingly close. The future vista of her life seemed an unending succession of scenes like this: under moonlight and pale starlight, and in the backs of warm limousines and in low, cosy roadsters stopped under sheltering trees – only the boy might change, and this one was *so* nice. He took her hand softly. With a sudden movement he turned it and, holding it to his lips, kissed the palm.

'Isabelle!' His whisper blended in the music, and they seemed to float nearer together. Her breath came faster. 'Can't I kiss you, Isabelle – Isabelle?' Lips half parted, she turned her head to him in the dark. Suddenly the ring of voices, the sound of running footsteps surged towards them. Quick as a flash Amory reached up and turned on the light, and when the door opened and three boys, the wrathy and dance-craving Froggy among them, rushed in, he was turning over the magazines on the table, while she sat without moving, serene and unembarrassed, and even greeted them with a welcoming smile. But her heart was beating wildly, and she felt somehow as if she had been deprived.

It was evidently over. There was a clamour for a dance, there was a glance that passed between them – on his side despair, on hers regret, and then the evening went on, with the reassured beaux and the eternal cutting in.

At quarter to twelve Amory shook hands with her gravely, in the midst of a small crowd assembled to wish him good-speed. For an instant he lost his poise, and she felt a bit rattled when a satirical voice from a concealed wit cried: 'Take her outside, Amory!' As he took her hand he pressed it a little, and she returned the pressure as she had done to twenty hands that evening – that was all.

At two o'clock back at the Weatherbys' Sally asked her if she and Amory had had a 'time' in the den. Isabelle turned to her quietly. In her eyes was the light of the idealist, the inviolate dreamer of Joan-like dreams.

'No,' she answered. 'I don't do that sort of thing any more; he asked me to, but I said no.'

As she crept into bed she wondered what he'd say in his special delivery tomorrow. He had such a good-looking mouth – would she ever – ?

'Fourteen angels were watching o'er them,' sang Sally sleepily from the next room.

'Damn!' muttered Isabelle, punching the pillow into a luxurious lump and exploring the cold sheets cautiously. 'Damn!'

CARNIVAL

Amory, by way of the *Princetonian*, had arrived. The minor snobs, finely balanced thermometers of success, warmed to him as the club elections grew nigh, and he and Tom were visited by groups of upperclassmen who arrived awkwardly, balanced on the edges of the furniture and talked of all subjects except the one of absorbing interest. Amory was amused at the intent eyes upon him, and, in case the visitors represented some club in which he was not interested, took great pleasure in shocking them with unorthodox remarks.

'Oh, let me see – ' he said one night to a flabbergasted delegation, 'what club do you represent?'

With visitors from Ivy and Cottage and Tiger Inn he played the 'nice, unspoilt, ingenuous boy' very much at ease and quite unaware of the object of the call.

When the fatal morning arrived, early in March, and the campus became a document in hysteria, he slid smoothly into Cottage with Alec Connage and watched his suddenly neurotic class with much wonder.

There were fickle groups that jumped from club to club; there were friends of two or three days who announced tearfully and wildly that they must join the same club, nothing should separate them; there were snarling disclosures of long-hidden grudges as the Suddenly Prominent remembered snubs of freshman year. Unknown men were elevated into importance when they received certain coveted bids; others who were considered 'all set' found that they had made unexpected enemies, felt themselves stranded and deserted, talked wildly of leaving college.

In his own crowd Amory saw men kept out for wearing green hats, for being 'a damn tailor's dummy', for having 'too much pull in heaven', for getting drunk one night 'not like a gentleman, by God', or for unfathomable secret reasons known to no one but the wielders of the black balls.

This orgy of sociability culminated in a gigantic party at the Nassau

Inn, where punch was dispensed from immense bowls, and the whole downstairs became a delirious, circulating, shouting pattern of faces and voices.

'Hi, Dibby – 'gratulations!'

'Goo' boy, Tom, you got a good bunch in Cap.'

'Say, Kerry – '

'Oh, Kerry – I hear you went Tiger with all the weight-lifters!' 'Well, I didn't go Cottage – the parlour-snakes' delight.'

'They say Overton fainted when he got his Ivy bid – Did he sign up the first day? – oh, *no*. Tore over to Murray-Dodge on a bicycle – afraid it was a mistake.'

'How'd you get into Cap – you old roué?'

' 'Gratulations!'

' 'Gratulations yourself. Hear you got a good crowd.'

When the bar closed, the party broke up into groups and streamed, singing, over the snow-clad campus, in a weird delusion that snobbishness and strain were over at last, and that they could do what they pleased for the next two years.

Long afterwards Amory thought of sophomore spring as the happiest time of his life. His ideas were in tune with life as he found it; he wanted no more than to drift and dream and enjoy a dozen new-found friendships through the April afternoons.

Alec Connage came into his room one morning and woke him up into the sunshine and peculiar glory of Campbell Hall shining in the window.

'Wake up, Original Sin, and scrape yourself together. Be in front of Renwick's in half an hour. Somebody's got a car.' He took the bureau cover and carefully deposited it, with its load of small articles, upon the bed.

'Where'd you get the car?' demanded Amory cynically.

'Sacred trust, but don't be a critical goopher or you can't go!'

'I think I'll sleep,' Amory said calmly, resettling himself and reaching beside the bed for a cigarette.

'Sleep!'

'Why not? I've got a class at eleven-thirty.'

'You damned gloom! Of course, if you don't want to go to the coast – '

With a bound Amory was out of bed, scattering the bureau cover's burden on the floor. The coast . . . he hadn't seen it for years, since he and his mother were on their pilgrimage.

'Who's going?' he demanded as he wriggled into his BVD's.

'Oh, Dick Humbird and Kerry Holiday and Jesse Ferrenby and – oh about five or six. Speed it up, kid!'

In ten minutes Amory was devouring cornflakes in Renwick's, and at nine-thirty they bowled happily out of town, headed for the sands of Deal Beach.

'You see,' said Kerry, 'the car belongs down there. In fact, it was stolen from Asbury Park by persons unknown, who deserted it in Princeton and left for the West. Heartless Humbird here got permission from the city council to deliver it.'

'Anybody got any money?' suggested Ferrenby, turning around from the front seat.

There was an emphatic negative chorus.

'That makes it interesting.'

'Money – what's money? We can sell the car.'

'Charge him salvage or something.'

'How're we going to get food?' asked Amory.

'Honestly,' answered Kerry, eying him reprovingly, 'do you doubt Kerry's ability for three short days? Some people have lived on nothing for years at a time. Read the *Boy Scout Monthly*.'

'Three days,' Amory mused, 'and I've got classes.'

'One of the days is the Sabbath.'

'Just the same, I can only cut six more classes, with over a month and a half to go.'

'Throw him out!'

'It's a long walk back.'

'Amory, you're running it out, if I may coin a new phrase.'

'Hadn't you better get some dope on yourself, Amory?'

Amory subsided resignedly and drooped into a contemplation of the scenery. Swinburne seemed to fit in somehow.

> Oh, winter's rains and ruins are over,
>   And all the seasons of snows and sins;
> The days dividing lover and lover,
>   The light that loses, the night that wins;
> And time remembered is grief forgotten,
> And frosts are slain and flowers begotten,
> And in green underwood and cover,
>   Blossom by blossom the spring begins.
>
> The full streams feed on flower of –

'What's the matter, Amory? Amory's thinking about poetry, about the pretty birds and flowers. I can see it in his eye.'

'No, I'm not,' he lied. 'I'm thinking about the *Princetonian*. I ought to make up tonight; but I can telephone back, I suppose.'

'Oh,' said Kerry respectfully, 'these important men –'

Amory flushed and it seemed to him that Ferrenby, a defeated competitor, winced a little. Of course, Kerry was only kidding, but he really mustn't mention the *Princetonian*.

It was a halcyon day, and as they neared the shore and the salt breezes scurried by, he began to picture the ocean and long, level stretches of sand and red roofs over blue sea. Then they hurried through the little town and it all flashed upon his consciousness to a mighty paean of emotion . . .

'Oh, good Lord! *Look* at it!' he cried.

'What?'

'Let me out, quick – I haven't seen it for eight years! Oh, gentlefolk, stop the car!'

'What an odd child!' remarked Alec.

'I do believe he's a bit eccentric.'

The car was obligingly drawn up at a curb, and Amory ran for the boardwalk. First, he realised that the sea was blue and that there was an enormous quantity of it, and that it roared and roared – really all the banalities about the ocean that one could realise, but if anyone had told him then that these things were banalities, he would have gaped in wonder.

'Now we'll get lunch,' ordered Kerry, wandering up with the crowd. 'Come on, Amory, tear yourself away and get practical.'

'We'll try the best hotel first,' he went on, 'and thence and so forth.'

They strolled along the boardwalk to the most imposing hostelry in sight, and, entering the dining-room, scattered about a table.

'Eight Bronxes,' commanded Alec, 'and a club sandwich and Juliennes. The food for one. Hand the rest around.'

Amory ate little, having seized a chair where he could watch the sea and feel the rock of it. When luncheon was over they sat and smoked quietly.

'What's the bill?'

Someone scanned it.

'Eight twenty-five.'

'Rotten overcharge. We'll give them two dollars and one for the waiter. Kerry, collect the small change.'

The waiter approached, and Kerry gravely handed him a dollar, tossed two dollars on the check, and turned away. They sauntered leisurely towards the door, pursued in a moment by the suspicious Ganymede.

'Some mistake, sir.'

Kerry took the bill and examined it critically.

'No mistake!' he said, shaking his head gravely, and, tearing it into four pieces, he handed the scraps to the waiter, who was so dumfounded that he stood motionless and expressionless while they walked out.

'Won't he send after us?'

'No,' said Kerry; 'for a minute he'll think we're the proprietor's sons or something; then he'll look at the check again and call the manager, and in the meantime – '

They left the car at Asbury and street-car'd to Allenhurst, where they investigated the crowded pavilions for beauty. At four there were refreshments in a lunch-room, and this time they paid an even smaller per cent on the total cost; something about the appearance and *savoir-faire* of the crowd made the thing go, and they were not pursued.

'You see, Amory, we're Marxian Socialists,' explained Kerry. 'We don't believe in property and we're putting it to the great test.'

'Night will descend,' Amory suggested.

'Watch, and put your trust in Holiday.'

They became jovial about five-thirty and, linking arms, strolled up and down the boardwalk in a row, chanting a monotonous ditty about the sad sea waves. Then Kerry saw a face in the crowd that attracted him and, rushing off, reappeared in a moment with one of the homeliest girls Amory had ever set eyes on. Her pale mouth extended from ear to ear, her teeth projected in a solid wedge, and she had little, squinty eyes that peeped ingratiatingly over the side sweep of her nose. Kerry presented them formally.

'Name of Kaluka, Hawaiian queen! Let me present Messrs Connage, Sloane, Humbird, Ferrenby and Blaine.'

The girl bobbed courtesies all around. Poor creature; Amory supposed she had never before been noticed in her life – possibly she was half-witted. While she accompanied them (Kerry had invited her to supper) she said nothing which could discountenance such a belief.

'She prefers her native dishes,' said Alec gravely to the waiter, 'but any coarse food will do.'

All through supper he addressed her in the most respectful language, while Kerry made idiotic love to her on the other side, and she giggled and grinned. Amory was content to sit and watch the by-play, thinking what a light touch Kerry had, and how he could transform the barest incident into a thing of curve and contour. They all seemed to have the spirit of it more or less, and it was a relaxation to be with them. Amory usually liked men individually, yet feared them in crowds unless the crowd was around him. He wondered how much each one contributed to the party, for there was somewhat of a spiritual tax levied. Alec and Kerry were the life of it, but not quite the centre. Somehow the quiet Humbird and Sloane, with his impatient superciliousness, were the centre.

Dick Humbird had, ever since freshman year, seemed to Amory a perfect type of aristocrat. He was slender but well-built – black curly hair, straight features, and rather a dark skin. Everything he said sounded intangibly appropriate. He possessed infinite courage, an averagely good mind, and a sense of honour with a clear charm and *noblesse oblige* that varied it from righteousness. He could dissipate without going to pieces, and even his most bohemian adventures never seemed 'running it out'. People dressed like him, tried to talk as he did . . . Amory decided that he probably held the world back, but he wouldn't have changed him . . .

He differed from the healthy type that was essentially middle class – he never seemed to perspire. Some people couldn't be familiar with a chauffeur without having it returned; Humbird could have lunched at Sherry's with a coloured man, yet people would have somehow known that it was all right. He was not a snob, though he knew only half his class. His friends ranged from the highest to the lowest, but it was impossible to 'cultivate' him. Servants worshipped him, and treated him like a god. He seemed the eternal example of what the upper class tries to be.

'He's like those pictures in the *Illustrated London News* of the English officers who have been killed,' Amory had said to Alec. 'Well,' Alec had answered, 'if you want to know the shocking truth, his father was a grocery clerk who made a fortune in Tacoma real estate and came to New York ten years ago.'

Amory had felt a curious sinking sensation.

This present type of party was made possible by the surging together of the class after club elections – as if to make a last desperate attempt to know itself, to keep together, to fight off the tightening spirit of the clubs. It was a let-down from the conventional heights they had all walked so rigidly.

After supper they saw Kaluka to the boardwalk, and then strolled back along the beach to Asbury. The evening sea was a new sensation, for all its colour and mellow age was gone, and it seemed the bleak waste that made the Norse sagas sad; Amory thought of Kipling's 'Beaches of Lukannon before the sealers came'.

It was still a music, though infinitely sorrowful.

Ten o'clock found them penniless. They had suppered greatly on their last eleven cents and, singing, strolled up through the casinos and lighted arches on the boardwalk, stopping to listen approvingly to all band concerts. In one place Kerry took up a collection for the French War Orphans which netted a dollar and twenty cents, and with this they bought some brandy in case they caught cold in the night. They finished the day in a moving-picture show and went into solemn systematic roars of laughter at an ancient comedy, to the startled annoyance of the rest of the audience. Their entrance was distinctly strategic, for each man as he entered pointed reproachfully at the one just behind him. Sloane, bringing up the rear, disclaimed all knowledge and responsibility as soon as the others were scattered inside; then as the irate ticket-taker rushed in he followed nonchalantly.

They reassembled later by the Casino and made arrangements for the night. Kerry wormed permission from the watchman to sleep on the platform and, having collected a huge pile of rugs from the booths to serve as mattresses and blankets, they talked until midnight, and then fell into a dreamless sleep, though Amory tried hard to stay awake and watch that marvellous moon settle on the sea.

So they progressed for two happy days, up and down the shore by street-car or machine, or by shoe-leather on the crowded boardwalk; sometimes eating with the wealthy, more frequently dining frugally at the expense of an unsuspecting restaurateur. They had their photos taken, eight poses, in a quick-development store. Kerry insisted on grouping them as a 'varsity' football team, and then as a tough gang from the East Side, with their coats inside out, and himself sitting in the middle on a cardboard moon. The photographer probably has them yet – at least, they never called for them. The weather was perfect, and again they slept outside, and again Amory fell unwillingly asleep.

Sunday broke stolid and respectable, and even the sea seemed to mumble and complain, so they returned to Princeton via the Fords of transient farmers, and broke up with colds in their heads, but otherwise none the worse for wandering.

Even more than in the year before, Amory neglected his work, not deliberately but lazily and through a multitude of other interests. Coordinate geometry and the melancholy hexameters of Corneille and Racine held forth small allurements, and even psychology, which he had eagerly awaited, proved to be a dull subject full of muscular reactions and biological phrases rather than the study of personality and influence. That was a noon class, and it always sent him dozing. Having found that, 'Subjective and objective, sir,' answered most of the questions, he used the phrase on all occasions, and it became the class joke when, on a query being levelled at him, he was nudged awake by Ferrenby or Sloane to gasp it out.

Mostly there were parties – to Orange or the Shore, more rarely to New York and Philadelphia, though one night they marshalled fourteen waitresses out of Childs' and took them to ride down Fifth Avenue on top of an auto bus. They all cut more classes than were allowed, which meant an additional course the following year, but spring was too rare to let anything interfere with their colourful ramblings. In May Amory was elected to the Sophomore Prom Committee, and when after a long evening's discussion with Alec they made out a tentative list of class probabilities for the Senior Council, they placed themselves among the surest. The Senior Council was composed presumably of the eighteen most representative seniors, and in view of Alec's football managership and Amory's chance of nosing out Burne Holiday as *Princetonian* chairman, they seemed fairly justified in this presumption. Oddly enough, they both placed D'Invilliers as among the possibilities, a guess that a year before the class would have gaped at.

All through the spring Amory had kept up an intermittent correspondence with Isabelle Borge, punctuated by violent squabbles and chiefly enlivened by his attempts to find new words for love. He discovered Isabelle to be discreetly and aggravatingly unsentimental in letters, but he hoped against hope that she would prove not too exotic a bloom to fit the large spaces of spring as she had fitted the den in the Minnehaha Club. During May he wrote thirty-page documents almost nightly, and sent them to her in bulky envelopes exteriorly labelled 'Part I' and 'Part II'.

'Oh, Alec, I believe I'm tired of college,' he said sadly, as they walked the dusk together.

'I think I am, too, in a way.'

'All I'd like would be a little home in the country, some warm country, and a wife, and just enough to do to keep from rotting.'

'Me, too.'

'I'd like to quit.'

'What does your girl say?'

'Oh!' Amory gasped in horror. 'She wouldn't *think* of marrying . . . that is, not now. I mean the future, you know.'

'My girl would. I'm engaged.'

'Are you really?'

'Yes. Don't say a word to anybody, please, but I am. I may not come back next year.'

'But you're only twenty! Give up college?'

'Why, Amory, you were saying a minute ago – '

'Yes,' Amory interrupted, 'but I was just wishing. I wouldn't think of leaving college. It's just that I feel so sad these wonderful nights. I sort of feel they're never coming again, and I'm not really getting all I could out of them. I wish my girl lived here. But marry – not a chance. Especially as father says the money isn't forthcoming as it used to be.'

'What a waste these nights are!' agreed Alec.

But Amory sighed and made use of the nights. He had a snapshot of Isabelle, enshrined in an old watch, and at eight almost every night he would turn off all the lights except the desk lamp and, sitting by the open windows with the picture before him, write her rapturous letters.

> . . . Oh it's so hard to write you what I really *feel* when I think about you so much; you've gotten to mean to me a *dream* that I can't put on paper any more. Your last letter came and it was wonderful! I read it over about six times, especially the *last* part, but I do wish, sometimes, you'd be more *frank* and tell me what you really do think of me, yet your last letter was too good to be true, and I can hardly wait until June! Be sure and be able to come to the prom. It'll be fine, I think, and I want to bring *you* just at the end of a wonderful year. I often think over what you said on that night and wonder how much you meant. If it were anyone but you – but you see I *thought* you were fickle the first time I saw you and you are so popular and everything that I can't imagine you really liking me *best*.
>
> Oh, Isabelle, dear – it's a wonderful night. Somebody is playing 'Love Moon' on a mandolin far across the campus, and the music seems to bring you into the window. Now he's playing 'Goodbye, Boys, I'm Through', and how well it suits me. For I *am* through with everything. I have decided never to take a cocktail again, and I know I'll never again fall in love – I couldn't – you've been too much

a part of my days and nights to ever let me think of another girl. I meet them all the time and they don't interest me. I'm not pretending to be blasé, because it's not that. It's just that I'm in love. Oh, *dearest* Isabelle (somehow I can't call you just Isabelle, and I'm afraid I'll come out with the 'dearest' before your family this June), you've got to come to the prom, and then I'll come up to your house for a day and everything'll be perfect . . .

And so on in an eternal monotone that seemed to both of them infinitely charming, infinitely new.

June came and the days grew so hot and lazy that they could not worry even about exams, but spent dreamy evenings on the court of Cottage, talking of long subjects until the sweep of country towards Stony Brook became a blue haze and the lilacs were white around tennis-courts, and words gave way to silent cigarettes . . . Then down deserted Prospect and along McCosh with song everywhere around them, up to the hot joviality of Nassau Street.

Tom D'Invilliers and Amory walked late in those days. A gambling fever swept through the sophomore class and they bent over the bones till three o'clock many a sultry night. After one session they came out of Sloane's room to find the dew fallen and the stars old in the sky.

'Let's borrow bicycles and take a ride,' Amory suggested.

'All right. I'm not a bit tired and this is almost the last night of the year, really, because the prom stuff starts Monday.'

They found two unlocked bicycles in Holder Court and rode out about half-past three along the Lawrenceville Road.

'What are you going to do this summer, Amory?'

'Don't ask me – same old things, I suppose. A month or two in Lake Geneva – I'm counting on you to be there in July, you know – then there'll be Minneapolis, and that means hundreds of summer hops, parlour-snaking, getting bored – But oh, Tom,' he added suddenly, 'hasn't this year been slick!'

'No,' declared Tom emphatically, a new Tom, clothed by Brooks, shod by Franks, 'I've won this game, but I feel as if I never want to play another. You're all right – you're a rubber ball, and somehow it suits you, but I'm sick of adapting myself to the local snobbishness of this corner of the world. I want to go where people aren't barred because of the colour of their neckties and the roll of their coats.'

'You can't, Tom,' argued Amory, as they rolled along through the scattering night; 'wherever you go now you'll always unconsciously apply these standards of "having it" or "lacking it". For better or worse we've stamped you; you're a Princeton type!'

'Well, then,' complained Tom, his cracked voice rising plaintively, 'why do I have to come back at all? I've learned all that Princeton has to offer. Two years more of mere pedantry and lying around a club aren't going to help. They're just going to disorganise me, conventionalise me completely. Even now I'm so spineless that I wonder how I get away with it.'

'Oh, but you're missing the real point, Tom,' Amory interrupted. 'You've just had your eyes opened to the snobbishness of the world in a rather abrupt manner. Princeton invariably gives the thoughtful man a social sense.'

'You consider you taught me that, don't you?' he asked quizzically, eying Amory in the half dark.

Amory laughed quietly.

'Didn't I?'

'Sometimes,' he said slowly, 'I think you're my bad angel. I might have been a pretty fair poet.'

'Come on, that's rather hard. You chose to come to an Eastern college. Either your eyes were opened to the mean scrambling quality of people, or you'd have gone through blind, and you'd hate to have done that – been like Marty Kaye.'

'Yes,' he agreed, 'you're right. I wouldn't have liked it. Still, it's hard to be made a cynic at twenty.'

'I was born one,' Amory murmured. 'I'm a cynical idealist.' He paused and wondered if that meant anything.

They reached the sleeping school of Lawrenceville, and turned to ride back.

'It's good, this ride, isn't it?' Tom said presently.

'Yes; it's a good finish, it's knock-out; everything's good tonight. Oh, for a hot, languorous summer and Isabelle!'

'Oh, you and your Isabelle! I'll bet she's a simple one . . . let's say some poetry.'

So Amory declaimed the 'Ode to a Nightingale' to the bushes they passed.

'I'll never be a poet,' said Amory as he finished. 'I'm not enough of a sensualist really; there are only a few obvious things that I notice as primarily beautiful: women, spring evenings, music at night, the sea; I don't catch the subtle things like "silver-snarling trumpets". I may turn out an intellectual, but I'll never write anything but mediocre poetry.'

They rode into Princeton as the sun was making coloured maps of the sky behind the graduate school, and hurried to the refreshment of a shower that would have to serve in place of sleep. By noon the bright-costumed alumni crowded the streets with their bands and choruses, and in the tents there was great reunion under the orange-and-black banners that curled and strained in the wind. Amory looked long at one house which bore the legend 'Sixty-nine'. There a few grey-haired men sat and talked quietly while the classes swept by in panorama of life.

UNDER THE ARC-LIGHT

Then tragedy's emerald eyes glared suddenly at Amory over the edge of June. On the night after his ride to Lawrenceville a crowd sallied to New York in quest of adventure, and started back to Princeton about twelve o'clock in two machines. It had been a gay party and different stages of sobriety were represented. Amory was in the car behind; they had taken the wrong road and lost the way, and so were hurrying to catch up.

It was a clear night and the exhilaration of the road went to Amory's head. He had the ghost of two stanzas of a poem forming in his mind . . .

> So the grey car crept nightwards in the dark and there was no life stirred as it went by . . . As the still ocean paths before the shark in starred and glittering waterways, beauty-high, the moon-swathed trees divided, pair on pair, while flapping nightbirds cried across the air . . .
>
> A moment by an inn of lamps and shades, a yellow inn under a yellow moon – then silence, where crescendo laughter fades . . . the car swung out again to the winds of June, mellowed the shadows where the distance grew, then crushed the yellow shadows into blue . . .

They jolted to a stop, and Amory peered up, startled. A woman was standing beside the road, talking to Alec at the wheel. Afterwards he remembered the harpy effect that her old kimono gave her, and the cracked hollowness of her voice as she spoke: 'You Princeton boys?'

'Yes.'

'Well, there's one of you killed here, and two others about dead.'

'*My God!*'

'Look!' She pointed and they gazed in horror. Under the full light of a roadside arc-light lay a form, face downward in a widening circle of blood.

They sprang from the car. Amory thought of the back of that head – that hair – that hair . . . and then they turned the form over.

'It's Dick – Dick Humbird!'

'Oh, Christ!'

'Feel his heart!'

Then the insistent voice of the old crone in a sort of croaking triumph: 'He's quite dead, all right. The car turned over. Two of the men that weren't hurt just carried the others in, but this one's no use.'

Amory rushed into the house and the rest followed with a limp mass that they laid on the sofa in the shoddy little front parlour. Sloane, with his shoulder punctured, was on another lounge. He was half delirious, and kept calling something about a chemistry lecture at 8:10.

'I don't know what happened,' said Ferrenby in a strained voice. 'Dick was driving and he wouldn't give up the wheel; we told him he'd been drinking too much – then there was this damn curve – oh, my *God*! . . . ' He threw himself face downwards on the floor and broke into dry sobs.

The doctor had arrived, and Amory went over to the couch, where someone handed him a sheet to put over the body. With a sudden hardness, he raised one of the hands and let it fall back inertly. The brow was cold but the face not expressionless. He looked at the shoelaces – Dick had tied them that morning. *He* had tied them – and now he was this heavy white mass. All that remained of the charm and personality of the Dick Humbird he had known – oh, it was all so horrible and unaristocratic and close to the earth. All tragedy has that strain of the grotesque and squalid – so useless, futile . . . the way animals die . . . Amory was reminded of a cat that had lain horribly mangled in some alley of his childhood.

'Someone go to Princeton with Ferrenby.'

Amory stepped outside the door and shivered slightly at the late night wind – a wind that stirred a broken fender on the mass of bent metal to a plaintive, tinny sound.

CRESCENDO!

Next day, by a merciful chance, passed in a whirl. When Amory was by himself his thoughts zigzagged inevitably to the picture of that red mouth yawning incongruously in the white face, but with a determined effort he piled present excitement upon the memory of it and shut it coldly away from his mind.

Isabelle and her mother drove into town at four, and they rode up smiling Prospect Avenue, through the gay crowd, to have tea at Cottage. The clubs had their annual dinners that night, so at seven he loaned her to a freshman and arranged to meet her in the gymnasium at eleven, when the upperclassmen were admitted to the freshman dance. She was all he had expected, and he was happy and eager to make that night the centre of every dream. At nine the upper classes stood in front of the clubs as the freshman torchlight parade rioted past, and Amory wondered if the dress-suited groups against the dark, stately backgrounds and under the flare of the torches made the night as brilliant to the staring, cheering freshmen as it had been to him the year before.

The next day was another whirl. They lunched in a gay party of six in a private dining-room at the club, while Isabelle and Amory looked at each other tenderly over the fried chicken and knew that their love was to be eternal. They danced away the prom until five, and the stags cut in on Isabelle with joyous abandon, which grew more and more enthusiastic as the hour grew late, and their wines, stored in overcoat pockets in the coat room, made old weariness wait until another day. The stag line is a most homogeneous mass of men. It fairly sways with a single soul. A dark-haired beauty dances by and there is a half-gasping sound as the ripple surges forward and someone sleeker than the rest darts out and cuts in. Then when the six-foot girl (brought by Kaye in your class, and to whom he has been trying to introduce you all evening) gallops by, the line surges back and the groups face about and become intent on far corners of the hall, for Kaye, anxious and perspiring, appears elbowing through the crowd in search of familiar faces.

'I say, old man, I've got an awfully nice – '

'Sorry, Kaye, but I'm set for this one. I've got to cut in on a fella.'

'Well, the next one?'

'What – ah – er – I swear I've got to go cut in – look me up when she's got a dance free.'

It delighted Amory when Isabelle suggested that they leave for a while and drive around in her car. For a delicious hour that passed too soon they glided the silent roads about Princeton and talked from the surface of their hearts in shy excitement. Amory felt strangely ingenuous and made no attempt to kiss her.

Next day they rode up through the Jersey country, had luncheon in New York, and in the afternoon went to see a problem play at which Isabelle wept all through the second act, rather to Amory's embarrassment – though it filled him with tenderness to watch her. He was tempted to lean over and kiss away her tears, and she slipped her hand into his under cover of darkness to be pressed softly.

Then at six they arrived at the Borges' summer place on Long Island, and Amory rushed upstairs to change into a dinner coat. As he put in his studs he realised that he was enjoying life as he would probably never enjoy it again. Everything was hallowed by the haze of his own youth. He had arrived, abreast of the best in his generation at Princeton. He was in love and his love was returned. Turning on all the lights, he looked at himself in the mirror, trying to find in his own face the qualities that made him see clearer than the great crowd of people, that made him decide firmly, and able to influence and follow his own will. There was little in his life now that he would have changed . . . Oxford might have been a bigger field.

Silently he admired himself. How conveniently well he looked, and how well a dinner coat became him. He stepped into the hall and then waited at the top of the stairs, for he heard footsteps coming. It was Isabelle, and from the top of her shining hair to her little golden slippers she had never seemed so beautiful.

'Isabelle!' he cried, half involuntarily, and held out his arms. As in the storybooks, she ran into them, and on that half-minute, as their lips first touched, rested the high point of vanity, the crest of his young egotism.

3

The Egotist Considers

'Ouch! Let me go!'

He dropped his arms to his sides.

'What's the matter?'

'Your shirt stud – it hurt me – look!' She was looking down at her neck, where a little blue spot about the size of a pea marred its pallor.

'Oh, Isabelle,' he reproached himself, 'I'm a goopher. Really, I'm sorry – I shouldn't have held you so close.'

She looked up impatiently.

'Oh, Amory, of course you couldn't help it, and it didn't hurt much; but what *are* we going to do about it?'

'*Do* about it?' he asked. 'Oh – that spot; it'll disappear in a second.'

'It isn't,' she said, after a moment of concentrated gazing, 'it's still there – and it looks like Old Nick – oh, Amory, what'll we do! It's *just* the height of your shoulder.'

'Massage it,' he suggested, repressing the faintest inclination to laugh.

She rubbed it delicately with the tips of her fingers, and then a tear gathered in the corner of her eye, and slid down her cheek.

'Oh, Amory,' she said despairingly, lifting up a most pathetic face, 'I'll just make my whole neck *flame* if I rub it. What'll I do?'

A quotation sailed into his head and he couldn't resist repeating it aloud.

'All the perfumes of Arabia will not whiten this little hand.'

She looked up and the sparkle of the tear in her eye was like ice.

'You're not very sympathetic.'

Amory mistook her meaning.

'Isabelle, darling, I think it'll – '

'Don't touch me!' she cried. 'Haven't I enough on my mind and you stand there and *laugh*!'

Then he slipped again.

'Well, it *is* funny, Isabelle, and we were talking the other day about a sense of humour being – '

She was looking at him with something that was not a smile, rather the faint, mirthless echo of a smile, in the corners of her mouth.

'Oh, shut up!' she cried suddenly, and fled down the hallway towards her room. Amory stood there, covered with remorseful confusion.

'Damn!'

When Isabelle reappeared she had thrown a light wrap about her shoulders, and they descended the stairs in a silence that endured through dinner.

'Isabelle,' he began rather testily, as they arranged themselves in the car, bound for a dance at the Greenwich Country Club, 'you're angry, and I'll be, too, in a minute. Let's kiss and make up.'

Isabelle considered glumly.

'I hate to be laughed at,' she said finally.

'I won't laugh any more. I'm not laughing now, am I?'

'You did.'

'Oh, don't be so darned feminine.'

Her lips curled slightly. 'I'll be anything I want.'

Amory kept his temper with difficulty. He became aware that he had not an ounce of real affection for Isabelle, but her coldness piqued him. He wanted to kiss her, kiss her a lot, because then he knew he could leave in the morning and not care. On the contrary, if he didn't kiss her, it would worry him . . . It would interfere vaguely with his idea of himself as a conqueror. It wasn't dignified to come off second best, *pleading*, with a doughty warrior like Isabelle.

Perhaps she suspected this. At any rate, Amory watched the night that should have been the consummation of romance glide by with great moths overhead and the heavy fragrance of roadside gardens, but without those broken words, those little sighs . . .

Afterwards they suppered on ginger ale and devil's food in the pantry, and Amory announced a decision.

'I'm leaving early in the morning.'

'Why?'

'Why not?' he countered.

'There's no need.'

'However, I'm going.'

'Well, if you insist on being ridiculous – '

'Oh, don't put it that way,' he objected.

' – just because I won't let you kiss me. Do you think – '

'Now, Isabelle,' he interrupted, 'you know it's not that – even suppose it is. We've reached the stage where we either ought to kiss – or – or – nothing. It isn't as if you were refusing on moral grounds.'

She hesitated.

'I really don't know what to think about you,' she began, in a feeble, perverse attempt at conciliation. 'You're so funny.'

'How?'

'Well, I thought you had a lot of self-confidence and all that; remember you told me the other day that you could do anything you wanted, or get anything you wanted?'

Amory flushed. He *had* told her a lot of things.

'Yes.'

'Well, you didn't seem to feel so self-confident tonight. Maybe you're just plain conceited.'

'No, I'm not,' he hesitated. 'At Princeton – '

'Oh, you and Princeton! You'd think that was the world, the way you talk! Perhaps you *can* write better than anybody else on your old *Princetonian*; maybe the freshmen *do* think you're important – '

'You don't understand – '

'Yes, I do,' she interrupted. 'I *do*, because you're always talking about yourself and I used to like it; now I don't.'

'Have I tonight?'

'That's just the point,' insisted Isabelle. 'You got all upset tonight. You just sat and watched my eyes. Besides, I have to think all the time I'm talking to you – you're so critical.'

'I make you think, do I?' Amory repeated with a touch of vanity.

'You're a nervous strain' – this emphatically – 'and when you analyse every little emotion and instinct I just don't have 'em.'

'I know.' Amory admitted her point and shook his head helplessly.

'Let's go.' She stood up.

He rose abstractedly and they walked to the foot of the stairs.

'What train can I get?'

'There's one about 9:11 if you really must go.'

'Yes, I've got to go, really. Good-night.'

'Good-night.'

They were at the head of the stairs, and as Amory turned into his room he thought he caught just the faintest cloud of discontent in her face. He lay awake in the darkness and wondered how much he cared – how much of his sudden unhappiness was hurt vanity – whether he was, after all, temperamentally unfitted for romance.

When he awoke, it was with a glad flood of consciousness. The early wind stirred the chintz curtains at the windows and he was idly puzzled not to be in his room at Princeton with his school football picture over the bureau and the Triangle Club on the wall opposite. Then the grandfather's clock in the hall outside struck eight, and the memory of the night before came to him. He was out of bed, dressing, like the wind; he must get out of the house before he saw Isabelle. What had seemed a melancholy happening, now seemed a tiresome anticlimax. He was dressed at half-past, so he sat down by the window; felt that the sinews of his heart were twisted somewhat more than he had thought. What an ironic mockery the morning seemed! – bright and sunny, and full of the smell of the garden; hearing Mrs Borge's voice in the sun-parlour below, he wondered where was Isabelle.

There was a knock at the door.

'The car will be around at ten minutes of nine, sir.'

He returned to his contemplation of the outdoors, and began repeating over and over, mechanically, a verse from Browning, which he had once quoted to Isabelle in a letter:

'Each life unfulfilled, you see,
It hangs still, patchy and scrappy;
We have not sighed deep, laughed free,
Starved, feasted, despaired – been happy.'

But his life would not be unfulfilled. He took a sombre satisfaction in thinking that perhaps all along she had been nothing except what he had read into her; that this was her high point, that no one else would ever make her think. Yet that was what she had objected to in him; and Amory was suddenly tired of thinking, thinking!

'Damn her!' he said bitterly, 'she's spoiled my year!'

THE SUPERMAN GROWS CARELESS

On a dusty day in September Amory arrived in Princeton and joined the sweltering crowd of conditioned men who thronged the streets. It seemed a stupid way to commence his upper-class years, to spend four hours a morning in the stuffy room of a tutoring school, imbibing the infinite boredom of conic sections. Mr Rooney, pander to the dull, conducted the class and smoked innumerable Pall Malls as he drew diagrams and worked equations from six in the morning until midnight.

'Now, Langueduc, if I used that formula, where would my *A* point be?'

Langueduc lazily shifts his six-foot-three of football material and tries to concentrate.

'Oh – ah – I'm damned if I know, Mr Rooney.'

'Oh, why of course, of course you can't *use* that formula. *That's* what I wanted you to say.'

'Why, sure, of course.'

'Do you see why?'

'You bet – I suppose so.'

'If you don't see, tell me. I'm here to show you.'

'Well, Mr Rooney, if you don't mind, I wish you'd go over that again.'

'Gladly. Now here's *A* . . . '

The room was a study in stupidity – two huge stands for paper, Mr Rooney in his shirt-sleeves in front of them, and slouched around on chairs, a dozen men: Fred Sloane, the pitcher, who absolutely *had* to get eligible; 'Slim' Langueduc, who would beat Yale this fall, if only he could master a poor fifty per cent; McDowell, gay young sophomore, who thought it was quite a sporting thing to be tutoring here with all these prominent athletes.

'Those poor birds who haven't a cent to tutor, and have to study during the term are the ones I pity,' he announced to Amory one day, with a flaccid camaraderie in the droop of the cigarette from his pale lips. 'I should think it would be such a bore, there's so much else to do in New York during the term. I suppose they don't know what they miss, anyhow.' There was such an air of 'you and I' about Mr McDowell that Amory very nearly pushed him out of the open window when he said this . . . Next February his mother would wonder why he didn't make a club and increase his allowance . . . simple little nut . . .

Through the smoke and the air of solemn, dense earnestness that filled the room would come the inevitable helpless cry: 'I don't get it! Repeat that, Mr Rooney!' Most of them were so stupid or careless that they wouldn't admit when they didn't understand, and Amory was of the latter. He found it impossible to study conic sections; something in their calm and tantalising respectability breathing defiantly through Mr Rooney's fetid parlours distorted their equations into insoluble anagrams. He made a last night's effort with the proverbial wet towel, and then blissfully took the exam, wondering unhappily why all the colour and ambition of the spring before had faded out. Somehow, with the defection of Isabelle the idea of undergraduate success had loosed its grasp on his imagination, and he contemplated a possible failure to pass off his condition with equanimity, even though it would arbitrarily mean his removal from the *Princetonian* board and the slaughter of his chances for the Senior Council.

There was always his luck.

He yawned, scribbled his honour pledge on the cover, and sauntered from the room.

'If you don't pass it,' said the newly arrived Alec as they sat on the window-seat of Amory's room and mused upon a scheme of wall decoration, 'you're the world's worst goopher. Your stock will go down like an elevator at the club and on the campus.'

'Oh, hell, I know it. Why rub it in?'

' 'Cause you deserve it. Anybody that'd risk what you were in line for *ought* to be ineligible for *Princetonian* chairman.'

'Oh, drop the subject,' Amory protested. 'Watch and wait and shut up. I don't want everyone at the club asking me about it, as if I were a prize potato being fattened for a vegetable show.' One evening a week later Amory stopped below his own window on the way to Renwick's, and, seeing a light, called up: 'Oh, Tom, any mail?'

Alec's head appeared against the yellow square of light.

'Yes, your result's here.'

His heart clamoured violently.

'What is it, blue or pink?'

'Don't know. Better come up.'

He walked into the room and straight over to the table, and then suddenly noticed that there were other people in the room.

' 'Lo, Kerry.' He was most polite. 'Ah, men of Princeton.' They seemed to be mostly friends, so he picked up the envelope marked 'Registrar's Office', and weighed it nervously.

'We have here quite a slip of paper.'

'Open it, Amory.'

'Just to be dramatic, I'll let you know that if it's blue, my name is withdrawn from the editorial board of the *Prince*, and my short career is over.'

He paused, and then saw for the first time Ferrenby's eyes, wearing a hungry look and watching him eagerly. Amory returned the gaze pointedly.

'Watch my face, gentlemen, for the primitive emotions.'

He tore it open and held the slip up to the light.

'Well?'

'Pink or blue?'

'Say what it is.'

'We're all ears, Amory.'

'Smile or swear – or something.'

There was a pause . . . a small crowd of seconds swept by . . . then he looked again and another crowd went on into time.

'Blue as the sky, gentlemen . . . '

AFTERMATH

What Amory did that year from early September to late in the spring was so purposeless and inconsecutive that it seems scarcely worth recording. He was, of course, immediately sorry for what he had lost. His philosophy of success had tumbled down upon him, and he looked for the reasons.

'Your own laziness,' said Alec later.

'No – something deeper than that. I've begun to feel that I was meant to lose this chance.'

'They're rather off you at the club, you know; every man that doesn't come through makes our crowd just so much weaker.'

'I hate that point of view.'

'Of course, with a little effort you could still stage a comeback.'

'No – I'm through – as far as ever being a power in college is concerned.'

'But, Amory, honestly, what makes me the angriest isn't the fact that you won't be chairman of the *Prince* and on the Senior Council, but just that you didn't get down and pass that exam.'

'Not me,' said Amory slowly; 'I'm mad at the concrete thing. My own idleness was quite in accord with my system, but the luck broke.'

'Your system broke, you mean.'

'Maybe.'

'Well, what are you going to do? Get a better one quick, or just bum around for two more years as a has-been?'

'I don't know yet . . . '

'Oh, Amory, buck up!'

'Maybe.'

Amory's point of view, though dangerous, was not far from the true one. If his reactions to his environment could be tabulated, the chart would have appeared like this, beginning with his earliest years:

1 The fundamental Amory.
2 Amory plus Beatrice.
3 Amory plus Beatrice plus Minneapolis.

Then St Regis's had pulled him to pieces and started him over again:

4 Amory plus St Regis's.
5 Amory plus St Regis's plus Princeton.

That had been his nearest approach to success through conformity. The fundamental Amory, idle, imaginative, rebellious, had been nearly snowed under. He had conformed, he had succeeded, but as his imagination was neither satisfied nor grasped by his own success, he had listlessly, half-accidentally chucked the whole thing and become again:

6 The fundamental Amory.

FINANCIAL

His father died quietly and inconspicuously at Thanksgiving. The incongruity of death with either the beauties of Lake Geneva or with his mother's dignified, reticent attitude diverted him, and he looked at the funeral with an amused tolerance. He decided that burial was after all preferable to cremation, and he smiled at his old boyhood choice, slow oxidation in the top of a tree. The day after the ceremony he was amusing himself in the great library by sinking back on a couch in graceful mortuary attitudes, trying to determine whether he would, when his day came, be found with his arms crossed piously over his chest (Monsignor Darcy had once advocated this posture as being the most distinguished) or with his hands clasped behind his head, a more pagan and Byronic attitude.

What interested him much more than the final departure of his father from things mundane was a tri-cornered conversation between Beatrice, Mr Barton, of Barton and Krogman, their lawyers, and himself that took place several days after the funeral. For the first time he came into actual cognisance of the family finances, and realised what a tidy fortune had once been under his father's management. He took a ledger labelled '1906' and ran through it rather carefully. The total expenditure that year had come to something over one hundred and ten thousand dollars. Forty thousand of this had been Beatrice's own income, and there had been no attempt to account for it: it was all under the heading, 'Drafts, cheques and letters of credit forwarded to Beatrice Blaine'. The dispersal of the rest was rather minutely itemised: the taxes and improvements on the Lake Geneva estate had come to almost nine thousand dollars; the general upkeep, including Beatrice's electric and a French car, bought that year, was over thirty-five thousand dollars. The rest was fully taken care of, and there were invariably items which failed to balance on the right side of the ledger.

In the volume for 1912 Amory was shocked to discover the decrease in the number of bond holdings and the great drop in the income. In the case of Beatrice's money this was not so pronounced, but it was obvious that his father had devoted the previous year to several unfortunate gambles in oil. Very little of the oil had been burned, but Stephen Blaine had been rather badly singed. The next year and the next and the next showed similar decreases, and Beatrice had for the first time begun using her own money for keeping up the house. Yet her doctor's bill for 1913 had been over nine thousand dollars.

About the exact state of things Mr Barton was quite vague and confused. There had been recent investments, the outcome of which was for the present problematical, and he had an idea there were further speculations and exchanges concerning which he had not been consulted.

It was not for several months that Beatrice wrote Amory the full situation. The entire residue of the Blaine and O'Hara fortunes consisted of the place at Lake Geneva and approximately a half million dollars, invested now in fairly conservative six-per-cent holdings. In fact, Beatrice wrote that she was putting the money into railroad and street-car bonds as fast as she could conveniently transfer it.

> I am quite sure [she wrote to Amory] that if there is one thing we can be positive of, it is that people will not stay in one place. This Ford person has certainly made the most of that idea. So I am instructing Mr Barton to specialise on such things as Northern Pacific and these Rapid Transit Companies, as they call the street-cars. I shall never forgive myself for not buying Bethlehem Steel. I've heard the most *fascinating* stories. You must go into finance, Amory. I'm sure you would revel in it. You start as a messenger or a teller, I believe, and from that you go up – almost indefinitely. I'm sure if I were a man I'd love the handling of money; it has become quite a senile passion with me. Before I get any farther I want to discuss something. A Mrs Bispam, an over-cordial little lady whom I met at a tea the other day, told me that her son, he is at Yale, wrote her that all the boys there wore their summer underwear *all during the winter*, and also went about with their heads wet and in low shoes on the *coldest days*. Now, Amory, I don't know whether that is a fad at Princeton too, but I don't want you to be so foolish. It not only

inclines a young man to *pneumonia* and *infantile paralysis*, but to all forms of lung trouble, to which you are particularly *inclined*. You cannot experiment with your health. I have found that out. I will not make myself ridiculous, as some mothers no doubt do, by insisting that you wear overshoes, though I remember one Christmas you wore them around *constantly* without a single buckle latched, making such a curious swishing sound, and you refused to buckle them because it was not the thing to do. The very *next* Christmas you would not wear even *rubbers*, though I begged you. You are nearly twenty years old now, dear, and I can't be with you constantly to find whether you are doing the sensible thing.

This has been a very *practical* letter. I warned you in my last that the lack of money to do the things one wants to makes one quite prosy and domestic, but there is still plenty for everything if we are not too extravagant. Take care of yourself, my dear boy, and do try to write at least *once* a week, because I imagine all sorts of horrible things if I don't hear from you.

Affectionately,

MOTHER

FIRST APPEARANCE OF THE TERM 'PERSONAGE'

Monsignor Darcy invited Amory up to the Stuart palace on the Hudson for a week at Christmas, and they had enormous conversations around the open fire. Monsignor was growing a trifle stouter and his personality had expanded even with that, and Amory felt both rest and security in sinking into a squat, cushioned chair and joining him in the middle-aged sanity of a cigar.

'I've felt like leaving college, Monsignor.'

'Why?'

'All my career's gone up in smoke; you think it's petty and all that, but – '

'Not at all petty. I think it's most important. I want to hear the whole thing. Everything you've been doing since I saw you last.'

Amory talked; he went thoroughly into the destruction of his egotistic highways, and in a half-hour the listless quality had left his voice.

'What would you do if you left college?' asked Monsignor.

'Don't know. I'd like to travel, but of course this tiresome war prevents that. Anyways, mother would hate not having me graduate.

I'm just at sea. Kerry Holiday wants me to go over with him and join the Lafayette Escadrille.'

'You know you wouldn't like to go.'

'Sometimes I would – tonight I'd go in a second.'

'Well, you'd have to be very much more tired of life than I think you are. I know you.'

'I'm afraid you do,' agreed Amory reluctantly. 'It just seemed an easy way out of everything – when I think of another useless, draggy year.'

'Yes, I know; but to tell you the truth, I'm not worried about you; you seem to me to be progressing perfectly naturally.'

'No,' Amory objected. 'I've lost half my personality in a year.'

'Not a bit of it!' scoffed Monsignor. 'You've lost a great amount of vanity and that's all.'

'Lordy! I feel, anyway, as if I'd gone through another fifth form at St Regis's.'

'No.' Monsignor shook his head. 'That was a misfortune; this has been a good thing. Whatever worth while comes to you won't be through the channels you were searching last year.'

'What could be more unprofitable than my present lack of pep?'

'Perhaps in itself . . . but you're developing. This has given you time to think and you're casting off a lot of your old luggage about success and the superman and all. People like us can't adopt whole theories, as you did. If we can do the next thing, and have an hour a day to think in, we can accomplish marvels, but as far as any high-handed scheme of blind dominance is concerned – we'd just make asses of ourselves.'

'But, Monsignor, I can't do the next thing.'

'Amory, between you and me, I have only just learned to do it myself. I can do the one hundred things beyond the next thing, but I stub my toe on that, just as you stubbed your toe on mathematics this fall.'

'Why do we have to do the next thing? It never seems the sort of thing I should do.'

'We have to do it because we're not personalities, but personages.'

'That's a good line – what do you mean?'

'A personality is what you thought you were, what this Kerry and Sloane you tell me of evidently are. Personality is a physical matter almost entirely; it lowers the people it acts on – I've seen it vanish in a long sickness. But while a personality is active, it overrides "the next thing". Now a personage, on the other hand, gathers. He is never thought of apart from what he's done. He's a bar on which a thousand things have been hung – glittering things sometimes, as ours are; but he uses those things with a cold mentality back of them.'

'And several of my most glittering possessions had fallen off when I needed them.' Amory continued the metaphor eagerly.

'Yes, that's it; when you feel that your garnered prestige and talents and all that are hung out, you need never bother about anybody; you can cope with them without difficulty.'

'But, on the other hand, if I haven't my possessions, I'm helpless!'

'Absolutely.'

'That's certainly an idea.'

'Now you've a clean start – a start Kerry or Sloane can constitutionally never have. You brushed three or four ornaments down, and, in a fit of pique, knocked off the rest of them. The thing now is to collect some new ones, and the farther you look ahead in the collecting the better. But remember, do the next thing!'

'How clear you can make things!'

So they talked, often about themselves, sometimes of philosophy and religion, and life as respectively a game or a mystery. The priest seemed to guess Amory's thoughts before they were clear in his own head, so closely related were their minds in form and groove.

'Why do I make lists?' Amory asked him one night. 'Lists of all sorts of things?'

'Because you're a mediaevalist,' Monsignor answered. 'We both are. It's the passion for classifying and finding a type.'

'It's a desire to get something definite.'

'It's the nucleus of scholastic philosophy.'

'I was beginning to think I was growing eccentric till I came up here. It was a pose, I guess.'

'Don't worry about that; for you not posing may be the biggest pose of all. Pose – '

'Yes?'

'But do the next thing.'

After Amory returned to college he received several letters from Monsignor which gave him more egotistic food for consumption.

> I am afraid that I gave you too much assurance of your inevitable safety, and you must remember that I did that through faith in your springs of effort; not in the silly conviction that you will arrive without struggle. Some nuances of character you will have to take

for granted in yourself, though you must be careful in confessing them to others. You are unsentimental, almost incapable of affection, astute without being cunning and vain without being proud.

Don't let yourself feel worthless; often through life you will really be at your worst when you seem to think best of yourself; and don't worry about losing your 'personality', as you persist in calling it; at fifteen you had the radiance of early morning, at twenty you will begin to have the melancholy brilliance of the moon, and when you are my age you will give out, as I do, the genial golden warmth of 4 p.m.

If you write me letters, please let them be natural ones. Your last, that dissertation on architecture, was perfectly awful – so 'highbrow' that I picture you living in an intellectual and emotional vacuum; and beware of trying to classify people too definitely into types; you will find that all through their youth they will persist annoyingly in jumping from class to class, and by pasting a supercilious label on everyone you meet you are merely packing a Jack-in-the-box that will spring up and leer at you when you begin to come into really antagonistic contact with the world. An idealisation of some such a man as Leonardo da Vinci would be a more valuable beacon to you at present.

You are bound to go up and down, just as I did in my youth, but do keep your clarity of mind, and if fools or sages dare to criticise don't blame yourself too much.

You say that convention is all that really keeps you straight in this 'woman proposition'; but it's more than that, Amory; it's the fear that what you begin you can't stop; you would run amuck, and I know whereof I speak; it's that half-miraculous sixth sense by which you detect evil, it's the half-realised fear of God in your heart.

Whatever your *métier* proves to be – religion, architecture, literature – I'm sure you would be much safer anchored to the Church, but I won't risk my influence by arguing with you even though I am secretly sure that the 'black chasm of Romanism' yawns beneath you. Do write me soon.

With affectionate regards,

THAYER DARCY

Even Amory's reading paled during this period; he delved further into the misty side streets of literature: Huysmans, Walter Pater, Théophile Gautier, and the racier sections of Rabelais, Boccaccio, Petronius and Suetonius. One week, through general curiosity, he inspected the private libraries of his classmates and found Sloane's as typical as any: sets of Kipling, O. Henry, John Fox Jr and Richard Harding Davis; *What Every Middle-Aged Woman Ought to Know*, *The Spell of the Yukon*; a 'gift' copy of James Whitcomb Riley, an assortment of battered, annotated schoolbooks, and, finally, to his surprise, one of his own late discoveries, the collected poems of Rupert Brooke.

Together with Tom D'Invilliers, he sought among the lights of Princeton for someone who might found the Great American Poetic Tradition.

The undergraduate body itself was rather more interesting that year than had been the entirely Philistine Princeton of two years before. Things had livened surprisingly, though at the sacrifice of much of the spontaneous charm of freshman year. In the old Princeton they would never have discovered Tanaduke Wylie. Tanaduke was a sophomore, with tremendous ears and a way of saying, 'The earth swirls down through the ominous moons of preconsidered generations!' that made them vaguely wonder why it did not sound quite clear but never question that it was the utterance of a supersoul. At least so Tom and Amory took him. They told him in all earnestness that he had a mind like Shelley's, and featured his ultrafree free verse and prose poetry in the *Nassau Literary Magazine*. But Tanaduke's genius absorbed the many colours of the age, and he took to the Bohemian life, to their great disappointment. He talked of Greenwich Village now instead of 'noon-swirled moons', and met winter muses, unacademic and cloistered by Forty-Second Street and Broadway, instead of the Shelleyan dream-children with whom he had regaled their expectant appreciation. So they surrendered Tanaduke to the futurists, deciding that he and his flaming ties would do better there. Tom gave him the final advice that he should stop writing for two years and read the complete works of Alexander Pope four times, but on Amory's suggestion that Pope for Tanaduke was like foot-ease for stomach trouble, they withdrew in laughter, and called it a coin's toss whether this genius was too big or too petty for them.

Amory rather scornfully avoided the popular professors who dispensed easy epigrams and thimblefuls of Chartreuse to groups of admirers every night. He was disappointed, too, at the air of general uncertainty on every subject that seemed linked with the pedantic temperament; his opinions took shape in a miniature satire called 'In a Lecture-Room', which he persuaded Tom to print in the *Nassau Lit*.

Good-morning, Fool . . .
            Three times a week
You hold us helpless while you speak,
Teasing our thirsty souls with the
Sleek 'yeas' of your philosophy . . .
Well, here we are, your hundred sheep,
Tune up, play on, pour forth . . . we sleep . . .
You are a student, so they say;
You hammered out the other day
A syllabus, from what we know
Of some forgotten folio;
You'd sniffled through an era's must,
Filling your nostrils up with dust,
And then, arising from your knees,
Published, in one gigantic sneeze . . .
But here's a neighbour on my right,
An *Eager Ass*, considered bright;
Asker of questions . . . How he'll stand,
With earnest air and fidgy hand,
After this hour, telling you
He sat all night and burrowed through
Your book . . . Oh, you'll be coy and he
Will simulate precosity,
And pedants both, you'll smile and smirk,
And leer, and hasten back to work . . .

'Twas this day week, sir, you returned
A theme of mine, from which I learned
(Through various comment on the side
Which you had scrawled) that I defied
The *highest rules of criticism*
For *cheap* and *careless* witticism . . .
        'Are you quite sure that this could be?'
And
    'Shaw is no authority!'
But *Eager Ass*, with what he's sent,
Plays havoc with your best per cent.

Still – still I meet you here and there . . .
When Shakespeare's played you hold a chair,

And some defunct, moth-eaten star
Enchants the mental prig you are . . .
A radical comes down and shocks
The *atheistic orthodox*?
You're representing *Common Sense*,
Mouth open, in the audience.

And, sometimes, even chapel lures
That conscious tolerance of yours,
That broad and beaming view of truth
(Including *Kant* and *General Booth* . . .)
And so from shock to shock you live,
A hollow, pale affirmative . . .

The hour's up . . . and roused from rest
One hundred children of the blest
Cheat you a word or two with feet
That down the noisy aisle-ways beat . . .
Forget on *narrow-minded earth*
The Mighty Yawn that gave you birth.

In April, Kerry Holiday left college and sailed for France to enroll in the Lafayette Escadrille. Amory's envy and admiration of this step was drowned in an experience of his own to which he never succeeded in giving an appropriate value, but which, nevertheless, haunted him for three years afterwards.

THE DEVIL

Healy's they left at twelve and taxied to Bistolary's. There were Axia Marlowe and Phoebe Column, from the Summer Garden show, Fred Sloane and Amory. The evening was so very young that they felt ridiculous with surplus energy, and burst into the café like Dionysian revellers.

'Table for four in the middle of the floor,' yelled Phoebe. 'Hurry, old dear, tell 'em we're here!'

'Tell 'em to play "Admiration"!' shouted Sloane. 'You two order; Phoebe and I are going to shake a wicked calf,' and they sailed off in the muddled crowd. Axia and Amory, acquaintances of an hour, jostled behind a waiter to a table at a point of vantage; there they took seats and watched.

'There's Findle Margotson, from New Haven!' she cried above the uproar. ' 'Lo, Findle! Whoo-ee!'

'Oh, Axia!' he shouted in salutation. 'C'mon over to our table.'

'No!' Amory whispered.

'Can't do it, Findle; I'm with somebody else! Call me up tomorrow about one o'clock!'

Findle, a nondescript man-about-Bisty's, answered incoherently and turned back to the brilliant blonde whom he was endeavouring to steer around the room.

'There's a natural damn fool,' commented Amory.

'Oh, he's all right. Here's the old jitney waiter. If you ask me, I want a double daiquiri.'

'Make it four.'

The crowd whirled and changed and shifted. They were mostly from the colleges, with a scattering of the male refuse of Broadway, and women of two types, the higher of which was the chorus girl. On the whole it was a typical crowd, and their party as typical as any. About three-fourths of the whole business was for effect and therefore, harmless, ended at the door of the café soon enough for the five-o'clock train back to Yale or Princeton; about one-fourth continued on into the dimmer hours and gathered strange dust from strange places. Their party was scheduled to be one of the harmless kind. Fred Sloane and Phoebe Column were old friends; Axia and Amory new ones. But strange things are prepared even in the dead of night, and the unusual, which lurks least in the café, home of the prosaic and inevitable, was preparing to spoil for him the waning romance of Broadway. The way it took was so inexpressibly terrible, so unbelievable, that afterwards he never thought of it as experience; but it was a scene from a misty tragedy, played far behind the veil, and that it meant something definite he knew.

About one o'clock they moved to Maxim's, and two found them in Devinière's. Sloane had been drinking consecutively and was in a state of unsteady exhilaration, but Amory was quite tiresomely sober; they had run across none of those ancient, corrupt buyers of champagne who usually assisted their New York parties. They were just through dancing and were making their way back to their chairs when Amory became aware that someone at a nearby table was looking at him. He turned and glanced casually . . . a middle-aged man dressed in a brown sack suit, it was, sitting a little apart at a table by himself and watching their party intently. At Amory's glance he smiled faintly. Amory turned to Fred, who was just sitting down.

'Who's that pale fool watching us?' he complained indignantly.

'Where?' cried Sloane. 'We'll have him thrown out!' He rose to his feet and swayed back and forth, clinging to his chair. 'Where is he?'

Axia and Phoebe suddenly leaned and whispered to each other across the table, and before Amory realised it they found themselves on their way to the door.

'Where now?'

'Up to the flat,' suggested Phoebe. 'We've got brandy and fizz – and everything's slow down here tonight.'

Amory considered quickly. He hadn't been drinking, and decided that if he took no more, it would be reasonably discreet for him to trot along in the party. In fact, it would be, perhaps, the thing to do in order to keep an eye on Sloane, who was not in a state to do his own thinking. So he took Axia's arm, and piling intimately into a taxicab, they drove out over the Hundreds and drew up at a tall, white-stone apartment-house . . . Never would he forget that street . . . It was a broad street, lined on both sides with just such tall, white-stone buildings, dotted with dark windows; they stretched along as far as the eye could see, flooded with a bright moonlight that gave them a calcium pallor. He imagined each one to have an elevator and a coloured hall-boy and a key-rack; each one to be eight storeys high and full of three- and four-room suites. He was rather glad to walk into the cheeriness of Phoebe's living-room and sink on to a sofa, while the girls went rummaging for food.

'Phoebe's great stuff,' confided Sloane, *sotto voce*.

'I'm only going to stay half an hour,' Amory said sternly. He wondered if it sounded priggish.

'Hell y' say,' protested Sloane. 'We're here now – don't le's rush.'

'I don't like this place,' Amory said sulkily, 'and I don't want any food.'

Phoebe reappeared with sandwiches, brandy bottle, siphon and four glasses.

'Amory, pour 'em out,' she said, 'and we'll drink to Fred Sloane, who has a rare, distinguished edge.'

'Yes,' said Axia, coming in, 'and Amory. I like Amory.' She sat down beside him and laid her yellow head on his shoulder.

'I'll pour,' said Sloane; 'you use siphon, Phoebe.'

They filled the tray with glasses.

'Ready, here she goes!'

Amory hesitated, glass in hand.

There was a minute while temptation crept over him like a warm wind, and his imagination turned to fire, and he took the glass from Phoebe's hand. That was all; for at the second that his decision came, he looked up and saw, ten yards from him, the man who had been in the café, and with his jump of astonishment the glass fell from his uplifted hand. There the man half sat, half leaned against a pile of pillows on the corner divan. His face was cast in the same yellow wax as in the café, neither the dull, pasty colour of a dead man – rather a sort of virile pallor – nor unhealthy, you'd have called it; but like a strong man who'd worked in a mine or done night shifts in a damp climate. Amory looked him over carefully and later he could have drawn him after a fashion, down to the merest details. His mouth was the kind that is called frank, and he had steady grey eyes that moved slowly from one to the other of their group, with just the shade of a questioning expression. Amory noticed his hands; they weren't fine at all, but they had versatility and a tenuous strength . . . they were nervous hands that sat lightly along the cushions and moved constantly with little jerky openings and closings. Then, suddenly, Amory perceived the feet, and with a rush of blood to the head he realised he was afraid. The feet were all wrong . . . with a sort of wrongness that he felt rather than knew . . . It was like weakness in a good woman, or blood on satin; one of those terrible incongruities that shake little things in the back of the brain. He wore no shoes, but, instead, a sort of half moccasin, pointed, though, like the shoes they wore in the fourteenth century, and with the little ends curling up. They were a darkish brown and his toes seemed to fill them to the end . . . They were unutterably terrible . . .

He must have said something, or looked something, for Axia's voice came out of the void with a strange goodness.

'Well, look at Amory! Poor old Amory's sick – old head going round?'

'Look at that man!' cried Amory, pointing towards the corner divan.

'You mean that purple zebra!' shrieked Axia facetiously. 'Ooo-ee! Amory's got a purple zebra watching him!'

Sloane laughed vacantly.

'Ole zebra gotcha, Amory?'

There was a silence . . . The man regarded Amory quizzically . . . Then the human voices fell faintly on his ear: 'Thought you weren't drinking,' remarked Axia sardonically, but her voice was good to hear; the whole divan that held the man was alive; alive like heat waves over asphalt, like wriggling worms . . .

'Come back! Come back!' Axia's arm fell on his. 'Amory, dear, you aren't going, Amory!' He was halfway to the door.

'Come on, Amory, stick 'th us!'

'Sick, are you?'

'Sit down a second!'

'Take some water.'

'Take a little brandy . . . '

The elevator was close, and the coloured boy was half asleep, paled to a livid bronze . . . Axia's beseeching voice floated down the shaft. Those feet . . . those feet . . .

As they settled to the lower floor the feet came into view in the sickly electric light of the paved hall.

IN THE ALLEY

Down the long street came the moon, and Amory turned his back on it and walked. Ten, fifteen steps away sounded the footsteps. They were like a slow dripping, with just the slightest insistence in their fall. Amory's shadow lay perhaps ten feet ahead of him, and soft shoes was presumably that far behind. With the instinct of a child Amory edged in under the blue darkness of the white buildings, cleaving the moonlight for haggard seconds, once bursting into a slow run with clumsy stumblings. After that he stopped suddenly; he must keep hold, he thought. His lips were dry and he licked them.

If he met anyone good – were there any good people left in the world or did they all live in white apartment-houses now? Was everyone followed in the moonlight? But if he met someone good who'd know what he meant and hear this damned scuffle . . . then the scuffling grew suddenly nearer, and a black cloud settled over the moon. When again the pale sheen skimmed the cornices, it was almost beside him, and Amory thought he heard a quiet breathing. Suddenly he realised that the footsteps were not behind, had never been behind, they were ahead and he was not eluding but following . . . following. He began to run, blindly, his heart knocking heavily, his hands clenched. Far ahead a black dot showed itself, resolved slowly into a human shape. But Amory was beyond that now; he turned off the street and darted into an alley, narrow and dark and smelling of old rottenness. He twisted down a long, sinuous blackness, where the moonlight was shut away except for tiny glints and patches . . . then suddenly sank panting into a corner by a fence, exhausted. The steps ahead stopped, and he could hear them shift slightly with a continuous motion, like waves around a dock.

He put his face in his hands and covered eyes and ears as well as he could. During all this time it never occurred to him that he was delirious or drunk. He had a sense of reality such as material things could never give him. His intellectual content seemed to submit passively to it, and it fitted like a glove everything that had ever preceded it in his life. It did not muddle him. It was like a problem whose answer he knew on paper, yet whose solution he was unable to grasp. He was far beyond horror. He had sunk through the thin surface of that, now moved in a region where the feet and the fear of white walls were real, living things, things he must accept. Only far inside his soul a little fire leaped and cried that something was pulling him down, trying to get him inside a door and slam it behind him. After that door was slammed there would be only footfalls and white buildings in the moonlight, and perhaps he would be one of the footfalls.

During the five or ten minutes he waited in the shadow of the fence, there was somehow this fire . . . that was as near as he could name it afterwards. He remembered calling aloud: 'I want someone stupid. Oh, send someone stupid!' This to the black fence opposite him, in whose shadows the footsteps shuffled . . . shuffled. He supposed 'stupid' and 'good' had become somehow intermingled through previous association. When he called thus it was not an act of will at all – will had turned him away from the moving figure in the street; it was almost instinct that called, just the pile on pile of inherent tradition or some wild prayer from way over the night. Then something clanged like a low gong struck at a distance, and before his eyes a face flashed over the two feet, a face pale and distorted with a sort of infinite evil that twisted it like flame in the wind; *but he knew, for the half instant that the gong tanged and hummed, that it was the face of Dick Humbird.*

Minutes later he sprang to his feet, realising dimly that there was no more sound, and that he was alone in the greying alley. It was cold, and he started on a steady run for the light that showed the street at the other end.

It was late morning when he woke and found the telephone beside his bed in the hotel tolling frantically, and remembered that he had left word to be called at eleven. Sloane was snoring heavily, his clothes in a pile by his bed. They dressed and ate breakfast in silence, and then sauntered out to get some air. Amory's mind was working slowly, trying to assimilate what had happened and separate from the chaotic imagery that stacked his memory the bare shreds of truth. If the morning had been cold and grey he could have grasped the reins of the past in an instant, but it was one of those days that New York gets sometimes in May, when the air on Fifth Avenue is a soft, light wine. How much or how little Sloane remembered Amory did not care to know; he apparently had none of the nervous tension that was gripping Amory and forcing his mind back and forth like a shrieking saw.

Then Broadway broke upon them, and with the babel of noise and the painted faces a sudden sickness rushed over Amory.

'For God's sake, let's go back! Let's get off of this – this place!'

Sloane looked at him in amazement.

'What do you mean?'

'This street, it's ghastly! Come on! let's get back to the Avenue!'

'Do you mean to say,' said Sloane stolidly, 'that 'cause you had some sort of indigestion that made you act like a maniac last night, you're never coming on Broadway again?'

Simultaneously Amory classed him with the crowd, and he seemed no longer Sloane of the debonair humour and the happy personality, but only one of the evil faces that whirled along the turbid stream.

'Man!' he shouted so loud that the people on the corner turned and followed them with their eyes, 'it's filthy, and if you can't see it, you're filthy, too!'

'I can't help it,' said Sloane doggedly. 'What's the matter with you? Old remorse getting you? You'd be in a fine state if you'd gone through with our little party.'

'I'm going, Fred,' said Amory slowly. His knees were shaking under him, and he knew that if he stayed another minute on this street he would keel over where he stood. 'I'll be at the Vanderbilt for lunch.' And he strode rapidly off and turned over to Fifth Avenue. Back at the hotel he felt better, but as he walked into the barbershop, intending to get a head massage, the smell of the powders and tonics brought back Axia's sidelong, suggestive smile, and he left hurriedly. In the doorway of his room a sudden blackness flowed around him like a divided river.

When he came to himself he knew that several hours had passed. He pitched on to the bed and rolled over on his face with a deadly fear that he was going mad. He wanted people, someone sane and stupid and good. He lay for he knew not how long without moving. He could feel the little hot veins on his forehead standing out, and his terror had hardened on him like plaster. He felt he was passing up again through the thin crust of horror, and now only could he distinguish the shadowy twilight he was leaving. He must have fallen asleep again, for when he next recollected himself he had paid the hotel bill and was stepping into a taxi at the door. It was raining torrents.

On the train for Princeton he saw no one he knew, only a crowd of fagged-looking Philadelphians. The presence of a painted woman across the aisle filled him with a fresh burst of sickness and he changed to another car, tried to concentrate on an article in a popular magazine. He found himself reading the same paragraphs over and over, so he abandoned this attempt and leaning over wearily pressed his hot forehead against the damp window-pane. The car, a smoker, was hot and stuffy with most of the smells of the state's alien population; he opened a window and shivered against the cloud of fog that drifted in over him. The two hours' ride was like days, and he nearly cried aloud with joy when the towers of Princeton loomed up beside him and the yellow squares of light filtered through the blue rain.

Tom was standing in the centre of the room, pensively relighting a cigar-stub. Amory fancied he looked rather relieved on seeing him.

'Had a hell of a dream about you last night,' came in the cracked voice through the cigar smoke. 'I had an idea you were in some trouble.'

'Don't tell me about it!' Amory almost shrieked. 'Don't say a word; I'm tired and pepped out.'

Tom looked at him queerly and then sank into a chair and opened his Italian notebook. Amory threw his coat and hat on the floor, loosened his collar, and took a Wells novel at random from the shelf. 'Wells is sane,' he thought, 'and if he won't do I'll read Rupert Brooke.'

Half an hour passed. Outside the wind came up, and Amory started as the wet branches moved and clawed with their fingernails at the window-pane. Tom was deep in his work, and inside the room only the occasional scratch of a match or the rustle of leather as they shifted in their chairs broke the stillness. Then like a zigzag of lightning came the change. Amory sat bolt upright, frozen cold in his chair. Tom was looking at him with his mouth drooping, eyes fixed.

'God help us!' Amory cried.

'Oh, my heavens!' shouted Tom, 'look behind!' Quick as a flash Amory whirled around. He saw nothing but the dark window-pane. 'It's gone now,' came Tom's voice after a second in a still terror. 'Something was looking at you.'

Trembling violently, Amory dropped into his chair again.

'I've got to tell you,' he said. 'I've had one hell of an experience. I think I've – I've seen the devil or – something like him. What face did you just see? – or no,' he added quickly, 'don't tell me!'

And he gave Tom the story. It was midnight when he finished, and after that, with all lights burning, two sleepy, shivering boys read to each other from *The New Machiavelli*, until dawn came up out of Witherspoon Hall, and the *Princetonian* fell against the door, and the May birds hailed the sun on last night's rain.

4

Narcissus Off Duty

During Princeton's transition period, that is, during Amory's last two years there, while he saw it change and broaden and live up to its Gothic beauty by better means than night parades, certain individuals arrived who stirred it to its plethoric depths. Some of them had been freshmen, and wild freshmen, with Amory; some were in the class below; and it was in the beginning of his last year and around small tables at the Nassau Inn that they began questioning aloud the institutions that Amory and countless others before him had questioned so long in secret. First, and partly by accident, they struck on certain books, a definite type of biographical novel that Amory christened 'quest' books. In the 'quest' book the hero set off in life armed with the best weapons and avowedly intending to use them as such weapons are usually used, to push their possessors ahead as selfishly and blindly as possible, but the heroes of the 'quest' books discovered that there might be a more magnificent use for them. *None Other Gods*, *Sinister Street* and *The Research Magnificent* were examples of such books; it was the latter of these three that gripped Burne Holiday and made him wonder in the beginning of senior year how much it was worth while being a diplomatic autocrat around his club on Prospect Avenue and basking in the highlights of class office. It was distinctly through the channels of aristocracy that Burne found his way. Amory, through Kerry, had had a vague drifting acquaintance with him, but not until January of senior year did their friendship commence.

'Heard the latest?' said Tom, coming in late one drizzly evening with that triumphant air he always wore after a successful conversational bout.

'No. Somebody flunked out? Or another ship sunk?'

'Worse than that. About one-third of the junior class are going to resign from their clubs.'

'What!'

'Actual fact!'

'Why!'

'Spirit of reform and all that. Burne Holiday is behind it. The club presidents are holding a meeting tonight to see if they can find a joint means of combating it.'

'Well, what's the idea of the thing?'

'Oh, clubs injurious to Princeton democracy; cost a lot; draw social lines, take time; the regular line you get sometimes from disappointed sophomores. Woodrow thought they should be abolished and all that.'

'But this is the real thing?'

'Absolutely. I think it'll go through.'

'For Pete's sake, tell me more about it.'

'Well,' began Tom, 'it seems that the idea developed simultaneously in several heads. I was talking to Burne awhile ago, and he claims that it's a logical result if an intelligent person thinks long enough about the social system. They had a "discussion crowd" and the point of abolishing the clubs was brought up by someone – everybody there leaped at it – it had been in each one's mind, more or less, and it just needed a spark to bring it out.'

'Fine! I swear I think it'll be most entertaining. How do they feel up at Cap and Gown?'

'Wild, of course. Everyone's been sitting and arguing and swearing and getting mad and getting sentimental and getting brutal. It's the same at all the clubs; I've been the rounds. They get one of the radicals in the corner and fire questions at him.'

'How do the radicals stand up?'

'Oh, moderately well. Burne's a damn good talker, and so obviously sincere that you can't get anywhere with him. It's so evident that resigning from his club means so much more to him than preventing it does to us that I felt futile when I argued; finally took a position that was brilliantly neutral. In fact, I believe Burne thought for a while that he'd converted me.'

'And you say almost a third of the junior class are going to resign?'

'Call it a fourth and be safe.'

'Lord – who'd have thought it possible!'

There was a brisk knock at the door, and Burne himself came in. 'Hello, Amory – hello, Tom.'

Amory rose.

' 'Evening, Burne. Don't mind if I seem to rush; I'm going to Renwick's.'

Burne turned to him quickly.

'You probably know what I want to talk to Tom about, and it isn't a bit private. I wish you'd stay.'

'I'd be glad to.' Amory sat down again, and as Burne perched on a table and launched into argument with Tom, he looked at this revolutionary more carefully than he ever had before. Broad-browed and strong-chinned, with a fineness in the honest grey eyes that were like Kerry's, Burne was a man who gave an immediate impression of bigness and security – stubborn, that was evident, but his stubbornness wore no stolidity, and when he had talked for five minutes Amory knew that this keen enthusiasm had in it no quality of dilettantism.

The intense power Amory felt later in Burne Holiday differed from the admiration he had had for Humbird. This time it began as purely a mental interest. With other men whom he had thought of as primarily first-class, he had been attracted first by their personalities, and in Burne he missed that immediate magnetism to which he usually swore allegiance. But that night Amory was struck by Burne's intense earnestness, a quality he was accustomed to associate only with the dread stupidity, and by the great enthusiasm that struck dead chords in his heart. Burne stood vaguely for a land Amory hoped he was drifting towards – and it was almost time that land was in sight. Tom and Amory and Alec had reached an impasse; never did they seem to have new experiences in common, for Tom and Alec had been as blindly busy with their committees and boards as Amory had been blindly idling, and the things they had for dissection – college, contemporary personality and the like – they had hashed and rehashed for many a frugal conversational meal.

That night they discussed the clubs until twelve, and, in the main, they agreed with Burne. To the roommates it did not seem such a vital subject as it had in the two years before, but the logic of Burne's objections to the social system dovetailed so completely with everything they had thought, that they questioned rather than argued, and envied the sanity that enabled this man to stand out so against all traditions.

Then Amory branched off and found that Burne was deep in other things as well. Economics had interested him and he was turning socialist. Pacifism played in the back of his mind, and he read the *Masses* and Lyof Tolstoy faithfully.

'How about religion?' Amory asked him.

'Don't know. I'm in a muddle about a lot of things – I've just discovered that I've a mind, and I'm starting to read.'

'Read what?'

'Everything. I have to pick and choose, of course, but mostly things to make me think. I'm reading the four gospels now, and *The Varieties of Religious Experience*.'

'What chiefly started you?'

'Wells, I guess, and Tolstoy, and a man named Edward Carpenter. I've been reading for over a year now – on a few lines, on what I consider the essential lines.'

'Poetry?'

'Well, frankly, not what you call poetry, or for your reasons – you two write, of course, and look at things differently. Whitman is the man that attracts me.'

'Whitman?'

'Yes; he's a definite ethical force.'

'Well, I'm ashamed to say that I'm a blank on the subject of Whitman. How about you, Tom?'

Tom nodded sheepishly.

'Well,' continued Burne, 'you may strike a few poems that are tiresome, but I mean the mass of his work. He's tremendous – like Tolstoy. They both look things in the face, and, somehow, different as they are, stand for somewhat the same things.'

'You have me stumped, Burne,' Amory admitted. 'I've read *Anna Karenina* and *The Kreutzer Sonata* of course, but Tolstoy is mostly in the original Russian as far as I'm concerned.'

'He's the greatest man in hundreds of years,' cried Burne enthusiastically. 'Did you ever see a picture of that shaggy old head of his?'

They talked until three, from biology to organised religion, and when Amory crept shivering into bed it was with his mind aglow with ideas and a sense of shock that someone else had discovered the path he might have followed. Burne Holiday was so evidently developing – and Amory had considered that he was doing the same. He had fallen into a deep cynicism over what had crossed his path, plotted the imperfectability of man and read Shaw and Chesterton enough to keep his mind from the edges of decadence – now suddenly all his mental processes of the last year and a half seemed stale and futile – a petty consummation of himself . . . and like a sombre background lay that incident of the spring before, that filled half his nights with a dreary terror and made him unable to pray. He was not even a Catholic, yet that was the only ghost of a code that he had, the gaudy, ritualistic, paradoxical Catholicism whose prophet was Chesterton, whose claqueurs were such reformed rakes of literature as Huysmans and Bourget, whose American sponsor was Ralph Adams Cram, with his adulation of thirteenth-century cathedrals – a Catholicism which Amory found convenient and ready-made, without priest or sacraments or sacrifice.

He could not sleep, so he turned on his reading-lamp and, taking down *The Kreutzer Sonata*, searched it carefully for the germs of Burne's enthusiasm. Being Burne was suddenly so much realler than being clever. Yet he sighed . . . here were other possible clay feet.

He thought back through two years, of Burne as a hurried, nervous freshman, quite submerged in his brother's personality. Then he remembered an incident of sophomore year, in which Burne had been suspected of the leading role.

Dean Hollister had been heard by a large group arguing with a taxi-driver, who had driven him from the junction. In the course of the altercation the dean remarked that he 'might as well buy the taxicab'. He paid and walked off, but next morning he entered his private office to find the taxicab itself in the space usually occupied by his desk, bearing a sign which read 'Property of Dean Hollister. Bought and Paid for' . . . It took two expert mechanics half a day to disassemble it into its minutest parts and remove it, which only goes to prove the rare energy of sophomore humour under efficient leadership.

Then again, that very fall, Burne had caused a sensation. A certain Phyllis Styles, an intercollegiate prom-trotter, had failed to get her yearly invitation to the Harvard-Princeton game.

Jesse Ferrenby had brought her to a smaller game a few weeks before, and had pressed Burne into service – to the ruination of the latter's misogyny.

'Are you coming to the Harvard game?' Burne had asked indiscreetly, merely to make conversation.

'If you ask me,' cried Phyllis quickly.

'Of course I do,' said Burne feebly. He was unversed in the arts of Phyllis, and was sure that this was merely a vapid form of kidding. Before an hour had passed he knew that he was indeed involved. Phyllis had pinned him down and served him up, informed him the train she was arriving by, and depressed him thoroughly. Aside from loathing Phyllis, he had particularly wanted to stag that game and entertain some Harvard friends.

'She'll see,' he informed a delegation who arrived in his room to josh him. 'This will be the last game she ever persuades any young innocent to take her to!'

'But, Burne – why did you *invite* her if you didn't want her?'

'Burne, you *know* you're secretly mad about her – that's the *real* trouble.'

'What can *you* do, Burne? What can *you* do against Phyllis?'

But Burne only shook his head and muttered threats which consisted largely of the phrase: 'She'll see, she'll see!'

The blithesome Phyllis bore her twenty-five summers gayly from the train, but on the platform a ghastly sight met her eyes. There were Burne and Fred Sloane arrayed to the last dot like the lurid figures on college posters. They had bought flaring suits with huge peg-top trousers and gigantic padded shoulders. On their heads were rakish college hats, pinned up in front and sporting bright orange-and-black bands, while from their celluloid collars blossomed flaming orange ties. They wore black armbands with orange 'Ps', and carried canes flying Princeton pennants, the effect completed by socks and peeping handkerchiefs in the same colour motifs. On a clanking chain they led a large, angry tomcat, painted to represent a tiger.

A good half of the station crowd was already staring at them, torn between horrified pity and riotous mirth, and as Phyllis, with her svelte jaw dropping, approached, the pair bent over and emitted a college cheer in loud, far-carrying voices, thoughtfully adding the name 'Phyllis' to the end. She was vociferously greeted and escorted enthusiastically across the campus, followed by half a hundred village urchins – to the stifled laughter of hundreds of alumni and visitors, half of whom had no idea that this was a practical joke, but thought that Burne and Fred were two varsity sports showing their girl a collegiate time.

Phyllis's feelings as she was paraded by the Harvard and Princeton stands, where sat dozens of her former devotees, can be imagined. She tried to walk a little ahead, she tried to walk a little behind – but they stayed close, that there should be no doubt whom she was with, talking in loud voices of their friends on the football team, until she could almost hear her acquaintances whispering: 'Phyllis Styles must be *awfully hard up* to have to come with *those two*.'

That had been Burne, dynamically humorous, fundamentally serious. From that root had blossomed the energy that he was now trying to orient with progress . . .

So the weeks passed and March came and the clay feet that Amory looked for failed to appear. About a hundred juniors and seniors resigned from their clubs in a final fury of righteousness, and the clubs in helplessness turned upon Burne their finest weapon: ridicule.

Everyone who knew him liked him – but what he stood for (and he began to stand for more all the time) came under the lash of many tongues, until a frailer man than he would have been snowed under.

'Don't you mind losing prestige?' asked Amory one night. They had taken to exchanging calls several times a week.

'Of course I don't. What's prestige, at best?'

'Some people say that you're just a rather original politician.'

He roared with laughter.

'That's what Fred Sloane told me today. I suppose I have it coming.'

One afternoon they dipped into a subject that had interested Amory for a long time – the matter of the bearing of physical attributes on a man's make-up. Burne had gone into the biology of this, and then: 'Of course health counts – a healthy man has twice the chance of being good,' he said.

'I don't agree with you – I don't believe in "muscular Christianity".'

'I do – I believe Christ had great physical vigour.'

'Oh, no,' Amory protested. 'He worked too hard for that. I imagine that when he died he was a broken-down man – and the great saints haven't been strong.'

'Half of them have.'

'Well, even granting that, I don't think health has anything to do with goodness; of course, it's valuable to a great saint to be able to stand enormous strains, but this fad of popular preachers rising on their toes in simulated virility, bellowing that calisthenics will save the world – no, Burne, I can't go that.'

'Well, let's waive it – we won't get anywhere, and besides I haven't quite made up my mind about it myself. Now, here's something I *do* know – personal appearance has a lot to do with it.'

'Colouring?' Amory asked eagerly.

'Yes.'

'That's what Tom and I figured,' Amory agreed. 'We took the year-books for the last ten years and looked at the pictures of the Senior Council. I know you don't think much of that august body, but it does represent success here in a general way. Well, I suppose only about thirty-five per cent of every class here are blonds, are really light – yet *two-thirds* of every Senior Council are light. We looked at pictures of ten years of them, mind you; that means that out of every *fifteen* light-haired men in the senior class *one* is on the Senior Council, and of the dark-haired men it's only one in *fifty*.'

'It's true,' Burne agreed. 'The light-haired man *is* a higher type, generally speaking. I worked the thing out with the Presidents of the United States once, and found that way over half of them were light-haired – yet think of the preponderant number of brunettes in the race.'

'People unconsciously admit it,' said Amory. 'You'll notice a blond person is *expected* to talk. If a blonde girl doesn't talk we call her a "doll"; if a light-haired man is silent he's considered stupid. Yet the world is full of "dark silent men" and "languorous brunettes" who haven't a brain in their heads, but somehow are never accused of the dearth.'

'And the large mouth and broad chin and rather big nose undoubtedly make the superior face.'

'I'm not so sure.' Amory was all for classical features.

'Oh, yes – I'll show you,' and Burne pulled out of his desk a photographic collection of heavily bearded, shaggy celebrities – Tolstoy, Whitman, Carpenter, and others.

'Aren't they wonderful?'

Amory tried politely to appreciate them, and gave up laughingly.

'Burne, I think they're the ugliest-looking crowd I ever came across. They look like an old men's home.'

'Oh, Amory, look at that forehead on Emerson; look at Tolstoy's eyes.' His tone was reproachful.

Amory shook his head.

'No! Call them remarkable-looking or anything you want – but ugly they certainly are.'

Unabashed, Burne ran his hand lovingly across the spacious foreheads, and piling up the pictures put them back in his desk.

Walking at night was one of his favourite pursuits, and one night he persuaded Amory to accompany him.

'I hate the dark,' Amory objected. 'I didn't use to – except when I was particularly imaginative, but now, I really do – I'm a regular fool about it.'

'That's useless, you know.'

'Quite possibly.'

'We'll go east,' Burne suggested, 'and down that string of roads through the woods.'

'Doesn't sound very appealing to me,' admitted Amory reluctantly, 'but let's go.'

They set off at a good gait, and for an hour swung along in a brisk argument until the lights of Princeton were luminous white blots behind them.

'Any person with any imagination is bound to be afraid,' said Burne earnestly. 'And this very walking at night is one of the things I was afraid about. I'm going to tell you why I can walk anywhere now and not be afraid.'

'Go on,' Amory urged eagerly. They were striding towards the woods, Burne's nervous, enthusiastic voice warming to his subject.

'I used to come out here alone at night, oh, three months ago, and I always stopped at that crossroads we just passed. There were the woods looming up ahead, just as they do now, there were dogs howling and the shadows and no human sound. Of course, I peopled the woods with everything ghastly, just like you do; don't you?'

'I do,' Amory admitted.

'Well, I began analysing it – my imagination persisted in sticking horrors into the dark – so I stuck my imagination into the dark instead, and let it look out at me – I let it play stray dog or escaped convict or ghost, and then saw myself coming along the road. That made it all right – as it always makes everything all right to project yourself completely into another's place. I knew that if I were the dog or the convict or the ghost I wouldn't be a menace to Burne Holiday any more than he was a menace to me. Then I thought of my watch. I'd better go back and leave it and then essay the woods. No; I decided, it's better on the whole that I should lose a watch than that I should turn back – and I did go into them – not only followed the road through them, but walked into them until I wasn't frightened any more – did it until one night I sat down and dozed off in there; then I knew I was through being afraid of the dark.'

'Lordy,' Amory breathed. 'I couldn't have done that. I'd have come out halfway, and the first time an automobile passed and made the dark thicker when its lamps disappeared, I'd have come in.'

'Well,' Burne said suddenly, after a few moments' silence, 'we're halfway through, let's turn back.'

On the return he launched into a discussion of will.

'It's the whole thing,' he asserted. 'It's the one dividing line between good and evil. I've never met a man who led a rotten life and didn't have a weak will.'

'How about great criminals?'

'They're usually insane. If not, they're weak. There is no such thing as a strong, sane criminal.'

'Burne, I disagree with you altogether; how about the superman?'

'Well?'

'He's evil, I think, yet he's strong and sane.'

'I've never met him. I'll bet, though, that he's stupid or insane.'

'I've met him over and over and he's neither. That's why I think you're wrong.'

'I'm sure I'm not – and so I don't believe in imprisonment except for the insane.'

On this point Amory could not agree. It seemed to him that life and history were rife with the strong criminal, keen, but often self-deluding; in politics and business one found him and among the old statesmen and kings and generals; but Burne never agreed and their courses began to split on that point.

Burne was drawing further and further away from the world about him. He resigned the vice-presidency of the senior class and took to reading and walking as almost his only pursuits. He voluntarily attended graduate lectures in philosophy and biology, and sat in all of them with a rather pathetically intent look in his eyes, as if waiting for something the lecturer would never quite come to. Sometimes Amory would see him squirm in his seat; and his face would light up; he was on fire to debate a point.

He grew more abstracted on the street and was even accused of becoming a snob, but Amory knew it was nothing of the sort, and once when Burne passed him four feet off, absolutely unseeingly, his mind a thousand miles away, Amory almost choked with the romantic joy of watching him. Burne seemed to be climbing heights where others would be forever unable to get a foothold.

'I tell you,' Amory declared to Tom, 'he's the first contemporary I've ever met whom I'll admit is my superior in mental capacity.'

'It's a bad time to admit it – people are beginning to think he's odd.'

'He's way over their heads – you know you think so yourself when you talk to him – Good Lord, Tom, you *used* to stand out against "people". Success has completely conventionalised you.'

Tom grew rather annoyed.

'What's he trying to do – be excessively holy?'

'No! not like anybody you've ever seen. Never enters the Philadelphian Society. He has no faith in that rot. He doesn't believe that public swimming-pools and a kind word in time will right the wrongs of the world; moreover, he takes a drink whenever he feels like it.'

'He certainly is getting in wrong.'

'Have you talked to him lately?'

'No.'

'Then you haven't any conception of him.'

The argument ended nowhere, but Amory noticed more than ever how the sentiment towards Burne had changed on the campus.

'It's odd,' Amory said to Tom one night when they had grown more amicable on the subject, 'that the people who violently disapprove of Burne's radicalism are distinctly the Pharisee class – I mean they're the best-educated men in college – the editors of the papers, like yourself and Ferrenby, the younger professors . . . The illiterate athletes like Langueduc think he's getting eccentric, but they just say, "Good old Burne has got some queer ideas in his head," and pass on – the Pharisee class – Gee! they ridicule him unmercifully.'

The next morning he met Burne hurrying along McCosh walk after a recitation.

'Whither bound, Tsar?'

'Over to the *Prince* office to see Ferrenby,' he waved a copy of the morning's *Princetonian* at Amory. 'He wrote this editorial.'

'Going to flay him alive?'

'No – but he's got me all balled up. Either I've misjudged him or he's suddenly become the world's worst radical.'

Burne hurried on, and it was several days before Amory heard an account of the ensuing conversation. Burne had come into the editor's sanctum displaying the paper cheerfully.

'Hello, Jesse.'

'Hello there, Savonarola.'

'I just read your editorial.'

'Good boy – didn't know you stooped that low.'

'Jesse, you startled me.'

'How so?'

'Aren't you afraid the faculty'll get after you if you pull this irreligious stuff?'

'What?'

'Like this morning.'

'What the devil – that editorial was on the coaching system.'

'Yes, but that quotation – '

Jesse sat up.

'What quotation?'

'You know: "He who is not with me is against me." '

'Well – what about it?'

Jesse was puzzled but not alarmed.

'Well, you say here – let me see.' Burne opened the paper and read: ' "*He who is not with me is against me*, as that gentleman said who was notoriously capable of only coarse distinctions and puerile generalities." '

'What of it?' Ferrenby began to look alarmed. 'Oliver Cromwell said it, didn't he? or was it Washington, or one of the saints? Good Lord, I've forgotten.'

Burne roared with laughter.

'Oh, Jesse, oh, good, kind Jesse.'

'Who said it, for Pete's sake?'

'Well,' said Burne, recovering his voice, 'St Matthew attributes it to Christ.'

'My God!' cried Jesse, and collapsed backwards into the waste-basket.

AMORY WRITES A POEM

The weeks tore by. Amory wandered occasionally to New York on the chance of finding a new shining green auto-bus, that its stick-of-candy glamour might penetrate his disposition. One day he ventured into a stock-company revival of a play whose name was faintly familiar. The curtain rose – he watched casually as a girl entered. A few phrases rang in his ear and touched a faint chord of memory. Where – ? When – ?

Then he seemed to hear a voice whispering beside him, a very soft, vibrant voice: 'Oh, I'm such a poor little fool; *do* tell me when I do wrong.'

The solution came in a flash and he had a quick, glad memory of Isabelle.

He found a blank space on his programme, and began to scribble rapidly:

'Here in the figured dark I watch once more,
  There, with the curtain, roll the years away;
  Two years of years – there was an idle day
Of ours, when happy endings didn't bore
Our unfermented souls; I could adore
  Your eager face beside me, wide-eyed, gay,
  Smiling a repertoire while the poor play
Reached me as a faint ripple reaches shore.
  Yawning and wondering an evening through,
  I watch alone . . . and chatterings, of course,
  Spoil the one scene which, somehow, *did* have charms;
You wept a bit, and I grew sad for you
  Right here! Where Mr X defends divorce
  And What's-Her-Name falls fainting in his arms.'

'Ghosts are such dumb things,' said Alec, 'they're slow-witted. I can always out-guess a ghost.'

'How?' asked Tom.

'Well, it depends where. Take a bedroom, for example. If you use *any* discretion a ghost can never get you in a bedroom.'

'Go on, s'pose you think there's maybe a ghost in your bedroom – what measures do you take on getting home at night?' demanded Amory, interested.

'Take a stick,' answered Alec, with ponderous reverence, 'one about the length of a broom-handle. Now, the first thing to do is to get the room *cleared* – to do this you rush with your eyes closed into your study and turn on the lights – next, approaching the closet, carefully run the stick in the door three or four times. Then, if nothing happens, you can look in. *Always, always* run the stick in viciously first – *never* look first!'

'Of course, that's the ancient Celtic school,' said Tom gravely.

'Yes – but they usually pray first. Anyway, you use this method to clear the closets and also for behind all doors – '

'And the bed,' Amory suggested.

'Oh, Amory, no!' cried Alec in horror. 'That isn't the way – the bed requires different tactics – let the bed alone, as you value your reason – if there is a ghost in the room and that's only about a third of the time, it is *almost always* under the bed.'

'Well – ' Amory began.

Alec waved him into silence.

'Of *course* you never look. You stand in the middle of the floor and before he knows what you're going to do make a sudden leap for the bed – never walk near the bed; to a ghost your ankle is your most vulnerable part – once in bed, you're safe; he may lie around under the bed all night, but you're safe as daylight. If you still have doubts pull the blanket over your head.'

'All that's very interesting, Alec.'

'Isn't it?' Alec beamed proudly. 'All my own, too – the Sir Oliver Lodge of the new world.'

Amory was enjoying college immensely again. The sense of going forward in a direct, determined line had come back; youth was stirring and shaking out a few new feathers. He had even stored enough surplus energy to sally into a new pose.

'What's the idea of all this "distracted" stuff, Amory?' asked Alec one day, and then as Amory pretended to be cramped over his book in a daze: 'Oh, don't try to act Burne, the mystic, to me.'

Amory looked up innocently.

'What?'

'What?' mimicked Alec. 'Are you trying to read yourself into a rhapsody with – let's see the book.'

He snatched it; regarded it derisively.

'Well?' said Amory a little stiffly.

'*The Life of St Teresa*,' read Alec aloud. 'Oh, my gosh!'

'Say, Alec.'

'What?'

'Does it bother you?'

'Does what bother me?'

'My acting dazed and all that?'

'Why, no – of course it doesn't *bother* me.'

'Well, then, don't spoil it. If I enjoy going around telling people guilelessly that I think I'm a genius, let me do it.'

'You're getting a reputation for being eccentric,' said Alec, laughing, 'if that's what you mean.'

Amory finally prevailed, and Alec agreed to accept his face value in the presence of others if he was allowed rest periods when they were alone; so Amory 'ran it out' at a great rate, bringing the most eccentric characters to dinner, wild-eyed grad students, preceptors with strange theories of God and government, to the cynical amazement of the supercilious Cottage Club.

As February became slashed by sun and moved cheerfully into March, Amory went several times to spend weekends with Monsignor; once he took Burne, with great success, for he took equal pride and delight in displaying them to each other. Monsignor took him several times to see Thornton Hancock, and once or twice to the house of a Mrs Lawrence, a type of Rome-haunting American whom Amory liked immediately.

Then one day came a letter from Monsignor, which appended an interesting postscript:

> Do you know [it ran] that your third cousin, Clara Page, widowed six months and very poor, is living in Philadelphia? I don't think you've ever met her, but I wish, as a favour to me, you'd go to see her. To my mind, she's rather a remarkable woman, and just about your age.

Amory sighed and decided to go, as a favour . . .

CLARA

She was immemorial . . . Amory wasn't good enough for Clara, Clara of ripply golden hair, but then no man was. Her goodness was above the proxy morals of the husband-seeker, apart from the dull literature of female virtue.

Sorrow lay lightly around her, and when Amory found her in Philadelphia he thought her steely blue eyes held only happiness; a latent strength, a realism, was brought to its fullest development by the facts that she was compelled to face. She was alone in the world, with two small children, little money, and, worst of all, a host of friends. He saw her that winter in Philadelphia entertaining a houseful of men for an evening, when he knew she had not a servant in the house except the little coloured girl guarding the babies overhead. He saw one of the greatest libertines in that city, a man who was habitually drunk and notorious at home and abroad, sitting opposite her for an evening, discussing *girls' boarding-schools* with a sort of innocent excitement. What a twist Clara had to her mind! She could make fascinating and almost brilliant conversation out of the thinnest air that ever floated through a drawing-room.

The idea that the girl was poverty-stricken had appealed to Amory's sense of situation. He arrived in Philadelphia expecting to be told that 921 Ark Street was in a miserable lane of hovels. He was even disappointed when it proved to be nothing of the sort. It was an old house that had been in her husband's family for years. An elderly aunt, who objected to having it sold, had put ten years' taxes with a lawyer and pranced off to Honolulu, leaving Clara to struggle with the heating-problem as best she could. So no wild-haired woman with a hungry baby at her breast and a sad Amelia-like look greeted him. Instead, Amory would have thought from his reception that she had not a care in the world.

A calm virility and a dreamy humour, marked contrasts to her level-headedness – into these moods she slipped sometimes as a refuge. She could do the most prosy things (though she was wise enough never to stultify herself with such 'household arts' as *knitting* and *embroidery*), yet immediately afterwards pick up a book and let her imagination rove as a formless cloud with the wind. Deepest of all in her personality was the golden radiance that she diffused around her. As an open fire in a dark room throws romance and pathos into the quiet faces at its edge, so she cast her lights and shadows around the rooms that held her, until she made of her prosy old uncle a man of quaint and meditative charm, metamorphosed the stray telegraph boy into a Puck-like creature of delightful originality. At first this quality of hers somehow irritated Amory. He considered his own uniqueness sufficient, and it rather embarrassed him when she tried to read new interests into him for the benefit of what other adorers were present. He felt as if a polite but insistent stage-manager were attempting to make him give a new interpretation of a part he had conned for years.

But Clara talking, Clara telling a slender tale of a hatpin and an inebriated man and herself . . . People tried afterwards to repeat her anecdotes but for the life of them they could make them sound like nothing whatever. They gave her a sort of innocent attention and the best smiles many of them had smiled for long; there were few tears in Clara, but people smiled misty-eyed at her.

Very occasionally Amory stayed for little half-hours after the rest of the court had gone, and they would have bread and jam and tea late in the afternoon or 'maple-sugar lunches', as she called them, at night.

'You *are* remarkable, aren't you!' Amory was becoming trite from where he perched in the centre of the dining-room table one six o'clock.

'Not a bit,' she answered. She was searching out napkins in the sideboard. 'I'm really most humdrum and commonplace. One of those people who have no interest in anything but their children.'

'Tell that to somebody else,' scoffed Amory. 'You know you're perfectly effulgent.' He asked her the one thing that he knew might embarrass her. It was the remark that the first bore made to Adam.

'Tell me about yourself.'

And she gave the answer that Adam must have given.

'There's nothing to tell.'

But eventually Adam probably told the bore all the things he thought about at night when the locusts sang in the sandy grass, and he must have remarked patronisingly how *different* he was from Eve, forgetting how different she was from him . . . at any rate, Clara told Amory much about herself that evening. She had had a harried life from sixteen on, and her education had stopped sharply with her leisure. Browsing in her library, Amory found a tattered grey book out of which fell a yellow sheet that he impudently opened. It was a poem that she had written at school about a grey convent wall on a grey day, and a girl with her cloak blown by the wind sitting atop it and thinking about the many-coloured world. As a rule such sentiment bored him, but this was done with so much simplicity and atmosphere, that it brought a picture of Clara to his mind, of Clara on such a cool, grey day with her keen blue eyes staring out, trying to see her tragedies come marching over the gardens outside. He envied that poem. How he would have loved to have come along and seen her on the wall and talked nonsense or romance to her, perched above him in the air. He began to be frightfully jealous of everything about Clara: of her past, of her babies, of the men and women who flocked to drink deep of her cool kindness and rest their tired minds as at an absorbing play.

'*Nobody* seems to bore you,' he objected.

'About half the world do,' she admitted, 'but I think that's a pretty good average, don't you?' and she turned to find something in Browning that bore on the subject. She was the only person he ever met who could look up passages and quotations to show him in the middle of the conversation, and yet not be irritating to distraction. She did it constantly, with such a serious enthusiasm that he grew fond of watching her golden hair bent over a book, brow wrinkled ever so little at hunting her sentence.

Through early March he took to going to Philadelphia for weekends. Almost always there was someone else there and she seemed not anxious to see him alone, for many occasions presented themselves when a word from her would have given him another delicious half-hour of adoration. But he fell gradually in love and began to speculate wildly on marriage. Though this design flowed through his brain even to his lips, still he knew afterwards that the desire had not been deeply rooted. Once he dreamt that it had come true and woke up in a cold panic, for in his dream she had been a silly, flaxen Clara, with the gold gone out of her hair and platitudes falling insipidly from her changeling tongue. But she was the first fine woman he ever knew and one of the few good people who ever interested him. She made her goodness such an asset. Amory had decided that most good people either dragged theirs after them as a liability, or else distorted it to artificial geniality, and of course there were the ever-present prig and Pharisee – (but Amory never included *them* as being among the saved).

ST CECILIA

Over her grey and velvet dress,
    Under her molten, beaten hair,
Colour of rose in mock distress
    Flushes and fades and makes her fair;
Fills the air from her to him
    With light and languor and little sighs,
Just so subtly he scarcely knows . . .
    Laughing, lightning, colour of rose.

'Do you like me?'

'Of course I do,' said Clara seriously.

'Why?'

'Well, we have some qualities in common. Things that are spontaneous in each of us – or were originally.'

'You're implying that I haven't used myself very well?'

Clara hesitated.

'Well, I can't judge. A man, of course, has to go through a lot more, and I've been sheltered.'

'Oh, don't stall, please, Clara,' Amory interrupted; 'but do talk about me a little, won't you?'

'Surely, I'd adore to.' She didn't smile.

'That's sweet of you. First answer some questions. Am I painfully conceited?'

'Well – no, you have tremendous vanity, but it'll amuse the people who notice its preponderance.'

'I see.'

'You're really humble at heart. You sink to the third hell of depression when you think you've been slighted. In fact, you haven't much self-respect.'

'Centre of target twice, Clara. How do you do it? You never let me say a word.'

'Of course not – I can never judge a man while he's talking. But I'm not through; the reason you have so little real self-confidence, even though you gravely announce to the occasional philistine that you think you're a genius, is that you've attributed all sorts of atrocious faults to yourself and are trying to live up to them. For instance, you're always saying that you are a slave to highballs.'

'But I am, potentially.'

'And you say you're a weak character, that you've no will.'

'Not a bit of will – I'm a slave to my emotions, to my likes, to my hatred of boredom, to most of my desires – '

'You are not!' She brought one little fist down on to the other. 'You're a slave, a bound helpless slave to one thing in the world, your imagination.'

'You certainly interest me. If this isn't boring you, go on.'

'I notice that when you want to stay over an extra day from college you go about it in a sure way. You never decide at first while the merits of going or staying are fairly clear in your mind. You let your imagination shinny on the side of your desires for a few hours, and then you decide. Naturally your imagination, after a little freedom, thinks up a million reasons why you should stay, so your decision when it comes isn't true. It's biassed.'

'Yes,' objected Amory, 'but isn't it lack of willpower to let my imagination shinny on the wrong side?'

'My dear boy, there's your big mistake. This has nothing to do with willpower; that's a crazy, useless word, anyway; you lack judgement – the judgement to decide at once when you know your imagination will play you false, given half a chance.'

'Well, I'll be darned!' exclaimed Amory in surprise, 'that's the last thing I expected.'

Clara didn't gloat. She changed the subject immediately. But she had started him thinking and he believed she was partly right. He felt like a factory-owner who after accusing a clerk of dishonesty finds that his own son, in the office, is changing the books once a week. His poor, mistreated will that he had been holding up to the scorn of himself and his friends, stood before him innocent, and his judgement walked off to prison with the unconfinable imp, imagination, dancing in mocking glee beside him. Clara's was the only advice he ever asked without dictating the answer himself – except, perhaps, in his talks with Monsignor Darcy.

How he loved to do any sort of thing with Clara! Shopping with her was a rare, epicurean dream. In every store where she had ever traded she was whispered about as the beautiful Mrs Page.

'I'll bet she won't stay single long.'

'Well, don't scream it out. She ain't lookin' for no advice.'

'*Ain't* she beautiful!'

(*Enter a floor-walker – silence till he moves forward, smirking.*)

'Society person, ain't she?'

'Yeah, but poor now, I guess; so they say.'

'Gee! girls, *ain't* she some kid!'

And Clara beamed on all alike. Amory believed that tradespeople gave her discounts, sometimes to her knowledge and sometimes without it. He knew she dressed very well, had always the best of everything in the house, and was inevitably waited upon by the head floor-walker at the very least.

Sometimes they would go to church together on Sunday and he would walk beside her and revel in her cheeks moist from the soft water in the new air. She was very devout, always had been, and God knows what heights she attained and what strength she drew down to herself when she knelt and bent her golden hair into the stained-glass light.

'St Cecelia,' he cried aloud one day, quite involuntarily, and the people turned and peered, and the priest paused in his sermon and Clara and Amory turned to fiery red.

That was the last Sunday they had, for he spoiled it all that night. He couldn't help it.

They were walking through the March twilight where it was as warm as June, and the joy of youth filled his soul so that he felt he must speak.

'I think,' he said and his voice trembled, 'that if I lost faith in you I'd lose faith in God.'

She looked at him with such a startled face that he asked her the matter.

'Nothing,' she said slowly, 'only this: five men have said that to me before, and it frightens me.'

'Oh, Clara, is that your fate!'

She did not answer.

'I suppose love to you is –' he began.

She turned like a flash.

'I have never been in love.'

They walked along, and he realised slowly how much she had told him . . . never in love . . . She seemed suddenly a daughter of light alone. His entity dropped out of her plane and he longed only to touch her dress with almost the realisation that Joseph must have had of Mary's eternal significance. But quite mechanically he heard himself saying: 'And I love you – any latent greatness that I've got is . . . oh, I can't talk, but Clara, if I come back in two years in a position to marry you – '

She shook her head.

'No,' she said; 'I'd never marry again. I've got my two children and I want myself for them. I like you – I like all clever men, you more than any – but you know me well enough to know that I'd never marry a clever man – '

She broke off suddenly.

'Amory.'

'What?'

'You're not in love with me. You never wanted to marry me, did you?'

'It was the twilight,' he said wonderingly. 'I didn't feel as though I were speaking aloud. But I love you – or adore you – or worship you – '

'There you go – running through your catalogue of emotions in five seconds.'

He smiled unwillingly.

'Don't make me out such a lightweight, Clara; you *are* depressing sometimes.'

'You're not a lightweight, of all things,' she said intently, taking his arm and opening wide her eyes – he could see their kindliness in the fading dusk. 'A lightweight is an eternal nay.'

'There's so much spring in the air – there's so much lazy sweetness in your heart.'

She dropped his arm.

'You're all fine now, and I feel glorious. Give me a cigarette. You've never seen me smoke, have you? Well, I do, about once a month.'

And then that wonderful girl and Amory raced to the corner like two mad children gone wild with pale-blue twilight.

'I'm going to the country for tomorrow,' she announced, as she stood panting, safe beyond the flare of the corner lamp-post. 'These days are too magnificent to miss, though perhaps I feel them more in the city.'

'Oh, Clara!' Amory said; 'what a devil you could have been if the Lord had just bent your soul a little the other way!'

'Maybe,' she answered; 'but I think not. I'm never really wild and never have been. That little outburst was pure spring.'

'And you are, too,' said he.

They were walking along now.

'No – you're wrong again, how can a person of your own self-reputed brains be so constantly wrong about me? I'm the opposite of everything spring ever stood for. It's unfortunate, if I happen to look like what pleased some soppy old Greek sculptor, but I assure you that if it weren't for my face I'd be a quiet nun in the convent without' – then she broke into a run and her raised voice floated back to him as he followed – 'my precious babies, which I must go back and see.'

She was the only girl he ever knew with whom he could understand how another man might be preferred. Often Amory met wives whom he had known as débutantes, and looking intently at them imagined that he found something in their faces which said: 'Oh, if I could only have gotten *you*!' Oh, the enormous conceit of the man!

But that night seemed a night of stars and singing and Clara's bright soul still gleamed on the ways they had trod.

'*Golden, golden is the air* – ' he chanted to the little pools of water . . . '*Golden is the air, golden notes from golden mandolins, golden frets of golden violins, fair, oh, wearily fair . . . Skeins from braided baskets mortals may not hold; oh, what young extravagant God, who would know or ask it? . . . who could give such gold . . .*'

AMORY IS RESENTFUL

Slowly and inevitably, yet with a sudden surge at the last, while Amory talked and dreamed, war rolled swiftly up the beach and washed the sands where Princeton played. Every night the gymnasium echoed as platoon after platoon swept over the floor and shuffled out the basketball markings. When Amory went to Washington the next weekend he caught some of the spirit of crisis which changed to repulsion in the Pullman car coming back, for the berths across from him were occupied by stinking aliens – Greeks, he guessed, or Russians. He thought how much easier patriotism had been to a homogeneous race, how much easier it would have been to fight as the Colonies fought, or as the Confederacy fought. And he did no sleeping that night, but listened to the aliens guffaw and snore while they filled the car with the heavy scent of latest America.

In Princeton everyone bantered in public and told themselves privately that their deaths at least would be heroic. The literary students read Rupert Brooke passionately; the lounge-lizards worried over whether the government would permit the English-cut uniform for officers; a few of the hopelessly lazy wrote to the obscure branches of the War Department, seeking an easy commission and a soft berth.

Then, after a week, Amory saw Burne and knew at once that argument would be futile – Burne had come out as a pacifist. The socialist magazines, a great smattering of Tolstoy, and his own intense longing for a cause that would bring out whatever strength lay in him, had finally decided him to preach peace as a subjective ideal.

'When the German army entered Belgium,' he began, 'if the inhabitants had gone peaceably about their business, the German army would have been disorganised in – '

'I know,' Amory interrupted, 'I've heard it all. But I'm not going to talk propaganda with you. There's a chance that you're right – but even so we're hundreds of years before the time when non-resistance can touch us as a reality.'

'But, Amory, listen – '

'Burne, we'd just argue – '

'Very well.'

'Just one thing – I don't ask you to think of your family or friends, because I know they don't count a picayune with you beside your sense of duty – but, Burne, how do you know that the magazines you read and the societies you join and these idealists you meet aren't just plain *German*?'

'Some of them are, of course.'

'How do you know they aren't *all* pro-German – just a lot of weak ones – with German-Jewish names.'

'That's the chance, of course,' he said slowly. 'How much or how little I'm taking this stand because of propaganda I've heard, I don't know; naturally I think that it's my most innermost conviction – it seems a path spread before me just now.'

Amory's heart sank.

'But think of the cheapness of it – no one's really going to martyr you for being a pacifist – it's just going to throw you in with the worst – '

'I doubt it,' he interrupted.

'Well, it all smells of Bohemian New York to me.'

'I know what you mean, and that's why I'm not sure I'll agitate.'

'You're one man, Burne – going to talk to people who won't listen – with all God's given you.'

'That's what Stephen must have thought many years ago. But he preached his sermon and they killed him. He probably thought as he was dying what a waste it all was. But you see, I've always felt that Stephen's death was the thing that occurred to Paul on the road to Damascus, and sent him to preach the word of Christ all over the world.'

'Go on.'

'That's all – this is my particular duty. Even if right now I'm just a pawn – just sacrificed. God! Amory – you don't think I like the Germans!'

'Well, I can't say anything else – I get to the end of all the logic about non-resistance, and there, like an excluded middle, stands the huge spectre of man as he is and always will be. And this spectre stands right beside the one logical necessity of Tolstoy's, and the other logical necessity of Nietzsche's – ' Amory broke off suddenly. 'When are you going?'

'I'm going next week.'

'I'll see you, of course.'

As he walked away it seemed to Amory that the look in his face bore a great resemblance to that in Kerry's when he had said goodbye under Blair Arch two years before. Amory wondered unhappily why he could never go into anything with the primal honesty of those two.

'Burne's a fanatic,' he said to Tom, 'and he's dead wrong and, I'm inclined to think, just an unconscious pawn in the hands of anarchistic publishers and German-paid rag wavers – but he haunts me – just leaving everything worth while – '

Burne left in a quietly dramatic manner a week later. He sold all his possessions and came down to the room to say goodbye, with a battered old bicycle, on which he intended to ride to his home in Pennsylvania.

'Peter the Hermit bidding farewell to Cardinal Richelieu,' suggested Alec, who was lounging in the window-seat as Burne and Amory shook hands.

But Amory was not in a mood for that, and as he saw Burne's long legs propel his ridiculous bicycle out of sight beyond Alexander Hall, he knew he was going to have a bad week. Not that he doubted the war – Germany stood for everything repugnant to him; for materialism and the direction of tremendous licentious force; it was just that Burne's face stayed in his memory and he was sick of the hysteria he was beginning to hear.

'What on earth is the use of suddenly running down Goethe,' he declared to Alec and Tom. 'Why write books to prove he started the war – or that that stupid, overestimated Schiller is a demon in disguise?'

'Have you ever read anything of theirs?' asked Tom shrewdly.

'No,' Amory admitted.

'Neither have I,' he said laughing.

'People will shout,' said Alec quietly, 'but Goethe's on his same old shelf in the library – to bore anyone that wants to read him!'

Amory subsided, and the subject dropped.

'What are you going to do, Amory?'

'Infantry or aviation, I can't make up my mind – I hate mechanics, but then of course aviation's the thing for me – '

'I feel as Amory does,' said Tom. 'Infantry or aviation – aviation sounds like the romantic side of the war, of course – like cavalry used to be, you know; but like Amory I don't know a horsepower from a piston-rod.'

Somehow Amory's dissatisfaction with his lack of enthusiasm culminated in an attempt to put the blame for the whole war on the ancestors of his generation . . . all the people who cheered for Germany in 1870 . . . All the materialists rampant, all the idolisers of German science and efficiency. So he sat one day in an English lecture and heard *Locksley Hall* quoted and fell into a brown study with contempt for Tennyson and all he stood for – for he took him as a representative of the Victorians.

> 'Victorians, Victorians, who never learned to weep,
> Who sowed the bitter harvest that your children go to reap – '

scribbled Amory in his notebook. The lecturer was saying something about Tennyson's solidity and fifty heads were bent to take notes. Amory turned over to a fresh page and began scrawling again.

> 'They shuddered when they found what Mr Darwin was about,
> They shuddered when the waltz came in and Newman
> hurried out – '

But the waltz came in much earlier; he crossed that out.

'And entitled "A Song in Time of Order",' came the professor's voice, droning far away. 'Time of Order' – Good Lord! Everything crammed in the box and the Victorians sitting on the lid smiling serenely . . . With Browning in his Italian villa crying bravely: 'All's for the best.' Amory scribbled again.

> 'You knelt up in the temple and he bent to hear you pray,
> You thanked him for your "glorious gains" – reproached
> him for "Cathay".'

Why could he never get more than a couplet at a time?

Now he needed something to rhyme with:

> 'You would keep Him straight with science, tho' He had
> gone wrong before . . . '

Well, anyway . . .

'You met your children in your home – "I've fixed it up!" you cried,
Took your fifty years of Europe, and then virtuously – died.'

'That was to a great extent Tennyson's idea,' came the lecturer's voice. 'Swinburne's "Song in Time of Order" might well have been Tennyson's title. He idealised order against chaos, against waste.'

At last Amory had it. He turned over another page and scrawled vigorously for the twenty minutes that were left of the hour. Then he walked up to the desk and deposited a page torn out of his notebook.

'Here's a poem to the Victorians, sir,' he said coldly.

The professor picked it up curiously while Amory backed rapidly through the door.

Here is what he had written:

'Songs in the time of order
You left for us to sing,
Proofs with excluded middles,
Answers to life in rhyme,

Keys of the prison warder
And ancient bells to ring,
Time was the end of riddles,
We were the end of time . . .

Here were domestic oceans
And a sky that we might reach,
Guns and a guarded border,
Gauntlets – but not to fling,

Thousands of old emotions
And a platitude for each,
Songs in the time of order –
And tongues, that we might sing.'

THE END OF MANY THINGS

Early April slipped by in a haze – a haze of long evenings on the club veranda with the graphophone playing 'Poor Butterfly' inside . . . for 'Poor Butterfly' had been the song of that last year. The war seemed scarcely to touch them and it might have been one of the senior springs of the past, except for the drilling every other afternoon, yet

Amory realised poignantly that this was the last spring under the old regime.

'This is the great protest against the superman,' said Amory.

'I suppose so,' Alec agreed.

'He's absolutely irreconcilable with any Utopia. As long as he occurs, there's trouble and all the latent evil that makes a crowd list and sway when he talks.'

'And of course all that he is is a gifted man without a moral sense.'

'That's all. I think the worst thing to contemplate is this – it's all happened before, how soon will it happen again? Fifty years after Waterloo, Napoleon was as much a hero to English schoolchildren as Wellington. How do we know our grandchildren won't idolise Von Hindenburg the same way?'

'What brings it about?'

'Time, damn it, and the historian. If we could only learn to look on evil as evil, whether it's clothed in filth or monotony or magnificence.'

'God! Haven't we raked the universe over the coals for four years?'

Then the night came that was to be the last. Tom and Amory, bound in the morning for different training-camps, paced the shadowy walks as usual and seemed still to see around them the faces of the men they knew.

'The grass is full of ghosts tonight.'

'The whole campus is alive with them.'

They paused by Little and watched the moon rise, to make silver of the slate roof of Dodd and blue the rustling trees.

'You know,' whispered Tom, 'what we feel now is the sense of all the gorgeous youth that has rioted through here in two hundred years.'

A last burst of singing flooded up from Blair Arch – broken voices for some long parting.

'And what we leave here is more than this class; it's the whole heritage of youth. We're just one generation – we're breaking all the links that seemed to bind us here to top-booted and high-stocked generations. We've walked arm and arm with Burr and Light-Horse Harry Lee through half these deep-blue nights.'

'That's what they are,' Tom tangented off, 'deep blue – a bit of colour would spoil them, make them exotic. Spires, against a sky that's a promise of dawn, and blue light on the slate roofs – it hurts . . . rather – '

'Goodbye, Aaron Burr,' Amory called towards deserted Nassau Hall, 'you and I knew strange corners of life.'

His voice echoed in the stillness.

'The torches are out,' whispered Tom. 'Ah, Messalina, the long shadows are building minarets on the stadium – '

For an instant the voices of freshman year surged around them and then they looked at each other with faint tears in their eyes.

'Damn!'

'Damn!'

The last light fades and drifts across the land – the low, long land, the sunny land of spires; the ghosts of evening tune again their lyres and wander singing in a plaintive band down the long corridors of trees; pale fires echo the night from tower top to tower: Oh, sleep that dreams, and dream that never tires, press from the petals of the lotus flower something of this to keep, the essence of an hour.

No more to wait the twilight of the moon in this sequestered vale of star and spire, for one eternal morning of desire passes to time and earthy afternoon. Here, Heraclitus, did you find in fire and shifting things the prophecy you hurled down the dead years; this midnight my desire will see, shadowed among the embers, furled in flame, the splendour and the sadness of the world.

INTERLUDE

May 1917–February 1919

A letter dated January 1918, written by Monsignor Darcy to Amory, who is a second lieutenant in the 171st Infantry, Port of Embarkation, Camp Mills, Long Island.

My Dear Boy – All you need tell me of yourself is that you still are; for the rest I merely search back in a restive memory, a thermometer that records only fevers, and match you with what I was at your age. But men will chatter and you and I will still shout our futilities to each other across the stage until the last silly curtain falls *plump!* upon our bobbing heads. But you are starting the spluttering magic-lantern show of life with much the same array of slides as I had, so I need to write you if only to shriek the colossal stupidity of *people* . . .

This is the end of one thing: for better or worse you will never again be quite the Amory Blaine that I knew, never again will we meet as we have met, because your generation is growing hard, much harder than mine ever grew, nourished as they were on the stuff of the nineties.

Amory, lately I reread Aeschylus and there in the divine irony of the *Agamemnon* I find the only answer to this bitter age – all the world tumbled about our ears, and the closest parallel ages back in that hopeless resignation. There are times when I think of the men out there as Roman legionaries, miles from their corrupt city, stemming back the hordes . . . hordes a little more menacing, after all, than the corrupt city . . . another blind blow at the race, furies that we passed with ovations years ago, over whose corpses we bleated triumphantly all through the Victorian era . . .

And afterwards an out-and-out materialistic world – and the Catholic Church. I wonder where you'll fit in. Of one thing I'm sure – Celtic you'll live and Celtic you'll die; so if you don't use heaven as a continual referendum for your ideas you'll find earth a continual recall to your ambitions.

Amory, I've discovered suddenly that I'm an old man. Like all old men, I've had dreams sometimes and I'm going to tell you of them. I've enjoyed imagining that you were my son, that perhaps when I was young I went into a state of coma and begat you, and when I came to, had no recollection of it . . . it's the paternal instinct, Amory – celibacy goes deeper than the flesh . . .

Sometimes I think that the explanation of our deep resemblance is some common ancestor, and I find that the only blood that the Darcys and the O'Haras have in common is that of the O'Donahues . . . Stephen was his name, I think . . .

When the lightning strikes one of us it strikes both: you had hardly arrived at the port of embarkation when I got my papers to start for Rome, and I am waiting every moment to be told where to take ship. Even before you get this letter I shall be on the ocean; then will come your turn. You went to war as a gentleman should, just as you went to school and college, because it was the thing to do. It's better to leave the blustering and tremulo-heroism to the middle classes; they do it so much better.

Do you remember that weekend last March when you brought Burne Holiday from Princeton to see me? What a magnificent boy he is! It gave me a frightful shock afterwards when you wrote that he thought me splendid; how could he be so deceived? Splendid is the one thing that neither you nor I are. We are many other things – we're extraordinary, we're clever, we could be said, I suppose, to be brilliant. We can attract people, we can make atmosphere, we can almost lose our Celtic souls in Celtic subtleties, we can almost always have our own way; but splendid – rather not!

I am going to Rome with a wonderful dossier and letters of introduction that cover every capital in Europe, and there will be 'no small stir' when I get there. How I wish you were with me! This sounds like a rather cynical paragraph, not at all the sort of thing that a middle-aged clergyman should write to a youth about to depart for the war; the only excuse is that the middle-aged clergyman is talking to himself. There are deep things in us and you know what they are as well as I do. We have great faith, though yours at present is uncrystallised; we have a terrible honesty that all our sophistry cannot destroy and, above all, a childlike simplicity that keeps us from ever being really malicious.

I have written a keen for you which follows. I am sorry your cheeks are not up to the description I have written of them, but you *will* smoke and read all night –

At any rate here it is:

A Lament for a Foster Son,
and He going to the War against the King of Foreign

Ochone
He is gone from me the son of my mind
And he in his golden youth like Angus Oge
Angus of the bright birds
And his mind strong and subtle like the mind of
Cuchulin on Muirtheme.

Awirra sthrue
His brow is as white as the milk of the cows of Maeve
And his cheeks like the cherries of the tree
And it bending down to Mary and she feeding
the Son of God.

Aveelia Vrone
His hair is like the golden collar of the Kings at Tara
And his eyes like the four grey seas of Erin.
And they swept with the mists of rain.

Mavrone go Gudyo
He to be in the joyful and red battle
Amongst the chieftains and they doing great deeds of valour
His life to go from him
It is the chords of my own soul would be loosed.

A Vich Deelish
My heart is in the heart of my son
And my life is in his life surely
A man can be twice young
In the life of his sons only.

Jia du Vaha Alanav
May the Son of God be above him and beneath him,
before him and behind him
May the King of the elements cast a mist over the eyes of
the King of Foreign,
May the Queen of the Graces lead him by the hand the
way he can go through the midst of his enemies and they
not seeing him

May Patrick of the Gael and Collumb of the Churches
and the five thousand Saints of Erin be better than
a shield to him
And he got into the fight.
Och Ochone.

Amory – Amory – I feel, somehow, that this is all; one or both of us is not going to last out this war . . . I've been trying to tell you how much this reincarnation of myself in you has meant in the last few years . . . curiously alike we are . . . curiously unlike.

Goodbye, dear boy, and God be with you.

THAYER DARCY

EMBARKING AT NIGHT

Amory moved forward on the deck until he found a stool under an electric light. He searched in his pocket for notebook and pencil and then began to write, slowly, laboriously:

We leave tonight . . .
Silent, we filled the still, deserted street,
A column of dim grey,
And ghosts rose startled at the muffled beat
Along the moonless way;
The shadowy shipyards echoed to the feet
That turned from night and day.

And so we linger on the windless decks,
See on the spectre shore
Shades of a thousand days, poor grey-ribbed wrecks . . .
Oh, shall we then deplore
Those futile years!
See how the sea is white!
The clouds have broken and the heavens burn
To hollow highways, paved with gravelled light
The churning of the waves about the stern
Rises to one voluminous nocturne,
. . . We leave tonight.'

A letter from Amory, headed 'Brest, March 11th, 1919', to Lieutenant T. P. D'Invilliers, Camp Gordon, Ga.

Dear Baudelaire – We meet in Manhattan on the 30th of this very mo.; we then proceed to take a very sporty apartment, you and I and Alec, who is at my elbow as I write. I don't know what I'm going to do but I have a vague dream of going into politics. Why is it that the pick of the young Englishmen from Oxford and Cambridge go into politics and in the USA we leave it to the muckers? – raised in the ward, educated in the assembly and sent to Congress, fat-paunched bundles of corruption, devoid of 'both ideas and ideals' as the debaters used to say. Even forty years ago we had good men in politics, but we, we are brought up to pile up a million and 'show what we are made of'. Sometimes I wish I'd been an Englishman; American life is so damned dumb and stupid and healthy.

Since poor Beatrice died I'll probably have a little money, but very darn little. I can forgive mother almost everything except the fact that in a sudden burst of religiosity towards the end, she left half of what remained to be spent in stained-glass windows and seminary endowments. Mr Barton, my lawyer, writes me that my thousands are mostly in street railways and that the said Street R.R.s are losing money because of the five-cent fares. Imagine a salary list that gives $350 a month to a man that can't read and write! – yet I believe in it, even though I've seen what was once a sizable fortune melt away between speculation, extravagance, the democratic administration, and the income tax – modern, that's me all over, Mabel.

At any rate we'll have really knock-out rooms – you can get a job on some fashion magazine, and Alec can go into the Zinc Company or whatever it is that his people own – he's looking over my shoulder and he says it's a brass company, but I don't think it matters much, do you? There's probably as much corruption in zinc-made money as brass-made money. As for the well-known Amory, he would write immortal literature if he were sure enough about anything to risk telling anyone else about it. There is no more dangerous gift to posterity than a few cleverly turned platitudes.

Tom, why don't you become a Catholic? Of course to be a good one you'd have to give up those violent intrigues you used to tell me about, but you'd write better poetry if you were linked up to tall golden candlesticks and long, even chants, and even if the American priests are rather burgeois, as Beatrice used to say, still you need only go to the sporty churches, and I'll introduce you to Monsignor Darcy who really is a wonder.

Kerry's death was a blow, so was Jesse's to a certain extent. And I have a great curiosity to know what queer corner of the world has swallowed Burne. Do you suppose he's in prison under some false name? I confess that the war instead of making me orthodox, which is the correct reaction, has made me a passionate agnostic. The Catholic Church has had its wings clipped so often lately that its part was timidly negligible, and they haven't any good writers any more. I'm sick of Chesterton.

I've only discovered one soldier who passed through the much-advertised spiritual crisis, like this fellow, Donald Hankey, and the one I knew was already studying for the ministry, so he was ripe for it. I honestly think that's all pretty much rot, though it seemed to give sentimental comfort to those at home; and may make fathers and mothers appreciate their children. This crisis-inspired religion is rather valueless and fleeting at best. I think four men have discovered Paris to one that discovered God.

But us – you and me and Alec – oh, we'll get a Jap butler and dress for dinner and have wine on the table and lead a contemplative, emotionless life until we decide to use machine-guns with the property owners – or throw bombs with the Bolshevik. God! Tom, I hope something happens. I'm restless as the devil and have a horror of getting fat or falling in love and growing domestic.

The place at Lake Geneva is now for rent but when I land I'm going West to see Mr Barton and get some details. Write me care of the Blackstone, Chicago.

S'ever, dear Boswell,

SAMUEL JOHNSON

only go to the sporty churches and I'll introduce you to Monsignor Darcy who really is a wonder.

Kerry's death was a blow so was Jesse's to a certain extent. And I have a great curiosity to know what queer corner of the world has swallowed Burne. Do you suppose he's in prison under some false name? I confess that the war instead of making me orthodox, which is the correct reaction, has made me a passionate agnostic. The Catholic Church has had its wings clipped so often lately that its part was timidly negligible, and they haven't any good writers any more. I'm sick of Chesterton.

I've only discovered one soldier who passed through the much advertised spiritual crisis, like this fellow, Donald Hankey, and the one I knew was already studying for the ministry, so he was ripe for it. I honestly think that's all pretty much rot, though it seemed to give sentimental comfort to those at home; and may make fathers and mothers appreciate their children. This crisis-inspired religion is rather valueless and fleeting at best. I think four men have discovered Paris to one that discovered God.

But us—you and the undersigned—[illegible]

[illegible]

[illegible]

Yours [illegible]

[illegible]

BOOK TWO

The Education of a Personage

1

The Débutante

The time is February. The place is a large, dainty bedroom in the Connage house on Sixty-Eighth Street, New York. A girl's room: pink walls and curtains and a pink bedspread on a cream-coloured bed. Pink and cream are the motifs of the room, but the only article of furniture in full view is a luxurious dressing-table with a glass top and a three-sided mirror. On the walls there is an expensive print of Cherry Ripe, *a few polite dogs by Landseer, and the* King of the Black Isles *by Maxfield Parrish.*

(Great disorder consisting of the following items: (1) seven or eight empty cardboard boxes, with tissue-paper tongues hanging panting from their mouths; (2) an assortment of street dresses mingled with their sisters of the evening, all upon the table, all evidently new; (3) a roll of tulle, which has lost its dignity and wound itself tortuously around everything in sight, and (4) upon the two small chairs, a collection of lingerie that beggars description. One would enjoy seeing the bill called forth by the finery displayed and one is possessed by a desire to see the princess for whose benefit – Look! There's someone! Disappointment! This is only a maid hunting for something. She lifts a heap from a chair – not there; another heap, the dressing-table, the chiffonier drawers. She brings to light several beautiful chemises and an amazing pair of pyjamas but this does not satisfy her – she goes out.

An indistinguishable mumble from the next room.

Now, we are getting warm. This is Alec's mother, MRS CONNAGE, *ample, dignified, rouged to the dowager point and quite worn out. Her lips move significantly as she looks for* IT. *Her search is less thorough than the maid's but there is a touch of fury in it that quite makes up for its sketchiness. She stumbles on the tulle and her 'damn' is quite audible. She retires, empty-handed.*

More chatter outside and a girl's voice, a very spoiled voice, says: 'Of all the stupid people – '

After a pause a third seeker enters, not she of the spoiled voice, but a younger edition. This is CECILIA CONNAGE, *sixteen, pretty, shrewd, and constitutionally good-humoured. She is dressed for the evening in a gown the obvious simplicity of which probably bores her. She goes to the nearest pile, selects a small pink garment and holds it up appraisingly.*

CECILIA: Pink?

ROSALIND (*outside*): Yes!

CECILIA: *Very* snappy?

ROSALIND: Yes!

CECILIA: I've got it!

(*She sees herself in the mirror of the dressing-table and commences to shimmy enthusiastically.*)

ROSALIND (*outside*): What are you doing – trying it on?

(CECILIA *ceases and goes out carrying the garment at the right shoulder. From the other door, enters* ALEC CONNAGE. *He looks around quickly and in a huge voice shouts:* 'Mama!' *There is a chorus of protest from next door and encouraged he starts towards it, but is repelled by another chorus.*)

ALEC: So *that's* where you all are! Amory Blaine is here.

CECILIA (*quickly*): Take him downstairs.

ALEC: Oh, he *is* downstairs.

MRS CONNAGE: Well, you can show him where his room is. Tell him I'm sorry that I can't meet him now.

ALEC: He's heard a lot about you all. I wish you'd hurry. Father's telling him all about the war and he's restless. He's sort of temperamental.

(*This last suffices to draw* CECILIA *into the room.*)

CECILIA (*seating herself high upon lingerie*): How do you mean – temperamental? You used to say that about him in letters.

ALEC: Oh, he writes stuff.

CECILIA: Does he play the piano?

ALEC: Don't think so.

CECILIA (*speculatively*): Drink?

ALEC: Yes – nothing queer about him.

CECILIA: Money?

ALEC: Good Lord – ask him, he used to have a lot, and he's got some income now.

(MRS CONNAGE *appears.*)

MRS CONNAGE: Alec, of course we're glad to have any friend of yours –

ALEC: You certainly ought to meet Amory.

MRS CONNAGE: Of course, I want to. But I think it's so childish of you to leave a perfectly good home to go and live with two other boys in some impossible apartment. I hope it isn't in order that you can all drink as much as you want. (*She pauses.*) He'll be a little neglected tonight. This is Rosalind's week, you see. When a girl comes out, she needs *all* the attention.

ROSALIND (*outside*): Well, then, prove it by coming here and hooking me.

(MRS CONNAGE *goes.*)

ALEC: Rosalind hasn't changed a bit.

CECILIA (*in a lower tone*): She's awfully spoiled.

ALEC: She'll meet her match tonight.

CECILIA: Who – Mr Amory Blaine?

(ALEC *nods.*)

CECILIA: Well, Rosalind has still to meet the man she can't outdistance. Honestly, Alec, she treats men terribly. She abuses them and cuts them and breaks dates with them and yawns in their faces – and they come back for more.

ALEC: They love it.

CECILIA: They hate it. She's a – she's a sort of vampire, I think – and she can make girls do what she wants usually – only she hates girls.

ALEC: Personality runs in our family.

CECILIA (*resignedly*): I guess it ran out before it got to me.

ALEC: Does Rosalind behave herself?

CECILIA: Not particularly well. Oh, she's average – smokes sometimes, drinks punch, frequently kissed – Oh, yes – common knowledge – one of the effects of the war, you know.

(MRS CONNAGE *emerges.*)

MRS CONNAGE: Rosalind's almost finished so I can go down and meet your friend.

(ALEC *and his mother go out.*)

ROSALIND (*outside*): Oh, mother –

CECILIA: Mother's gone down.

(*And now* ROSALIND *enters.* ROSALIND *is – utterly* ROSALIND. *She is one of those girls who need never make the slightest effort to have men fall in love with them. Two types of men seldom do: dull men are usually afraid of her cleverness and intellectual men are usually afraid of her beauty. All others are hers by natural prerogative.*

If ROSALIND *could be spoiled the process would have been complete by this time, and as a matter of fact, her disposition is not all it should be; she wants what she wants when she wants it and she is prone to make everyone around her pretty miserable when she doesn't get it – but in the true sense she is not spoiled. Her fresh enthusiasm, her will to grow and learn, her endless faith in the inexhaustibility of romance, her courage and fundamental honesty – these things are not spoiled.*

There are long periods when she cordially loathes her whole family. She is quite unprincipled; her philosophy is carpe diem *for herself and* laissez-faire *for others. She loves shocking stories: she has that coarse streak that usually goes with natures that are both fine and big. She wants people to like her, but if they do not it never worries her or changes her. She is by no means a model character.*

The education of all beautiful women is the knowledge of men. ROSALIND *had been disappointed in man after man as individuals, but she had great faith in man as a sex. Women she detested. They represented qualities that she felt and despised in herself – incipient meanness, conceit, cowardice, and petty dishonesty. She once told a roomful of her mother's friends that the only excuse for women was the necessity for a disturbing element among men. She danced exceptionally well, drew cleverly but hastily, and had a startling facility with words, which she used only in love-letters.*

But all criticism of ROSALIND *ends in her beauty. There was that shade of glorious yellow hair, the desire to imitate which supports the dye industry. There was the eternal kissable mouth, small, slightly sensual and utterly disturbing. There were grey eyes and an unimpeachable skin with two spots of vanishing colour. She was slender and athletic, without underdevelopment, and it was a delight to watch her move about a room, walk along a street, swing a golf club or turn a 'cartwheel'.*

A last qualification – her vivid, instant personality escaped that conscious, theatrical quality that AMORY *had found in* ISABELLE. MONSIGNOR DARCY *would have been quite up a tree whether to call her a personality or a personage. She was perhaps the delicious, inexpressible, once-in-a-century blend.*

On the night of her début she is, for all her strange, stray wisdom, quite like a happy little girl. Her mother's maid has just done her hair, but she has decided impatiently that she can do a better job herself. She is too nervous just now to stay in one place. To that we owe her presence in this littered room. She is going to speak. ISABELLE*'s alto tones had been like a violin, but if you could hear* ROSALIND, *you would say her voice was musical as a waterfall.)*

ROSALIND*:* Honestly, there are only two costumes in the world that I really enjoy being in – (*combing her hair at the dressing-table.*) One's a hoop skirt with pantaloons; the other's a one-piece bathing-suit. I'm quite charming in both of them.

CECILIA: Glad you're coming out?

ROSALIND: Yes; aren't you?

CECILIA (*cynically*): You're glad so you can get married and live on Long Island with the *fast younger married set*. You want life to be a chain of flirtation with a man for every link.

ROSALIND: *Want* it to be one! You mean I've *found* it one.

CECILIA: Ha!

ROSALIND: Cecelia, darling, you don't know what a trial it is to be – like me. I've got to keep my face like steel in the street to keep men from winking at me. If I laugh hard from a front row in the theatre, the comedian plays to me for the rest of the evening. If I drop my voice, my eyes, my handkerchief at a dance, my partner calls me up on the phone every day for a week.

CECILIA: It must be an awful strain.

ROSALIND: The unfortunate part is that the only men who interest me at all are the totally ineligible ones. Now – if I were poor I'd go on the stage.

CECILIA: Yes, you might as well get paid for the amount of acting you do.

ROSALIND: Sometimes when I've felt particularly radiant I've thought, why should this be wasted on one man?

CECILIA: Often when you're particularly sulky, I've wondered why it should all be wasted on just one family. (*getting up*) I think I'll go down and meet Mr Amory Blaine. I like temperamental men.

ROSALIND: There aren't any. Men don't know how to be really angry or really happy – and the ones that do, go to pieces.

CECILIA: Well, I'm glad I don't have all your worries. I'm engaged.

ROSALIND (*with a scornful smile*): Engaged? Why, you little lunatic! If mother heard you talking like that she'd send you off to boarding-school, where you belong.

CECILIA: You won't tell her, though, because I know things I could tell – and you're too selfish!

ROSALIND (*a little annoyed*): Run along, little girl! Who are you engaged to, the iceman? The man that keeps the candy-store?

CECILIA: Cheap wit – goodbye, darling, I'll see you later.

ROSALIND: Oh, be *sure* and do that – you're such a help.

(*Exit* CECILIA. ROSALIND *finishes her hair and rises, humming. She goes up to the mirror and starts to dance in front of it on the soft carpet. She watches not her feet, but her eyes – never casually but always intently, even when she smiles. The door suddenly opens and then slams behind* AMORY, *very cool and handsome as usual. He melts into instant confusion.*)

HE: Oh, I'm sorry. I thought –

SHE (*smiling radiantly*): Oh, you're Amory Blaine, aren't you?

HE (*regarding her closely*): And you're Rosalind?

SHE: I'm going to call you Amory – oh, come in – it's all right – mother'll be right in – (*under her breath*) unfortunately.

HE (*gazing around*): This is sort of a new wrinkle for me.

SHE: This is no man's land.

HE: This is where you – you – (*pause*)

SHE: Yes – all those things. (*She crosses to the bureau.*) See, here's my rouge – eye pencils.

HE: I didn't know you were that way.

SHE: What did you expect?

HE: I thought you'd be sort of – sort of – sexless; you know, swim and play golf.

SHE: Oh, I do – but not in business hours.

HE: Business?

SHE: Six to two – strictly.

HE: I'd like to have some stock in the corporation.

SHE: Oh, it's not a corporation – it's just 'Rosalind, Unlimited'. Fifty-one shares, name, goodwill and everything goes at $25,000 a year.

HE (*disapprovingly*): Sort of a chilly proposition.

SHE: Well, Amory, you don't mind – do you? When I meet a man that doesn't bore me to death after two weeks, perhaps it'll be different.

HE: Odd, you have the same point of view on men that I have on women.

SHE: I'm not really feminine, you know – in my mind.

HE (*interested*): Go on.

SHE: No, you – you go on – you've made me talk about myself. That's against the rules.

HE: Rules?

SHE: My own rules – but you – Oh, Amory, I hear you're brilliant. The family expects *so* much of you.

HE: How encouraging!

SHE: Alec said you'd taught him to think. Did you? I didn't believe anyone could.

HE: No. I'm really quite dull.

(*He evidently doesn't intend this to be taken seriously.*)

SHE: Liar.

HE: I'm – I'm religious – I'm literary. I've – I've even written poems.

SHE: *Vers libre* – splendid! (*She declaims.*)

The trees are green,
The birds are singing in the trees,
The girl sips her poison,
The bird flies away the girl dies.

HE (*laughing*): No, not that kind.
SHE: (*suddenly*): I like you.
HE: Don't.
SHE: Modest too –
HE: I'm afraid of you. I'm always afraid of a girl – until I've kissed her.
SHE (*emphatically*): My dear boy, the war is over.
HE: So I'll always be afraid of you.
SHE (*rather sadly*): I suppose you will.
(*a slight hesitation on both their parts*)
HE (*after due consideration*): Listen. This is a frightful thing to ask.
SHE (*knowing what's coming*): After five minutes.
HE: But will you – kiss me? Or are you afraid?
SHE: I'm never afraid – but your reasons are so poor.
HE: Rosalind, I really *want* to kiss you.
SHE: So do I.
(*They kiss – definitely and thoroughly.*)
HE (*after a breathless second*): Well, is your curiosity satisfied?
SHE: Is yours?
HE: No, it's only aroused.
(*He looks it.*)
SHE (*dreamily*): I've kissed dozens of men. I suppose I'll kiss dozens more.
HE (*abstractedly*): Yes, I suppose you could – like that.
SHE: Most people like the way I kiss.
HE (*remembering himself*): Good Lord, yes. Kiss me once more, Rosalind.
SHE: No – my curiosity is generally satisfied at one.
HE: (*discouraged*): Is that a rule?
SHE: I make rules to fit the cases.
HE: You and I are somewhat alike – except that I'm years older in experience.
SHE: How old are you?
HE: Almost twenty-three. You?
SHE: Nineteen – just.
HE: I suppose you're the product of a fashionable school.

SHE: No – I'm fairly raw material. I was expelled from Spence – I've forgotten why.

HE: What's your general trend?

SHE: Oh, I'm bright, quite selfish, emotional when aroused, fond of admiration –

HE (*suddenly*): I don't want to fall in love with you –

SHE (*raising her eyebrows*): Nobody asked you to.

HE (*continuing coldly*): But I probably will. I love your mouth.

SHE: Hush! Please don't fall in love with my mouth – hair, eyes, shoulders, slippers – but *not* my mouth. Everybody falls in love with my mouth.

HE: It's quite beautiful.

SHE: It's too small.

HE: No it isn't – let's see.

(*He kisses her again with the same thoroughness.*)

SHE (*rather moved*): Say something sweet.

HE (*frightened*): Lord help me.

SHE (*drawing away*): Well, don't – if it's so hard.

HE: Shall we pretend? So soon?

SHE: We haven't the same standards of time as other people.

HE: Already it's – other people.

SHE: Let's pretend.

HE: No – I can't – it's sentiment.

SHE: You're not sentimental?

HE: No, I'm romantic – a sentimental person thinks things will last – a romantic person hopes against hope that they won't. Sentiment is emotional.

SHE: And you're not? (*with her eyes half-closed*) You probably flatter yourself that that's a superior attitude.

HE: Well – Rosalind, Rosalind, don't argue – kiss me again.

SHE (*quite chilly now*): No – I have no desire to kiss you.

HE (*openly taken aback*): You wanted to kiss me a minute ago.

SHE: This is now.

HE: I'd better go.

SHE: I suppose so.

(*He goes towards the door.*)

SHE: Oh!

(*He turns.*)

SHE (*laughing*): Score – Home Team: One hundred; Opponents: Zero.

(*He starts back.*)

SHE (*quickly*): Rain – no game.

(*He goes out. She goes quietly to the chiffonier, takes out a cigarette-case and hides it in the side drawer of a desk. Her mother enters, notebook in hand.*)

MRS CONNAGE: Good – I've been wanting to speak to you alone before we go downstairs.

ROSALIND: Heavens! you frighten me!

MRS CONNAGE: Rosalind, you've been a very expensive proposition.

ROSALIND (*resignedly*): Yes.

MRS CONNAGE: And you know your father hasn't what he once had.

ROSALIND (*making a wry face*): Oh, please don't talk about money.

MRS CONNAGE: You can't do anything without it. This is our last year in this house – and unless things change Cecelia won't have the advantages you've had.

ROSALIND (*impatiently*): Well – what is it?

MRS CONNAGE: So I ask you to please mind me in several things I've put down in my notebook. The first one is: don't disappear with young men. There may be a time when it's valuable, but at present I want you on the dance-floor where I can find you. There are certain men I want to have you meet and I don't like finding you in some corner of the conservatory exchanging silliness with anyone – or listening to it.

ROSALIND (*sarcastically*): Yes, listening to it *is* better.

MRS CONNAGE: And don't waste a lot of time with the college set – little boys nineteen and twenty years old. I don't mind a prom or a football game, but staying away from advantageous parties to eat in little cafés downtown with Tom, Dick and Harry –

ROSALIND (*offering her code, which is, in its way, quite as high as her mother's*): Mother, it's done – you can't run everything now the way you did in the early nineties.

MRS CONNAGE (*paying no attention*): There are several bachelor friends of your father's that I want you to meet tonight – youngish men.

ROSALIND (*nodding wisely*): About forty-five?

MRS CONNAGE (*sharply*): Why not?

ROSALIND: Oh, *quite* all right – they know life and are so adorably tired looking (*shakes her head*) – but they *will* dance.

MRS CONNAGE: I haven't met Mr Blaine – but I don't think you'll care for him. He doesn't sound like a money-maker.

ROSALIND: Mother, I never *think* about money.

MRS CONNAGE: You never keep it long enough to think about it.

ROSALIND (*sighs*): Yes, I suppose someday I'll marry a ton of it – out of sheer boredom.

MRS CONNAGE (*referring to notebook*): I had a wire from Hartford. Dawson Ryder is coming up. Now there's a young man I like, and he's floating in money. It seems to me that since you seem tired of Howard Gillespie you might give Mr Ryder some encouragement. This is the third time he's been up in a month.

ROSALIND: How did you know I was tired of Howard Gillespie?

MRS CONNAGE: The poor boy looks so miserable every time he comes.

ROSALIND: That was one of those romantic, pre-battle affairs. They're all wrong.

MRS CONNAGE (*having said her say*): At any rate, make us proud of you tonight.

ROSALIND: Don't you think I'm beautiful?

MRS CONNAGE: You know you are.

(*From downstairs is heard the moan of a violin being tuned, the roll of a drum.* MRS CONNAGE *turns quickly to her daughter.*)

MRS CONNAGE: Come!

ROSALIND: One minute!

(*Her mother leaves.* ROSALIND *goes to the glass where she gazes at herself with great satisfaction. She kisses her hand and touches her mirrored mouth with it. Then she turns out the lights and leaves the room. Silence for a moment. A few chords from the piano, the discreet patter of faint drums, the rustle of new silk, all blend on the staircase outside and drift in through the partly opened door. Bundled figures pass in the lighted hall. The laughter heard below becomes doubled and multiplied. Then someone comes in, closes the door, and switches on the lights. It is* CECILIA. *She goes to the chiffonier, looks in the drawers, hesitates – then to the desk whence she takes the cigarette-case and extracts one. She lights it and then, puffing and blowing, walks towards the mirror.*)

CECILIA (*in tremendously sophisticated accents*): Oh, yes, coming out is *such* a farce nowadays, you know. One really plays around so much before one is seventeen that it's positively an anticlimax. (*She shakes hands with a visionary middle-aged nobleman.*) Yes, your grace – I b'lieve I've heard my sister speak of you. Have a puff – they're very good. They're – they're Coronas. You don't smoke? What a pity! The king doesn't allow it, I suppose. Yes, I'll dance.

(*So she dances around the room to a tune from downstairs, her arms outstretched to an imaginary partner, the cigarette waving in her hand.*)

SEVERAL HOURS LATER

The corner of a den downstairs, filled by a very comfortable leather lounge. A small light is on each side above, and in the middle, over the couch hangs a painting of a very old, very dignified gentleman, period 1860. Outside the music is heard in a fox-trot.

ROSALIND *is seated on the lounge and on her left is* HOWARD GILLESPIE, *a vapid youth of about twenty-four. He is obviously very unhappy, and she is quite bored.*

GILLESPIE (*feebly*): What do you mean I've changed. I feel the same towards you.

ROSALIND: But you don't look the same to me.

GILLESPIE: Three weeks ago you used to say that you liked me because I was so blasé, so indifferent – I still am.

ROSALIND: But not about me. I used to like you because you had brown eyes and thin legs.

GILLESPIE (*helplessly*): They're still thin and brown. You're a vampire, that's all.

ROSALIND: The only thing I know about vamping is what's on the piano score. What confuses men is that I'm perfectly natural. I used to think you were never jealous. Now you follow me with your eyes wherever I go.

GILLESPIE: I love you.

ROSALIND (*coldly*): I know it.

GILLESPIE: And you haven't kissed me for two weeks. I had an idea that after a girl was kissed she was – was – won.

ROSALIND: Those days are over. I have to be won all over again every time you see me.

GILLESPIE: Are you serious?

ROSALIND: About as usual. There used to be two kinds of kisses: first when girls were kissed and deserted; second, when they were engaged. Now there's a third kind, where the man is kissed and deserted. If Mr Jones of the nineties bragged he'd kissed a girl, everyone knew he was through with her. If Mr Jones of 1919 brags the same everyone knows it's because he can't kiss her any more. Given a decent start any girl can beat a man nowadays.

GILLESPIE: Then why do you play with men?

ROSALIND (*leaning forward confidentially*): For that first moment, when he's interested. There is a moment – oh, just before the first kiss, a whispered word – something that makes it worth while.

GILLESPIE: And then?

ROSALIND: Then after that you make him talk about himself. Pretty soon he thinks of nothing but being alone with you – he sulks, he won't fight, he doesn't want to play – Victory!

(*Enter* DAWSON RYDER, *twenty-six, handsome, wealthy, faithful to his own; a bore perhaps, but steady and sure of success.*)

RYDER: I believe this is my dance, Rosalind.

ROSALIND: Well, Dawson, so you recognise me. Now I know I haven't got too much paint on. Mr Ryder, this is Mr Gillespie.

(*They shake hands and* GILLESPIE *leaves, tremendously downcast.*)

RYDER: Your party is certainly a success.

ROSALIND: Is it – I haven't seen it lately. I'm weary – Do you mind sitting out a minute?

RYDER: Mind – I'm delighted. You know I loathe this 'rushing' idea. See a girl yesterday, today, tomorrow.

ROSALIND: Dawson!

RYDER: What?

ROSALIND: I wonder if you know you love me.

RYDER (*startled*): What? Oh – you know you're remarkable!

ROSALIND: Because you know I'm an awful proposition. Anyone who marries me will have his hands full. I'm mean – mighty mean.

RYDER: Oh, I wouldn't say that.

ROSALIND: Oh, yes, I am – especially to the people nearest to me. (*She rises.*) Come, let's go. I've changed my mind and I want to dance. Mother is probably having a fit.

(*Exeunt. Enter* ALEC and CECILIA.)

CECILIA: Just my luck to get my own brother for an intermission.

ALEC (*gloomily*): I'll go if you want me to.

CECILIA: Good heavens, no – with whom would I begin the next dance? (*sighs*) There's no colour in a dance since the French officers went back.

ALEC (*thoughtfully*): I don't want Amory to fall in love with Rosalind.

CECILIA: Why, I had an idea that that was just what you did want.

ALEC: I did, but since seeing these girls – I don't know. I'm awfully attached to Amory. He's sensitive and I don't want him to break his heart over somebody who doesn't care about him.

CECILIA: He's very good looking.

ALEC (*still thoughtfully*): She won't marry him, but a girl doesn't have to marry a man to break his heart.

CECILIA: What does it? I wish I knew the secret.

ALEC: Why, you cold-blooded little kitty. It's lucky for some that the Lord gave you a pug nose.

(*Enter* MRS CONNAGE.)

MRS CONNAGE: Where on earth is Rosalind?

ALEC (*brilliantly*): Of course you've come to the best people to find out. She'd naturally be with us.

MRS CONNAGE: Her father has marshalled eight bachelor millionaires to meet her.

ALEC: You might form a squad and march through the halls.

MRS CONNAGE: I'm perfectly serious – for all I know she may be at the Cocoanut Grove with some football player on the night of her début. You look left and I'll –

ALEC (*flippantly*): Hadn't you better send the butler through the cellar?

MRS CONNAGE (*perfectly serious*): Oh, you don't think she'd be there?

CECILIA: He's only joking, mother.

ALEC: Mother had a picture of her tapping a keg of beer with some high hurdler.

MRS CONNAGE: Let's look right away.

(*They go out.* ROSALIND *comes in with* GILLESPIE.)

GILLESPIE: Rosalind – Once more I ask you. Don't you care a blessed thing about me?

(AMORY *walks in briskly.*)

AMORY: My dance.

ROSALIND : Mr Gillespie, this is Mr Blaine.

GILLESPIE: I've met Mr Blaine. From Lake Geneva, aren't you?

AMORY: Yes.

GILLESPIE (*desperately*): I've been there. It's in the – the Middle West, isn't it?

AMORY (*spicily*): Approximately. But I always felt that I'd rather be provincial hot-tamale than soup without seasoning.

GILLESPIE: What!

AMORY: Oh, no offence.

(GILLESPIE *bows and leaves.*)

ROSALIND: He's too much *people*.

AMORY: I was in love with a *people* once.

ROSALIND: So?

AMORY: Oh, yes – her name was Isabelle – nothing at all to her except what I read into her.

ROSALIND: What happened?

AMORY: Finally I convinced her that she was smarter than I was – then she threw me over. Said I was critical and impractical, you know.

ROSALIND: What do you mean impractical?

AMORY: Oh – drive a car, but can't change a tyre.

ROSALIND: What are you going to do?

AMORY: Can't say – run for President, write –

ROSALIND: Greenwich Village?

AMORY: Good heavens, no – I said write – not drink.

ROSALIND: I like businessmen. Clever men are usually so homely.

AMORY: I feel as if I'd known you for ages.

ROSALIND: Oh, are you going to commence the 'pyramid' story?

AMORY: No – I was going to make it French. I was Louis XIV and you were one of my – my – (*changing his tone*) Suppose – we fell in love.

ROSALIND: I've suggested pretending.

AMORY: If we did it would be very big.

ROSALIND: Why?

AMORY: Because selfish people are in a way terribly capable of great loves.

ROSALIND (*turning her lips up*): Pretend.

(*Very deliberately they kiss.*)

AMORY: I can't say sweet things. But you *are* beautiful.

ROSALIND: Not that.

AMORY: What then?

ROSALIND (*sadly*): Oh, nothing – only I want sentiment, real sentiment – and I never find it.

AMORY: I never find anything else in the world – and I loathe it.

ROSALIND: It's so hard to find a male to gratify one's artistic taste.

(*Someone has opened a door and the music of a waltz surges into the room.* ROSALIND *rises.*)

ROSALIND: Listen! they're playing 'Kiss Me Again'.

(*He looks at her.*)

AMORY: Well?

ROSALIND: Well?

AMORY (*softly – the battle lost*): I love you.

ROSALIND: I love you – now.

(*They kiss.*)

AMORY: Oh, God, what have I done?

ROSALIND: Nothing. Oh, don't talk. Kiss me again.
AMORY: I don't know why or how, but I love you – from the moment I saw you.
ROSALIND: Me too – I – I – oh, tonight's tonight.
(*Her brother strolls in, starts and then in a loud voice says:* 'Oh, excuse me,' *and goes.*)
ROSALIND (*her lips scarcely stirring*): Don't let me go – I don't care who knows what I do.
AMORY: Say it!
ROSALIND: I love you – now. (*They part.*) Oh – I am very youthful, thank God – and rather beautiful, thank God – and happy, thank God, thank God – (*She pauses and then, in an odd burst of prophecy, adds*) Poor Amory!
(*He kisses her again.*)

KISMET

Within two weeks Amory and Rosalind were deeply and passionately in love. The critical qualities which had spoiled for each of them a dozen romances were dulled by the great wave of emotion that washed over them.

'It may be an insane love-affair,' she told her anxious mother, 'but it's not inane.'

The wave swept Amory into an advertising agency early in March, where he alternated between astonishing bursts of rather exceptional work and wild dreams of becoming suddenly rich and touring Italy with Rosalind.

They were together constantly, for lunch, for dinner, and nearly every evening – always in a sort of breathless hush, as if they feared that any minute the spell would break and drop them out of this paradise of rose and flame. But the spell became a trance, seemed to increase from day to day; they began to talk of marrying in July – in June. All life was transmitted into terms of their love, all experience, all desires, all ambitions, were nullified – their senses of humour crawled into corners to sleep; their former love-affairs seemed faintly laughable and scarcely regretted juvenilia.

For the second time in his life Amory had had a complete bouleversement and was hurrying into line with his generation.

A LITTLE INTERLUDE

Amory wandered slowly up the avenue and thought of the night as inevitably his – the pageantry and carnival of rich dusk and dim streets . . . it seemed that he had closed the book of fading harmonies at last and stepped into the sensuous vibrant walks of life. Everywhere these countless lights, this promise of a night of streets and singing – he moved in a half-dream through the crowd as if expecting to meet Rosalind hurrying towards him with eager feet from every corner . . . How the unforgettable faces of dusk would blend to her, the myriad footsteps, a thousand overtures, would blend to her footsteps; and there would be more drunkenness than wine in the softness of her eyes on his. Even his dreams now were faint violins drifting like summer sounds upon the summer air.

The room was in darkness except for the faint glow of Tom's cigarette where he lounged by the open window. As the door shut behind him, Amory stood a moment with his back against it.

'Hello, Benvenuto Blaine. How went the advertising business today?'

Amory sprawled on a couch.

'I loathed it as usual!' The momentary vision of the bustling agency was displaced quickly by another picture. 'My God! She's wonderful!'

Tom sighed.

'I can't tell you,' repeated Amory, 'just how wonderful she is. I don't want you to know. I don't want anyone to know.'

Another sigh came from the window – quite a resigned sigh.

'She's life and hope and happiness, my whole world now.'

He felt the quiver of a tear on his eyelid.

'Oh, *golly*, Tom!'

BITTER SWEET

'Sit like we do,' she whispered.

He sat in the big chair and held out his arms so that she could nestle inside them.

'I knew you'd come tonight,' she said softly, 'like summer, just when I needed you most . . . darling . . . darling . . .'

His lips moved lazily over her face.

'You *taste* so good,' he sighed.

'How do you mean, lover?'

'Oh, just sweet, just sweet . . . ' he held her closer.

'Amory,' she whispered, 'when you're ready for me I'll marry you.'

'We won't have much at first.'

'Don't!' she cried. 'It hurts when you reproach yourself for what you can't give me. I've got your precious self – and that's enough for me.'

'Tell me . . . '

'You know, don't you? Oh, you know.'

'Yes, but I want to hear you say it.'

'I love you, Amory, with all my heart.'

'Always, will you?'

'All my life – Oh, Amory – '

'What?'

'I want to belong to you. I want your people to be my people. I want to have your babies.'

'But I haven't any people.'

'Don't laugh at me, Amory. Just kiss me.'

'I'll do what you want,' he said.

'No, I'll do what *you* want. We're *you* – not me. Oh, you're so much a part, so much all of me . . . '

He closed his eyes.

'I'm so happy that I'm frightened. Wouldn't it be awful if this was – was the high point? . . . '

She looked at him dreamily.

'Beauty and love pass, I know . . . Oh, there's sadness, too. I suppose all great happiness is a little sad. Beauty means the scent of roses and then the death of roses – '

'Beauty means the agony of sacrifice and the end of agony . . . '

'And, Amory, we're beautiful, I know. I'm sure God loves us – '

'He loves you. You're his most precious possession.'

'I'm not his, I'm yours. Amory, I belong to you. For the first time I regret all the other kisses; now I know how much a kiss can mean.'

Then they would smoke and he would tell her about his day at the office – and where they might live. Sometimes, when he was particularly loquacious, she went to sleep in his arms, but he loved that Rosalind – all Rosalinds – as he had never in the world loved anyone else. Intangibly fleeting, unrememberable hours.

AQUATIC INCIDENT

One day Amory and Howard Gillespie meeting by accident downtown took lunch together, and Amory heard a story that delighted him. Gillespie after several cocktails was in a talkative mood; he began by telling Amory that he was sure Rosalind was slightly eccentric.

He had gone with her on a swimming party up in Westchester County, and someone mentioned that Annette Kellerman had been there one day on a visit and had dived from the top of a rickety, thirty-foot summer-house. Immediately Rosalind insisted that Howard should climb up with her to see what it looked like.

A minute later, as he sat and dangled his feet on the edge, a form shot by him; Rosalind, her arms spread in a beautiful swan dive, had sailed through the air into the clear water.

'Of course, *I* had to go, after that – and I nearly killed myself. I thought I was pretty good to even try it. Nobody else in the party tried it. Well, afterwards Rosalind had the nerve to ask me why I stooped over when I dived. "It didn't make it any easier," she said, "it just took all the courage out of it." I ask you, what can a man do with a girl like that? Unnecessary, I call it.'

Gillespie failed to understand why Amory was smiling delightedly all through lunch. He thought perhaps he was one of these hollow optimists.

FIVE WEEKS LATER

Again the library of the Connage house.

(ROSALIND *is alone, sitting on the lounge staring very moodily and unhappily at nothing. She has changed perceptibly – she is a trifle thinner for one thing; the light in her eyes is not so bright; she looks easily a year older. Her mother comes in, muffled in an opera-cloak. She takes in* ROSALIND *with a nervous glance.*)

MRS CONNAGE: Who is coming tonight?

(ROSALIND *fails to hear her, at least takes no notice.*)

MRS CONNAGE: Alec is coming up to take me to this Barrie play, *Et tu, Brutus*. (*She perceives that she is talking to herself.*) Rosalind! I asked you who is coming tonight?

ROSALIND (*starting*): Oh – what – oh – Amory –

MRS CONNAGE (*sarcastically*): You have so *many* admirers lately that I couldn't imagine *which* one. (ROSALIND *doesn't answer.*) Dawson Ryder is more patient than I thought he'd be. You haven't given him an evening this week.

ROSALIND (*with a very weary expression that is quite new to her face*): Mother – please –

MRS CONNAGE: Oh, *I* won't interfere. You've already wasted over two months on a theoretical genius who hasn't a penny to his name, but *go* ahead, waste your life on him. *I* won't interfere.

ROSALIND (*as if repeating a tiresome lesson*): You know he has a little income – and you know he's earning thirty-five dollars a week in advertising –

MRS CONNAGE: And it wouldn't buy your clothes. (*She pauses but* ROSALIND *makes no reply.*) I have your best interests at heart when I tell you not to take a step you'll spend your days regretting. It's not as if your father could help you. Things have been hard for him lately and he's an old man. You'd be dependent absolutely on a dreamer, a nice, well-born boy, but a dreamer – merely *clever.*

(*She implies that this quality in itself is rather vicious.*)

ROSALIND: For heaven's sake, mother –

(*A maid appears, announces Mr Blaine who follows immediately.* AMORY'S *friends have been telling him for ten days that he 'looks like the wrath of God', and he does. As a matter of fact he has not been able to eat a mouthful in the last thirty-six hours.*)

AMORY: Good-evening, Mrs Connage.

MRS CONNAGE (*not unkindly*): Good-evening, Amory.

(AMORY and ROSALIND *exchange glances – and* ALEC *comes in.* ALEC'S *attitude throughout has been neutral. He believes in his heart that the marriage would make* AMORY *mediocre and* ROSALIND *miserable, but he feels a great sympathy for both of them.*)

ALEC: Hi, Amory!

AMORY: Hi, Alec! Tom said he'd meet you at the theatre.

ALEC: Yeah, just saw him. How's the advertising today? Write some brilliant copy?

AMORY: Oh, it's about the same. I got a rise – (*Everyone looks at him rather eagerly*) – of two dollars a week. (*general collapse*)

MRS CONNAGE: Come, Alec, I hear the car.

(*A good-night, rather chilly in sections. After* MRS CONNAGE *and* ALEC *go out there is a pause.* ROSALIND *still stares moodily at the fireplace.* AMORY *goes to her and puts his arm around her.*)

AMORY: Darling girl.

(*They kiss. Another pause and then she seizes his hand, covers it with kisses and holds it to her breast.*)

ROSALIND (*sadly*): I love your hands, more than anything. I see them often when you're away from me – so tired; I know every line of them. Dear hands!

(*Their eyes meet for a second and then she begins to cry – a tearless sobbing.*)

AMORY: Rosalind!

ROSALIND: Oh, we're so darned pitiful!

AMORY: Rosalind!

ROSALIND: Oh, I want to die!

AMORY: Rosalind, another night of this and I'll go to pieces. You've been this way four days now. You've got to be more encouraging or I can't work or eat or sleep. (*He looks around helplessly as if searching for new words to clothe an old, shopworn phrase.*) We'll have to make a start. I *like* having to make a start together. (*His forced hopefulness fades as he sees her unresponsive.*) What's the matter? (*He gets up suddenly and starts to pace the floor.*) It's Dawson Ryder, that's what it is. He's been working on your nerves. You've been with him every afternoon for a week. People come and tell me they've seen you together, and I have to smile and nod and pretend it hasn't the slightest significance for me. And you won't tell me anything as it develops.

ROSALIND: Amory, if you don't sit down I'll scream.

AMORY (*sitting down suddenly beside her*): Oh, Lord.

ROSALIND (*taking his hand gently*): You know I love you, don't you?

AMORY: Yes.

ROSALIND: You know I'll always love you –

AMORY: Don't talk that way; you frighten me. It sounds as if we weren't going to have each other. (*She cries a little and rising from the couch goes to the armchair.*) I've felt all afternoon that things were worse. I nearly went wild down at the office – couldn't write a line. Tell me everything.

ROSALIND: There's nothing to tell, I say. I'm just nervous.

AMORY: Rosalind, you're playing with the idea of marrying Dawson Ryder.

ROSALIND (*after a pause*): He's been asking me to all day.

AMORY: Well, he's got his nerve!

ROSALIND (*after another pause*): I like him.

AMORY: Don't say that. It hurts me.

ROSALIND: Don't be a silly idiot. You know you're the only man I've ever loved, ever will love.

AMORY (*quickly*): Rosalind, let's get married – next week.

ROSALIND: We can't.

AMORY: Why not?

ROSALIND: Oh, we can't. I'd be your squaw – in some horrible place.

AMORY: We'll have two hundred and seventy-five dollars a month all told.

ROSALIND: Darling, I don't even do my own hair, usually.

AMORY: I'll do it for you.

ROSALIND (*between a laugh and a sob*): Thanks.

AMORY: Rosalind, you *can't* be thinking of marrying someone else. Tell me! You leave me in the dark. I can help you fight it out if you'll only tell me.

ROSALIND: It's just – us. We're pitiful, that's all. The very qualities I love you for are the ones that will always make you a failure.

AMORY (*grimly*): Go on.

ROSALIND: Oh – it *is* Dawson Ryder. He's so reliable, I almost feel that he'd be a – a background.

AMORY: You don't love him.

ROSALIND: I know, but I respect him, and he's a good man and a strong one.

AMORY (*grudgingly*): Yes – he's that.

ROSALIND: Well – here's one little thing. There was a little poor boy we met in Rye on Tuesday afternoon – and, oh, Dawson took him on his lap and talked to him and promised him an Indian suit – and next day he remembered and bought it – and, oh, it was so sweet and I couldn't help thinking he'd be so nice to – to our children – take care of them – and I wouldn't have to worry.

AMORY (*in despair*): Rosalind! Rosalind!

ROSALIND (*with a faint roguishness*): Don't look so consciously suffering.

AMORY: What power we have of hurting each other!

ROSALIND (*commencing to sob again*): It's been so perfect – you and I. So like a dream that I'd longed for and never thought I'd find. The first real unselfishness I've ever felt in my life. And I can't see it fade out in a colourless atmosphere!

AMORY: It won't – it won't!

ROSALIND: I'd rather keep it as a beautiful memory – tucked away in my heart.

AMORY: Yes, women can do that – but not men. I'd remember always, not the beauty of it while it lasted, but just the bitterness, the long bitterness.

ROSALIND: Don't!

AMORY: All the years never to see you, never to kiss you, just a gate shut and barred – you don't dare be my wife.

ROSALIND: No – no – I'm taking the hardest course, the strongest course. Marrying you would be a failure and I never fail – if you don't stop walking up and down I'll scream!

(*Again he sinks despairingly on to the lounge.*)

AMORY: Come over here and kiss me.

ROSALIND: No.

AMORY: Don't you *want* to kiss me?

ROSALIND: Tonight I want you to love me calmly and coolly.

AMORY: The beginning of the end.

ROSALIND (*with a burst of insight*): Amory, you're young. I'm young. People excuse us now for our poses and vanities, for treating people like Sancho and yet getting away with it. They excuse us now. But you've got a lot of knocks coming to you –

AMORY: And you're afraid to take them with me.

ROSALIND: No, not that. There was a poem I read somewhere – you'll say Ella Wheeler Wilcox and laugh – but listen:

For this is wisdom – to love and live,
To take what fate or the gods may give,
To ask no question, to make no prayer,
To kiss the lips and caress the hair,
Speed passion's ebb as we greet its flow,
To have and to hold and in time – let go.

AMORY: But we haven't had.

ROSALIND: Amory, I'm yours – you know it. There have been times in the last month I'd have been completely yours if you'd said so. But I can't marry you and ruin both our lives.

AMORY: We've got to take our chance for happiness.

ROSALIND: Dawson says I'd learn to love him.

(AMORY *with his head sunk in his hands does not move. The life seems suddenly gone out of him.*)

ROSALIND: Lover! Lover! I can't do with you, and I can't imagine life without you.

AMORY: Rosalind, we're on each other's nerves. It's just that we're both high-strung, and this week –

(*His voice is curiously old. She crosses to him and taking his face in her hands, kisses him.*)

ROSALIND: I can't, Amory. I can't be shut away from the trees and flowers, cooped up in a little flat, waiting for you. You'd hate me in a narrow atmosphere. I'd make you hate me.

(*Again she is blinded by sudden uncontrolled tears.*)

AMORY: Rosalind –

ROSALIND: Oh, darling, go – Don't make it harder! I can't stand it –

AMORY (*his face drawn, his voice strained*): Do you know what you're saying? Do you mean for ever?

(*There is a difference somehow in the quality of their suffering.*)

ROSALIND: Can't you see –

AMORY: I'm afraid I can't if you love me. You're afraid of taking two years' knocks with me.

ROSALIND: I wouldn't be the Rosalind you love.

AMORY (*a little hysterically*): I can't give you up! I can't, that's all! I've got to have you!

ROSALIND (*a hard note in her voice*): You're being a baby now.

AMORY (*wildly*): I don't care! You're spoiling our lives!

ROSALIND: I'm doing the wise thing, the only thing.

AMORY: Are you going to marry Dawson Ryder?

ROSALIND: Oh, don't ask me. You know I'm old in some ways – in others – well, I'm just a little girl. I like sunshine and pretty things and cheerfulness – and I dread responsibility. I don't want to think about pots and kitchens and brooms. I want to worry whether my legs will get slick and brown when I swim in the summer.

AMORY: And you love me.

ROSALIND: That's just why it has to end. Drifting hurts too much. We can't have any more scenes like this.

(*She draws his ring from her finger and hands it to him. Their eyes are blind again with tears.*)

AMORY (*his lips against her wet cheek*): Don't! Keep it, please – oh, don't break my heart!

(*She presses the ring softly into his hand.*)

ROSALIND (*brokenly*): You'd better go.

AMORY: Goodbye –

(*She looks at him once more, with infinite longing, infinite sadness.*)

ROSALIND: Don't ever forget me, Amory –

AMORY: Goodbye –

(*He goes to the door, fumbles for the knob, finds it – she sees him throw back his head – and he is gone. Gone – she half starts from the lounge and then sinks forward on her face into the pillows.*)

ROSALIND: Oh, God, I want to die! (*After a moment she rises and with her eyes closed feels her way to the door. Then she turns and looks once more at the room. Here they had sat and dreamed: that tray she had so often filled with matches for him; that shade that they had discreetly lowered one long Sunday afternoon. Misty-eyed she stands and remembers; she speaks aloud.*) Oh, Amory, what have I done to you?

(*And deep under the aching sadness that will pass in time, Rosalind feels that she has lost something, she knows not what, she knows not why.*)

2

Experiments in Convalescence

The Knickerbocker Bar, beamed upon by Maxfield Parrish's jovial, colourful *Old King Cole*, was well crowded. Amory stopped in the entrance and looked at his wristwatch; he wanted particularly to know the time, for something in his mind that catalogued and classified liked to chip things off cleanly. Later it would satisfy him in a vague way to be able to think, 'That thing ended at exactly twenty minutes after eight on Thursday, June 10, 1919.' This was allowing for the walk from her house – a walk concerning which he had afterwards not the faintest recollection.

He was in rather grotesque condition: two days of worry and nervousness, of sleepless nights, of untouched meals, culminating in the emotional crisis and Rosalind's abrupt decision – the strain of it had drugged the foreground of his mind into a merciful coma. As he fumbled clumsily with the olives at the free-lunch table, a man approached and spoke to him, and the olives dropped from his nervous hands.

'Well, Amory . . . '

It was someone he had known at Princeton; he had no idea of the name.

'Hello, old boy – ' he heard himself saying.

'Name's Jim Wilson – you've forgotten.'

'Sure, you bet, Jim. I remember.'

'Going to reunion?'

'You know!' Simultaneously he realised that he was not going to reunion.

'Get overseas?'

Amory nodded, his eyes staring oddly. Stepping back to let someone pass, he knocked the dish of olives to a crash on the floor. 'Too bad,' he muttered. 'Have a drink?'

Wilson, ponderously diplomatic, reached over and slapped him on the back. 'You've had plenty, old boy.'

Amory eyed him dumbly until Wilson grew embarrassed under the scrutiny.

'Plenty, hell!' said Amory finally. 'I haven't had a drink today.'

Wilson looked incredulous.

'Have a drink or not?' cried Amory rudely.

Together they sought the bar.

'Rye high.'

'I'll just take a Bronx.'

Wilson had another; Amory had several more. They decided to sit down. At ten o'clock Wilson was displaced by Carling, class of '15. Amory, his head spinning gorgeously, layer upon layer of soft satisfaction setting over the bruised spots of his spirit, was discoursing volubly on the war.

' 'S a mental was'e,' he insisted with owl-like wisdom. 'Two years my life spent inalleshual vacuity. Los' idealism, got be physcal anmal,' he shook his fist expressively at Old King Cole, 'got be Prussian 'bout ev'thing, women 'specially. Use' be straight 'bout women college. Now don'givadam.' He expressed his lack of principle by sweeping a seltzer bottle with a broad gesture to noisy extinction on the floor, but this did not interrupt his speech. 'Seek pleasure where find it for tomorrow die. 'At's philos'phy for me now on.'

Carling yawned, but Amory, waxing brilliant, continued: 'Use' wonder 'bout things – people satisfied compromise, fif'y-fif'y att'tude on life. Now don' wonder, don' wonder – ' He became so emphatic in impressing on Carling the fact that he didn't wonder that he lost the thread of his discourse and concluded by announcing to the bar at large that he was a 'physcal anmal'.

'What are you celebrating, Amory?'

Amory leaned forward confidentially.

'Cel'brating blowmylife. Great moment blow my life. Can't tell you 'bout it – '

He heard Carling addressing a remark to the bartender: 'Give him a bromo-seltzer.'

Amory shook his head indignantly.

'None that stuff!'

'But listen, Amory, you're making yourself sick. You're white as a ghost.'

Amory considered the question. He tried to look at himself in the mirror but even by squinting up one eye could only see as far as the row of bottles behind the bar.

'Like som'n solid. We go get some – some salad.'

He settled his coat with an attempt at nonchalance, but letting go of the bar was too much for him, and he slumped against a chair.

'We'll go over to Shanley's,' suggested Carling, offering an elbow.

With this assistance Amory managed to get his legs in motion enough to propel him across Forty-Second Street.

Shanley's was very dim. He was conscious that he was talking in a loud voice, very succinctly and convincingly, he thought, about a desire to crush people under his heel. He consumed three club sandwiches, devouring each as though it were no larger than a chocolate-drop. Then Rosalind began popping into his mind again, and he found his lips forming her name over and over. Next he was sleepy, and he had a hazy, listless sense of people in dress suits, probably waiters, gathering around the table . . .

. . . He was in a room and Carling was saying something about a knot in his shoelace.

'Nemmine,' he managed to articulate drowsily. 'Sleep in 'em . . . '

STILL ALCOHOLIC

He awoke laughing and his eyes lazily roamed his surroundings, evidently a bedroom and bath in a good hotel. His head was whirring and picture after picture was forming and blurring and melting before his eyes, but beyond the desire to laugh he had no entirely conscious reaction. He reached for the phone beside his bed.

'Hello – what hotel is this – ? Knickerbocker? All right, send up two rye highballs – '

He lay for a moment and wondered idly whether they'd send up a bottle or just two of those little glass containers. Then, with an effort, he struggled out of bed and ambled into the bathroom.

When he emerged, rubbing himself lazily with a towel, he found the bar boy with the drinks and had a sudden desire to kid him. On reflection he decided that this would be undignified, so he waved him away.

As the new alcohol tumbled into his stomach and warmed him, the isolated pictures began slowly to form a cinema reel of the day before. Again he saw Rosalind curled weeping among the pillows, again he felt her tears against his cheek. Her words began ringing in his ears: 'Don't ever forget me, Amory – don't ever forget me – '

'Hell!' he faltered aloud, and then he choked and collapsed on the bed in a shaken spasm of grief. After a minute he opened his eyes and regarded the ceiling.

'Damned fool!' he exclaimed in disgust, and with a voluminous sigh rose and approached the bottle. After another glass he gave way loosely to the luxury of tears. Purposely he called up into his mind little incidents of the vanished spring, phrased to himself emotions that would make him react even more strongly to sorrow.

'We were so happy,' he intoned dramatically, 'so very happy.' Then he gave way again and knelt beside the bed, his head half-buried in the pillow.

'My own girl – my own – Oh – '

He clenched his teeth so that the tears streamed in a flood from his eyes.

'Oh . . . my baby girl, all I had, all I wanted! . . . Oh, my girl, come back, come back! I need you . . . need you . . . we're so pitiful . . . just misery we brought each other . . . She'll be shut away from me . . . I can't see her; I can't be her friend. It's got to be that way – it's got to be – '

And then again: 'We've been so happy, so very happy . . . '

He rose to his feet and threw himself on the bed in an ecstasy of sentiment, and then lay exhausted while he realised slowly that he had been very drunk the night before, and that his head was spinning again wildly. He laughed, rose, and crossed again to Lethe . . .

At noon he ran into a crowd in the Biltmore bar, and the riot began again. He had a vague recollection afterwards of discussing French poetry with a British officer who was introduced to him as 'Captain Corn, of His Majesty's Foot', and he remembered attempting to recite 'Clair de Lune' at luncheon; then he slept in a big, soft chair until almost five o'clock when another crowd found and woke him; there followed an alcoholic dressing of several temperaments for the ordeal of dinner. They selected theatre tickets at Tyson's for a play that had a four-drink programme – a play with two monotonous voices, with turbid, gloomy scenes, and lighting effects that were hard to follow when his eyes behaved so amazingly. He imagined afterwards that it must have been *The Jest* . . .

. . . Then the Cocoanut Grove, where Amory slept again on a little balcony outside. Out in Shanley's, Yonkers, he became almost logical, and by a careful control of the number of highballs he drank, grew quite lucid and garrulous. He found that the party consisted of five men, two of whom he knew slightly; he became righteous about paying his share of the expense and insisted in a loud voice on arranging everything then and there, to the amusement of the tables around him . . .

Someone mentioned that a famous cabaret star was at the next table, so Amory rose and, approaching gallantly, introduced himself . . . this involved him in an argument, first with her escort and then with the head waiter – Amory's attitude being a lofty and exaggerated courtesy . . . he consented, after being confronted with irrefutable logic, to being led back to his own table.

'Decided to commit suicide,' he announced suddenly.

'When? Next year?'

'Now. Tomorrow morning. Going to take a room at the Commodore, get into a hot bath and open a vein.'

'He's getting morbid!'

'You need another rye, old boy!'

'We'll all talk it over tomorrow.'

But Amory was not to be dissuaded, from argument at least.

'Did you ever get that way?' he demanded confidentially *fortaccio.*

'Sure!'

'Often?'

'My chronic state.'

This provoked discussion. One man said that he got so depressed sometimes that he seriously considered it. Another agreed that there was nothing to live for. 'Captain Corn', who had somehow rejoined the party, said that in his opinion it was when one's health was bad that one felt that way most. Amory's suggestion was that they should each order a Bronx, mix broken glass in it, and drink it off. To his relief no one applauded the idea, so having finished his highball, he balanced his chin in his hand and his elbow on the table – a most delicate, scarcely noticeable sleeping position, he assured himself – and went into a deep stupor . . .

He was awakened by a woman clinging to him, a pretty woman, with brown, disarranged hair and dark blue eyes.

'Take me home!' she cried.

'Hello!' said Amory, blinking.

'I like you,' she announced tenderly.

'I like you too.'

He noticed that there was a noisy man in the background and that one of his party was arguing with him.

'Fella I was with's a damn fool,' confided the blue-eyed woman. 'I hate him. I want to go home with you.'

'You drunk?' queried Amory with intense wisdom.

She nodded coyly.

'Go home with him,' he advised gravely. 'He brought you.'

At this point the noisy man in the background broke away from his detainers and approached.

'Say!' he said fiercely. 'I brought this girl out here and you're butting in!'

Amory regarded him coldly, while the girl clung to him closer.

'You let go that girl!' cried the noisy man.

Amory tried to make his eyes threatening.

'You go to hell!' he directed finally, and turned his attention to the girl. 'Love first sight,' he suggested.

'I love you,' she breathed and nestled close to him. She *did* have beautiful eyes.

Someone leaned over and spoke in Amory's ear.

'That's just Margaret Diamond. She's drunk and this fellow here brought her. Better let her go.'

'Let him take care of her, then!' shouted Amory furiously. 'I'm no WYCA worker, am I? – am I?'

'Let her go!'

'It's *her* hanging on, damn it! Let her hang!'

The crowd around the table thickened. For an instant a brawl threatened, but a sleek waiter bent back Margaret Diamond's fingers until she released her hold on Amory, whereupon she slapped the waiter furiously in the face and flung her arms about her raging original escort.

'Oh, Lord!' cried Amory.

'Let's go!'

'Come on, the taxis are getting scarce!'

'Check, waiter.'

'C'mon, Amory. Your romance is over.'

Amory laughed.

'You don't know how true you spoke. No idea. 'At's the whole trouble.'

AMORY ON THE LABOUR QUESTION

Two mornings later he knocked at the president's door at Bascome and Barlow's Advertising Agency.

'Come in!'

Amory entered unsteadily.

' 'Morning, Mr Barlow.'

Mr Barlow brought his glasses to the inspection and set his mouth slightly ajar that he might better listen.

'Well, Mr Blaine. We haven't seen you for several days.'

'No,' said Amory. 'I'm quitting.'

'Well – well – this is – '

'I don't like it here.'

'I'm sorry. I thought our relations had been quite – ah – pleasant. You seemed to be a hard worker – a little inclined perhaps to write fancy copy – '

'I just got tired of it,' interrupted Amory rudely. 'It didn't matter a damn to me whether Harebell's flour was any better than anyone else's. In fact, I never ate any of it. So I got tired of telling people about it – oh, I know I've been drinking – '

Mr Barlow's face steeled by several ingots of expression.

'You asked for a position – '

Amory waved him to silence.

'And I think I was rottenly underpaid. Thirty-five dollars a week – less than a good carpenter.'

'You had just started. You'd never worked before,' said Mr Barlow coolly.

'But it took about ten thousand dollars to educate me where I could write your darned stuff for you. Anyway, as far as length of service goes, you've got stenographers here you've paid fifteen a week for five years.'

'I'm not going to argue with you, sir,' said Mr Barlow rising.

'Neither am I. I just wanted to tell you I'm quitting.'

They stood for a moment looking at each other impassively and then Amory turned and left the office.

A LITTLE LULL

Four days after that he returned at last to the apartment. Tom was engaged on a book review for the *New Democracy* on the staff of which he was employed. They regarded each other for a moment in silence.

'Well?'

'Well?'

'Good Lord, Amory, where'd you get the black eye – and the jaw?'

Amory laughed.

'That's a mere nothing.'

He peeled off his coat and bared his shoulders.

'Look here!'

Tom emitted a low whistle.

'What hit you?'

Amory laughed again.

'Oh, a lot of people. I got beaten up. Fact.' He slowly replaced his shirt. 'It was bound to come sooner or later and I wouldn't have missed it for anything.'

'Who was it?'

'Well, there were some waiters and a couple of sailors and a few stray pedestrians, I guess. It's the strangest feeling. You ought to get beaten up just for the experience of it. You fall down after a while and everybody sort of slashes in at you before you hit the ground – then they kick you.'

Tom lighted a cigarette.

'I spent a day chasing you all over town, Amory. But you always kept a little ahead of me. I'd say you've been on some party.'

Amory tumbled into a chair and asked for a cigarette.

'You sober now?' asked Tom quizzically.

'Pretty sober. Why?'

'Well, Alec has left. His family had been after him to go home and live, so he – '

A spasm of pain shook Amory.

'Too bad.'

'Yes, it is too bad. We'll have to get someone else if we're going to stay here. The rent's going up.'

'Sure. Get anybody. I'll leave it to you, Tom.'

Amory walked into his bedroom. The first thing that met his glance was a photograph of Rosalind that he had intended to have framed, propped up against a mirror on his dresser. He looked at it unmoved. After the vivid mental pictures of her that were his portion at present, the portrait was curiously unreal. He went back into the study.

'Got a cardboard box?'

'No,' answered Tom, puzzled. 'Why should I have? Oh, yes – there may be one in Alec's room.'

Eventually Amory found what he was looking for and, returning to his dresser, opened a drawer full of letters, notes, part of a chain, two little handkerchiefs and some snapshots. As he transferred them carefully to the box his mind wandered to some place in a book where the hero, after preserving for a year a cake of his lost love's soap, finally washed his hands with it. He laughed and began to hum 'After you've gone' . . . ceased abruptly . . .

The string broke twice, and then he managed to secure it, dropped the package into the bottom of his trunk, and having slammed the lid returned to the study.

'Going out?' Tom's voice held an undertone of anxiety.

'Uh-huh.'

'Where?'

'Couldn't say, old keed.'

'Let's have dinner together.'

'Sorry. I told Sukey Brett I'd eat with him.'

'Oh.'

'Bye-bye.'

Amory crossed the street and had a highball; then he walked to Washington Square and found a top seat on a bus. He disembarked at Forty-Third Street and strolled to the Biltmore bar.

'Hi, Amory!'

'What'll you have?'

'Yo-ho! Waiter!'

TEMPERATURE NORMAL

The advent of Prohibition with the 'thirsty-first' put a sudden stop to the submerging of Amory's sorrows, and when he awoke one morning to find that the old bar-to-bar days were over, he had neither remorse for the past three weeks nor regret that their repetition was impossible. He had taken the most violent, if the weakest, method to shield himself from the stabs of memory, and while it was not a course he would have prescribed for others, he found in the end that it had done its business: he was over the first flush of pain.

Don't misunderstand! Amory had loved Rosalind as he would never love another living person. She had taken the first flush of his youth and brought from his unplumbed depths tenderness that had surprised him, gentleness and unselfishness that he had never given to another creature. He had later love-affairs, but of a different sort: in those he went back to that, perhaps, more typical frame of mind, in which the girl became the mirror of a mood in him. Rosalind had drawn out what was more than passionate admiration; he had a deep, undying affection for Rosalind.

But there had been, near the end, so much dramatic tragedy,

culminating in the arabesque nightmare of his three weeks' spree, that he was emotionally worn out. The people and surroundings that he remembered as being cool or delicately artificial, seemed to promise him a refuge. He wrote a cynical story which featured his father's funeral and dispatched it to a magazine, receiving in return a cheque for sixty dollars and a request for more of the same tone. This tickled his vanity, but inspired him to no further effort.

He read enormously. He was puzzled and depressed by *A Portrait of the Artist as a Young Man*, intensely interested by *Joan and Peter* and *The Undying Fire*, and rather surprised by his discovery through a critic named Mencken of several excellent American novels: *Vandover and the Brute*, *The Damnation of Theron Ware* and *Jennie Gerhardt*. Mackenzie, Chesterton, Galsworthy, Bennett, had sunk in his appreciation from sagacious, life-saturated geniuses to merely diverting contemporaries. Shaw's aloof clarity and brilliant consistency and the gloriously intoxicated efforts of H. G. Wells to fit the key of romantic symmetry into the elusive lock of truth alone won his rapt attention.

He wanted to see Monsignor Darcy, to whom he had written when he landed, but he had not heard from him; besides he knew that a visit to Monsignor would entail the story of Rosalind, and the thought of repeating it turned him cold with horror.

In his search for cool people he remembered Mrs Lawrence, a very intelligent, very dignified lady, a convert to the Church, and a great devotee of Monsignor's.

He called her on the phone one day. Yes, she remembered him perfectly; no, Monsignor wasn't in town, was in Boston she thought; he'd promised to come to dinner when he returned. Couldn't Amory take luncheon with her?

'I thought I'd better catch up, Mrs Lawrence,' he said rather ambiguously when he arrived.

'Monsignor was here just last week,' said Mrs Lawrence regretfully. 'He was very anxious to see you, but he'd left your address at home.'

'Did he think I'd plunged into Bolshevism?' asked Amory, interested.

'Oh, he's having a frightful time.'

'Why?'

'About the Irish Republic. He thinks it lacks dignity.'

'So?'

'He went to Boston when the Irish President arrived and he was greatly distressed because the receiving committee, when they rode in an automobile, *would* put their arms around the President.'

'I don't blame him.'

'Well, what impressed you more than anything while you were in the army? You look a great deal older.'

'That's from another, more disastrous battle,' he answered, smiling in spite of himself. 'But the army – let me see – well, I discovered that physical courage depends to a great extent on the physical shape a man is in. I found that I was as brave as the next man – it used to worry me before.'

'What else?'

'Well, the idea that men can stand anything if they get used to it, and the fact that I got a high mark in the psychological examination.'

Mrs Lawrence laughed. Amory was finding it a great relief to be in this cool house on Riverside Drive, away from more condensed New York and the sense of people expelling great quantities of breath into a little space. Mrs Lawrence reminded him vaguely of Beatrice, not in temperament, but in her perfect grace and dignity. The house, its furnishings, the manner in which dinner was served, were in immense contrast to what he had met in the great places on Long Island, where the servants were so obtrusive that they had positively to be bumped out of the way, or even in the houses of more conservative 'Union Club' families. He wondered if this air of symmetrical restraint, this grace, which he felt was continental, was distilled through Mrs Lawrence's New England ancestry or acquired in long residence in Italy and Spain.

Two glasses of sauterne at luncheon loosened his tongue, and he talked, with what he felt was something of his old charm, of religion and literature and the menacing phenomena of the social order. Mrs Lawrence was ostensibly pleased with him, and her interest was especially in his mind; he wanted people to like his mind again – after a while it might be such a nice place in which to live.

'Monsignor Darcy still thinks that you're his reincarnation, that your faith will eventually clarify.'

'Perhaps,' he assented. 'I'm rather pagan at present. It's just that religion doesn't seem to have the slightest bearing on life at my age.'

When he left her house he walked down Riverside Drive with a feeling of satisfaction. It was amusing to discuss again such subjects as this young poet, Stephen Vincent Benet, or the Irish Republic. Between the rancid accusations of Edward Carson and Justice Cohalan he had completely tired of the Irish question; yet there had been a time when his own Celtic traits were pillars of his personal philosophy.

There seemed suddenly to be much left in life, if only this revival of old interests did not mean that he was backing away from it again – backing away from life itself.

RESTLESSNESS

'I'm tres old and tres bored, Tom,' said Amory one day, stretching himself at ease in the comfortable window-seat. He always felt most natural in a recumbent position.

'You used to be entertaining before you started to write,' he continued. 'Now you save any idea that you think would do to print.'

Existence had settled back to an ambitionless normality. They had decided that with economy they could still afford the apartment, which Tom, with the domesticity of an elderly cat, had grown fond of. The old English hunting prints on the wall were Tom's, and the large tapestry by courtesy, a relic of decadent days in college, and the great profusion of orphaned candlesticks and the carved Louis XIV chair in which no one could sit more than a minute without acute spinal disorders – Tom claimed that this was because one was sitting in the lap of Montespan's wraith – at any rate, it was Tom's furniture that decided them to stay.

They went out very little: to an occasional play, or to dinner at the Ritz or the Princeton Club. With Prohibition the great rendezvous had received their death wounds; no longer could one wander to the Biltmore bar at twelve or five and find congenial spirits, and both Tom and Amory had outgrown the passion for dancing with Midwestern or New Jersey debbies at the Club-de-Vingt (surnamed the 'Club de Gink') or the Plaza Rose Room – besides even that required several cocktails 'to come down to the intellectual level of the women present', as Amory had once put it to a horrified matron.

Amory had lately received several alarming letters from Mr Barton – the Lake Geneva house was too large to be easily rented; the best rent obtainable at present would serve this year to do little more than pay for the taxes and necessary improvements; in fact, the lawyer suggested that the whole property was simply a white elephant on Amory's hands. Nevertheless, even though it might not yield a cent for the next three years, Amory decided with a vague sentimentality that for the present, at any rate, he would not sell the house.

This particular day on which he announced his ennui to Tom had been quite typical. He had risen at noon, lunched with Mrs Lawrence, and then ridden abstractedly homeward atop one of his beloved buses.

'Why shouldn't you be bored,' yawned Tom. 'Isn't that the conventional frame of mind for the young man of your age and condition?'

'Yes,' said Amory speculatively, 'but I'm more than bored; I am restless.'

'Love and war did for you.'

'Well,' Amory considered, 'I'm not sure that the war itself had any great effect on either you or me – but it certainly ruined the old backgrounds, sort of killed individualism out of our generation.'

Tom looked up in surprise.

'Yes it did,' insisted Amory. 'I'm not sure it didn't kill it out of the whole world. Oh, Lord, what a pleasure it used to be to dream I might be a really great dictator or writer or religious or political leader – and now even a Leonardo da Vinci or Lorenzo de Medici couldn't be a real old-fashioned bolt in the world. Life is too huge and complex. The world is so overgrown that it can't lift its own fingers, and I was planning to be such an important finger – '

'I don't agree with you,' Tom interrupted. 'There never were men placed in such egotistic positions since – oh, since the French Revolution.'

Amory disagreed violently.

'You're mistaking this period when every nut is an individualist for a period of individualism. Wilson has only been powerful when he has represented; he's had to compromise over and over again. Just as soon as Trotsky and Lenin take a definite, consistent stand they'll become merely two-minute figures like Kerensky. Even Foch hasn't half the significance of Stonewall Jackson. War used to be the most individualistic pursuit of man, and yet the popular heroes of the war had neither authority nor responsibility: Guynemer and Sergeant York. How could a schoolboy make a hero of Pershing? A big man has no time really to do anything but just sit and be big.'

'Then you don't think there will be any more permanent world heroes?'

'Yes – in history – not in life. Carlyle would have difficulty getting material for a new chapter on *The Hero as a Big Man*.'

'Go on. I'm a good listener today.'

'People try so hard to believe in leaders now, pitifully hard. But we no sooner get a popular reformer or politician or soldier or writer or philosopher – a Roosevelt, a Tolstoy, a Wood, a Shaw, a Nietzsche –

than the cross-currents of criticism wash him away. My Lord, no man can stand prominence these days. It's the surest path to obscurity. People get sick of hearing the same name over and over.'

'Then you blame it on the press?'

'Absolutely. Look at you; you're on the *New Democracy*, considered the most brilliant weekly in the country, read by the men who do things and all that. What's your business? Why, to be as clever, as interesting, and as brilliantly cynical as possible about every man, doctrine, book, or policy that is assigned you to deal with. The more strong lights, the more spiritual scandal you can throw on the matter, the more money they pay you, the more the people buy the issue. You, Tom d'Invilliers, a blighted Shelley, changing, shifting, clever, unscrupulous, represent the critical consciousness of the race – Oh, don't protest, I know the stuff. I used to write book reviews in college; I considered it rare sport to refer to the latest honest, conscientious effort to propound a theory or a remedy as a "welcome addition to our light summer reading". Come on now, admit it.'

Tom laughed, and Amory continued triumphantly.

'We *want* to believe. Young students try to believe in older authors, constituents try to believe in their Congressmen, countries try to believe in their statesmen, but they *can't*. Too many voices, too much scattered, illogical, ill-considered criticism. It's worse in the case of newspapers. Any rich, unprogressive old party with that particularly grasping, acquisitive form of mentality known as financial genius can own a paper that is the intellectual meat and drink of thousands of tired, hurried men, men too involved in the business of modern living to swallow anything but predigested food. For two cents the voter buys his politics, prejudices and philosophy. A year later there is a new political ring or a change in the paper's ownership, consequence: more confusion, more contradiction, a sudden inrush of new ideas, their tempering, their distillation, the reaction against them – '

He paused only to get his breath.

'And that is why I have sworn not to put pen to paper until my ideas either clarify or depart entirely; I have quite enough sins on my soul without putting dangerous, shallow epigrams into people's heads; I might cause a poor, inoffensive capitalist to have a vulgar liaison with a bomb, or get some innocent little Bolshevik tangled up with a machine-gun bullet – '

Tom was growing restless under this lampooning of his connection with the *New Democracy*.

'What's all this got to do with your being bored?'

Amory considered that it had much to do with it.

'How'll I fit in?' he demanded. 'What am I for? To propagate the race? According to the American novels we are led to believe that the "healthy American boy" from nineteen to twenty-five is an entirely sexless animal. As a matter of fact, the healthier he is the less that's true. The only alternative to letting it get you is some violent interest. Well, the war is over; I believe too much in the responsibilities of authorship to write just now; and business, well, business speaks for itself. It has no connection with anything in the world that I've ever been interested in, except a slim, utilitarian connection with economics. What I'd see of it, lost in a clerkship, for the next and best ten years of my life would have the intellectual content of an industrial movie.'

'Try fiction,' suggested Tom.

'Trouble is I get distracted when I start to write stories – get afraid I'm doing it instead of living – get thinking maybe life is waiting for me in the Japanese Gardens at the Ritz or at Atlantic City or on the lower East Side.

'Anyway,' he continued, 'I haven't the vital urge. I wanted to be a regular human being but the girl couldn't see it that way.'

'You'll find another.'

'God! Banish the thought. Why don't you tell me that "if the girl had been worth having she'd have waited for you"? No, sir, the girl really worth having won't wait for anybody. If I thought there'd be another I'd lose my remaining faith in human nature. Maybe I'll play – but Rosalind was the only girl in the wide world that could have held me.'

'Well,' yawned Tom, 'I've played confidant a good hour by the clock. Still, I'm glad to see you're beginning to have violent views again on something.'

'I am,' agreed Amory reluctantly. 'Yet when I see a happy family it makes me sick at my stomach – '

'Happy families try to make people feel that way,' said Tom cynically.

TOM THE CENSOR

There were days when Amory listened. These were when Tom, wreathed in smoke, indulged in the slaughter of American literature. Words failed him.

'Fifty thousand dollars a year,' he would cry. 'My God! Look at them, look at them – Edna Ferber, Gouverneur Morris, Fannie Hurst, Mary Roberts Rinehart – not producing among 'em one story or novel that will last ten years. This man Cobb – I don't think he's either clever or amusing – and what's more, I don't think very many people do, except the editors. He's just groggy with advertising. And – oh Harold Bell Wright – oh Zane Grey – '

'They try.'

'No, they don't even try. Some of them *can* write, but they won't sit down and do one honest novel. Most of them *can't* write, I'll admit. I believe Rupert Hughes tries to give a real, comprehensive picture of American life, but his style and perspective are barbarous. Ernest Poole and Dorothy Canfield try but they're hindered by their absolute lack of any sense of humour; but at least they crowd their work instead of spreading it thin. Every author ought to write every book as if he were going to be beheaded the day he finished it.'

'Is that *double entente*?'

'Don't slow me up! Now there's a few of 'em that seem to have some cultural background, some intelligence and a good deal of literary felicity but they just simply won't write honestly; they'd all claim there was no public for good stuff. Then why the devil is it that Wells, Conrad, Galsworthy, Shaw, Bennett, and the rest depend on America for over half their sales?'

'How does little Tommy like the poets?'

Tom was overcome. He dropped his arms until they swung loosely beside the chair and emitted faint grunts.

'I'm writing a satire on 'em now, calling it "Boston Bards and Hearst Reviewers".'

'Let's hear it,' said Amory eagerly.

'I've only got the last few lines done.'

'That's very modern. Let's hear 'em, if they're funny.'

Tom produced a folded paper from his pocket and read aloud, pausing at intervals so that Amory could see that it was free verse:

> 'So
> Walter Arensberg,
> Alfred Kreymborg,
> Carl Sandburg,
> Louis Untermeyer,
> Eunice Tietjens,
> Clara Shanafelt,

James Oppenheim,
Maxwell Bodenheim,
Richard Glaenzer,
Scharmel Iris,
Conrad Aiken,
I place your names here
So that you may live
If only as names,
Sinuous, mauve-coloured names,
In the Juvenilia
Of my collected editions.'

Amory roared.

'You win the iron pansy. I'll buy you a meal on the arrogance of the last two lines.'

Amory did not entirely agree with Tom's sweeping damnation of American novelists and poets. He enjoyed both Vachel Lindsay and Booth Tarkington, and admired the conscientious, if slender, artistry of Edgar Lee Masters.

'What I hate is this idiotic drivel about "I am God – I am man – I ride the winds – I look through the smoke – I am the life sense".'

'It's ghastly!'

'And I wish American novelists would give up trying to make business romantically interesting. Nobody wants to read about it, unless it's crooked business. If it was an entertaining subject they'd buy the life of James J. Hill and not one of these long office tragedies that harp along on the significance of smoke – '

'And gloom,' said Tom. 'That's another favourite, though I'll admit the Russians have the monopoly. Our speciality is stories about little girls who break their spines and get adopted by grouchy old men because they smile so much. You'd think we were a race of cheerful cripples and that the common end of the Russian peasant was suicide – '

'Six o'clock,' said Amory, glancing at his wristwatch. 'I'll buy you a grea' big dinner on the strength of the Juvenilia of your collected editions.'

LOOKING BACKWARD

July sweltered out with a last hot week, and Amory in another surge of unrest realised that it was just five months since he and Rosalind had met. Yet it was already hard for him to visualise the heart-whole boy who had stepped off the transport, passionately desiring the adventure of life. One night while the heat, overpowering and enervating, poured into the windows of his room he struggled for several hours in a vague effort to immortalise the poignancy of that time.

The February streets, wind-washed by night, blow full of strange half-intermittent damps, bearing on wasted walks in shining sight wet snow plashed into gleams under the lamps, like golden oil from some divine machine, in an hour of thaw and stars.

Strange damps – full of the eyes of many men, crowded with life borne in upon a lull . . . Oh, I was young, for I could turn again to you, most finite and most beautiful, and taste the stuff of half-remembered dreams, sweet and new on your mouth.

. . . There was a tanging in the midnight air – silence was dead and sound not yet awoken – Life cracked like ice! – one brilliant note and there, radiant and pale, you stood . . . and spring had broken. (The icicles were short upon the roofs and the changeling city swooned.)

Our thoughts were frosty mist along the eaves; our two ghosts kissed, high on the long, mazed wires – eerie half-laughter echoes here and leaves only a fatuous sigh for young desires; regret has followed after things she loved, leaving the great husk.

ANOTHER ENDING

In mid-August came a letter from Monsignor Darcy, who had evidently just stumbled on his address:

My Dear Boy – Your last letter was quite enough to make me worry about you. It was not a bit like yourself. Reading between the lines I should imagine that your engagement to this girl is making you rather unhappy, and I see you have lost all the feeling of romance that you had before the war. You make a great mistake if you think you can be romantic without religion. Sometimes I think that with both of us the secret of success, when we find it, is the mystical element in us: something flows into us that enlarges our personalities, and when it ebbs out our personalities shrink; I should call your last two letters rather shrivelled. Beware of losing yourself in the personality of another being, man or woman.

His Eminence Cardinal O'Neill and the Bishop of Boston are staying with me at present, so it is hard for me to get a moment to write, but I wish you would come up here later if only for a weekend. I go to Washington this week.

What I shall do in the future is hanging in the balance. Absolutely between ourselves I should not be surprised to see the red hat of a cardinal descend upon my unworthy head within the next eight months. In any event, I should like to have a house in New York or Washington where you could drop in for weekends.

Amory, I'm very glad we're both alive; this war could easily have been the end of a brilliant family. But in regard to matrimony, you are now at the most dangerous period of your life. You might marry in haste and repent at leisure, but I think you won't. From what you write me about the present calamitous state of your finances, what you want is naturally impossible. However, if I judge you by the means I usually choose, I should say that there will be something of an emotional crisis within the next year.

Do write me. I feel annoyingly out of date on you.

With greatest affection,

THAYER DARCY

Within a week after the receipt of this letter their little household fell precipitously to pieces. The immediate cause was the serious and probably chronic illness of Tom's mother. So they stored the furniture, gave instructions to sublet and shook hands gloomily in the Pennsylvania Station. Amory and Tom seemed always to be saying goodbye.

Feeling very much alone, Amory yielded to an impulse and set off southward, intending to join Monsignor in Washington. They missed connections by two hours, and, deciding to spend a few days with an ancient, remembered uncle, Amory journeyed up through the luxuriant fields of Maryland into Ramilly County. But instead of two days his stay lasted from mid-August nearly through September, for in Maryland he met Eleanor.

3

Young Irony

For years afterwards when Amory thought of Eleanor he seemed still to hear the wind sobbing around him and sending little chills into the places beside his heart. The night when they rode up the slope and watched the cold moon float through the clouds, he lost a further part of him that nothing could restore; and when he lost it he lost also the power of regretting it. Eleanor was, say, the last time that evil crept close to Amory under the mask of beauty, the last weird mystery that held him with wild fascination and pounded his soul to flakes.

With her his imagination ran riot and that is why they rode to the highest hill and watched an evil moon ride high, for they knew then that they could see the devil in each other. But Eleanor – did Amory dream her? Afterwards their ghosts played, yet both of them hoped from their souls never to meet. Was it the infinite sadness of her eyes that drew him or the mirror of himself that he found in the gorgeous clarity of her mind? She will have no other adventure like Amory, and if she reads this she will say: 'And Amory will have no other adventure like me.'

Nor will she sigh, any more than he would sigh.

Eleanor tried to put it on paper once:

The fading things we only know
　We'll have forgotten . . .
　　Put away . . .
Desires that melted with the snow,
　And dreams begotten
　　This today:
The sudden dawns we laughed to greet,
　That all could see, that none could share,
Will be but dawns . . . and if we meet
　We shall not care.

Dear . . . not one tear will rise for this . . .
　A little while hence
　　No regret

Will stir for a remembered kiss –
  Not even silence,
    When we've met,
Will give old ghosts a waste to roam,
  Or stir the surface of the sea . . .
If grey shapes drift beneath the foam
    We shall not see.

They quarrelled dangerously because Amory maintained that *sea* and *see* couldn't possibly be used as a rhyme. And then Eleanor had part of another verse that she couldn't find a beginning for:

. . . But wisdom passes . . . still the years
Will feed us wisdom . . . Age will go
Back to the old – For all our tears
            We shall not know.

Eleanor hated Maryland passionately. She belonged to the oldest of the old families of Ramilly County and lived in a big, gloomy house with her grandfather. She had been born and brought up in France . . . I see I am starting wrong. Let me begin again.

Amory was bored, as he usually was in the country. He used to go for far walks by himself – and wander along reciting 'Ulalume' to the cornfields, and congratulating Poe for drinking himself to death in that atmosphere of smiling complacency. One afternoon he had strolled for several miles along a road that was new to him, and then through a wood on bad advice from a coloured woman . . . losing himself entirely. A passing storm decided to break out, and to his great impatience the sky grew black as pitch and the rain began to splatter down through the trees, become suddenly furtive and ghostly. Thunder rolled with menacing crashes up the valley and scattered through the woods in intermittent batteries. He stumbled blindly on, hunting for a way out, and finally, through webs of twisted branches, caught sight of a rift in the trees where the unbroken lightning showed open country. He rushed to the edge of the woods and then hesitated whether or not to cross the fields and try to reach the shelter of the little house marked by a light far down the valley. It was only half-past five, but he could see scarcely ten steps before him, except when the lightning made everything vivid and grotesque for great sweeps around.

Suddenly a strange sound fell on his ears. It was a song, in a low, husky voice, a girl's voice, and whoever was singing was very close to him. A year before he might have laughed, or trembled; but in his restless mood he only stood and listened while the words sank into his consciousness:

'Les sanglots longs
Des violons
  De l'automne
Blessent mon coeur
D'une langueur
  Monotone.'

The lightning split the sky, but the song went on without a quaver. The girl was evidently in the field and the voice seemed to come vaguely from a haystack about twenty feet in front of him.

Then it ceased: ceased and began again in a weird chant that soared and hung and fell and blended with the rain:

'Tout suffocant
Et blême quand
  Sonne l'heure
Je me souviens
Des jours anciens
  Et je pleure . . . '

'Who the devil is there in Ramilly County,' muttered Amory aloud, 'who would deliver Verlaine in an extemporaneous tune to a soaking haystack?'

'Somebody's there!' cried the voice unalarmed. 'Who are you? – Manfred, St Christopher or Queen Victoria?'

'I'm Don Juan!' Amory shouted on impulse, raising his voice above the noise of the rain and the wind.

A delighted shriek came from the haystack.

'I know who you are – you're the blond boy that likes "Ulalume" – I recognise your voice.'

'How do I get up?' he cried from the foot of the haystack, whither he had arrived, dripping wet. A head appeared over the edge – it was so dark that Amory could just make out a patch of damp hair and two eyes that gleamed like a cat's.

'Run back!' came the voice, 'and jump and I'll catch your hand – no, not there – on the other side.'

He followed directions and as he sprawled up the side, knee-deep in hay, a small, white hand reached out, gripped his, and helped him on to the top.

'Here you are, Juan,' cried she of the damp hair. 'Do you mind if I drop the Don?'

'You've got a thumb like mine!' he exclaimed.

'And you're holding my hand, which is dangerous without seeing my face.' He dropped it quickly.

As if in answer to his prayers came a flash of lightning and he looked eagerly at her who stood beside him on the soggy haystack, ten feet above the ground. But she had covered her face and he saw nothing but a slender figure, dark, damp, bobbed hair, and the small white hands with the thumbs that bent back like his.

'Sit down,' she suggested politely, as the dark closed in on them. 'If you'll sit opposite me in this hollow you can have half of the raincoat, which I was using as a waterproof tent until you so rudely interrupted me.'

'I was asked,' Amory said joyfully; 'you asked me – you know you did.'

'Don Juan always manages that,' she said, laughing, 'but I shan't call you that any more, because you've got reddish hair. Instead you can recite "Ulalume" and I'll be Psyche, your soul.'

Amory flushed, happily invisible under the curtain of wind and rain. They were sitting opposite each other in a slight hollow in the hay with the raincoat spread over most of them, and the rain doing for the rest. Amory was trying desperately to see Psyche, but the lightning refused to flash again, and he waited impatiently. Good Lord! supposing she wasn't beautiful – supposing she was forty and pedantic – heavens! Suppose, only suppose, she was mad. But he knew the last was unworthy. Here had Providence sent a girl to amuse him, just as it sent Benvenuto Cellini men to murder, and he was wondering if she was mad, just because she exactly filled his mood.

'I'm not,' she said.

'Not what?'

'Not mad. I didn't think you were mad when I first saw you, so it isn't fair that you should think so of me.'

'How on earth – '

As long as they knew each other Eleanor and Amory could be 'on a subject' and stop talking with the definite thought of it in their heads, yet ten minutes later speak aloud and find that their minds had followed the same channels and led them each to a parallel idea, an idea that others would have found absolutely unconnected with the first.

'Tell me,' he demanded, leaning forward eagerly, 'how do you know about "Ulalume" – how did you know the colour of my hair? What's your name? What were you doing here? Tell me all at once!'

Suddenly the lightning flashed in with a leap of overreaching light and he saw Eleanor, and looked for the first time into those eyes of hers. Oh, she was magnificent – pale skin, the colour of marble in starlight, slender brows, and eyes that glittered green as emeralds in the blinding glare. She was a witch, of perhaps nineteen, he judged, alert and dreamy and with the tell-tale white line over her upper lip that was a weakness and a delight. He sank back with a gasp against the wall of hay.

'Now you've seen me,' she said calmly, 'and I suppose you're about to say that my green eyes are burning into your brain.'

'What colour is your hair?' he asked intently. 'It's bobbed, isn't it?'

'Yes, it's bobbed. I don't know what colour it is,' she answered, musing, 'so many men have asked me. It's medium, I suppose – No one ever looks long at my hair. I've got beautiful eyes, though, haven't I? I don't care what you say, I have beautiful eyes.'

'Answer my question, Madeline.'

'Don't remember them all – besides my name isn't Madeline, it's Eleanor.'

'I might have guessed it. You *look* like Eleanor – you have that Eleanor look. You know what I mean.'

There was a silence as they listened to the rain.

'It's going down my neck, fellow lunatic,' she offered finally.

'Answer my questions.'

'Well – name of Savage, Eleanor; live in big old house mile down road; nearest living relation to be notified, grandfather – Ramilly Savage; height, five feet four inches; number on watch-case, 3077 W; nose, delicate aquiline; temperament, uncanny – '

'And me,' Amory interrupted, 'where did you see me?'

'Oh, you're one of *those* men,' she answered haughtily, 'must lug old self into conversation. Well, my boy, I was behind a hedge sunning myself one day last week, and along comes a man saying in a pleasant, conceited way of talking:

"And now when the night was senescent"
(says he)
"And the star dials pointed to morn,
At the end of the path a liquescent"
(says he)
"And nebulous lustre was born."

'So I poked my eyes up over the hedge, but you had started to run, for some unknown reason, and so I saw but the back of your beautiful head. "Oh!" says I, "there's a man for whom many of us might sigh," and I continued in my best Irish – '

'All right,' Amory interrupted. 'Now go back to yourself.'

'Well, I will. I'm one of those people who go through the world giving other people thrills, but getting few myself except those I read into men on such nights as these. I have the social courage to go on the stage, but not the energy; I haven't the patience to write books; and I never met a man I'd marry. However, I'm only eighteen.'

The storm was dying down softly and only the wind kept up its ghostly surge and made the stack lean and gravely settle from side to side. Amory was in a trance. He felt that every moment was precious. He had never met a girl like this before – she would never seem quite the same again. He didn't at all feel like a character in a play, the appropriate feeling in an unconventional situation – instead, he had a sense of coming home.

'I have just made a great decision,' said Eleanor after another pause, 'and that is why I'm here, to answer another of your questions. I have just decided that I don't believe in immortality.'

'Really! how banal!'

'Frightfully so,' she answered, 'but depressing with a stale, sickly depression, nevertheless. I came out here to get wet – like a wet hen; wet hens always have great clarity of mind,' she concluded.

'Go on,' Amory said politely.

'Well – I'm not afraid of the dark, so I put on my slicker and rubber boots and came out. You see I was always afraid, before, to say I didn't believe in God – because the lightning might strike me – but here I am and it hasn't, of course, but the main point is that this time I wasn't any more afraid of it than I had been when I was a Christian Scientist, like I was last year. So now I know I'm a materialist and I was fraternising with the hay when you came out and stood by the woods, scared to death.'

'Why, you little wretch – ' cried Amory indignantly. 'Scared of what?'

'*Yourself!*' she shouted, and he jumped. She clapped her hands and laughed. 'See – see! Conscience – kill it like me! Eleanor Savage, materiologist – no jumping, no starting, come early – '

'But I *have* to have a soul,' he objected. 'I can't be rational – and I won't be molecular.'

She leaned towards him, her burning eyes never leaving his own, and whispered with a sort of romantic finality: 'I thought so, Juan, I feared so – you're sentimental. You're not like me. I'm a romantic little materialist.'

'I'm not sentimental – I'm as romantic as you are. The idea, you know, is that the sentimental person thinks things will last – the romantic person has a desperate confidence that they won't.' (This was an ancient distinction of Amory's.)

'Epigrams. I'm going home,' she said sadly. 'Let's get off the haystack and walk to the crossroads.'

They slowly descended from their perch. She would not let him help her down and motioning him away arrived in a graceful lump in the soft mud where she sat for an instant, laughing at herself. Then she jumped to her feet and slipped her hand into his, and they tiptoed across the fields, jumping and swinging from dry spot to dry spot. A transcendent delight seemed to sparkle in every pool of water, for the moon had risen and the storm had scurried away into western Maryland. When Eleanor's arm touched his he felt his hands grow cold with deadly fear lest he should lose the shadow brush with which his imagination was painting wonders of her. He watched her from the corners of his eyes as ever he did when he walked with her – she was a feast and a folly and he wished it had been his destiny to sit for ever on a haystack and see life through her green eyes. His paganism soared that night and when she faded out like a grey ghost down the road, a deep singing came out of the fields and filled his way homeward. All night the summer moths flitted in and out of Amory's window; all night large looming sounds swayed in mystic reverie through the silver grain – and he lay awake in the clear darkness.

Amory selected a blade of grass and nibbled at it scientifically.

'I never fall in love in August or September,' he proffered.

'When then?'

'Christmas or Easter. I'm a liturgist.'

'Easter!' She turned up her nose. 'Huh! Spring in corsets!'

'Easter *would* bore spring, wouldn't she? Easter has her hair braided, wears a tailored suit.'

> 'Bind on thy sandals, oh, thou most fleet.
> Over the splendour and speed of thy feet – '

quoted Eleanor softly, and then added: 'I suppose Hallowe'en is a better day for autumn than Thanksgiving.'

'Much better – and Christmas Eve does very well for winter, but summer . . . '

'Summer has no day,' she said. 'We can't possibly have a summer love. So many people have tried that the name's become proverbial. Summer is only the unfulfilled promise of spring, a charlatan in place of the warm balmy nights I dream of in April. It's a sad season of life without growth . . . It has no day.'

'Fourth of July,' Amory suggested facetiously.

'Don't be funny!' she said, raking him with her eyes.

'Well, what could fulfil the promise of spring?'

She thought a moment.

'Oh, I suppose heaven would, if there was one,' she said finally, 'a sort of pagan heaven – you ought to be a materialist,' she continued irrelevantly.

'Why?'

'Because you look a good deal like the pictures of Rupert Brooke.'

To some extent Amory tried to play Rupert Brooke as long as he knew Eleanor. What he said, his attitude towards life, towards her, towards himself, were all reflexes of the dead Englishman's literary moods. Often she sat in the grass, a lazy wind playing with her short hair, her voice husky as she ran up and down the scale from Grantchester to Waikiki. There was something most passionate in Eleanor's reading aloud. They seemed nearer, not only mentally, but physically, when they read, than when she was in his arms, and this was often, for they fell half into love almost from the first. Yet was Amory capable of love now? He could, as always, run through the emotions in a half-hour, but even while they revelled in their imaginations, he knew that neither of them could care as he had cared once before – I suppose that was why they turned to Brooke, and Swinburne, and Shelley. Their chance was to make everything fine and finished and rich and imaginative; they must bend tiny golden tentacles from his imagination to hers, that would take the place of the great, deep love that was never so near, yet never so much of a dream.

One poem they read over and over, Swinburne's 'Triumph of Time', and four lines of it rang in his memory afterwards on warm nights when he saw the fireflies among dusky tree trunks and heard the low drone of many frogs. Then Eleanor seemed to come out of the night and stand by him, and he heard her throaty voice, with its tone of a fleecy-headed drum, repeating:

'Is it worth a tear, is it worth an hour,
To think of things that are well outworn;
Of fruitless husk and fugitive flower,
The dream forgone and the deed forborne?'

They were formally introduced two days later, and his aunt told him her history. The Ramillys were two: old Mr Ramilly and his granddaughter, Eleanor. She had lived in France with a restless mother whom Amory imagined to have been very like his own, on whose death she had come to America, to live in Maryland. She had gone to Baltimore first, to stay with a bachelor uncle, and there she insisted on being a débutante at the age of seventeen. She had a wild winter and arrived in the country in March, having quarrelled frantically with all her Baltimore relatives, and shocked them into fiery protest. A rather fast crowd had come out, who drank cocktails in limousines and were promiscuously condescending and patronising towards older people, and Eleanor with an *esprit* that hinted strongly of the boulevards, led many innocents, still redolent of St Timothy's and Farmington, into paths of Bohemian naughtiness. When the story came to her uncle, a forgetful cavalier of a more hypocritical era, there was a scene, from which Eleanor emerged, subdued but rebellious and indignant, to seek haven with her grandfather who hovered in the country on the near side of senility. That's as far as her story went; she told him the rest herself, but that was later.

Often they swam and as Amory floated lazily in the water he shut his mind to all thoughts except those of hazy soap-bubble lands where the sun splattered through wind-drunk trees. How could anyone possibly think or worry, or do anything except splash and dive and loll there on the edge of time while the flower months failed. Let the days move over – sadness and memory and pain recurred outside, and here, once more, before he went on to meet them, he wanted to drift and be young.

There were days when Amory resented that life had changed from an even progress along a road stretching ever in sight, with the scenery merging and blending, into a succession of quick, unrelated scenes – two years of sweat and blood; that sudden absurd instinct for paternity that Rosalind had stirred; the half-sensual, half-neurotic quality of this autumn with Eleanor. He felt that it would take all time, more than he could ever spare, to glue these strange cumbersome pictures into the scrapbook of his life. It was all like a banquet where he sat for this half-hour of his youth and tried to enjoy brilliant epicurean courses.

Dimly he promised himself a time where all should be welded together. For months it seemed that he had alternated between being borne along a stream of love or fascination, or left in an eddy, and in the eddies he had not desired to think, rather to be picked up on a wave's top and swept along again.

'The despairing, dying autumn and our love – how well they harmonise!' said Eleanor sadly one day as they lay dripping by the water.

'The Indian summer of our hearts – ' he ceased.

'Tell me,' she said finally, 'was she light or dark?'

'Light.'

'Was she more beautiful than I am?'

'I don't know,' said Amory shortly.

One night they walked while the moon rose and poured a great burden of glory over the garden until it seemed fairyland with Amory and Eleanor, dim phantasmal shapes, expressing eternal beauty in curious elfin love moods. Then they turned out of the moonlight into the trellised darkness of a vine-hung pagoda, where there were scents so plaintive as to be nearly musical.

'Light a match,' she whispered. 'I want to see you.'

Scratch! Flare!

The night and the scarred trees were like scenery in a play, and to be there with Eleanor, shadowy and unreal, seemed somehow oddly familiar. Amory thought how it was only the past that ever seemed strange and unbelievable. The match went out.

'It's black as pitch.'

'We're just voices now,' murmured Eleanor, 'little lonesome voices. Light another.'

'That was my last match.'

Suddenly he caught her in his arms.

'You *are* mine – you know you're mine!' he cried wildly . . . the moonlight twisted in through the vines and listened . . . the fireflies hung upon their whispers as if to win his glance from the glory of her eyes.

THE END OF SUMMER

'No wind is stirring in the grass; not one wind stirs . . . the water in the hidden pools, as glass, fronts the full moon and so inters the golden token in its icy mass,' chanted Eleanor to the trees that skeletoned the body of the night. 'Isn't it ghostly here? If you can hold your horse's feet up, let's cut through the woods and find the hidden pools.'

'It's after one, and you'll get the devil,' he objected, 'and I don't know enough about horses to put one away in the pitch dark.'

'Shut up, you old fool,' she whispered irrelevantly, and, leaning over, she patted him lazily with her riding-crop. 'You can leave your old plug in our stable and I'll send him over tomorrow.'

'But my uncle has got to drive me to the station with this old plug at seven o'clock.'

'Don't be a spoil-sport – remember, you have a tendency towards wavering that prevents you from being the entire light of my life.'

Amory drew his horse up close beside, and, leaning towards her, grasped her hand.

'Say I am – *quick*, or I'll pull you over and make you ride behind me.'

She looked up and smiled and shook her head excitedly.

'Oh, do! – or rather, don't! Why are all the exciting things so uncomfortable, like fighting and exploring and skiing in Canada? By the way, we're going to ride up Harper's Hill. I think that comes in our programme about five o'clock.'

'You little devil,' Amory growled. 'You're going to make me stay up all night and sleep in the train like an immigrant all day tomorrow, going back to New York.'

'Hush! someone's coming along the road – let's go! *Whoo-ee-oop!*' And with a shout that probably gave the belated traveller a series of shivers, she turned her horse into the woods and Amory followed slowly, as he had followed her all day for three weeks.

The summer was over, but he had spent the days in watching Eleanor, a graceful, facile Manfred, build herself intellectual and imaginative pyramids while she revelled in the artificialities of the temperamental teens and they wrote poetry at the dinner-table.

When Vanity kissed Vanity, a hundred happy Junes ago, he pondered o'er her breathlessly, and, that all men might ever know, he rhymed her eyes with life and death: 'Thru Time I'll save my love!' he said . . . yet Beauty vanished with his breath, and, with her lovers, she was dead . . .

– Ever his wit and not her eyes, ever his art and not her hair: 'Who'd learn a trick in rhyme, be wise and pause before his sonnet there' . . . So all my words, however true, might sing you to a thousandth June, and no one ever *know* that you were Beauty for an afternoon.

So he wrote one day, when he pondered how coldly we thought of the 'Dark Lady of the Sonnets', and how little we remembered her as the great man wanted her remembered. For what Shakespeare *must* have desired, to have been able to write with such divine despair, was that the lady should live . . . and now we have no real interest in her . . . The irony of it is that if he had cared *more* for the poem than for the lady the sonnet would be only obvious, imitative rhetoric and no one would ever have read it after twenty years . . .

This was the last night Amory ever saw Eleanor. He was leaving in the morning and they had agreed to take a long farewell trot by the cold moonlight. She wanted to talk, she said – perhaps the last time in her life that she could be rational (she meant pose with comfort). So they had turned into the woods and rode for half an hour with scarcely a word, except when she whispered, 'Damn!' at a bothersome branch – whispered it as no other girl was ever able to whisper it. Then they started up Harper's Hill, walking their tired horses.

'Good Lord! It's quiet here!' whispered Eleanor; 'much more lonesome than the woods.'

'I hate woods,' Amory said, shuddering. 'Any kind of foliage or underbrush at night. Out here it's so broad and easy on the spirit.'

'The long slope of a long hill.'

'And the cold moon rolling moonlight down it.'

'And thee and me, last and most important.'

It was quiet that night – the straight road they followed up to the edge of the cliff knew few footsteps at any time. Only an occasional

Negro cabin, silver-grey in the rock-ribbed moonlight, broke the long line of bare ground; behind lay the black edge of the woods like a dark frosting on white cake, and ahead the sharp, high horizon. It was much colder – so cold that it settled on them and drove all the warm nights from their minds.

'The end of summer,' said Eleanor softly. 'Listen to the beat of our horses' hoofs – tump-tump-tump-a-tump.' Have you ever been feverish and had all noises divide into "tump-tump-tump" until you could swear eternity was divisible into so many tumps? That's the way I feel – old horses go tump-tump . . . I guess that's the only thing that separates horses and clocks from us. Human beings can't go "tump-tump-tump" without going crazy.'

The breeze freshened and Eleanor pulled her cape around her and shivered.

'Are you very cold?' asked Amory.

'No, I'm thinking about myself – my black old inside self, the real one, with the fundamental honesty that keeps me from being absolutely wicked by making me realise my own sins.'

They were riding up close by the cliff and Amory gazed over. Where the fall met the ground a hundred feet below, a black stream made a sharp line, broken by tiny glints in the swift water.

'Rotten, rotten old world,' broke out Eleanor suddenly, 'and the wretchedest thing of all is me – oh, *why* am I a girl? Why am I not a stupid – ? Look at you; you're stupider than I am, not much, but some, and you can lope about and get bored and then lope somewhere else, and you can play around with girls without being involved in meshes of sentiment, and you can do anything and be justified – and here am I with the brains to do everything, yet tied to the sinking ship of future matrimony. If I were born a hundred years from now, well and good, but now what's in store for me – I have to marry, that goes without saying. Who? I'm too bright for most men, and yet I have to descend to their level and let them patronise my intellect in order to get their attention. Every year that I don't marry I've got less chance of a first-class man. At the best I can have my choice from one or two cities and, of course, I have to marry into a dinner-coat.

'Listen,' she leaned close again, 'I like clever men and good-looking men, and, of course, no one cares more for personality than I do. Oh, just one person in fifty has any glimmer of what sex is. I'm hipped on Freud and all that, but it's rotten that every bit of *real* love in the world is ninety-nine per cent passion and one little soupçon of jealousy.' She finished as suddenly as she began.

'Of course, you're right,' Amory agreed. 'It's a rather unpleasant overpowering force that's part of the machinery under everything. It's like an actor that lets you see his mechanics! Wait a minute till I think this out . . .'

He paused and tried to get a metaphor. They had turned from the cliff and were riding along the road about fifty feet to the left.

'You see everyone's got to have some cloak to throw around it. The mediocre intellects, Plato's second class, use the remnants of romantic chivalry diluted with Victorian sentiment – and we who consider ourselves the intellectuals cover it up by pretending that it's another side of us, has nothing to do with our shining brains; we pretend that the fact that we realise it is really absolving us from being a prey to it. But the truth is that sex is right in the middle of our purest abstractions, so close that it obscures vision . . . I can kiss you now and will . . . ' He leaned towards her in his saddle, but she drew away.

'I can't – I can't kiss you now – I'm more sensitive.'

'You're more stupid then,' he declared rather impatiently. 'Intellect is no protection from sex any more than convention is . . . '

'What is?' she fired up. 'The Catholic Church or the maxims of Confucius?'

Amory looked up, rather taken aback.

'That's your panacea, isn't it?' she cried. 'Oh, you're just an old hypocrite, too. Thousands of scowling priests keeping the degenerate Italians and illiterate Irish repentant with gabble-gabble about the sixth and ninth commandments. It's just all cloaks, sentiment and spiritual rouge and panaceas. I'll tell you there *is* no God, not even a definite abstract goodness; so it's all got to be worked out for the individual by the individual here in high white foreheads like mine, and you're too much the prig to admit it.' She let go her reins and shook her little fists at the stars.

'If there's a God let him strike me – strike me!'

'Talking about God again after the manner of atheists,' Amory said sharply. His materialism, always a thin cloak, was torn to shreds by Eleanor's blasphemy . . . She knew it and it angered him that she knew it.

'And like most intellectuals who don't find faith convenient,' he continued coldly, 'like Napoleon and Oscar Wilde and the rest of your type, you'll yell loudly for a priest on your deathbed.'

Eleanor drew her horse up sharply and he reined in beside her.

'Will I?' she said in a queer voice that scared him. 'Will I? Watch! *I'm going over the cliff!*' And before he could interfere she had turned and was riding breakneck for the end of the plateau.

He wheeled and started after her, his body like ice, his nerves in a vast clangour. There was no chance of stopping her. The moon was under a cloud and her horse would step blindly over. Then some ten feet from the edge of the cliff she gave a sudden shriek and flung herself sideways – plunged from her horse and, rolling over twice, landed in a pile of brush five feet from the edge. The horse went over with a frantic whinny. In a minute he was by Eleanor's side and saw that her eyes were open.

'Eleanor!' he cried.

She did not answer, but her lips moved and her eyes filled with sudden tears.

'Eleanor, are you hurt?'

'No; I don't think so,' she said faintly, and then began weeping. 'My horse dead?'

'Good God – Yes!'

'Oh!' she wailed. 'I thought I was going over. I didn't know – '

He helped her gently to her feet and boosted her on to his saddle. So they started homeward; Amory walking and she bent forward on the pommel, sobbing bitterly.

'I've got a crazy streak,' she faltered, 'twice before I've done things like that. When I was eleven mother went – went mad – stark raving crazy. We were in Vienna – '

All the way back she talked haltingly about herself, and Amory's love waned slowly with the moon. At her door they started from habit to kiss good-night, but she could not run into his arms, nor were they stretched to meet her as in the week before. For a minute they stood there, hating each other with a bitter sadness. But as Amory had loved himself in Eleanor, so now what he hated was only a mirror. Their poses were strewn about the pale dawn like broken glass. The stars were long gone and there were left only the little sighing gusts of wind and the silences between . . . but naked souls are poor things ever, and soon he turned homeward and let new lights come in with the sun.

A POEM THAT ELEANOR SENT AMORY SEVERAL YEARS LATER

Here, Earth-born, over the lilt of the water,
  Lisping its music and bearing a burden of light,
Bosoming day as a laughing and radiant daughter . . .
  Here we may whisper unheard, unafraid of the night.
Walking alone . . . was it splendour, or what, we were bound with,
  Deep in the time when summer lets down her hair?
Shadows we loved and the patterns they covered the ground with,
  Tapestries, mystical, faint in the breathless air.

That was the day . . . and the night for another story,
  Pale as a dream and shadowed with pencilled trees –
Ghosts of the stars came by who had sought for glory,
  Whispered to us of peace in the plaintive breeze,
Whispered of old dead faiths that the day had shattered,
  Youth the penny that bought delight of the moon;
That was the urge that we knew and the language that mattered
  That was the debt that we paid to the usurer June.

Here, deepest of dreams, by the waters that bring not
  Anything back of the past that we need not know,
What if the light is but sun and the little streams sing not,
  We are together, it seems . . . I have loved you so . . .
What did the last night hold, with the summer over,
  Drawing us back to the home in the changing glade?
What leered out of the dark in the ghostly clover?

  God! . . . till you stirred in your sleep . . . and were wild afraid . . .
Well . . . we have passed . . . we are chronicle now to the eerie.
  Curious metal from meteors that failed in the sky;
Earth-born the tireless is stretched by the water, quite weary,
  Close to this ununderstandable changeling that's I . . .
Fear is an echo we traced to Security's daughter;
  Now we are faces and voices . . . and less, too soon,
Whispering half-love over the lilt of the water . . .
  Youth the penny that bought delight of the moon.

A POEM AMORY SENT TO ELEANOR AND WHICH HE CALLED 'SUMMER STORM'

Faint winds, and a song fading and leaves falling,
Faint winds, and far away a fading laughter . . .
And the rain and over the fields a voice calling . . .

Our grey blown cloud scurries and lifts above,
Slides on the sun and flutters there to waft her
Sisters on. The shadow of a dove
Falls on the cote, the trees are filled with wings;
And down the valley through the crying trees
The body of the darker storm flies; brings
With its new air the breath of sunken seas
And slender tenuous thunder . . .
But I wait . . .

Wait for the mists and for the blacker rain –
Heavier winds that stir the veil of fate,
Happier winds that pile her hair;
Again
They tear me, teach me, strew the heavy air
Upon me, winds that I know, and storm.

There was a summer every rain was rare;
There was a season every wind was warm . . .
And now *you* pass me in the mist . . . your hair
Rain-blown about you, damp lips curved once more
In that wild irony, that gay despair
That made you old when we have met before;
Wraith-like you drift on out before the rain,
Across the fields, blown with the stemless flowers,
With your old hopes, dead leaves and loves again –
Dim as a dream and wan with all old hours
(Whispers will creep into the growing dark . . .
Tumult will die over the trees)
Now night
Tears from her wetted breast the splattered blouse
Of day, glides down the dreaming hills, tear-bright,
To cover with her hair the eerie green . . .
Love for the dusk . . . Love for the glistening after;
Quiet the trees to their last tops . . . serene . . .

Faint winds, and far away a fading laughter . . .

4

The Supercilious Sacrifice

Atlantic City. Amory paced the boardwalk at day's end, lulled by the everlasting surge of changing waves, smelling the half-mournful odour of the salt breeze. The sea, he thought, had treasured its memories deeper than the faithless land. It seemed still to whisper of Norse galleys ploughing the water world under raven-figured flags, of the British dreadnoughts, grey bulwarks of civilisation, steaming up through the fog of one dark July into the North Sea.

'Well – Amory Blaine!'

Amory looked down into the street below. A low racing car had drawn to a stop and a familiar cheerful face protruded from the driver's seat.

'Come on down, goopher!' cried Alec.

Amory called a greeting and descending a flight of wooden steps approached the car. He and Alec had been meeting intermittently, but the barrier of Rosalind lay always between them. He was sorry for this; he hated to lose Alec.

'Mr Blaine, this is Miss Waterson, Miss Wayne and Mr Tully.'

'How d'y do?'

'Amory,' said Alec exuberantly, 'if you'll jump in we'll take you to some secluded nook and give you a wee jolt of Bourbon.'

Amory considered.

'That's an idea.'

'Step in – move over, Jill, and Amory will smile very handsomely at you.'

Amory squeezed into the back seat beside a gaudy, vermilion-lipped blonde.

'Hello, Doug Fairbanks,' she said flippantly. 'Walking for exercise or hunting for company?'

'I was counting the waves,' replied Amory gravely. 'I'm going in for statistics.'

'Don't kid me, Doug.'

When they reached an unfrequented side street Alec stopped the car among deep shadows.

'What you doing down here these cold days, Amory?' he demanded, as he produced a quart of Bourbon from under the fur rug.

Amory avoided the question. Indeed, he had had no definite reason for coming to the coast.

'Do you remember that party of ours, sophomore year?' he asked instead.

'Do I? When we slept in the pavilions up in Asbury Park – '

'Lord, Alec! It's hard to think that Jesse and Dick and Kerry are all three dead.'

Alec shivered.

'Don't talk about it. These dreary fall days depress me enough.'

Jill seemed to agree.

'Doug here is sorta gloomy anyways,' she commented. 'Tell him to drink deep – it's good and scarce these days.'

'What I really want to ask you, Amory, is where you are – '

'Why, New York, I suppose – '

'I mean tonight, because if you haven't got a room yet you'd better help me out.'

'Glad to.'

'You see, Tully and I have two rooms with bath between at the Ranier, and he's got to go back to New York. I don't want to have to move. Question is, will you occupy one of the rooms?'

Amory was willing, if he could get in right away.

'You'll find the key in the office; the rooms are in my name.'

Declining further locomotion or further stimulation, Amory left the car and sauntered back along the boardwalk to the hotel.

He was in an eddy again, a deep, lethargic gulf, without desire to work or write, love or dissipate. For the first time in his life he rather longed for death to roll over his generation, obliterating their petty fevers and struggles and exultations. His youth seemed never so vanished as now in the contrast between the utter loneliness of this visit and that riotous, joyful party of four years before. Things that had been the merest commonplaces of his life then, deep sleep, the sense of beauty around him, all desire, had flown away and the gaps they left were filled only with the great listlessness of his disillusion.

'To hold a man a woman has to appeal to the worst in him.' This sentence was the thesis of most of his bad nights, of which he felt this was to be one. His mind had already started to play variations on the subject. Tireless passion, fierce jealousy, longing to possess and crush – these alone were left of all his love for Rosalind; these remained to him as payment for the loss of his youth – bitter calomel under the thin sugar of love's exaltation.

In his room he undressed and wrapping himself in blankets to keep out the chill October air drowsed in an armchair by the open window. He remembered a poem he had read months before:

> Oh staunch old heart who toiled so long for me,
> I waste my years sailing along the sea –

Yet he had no sense of waste, no sense of the present hope that waste implied. He felt that life had rejected him.

'Rosalind! Rosalind!' He poured the words softly into the half-darkness until she seemed to permeate the room; the wet salt breeze filled his hair with moisture, the rim of a moon seared the sky and made the curtains dim and ghostly. He fell asleep.

When he awoke it was very late and quiet. The blanket had slipped partly off his shoulders and he touched his skin to find it damp and cold.

Then he became aware of a tense whispering not ten feet away.

He became rigid.

'*Don't make a sound!*' It was Alec's voice. '*Jill – do you hear me?*'

'Yes – ' breathed very low, very frightened. They were in the bathroom.

Then his ears caught a louder sound from somewhere along the corridor outside. It was a mumbling of men's voices and a repeated muffled rapping. Amory threw off the blankets and moved close to the bathroom door.

'My God!' came the girl's voice again. 'You'll have to let them in.'

'*Sh!*'

Suddenly a steady, insistent knocking began at Amory's hall door and simultaneously out of the bathroom came Alec, followed by the vermilion-lipped girl. They were both clad in pyjamas.

'Amory!' an anxious whisper.

'What's the trouble?'

'It's house detectives. My God, Amory – they're just looking for a test-case – '

'Well, better let them in.'

'You don't understand. They can get me under the Mann Act.'

The girl followed him slowly, a rather miserable, pathetic figure in the darkness.

Amory tried to plan quickly.

'You make a racket and let them in your room,' he suggested anxiously, 'and I'll get her out by this door.'

'They're here too, though. They'll watch this door.'

'Can't you give a wrong name?'

'No chance. I registered under my own name; besides, they'd trail the auto licence number.'

'Say you're married.'

'Jill says one of the house detectives knows her.'

The girl had stolen to the bed and tumbled upon it; lay there listening wretchedly to the knocking which had grown gradually to a pounding. Then came a man's voice, angry and imperative: 'Open up or we'll break the door in!'

In the silence when this voice ceased Amory realised that there were other things in the room besides people . . . over and around the figure crouched on the bed there hung an aura, gossamer as a moonbeam, tainted as stale, weak wine, yet a horror, diffusively brooding already over the three of them . . . and over by the window among the stirring curtains stood something else, featureless and indistinguishable, yet strangely familiar . . . Simultaneously two great cases presented themselves side by side to Amory; all that took place in his mind, then, occupied in actual time less than ten seconds.

The first fact that flashed radiantly on his comprehension was the great impersonality of sacrifice – he perceived that what we call love and hate, reward and punishment, had no more to do with it than the date of the month. He quickly recapitulated the story of a sacrifice he had heard of in college: a man had cheated in an examination; his roommate in a gust of sentiment had taken the entire blame and due to the shame of it the innocent one's entire future seemed shrouded in regret and failure, capped by the ingratitude of the real culprit. He had finally taken his own life – years afterwards the facts had come out. At the time the story had both puzzled and worried Amory. Now he realised the truth; that sacrifice was no purchase of freedom. It was like a great elective office, it was like an inheritance of power – to certain people at certain times an essential luxury, carrying with it not a guarantee but a responsibility, not a security but an infinite risk. Its very momentum might drag him down to ruin – the passing of the emotional wave that made it possible might leave the one who made it high and dry for ever on an island of despair.

. . . Amory knew that afterwards Alec would secretly hate him for having done so much for him . . .

. . . All this was flung before Amory like an opened scroll, while ulterior to him and speculating upon him were those two breathless, listening forces: the gossamer aura that hung over and about the girl and that familiar thing by the window.

Sacrifice by its very nature was arrogant and impersonal; sacrifice should be eternally supercilious.

Weep not for me but for thy children.

That – thought Amory – would be somehow the way God would talk to me.

Amory felt a sudden surge of joy and then like a face in a motion-picture the aura over the bed faded out; the dynamic shadow by the window, that was as near as he could name it, remained for the fraction of a moment and then the breeze seemed to lift it swiftly out of the room. He clenched his hands in quick ecstatic excitement . . . the ten seconds were up . . .

'Do what I say, Alec – do what I say. Do you understand?'

Alec looked at him dumbly – his face a tableau of anguish.

'You have a family,' continued Amory slowly. 'You have a family and it's important that you should get out of this. Do you hear me?' He repeated clearly what he had said. 'Do you hear me?'

'I hear you.' The voice was curiously strained, the eyes never for a second left Amory's.

'Alec, you're going to lie down here. If anyone comes in you act drunk. You do what I say – if you don't I'll probably kill you.'

There was another moment while they stared at each other. Then Amory went briskly to the bureau and, taking his pocketbook, beckoned peremptorily to the girl. He heard one word from Alec that sounded like 'penitentiary', then he and Jill were in the bathroom with the door bolted behind them.

'You're here with me,' he said sternly. 'You've been with me all evening.'

She nodded, gave a little half cry.

In a second he had the door of the other room open and three men entered. There was an immediate flood of electric light and he stood there blinking.

'You've been playing a little too dangerous a game, young man!'

Amory laughed.

'Well?'

The leader of the trio nodded authoritatively at a burly man in a check suit.

'All right, Olson.'

'I got you, Mr O'May,' said Olson, nodding. The other two took a curious glance at their quarry and then withdrew, closing the door angrily behind them.

The burly man regarded Amory contemptuously.

'Didn't you ever hear of the Mann Act? Coming down here with her,' he indicated the girl with his thumb, 'with a New York licence on your car – to a hotel like *this*.' He shook his head implying that he had struggled over Amory but now gave him up.

'Well,' said Amory rather impatiently, 'what do you want us to do?'

'Get dressed, quick – and tell your friend not to make such a racket.' Jill was sobbing noisily on the bed, but at these words she subsided sulkily and, gathering up her clothes, retired to the bathroom. As Amory slipped into Alec's BVDs he found that his attitude towards the situation was agreeably humorous. The aggrieved virtue of the burly man made him want to laugh.

'Anybody else here?' demanded Olson, trying to look keen and ferret-like.

'Fellow who had the rooms,' said Amory carelessly. 'He's drunk as an owl, though. Been in there asleep since six o'clock.'

'I'll take a look at him presently.'

'How did you find out?' asked Amory curiously.

'Night clerk saw you go upstairs with this woman.'

Amory nodded; Jill reappeared from the bathroom, completely if rather untidily arrayed.

'Now then,' began Olson, producing a notebook, 'I want your real names – no damn John Smith or Mary Brown.'

'Wait a minute,' said Amory quietly. 'Just drop that big-bully stuff. We merely got caught, that's all.'

Olson glared at him.

'Name?' he snapped.

Amory gave his name and New York address.

'And the lady?'

'Miss Jill – '

'Say,' cried Olson indignantly, 'just ease up on the nursery rhymes. What's your name? Sarah Murphy? Minnie Jackson?'

'Oh, my God!' cried the girl cupping her tear-stained face in her hands. 'I don't want my mother to know. I don't want my mother to know.'

'Come on now!'

'Shut up!' cried Amory at Olson.

An instant's pause.

'Stella Robbins,' she faltered finally. 'General Delivery, Rugway, New Hampshire.'

Olson snapped his notebook shut and looked at them very ponderously.

'By rights the hotel could turn the evidence over to the police and you'd go to penitentiary, you would, for bringin' a girl from one state to 'nother f'r immoral purp'ses – ' He paused to let the majesty of his words sink in. 'But – the hotel is going to let you off.'

'It doesn't want to get in the papers,' cried Jill fiercely. 'Let us off! Huh!'

A great lightness surrounded Amory. He realised that he was safe and only then did he appreciate the full enormity of what he might have incurred.

'However,' continued Olson, 'there's a protective association among the hotels. There's been too much of this stuff, and we got a 'rangement with the newspapers so that you get a little free publicity. Not the name of the hotel, but just a line sayin' that you had a little trouble in 'lantic City. See?'

'I see.'

'You're gettin' off light – damn light – but – '

'Come on,' said Amory briskly. 'Let's get out of here. We don't need a valedictory.'

Olson walked through the bathroom and took a cursory glance at Alec's still form. Then he extinguished the lights and motioned them to follow him. As they walked into the elevator Amory considered a piece of bravado – yielded finally. He reached out and tapped Olson on the arm.

'Would you mind taking off your hat? There's a lady in the elevator.'

Olson's hat came off slowly. There was a rather embarrassing two minutes under the lights of the lobby while the night clerk and a few belated guests stared at them curiously; the loudly dressed girl with bent head, the handsome young man with his chin several points aloft; the inference was quite obvious. Then the chill outdoors – where the salt air was fresher and keener still with the first hints of morning.

'You can get one of those taxis and beat it,' said Olson, pointing to the blurred outline of two machines whose drivers were presumably asleep inside.

'Goodbye,' said Olson. He reached in his pocket suggestively, but Amory snorted, and, taking the girl's arm, turned away.

'Where did you tell the driver to go?' she asked as they whirled along the dim street.

'The station.'

'If that guy writes my mother – '

'He won't. Nobody'll ever know about this – except our friends and enemies.'

Dawn was breaking over the sea.

'It's getting blue,' she said.

'It does very well,' agreed Amory critically, and then as an afterthought: 'It's almost breakfast-time – do you want something to eat?'

'Food – ' she said with a cheerful laugh. 'Food is what queered the party. We ordered a big supper to be sent up to the room about two o'clock. Alec didn't give the waiter a tip, so I guess the little bastard snitched.'

Jill's low spirits seemed to have gone faster than the scattering night. 'Let me tell you,' she said emphatically, 'when you want to stage that sorta party stay away from liquor, and when you want to get tight stay away from bedrooms.'

'I'll remember.'

He tapped suddenly at the glass and they drew up at the door of an all-night restaurant.

'Is Alec a great friend of yours?' asked Jill as they perched themselves on high stools inside, and set their elbows on the dingy counter.

'He used to be. He probably won't want to be any more – and never understand why.'

'It was sorta crazy you takin' all that blame. Is he pretty important? Kinda more important than you are?'

Amory laughed.

'That remains to be seen,' he answered. 'That's the question.'

THE COLLAPSE OF SEVERAL PILLARS

Two days later back in New York Amory found in a newspaper what he had been searching for – a dozen lines which announced to whom it might concern that Mr Amory Blaine, who 'gave his address' as, etc., had been requested to leave his hotel in Atlantic City because of entertaining in his room a lady *not* his wife.

Then he started, and his fingers trembled, for directly above was a longer paragraph of which the first words were: 'Mr and Mrs Leland R. Connage are announcing the engagement of their daughter, Rosalind, to Mr J. Dawson Ryder, of Hartford, Connecticut – '

He dropped the paper and lay down on his bed with a frightened, sinking sensation in the pit of his stomach. She was gone, definitely, finally gone. Until now he had half unconsciously cherished the hope deep in his heart that someday she would need him and send for him, cry that it had been a mistake, that her heart ached only for the pain she had caused him. Never again could he find even the sombre luxury of wanting her – not this Rosalind, harder, older – nor any beaten, broken woman that his imagination brought to the door of his forties; Amory had wanted her youth, the fresh radiance of her mind and body, the stuff that she was selling now once and for all. So far as he was concerned, young Rosalind was dead.

A day later came a crisp, terse letter from Mr Barton in Chicago, which informed him that as three more street-car companies had gone into the hands of receivers he could expect for the present no further remittances. Last of all, on a dazed Sunday night, a telegram told him of Monsignor Darcy's sudden death in Philadelphia five days before.

He knew then what it was that he had perceived among the curtains of the room in Atlantic City.

5

The Egotist Becomes a Personage

A fathom deep in sleep I lie
  With old desires, restrained before,
To clamour lifeward with a cry,
  As dark flies out the greying door;
And so in quest of creeds to share
  I seek assertive day again . . .
But old monotony is there:
  Endless avenues of rain.

Oh, might I rise again! Might I
  Throw off the heat of that old wine,
See the new morning mass the sky
  With fairy towers, line on line;
Find each mirage in the high air
  A symbol, not a dream again . . .
But old monotony is there:
  Endless avenues of rain.

Under the glass port cochère of a theatre Amory stood, watching the first great drops of rain splatter down and flatten to dark stains on the sidewalk. The air became grey and opalescent; a solitary light suddenly outlined a window over the way; then another light; then a hundred more danced and glimmered into vision. Under his feet a thick, iron-studded skylight turned yellow; in the street the lamps of the taxicabs sent out glistening sheens along the already black pavement. The unwelcome November rain had perversely stolen the day's last hour and pawned it with that ancient fence, the night.

The silence of the theatre behind him ended with a curious snapping sound, followed by the heavy roaring of a rising crowd and the interlaced clatter of many voices. The matinée was over.

He stood aside, edged a little into the rain to let the throng pass. A small boy rushed out, sniffed in the damp, fresh air and turned up the collar of his coat; came three or four couples in a great hurry; came a further scattering of people whose eyes as they emerged glanced invariably, first at the wet street, then at the rain-filled air, finally at the dismal sky; last a dense, strolling mass that depressed him with its heavy odour compounded of the tobacco smell of the men and the fetid sensuousness of stale powder on women. After the thick crowd came another scattering; a stray half-dozen; a man on crutches; finally the rattling bang of folding seats inside announced that the ushers were at work.

New York seemed not so much awakening as turning over in its bed. Pallid men rushed by, pinching together their coat-collars; a great swarm of tired, magpie girls from a department-store crowded along with shrieks of strident laughter, three to an umbrella; a squad of marching policemen passed, already miraculously protected by oilskin capes.

The rain gave Amory a feeling of detachment, and the numerous unpleasant aspects of city life without money occurred to him in threatening procession. There was the ghastly, stinking crush of the subway – the car cards thrusting themselves at one, leering out like dull bores who grab your arm with another story; the querulous worry as to whether someone isn't leaning on you; a man deciding not to give his seat to a woman, hating her for it; the woman hating him for not doing it; at worst a squalid phantasmagoria of breath, and old cloth on human bodies and the smells of the food men ate – at best just people – too hot or too cold, tired, worried.

He pictured the rooms where these people lived – where the patterns of the blistered wallpapers were heavy reiterated sunflowers on green and yellow backgrounds, where there were tin bathtubs and gloomy hallways and verdureless, unnamable spaces in back of the buildings; where even love dressed as seduction – a sordid murder around the corner, illicit motherhood in the flat above. And always there was the economical stuffiness of indoor winter, and the long summers, nightmares of perspiration between sticky enveloping walls . . . dirty restaurants where careless, tired people helped themselves to sugar with their own used coffee-spoons, leaving hard brown deposits in the bowl.

It was not so bad where there were only men or else only women; it was when they were vilely herded that it all seemed so rotten. It was some shame that women gave off at having men see them tired and poor – it was some disgust that men had for women who were tired and poor. It was dirtier than any battlefield he had seen, harder to contemplate than any actual hardship moulded of mire and sweat and danger, it was an atmosphere wherein birth and marriage and death were loathsome, secret things.

He remembered one day in the subway when a delivery boy had brought in a great funeral wreath of fresh flowers, how the smell of it had suddenly cleared the air and given everyone in the car a momentary glow.

'I detest poor people,' thought Amory suddenly. 'I hate them for being poor. Poverty may have been beautiful once, but it's rotten now. It's the ugliest thing in the world. It's essentially cleaner to be corrupt and rich than it is to be innocent and poor.' He seemed to see again a figure whose significance had once impressed him – a well-dressed young man gazing from a club window on Fifth Avenue and saying something to his companion with a look of utter disgust. Probably, thought Amory, what he said was: 'My God! Aren't people horrible!'

Never before in his life had Amory considered poor people. He thought cynically how completely he was lacking in all human sympathy. O. Henry had found in these people romance, pathos, love, hate – Amory saw only coarseness, physical filth and stupidity. He made no self-accusations: never any more did he reproach himself for feelings that were natural and sincere. He accepted all his reactions as a part of him, unchangeable, unmoral. This problem of poverty transformed, magnified, attached to some grander, more dignified attitude might someday even be his problem; at present it roused only his profound distaste.

He walked over to Fifth Avenue, dodging the blind, black menace of umbrellas, and standing in front of Delmonico's hailed an auto-bus. Buttoning his coat closely around him he climbed to the roof, where he rode in solitary state through the thin, persistent rain, stung into alertness by the cool moisture perpetually reborn on his cheek. Somewhere in his mind a conversation began, rather resumed its place in his attention. It was composed not of two voices, but of one, which acted alike as questioner and answerer:

Q. – Well – what's the situation?
A. – That I have about twenty-four dollars to my name.
Q. – You have the Lake Geneva estate.
A. – But I intend to keep it.
Q. – Can you live?

A. – I can't imagine not being able to. People make money in books and I've found that I can always do the things that people do in books. Really they are the only things I can do.

Q. – Be definite.

A. – I don't know what I'll do – nor have I much curiosity. Tomorrow I'm going to leave New York for good. It's a bad town unless you're on top of it.

Q. – Do you want a lot of money?

A. – No. I am merely afraid of being poor.

Q. – Very afraid?

A. – Just passively afraid.

Q. – Where are you drifting?

A. – Don't ask *me*!

Q. – Don't you care?

A. – Rather. I don't want to commit moral suicide.

Q. – Have you no interests left?

A. – None. I've no more virtue to lose. Just as a cooling pot gives off heat, so all through youth and adolescence we give off calories of virtue. That's what's called ingenuousness.

Q. – An interesting idea.

A. – That's why a 'good man going wrong' attracts people. They stand around and literally *warm themselves* at the calories of virtue he gives off. Sarah makes an unsophisticated remark and the faces simper in delight – 'How *innocent* the poor child is!' They're warming themselves at her virtue. But Sarah sees the simper and never makes that remark again. Only she feels a little colder after that.

Q. – All your calories gone?

A. – All of them. I'm beginning to warm myself at other people's virtue.

Q. – Are you corrupt?

A. – I think so. I'm not sure. I'm not sure about good and evil at all any more.

Q. – Is that a bad sign in itself?

A. – Not necessarily.

Q. – What would be the test of corruption?

A. – Becoming really insincere – calling myself 'not such a bad fellow', thinking I regretted my lost youth when I only envy the delights of losing it. Youth is like having a big plate of candy. Sentimentalists think they want to be in the pure, simple state they were in before they ate the candy. They don't. They just want the fun of eating it all over again. The matron doesn't want to repeat her girlhood – she wants to repeat her honeymoon. I don't want to repeat my innocence. I want the pleasure of losing it again.

Q. – Where are you drifting?

This dialogue merged grotesquely into his mind's most familiar state – a grotesque blending of desires, worries, exterior impressions and physical reactions.

One Hundred and Twenty-Seventh Street – or One Hundred and Thirty-Seventh Street . . . Two and three look alike – no, not much. Seat damp . . . are clothes absorbing wetness from seat, or seat absorbing dryness from clothes? . . . Sitting on wet substance gave appendicitis, so Froggy Parker's mother said. Well, he'd had it – I'll sue the steamboat company, Beatrice said, and my uncle has a quarter interest – did Beatrice go to heaven? . . . probably not. He represented Beatrice's immortality, also love-affairs of numerous dead men who surely had never thought of him . . . if it wasn't appendicitis, influenza maybe. What? One Hundred and Twentieth Street? That must have been One Hundred and Twelfth back there. One One Two instead of One Two Seven. Rosalind not like Beatrice, Eleanor like Beatrice, only wilder and brainier. Apartments along here expensive – probably hundred and fifty a month – maybe two hundred. Uncle had only paid hundred a month for whole great big house in Minneapolis. Question – were the stairs on the left or right as you came in? Anyway, in 12 Univee they were straight back and to the left. What a dirty river – want to go down there and see if it's dirty – French rivers all brown or black, so were Southern rivers. Twenty-four dollars meant four hundred and eighty doughnuts. He could live on it three months and sleep in the park. Wonder where Jill was – Jill Bayne, Fayne, Sayne – what the devil – neck hurts, darned uncomfortable seat. No desire to sleep with Jill, what could Alec see in her? Alec had a coarse taste in women. Own taste the best; Isabelle, Clara, Rosalind, Eleanor, were all-American. Eleanor would pitch, probably southpaw. Rosalind was outfield, wonderful hitter. Clara first base, maybe. Wonder what Humbird's body looked like now. If he himself hadn't been bayonet instructor he'd have gone up to line three months sooner, probably been killed. Where's the darned bell –

The street numbers of Riverside Drive were obscured by the mist and dripping trees from anything but the swiftest scrutiny, but Amory had finally caught sight of one – One Hundred and Twenty-Seventh Street. He got off and with no distinct destination followed a winding, descending sidewalk and came out facing the river, in particular a long pier and a partitioned litter of shipyards for miniature craft: small launches, canoes, rowboats and catboats. He turned northward and followed the shore, jumped a small wire fence and found himself in a great disorderly yard adjoining a dock. The hulls of many boats in various stages of repair were around him; he smelled sawdust and paint and the scarcely distinguishable flat odour of the Hudson. A man approached through the heavy gloom.

'Hello,' said Amory.

'Got a pass?'

'No. Is this private?'

'This is the Hudson River Sporting and Yacht Club.'

'Oh! I didn't know. I'm just resting.'

'Well – ' began the man dubiously.

'I'll go if you want me to.'

The man made non-committal noises in his throat and passed on. Amory seated himself on an overturned boat and leaned forward thoughtfully until his chin rested in his hand.

'Misfortune is liable to make me a damn bad man,' he said slowly.

IN THE DROOPING HOURS

While the rain drizzled on Amory looked futilely back at the stream of his life, all its glitterings and dirty shallows. To begin with, he was still afraid – not physically afraid any more, but afraid of people and prejudice and misery and monotony. Yet, deep in his bitter heart, he wondered if he was after all worse than this man or the next. He knew that he could sophisticate himself finally into saying that his own weakness was just the result of circumstances and environment; that often when he raged at himself as an egotist something would whisper ingratiatingly: 'No. Genius!' That was one manifestation of fear, that voice which whispered that he could not be both great and good, that genius was the exact combination of those inexplicable grooves and twists in his mind, that any discipline would curb it to mediocrity. Probably more than any concrete vice or failing Amory despised his own personality – he loathed knowing that tomorrow and the thousand days after he would swell pompously at a compliment and sulk at an ill word like a third-rate musician or a first-class actor. He was ashamed of the fact that very simple and honest people usually distrusted him; that he had been cruel, often, to those who had sunk their personalities in him – several girls, and a man here and there through college, that he had been an evil influence on; people who had followed him here and there into mental adventures from which he alone rebounded unscathed.

Usually, on nights like this, for there had been many lately, he could escape from this consuming introspection by thinking of children and the infinite possibilities of children – he leaned and listened and he heard a startled baby awake in a house across the street and lend a tiny whimper to the still night. Quick as a flash he turned away, wondering with a touch of panic whether something in the brooding despair of his mood had made a darkness in its tiny soul. He shivered. What if some day the balance was overturned, and he became a thing that frightened children and crept into rooms in the dark, approached dim communion with those phantoms who whispered shadowy secrets to the mad of that dark continent upon the moon . . .

Amory smiled a bit.

'You're too much wrapped up in yourself,' he heard someone say. And again – 'Get out and do some real work – '

'Stop worrying – '

He fancied a possible future comment of his own.

'Yes – I was perhaps an egotist in youth, but I soon found it made me morbid to think too much about myself.'

Suddenly he felt an overwhelming desire to let himself go to the devil – not to go violently as a gentleman should, but to sink safely and sensuously out of sight. He pictured himself in an adobe house in Mexico, half-reclining on a rug-covered couch, his slender, artistic fingers closed on a cigarette while he listened to guitars strumming melancholy undertones to an age-old dirge of Castile and an olive-skinned, carmine-lipped girl caressed his hair. Here he might live a strange litany, delivered from right and wrong and from the hound of heaven and from every God (except the exotic Mexican one who was pretty slack himself and rather addicted to Oriental scents) – delivered from success and hope and poverty into that long chute of indulgence which led, after all, only to the artificial lake of death.

There were so many places where one might deteriorate pleasantly:

Port Said, Shanghai, parts of Turkestan, Constantinople, the South Seas – all lands of sad, haunting music and many odours, where lust could be a mode and expression of life, where the shades of night skies and sunsets would seem to reflect only moods of passion: the colours of lips and poppies.

STILL WEEDING

Once he had been miraculously able to scent evil as a horse detects a broken bridge at night, but the man with the queer feet in Phoebe's room had diminished to the aura over Jill. His instinct perceived the fetidness of poverty, but no longer ferreted out the deeper evils in pride and sensuality.

There were no more wise men; there were no more heroes; Burne Holiday was sunk from sight as though he had never lived; Monsignor was dead. Amory had grown up to a thousand books, a thousand lies; he had listened eagerly to people who pretended to know, who knew nothing. The mystical reveries of saints that had once filled him with awe in the still hours of night, now vaguely repelled him. The Byrons and Brookes who had defied life from mountain tops were in the end but *flâneurs* and poseurs, at best mistaking the shadow of courage for the substance of wisdom. The pageantry of his disillusion took shape in a world-old procession of Prophets, Athenians, Martyrs, Saints, Scientists, Don Juans, Jesuits, Puritans, Fausts, Poets, Pacifists; like costumed alumni at a college reunion they streamed before him as their dreams, personalities and creeds had in turn thrown coloured lights on his soul; each had tried to express the glory of life and the tremendous significance of man; each had boasted of synchronising what had gone before into his own rickety generalities; each had depended after all on the set stage and the convention of the theatre, which is that man in his hunger for faith will feed his mind with the nearest and most convenient food.

Women – of whom he had expected so much; whose beauty he had hoped to transmute into modes of art; whose unfathomable instincts, marvellously incoherent and inarticulate, he had thought to perpetuate in terms of experience – had become merely consecrations to their own posterity. Isabelle, Clara, Rosalind, Eleanor, were all removed by their very beauty, around which men had swarmed, from the possibility of contributing anything but a sick heart and a page of puzzled words to write.

Amory based his loss of faith in help from others on several sweeping syllogisms. Granted that his generation, however bruised and decimated from this Victorian war, were the heirs of progress. Waving aside petty differences of conclusions which, although they might occasionally cause the deaths of several millions of young men, might be explained away – supposing that after all Bernard Shaw and Bernhardi, Bonar Law and Bethmann-Hollweg were mutual heirs of progress if only in agreeing against the ducking of witches – waiving the antitheses and approaching individually these men who seemed to be the leaders, he was repelled by the discrepancies and contradictions in the men themselves.

There was, for example, Thornton Hancock, respected by half the intellectual world as an authority on life, a man who had verified and believed the code he lived by, an educator of educators, an adviser to Presidents – yet Amory knew that this man had, in his heart, leaned on the priest of another religion.

And Monsignor, upon whom a cardinal rested, had moments of strange and horrible insecurity – inexplicable in a religion that explained even disbelief in terms of its own faith: if you doubted the devil it was the devil that made you doubt him. Amory had seen Monsignor go to the houses of stolid philistines, read popular novels furiously, saturate himself in routine, to escape from that horror.

And this priest, a little wiser, somewhat purer, had been, Amory knew, not essentially older than he.

Amory was alone – he had escaped from a small enclosure into a great labyrinth. He was where Goethe was when he began *Faust*; he was where Conrad was when he wrote *Almayer's Folly*.

Amory said to himself that there were essentially two sorts of people who through natural clarity or disillusion left the enclosure and sought the labyrinth. There were men like Wells and Plato, who had, half unconsciously, a strange, hidden orthodoxy, who would accept for themselves only what could be accepted for all men – incurable romanticists who never, for all their efforts, could enter the labyrinth as stark souls; there were on the other hand sword-like pioneering personalities, Samuel Butler, Renan, Voltaire, who progressed much slower, yet eventually much further, not in the direct pessimistic line of speculative philosophy but concerned in the eternal attempt to attach a positive value to life . . .

Amory stopped. He began for the first time in his life to have a strong distrust of all generalities and epigrams. They were too easy, too dangerous to the public mind. Yet all thought usually reached the public after thirty years in some such form: Benson and Chesterton had popularised Huysmans and Newman; Shaw had sugar-coated Nietzsche and Ibsen and Schopenhauer. The man in the street heard the conclusions of dead genius through someone else's clever paradoxes and didactic epigrams.

Life was a damned muddle . . . a football game with everyone offside and the referee got rid of – everyone claiming the referee would have been on his side . . .

Progress was a labyrinth . . . people plunging blindly in and then rushing wildly back, shouting that they had found it . . . the invisible king – the *élan vital* – the principle of evolution . . . writing a book, starting a war, founding a school . . .

Amory, even had he not been a selfish man, would have started all enquiries with himself. He was his own best example – sitting in the rain, a human creature of sex and pride, foiled by chance and his own temperament of the balm of love and children, preserved to help in building up the living consciousness of the race.

In self-reproach and loneliness and disillusion he came to the entrance of the labyrinth.

Another dawn flung itself across the river, a belated taxi hurried along the street, its lamps still shining like burning eyes in a face white from a night's carouse. A melancholy siren sounded far down the river.

MONSIGNOR

Amory kept thinking how Monsignor would have enjoyed his own funeral. It was magnificently Catholic and liturgical. Bishop O'Neill sang solemn high mass and the cardinal gave the final absolutions. Thornton Hancock, Mrs Lawrence, the British and Italian ambassadors, the papal delegate, and a host of friends and priests were there – yet the inexorable shears had cut through all these threads that Monsignor had gathered into his hands. To Amory it was a haunting grief to see him lying in his coffin, with closed hands upon his purple vestments. His face had not changed, and, as he never knew he was dying, it showed no pain or fear. It was Amory's dear old friend, his and the others' – for the church was full of people with daft, staring faces, the most exalted seeming the most stricken.

The cardinal, like an archangel in cope and mitre, sprinkled the holy water; the organ broke into sound; the choir began to sing the *Requiem aeternam*.

All these people grieved because they had to some extent depended upon Monsignor. Their grief was more than sentiment for the 'crack in his voice or a certain break in his walk', as Wells put it. These people had leaned on Monsignor's faith, his way of finding cheer, of making religion a thing of lights and shadows, making all light and shadow merely aspects of God. People felt safe when he was near.

Of Amory's attempted sacrifice had been born merely the full realisation of his disillusion, but of Monsignor's funeral was born the romantic elf who was to enter the labyrinth with him. He found something that he wanted, had always wanted and always would want – not to be admired, as he had feared; not to be loved, as he had made himself believe; but to be necessary to people, to be indispensable; he remembered the sense of security he had found in Burne.

Life opened up in one of its amazing bursts of radiance and Amory suddenly and permanently rejected an old epigram that had been playing listlessly in his mind: 'Very few things matter and nothing matters very much.'

On the contrary, Amory felt an immense desire to give people a sense of security.

THE BIG MAN WITH GOGGLES

On the day that Amory started on his walk to Princeton the sky was a colourless vault, cool, high and barren of the threat of rain. It was a grey day, that least fleshly of all weathers; a day of dreams and far hopes and clear visions. It was a day easily associated with those abstract truths and purities that dissolve in the sunshine or fade out in mocking laughter by the light of the moon. The trees and clouds were carved in classical severity; the sounds of the countryside had harmonised to a monotone, metallic as a trumpet, breathless as the Grecian urn.

The day had put Amory in such a contemplative mood that he caused much annoyance to several motorists who were forced to slow up considerably or else run him down. So engrossed in his thoughts was he that he was scarcely surprised at that strange phenomenon – cordiality manifested within fifty miles of Manhattan – when a passing car slowed down beside him and a voice hailed him. He looked up and saw a magnificent Locomobile in which sat two middle-aged men, one of them small and anxious looking, apparently an artificial growth on the other, who was large and begoggled and imposing.

'Do you want a lift?' asked the apparently artificial growth, glancing from the corner of his eye at the imposing man as if for some habitual, silent corroboration.

'You bet I do. Thanks.'

The chauffeur swung open the door, and, climbing in, Amory settled himself in the middle of the back seat. He took in his companions curiously. The chief characteristic of the big man seemed to be a great confidence in himself set off against a tremendous boredom with everything around him. That part of his face which protruded under the goggles was what is generally termed 'strong'; rolls of not undignified fat had collected near his chin; somewhere above was a wide thin mouth and the rough model for a Roman nose, and, below, his shoulders collapsed without a struggle into the powerful bulk of his chest and belly. He was excellently and quietly dressed. Amory noticed that he was inclined to stare straight at the back of the chauffeur's head as if speculating steadily but hopelessly some baffling hirsute problem.

The smaller man was remarkable only for his complete submersion in the personality of the other. He was of that lower secretarial type who at forty have engraved upon their business cards: 'Assistant to the President', and without a sigh consecrate the rest of their lives to second-hand mannerisms.

'Going far?' asked the smaller man in a pleasant disinterested way.

'Quite a stretch.'

'Hiking for exercise?'

'No,' responded Amory succinctly, 'I'm walking because I can't afford to ride.'

'Oh.'

Then again: 'Are you looking for work? Because there's lots of work,' he continued rather testily. 'All this talk of lack of work. The West is especially short of labour.' He expressed the West with a sweeping, lateral gesture.

Amory nodded politely.

'Have you a trade?'

No – Amory had no trade.

'Clerk, eh?'

No – Amory was not a clerk.

'Whatever your line is,' said the little man, seeming to agree wisely with something Amory had said, 'now is the time of opportunity and business openings.' He glanced again towards the big man, as a lawyer grilling a witness glances involuntarily at the jury.

Amory decided that he must say something and for the life of him could think of only one thing to say.

'Of course I want a great lot of money – '

The little man laughed mirthlessly but conscientiously.

'That's what everyone wants nowadays, but they don't want to work for it.'

'A very natural, healthy desire. Almost all normal people want to be rich without great effort – except the financiers in problem plays, who want to "crash their way through". Don't you want easy money?'

'Of course not,' said the secretary indignantly.

'But,' continued Amory disregarding him, 'being very poor at present I am contemplating socialism as possibly my forte.'

Both men glanced at him curiously.

'These bomb throwers – ' The little man ceased as words lurched ponderously from the big man's chest. 'If I thought you were a bomb thrower I'd run you over to the Newark jail. That's what I think of Socialists.'

Amory laughed.

'What are you,' asked the big man, 'one of these parlour Bolsheviks, one of these idealists? I must say I fail to see the difference. The idealists loaf around and write the stuff that stirs up the poor immigrants.'

'Well,' said Amory, 'if being an idealist is both safe and lucrative, I might try it.'

'What's your difficulty? Lost your job?'

'Not exactly, but – well, call it that.'

'What was it?'

'Writing copy for an advertising agency.'

'Lots of money in advertising.'

Amory smiled discreetly.

'Oh, I'll admit there's money in it eventually. Talent doesn't starve any more. Even art gets enough to eat these days. Artists draw your magazine covers, write your advertisements, hash out ragtime for your theatres. By the great commercialising of printing you've found a harmless, polite occupation for every genius who might have carved his own niche. But beware the artist who's an intellectual also. The artist who doesn't fit – the Rousseau, the Tolstoy, the Samuel Butler, the Amory Blaine – '

'Who's he?' demanded the little man suspiciously.

'Well,' said Amory, 'he's a – he's an intellectual personage not very well known at present.'

The little man laughed his conscientious laugh, and stopped rather suddenly as Amory's burning eyes turned on him.

'What are you laughing at?'

'These *intellectual* people – '

'Do you know what it means?'

The little man's eyes twitched nervously.

'Why, it *usually* means – '

'It *always* means brainy and well educated,' interrupted Amory. 'It means having an active knowledge of the race's experience.' Amory decided to be very rude. He turned to the big man. 'The young man,' he indicated the secretary with his thumb, and said young man as one says bellboy, with no implication of youth, 'has the usual muddled connotation of all popular words.'

'You object to the fact that capital controls printing?' said the big man, fixing him with his goggles.

'Yes – and I object to doing their mental work for them. It seemed to me that the root of all the business I saw around me consisted in overworking and underpaying a bunch of dubs who submitted to it.'

'Here now,' said the big man, 'you'll have to admit that the labouring man is certainly highly paid – five- and six-hour days – it's ridiculous. You can't buy an honest day's work from a man in the trade unions.'

'You've brought it on yourselves,' insisted Amory. 'You people never make concessions until they're wrung out of you.'

'What people?'

'Your class; the class I belonged to until recently; those who by inheritance or industry or brains or dishonesty have become the moneyed class.'

'Do you imagine that if that road-mender over there had the money he'd be any more willing to give it up?'

'No, but what's that got to do with it?'

The older man considered.

'No, I'll admit it hasn't. It rather sounds as if it had though.'

'In fact,' continued Amory, 'he'd be worse. The lower classes are narrower, less pleasant and personally more selfish – certainly more stupid. But all that has nothing to do with the question.'

'Just exactly what is the question?'

Here Amory had to pause to consider exactly what the question was.

'When life gets hold of a brainy man of fair education,' began Amory slowly, 'that is, when he marries he becomes, nine times out of ten, a conservative as far as existing social conditions are concerned. He may be unselfish, kind-hearted, even just in his own way, but his first job is to provide and to hold fast. His wife shoos him on, from ten thousand a year to twenty thousand a year, on and on, in an enclosed treadmill that hasn't any windows. He's done! Life's got him! He's no help! He's a spiritually married man.'

Amory paused and decided that it wasn't such a bad phrase.

'Some men,' he continued, 'escape the grip. Maybe their wives have no social ambitions; maybe they've hit a sentence or two in a "dangerous book" that pleased them; maybe they started on the treadmill as I did and were knocked off. Anyway, they're the congressmen you can't bribe, the Presidents who aren't politicians, the writers, speakers, scientists, statesmen who aren't just popular grab-bags for a half-dozen women and children.'

'He's the natural radical?'

'Yes,' said Amory. 'He may vary from the disillusioned critic, like old Thornton Hancock, all the way to Trotsky. Now this spiritually unmarried man hasn't direct power, for unfortunately the spiritually married man, as a by-product of his money chase, has garnered in the great newspaper, the popular magazine, the influential weekly – so that Mrs Newspaper, Mrs Magazine, Mrs Weekly can have a better limousine than those oil people across the street or those cement people round the corner.

'Why not?'

'It makes wealthy men the keepers of the world's intellectual conscience and, of course, a man who has money under one set of social institutions quite naturally can't risk his family's happiness by letting the clamour for another appear in his newspaper.'

'But it appears,' said the big man.

'Where? – in the discredited mediums. Rotten cheap-papered weeklies.'

'All right – go on.'

'Well, my first point is that through a mixture of conditions of which the family is the first, there are these two sorts of brains. One sort takes human nature as it finds it, uses its timidity, its weakness and its strength for its own ends. Opposed is the man who, being spiritually unmarried, continually seeks for new systems that will control or counteract human nature. His problem is harder. It is not life that's complicated, it's the struggle to guide and control life. That is his struggle. He is a part of progress – the spiritually married man is not.'

The big man produced three big cigars, and proffered them on his huge palm. The little man took one, Amory shook his head and reached for a cigarette.

'Go on talking,' said the big man. 'I've been wanting to hear one of you fellows.'

GOING FASTER

'Modern life,' began Amory again, 'changes no longer century by century, but year by year, ten times faster than it ever has before – populations doubling, civilisations unified more closely with other civilisations, economic interdependence, racial questions, and – we're *dawdling* along. My idea is that we've got to go very much faster.' He slightly emphasised the last words and the chauffeur unconsciously increased the speed of the car. Amory and the big man laughed; the little man laughed, too, after a pause.

'Every child,' said Amory, 'should have an equal start. If his father can endow him with a good physique and his mother with some common sense in his early education, that should be his heritage. If the father can't give him a good physique, if the mother has spent in chasing men the years in which she should have been preparing herself to educate her children, so much the worse for the child. He shouldn't be artificially bolstered up with money, sent to these horrible tutoring schools, dragged through college . . . Every boy ought to have an equal start.'

'All right,' said the big man, his goggles indicating neither approval nor objection.

'Next I'd have a fair trial of government ownership of all industries.'

'That's been proved a failure.'

'No – it merely failed. If we had government ownership we'd have the best analytical business minds in the government working for something besides themselves. We'd have Mackays instead of Burlesons; we'd have Morgans in the Treasury Department; we'd have Hills running interstate commerce. We'd have the best lawyers in the Senate.'

'They wouldn't give their best efforts for nothing. McAdoo – '

'No,' said Amory, shaking his head. 'Money isn't the only stimulus that brings out the best that's in a man, even in America.'

'You said a while ago that it was.'

'It is, right now. But if it were made illegal to have more than a certain amount the best men would all flock for the one other reward which attracts humanity – honour.'

The big man made a sound that was very like *boo*. 'That's the silliest thing you've said yet.'

'No, it isn't silly. It's quite plausible. If you'd gone to college you'd have been struck by the fact that the men there would work twice as hard for any one of a hundred petty honours as those other men did who were earning their way through.'

'Kid's – child's play!' scoffed his antagonist.

'Not by a darned sight – unless we're all children. Did you ever see a grown man when he's trying for a secret society – or a rising family whose name is up at some club? They'll jump when they hear the sound of the word. The idea that to make a man work you've got to hold gold in front of his eyes is a growth, not an axiom. We've done that for so long that we've forgotten there's any other way. We've made a world where that's necessary. Let me tell you' – Amory became emphatic – 'if there were ten men insured against either wealth or starvation, and offered a green ribbon for five hours' work a day and a blue ribbon for ten hours' work a day nine out of ten of them would be trying for the blue ribbon. That competitive instinct only wants a badge. If the size of their house is the badge they'll sweat their heads off for that. If it's only a blue ribbon, I damn near believe they'll work just as hard. They have in other ages.'

'I don't agree with you.'

'I know it,' said Amory nodding sadly. 'It doesn't matter any more though. I think these people are going to come and take what they want pretty soon.'

A fierce hiss came from the little man.

'*Machine-guns!*'

'Ah, but you've taught them their use.'

The big man shook his head.

'In this country there are enough property owners not to permit that sort of thing.'

Amory wished he knew the statistics of property owners and non-property owners; he decided to change the subject.

But the big man was aroused.

'When you talk of "taking things away", you're on dangerous ground.'

'How can they get it without taking it? For years people have been stalled off with promises. Socialism may not be progress, but the threat of the red flag is certainly the inspiring force of all reform. You've got to be sensational to get attention.'

'Russia is your example of a beneficent violence, I suppose?'

'Quite possibly,' admitted Amory. 'Of course, it's overflowing just as the French Revolution did, but I've no doubt that it's really a great experiment and well worth while.'

'Don't you believe in moderation?'

'You won't listen to the moderates, and it's almost too late. The truth is that the public has done one of those startling and amazing things that they do about once in a hundred years. They've seized an idea.'

'What is it?'

'That however the brains and abilities of men may differ, their stomachs are essentially the same.'

THE LITTLE MAN GETS HIS

'If you took all the money in the world,' said the little man with much profundity, 'and divided it up in equ – '

'Oh, shut up!' said Amory briskly and, paying no attention to the little man's enraged stare, he went on with his argument.

'The human stomach – ' he began; but the big man interrupted rather impatiently.

'I'm letting you talk, you know,' he said, 'but please avoid stomachs. I've been feeling mine all day. Anyway, I don't agree with one-half you've said. Government ownership is the basis of your whole argument, and it's invariably a beehive of corruption. Men won't work for blue ribbons, that's all rot.'

When he ceased the little man spoke up with a determined nod, as if resolved this time to have his say out.

'There are certain things which are human nature,' he asserted with an owl-like look, 'which always have been and always will be, which can't be changed.'

Amory looked from the small man to the big man helplessly.

'Listen to that! *That's* what makes me discouraged with progress. *Listen* to that! I can name offhand over one hundred natural phenomena that have been changed by the will of man – a hundred instincts in man that have been wiped out or are now held in check by civilisation.

What this man here just said has been for thousands of years the last refuge of the associated mutton-heads of the world. It negates the efforts of every scientist, statesman, moralist, reformer, doctor and philosopher that ever gave his life to humanity's service. It's a flat impeachment of all that's worth while in human nature. Every person over twenty-five years old who makes that statement in cold blood ought to be deprived of the franchise.'

The little man leaned back against the seat, his face purple with rage. Amory continued, addressing his remarks to the big man.

'These quarter-educated, stale-minded men such as your friend here, who *think* they think, every question that comes up, you'll find his type in the usual ghastly muddle. One minute it's "the brutality and inhumanity of these Prussians" – the next it's "we ought to exterminate the whole German people". They always believe that "things are in a bad way now", but they "haven't any faith in these idealists". One minute they call Wilson "just a dreamer, not practical" – a year later they rail at him for making his dreams realities. They haven't clear logical ideas on one single subject except a sturdy, stolid opposition to all change. They don't think uneducated people should be highly paid, but they won't see that if they don't pay the uneducated people their children are going to be uneducated too, and we're going round and round in a circle. That – is the great middle class!'

The big man with a broad grin on his face leaned over and smiled at the little man.

'You're catching it pretty heavy, Garvin; how do you feel?'

The little man made an attempt to smile and act as if the whole matter were so ridiculous as to be beneath notice. But Amory was not through.

'The theory that people are fit to govern themselves rests on this man. If he can be educated to think clearly, concisely and logically, freed of his habit of taking refuge in platitudes and prejudices and sentimentalisms, then I'm a militant Socialist. If he can't, then I don't think it matters much what happens to man or his systems, now or hereafter.'

'I am both interested and amused,' said the big man. 'You are very young.'

'Which may only mean that I have neither been corrupted nor made timid by contemporary experience. I possess the most valuable experience, the experience of the race, for in spite of going to college I've managed to pick up a good education.'

'You talk glibly.'

'It's not all rubbish,' cried Amory passionately. 'This is the first time in my life I've argued Socialism. It's the only panacea I know. I'm restless. My whole generation is restless. I'm sick of a system where the richest man gets the most beautiful girl if he wants her, where the artist without an income has to sell his talents to a button manufacturer. Even if I had no talents I'd not be content to work ten years, condemned either to celibacy or a furtive indulgence, to give some man's son an automobile.'

'But, if you're not sure – '

'That doesn't matter,' exclaimed Amory. 'My position couldn't be worse. A social revolution might land me on top. Of course I'm selfish. It seems to me I've been a fish out of water in too many outworn systems. I was probably one of the two dozen men in my class at college who got a decent education; still they'd let any well-tutored flathead play football and *I* was ineligible, because some silly old men thought we should *all* profit by conic sections. I loathed the army. I loathed business. I'm in love with change and I've killed my conscience – '

'So you'll go along crying that we must go faster.'

'That, at least, is true,' Amory insisted. 'Reform won't catch up to the needs of civilisation unless it's made to. A *laissez-faire* policy is like spoiling a child by saying he'll turn out all right in the end. He will – if he's made to.'

'But you don't believe all this Socialist patter you talk.'

'I don't know. Until I talked to you I hadn't thought seriously about it. I wasn't sure of half of what I said.'

'You puzzle me,' said the big man, 'but you're all alike. They say Bernard Shaw, in spite of his doctrines, is the most exacting of all dramatists about his royalties. To the last farthing.'

'Well,' said Amory, 'I simply state that I'm a product of a versatile mind in a restless generation – with every reason to throw my mind and pen in with the radicals. Even if, deep in my heart, I thought we were all blind atoms in a world as limited as a stroke of a pendulum, I and my sort would struggle against tradition; try, at least, to displace old cants with new ones. I've thought I was right about life at various times, but faith is difficult. One thing I know. If living isn't a seeking for the grail it may be a damned amusing game.'

For a minute neither spoke and then the big man asked: 'What was your university?'

'Princeton.'

The big man became suddenly interested; the expression of his goggles altered slightly.

'I sent my son to Princeton.'

'Did you?'

'Perhaps you knew him. His name was Jesse Ferrenby. He was killed last year in France.'

'I knew him very well. In fact, he was one of my particular friends.'

'He was – a – quite a fine boy. We were very close.'

Amory began to perceive a resemblance between the father and the dead son and he told himself that there had been all along a sense of familiarity. Jesse Ferrenby, the man who in college had borne off the crown that he had aspired to. It was all so far away. What little boys they had been, working for blue ribbons –

The car slowed up at the entrance to a great estate, ringed around by a huge hedge and a tall iron fence.

'Won't you come in for lunch?'

Amory shook his head.

'Thank you, Mr Ferrenby, but I've got to get on.'

The big man held out his hand. Amory saw that the fact that he had known Jesse more than outweighed any disfavour he had created by his opinions. What ghosts were people with which to work! Even the little man insisted on shaking hands.

'Goodbye!' shouted Mr Ferrenby, as the car turned the corner and started up the drive. 'Good luck to you and bad luck to your theories.'

'Same to you, sir,' cried Amory, smiling and waving his hand.

'OUT OF THE FIRE, OUT OF THE LITTLE ROOM'

Eight hours from Princeton Amory sat down by the Jersey roadside and looked at the frost-bitten country. Nature as a rather coarse phenomenon composed largely of flowers that, when closely inspected, appeared moth-eaten, and of ants that endlessly traversed blades of grass, was always disillusioning; nature represented by skies and waters and far horizons was more likable. Frost and the promise of winter thrilled him now, made him think of a wild battle between St Regis's and Groton, ages ago, seven years ago – and of an autumn day in France twelve months before when he had lain in tall grass, his platoon flattened down close around him, waiting to tap the shoulders of a Lewis gunner. He saw the two pictures together with somewhat the same primitive exaltation – two games he had played, differing in quality of acerbity, linked in a way that differed them from Rosalind or the subject of labyrinths which were, after all, the business of life.

'I am selfish,' he thought.

'This is not a quality that will change when I "see human suffering" or "lose my parents" or "help others".

'This selfishness is not only part of me. It is the most living part.

'It is by somehow transcending rather than by avoiding that selfishness that I can bring poise and balance into my life.

'There is no virtue of unselfishness that I cannot use. I can make sacrifices, be charitable, give to a friend, endure for a friend, lay down my life for a friend – all because these things may be the best possible expression of myself; yet I have not one drop of the milk of human kindness.'

The problem of evil had solidified for Amory into the problem of sex. He was beginning to identify evil with the strong phallic worship in Brooke and the early Wells. Inseparably linked with evil was beauty – beauty, still a constant rising tumult; soft in Eleanor's voice, in an old song at night, rioting deliriously through life like superimposed waterfalls, half rhythm, half darkness. Amory knew that every time he had reached towards it longingly it had leered out at him with the grotesque face of evil. Beauty of great art, beauty of all joy, most of all the beauty of women.

After all, it had too many associations with licence and indulgence. Weak things were often beautiful, weak things were never good. And in this new loneness of his that had been selected for what greatness he might achieve, beauty must be relative or, itself a harmony, it would make only a discord.

In a sense this gradual renunciation of beauty was the second step after his disillusion had been made complete. He felt that he was leaving behind him his chance of being a certain type of artist. It seemed so much more important to be a certain sort of man.

His mind turned a corner suddenly and he found himself thinking of the Catholic Church. The idea was strong in him that there was a certain intrinsic lack in those to whom orthodox religion was necessary, and religion to Amory meant the Church of Rome. Quite conceivably it was an empty ritual but it was seemingly the only assimilative, traditionary bulwark against the decay of morals. Until the great mobs could be educated into a moral sense someone must cry: 'Thou shalt not!' Yet any acceptance was, for the present, impossible. He wanted time and the absence of ulterior pressure. He wanted to keep the tree without ornaments, realise fully the direction and momentum of this new start.

The afternoon waned from the purging good of three o'clock to the golden beauty of four. Afterwards he walked through the dull ache of a setting sun when even the clouds seemed bleeding and at twilight he came to a graveyard. There was a dusky, dreamy smell of flowers and the ghost of a new moon in the sky and shadows everywhere. On an impulse he considered trying to open the door of a rusty iron vault built into the side of a hill; a vault washed clean and covered with late-blooming, weepy watery-blue flowers that might have grown from dead eyes, sticky to the touch with a sickening odour.

Amory wanted to *feel* 'William Dayfield, 1864'.

He wondered that graves ever made people consider life in vain. Somehow he could find nothing hopeless in having lived. All the broken columns and clasped hands and doves and angels meant romances. He fancied that in a hundred years he would like having young people speculate as to whether his eyes were brown or blue, and he hoped quite passionately that his grave would have about it an air of many, many years ago. It seemed strange that out of a row of Union soldiers two or three made him think of dead loves and dead lovers, when they were exactly like the rest, even to the yellowish moss.

Long after midnight the towers and spires of Princeton were visible, with here and there a late-burning light – and suddenly out of the clear darkness the sound of bells. As an endless dream it went on; the spirit of the past brooding over a new generation, the chosen youth from the muddled, unchastened world, still fed romantically on the mistakes and half-forgotten dreams of dead statesmen and poets. Here was a new generation, shouting the old cries, learning the old creeds, through a reverie of long days and nights; destined finally to go out into that dirty grey turmoil to follow love and pride; a new generation dedicated more than the last to the fear of poverty and the worship of success; grown up to find all gods dead, all wars fought, all faiths in man shaken . . .

Amory, sorry for them, was still not sorry for himself – art, politics, religion, whatever his medium should be, he knew he was safe now, free from all hysteria – he could accept what was acceptable, roam, grow, rebel, sleep deep through many nights . . .

There was no God in his heart, he knew; his ideas were still in riot; there was ever the pain of memory; the regret for his lost youth – yet the waters of disillusion had left a deposit on his soul, responsibility and a love of life, the faint stirring of old ambitions and unrealised dreams. But – oh, Rosalind! Rosalind! . . .

'It's all a poor substitute at best,' he said sadly.

And he could not tell why the struggle was worth while, why he had determined to use to the utmost himself and his heritage from the personalities he had passed . . .

He stretched out his arms to the crystalline, radiant sky.

'I know myself,' he cried, 'but that is all.'

There was no God in his heart, he knew; his ideas were still in riot; there was ever the pain of memory; the regret for his lost youth – yet the waters of disillusion had left a deposit on his soul, responsibility and a love of life, the faint stirring of old ambitions and unrealized dreams. But – oh, Rosalind! Rosalind!…

'It's all a poor substitute at best,' he said sadly.

And he could not tell why the struggle was worth while, why he had determined to use to the utmost himself and his heritage from the personalities he had passed…

He stretched out his arms to the crystalline, radiant sky.

'I know myself,' he cried, 'but that is all.'

THE BEAUTIFUL AND DAMNED

The Beautiful and Damned

A novel first published in 1922

TO SHANE LESLIE,
GEORGE JEAN NATHAN AND
MAXWELL PERKINS
in appreciation of much literary
help and encouragement

CONTENTS

BOOK ONE

BOOK TWO

BOOK THREE

The victor belongs to the spoils.

Anthony Patch

BOOK ONE

Chapter 1

Anthony Patch

In 1913, when Anthony Patch was twenty-five, two years were already gone since irony, the Holy Ghost of this later day, had, theoretically at least, descended upon him. Irony was the final polish of the shoe, the ultimate dab of the clothes-brush, a sort of intellectual 'There!' – yet at the brink of this story he has as yet gone no further than the conscious stage. As you first see him he wonders frequently whether he is not without honour and slightly mad, a shameful and obscene thinness glistening on the surface of the world like oil on a clean pond, these occasions being varied, of course, with those in which he thinks himself rather an exceptional young man, thoroughly sophisticated, well adjusted to his environment, and somewhat more significant than anyone else he knows.

This was his healthy state and it made him cheerful, pleasant, and very attractive to intelligent men and to all women. In this state he considered that he would one day accomplish some quiet subtle thing that the elect would deem worthy and, passing on, would join the dimmer stars in a nebulous, indeterminate heaven halfway between death and immortality. Until the time came for this effort he would be Anthony Patch – not a portrait of a man but a distinct and dynamic personality, opinionated, contemptuous, functioning from within outwards – a man who was aware that there could be no honour and yet had honour, who knew the sophistry of courage and yet was brave.

A WORTHY MAN AND HIS GIFTED SON

Anthony drew as much consciousness of social security from being the grandson of Adam J. Patch as he would have had from tracing his line over the sea to the Crusaders. This is inevitable; Virginians and Bostonians to the contrary notwithstanding, an aristocracy founded sheerly on money postulates wealth in the particular.

Now Adam J. Patch, more familiarly known as 'Cross Patch', left his father's farm in Tarrytown early in sixty-one to join a New York cavalry regiment. He came home from the war a major, charged into Wall Street, and amid much fuss, fume, applause and ill will he gathered to himself some seventy-five million dollars.

This occupied his energies until he was fifty-seven years old. It was then that he determined, after a severe attack of sclerosis, to consecrate the remainder of his life to the moral regeneration of the world. He became a reformer among reformers. Emulating the magnificent efforts of Anthony Comstock, after whom his grandson was named, he levelled a varied assortment of uppercuts and body-blows at liquor, literature, vice, art, patent medicines and Sunday theatres. His mind, under the influence of that insidious mildew which eventually forms on all but the few, gave itself up furiously to every indignation of the age. From an armchair in the office of his Tarrytown estate he directed against the enormous hypothetical enemy, unrighteousness, a campaign which went on through fifteen years, during which he displayed himself a rabid monomaniac, an unqualified nuisance and an intolerable bore. The year in which this story opens found him wearying; his campaign had grown desultory; 1861 was creeping up slowly on 1895; his thoughts ran a great deal on the Civil War, somewhat on his dead wife and son, almost infinitesimally on his grandson Anthony.

Early in his career Adam Patch had married an anaemic lady of thirty, Alicia Withers, who brought him one hundred thousand dollars and an impeccable entré into the banking circles of New York. Immediately and rather spunkily she had borne him a son and, as if completely devitalised by the magnificence of this performance, she had thenceforth effaced herself within the shadowy dimensions of the nursery. The boy, Adam Ulysses Patch, became an inveterate joiner of clubs, connoisseur of good form and driver of tandems – at the astonishing age of twenty-six he began his memoirs under the title *New York Society as I Have Seen It*. On the rumour of its conception this work was eagerly bid for among publishers, but as it proved after his death to be immoderately verbose and overpoweringly dull, it never obtained even a private printing.

This Fifth Avenue Chesterfield married at twenty-two. His wife was Henrietta Lebrune, the Boston 'Society Contralto', and the single child of the union was, at the request of his grandfather, christened Anthony Comstock Patch. When he went to Harvard, the Comstock dropped out of his name to a nether hell of oblivion and was never heard of thereafter.

Young Anthony had one picture of his father and mother together – so often had it faced his eyes in childhood that it had acquired the impersonality of furniture, but everyone who came into his bedroom regarded it with interest. It showed a dandy of the nineties, spare and handsome, standing beside a tall dark lady with a muff and the suggestion of a bustle. Between them was a little boy with long brown curls, dressed in a velvet Lord Fauntleroy suit. This was Anthony at five, the year of his mother's death.

His memories of the Boston Society Contralto were nebulous and musical. She was a lady who sang, sang, sang, in the music room of their house on Washington Square – sometimes with guests scattered all about her, the men with their arms folded, balanced breathlessly on the edges of sofas, the women with their hands in their laps, occasionally making little whispers to the men and always clapping very briskly and uttering cooing cries after each song – and often she sang to Anthony alone, in Italian or French or in a strange and terrible dialect which she imagined to be the speech of the Southern Negro.

His recollections of the gallant Ulysses, the first man in America to roll the lapels of his coat, were much more vivid. After Henrietta Lebrune Patch had 'joined another choir', as her widower huskily remarked from time to time, father and son lived up at grampa's in Tarrytown, and Ulysses came daily to Anthony's nursery and expelled pleasant, thick-smelling words for sometimes as much as an hour. He was continually promising Anthony hunting trips and fishing trips and excursions to Atlantic City, 'oh, sometime soon now'; but none of them ever materialised. One trip they did take; when Anthony was eleven they went abroad, to England and Switzerland, and there in the best hotel in Lucerne his father died with much sweating and grunting and crying aloud for air. In a panic of despair and terror Anthony was brought back to America, wedded to a vague melancholy that was to stay beside him through the rest of his life.

PAST AND PERSON OF THE HERO

At eleven he had a horror of death. Within six impressionable years his parents had died and his grandmother had faded off almost imperceptibly, until, for the first time since her marriage, her person held for one day an unquestioned supremacy over her own drawing-room. So to Anthony life was a struggle against death, that waited at every corner. It was as a concession to his hypochondriacal imagination that he formed the habit of reading in bed – it soothed him. He read until he was tired and often fell asleep with the lights still on.

His favourite diversion until he was fourteen was his stamp collection; enormous, as nearly exhaustive as a boy's could be – his grandfather considered fatuously that it was teaching him geography. So Anthony kept up a correspondence with a half-dozen 'Stamp and Coin' companies and it was rare that the mail failed to bring him new stamp-books or packages of glittering approval sheets – there was a mysterious fascination in transferring his acquisitions interminably from one book to another. His stamps were his greatest happiness and he bestowed impatient frowns on anyone who interrupted him at play with them; they devoured his allowance every month, and he lay awake at night musing untiringly on their variety and many-coloured splendour.

At sixteen he had lived almost entirely within himself, an inarticulate boy, thoroughly un-American, and politely bewildered by his contemporaries. The two preceding years had been spent in Europe with a private tutor, who persuaded him that Harvard was the thing; it would 'open doors', it would be a tremendous tonic, it would give him innumerable self-sacrificing and devoted friends. So he went to Harvard – there was no other logical thing to be done with him.

Oblivious to the social system, he lived for a while alone and unsought in a high room in Beck Hall – a slim dark boy of medium height with a shy sensitive mouth. His allowance was more than liberal. He laid the foundations for a library by purchasing from a wandering bibliophile first editions of Swinburne, Meredith and Hardy, and a yellowed illegible autograph letter of Keats's, finding later that he had been amazingly overcharged. He became an exquisite dandy, amassed a rather pathetic collection of silk pyjamas, brocaded dressing-gowns, and neckties too flamboyant to wear; in this secret finery he would parade before a mirror in his room or lie stretched in satin along his window-seat looking down on the yard and realising dimly this clamour, breathless and immediate, in which it seemed he was never to have a part.

Curiously enough he found in senior year that he had acquired a position in his class. He learned that he was looked upon as a rather romantic figure, a scholar, a recluse, a tower of erudition. This amused him but secretly pleased him – he began going out, at first a little and then a great deal. He made the Pudding. He drank – quietly and in the proper tradition. It was said of him that had he not come to college so young he might have 'done extremely well'. In 1909, when he graduated, he was only twenty years old.

Then abroad again – to Rome this time, where he dallied with architecture and painting in turn, took up the violin, and wrote some ghastly Italian sonnets, supposedly the ruminations of a thirteenth-century monk on the joys of the contemplative life. It became established among his Harvard intimates that he was in Rome, and those of them who were abroad that year looked him up and discovered with him, on many moonlight excursions, much in the city that was older than the Renaissance or indeed than the republic. Maury Noble, from Philadelphia, for instance, remained two months, and together they realised the peculiar charm of Latin women and had a delightful sense of being very young and free in a civilisation that was very old and free. Not a few acquaintances of his grandfather's called on him, and had he so desired he might have been *persona grata* with the diplomatic set – indeed, he found that his inclinations tended more and more towards conviviality, but that long adolescent aloofness and consequent shyness still dictated to his conduct.

He returned to America in 1912 because of one of his grandfather's sudden illnesses, and after an excessively tiresome talk with the perpetually convalescent old man he decided to put off until his grandfather's death the idea of living permanently abroad. After a prolonged search he took an apartment on Fifty-Second Street and to all appearances settled down.

In 1913 Anthony Patch's adjustment of himself to the universe was in process of consummation. Physically, he had improved since his undergraduate days – he was still too thin but his shoulders had widened and his brunette face had lost the frightened look of his freshman year. He was secretly orderly and in person spick and span – his friends declared that they had never seen his hair rumpled. His nose was too sharp; his mouth was one of those unfortunate mirrors of mood inclined to droop perceptibly in moments of unhappiness, but his blue eyes were charming, whether alert with intelligence or half closed in an expression of melancholy humour.

One of those men devoid of the symmetry of feature essential to the Aryan ideal, he was yet, here and there, considered handsome – moreover, he was very clean, in appearance and in reality, with that especial cleanness borrowed from beauty.

THE REPROACHLESS APARTMENT

Fifth and Sixth Avenues, it seemed to Anthony, were the uprights of a gigantic ladder stretching from Washington Square to Central Park. Coming uptown on top of a bus towards Fifty-Second Street invariably gave him the sensation of hoisting himself hand by hand on a series of treacherous rungs, and when the bus jolted to a stop at his own rung he found something akin to relief as he descended the reckless metal steps to the sidewalk.

After that, he had but to walk down Fifty-Second Street half a block, pass a stodgy family of brownstone houses – and then in a jiffy he was under the high ceilings of his great front room. This was entirely satisfactory. Here, after all, life began. Here he slept, breakfasted, read and entertained.

The house itself was of murky material, built in the late nineties; in response to the steadily growing need for small apartments each floor had been thoroughly remodelled and rented individually. Of the four apartments Anthony's, on the second floor, was the most desirable.

The front room had fine high ceilings and three large windows that loomed down pleasantly upon Fifty-Second Street. In its appointments it escaped by a safe margin being of any particular period; it escaped stiffness, stuffiness, bareness and decadence. It smelt neither of smoke nor of incense – it was tall and faintly blue. There was a deep lounge of the softest brown leather with somnolence drifting about it like a haze. There was a high screen of Chinese lacquer chiefly concerned with geometrical fishermen and huntsmen in black and gold; this made a corner alcove for a voluminous chair guarded by an orange-coloured standing lamp. Deep in the fireplace a quartered shield was burned to a murky black.

Passing through the dining-room, which, as Anthony took only breakfast at home, was merely a magnificent potentiality, and down a comparatively long hall, one came to the heart and core of the apartment – Anthony's bedroom and bath.

Both of them were immense. Under the ceilings of the former even the great canopied bed seemed of only average size. On the floor an exotic rug of crimson velvet was soft as fleece on his bare feet. His bathroom, in contrast to the rather portentous character of his bedroom, was gay, bright, extremely habitable and even faintly facetious. Framed around the walls were photographs of four celebrated thespian beauties of the day: Julia Sanderson as 'The Sunshine Girl', Ina Claire as 'The Quaker Girl', Billie Burke as 'The Mind-the-Paint Girl', and Hazel Dawn as 'The Pink Lady'. Between Billie Burke and Hazel Dawn hung a print representing a great stretch of snow presided over by a cold and formidable sun – this, claimed Anthony, symbolised the cold shower.

The bathtub, equipped with an ingenious bookholder, was low and large. Beside it a wall wardrobe bulged with sufficient linen for three men and with a generation of neckties. There was no skimpy glorified towel of a carpet – instead, a rich rug, like the one in his bedroom a miracle of softness, that seemed almost to massage the wet foot emerging from the tub . . .

All in all a room to conjure with – it was easy to see that Anthony dressed there, arranged his immaculate hair there, in fact did everything but sleep and eat there. It was his pride, this bathroom. He felt that if he had a love he would have hung her picture just facing the tub so that, lost in the soothing steamings of the hot water, he might lie and look up at her and muse warmly and sensuously on her beauty.

NOR DOES HE SPIN

The apartment was kept clean by an English servant with the singularly, almost theatrically, appropriate name of Bounds, whose technique was marred only by the fact that he wore a soft collar. Had he been entirely Anthony's Bounds this defect would have been summarily remedied, but he was also the Bounds of two other gentlemen in the neighbourhood. From eight until eleven in the morning he was entirely Anthony's. He arrived with the mail and cooked breakfast. At nine-thirty he pulled the edge of Anthony's blanket and spoke a few terse words – Anthony never remembered clearly what they were and rather suspected they were deprecative; then he served breakfast on a card-table in the front room, made the bed and, after asking with some hostility if there was anything else, withdrew.

In the mornings, at least once a week, Anthony went to see his broker. His income was slightly under seven thousand a year, the interest on money inherited from his mother. His grandfather, who had never allowed his own son to graduate from a very liberal allowance, judged that this sum was sufficient for young Anthony's needs. Every Christmas he sent him a five-hundred-dollar bond, which Anthony usually sold, if possible, as he was always a little, not very, hard up.

The visits to his broker varied from semi-social chats to discussions of the safety of eight-per-cent investments, and Anthony always enjoyed them. The big trust-company building seemed to link him definitively to the great fortunes whose solidarity he respected and to assure him that he was adequately chaperoned by the hierarchy of finance. From these hurried men he derived the same sense of safety that he had in contemplating his grandfather's money – even more, for the latter appeared, vaguely, a demand loan made by the world to Adam Patch's own moral righteousness, while this money downtown seemed rather to have been grasped and held by sheer indomitable strengths and tremendous feats of will; in addition, it seemed more definitely and explicitly – money.

Closely as Anthony trod on the heels of his income, he considered it to be enough. Some golden day, of course, he would have many millions; meanwhile he possessed a *raison d'être* in the theoretical creation of essays on the popes of the Renaissance. This flashes back to the conversation with his grandfather immediately upon his return from Rome.

He had hoped to find his grandfather dead, but had learned by telephoning from the pier that Adam Patch was comparatively well again – the next day he had concealed his disappointment and gone out to Tarrytown. Five miles from the station his taxicab entered an elaborately groomed drive that threaded a veritable maze of walls and wire fences guarding the estate – this, said the public, was because it was definitely known that if the Socialists had their way, one of the first men they'd assassinate would be old Cross Patch.

Anthony was late and the venerable philanthropist was awaiting him in a glass-walled sun parlour, where he was glancing through the morning papers for the second time. His secretary, Edward Shuttleworth – who before his regeneration had been gambler, saloon-keeper and general reprobate – ushered Anthony into the room, exhibiting his redeemer and benefactor as though he were displaying a treasure of immense value.

They shook hands gravely. 'I'm awfully glad to hear you're better,' Anthony said.

The senior Patch, with an air of having seen his grandson only last week, pulled out his watch.

'Train late?' he asked mildly.

It had irritated him to wait for Anthony. He was under the delusion not only that in his youth he had handled his practical affairs with the utmost scrupulousness, even to keeping every engagement on the dot, but also that this was the direct and primary cause of his success.

'It's been late a good deal this month,' he remarked with a shade of meek accusation in his voice – and then after a long sigh, 'Sit down.'

Anthony surveyed his grandfather with that tacit amazement which always attended the sight. That this feeble, unintelligent old man was possessed of such power that, yellow journals to the contrary, the men in the republic whose souls he could not have bought directly or indirectly would scarcely have populated White Plains, seemed as impossible to believe as that he had once been a pink-and-white baby.

The span of his seventy-five years had acted as a magic bellows – the first quarter-century had blown him full with life, and the last had sucked it all back. It had sucked in the cheeks and the chest and the girth of arm and leg. It had tyrannously demanded his teeth, one by one, suspended his small eyes in dark-bluish sacks, tweeked out his hairs, changed him from grey to white in some places, from pink to yellow in others – callously transposing his colours like a child trying over a paintbox. Then through his body and his soul it had attacked his brain. It had sent him night-sweats and tears and unfounded dreads. It had split his intense normality into credulity and suspicion. Out of the coarse material of his enthusiasm it had cut dozens of meek but petulant obsessions; his energy was shrunk to the bad temper of a spoiled child, and for his will to power was substituted a fatuous puerile desire for a land of harps and canticles on earth.

The amenities having been gingerly touched upon, Anthony felt that he was expected to outline his intentions – and simultaneously a glimmer in the old man's eye warned him against broaching, for the present, his desire to live abroad. He wished that Shuttleworth would have tact enough to leave the room – he detested Shuttleworth – but the secretary had settled blandly in a rocker and was dividing between the two Patches the glances of his faded eyes.

'Now that you're here you ought to *do* something,' said his grandfather softly, 'accomplish something.'

Anthony waited for him to speak of 'leaving something done when you pass on'.

Then he made a suggestion: 'I thought – it seemed to me that perhaps I'm best qualified to write – '

Adam Patch winced, visualising a family poet with long hair and three mistresses.

' – history,' finished Anthony.

'History? History of what? The Civil War? The Revolution?'

'Why – no, sir. A history of the Middle Ages.' Simultaneously an idea was born for a history of the Renaissance popes, written from some novel angle. Still, he was glad he had said 'Middle Ages'.

'Middle Ages? Why not your own country? Something you know about?'

'Well, you see I've lived so much abroad – '

'Why you should write about the Middle Ages, I don't know. Dark Ages, we used to call 'em. Nobody knows what happened, and nobody cares, except that they're over now.' He continued for some minutes on the uselessness of such information, touching, naturally, on the Spanish Inquisition and the 'corruption of the monasteries'. Then: 'Do you think you'll be able to do any work in New York – or do you really intend to work at all?' This last with soft, almost imperceptible, cynicism.

'Why, yes, I do, sir.'

'When'll you be done?'

'Well, there'll be an outline, you see – and a lot of preliminary reading.'

'I should think you'd have done enough of that already.'

The conversation worked itself jerkily towards a rather abrupt conclusion, when Anthony rose, looked at his watch, and remarked that he had an engagement with his broker that afternoon. He had intended to stay a few days with his grandfather, but he was tired and irritated from a rough crossing, and quite unwilling to stand a subtle and sanctimonious browbeating. He would come out again in a few days, he said.

Nevertheless, it was due to this encounter that work had come into his life as a permanent idea. During the year that had passed since then, he had made several lists of authorities, he had even experimented with chapter titles and the division of his work into periods, but not one line of actual writing existed at present, or seemed likely ever to exist. He did nothing – and contrary to the most accredited copybook logic, he managed to divert himself with more than average content.

AFTERNOON

It was October in 1913, midway in a week of pleasant days, with the sunshine loitering in the cross-streets and the atmosphere so languid as to seem weighted with ghostly falling leaves. It was pleasant to sit lazily by the open window finishing a chapter of *Erewhon*. It was pleasant to yawn about five, toss the book on a table, and saunter humming along the hall to his bath.

> 'To . . . you . . . beaut-if-ul lady,'

he was singing as he turned on the tap.

> 'I raise . . . my . . . eyes;
> To . . . you . . . beaut-if-ul la-a-dy
> My . . . heart . . . cries – '

He raised his voice to compete with the flood of water pouring into the tub, and as he looked at the picture of Hazel Dawn upon the wall he put an imaginary violin to his shoulder and softly caressed it with a phantom bow. Through his closed lips he made a humming noise, which he vaguely imagined resembled the sound of a violin. After a moment his hands ceased their gyrations and wandered to his shirt, which he began to unfasten. Stripped, and adopting an athletic posture like the tiger-skin man in the advertisement, he regarded himself with some satisfaction in the mirror, breaking off to dabble a tentative foot in the tub. Readjusting a faucet and indulging in a few preliminary grunts, he slid in.

Once accustomed to the temperature of the water he relaxed into a state of drowsy content. When he finished his bath he would dress leisurely and walk down Fifth Avenue to the Ritz, where he had an appointment for dinner with his two most frequent companions, Dick Caramel and Maury Noble. Afterwards he and Maury were going to the theatre – Caramel would probably trot home and work on his book, which ought to be finished pretty soon.

Anthony was glad *he* wasn't going to work on *his* book. The notion of sitting down and conjuring up, not only words in which to clothe thoughts but thoughts worthy of being clothed – the whole thing was absurdly beyond his desires.

Emerging from his bath he polished himself with the meticulous attention of a bootblack. Then he wandered into the bedroom, and whistling the while a weird, uncertain melody, strolled here and there buttoning, adjusting, and enjoying the warmth of the thick carpet on his feet.

He lit a cigarette, tossed the match out the open top of the window, then paused in his tracks with the cigarette two inches from his mouth – which fell faintly ajar. His eyes were focused upon a spot of brilliant colour on the roof of a house farther down the alley.

It was a girl in a red négligé, silk surely, drying her hair by the still hot sun of late afternoon. His whistle died upon the stiff air of the room; he walked cautiously another step nearer the window with a sudden impression that she was beautiful. Sitting on the stone parapet beside her was a cushion the same colour as her garment and she was leaning both arms upon it as she looked down into the sunny area-way, where Anthony could hear children playing.

He watched her for several minutes. Something was stirred in him, something not accounted for by the warm smell of the afternoon or the triumphant vividness of red. He felt persistently that the girl was beautiful – then of a sudden he understood: it was her distance, not a rare and precious distance of soul but still distance, if only in terrestrial yards. The autumn air was between them, and the roofs and the blurred voices. Yet for a not altogether explained second, posing perversely in time, his emotion had been nearer to adoration than in the deepest kiss he had ever known.

He finished his dressing, found a black bow tie and adjusted it carefully by the three-sided mirror in the bathroom. Then yielding to an impulse he walked quickly into the bedroom and again looked out the window. The woman was standing up now; she had tossed her hair back and he had a full view of her. She was fat, full thirty-five, utterly undistinguished. Making a clicking noise with his mouth he returned to the bathroom and reparted his hair.

'To . . . you . . . beaut-if-ul lady,'

he sang lightly,

'I raise . . . my . . . eyes – '

Then with a last soothing brush that left an iridescent surface of sheer gloss he left his bathroom and his apartment and walked down Fifth Avenue to the Ritz-Carlton.

THREE MEN

At seven Anthony and his friend Maury Noble are sitting at a corner table on the cool roof. Maury Noble is like nothing so much as a large slender and imposing cat. His eyes are narrow and full of incessant, protracted blinks. His hair is smooth and flat, as though it has been licked by a possible – and, if so, Herculean – mother-cat. During Anthony's time at Harvard he had been considered the most unique figure in his class, the most brilliant, the most original – smart, quiet and among the saved.

This is the man whom Anthony considers his best friend. This is the only man of all his acquaintance whom he admires and, to a bigger extent than he likes to admit to himself, envies.

They are glad to see each other now – their eyes are full of kindness as each feels the full effect of novelty after a short separation. They are drawing a relaxation from each other's presence, a new serenity; Maury Noble behind that fine and absurdly catlike face is all but purring. And Anthony, nervous as a will-o'-the-wisp, restless – he is at rest now.

They are engaged in one of those easy short-speech conversations that only men under thirty or men under great stress indulge in.

ANTHONY: Seven o'clock. Where's the Caramel? (*impatiently*) I wish he'd finish that interminable novel. I've spent more time hungry –

MAURY: He's got a new name for it. *The Demon Lover* – not bad, eh?

ANTHONY (*interested*): *The Demon Lover*? Oh 'woman wailing' – No – not a bit bad! Not bad at all – d'you think?

MAURY: Rather good. What time did you say?

ANTHONY: Seven.

MAURY (*his eyes narrowing – not unpleasantly, but to express a faint disapproval*): Drove me crazy the other day.

ANTHONY: How?

MAURY: That habit of taking notes.

ANTHONY: Me, too. Seems I'd said something night before that he considered material but he'd forgotten it – so he had at me. He'd say, 'Can't you try to concentrate?' And I'd say, 'You bore me to tears. How do I remember?'

(MAURY *laughs noiselessly, by a sort of bland and appreciative widening of his features.*)

MAURY: Dick doesn't necessarily see more than anyone else. He merely can put down a larger proportion of what he sees.

ANTHONY: That rather impressive talent –

MAURY: Oh, yes. Impressive!

ANTHONY: And energy – ambitious, well-directed energy. He's so entertaining – he's so tremendously stimulating and exciting. Often there's something breathless in being with him.

MAURY: Oh, yes. (*Silence reigns briefly,*)

ANTHONY (*with his thin, somewhat uncertain face at its most convinced*):

But not indomitable energy. Some day, bit by bit, it'll blow away, and his rather impressive talent with it, and leave only a wisp of a man, fretful and egotistic and garrulous.

MAURY (*with laughter*): Here we sit vowing to each other that little Dick sees less deeply into things than we do. And I'll bet he feels a measure of superiority on his side – creative mind over merely critical mind and all that.

ANTHONY: Oh, yes. But he's wrong. He's inclined to fall for a million silly enthusiasms. If it wasn't that he's absorbed in realism and therefore has to adopt the garments of the cynic he'd be – he'd be credulous as a college religious leader. He's an idealist. Oh, yes. He thinks he's not, because he's rejected Christianity. Remember him in college? Just swallowed every writer whole, one after another, ideas, technique and characters, Chesterton, Shaw, Wells, each one as easily as the last.

MAURY (*still considering his own last observation*): I remember.

ANTHONY: It's true. Natural born fetish-worshipper. Take art –

MAURY: Let's order. He'll be –

ANTHONY: Sure. Let's order. I told him –

MAURY: Here he comes. Look – he's going to bump that waiter. (*He lifts his finger as a signal – lifts it as though it were a soft and friendly claw.*) Here y'are, Caramel.

A NEW VOICE (*fiercely*): Hello, Maury. Hello, Anthony Comstock Patch. How is old Adam's grandson? Débutantes still after you, eh?

(*In person* RICHARD CARAMEL *is short and fair – he is to be bald at thirty-five. He has yellowish eyes – one of them startlingly clear, the other opaque as a muddy pool – and a bulging brow like a funny-paper baby. He bulges in other places – his paunch bulges, prophetically, his words have an air of bulging from his mouth, even his dinner-coat pockets bulge, as though from contamination, with a dog-eared collection of time-tables, programmes and miscellaneous scraps – on these he takes his notes with great screwings up of his unmatched yellow eyes and motions of silence with his disengaged left hand.*

When he reaches the table he shakes hands with ANTHONY*and* MAURY. *He is one of those men who invariably shake hands, even with people whom they have seen an hour before.*)

ANTHONY: Hello, Caramel. Glad you're here. We needed a comic relief.

MAURY: You're late. Been racing the postman down the block? We've been clawing over your character.

DICK (*fixing* ANTHONY *eagerly with the bright eye*): What'd you say? Tell me and I'll write it down. Cut three thousand words out of Part One this afternoon.

MAURY: Noble aesthete. And I poured alcohol into my stomach.

DICK: I don't doubt it. I bet you two have been sitting here for an hour talking about liquor.

ANTHONY: We never pass out, my beardless boy.

MAURY: We never go home with ladies we meet when we're lit.

ANTHONY: All in all our parties are characterised by a certain haughty distinction.

DICK: The particularly silly sort who boast about being 'tanks'! Trouble is you're both in the eighteenth century. School of the Old English Squire. Drink quietly until you roll under the table. Never have a good time. Oh, no, that isn't done at all.

ANTHONY: This from Chapter Six, I'll bet.

DICK: Going to the theatre?

MAURY: Yes. We intend to spend the evening doing some deep thinking over life's problems. The thing is tersely called *The Woman*. I presume that she will 'pay'.

ANTHONY: My God! Is that what it is? Let's go to the Follies again.

MAURY: I'm tired of it. I've seen it three times. (*To* DICK): The first time, we went out after Act One and found a most amazing bar. When we came back we entered the wrong theatre.

ANTHONY: Had a protracted dispute with a scared young couple we thought were in our seats.

DICK (*as though talking to himself*): I think – that when I've done another novel and a play, and maybe a book of short stories, I'll do a musical comedy.

MAURY: I know – with intellectual lyrics that no one will listen to. And all the critics will groan and grunt about 'dear old *Pinafore*'. And I shall go on shining as a brilliantly meaningless figure in a meaningless world.

DICK (*pompously*): Art isn't meaningless.

MAURY: It is in itself. It isn't in that it tries to make life less so.

ANTHONY: In other words, Dick, you're playing before a grandstand peopled with ghosts.

MAURY: Give a good show anyhow.

ANTHONY (*to* MAURY): On the contrary, I'd feel, it being a meaningless world, why write? The very attempt to give it purpose is purposeless.

DICK: Well, even admitting all that, be a decent pragmatist and grant a poor man the instinct to live. Would you want everyone to accept that sophistic rot?

ANTHONY: Yeah, I suppose so.

MAURY: No, sir! I believe that everyone in America but a selected thousand should be compelled to accept a very rigid system of morals – Roman Catholicism, for instance. I don't complain of conventional morality. I complain rather of the mediocre heretics who seize upon the findings of sophistication and adopt the pose of a moral freedom to which they are by no means entitled by their intelligences.

(*Here the soup arrives and what* MAURY *might have gone on to say is lost for all time.*)

NIGHT

Afterwards they visited a ticket speculator and, at a price, obtained seats for a new musical comedy called *High Jinks*. In the foyer of the theatre they waited a few moments to see the first-night crowd come in. There were opera cloaks, stitched of myriad, many-coloured silks, and furs; there were jewels dripping from arms and throats and ear-tips of white and rose; there were innumerable broad shimmers down the middles of innumerable silk hats; there were shoes of gold and bronze and red and shining black; there were the high-piled, tight-packed coiffures of many women and the slick, watered hair of well-kept men – most of all there was the ebbing, flowing, chattering, chuckling, foaming, slow-rolling wave effect of this cheerful sea of people as tonight it poured its glittering torrent into the artificial lake of laughter . . .

After the play they parted – Maury was going to a dance at Sherry's, Anthony homeward and to bed.

He found his way slowly over the jostled evening mass of Times Square, which the chariot race and its thousand satellites made rarely beautiful and bright and intimate with carnival. Faces swirled about him, a kaleidoscope of girls, ugly, ugly as sin – too fat, too lean, yet floating upon this autumn air as upon their own warm and passionate breaths poured out into the night. Here, for all their vulgarity, he thought, they were faintly and subtly mysterious. He inhaled carefully, swallowing into his lungs perfume and the not unpleasant scent of many cigarettes. He caught the glance of a dark young beauty sitting alone in a closed taxicab. Her eyes in the half-light suggested night and violets, and for a moment he stirred again to that half-forgotten remoteness of the afternoon.

Two young Jewish men passed him, talking in loud voices and craning their necks here and there in fatuous supercilious glances. They were dressed in suits of the exaggerated tightness then semi-fashionable; their turned over collars were notched at the Adam's apple; they wore grey spats and carried grey gloves on their cane handles.

Passed a bewildered old lady borne along like a basket of eggs between two men who exclaimed to her of the wonders of Times Square – explained them so quickly that the old lady, trying to be impartially interested, waved her head here and there like a piece of wind-worried old orange-peel. Anthony heard a snatch of their conversation: 'There's the Astor, mama!'

'Look! See the chariot race sign – '

'There's where we were today. No, *there*!'

'Good gracious! . . . '

'You should worry and grow thin like a dime.' He recognised the current witticism of the year as it issued stridently from one of the pairs at his elbow.

'And I says to him, I says – '

The soft rush of taxis by him, and laughter, laughter hoarse as a crow's, incessant and loud, with the rumble of the subways underneath – and over all, the revolutions of light, the growings and recedings of light – light dividing like pearls – forming and reforming in glittering bars and circles and monstrous grotesque figures cut amazingly on the sky.

He turned thankfully down the hush that blew like a dark wind out of a cross-street, passed a bakery-restaurant in whose windows a dozen roast chickens turned over and over on an automatic spit. From the door came a smell that was hot, doughy and pink. A drugstore next, exhaling medicines, spilt soda water and a pleasant undertone from the cosmetic counter; then a Chinese laundry, still open, steamy and stifling, smelling folded and vaguely yellow. All these depressed him; reaching Sixth Avenue he stopped at a corner cigar store and emerged feeling better – the cigar store was cheerful, humanity in a navy blue mist, buying a luxury . . .

Once in his apartment he smoked a last cigarette, sitting in the dark by his open front window. For the first time in over a year he found himself thoroughly enjoying New York. There was a rare pungency in it certainly, a quality almost Southern. A lonesome town, though. He who had grown up alone had lately learned to avoid solitude. During the past several months he had been careful, when he had no engagement for the evening, to hurry to one of his clubs and find someone. Oh, there was a loneliness here –

His cigarette, its smoke bordering the thin folds of curtain with rims of faint white spray, glowed on until the clock in St Anne's down the street struck one with a querulous fashionable beauty. The elevated, half a quiet block away, sounded a rumble of drums – and should he lean from his window he would see the train, like an angry eagle, breasting the dark curve at the corner. He was reminded of a fantastic romance he had lately read in which cities had been bombed from aerial trains, and for a moment he fancied that Washington Square had declared war on Central Park and that this was a northbound menace loaded with battle and sudden death. But as it passed the illusion faded; it diminished to the faintest of drums – then to a faraway droning eagle.

There were the bells and the continued low blur of auto horns from Fifth Avenue, but his own street was silent and he was safe in here from all the threat of life, for there was his door and the long hall and his guardian bedroom – safe, safe! The arc-light shining into his window seemed for this hour like the moon, only brighter and more beautiful than the moon.

A FLASHBACK IN PARADISE

Beauty, who was born anew every hundred years, sat in a sort of outdoor waiting-room through which blew gusts of white wind and occasionally a breathless hurried star. The stars winked at her intimately as they went by and the winds made a soft incessant flurry in her hair. She was incomprehensible, for, in her, soul and spirit were one – the beauty of her body was the essence of her soul. She was that unity sought for by philosophers through many centuries. In this outdoor waiting-room of winds and stars she had been sitting for a hundred years, at peace in the contemplation of herself.

It became known to her, at length, that she was to be born again. Sighing, she began a long conversation with a voice that was in the white wind, a conversation that took many hours and of which I can give only a fragment here.

BEAUTY (*her lips scarcely stirring, her eyes turned, as always, inward upon herself*): Whither shall I journey now?

THE VOICE: To a new country – a land you have never seen before.

BEAUTY (*petulantly*): I loathe breaking into these new civilisations. How long a stay this time?

THE VOICE: Fifteen years.

BEAUTY: And what's the name of the place?

THE VOICE: It is the most opulent, most gorgeous land on earth – a land whose wisest are but little wiser than its dullest; a land where the rulers have minds like little children and the law-givers believe in Santa Claus; where ugly women control strong men –

BEAUTY (*in astonishment*): What?

THE VOICE (*very much depressed*): Yes, it is truly a melancholy spectacle. Women with receding chins and shapeless noses go about in broad daylight saying, 'Do this!' and, 'Do that!' and all the men, even those of great wealth, obey implicitly their women to whom they refer sonorously either as 'Mrs So-and-so' or as 'the wife'.

BEAUTY: But this can't be true! I can understand, of course, their obedience to women of charm – but to fat women? to bony women? to women with scrawny cheeks?

THE VOICE: Even so.

BEAUTY: What of me? What chance shall I have?

THE VOICE: It will be 'harder going', if I may borrow a phrase.

BEAUTY (*after a dissatisfied pause*): Why not the old lands, the land of grapes and soft-tongued men or the land of ships and seas?

THE VOICE: It's expected that they'll be very busy shortly.

BEAUTY: Oh!

THE VOICE: Your life on earth will be, as always, the interval between two significant glances in a mundane mirror.

BEAUTY: What will I be? Tell me?

THE VOICE: At first it was thought that you would go this time as an actress in the motion pictures but, after all, it's not advisable. You will be disguised during your fifteen years as what is called a 'susciety gurl'.

BEAUTY: What's that?

(*There is a new sound in the wind which must for our purposes be interpreted as* THE VOICE *scratching its head.*)

THE VOICE (*at length*): It's a sort of bogus aristocrat.

BEAUTY: Bogus? What is bogus?

THE VOICE: That, too, you will discover in this land. You will find much that is bogus. Also, you will do much that is bogus.

BEAUTY (*placidly*): It all sounds so vulgar.

THE VOICE: Not half as vulgar as it is. You will be known during your fifteen years as a ragtime kid, a flapper, a jazz-baby and a baby vamp. You will dance new dances neither more nor less gracefully than you danced the old ones.

BEAUTY (*in a whisper*): Will I be paid?

THE VOICE: Yes, as usual – in love.

BEAUTY (*with a faint laugh which disturbs only momentarily the immobility of her lips*): And will I like being called a jazz-baby?

THE VOICE (*soberly*): You will love it . . .

(*The dialogue ends here, with* BEAUTY *still sitting quietly, the stars pausing in an ecstasy of appreciation, the wind, white and gusty, blowing through her hair.*

All this took place seven years before ANTHONY *sat by the front windows of his apartment and listened to the chimes of St Anne's.*)

Chapter 2

Portrait of a Siren

Crispness folded down upon New York a month later, bringing November and the three big football games and a great fluttering of furs along Fifth Avenue. It brought, also, a sense of tension to the city, and suppressed excitement. Every morning now there were invitations in Anthony's mail. Three dozen virtuous females of the first layer were proclaiming their fitness, if not their specific willingness, to bear children unto three dozen millionaires. Five dozen virtuous females of the second layer were proclaiming not only this fitness, but in addition a tremendous undaunted ambition towards the first three dozen young men, who were of course invited to each of the ninety-six parties – as were the young lady's group of family friends, acquaintances, college boys, and eager young outsiders. To continue, there was a third layer from the skirts of the city, from Newark and the Jersey suburbs up to bitter Connecticut and the ineligible sections of Long Island – and doubtless contiguous layers down to the city's shoes: Jewesses were coming out into a society of Jewish men and women, from Riverside to the Bronx, and looking forward to a rising young broker or jeweller and a kosher wedding; Irish girls were casting their eyes, with licence at last to do so, upon a society of young Tammany politicians, pious undertakers and grown-up choirboys.

And, naturally, the city caught the contagious air of entrée – the working girls, poor ugly souls, wrapping soap in the factories and showing finery in the big stores, dreamed that perhaps in the spectacular excitement of this winter they might obtain for themselves the coveted male – as in a muddled carnival crowd an inefficient pickpocket may consider his chances increased. And the chimneys commenced to smoke and the subway's foulness was freshened. And the actresses came out in new plays and the publishers came out with new books and the Castles came out with new dances. And the railroads came out with new schedules containing new mistakes instead of the old ones that the commuters had grown used to . . .

The City was coming out!

Anthony, walking along Forty-Second Street one afternoon under a steel-grey sky, ran unexpectedly into Richard Caramel emerging from the Manhattan Hotel barbershop. It was a cold day, the first definitely cold day, and Caramel had on one of those knee-length, sheep-lined coats, long worn by the working men of the Middle West, that were just coming into fashionable approval. His soft hat was of a discreet dark brown, and from under it his clear eye flamed like a topaz. He stopped Anthony enthusiastically, slapping him on the arms more from a desire to keep himself warm than from playfulness, and, after his inevitable hand shake, exploded into sound.

'Cold as the devil – Good Lord, I've been working like the deuce all day till my room got so cold I thought I'd get pneumonia. Darn landlady economising on coal came up when I yelled over the stairs for her for half an hour. Began explaining why and all. God! First she drove me crazy, then I began to think she was sort of a character, and took notes while she talked – so she couldn't see me, you know, just as though I were writing casually – '

He had seized Anthony's arm and was walking him briskly up Madison Avenue.

'Where to?'

'Nowhere in particular.'

'Well, then what's the use?' demanded Anthony.

They stopped and stared at each other, and Anthony wondered if the cold made his own face as repellent as Dick Caramel's, whose nose was crimson, whose bulging brow was blue, whose yellow unmatched eyes were red and watery at the rims. After a moment they began walking again.

'Done some good work on my novel.' Dick was looking and talking emphatically at the sidewalk. 'But I have to get out once in a while.' He glanced at Anthony apologetically, as though craving encouragement.

'I have to talk. I guess very few people ever really *think*, I mean sit down and ponder and have ideas in sequence. I do my thinking in writing or conversation. You've got to have a start, sort of – something to defend or contradict – don't you think?'

Anthony grunted and withdrew his arm gently.

'I don't mind carrying you, Dick, but with that coat – '

'I mean,' continued Richard Caramel gravely, 'that on paper your first paragraph contains the idea you're going to damn or enlarge on. In conversation you've got your vis-à-vis's last statement – but when you simply *ponder*, why, your ideas just succeed each other like magic-lantern pictures and each one forces out the last.'

They passed Forty-Fifth Street and slowed down slightly. Both of them lit cigarettes and blew tremendous clouds of smoke and frosted breath into the air.

'Let's walk up to the Plaza and have an egg-nog,' suggested Anthony. 'Do you good. Air'll get the rotten nicotine out of your lungs. Come on – I'll let you talk about your book all the way.'

'I don't want to if it bores you. I mean you needn't do it as a favour.' The words tumbled out in haste, and though he tried to keep his face casual it screwed up uncertainly. Anthony was compelled to protest: 'Bore me? I should say not!'

'Got a cousin – ' began Dick, but Anthony interrupted by stretching out his arms and breathing forth a low cry of exultation.

'Good weather!' he exclaimed, 'isn't it? Makes me feel about ten. I mean it makes me feel as I should have felt when I was ten. Murderous! Oh, God! one minute it's my world, and the next I'm the world's fool. Today it's my world and everything's easy, easy. Even Nothing is easy!'

'Got a cousin up at the Plaza. Famous girl. We can go up and meet her. She lives there in the winter – has lately anyway – with her mother and father.'

'Didn't know you had cousins in New York.'

'Her name's Gloria. She's from home – Kansas City. Her mother's a practising Bilphist, and her father's quite dull but a perfect gentleman.'

'What are they? Literary material?'

'They try to be. All the old man does is tell me he just met the most wonderful character for a novel. Then he tells me about some idiotic friend of his and then he says: "*There's* a character for you! Why don't you write him up? Everybody'd be interested in *him*." Or else he tells me about Japan or Paris, or some other very obvious place, and says: "Why don't you write a story about that place? That'd be a wonderful setting for a story!" '

'How about the girl?' enquired Anthony casually, 'Gloria – Gloria what?'

'Gilbert. Oh, you've heard of her – Gloria Gilbert. Goes to dances at colleges – all that sort of thing.'

'I've heard her name.'

'Good-looking – in fact damned attractive.'

They reached Fiftieth Street and turned over towards the Avenue.

'I don't care for young girls as a rule,' said Anthony, frowning.

This was not strictly true. While it seemed to him that the average débutante spent every hour of her day thinking and talking about what the great world had mapped out for her to do during the next hour, any girl who made a living directly on her prettiness interested him enormously.

'Gloria's darn nice – not a brain in her head.'

Anthony laughed in a one-syllabled snort.

'By that you mean that she hasn't a line of literary patter.'

'No, I don't.'

'Dick, you know what passes as brains in a girl for you. Earnest young women who sit with you in a corner and talk earnestly about life. The kind who when they were sixteen argued with grave faces as to whether kissing was right or wrong – and whether it was immoral for freshmen to drink beer.'

Richard Caramel was offended. His scowl crinkled like crushed paper.

'No – ' he began, but Anthony interrupted ruthlessly.

'Oh, yes; kind who just at present sit in corners and confer on the latest Scandinavian Dante available in English translation.'

Dick turned to him, a curious falling in his whole countenance. His question was almost an appeal.

'What's the matter with you and Maury? You talk sometimes as though I were a sort of inferior.'

Anthony was confused, but he was also cold and a little uncomfortable, so he took refuge in attack.

'I don't think your brains matter, Dick.'

'Of course they matter!' exclaimed Dick angrily. 'What do you mean? Why don't they matter?'

'You might know too much for your pen.'

'I couldn't possibly.'

'I can imagine,' insisted Anthony, 'a man knowing too much for his talent to express. Like me. Suppose, for instance, I have more wisdom than you, and less talent. It would tend to make me inarticulate. You, on the contrary, have enough water to fill the pail and a big enough pail to hold the water.'

'I don't follow you at all,' complained Dick in a crestfallen tone. Infinitely dismayed, he seemed to bulge in protest. He was staring intently at Anthony and caroming off a succession of passers-by, who reproached him with fierce, resentful glances.

'I simply mean that a talent like Wells's could carry the intelligence of a Spencer. But an inferior talent can only be graceful when it's carrying inferior ideas. And the more narrowly you can look at a thing the more entertaining you can be about it.'

Dick considered, unable to decide the exact degree of criticism intended by Anthony's remarks. But Anthony, with that facility which seemed so frequently to flow from him, continued, his dark eyes gleaming in his thin face, his chin raised, his voice raised, his whole physical being raised: 'Say I am proud and sane and wise – an Athenian among Greeks. Well, I might fail where a lesser man would succeed. He could imitate, he could adorn, he could be enthusiastic, he could be hopefully constructive. But this hypothetical me would be too proud to imitate, too sane to be enthusiastic, too sophisticated to be Utopian, too Grecian to adorn.'

'Then you don't think the artist works from his intelligence?'

'No. He goes on improving, if he can, what he imitates in the way of style, and choosing from his own interpretation of the things around him what constitutes material. But after all every writer writes because it's his mode of living. Don't tell me you like this "Divine Function of the Artist" business?'

'I'm not accustomed even to refer to myself as an artist.'

'Dick,' said Anthony, changing his tone, 'I want to beg your pardon.'

'Why?'

'For that outburst. I'm honestly sorry. I was talking for effect.'

Somewhat mollified, Dick rejoined: 'I've often said you were a Philistine at heart.'

It was a crackling dusk when they turned in under the white façade of the Plaza and tasted slowly the foam and yellow thickness of an egg-nog. Anthony looked at his companion. Richard Caramel's nose and brow were slowly approaching a like pigmentation; the red was leaving the one, the blue deserting the other. Glancing in a mirror, Anthony was glad to find that his own skin had not discoloured. On the contrary, a faint glow had kindled in his cheeks – he fancied that he had never looked so well.

'Enough for me,' said Dick, his tone that of an athlete in training. 'I want to go up and see the Gilberts. Won't you come?'

'Why – yes. If you don't dedicate me to the parents and dash off in the corner with Dora.'

'Not Dora – Gloria.'

A clerk announced them over the phone, and ascending to the tenth floor they followed a winding corridor and knocked at 1088. The door was answered by a middle-aged lady – Mrs Gilbert herself.

'How do you do?' She spoke in the conventional American lady-lady language. 'Well, I'm *aw*fully glad to see you – '

Hasty interjections by Dick, and then: 'Mr Pats? Well, do come in, and leave your coat there.' She pointed to a chair and changed her inflection to a deprecatory laugh full of minute gasps. 'This is really lovely – lovely. Why, Richard, you haven't been here for *so* long – no! – no!' The latter monosyllables served half as responses, half as periods, to some vague starts from Dick. 'Well, do sit down and tell me what you've been doing.'

One crossed and recrossed; one stood and bowed ever so gently; one smiled again and again with helpless stupidity; one wondered if she would ever sit down – at length one slid thankfully into a chair and settled for a pleasant call.

'I suppose it's because you've been busy – as much as anything else,' smiled Mrs Gilbert somewhat ambiguously. The 'as much as anything else' she used to balance all her more rickety sentences. She had two other ones: 'at least that's the way I look at it' and 'pure and simple' – these three, alternated, gave each of her remarks an air of being a general reflection on life, as though she had calculated all causes and, at length, put her finger on the ultimate one.

Richard Caramel's face, Anthony saw, was now quite normal. The brow and cheeks were of a flesh colour, the nose politely inconspicuous. He had fixed his aunt with the bright-yellow eye, giving her that acute and exaggerated attention that young males are accustomed to render to all females who are of no further value.

'Are you a writer too, Mr Pats? . . . Well, perhaps we can all bask in Richard's fame.' – Gentle laughter led by Mrs Gilbert.

'Gloria's out,' she said, with an air of laying down an axiom from which she would proceed to derive results. 'She's dancing somewhere. Gloria goes, goes, goes. I tell her I don't see how she stands it. She dances all afternoon and all night, until I think she's going to wear herself to a shadow. Her father is very worried about her.'

She smiled from one to the other. They both smiled.

She was composed, Anthony perceived, of a succession of semi-circles and parabolas, like those figures that gifted folk make on the typewriter: head, arms, bust, hips, thighs and ankles were in a bewildering tier of roundnesses. Well ordered and clean she was, with hair of an artificially rich grey; her large face sheltered weather-beaten blue eyes and was adorned with just the faintest white moustache.

'I always say,' she remarked to Anthony, 'that Richard is an ancient soul.'

In the tense pause that followed, Anthony considered a pun – something about Dick having been much walked upon.

'We all have souls of different ages,' continued Mrs Gilbert radiantly; 'at least that's what I say.'

'Perhaps so,' agreed Anthony with an air of quickening to a hopeful idea.

The voice bubbled on: 'Gloria has a very young soul – irresponsible, as much as anything else. She has no sense of responsibility.'

'She's sparkling, Aunt Catherine,' said Richard pleasantly. 'A sense of responsibility would spoil her. She's too pretty.'

'Well,' confessed Mrs Gilbert, 'all I know is that she goes and goes and goes – '

The number of goings to Gloria's discredit was lost in the rattle of the doorknob as it turned to admit Mr Gilbert.

He was a short man with a moustache resting like a small white cloud beneath his undistinguished nose. He had reached the stage where his value as a social creature was a black and imponderable negative. His ideas were the popular delusions of twenty years before; his mind steered a wobbly and anaemic course in the wake of the daily newspaper editorials. After graduating from a small but terrifying Western university, he had entered the celluloid business, and as this required only the minute measure of intelligence he brought to it, he did well for several years – in fact until about 1911, when he began exchanging contracts for vague agreements with the moving-picture industry. The moving-picture industry had decided about 1912 to gobble him up, and at this time he was, so to speak, delicately balanced on its tongue. Meanwhile he was supervising manager of the Associated Midwestern Film Materials Company, spending six months of each year in New York and the remainder in Kansas City and St Louis. He felt credulously that there was a good thing coming to him – and his wife thought so, and his daughter thought so too.

He disapproved of Gloria: she stayed out late, she never ate her meals, she was always in a mix-up – he had irritated her once and she had used towards him words that he had not thought were part of her vocabulary. His wife was easier. After fifteen years of incessant guerrilla warfare he had conquered her – it was a war of muddled optimism against organised dullness, and something in the number of yeses with which he could poison a conversation had won him the victory.

'Yes-yes-yes-yes,' he would say, 'yes-yes-yes-yes. Let me see. That was the summer of – let me see – ninety-one or ninety-two – Yes-yes-yes-yes – '

Fifteen years of yeses had beaten Mrs Gilbert. Fifteen further years of that incessant unaffirmative affirmative, accompanied by the perpetual flicking of ash-mushrooms from thirty-two thousand cigars, had broken her. To this husband of hers she made the last concession of married life, which is more complete, more irrevocable, than the first – she listened to him. She told herself that the years had brought her tolerance – actually they had slain what measure she had ever possessed of moral courage.

She introduced him to Anthony.

'This is Mr Pats,' she said.

The young man and the old touched flesh; Mr Gilbert's hand was soft, worn away to the pulpy semblance of a squeezed grapefruit. Then husband and wife exchanged greetings – he told her it had grown colder out; he said he had walked down to a news-stand on Forty-Fourth Street for a Kansas City paper. He had intended to ride back in the bus but he had found it too cold, yes, yes, yes, yes, too cold.

Mrs Gilbert added flavour to his adventure by being impressed with his courage in braving the harsh air.

'Well, you *are* spunky!' she exclaimed admiringly. 'You *are* spunky. I wouldn't have gone out for anything.'

Mr Gilbert with true masculine impassivity disregarded the awe he had excited in his wife. He turned to the two young men and triumphantly routed them on the subject of the weather. Richard Caramel was called on to remember the month of November in Kansas. No sooner had the theme been pushed towards him, however, than it was violently fished back to be lingered over, pawed over, elongated, and generally devitalised by its sponsor.

The immemorial thesis that the days somewhere were warm but the nights very pleasant was successfully propounded and they decided the exact distance on an obscure railroad between two points that Dick had inadvertently mentioned. Anthony fixed Mr Gilbert with a steady stare and went into a trance through which, after a moment, Mrs Gilbert's smiling voice penetrated: 'It seems as though the cold were damper here – it seems to eat into my bones.'

As this remark, adequately yessed, had been on the tip of Mr Gilbert's tongue, he could not be blamed for rather abruptly changing the subject.

'Where's Gloria?'

'She ought to be here any minute.'

'Have you met my daughter, Mr – ?'

'Haven't had the pleasure. I've heard Dick speak of her often.'

'She and Richard are cousins.'

'Yes?' Anthony smiled with some effort. He was not used to the society of his seniors, and his mouth was stiff from superfluous cheerfulness. It was such a pleasant thought about Gloria and Dick being cousins. He managed within the next minute to throw an agonised glance at his friend.

Richard Caramel was afraid they'd have to toddle off.

Mrs Gilbert was tremendously sorry.

Mr Gilbert thought it was too bad.

Mrs Gilbert had a further idea – something about being glad they'd come, anyhow, even if they'd only seen an old lady 'way too old to flirt with them. Anthony and Dick evidently considered this a sly sally, for they laughed one bar in three-four time.

Would they come again soon?

'Oh, yes.'

Gloria would be *aw*fully sorry!

'Goodbye – '

'Goodbye – '

Smiles!

Smiles!

Bang!

Two disconsolate young men walking down the tenth-floor corridor of the Plaza in the direction of the elevator.

A LADY'S LEGS

Behind Maury Noble's attractive indolence, his irrelevance and his easy mockery, lay a surprising and relentless maturity of purpose. His intention, as he stated it in college, had been to use three years in travel, three years in utter leisure – and then to become immensely rich as quickly as possible.

His three years of travel were over. He had accomplished the globe with an intensity and curiosity that in anyone else would have seemed pedantic, without redeeming spontaneity, almost the self-editing of a human Baedeker; but, in this case, it assumed an air of mysterious purpose and significant design – as though Maury Noble were some predestined anti-Christ, urged by a preordination to go everywhere there was to go along the earth and to see all the billions of humans who bred and wept and slew each other here and there upon it.

Back in America, he was sallying into the search for amusement with the same consistent absorption. He who had never taken more than a few cocktails or a pint of wine at a sitting, taught himself to drink as he would have taught himself Greek – like Greek it would be the gateway to a wealth of new sensations, new psychic states, new reactions in joy or misery.

His habits were a matter for esoteric speculation. He had three rooms in a bachelor apartment on Forty-Forth Street, but he was seldom to be found there. The telephone girl had received the most positive instructions that no one should even have his ear without first giving a name to be passed on. She had a list of half a dozen people to whom he was never at home, and of the same number to whom he was always at home. Foremost on the latter list were Anthony Patch and Richard Caramel.

Maury's mother lived with her married son in Philadelphia, and there Maury went usually for the weekends, so one Saturday night when Anthony, prowling the chilly streets in a fit of utter boredom, dropped in at the Molton Arms he was overjoyed to find that Mr Noble was at home.

His spirits soared faster than the flying elevator. This was so good, so extremely good, to be about to talk to Maury – who would be equally happy at seeing him. They would look at each other with a deep affection just behind their eyes which both would conceal beneath some attenuated raillery. Had it been summer they would have gone out together and indolently sipped two long Tom Collinses, as they wilted their collars and watched the faintly diverting round of some lazy August cabaret. But it was cold outside, with wind around the edges of the tall buildings and December just up the street, so better far an evening together under the soft lamplight and a drink or two of Bushmill's, or a thimbleful of Maury's Grand Marnier, with the books gleaming like ornaments against the walls, and Maury radiating a divine inertia as he rested, large and catlike, in his favourite chair.

There he was! The room closed about Anthony, warmed him. The glow of that strong persuasive mind, that temperament almost Oriental in its outward impassivity, warmed Anthony's restless soul and brought him a peace that could be likened only to the peace a stupid woman gives. One must understand all – else one must take all for granted. Maury filled the room, tigerlike, godlike. The winds outside were stilled; the brass candlesticks on the mantel glowed like tapers before an altar.

'What keeps you here today?' Anthony spread himself over a yielding sofa and made an elbow-rest among the pillows.

'Just been here an hour. Tea dance – and I stayed so late I missed my train to Philadelphia.'

'Strange to stay so long,' commented Anthony curiously.

'Rather. What'd you do?'

'Geraldine. Little usher at Keith's. I told you about her.'

'Oh!'

'Paid me a call about three and stayed till five. Peculiar little soul – she gets me. She's so utterly stupid.'

Maury was silent.

'Strange as it may seem,' continued Anthony, 'so far as I'm concerned, and even so far as I know, Geraldine is a paragon of virtue.'

He had known her a month, a girl of nondescript and nomadic habits. Someone had casually passed her on to Anthony, who considered her amusing and rather liked the chaste and fairylike kisses she had given him on the third night of their acquaintance, when they had driven in a taxi through the Park. She had a vague family – a shadowy aunt and uncle who shared with her an apartment in the labyrinthine hundreds. She was company, familiar and faintly intimate and restful. Further than that he did not care to experiment – not from any moral compunction, but from a dread of allowing any entanglement to disturb what he felt was the growing serenity of his life.

'She has two stunts,' he informed Maury; 'one of them is to get her hair over her eyes some way and then blow it out, and the other is to say "You cra-a-azy!" when someone makes a remark that's over her head. It fascinates me. I sit there hour after hour, completely intrigued by the maniacal symptoms she finds in my imagination.'

Maury stirred in his chair and spoke.

'Remarkable that a person can comprehend so little and yet live in such a complex civilisation. A woman like that actually takes the whole universe in the most matter-of-fact way. From the influence of Rousseau to the bearing of the tariff rates on her dinner, the whole phenomenon is utterly strange to her. She's just been carried along from an age of spearheads and plunked down here with the equipment of an archer for going into a pistol duel. You could sweep away the entire crust of history and she'd never know the difference.'

'I wish our Richard would write about her.'

'Anthony, surely you don't think she's worth writing about.'

'As much as anybody,' he answered, yawning. 'You know I was thinking today that I have a great confidence in Dick. So long as he sticks to people and not to ideas, and as long as his inspirations come from life and not from art, and always granting a normal growth, I believe he'll be a big man.'

'I should think the appearance of the black notebook would prove that he's going to life.'

Anthony raised himself on his elbow and answered eagerly: 'He tries to go to life. So does every author except the very worst, but after all most of them live on predigested food. The incident or character may be from life, but the writer usually interprets it in terms of the last book he read. For instance, suppose he meets a sea captain and thinks he's an original character. The truth is that he sees the resemblance between the sea captain and the last sea captain Dana created, or whoever creates sea captains, and therefore he knows how to set this sea captain on paper. Dick, of course, can set down any consciously picturesque, character-like character, but could he accurately transcribe his own sister?'

Then they were off for half an hour on literature.

'A classic,' suggested Anthony, 'is a successful book that has survived the reaction of the next period or generation. Then it's safe, like a style in architecture or furniture. It's acquired a picturesque dignity to take the place of its fashion . . . '

After a time the subject temporarily lost its tang. The interest of the two young men was not particularly technical. They were in love with generalities. Anthony had recently discovered Samuel Butler and the brisk aphorisms in the *Notebooks* seemed to him the quintessence of criticism. Maury, his whole mind so thoroughly mellowed by the very hardness of his scheme of life, seemed inevitably the wiser of the two, yet in the actual stuff of their intelligences they were not, it seemed, fundamentally different.

They drifted from letters to the curiosities of each other's day.

'Whose tea was it?'

'People named Abercrombie.'

'Why'd you stay late? Meet a luscious débutante?'

'Yes.'

'Did you really?' Anthony's voice lifted in surprise.

'Not a débutante exactly. Said she came out two winters ago in Kansas City.'

'Sort of left over?'

'No,' answered Maury with some amusement, 'I think that's the last thing I'd say about her. She seemed – well, somehow the youngest person there.'

'Not too young to make you miss a train.'

'Young enough. Beautiful child.'

Anthony chuckled in his one-syllable snort.

'Oh, Maury, you're in your second childhood. What do you mean by beautiful?'

Maury gazed helplessly into space.

'Well, I can't describe her exactly – except to say that she was beautiful. She was – tremendously alive. She was eating gumdrops.'

'What!'

'It was a sort of attenuated vice. She's a nervous kind – said she always ate gumdrops at teas because she had to stand around so long in one place.'

'What'd you talk about – Bergson? Bilphism? Whether the one-step is immoral?'

Maury was unruffled; his fur seemed to run all ways.

'As a matter of fact we did talk on Bilphism. Seems her mother's a Bilphist. Mostly, though, we talked about legs.'

Anthony rocked in glee.

'My God! Whose legs?'

'Hers. She talked a lot about hers. As though they were a sort of choice bric-à-brac. She aroused a great desire to see them.'

'What is she – a dancer?'

'No, I found she was a cousin of Dick's.'

Anthony sat upright so suddenly that the pillow he released stood on end like a live thing and dived to the floor.

'Name's Gloria Gilbert?' he cried.

'Yes. Isn't she remarkable?'

'I'm sure I don't know – but for sheer dullness her father – '

'Well,' interrupted Maury with implacable conviction, 'her family may be as sad as professional mourners but I'm inclined to think that she's a quite authentic and original character. The outer signs of the cut-and-dried Yale prom girl and all that – but different, very emphatically different.'

'Go on, go on!' urged Anthony. 'Soon as Dick told me she didn't have a brain in her head I knew she must be pretty good.'

'Did he say that?'

'Swore to it,' said Anthony with another snorting laugh.

'Well, what he means by brains in a woman is – '

'I know,' interrupted Anthony eagerly, 'he means a smattering of literary misinformation.'

'That's it. The kind who believes that the annual moral let-down of the country is a very good thing or the kind who believes it's a very ominous thing. Either pince-nez or postures. Well, this girl talked about legs. She talked about skin too – her own skin. Always her own. She told me the sort of tan she'd like to get in the summer and how closely she usually approximated it.'

'You sat enraptured by her low alto?'

'By her low alto! No, by tan! I began thinking about tan. I began to think what colour I turned when I made my last exposure about two years ago. I did use to get a pretty good tan. I used to get a sort of bronze, if I remember rightly.'

Anthony retired into the cushions, shaken with laughter.

'She's got you going – oh, Maury! Maury the Connecticut life-saver. The human nutmeg. Extra! Heiress elopes with coastguard because of his luscious pigmentation! Afterwards found to be Tasmanian strain in his family!'

Maury sighed; rising he walked to the window and raised the shade.

'Snowing hard.'

Anthony, still laughing quietly to himself, made no answer.

'Another winter.' Maury's voice from the window was almost a whisper. 'We're growing old, Anthony. I'm twenty-seven, by God! Three years to thirty, and then I'm what an undergraduate calls a middle-aged man.'

Anthony was silent for a moment.

'You *are* old, Maury,' he agreed at length. 'The first signs of a very dissolute and wobbly senescence – you have spent the afternoon talking about tan and a lady's legs.'

Maury pulled down the shade with a sudden harsh snap.

'Idiot!' he cried, 'that from you! Here I sit, young Anthony, as I'll sit for a generation or more and watch such gay souls as you and Dick and Gloria Gilbert go past me, dancing and singing and loving and hating one another and being moved, being eternally moved. And I am moved only by my lack of emotion. I shall sit and the snow will come – oh, for a Caramel to take notes – and another winter and I shall be thirty and you and Dick and Gloria will go on being eternally moved and dancing by me and singing. But after you've all gone I'll be saying things for new Dicks to write down, and listening to the disillusions and cynicisms and emotions of new Anthonys – yes, and talking to new Glorias about the tans of summers yet to come.'

The firelight flurried up on the hearth. Maury left the window, stirred the blaze with a poker, and dropped a log upon the andirons. Then he sat back in his chair and the remnants of his voice faded in the new fire that spit red and yellow along the bark.

'After all, Anthony, it's you who are very romantic and young. It's you who are infinitely more susceptible and afraid of your calm being broken. It's me who tries again and again to be moved – let myself go a thousand times and I'm always me. Nothing – quite – stirs me.

'Yet,' he murmured after another long pause, 'there was something about that little girl with her absurd tan that was eternally old – like me.'

TURBULENCE

Anthony turned over sleepily in his bed, greeting a patch of cold sun on his counterpane, criss-crossed with the shadows of the leaded window. The room was full of morning. The carved chest in the corner, the ancient and inscrutable wardrobe, stood about the room like dark symbols of the obliviousness of matter; only the rug was beckoning and perishable to his perishable feet, and Bounds, horribly inappropriate in his soft collar, was of stuff as fading as the gauze of frozen breath he uttered. He was close to the bed, his hand still lowered where he had been jerking at the upper blanket, his dark-brown eyes fixed imperturbably upon his master.

'Bows!' muttered the drowsy god. 'Thachew, Bows?'

'It's I, sir.'

Anthony moved his head, forced his eyes wide, and blinked triumphantly.

'Bounds.'

'Yes, sir?'

'Can you get off – yeow-ow-oh-oh-oh God! – ' Anthony yawned insufferably and the contents of his brain seemed to fall together in a dense hash. He made a fresh start.

'Can you come around about four and serve some tea and sandwiches or something?'

'Yes, sir.'

Anthony considered with chilling lack of inspiration. 'Some

sandwiches,' he repeated helplessly, 'oh, some cheese sandwiches and jelly ones and chicken and olive, I guess. Never mind breakfast.'

The strain of invention was too much. He shut his eyes wearily, let his head roll to rest inertly, and quickly relaxed what he had regained of muscular control. Out of a crevice of his mind crept the vague but inevitable spectre of the night before – but it proved in this case to be nothing but a seemingly interminable conversation with Richard Caramel, who had called on him at midnight; they had drunk four bottles of beer and munched dry crusts of bread while Anthony listened to a reading of the first part of *The Demon Lover*.

– Came a voice now after many hours. Anthony disregarded it, as sleep closed over him, folded down upon him, crept up into the byways of his mind.

Suddenly he was awake, saying: 'What?'

'For how many, sir?' It was still Bounds, standing patient and motionless at the foot of the bed – Bounds who divided his manner among three gentlemen.

'How many what?'

'I think, sir, I'd better know how many are coming. I'll have to plan for the sandwiches, sir.'

'Two,' muttered Anthony huskily; 'lady and a gentleman.'

Bounds said, 'Thank you, sir,' and moved away, bearing with him his humiliating reproachful soft collar, reproachful to each of the three gentlemen, who only demanded of him a third.

After a long time Anthony arose and drew an opalescent dressing grown of brown and blue over his slim pleasant figure. With a last yawn he went into the bathroom, and turning on the dresser light (the bathroom had no outside exposure) he contemplated himself in the mirror with some interest. A wretched apparition, he thought; he usually thought so in the morning – sleep made his face unnaturally pale. He lit a cigarette and glanced through several letters and the morning *Tribune*.

An hour later, shaven and dressed, he was sitting at his desk looking at a small piece of paper he had taken out of his wallet. It was scrawled with semi-legible memoranda: 'See Mr Howland at five. Get haircut. See about Rivers' bill. Go bookstore.'

– And under the last: 'Cash in bank, $690 [crossed out], $612 [crossed out], $607.'

Finally, down at the bottom and in a hurried scrawl: 'Dick and Gloria Gilbert for tea.'

This last item brought him obvious satisfaction. His day, usually a jellylike creature, a shapeless, spineless thing, had attained Mesozoic structure. It was marching along surely, even jauntily, towards a climax, as a play should, as a day should. He dreaded the moment when the backbone of the day should be broken, when he should have met the girl at last, talked to her, and then bowed her laughter out the door, returning only to the melancholy dregs in the teacups and the gathering staleness of the uneaten sandwiches.

There was a growing lack of colour in Anthony's days. He felt it constantly and sometimes traced it to a talk he had had with Maury Noble a month before. That anything so ingenuous, so priggish, as a sense of waste should oppress him was absurd, but there was no denying the fact that some unwelcome survival of a fetish had drawn him three weeks before down to the public library, where, by the token of Richard Caramel's card, he had drawn out half a dozen books on the Italian Renaissance. That these books were still piled on his desk in the original order of carriage, that they were daily increasing his liabilities by twelve cents, was no mitigation of their testimony. They were cloth and morocco witnesses to the fact of his defection. Anthony had had several hours of acute and startling panic.

In justification of his manner of living there was first, of course, The Meaninglessness of Life. As aides and ministers, pages and squires, butlers and lackeys to this great Khan there were a thousand books glowing on his shelves, there was his apartment and all the money that was to be his when the old man up the river should choke on his last morality. From a world fraught with the menace of débutantes and the stupidity of many Geraldines he was thankfully delivered – rather should he emulate the feline immobility of Maury and wear proudly the culminative wisdom of the numbered generations.

Over and against these things was something which his brain persistently analysed and dealt with as a tiresome complex but which, though logically disposed of and bravely trampled under foot, had sent him out through the soft slush of late November to a library which had none of the books he most wanted. It is fair to analyse Anthony as far as he could analyse himself; further than that it is, of course, presumption. He found in himself a growing horror and loneliness. The idea of eating alone frightened him; in preference he dined often with men he detested. Travel, which had once charmed him, seemed at length, unendurable, a business of colour without substance, a phantom chase after his own dream's shadow.

– If I am essentially weak, he thought, I need work to do, work to do. It worried him to think that he was, after all, a facile mediocrity, with neither the poise of Maury nor the enthusiasm of Dick. It seemed a tragedy to want nothing – and yet he wanted something, something. He knew in flashes what it was – some path of hope to lead him towards what he thought was an imminent and ominous old age.

After cocktails and luncheon at the University Club Anthony felt better. He had run into two men from his class at Harvard, and in contrast to the grey heaviness of their conversation his life assumed colour. Both of them were married: one spent his coffee time in sketching an extra-nuptial adventure to the bland and appreciative smiles of the other. Both of them, he thought, were Mr Gilberts in embryo; the number of their yeses would have to be quadrupled, their natures crabbed by twenty years – then they would be no more than obsolete and broken machines, pseudo-wise and valueless, nursed to an utter senility by the women they had broken.

Ah, he was more than that, as he paced the long carpet in the lounge after dinner, pausing at the window to look into the harried street. He was Anthony Patch, brilliant, magnetic, the heir of many years and many men. This was his world now – and that last strong irony he craved lay in the offing.

With a stray boyishness he saw himself a power upon the earth; with his grandfather's money he might build his own pedestal and be a Talleyrand, a Lord Verulam. The clarity of his mind, its sophistication, its versatile intelligence, all at their maturity and dominated by some purpose yet to be born would find him work to do. On this minor his dream faded – work to do: he tried to imagine himself in Congress rooting around in the litter of that incredible pigsty with the narrow and porcine brows he saw pictured sometimes in the rotogravure sections of the Sunday newspapers, those glorified proletarians babbling blandly to the nation the ideas of high-school seniors! Little men with copybook ambitions who by mediocrity had thought to emerge from mediocrity into the lustreless and unromantic heaven of a government by the people – and the best, the dozen shrewd men at the top, egotistic and cynical, were content to lead this choir of white ties and wire collar-buttons in a discordant and amazing hymn, compounded of a vague confusion between wealth as a reward of virtue and wealth as a proof of vice, and continued cheers for God, the Constitution and the Rocky Mountains!

Lord Verulam! Talleyrand!

Back in his apartment the greyness returned. His cocktails had died, making him sleepy, somewhat befogged and inclined to be surly. Lord Verulam – he? The very thought was bitter. Anthony Patch with no record of achievement, without courage, without strength to be satisfied with truth when it was given him. Oh, he was a pretentious fool, making careers out of cocktails and meanwhile regretting, weakly and secretly, the collapse of an insufficient and wretched idealism. He had garnished his soul in the subtlest taste and now he longed for the old rubbish. He was empty, it seemed, empty as an old bottle –

The buzzer rang at the door. Anthony sprang up and lifted the tube to his ear. It was Richard Caramel's voice, stilted and facetious: 'Announcing Miss Gloria Gilbert.'

'How do you do?' he said, smiling and holding the door ajar.

Dick bowed.

'Gloria, this is Anthony.'

'Well!' she cried, holding out a little gloved hand. Under her fur coat her dress was Alice-blue, with white lace crinkled stiffly about her throat.

'Let me take your things.'

Anthony stretched out his arms and the brown mass of fur tumbled into them.

'Thanks.'

'What do you think of her, Anthony?' Richard Caramel demanded barbarously. 'Isn't she beautiful?'

'Well!' cried the girl defiantly – withal unmoved.

She was dazzling – alight; it was agony to comprehend her beauty in a glance. Her hair, full of a heavenly glamour, was gay against the winter colour of the room.

Anthony moved about, magician-like, turning the mushroom lamp into an orange glory. The stirred fire burnished the copper andirons on the hearth –

'I'm a solid block of ice,' murmured Gloria casually, glancing around with eyes whose irises were of the most delicate and transparent bluish white. 'What a slick fire! We found a place where you could stand on an iron-bar grating, sort of, and it blew warm air up at you – but Dick wouldn't wait there with me. I told him to go on alone and let me be happy.'

Conventional enough this. She seemed talking for her own pleasure, without effort. Anthony, sitting at one end of the sofa, examined her profile against the foreground of the lamp: the exquisite regularity of nose and upper lip, the chin, faintly decided, balanced beautifully on a rather short neck. On a photograph she must have been completely classical, almost cold – but the glow of her hair and cheeks, at once flushed and fragile, made her the most living person he had ever seen.

'. . . Think you've got the best name I've heard,' she was saying, still apparently to herself; her glance rested on him a moment and then flitted past him – to the Italian bracket-lamps clinging like luminous yellow turtles at intervals along the walls, to the books row upon row, then to her cousin on the other side. 'Anthony Patch. Only you ought to look sort of like a horse, with a long narrow face – and you ought to be in tatters.'

'That's all the Patch part, though. How should Anthony look?'

'You look like Anthony,' she assured him seriously – he thought she had scarcely seen him – 'rather majestic,' she continued, 'and solemn.'

Anthony indulged in a disconcerted smile.

'Only I like alliterative names,' she went on, 'all except mine. Mine's too flamboyant. I used to know two girls named Jinks, though, and just think if they'd been named anything except what they were named – Judy Jinks and Jerry Jinks. Cute, what? Don't you think?' Her childish mouth was parted, awaiting a rejoinder.

'Everybody in the next generation,' suggested Dick, 'will be named Peter or Barbara – because at present all the piquant literary characters are named Peter or Barbara.'

Anthony continued the prophecy: 'Of course Gladys and Eleanor, having graced the last generation of heroines and being at present in their social prime, will be passed on to the next generation of shop-girls – '

'Displacing Ella and Stella,' interrupted Dick.

'And Pearl and Jewel,' Gloria added cordially, 'and Earl and Elmer and Minnie.'

'And then I'll come along,' remarked Dick, 'and picking up the obsolete name, Jewel, I'll attach it to some quaint and attractive character and it'll start its career all over again.'

Her voice took up the thread of subject and wove along with faintly upturning, half-humorous intonations for sentence ends – as though defying interruption – and intervals of shadowy laughter. Dick had told her that Anthony's man was named Bounds – she thought that was wonderful! Dick had made some sad pun about Bounds doing patchwork, but if there was one thing worse than a pun, she said, it was a person who, as the inevitable come-back to a pun, gave the perpetrator a mock-reproachful look.

'Where are you from?' enquired Anthony. He knew, but beauty had rendered him thoughtless.

'Kansas City, Missouri.'

'They put her out the same time they barred cigarettes.'

'Did they bar cigarettes? I see the hand of my holy grandfather.'

'He's a reformer or something, isn't he?'

'I blush for him.'

'So do I,' she confessed. 'I detest reformers, especially the sort who try to reform me.'

'Are there many of those?'

'Dozens. It's, "Oh, Gloria, if you smoke so many cigarettes you'll lose your pretty complexion!" and, "Oh, Gloria, why don't you marry and settle down?" '

Anthony agreed emphatically while he wondered who had had the temerity to speak thus to such a personage.

'And then,' she continued, 'there are all the subtle reformers who tell you the wild stories they've heard about you and how they've been sticking up for you.'

He saw, at length, that her eyes were grey, very level and cool, and when they rested on him he understood what Maury had meant by saying she was very young and very old. She talked always about herself as a very charming child might talk, and her comments on her tastes and distastes were unaffected and spontaneous.

'I must confess,' said Anthony gravely, 'that even *I*'ve heard one thing about you.'

Alert at once, she sat up straight. Those eyes, with the greyness and eternity of a cliff of soft granite, caught his.

'Tell me. I'll believe it. I always believe anything anyone tells me about myself – don't you?'

'Invariably!' agreed the two men in unison.

'Well, tell me.'

'I'm not sure that I ought to,' teased Anthony, smiling unwillingly. She was so obviously interested, in a state of almost laughable self-absorption.

'He means your nickname,' said her cousin.

'What name?' enquired Anthony, politely puzzled.

Instantly she was shy – then she laughed, rolled back against the cushions, and turned her eyes up as she spoke: 'Coast-to-Coast Gloria.'

Her voice was full of laughter, laughter undefined as the varying shadows playing between fire and lamp upon her hair. 'O Lord!'

Still Anthony was puzzled.

'What do you mean?'

'*Me*, I mean. That's what some silly boys coined for *me*.'

'Don't you see, Anthony,' explained Dick, 'traveller of a nationwide notoriety and all that. Isn't that what you've heard? She's been called that for years – since she was seventeen.'

Anthony's eyes became sad and humorous.

'Who's this female Methuselah you've brought in here, Caramel?'

She disregarded this, possibly rather resented it, for she switched back to the main topic.

'What *have* you heard of me?'

'Something about your physique.'

'Oh,' she said, coolly disappointed, 'that all?'

'Your tan.'

'My tan?' She was puzzled. Her hand rose to her throat, rested there an instant as though the fingers were feeling variants of colour.

'Do you remember Maury Noble? Man you met about a month ago. You made a great impression.'

She thought a moment.

'I remember – but he didn't call me up.'

'He was afraid to, I don't doubt.'

It was black dark without now and Anthony wondered that his apartment had ever seemed grey – so warm and friendly were the books and pictures on the walls and the good Bounds offering tea from a respectful shadow and the three nice people giving out waves of interest and laughter back and forth across the happy fire.

DISSATISFACTION

On Thursday afternoon Gloria and Anthony had tea together in the grill room at the Plaza. Her fur-trimmed suit was grey – 'because with grey you *have* to wear a lot of paint,' she explained – and a small toque sat rakishly on her head, allowing yellow ripples of hair to wave out in jaunty glory. In the higher light it seemed to Anthony that her personality was infinitely softer – she seemed so young, scarcely eighteen; her form under the tight sheath, known then as a hobble-skirt, was amazingly supple and slender, and her hands, neither 'artistic' nor stubby, were small as a child's hands should be.

As they entered, the orchestra were sounding the preliminary whimpers to a maxixe, a tune full of castanets and facile faintly languorous violin harmonies, appropriate to the crowded winter grill teeming with an excited college crowd, high-spirited at the approach of the holidays. Carefully, Gloria considered several locations, and rather to Anthony's annoyance paraded him circuitously to a table for two at the far side of the room. Reaching it she again considered. Would she sit on the right or on the left? Her beautiful eyes and lips were very grave as she made her choice, and Anthony thought again how naïve was her every gesture; she took all the things of life for hers to choose from and apportion, as though she were continually picking out presents for herself from an inexhaustible counter.

Abstractedly she watched the dancers for a few moments, commenting murmurously as a couple eddied near.

'There's a pretty girl in blue' – and as Anthony looked obediently – 'there! No. behind you – there!'

'Yes,' he agreed helplessly.

'You didn't see her.'

'I'd rather look at you.'

'I know, but she was pretty. Except that she had big ankles.'

'Was she? – I mean, did she?' he said indifferently.

A girl's salutation came from a couple dancing close to them.

'Hello, Gloria! O Gloria!'

'Hello there.'

'Who's that?' he demanded.

'I don't know. Somebody.' She caught sight of another face. 'Hello, Muriel!' Then to Anthony: 'There's Muriel Kane. Now I think she's attractive, 'cept not very.'

Anthony chuckled appreciatively.

' "Attractive, 'cept not very",' he repeated.

She smiled – was interested immediately.

'Why is that funny?' Her tone was pathetically intent.

'It just was.'

'Do you want to dance?'

'Do you?'

'Sort of. But let's sit,' she decided.

'And talk about you? You love to talk about you, don't you?'

'Yes.' Caught in a vanity, she laughed.

'I imagine your autobiography would be a classic.'

'Dick says I haven't got one.'

'Dick!' he exclaimed. 'What does he know about you?'

'Nothing. But he says the biography of every woman begins with the first kiss that counts, and ends when her last child is laid in her arms.'

'He's talking from his book.'

'He says unloved women have no biographies – they have histories.'

Anthony laughed again.

'Surely you don't claim to be unloved!'

'Well, I suppose not.'

'Then why haven't you a biography? Haven't you ever had a kiss that counted?' As the words left his lips he drew in his breath sharply as though to suck them back. This *baby*!

'I don't know what you mean "counts",' she objected.

'I wish you'd tell me how old you are.'

'Twenty-two,' she said, meeting his eyes gravely. 'How old did you think?'

'About eighteen.'

'I'm going to start being that. I don't like being twenty-two. I hate it more than anything in the world.'

'Being twenty-two?'

'No. Getting old and everything. Getting married.'

'Don't you ever want to marry?'

'I don't want to have responsibility and a lot of children to take care of.'

Evidently she did not doubt that on her lips all things were good. He waited rather breathlessly for her next remark, expecting it to follow up her last. She was smiling, without amusement but pleasantly, and after an interval half a dozen words fell into the space between them: 'I wish I had some gumdrops.'

'You shall!' He beckoned to a waiter and sent him to the cigar counter.

'D'you mind? I love gumdrops. Everybody kids me about it because I'm always whacking away at one – whenever my daddy's not around.'

'Not at all. – Who are all these children?' he asked suddenly. 'Do you know them all?'

'Why – no, but they're from – oh, from everywhere, I suppose. Don't you ever come here?'

'Very seldom. I don't care particularly for "nice girls".'

Immediately he had her attention. She turned a definite shoulder to the dancers, relaxed in her chair, and demanded: 'What *do* you do with yourself?'

Thanks to a cocktail Anthony welcomed the question. In a mood to talk, he wanted, moreover, to impress this girl whose interest seemed so tantalisingly elusive – she stopped to browse in unexpected pastures, hurried quickly over the inobviously obvious. He wanted to pose. He wanted to appear suddenly to her in novel and heroic colours. He wanted to stir her from that casualness she showed towards everything except herself.

'I do nothing,' he began, realising simultaneously that his words were to lack the debonair grace he craved for them. 'I do nothing, for there's nothing I can do that's worth doing.'

'Well?' He had neither surprised her nor even held her, yet she had certainly understood him, if indeed he had said aught worth understanding.

'Don't you approve of lazy men?'

She nodded.

'I suppose so, if they're gracefully lazy. Is that possible for an American?'

'Why not?' he demanded, discomfited.

But her mind had left the subject and wandered up ten floors.

'My daddy's mad at me,' she observed dispassionately.

'Why? But I want to know just why it's impossible for an American to be gracefully idle' – his words gathered conviction – 'it astonishes me. It – it – I don't understand why people think that every young man ought to go downtown and work ten hours a day for the best twenty years of his life at dull, unimaginative work, certainly not altruistic work.'

He broke off. She watched him inscrutably. He waited for her to agree or disagree, but she did neither.

'Don't you ever form judgements on things?' he asked with some exasperation.

She shook her head and her eyes wandered back to the dancers as she answered: 'I don't know. I don't know anything about – what you should do, or what anybody should do.'

She confused him and hindered the flow of his ideas. Self-expression had never seemed at once so desirable and so impossible.

'Well,' he admitted apologetically, 'neither do I, of course, but – '

'I just think of people,' she continued, 'whether they seem right where they are and fit into the picture. I don't mind if they don't do anything. I don't see why they should; in fact it always astonishes me when anybody does anything.'

'You don't want to do anything?'

'I want to sleep.'

For a second he was startled, almost as though she had meant this literally.

'Sleep?'

'Sort of. I want to just be lazy and I want some of the people around me to be doing things, because that makes me feel comfortable and safe – and I want some of them to be doing nothing at all, because they can be graceful and companionable for me. But I never want to change people or get excited over them.'

'You're a quaint little determinist,' laughed Anthony. 'It's your world, isn't it?'

'Well – ' she said with a quick upward glance, 'isn't it? As long as I'm – young.'

She had paused slightly before the last word and Anthony suspected that she had started to say 'beautiful'. It was undeniably what she had intended.

Her eyes brightened and he waited for her to enlarge on the theme. He had drawn her out, at any rate – he bent forward slightly to catch the words.

But 'Let's dance!' was all she said.

That winter afternoon at the Plaza was the first of a succession of 'dates' Anthony made with her in the blurred and stimulating days before Christmas. Invariably she was busy. What particular strata of the city's social life claimed her he was a long time finding out. It seemed to matter very little. She attended the semi-public charity dances at the big hotels; he saw her several times at dinner parties in Sherry's, and once, as he waited for her to dress, Mrs Gilbert, apropos of her daughter's habit of 'going', rattled off an amazing holiday programme that included half a dozen dances to which Anthony had received cards.

He made engagements with her several times for lunch and tea – the former were hurried and, to him at least, rather unsatisfactory occasions, for she was sleepy-eyed and casual, incapable of concentrating upon anything or of giving consecutive attention to his remarks. When after two of these sallow meals he accused her of tendering him the skin and bones of the day she laughed and gave him a tea-time three days off. This was infinitely more satisfactory.

One Sunday afternoon just before Christmas he called up and found her in the lull directly after some important but mysterious quarrel:

she informed him in a tone of mingled wrath and amusement that she had sent a man out of her apartment – here Anthony speculated violently – and that the man had been giving a little dinner for her that very night and that of course she wasn't going. So Anthony took her to supper.

'Let's go to something!' she proposed as they went down in the elevator. 'I want to see a show, don't you?'

Enquiry at the hotel ticket desk disclosed only two Sunday night 'concerts'.

'They're always the same,' she complained unhappily, 'same old Yiddish comedians. Oh, let's go somewhere!'

To conceal a guilty suspicion that he should have arranged a performance of some kind for her approval Anthony affected a knowing cheerfulness.

'We'll go to a good cabaret.'

'I've seen every one in town.'

'Well, we'll find a new one.'

She was in wretched humour; that was evident. Her grey eyes were granite now indeed. When she wasn't speaking she stared straight in front of her as if at some distasteful abstraction in the lobby.

'Well, come on, then.'

He followed her, a graceful girl even in her enveloping fur, out to a taxicab, and, with an air of having a definite place in mind, instructed the driver to go over to Broadway and then turn south. He made several casual attempts at conversation but as she adopted an impenetrable armour of silence and answered him in sentences as morose as the cold darkness of the taxicab he gave up, and assuming a like mood fell into a dim gloom.

A dozen blocks down Broadway Anthony's eyes were caught by a large and unfamiliar electric sign spelling 'Marathon' in glorious yellow script, adorned with electrical leaves and flowers that alternately vanished and beamed upon the wet and glistening street. He leaned and rapped on the taxi-window and in a moment was receiving information from a coloured doorman: Yes, this was a cabaret. Fine cabaret. Bes' showina city!

'Shall we try it?'

With a sigh Gloria tossed her cigarette out the open door and prepared to follow it; then they had passed under the screaming sign, under the wide portal, and up by a stuffy elevator into this unsung palace of pleasure.

The gay habitats of the very rich and the very poor, the very dashing and the very criminal, not to mention the lately exploited very Bohemian, are made known to the awed high-school girls of Augusta, Georgia, and Redwing, Minnesota, not only through the bepictured and entrancing spreads of the Sunday theatrical supplements but through the shocked and alarmful eyes of Mr Rupert Hughes and other chroniclers of the mad pace of America. But the excursions of Harlem on to Broadway, the deviltries of the dull and the revelries of the respectable are a matter of esoteric knowledge only to the participants themselves.

A tip circulates – and in the place knowingly mentioned, gather the lower moral-classes on Saturday and Sunday nights – the little troubled men who are pictured in the comics as 'the Consumer' or 'the Public'. They have made sure that the place has three qualifications: it is cheap; it imitates with a sort of shoddy and mechanical wistfulness the glittering antics of the great cafés in the theatre district; and – this, above all, important – it is a place where they can 'take a nice girl', which means, of course, that everyone has become equally harmless, timid and uninteresting through lack of money and imagination.

There on Sunday nights gather the credulous, sentimental, underpaid, overworked people with hyphenated occupations – book-keepers, ticket-sellers, office-managers, sales-men – and, most of all, clerks – clerks of the express, of the mail, of the grocery, of the brokerage, of the bank. With them are their giggling, over-gestured, pathetically pretentious women, who grow fat with them, bear them too many babies, and float helpless and uncontent in a colourless sea of drudgery and broken hopes.

They name these brummagem cabarets after Pullman cars. The 'Marathon'! Not for them the salacious similes borrowed from the cafés of Paris! This is where their docile patrons bring their 'nice women', whose starved fancies are only too willing to believe that the scene is comparatively gay and joyous, and even faintly immoral. This is life! Who cares for the morrow?

Abandoned people!

Anthony and Gloria, seated, looked about them. At the next table a party of four were in process of being joined by a party of three, two men and a girl, who were evidently late – and the manner of the girl was a study in national sociology. She was meeting some new men – and she was pretending desperately. By gesture she was pretending and by words and by the scarcely perceptible motionings of her eyelids that she belonged to a class a little superior to the class with which she now had to do, that a while ago she had been, and presently would again be, in a higher, rarer air. She was almost painfully refined – she wore a last year's hat covered with violets no more yearningly pretentious and palpably artificial than herself.

Fascinated, Anthony and Gloria watched the girl sit down and radiate the impression that she was only condescendingly present. For *me*, her eyes said, this is practically a slumming expedition, to be cloaked with belittling laughter and semi-apologetics.

– And the other women passionately poured out the impression that though they were in the crowd they were not of it. This was not the sort of place to which they were accustomed; they had dropped in because it was near by and convenient – every party in the restaurant poured out that impression . . . who knew? They were forever changing class, all of them – the women often marrying above their opportunities, the men striking suddenly a magnificent opulence: a sufficiently preposterous advertising scheme, a celestialised ice-cream cone. Meanwhile, they met here to eat, closing their eyes to the economy displayed in infrequent changings of tablecloths, in the casualness of the cabaret performers, most of all in the colloquial carelessness and familiarity of the waiters. One was sure that these waiters were not impressed by their patrons. One expected that presently they would sit at the tables . . .

'Do you object to this?' enquired Anthony.

Gloria's face warmed and for the first time that evening she smiled. 'I love it,' she said frankly. It was impossible to doubt her. Her grey eyes roved here and there, drowsing, idle or alert, on each group, passing to the next with unconcealed enjoyment, and to Anthony were made plain the different values of her profile, the wonderfully alive expressions of her mouth, and the authentic distinction of face and form and manner that made her like a single flower amidst a collection of cheap bric-à-brac. At her happiness, a gorgeous sentiment welled into his eyes, choked him up, set his nerves a-tingle, and filled his throat with husky and vibrant emotion. There was a hush upon the room. The careless violins and saxophones, the shrill rasping complaint of a child near by, the voice of the violet-hatted girl at the next table, all moved slowly out, receded, and fell away like shadowy reflections on the shining floor – and they two, it seemed to him, were alone and infinitely remote, quiet. Surely the freshness of her cheeks was a gossamer projection from a land of delicate and undiscovered shades;

her hand gleaming on the stained tablecloth was a shell from some far and wildly virginal sea . . .

Then the illusion snapped like a nest of threads; the room grouped itself around him, voices, faces, movement; the garish shimmer of the lights overhead became real, became portentous; breath began, the slow respiration that she and he took in time with this docile hundred, the rise and fall of bosoms, the eternal meaningless play and interplay and tossing and reiterating of word and phrase – all these wrenched his senses open to the suffocating pressure of life – and then her voice came at him, cool as the suspended dream he had left behind.

'I belong here,' she murmured, 'I'm like these people.'

For an instant this seemed a sardonic and unnecessary paradox hurled at him across the impassable distances she created about herself. Her entrancement had increased – her eyes rested upon a Semitic violinist who swayed his shoulders to the rhythm of the year's mellowest foxtrot:

Something – goes
Ring-a-ting-a-ling-a-ling
Right in-your ear – '

Again she spoke, from the centre of this pervasive illusion of her own. It amazed him. It was like blasphemy from the mouth of a child.

'I'm like they are – like Japanese lanterns and crêpe paper, and the music of that orchestra.'

'You're a young idiot!' he insisted wildly. She shook her blonde head.

'No, I'm not. I *am* like them . . . You ought to see . . . You don't know me.' She hesitated and her eyes came back to him, rested abruptly on his, as though surprised at the last to see him there. 'I've got a streak of what you'd call cheapness. I don't know where I get it but it's – oh, things like this and bright colours and gaudy vulgarity. I seem to belong here. These people could appreciate me and take me for granted, and these men would fall in love with me and admire me, whereas the clever men I meet would just analyse me and tell me I'm this because of this or that because of that.'

– Anthony for the moment wanted fiercely to paint her, to set her down *now*, as she was, as with each relentless second she could never be again.

'What were you thinking?' she asked.

'Just that I'm not a realist,' he said, and then: 'No, only the romanticist preserves the things worth preserving.'

Out of the deep sophistication of Anthony an understanding formed, nothing atavistic or obscure, indeed scarcely physical at all, an understanding remembered from the romancings of many generations of minds that as she talked and caught his eyes and turned her lovely head, she moved him as he had never been moved before. The sheath that held her soul had assumed significance – that was all. She was a sun, radiant, growing, gathering light and storing it – then after an eternity pouring it forth in a glance, the fragment of a sentence, to that part of him that cherished all beauty and all illusion.

Chapter 3

The Connoisseur of Kisses

From his undergraduate days as editor of the *Harvard Crimson* Richard Caramel had desired to write. But as a senior he had picked up the glorified illusion that certain men were set aside for 'service' and, going into the world, were to accomplish a vague yearnful something which would react either in eternal reward or, at the least, in the personal satisfaction of having striven for the greatest good of the greatest number.

This spirit has long rocked the colleges in America. It begins, as a rule, during the immaturities and facile impressions of freshman year – sometimes back in preparatory school. Prosperous apostles known for their emotional acting go the rounds of the universities and, by frightening the amiable sheep and dulling the quickening of interest and intellectual curiosity which is the purpose of all education, distil a mysterious conviction of sin, harking back to childhood crimes and to the ever-present menace of 'women'. To these lectures go the wicked youths to cheer and joke and the timid to swallow the tasty pills, which would be harmless if administered to farmers' wives and pious drug-clerks but are rather dangerous medicine for these 'future leaders of men'.

This octopus was strong enough to wind a sinuous tentacle about Richard Caramel. The year after his graduation it called him into the slums of New York to muck about with bewildered Italians as secretary to an 'Alien Young Men's Rescue Association'. He laboured at it over a year before the monotony began to weary him. The aliens kept coming inexhaustibly – Italians, Poles, Scandinavians, Czechs, Armenians – with the same wrongs, the same exceptionally ugly faces and very much the same smells, though he fancied that these grew more profuse and diverse as the months passed. His eventual conclusions about the expediency of service were vague, but concerning his own relation to it they were abrupt and decisive. Any amiable young man, his head ringing with the latest crusade, could accomplish as much as he could with the débris of Europe – and it was time for him to write.

He had been living in a downtown YMCA, but when he quit the

task of making sow-ear purses out of sows' ears, he moved uptown and went to work immediately as a reporter for the *Sun*. He kept at this for a year, doing desultory writing on the side, with little success, and then one day an infelicitous incident peremptorily closed his newspaper career. On a February afternoon he was assigned to report a parade of Squadron A. Snow threatening, he went to sleep instead before a hot fire, and when he woke up did a smooth column about the muffled beats of the horses' hoofs in the snow . . . This he handed in. Next morning a marked copy of the paper was sent down to the City Editor with a scrawled note: 'Fire the man who wrote this.' It seemed that Squadron A had also seen the snow threatening – and had postponed the parade until another day.

A week later he had begun *The Demon Lover* . . .

In January, the Monday of the months, Richard Caramel's nose was blue constantly, a sardonic blue, vaguely suggestive of the flames licking around a sinner. His book was nearly ready, and as it grew in completeness it seemed to grow also in its demands, sapping him, overpowering him, until he walked haggard and conquered in its shadow. Not only to Anthony and Maury did he pour out his hopes and boasts and indecisions, but to anyone who could be prevailed upon to listen. He called on polite but bewildered publishers, he discussed it with his casual vis-à-vis at the Harvard Club; it was even claimed by Anthony that he had been discovered, one Sunday night, debating the transposition of Chapter Two with a literary ticket-collector in the chill and dismal recesses of a Harlem subway station. And latest among his confidantes was Mrs Gilbert, who sat with him by the hour and alternated between Bilphism and literature in an intense cross-fire.

'Shakespeare was a Bilphist,' she assured him through a fixed smile. 'Oh, yes! He was a Bilphist. It's been proved.'

At this Dick would look a bit blank.

'If you've read *Hamlet* you can't help but see.'

'Well, he – he lived in a more credulous age – a more religious age.'

But she demanded the whole loaf: 'Oh, yes, but you see Bilphism isn't a religion. It's the science of all religions.' She smiled defiantly at him. This was the *bon mot* of her belief. There was something in the arrangement of words which grasped her mind so definitely that the statement became superior to any obligation to define itself. It is not unlikely that she would have accepted any idea encased in this radiant formula – which was perhaps not a formula; it was the *reductio ad absurdum* of all formulas.

Then eventually, but gorgeously, would come Dick's turn.

'You've heard of the new poetry movement. You haven't? Well, it's a lot of young poets that are breaking away from the old forms and doing a lot of good. Well, what I was going to say was that my book is going to start a new prose movement, a sort of renaissance.'

'I'm sure it will,' beamed Mrs Gilbert. 'I'm *sure* it will. I went to Jenny Martin last Tuesday, the palmist, you know, that everyone's *mad* about. I told her my nephew was engaged upon a work and she said she knew I'd be glad to hear that his success would be *extraordinary*. But she'd never seen you or known anything about you – not even your *name*.'

Having made the proper noises to express his amazement at this astounding phenomenon, Dick waved her theme by him as though he were an arbitrary traffic policeman, and, so to speak, beckoned forward his own traffic.

'I'm absorbed, Aunt Catherine,' he assured her, 'I really am. All my friends are joshing me – oh, I see the humour in it and I don't care. I think a person ought to be able to take joshing. But I've got a sort of conviction,' he concluded gloomily.

'You're an ancient soul, I always say.'

'Maybe I am.' Dick had reached the stage where he no longer fought, but submitted. He *must* be an ancient soul, he fancied grotesquely; so old as to be absolutely rotten. However, the reiteration of the phrase still somewhat embarrassed him and sent uncomfortable shivers up his back. He changed the subject.

'Where is my distinguished cousin Gloria?'

'She's on the go somewhere, with someone.'

Dick paused, considered, and then, screwing up his face into what was evidently begun as a smile but ended as a terrifying frown, delivered a comment.

'I think my friend Anthony Patch is in love with her.'

Mrs Gilbert started, beamed half a second too late, and breathed her 'Really?' in the tone of a detective-play whisper.

'I *think* so,' corrected Dick gravely. 'She's the first girl I've ever seen him with, so much.'

'Well, of course,' said Mrs Gilbert with meticulous carelessness, 'Gloria never makes me her confidante. She's very secretive. Between you and me' – she bent forward cautiously, obviously determined that only heaven and her nephew should share her confession – 'between you and me, I'd like to see her settle down.'

Dick arose and paced the floor earnestly, a small, active, already rotund young man, his hands thrust unnaturally into his bulging pockets.

'I'm not claiming I'm right, mind you,' he assured the infinitely-of-the-hotel steel-engraving which smirked respectably back at him. 'I'm saying nothing that I'd want Gloria to know. But I think Mad Anthony is interested – tremendously so. He talks about her constantly. In anyone else that'd be a bad sign.'

'Gloria is a very young soul – ' began Mrs Gilbert eagerly, but her nephew interrupted with a hurried sentence: 'Gloria'd be a very young nut not to marry him.' He stopped and faced her, his expression a battle map of lines and dimples, squeezed and strained to its ultimate show of intensity – this as if to make up by his sincerity for any indiscretion in his words. 'Gloria's a wild one, Aunt Catherine. She's uncontrollable. How she's done it I don't know, but lately she's picked up a lot of the funniest friends. She doesn't seem to care. And the men she used to go with around New York were – ' He paused for breath.

'Yes-yes-yes,' interjected Mrs Gilbert, with an anaemic attempt to hide the immense interest with which she listened.

'Well,' continued Richard Caramel gravely, 'there it is. I mean that the men she went with and the people she went with used to be first rate. Now they aren't.'

Mrs Gilbert blinked very fast – her bosom trembled, inflated, remained so for an instant, and with the exhalation her words flowed out in a torrent.

She knew, she cried in a whisper; oh, yes, mothers see these things. But what could she do? He knew Gloria. He'd seen enough of Gloria to know how hopeless it was to try to deal with her. Gloria had been so spoiled – in a rather complete and unusual way. She had been suckled until she was three, for instance, when she could probably have chewed sticks. Perhaps – one never knew – it was this that had given that health and *hardiness* to her whole personality. And then ever since she was twelve years old she'd had boys about her so thick – oh, so thick one couldn't *move*. At sixteen she began going to dances at preparatory schools, and then came the colleges; and everywhere she went, boys, boys, boys. At first, oh, until she was eighteen there had been so many that it never seemed one any more than the others, but then she began to single them out.

She knew there had been a string of affairs spread over about three years, perhaps a dozen of them altogether. Sometimes the men were undergraduates, sometimes just out of college – they lasted on an average of several months each, with short attractions in between. Once or twice they had endured longer and her mother had hoped she would be engaged, but always a new one came – a new one –

The men? Oh, she made them miserable, literally! There was only one who had kept any sort of dignity, and he had been a mere child, young Carter Kirby, of Kansas City, who was so conceited anyway that he just sailed out on his vanity one afternoon and left for Europe next day with his father. The others had been – wretched. They never seemed to know when she was tired of them, and Gloria had seldom been deliberately unkind. They would keep phoning, writing letters to her, trying to see her, making long trips after her around the country. Some of them had confided in Mrs Gilbert, told her with tears in their eyes that they would never get over Gloria . . . at least two of them had since married, though . . . But Gloria, it seemed, struck to kill – to this day Mr Carstairs called up once a week, and sent her flowers which she no longer bothered to refuse.

Several times, twice, at least, Mrs Gilbert knew it had gone as far as a private engagement – with Tudor Baird and that Holcome boy at Pasadena. She was sure it had, because – this must go no further – she had come in unexpectedly and found Gloria acting, well, very much engaged indeed. She had not spoken to her daughter, of course. She had had a certain sense of delicacy and, besides, each time she had expected an announcement in a few weeks. But the announcement never came; instead, a new man came.

Scenes! Young men walking up and down the library like caged tigers! Young men glaring at each other in the hall as one came and the other left! Young men calling up on the telephone and being hung up upon in desperation! Young men threatening South America! . . . Young men writing the most pathetic letters! (She said nothing to this effect, but Dick fancied that Mrs Gilbert's eyes had seen some of these letters.)

. . . And Gloria, between tears and laughter, sorry, glad, out of love and in love, miserable, nervous, cool, amidst a great returning of presents, substitution of pictures in immemorial frames, and taking of hot baths and beginning again – with the next.

That state of things continued, assumed an air of permanency. Nothing harmed Gloria or changed her or moved her. And then out of a clear sky one day she informed her mother that undergraduates wearied her. She was absolutely going to no more college dances.

This had begun the change – not so much in her actual habits, for she danced, and had as many 'dates' as ever – but they were dates in a different spirit. Previously it had been a sort of pride, a matter of her own vainglory. She had been, probably, the most celebrated and sought-after young beauty in the country. Gloria Gilbert of Kansas City! She had fed on it ruthlessly – enjoying the crowds around her, the manner in which the most desirable men singled her out; enjoying the fierce jealousy of other girls; enjoying the fabulous, not to say scandalous, and, her mother was glad to say, entirely unfounded rumours about her – for instance, that she had gone in the Yale swimming-pool one night in a chiffon evening dress.

And from loving it with a vanity that was almost masculine – it had been in the nature of a triumphant and dazzling career – she became suddenly anaesthetic to it. She retired. She who had dominated countless parties, who had blown fragrantly through many ballrooms to the tender tribute of many eyes, seemed to care no longer. He who fell in love with her now was dismissed utterly, almost angrily. She went listlessly with the most indifferent men. She continually broke engagements, not as in the past from a cool assurance that she was irreproachable, that the man she insulted would return like a domestic animal – but indifferently, without contempt or pride. She rarely stormed at men any more – she yawned at them. She seemed – and it was so strange – she seemed to her mother to be growing cold.

Richard Caramel listened. At first he had remained standing, but as his aunt's discourse waxed in content – it stands here pruned by half, of all side references to the youth of Gloria's soul and to Mrs Gilbert's own mental distresses – he drew a chair up and attended rigorously as she floated, between tears and plaintive helplessness, down the long story of Gloria's life. When she came to the tale of this last year, a tale of the ends of cigarettes left all over New York in little trays marked 'Midnight Frolic' and 'Justine Johnson's Little Club', he began nodding his head slowly, then faster and faster, until, as she finished on a staccato note, it was bobbing briskly up and down, absurdly like a doll's wired head, expressing – almost anything.

In a sense Gloria's past was an old story to him. He had followed it with the eyes of a journalist, for he was going to write a book about her someday. But his interests, just at present, were family interests. He wanted to know, in particular, who was this Joseph Bloeckman that he had seen her with several times; and those two girls she was with constantly, 'this' Rachael Jerryl and 'this' Miss Kane – surely Miss Kane wasn't exactly the sort one would associate with Gloria!

But the moment had passed. Mrs Gilbert having climbed the hill of exposition was about to glide swiftly down the ski-jump of collapse. Her eyes were like a blue sky seen through two round, red window-casements. The flesh about her mouth was trembling.

And at that moment the door opened, admitting into the room Gloria and the two young ladies lately mentioned.

TWO YOUNG WOMEN

'Well!'

'How do you do, Mrs Gilbert!'

Miss Kane and Miss Jerryl are presented to Mr Richard Caramel. 'This is Dick' (laughter).

'I've heard so much about you,' says Miss Kane between a giggle and a shout.

'How do you do,' says Miss Jerryl shyly.

Richard Caramel tries to move about as if his figure were better. He is torn between his innate cordiality and the fact that he considers these girls rather common – not at all the Farmover type.

Gloria has disappeared into the bedroom.

'Do sit down,' beams Mrs Gilbert, who is by now quite herself. 'Take off your things.' Dick is afraid she will make some remark about the age of his soul, but he forgets his qualms in completing a conscientious, novelist's examination of the two young women.

Muriel Kane had originated in a rising family of East Orange. She was short rather than small, and hovered audaciously between plumpness and width. Her hair was black and elaborately arranged. This, in conjunction with her handsome, rather bovine eyes, and her over-red lips, combined to make her resemble Theda Bara, the prominent motion-picture actress. People told her constantly that she was a 'vampire', and she believed them. She suspected hopefully that they were afraid of her, and she did her utmost under all circumstances to give the impression of danger. An imaginative man could see the red flag that she constantly carried, waving it wildly, beseechingly – and, alas, to little spectacular avail. She was also tremendously timely: she knew the latest songs, all the latest songs – when one of them was played on the phonograph she would rise to her feet and rock her shoulders back and forth and snap her fingers, and if there was no music she would accompany herself by humming.

Her conversation was also timely: 'I don't care,' she would say, 'I should worry and lose my figure' – and again: 'I can't make my feet behave when I hear that tune. Oh, baby!'

Her fingernails were too long and ornate, polished to a pink and unnatural fever. Her clothes were too tight, too stylish, too vivid, her eyes too roguish, her smile too coy. She was almost pitifully over-emphasised from head to foot.

The other girl was obviously a more subtle personality. She was an exquisitely dressed Jewess with dark hair and a lovely milky pallor. She seemed shy and vague, and these two qualities accentuated a rather delicate charm that floated about her. Her family were 'Episcopalians', owned three smart women's shops along Fifth Avenue, and lived in a magnificent apartment on Riverside Drive. It seemed to Dick, after a few moments, that she was attempting to imitate Gloria – he wondered that people invariably chose inimitable people to imitate.

'We had the most *hectic* time!' Muriel was exclaiming enthusiastically. 'There was a crazy woman behind us on the bus. She was absitively, posolutely *nutty*! She kept talking to herself about something she'd like to do to somebody or something. I was *pet*rified, but Gloria simply *wouldn't* get off.'

Mrs Gilbert opened her mouth, properly awed.

'Really?'

'Oh, she was crazy. But we should worry, she didn't hurt us. Ugly! Gracious! The man across from us said her face ought to be on a night-nurse in a home for the blind, and we all *howled*, naturally, so the man tried to pick us up.'

Presently Gloria emerged from her bedroom and in unison every eye turned on her. The two girls receded into a shadowy background, unperceived, unmissed.

'We've been talking about you,' said Dick quickly, ' – your mother and I.'

'Well,' said Gloria.

A pause – Muriel turned to Dick.

'You're a great writer, aren't you?'

'I'm a writer,' he confessed sheepishly.

'I always say,' said Muriel earnestly, 'that if I ever had time to write down all my experiences it'd make a wonderful book.'

Rachael giggled sympathetically; Richard Caramel's bow was almost stately. Muriel continued: 'But I don't see how you can sit down and do it. And poetry! Lordy, I can't make two lines rhyme. Well, I should worry!'

Richard Caramel with difficulty restrained a shout of laughter. Gloria was chewing an amazing gum-drop and staring moodily out the window. Mrs Gilbert cleared her throat and beamed.

'But you see,' she said in a sort of universal exposition, 'you're not an ancient soul – like Richard.'

The Ancient Soul breathed a gasp of relief – it was out at last.

Then as if she had been considering it for five minutes, Gloria made a sudden announcement: 'I'm going to give a party.'

'Oh, can I come?' cried Muriel with facetious daring.

'A dinner. Seven people: Muriel and Rachael and I, and you, Dick, and Anthony, and that man named Noble – I liked him – and Bloeckman.'

Muriel and Rachael went into soft and purring ecstasies of enthusiasm. Mrs Gilbert blinked and beamed. With an air of casualness Dick broke in with a question: 'Who is this fellow Bloeckman, Gloria?'

Scenting a faint hostility, Gloria turned to him.

'Joseph Bloeckman? He's the moving-picture man. Vice-president of Films Par Excellence. He and father do a lot of business.'

'Oh!'

'Well, will you all come?'

They would all come. A date was arranged within the week. Dick rose, adjusted hat, coat and muffler, and gave out a general smile.

'Bye-bye,' said Muriel, waving her hand gaily, 'call me up sometime.'

Richard Caramel blushed for her.

DEPLORABLE END OF THE CHEVALIER O'KEEFE

It was Monday and Anthony took Geraldine Burke to luncheon at the Beaux Arts – afterwards they went up to his apartment and he wheeled out the little rolling-table that held his supply of liquor, selecting vermouth, gin and absinthe for a proper stimulant.

Geraldine Burke, usher at Keith's, had been an amusement of several months. She demanded so little that he liked her, for since a lamentable affair with a débutante the preceding summer, when he had discovered that after half a dozen kisses a proposal was expected, he had been wary of girls of his own class. It was only too easy to turn a critical eye on their imperfections – some physical harshness or a general lack of personal delicacy – but a girl who was usher at Keith's was approached with a different attitude. One could tolerate qualities in an intimate valet that would be unforgivable in a mere acquaintance on one's social level.

Geraldine, curled up at the foot of the lounge, considered him with narrow slanting eyes.

'You drink all the time, don't you?' she said suddenly.

'Why, I suppose so,' replied Anthony in some surprise. 'Don't you?'

'Nope. I go on parties sometimes – you know, about once a week, but I only take two or three drinks. You and your friends keep on drinking all the time. I should think you'd ruin your health.'

Anthony was somewhat touched.

'Why, aren't you sweet to worry about me!'

'Well, I do.'

'I don't drink so very much,' he declared. 'Last month I didn't touch a drop for three weeks. And I only get really tight about once a week.'

'But you have something to drink every day and you're only twenty-five. Haven't you any ambition? Think what you'll be at forty?'

'I sincerely trust that I won't live that long.'

She clicked her teeth with her tongue.

'You cra-azy!' she said as he mixed another cocktail – and then: 'Are you any relation to Adam Patch?'

'Yes, he's my grandfather.'

'Really?' She was obviously thrilled.

'Absolutely.'

'That's funny. My daddy used to work for him.'

'He's a queer old man.'

'Is he nice?' she demanded.

'Well, in private life he's seldom unnecessarily disagreeable.'

'Tell us about him.'

'Why,' Anthony considered ' – he's all shrunken up and he's got the remains of some grey hair that always looks as though the wind were in it. He's very moral.'

'He's done a lot of good,' said Geraldine with intense gravity.

'Rot!' scoffed Anthony. 'He's a pious ass – a chicken-brain.'

Her mind left the subject and flitted on.

'Why don't you live with him?'

'Why don't I board in a Methodist parsonage?'

'You cra-azy!'

Again she made a little clicking sound to express disapproval. Anthony thought how moral was this little waif at heart – how completely moral she would still be after the inevitable wave came that would wash her off the sands of respectability.

'Do you hate him?'

'I wonder. I never liked him. You never like people who do things for you.'

'Does he hate you?'

'My dear Geraldine,' protested Anthony, frowning humorously, 'do have another cocktail. I annoy him. If I smoke a cigarette he comes into the room sniffing. He's a prig, a bore and something of a hypocrite. I probably wouldn't be telling you this if I hadn't had a few drinks, but I don't suppose it matters.'

Geraldine was persistently interested. She held her glass, untasted, between finger and thumb and regarded him with eyes in which there was a touch of awe.

'How do you mean a hypocrite?'

'Well,' said Anthony impatiently, 'maybe he's not. But he doesn't like the things that I like, and so, as far as I'm concerned, he's uninteresting.'

'Hm.' Her curiosity seemed, at length, satisfied. She sank back into the sofa and sipped her cocktail.

'You're a funny one,' she commented thoughtfully. 'Does everybody want to marry you because your grandfather is rich?'

'They don't – but I shouldn't blame them if they did. Still, you see, I never intend to marry.'

She scorned this.

'You'll fall in love someday. Oh, you will – I know.' She nodded wisely.

'It'd be idiotic to be overconfident. That's what ruined the Chevalier O'Keefe.'

'Who was he?'

'A creature of my splendid mind. He's my one creation, the Chevalier.'

'Cra-a-azy!' she murmured pleasantly, using the clumsy rope-ladder with which she bridged all gaps and climbed after her mental superiors. Subconsciously she felt that it eliminated distances and brought the person whose imagination had eluded her back within range.

'Oh, no!' objected Anthony, 'oh, no, Geraldine. You mustn't play the alienist upon the Chevalier. If you feel yourself unable to understand him I won't bring him in. Besides, I should feel a certain uneasiness because of his regrettable reputation.'

'I guess I can understand anything that's got any sense to it,' answered Geraldine a bit testily.

'In that case there are various episodes in the life of the Chevalier which might prove diverting.'

'Well?'

'It was his untimely end that caused me to think of him and made him apropos in the conversation. I hate to introduce him end foremost, but it seems inevitable that the Chevalier must back into your life.'

'Well, what about him? Did he die?'

'He did! In this manner. He was an Irishman, Geraldine, a semi-fictional Irishman – the wild sort with a genteel brogue and "reddish hair". He was exiled from Erin in the late days of chivalry and, of course, crossed over to France. Now the Chevalier O'Keefe, Geraldine, had, like me, one weakness. He was enormously susceptible to all sorts and conditions of women. Besides being a sentimentalist he was a romantic, a vain fellow, a man of wild passions, a little blind in one eye and almost stone-blind in the other. Now a male roaming the world in this condition is as helpless as a lion without teeth, and in consequence the Chevalier was made utterly miserable for twenty years by a series of women who hated him, used him, bored him, aggravated him, sickened him, spent his money, made a fool of him – in brief, as the world has it, loved him.

'This was bad, Geraldine, and as the Chevalier, save for this one weakness, this exceeding susceptibility, was a man of penetration, he decided that he would rescue himself once and for all from these drains upon him. With this purpose he went to a very famous monastery in Champagne called – well, anachronistically known as St Voltaire's. It was the rule at St Voltaire's that no monk could descend to the ground storey of the monastery so long as he lived, but should exist engaged in prayer and contemplation in one of the four towers, which were called after the four commandments of the monastery rule: Poverty, Chastity, Obedience and Silence.

'When the day came that was to witness the Chevalier's farewell to the world he was utterly happy. He gave all his Greek books to his landlady, and his sword he sent in a golden sheath to the King of France, and all his mementos of Ireland he gave to the young Huguenot who sold fish in the street where he lived.

'Then he rode out to St Voltaire's, slew his horse at the door, and presented the carcass to the monastery cook.

'At five o'clock that night he felt, for the first time, free – for ever free from sex. No woman could enter the monastery; no monk could descend below the second storey. So as he climbed the winding stair that led to his cell at the very top of the Tower of Chastity he paused for a moment by an open window which looked down fifty feet on to a road below. It was all so beautiful, he thought, this world that he was leaving, the golden shower of sun beating down upon the long fields, the spray of trees in the distance, the vineyards, quiet and green, freshening wide miles before him. He leaned his elbows on the window casement and gazed at the winding road.

'Now, as it happened, Thérèse, a peasant girl of sixteen from a neighbouring village, was at that moment passing along this same road that ran in front of the monastery. Five minutes before, the little piece of ribbon which held up the stocking on her pretty left leg had worn through and broken. Being a girl of rare modesty she had thought to wait until she arrived home before repairing it, but it had bothered her to such an extent that she felt she could endure it no longer. So, as she passed the Tower of Chastity, she stopped and with a pretty gesture lifted her skirt – as little as possible, be it said to her credit – to adjust her garter.

'Up in the tower the newest arrival in the ancient monastery of St Voltaire, as though pulled forward by a gigantic and irresistible hand, leaned from the window. Farther he leaned and farther until suddenly one of the stones loosened under his weight, broke from its cement with a soft powdery sound – and, first headlong, then head over heels, finally in a vast and impressive revolution tumbled the Chevalier O'Keefe, bound for the hard earth and eternal damnation.

'Thèrése was so much upset by the occurrence that she ran all the way home and for ten years spent an hour a day in secret prayer for the soul of the monk whose neck and vows were simultaneously broken on that unfortunate Sunday afternoon.

'And the Chevalier O'Keefe, being suspected of suicide, was not buried in consecrated ground, but tumbled into a field near by, where he doubtless improved the quality of the soil for many years afterwards. Such was the untimely end of a very brave and gallant gentleman. What do you think, Geraldine?'

But Geraldine, lost long before, could only smile roguishly, wave her first finger at him, and repeat her bridge-all, her explain-all: 'Crazy!' she said, 'you cra-a-azy!'

His thin face was kindly, she thought, and his eyes quite gentle. She liked him because he was arrogant without being conceited, and because, unlike the men she met about the theatre, he had a horror of being conspicuous. What an odd, pointless story! But she had enjoyed the part about the stocking!

After the fifth cocktail he kissed her, and between laughter and bantering caresses and a half-stifled flare of passion they passed an hour. At four-thirty she claimed an engagement, and going into the bathroom she rearranged her hair. Refusing to let him order her a taxi she stood for a moment in the doorway.

'You *will* get married,' she was insisting, 'you wait and see.'

Anthony was playing with an ancient tennis ball, and he bounced it carefully on the floor several times before he answered with a soupçon of acidity: 'You're a little idiot, Geraldine.'

She smiled provokingly.

'Oh, I am, am I? Want to bet?'

'That'd be silly too.'

'Oh, it would, would it? Well, I'll just bet you'll marry somebody inside of a year.'

Anthony bounced the tennis ball very hard. This was one of his handsome days, she thought; a sort of intensity had displaced the melancholy in his dark eyes.

'Geraldine,' he said, at length, 'in the first place I have no one I want to marry; in the second place I haven't enough money to support two people; in the third place I am entirely opposed to marriage for people of my type; in the fourth place I have a strong distaste for even the abstract consideration of it.'

But Geraldine only narrowed her eyes knowingly, made her clicking sound, and said she must be going. It was late.

'Call me up soon,' she reminded him as he kissed her goodbye, 'you haven't for three weeks, you know.'

'I will,' he promised fervently.

He shut the door and coming back into the room stood for a moment lost in thought with the tennis ball still clasped in his hand. There was one of his lonelinesses coming, one of those times when he walked the streets or sat, aimless and depressed, biting a pencil at his desk. It was a self-absorption with no comfort, a demand for expression with no outlet, a sense of time rushing by, ceaselessly and wastefully – assuaged only by that conviction that there was nothing to waste, because all efforts and attainments were equally valueless.

He thought with emotion – aloud, ejaculative, for he was hurt and confused.

'No *idea* of getting married, by *God*!'

Of a sudden he hurled the tennis ball violently across the room, where it barely missed the lamp, and, rebounding here and there for a moment, lay still upon the floor.

SIGNLIGHT AND MOONLIGHT

For her dinner Gloria had taken a table in the Cascades at the Biltmore, and when the men met in the hall outside, a little after eight, 'that person Bloeckman' was the target of six masculine eyes. He was a stoutening, ruddy Jew of about thirty-five, with an expressive face under smooth sandy hair – and, no doubt, in most business gatherings his personality would have been considered ingratiating. He sauntered up to the three younger men, who stood in a group smoking as they waited for their hostess, and introduced himself with a little too evident assurance – nevertheless it is to be doubted whether he received the intended impression of faint and ironic chill: there was no hint of understanding in his manner.

'You related to Adam J. Patch?' he enquired of Anthony, emitting two slender strings of smoke from nostrils over-wide.

Anthony admitted it with the ghost of a smile.

'He's a fine man,' pronounced Bloeckman profoundly. 'He's a fine example of an American.'

'Yes,' agreed Anthony, 'he certainly is.'

– I detest these underdone men, he thought coldly. Boiled looking! Ought to be shoved back in the oven; just one more minute would do it.

Bloeckman squinted at his watch.

'Time these girls were showing up . . .'

– Anthony waited breathlessly; it came –

' . . . but then,' with a widening smile, 'you know how women are.'

The three young men nodded; Bloeckman looked casually about him, his eyes resting critically on the ceiling and then passing lower. His expression combined that of a Middle-Western farmer appraising his wheat crop and that of an actor wondering whether he is observed – the public manner of all good Americans. As he finished his survey he turned back quickly to the reticent trio, determined to strike to their very heart and core.

'You college men? . . . Harvard, eh. I see the Princeton boys beat you fellows in hockey.'

Unfortunate man. He had drawn another blank. They had been three years out and heeded only the big football games. Whether, after the failure of this sally, Mr Bloeckman would have perceived himself to be in a cynical atmosphere is problematical, for –

Gloria arrived. Muriel arrived. Rachael arrived. After a hurried, 'Hello, people!' uttered by Gloria and echoed by the other two, the three swept by into the dressing-room.

A moment later Muriel appeared in a state of elaborate undress and *crept* towards them. She was in her element: her ebony hair was slicked straight back on her head; her eyes were artificially darkened; she reeked of insistent perfume. She was got up to the best of her ability as a siren, more popularly a 'vamp' – a picker up and thrower away of men, an unscrupulous and fundamentally unmoved toyer with affections. Something in the exhaustiveness of her attempt fascinated Maury at first sight – a woman with wide hips affecting a panther-like litheness! As they waited the extra three minutes for Gloria, and, by polite assumption, for Rachael, he was unable to take his eyes from her. She would turn her head away, lowering her eyelashes and biting her nether lip in an amazing exhibition of coyness. She would rest her hands on her hips and sway from side to side in tune to the music, saying: 'Did you ever hear such perfect ragtime? I just can't make my shoulders behave when I hear that.'

Mr Bloeckman clapped his hands gallantly.

'You ought to be on the stage.'

'I'd like to be!' cried Muriel; 'will you back me?'

'I sure will.'

With becoming modesty Muriel ceased her motions and turned to Maury, asking what he had 'seen' this year. He interpreted this as referring to the dramatic world, and they had a gay and exhilarating exchange of titles, after this manner.

MURIEL: Have you seen *Peg o' My Heart*?

MAURY: No, I haven't.

MURIEL (*eagerly*): It's wonderful! You want to see it.

MAURY: Have you seen *Omar, the Tentmaker*?

MURIEL: No, but I hear it's wonderful. I'm very anxious to see it. Have you seen *Fair and Warmer*?

MAURY (*hopefully*): Yes.

MURIEL: I don't think it's very good. It's trashy.

MAURY (*faintly*): Yes, that's true.

MURIEL: But I went to *Within the Law* last night and I thought it was fine. Have you seen *The Little Café*? . . .

This continued until they ran out of plays. Dick, meanwhile, turned to Mr Bloeckman, determined to extract what gold he could from this unpromising load.

'I hear all the new novels are sold to the moving pictures as soon as they come out.'

'That's true. Of course the main thing in a moving picture is a strong story.'

'Yes, I suppose so.'

'So many novels are all full of talk and psychology. Of course those aren't as valuable to us. It's impossible to make much of that interesting on the screen.'

'You want plots first,' said Richard brilliantly.

'Of course. Plots first – ' He paused, shifted his gaze. His pause spread, included the others with all the authority of a warning finger. Gloria followed by Rachael was coming out of the dressing-room.

Among other things it developed during dinner that Joseph Bloeckman never danced, but spent the music time watching the others with the bored tolerance of an elder among children. He was a dignified man and a proud one. Born in Munich he had begun his American career as a peanut vender with a travelling circus. At eighteen he was a sideshow ballyhoo; later, the manager of the sideshow; and, soon after, the proprietor of a second-class vaudeville house. Just when the moving picture had passed out of the stage of a curiosity and become a promising industry he was an ambitious young man of twenty-six with some money to invest, nagging financial ambitions and a good working knowledge of the popular show business. That had been nine years before. The moving-picture industry had borne him up with it where it threw off dozens of men with more financial ability, more imagination and more practical ideas . . . and now he sat here and contemplated the immortal Gloria for whom young Stuart Holcome had gone from New York to Pasadena – watched her, and knew that presently she would cease dancing and come back to sit on his left hand.

He hoped she would hurry. The oysters had been standing some minutes.

Meanwhile Anthony, who had been placed on Gloria's left hand, was dancing with her, always in a certain fourth of the floor. This, had there been stags, would have been a delicate tribute to the girl, meaning, 'Damn you, don't cut in!' It was very consciously intimate.

'Well,' he began, looking down at her, 'you look mighty sweet tonight.'

She met his eyes over the horizontal half foot that separated them.

'Thank you – Anthony.'

'In fact you're uncomfortably beautiful,' he added. There was no smile this time.

'And you're very charming.'

'Isn't this nice?' he laughed. 'We actually approve of each other.'

'Don't you, usually?' She had caught quickly at his remark, as she always did at any unexplained allusion to herself, however faint.

He lowered his voice, and when he spoke there was in it no more than a wisp of badinage.

'Does a priest approve the Pope?'

'I don't know – but that's probably the vaguest compliment I ever received.'

'Perhaps I can muster a few bromides.'

'Well, I wouldn't have you strain yourself. Look at Muriel! Right here next to us.'

He glanced over his shoulder. Muriel was resting her brilliant cheek against the lapel of Maury Noble's dinner-coat and her powdered left arm was apparently twisted around his head. One was impelled to wonder why she failed to seize the nape of his neck with her hand. Her eyes, turned ceiling-ward, rolled largely back and forth; her hips swayed, and as she danced she kept up a constant low singing. This at first seemed to be a translation of the song into some foreign tongue but became eventually apparent as an attempt to fill out the metre of the song with the only words she knew – the words of the title –

He's a rag-picker,
A rag-picker;
A ragtime picking man,
Rag-picking, picking, pick, pick,
Rag-pick, pick, pick.

– and so on, into phrases still more strange and barbaric. When she caught the amused glances of Anthony and Gloria she acknowledged them only with a faint smile and a half-closing of her eyes, to indicate that the music entering into her soul had put her into an ecstatic and exceedingly seductive trance.

The music ended and they returned to their table, whose solitary but dignified occupant arose and tendered each of them a smile so ingratiating that it was as if he were shaking their hands and congratulating them on a brilliant performance.

'Blockhead never will dance! I think he has a wooden leg,' remarked Gloria to the table at large. The three young men started and the gentleman referred to winced perceptibly.

This was the one rough spot in the course of Bloeckman's acquaintance with Gloria. She relentlessly punned on his name. First it had been 'Blockhouse'. Lately, the more invidious 'Blockhead'. He had requested with a strong undertone of irony that she use his first name, and this she had done obediently several times – before slipping, helpless, repentant but dissolved in laughter, back into 'Blockhead'.

It was a very sad and thoughtless thing.

'I'm afraid Mr Bloeckman thinks we're a frivolous crowd,' sighed Muriel, waving a balanced oyster in his direction.

'He has that air,' murmured Rachael. Anthony tried to remember whether she had said anything before. He thought not. It was her initial remark.

Mr Bloeckman suddenly cleared his throat and said in a loud, distinct voice: 'On the contrary. When a man speaks he's merely tradition. He has at best a few thousand years back of him. But woman, why, she is the miraculous mouthpiece of posterity.'

In the stunned pause that followed this astounding remark, Anthony choked suddenly on an oyster and hurried his napkin to his face. Rachael and Muriel raised a mild if somewhat surprised laugh, in which Dick and Maury joined, both of them red in the face and restraining uproariousness with the most apparent difficulty.

' – My God!' thought Anthony. 'It's a subtitle from one of his movies. The man's memorised it!'

Gloria alone made no sound. She fixed Mr Bloeckman with a glance of silent reproach.

'Well, for the love of heaven! Where on earth did you dig that up?'

Bloeckman looked at her uncertainly, not sure of her intention. But in a moment he recovered his poise and assumed the bland and consciously tolerant smile of an intellectual among spoiled and callow youth.

The soup came up from the kitchen – but simultaneously the

orchestra leader came up from the bar, where he had absorbed the tone colour inherent in a seidel of beer. So the soup was left to cool during the delivery of a ballad entitled 'Everything's at Home Except Your Wife'.

Then the champagne – and the party assumed more amusing proportions. The men, except Richard Caramel, drank freely; Gloria and Muriel sipped a glass apiece; Rachael Jerryl took none. They sat out the waltzes but danced to everything else – all except Gloria, who seemed to tire after a while and preferred to sit smoking at the table, her eyes now lazy, now eager, according to whether she listened to Bloeckman or watched a pretty woman among the dancers. Several times Anthony wondered what Bloeckman was telling her. He was chewing a cigar back and forth in his mouth, and had expanded after dinner to the extent of violent gestures.

Ten o'clock found Gloria and Anthony beginning a dance. Just as they were out of earshot of the table she said in a low voice: 'Dance over by the door. I want to go down to the drugstore.'

Obediently Anthony guided her through the crowd in the designated direction; in the hall she left him for a moment, to reappear with a cloak over her arm.

'I want some gumdrops,' she said, humorously apologetic; 'you can't guess what for this time. It's just that I want to bite my fingernails, and I will if I don't get some gumdrops.' She sighed, and resumed as they stepped into the empty elevator: 'I've been biting 'em all day. A bit nervous, you see. Excuse the pun. It was unintentional – the words just arranged themselves. Gloria Gilbert, the female wag.'

Reaching the ground floor they naïvely avoided the hotel candy counter, descended the wide front staircase, and walking through several corridors found a drugstore in the Grand Central Station. After an intense examination of the perfume counter she made her purchase. Then on some mutual unmentioned impulse they strolled, arm in arm, not in the direction from which they had come, but out into Forty-Third Street.

The night was alive with thaw; it was so nearly warm that a breeze drifting low along the sidewalk brought to Anthony a vision of an unhoped-for hyacinthine spring. Above in the blue oblong of sky, around them in the caress of the drifting air, the illusion of a new season carried relief from the stiff and breathed-over atmosphere they had left, and for a hushed moment the traffic sounds and the murmur of water flowing in the gutters seemed an illusive and rarefied prolongation of that music to which they had lately danced. When Anthony spoke it was with surety that his words came from something breathless and desirous that the night had conceived in their two hearts.

'Let's take a taxi and ride around a bit!' he suggested, without looking at her.

Oh, Gloria, Gloria!

A cab yawned at the curb. As it moved off like a boat on a labyrinthine ocean and lost itself among the inchoate night masses of the great buildings, among the now stilled, now strident, cries and clangings, Anthony put his arm around the girl, drew her over to him and kissed her damp, childish mouth.

She was silent. She turned her face up to him, pale under the wisps and patches of light that trailed in like moonshine through foliage. Her eyes were gleaming ripples in the white lake of her face; the shadows of her hair bordered the brow with a persuasive unintimate dusk. No love was there, surely; nor the imprint of any love. Her beauty was cool as this damp breeze, as the moist softness of her own lips.

'You're such a swan in this light,' he whispered after a moment. There were silences as murmurous as sound. There were pauses that seemed about to shatter and were only to be snatched back to oblivion by the tightening of his arms about her and the sense that she was resting there as a caught, gossamer feather, drifted in out of the dark. Anthony laughed, noiselessly and exultantly, turning his face up and away from her, half in an overpowering rush of triumph, half lest her sight of him should spoil the splendid immobility of her expression. Such a kiss – it was a flower held against the face, never to be described, scarcely to be remembered; as though her beauty were giving off emanations of itself which settled transiently and already dissolving upon his heart.

. . . The buildings fell away in melted shadows; this was the Park now, and after a long while the great white ghost of the Metropolitan Museum moved majestically past, echoing sonorously to the rush of the cab.

'Why, Gloria! Why, Gloria!'

Her eyes appeared to regard him out of many thousand years: all emotion she might have felt, all words she might have uttered, would have seemed inadequate beside the adequacy of her silence, ineloquent against the eloquence of her beauty – and of her body, close to him, slender and cool.

'Tell him to turn around,' she murmured, 'and drive pretty fast going back . . . '

Up in the supper room the air was hot. The table, littered with napkins and ashtrays, was old and stale. It was between dances as they entered, and Muriel Kane looked up with roguishness extraordinary.

'Well, where have *you* been?'

'To call up mother,' answered Gloria coolly. 'I promised her I would. Did we miss a dance?'

Then followed an incident that though slight in itself Anthony had cause to reflect on many years afterwards. Joseph Bloeckman, leaning well back in his chair, fixed him with a peculiar glance, in which several emotions were curiously and inextricably mingled. He did not greet Gloria except by rising, and he immediately resumed a conversation with Richard Caramel about the influence of literature on the moving pictures.

MAGIC

The stark and unexpected miracle of a night fades out with the lingering death of the last stars and the premature birth of the first newsboys. The flame retreats to some remote and platonic fire; the white heat has gone from the iron and the glow from the coal.

Along the shelves of Anthony's library, filling a wall amply, crept a chill and insolent pencil of sunlight touching with frigid disapproval Thérèse of France and Ann the Superwoman, Jenny of the Orient Ballet and Zuleika the Conjurer – and Hoosier Cora – then down a shelf and into the years, resting pityingly on the over-invoked shades of Helen, Thaïs, Salome and Cleopatra.

Anthony, shaved and bathed, sat in his most deeply cushioned chair and watched it until at the steady rising of the sun it lay glinting for a moment on the silk ends of the rug – and went out.

It was ten o'clock. The *Sunday Times*, scattered about his feet, proclaimed by rotogravure and editorial, by social revelation and sporting sheet, that the world had been tremendously engrossed during the past week in the business of moving towards some splendid if somewhat indeterminate goal. For his part Anthony had been once to his grandfather's, twice to his broker's and three times to his tailor's – and in the last hour of the week's last day he had kissed a very beautiful and charming girl.

When he reached home his imagination had been teeming with high-pitched, unfamiliar dreams. There was suddenly no question on his mind, no eternal problem for a solution and resolution. He had experienced an emotion that was neither mental nor physical, nor merely a mixture of the two, and the love of life absorbed him for the present to the exclusion of all else. He was content to let the experiment remain isolated and unique. Almost impersonally he was convinced that no woman he had ever met compared in any way with Gloria. She was deeply herself; she was immeasurably sincere – of these things he was certain. Beside her the two dozen schoolgirls and débutantes, young married women and waifs and strays whom he had known were so many *females*, in the word's most contemptuous sense, breeders and bearers, exuding still that faintly odorous atmosphere of the cave and the nursery.

So far as he could see, she had neither submitted to any will of his nor caressed his vanity – except as her pleasure in his company was a caress. Indeed he had no reason for thinking she had given him aught that she did not give to others. This was as it should be. The idea of an entanglement growing out of the evening was as remote as it would have been repugnant. And she had disclaimed and buried the incident with a decisive untruth. Here were two young people with fancy enough to distinguish a game from its reality – who by the very casualness with which they met and passed on would proclaim themselves unharmed.

Having decided this he went to the phone and called up the Plaza Hotel.

Gloria was out. Her mother knew neither where she had gone nor when she would return.

It was somehow at this point that the first wrongness in the case asserted itself. There was an element of callousness, almost of indecency, in Gloria's absence from home. He suspected that by going out she had intrigued him into a disadvantage. Returning she would find his name, and smile. Most discreetly! He should have waited a few hours in order to drive home the utter inconsequence with which he regarded the incident. What an asinine blunder! She would think he considered himself particularly favoured. She would think he was reacting with the most inept intimacy to a quite trivial episode.

He remembered that during the previous month his janitor, to whom he had delivered a rather muddled lecture on the 'brother-hoo've man', had come up next day and, on the basis of what had happened the night before, seated himself in the window seat for a cordial and chatty half-hour. Anthony wondered in horror if Gloria would regard him as he had regarded that man. Him – Anthony Patch! Horror!

It never occurred to him that he was a passive thing, acted upon by an influence above and beyond Gloria, that he was merely the sensitive plate on which the photograph was made. Some gargantuan photographer had focused the camera on Gloria and *snap*! – the poor plate could but develop, confined like all things to its nature.

But Anthony, lying upon his couch and staring at the orange lamp, passed his thin fingers incessantly through his dark hair and made new symbols for the hours. She was in a shop now, it seemed, moving lithely among the velvets and the furs, her own dress making, as she walked, a debonair rustle in that world of silken rustles and cool soprano laughter and scents of many slain but living flowers. The Minnies and Pearls and Jewels and Jennies would gather round her like courtiers, bearing wispy frailties of georgette crêpe, delicate chiffon to echo her cheeks in faint pastel, milky lace to rest in pale disarray against her neck – damask was used but to cover priests and divans in these days, and cloth of Samarkand was remembered only by the romantic poets.

She would go elsewhere after a while, tilting her head a hundred ways under a hundred bonnets, seeking in vain for mock cherries to match her lips or plumes that were graceful as her own supple body.

Noon would come – she would hurry along Fifth Avenue, a Nordic Ganymede, her fur coat swinging fashionably with her steps, her cheeks redder by a stroke of the wind's brush, her breath a delightful mist upon the bracing air – and the doors of the Ritz would revolve, the crowd would divide, fifty masculine eyes would start, stare, as she gave back forgotten dreams to the husbands of many obese and comic women.

One o'clock. With her fork she would tantalise the heart of an adoring artichoke, while her escort served himself up in the thick, dripping sentences of an enraptured man.

Four o'clock: her little feet moving to melody, her face distinct in the crowd, her partner happy as a petted puppy and mad as the immemorial hatter . . . Then – then night would come drifting down and perhaps another damp. The signs would spill their light into the street. Who knew? No wiser than he, they haply sought to recapture that picture done in cream and shadow they had seen on the hushed Avenue the night before. And they might, ah, they might! A thousand taxis would yawn at a thousand corners, and only to him was that kiss for ever lost and done. In a thousand guises Thaïs would hail a cab and turn up her face for loving. And her pallor would be virginal and lovely, and her kiss chaste as the moon . . .

He sprang excitedly to his feet. How inappropriate that she should be out! He had realised at last what he wanted – to kiss her again, to find rest in her great immobility. She was the end of all restlessness, all malcontent.

Anthony dressed and went out, as he should have done long before, and down to Richard Caramel's room to hear the last revision of the last chapter of *The Demon Lover*. He did not call Gloria again until six. He did not find her in until eight and – oh, climax of anticlimaxes! – she could give him no engagement until Tuesday afternoon. A broken piece of gutta-percha clattered to the floor as he banged up the phone.

BLACK MAGIC

Tuesday was freezing cold. He called at a bleak two o'clock and as they shook hands he wondered confusedly whether he had ever kissed her; it was almost unbelievable – he seriously doubted if she remembered it.

'I called you four times on Sunday,' he told her.

'Did you?'

There was surprise in her voice and interest in her expression. Silently he cursed himself for having told her. He might have known her pride did not deal in such petty triumphs. Even then he had not guessed at the truth – that never having had to worry about men she had seldom used the wary subterfuges, the playings out and haulings in, that were the stock in trade of her sisterhood. When she liked a man, that was trick enough. Did she think she loved him – there was an ultimate and fatal thrust. Her charm endlessly preserved itself.

'I was anxious to see you,' he said simply. 'I want to talk to you – I mean really talk, somewhere where we can be alone. May I?'

'What do you mean?'

He swallowed a sudden lump of panic. He felt that she knew what he wanted.

'I mean, not at a tea-table,' he said.

'Well, all right, but not today. I want to get some exercise. Let's walk!'

It was bitter and raw. All the evil hate in the mad heart of February was wrought into the forlorn and icy wind that cut its way cruelly across Central Park and down along Fifth Avenue. It was almost impossible to talk, and discomfort made him distracted, so much so that he turned at Sixty-First Street to find that she was no longer beside him. He looked around. She was forty feet in the rear standing motionless, her face half hidden in her fur-coat collar, moved either by anger or laughter – he could not determine which. He started back.

'Don't let me interrupt your walk!' she called.

'I'm mighty sorry,' he answered in confusion. 'Did I go too fast?'

'I'm cold,' she announced. 'I want to go home. And you walk too fast.'

'I'm very sorry.'

Side by side they started for the Plaza. He wished he could see her face.

'Men don't usually get so absorbed in themselves when they're with me.'

'I'm sorry.'

'That's very interesting.'

'It *is* rather too cold to walk,' he said, briskly, to hide his annoyance.

She made no answer and he wondered if she would dismiss him at the hotel entrance. She walked in without speaking, however, and to the elevator, throwing him a single remark as she entered it: 'You'd better come up.'

He hesitated for the fraction of a moment.

'Perhaps I'd better call some other time.'

'Just as you say.' Her words were murmured as an aside. The main concern of life was the adjusting of some stray wisps of hair in the elevator mirror. Her cheeks were brilliant, her eyes sparkled – she had never seemed so lovely, so exquisitely to be desired.

Despising himself, he found that he was walking down the tenth-floor corridor a subservient foot behind her; was in the sitting-room while she disappeared to shed her furs. Something had gone wrong – in his own eyes he had lost a shred of dignity; in an unpremeditated yet significant encounter he had been completely defeated.

However, by the time she reappeared in the sitting-room he had explained himself to himself with sophistic satisfaction. After all he had done the strongest thing, he thought. He had wanted to come up, he had come. Yet what happened later on that afternoon must be traced to the indignity he had experienced in the elevator; the girl was worrying him intolerably, so much so that when she came out he involuntarily drifted into criticism.

'Who's this Bloeckman, Gloria?'

'A business friend of father's.'

'Odd sort of fellow!'

'He doesn't like you either,' she said with a sudden smile.

Anthony laughed.

'I'm flattered at his notice. He evidently considers me a –' He broke off with, 'Is he in love with you?'

'I don't know.'

'The deuce you don't,' he insisted. 'Of course he is. I remember the look he gave me when we got back to the table. He'd probably have had me quietly assaulted by a delegation of movie supes if you hadn't invented that phone call.'

'He didn't mind. I told him afterwards what really happened.'

'You told him!'

'He asked me.'

'I don't like that very well,' he remonstrated.

She laughed again.

'Oh, you don't?'

'What business is it of his?'

'None. That's why I told him.'

Anthony in a turmoil bit savagely at his mouth.

'Why should I lie?' she demanded directly. 'I'm not ashamed of anything I do. It happened to interest him to know that I kissed you, and I happened to be in a good humour, so I satisfied his curiosity by a simple and precise "yes". Being rather a sensible man, after his fashion, he dropped the subject.'

'Except to say that he hated me.'

'Oh, it worries you? Well, if you must probe this stupendous matter to its depths he didn't say he hated you. I simply know he does.'

'It doesn't wor –'

'Oh, let's drop it!' she cried spiritedly. 'It's a most uninteresting matter to me.'

With a tremendous effort Anthony made his acquiescence a twist of subject, and they drifted into an ancient question-and-answer game concerned with each other's pasts, gradually warming as they discovered the age-old, immemorial resemblances in tastes and ideas. They said things that were more revealing than they intended – but each pretended to accept the other at face, or rather word, value.

The growth of intimacy is like that. First one gives off his best picture, the bright and finished product mended with bluff and falsehood and humour. Then more details are required and one paints a second portrait, and a third – before long the best lines cancel out – and the secret is exposed at last; the planes of the pictures have intermingled and given us away, and though we paint and paint we can no longer sell a picture. We must be satisfied with hoping that such fatuous accounts of ourselves as we make to our wives and children and business associates are accepted as true.

'It seems to me,' Anthony was saying earnestly, 'that the position of a man with neither necessity nor ambition is unfortunate. Heaven knows it'd be pathetic of me to be sorry for myself – yet, sometimes I envy Dick.'

Her silence was encouragement. It was as near as she ever came to an intentional lure.

' – And there used to be dignified occupations for a gentleman who had leisure, things a little more constructive than filling up the landscape with smoke or juggling someone else's money. There's science, of course: sometimes I wish I'd taken a good foundation, say at Boston Tech. But now, by golly, I'd have to sit down for two years and struggle through the fundamentals of physics and chemistry.'

She yawned.

'I've told you I don't know what anybody ought to do,' she said ungraciously, and at her indifference his rancour was born again.

'Aren't you interested in anything except yourself?'

'Not much.'

He glared; his growing enjoyment in the conversation was ripped to shreds. She had been irritable and vindictive all day, and it seemed to him that for this moment he hated her hard selfishness. He stared morosely at the fire.

Then a strange thing happened. She turned to him and smiled, and as he saw her smile every rag of anger and hurt vanity dropped from him – as though his very moods were but the outer ripples of her own, as though emotion rose no longer in his breast unless she saw fit to pull an omnipotent controlling thread.

He moved closer and taking her hand pulled her ever so gently towards him until she half lay against his shoulder. She smiled up at him as he kissed her.

'Gloria,' he whispered very softly. Again she had made a magic, subtle and pervading as a spilt perfume, irresistible and sweet.

Afterwards, neither the next day nor after many years, could he remember the important things of that afternoon. Had she been moved? In his arms had she spoken a little – or at all? What measure of enjoyment had she taken in his kisses? And had she at any time lost herself ever so little?

Oh, for him there was no doubt. He had risen and paced the floor in sheer ecstasy. That such a girl should be; should poise curled in a corner of the couch like a swallow newly landed from a clean swift flight, watching him with inscrutable eyes. He would stop his pacing and, half shy each time at first, drop his arm around her and find her kiss.

She was fascinating, he told her. He had never met anyone like her before. He besought her jauntily but earnestly to send him away; he didn't want to fall in love. He wasn't coming to see her any more – already she had haunted too many of his ways.

What delicious romance! His true reaction was neither fear nor sorrow – only this deep delight in being with her that coloured the banality of his words and made the mawkish seem sad and the posturing seem wise. He *would* come back – eternally. He should have known!

'This is all. It's been very rare to have known you, very strange and wonderful. But this wouldn't do – and wouldn't last.' As he spoke there was in his heart that tremulousness that we take for sincerity in ourselves.

Afterwards he remembered one reply of hers to something he had asked her. He remembered it in this form – perhaps he had unconsciously arranged and polished it: 'A woman should be able to kiss a man beautifully and romantically without any desire to be either his wife or his mistress.'

As always when he was with her she seemed to grow gradually older until at the end ruminations too deep for words would be wintering in her eyes.

An hour passed, and the fire leaped up in little ecstasies as though its fading life was sweet. It was five now, and the clock over the mantel became articulate in sound. Then as if a brutish sensibility in him was reminded by those thin, tinny beats that the petals were falling from the flowered afternoon, Anthony pulled her quickly to her feet and held her helpless, without breath, in a kiss that was neither a game nor a tribute.

Her arms fell to her side. In an instant she was free.

'Don't!' she said quietly. 'I don't want that.'

She sat down on the far side of the lounge and gazed straight before her. A frown had gathered between her eyes. Anthony sank down beside her and closed his hand over hers. It was lifeless and unresponsive.

'Why, Gloria!' He made a motion as if to put his arm about her but she drew away.

'I don't want that,' she repeated.

'I'm very sorry,' he said, a little impatiently. 'I – I didn't know you made such fine distinctions.'

She did not answer.

'Won't you kiss me, Gloria?'

'I don't want to.' It seemed to him she had not moved for hours.

'A sudden change, isn't it?' Annoyance was growing in his voice.

'Is it?' She appeared uninterested. It was almost as though she were looking at someone else.

'Perhaps I'd better go.'

No reply. He rose and regarded her angrily, uncertainly. Again he sat down.

'Gloria, Gloria, won't you kiss me?'

'No.' Her lips, parting for the word, had just faintly stirred.

Again he got to his feet, this time with less decision, less confidence.

'Then I'll go.'

Silence.

'All right – I'll go.'

He was aware of a certain irremediable lack of originality in his remarks. Indeed he felt that the whole atmosphere had grown oppressive. He wished she would speak, rail at him, cry out upon him, anything but this pervasive and chilling silence. He cursed himself for a weak fool; his clearest desire was to move her, to hurt her, to see her wince. Helplessly, involuntarily, he erred again.

'If you're tired of kissing me I'd better go.'

He saw her lips curl slightly and his last dignity left him. She spoke, at length: 'I believe you've made that remark several times before.'

He looked about him immediately, saw his hat and coat on a chair – blundered into them, during an intolerable moment. Looking again at the couch he perceived that she had not turned, not even moved. With a shaken, immediately regretted 'goodbye' he went quickly but without dignity from the room.

For over a moment Gloria made no sound. Her lips were still curled; her glance was straight, proud, remote. Then her eyes blurred a little, and she murmured three words half aloud to the death-bound fire: 'Goodbye, you ass!' she said.

The man had had the hardest blow of his life. He knew at last what he wanted, but in finding it out it seemed that he had put it for ever beyond his grasp. He reached home in misery, dropped into an armchair without even removing his overcoat, and sat there for over an hour, his mind racing the paths of fruitless and wretched self-absorption. She had sent him away! That was the reiterated burden of his despair. Instead of seizing the girl and holding her by sheer strength until she became passive to his desire, instead of beating down her will by the force of his own, he had walked, defeated and powerless, from her door, with the corners of his mouth drooping and what force there might have been in his grief and rage hidden behind the manner of a whipped schoolboy. At one minute she had liked him tremendously – ah, she had nearly loved him. In the next he had become a thing of indifference to her, an insolent and efficiently humiliated man.

He had no great self-reproach – some, of course, but there were other things dominant in him now, far more urgent. He was not so much in love with Gloria as mad for her. Unless he could have her near him again, kiss her, hold her close and acquiescent, he wanted nothing more from life. By her three minutes of utter unwavering indifference the girl had lifted herself from a high but somehow casual position in his mind, to be instead his complete preoccupation. However much his wild thoughts varied between a passionate desire for her kisses and an equally passionate craving to hurt and mar her, the residue of his mind craved in finer fashion to possess the triumphant soul that had shone through those three minutes. She was beautiful – but especially she was without mercy. He must own that strength that could send him away.

At present no such analysis was possible to Anthony. His clarity of mind, all those endless resources which he thought his irony had brought him were swept aside. Not only for that night but for the days and weeks that followed his books were to be but furniture and his friends only people who lived and walked in a nebulous outer world from which he was trying to escape – that world was cold and full of bleak wind, and for a little while he had seen into a warm house where fires shone.

About midnight he began to realise that he was hungry. He went down into Fifty-Second Street, where it was so cold that he could scarcely see; the moisture froze on his lashes and in the corners of his lips. Everywhere dreariness had come down from the north, settling upon the thin and cheerless street, where black bundled figures blacker still against the night, moved stumbling along the sidewalk through the shrieking wind, sliding their feet cautiously ahead as though they were on skis. Anthony turned over towards Sixth Avenue, so absorbed in his thoughts as not to notice that several passers-by had stared at him. His overcoat was wide open, and the wind was biting in, hard and full of merciless death.

. . . After a while a waitress spoke to him, a fat waitress with black-rimmed eye-glasses from which dangled a long black cord.

'Order, please!'

Her voice, he considered, was unnecessarily loud. He looked up resentfully.

'You wanna order or doncha?'

'Of course,' he protested.

'Well, I ast you three times. This ain't no rest-room.'

He glanced at the big clock and discovered with a start that it was after two. He was down around Thirtieth Street somewhere, and after a moment he found and translated the

CHILD'S

in a white semicircle of letters upon the glass front. The place was inhabited sparsely by three or four bleak and half-frozen night-hawks.

'Give me some bacon and eggs and coffee, please.'

The waitress bent upon him a last disgusted glance and, looking ludicrously intellectual in her corded glasses, hurried away.

God! Gloria's kisses had been such flowers. He remembered as though it had been years ago the low freshness of her voice, the beautiful lines of her body shining through her clothes, her face lily-coloured under the lamps of the street – under the lamps.

Misery struck at him again, piling a sort of terror upon the ache and yearning. He had lost her. It was true – no denying it, no softening it. But a new idea had seared his sky – what of Bloeckman! What would happen now? There was a wealthy man, middle-aged enough to be tolerant with a beautiful wife, to baby her whims and indulge her unreason, to wear her as she perhaps wished to be worn – a bright flower in his buttonhole, safe and secure from the things she feared. He felt that she had been playing with the idea of marrying Bloeckman, and it was well possible that this disappointment in

Anthony might throw her on sudden impulse into Bloeckman's arms.

The idea drove him childishly frantic. He wanted to kill Bloeckman and make him suffer for his hideous presumption. He was saying this over and over to himself with his teeth tight shut, and a perfect orgy of hate and fright in his eyes.

But, behind this obscene jealousy, Anthony was in love at last, profoundly and truly in love, as the word goes between man and woman.

His coffee appeared at his elbow and gave off for a certain time a gradually diminishing wisp of steam. The night manager, seated at his desk, glanced at the motionless figure alone at the last table, and then with a sigh moved down upon him just as the hour hand crossed the figure three on the big clock.

WISDOM

After another day the turmoil subsided and Anthony began to exercise a measure of reason. He was in love – he cried it passionately to himself. The things that a week before would have seemed insuperable obstacles, his limited income, his desire to be irresponsible and independent, had in this forty hours become the merest chaff before the wind of his infatuation. If he did not marry her his life would be a feeble parody on his own adolescence. To be able to face people and to endure the constant reminder of Gloria that all existence had become, it was necessary for him to have hope. So he built hope desperately and tenaciously out of the stuff of his dream, a hope flimsy enough, to be sure, a hope that was cracked and dissipated a dozen times a day, a hope mothered by mockery, but, nevertheless, a hope that would be brawn and sinew to his self-respect.

Out of this developed a spark of wisdom, a true perception of his own from out the effortless past.

'Memory is short,' he thought.

So very short. At the crucial point the Trust President is on the stand, a potential criminal needing but one push to be a jailbird, scorned by the upright for leagues around. Let him be acquitted – and in a year all is forgotten. 'Yes, he did have some trouble once, just a technicality, I believe.' Oh, memory is very short!

Anthony had seen Gloria altogether about a dozen times, say two dozen hours. Supposing he left her alone for a month, made no attempt to see her or speak to her, and avoided every place where she might possibly be. Wasn't it possible, the more possible because she had never loved him, that at the end of that time the rush of events would efface his personality from her conscious mind, and with his personality his offence and humiliation? She would forget, for there would be other men. He winced. The implication struck out at him – other men. Two months – God! Better three weeks, two weeks –

He thought this the second evening after the catastrophe when he was undressing, and at this point he threw himself down on the bed and lay there, trembling very slightly and looking at the top of the canopy.

Two weeks – that was worse than no time at all. In two weeks he would approach her much as he would have to now, without personality or confidence – remaining still the man who had gone too far and then for a period that in time was but a moment but in fact an eternity, whined. No, two weeks was too short a time. Whatever poignancy there had been for her in that afternoon must have time to dull. He must give her a period when the incident should fade, and then a new period when she should gradually begin to think of him, no matter how dimly, with a true perspective that would remember his pleasantness as well as his humiliation.

He fixed, finally, on six weeks as approximately the interval best suited to his purpose, and on a desk calendar he marked the days off, finding that it would fall on the ninth of April. Very well, on that day he would phone and ask her if he might call. Until then – silence.

After his decision a gradual improvement was manifest. He had taken at least a step in the direction to which hope pointed, and he realised that the less he brooded upon her the better he would be able to give the desired impression when they met.

In another hour he fell into a deep sleep.

THE INTERVAL

Nevertheless, though, as the days passed, the glory of her hair dimmed perceptibly for him and in a year of separation might have departed completely, the six weeks held many abominable days. He dreaded the sight of Dick and Maury, imagining wildly that they knew all – but when the three met it was Richard Caramel and not Anthony who was the centre of attention; *The Demon Lover* had been accepted for immediate publication. Anthony felt that from now on he moved apart. He no longer craved the warmth and security of Maury's society which had cheered him no further back than November. Only Gloria could give that now and no one else ever again. So Dick's success rejoiced him only casually and worried him not a little. It meant that the world was going ahead – writing and reading and publishing – and living. And he wanted the world to wait motionless and breathless for six weeks – while Gloria forgot.

TWO ENCOUNTERS

His greatest satisfaction was in Geraldine's company. He took her once to dinner and the theatre and entertained her several times in his apartment. When he was with her she absorbed him, not as Gloria had, but quieting those erotic sensibilities in him that worried over Gloria. It didn't matter how he kissed Geraldine. A kiss was a kiss – to be enjoyed to the utmost for its short moment. To Geraldine things belonged in definite pigeon-holes: a kiss was one thing, anything further was quite another; a kiss was all right; the other things were 'bad'.

When half the interval was up two incidents occurred on successive days that upset his increasing calm and caused a temporary relapse.

The first was – he saw Gloria. It was a short meeting. Both bowed. Both spoke, yet neither heard the other. But when it was over Anthony read down a column of the *Sun* three times in succession without understanding a single sentence.

One would have thought Sixth Avenue a safe street! Having forsworn his barber at the Plaza he went around the corner one morning to be shaved, and while waiting his turn he took off coat and vest, and with his soft collar open at the neck stood near the front of the shop. The day was an oasis in the cold desert of March and the sidewalk was cheerful with a population of strolling sun-worshippers. A stout woman upholstered in velvet, her flabby cheeks too much massaged, swirled by with her poodle straining at its leash – the effect being given of a tug bringing in an ocean liner. Just behind them a man in a striped blue suit, walking slue-footed in white-spatted feet, grinned at the sight and catching Anthony's eye, winked through the glass. Anthony laughed, thrown immediately into that humour in which men and women were graceless and absurd phantasms, grotesquely curved and rounded in a rectangular world of their own building. They inspired the same sensations in him as did those strange and monstrous fish who inhabit the esoteric world of green in the aquarium.

Two more strollers caught his eye casually, a man and a girl – then in a horrified instant the girl resolved herself into Gloria. He stood there powerless; they came nearer and Gloria, glancing in, saw him. Her eyes widened and she smiled politely. Her lips moved. She was less than five feet away.

'How do you do?' he muttered inanely.

Gloria, happy, beautiful, and young – with a man he had never seen before!

It was then that the barber's chair was vacated and he read down the newspaper column three times in succession.

The second incident took place the next day. Going into the Manhattan bar about seven he was confronted with Bloeckman. As it happened, the room was nearly deserted, and before the mutual recognition he had stationed himself within a foot of the older man and ordered his drink, so it was inevitable that they should converse.

'Hello, Mr Patch,' said Bloeckman amiably enough.

Anthony took the proffered hand and exchanged a few aphorisms on the fluctuations of the mercury.

'Do you come in here much?' enquired Bloeckman.

'No, very seldom.' He omitted to add that the Plaza bar had, until lately, been his favourite.

'Nice bar. One of the best bars in town.'

Anthony nodded. Bloeckman emptied his glass and picked up his cane. He was in evening dress.

'Well, I'll be hurrying on. I'm going to dinner with Miss Gilbert.'

Death looked suddenly out at him from two blue eyes. Had he announced himself as his vis-à-vis's prospective murderer he could not have struck a more vital blow at Anthony. The younger man must have reddened visibly, for his every nerve was in instant clamour. With tremendous effort he mustered a rigid – oh, so rigid – smile, and said a conventional goodbye. But that night he lay awake until after four, half wild with grief and fear and abominable imaginings.

WEAKNESS

And one day in the fifth week he called her up. He had been sitting in his apartment trying to read *L'Éducation sentimentale*, and something in the book had sent his thoughts racing in the direction that, set free, they always took, like horses racing for a home stable. With suddenly quickened breath he walked to the telephone. When he gave the number it seemed to him that his voice faltered and broke like a schoolboy's. The Central must have heard the pounding of his heart. The sound of the receiver being taken up at the other end was a crack of doom, and Mrs Gilbert's voice, soft as maple syrup running into a glass container, had for him a quality of horror in its single 'Hello-o-ah?'

'Miss Gloria's not feeling well. She's lying down, asleep. Who shall I say called?'

'Nobody!' he shouted.

In a wild panic he slammed down the receiver; collapsed into his armchair in the cold sweat of breathless relief.

SERENADE

The first thing he said to her was: 'Why, you've bobbed your hair!' and she answered: 'Yes, isn't it gorgeous?'

It was not fashionable then. It was to be fashionable in five or six years. At that time it was considered extremely daring.

'It's all sunshine outdoors,' he said gravely. 'Don't you want to take a walk?'

She put on a light coat and a quaintly piquant Napoleon-hat of Alice-blue, and they walked along the Avenue and into the Zoo, where they properly admired the grandeur of the elephant and the collar-height of the giraffe, but did not visit the monkey house because Gloria said that monkeys smelt so bad.

Then they returned towards the Plaza, talking about nothing, but glad for the spring singing in the air and for the warm balm that lay upon the suddenly golden city. To their right was the Park, while at the left a great bulk of granite and marble muttered dully a millionaire's chaotic message to whosoever would listen: something about, 'I worked and I saved and I was sharper than all Adam and here I sit, by golly, by golly!'

All the newest and most beautiful designs in automobiles were out on Fifth Avenue, and ahead of them the Plaza loomed up rather unusually white and attractive. The supple, indolent Gloria walked a short shadow's length ahead of him, pouring out lazy casual comments that floated a moment on the dazzling air before they reached his ear.

'Oh!' she cried, 'I want to go south to Hot Springs! I want to get out in the air and just roll around on the new grass and forget there's ever been any winter.'

'Don't you, though!'

'I want to hear a million robins making a frightful racket. I sort of like birds.'

'All women *are* birds,' he ventured.

'What kind am I?' – quick and eager.

'A swallow, I think, and sometimes a bird of paradise. Most girls are sparrows, of course – see that row of nursemaids over there? They're sparrows – or are they magpies? And of course you've met canary girls – and robin girls.'

'And swan girls and parrot girls. All grown women are hawks, I think, or owls.'

'What am I – a buzzard?'

She laughed and shook her head.

'Oh, no, you're not a bird at all, do you think? You're a Russian wolfhound.'

Anthony remembered that they were white and always looked unnaturally hungry. But then they were usually photographed with dukes and princesses, so he was properly flattered.

'Dick's a fox terrier, a trick fox terrier,' she continued.

'And Maury's a cat.' Simultaneously it occurred to him how like Bloeckman was to a robust and offensive hog. But he preserved a discreet silence.

Later, as they parted, Anthony asked when he might see her again.

'Don't you ever make long engagements,' he pleaded, 'even if it's a week ahead? I think it'd be fun to spend a whole day together, morning and afternoon both.'

'It would be, wouldn't it?' She thought for a moment. 'Let's do it next Sunday.'

'All right. I'll map out a programme that'll take up every minute.'

He did. He even figured to a nicety what would happen in the two hours when she would come to his apartment for tea: how the good Bounds would have the windows wide to let in the fresh breeze – but a fire going also lest there be chill in the air – and how there would be clusters of flowers about in big cool bowls that he would buy for the occasion. They would sit on the lounge.

And when the day came they did sit upon the lounge. After a while Anthony kissed her because it came about quite naturally; he found sweetness sleeping still upon her lips, and felt that he had never been away. The fire was bright and the breeze sighing in through the curtains brought a mellow damp, promising May and a world of summer. His soul thrilled to remote harmonies; he heard the strum of far guitars and waters lapping on a warm Mediterranean shore – for he was young now as he would never be again, and more triumphant than death.

Six o'clock stole down too soon and rang the querulous melody of St Anne's chimes on the corner. Through the gathering dusk they strolled to the Avenue, where the crowds, like prisoners released, were walking with elastic step at last after the long winter, and the tops of the buses were thronged with congenial kings and the shops full of fine soft things for the summer, the rare summer, the gay promising summer that seemed for love what the winter was for money. Life was singing for his supper on the corner! Life was handing round cocktails in the street! Old women there were in that crowd who felt that they could have run and won a hundred-yard dash!

In bed that night with the lights out and the cool room swimming with moonlight, Anthony lay awake and played with every minute of the day like a child playing in turn with each one of a pile of long-wanted Christmas toys. He had told her gently, almost in the middle of a kiss, that he loved her, and she had smiled and held him closer and murmured, 'I'm glad,' looking into his eyes. There had been a new quality in her attitude, a new growth of sheer physical attraction towards him and a strange emotional tenseness that was enough to make him clench his hands and draw in his breath at the recollection. He had felt nearer to her than ever before. In a rare delight he cried aloud to the room that he loved her.

He phoned next morning – no hesitation now, no uncertainty – instead a delirious excitement that doubled and trebled when he heard her voice: 'Good-morning – Gloria.'

'Good-morning.'

'That's all I called you up to say – dear.'

'I'm glad you did.'

'I wish I could see you.'

'You will, tomorrow night.'

'That's a long time, isn't it?'

'Yes – ' Her voice was reluctant. His hand tightened on the receiver.

'Couldn't I come tonight?' He dared anything in the glory and revelation of that almost whispered 'yes'.

'I have a date.'

'Oh – '

'But I might – I might be able to break it.'

'Oh!' – a sheer cry, a rhapsody. 'Gloria?'

'What?'

'I love you.'

Another pause and then: 'I – I'm glad.'

Happiness, remarked Maury Noble one day, is only the first hour after the alleviation of some especially intense misery. But oh, Anthony's face as he walked down the tenth-floor corridor of the Plaza that night! His dark eyes were gleaming – around his mouth were lines it was a kindness to see. He was handsome then if never before, bound for one of those immortal moments which come so radiantly that their remembered light is enough to see by for years.

He knocked and, at a word, entered. Gloria, dressed in simple pink, starched and fresh as a flower, was across the room, standing very still, and looking at him wide-eyed.

As he closed the door behind him she gave a little cry and moved swiftly over the intervening space, her arms rising in a premature caress as she came near. Together they crushed out the stiff folds of her dress in one triumphant and enduring embrace.

BOOK TWO

Chapter 1

The Radiant Hour

After a fortnight Anthony and Gloria began to indulge in 'practical discussions', as they called those sessions when under the guise of severe realism they walked in an eternal moonlight.

'Not as much as I do you,' the critic of *belles-lettres* would insist. 'If you really loved me you'd want everyone to know it.'

'I do,' she protested; 'I want to stand on the street corner like a sandwich man, informing all the passers-by.'

'Then tell me all the reasons why you're going to marry me in June.'

'Well, because you're so clean. You're sort of blowy clean, like I am. There's two sorts, you know. One's like Dick: he's clean like polished pans. You and I are clean like streams and winds. I can tell whenever I see a person whether he is clean, and if so, which kind of clean he is.'

'We're twins.'

Ecstatic thought!

'Mother says' – she hesitated uncertainly – 'mother says that two souls are sometimes created together and – and in love before they're born.'

Bilphism gained its easiest convert . . . After a while he lifted up his head and laughed soundlessly towards the ceiling. When his eyes came back to her he saw that she was angry.

'Why did you laugh?' she cried, 'you've done that twice before. There's nothing funny about our relation to each other. I don't mind playing the fool, and I don't mind having you do it, but I can't stand it when we're together.'

'I'm sorry.'

'Oh, don't say you're sorry! If you can't think of anything better than that, just keep quiet!'

'I love you.'

'I don't care.'

There was a pause. Anthony was depressed . . . At length Gloria murmured: 'I'm sorry I was mean.'

'You weren't. I was the one.'

Peace was restored – the ensuing moments were so much more sweet and sharp and poignant. They were stars on this stage, each playing to an audience of two: the passion of their pretence created the actuality. Here, finally, was the quintessence of self-expression – yet it was probable that for the most part their love expressed Gloria rather than Anthony. He felt often like a scarcely tolerated guest at a party she was giving.

Telling Mrs Gilbert had been an embarrassed matter. She sat stuffed into a small chair and listened with an intense and very blinky sort of concentration. She must have known it – for three weeks Gloria had seen no one else – and she must have noticed that this time there was an authentic difference in her daughter's attitude. She had been given special deliveries to post; she had heeded, as all mothers seem to heed, the hither end of telephone conversations, disguised but still rather warm –

– Yet she had delicately professed surprise and declared herself immensely pleased; she doubtless was; so were the geranium plants blossoming in the window-boxes, and so were the cabbies when the lovers sought the romantic privacy of hansom cabs – quaint device – and the staid bills of fare on which they scribbled 'you know I do', pushing it over for the other to see.

But between kisses Anthony and this golden girl quarrelled incessantly.

'Now, Gloria,' he would cry, 'please let me explain!'

'Don't explain. Kiss me.'

'I don't think that's right. If I hurt your feelings we ought to discuss it. I don't like this kiss-and-forget.'

'But I don't want to argue. I think it's wonderful that we *can* kiss and forget, and when we can't it'll be time to argue.'

At one time some gossamer difference attained such bulk that Anthony arose and punched himself into his overcoat – for a moment it appeared that the scene of the preceding February was to be repeated, but knowing how deeply she was moved he retained his dignity with his pride, and in a moment Gloria was sobbing in his arms, her lovely face miserable as a frightened little girl's.

Meanwhile they kept unfolding to each other, unwillingly, by curious reactions and evasions, by distastes and prejudices and unintended hints of the past. The girl was proudly incapable of jealousy and, because he was extremely jealous, this virtue piqued him. He told her recondite incidents of his own life on purpose to arouse some spark of it, but to no avail. She possessed him now – nor did she desire the dead years.

'Oh, Anthony,' she would say, 'always when I'm mean to you I'm sorry afterwards. I'd give my right hand to save you one little moment's pain.'

And in that instant her eyes were brimming and she was not aware that she was voicing an illusion. Yet Anthony knew that there were days when they hurt each other purposely – taking almost a delight in the thrust. Incessantly she puzzled him: one hour so intimate and charming, striving desperately towards an unguessed, transcendent union; the next, silent and cold, apparently unmoved by any consideration of their love or anything he could say. Often he would eventually trace these portentous reticences to some physical discomfort – of these she never complained until they were over – or to some carelessness or presumption in him, or to an unsatisfactory dish at dinner, but even then the means by which she created the infinite distances she spread about herself were a mystery, buried somewhere back in those twenty-two years of unwavering pride.

'Why do you like Muriel?' he demanded one day.

'I don't very much.'

'Then why do you go with her?'

'Just for someone to go with. They're no exertion, those girls. They sort of believe everything I tell them – but I rather like Rachael. I think she's cute – and so clean and slick, don't you? I used to have other friends – in Kansas City and at school – casual, all of them, girls who just flitted into my range and out of it for no more reason than that boys took us places together. They didn't interest me after environment stopped throwing us together. Now they're mostly married. What does it matter – they were all just people.'

'You like men better, don't you?'

'Oh, much better. I've got a man's mind.'

'You've got a mind like mine. Not strongly gendered either way.'

Later she told him about the beginnings of her friendship with Bloeckman. One day in Delmonico's, Gloria and Rachael had come upon Bloeckman and Mr Gilbert having luncheon and curiosity had impelled her to make it a party of four. She had liked him – rather. He was a relief from younger men, satisfied as he was with so little. He humoured her and he laughed, whether he understood her or not. She met him several times, despite the open disapproval of her parents, and within a month he had asked her to marry him, tendering her everything from a villa in Italy to a brilliant career on the screen. She had laughed in his face – and he had laughed too.

But he had not given up. To the time of Anthony's arrival in the arena he had been making steady progress. She treated him rather well – except that she had called him always by an invidious nickname – perceiving, meanwhile, that he was figuratively following along beside her as she walked the fence, ready to catch her if she should fall.

The night before the engagement was announced she told Bloeckman. It was a heavy blow. She did not enlighten Anthony as to the details, but she implied that he had not hesitated to argue with her. Anthony gathered that the interview had terminated on a stormy note, with Gloria very cool and unmoved lying in her corner of the sofa and Joseph Bloeckman of 'Films Par Excellence' pacing the carpet with eyes narrowed and head bowed. Gloria had been sorry for him but she had judged it best not to show it. In a final burst of kindness she had tried to make him hate her, there at the last. But Anthony, understanding that Gloria's indifference was her strongest appeal, judged how futile this must have been. He wondered, often but quite casually, about Bloeckman – finally he forgot him entirely.

HEYDAY

One afternoon they found front seats on the sunny roof of a bus and rode for hours from the fading Square up along the sullied river, and then, as the stray beams fled the westward streets, sailed down the turgid Avenue, darkening with ominous bees from the department stores. The traffic was clotted and gripped in a patternless jam; the buses were packed four deep like platforms above the crowd as they waited for the moan of the traffic whistle.

'Isn't it good!' cried Gloria. 'Look!'

A miller's wagon, stark white with flour, driven by a powdery clown, passed in front of them behind a white horse and his black team-mate.

'What a pity!' she complained; 'they'd look so beautiful in the dusk if only both horses were white. I'm mighty happy just this minute, in this city.'

Anthony shook his head in disagreement.

'I think the city's a mountebank. Always struggling to approach the tremendous and impressive urbanity ascribed to it. Trying to be romantically metropolitan.'

'I don't. I think it is impressive.'

'Momentarily. But it's really a transparent, artificial sort of spectacle. It's got its press-agented stars and its flimsy, unenduring stage settings, and, I'll admit, the greatest army of supers ever assembled – ' He paused, laughed shortly, and added: 'Technically excellent, perhaps, but not convincing.'

'I'll bet policemen think people are fools,' said Gloria thoughtfully, as she watched a large but cowardly lady being helped across the street. 'He always sees them frightened and inefficient and old – they are,' she added. And then: 'We'd better get off. I told mother I'd have an early supper and go to bed. She says I look tired, damn it.'

'I wish we were married,' he muttered soberly; 'there'll be no good-night then and we can do just as we want.'

'Won't it be good! I think we ought to travel a lot. I want to go to the Mediterranean and Italy. And I'd like to go on the stage some time – say for about a year.'

'You bet. I'll write a play for you.'

'Won't that be good! And I'll act in it. And then sometime when we have more money' – old Adam's death was always thus tactfully alluded to – 'we'll build a magnificent estate, won't we?'

'Oh, yes, with private swimming pools.'

'Dozens of them. And private rivers. Oh, I wish it were now.'

Odd coincidence – he had just been wishing that very thing. They plunged like divers into the dark eddying crowd and emerging in the cool Fifties sauntered indolently homeward, infinitely romantic to each other . . . both were walking alone in a dispassionate garden with a ghost found in a dream.

Halcyon days like boats drifting along slow-moving rivers; spring evenings full of a plaintive melancholy that made the past beautiful and bitter, bidding them look back and see that the loves of other summers long gone were dead with the forgotten waltzes of their years. Always the most poignant moments were when some artificial barrier kept them apart: in the theatre their hands would steal together, join, give and return gentle pressures through the long dark; in crowded rooms they would form words with their lips for each other's eyes – not knowing that they were but following in the footsteps of dusty generations but comprehending dimly that if truth is the end of life, happiness is a mode of it, to be cherished in its brief and tremulous moment. And then, one fairy night, May became June. Sixteen days now – fifteen – fourteen –

THREE DIGRESSIONS

Just before the engagement was announced Anthony had gone up to Tarrytown to see his grandfather, who, a little more wizened and grizzly as time played its ultimate chuckling tricks, greeted the news with profound cynicism.

'Oh, you're going to get married, are you?' He said this with such a dubious mildness and shook his head up and down so many times that Anthony was not a little depressed. While he was unaware of his grandfather's intentions he presumed that a large part of the money would come to him. A good deal would go in charities, of course; a good deal to carry on the business of reform.

'Are you going to work?'

'Why – ' temporised Anthony, somewhat disconcerted. 'I *am* working. You know – '

'Ah, I mean work,' said Adam Patch dispassionately.

'I'm not quite sure yet what I'll do. I'm not exactly a beggar, grampa,' he asserted with some spirit.

The old man considered this with eyes half closed. Then almost apologetically he asked: 'How much do you save a year?'

'Nothing so far – '

'And so after just managing to get along on your money you've decided that by some miracle two of you can get along on it.'

'Gloria has some money of her own. Enough to buy clothes.'

'How much?'

Without considering this question impertinent, Anthony answered it. 'About a hundred a month.'

'That's altogether about seventy-five hundred a year.' Then he added softly: 'It ought to be plenty. If you have any sense it ought to be plenty. But the question is whether you have any or not.'

'I suppose it is.' It was shameful to be compelled to endure this pious browbeating from the old man, and his next words were stiffened with vanity. 'I can manage very well. You seem convinced that I'm utterly worthless. At any rate I came up here simply to tell you that I'm getting married in June. Goodbye, sir.' With this he turned away and headed for the door, unaware that in that instant his grandfather, for the first time, rather liked him.

'Wait!' called Adam Patch, 'I want to talk to you.'

Anthony faced about.

'Well, sir?'

'Sit down. Stay all night.'

Somewhat mollified, Anthony resumed his seat.

'I'm sorry, sir, but I'm going to see Gloria tonight.'

'What's her name?'

'Gloria Gilbert.'

'New York girl? Someone you know?'

'She's from the Middle West.'

'What business is her father in?'

'In a celluloid corporation or trust or something. They're from Kansas City.'

'You going to be married out there?'

'Why, no, sir. We thought we'd be married in New York – rather quietly.'

'Like to have the wedding out here?'

Anthony hesitated. The suggestion made no appeal to him, but it was certainly the part of wisdom to give the old man, if possible, a proprietary interest in his married life. In addition Anthony was a little touched.

'That's very kind of you, grampa, but wouldn't it be a lot of trouble?'

'Everything's a lot of trouble. Your father was married here – but in the old house.'

'Why – I thought he was married in Boston.'

Adam Patch considered.

'That's true. He *was* married in Boston.'

Anthony felt a moment's embarrassment at having made the correction, and he covered it up with words.

'Well, I'll speak to Gloria about it. Personally I'd like to, but of course it's up to the Gilberts, you see.'

His grandfather drew a long sigh, half closed his eyes, and sank back in his chair.

'In a hurry?' he asked in a different tone.

'Not especially.'

'I wonder,' began Adam Patch, looking out with a mild, kindly glance at the lilac bushes that rustled against the windows, 'I wonder if you ever think about the afterlife.'

'Why – sometimes.'

'I think a great deal about the afterlife.' His eyes were dim but his voice was confident and clear. 'I was sitting here today thinking about what's lying in wait for us, and somehow I began to remember an afternoon nearly sixty-five years ago, when I was playing with my little sister Annie, down where that summer-house is now.' He pointed out into the long flower-garden, his eyes trembling with tears, his voice shaking.

'I began thinking – and it seemed to me that *you* ought to think a little more about the afterlife. You ought to be – steadier' – he paused and seemed to grope about for the right word – 'more industrious – why – '

Then his expression altered, his entire personality seemed to snap together like a trap, and when he continued the softness had gone from his voice.

' – Why, when I was just two years older than you,' he rasped with a cunning chuckle, 'I sent three members of the firm of Wrenn and Hunt to the poorhouse.'

Anthony started with embarrassment.

'Well, goodbye,' added his grandfather suddenly, 'you'll miss your train.'

Anthony left the house unusually elated, and strangely sorry for the old man; not because his wealth could buy him 'neither youth nor digestion' but because he had asked Anthony to be married there, and because he had forgotten something about his son's wedding that he should have remembered.

Richard Caramel, who was one of the ushers, caused Anthony and Gloria much distress in the last few weeks by continually stealing the rays of their spotlight. *The Demon Lover* had been published in April, and it interrupted the love affair as it may be said to have interrupted everything its author came in contact with. It was a highly original, rather over-written piece of sustained description concerned with a Don Juan of the New York slums. As Maury and Anthony had said before, as the more hospitable critics were saying then, there was no writer in America with such power to describe the atavistic and unsubtle reactions of that section of society.

The book hesitated and then suddenly 'went'. Editions, small at first, then larger, crowded each other week by week. A spokesman of the Salvation Army denounced it as a cynical misrepresentation of all the uplift taking place in the underworld. Clever press-agenting spread the unfounded rumour that 'Gypsy' Smith was beginning a libel suit because one of the principal characters was a burlesque of himself. It was barred from the public library of Burlington, Iowa, and a Mid-western columnist announced by innuendo that Richard Caramel was in a sanatorium with delirium tremens.

The author, indeed, spent his days in a state of pleasant madness. The book was in his conversation three-fourths of the time – he wanted to know if one had heard 'the latest'; he would go into a store and in a loud voice order books to be charged to him, in order to catch a chance morsel of recognition from clerk or customer. He knew to a town in what sections of the country it was selling best; he knew exactly what he cleared on each edition, and when he met anyone who had not read it, or, as it happened only too often, had not heard of it, he succumbed to moody depression.

So it was natural for Anthony and Gloria to decide, in their jealousy, that he was so swollen with conceit as to be a bore. To Dick's great annoyance Gloria publicly boasted that she had never read *The Demon Lover*, and didn't intend to until everyone stopped talking about it. As a matter of fact, she had no time to read now, for the presents were pouring in – first a scattering, then an avalanche, varying from the bric-à-brac of forgotten family friends to the photographs of forgotten poor relations.

Maury gave them an elaborate 'drinking set', which included silver goblets, cocktail shaker and bottle-openers. The extortion from Dick was more conventional – a tea-set from Tiffany's. From Joseph Bloeckman came a simple and exquisite travelling clock, with his card. There was even a cigarette-holder from Bounds; this touched Anthony and made him want to weep – indeed, any emotion short of hysteria seemed natural in the half-dozen people who were swept up by this tremendous sacrifice to convention. The room set aside in the Plaza bulged with offerings sent by Harvard friends and by associates of his grandfather, with remembrances of Gloria's Farmover days, and with rather pathetic trophies from her former beaux, which last arrived with esoteric, melancholy messages, written on cards tucked carefully inside, beginning 'I little thought when – ' or 'I'm sure I wish you all the happiness – ' or even 'When you get this I shall be on my way to – '

The most munificent gift was simultaneously the most disappointing. It was a concession of Adam Patch's – a check for five thousand dollars.

To most of the presents Anthony was cold. It seemed to him that they would necessitate keeping a chart of the marital status of all their acquaintances during the next half-century. But Gloria exulted in each one, tearing at the tissue-paper and excelsior with the rapaciousness of a dog digging for a bone, breathlessly seizing a ribbon or an edge of metal and finally bringing to light the whole article and holding it up critically, no emotion except rapt interest in her unsmiling face.

'Look, Anthony!'

'Darn nice, isn't it!'

No answer until an hour later when she would give him a careful account of her precise reaction to the gift, whether it would have been improved by being smaller or larger, whether she was surprised at getting it, and, if so, just how much surprised.

Mrs Gilbert arranged and rearranged a hypothetical house, distributing the gifts among the different rooms, tabulating articles as 'second-best clock' or 'silver to use *every* day', and embarrassing Anthony and Gloria by semi-facetious references to a room she called the nursery. She was pleased by old Adam's gift and thereafter had it that he was a very ancient soul, 'as much as anything else'. As Adam Patch never quite decided whether she referred to the advancing senility of his mind or to some private and psychic schema of her own, it cannot be said to have pleased him. Indeed he always spoke of her to Anthony as 'that old woman, the mother', as though she were a character in a comedy he had seen staged many times before. Concerning Gloria he was unable to make up his mind. She attracted him but, as she herself told Anthony, he had decided that she was frivolous and was afraid to approve of her.

Five days! – A dancing platform was being erected on the lawn at Tarrytown. Four days! – A special train was chartered to convey the guests to and from New York. Three days! –

THE DIARY

She was dressed in blue silk pyjamas and standing by her bed with her hand on the light to put the room in darkness, when she changed her mind and opening a table drawer brought out a little black book – a 'line-a-day' diary. This she had kept for seven years. Many of the pencil entries were almost illegible and there were notes and references to nights and afternoons long since forgotten, for it was not an intimate diary, even though it began with the immemorial, 'I am going to keep a diary for my children.' Yet as she thumbed over the pages the eyes of many men seemed to look out at her from their half-obliterated names. With one she had gone to New Haven for the first time – in 1908, when she was sixteen and padded shoulders were fashionable at Yale – she had been flattered because 'Touchdown' Michaud had 'rushed' her all evening. She sighed, remembering the grown-up satin dress she had been so proud of and the orchestra playing 'Yama-Yama, My Yama

Man' and 'Jungle-Town'. So long ago! – the names: Eltynge Reardon, Jim Parsons, 'Curly' McGregor, Kenneth Cowan, 'Fish-Eye' Fry (whom she had liked for being so ugly), Carter Kirby – he had sent her a present; so had Tudor Baird; – Marty Reffer, the first man she had been in love with for more than a day, and Stuart Holcome, who had run away with her in his automobile and tried to make her marry him by force. And Larry Fenwick, whom she had always admired because he had told her one night that if she wouldn't kiss him she could get out of his car and walk home. What a list!

. . . And, after all, an obsolete list. She was in love now, set for the eternal romance that was to be the synthesis of all romance, yet sad for these men and these moonlights and for the 'thrills' she had had – and the kisses. The past – her past, oh, what a joy! She had been exuberantly happy.

Turning over the pages her eyes rested idly on the scattered entries of the past four months. She read the last few carefully.

April 1st – I know Bill Carstairs hates me because I was so disagreeable, but I hate to be sentimentalised over sometimes. We drove out to the Rockyear Country Club and the most wonderful moon kept shining through the trees. My silver dress is getting tarnished. Funny how one forgets the other nights at Rockyear – with Kenneth Cowan when I loved him so!

April 3rd – After two hours of Schroeder who, they inform me, has millions, I've decided that this matter of sticking to things wears one out, particularly when the things concerned are men. There's nothing so often overdone and from today I swear to be amused. We talked about 'love' – how banal! With how many men have I talked about love?

April 11th – Patch actually called up today! and when he forswore me about a month ago he fairly raged out the door. I'm gradually losing faith in any man being susceptible to fatal injuries.

April 20th – Spent the day with Anthony. Maybe I'll marry him sometime. I kind of like his ideas – he stimulates all the originality in me. Blockhead came around about ten in his new car and took me out to Riverside Drive. I liked him tonight: he's so considerate. He knew I didn't want to talk so he was quiet all during the ride.

April 21st – Woke up thinking of Anthony and sure enough he called and sounded sweet on the phone – so I broke a date for him. Today I feel I'd break anything for him, including the ten commandments and my neck. He's coming at eight and I shall wear pink and look very fresh and starched –

She paused here, remembering that after he had gone that night she had undressed with the shivering April air streaming in the windows. Yet it seemed she had not felt the cold, warmed by the profound banalities burning in her heart.

The next entry occurred a few days later:

April 24th – I want to marry Anthony, because husbands are so often 'husbands' and I must marry a lover.

There are four general types of husbands.

(1) The husband who always wants to stay in in the evening, has no vices and works for a salary. Totally undesirable!
(2) The atavistic master whose mistress one is, to wait on his pleasure. This sort always considers every pretty woman 'shallow', a sort of peacock with arrested development.
(3) Next comes the worshipper, the idolater of his wife and all that is his, to the utter oblivion of everything else. This sort demands an emotional actress for a wife. God! it must be an exertion to be thought righteous.
(4) And Anthony – a temporarily passionate lover with wisdom enough to realise when it has flown and that it must fly. And I want to get married to Anthony.

What grubworms women are to crawl on their bellies through colourless marriages! Marriage was created not to be a background but to need one. Mine is going to be outstanding. It can't, shan't be the setting – it's going to be the performance, the live, lovely, glamorous performance, and the world shall be the scenery. I refuse to dedicate my life to posterity. Surely one owes as much to the current generation as to one's unwanted children. What a fate – to grow rotund and unseemly, to lose my self-love, to think in terms of milk, oatmeal, nurse, diapers . . . Dear dream children, how much more beautiful you are, dazzling little creatures who flutter (all dream children must flutter) on golden, golden wings –

Such children, however, poor dear babies, have little in common with the wedded state.

June 7th – Moral question: Was it wrong to make Bloeckman love me? Because I did really make him. He was almost sweetly sad tonight. How opportune it was that my throat is swollen plunk together and tears were easy to muster. But he's just the past – buried already in my plentiful lavender.

June 8th – And today I've promised not to chew my mouth. Well, I won't, I suppose – but if he'd only asked me not to eat!

Blowing bubbles – that's what we're doing, Anthony and me. And we blew such beautiful ones today, and they'll explode and then we'll blow more and more, I guess – bubbles just as big and just as beautiful, until all the soap and water is used up.

On this note the diary ended. Her eyes wandered up the page, over the June 8ths of 1912, 1910, 1907. The earliest entry was scrawled in the plump, bulbous hand of a sixteen-year-old girl – it was the name, Bob Lamar, and a word she could not decipher. Then she knew what it was – and, knowing, she found her eyes misty with tears. There in a greying blur was the record of her first kiss, faded as its intimate afternoon, on a rainy veranda seven years before. She seemed to remember something one of them had said that day and yet she could not remember. Her tears came faster, until she could scarcely see the page. She was crying, she told herself, because she could remember only the rain and the wet flowers in the yard and the smell of the damp grass.

. . . After a moment she found a pencil and holding it unsteadily drew three parallel lines beneath the last entry. Then she printed FINIS in large capitals, put the book back in the drawer, and crept into bed.

BREATH OF THE CAVE

Back in his apartment after the bridal dinner, Anthony snapped out his lights and, feeling impersonal and fragile as a piece of china waiting on a serving-table, got into bed. It was a warm night – a sheet was enough for comfort – and through his wide-open windows came sound, evanescent and summery, alive with remote anticipation. He was thinking that the young years behind him, hollow and colourful, had been lived in facile and vacillating cynicism upon the recorded emotions of men long dust. And there was something beyond that; he knew now. There was the union of his soul with Gloria's, whose radiant fire and freshness was the living material of which the dead beauty of books was made.

From the night into his high-walled room there came, persistently, that evanescent and dissolving sound – something the city was tossing up and calling back again, like a child playing with a ball. In Harlem, the Bronx, Gramercy Park and along the waterfronts, in little parlours or on pebble-strewn, moon-flooded roofs, a thousand lovers were making this sound, crying little fragments of it into the air. All the city was playing with this sound out there in the blue summer dark, throwing it up and calling it back, promising that, in a little while, life would be beautiful as a story, promising happiness – and by that promise giving it. It gave love hope in its own survival. It could do no more.

It was then that a new note separated itself jarringly from the soft crying of the night. It was a noise from an area-way within a hundred feet from his rear window, the noise of a woman's laughter. It began low, incessant and whining – some servant-maid with her fellow, he thought – and then it grew in volume and became hysterical, until it reminded him of a girl he had seen overcome with nervous laughter at a vaudeville performance. Then it sank, receded, only to rise again and include words – a coarse joke, some bit of obscure horseplay he could not distinguish. It would break off for a moment and he would just catch the low rumble of a man's voice, then begin again – interminably; at first annoying, then strangely terrible. He shivered, and getting up out of bed went to the window. It had reached a high point, tensed and stifled, almost the quality of a scream – then it ceased and left behind it a silence empty and menacing as the greater silence overhead. Anthony stood by the window a moment longer before he returned to his bed. He found himself upset and shaken. Try as he might to strangle his reaction, some animal quality in that unrestrained laughter had grasped at his imagination, and for the first time in four months aroused his old aversion and horror towards all the business of life. The room had grown smothery. He wanted to be out in some cool and bitter breeze, miles above the cities, and to live serene and detached back in the corners of his mind. Life was that sound out there, that ghastly reiterated female sound.

'Oh, my *God*!' he cried, drawing in his breath sharply.

Burying his face in the pillows he tried in vain to concentrate upon the details of the next day.

MORNING

In the grey light he found that it was only five o'clock. He regretted nervously that he had awakened so early – he would appear fagged at the wedding. He envied Gloria who could hide her fatigue with careful pigmentation.

In his bathroom he contemplated himself in the mirror and saw that he was unusually white – half a dozen small imperfections stood out against the morning pallor of his complexion, and overnight he had grown the faint stubble of a beard – the general effect, he fancied, was unprepossessing, haggard, half unwell.

On his dressing-table were spread a number of articles which he told over carefully with suddenly fumbling fingers – their tickets to California, the book of traveller's checks, his watch, set to the half-minute, the key to his apartment, which he must not forget to give to Maury, and, most important of all, the ring. It was of platinum set around with small emeralds; Gloria had insisted on this; she had always wanted an emerald wedding ring, she said.

It was the third present he had given her; first had come the engagement ring, and then a little gold cigarette-case. He would be giving her many things now – clothes and jewels and friends and excitement. It seemed absurd that from now on he would pay for all her meals. It was going to cost: he wondered if he had not underestimated for this trip, and if he had not better cash a larger cheque. The question worried him.

Then the breathless impendency of the event swept his mind clear of details. This was the day – unsought, unsuspected six months before, but now breaking in yellow light through his east window, dancing along the carpet as though the sun were smiling at some ancient and reiterated gag of his own.

Anthony laughed in a nervous one-syllable snort.

'By God!' he muttered to himself, 'I'm as good as married!'

THE USHERS

Six young men in CROSS PATCH*'s library growing more and more cheery under the influence of Mumm's Extra Dry, set surreptitiously in cold pails by the bookcases.*

THE FIRST YOUNG MAN: By golly! Believe me, in my next book I'm going to do a wedding scene that'll knock 'em cold!

THE SECOND YOUNG MAN: Met a débutante th'other day said she thought your book was powerful. As a rule young girls cry for this primitive business.

THE THIRD YOUNG MAN: Where's Anthony?

THE FOURTH YOUNG MAN: Walking up and down outside talking to himself.

SECOND YOUNG MAN: Lord! Did you see the minister? Most peculiar looking teeth.

FIFTH YOUNG MAN: Think they're natural. Funny thing people having gold teeth.

SIXTH YOUNG MAN: They say they love 'em. My dentist told me once a woman came to him and insisted on having two of her teeth covered with gold. No reason at all. All right the way they were.

FOURTH YOUNG MAN: Hear you got out a book, Dicky. 'Gratulations!

DICK (*stiffly*): Thanks.

FOURTH YOUNG MAN (*innocently*): What is it? College stories?

DICK (*more stiffly*): No. Not college stories.

FOURTH YOUNG MAN: Pity! Hasn't been a good book about Harvard for years.

DICK (*touchily*): Why don't you supply the lack?

THIRD YOUNG MAN: I think I saw a squad of guests turn the drive in a Packard just now.

SIXTH YOUNG MAN: Might open a couple more bottles on the strength of that.

THIRD YOUNG MAN: It was the shock of my life when I heard the old man was going to have a wet wedding. Rabid Prohibitionist, you know.

FOURTH YOUNG MAN (*snapping his fingers excitedly*): By gad! I knew I'd forgotten something. Kept thinking it was my vest.

DICK: What was it?

FOURTH YOUNG MAN: By gad! By gad!

SIXTH YOUNG MAN: Here! Here! Why the tragedy?

SECOND YOUNG MAN: What'd you forget? The way home?

DICK (*maliciously*): He forgot the plot for his book of Harvard stories.

FOURTH YOUNG MAN: No, sir, I forgot the present, by George! I forgot to buy old Anthony a present. I kept putting it off and putting it off, and by gad I've forgotten it! What'll they think?

SIXTH YOUNG MAN (*facetiously*): That's probably what's been holding up the wedding.

(THE FOURTH YOUNG MAN *looks nervously at his watch. Laughter.*)

FOURTH YOUNG MAN: By gad! What an ass I am!

SECOND YOUNG MAN: What d'you make of the bridesmaid who thinks she's Nora Bayes? Kept telling me she wished this was a ragtime wedding. Name's Haines or Hampton.

DICK (*hurriedly spurring his imagination*): Kane, you mean, Muriel Kane. She's a sort of debt of honour, I believe. Once saved Gloria from drowning, or something of the sort.

SECOND YOUNG MAN: I didn't think she could stop that perpetual swaying long enough to swim. Fill up my glass, will you? Old man and I had a long talk about the weather just now.

MAURY: Who? Old Adam?

SECOND YOUNG MAN: No, the bride's father. He must be with a weather bureau.

DICK: He's my uncle, Otis.

OTIS: Well, it's an honourable profession. (*Laughter*.)

SIXTH YOUNG MAN: Bride your cousin, isn't she?

DICK: Yes, Cable, she is.

CABLE: She certainly is a beauty. Not like you, Dicky. Bet she brings old Anthony to terms.

MAURY: Why are all grooms given the title of 'old'? I think marriage is an error of youth.

DICK: Maury, the professional cynic.

MAURY: Why, you intellectual faker!

FIFTH YOUNG MAN: Battle of the highbrows here, Otis. Pick up what crumbs you can.

DICK: Faker yourself! What do *you* know?

MAURY: What do *you* know?

DICK: Ask me anything. Any branch of knowledge.

MAURY: All right. What's the fundamental principle of biology?

DICK: You don't know yourself.

MAURY: Don't hedge!

DICK: Well, natural selection?

MAURY: Wrong.

DICK: I give it up.

MAURY: Ontogeny recapitulates phyllogeny.

FIFTH YOUNG MAN: Take your base!

MAURY: Ask you another. What's the influence of mice on the clover crop? (*Laughter*.)

FOURTH YOUNG MAN: What's the influence of rats on the Decalogue?

MAURY: Shut up, you saphead. There *is* a connection.

DICK: What is it then?

MAURY (*pausing a moment in growing disconcertion*): Why, let's see. I seem to have forgotten exactly. Something about the bees eating the clover.

FOURTH YOUNG MAN: And the clover eating the mice! Haw! Haw!

MAURY (*frowning*): Let me just think a minute.

DICK (*sitting up suddenly*): Listen!

(*A volley of chatter explodes in the adjoining room. The six young men arise, feeling at their neckties.*)

DICK (*weightily*): We'd better join the firing squad. They're going to take the picture, I guess. No, that's afterwards.

OTIS: Cable, you take the ragtime bridesmaid.

FOURTH YOUNG MAN: I wish to God I'd sent that present.

MAURY: If you'll give me another minute I'll think of that about the mice.

OTIS: I was usher last month for old Charlie McIntyre and –

(*They move slowly towards the door as the chatter becomes a babel and the practising preliminary to the overture issues in long pious groans from* ADAM PATCH*'s organ.*)

ANTHONY

There were five hundred eyes boring through the back of his cutaway and the sun glinting on the clergyman's inappropriately bourgeois teeth. With difficulty he restrained a laugh. Gloria was saying something in a clear proud voice and he tried to think that the affair was irrevocable, that every second was significant, that his life was being slashed into two periods and that the face of the world was changing before him. He tried to recapture that ecstatic sensation of ten weeks before. All these emotions eluded him, he did not even feel the physical nervousness of that very morning – it was all one gigantic aftermath. And those gold teeth! He wondered if the clergyman were married; he wondered perversely if a clergyman could perform his own marriage service . . .

But as he took Gloria into his arms he was conscious of a strong reaction. The blood was moving in his veins now. A languorous and pleasant content settled like a weight upon him, bringing responsibility and possession. He was married.

GLORIA

So many, such mingled emotions, that no one of them was separable from the others! She could have wept for her mother, who was crying quietly back there ten feet, and for the loveliness of the June sunlight flooding in at the windows. She was beyond all conscious perceptions. Only a sense, coloured with delirious wild excitement, that the ultimately important was happening – and a trust, fierce and passionate, burning in her like a prayer, that in a moment she would be for ever and securely safe.

Late one night they arrived in Santa Barbara, where the night clerk at the Hotel Lafcadio refused to admit them, on the grounds that they were not married.

The clerk thought that Gloria was beautiful. He did not think that anything so beautiful as Gloria could be moral.

'CON AMORE'

That first half-year – the trip West, the long months' loiter along the California coast and the grey house near Greenwich where they lived until late autumn made the country dreary – those days, those places, saw the enraptured hours. The breathless idyl of their engagement gave way, first, to the intense romance of the more passionate relationship. The breathless idyl left them, fled on to other lovers; they looked around one day and it was gone, how they scarcely knew. Had either of them lost the other in the days of the idyl, the love lost would have been ever to the loser that dim desire without fulfilment which stands back of all life. But magic must hurry on, and the lovers remain . . .

The idyl passed, bearing with it its extortion of youth. Came a day when Gloria found that other men no longer bored her; came a day when Anthony discovered that he could sit again late into the evening, talking with Dick of those tremendous abstractions that had once occupied his world. But, knowing they had had the best of love, they clung to what remained. Love lingered – by way of long conversations at night into those stark hours when the mind thins and sharpens and the borrowings from dreams become the stuff of all life, by way of deep and intimate kindnesses they developed towards each other, by way of their laughing at the same absurdities and thinking the same things noble and the same things sad.

It was, first of all, a time of discovery. The things they found in each other were so diverse, so intermixed and, moreover, so sugared with love as to seem at the time not so much discoveries as isolated phenomena – to be allowed for, and to be forgotten. Anthony found that he was living with a girl of tremendous nervous tension and of the most high-handed selfishness. Gloria knew within a month that her husband was an utter coward towards any one of a million phantasms created by his imagination. Her perception was intermittent, for this cowardice sprang out, became almost obscenely evident, then faded and vanished as though it had been only a creation of her own mind. Her reactions to it were not those attributed to her sex – it roused her neither to disgust nor to a premature feeling of motherhood. Herself almost completely without physical fear, she was unable to understand, and so she made the most of what she felt to be his fear's redeeming feature, which was that though he was a coward under a shock and a coward under a strain – when his imagination was given play – he had yet a sort of dashing recklessness that moved her on its brief occasions almost to admiration, and a pride that usually steadied him when he thought he was observed.

The trait first showed itself in a dozen incidents of little more than nervousness – his warning to a taxi-driver against fast driving, in Chicago; his refusal to take her to a certain tough café she had always wished to visit; these of course admitted the conventional interpretation – that it was of her he had been thinking; nevertheless, their cumulative weight disturbed her. But something that occurred in a San Francisco hotel, when they had been married a week, gave the matter certainty.

It was after midnight and pitch dark in their room. Gloria was dozing off and Anthony's even breathing beside her made her suppose that he was asleep, when suddenly she saw him raise himself on his elbow and stare at the window.

'What is it, dearest?' she murmured.

'Nothing' – he had relaxed to his pillow and turned towards her – 'nothing, my darling wife.'

'Don't say "wife". I'm your mistress. Wife's such an ugly word. Your "permanent mistress" is so much more tangible and desirable . . . Come into my arms,' she added in a rush of tenderness; 'I can sleep so well, so well with you in my arms.'

Coming into Gloria's arms had a quite definite meaning. It required that he should slide one arm under her shoulder, lock both arms about her, and arrange himself as nearly as possible as a sort of three-sided crib for her luxurious ease. Anthony, who tossed, whose arms went tinglingly to sleep after half an hour of that position, would wait until she was asleep and roll her gently over to her side of the bed – then, left to his own devices, he would curl himself into his usual knots.

Gloria, having attained sentimental comfort, retired into her doze. Five minutes ticked away on Bloeckman's travelling clock; silence lay all about the room, over the unfamiliar, impersonal furniture and the half-oppressive ceiling that melted imperceptibly into invisible walls on both sides. Then there was suddenly a rattling flutter at the window, staccato and loud upon the hushed, pent air.

With a leap Anthony was out of the bed and standing tense beside it.

'Who's there?' he cried in an awful voice.

Gloria lay very still, wide awake now and engrossed not so much in the rattling as in the rigid breathless figure whose voice had reached from the bedside into that ominous dark.

The sound stopped; the room was quiet as before – then Anthony pouring words in at the telephone.

'Someone just tried to get into the room! . . . There's someone at the window!' His voice was emphatic now, faintly terrified. 'All right! Hurry!' He hung up the receiver; stood motionless.

. . . There was a rush and commotion at the door, a knocking – Anthony went to open it upon an excited night clerk with three bell-boys grouped staring behind him. Between thumb and finger the night clerk held a wet pen with the threat of a weapon; one of the bellboys had seized a telephone directory and was looking at it sheepishly. Simultaneously the group was joined by the hastily summoned house-detective, and as one man they surged into the room.

Lights sprang on with a click. Gathering a piece of sheet about her Gloria dived away from sight, shutting her eyes to keep out the horror of this unpremeditated visitation. There was no vestige of an idea in her stricken sensibilities save that her Anthony was at grievous fault.

. . . The night clerk was speaking from the window, his tone half of the servant, half of the teacher reproving a schoolboy.

'Nobody out there,' he declared conclusively; 'my golly, nobody *could* be out there. This here's a sheer fall to the street of fifty feet. It was the wind you heard, tugging at the blind.'

'Oh.'

Then she was sorry for him. She wanted only to comfort him and draw him back tenderly into her arms, to tell them to go away because the thing their presence connotated was odious. Yet she could not raise her head for shame. She heard a broken sentence, apologies, conventions of the employee and one unrestrained snicker from a bellboy.

'I've been nervous as the devil all evening,' Anthony was saying; 'somehow that noise just shook me – I was only about half awake.'

'Sure, I understand,' said the night clerk with comfortable tact; 'been that way myself.'

The door closed; the lights snapped out; Anthony crossed the floor quietly and crept into bed. Gloria, feigning to be heavy with sleep, gave a quiet little sigh and slipped into his arms.

'What was it, dear?'

'Nothing,' he answered, his voice still shaken; 'I thought there was somebody at the window, so I looked out, but I couldn't see anyone and the noise kept up, so I phoned downstairs. Sorry if I disturbed you, but I'm awfully darn nervous tonight.'

Catching the lie, she gave an interior start – he had not gone to the window, nor near the window. He had stood by the bed and then sent in his call of fear.

'Oh,' she said – and then: 'I'm so sleepy.'

For an hour they lay awake side by side, Gloria with her eyes shut so tight that blue moons formed and revolved against backgrounds of deepest mauve, Anthony staring blindly into the darkness overhead.

After many weeks it came gradually out into the light, to be laughed and joked at. They made a tradition to fit over it – whenever that overpowering terror of the night attacked Anthony, she would put her arms about him and croon, soft as a song: 'I'll protect my Anthony. Oh, nobody's ever going to harm my Anthony!'

He would laugh as though it were a jest they played for their mutual amusement, but to Gloria it was never quite a jest. It was, at first, a keen disappointment; later, it was one of the times when she controlled her temper.

The management of Gloria's temper, whether it was aroused by a lack of hot water for her bath or by a skirmish with her husband, became almost the primary duty of Anthony's day. It must be done just so – by this much silence, by that much pressure, by this much yielding, by that much force. It was in her angers with their attendant cruelties that her inordinate egotism chiefly displayed itself. Because she was brave, because she was 'spoiled', because of her outrageous and commendable independence of judgement, and finally because of her arrogant consciousness that she had never seen a girl as beautiful as herself, Gloria had developed into a consistent, practising Nietzschean. This, of course, with overtones of profound sentiment.

There was, for example, her stomach. She was used to certain dishes, and she had a strong conviction that she could not possibly eat anything else. There must be a lemonade and a tomato sandwich late in the morning, then a light lunch with a stuffed tomato. Not only did she require food from a selection of a dozen dishes, but in addition this food must be prepared in just a certain way. One of the most annoying half-hours of the first fortnight occurred in Los Angeles, when an unhappy waiter brought her a tomato stuffed with chicken salad instead of celery.

'We always serve it that way, madame,' he quavered to the grey eyes that regarded him wrathfully.

Gloria made no answer, but when the waiter had turned discreetly away she banged both fists upon the table until the china and silver rattled.

'Poor Gloria!' laughed Anthony unwittingly, 'you can't get what you want ever, can you?'

'I can't eat *stuff*!' she flared up.

'I'll call back the waiter.'

'I don't want you to! He doesn't know anything, the darn *fool*!'

'Well, it isn't the hotel's fault. Either send it back, forget it, or be a sport and eat it.'

'Shut up!' she said succinctly.

'Why take it out on me?'

'Oh, I'm *not*,' she wailed, 'but I simply *can't* eat it.'

Anthony subsided helplessly.

'We'll go somewhere else,' he suggested.

'I don't *want* to go anywhere else. I'm tired of being trotted around to a dozen cafés and not getting one thing fit to eat.'

'When did we go around to a dozen cafés?'

'You'd *have* to in *this* town,' insisted Gloria with ready sophistry.

Anthony, bewildered, tried another tack.

'Why don't you try to eat it? It can't be as bad as you think.'

'Just – because – I – don't – like – chicken!'

She picked up her fork and began poking contemptuously at the tomato, and Anthony expected her to begin flinging the stuffings in all directions. He was sure that she was approximately as angry as she had ever been – for an instant he had detected a spark of hate directed as much towards him as towards anyone else – and Gloria angry was, for the present, unapproachable.

Then, surprisingly, he saw that she had tentatively raised the fork to her lips and tasted the chicken salad. Her frown had not abated and he stared at her anxiously, making no comment and daring scarcely to breathe. She tasted another forkful – in another moment she was eating. With difficulty Anthony restrained a chuckle; when at length he spoke his words had no possible connection with chicken salad.

This incident, with variations, ran like a lugubrious fugue through the first year of marriage; always it left Anthony baffled, irritated, and depressed. But another rough brushing of temperaments, a question of laundry-bags, he found even more annoying as it ended inevitably in a decisive defeat for him.

One afternoon in Coronado, where they made the longest stay of their trip, more than three weeks, Gloria was arraying herself brilliantly for tea. Anthony, who had been downstairs listening to the latest rumour bulletins of war in Europe, entered the room, kissed the back of her powdered neck, and went to his dresser. After a great pulling out and pushing in of drawers, evidently unsatisfactory, he turned around to the Unfinished Masterpiece.

'Got any handkerchiefs, Gloria?' he asked. Gloria shook her golden head.

'Not a one. I'm using one of yours.'

'The last one, I deduce.' He laughed dryly.

'Is it?' She applied an emphatic though very delicate contour to her lips.

'Isn't the laundry back?'

'I don't know.'

Anthony hesitated – then, with sudden discernment, opened the closet door. His suspicions were verified. On the hook provided hung the blue bag furnished by the hotel. This was full of his clothes – he had put them there himself. The floor beneath it was littered with an astonishing mass of finery – lingerie, stockings, dresses, nightgowns and pyjamas – most of it scarcely worn but all of it coming indubitably under the general heading of Gloria's laundry.

He stood holding the closet door open.

'Why, Gloria!'

'What?'

The lip-line was being erased and corrected according to some mysterious perspective; not a finger trembled as she manipulated the lipstick, not a glance wavered in his direction. It was a triumph of concentration.

'Haven't you ever sent out the laundry?'

'Is it there?'

'It most certainly is.'

'Well, I guess I haven't, then.'

'Gloria,' began Anthony, sitting down on the bed and trying to catch her mirrored eyes, 'you're a nice fellow, you are! I've sent it out every time it's been sent since we left New York, and over a week ago you promised you'd do it for a change. All you'd have to do would be to cram your own junk into that bag and ring for the chambermaid.'

'Oh, why fuss about the laundry?' exclaimed Gloria petulantly, 'I'll take care of it.'

'I haven't fussed about it. I'd just as soon divide the bother with you, but when we run out of handkerchiefs it's darn near time something's done.'

Anthony considered that he was being extraordinarily logical. But Gloria, unimpressed, put away her cosmetics and casually offered him her back.

'Hook me up,' she suggested; 'Anthony, dearest, I forgot all about it. I meant to, honestly, and I will today. Don't be cross with your sweetheart.'

What could Anthony do then but draw her down upon his knee and kiss a shade of colour from her lips.

'But I don't mind,' she murmured with a smile, radiant and magnanimous. 'You can kiss all the paint off my lips any time you want.'

They went down to tea. They bought some handkerchiefs in a notion store near by. All was forgotten.

But two days later Anthony looked in the closet and saw the bag still hung limp upon its hook and that the gay and vivid pile on the floor had increased surprisingly in height.

'Gloria!' he cried.

'Oh – ' Her voice was full of real distress. Despairingly Anthony went to the phone and called the chambermaid.

'It seems to me,' he said impatiently, 'that you expect me to be some sort of French valet to you.'

Gloria laughed, so infectiously that Anthony was unwise enough to smile. Unfortunate man! In some intangible manner his smile made her mistress of the situation – with an air of injured righteousness she went emphatically to the closet and began pushing her laundry violently into the bag. Anthony watched her – ashamed of himself.

'There!' she said, implying that her fingers had been worked to the bone by a brutal taskmaster.

He considered, nevertheless, that he had given her an object-lesson and that the matter was closed, but on the contrary it was merely beginning. Laundry pile followed laundry pile – at long intervals; dearth of handkerchief followed dearth of handkerchief – at short ones; not to mention dearth of sock, of shirt, of everything. And Anthony found at length that either he must send it out himself or go through the increasingly unpleasant ordeal of a verbal battle with Gloria.

GLORIA AND GENERAL LEE

On their way East they stopped two days in Washington, strolling about with some hostility towards its atmosphere of harsh repellent light, of distance without freedom, of pomp without splendour – it seemed a pasty-pale and self-conscious city. The second day they made an ill-advised trip to General Lee's old home at Arlington.

The bus which bore them was crowded with hot, unprosperous people, and Anthony, intimate to Gloria, felt a storm brewing. It broke at the Zoo, where the party stopped for ten minutes. The Zoo, it seemed, smelt of monkeys. Anthony laughed; Gloria called down the curse of heaven upon monkeys, including in her malevolence all the passengers of the bus and their perspiring offspring who had hied themselves monkey-ward.

Eventually the bus moved on to Arlington. There it met other buses and immediately a swarm of women and children were leaving a trail of peanut-shells through the halls of General Lee and crowding at length into the room where he was married. On the wall of this room a pleasing sign announced in large red letters 'Ladies' Toilet'. At this final blow Gloria broke down.

'I think it's perfectly terrible!' she said furiously, 'the idea of letting these people come here! And of encouraging them by making these houses show-places.'

'Well,' objected Anthony, 'if they weren't kept up they'd go to pieces.'

'What if they did!' she exclaimed as they sought the wide pillared porch. 'Do you think they've left a breath of 1860 here? This has become a thing of 1914.'

'Don't you want to preserve old things?'

'But you *can't*, Anthony. Beautiful things grow to a certain height and then they fail and fade off, breathing out memories as they decay. And just as any period decays in our minds, the things of that period should decay too, and in that way they're preserved for a while in the few hearts like mine that react to them. That graveyard at Tarrytown, for instance. The asses who give money to preserve things have spoiled that too. Sleepy Hollow's gone; Washington Irving's dead and his books are rotting in our estimation year by year – then let the graveyard rot too, as it should, as all things should. Trying to preserve a century by keeping its relics up to date is like keeping a dying man alive by stimulants.'

'So you think that just as a time goes to pieces its houses ought to go too?'

'Of course! Would you value your Keats letter if the signature was traced over to make it last longer? It's just because I love the past that I want this house to look back on its glamorous moment of youth and beauty, and I want its stairs to creak as if to the footsteps of women with hoop skirts and men in boots and spurs. But they've made it into a blondined, rouged-up old woman of sixty. It hasn't any right to look so prosperous. It might care enough for Lee to drop a brick now and then. How many of these – these *animals*' – she waved her hand around – 'get anything from this, for all the histories and guidebooks and restorations in existence? How many of them who think that, at best, appreciation is talking in undertones and walking on tiptoes would even come here if it was any trouble? I want it to smell of magnolias instead of peanuts and I want my shoes to crunch on the same gravel that Lee's boots crunched on. There's no beauty without poignancy and there's no poignancy without the feeling that it's going, men, names, books, houses – bound for dust – mortal – '

A small boy appeared beside them and, swinging a handful of banana-peels, flung them valiantly in the direction of the Potomac.

SENTIMENT

Simultaneously with the fall of Liège, Anthony and Gloria arrived in New York. In retrospect the six weeks seemed miraculously happy. They had found to a great extent, as most young couples find in some measure, that they possessed in common many fixed ideas and curiosities and odd quirks of mind; they were essentially companionable.

But it had been a struggle to keep many of their conversations on the level of discussions. Arguments were fatal to Gloria's disposition. She had all her life been associated either with her mental inferiors or with men who, under the almost hostile intimidation of her beauty, had not dared to contradict her; naturally, then, it irritated her when Anthony emerged from the state in which her pronouncements were an infallible and ultimate decision.

He failed to realise, at first, that this was the result partly of her 'female' education and partly of her beauty, and he was inclined to include her with her entire sex as curiously and definitely limited. It maddened him to find she had no sense of justice. But he discovered that, when a subject did interest her, her brain tired less quickly than his. What he chiefly missed in her mind was the pedantic teleology – the sense of order and accuracy, the sense of life as a mysteriously correlated piece of patchwork, but he understood after a while that such a quality in her would have been incongruous.

Of the things they possessed in common, greatest of all was their almost uncanny pull at each other's hearts. The day they left the hotel in Coronado she sat down on one of the beds while they were packing, and began to weep bitterly.

'Dearest – ' His arms were around her; he pulled her head down upon his shoulder. 'What is it, my own Gloria? Tell me.'

'We're going away,' she sobbed. 'Oh, Anthony, it's sort of the first place we've lived together. Our two little beds here – side by side – they'll be always waiting for us, and we're never coming back to 'em any more.'

She was tearing at his heart as she always could. Sentiment came over him, rushed into his eyes.

'Gloria, why, we're going on to another room. And two other little beds. We're going to be together all our lives.'

Words flooded from her in a low husky voice.

'But it won't be – like our two beds – ever again. Everywhere we go and move on and change, something's lost – something's left behind. You can't ever quite repeat anything, and I've been so yours, here – '

He held her passionately near, discerning, far beyond any criticism of her sentiment, a wise grasping of the minute, if only an indulgence of her desire to cry – Gloria the idler, caresser of her own dreams, extracting poignancy from the memorable things of life and youth.

Later in the afternoon when he returned from the station with the tickets he found her asleep on one of the beds, her arm curled about a black object which he could not at first identify. Coming closer he found it was one of his shoes, not a particularly new one, nor clean one, but her face, tear-stained, was pressed against it, and he understood her ancient and most honourable message. There was almost ecstasy in waking her and seeing her smile at him, shy but well aware of her own nicety of imagination.

With no appraisal of the worth or dross of these two things, it seemed to Anthony that they lay somewhere near the heart of love.

THE GREY HOUSE

It is in the twenties that the actual momentum of life begins to slacken, and it is a simple soul indeed to whom as many things are significant and meaningful at thirty as at ten years before. At thirty an organ-grinder is a more or less moth-eaten man who grinds an organ – and once he was an organ-grinder! The unmistakable stigma of humanity touches all those impersonal and beautiful things that only youth ever grasps in their impersonal glory. A brilliant ball, gay with light romantic laughter, wears through its own silks and satins to show the bare framework of a man-made thing – oh, that eternal hand! – a play, most tragic and most divine, becomes merely a succession of speeches, sweated over by the eternal plagiarist in the clammy hours and acted by men subject to cramps, cowardice, and manly sentiment.

And this time with Gloria and Anthony came in this first year of marriage, and the grey house caught them in that stage when the organ-grinder was slowly undergoing his inevitable metamorphosis. She was twenty-three; he was twenty-six.

The grey house was, at first, of sheerly pastoral intent. They lived impatiently in Anthony's apartment for the first fortnight after the return from California, in a stifled atmosphere of open trunks, too many callers, and the eternal laundry-bags. They discussed with their friends the stupendous problem of their future. Dick and Maury would sit with them agreeing solemnly, almost thoughtfully, as Anthony ran through his list of what they 'ought' to do, and where they 'ought' to live.

'I'd like to take Gloria abroad,' he complained, 'except for this damn war – and next to that I'd sort of like to have a place in the country, somewhere near New York, of course, where I could write – or whatever I decide to do.'

Gloria laughed.

'Isn't he cute?' she required of Maury. ' "Whatever he decides to do!" But what am *I* going to do if he works? Maury, will you take me around if Anthony works?'

'Anyway, I'm not going to work yet,' said Anthony quickly.

It was vaguely understood between them that on some misty day he would enter a sort of glorified diplomatic service and be envied by princes and prime ministers for his beautiful wife.

'Well,' said Gloria helplessly, 'I'm sure I don't know. We talk and talk and never get anywhere, and we ask all our friends and they just answer the way we want 'em to. I wish somebody'd take care of us.'

'Why don't you go out to – out to Greenwich or something?' suggested Richard Caramel.

'I'd like that,' said Gloria, brightening. 'Do you think we could get a house there?'

Dick shrugged his shoulders and Maury laughed.

'You two amuse me,' he said. 'Of all the unpractical people! As soon as a place is mentioned you expect us to pull great piles of photographs out of our pockets showing the different styles of architecture available in bungalows.'

'That's just what I don't want,' wailed Gloria, 'a hot stuffy bungalow, with a lot of babies next door and their father cutting the grass in his shirt sleeves – '

'For heaven's sake, Gloria,' interrupted Maury, 'nobody wants to lock you up in a bungalow. Who in God's name brought bungalows into the conversation? But you'll never get a place anywhere unless you go out and hunt for it.'

'Go where? You say "go out and hunt for it", but where?'

With dignity Maury waved his hand paw-like about the room.

'Out anywhere. Out in the country. There're lots of places.'

'Thanks.'

'Look here!' Richard Caramel brought his yellow eye rakishly into play. 'The trouble with you two is that you're all disorganised. Do you know anything about New York State? Shut up, Anthony, I'm talking to Gloria.'

'Well,' she admitted finally, 'I've been to two or three house parties in Portchester and around in Connecticut – but, of course, that isn't in

New York State, is it? And neither is Morristown,' she finished with drowsy irrelevance.

There was a shout of laughter.

'Oh, Lord!' cried Dick, 'neither is Morristown! No, and neither is Santa Barbara, Gloria. Now listen. To begin with, unless you have a fortune there's no use considering any place like Newport or Southampton or Tuxedo. They're out of the question.'

They all agreed to this solemnly.

'And personally I hate New Jersey. Then, of course, there's upper New York, above Tuxedo.'

'Too cold,' said Gloria briefly. 'I was there once in an automobile.'

'Well, it seems to me there're a lot of towns like Rye between New York and Greenwich where you could buy a little grey house of some – '

Gloria leaped at the phrase triumphantly. For the first time since their return East she knew what she wanted.

'Oh, *yes*!' she cried. 'Oh, *yes*! that's it: a little grey house with sort of white around and a whole lot of swamp maples just as brown and gold as an October picture in a gallery. Where can we find one?'

'Unfortunately, I've mislaid my list of little grey houses with swamp maples around them – but I'll try to find it. Meanwhile you take a piece of paper and write down the names of seven possible towns. And every day this week you take a trip to one of those towns.'

'Oh, gosh!' protested Gloria, collapsing mentally, 'why won't you do it for us? I hate trains.'

'Well, hire a car, and – '

Gloria yawned.

'I'm tired of discussing it. Seems to me all we do is talk about where to live.'

'My exquisite wife wearies of thought,' remarked Anthony ironically. 'She must have a tomato sandwich to stimulate her jaded nerves. Let's go out to tea.'

As the unfortunate upshot of this conversation, they took Dick's advice literally, and two days later went out to Rye, where they wandered around with an irritated real-estate agent, like bewildered babes in the wood. They were shown houses at a hundred a month which closely adjoined other houses at a hundred a month; they were shown isolated houses to which they invariably took violent dislikes, though they submitted weakly to the agent's desire that they 'look at that stove – some stove!' and to a great shaking of doorposts and tapping of walls, intended evidently to show that the house would not immediately collapse, no matter how convincingly it gave that impression. They gazed through windows into interiors furnished either 'commercially' with slab-like chairs and unyielding settees, or 'homelike' with the melancholy bric-à-brac of other summers – crossed tennis rackets, fit-form couches, and depressing Gibson girls. With a feeling of guilt they looked at a few really nice houses, aloof, dignified and cool – at three hundred a month. They went away from Rye thanking the real-estate agent very much indeed.

On the crowded train back to New York the seat behind was occupied by a super-respirating Latin whose last few meals had obviously been composed entirely of garlic. They reached the apartment gratefully, almost hysterically, and Gloria rushed for a hot bath in the reproachless bathroom. So far as the question of a future abode was concerned both of them were incapacitated for a week.

The matter eventually worked itself out with unhoped-for romance. Anthony ran into the living-room one afternoon fairly radiating 'the idea'.

'I've got it,' he was exclaiming as though he had just caught a mouse. 'We'll get a car.'

'Gee whiz! Haven't we got troubles enough taking care of ourselves?'

'Give me a second to explain, can't you? just let's leave our stuff with Dick and just pile a couple of suitcases in our car, the one we're going to buy – we'll have to have one in the country anyway – and just start out in the direction of New Haven. You see, as we get out of commuting distance from New York, the rents'll get cheaper, and as soon as we find a house we want we'll just settle down.'

By his frequent and soothing interpolation of the word 'just' he aroused her lethargic enthusiasm. Strutting violently about the room, he simulated a dynamic and irresistible efficiency. 'We'll buy a car tomorrow.'

Life, limping after imagination's ten-league boots, saw them out of town a week later in a cheap but sparkling new roadster, saw them through the chaotic unintelligible Bronx, then over a wide murky district which alternated cheerless blue-green wastes with suburbs of tremendous and sordid activity. They left New York at eleven and it was well past a hot and beatific noon when they moved rakishly through Pelham.

'These aren't towns,' said Gloria scornfully, 'these are just city blocks plumped down coldly into waste acres. I imagine all the men here have their moustaches stained from drinking their coffee too quickly in the morning.'

'And play pinochle on the commuting trains.'

'What's pinochle?'

'Don't be so literal. How should I know? But it sounds as though they ought to play it.'

'I like it. It sounds as if it were something where you sort of cracked your knuckles or something . . . Let me drive.'

Anthony looked at her suspiciously.

'You swear you're a good driver?'

'Since I was fourteen.'

He stopped the car cautiously at the side of the road and they changed seats. Then with a horrible grinding noise the car was put in gear, Gloria adding an accompaniment of laughter which seemed to Anthony disquieting and in the worst possible taste.

'Here we go!' she yelled. 'Whoo-oop!'

Their heads snapped back like marionettes on a single wire as the car leaped ahead and curved retchingly about a standing milk-wagon, whose driver stood up on his seat and bellowed after them. In the immemorial tradition of the road, Anthony retorted with a few brief epigrams as to the grossness of the milk-delivering profession. He cut his remarks short, however, and turned to Gloria with the growing conviction that he had made a grave mistake in relinquishing control and that Gloria was a driver of many eccentricities and of infinite carelessness.

'Remember now!' he warned her nervously, 'the man said we oughtn't to go over twenty miles an hour for the first five thousand miles.'

She nodded briefly, but evidently intending to accomplish the prohibitive distance as quickly as possible, slightly increased her speed. A moment later he made another attempt.

'See that sign? Do you want to get us pinched?'

'Oh, for heaven's sake,' cried Gloria in exasperation, 'you *always* exaggerate things so!'

'Well, I don't want to get arrested.'

'Who's arresting you? You're so persistent – just like you were about my cough medicine last night.'

'It was for your own good.'

'Ha! I might as well be living with mama.'

'What a thing to say to me!'

A standing policeman swerved into view, was hastily passed.

'See him?' demanded Anthony.

'Oh, you drive me crazy! He didn't arrest us, did he?'

'When he does it'll be too late,' countered Anthony brilliantly.

Her reply was scornful, almost injured.

'Why, this old thing won't *go* over thirty-five.'

'It isn't old.'

'It is in spirit.'

That afternoon the car joined the laundry-bags and Gloria's appetite as one of the trinity of contention. He warned her of railroad tracks; he pointed out approaching automobiles; finally he insisted on taking the wheel and a furious, insulted Gloria sat silently beside him between the towns of Larchmont and Rye.

But it was due to this furious silence of hers that the grey house materialised from its abstraction, for just beyond Rye he surrendered gloomily to it and re-relinquished the wheel. Mutely he beseeched her and Gloria, instantly cheered, vowed to be more careful. But because a discourteous street-car persisted callously in remaining upon its track Gloria ducked down a side-street – and thereafter that afternoon was never able to find her way back to the Post Road. The street they finally mistook for it lost its Post-Road aspect when it had gone five miles from Cos Cob. Its macadam became gravel, then dirt – moreover, it narrowed and developed a border of maple trees, through which filtered the westering sun, making its endless experiments with shadow designs upon the long grass.

'We're lost now,' complained Anthony.

'Read that sign!'

' "Marietta – Five Miles". What's Marietta?'

'Never heard of it, but let's go on. We can't turn here and there's probably a detour back to the Post Road.'

The way became scarred with deepening ruts and insidious shoulders of stone. Three farmhouses faced them momentarily, slid by. A town sprang up in a cluster of dull roofs around a white tall steeple.

Then Gloria, hesitating between two approaches, and making her choice too late, drove over a fire-hydrant and ripped the transmission violently from the car.

It was dark when the real-estate agent of Marietta showed them the grey house. They came upon it just west of the village, where it rested against a sky that was a warm blue cloak buttoned with tiny stars. The grey house had been there when women who kept cats were probably witches, when Paul Revere made false teeth in Boston preparatory to arousing the great commercial people, when our ancestors were gloriously deserting Washington in droves. Since those days the house had been bolstered up in a feeble corner, considerably repartitioned and newly plastered inside, amplified by a kitchen and added to by a side-porch – but, save for where some jovial oaf had roofed the new kitchen with red tin, Colonial it defiantly remained.

'How did you happen to come to Marietta?' demanded the real-estate agent in a tone that was first cousin to suspicion. He was showing them through four spacious and airy bedrooms.

'We broke down,' explained Gloria. 'I drove over a fire-hydrant and we had ourselves towed to the garage and then we saw your sign.'

The man nodded, unable to follow such a sally of spontaneity. There was something subtly immoral in doing anything without several months' consideration.

They signed a lease that night and, in the agent's car, returned jubilantly to the somnolent and dilapidated Marietta Inn, which was too broken for even the chance immoralities and consequent gaieties of a country road house. Half the night they lay awake planning the things they were to do there. Anthony was going to work at an astounding pace on his history and thus ingratiate himself with his cynical grandfather . . . When the car was repaired they would explore the country and join the nearest 'really nice' club, where Gloria would play golf 'or something' while Anthony wrote. This, of course, was Anthony's idea – Gloria was sure she wanted but to read and dream and be fed tomato sandwiches and lemonades by some angelic servant still in a shadowy hinterland. Between paragraphs Anthony would come and kiss her as she lay indolently in the hammock . . . The hammock! a host of new dreams in tune to its imagined rhythm, while the wind stirred it and waves of sun undulated over the shadows of blown wheat, or the dusty road freckled and darkened with quiet summer rain . . .

And guests – here they had a long argument, both of them trying to be extraordinarily mature and far-sighted. Anthony claimed that they would need people at least every other weekend 'as a sort of change'. This provoked an involved and extremely sentimental conversation as to whether Anthony did not consider Gloria change enough. Though he assured her that he did, she insisted upon doubting him . . . Eventually the conversation assumed its eternal monotone: 'What then? Oh, what'll we do then?'

'Well, we'll have a dog,' suggested Anthony.

'I don't want one. I want a kitty.' She went thoroughly and with great enthusiasm into the history, habits and tastes of a cat she had once possessed. Anthony considered that it must have been a horrible character with neither personal magnetism nor a loyal heart.

Later they slept, to wake an hour before dawn with the grey house dancing in phantom glory before their dazzled eyes.

THE SOUL OF GLORIA

For that autumn the grey house welcomed them with a rush of sentiment that falsified its cynical old age. True, there were the laundry-bags, there was Gloria's appetite, there was Anthony's tendency to brood and his imaginative 'nervousness', but there were intervals also of an unhoped-for serenity. Close together on the porch they would wait for the moon to stream across the silver acres of farmland, jump a thick wood and tumble waves of radiance at their feet. In such a moonlight Gloria's face was of a pervading, reminiscent white, and with a modicum of effort they would slip off the blinders of custom and each would find in the other almost the quintessential romance of the vanished June.

One night while her head lay upon his heart and their cigarettes glowed in swerving buttons of light through the dome of darkness over the bed, she spoke for the first time and fragmentarily of the men who had hung for brief moments on her beauty.

'Do you ever think of them?' he asked her.

'Only occasionally – when something happens that recalls a particular man.'

'What do you remember – their kisses?'

'All sorts of things . . . Men are different with women.'

'Different in what way?'

'Oh, entirely – and quite inexpressibly. Men who had the most firmly rooted reputation for being this way or that would sometimes be surprisingly inconsistent with me. Brutal men were tender, negligible men were astonishingly loyal and lovable, and, often, honourable men took attitudes that were anything but honourable.'

'For instance?'

'Well, there was a boy named Percy Wolcott from Cornell who was quite a hero in college, a great athlete, and saved a lot of people from a fire or something like that. But I soon found he was stupid in a rather dangerous way.'

'What way?'

'It seems he had some naïve conception of a woman "fit to be his wife", a particular conception that I used to run into a lot and that always drove me wild. He demanded a girl who'd never been kissed and who liked to sew and sit at home and pay tribute to his self-esteem. And I'll bet a hat if he's got an idiot to sit and be stupid with him he's tearing out on the side with some much speedier lady.'

'I'd be sorry for his wife.'

'I wouldn't. Think what an ass she'd be not to realise it before she married him. He's the sort whose idea of honouring and respecting a woman would be never to give her any excitement. With the best intentions, he was deep in the Dark Ages.'

'What was his attitude towards you?'

'I'm coming to that. As I told you – or did I tell you? – he was mighty good-looking: big brown honest eyes and one of those smiles that guarantee the heart behind it is twenty-carat gold. Being young and credulous, I thought he had some discretion, so I kissed him fervently one night when we were riding around after a dance at the Homestead at Hot Springs. It had been a wonderful week, I remember – with the most luscious trees spread like green lather, sort of, all over the valley and a mist rising out of them on October mornings like bonfires lit to turn them brown – '

'How about your friend with the ideals?' interrupted Anthony.

'It seems that when he kissed me he began to think that perhaps he could get away with a little more, that I needn't be "respected" like this Beatrice Fairfax glad-girl of his imagination.'

'What'd he do?'

'Not much. I pushed him off a sixteen-foot embankment before he was well started.'

'Hurt him?' enquired Anthony with a laugh.

'Broke his arm and sprained his ankle. He told the story all over Hot Springs, and when his arm healed a man named Barley who liked me fought him and broke it over again. Oh, it was all an awful mess. He threatened to sue Barley, and Barley – he was from Georgia – was seen buying a gun in town. But before that mama had dragged me North again, much against my will, so I never did find out all that happened – though I saw Barley once in the Vanderbilt lobby.'

Anthony laughed long and loud.

'What a career! I suppose I ought to be furious because you've kissed so many men. I'm not, though.'

At this she sat up in bed.

'It's funny, but I'm so sure that those kisses left no mark on me – no taint of promiscuity, I mean – even though a man once told me in all seriousness that he hated to think I'd been a public drinking glass.'

'He had his nerve.'

'I just laughed and told him to think of me rather as a loving-cup that goes from hand to hand but should be valued none the less.'

'Somehow it doesn't bother me – on the other hand it would, of course, if you'd done any more than kiss them. But I believe *you* are absolutely incapable of jealousy except as hurt vanity. Why don't you care what I've done? Wouldn't you prefer it if I'd been absolutely innocent?'

'It's all in the impression it might have made on you. *My* kisses were because the man was good-looking, or because there was a slick moon, or even because I've felt vaguely sentimental and a little stirred. But that's all – it's had utterly no effect on me. But you'd remember and let memories haunt you and worry you.'

'Haven't you ever kissed anyone like you've kissed me?'

'No,' she answered simply. 'As I've told you, men have tried – oh, lots of things. Any pretty girl has that experience . . . You see,' she resumed, 'it doesn't matter to me how many women you've stayed with in the past, so long as it was merely a physical satisfaction, but I don't believe I could endure the idea of your ever having lived with another woman for a protracted period or even having wanted to marry some possible girl. It's different somehow. There'd be all the little intimacies remembered – and they'd dull that freshness that after all is the most precious part of love.'

Rapturously he pulled her down beside him on the pillow.

'Oh, my darling,' he whispered, 'as if I remembered anything but your dear kisses.'

Then Gloria, in a very mild voice: 'Anthony, did I hear anybody say they were thirsty?'

Anthony laughed abruptly and with a sheepish and amused grin got out of bed.

'With just a *little* piece of ice in the water,' she added. 'Do you suppose I could have that?'

Gloria used the adjective 'little' whenever she asked a favour – it made the favour sound less arduous. But Anthony laughed again –

whether she wanted a cake of ice or a marble of it, he must go downstairs to the kitchen . . . Her voice followed him through the hall: 'And just a *little* cracker with just a *little* marmalade on it . . .'

'Oh, gosh!' sighed Anthony in rapturous slang, 'she's wonderful, that girl! She *has* it!'

'When we have a baby,' she began one day – this, it had already been decided, was to be after three years – 'I want it to look like you.'

'Except its legs,' he insinuated slyly.

'Oh, yes, except his legs. He's got to have my legs. But the rest of him can be you.'

'My nose?'

Gloria hesitated.

'Well, perhaps my nose. But certainly your eyes – and my mouth, and I guess my shape of the face. I wonder; I think he'd be sort of cute if he had my hair.'

'My dear Gloria, you've appropriated the whole baby.'

'Well, I didn't mean to,' she apologised cheerfully.

'Let him have my neck at least,' he urged, regarding himself gravely in the glass. 'You've often said you liked my neck because the Adam's apple doesn't show, and, besides, your neck's too short.'

'Why, it is *not*!' she cried indignantly, turning to the mirror, 'it's just right. I don't believe I've ever seen a better neck.'

'It's too short,' he repeated teasingly.

'Short?' Her tone expressed exasperated wonder. 'Short? You're crazy!' She elongated and contracted it to convince herself of its reptilian sinuousness. 'Do you call *that* a short neck?'

'One of the shortest I've ever seen.'

For the first time in weeks tears started from Gloria's eyes and the look she gave him had a quality of real pain.

'Oh, Anthony – '

'My Lord, Gloria!' He approached her in bewilderment and took her elbows in his hands. 'Don't cry, *please*! Didn't you know I was only kidding? Gloria, look at me! Why, dearest, you've got the longest neck I've ever seen. Honestly.'

Her tears dissolved in a twisted smile.

'Well – you shouldn't have said that, then. Let's talk about the b-baby.'

Anthony paced the floor and spoke as though rehearsing for a debate.

'To put it briefly, there are two babies we could have, two distinct and logical babies, utterly differentiated. There's the baby that's the combination of the best of both of us. Your body, my eyes, my mind, your intelligence – and then there is the baby which is our worst – my body, your disposition, and my irresolution.'

'I like that second baby,' she said.

'What I'd really like,' continued Anthony, 'would be to have two sets of triplets one year apart and then experiment with the six boys – '

'Poor me,' she interjected.

' – I'd educate them each in a different country and by a different system and when they were twenty-three I'd call them together and see what they were like.'

'Let's have 'em all with my neck,' suggested Gloria.

THE END OF A CHAPTER

The car was at length repaired and with a deliberate vengeance took up where it left off the business of causing infinite dissension. Who should drive? How fast should Gloria go? These two questions and the eternal recriminations involved ran through the days. They motored to the Post-Road towns, Rye, Portchester and Greenwich, and called on a dozen friends, mostly Gloria's, who all seemed to be in different stages of having babies and in this respect as well as in others bored her to a point of nervous distraction. For an hour after each visit she would bite her fingers furiously and be inclined to take out her rancour on Anthony.

'I loathe women,' she cried in a mild temper. 'What on earth can you say to them – except talk "lady-lady"? I've enthused over a dozen babies that I've wanted only to choke. And every one of those girls is either incipiently jealous and suspicious of her husband if he's charming or beginning to be bored with him if he isn't.'

'Don't you ever intend to see any women?'

'I don't know. They never seem clean to me – never – never. Except just a few. Constance Shaw – you know, the Mrs Merriam who came over to see us last Tuesday – is almost the only one. She's so tall and fresh-looking and stately.'

'I don't like them so tall.'

Though they went to several dinner dances at various country clubs, they decided that the autumn was too nearly over for them to 'go out' on any scale, even had they been so inclined. He hated golf; Gloria liked it only mildly, and though she enjoyed a violent rush that some undergraduates gave her one night and was glad that Anthony should be proud of her beauty, she also perceived that their hostess for the evening, a Mrs Granby, was somewhat disquieted by the fact that Anthony's classmate, Alec Granby, joined with enthusiasm in the rush. The Granbys never phoned again, and though Gloria laughed, it piqued her not a little.

'You see,' she explained to Anthony, 'if I wasn't married it wouldn't worry her – but she's been to the movies in her day and she thinks I may be a vampire. But the point is that placating such people requires an effort that I'm simply unwilling to make . . . And those cute little freshmen making eyes at me and paying me idiotic compliments! I've grown up, Anthony.'

Marietta itself offered little social life. Half a dozen farm-estates formed a hexagon around it, but these belonged to ancient men who displayed themselves only as inert, grey-thatched lumps in the back of limousines on their way to the station, whither they were sometimes accompanied by equally ancient and doubly massive wives. The townspeople were a particularly uninteresting type – unmarried females were predominant for the most part – with school-festival horizons and souls bleak as the forbidding white architecture of the three churches. The only native with whom they came into close contact was the broad-hipped, broad-shouldered Swedish girl who came every day to do their work. She was silent and efficient, and Gloria, after finding her weeping violently into her bowed arms upon the kitchen table, developed an uncanny fear of her and stopped complaining about the food. Because of her untold and esoteric grief the girl stayed on.

Gloria's penchant for premonitions and her bursts of vague supernaturalism were a surprise to Anthony. Either some complex, properly and scientifically inhibited in the early years with her Bilphistic mother, or some inherited hypersensitiveness, made her susceptible to any suggestion of the psychic, and, far from gullible about the motives of people, she was inclined to credit any extraordinary happening attributed to the whimsical perambulations of the buried. The desperate squeakings about the old house on windy nights that to Anthony were burglars with revolvers ready in hand represented to Gloria the auras, evil and restive, of dead generations, expiating the inexpiable upon the ancient and romantic hearth. One night, because of two swift bangs downstairs, which Anthony fearfully but unavailingly investigated, they lay awake nearly until dawn asking each other examination-paper questions about the history of the world.

In October Muriel came out for a two weeks' visit. Gloria had called her on long-distance, and Miss Kane ended the conversation characteristically by saying 'All-ll-ll righty. I'll be there with bells!' She arrived with a dozen popular songs under her arm.

'You ought to have a phonograph out here in the country,' she said, 'just a little Vic – they don't cost much. Then whenever you're lonesome you can have Caruso or Al Jolson right at your door.'

She worried Anthony to distraction by telling him that 'he was the first clever man she had ever known and she got so tired of shallow people'. He wondered that people fell in love with such women. Yet he supposed that under a certain impassioned glance even she might take on a softness and promise.

But Gloria, violently showing off her love for Anthony, was diverted into a state of purring content.

Finally Richard Caramel arrived for a garrulous and to Gloria painfully literary weekend, during which he discussed himself with Anthony long after she lay in childlike sleep upstairs.

'It's been mighty funny, this success and all,' said Dick. 'Just before the novel appeared I'd been trying, without success, to sell some short stories. Then, after my book came out, I polished up three and had them accepted by one of the magazines that had rejected them before. I've done a lot of them since; publishers don't pay me for my book till this winter.'

'Don't let the victor belong to the spoils.'

'You mean write trash?' He considered. 'If you mean deliberately injecting a slushy fade-out into each one, I'm not. But I don't suppose I'm being so careful. I'm certainly writing faster and I don't seem to be thinking as much as I used to. Perhaps it's because I don't get any conversation, now that you're married and Maury's gone to Philadelphia. Haven't the old urge and ambition. Early success and all that.'

'Doesn't it worry you?'

'Frantically. I get a thing I call sentence-fever that must be like buck-fever – it's a sort of intense literary self-consciousness that comes when I try to force myself. But the really awful days aren't when I think I can't write. They're when I wonder whether any writing is worth while at all – I mean whether I'm not a sort of glorified buffoon.'

'I like to hear you talk that way,' said Anthony with a touch of his old patronising insolence. 'I was afraid you'd got a bit idiotic over your work. Read the damnedest interview you gave out – '

Dick interrupted with an agonised expression.

'Good Lord! Don't mention it. Young lady wrote it – most admiring young lady. Kept telling me my work was "strong", and I sort of lost my head and made a lot of strange pronouncements. Some of it was good, though, don't you think?'

'Oh, yes; that part about the wise writer writing for the youth of his generation, the critic of the next, and the schoolmaster of ever afterwards.'

'Oh, I believe a lot of it,' admitted Richard Caramel with a faint beam. 'It simply was a mistake to give it out.'

In November they moved into Anthony's apartment, from which they sallied triumphantly to the Yale–Harvard and Harvard–Princeton football games, to the St Nicholas ice-skating rink, to a thorough round of the theatres and to a miscellany of entertainments – from small, staid dances to the great affairs that Gloria loved, held in those few houses where lackeys with powdered wigs scurried around in magnificent Anglomania under the direction of gigantic major-domos. Their intention was to go abroad the first of the year or, at any rate, when the war was over. Anthony had actually completed a Chestertonian essay on the twelfth century by way of introduction to his proposed book and Gloria had done some extensive research work on the question of Russian sable coats – in fact the winter was approaching quite comfortably, when the Bilphistic demiurge decided suddenly in mid-December that Mrs Gilbert's soul had aged sufficiently in its present incarnation. In consequence Anthony took a miserable and hysterical Gloria out to Kansas City, where, in the fashion of mankind, they paid the terrible and mind-shaking deference to the dead.

Mr Gilbert became, for the first and last time in his life, a truly pathetic figure. That woman he had broken to wait upon his body and play congregation to his mind had ironically deserted him – just when he could not much longer have supported her. Never again would he be able so satisfactorily to bore and bully a human soul.

Chapter 2

Symposium

Gloria had lulled Anthony's mind to sleep. She, who seemed of all women the wisest and the finest, hung like a brilliant curtain across his doorways, shutting out the light of the sun. In those first years what he believed bore invariably the stamp of Gloria; he saw the sun always through the pattern of the curtain.

It was a sort of lassitude that brought them back to Marietta for another summer. Through a golden enervating spring they had loitered, restive and lazily extravagant, along the California coast, joining other parties intermittently and drifting from Pasadena to Coronado, from Coronado to Santa Barbara, with no purpose more apparent than Gloria's desire to dance to different music or catch some infinitesimal variant among the changing colours of the sea. Out of the Pacific there rose to greet them savage rocklands and equally barbaric hostelries built that at tea-time one might drowse into a languid wicker bazaar glorified by the polo costumes of Southhampton and Lake Forest and Newport and Palm Beach. And, as the waves met and splashed and glittered in the most placid of the bays, so they joined this group and that, and with them shifted stations, murmuring ever of those strange unsubstantial gaieties in wait just over the next green and fruitful valley.

A simple healthy leisure class it was – the best of the men not unpleasantly undergraduate – they seemed to be on a perpetual candidates list for some etherealised 'Porcellian' or 'Skull and Bones' extended out indefinitely into the world; the women, of more than average beauty, fragilely athletic, somewhat idiotic as hostesses but charming and infinitely decorative as guests. Sedately and gracefully they danced the steps of their selection in the balmy tea hours, accomplishing with a certain dignity the movements so horribly burlesqued by clerk and chorus girl the country over. It seemed ironic that in this lone and discredited offspring of the arts Americans should excel, unquestionably.

Having danced and splashed through a lavish spring, Anthony and Gloria found that they had spent too much money and for this must go into retirement for a certain period. There was Anthony's 'work', they said. Almost before they knew it they were back in the grey house, more aware now that other lovers had slept there, other names had been called over the banisters, other couples had sat upon the porch steps watching the grey-green fields and the black bulk of woods beyond.

It was the same Anthony, more restless, inclined to quicken only under the stimulus of several highballs, faintly, almost imperceptibly, apathetic towards Gloria. But Gloria – she would be twenty-four in August and was in an attractive but sincere panic about it. Six years to thirty! Had she been less in love with Anthony her sense of the flight of time would have expressed itself in a reawakened interest in other men, in a deliberate intention of extracting a transient gleam of romance from every potential lover who glanced at her with lowered brows over a shining dinner table. She said to Anthony one day: 'How I feel is that if I wanted anything I'd take it. That's what I've always thought all my life. But it happens that I want you, and so I just haven't room for any other desires.'

They were bound eastward through a parched and lifeless Indiana, and she had looked up from one of her beloved moving-picture magazines to find a casual conversation suddenly turned grave.

Anthony frowned out of the car window. As the track crossed a country road a farmer appeared momentarily in his wagon; he was chewing on a straw and was apparently the same farmer they had passed a dozen times before, sitting in silent and malignant symbolism. As Anthony turned to Gloria his frown intensified.

'You worry me,' he objected; 'I can imagine *wanting* another woman under certain transitory circumstances, but I can't imagine taking her.'

'But I don't feel that way, Anthony. I can't be bothered resisting things I want. My way is not to want them – to want nobody but you.'

'Yet when I think that if you just happened to take a fancy to someone – '

'Oh, don't be an idiot!' she exclaimed. 'There'd be nothing casual about it. And I can't even imagine the possibility.'

This emphatically closed the conversation. Anthony's unfailing appreciation made her happier in his company than in anyone's else. She definitely enjoyed him – she loved him. So the summer began very much as had the one before.

There was, however, one radical change in the *ménage*. The icy-hearted Scandinavian, whose austere cooking and sardonic manner of waiting on table had so depressed Gloria, gave way to an exceedingly efficient Japanese whose name was Tanalahaka, but who confessed that he heeded any summons which included the dissyllable 'Tana'.

Tana was unusually small even for a Japanese, and displayed a somewhat naïve conception of himself as a man of the world. On the day of his arrival from 'R. Gugimoniki, Japanese Reliable Employment Agency', he called Anthony into his room to see the treasures of his trunk. These included a large collection of Japanese postcards, which he was all for explaining to his employer at once, individually and at great length. Among them were half a dozen of pornographic intent and plainly of American origin, though the makers had modestly omitted both their names and the form for mailing. He next brought out some of his own handiwork – a pair of American pants, which he had made himself, and two suits of solid silk underwear. He informed Anthony confidentially as to the purpose for which these latter were reserved. The next exhibit was a rather good copy of an etching of Abraham Lincoln, to whose face he had given an unmistakable Japanese cast. Last came a flute; he had made it himself but it was broken: he was going to fix it soon.

After these polite formalities, which Anthony conjectured must be native to Japan, Tana delivered a long harangue in splintered English on the relation of master and servant from which Anthony gathered that he had worked on large estates but had always quarrelled with the other servants because they were not honest. They had a great time over the word 'honest', and in fact became rather irritated with each other, because Anthony persisted stubbornly that Tana was trying to say 'hornets', and even went to the extent of buzzing in the manner of a bee and flapping his arms to imitate wings.

After three-quarters of an hour Anthony was released with the warm assurance that they would have other nice chats in which Tana would tell 'how we do in my countree'.

Such was Tana's garrulous première in the grey house – and he fulfilled its promise. Though he was conscientious and honourable, he was unquestionably a terrific bore. He seemed unable to control his tongue, sometimes continuing from paragraph to paragraph with a look akin to pain in his small brown eyes.

Sunday and Monday afternoons he read the comic sections of the newspapers. One cartoon which contained a facetious Japanese butler diverted him enormously, though he claimed that the protagonist, who to Anthony appeared clearly Oriental, had really an American face.

The difficulty with the funny paper was that when, aided by Anthony, he had spelled out the last three pictures and assimilated their context with a concentration surely adequate for Kant's *Critique*, he had entirely forgotten what the first pictures were about.

In the middle of June, Anthony and Gloria celebrated their first anniversary by having a 'date'. Anthony knocked at the door and she ran to let him in. Then they sat together on the couch calling over those names they had made for each other, new combinations of endearments ages old. Yet to this 'date' was appended no attenuated good-night with its ecstasy of regret.

Later in June horror leered out at Gloria, struck at her and frightened her bright soul back half a generation. Then slowly it faded out, faded back into that impenetrable darkness whence it had come – taking relentlessly its modicum of youth.

With an infallible sense of the dramatic it chose a little railroad station in a wretched village near Portchester. The station platform lay all day bare as a prairie, exposed to the dusty yellow sun and to the glance of that most obnoxious type of countryman who lives near a metropolis and has attained its cheap smartness without its urbanity. A dozen of these yokels, red-eyed, cheerless as scarecrows, saw the incident. Dimly it passed across their confused and uncomprehending minds, taken at its broadest for a coarse joke, at its subtlest for a 'shame'. Meanwhile there upon the platform a measure of brightness faded from the world.

With Eric Merriam, Anthony had been sitting over a decanter of Scotch all the hot summer afternoon, while Gloria and Constance Merriam swam and sunned themselves at the Beach Club, the latter under a striped parasol-awning, Gloria stretched sensuously upon the soft hot sand, tanning her inevitable legs. Later they had all four played with inconsequential sandwiches; then Gloria had risen, tapping Anthony's knee with her parasol to get his attention.

'We've got to go, dear.'

'Now?' He looked at her unwillingly. At that moment nothing seemed of more importance than to idle on that shady porch drinking mellowed Scotch, while his host reminisced interminably on the by-play of some forgotten political campaign.

'We've really got to go,' repeated Gloria. 'We can get a taxi to the station . . . Come on, Anthony!' she commanded a bit more imperiously.

'Now see here – ' Merriam, his yarn cut off, made conventional objections, meanwhile provocatively filling his guest's glass with a highball that should have been sipped through ten minutes. But at Gloria's annoyed, 'We really *must*!' Anthony drank it off, got to his feet and made an elaborate bow to his hostess.

'It seems we "must",' he said, with little grace.

In a minute he was following Gloria down a garden-walk between tall rose bushes, her parasol brushing gently the June-blooming leaves. Most inconsiderate, he thought, as they reached the road. He felt with injured naïvety that Gloria should not have interrupted such innocent and harmless enjoyment. The whiskey had both soothed and clarified the restless things in his mind. It occurred to him that she had taken this same attitude several times before. Was he always to retreat from pleasant episodes at a touch of her parasol or a flicker of her eye? His unwillingness blurred to ill will, which rose within him like a resistless bubble. He kept silent, perversely inhibiting a desire to reproach her. They found a taxi in front of the Inn; rode silently to the little station . . .

Then Anthony knew what he wanted – to assert his will against this cool and impervious girl, to obtain with one magnificent effort a mastery that seemed infinitely desirable.

'Let's go over to see the Barneses,' he said without looking at her. 'I don't feel like going home.'

– Mrs Barnes, née Rachael Jerryl, had a summer place several miles from Redgate.

'We went there day before yesterday,' she answered shortly.

'I'm sure they'd be glad to see us.' He felt that that was not a strong enough note, braced himself stubbornly, and added: 'I want to see the Barneses. I haven't any desire to go home.'

'Well, I haven't any desire to go to the Barneses.'

Suddenly they stared at each other.

'Why, Anthony,' she said with annoyance, 'this is Sunday night and they probably have guests for supper. Why we should go in at this hour – '

'Then why couldn't we have stayed at the Merriams'?' he burst out. 'Why go home when we were having a perfectly decent time? They asked us to supper.'

'They had to. Give me the money and I'll get the railroad tickets.'

'I certainly will not! I'm in no humour for a ride in that damn hot train.'

Gloria stamped her foot on the platform.

'Anthony, you act as if you're tight!'

'On the contrary, I'm perfectly sober.'

But his voice had slipped into a husky key and she knew with certainty that this was untrue.

'If you're sober you'll give me the money for the tickets.'

But it was too late to talk to him that way. In his mind was but one idea – that Gloria was being selfish, that she was always being selfish and would continue to be unless here and now he asserted himself as her master. This was the occasion of all occasions, since for a whim she had deprived him of a pleasure. His determination solidified, approached momentarily a dull and sullen hate.

'I won't go in the train,' he said, his voice trembling a little with anger. 'We're going to the Barneses.'

'I'm not!' she cried. 'If you go, I'm going home alone.'

'Go on, then.'

Without a word she turned towards the ticket office; simultaneously he remembered that she had some money with her and that this was not the sort of victory he wanted, the sort he must have. He took a step after her and seized her arm.

'See here!' he muttered, 'you're *not* going alone!'

'I certainly am – why, Anthony!' This exclamation as she tried to pull away from him and he only tightened his grasp.

He looked at her with narrowed and malicious eyes.

'Let go!' Her cry had a quality of fierceness. 'If you have *any* decency you'll let go.'

'Why?' He knew why. But he took a confused and not quite confident pride in holding her there.

'I'm going home, do you understand? And you're going to let me go!'

'No, I'm not.'

Her eyes were burning now.

'Are you going to make a scene here?'

'I say you're not going! I'm tired of your eternal selfishness!'

'I only want to go home.' Two wrathful tears started from her eyes.

'This time you're going to do what *I* say.'

Slowly her body straightened: her head went back in a gesture of infinite scorn.

'I hate you!' Her low words were expelled like venom through her clenched teeth. 'Oh, *let* me go! Oh, I *hate* you!' She tried to jerk herself away but he only grasped the other arm. 'I hate you! I hate you!'

At Gloria's fury his uncertainty returned, but he felt that now he had gone too far to give in. It seemed that he had always given in and that in her heart she had despised him for it. Ah, she might hate him now, but afterwards she would admire him for his dominance.

The approaching train gave out a premonitory siren that tumbled melodramatically towards them down the glistening blue tracks. Gloria tugged and strained to free herself, and words older than the Book of Genesis came to her lips.

'Oh, you brute!' she sobbed. 'Oh, you brute! Oh, I hate you! Oh, you brute! Oh – '

On the station platform other prospective passengers were beginning to turn and stare; the drone of the train was audible, it increased to a clamour. Gloria's efforts redoubled, then ceased altogether, and she stood there trembling and hot-eyed at this helpless humiliation, as the engine roared and thundered into the station.

Low, below the flood of steam and the grinding of the brakes came her voice: 'Oh, if there was one *man* here you couldn't do this! You couldn't do this! You coward! You coward, oh, you coward!'

Anthony, silent, trembling himself, gripped her rigidly, aware that faces, dozens of them, curiously unmoved, shadows of a dream, were regarding him. Then the bells distilled metallic crashes that were like physical pain, the smoke-stacks volleyed in slow acceleration at the sky, and in a moment of noise and grey gaseous turbulence the line of faces ran by, moved off, became indistinct – until suddenly there was only the sun slanting east across the tracks and a volume of sound decreasing far off like a train made out of tin thunder. He dropped her arms. He had won.

Now, if he wished, he might laugh. The test was done and he had sustained his will with violence. Let leniency walk in the wake of victory.

'We'll hire a car here and drive back to Marietta,' he said with fine reserve.

For answer Gloria seized his hand with both of hers and raising it to her mouth bit deeply into his thumb. He scarcely noticed the pain; seeing the blood spurt, he absent-mindedly drew out his handkerchief and wrapped the wound. That too was part of the triumph he supposed – it was inevitable that defeat should thus be resented – and as such was beneath notice.

She was sobbing, almost without tears, profoundly and bitterly.

'I won't go! I won't go! You – can't – make – me – go! You've – you've killed any love I ever had for you, and any respect. But all that's left in me would die before I'd move from this place. Oh, if I'd thought *you'd* lay your hands on me – '

'You're going with me,' he said brutally, 'if I have to carry you.'

He turned, beckoned to a taxicab, told the driver to go to Marietta. The man dismounted and swung the door open. Anthony faced his wife and said between his clenched teeth: 'Will you get in? – or will I *put* you in?'

With a subdued cry of infinite pain and despair she yielded herself up and got into the car.

All the long ride, through the increasing dark of twilight, she sat huddled in her side of the car, her silence broken by an occasional dry and solitary sob. Anthony stared out the window, his mind working dully on the slowly changing significance of what had occurred. Something was wrong – that last cry of Gloria's had struck a chord which echoed posthumously and with incongruous disquiet in his heart. He must be right – yet, she seemed such a pathetic little thing now, broken and dispirited, humiliated beyond the measure of her lot to bear. The sleeves of her dress were torn; her parasol was gone, forgotten on the platform. It was a new costume, he remembered, and she had been so proud of it that very morning when they had left the house . . . He began wondering if anyone they knew had seen the incident. And persistently there recurred to him her cry: 'All that's left in me would die – '

This gave him a confused and increasing worry. It fitted so well with the Gloria who lay in the corner – no longer a proud Gloria, nor any Gloria he had known. He asked himself if it were possible. While he did not believe she would cease to love him – this, of course, was unthinkable – it was yet problematical whether Gloria without her arrogance, her independence, her virginal confidence and courage, would be the girl of his glory, the radiant woman who was precious and charming because she was ineffably, triumphantly herself.

He was very drunk even then, so drunk as not to realise his own drunkenness. When they reached the grey house he went to his own room and, his mind still wrestling helplessly and sombrely with what he had done, fell into a deep stupor on his bed.

It was after one o'clock and the hall seemed extraordinarily quiet when Gloria, wide-eyed and sleepless, traversed it and pushed open the door of his room. He had been too befuddled to open the windows and the air was stale and thick with whiskey. She stood for a moment by his bed, a slender, exquisitely graceful figure in her boyish silk pyjamas – then with abandon she flung herself upon him, half waking him in the frantic emotion of her embrace, dropping her warm tears upon his throat.

'Oh, Anthony!' she cried passionately, 'oh, my darling, you don't know what you did!'

Yet in the morning, coming early into her room, he knelt down by her bed and cried like a little boy, as though it was his heart that had been broken.

'It seemed, last night,' she said gravely, her fingers playing in his hair, 'that all the part of me you loved, the part that was worth knowing, all the pride and fire, was gone. I knew that what was left of me would always love you, but never in quite the same way.'

Nevertheless, she was aware even then that she would forget in time and that it is the manner of life seldom to strike but always to wear away. After that morning the incident was never mentioned and its deep wound healed with Anthony's hand – and if there was triumph some darker force than theirs possessed it, possessed the knowledge and the victory.

Gloria's independence, like all sincere and profound qualities, had begun unconsciously, but, once brought to her attention by Anthony's fascinated discovery of it, it assumed more nearly the proportions of a formal code. From her conversation it might be assumed that all her energy and vitality went into a violent affirmation of the negative principle 'Never give a damn.'

'Not for anything or anybody,' she said, 'except myself and, by implication, for Anthony. That's the rule of all life and if it weren't I'd be that way anyhow. Nobody'd do anything for me if it didn't gratify them to, and I'd do as little for them.'

She was on the front porch of the nicest lady in Marietta when she said this, and as she finished she gave a curious little cry and sank in a dead faint to the porch floor.

The lady brought her to and drove her home in her car. It had occurred to the estimable Gloria that she was probably with child.

She lay upon the long lounge downstairs. Day was slipping warmly out of the window, touching the late roses on the porch pillars.

'All I think of ever is that I love you,' she wailed. 'I value my body because you think it's beautiful. And this body of mine – of yours – to have it grow ugly and shapeless? It's simply intolerable. Oh, Anthony, I'm not afraid of the pain.'

He consoled her desperately – but in vain. She continued: 'And then afterwards I might have wide hips and be pale, with all my freshness gone and no radiance in my hair.'

He paced the floor with his hands in his pockets, asking: 'Is it certain?'

'*I* don't know anything. I've always hated obstrics, or whatever you call them. I thought I'd have a child sometime. But not now.'

'Well, for God's sake don't lie there and go to pieces.'

Her sobs lapsed. She drew down a merciful silence from the twilight which filled the room. 'Turn on the lights,' she pleaded. 'These days seem so short – June seemed – to – have – longer days when I was a little girl.'

The lights snapped on and it was as though blue drapes of softest silk had been dropped behind the windows and the door. Her pallor, her immobility, without grief now, or joy, awoke his sympathy.

'Do you want me to have it?' she asked listlessly.

'I'm indifferent. That is, I'm neutral. If you have it I'll probably be glad. If you don't – well, that's all right too.'

'I wish you'd make up your mind one way or the other!'

'Suppose you make up *your* mind.'

She looked at him contemptuously, scorning to answer.

'You'd think you'd been singled out of all the women in the world for this crowning indignity.'

'What if I do!' she cried angrily. 'It isn't an indignity for them. It's their one excuse for living. It's the one thing they're good for. It *is* an indignity for *me*.

'See here, Gloria, I'm with you whatever you do, but for God's sake be a sport about it.'

'Oh, don't *fuss* at me!' she wailed.

They exchanged a mute look of no particular significance but of much stress. Then Anthony took a book from the shelf and dropped into a chair.

Half an hour later her voice came out of the intense stillness that pervaded the room and hung like incense on the air.

'I'll drive over and see Constance Merriam tomorrow.'

'All right. And I'll go to Tarrytown and see grampa.'

' – You see,' she added, 'it isn't that I'm afraid – of this or anything else. I'm being true to me, you know.'

'I know,' he agreed.

THE PRACTICAL MEN

Adam Patch, in a pious rage against the Germans, subsisted on the war news. Pin-maps plastered his walls; atlases were piled deep on tables convenient to his hand together with 'Photographic Histories of the World War', official Explain-alls, and the 'Personal Impressions' of war correspondents and of Privates X, Y and Z. Several times during Anthony's visit his grandfather's secretary, Edward Shuttleworth, the one-time 'accomplished gin-physician' of 'Pat's Place' in Hoboken, now shod with righteous indignation, would appear with an extra. The old man attacked each paper with untiring fury, tearing out those columns which appeared to him of sufficient pregnancy for preservation and thrusting them into one of his already bulging files.

'Well, what have you been doing?' he asked Anthony blandly. 'Nothing? Well, I thought so. I've been intending to drive over and see you, all summer.'

'I've been writing. Don't you remember the essay I sent you – the one I sold to *The Florentine* last winter?'

'Essay? You never sent *me* any essay.'

'Oh, yes, I did. We talked about it.'

Adam Patch shook his head mildly.

'Oh, no. You never sent *me* any essay. You may have thought you sent it but it never reached me.'

'Why, you read it, grampa,' insisted Anthony, somewhat exasperated, 'you read it and disagreed with it.'

The old man suddenly remembered, but this was made apparent only by a partial falling open of his mouth, displaying rows of grey gums. Eying Anthony with a green and ancient stare he hesitated between confessing his error and covering it up.

'So you're writing,' he said quickly. 'Well, why don't you go over and write about these Germans? Write something real, something about what's going on, something people can read.'

'Anybody can't be a war correspondent,' objected Anthony. 'You have to have some newspaper willing to buy your stuff. And I can't spare the money to go over as a freelance.'

'I'll send you over,' suggested his grandfather surprisingly. 'I'll get you over as an authorised correspondent of any newspaper you pick out.'

Anthony recoiled from the idea – almost simultaneously he bounded towards it.

'I – don't – know – '

He would have to leave Gloria, whose whole life yearned towards him and enfolded him. Gloria was in trouble. Oh, the thing wasn't feasible – yet; he saw himself in khaki, leaning, as all war correspondents lean, upon a heavy stick, portfolio at shoulder – trying to look like an Englishman. 'I'd like to think it over,' he, confessed. 'It's certainly very kind of you. I'll think it over and I'll let you know.'

Thinking it over absorbed him on the journey to New York. He had had one of those sudden flashes of illumination vouchsafed to all men who are dominated by a strong and beloved woman, which show them a world of harder men, more fiercely trained and grappling with the abstractions of thought and war. In that world the arms of Gloria would exist only as the hot embrace of a chance mistress, coolly sought and quickly forgotten . . .

These unfamiliar phantoms were crowding closely about him when he boarded his train for Marietta, in the Grand Central Station. The car was crowded; he secured the last vacant seat and it was only after several minutes that he gave even a casual glance to the man beside him. When he did he saw a heavy lay of jaw and nose, a curved chin and small, puffed-under eyes. In a moment he recognised Joseph Bloeckman.

Simultaneously they both half rose, were half embarrassed, and exchanged what amounted to a half handshake. Then, as though to complete the matter, they both half laughed.

'Well,' remarked Anthony without inspiration, 'I haven't seen you for a long time.' Immediately he regretted his words and started to add: 'I didn't know you lived out this way.' But Bloeckman anticipated him by asking pleasantly: 'How's your wife? . . . '

'She's very well. How've you been?'

'Excellent.' His tone amplified the grandeur of the word.

It seemed to Anthony that during the last year Bloeckman had grown tremendously in dignity. The boiled look was gone, he seemed 'done' at last. In addition he was no longer overdressed. The inappropriate facetiousness he had affected in ties had given way to a sturdy dark pattern, and his right hand, which had formerly displayed two heavy rings, was now innocent of ornament and even without the raw glow of a manicure.

This dignity appeared also in his personality. The last aura of the successful travelling-man had faded from him, that deliberate ingratiation of which the lowest form is the bawdy joke in the Pullman smoker. One imagined that, having been fawned upon financially, he had attained aloofness; having been snubbed socially, he had acquired reticence. But whatever had given him weight instead of bulk, Anthony no longer felt a correct superiority in his presence.

'D'you remember Caramel, Richard Caramel? I believe you met him one night.'

'I remember. He was writing a book.'

'Well, he sold it to the movies. Then they had some scenario man named Jordan work on it. Well, Dick subscribes to a clipping bureau and he's furious because about half the movie reviewers speak of the "power and strength of William Jordan's *Demon Lover*". Didn't mention old Dick at all. You'd think this fellow Jordan had actually conceived and developed the thing.'

Bloeckman nodded comprehensively.

'Most of the contracts state that the original writer's name goes into all the paid publicity. Is Caramel still writing?'

'Oh, yes. Writing hard. Short stories.'

'Well, that's fine, that's fine . . . You on this train often?'

'About once a week. We live in Marietta.'

'Is that so? Well, well! I live near Cos Cob myself. Bought a place there only recently. We're only five miles apart.'

'You'll have to come and see us.' Anthony was surprised at his own courtesy. 'I'm sure Gloria'd be delighted to see an old friend. Anybody'll tell you where the house is – it's our second season there.'

'Thank you.' Then, as though returning a complementary politeness: 'How is your grandfather?'

'He's been well. I had lunch with him today.'

'A great character,' said Bloeckman severely. 'A fine example of an American.'

THE TRIUMPH OF LETHARGY

Anthony found his wife deep in the porch hammock voluptuously engaged with a lemonade and a tomato sandwich and carrying on an apparently cheery conversation with Tana upon one of Tana's complicated themes.

'In my countree,' Anthony recognised his invariable preface, 'all time – peoples – eat rice – because haven't got. Cannot eat what no have got.' Had his nationality not been desperately apparent one would have thought he had acquired his knowledge of his native land from American primary-school geographies.

When the Oriental had been squelched and dismissed to the kitchen, Anthony turned questioningly to Gloria: 'It's all right,' she announced, smiling broadly. 'And it surprised me more than it does you.'

'There's no doubt?'

'None! Couldn't be!'

They rejoiced happily, gay again with reborn irresponsibility. Then he told her of his opportunity to go abroad, and that he was almost ashamed to reject it.

'What do *you* think? Just tell me frankly.'

'Why, Anthony!' Her eyes were startled. 'Do you want to go? Without me?'

His face fell – yet he knew, with his wife's question, that it was too late. Her arms, sweet and strangling, were around him, for he had made all such choices back in that room in the Plaza the year before. This was an anachronism from an age of such dreams.

'Gloria,' he lied, in a great burst of comprehension, 'of course I don't. I was thinking you might go as a nurse or something.' He wondered dully if his grandfather would consider this.

As she smiled he realised again how beautiful she was, a gorgeous girl of miraculous freshness and sheerly honourable eyes. She embraced his suggestion with luxurious intensity, holding it aloft like a sun of her own making and basking in its beams. She strung together an amazing synopsis for an extravaganza of martial adventure.

After supper, surfeited with the subject, she yawned. She wanted not to talk but only to read *Penrod*, stretched upon the lounge until at midnight she fell asleep. But Anthony, after he had carried her romantically up the stairs, stayed awake to brood upon the day, vaguely angry with her, vaguely dissatisfied.

'What am I going to do?' he began at breakfast. 'Here we've been married a year and we've just worried around without even being efficient people of leisure.'

'Yes, you ought to do something,' she admitted, being in an agreeable and loquacious humour. This was not the first of these discussions, but as they usually developed Anthony in the role of protagonist, she had come to avoid them.

'It's not that I have any moral compunctions about work,' he continued, 'but grampa may die tomorrow and he may live for ten years. Meanwhile we're living above our income and all we've got to show for it is a farmer's car and a few clothes. We keep an apartment that we've only lived in three months and a little old house way off in nowhere. We're frequently bored and yet we won't make any effort to know anyone except the same crowd who drift around California all summer wearing sports clothes and waiting for their families to die.'

'How you've changed!' remarked Gloria. 'Once you told me you didn't see why an American couldn't loaf gracefully.'

'Well, damn it, I wasn't married. And the old mind was working at top speed and now it's going round and round like a cog-wheel with nothing to catch it. As a matter of fact I think that if I hadn't met you I *would* have done something. But you make leisure so subtly attractive – '

'Oh, it's all my fault – '

'I didn't mean that, and you know I didn't. But here I'm almost twenty-seven and – '

'Oh,' she interrupted in vexation, 'you make me tired! Talking as though I were objecting or hindering you!'

'I was just discussing it, Gloria. Can't I discuss – '

'I should think you'd be strong enough to settle – '

' – something with you without – '

' – your own problems without coming to me. You *talk* a lot about going to work. I could use more money very easily, but *I'm* not complaining. Whether you work or not I love you.' Her last words were gentle as fine snow upon hard ground. But for the moment neither was attending to the other – they were each engaged in polishing and perfecting their own attitude.

'I have worked – some.' This by Anthony was an imprudent bringing up of raw reserves. Gloria laughed, torn between delight and derision; she resented his sophistry as at the same time she admired his nonchalance. She would never blame him for being the ineffectual idler so long as he did it sincerely, from the attitude that nothing much was worth doing.

'Work!' she scoffed. 'Oh, you sad bird! You bluffer! Work – that means a great arranging of the desk and the lights, a great sharpening of pencils, and "Gloria, don't sing!" and "Please keep that damn Tana away from me", and "Let me read you my opening sentence", and "I won't be through for a long time, Gloria, so don't stay up for me", and a tremendous consumption of tea or coffee. And that's all. In just about an hour I hear the old pencil stop scratching and look over. You've got out a book and you're "looking up" something. Then you're reading. Then yawns – then bed and a great tossing about because you're all full of caffeine and can't sleep. Two weeks later the whole performance over again.'

With much difficulty Anthony retained a scanty breech-clout of dignity.

'Now that's a *slight* exaggeration. You know *darn well* I sold an essay to *The Florentine* – and it attracted a lot of attention considering the circulation of *The Florentine*. And what's more, Gloria, you know I sat up till five o'clock in the morning finishing it.'

She lapsed into silence, giving him rope. And if he had not hanged himself he had certainly come to the end of it.

'At least,' he concluded feebly, 'I'm perfectly willing to be a war correspondent.'

But so was Gloria. They were both willing – anxious; they assured each other of it. The evening ended on a note of tremendous sentiment, the majesty of leisure, the ill health of Adam Patch, love at any cost.

'Anthony!' she called over the bannister one afternoon a week later, 'there's someone at the door.' Anthony, who had been lolling in the hammock on the sun-speckled south porch, strolled around to the front of the house. A foreign car, large and impressive, crouched like an immense and saturnine bug at the foot of the path. A man in a soft pongee suit, with cap to match, hailed him.

'Hello there, Patch. Ran over to call on you.'

It was Bloeckman; as always, infinitesimally improved, of subtler intonation, of more convincing ease.

'I'm awfully glad you did.' Anthony raised his voice to a vine-covered window: 'Glor-i-*a*! We've got a visitor!'

'I'm in the tub,' wailed Gloria politely.

With a smile the two men acknowledged the triumph of her alibi.

'She'll be down. Come round here on the side-porch. Like a drink? Gloria's always in the tub – good third of every day.'

'Pity she doesn't live on the Sound.'

'Can't afford it.'

As coming from Adam Patch's grandson, Bloeckman took this as a form of pleasantry. After fifteen minutes filled with estimable brilliancies, Gloria appeared, fresh in starched yellow, bringing atmosphere and an increase of vitality.

'I want to be a successful sensation in the movies,' she announced. 'I hear that Mary Pickford makes a million dollars annually.'

'You could, you know,' said Bloeckman. 'I think you'd film very well.'

'Would you let me, Anthony? If I only play unsophisticated roles?'

As the conversation continued in stilted commas, Anthony wondered that to him and Bloeckman both this girl had once been the most stimulating, the most tonic personality they had ever known – and now the three sat like over-oiled machines, without conflict, without fear, without elation, heavily enamelled little figures secure beyond enjoyment in a world where death and war, dull emotion and noble savagery were covering a continent with the smoke of terror.

In a moment he would call Tana and they would pour into themselves a gay and delicate poison which would restore them momentarily to the pleasurable excitement of childhood, when every face in a crowd had carried its suggestion of splendid and significant transactions taking place somewhere to some magnificent and illimitable purpose . . . Life was no more than this summer afternoon; a faint wind stirring the lace collar of Gloria's dress; the slow baking drowsiness of the veranda . . . Intolerably unmoved they all seemed, removed from any romantic imminency of action. Even Gloria's beauty needed wild emotions, needed poignancy, needed death . . .

' . . . Any day next week,' Bloeckman was saying to Gloria. 'Here – take this card. What they do is to give you a test of about three hundred feet of film, and they can tell pretty accurately from that.'

'How about Wednesday?'

'Wednesday's fine. Just phone me and I'll go around with you – '

He was on his feet, shaking hands briskly – then his car was a wraith of dust down the road. Anthony turned to his wife in bewilderment.

'Why, Gloria!'

'You don't mind if I have a trial, Anthony. Just a trial? I've got to go to town Wednesday, *any*how.'

'But it's so silly! You don't want to go into the movies – moon around a studio all day with a lot of cheap chorus people.'

'Lot of mooning around Mary Pickford does!'

'Everybody isn't a Mary Pickford.'

'Well, I can't see how you'd object to my *try*ing.'

'I do, though. I hate actors.'

'Oh, you make me tired. Do you imagine I have a very thrilling time dozing on this damn porch?'

'You wouldn't mind if you loved me.'

'Of course I love you,' she said impatiently, making out a quick case for herself. 'It's just because I do that I hate to see you go to pieces by just lying around and saying you ought to work. Perhaps if I *did* go into this for a while it'd stir you up so you'd do something.'

'It's just your craving for excitement, that's all it is.'

'Maybe it is! It's a perfectly natural craving, isn't it?'

'Well, I'll tell you one thing. If you go into the movies I'm going to Europe.'

'Well, go on then! *I'm* not stopping you!'

To show she was not stopping him she melted into melancholy tears. Together they marshalled the armies of sentiment – words, kisses, endearments, self-reproaches. They attained nothing. Inevitably they attained nothing. Finally, in a burst of gargantuan emotion each of them sat down and wrote a letter. Anthony's was to his grandfather; Gloria's was to Joseph Bloeckman. It was a triumph of lethargy.

One day early in July Anthony, returned from an afternoon in New York, called upstairs to Gloria. Receiving no answer he guessed she was asleep and so went into the pantry for one of the little sandwiches that were always prepared for them. He found Tana seated at the kitchen table before a miscellaneous assortment of odds and ends – cigar-boxes, knives, pencils, the tops of cans, and some scraps of paper covered with elaborate figures and diagrams.

'What the devil you doing?' demanded Anthony curiously.

Tana politely grinned.

'I show you,' he exclaimed enthusiastically. 'I tell – '

'You making a dog-house?'

'No, sa.' Tana grinned again. 'Make typewutta.'

'Typewriter?'

'Yes, sa. I think, oh all time I think, lie in bed think 'bout typewutta.'

'So you thought you'd make one, eh?'

'Wait. I tell.'

Anthony, munching a sandwich, leaned leisurely against the sink.

Tana opened and closed his mouth several times as though testing its capacity for action. Then with a rush he began: 'I been think – typewutta – has, oh, many many many many *thing*. Oh many many many many.'

'Many keys. I see.'

'No-o? *Yes* – key! Many many many many lettah. Like so a-b-c.'

'Yes, you're right.'

'Wait. I tell.' He screwed his face up in a tremendous effort to express himself: 'I been think – many words – end same. Like e-n-g.'

'You bet. A whole raft of them.'

'So – I make – typewutta – quick. Not so many lettah – '

'That's a great idea, Tana. Save time. You'll make a fortune. Press one key and there's "ing". Hope you work it out.'

Tana laughed disparagingly. 'Wait. I tell – '

'Where's Mrs Patch?'

'She out. Wait, I tell – ' Again he screwed up his face for action. '*My* typewutta – '

'Where is she?'

'Here – I make.' He pointed to the miscellany of junk on the table.

'I mean Mrs Patch.'

'She out.' Tana reassured him. 'She be back five o'clock, she say.'

'Down in the village?'

'No. Went off before lunch. She go Mr Bloeckman.'

Anthony started.

'Went out with Mr Bloeckman?'

'She be back five.'

Without a word Anthony left the kitchen with Tana's disconsolate 'I tell' trailing after him. So this was Gloria's idea of excitement, by God! His fists were clenched; within a moment he had worked himself up to a tremendous pitch of indignation. He went to the door and looked out; there was no car in sight and his watch stood at four minutes of five. With furious energy he dashed down to the end of the path – as far as the bend of the road a mile off he could see no car – except – but it was a farmer's flivver. Then, in an undignified pursuit of dignity, he rushed back to the shelter of the house as quickly as he had rushed out.

Pacing up and down the living-room he began an angry rehearsal of the speech he would make to her when she came in –

'So this is love!' he would begin – or no, it sounded too much like the popular phrase 'So this is Paris!' He must be dignified, hurt, grieved. Anyhow – 'So this is what *you* do when I have to go up and trot all day around the hot city on business. No wonder I can't write! No wonder I don't dare let you out of my sight!' He was expanding now, warming to his subject. 'I'll tell you,' he continued, 'I'll tell you – ' He paused, catching a familiar ring in the words – then he realised – it was Tana's 'I tell'.

Yet Anthony neither laughed nor seemed absurd to himself. To his frantic imagination it was already six – seven – eight, and she was never coming! Bloeckman finding her bored and unhappy had persuaded her to go to California with him . . .

– There was a great to-do out in front, a joyous, 'Yoho, Anthony!' and he rose trembling, weakly happy to see her fluttering up the path. Bloeckman was following, cap in hand.

'Dearest!' she cried. 'We've been for the best jaunt – all over New York State.'

'I'll have to be starting home,' said Bloeckman, almost immediately. 'Wish you'd both been here when I came.'

'I'm sorry I wasn't,' answered Anthony dryly. When he had departed Anthony hesitated. The fear was gone from his heart, yet he felt that some protest was ethically apropos. Gloria resolved his uncertainty.

'I knew you wouldn't mind. He came just before lunch and said he had to go to Garrison on business and wouldn't I go with him. He looked so lonesome, Anthony. And I drove his car all the way.'

Listlessly Anthony dropped into a chair, his mind tired – tired with nothing, tired with everything, with the world's weight he had never chosen to bear. He was ineffectual and vaguely helpless here as he had always been. One of those personalities who, in spite of all their words, are inarticulate, he seemed to have inherited only the vast tradition of human failure – that, and the sense of death.

'I suppose I don't care,' he answered.

One must be broad about these things, and Gloria being young, being beautiful, must have reasonable privileges. Yet it wearied him that he failed to understand.

WINTER

She rolled over on her back and lay still for a moment in the great bed watching the February sun suffer one last attenuated refinement in its passage through the leaded panes into the room. For a time she had no accurate sense of her whereabouts or of the events of the day before, or the day before that; then, like a suspended pendulum, memory began to beat out its story, releasing with each swing a burdened quota of time until her life was given back to her.

She could hear, now, Anthony's troubled breathing beside her; she could smell whiskey and cigarette smoke. She noticed that she lacked complete muscular control; when she moved it was not a sinuous motion with the resultant strain distributed easily over her body – it was a tremendous effort of her nervous system as though each time she were hypnotising herself into performing an impossible action . . .

She was in the bathroom, brushing her teeth to get rid of that intolerable taste; then back by the bedside listening to the rattle of Bounds's key in the outer door.

'Wake up, Anthony!' she said sharply.

She climbed into bed beside him and closed her eyes. Almost the last thing she remembered was a conversation with Mr and Mrs Lacy. Mrs Lacy had said, 'Sure you don't want us to get you a taxi?' and Anthony had replied that he guessed they could walk over to Fifth all right. Then they had both attempted, imprudently, to bow – and collapsed absurdly into a battalion of empty milk bottles just outside the door. There must have been two dozen milk bottles standing open-mouthed in the dark. She could conceive of no plausible explanation for those milk bottles. Perhaps they had been attracted by the singing in the Lacy house and had hurried over agape with wonder to see the fun. Well, they'd had the worst of it – though it seemed that she and Anthony never would get up, the perverse things rolled so . . .

Still, they had found a taxi. 'My meter's broken and it'll cost you a dollar and a half to get home,' said the taxi driver. 'Well,' said Anthony, 'I'm young Packy McFarland and if you'll come down here I'll beat you till you can't stand up' . . . At that point the man had driven off without them. They must have found another taxi, for they were in the apartment . . .

'What time is it?' Anthony was sitting up in bed, staring at her with owlish precision.

This was obviously a rhetorical question. Gloria could think of no reason why she should be expected to know the time.

'Golly, I feel like the devil!' muttered Anthony dispassionately. Relaxing, he tumbled back upon his pillow. 'Bring on your grim reaper!'

'Anthony, how'd we finally get home last night?'

'Taxi.'

'Oh!' Then, after a pause: 'Did you put me to bed?'

'I don't know. Seems to me you put *me* to bed. What day is it?'

'Tuesday.'

'Tuesday? I hope so. If it's Wednesday, I've got to start work at that idiotic place. Supposed to be down at nine or some such ungodly hour.'

'Ask Bounds,' suggested Gloria feebly.

'Bounds!' he called.

Sprightly, sober – a voice from a world that it seemed in the past two days they had left for ever, Bounds sprang in short steps down the hall and appeared in the half-darkness of the door.

'What day, Bounds?'

'February the twenty-second, I think, sir.'

'I mean day of the week.'

'Tuesday, sir.'

'Thanks.'

After a pause: 'Are you ready for breakfast, sir?'

'Yes, and Bounds, before you get it, will you make a pitcher of water, and set it here beside the bed? I'm a little thirsty.'

'Yes, sir.'

Bounds retreated in sober dignity down the hallway.

'Lincoln's birthday,' affirmed Anthony without enthusiasm, 'or St Valentine's or somebody's. When did we start on this insane party?'

'Sunday night.'

'After prayers?' he suggested sardonically.

'We raced all over town in those hansoms and Maury sat up with his driver, don't you remember? Then we came home and he tried to cook some bacon – came out of the pantry with a few blackened remains, insisting it was "fried to the proverbial crisp".'

Both of them laughed, spontaneously but with some difficulty, and lying there side by side reviewed the chain of events that had ended in this rusty and chaotic dawn.

They had been in New York for almost four months, since the country had grown too cool in late October. They had given up California this year, partly because of lack of funds, partly with the idea of going abroad should this interminable war, persisting now into its second year, end during the winter. Of late their income had lost elasticity; no longer did it stretch to cover gay whims and pleasant extravagances, and Anthony had spent many puzzled and unsatisfactory hours over a densely figured pad, making remarkable budgets that left huge margins for 'amusements, trips, etc.', and trying to apportion, even approximately, their past expenditures.

He remembered a time when in going on a 'party' with his two best friends, he and Maury had invariably paid more than their share of the expenses. They would buy the tickets for the theatre or squabble between themselves for the dinner check. It had seemed fitting; Dick, with his naïvety and his astonishing fund of information about himself, had been a diverting, almost juvenile, figure – court jester to their royalty. But this was no longer true. It was Dick who always had money; it was Anthony who entertained within limitations – always excepting occasional wild, wine-inspired, cheque-cashing parties – and it was Anthony who was solemn about it next morning and told the scornful and disgusted Gloria that they'd have to be 'more careful next time'.

In the two years since the publication of *The Demon Lover*, Dick had made over twenty-five thousand dollars, most of it lately, when the reward of the author of fiction had begun to swell unprecedentedly as a result of the voracious hunger of the motion pictures for plots. He received seven hundred dollars for every story, at that time a large emolument for such a young man – he was not quite thirty – and for every one that contained enough 'action' (kissing, shooting and sacrificing) for the movies, he obtained an additional thousand. His stories varied; there was a measure of vitality and a sort of instinctive technique in all of them, but none attained the personality of *The Demon Lover*, and there were several that Anthony considered downright cheap. These, Dick explained severely, were to widen his audience. Wasn't it true that men who had attained real permanence from Shakespeare to Mark Twain had appealed to the many as well as to the elect?

Though Anthony and Maury disagreed, Gloria told him to go ahead and make as much money as he could – that was the only thing that counted anyhow . . .

Maury, a little stouter, faintly mellower, and more complaisant, had gone to work in Philadelphia. He came to New York once or twice a month and on such occasions the four of them travelled the popular routes from dinner to the theatre, thence to the Frolic or, perhaps, at the urging of the ever-curious Gloria, to one of the cellars of Greenwich Village, notorious through the furious but short-lived vogue of the 'new poetry movement'.

In January, after many monologues directed at his reticent wife, Anthony determined to 'get something to do', for the winter at any rate. He wanted to please his grandfather and even, in a measure, to see how he liked it himself. He discovered during several tentative semi-social calls that employers were not interested in a young man who was only going to 'try it for a few months or so'. As the grandson of Adam Patch he was received everywhere with marked courtesy, but the old man was a back number now – the heyday of his fame as first an 'oppressor' and then an uplifter of the people had been during the twenty years preceding his retirement. Anthony even found several of the younger men who were under the impression that Adam Patch had been dead for some years.

Eventually Anthony went to his grandfather and asked his advice, which turned out to be that he should enter the bond business as a salesman, a tedious suggestion to Anthony, but one that in the end he determined to follow. Sheer money in deft manipulation had fascinations under all circumstances, while almost any side of manufacturing would be insufferably dull. He considered newspaper work but decided that the hours were not ordered for a married man. And he lingered over pleasant fancies of himself either as editor of a brilliant weekly of opinion, an American *Mercure de France*, or as scintillant producer of satiric comedy and Parisian musical revue. However, the approaches to these latter guilds seemed to be guarded by professional secrets. Men drifted into them by the devious highways of writing and acting. It was palpably impossible to get on a magazine unless you had been on one before.

So in the end he entered, by way of his grandfather's letter, that Sanctum Americanum where sat the president of Wilson, Hiemer and Hardy at his 'cleared desk', and issued therefrom employed. He was to begin work on the twenty-third of February.

In tribute to the momentous occasion this two-day revel had been planned, since, he said, after he began working he'd have to get to bed early during the week. Maury Noble had arrived from Philadelphia on a trip that had to do with seeing some man in Wall Street (whom, incidentally, he failed to see), and Richard Caramel had been half persuaded, half tricked into joining them. They had condescended to a wet and fashionable wedding on Monday afternoon, and in the evening had occurred the dénouement: Gloria, going beyond her accustomed limit of four precisely timed cocktails, led them on as gay and joyous a bacchanal as they had ever known, disclosing an astonishing knowledge of ballet steps, and singing songs which she confessed had been taught her by her cook when she was innocent and seventeen. She repeated these by request at intervals throughout the evening with such frank conviviality that Anthony, far from being annoyed, was gratified at this fresh source of entertainment. The occasion was memorable in other ways – a long conversation between Maury and a defunct crab, which he was dragging around on the end of a string, as to whether the crab was fully conversant with the applications of the binomial theorem, and the aforementioned race in two hansom cabs with the sedate and impressive shadows of Fifth Avenue for audience, ending in a labyrinthine escape into the darkness of Central Park. Finally Anthony and Gloria had paid a call on some wild young married people – the Lacys – and collapsed in the empty milk bottles.

Morning now – theirs to add up the cheques cashed here and there in clubs, stores, restaurants. Theirs to air the dank staleness of wine and cigarettes out of the tall blue front room, to pick up the broken glass and brush at the stained fabric of chairs and sofas; to give Bounds suits and dresses for the cleaners; finally, to take their smothery half-feverish bodies and faded depressed spirits out into the chill air of February, that life might go on and Wilson, Hiemer and Hardy obtain the services of a vigorous man at nine next morning.

'Do you remember,' called Anthony from the bathroom, 'when Maury got out at the corner of One Hundred and Tenth Street and acted as a traffic cop, beckoning cars forward and motioning them back? They must have thought he was a private detective.'

After each reminiscence they both laughed inordinately, their overwrought nerves responding as acutely and janglingly to mirth as to depression.

Gloria at the mirror was wondering at the splendid colour and freshness of her face – it seemed that she had never looked so well, though her stomach hurt her and her head was aching furiously.

The day passed slowly. Anthony, riding in a taxi to his broker's to borrow money on a bond, found that he had only two dollars in his pocket. The fare would cost all of that, but he felt that on this particular afternoon he could not have endured the subway. When the taximetre reached his limit he must get out and walk.

With this his mind drifted off into one of its characteristic day-dreams . . . In this dream he discovered that the metre was going too fast – the driver had dishonestly adjusted it. Calmly he reached his destination and then nonchalantly handed the man what he justly owed him. The man showed fight, but almost before his hands were up Anthony had knocked him down with one terrific blow. And when he rose Anthony quickly sidestepped and floored him definitively with a crack to the temple.

. . . He was in court now. The judge had fined him five dollars and he had no money. Would the court take his cheque? Ah, but the court did not know him. Well, he could identify himself by having them call his apartment.

. . . They did so. Yes, it was Mrs Anthony Patch speaking – but how did she know that this man was her husband? How could she know? Let the police sergeant ask her if she remembered the milk bottles . . .

He leaned forward hurriedly and tapped at the glass. The taxi was only at Brooklyn Bridge, but the metre showed a dollar and eighty cents, and Anthony would never have omitted the ten-per-cent tip.

Later in the afternoon he returned to the apartment. Gloria had also been out – shopping – and was asleep, curled in a corner of the sofa with her purchase locked securely in her arms. Her face was as untroubled as a little girl's, and the bundle that she pressed tightly to her bosom was a child's doll, a profound and infinitely healing balm to her disturbed and childish heart.

DESTINY

It was with this party, more especially with Gloria's part in it, that a decided change began to come over their way of living. The magnificent attitude of not giving a damn altered overnight; from being a mere tenet of Gloria's it became the entire solace and justification for what they chose to do and what consequence it brought. Not to be sorry, not to loose one cry of regret, to live according to a clear code of honour towards each other, and to seek the moment's happiness as fervently and persistently as possible.

'No one cares about us but ourselves, Anthony,' she said one day. 'It'd be ridiculous for me to go about pretending I felt any obligations towards the world, and as for worrying what people think about me, I simply *don't*, that's all. Since I was a little girl in dancing-school I've been criticised by the mothers of all the little girls who weren't as popular as I was, and I've always looked on criticism as a sort of envious tribute.'

This was because of a party in the Boul' Mich' one night, where Constance Merriam had seen her as one of a highly stimulated party of four. Constance Merriam, 'as an old school friend', had gone to the trouble of inviting her to lunch next day in order to inform her how terrible it was.

'I told her I couldn't see it,' Gloria told Anthony. 'Eric Merriam is a sort of sublimated Percy Wolcott – you remember that man in Hot Springs I told you about – his idea of respecting Constance is to leave her at home with her sewing and her baby and her book, and such innocuous amusements, whenever he's going on a party that promises to be anything but deathly dull.'

'Did you tell her that?'

'I certainly did. And I told her that what she really objected to was that I was having a better time than she was.'

Anthony applauded her. He was tremendously proud of Gloria, proud that she never failed to eclipse whatever other women might be in the party, proud that men were always glad to revel with her in great rowdy groups, without any attempt to do more than enjoy her beauty and the warmth of her vitality.

These 'parties' gradually became their chief source of entertainment. Still in love, still enormously interested in each other, they yet found as spring drew near that staying at home in the evening palled on them; books were unreal; the old magic of being alone had long since vanished – instead they preferred to be bored by a stupid musical comedy, or to go to dinner with the most uninteresting of their acquaintances, so long as there would be enough cocktails to keep the conversation from becoming utterly intolerable. A scattering of younger married people who had been their friends in school or college, as well as a varied assortment of single men, began to think instinctively of them whenever colour and excitement were needed, so there was scarcely a day without its phone call, its, 'Wondered what you were doing this evening.' Wives, as a rule, were afraid of Gloria – her facile attainment of the centre of the stage, her innocent but nevertheless disturbing way of becoming a favourite with husbands – these things drove them instinctively into an attitude of profound distrust, heightened by the fact that Gloria was largely unresponsive to any intimacy shown her by a woman.

On the appointed Wednesday in February Anthony had gone to the imposing offices of Wilson, Hiemer and Hardy and listened to many vague instructions delivered by an energetic young man of about his own age, named Kahler, who wore a defiant yellow pompadour, and in announcing himself as an assistant secretary gave the impression that it was a tribute to exceptional ability.

'There's two kinds of men here, you'll find,' he said. 'There's the man who gets to be an assistant secretary or treasurer, gets his name on our folder here, before he's thirty, and there's the man who gets his name there at forty-five. The man who gets his name there at forty-five stays there the rest of his life.'

'How about the man who gets it there at thirty?' enquired Anthony politely.

'Why, he gets up here, you see.' He pointed to a list of assistant vice-presidents upon the folder. 'Or maybe he gets to be president or secretary or treasurer.'

'And what about these over here?'

'Those? Oh, those are the trustees – the men with capital.'

'I see.'

'Now some people,' continued Kahler, 'think that whether a man gets started early or late depends on whether he's got a college education. But they're wrong.'

'I see.'

'I had one; I was Buckleigh, class of nineteen-eleven, but when I came down to the Street I soon found that the things that would help me here weren't the fancy things I learned in college. In fact, I had to get a lot of fancy stuff out of my head.'

Anthony could not help wondering what possible 'fancy stuff' he had learned at Buckleigh in nineteen-eleven. An irrepressible idea that it was some sort of needlework recurred to him throughout the rest of the conversation.

'See that fellow over there?' Kahler pointed to a youngish-looking man with handsome grey hair, sitting at a desk inside a mahogany railing. 'That's Mr Ellinger, the first vice-president. Been everywhere, seen everything; got a fine education.'

In vain did Anthony try to open his mind to the romance of finance; he could think of Mr Ellinger only as one of the buyers of the handsome leather sets of Thackeray, Balzac, Hugo and Gibbon that lined the walls of the big bookstores.

Through the damp and uninspiring month of March he was prepared for salesmanship. Lacking enthusiasm he was capable of viewing the turmoil and bustle that surrounded him only as a fruitless circumambient striving towards an incomprehensible goal, tangibly evidenced only by the rival mansions of Mr Frick and Mr Carnegie on Fifth Avenue. That these portentous vice-presidents and trustees should be actually the fathers of the 'best men' he had known at Harvard seemed to him incongruous.

He ate in an employees' lunch-room upstairs with an uneasy suspicion that he was being uplifted, wondering through that first week if the dozens of young clerks, some of them alert and immaculate, and just out of college, lived in flamboyant hope of crowding on to that narrow slip of cardboard before the catastrophic thirties. The conversation that interwove with the pattern of the day's work was all much of a piece. One discussed how Mr Wilson had made his money, what method Mr Hiemer had employed and the means resorted to by Mr Hardy. One related age-old but eternally breathless anecdotes of the fortunes stumbled on precipitously in the Street by a 'butcher' or a 'bartender', or 'a darn *mess*enger boy, by golly!' and then one talked of the current gambles, and whether it was best to go out for a hundred thousand a year or be content with twenty. During the preceding year one of the assistant secretaries had invested all his savings in Bethlehem Steel. The story of his spectacular magnificence, of his haughty resignation in January, and of the triumphal palace he was now building in California, was the favourite office subject. The man's very name had acquired a magic significance, symbolising as he did the aspirations of all good Americans. Anecdotes were told about him – how one of the vice-presidents had advised him to sell, by golly, but he had hung on, even bought on margin, 'and *now* look where he is!'

Such, obviously, was the stuff of life – a dizzy triumph dazzling the eyes of all of them, a gypsy siren to content them with meagre wage and with the arithmetical improbability of their eventual success.

To Anthony the notion became appalling. He felt that to succeed here the idea of success must grasp and limit his mind. It seemed to him that the essential element in these men at the top was their faith that their affairs were the very core of life. All other things being equal, self-assurance and opportunism won out over technical knowledge; it was obvious that the more expert work went on near the bottom – so, with appropriate efficiency, the technical experts were kept there.

His determination to stay in at night during the week did not survive, and a good half of the time he came to work with a splitting, sickish headache and the crowded horror of the morning subway ringing in his ears like an echo of hell.

Then, abruptly, he quit. He had remained in bed all one Monday, and late in the evening, overcome by one of those attacks of moody despair to which he periodically succumbed, he wrote and mailed a letter to Mr Wilson, confessing that he considered himself ill adapted to the work. Gloria, coming in from the theatre with Richard Caramel, found him on the lounge, silently staring at the high ceiling, more depressed and discouraged than he had been at any time since their marriage.

She wanted him to whine. If he had she would have reproached him bitterly, for she was not a little annoyed, but he only lay there so utterly miserable that she felt sorry for him, and kneeling down she stroked his head, saying how little it mattered, how little anything mattered so long as they loved each other. It was like their first year, and Anthony, reacting to her cool hand, to her voice that was soft as breath itself upon his ear, became almost cheerful, and talked with her of his future plans. He even regretted, silently, before he went to bed that he had so hastily mailed his resignation.

'Even when everything seems rotten you can't trust that judgement,' Gloria had said. 'It's the sum of all your judgements that counts.'

In mid-April came a letter from the real-estate agent in Marietta, encouraging them to take the grey house for another year at a slightly increased rental, and enclosing a lease made out for their signatures. For a week lease and letter lay carelessly neglected on Anthony's desk. They had no intention of returning to Marietta. They were weary of the place, and had been bored most of the preceding summer. Besides, their car had deteriorated to a rattling mass of hypochondriacal metal, and a new one was financially inadvisable.

But because of another wild revel, enduring through four days and participated in, at one time or another, by more than a dozen people, they did sign the lease; to their utter horror they signed it and sent it, and immediately it seemed as though they heard the grey house, drably malevolent at last, licking its white chops and waiting to devour them.

'Anthony, where's that lease?' she called in high alarm one Sunday morning, sick and sober to reality. 'Where did you leave it? It was here!'

Then she knew where it was. She remembered the house party they had planned on the crest of their exuberance; she remembered a room full of men to whose less exhilarated moments she and Anthony were of no importance, and Anthony's boast of the transcendent merit and seclusion of the grey house, that it was so isolated that it didn't matter how much noise went on there. Then Dick, who had visited them, cried enthusiastically that it was the best little house imaginable, and that they were idiotic not to take it for another summer. It had been easy to work themselves up to a sense of how hot and deserted the city was getting, of how cool and ambrosial were the charms of Marietta. Anthony had picked up the lease and waved it wildly, found Gloria happily acquiescent, and with one last burst of garrulous decision during which all the men agreed with solemn handshakes that they would come out for a visit . . .

'Anthony,' she cried, 'we've signed and sent it!'

'What?'

'The lease!'

'What the devil!'

'Oh, *An*thony!' There was utter misery in her voice. For the summer, for eternity, they had built themselves a prison. It seemed to strike at the last roots of their stability. Anthony thought they might arrange it with the real-estate agent. They could no longer afford the double rent, and going to Marietta meant giving up his apartment, his reproachless apartment with the exquisite bath and the rooms for which he had bought his furniture and hangings – it was the closest to a home that he had ever had – familiar with memories of four colourful years.

But it was not arranged with the real-estate agent, nor was it arranged at all. Dispiritedly, without even any talk of making the best of it, without even Gloria's all-sufficing 'I don't care', they went back to the house that they now knew heeded neither youth nor love – only those austere and incommunicable memories that they could never share.

THE SINISTER SUMMER

There was a horror in the house that summer. It came with them and settled itself over the place like a sombre pall, pervasive through the lower rooms, gradually spreading and climbing up the narrow stairs until it oppressed their very sleep. Anthony and Gloria grew to hate being there alone. Her bedroom, which had seemed so pink and young and delicate, appropriate to her pastel-shaded lingerie tossed here and there on chair and bed, seemed now to whisper with its rustling curtains: 'Ah, my beautiful young lady, yours is not the first daintiness and delicacy that has faded here under the summer suns . . . generations of unloved women have adorned themselves by that glass for rustic lovers who paid no heed . . . Youth has come into this room in palest blue and left it in the grey cerements of despair, and through long nights many girls have lain awake where that bed stands pouring out waves of misery into the darkness.'

Gloria finally tumbled all her clothes and unguents ingloriously out of it, declaring that she had come to live with Anthony, and making the excuse that one of her screens was rotten and admitted bugs. So her room was abandoned to insensitive guests, and they dressed and slept in her husband's chamber, which Gloria considered somehow 'good', as though Anthony's presence there had acted as exterminator of any uneasy shadows of the past that might have hovered about its walls.

The distinction between 'good' and 'bad', ordered early and summarily out of both their lives, had been reinstated in another form. Gloria insisted that anyone invited to the grey house must be 'good', which, in the case of a girl, meant that she must be either simple and reproachless or, if otherwise, must possess a certain solidity and strength. Always intensely sceptical of her sex, her judgements were now concerned with the question of whether women were or were not clean. By uncleanliness she meant a variety of things, a lack of pride, a slackness in fibre and, most of all, the unmistakable aura of promiscuity.

'Women soil easily,' she said, 'far more easily than men. Unless a girl's very young and brave it's almost impossible for her to go downhill without a certain hysterical animality, the cunning, dirty sort of animality. A man's different – and I suppose that's why one of the commonest characters of romance is a man going gallantly to the devil.'

She was disposed to like many men, preferably those who gave her frank homage and unfailing entertainment – but often with a flash of insight she told Anthony that some one of his friends was merely using him, and consequently had best be left alone. Anthony customarily demurred, insisting that the accused was a 'good one', but he found that his judgement was more fallible than hers, memorably when, as it happened on several occasions, he was left with a succession of restaurant checks for which to render a solitary account.

More from their fear of solitude than from any desire to go through the fuss and bother of entertaining, they filled the house with guests every weekend, and often on through the week. The weekend parties were much the same. When the three or four men invited had arrived, drinking was more or less in order, followed by a hilarious dinner and a ride to the Cradle Beach Country Club, which they had joined because it was inexpensive, lively if not fashionable, and almost a necessity for just such occasions as these. Moreover, it was of no great moment what one did there, and so long as the Patch party were reasonably inaudible, it mattered little whether or not the social dictators of Cradle Beach saw the gay Gloria imbibing cocktails in the supper room at frequent intervals during the evening.

Saturday ended, generally, in a glamorous confusion – it proving often necessary to assist a muddled guest to bed. Sunday brought the New York papers and a quiet morning of recuperating on the porch – and Sunday afternoon meant goodbye to the one or two guests who must return to the city, and a great revival of drinking among the one or two who remained until next day, concluding in a convivial if not hilarious evening.

The faithful Tana, pedagogue by nature and man of all work by profession, had returned with them. Among their more frequent guests a tradition had sprung up about him. Maury Noble remarked one afternoon that his real name was Tannenbaum, and that he was a German agent kept in this country to disseminate Teutonic propaganda through Westchester County, and, after that, mysterious letters began to arrive from Philadelphia addressed to the bewildered Oriental as 'Lieutenant Emile Tannenbaum', containing a few cryptic messages signed 'General Staff', and adorned with an atmospheric double column of facetious Japanese. Anthony always handed them to Tana without a smile; hours afterwards the recipient could be found puzzling over them in the kitchen and declaring earnestly that the perpendicular symbols were not Japanese, nor anything resembling Japanese.

Gloria had taken a strong dislike to the man ever since the day when, returning unexpectedly from the village, she had discovered him reclining on Anthony's bed, puzzling out a newspaper. It was the instinct of all servants to be fond of Anthony and to detest Gloria, and Tana was no exception to the rule. But he was thoroughly afraid of her and made plain his aversion only in his moodier moments by subtly addressing Anthony with remarks intended for her ear: 'What Miz Pats want dinner?' he would say, looking at his master. Or else he would comment about the bitter selfishness of ' 'Merican peoples' in such manner that there was no doubt who were the 'peoples' referred to.

But they dared not dismiss him. Such a step would have been abhorrent to their inertia. They endured Tana as they endured ill weather and sickness of the body and the estimable Will of God – as they endured all things, even themselves.

IN DARKNESS

One sultry afternoon late in July Richard Caramel telephoned from New York that he and Maury were coming out, bringing a friend with them. They arrived about five, a little drunk, accompanied by a small, stocky man of thirty-five, whom they introduced as Mr Joe Hull, one of the best fellows that Anthony and Gloria would ever meet.

Joe Hull had a yellow beard continually fighting through his skin and a low voice which varied between *basso profundo* and a husky whisper. Anthony, carrying Maury's suitcase upstairs, followed him into the room and carefully closed the door.

'Who is this fellow?' he demanded.

Maury chuckled enthusiastically.

'Who, Hull? Oh, *he's* all right. He's a good one.'

'Yes, but who is he?'

'Hull? He's just a good fellow. He's a prince.' His laughter redoubled, culminating in a succession of pleasant catlike grins.

Anthony hesitated between a smile and a frown. 'He looks sort of funny to me. Weird-looking clothes' – he paused – 'I've got a sneaking suspicion you two picked him up somewhere last night.'

'Ridiculous,' declared Maury. 'Why, I've known him all my life.' However, as he capped this statement with another series of chuckles, Anthony was impelled to remark: 'The devil you have!'

Later, just before dinner, while Maury and Dick were conversing uproariously, with Joe Hull listening in silence as he sipped his drink, Gloria drew Anthony into the dining-room: 'I don't like this man Hull,' she said. 'I wish he'd use Tana's bathtub.'

'I can't very well ask him to.'

'Well, I don't want him in ours.'

'He seems to be a simple soul.'

'He's got on white shoes that look like gloves. I can see his toes right through them. Uh! Who is he, anyway?'

'You've got me.'

'Well, I think they've got their nerve to bring him out here. This isn't a Sailor's Rescue Home!'

'They were tight when they phoned. Maury said they've been on a party since yesterday afternoon.'

Gloria shook her head angrily, and saying no more returned to the porch. Anthony saw that she was trying to forget her uncertainty and devote herself to enjoying the evening.

It had been a tropical day, and even into late twilight the heat-waves emanating from the dry road were quivering faintly like undulating panes of isinglass. The sky was cloudless, but far beyond the woods in the direction of the Sound a faint and persistent rolling had commenced. When Tana announced dinner the men, at a word from Gloria, remained coatless and went inside.

Maury began a song, which they accomplished in harmony during the first course. It had two lines and was sung to a popular air called Daisy Dear. The lines were:

> The – pan-ic – has – come – over us,
> So *ha-a-as* – the moral de*cline*!'

Each rendition was greeted with bursts of enthusiasm and prolonged applause.

'Cheer up, Gloria!' suggested Maury. 'You seem the least bit depressed.'

'I'm not,' she lied.

'Here, Tannenbaum!' he called over his shoulder. 'I've filled you a drink. Come on!'

Gloria tried to stay his arm.

'Please don't, Maury!'

'Why not? Maybe he'll play the flute for us after dinner. Here, Tana.'

Tana, grinning, bore the glass away to the kitchen. In a few moments Maury gave him another.

'Cheer up, Gloria!' he cried. 'For heaven's sakes everybody, cheer up Gloria.'

'Dearest, have another drink,' counselled Anthony.

'Do, please!'

'Cheer up, Gloria,' said Joe Hull easily.

Gloria winced at this uncalled-for use of her first name, and glanced around to see if anyone else had noticed it. The word coming so glibly from the lips of a man to whom she had taken an inordinate dislike repelled her. A moment later she noticed that Joe Hull had given Tana another drink, and her anger increased, heightened somewhat from the effects of the alcohol.

' – and once,' Maury was saying, 'Peter Granby and I went into a Turkish bath in Boston, about two o'clock at night. There was no one there but the proprietor, and we jammed him into a closet and locked the door. Then a fella came in and wanted a Turkish bath. Thought we were the rubbers, by golly! Well, we just picked him up and tossed him into the pool with all his clothes on. Then we dragged him out and laid him on a slab and slapped him until he was black and blue. "Not so rough, fellows!" he'd say in a little squeaky voice, "please! . . ." '

– Was this Maury? thought Gloria. From anyone else the story would have amused her, but from Maury, the infinitely appreciative, the apotheosis of tact and consideration . . .

> The – pan-ic – has – come – over us,
> So *ha-a-as* – '

A drum of thunder from outside drowned out the rest of the

song; Gloria shivered and tried to empty her glass, but the first taste nauseated her, and she set it down. Dinner was over and they all marched into the big room, bearing several bottles and decanters. Someone had closed the porch door to keep out the wind, and in consequence circular tentacles of cigar smoke were twisting already upon the heavy air.

'Paging Lieutenant Tannenbaum!' Again it was the changeling Maury. 'Bring us the flute!'

Anthony and Maury rushed into the kitchen; Richard Caramel started the phonograph and approached Gloria.

'Dance with your well-known cousin.'

'I don't want to dance.'

'Then I'm going to carry you around.'

As though he were doing something of overpowering importance, he picked her up in his fat little arms and started trotting gravely about the room.

'Set me down, Dick! I'm dizzy!' she insisted.

He dumped her in a bouncing bundle on the couch, and rushed off to the kitchen, shouting 'Tana! Tana!'

Then, without warning, she felt other arms around her, felt herself lifted from the lounge. Joe Hull had picked her up and was trying, drunkenly, to imitate Dick.

'Put me down!' she said sharply.

His maudlin laugh, and the sight of that prickly yellow jaw close to her face stirred her to intolerable disgust.

'At once!'

'The – pan-ic – ' he began, but got no further, for Gloria's hand swung around swiftly and caught him on the cheek. At this he all at once let go of her, and she fell to the floor, her shoulder hitting the table a glancing blow in transit . . .

Then the room seemed full of men and smoke. There was Tana in his white coat reeling about supported by Maury. Into his flute he was blowing a weird blend of sound that was known, cried Anthony, as the Japanese train-song. Joe Hull had found a box of candles and was juggling them, yelling 'One down!' every time he missed, and Dick was dancing by himself in a fascinated whirl around and about the room. It appeared to her that everything in the room was staggering in grotesque fourth-dimensional gyrations through intersecting planes of hazy blue.

Outside, the storm had come up amazingly – the lulls within were filled with the scrape of the tall bushes against the house and the roaring of the rain on the tin roof of the kitchen. The lightning was interminable, letting down thick drips of thunder like pig iron from the heart of a white-hot furnace. Gloria could see that the rain was spitting in at three of the windows – but she could not move to shut them . . .

. . . She was in the hall. She had said good-night but no one had heard or heeded her. It seemed for an instant as though something had looked down over the head of the bannister, but she could not have gone back into the living-room – better madness than the madness of that clamour . . . Upstairs she fumbled for the electric switch and missed it in the darkness; a roomful of lightning showed her the button plainly on the wall. But when the impenetrable black shut down, it again eluded her fumbling fingers, so she slipped off her dress and petticoat and threw herself weakly on the dry side of the half-drenched bed.

She shut her eyes. From downstairs arose the babel of the drinkers, punctured suddenly by a tinkling shiver of broken glass, and then another, and by a soaring fragment of unsteady, irregular song . . .

She lay there for something over two hours – so she calculated afterwards, sheerly by piecing together the bits of time. She was conscious, even aware, after a long while that the noise downstairs had lessened, and that the storm was moving off westward, throwing back lingering showers of sound that fell, heavy and lifeless as her soul, into the soggy fields. This was succeeded by a slow, reluctant scattering of the rain and wind, until there was nothing outside her windows but a gentle dripping and the swishing play of a cluster of wet vine against the sill. She was in a state halfway between sleeping and waking, with neither condition predominant . . . and she was harassed by a desire to rid herself of a weight pressing down upon her breast. She felt that if she could cry the weight would be lifted, and forcing the lids of her eyes together she tried to raise a lump in her throat . . . to no avail . . .

Drip! Drip! Drip! The sound was not unpleasant – like spring, like a cool rain of her childhood, that made cheerful mud in her backyard and watered the tiny garden she had dug with miniature rake and spade and hoe. Drip – dri-ip! It was like days when the rain came out of yellow skies that melted just before twilight and shot one radiant shaft of sunlight diagonally down the heavens into the damp green trees. So cool, so clear and clean – and her mother there at the centre of the world, at the centre of the rain, safe and dry and strong. She wanted her mother now, and her mother was dead, beyond sight and touch for ever. And this weight was pressing on her, pressing on her – oh, it pressed on her so!

She became rigid. Someone had come to the door and was standing regarding her, very quiet except for a slight swaying motion. She could see the outline of his figure distinct against some indistinguishable light. There was no sound anywhere, only a great persuasive silence – even the dripping had ceased . . . only this figure, swaying, swaying in the doorway, an indiscernible and subtly menacing terror, a personality filthy under its varnish, like smallpox spots under a layer of powder. Yet her tired heart, beating until it shook her breasts, made her sure that there was still life in her, desperately shaken, threatened . . .

The minute or succession of minutes prolonged itself interminably, and a swimming blur began to form before her eyes, which tried with childish persistence to pierce the gloom in the direction of the door. In another instant it seemed that some unimaginable force would shatter her out of existence . . . and then the figure in the doorway – it was Hull, she saw, Hull – turned deliberately and, still slightly swaying, moved back and off, as if absorbed into that incomprehensible light that had given him dimension.

Blood rushed back into her limbs, blood and life together. With a start of energy she sat upright, shifting her body until her feet touched the floor over the side of the bed. She knew what she must do – now, now, before it was too late. She must go out into this cool damp, out, away, to feel the wet swish of the grass around her feet and the fresh moisture on her forehead. Mechanically she struggled into her clothes, groping in the dark of the closet for a hat. She must go from this house where the thing hovered that pressed upon her bosom, or else made itself into stray, swaying figures in the gloom.

In a panic she fumbled clumsily at her coat, found the sleeve just as she heard Anthony's footsteps on the lower stair. She dared not wait; he might not let her go, and even Anthony was part of this weight, part of this evil house and the sombre darkness that was growing up about it . . .

Through the hall then . . . and down the back stairs, hearing Anthony's voice in the bedroom she had just left –

'Gloria! Gloria!'

But she had reached the kitchen now, passed out through the doorway into the night. A hundred drops, startled by a flare of wind from a dripping tree, scattered on her and she pressed them gladly to her face with hot hands.

'Gloria! Gloria!'

The voice was infinitely remote, muffled and made plaintive by the walls she had just left. She rounded the house and started down the front path towards the road, almost exultant as she turned into it, and followed the carpet of short grass alongside, moving with caution in the intense darkness.

'Gloria!'

She broke into a run, stumbled over the segment of a branch twisted off by the wind. The voice was outside the house now. Anthony, finding the bedroom deserted, had come on to the porch. But this thing was driving her forward; it was back there with Anthony, and she must go on in her flight under this dim and oppressive heaven, forcing herself through the silence ahead as though it were a tangible barrier before her.

She had gone some distance along the barely discernible road, probably half a mile, passed a single deserted barn that loomed up, black and foreboding, the only building of any sort between the grey house and Marietta; then she turned the fork, where the road entered the wood and ran between two high walls of leaves and branches that nearly touched overhead. She noticed suddenly a thin, longitudinal gleam of silver upon the road before her, like a bright sword half embedded in the mud. As she came closer she gave a little cry of satisfaction – it was a wagon-rut full of water, and glancing heavenward she saw a light rift of sky and knew that the moon was out.

'Gloria!'

She started violently. Anthony was not two hundred feet behind her.

'Gloria, wait for me!'

She shut her lips tightly to keep from screaming, and increased her gait. Before she had gone another hundred yards the woods disappeared, rolling back like a dark stocking from the leg of the road. Three minutes' walk ahead of her, suspended in the now high and limitless air, she saw a thin interlacing of attenuated gleams and glitters, centred in a regular undulation on some one invisible point. Abruptly she knew where she would go. That was the great cascade of wires that rose high over the river, like the legs of a gigantic spider whose eye was the little green light in the switch-house, and ran with the railroad bridge in the direction of the station. The station! There would be the train to take her away.

'Gloria, it's me! It's Anthony! Gloria, I won't try to stop you! For God's sake, where are you?'

She made no answer but began to run, keeping on the high side of the road and leaping the gleaming puddles – dimensionless pools of thin, unsubstantial gold. Turning sharply to the left, she followed a narrow wagon road, swerving to avoid a dark body on the ground. She looked up as an owl hooted mournfully from a solitary tree. Just ahead of her she could see the trestle that led to the railroad bridge and the steps mounting up to it. The station lay across the river.

Another sound startled her, the melancholy siren of an approaching train, and almost simultaneously, a repeated call, thin now and far away.

'Gloria! Gloria!'

Anthony must have followed the main road. She laughed with a sort of malicious cunning at having eluded him; she could spare the time to wait until the train went by.

The siren soared again, closer at hand, and then, with no anticipatory roar and clamour, a dark and sinuous body curved into view against the shadows far down the high-banked track, and with no sound but the rush of the cleft wind and the clocklike tick of the rails, moved towards the bridge – it was an electric train. Above the engine two vivid blurs of blue light formed incessantly a radiant crackling bar between them, which, like a spluttering flame in a lamp beside a corpse, lit for an instant the successive rows of trees and caused Gloria to draw back instinctively to the far side of the road. The light was tepid, the temperature of warm blood . . . The clicking blended suddenly with itself in a rush of even sound, and then, elongating in sombre elasticity, the thing roared blindly by her and thundered on to the bridge, racing the lurid shaft of fire it cast into the solemn river alongside. Then it contracted swiftly, sucking in its sound until it left only a reverberant echo, which died upon the farther bank.

Silence crept down again over the wet country; the faint dripping resumed, and suddenly a great shower of drops tumbled upon Gloria stirring her out of the trance-like torpor which the passage of the train had wrought. She ran swiftly down a descending level to the bank and began climbing the iron stairway to the bridge, remembering that it was something she had always wanted to do, and that she would have the added excitement of traversing the yard-wide plank that ran beside the tracks over the river.

There! This was better. She was at the top now and could see the lands about her as successive sweeps of open country, cold under the moon, coarsely patched and seamed with thin rows and heavy clumps of trees. To her right, half a mile down the river, which trailed away behind the light like the shiny, slimy path of a snail, winked the scattered lights of Marietta. Not two hundred yards away at the end of the bridge squatted the station, marked by a sullen lantern. The oppression was lifted now – the tree-tops below her were rocking the young starlight to a haunted doze. She stretched out her arms with a gesture of freedom. This was what she had wanted, to stand alone where it was high and cool.

'Gloria!'

Like a startled child she scurried along the plank, hopping, skipping, jumping, with an ecstatic sense of her own physical lightness. Let him come now – she no longer feared that, only she must first reach the station, because that was part of the game. She was happy. Her hat, snatched off, was clutched tightly in her hand, and her short curled hair bobbed up and down about her ears. She had thought she would never feel so young again, but this was her night, her world. Triumphantly she laughed as she left the plank and reaching the wooden platform flung herself down happily beside an iron roof-post.

'Here I am!' she called, gay as the dawn in her elation. 'Here I am, Anthony, dear – old, worried Anthony.'

'Gloria!' He reached the platform, ran towards her. 'Are you all right?' Coming up he knelt and took her in his arms.

'Yes.'

'What was the matter? Why did you leave?' he queried anxiously.

'I had to – there was something' – she paused and a flicker of uneasiness lashed at her mind – 'there was something sitting on me – here.' She put her hand on her breast. 'I had to go out and get away from it.'

'What do you mean by "something"?'

'I don't know – that man Hull –'

'Did he bother you?'

'He came to my door, drunk. I think I'd got sort of crazy by that time.'

'Gloria, dearest – '

Wearily she laid her head upon his shoulder.

'Let's go back,' he suggested.

She shivered.

'Uh! No, I couldn't. It'd come and sit on me again.' Her voice rose to a cry that hung plaintive on the darkness. 'That thing – '

'There – there,' he soothed her, pulling her close to him. 'We won't do anything you don't want to do. What do you want to do? Just sit here?'

'I want – I want to go away.'

'Where?'

'Oh – anywhere.'

'By golly, Gloria,' he cried, 'you're still tight!'

'No, I'm not. I haven't been, all evening. I went upstairs about, oh, I don't know, about half an hour after dinner . . . Ouch!'

He had inadvertently touched her right shoulder.

'It hurts me. I hurt it some way. I don't know – somebody picked me up and dropped me.'

'Gloria, come home. It's late and damp.'

'I can't,' she wailed. 'Oh, Anthony, don't ask me to! I will tomorrow. You go home and I'll wait here for a train. I'll go to a hotel – '

'I'll go with you.'

'No, I don't want you with me. I want to be alone. I want to sleep – oh, I want to sleep. And then tomorrow, when you've got all the smell of whiskey and cigarettes out of the house, and everything straight, and Hull is gone, then I'll come home. If I went now, that thing – oh – !' She covered her eyes with her hand; Anthony saw the futility of trying to persuade her.

'I was all sober when you left,' he said. 'Dick was asleep on the lounge and Maury and I were having a discussion. That fellow Hull had wandered off somewhere. Then I began to realise I hadn't seen you for several hours, so I went upstairs – '

He broke off as a salutatory, 'Hello, there!' boomed suddenly out of the darkness. Gloria sprang to her feet and he did likewise.

'It's Maury's voice,' she cried excitedly. 'If it's Hull with him, keep them away, keep them away!'

'Who's there?' Anthony called.

'Just Dick and Maury,' returned two voices reassuringly.

'Where's Hull?'

'He's in bed. Passed out.'

Their figures appeared dimly on the platform.

'What the devil are you and Gloria doing here?' enquired Richard Caramel with sleepy bewilderment.

'What are *you* two doing here?'

Maury laughed.

'Damned if I know. We followed you, and had the deuce of a time doing it. I heard you out on the porch yelling for Gloria, so I woke up the Caramel here and got it through his head, with some difficulty, that if there was a search-party we'd better be on it. He slowed me up by sitting down in the road at intervals and asking me what it was all about. We tracked you by the pleasant scent of Canadian Club.'

There was a rattle of nervous laughter under the low train-shed.

'How did you track us, really?'

'Well, we followed along down the road and then we suddenly lost you. Seems you turned off at a wagon-trail. After a while somebody hailed us and asked us if we were looking for a young girl. Well, we came up and found it was a little shivering old man, sitting on a fallen tree like somebody in a fairy tale. "She turned down here," he said, "and most steppud on me, goin' somewhere in an awful hustle, and then a fella in short golfin' pants come runnin' along and went after her. He throwed me this." The old fellow had a dollar bill he was waving around –'

'Oh, the poor old man!' ejaculated Gloria, moved.

'I threw him another and we went on, though he asked us to stay and tell him what it was all about.'

'Poor old man,' repeated Gloria dismally.

Dick sat down sleepily on a box.

'And now what?' he enquired in the tone of stoic resignation.

'Gloria's upset,' explained Anthony. 'She and I are going to the city by the next train.'

Maury in the darkness had pulled a timetable from his pocket.

'Strike a match.'

A tiny flare leaped out of the opaque background illuminating the four faces, grotesque and unfamiliar here in the open night.

'Let's see. Two, two-thirty – no, that's evening. By gad, you won't get a train till five-thirty.'

Anthony hesitated.

'Well,' he muttered uncertainly, 'we've decided to stay here and wait for it. You two might as well go back and sleep.'

'You go, too, Anthony,' urged Gloria; 'I want you to have some sleep, dear. You've been as pale as a ghost all day.'

'Why, you little idiot!'

Dick yawned.

'Very well. You stay, we stay.'

He walked out from under the shed and surveyed the heavens.

'Rather a nice night, after all. Stars are out and everything. Exceptionally tasty assortment of them.'

'Let's see.' Gloria moved after him and the other two followed her. 'Let's sit out here,' she suggested. 'I like it much better.'

Anthony and Dick converted a long box into a back-rest and found a board dry enough for Gloria to sit on. Anthony dropped down beside her and with some effort Dick hoisted himself on to an apple-barrel near them.

'Tana went to sleep in the porch hammock,' he remarked. 'We carried him in and left him next to the kitchen stove to dry. He was drenched to the skin.'

'That awful little man!' sighed Gloria.

'How do you do!' The voice, sonorous and funereal, had come from above, and they looked up startled to find that in some manner Maury had climbed to the roof of the shed, where he sat dangling his feet over the edge, outlined as a shadowy and fantastic gargoyle against the now brilliant sky.

'It must be for such occasions as this,' he began softly, his words having the effect of floating down from an immense height and settling softly upon his auditors, 'that the righteous of the land decorate the railroads with billboards asserting in red and yellow that "Jesus Christ is God", placing them, appropriately enough, next to announcements that "Gunter's Whiskey is Good".'

There was gentle laughter and the three below kept their heads tilted upward.

'I think I shall tell you the story of my education,' continued Maury, 'under these sardonic constellations.'

'Do! Please!'

'Shall I, really?'

They waited expectantly while he directed a ruminative yawn towards the white smiling moon.

'Well,' he began, 'as an infant I prayed. I stored up prayers against future wickedness. One year I stored up nineteen hundred "Now I lay me"s.'

'Throw down a cigarette,' murmured someone.

A small package reached the platform simultaneously with the stentorian command: 'Silence! I am about to unburden myself of many memorable remarks reserved for the darkness of such earths and the brilliance of such skies.'

Below, a lighted match was passed from cigarette to cigarette. The voice resumed: 'I was adept at fooling the deity. I prayed immediately after all crimes until eventually prayer and crime became indistinguishable to me. I believed that because a man cried out "My God!" when a safe fell on him, it proved that belief was rooted deep in the human breast. Then I went to school. For fourteen years half a hundred earnest men pointed to ancient flintlocks and cried to me: "There's the real thing. These new rifles are only shallow, superficial imitations." They damned the books I read and the things I thought by calling them immoral; later the fashion changed, and they damned things by calling them "clever".

'And so I turned, canny for my years, from the professors to the poets, listening – to the lyric tenor of Swinburne and the tenor *robusto* of Shelley, to Shakespeare with his first bass and his fine range, to Tennyson with his second bass and his occasional falsetto, to Milton and Marlow, *bassos profundos*. I gave ear to Browning chatting, Byron declaiming and Wordsworth droning. This, at least, did me no harm. I learned a little of beauty – enough to know that it had nothing to do with truth – and I found, moreover, that there was no great literary tradition; there was only the tradition of the eventual death of every literary tradition . . .

'Then I grew up, and the beauty of succulent illusions fell away from me. The fibre of my mind coarsened and my eyes grew miserably keen. Life rose around my island like a sea, and presently I was swimming.

'The transition was subtle – the thing had lain in wait for me for some time. It has its insidious, seemingly innocuous trap for everyone. With me? No – I didn't try to seduce the janitor's wife – nor did I run through the streets unclothed, proclaiming my virility. It is never quite passion that does the business – it is the dress that passion wears. I became bored – that was all. Boredom, which is another name and a frequent disguise for vitality, became the unconscious motive of all my acts. Beauty was behind me, do you understand? – I was grown.' He paused. 'End of school and college period. Opening of Part Two.'

Three quietly active points of light showed the location of his listeners. Gloria was now half sitting, half lying, in Anthony's lap. His arm was around her so tightly that she could hear the beating of his heart. Richard Caramel, perched on the apple-barrel, from time to time stirred and gave off a faint grunt.

'I grew up then, into this land of jazz, and fell immediately into a state of almost audible confusion. Life stood over me like an immoral schoolmistress, editing my ordered thoughts. But, with a mistaken faith in intelligence, I plodded on. I read Smith, who laughed at charity and insisted that the sneer was the highest form of self-expression – but Smith himself replaced charity as an obscurer of the light. I read Jones, who neatly disposed of individualism – and behold! Jones was still in my way. I did not think – I was a battleground for the thoughts of many men; rather was I one of those desirable but impotent countries over which the great powers surge back and forth.

'I reached maturity under the impression that I was gathering the experience to order my life for happiness. Indeed, I accomplished the not unusual feat of solving each question in my mind long before it presented itself to me in life – and of being beaten and bewildered just the same.

'But after a few tastes of this latter dish I had had enough. Here! I said, Experience is not worth the getting. It's not a thing that happens pleasantly to a passive you – it's a wall that an active you runs up against. So I wrapped myself in what I thought was my invulnerable scepticism and decided that my education was complete. But it was too late. Protect myself as I might by making no new ties with tragic and predestined humanity, I was lost with the rest. I had traded the fight against love for the fight against loneliness, the fight against life for the fight against death.'

He broke off to give emphasis to his last observation – after a moment he yawned and resumed.

'I suppose that the beginning of the second phase of my education was a ghastly dissatisfaction at being used in spite of myself for some inscrutable purpose of whose ultimate goal I was unaware – if, indeed, there *was* an ultimate goal. It was a difficult choice. The schoolmistress seemed to be saying, "We're going to play football and nothing but football. If you don't want to play football you can't play at all – "

'What was I to do – the playtime was so short!

'You see, I felt that we were even denied what consolation there might have been in being a figment of a corporate man rising from his knees. Do you think that I leaped at this pessimism, grasped it as a sweetly smug superior thing, no more depressing really than, say, a grey autumn day before a fire? – I don't think I did that. I was a great deal too warm for that, and too alive.

'For it seemed to me that there was no ultimate goal for man. Man was beginning a grotesque and bewildered fight with nature – nature, that by the divine and magnificent accident had brought us to where we could fly in her face. She had invented ways to rid the race of the inferior and thus give the remainder strength to fill her higher – or, let us say, her more amusing – though still unconscious and accidental intentions. And, actuated by the highest gifts of the enlightenment, we were seeking to circumvent her. In this republic I saw the black beginning to mingle with the white – in Europe there was taking place an economic catastrophe to save three or four diseased and wretchedly governed races from the one mastery that might organise them for material prosperity.

'We produce a Christ who can raise up the leper – and presently the breed of the leper is the salt of the earth. If anyone can find any lesson in that, let him stand forth.'

'There's only one lesson to be learned from life, anyway,' interrupted Gloria, not in contradiction but in a sort of melancholy agreement.

'What's that?' demanded Maury sharply.

'That there's no lesson to be learned from life.'

After a short silence Maury said: 'Young Gloria, the beautiful and merciless lady, first looked at the world with the fundamental sophistication I have struggled to attain, that Anthony never will attain, that Dick will never fully understand.'

There was a disgusted groan from the apple-barrel. Anthony, grown accustomed to the dark, could see plainly the flash of Richard Caramel's yellow eye and the look of resentment on his face as he cried: 'You're crazy! By your own statement I should have attained some experience by trying.'

'Trying what?' cried Maury fiercely. 'Trying to pierce the darkness of political idealism with some wild, despairing urge towards truth? Sitting day after day supine in a rigid chair and infinitely removed from life staring at the tip of a steeple through the trees, trying to separate, definitely and for all time, the knowable from the unknowable? Trying to take a piece of actuality and give it glamour from your own soul to make up for that inexpressible quality it possessed in life and lost in transit to paper or canvas? Struggling in a laboratory through weary years for one iota of relative truth in a mass of wheels or a test tube – '

'Have you?'

Maury paused, and in his answer, when it came, there was a measure of weariness, a bitter over-note that lingered for a moment in those three minds before it floated up and off like a bubble bound for the moon.

'Not I,' he said softly. 'I was born tired – but with the quality of mother wit, the gift of women like Gloria – to that, for all my talking and listening, my waiting in vain for the eternal generality that seems to lie just beyond every argument and every speculation, to that I have added not one jot.'

In the distance a deep sound that had been audible for some moments identified itself by a plaintive mooing like that of a gigantic cow and by the pearly spot of a headlight apparent half a mile away. It was a steam-driven train this time, rumbling and groaning, and as it tumbled by with a monstrous complaint it sent a shower of sparks and cinders over the platform.

'Not one jot!' Again Maury's voice dropped down to them as from a great height. 'What a feeble thing intelligence is, with its short steps, its waverings, its pacings back and forth, its disastrous retreats! Intelligence is a mere instrument of circumstances. There are people who say that intelligence must have built the universe – why, intelligence never built a steam engine! Circumstances built a steam engine. Intelligence is little more than a short foot-rule by which we measure the infinite achievements of Circumstances.

'I could quote you the philosophy of the hour – but, for all we know, fifty years may see a complete reversal of this abnegation that's absorbing the intellectuals today, the triumph of Christ over Anatole France – ' He hesitated, and then added: 'But all I know – the tremendous importance of myself to me, and the necessity of acknowledging that importance to myself – these things the wise and lovely Gloria was born knowing, these things and the painful futility of trying to know anything else.

'Well, I started to tell you of my education, didn't I? But I learned nothing, you see, very little even about myself. And if I had I should die with my lips shut and the guard on my fountain pen – as the wisest men have done since – oh, since the failure of a certain matter – a strange matter, by the way. It concerned some sceptics who thought they were far-sighted, just as you and I. Let me tell you about them by way of an evening prayer before you all drop off to sleep.

'Once upon a time all the men of mind and genius in the world became of one belief – that is to say, of no belief. But it wearied them to think that within a few years after their death many cults and systems and prognostications would be ascribed to them which they had never meditated nor intended. So they said to one another: ' "Let's join together and make a great book that will last for ever to mock the credulity of man. Let's persuade our more erotic poets to write about the delights of the flesh, and induce some of our robust journalists to contribute stories of famous amours. We'll include all the most preposterous old wives' tales now current. We'll choose the keenest satirist alive to compile a deity from all the deities worshipped by mankind, a deity who will be more magnificent than any of them, and yet so weakly human that he'll become a byword for laughter the world over – and we'll ascribe to him all sorts of jokes and vanities and rages, in which he'll be supposed to indulge for his own diversion, so that the people will read our book and ponder it, and there'll be no more nonsense in the world.

' "Finally, let us take care that the book possesses all the virtues of style, so that it may last for ever as a witness to our profound scepticism and our universal irony."

'So the men did, and they died.

'But the book lived always, so beautifully had it been written, and so astounding the quality of imagination with which these men of mind and genius had endowed it. They had neglected to give it a name, but after they were dead it became known as the Bible.'

When he concluded there was no comment. Some damp languor sleeping on the air of night seemed to have bewitched them all.

'As I said, I started on the story of my education. But my highballs are dead and the night's almost over, and soon there'll be an awful jabbering going on everywhere, in the trees and the houses, and the two little stores over there behind the station, and there'll be a great running up and down upon the earth for a few hours – Well,' he concluded with a laugh, 'thank God we four can all pass to our eternal rest knowing we've left the world a little better for having lived in it.'

A breeze sprang up, blowing with it faint wisps of life which flattened against the sky.

'Your remarks grow rambling and inconclusive,' said Anthony sleepily. 'You expected one of those miracles of illumination by which you say your most brilliant and pregnant things in exactly the setting that should provoke the ideal symposium. Meanwhile Gloria has shown her far-sighted detachment by falling asleep – I can tell that by the fact that she has managed to concentrate her entire weight upon my broken body.'

'Have I bored you?' enquired Maury, looking down with some concern.

'No, you have disappointed us. You've shot a lot of arrows but did you shoot any birds?'

'I leave the birds to Dick,' said Maury hurriedly. 'I speak erratically, in disassociated fragments.'

'You can get no rise from me,' muttered Dick. 'My mind is full of any number of material things. I want a warm bath too much to worry about the importance of my work or what proportion of us are pathetic figures.'

Dawn made itself felt in a gathering whiteness eastward over the river and an intermittent cheeping in the nearby trees.

'Quarter to five,' sighed Dick; 'almost another hour to wait. Look! Two gone.' He was pointing to Anthony, whose lids had sagged over his eyes. 'Sleep of the Patch family – '

But in another five minutes, despite the amplifying cheeps and chirrups, his own head had fallen forward, nodded down twice, thrice . . .

Only Maury Noble remained awake, seated upon the station roof, his eyes wide open and fixed with fatigued intensity upon the distant nucleus of morning. He was wondering at the unreality of ideas, at the fading radiance of existence, and at the little absorptions that were creeping avidly into his life, like rats into a ruined house. He was sorry for no one now – on Monday morning there would be his business, and later there would be a girl of another class whose whole life he was; these were the things nearest his heart. In the strangeness of the brightening day it seemed presumptuous that with this feeble, broken instrument of his mind he had ever tried to think.

There was the sun, letting down great glowing masses of heat; there was life, active and snarling, moving about them like a fly swarm – the dark pants of smoke from the engine, a crisp 'All aboard!' and a bell ringing. Confusedly Maury saw eyes in the milk-train staring curiously up at him, heard Gloria and Anthony in quick controversy as to whether he should go to the city with her, then another clamour and she was gone and the three men, pale as ghosts, were standing alone upon the platform while a grimy coal-heaver went down the road on top of a motor truck, carolling hoarsely at the summer morning.

Chapter 3

The Broken Lute

It is seven-thirty of an August evening. The windows in the living-room of the grey house are wide open, patiently exchanging the tainted inner atmosphere of liquor and smoke for the fresh drowsiness of the late hot dusk. There are dying flower scents upon the air, so thin, so fragile, as to hint already of a summer laid away in time. But August is still proclaimed relentlessly by a thousand crickets around the side-porch, and by one who has broken into the house and concealed himself confidently behind a bookcase, from time to time shrieking of his cleverness and his indomitable will.

The room itself is in messy disorder. On the table is a dish of fruit, which is real but appears artificial. Around it are grouped an ominous assortment of decanters, glasses and heaped ashtrays, the latter still raising wavy smoke-ladders into the stale air, the effect on the whole needing but a skull to resemble that venerable chromo, once a fixture in every 'den', which presents the appendages to the life of pleasure with delightful and awe-inspiring sentiment.

After a while the sprightly solo of the super-cricket is interrupted rather than joined by a new sound – the melancholy wail of an erratically fingered flute. It is obvious that the musician is practising rather than performing, for from time to time the gnarled strain breaks off and, after an interval of indistinct mutterings, recommences.

Just prior to the seventh false start a third sound contributes to the subdued discord. It is a taxi outside. A minute's silence, then the taxi again, its boisterous retreat almost obliterating the scrape of footsteps on the cinder walk. The doorbell shrieks alarmingly through the house.

From the kitchen enters a small, fatigued Japanese, hastily buttoning a servant's coat of white duck. He opens the front screen-door and admits a handsome young man of thirty, clad in the sort of well-intentioned clothes peculiar to those who serve mankind. To his whole personality clings a well-intentioned air: his glance about the room is compounded of curiosity and a determined optimism; when he looks at Tana the entire burden of uplifting the godless Oriental is in his eyes. His name is FREDERICK E. PARAMORE. *He was at Harvard with* ANTHONY, *where because of the initials of their surnames they were constantly placed next to each other in classes. A fragmentary acquaintance developed – but since that time they have never met.*

Nevertheless, PARAMORE *enters the room with a certain air of arriving for the evening.*

Tana is answering a question.

TANA (*grinning with ingratiation*): Gone to Inn for dinnah. Be back half-hour. Gone since ha' past six.

PARAMORE (*regarding the glasses on the table*): Have they company?

TANA: Yes. Company. Mistah Caramel, Mistah and Missays Barnes, Miss Kane, all stay here.

PARAMORE: I see. (*kindly*) They've been having a spree, I see.

TANA: I no un'stan'.

PARAMORE: They've been having a fling.

TANA: Yes, they have drink. Oh, many, many, many drink.

PARAMORE (*receding delicately from the subject*): Didn't I hear the sounds of music as I approached the house?

TANA (*with a spasmodic giggle*): Yes, I play.

PARAMORE: One of the Japanese instruments.

(*He is quite obviously a subscriber to the* National Geographic Magazine.)

TANA: I play flu-u-ute, Japanese flu-u-ute.

PARAMORE: What song were you playing? One of your Japanese melodies?

TANA (*his brow undergoing preposterous contraction*): I play train-song. How you call? – railroad song. So call in my countree. Like train. It go so-o-o; that mean whistle; train start. Then go so-o-o; that mean train go. Go like that. Vera nice song in my countree. Children song.

PARAMORE: It sounded very nice. (*It is apparent at this point that only a gigantic effort at control restrains Tana from rushing upstairs for his post-cards, including the six made in America.*)

TANA: I fix highball for gentleman?

PARAMORE: No, thanks. I don't use it. (*He smiles.*)

(TANA *withdraws into the kitchen, leaving the intervening door slightly ajar. From the crevice there suddenly issues again the melody of the Japanese train song – this time not a practice, surely, but a performance, a lusty, spirited performance.*

The phone rings. TANA, *absorbed in his harmonics, gives no heed, so* PARAMORE *takes up the receiver.*)

PARAMORE: Hello . . . Yes . . . No, he's not here now, but he'll be back any moment . . . Butterworth? Hello, I didn't quite catch the name . . . Hello, hello, hello. Hello! . . . Huh!

(*The phone obstinately refuses to yield up any more sound.* PARAMORE *replaces the receiver.*

At this point the taxi motif re-enters, wafting with it a second young man; he carries a suitcase and opens the front door without ringing the bell.)

MAURY (*in the hall*): Oh, Anthony! Yoho! (*He comes into the large room and sees* PARAMORE.) How do?

PARAMORE (*gazing at him with gathering intensity*): Is this – is this Maury Noble?

MAURY: That's it. (*He advances, smiling and holding out his hand.*) How are you, old boy? Haven't seen you for years.

(*He has vaguely associated the face with Harvard, but is not even positive about that. The name, if he ever knew it, he has long since forgotten. However, with a fine sensitiveness and an equally commendable charity* PARAMORE *recognises the fact and tactfully relieves the situation.*)

PARAMORE: You've forgotten Fred Paramore? We were both in old Unc Robert's history class.

MAURY: No, I haven't, Unc – I mean Fred. Fred was – I mean Unc was a great old fellow, wasn't he?

PARAMORE (*nodding his head humorously several times*): Great old character. Great old character.

MAURY (*after a short pause*): Yes – he was. Where's Anthony?

PARAMORE: The Japanese servant told me he was at some inn. Having dinner, I suppose.

MAURY (*looking at his watch*): Gone long?

PARAMORE: I guess so. The Japanese told me they'd be back shortly.

MAURY: Suppose we have a drink.

PARAMORE: No, thanks. I don't use it. (*He smiles.*)

MAURY: Mind if I do? (*yawning as he helps himself from a bottle*) What have you been doing since you left college?

PARAMORE: Oh, many things. I've led a very active life. Knocked about here and there. (*His tone implies anything from lion-stalking to organised crime.*)

MAURY: Oh, been over to Europe?

PARAMORE: No, I haven't – unfortunately.

MAURY: I guess we'll all go over before long.

PARAMORE: Do you really think so?

MAURY: Sure! Country's been fed on sensationalism for more than two years. Everybody getting restless. Want to have some fun.

PARAMORE: Then you don't believe any ideals are at stake?

MAURY: Nothing of much importance. People want excitement every so often.

PARAMORE (*intently*): It's very interesting to hear you say that. Now I was talking to a man who'd been over there –

(*During the ensuing testament, left to be filled in by the reader with such phrases as 'Saw with his own eyes', 'Splendid spirit of France' and 'Salvation of civilisation'*, MAURY *sits with lowered eyelids, dispassionately bored.*)

MAURY (*at the first available opportunity*): By the way, do you happen to know that there's a German agent in this very house?

PARAMORE (*smiling cautiously*): Are you serious?

MAURY: Absolutely. Feel it my duty to warn you.

PARAMORE (*convinced*): A governess?

MAURY (*in a whisper, indicating the kitchen with his thumb*): Tana! That's not his real name. I understand he constantly gets mail addressed to Lieutenant Emile Tannenbaum.

PARAMORE (*laughing with hearty tolerance*): You're kidding me.

MAURY: I may be accusing him falsely. But, you haven't told me what you've been doing.

PARAMORE: For one thing – writing.

MAURY: Fiction?

PARAMORE: No. Non-fiction.

MAURY: What's that? A sort of literature that's half fiction and half fact?

PARAMORE: Oh, I've confined myself to fact. I've been doing a good deal of social-service work.

MAURY: Oh!

(*An immediate glow of suspicion leaps into his eyes. It is as though* PARAMORE *had announced himself as an amateur pickpocket.*)

PARAMORE: At present I'm doing service work in Stamford. Only last week someone told me that Anthony Patch lived so near.

(*They are interrupted by a clamour outside, unmistakable as that of two sexes in conversation and laughter. Then there enter the room in a body* ANTHONY, GLORIA, RICHARD CARAMEL, MURIEL KANE, RACHAEL BARNES *and* RODMAN BARNES, *her husband. They surge about* MAURY, *illogically replying*, 'Fine!' *to his general*, 'Hello.' . . . ANTHONY, *meanwhile, approaches his other guest.*)

ANTHONY: Well, I'll be darned. How are you? Mighty glad to see you.

PARAMORE: It's good to see you, Anthony. I'm stationed in Stamford, so I thought I'd run over. (*roguishly*) We have to work to beat the devil most of the time, so we're entitled to a few hours' vacation.

(*In an agony of concentration* ANTHONY *tries to recall the name. After a struggle of parturition his memory gives up the fragment 'Fred', around which he hastily builds the sentence, 'Glad you did, Fred!' Meanwhile the slight hush prefatory to an introduction has fallen upon the company.* MAURY, *who could help, prefers to look on in malicious enjoyment.*)

ANTHONY (*in desperation*): Ladies and gentlemen, this is – this is Fred.

MURIEL (*with obliging levity*): Hello, Fred!

(RICHARD CARAMEL *and* PARAMORE *greet each other intimately by their first names, the latter recollecting that* DICK *was one of the men in his class who had never before troubled to speak to him.* DICK *fatuously imagines that* PARAMORE *is someone he has previously met in* ANTHONY'S house.

The three young women go upstairs.)

MAURY (*in an undertone to* DICK): Haven't seen Muriel since Anthony's wedding.

DICK: She's now in her prime. Her latest is, 'I'll say so!'

(ANTHONY *struggles for a while with* PARAMORE *and at length attempts to make the conversation general by asking everyone to have a drink.*)

MAURY: I've done pretty well on this bottle. I've gone from 'Proof' down to 'Distillery'. (*He indicates the words on the label.*)

ANTHONY (*to* PARAMORE): Never can tell when these two will turn up. Said goodbye to them one afternoon at five and darned if they didn't appear about two in the morning. A big hired touring-car from New York drove up to the door and out they stepped, drunk as lords, of course.

(*In an ecstasy of consideration* PARAMORE *regards the cover of a book which he holds in his hand.* MAURY *and* DICK *exchange a glance.*)

DICK (*innocently, to* PARAMORE): You work here in town?

PARAMORE: No, I'm in the Laird Street Settlement in Stamford. (*To* ANTHONY): You have no idea of the amount of poverty in these small Connecticut towns. Italians and other immigrants. Catholics mostly, you know, so it's very hard to reach them.

ANTHONY (*politely*): Lot of crime?

PARAMORE: Not so much crime as ignorance and dirt.

MAURY: That's my theory: immediate electrocution of all ignorant and dirty people. I'm all for the criminals – give colour to life. Trouble is if you started to punish ignorance you'd have to begin in the first families, then you could take up the moving-picture people, and finally Congress and the clergy.

PARAMORE (*smiling uneasily*): I was speaking of the more fundamental ignorance – of even our language.

MAURY (*thoughtfully*): I suppose it is rather hard. Can't even keep up with the new poetry.

PARAMORE: It's only when the settlement work has gone on for months that one realises how bad things are. As our secretary said to me, your fingernails never seem dirty until you wash your hands. Of course we're already attracting much attention.

MAURY (*rudely*): As your secretary might say, if you stuff paper into a grate it'll burn brightly for a moment.

(*At this point* GLORIA, *freshly tinted and lustful of admiration and entertainment, rejoins the party, followed by her two friends. For several moments the conversation becomes entirely fragmentary.* GLORIA *calls* ANTHONY *aside.*)

GLORIA: Please don't drink much, Anthony.

ANTHONY: Why?

GLORIA: Because you're so simple when you're drunk.

ANTHONY: Good Lord! What's the matter now?

GLORIA (*after a pause during which her eyes gaze coolly into his*): Several things. In the first place, why do you insist on paying for everything? Both those men have more money than you!

ANTHONY: Why, Gloria! They're my guests!

GLORIA: That's no reason why you should pay for a bottle of champagne Rachael Barnes smashed. Dick tried to fix that second taxi bill, and you wouldn't let him.

ANTHONY: Why, Gloria –

GLORIA: When we have to keep selling bonds even to pay our bills, it's time to cut down on excess generosities. Moreover, I wouldn't be quite so attentive to Rachael Barnes. Her husband doesn't like it any more than I do!

ANTHONY: Why, Gloria –

GLORIA (*mimicking him sharply*): 'Why, Gloria!' But that's happened a little too often this summer – with every pretty woman you meet. It's grown to be a sort of habit, and I'm *not* going to stand it! If you can play around, I can, too. (*then, as an afterthought*) By the way, this Fred person isn't a second Joe Hull, is he?

ANTHONY: Heavens, no! He probably came up to get me to wheedle some money out of my grandfather for his flock.

(GLORIA *turns away from a very depressed* ANTHONY *and returns to her guests.*

By nine o'clock these can be divided into two classes – those who have been drinking consistently and those who have taken little or nothing. In the second group are the BARNESES, MURIEL *and* FREDERICK E. PARAMORE.)

MURIEL: I wish I could write. I get these ideas but I never seem to be able to put them in words.

DICK: As Goliath said, he understood how David felt, but he couldn't express himself. The remark was immediately adopted for a motto by the Philistines.

MURIEL: I don't get you. I must be getting stupid in my old age.

GLORIA (*weaving unsteadily among the company like an exhilarated angel*): If anyone's hungry there's some French pastry on the dining-room table.

MAURY: Can't tolerate those Victorian designs it comes in.

MURIEL (*violently amused*): *I'd* say you're tight, Maury.

(*Her bosom is still a pavement that she offers to the hoofs of many passing stallions, hoping that their iron shoes may strike even a spark of romance in the darkness . . .*

Messrs BARNES *and* PARAMORE *have been engaged in conversation upon some wholesome subject, a subject so wholesome that* MR BARNES *has been trying for several moments to creep into the more tainted air around the central lounge. Whether* PARAMORE *is lingering in the grey house out of politeness or curiosity, or in order at some future time to make a sociological report on the decadence of American life, is problematical.*)

MAURY: Fred, I imagined you were very broad-minded.

PARAMORE: I am.

MURIEL: Me, too. I believe one religion's as good as another and everything.

PARAMORE: There's some good in all religions.

MURIEL: I'm a Catholic but, as I always say, I'm not working at it.

PARAMORE (*with a tremendous burst of tolerance*): The Catholic religion is a very – a very powerful religion.

MAURY: Well, such a broad-minded man should consider the raised plane of sensation and the stimulated optimism contained in this cocktail.

PARAMORE (*taking the drink, rather defiantly*): Thanks, I'll try – one.

MAURY: One? Outrageous! Here we have a class-of-nineteen-ten reunion, and you refuse to be even a little pickled. Come on!

> Here's a health to King Charles,
> Here's a health to King Charles,
> Bring the bowl that you boast –

(PARAMORE *joins in with a hearty voice.*)

MAURY: Fill the cup, Frederick. You know everything's subordinated to nature's purposes with us, and her purpose with you is to make you a rip-roaring tippler.

PARAMORE: If a fellow can drink like a gentleman –

MAURY: What is a gentleman, anyway?

ANTHONY: A man who never has pins under his coat lapel.

MAURY: Nonsense! A man's social rank is determined by the amount of bread he eats in a sandwich.

DICK: He's a man who prefers the first edition of a book to the last edition of a newspaper.

RACHAEL : A man who never gives an impersonation of a dope-fiend.

MAURY: An American who can fool an English butler into thinking he's one.

MURIEL: A man who comes from a good family and went to Yale or Harvard or Princeton, and has money and dances well, and all that.

MAURY: At last – the perfect definition! Cardinal Newman's is now a back number.

PARAMORE: I think we ought to look on the question more broad-mindedly. Was it Abraham Lincoln who said that a gentleman is one who never inflicts pain?

MAURY: It's attributed, I believe, to General Ludendorff.

PARAMORE: Surely you're joking.

MAURY: Have another drink.

PARAMORE: I oughtn't to. (*lowering his voice for* MAURY*'s ear alone*) What if I were to tell you this is the third drink I've ever taken in my life?

(DICK *starts the phonograph, which provokes* MURIEL *to rise and sway from side to side, her elbows against her ribs, her forearms perpendicular to her body and out like fins.*)

MURIEL: Oh, let's take up the rugs and dance!

(*This suggestion is received by* ANTHONY *and* GLORIA *with interior groans and sickly smiles of acquiescence.*)

MURIEL: Come on, you lazybones. Get up and move the furniture back.

DICK: Wait till I finish my drink.

MAURY (*intent on his purpose towards* PARAMORE): I'll tell you what. Let's each fill one glass, drink it off and then we'll dance.

(*A wave of protest breaks against the rock of* MAURY*'s insistence.*)

MURIEL: My head is simply going *round* now.

RACHAEL (*in an undertone to* ANTHONY): Did Gloria tell you to stay away from me?

ANTHONY (*confused*): Why, certainly not. Of course not.

(RACHAEL *smiles at him inscrutably. Two years have given her a sort of hard, well-groomed beauty.*)

MAURY (*holding up his glass*): Here's to the defeat of democracy and the fall of Christianity.

MURIEL: Now really!

(*She flashes a mock-reproachful glance at* MAURY *and then drinks.*

They all drink, with varying degrees of difficulty.)

MURIEL: Clear the floor!

(*It seems inevitable that this process is to be gone through, so* ANTHONY *and* GLORIA *join in the great moving of tables, piling of chairs, rolling of carpets, and breaking of lamps. When the furniture has been stacked in ugly masses at the sides, there appears a space about eight feet square.*)

MURIEL: Oh, let's have music!

MAURY: Tana will render the love song of an eye, ear, nose and throat specialist.

(*Amid some confusion due to the fact that* TANA *has retired for the night, preparations are made for the performance. The pyjamaed Japanese, flute in hand, is wrapped in a comforter and placed in a chair atop one of the tables, where he makes a ludicrous and grotesque spectacle.* PARAMORE *is perceptibly drunk and so enraptured with the notion that he increases the effect by simulating funny-paper staggers and even venturing on an occasional hiccup.*)

PARAMORE (*to* GLORIA): Want to dance with me?

GLORIA: No, sir! Want to do the swan dance. Can you do it?

PARAMORE: Sure. Do them all.

GLORIA: All right. You start from that side of the room and I'll start from this.

MURIEL: Let's go!

(*Then Bedlam creeps screaming out of the bottles:* TANA *plunges into the recondite mazes of the train-song, the plaintive 'tootle toot-toot' blending its melancholy cadences with the* 'Poor Butter-fly [*tink-atink*], by the blossoms waiting' *of the phonograph.* MURIEL *is too weak with laughter to do more than cling desperately to* BARNES, *who, dancing with the ominous rigidity of an army officer, tramps without humour around the small space.* ANTHONY *is trying to hear* RACHAEL'*s whisper – without attracting* GLORIA'*s attention . . .*

But the grotesque, the unbelievable, the histrionic incident is about to occur, one of those incidents in which life seems set upon the passionate imitation of the lowest forms of literature. PARAMORE *has been trying to emulate* GLORIA, *and as the commotion reaches its height he begins to spin round and round, more and more dizzily – he staggers, recovers, staggers again and then falls in the direction of the hall . . . almost into the arms of old* ADAM PATCH, *whose approach has been rendered inaudible by the pandemonium in the room.*

ADAM PATCH *is very white. He leans upon a stick. The man with him is* EDWARD SHUTTLEWORTH, *and it is he who seizes* PARAMORE *by the shoulder and deflects the course of his fall away from the venerable philanthropist.*

The time required for quiet to descend upon the room like a monstrous pall may be estimated at two minutes, though for a short period after that the phonograph gags and the notes of the Japanese train-song dribble from the end of TANA*'s flute. Of the nine people only* BARNES, PARAMORE *and* TANA *are unaware of the late-comer's identity. Of the nine not one is aware that* ADAM PATCH *has that morning made a contribution of fifty thousand dollars to the cause of national Prohibition.*

It is given to PARAMORE *to break the gathering silence; the high tide of his life's depravity is reached in his incredible remark.)*

PARAMORE (*crawling rapidly towards the kitchen on his hands and knees*): I'm not a guest here – I work here.

(*Again silence falls – so deep now, so weighted with intolerably contagious apprehension, that* RACHAEL *gives a nervous little giggle, and* DICK *finds himself telling over and over a line from Swinburne, grotesquely appropriate to the scene:*

'One gaunt bleak blossom of scentless breath.'

. . . Out of the hush the voice of ANTHONY, *sober and strained, saying something to* ADAM PATCH; *then this, too, dies away.)*

SHUTTLEWORTH (*passionately*): Your grandfather thought he would motor over to see your house. I phoned from Rye and left a message.

(*A series of little gasps, emanating, apparently, from nowhere, from no one, fall into the next pause.* ANTHONY *is the colour of chalk.* GLORIA*'s lips are parted and her level gaze at the old man is tense and frightened. There is not one smile in the room. Not one? Or does* CROSS PATCH*'s drawn mouth tremble slightly open, to expose the even rows of his thin teeth? He speaks – five mild and simple words.)*

ADAM PATCH: We'll go back now, Shuttleworth – (*And that is all. He turns, and assisted by his cane goes out through the hall, through the front door, and with hellish portentousness his uncertain footsteps crunch on the gravel path under the August moon.)*

In this extremity they were like two goldfish in a bowl from which all the water had been drawn; they could not even swim across to each other.

Gloria would be twenty-six in May. There was nothing, she had said, that she wanted, except to be young and beautiful for a long time, to be gay and happy, and to have money and love. She wanted what most women want, but she wanted it much more fiercely and passionately. She had been married over two years. At first there had been days of serene understanding, rising to ecstasies of proprietorship and pride. Alternating with these periods had occurred sporadic hates, enduring a short hour, and forgetfulnesses lasting no longer than an afternoon. That had been for half a year.

Then the serenity, the content, had become less jubilant, had become, grey – very rarely, with the spur of jealousy or forced separation, the ancient ecstasies returned, the apparent communion of soul and soul, the emotional excitement. It was possible for her to hate Anthony for as much as a full day, to be carelessly incensed at him for as long as a week. Recrimination had displaced affection as an indulgence, almost as an entertainment, and there were nights when they would go to sleep trying to remember who was angry and who should be reserved next morning. And as the second year waned there had entered two new elements. Gloria realised that Anthony had become capable of utter indifference towards her, a temporary indifference, more than half lethargic, but one from which she could no longer stir him by a whispered word, or a certain intimate smile. There were days when her caresses affected him as a sort of suffocation. She was conscious of these things; she never entirely admitted them to herself.

It was only recently that she perceived that in spite of her adoration of him, her jealousy, her servitude, her pride, she fundamentally despised him – and her contempt blended indistinguishably with her other emotions . . . All this was her love – the vital and feminine illusion that had directed itself towards him one April night, many months before.

On Anthony's part she was, in spite of these qualifications, his sole preoccupation. Had he lost her he would have been a broken man, wretchedly and sentimentally absorbed in her memory for the remainder of life. He seldom took pleasure in an entire day spent alone with her – except on occasions he preferred to have a third person with them. There were times when he felt that if he were not left absolutely alone he would go mad – there were a few times when he definitely hated her. In his cups he was capable of short attractions towards other women, the hitherto-suppressed outcroppings of an experimental temperament.

That spring, that summer, they had speculated upon future happiness – how they were to travel from summer land to summer land, returning eventually to a gorgeous estate and possible idyllic children, then entering diplomacy or politics, to accomplish, for a while, beautiful and important things, until finally as a white-haired (beautifully, silkily, white-haired) couple they were to loll about in serene glory, worshipped by the bourgeoisie of the land . . . These times were to begin 'when we get our money'; it was on such dreams rather than on any satisfaction with their increasingly irregular, increasingly dissipated life that their hope rested. On grey mornings when the jests of the night before had shrunk to ribaldries without wit or dignity, they could, after a fashion, bring out this batch of common hopes and count them over, then smile at each other and repeat, by way of clinching the matter, the terse yet sincere Nietzscheanism of Gloria's defiant 'I don't care!'

Things had been slipping perceptibly. There was the money question, increasingly annoying, increasingly ominous; there was the realisation that liquor had become a practical necessity to their amusement – not an uncommon phenomenon in the British aristocracy of a hundred years ago, but a somewhat alarming one in a civilisation steadily becoming more temperate and more circumspect. Moreover, both of them seemed vaguely weaker in fibre, not so much in what they did as in their subtle reactions to the civilisation about them. In Gloria had been born something that she had hitherto never needed – the skeleton, incomplete but nevertheless unmistakable, of her ancient abhorrence, a conscience. This admission to herself was coincidental with the slow decline of her physical courage.

Then, on the August morning after Adam Patch's unexpected call, they awoke, nauseated and tired, dispirited with life, capable only of one pervasive emotion – fear.

PANIC

'Well?' Anthony sat up in bed and looked down at her. The corners of his lips were drooping with depression, his voice was strained and hollow.

Her reply was to raise her hand to her mouth and begin a slow, precise nibbling at her finger.

'We've done it,' he said after a pause; then, as she was still silent, he became exasperated. 'Why don't you say something?'

'What on earth do you want me to say?'

'What are you thinking?'

'Nothing.'

'Then stop biting your finger!'

Ensued a short confused discussion of whether or not she had been thinking. It seemed essential to Anthony that she should muse aloud upon last night's disaster. Her silence was a method of settling the responsibility on him. For her part she saw no necessity for speech – the moment required that she should gnaw at her finger like a nervous child.

'I've got to fix up this damn mess with my grandfather,' he said with uneasy conviction. A faint newborn respect was indicated by his use of 'my grandfather' instead of 'grampa'.

'You can't,' she affirmed abruptly. 'You can't – *ever*. He'll never forgive you as long as he lives.'

'Perhaps not,' agreed Anthony miserably. 'Still – I might possibly square myself by some sort of reformation and all that sort of thing – '

'He looked sick,' she interrupted, 'pale as flour.'

'He *is* sick. I told you that three months ago.'

'I wish he'd died last week!' she said petulantly. 'Inconsiderate old fool!'

Neither of them laughed.

'But just let me say,' she added quietly, 'the next time I see you acting with any woman like you did with Rachael Barnes last night, I'll leave you – *just – like – that*! I'm simply *not* going to stand it!'

Anthony quailed. 'Oh, don't be absurd,' he protested. 'You know there's no woman in the world for me except you – none, dearest.'

His attempt at a tender note failed miserably – the more imminent danger stalked back into the foreground.

'If I went to him,' suggested Anthony, 'and said with appropriate biblical quotations that I'd walked too long in the way of unrighteousness and at last seen the light – ' He broke off and glanced with a whimsical expression at his wife. 'I wonder what he'd do?'

'I don't know.'

She was speculating as to whether or not their guests would have the acumen to leave directly after breakfast.

Not for a week did Anthony muster the courage to go to Tarrytown. The prospect was revolting and left alone he would have been incapable of making the trip – but if his will had deteriorated in these past three years, so had his power to resist urging. Gloria compelled him to go. It was all very well to wait a week, she said, for that would give his grandfather's violent animosity time to cool – but to wait longer would be an error – it would give it a chance to harden.

He went, in trepidation . . . and vainly. Adam Patch was not well, said Shuttleworth indignantly. Positive instructions had been given that no one was to see him. Before the ex-gin-physician's vindictive eye Anthony's front wilted. He walked out to his taxicab with what was almost a slink – recovering only a little of his self-respect as he boarded the train; glad to escape, boylike, to the wonder palaces of consolation that still rose and glittered in his own mind.

Gloria was scornful when he returned to Marietta. Why had he not forced his way in? That was what she would have done!

Between them they drafted a letter to the old man, and after considerable revision sent it off. It was half an apology, half a manufactured explanation. The letter was not answered.

Came a day in September, a day slashed with alternate sun and rain, sun without warmth, rain without freshness. On that day they left the grey house, which had seen the flower of their love. Four trunks and three monstrous crates were piled in the dismantled room where, two years before, they had sprawled lazily, thinking in terms of dreams, remote, languorous, content. The room echoed with emptiness. Gloria, in a new brown dress edged with fur, sat upon a trunk in silence, and Anthony walked nervously to and fro smoking, as they waited for the truck that would take their things to the city.

'What are those?' she demanded, pointing to some books piled upon one of the crates.

'That's my old stamp collection,' he confessed sheepishly. 'I forgot to pack it.'

'Anthony, it's so silly to carry it around.'

'Well, I was looking through it the day we left the apartment last spring, and I decided not to store it.'

'Can't you sell it? Haven't we enough junk?'

'I'm sorry,' he said humbly.

With a thunderous rattling the truck rolled up to the door. Gloria shook her fist defiantly at the four walls. 'I'm so glad to go!' she cried, 'so glad. Oh, my God, how I hate this house!'

So the brilliant and beautiful lady went up with her husband to New York. On the very train that bore them away they quarrelled – her bitter words had the frequency, the regularity, the inevitability of the stations they passed.

'Don't be cross,' begged Anthony piteously. 'We've got nothing but each other, after all.'

'We haven't even that, most of the time,' cried Gloria.

'When haven't we?'

'A lot of times – beginning with one occasion on the station platform at Redgate.'

'You don't mean to say that – '

'No,' she interrupted coolly, 'I don't brood over it. It came and went – and when it went it took something with it.'

She finished abruptly. Anthony sat in silence, confused, depressed. The drab visions of train-side Mamaroneck, Larchmont, Rye, Pelham Manor, succeeded each other with intervals of bleak and shoddy wastes posing ineffectually as country. He found himself remembering how on one summer morning they two had started from New York in search of happiness. They had never expected to find it, perhaps, yet in itself that quest had been happier than anything he expected for ever more. Life, it seemed, must be a setting up of props around one – otherwise it was disaster. There was no rest, no quiet. He had been futile in longing to drift and dream; no one drifted except to maelstroms, no one dreamed without his dreams becoming fantastic nightmares of indecision and regret.

Pelham! They had quarrelled in Pelham because Gloria must drive. And when she set her little foot on the accelerator the car had jumped off spunkily, and their two heads had jerked back like marionettes worked by a single string.

The Bronx – the houses gathering and gleaming in the sun, which was falling now through wide refulgent skies and tumbling caravans of light down into the streets. New York, he supposed, was home – the city of luxury and mystery, of preposterous hopes and exotic dreams. Here on the outskirts absurd stucco palaces reared themselves in the cool sunset, poised for an instant in cool unreality, glided off far away, succeeded by the mazed confusion of the Harlem River. The train moved in through the deepening twilight, above and past half a hundred cheerful sweating streets of the upper East Side, each one passing the car window like the space between the spokes of a gigantic wheel, each one with its vigorous colourful revelation of poor children swarming in feverish activity like vivid ants in alleys of red sand. From the tenement windows leaned rotund, moon-shaped mothers, as constellations of this sordid heaven; women like dark imperfect jewels, women like vegetables, women like great bags of abominably dirty laundry.

'I like these streets,' observed Anthony aloud. 'I always feel as though it's a performance being staged for me; as though the second I've passed they'll all stop leaping and laughing and, instead, grow very sad, remembering how poor they are, and retreat with bowed heads into their houses. You often get that effect abroad, but seldom in this country.'

Down in a tall busy street he read a dozen Jewish names on a line of stores; in the door of each stood a dark little man watching the passers-by from intent eyes – eyes gleaming with suspicion, with pride, with clarity, with cupidity, with comprehension. New York – he could not dissociate it now from the slow, upward creep of this people – the little stores, growing, expanding, consolidating, moving, watched over with a hawk's eyes and a bee's attention to detail – they slathered out on all sides. It was impressive – in perspective it was tremendous.

Gloria's voice broke in with strange appropriateness upon his thoughts.

'I wonder where Bloeckman's been this summer.'

THE APARTMENT

After the sureties of youth there sets in a period of intense and intolerable complexity. With the soda-jerker this period is so short as to be almost negligible. Men higher in the scale hold out longer in the attempt to preserve the ultimate niceties of relationship, to retain 'impractical' ideas of integrity. But by the late twenties the business has grown too intricate, and what has hitherto been imminent and confusing has become gradually remote and dim. Routine comes down like twilight on a harsh landscape, softening it until it is tolerable. The complexity is too subtle, too varied; the values are changing utterly with each lesion of vitality; it has begun to appear that we can learn nothing from the past with which to face the future – so we cease to be impulsive, convincible men, interested in what is ethically true by fine margins, we substitute rules of conduct for ideas of integrity, we value safety above romance, we become, quite unconsciously, pragmatic. It is left to the few to be persistently concerned with the nuances of relationships – and even this few only in certain hours especially set aside for the task.

Anthony Patch had ceased to be an individual of mental adventure, of curiosity, and had become an individual of bias and prejudice, with a longing to be emotionally undisturbed. This gradual change had taken place through the past several years, accelerated by a succession of anxieties preying on his mind. There was, first of all, the sense of waste, always dormant in his heart, now awakened by the circumstances of his position. In his moments of insecurity he was haunted by the suggestion that life might be, after all, significant. In his early twenties the conviction of the futility of effort, of the wisdom of abnegation, had been confirmed by the philosophies he had admired as well as by his association with Maury Noble, and later with his wife. Yet there had been occasions – just before his first meeting with Gloria, for example, and when his grandfather had suggested that he should go abroad as a war correspondent – upon which his dissatisfaction had driven him almost to a positive step.

One day just before they left Marietta for the last time, in carelessly turning over the pages of a *Harvard Alumni Bulletin*, he had found a column which told him what his contemporaries had been about in this six years since graduation. Most of them were in business, it was true, and several were converting the heathen of China or America to a nebulous Protestantism; but a few, he found, were working constructively at jobs that were neither sinecures nor routines. There was Calvin Boyd, for instance, who, though barely out of medical school, had discovered a new treatment for typhus, had shipped abroad and was mitigating some of the civilisation that the Great Powers had brought to Servia; there was Eugene Bronson, whose articles in the *New Democracy* were stamping him as a man with ideas transcending both vulgar timeliness and popular hysteria; there was a man named Daly who had been suspended from the faculty of a righteous university for preaching Marxian doctrines in the classroom: in art, science, politics, he saw the authentic personalities of his time emerging – there was even Severance, the quarter-back, who had given up his life rather neatly and gracefully with the Foreign Legion on the Aisne.

He laid down the magazine and thought for a while about these diverse men. In the days of his integrity he would have defended his attitude to the last – an Epicurus in Nirvana, he would have cried that to struggle was to believe, to believe was to limit. He would as soon have become a churchgoer because the prospect of immortality gratified him as he would have considered entering the leather business because the intensity of the competition would have kept him from unhappiness. But at present he had no such delicate scruples. This autumn, as his twenty-ninth year began, he was inclined to close his mind to many things, to avoid prying deeply into motive and first causes, and mostly to long passionately for security from the world and from himself. He hated to be alone, as has been said he often dreaded being alone with Gloria.

Because of the chasm which his grandfather's visit had opened before him, and the consequent revulsion from his late mode of life, it was inevitable that he should look around in this suddenly hostile city for the friends and environments that had once seemed the warmest and most secure. His first step was a desperate attempt to get back his old apartment.

In the spring of 1912 he had signed a four-year lease at seventeen hundred a year, with an option of renewal. This lease had expired the previous May. When he had first rented the rooms they had been mere potentialities, scarcely to be discerned as that, but Anthony had seen into these potentialities and arranged in the lease that he and the landlord should each spend a certain amount in improvements. Rents had gone up in the past four years, and last spring when Anthony had waived his option the landlord, a Mr Sohenberg, had realised that he could get a much bigger price for what was now a prepossessing apartment. Accordingly, when Anthony approached him on the subject in September he was met with Sohenberg's offer of a three-year lease at twenty-five hundred a year. This, it seemed to Anthony, was outrageous. It meant that well over a third of their income would be consumed in rent. In vain he argued that his own money, his own ideas on the repartitioning, had made the rooms attractive.

In vain he offered two thousand dollars – twenty-two hundred, though they could ill afford it: Mr Sohenberg was obdurate. It seemed that two other gentlemen were considering it; just that sort of an apartment was in demand at the moment, and it would scarcely be business to *give* it to Mr Patch. Besides, though he had never mentioned it before, several of the other tenants had complained of noise during the previous winter – singing and dancing late at night, that sort of thing.

Internally raging, Anthony hurried back to the Ritz to report his discomfiture to Gloria.

'I can just see you,' she stormed, 'letting him back you down!'

'What could I say?'

'You could have told him what he *was*. I wouldn't have *stood* it. No other man in the world would have stood it! You just let people order you around and cheat you and bully you and take advantage of you as if you were a silly little boy. It's absurd!'

'Oh, for heaven's sake, don't lose your temper.'

'I know, Anthony, but you *are* such an ass!'

'Well, possibly. Anyway, we can't afford that apartment. But we can afford it better than living here at the Ritz.'

'You were the one who insisted on coming here.'

'Yes, because I knew you'd be miserable in a cheap hotel.'

'Of course I would!'

'At any rate we've got to find a place to live.'

'How much can we pay?' she demanded.

'Well, we can pay even his price if we sell more bonds, but we agreed last night that until I had found something definite to do we – '

'Oh, I know all that. I asked you how much we can pay out of just our income.'

'They say you ought not to pay more than a fourth.'

'How much is a fourth?'

'One hundred and fifty a month.'

'Do you mean to say we've got only six hundred dollars coming in every month?' A subdued note crept into her voice.

'Of course!' he answered angrily. 'Do you think we've gone on spending more than twelve thousand a year without cutting way into our capital?'

'I knew we'd sold bonds, but – have we spent that much a year? How did we?' Her awe increased.

'Oh, I'll look in those careful account-books we kept,' he remarked ironically, and then added: 'Two rents a good part of the time, clothes, travel – why, each of those springs in California cost about four thousand dollars. That darn car was an expense from start to finish. And parties and amusements and – oh, one thing or another.'

They were both excited now and inordinately depressed. The situation seemed worse in the actual telling Gloria than it had when he had first made the discovery himself.

'You've got to make some money,' she said suddenly.

'I know it.'

'And you've got to make another attempt to see your grandfather.'

'I will.'

'When?'

'When we get settled.'

This eventuality occurred a week later. They rented a small apartment on Fifty-Seventh Street at one hundred and fifty a month. It included bedroom, living-room, kitchenette and bath, in a thin, white-stone apartment house, and though the rooms were too small to display Anthony's best furniture, they were clean, new and, in a blonde and sanitary way, not unattractive. Bounds had gone abroad to enlist in the British army, and in his place they tolerated rather than enjoyed the services of a gaunt, big-boned Irishwoman, whom Gloria loathed because she discussed the glories of Sinn Fein as she served breakfast. But they vowed they would have no more Japanese, and English servants were for the present hard to obtain. Like Bounds, the woman prepared only breakfast. Their other meals they took at restaurants and hotels.

What finally drove Anthony post-haste up to Tarrytown was an announcement in several New York papers that Adam Patch, the multi-millionaire, the philanthropist, the venerable uplifter, was seriously ill and not expected to recover.

THE KITTEN

Anthony could not see him. The doctors' instructions were that he was to talk to no one, said Mr Shuttleworth – who offered kindly to take any message that Anthony might care to entrust with him, and deliver it to Adam Patch when his condition permitted. But by obvious innuendo he confirmed Anthony's melancholy inference that the prodigal grandson would be particularly unwelcome at the bedside. At one point in the conversation Anthony, with Gloria's positive instructions in mind, made a move as though to brush by the secretary, but Shuttleworth with a smile squared his brawny shoulders, and Anthony saw how futile such an attempt would be.

Miserably intimidated, he returned to New York, where husband and wife passed a restless week. A little incident that occurred one evening indicated to what tension their nerves were drawn.

Walking home along a cross-street after dinner, Anthony noticed a night-bound cat prowling near a railing.

'I always have an instinct to kick a cat,' he said idly.

'I like them.'

'I yielded to it once.'

'When?'

'Oh, years ago; before I met you. One night between the acts of a show. Cold night, like this, and I was a little tight – one of the first times I was ever tight,' he added. 'The poor little beggar was looking for a place to sleep, I guess, and I was in a mean mood, so it took my fancy to kick it – '

'Oh, the poor kitty!' cried Gloria, sincerely moved. Inspired with the narrative instinct, Anthony enlarged on the theme.

'It was pretty bad,' he admitted. 'The poor little beast turned around and looked at me rather plaintively as though hoping I'd pick him up and be kind to him – he was really just a kitten – and before he knew it a big foot launched out at him and caught his little back – '

'Oh!' Gloria's cry was full of anguish.

'It was such a cold night,' he continued, perversely, keeping his voice upon a melancholy note. 'I guess it expected kindness from somebody, and it got only pain – '

He broke off suddenly – Gloria was sobbing. They had reached home, and when they entered the apartment she threw herself upon the lounge, crying as though he had struck at her very soul.

'Oh, the poor little kitty!' she repeated piteously, 'the poor little kitty. So cold – '

'Gloria'

'Don't come near me! Please, don't come near me. You killed the soft little kitty.'

Touched, Anthony knelt beside her.

'Dear,' he said. 'Oh, Gloria, darling. It isn't true. I invented it – every word of it.'

But she would not believe him. There had been something in the details he had chosen to describe that made her cry herself asleep that night, for the kitten, for Anthony, for herself, for the pain and bitterness and cruelty of all the world.

THE PASSING OF AN AMERICAN MORALIST

Old Adam died on a midnight of late November with a pious compliment to his God on his thin lips. He, who had been flattered so much, faded out flattering the Omnipotent Abstraction which he fancied he might have angered in the more lascivious moments of his youth. It was announced that he had arranged some sort of an armistice with the deity, the terms of which were not made public, though they were thought to have included a large cash payment. All the newspapers printed his biography, and two of them ran short editorials on his sterling worth, and his part in the drama of industrialism, with which he had grown up. They referred guardedly to the reforms he had sponsored and financed. The memories of Comstock and Cato the Censor were resuscitated and paraded like gaunt ghosts through the columns.

Every newspaper remarked that he was survived by a single grandson, Anthony Comstock Patch, of New York.

The burial took place in the family plot at Tarrytown. Anthony and Gloria rode in the first carriage, too worried to feel grotesque, both trying desperately to glean presage of fortune from the faces of retainers who had been with him at the end.

They waited a frantic week for decency, and then, having received no notification of any kind, Anthony called up his grandfather's lawyer. Mr Brett was not in – he was expected back in an hour. Anthony left his telephone number.

It was the last day of November, cool and crackling outside, with a lustreless sun peering bleakly in at the windows. While they waited for the call, ostensibly engaged in reading, the atmosphere, within and without, seemed pervaded with a deliberate rendition of the pathetic fallacy. After an interminable while, the bell jingled, and Anthony, starting violently, took up the receiver.

'Hello . . . ' His voice was strained and hollow. 'Yes – I did leave word. Who is this, please? . . . Yes . . . Why, it was about the estate. Naturally I'm interested, and I've received no word about the reading of the will – I thought you might not have my address . . . What? . . . Yes . . . '

Gloria fell on her knees. The intervals between Anthony's speeches were like tourniquets winding on her heart. She found herself helplessly twisting the large buttons from a velvet cushion. Then: 'That's – that's very, very odd – that's very odd – that's very odd. Not even any – ah – mention or any – ah – reason?'

His voice sounded faint and far away. She uttered a little sound, half gasp, half cry.

'Yes, I'll see . . . All right, thanks . . . thanks . . . '

The phone clicked. Her eyes looking along the floor saw his feet cut the pattern of a patch of sunlight on the carpet. She arose and faced him with a grey, level glance just as his arms folded about her.

'My dearest,' he whispered huskily. 'He did it, goddamn him!'

'Who are the heirs?' asked Mr Haight. 'You see when you can tell me so little about it – '

Mr Haight was tall and bent and beetle-browed. He had been recommended to Anthony as an astute and tenacious lawyer.

'I only know vaguely,' answered Anthony. 'A man named Shuttleworth, who was a sort of pet of his, has the whole thing in charge as administrator or trustee or something – all except the direct bequests to charity and the provisions for servants and for those two cousins in Idaho.'

'How distant are the cousins?'

'Oh, third or fourth, anyway. I never even heard of them.'

Mr Haight nodded comprehensively.

'And you want to contest a provision of the will?'

'I guess so,' admitted Anthony helplessly. 'I want to do what sounds most hopeful – that's what I want you to tell me.'

'You want them to refuse probate to the will?'

Anthony shook his head.

'You've got me. I haven't any idea what "probate" is. I want a share of the estate.'

'Suppose you tell me some more details. For instance, do you know why the testator disinherited you?'

'Why – yes,' began Anthony. 'You see he was always a sucker for moral reform, and all that – '

'I know,' interjected Mr Haight humourlessly.

' – and I don't suppose he ever thought I was much good. I didn't go into business, you see. But I feel certain that up to last summer I was one of the beneficiaries. We had a house out in Marietta, and one night grandfather got the notion he'd come over and see us. It just happened that there was a rather gay party going on and he arrived without any warning. Well, he took one look, he and this fellow Shuttleworth, and then turned around and tore right back to Tarrytown. After that he never answered my letters or even let me see him.'

'He was a Prohibitionist, wasn't he?'

'He was everything – regular religious maniac.'

'How long before his death was the will made that disinherited you?'

'Recently – I mean since August.'

'And you think that the direct reason for his not leaving you the majority of the estate was his displeasure with your recent actions?'

'Yes.'

Mr Haight considered. Upon what grounds was Anthony thinking of contesting the will?

'Why, isn't there something about evil influence?'

'Undue influence is one ground – but it's the most difficult. You would have to show that such pressure was brought to bear so that the deceased was in a condition where he disposed of his property contrary to his intentions – '

'Well, suppose this fellow Shuttleworth dragged him over to Marietta just when he thought some sort of a celebration was probably going on?'

'That wouldn't have any bearing on the case. There's a strong division between advice and influence. You'd have to prove that the secretary had a sinister intention. I'd suggest some other grounds. A will is automatically refused probate in case of insanity, drunkenness' – here Anthony smiled – 'or feeble-mindedness through premature old age.'

'But,' objected Anthony, 'his private physician, being one of the beneficiaries, would testify that he wasn't feeble-minded. And he wasn't. As a matter of fact he probably did just what he intended to with his money – it was perfectly consistent with everything he'd ever done in his life – '

'Well, you see, feeble-mindedness is a great deal like undue influence – it implies that the property wasn't disposed of as originally intended. The most common ground is duress – physical pressure.'

Anthony shook his head.

'Not much chance on that, I'm afraid. Undue influence sounds best to me.'

After more discussion, so technical as to be largely unintelligible to Anthony, he retained Mr Haight as counsel. The lawyer proposed an interview with Shuttleworth, who, jointly with Wilson, Hiemer and Hardy, was executor of the will. Anthony was to come back later in the week.

It transpired that the estate consisted of approximately forty million dollars. The largest bequest to an individual was of one million, to Edward Shuttleworth, who received in addition thirty thousand a year salary as administrator of the thirty-million-dollar trust fund, left to be doled out to various charities and reform societies practically at his own discretion. The remaining nine millions were proportioned among the two cousins in Idaho and about twenty-five other beneficiaries: friends, secretaries, servants and employees, who had, at one time or another, earned the seal of Adam Patch's approval.

At the end of another fortnight Mr Haight, on a retainer's fee of fifteen thousand dollars, had begun preparations for contesting the will.

THE WINTER OF DISCONTENT

Before they had been two months in the little apartment on Fifty-Seventh Street, it had assumed for both of them the same indefinable but almost material taint that had impregnated the grey house in Marietta. There was the odour of tobacco always – both of them smoked incessantly; it was in their clothes, their blankets, the curtains and the ash-littered carpets. Added to this was the wretched aura of stale wine, with its inevitable suggestion of beauty gone foul and revelry remembered in disgust. About a particular set of glass goblets on the sideboard the odour was particularly noticeable, and in the main room the mahogany table was ringed with white circles where glasses had been set down upon it. There had been many parties – people broke things; people became sick in Gloria's bathroom; people spilled wine; people made unbelievable messes of the kitchenette.

These things were a regular part of their existence. Despite the resolutions of many Mondays it was tacitly understood as the weekend approached that it should be observed with some sort of unholy excitement. When Saturday came they would not discuss the matter, but would call up this person or that from among their circle of sufficiently irresponsible friends, and suggest a rendezvous. Only after the friends had gathered and Anthony had set out decanters, would he murmur casually, 'I guess I'll have just one highball myself – '

Then they were off for two days – realising on a wintry dawn that they had been the noisiest and most conspicuous members of the noisiest and most conspicuous party at the Boul' Mich', or the Club Ramée, or at other resorts much less particular about the hilarity of their clientèle. They would find that they had, somehow, squandered eighty or ninety dollars, how, they never knew; they customarily attributed it to the general penury of the 'friends' who had accompanied them.

It began to be not unusual for the more sincere of their friends to remonstrate with them, in the very course of a party, and to predict a sombre end for them in the loss of Gloria's 'looks' and Anthony's 'constitution'.

The story of the summarily interrupted revel in Marietta had, of course, leaked out in detail – 'Muriel doesn't mean to tell everyone she knows,' said Gloria to Anthony, 'but she thinks everyone she tells is the only one she's going to tell' – and, diaphanously veiled, the tale had been given a conspicuous place in *Town Tattle*. When the terms of Adam Patch's will were made public and the newspapers printed items concerning Anthony's suit, the story was beautifully rounded out – to Anthony's infinite disparagement. They began to hear rumours about themselves from all quarters, rumours founded usually on a soupçon of truth, but overlaid with preposterous and sinister detail.

Outwardly they showed no signs of deterioration. Gloria at twenty-six was still the Gloria of twenty; her complexion a fresh damp setting for her candid eyes; her hair still a childish glory, darkening slowly from corn colour to a deep russet gold; her slender body suggesting ever a nymph running and dancing through Orphic groves. Masculine eyes, dozens of them, followed her with a fascinated stare when she walked through a hotel lobby or down the aisle of a theatre. Men asked to be introduced to her, fell into prolonged states of sincere admiration, made definite love to her – for she was still a thing of exquisite and unbelievable beauty. And for his part Anthony had rather gained than lost in appearance; his face had taken on a certain intangible air of tragedy, romantically contrasted with his trim and immaculate person.

Early in the winter, when all conversation turned on the probability of America's going into the war, when Anthony was making a desperate and sincere attempt to write, Muriel Kane arrived in New York and came immediately to see them. Like Gloria, she seemed never to change. She knew the latest slang, danced the latest dances, and talked of the latest songs and plays with all the fervour of her first season as a New York drifter. Her coyness was eternally new, eternally ineffectual; her clothes were extreme; her black hair was bobbed, now, like Gloria's.

'I've come up for the midwinter prom at New Haven,' she announced, imparting her delightful secret. Though she must have been older then than any of the boys in college, she managed always to secure some sort of invitation, imagining vaguely that at the next party would occur the flirtation which was to end at the romantic altar.

'Where've you been?' enquired Anthony, unfailingly amused.

'I've been at Hot Springs. It's been slick and peppy this fall – more *men*!'

'Are you in love, Muriel?'

'What do you mean "love"?' This was the rhetorical question of the year. 'I'm going to tell you something,' she said, switching the subject abruptly. 'I suppose it's none of my business, but I think it's time for you two to settle down.'

'Why, we are settled down.'

'Yes, you are!' she scoffed archly. 'Everywhere I go I hear stories of your escapades. Let me tell you, I have an awful time sticking up for you.'

'You needn't bother,' said Gloria coldly.

'Now, Gloria,' she protested, 'you know I'm one of your best friends.'

Gloria was silent. Muriel continued: 'It's not so much the idea of a woman drinking, but Gloria's so pretty, and so many people know her by sight all around, that it's naturally conspicuous – '

'What have you heard recently?' demanded Gloria, her dignity going down before her curiosity.

'Well, for instance, that that party in Marietta *killed* Anthony's grandfather.'

Instantly husband and wife were tense with annoyance.

'Why, I think that's outrageous.'

'That's what they say,' persisted Muriel stubbornly.

Anthony paced the room. 'It's preposterous!' he declared. 'The very people we take on parties shout the story around as a great joke – and eventually it gets back to us in some such form as this.'

Gloria began running her finger through a stray reddish curl. Muriel licked her veil as she considered her next remark.

'You ought to have a baby.'

Gloria looked up wearily.

'We can't afford it.'

'All the people in the slums have them,' said Muriel triumphantly.

Anthony and Gloria exchanged a smile. They had reached the stage of violent quarrels that were never made up, quarrels that smouldered and broke out again at intervals or died away from sheer indifference – but this visit of Muriel's drew them temporarily together. When the discomfort under which they were living was remarked upon by a third party, it gave them the impetus to face this hostile world together.

It was very seldom, now, that the impulse towards reunion sprang from within.

Anthony found himself associating his own existence with that of the apartment's night-elevator man, a pale, scraggly bearded person of about sixty, with an air of being somewhat above his station. It was probably because of this quality that he had secured the position; it made him a pathetic and memorable figure of failure. Anthony recollected, without humour, a hoary jest about the elevator man's career being a matter of ups and downs – it was, at any rate, an enclosed life of infinite dreariness. Each time Anthony stepped into the car he waited breathlessly for the old man's, 'Well, I guess we're going to have some sunshine today.' Anthony thought how little rain or sunshine he would enjoy shut into that close little cage in the smoke-coloured, windowless hall.

A darkling figure, he attained tragedy in leaving the life that had used him so shabbily. Three young gunmen came in one night, tied him up and left him on a pile of coal in the cellar while they went through the trunk room. When the janitor found him next morning he had collapsed from chill. He died of pneumonia four days later.

He was replaced by a glib Martinique Negro, with an incongruous British accent and a tendency to be surly, whom Anthony detested. The passing of the old man had approximately the same effect on him that the kitten story had had on Gloria. He was reminded of the cruelty of all life and, in consequence, of the increasing bitterness of his own.

He was writing – and in earnest at last. He had gone to Dick and listened for a tense hour to an elucidation of those minutiae of procedure which hitherto he had rather scornfully looked down upon. He needed money immediately – he was selling bonds every month to pay their bills. Dick was frank and explicit: 'So far as articles on literary subjects in these obscure magazines go, you couldn't make enough to pay your rent. Of course if a man has the gift of humour, or a chance at a big biography, or some specialised knowledge, he may strike it rich. But for you, fiction's the only thing. You say you need money right away?'

'I certainly do.'

'Well, it'd be a year and a half before you'd make any money out of a novel. Try some popular short stories. And, by the way, unless they're exceptionally brilliant they have to be cheerful and on the side of the heaviest artillery to make you any money.'

Anthony thought of Dick's recent output, which had been appearing in a well-known monthly. It was concerned chiefly with the preposterous actions of a class of sawdust effigies who, one was assured, were New York society people, and it turned, as a rule, upon questions of the heroine's technical purity, with mock-sociological overtones about the 'mad antics of the four hundred'.

'But your stories – ' exclaimed Anthony aloud, almost involuntarily.

'Oh, that's different,' Dick asserted astoundingly. 'I have a reputation, you see, so I'm expected to deal with strong themes.'

Anthony gave an interior start, realising with this remark how much Richard Caramel had fallen off. Did he actually think that these amazing latter productions were as good as his first novel?

Anthony went back to the apartment and set to work. He found that the business of optimism was no mean task. After half a dozen futile starts he went to the public library and for a week investigated the files of a popular magazine. Then, better equipped, he accomplished his first story, 'The Dictaphone of Fate'. It was founded upon one of his few remaining impressions of that six weeks in Wall Street the year before. It purported to be the sunny tale of an office boy who, quite by accident, hummed a wonderful melody into the dictaphone. The cylinder was discovered by the boss's brother, a well-known producer of musical comedy – and then immediately lost. The body of the story was concerned with the pursuit of the missing cylinder and the eventual marriage of the noble office boy (now a successful composer) to Miss Rooney, the virtuous stenographer, who was half Joan of Arc and half Florence Nightingale.

He had gathered that this was what the magazines wanted. He offered, in his protagonists, the customary denizens of the pink-and-blue literary world, immersing them in a saccharine plot that would offend not a single stomach in Marietta. He had it typed in double space – this last as advised by a booklet, *Success as a Writer Made Easy*, by R. Meggs Widdlestien, which assured the ambitious plumber of the futility of perspiration, since after a six-lesson course he could make at least a thousand dollars a month.

After reading it to a bored Gloria and coaxing from her the immemorial remark that it was 'better than a lot of stuff that gets published', he satirically affixed the *nom de plume* of 'Gilles de Sade', enclosed the proper return envelope, and sent it off.

Following the gigantic labour of conception he decided to wait until he heard from the first story before beginning another. Dick had told him that he might get as much as two hundred dollars. If by any chance it did happen to be unsuited, the editor's letter would, no doubt, give him an idea of what changes should be made.

'It is, without question, the most abominable piece of writing in existence,' said Anthony.

The editor quite conceivably agreed with him. He returned the manuscript with a rejection slip. Anthony sent it off elsewhere and began another story. The second one was called 'The Little Open Doors'; it was written in three days. It concerned the occult: an estranged couple were brought together by a medium in a vaudeville show.

There were six altogether, six wretched and pitiable efforts to 'write down' by a man who had never before made a consistent effort to write at all. Not one of them contained a spark of vitality, and their total yield of grace and felicity was less than that of an average newspaper column. During their circulation they collected, all told, thirty-one rejection slips, headstones for the packages that he would find lying like dead bodies at his door.

In mid-January Gloria's father died, and they went again to Kansas City – a miserable trip, for Gloria brooded interminably, not upon her father's death, but on her mother's. Russel Gilbert's affairs having been cleared up, they came into possession of about three thousand dollars, and a great amount of furniture. This was in storage, for he had spent his last days in a small hotel. It was due to his death that Anthony made a new discovery concerning Gloria. On the journey East she disclosed herself, astonishingly, as a Bilphist.

'Why, Gloria,' he cried, 'you don't mean to tell me you believe that stuff.'

'Well,' she said defiantly, 'why not?'

'Because it's – it's fantastic. You know that in every sense of the word you're an agnostic. You'd laugh at any orthodox form of Christianity – and then you come out with the statement that you believe in some silly rule of reincarnation.'

'What if I do? I've heard you and Maury, and everyone else for whose intellect I have the slightest respect, agree that life as it appears is utterly meaningless. But it's always seemed to me that if I were unconsciously learning something here it might not be so meaningless.'

'You're not learning anything – you're just getting tired. And if you must have a faith to soften things, take up one that appeals to the reason of someone beside a lot of hysterical women. A person like you oughtn't to accept anything unless it's decently demonstrable.'

'I don't care about truth. I want some happiness.'

'Well, if you've got a decent mind the second has got to be qualified by the first. Any simple soul can delude himself with mental garbage.'

'I don't care,' she held out stoutly, 'and, what's more, I'm not propounding any doctrine.'

The argument faded off, but reoccurred to Anthony several times thereafter. It was disturbing to find this old belief, evidently assimilated from her mother, inserting itself again under its immemorial disguise as an innate idea.

They reached New York in March after an expensive and ill-advised week spent in Hot Springs, and Anthony resumed his abortive attempts at fiction. As it became plainer to both of them that escape did not lie in the way of popular literature, there was a further slipping of their mutual confidence and courage. A complicated struggle went on incessantly between them. All efforts to keep down expenses died away from sheer inertia, and by March they were again using any pretext as an excuse for a 'party'. With an assumption of recklessness Gloria tossed out the suggestion that they should take all their money and go on a real spree while it lasted – anything seemed better than to see it go in unsatisfactory driblets.

'Gloria, you want parties as much as I do.'

'It doesn't matter about me. Everything I do is in accordance with my ideas: to use every minute of these years, when I'm young, in having the best time I possibly can.'

'How about after that?'

'After that I won't care.'

'Yes, you will.'

'Well, I may – but I won't be able to do anything about it. And I'll have had my good time.'

'You'll be the same then. After a fashion, we *have* had our good time, raised the devil, and we're in the state of paying for it.'

Nevertheless, the money kept going. There would be two days of gaiety, two days of moroseness – an endless, almost invariable round. The sharp pull-ups, when they occurred, resulted usually in a spurt of work for Anthony, while Gloria, nervous and bored, remained in bed or else chewed abstractedly at her fingers. After a day or so of this, they would make an engagement, and then – Oh, what did it matter? This night, this glow, the cessation of anxiety and the sense that if living was not purposeful it was, at any rate, essentially romantic! Wine gave a sort of gallantry to their own failure.

Meanwhile the suit progressed slowly, with interminable examinations of witnesses and marshallings of evidence. The preliminary proceedings of settling the estate were finished. Mr Haight saw no reason why the case should not come up for trial before summer.

Bloeckman appeared in New York late in March; he had been in England for nearly a year on matters concerned with 'Films Par Excellence'. The process of general refinement was still in progress – always he dressed a little better, his intonation was mellower, and in his manner there was perceptibly more assurance that the fine things of the world were his by a natural and inalienable right. He called at the apartment, remained only an hour, during which he talked chiefly of the war, and left telling them he was coming again. On his second visit Anthony was not at home, but an absorbed and excited Gloria greeted her husband later in the afternoon.

'Anthony,' she began, 'would you still object if I went in the movies?'

His whole heart hardened against the idea. As she seemed to recede from him, if only in threat, her presence became again not so much precious as desperately necessary.

'Oh, Gloria – !'

'Blockhead said he'd put me in – only if I'm ever going to do anything I'll have to start now. They only want young women. Think of the money, Anthony!'

'For you – yes. But how about me?'

'Don't you know that anything I have is yours too?'

'It's such a hell of a career!' he burst out, the moral, the infinitely circumspect Anthony, 'and such a hell of a bunch. And I'm so utterly tired of that fellow Bloeckman coming here and interfering. I hate theatrical things.'

'It isn't theatrical! It's utterly different.'

'What am I supposed to do? Chase you all over the country? Live on your money?'

'Then make some yourself.'

The conversation developed into one of the most violent quarrels they had ever had. After the ensuing reconciliation and the inevitable period of moral inertia, she realised that he had taken the life out of the project. Neither of them ever mentioned the probability that Bloeckman was by no means disinterested, but they both knew that it lay behind Anthony's objection.

In April war was declared with Germany. Wilson and his cabinet – a cabinet that in its lack of distinction was strangely reminiscent of the twelve apostles – let loose the carefully starved dogs of war, and the press began to whoop hysterically against the sinister morals, sinister philosophy and sinister music produced by the Teutonic temperament. Those who fancied themselves particularly broad-minded made the exquisite distinction that it was only the German government which aroused them to hysteria; the rest were worked up to a condition of retching indecency. Any song which contained the word 'mother' and the word 'kaiser' was assured of a tremendous success. At last everyone had something to talk about – and almost everyone fully enjoyed it, as though they had been cast for parts in a sombre and romantic play.

Anthony, Maury and Dick sent in their applications for officers' training-camps and the two latter went about feeling strangely exalted and reproachless; they chattered to each other, like college boys, of war's being the one excuse for, and justification of, the aristocrat, and conjured up an impossible caste of officers, to be composed, it appeared, chiefly of the more attractive alumni of three or four Eastern colleges. It seemed to Gloria that in this huge red light streaming across the nation even Anthony took on a new glamour.

The Tenth Infantry, arriving in New York from Panama, were escorted from saloon to saloon by patriotic citizens, to their great bewilderment. West Pointers began to be noticed for the first time in years, and the general impression was that everything was glorious, but not half so glorious as it was going to be pretty soon, and that everybody was a fine fellow, and every race a great race – always excepting the Germans – and in every strata of society outcasts and scapegoats had but to appear in uniform to be forgiven, cheered, and wept over by relatives, ex-friends and utter strangers.

Unfortunately, a small and precise doctor decided that there was something the matter with Anthony's blood-pressure. He could not conscientiously pass him for an officers' training-camp.

THE BROKEN LUTE

Their third anniversary passed, uncelebrated, unnoticed. The season warmed in thaw, melted into hotter summer, simmered and boiled away. In July the will was offered for probate, and upon the contestation was assigned by the surrogate to trial term for trial. The matter was prolonged into September – there was difficulty in empanelling an unbiassed jury because of the moral sentiments involved. To Anthony's disappointment a verdict was finally returned in favour of the testator, whereupon Mr Haight caused a notice of appeal to be served upon Edward Shuttleworth.

As the summer waned Anthony and Gloria talked of the things they were to do when the money was theirs, and of the places they were to go to after the war, when they would 'agree on things again', for both of them looked forward to a time when love, springing like the phoenix from its own ashes, should be born again in its mysterious and unfathomable haunts.

He was drafted early in the fall, and the examining doctor made no mention of low blood-pressure. It was all very purposeless and sad when Anthony told Gloria one night that he wanted, above all things, to be killed. But, as always, they were sorry for each other for the wrong things at the wrong times . . .

They decided that for the present she was not to go with him to the Southern camp where his contingent was ordered. She would remain in New York to 'use the apartment', to save money, and to watch the progress of the case – which was pending now in the Appellate Division, of which the calendar, Mr Haight told them, was far behind.

Almost their last conversation was a senseless quarrel about the proper division of the income – at a word either would have given it all to the other. It was typical of the muddle and confusion of their lives that on the October night when Anthony reported at the Grand Central Station for the journey to camp, she arrived only in time to catch his eye over the anxious heads of a gathered crowd. Through the dark light of the enclosed train-sheds their glances stretched across a hysterical area, foul with yellow sobbing and the smells of poor women. They must have pondered upon what they had done to one another, and they must each have accused themselves of drawing this sombre pattern through which they were tracing tragically and obscurely. At the last they were too far away for either to see the other's tears.

BOOK THREE

Chapter 1

A Matter of Civilisation

At a frantic command from some invisible source, Anthony groped his way inside. He was thinking that for the first time in more than three years he was to remain longer than a night away from Gloria. The finality of it appealed to him drearily. It was his clean and lovely girl that he was leaving.

They had arrived, he thought, at the most practical financial settlement: she was to have three hundred and seventy-five dollars a month – not too much considering that over half of that would go in rent – and he was taking fifty to supplement his pay. He saw no need for more: food, clothes and quarters would be provided – there were no social obligations for a private.

The car was crowded and already thick with breath. It was one of the type known as 'tourist' cars, a sort of brummagem Pullman, with a bare floor, and straw seats that needed cleaning. Nevertheless, Anthony greeted it with relief. He had vaguely expected that the trip South would be made in a freight-car, in one end of which would stand eight horses and in the other forty men. He had heard the 'hommes 40, chevaux 8' story so often that it had become confused and ominous.

As he rocked down the aisle with his barrack-bag slung at his shoulder like a monstrous blue sausage, he saw no vacant seats, but after a moment his eye fell on a single space at present occupied by the feet of a short swarthy Sicilian, who, with his hat drawn over his eyes, hunched defiantly in the corner. As Anthony stopped beside him he stared up with a scowl, evidently intended to be intimidating; he must have adopted it as a defence against this entire gigantic equation. At Anthony's sharp, 'That seat taken?' he very slowly lifted the feet as though they were a breakable package, and placed them with some care upon the floor. His eyes remained on Anthony, who meanwhile sat down and unbuttoned the uniform coat issued him at Camp Upton the day before. It chafed him under the arms.

Before Anthony could scrutinise the other occupants of the section a young second lieutenant blew in at the upper end of the car and wafted airily down the aisle, announcing in a voice of appalling acerbity: 'There will be no smoking in this car! No smoking! Don't smoke, men, in this car!'

As he sailed out at the other end a dozen little clouds of expostulation arose on all sides.

'Oh, cripe!'

'Jeese!'

'No *smokin'*?'

'Hey, come back here, fella!'

'What's 'ee idea?'

Two or three cigarettes were shot out through the open windows. Others were retained inside, though kept sketchily away from view. From here and there in accents of bravado, of mockery, of submissive humour, a few remarks were dropped that soon melted into the listless and pervasive silence.

The fourth occupant of Anthony's section spoke up suddenly.

'G'by, liberty,' he said sullenly. 'G'by, everything except bein' an officer's dog.'

Anthony looked at him. He was a tall Irishman with an expression moulded of indifference and utter disdain. His eyes fell on Anthony, as though he expected an answer, and then upon the others. Receiving only a defiant stare from the Italian he groaned and spat noisily on the floor by way of a dignified transition back into taciturnity.

A few minutes later the door opened again and the second lieutenant was borne in upon his customary official zephyr, this time singing out a different tiding: 'All right, men, smoke if you want to! My mistake, men! It's all right, men! Go on and smoke – my mistake!'

This time Anthony had a good look at him. He was young, thin, already faded; he was like his own moustache; he was like a great piece of shiny straw. His chin receded, faintly; this was offset by a magnificent and unconvincing scowl, a scowl that Anthony was to connect with the faces of many young officers during the ensuing year.

Immediately everyone smoked – whether they had previously desired to or not. Anthony's cigarette contributed to the hazy oxidation which seemed to roll back and forth in opalescent clouds with every motion of the train. The conversation, which had lapsed between the two impressive visits of the young officer, now revived tepidly; the men across the aisle began making clumsy experiments with their straw seats' capacity for comparative comfort; two card games, half-heartedly begun, soon drew several spectators to sitting positions on the arms of seats. In a few minutes Anthony became aware of a persistently obnoxious sound – the small, defiant Sicilian had fallen audibly asleep. It was wearisome to contemplate that animate protoplasm, reasonable by courtesy only, shut up in a car by an incomprehensible civilisation, taken somewhere, to do a vague something without aim or significance or consequence. Anthony sighed, opened a newspaper which he had no recollection of buying, and began to read by the dim yellow light.

Ten o'clock bumped stuffily into eleven; the hours clogged and caught and slowed down. Amazingly the train halted along the dark countryside, from time to time indulging in short, deceitful movements backwards or forwards, and whistling harsh paeans into the high October night. Having read his newspaper through, editorials, cartoons and war-poems, his eye fell on a half-column headed 'Shakespeareville, Kansas'. It seemed that the Shakespeareville Chamber of Commerce had recently held an enthusiastic debate as to whether the American soldiers should be known as 'Sammies' or 'Battling Christians'. The thought gagged him. He dropped the newspaper, yawned, and let his mind drift off at a tangent. He wondered why Gloria had been late. It seemed so long ago already – he had a pang of illusive loneliness. He tried to imagine from what angle she would regard her new position, what place in her considerations he would continue to hold. The thought acted as a further depressant – he opened his paper and began to read again.

The members of the Chamber of Commerce in Shakespeareville had decided upon 'Liberty Lads'.

For two nights and two days they rattled southward, making mysterious inexplicable stops in what were apparently arid wastes, and then rushing through large cities with a pompous air of hurry. The whimsicalities of this train foreshadowed for Anthony the whimsicalities of all army administration.

In the arid wastes they were served from the baggage-car with beans and bacon that at first he was unable to eat – he dined scantily on some milk chocolate distributed by a village canteen. But on the second day the baggage-car's output began to appear surprisingly palatable. On the third morning the rumour was passed along that within the hour they would arrive at their destination, Camp Hooker.

It had become intolerably hot in the car, and the men were all in shirt sleeves. The sun came in through the windows, a tired and ancient sun, yellow as parchment and stretched out of shape in transit. It tried to enter in triumphant squares and produced only warped splotches – but it was appallingly steady; so much so that it disturbed Anthony not to be the pivot of all the inconsequential sawmills and trees and telegraph poles that were turning around him so fast. Outside it played its heavy tremolo over olive roads and fallow cotton-fields, back of which ran a ragged line of woods broken with eminences of grey rock. The foreground was dotted sparsely with wretched, ill-patched shanties, among which there would flash by, now and then, a specimen of the languid yokelry of South Carolina, or else a strolling darky with sullen and bewildered eyes.

Then the woods moved off and they rolled into a broad space like the baked top of a gigantic cake, sugared with an infinity of tents arranged in geometric figures over its surface. The train came to an uncertain stop, and the sun and the poles and the trees faded, and his universe rocked itself slowly back to its old usualness, with Anthony Patch in the centre. As the men, weary and perspiring, crowded out of the car, he smelt that unforgettable aroma that impregnates all permanent camps – the odour of garbage.

Camp Hooker was an astonishing and spectacular growth, suggesting 'A Mining Town in 1870 – The Second Week'. It was a thing of wooden shacks and whitish-grey tents, connected by a pattern of roads, with hard tan drill-grounds fringed with trees. Here and there stood green YMCA houses, unpromising oases, with their muggy odour of wet flannels and closed telephone-booths – and across from each of them there was usually a canteen, swarming with life, presided over indolently by an officer who, with the aid of a side-car, usually managed to make his detail a pleasant and chatty sinecure.

Up and down the dusty roads sped the soldiers of the quartermaster corps, also in side-cars. Up and down drove the generals in their government automobiles, stopping now and then to bring unalert details to attention, to frown heavily upon captains marching at the heads of companies, to set the pompous pace in that gorgeous game of showing off which was taking place triumphantly over the entire area.

The first week after the arrival of Anthony's draft was filled with a series of interminable inoculations and physical examinations, and with the preliminary drilling. The days left him desperately tired. He had been issued the wrong-size shoes by a popular, easy-going supply-sergeant, and in consequence his feet were so swollen that the last hours of the afternoon were an acute torture. For the first time in his life he could throw himself down on his cot between dinner and afternoon drill-call, and seeming to sink with each moment deeper into a bottomless bed, drop off immediately to sleep, while the noise and laughter around him faded to a pleasant drone of drowsy summer sound. In the morning he awoke stiff and aching, hollow as a ghost, and hurried forth to meet the other ghostly figures who swarmed in the wan company streets, while a harsh bugle shrieked and spluttered at the grey heavens.

He was in a skeleton infantry company of about a hundred men. After the invariable breakfast of fatty bacon, cold toast and cereal, the entire hundred would rush for the latrines, which, however well-policed, seemed always intolerable, like the lavatories in cheap hotels. Out on the field, then, in ragged order – the lame man on his left grotesquely marring Anthony's listless efforts to keep in step, the platoon sergeants either showing off violently to impress the officers and recruits, or else quietly lurking in close to the line of march, avoiding both labour and unnecessary visibility.

When they reached the field, work began immediately – they peeled off their shirts for calisthenics. This was the only part of the day that Anthony enjoyed. Lieutenant Kretching, who presided at the antics, was sinewy and muscular, and Anthony followed his movements faithfully, with a feeling that he was doing something of positive value to himself. The other officers and sergeants walked about among the men with the malice of schoolboys, grouping here and there around some unfortunate who lacked muscular control, giving him confused instructions and commands. When they discovered a particularly forlorn, ill-nourished specimen, they would linger the full half-hour making cutting remarks and snickering among themselves.

One little officer named Hopkins, who had been a sergeant in the regular army, was particularly annoying. He took the war as a gift of revenge from the high gods to himself, and the constant burden of his harangues was that these rookies did not appreciate the full gravity and responsibility of 'the service'. He considered that by a combination of foresight and dauntless efficiency he had raised himself to his current magnificence. He aped the particular tyrannies of every officer under whom he had served in times gone by. His frown was frozen on his brow – before giving a private a pass to go to town he would ponderously weigh the effect of such an absence upon the company, the army, and the welfare of the military profession the world over.

Lieutenant Kretching, blond, dull and phlegmatic, introduced Anthony ponderously to the problems of attention, right face, about face, and at ease. His principal defect was his forgetfulness. He often kept the company straining and aching at attention for five minutes while he stood out in front and explained a new movement; as a result only the men in the centre knew what it was all about – those on both flanks had been too emphatically impressed with the necessity of staring straight ahead.

The drill continued until noon. It consisted of stressing a succession of infinitely remote details, and though Anthony perceived that this was consistent with the logic of war, it none the less irritated him. That the same faulty blood-pressure which would have been indecent in an officer did not interfere with the duties of a private was a preposterous incongruity. Sometimes, after listening to a sustained invective concerned with a dull and, on the face of it, absurd subject known as military 'courtesy', he suspected that the dim purpose of the war was to let the regular army officers – men with the mentality and aspirations of schoolboys – have their fling with some real slaughter. He was being grotesquely sacrificed to the twenty-year patience of a Hopkins!

Of his three tent-mates – a flat-faced, conscientious objector from Tennessee, a big, scared Pole, and the disdainful Celt whom he had sat beside on the train – the two former spent the evenings in writing eternal letters home, while the Irishman sat in the tent door whistling over and over to himself half a dozen shrill and monotonous bird-calls. It was rather to avoid an hour of their company than with any hope of diversion that, when the quarantine was lifted at the end of the week, he went into town. He caught one of the swarm of jitneys that overran the camp each evening, and in half an hour was set down in front of the Stonewall Hotel on the hot and drowsy main street.

Under the gathering twilight the town was unexpectedly attractive. The sidewalks were peopled by vividly dressed, over-painted girls, who chattered volubly in low, lazy voices, by dozens of taxi-drivers who assailed passing officers with, 'Take y' anywheh, *Lieu*tenant,' and by an intermittent procession of ragged, shuffling, subservient Negroes. Anthony, loitering along through the warm dusk, felt for the first time in years the slow, erotic breath of the South, imminent in the hot softness of the air, in the pervasive lull of thought and time.

He had gone about a block when he was arrested suddenly by a harsh command at his elbow.

'Haven't you been taught to salute officers?'

He looked dumbly at the man who addressed him, a stout, black-haired captain, who fixed him menacingly with brown pop-eyes.

'*Come to attention!*' The words were literally thundered. A few pedestrians near by stopped and stared. A soft-eyed girl in a lilac dress tittered to her companion.

Anthony came to attention.

'What's your regiment and company?'

Anthony told him.

'After this when you pass an officer on the street you straighten up and salute!'

'All right!'

'Say, "Yes, sir!" '

'Yes, sir.'

The stout officer grunted, turned sharply, and marched down the street. After a moment Anthony moved on; the town was no longer indolent and exotic; the magic was suddenly gone out of the dusk. His eyes were turned precipitately inward upon the indignity of his position. He hated that officer, every officer – life was unendurable.

After he had gone half a block he realised that the girl in the lilac dress who had giggled at his discomfiture was walking with her friend about ten paces ahead of him. Several times she had turned and stared at Anthony, with cheerful laughter in the large eyes that seemed the same colour as her gown.

At the corner she and her companion visibly slackened their pace – he must make his choice between joining them and passing obliviously by. He passed, hesitated, then slowed down. In a moment the pair were abreast of him again, dissolved in laughter now – not such strident mirth as he would have expected in the North from actresses in this familiar comedy, but a soft, low rippling, like the overflow from some subtle joke, into which he had inadvertently blundered.

'How do you do?' he said.

Her eyes were soft as shadows. Were they violet, or was it their blue darkness mingling with the grey hues of dusk?

'Pleasant evening,' ventured Anthony uncertainly.

'Sure is,' said the second girl.

'Hasn't been a very pleasant evening for you,' sighed the girl in lilac. Her voice seemed as much a part of the night as the drowsy breeze stirring the wide brim of her hat.

'He had to have a chance to show off,' said Anthony with a scornful laugh.

'Reckon so,' she agreed.

They turned the corner and moved lackadaisically up a side street, as if following a drifting cable to which they were attached. In this town it seemed entirely natural to turn corners like that, it seemed natural to be bound nowhere in particular, to be thinking nothing . . . The side street was dark, a sudden offshoot into a district of wild rose hedges and little quiet houses set far back from the street.

'Where're you going?' he enquired politely.

'Just goin'.' The answer was an apology, a question, an explanation.

'Can I stroll along with you?'

'Reckon so.'

It was an advantage that her accent was different. He could not have determined the social status of a Southerner from her talk – in New York a girl of a lower class would have been raucous, unendurable – except through the rosy spectacles of intoxication.

Dark was creeping down. Talking little – Anthony in careless, casual questions, the other two with provincial economy of phrase and burden – they sauntered past another corner, and another. In the middle of a block they stopped beneath a lamp-post.

'I live near here,' explained the other girl.

'I live around the block,' said the girl in lilac.

'Can I see you home?'

'To the corner, if you want to.'

The other girl took a few steps backwards. Anthony removed his hat.

'You're supposed to salute,' said the girl in lilac with a laugh. 'All the soldiers salute.'

'I'll learn,' he responded soberly.

The other girl said, 'Well – ' hesitated, then added, 'call me up tomorrow, Dot,' and retreated from the yellow circle of the street-lamp. Then, in silence, Anthony and the girl in lilac walked the three blocks to the small rickety house which was her home. Outside the wooden gate she hesitated.

'Well – thanks.'

'Must you go in so soon?'

'I ought to.'

'Can't you stroll around a little longer?'

She regarded him dispassionately. 'I don't even know you.'

Anthony laughed. 'It's not too late.'

'I reckon I better go in.'

'I thought we might walk down and see a movie.'

'I'd like to.'

'Then I could bring you home. I'd have just enough time. I've got to be in camp by eleven.'

It was so dark that he could scarcely see her now. She was a dress swayed infinitesimally by the wind, two limpid, reckless eyes . . .

'Why don't you come – Dot? Don't you like movies? Better come.'

She shook her head.

'I oughtn't to.'

He liked her, realising that she was temporising for the effect on him. He came closer and took her hand.

'If we get back by ten, can't you? Just to the movies?'

'Well – I reckon so –'

Hand in hand they walked back towards downtown, along a hazy, dusky street where a Negro newsboy was calling an extra in the cadence of the local venders' tradition, a cadence that was as musical as song.

Dot

Anthony's affair with Dorothy Raycroft was an inevitable result of his increasing carelessness about himself. He did not go to her desiring to possess the desirable, nor did he fall before a personality more vital, more compelling than his own, as he had done with Gloria four years before. He merely slid into the matter through his inability to make definite judgements. He could say 'No!' neither to man nor woman; borrower and temptress alike found him tender-minded and pliable. Indeed he seldom made decisions at all, and when he did they were but half-hysterical resolves formed in the panic of some aghast and irreparable awakening.

The particular weakness he indulged on this occasion was his need for excitement and stimulus from without. He felt that for the first time in four years he could express and interpret himself anew. The girl promised rest; the hours in her company each evening alleviated the morbid and inevitably futile poundings of his imagination. He had become a coward in earnest – completely the slave of a hundred disordered and prowling thoughts which were released by the collapse of the authentic devotion to Gloria that had been the chief jailer of his insufficiency.

On that first night, as they stood by the gate, he kissed Dorothy and made an engagement to meet her the following Saturday. Then he went out to camp, and with the light burning lawlessly in his tent, he wrote a long letter to Gloria, a glowing letter, full of the sentimental dark, full of the remembered breath of flowers, full of a true and exceeding tenderness – these things he had learned again for a moment in a kiss given and taken under a rich warm moonlight just an hour before.

When Saturday night came he found Dot waiting at the entrance of the Bijou Moving Picture Theatre. She was dressed as on the preceding Wednesday in her lilac gown of frailest organdy, but it had evidently been washed and starched since then, for it was fresh and unrumpled. Daylight confirmed the impression he had received that in a sketchy, faulty way she was lovely. She was clean, her features were small, irregular, but eloquent and appropriate to each other. She was a dark, unenduring little flower – yet he thought he detected in her some quality of spiritual reticence, of strength drawn from her passive acceptance of all things. In this he was mistaken.

Dorothy Raycroft was nineteen. Her father had kept a small, unprosperous corner store, and she had graduated from high school in the lowest fourth of her class two days before he died. At high school she had enjoyed a rather unsavoury reputation. As a matter of fact her behaviour at the class picnic, where the rumours started, had been merely indiscreet – she had retained her technical purity until over a year later. The boy had been a clerk in a store on Jackson Street, and on the day after the incident he departed unexpectedly to New York. He had been intending to leave for some time, but had tarried for the consummation of his amorous enterprise.

After a while she confided the adventure to a girl friend, and later, as she watched her friend disappear down the sleepy street of dusty sunshine she knew in a flash of intuition that her story was going out into the world. Yet after telling it she felt much better, and a little bitter, and made as near an approach to character as she was capable of by walking in another direction and meeting another man with the honest intention of gratifying herself again. As a rule things happened to Dot. She was not weak, because there was nothing in her to tell her she was being weak. She was not strong, because she never knew that some of the things she did were brave. She neither defied nor conformed nor compromised.

She had no sense of humour, but, to take its place, a happy disposition that made her laugh at the proper times when she was with men. She had no definite intentions – sometimes she regretted vaguely that her reputation precluded what chance she had ever had for security.

There had been no open discovery: her mother was interested only in starting her off on time each morning for the jewellery store where she earned fourteen dollars a week. But some of the boys she had known in high school now looked the other way when they were walking with 'nice girls', and these incidents hurt her feelings. When they occurred she went home and cried.

Besides the Jackson Street clerk there had been two other men, of whom the first was a naval officer, who passed through town during the early days of the war. He had stayed over a night to make a connection, and was leaning idly against one of the pillars of the Stonewall Hotel when she passed by. He remained in town four days. She thought she loved him – lavished on him that first hysteria of passion that would have gone to the pusillanimous clerk. The naval officer's uniform – there were few of them in those days – had made the magic. He left with vague promises on his lips, and, once on the train, rejoiced that he had not told her his real name.

Her resultant depression had thrown her into the arms of Cyrus Fielding, the son of a local clothier, who had hailed her from his roadster one day as she passed along the sidewalk. She had always known him by name. Had she been born to a higher stratum he would have known her before. She had descended a little lower – so he met her after all. After a month he had gone away to training-camp, a little afraid of the intimacy, a little relieved in perceiving that she had not cared deeply for him, and that she was not the sort who would ever make trouble. Dot romanticised this affair and conceded to her vanity that the war had taken these men away from her. She told herself that she could have married the naval officer. Nevertheless, it worried her that within eight months there had been three men in her life. She thought with more fear than wonder in her heart that she would soon be like those 'bad girls' on Jackson Street at whom she and her gum-chewing, giggling friends had stared with fascinated glances three years before.

For a while she attempted to be more careful. She let men 'pick her up'; she let them kiss her, and even allowed certain other liberties to be forced upon her, but she did not add to her trio. After several months the strength of her resolution – or rather the poignant expediency of her fears – was worn away. She grew restless drowsing there out of life and time while the summer months faded. The soldiers she met were either obviously below her or, less obviously, above her – in which case they desired only to use her; they were Yankees, harsh and ungracious;

they swarmed in large crowds . . . And then she met Anthony.

On that first evening he had been little more than a pleasantly unhappy face, a voice, the means with which to pass an hour, but when she kept her engagement with him on Saturday she regarded him with consideration. She liked him. Unknowingly she saw her own tragedies mirrored in his face.

Again they went to the movies, again they wandered along the shadowy, scented streets, hand in hand this time, speaking a little in hushed voices. They passed through the gate – up towards the little porch –

'I can stay a while, can't I?'

'Sh!' she whispered, 'we've got to be very quiet. Mother sits up reading *Snappy Stories*.' In confirmation he heard the faint crackling inside as a page was turned. The open-shutter slits emitted horizontal rods of light that fell in thin parallels across Dorothy's skirt. The street was silent save for a group on the steps of a house across the way, who, from time to time, raised their voices in a soft, bantering song.

' – When you wa-ake
You shall ha-ave
All the pretty little hawsiz – '

Then, as though it had been waiting on a nearby roof for their arrival, the moon came slanting suddenly through the vines and turned the girl's face to the colour of white roses.

Anthony had a start of memory, so vivid that before his closed eyes there formed a picture, distinct as a flashback on a screen – a spring night of thaw set out of time in a half-forgotten winter five years before – another face, radiant, flower-like, upturned to lights as transforming as the stars –

Ah, *la belle dame sans merci* who lived in his heart, made known to him in transitory fading splendour by dark eyes in the Ritz-Carlton, by a shadowy glance from a passing carriage in the Bois de Boulogne! But those nights were only part of a song, a remembered glory – here again were the faint winds, the illusions, the eternal present with its promise of romance.

'Oh,' she whispered, 'do you love me? Do you love me?'

The spell was broken – the drifted fragments of the stars became only light, the singing down the street diminished to a monotone, to the whimper of locusts in the grass. With almost a sigh he kissed her fervent mouth, while her arms crept up about his shoulders.

As the weeks dried up and blew away, the range of Anthony's travels extended until he grew to comprehend the camp and its environment. For the first time in his life he was in constant personal contact with the waiters to whom he had given tips, the chauffeurs who had touched their hats to him, the carpenters, plumbers, barbers and farmers who had previously been remarkable only in the subservience of their professional genuflections. During his first two months in camp he did not hold ten minutes' consecutive conversation with a single man.

On the service record his occupation stood as 'student'; on the original questionnaire he had prematurely written 'author'; but when men in his company asked his business he commonly gave it as bank clerk – had he told the truth, that he did no work, they would have been suspicious of him as a member of the leisure class.

His platoon sergeant, Pop Donnelly, was a scraggly 'old soldier', worn thin with drink. In the past he had spent unnumbered weeks in the guardhouse, but recently, thanks to the drill-master famine, he had been elevated to his present pinnacle. His complexion was full of shell-holes – it bore an unmistakable resemblance to those aerial photographs of 'the battlefield at Blank'. Once a week he got drunk downtown on white liquor, returned quietly to camp and collapsed upon his bunk, joining the company at reveille looking more than ever like a white mask of death.

He nursed the astounding delusion that he was astutely 'slipping it over' on the government – he had spent eighteen years in its service at a minute wage, and he was soon to retire (here he usually winked) on the impressive income of fifty-five dollars a month. He looked upon it as a gorgeous joke that he had played upon the dozens who had bullied and scorned him since he was a Georgia country boy of nineteen.

At present there were but two lieutenants – Hopkins and the popular Kretching. The latter was considered a good fellow and a fine leader, until a year later, when he disappeared with a mess fund of eleven hundred dollars and, like so many leaders, proved exceedingly difficult to follow.

Eventually there was Captain Dunning, god of this brief but self-sufficing microcosm. He was a reserve officer, nervous, energetic and enthusiastic. This latter quality, indeed, often took material form and was visible as fine froth in the corners of his mouth. Like most executives he saw his charges strictly from the front, and to his hopeful eyes his command seemed just such an excellent unit as such an excellent war deserved. For all his anxiety and absorption he was having the time of his life.

Baptiste, the little Sicilian of the train, fell foul of him the second week of drill. The captain had several times ordered the men to be clean-shaven when they fell in each morning. One day there was disclosed an alarming breech of this rule, surely a case of Teutonic connivance – during the night four men had grown hair upon their faces. The fact that three of the four understood a minimum of English made a practical object-lesson only the more necessary, so Captain Dunning resolutely sent a volunteer barber back to the company street for a razor. Whereupon for the safety of democracy a half-ounce of hair was scraped dry from the cheeks of three Italians and one Pole.

Outside the world of the company there appeared, from time to time, the colonel, a heavy man with snarling teeth, who circumnavigated the battalion drill-field upon a handsome black horse. He was a West Pointer, and, mimetically, a gentleman. He had a dowdy wife and a dowdy mind, and spent much of his time in town taking advantage of the army's lately exalted social position. Last of all was the general, who traversed the roads of the camp preceded by his flag – a figure so austere, so removed, so magnificent, as to be scarcely comprehensible.

December. Cool winds at night now, and damp, chilly mornings on the drill-grounds. As the heat faded, Anthony found himself increasingly glad to be alive. Renewed strangely through his body, he worried little and existed in the present with a sort of animal content. It was not that Gloria or the life that Gloria represented was less often in his thoughts – it was simply that she became, day by day, less real, less vivid. For a week they had corresponded passionately, almost hysterically – then by an unwritten agreement they had ceased to write more than twice, and then once, a week. She was bored, she said; if his brigade was to be there a long time she was coming down to join him. Mr Haight was going to be able to submit a stronger brief than he had expected, but doubted that the appealed case would come up until late spring. Muriel was in the city doing Red Cross work, and they went out together rather often. What would Anthony think if *she* went into the Red Cross? Trouble was she had heard that she might have to bathe Negroes in alcohol, and after that she hadn't felt so patriotic. The city was full of soldiers and she'd seen a lot of boys she hadn't laid eyes on for years . . .

Anthony did not want her to come South. He told himself that this was for many reasons – he needed a rest from her and she from him. She would be bored beyond measure in town, and she would be able to see Anthony for only a few hours each day. But in his heart he feared that it was because he was attracted to Dorothy. As a matter of fact he lived in terror that Gloria should learn by some chance or intention of the relation he had formed. By the end of a fortnight the entanglement began to give him moments of misery at his own faithlessness. Nevertheless, as each day ended he was unable to withstand the lure that would draw him irresistibly out of his tent and over to the telephone at the YMCA.

'Dot.'

'Yes?'

'I may be able to get in tonight.'

'I'm so glad.'

'Do you want to listen to my splendid eloquence for a few starry hours?'

'Oh, you funny – ' For an instant he had a memory of five years before – of Geraldine. Then –

'I'll arrive about eight.'

At seven he would be in a jitney bound for the city, where hundreds of little Southern girls were waiting on moonlit porches for their lovers. He would be excited already for her warm retarded kisses, for the amazed quietude of the glances she gave him – glances nearer to worship than any he had ever inspired. Gloria and he had been equals, giving without thought of thanks or obligation. To this girl his very caresses were an inestimable boon. Crying quietly she had confessed to him that he was not the first man in her life; there had been one other – he gathered that the affair had no sooner commenced than it had been over.

Indeed, so far as she was concerned, she spoke the truth. She had forgotten the clerk, the naval officer, the clothier's son, forgotten her vividness of emotion, which is true forgetting. She knew that in some opaque and shadowy existence someone had taken her – it was as though it had occurred in sleep.

Almost every night Anthony came to town. It was too cool now for the porch, so her mother surrendered to them the tiny sitting-room, with its dozens of cheaply framed chromos, its yard upon yard of decorative fringe, and its thick atmosphere of several decades in the proximity of the kitchen. They would build a fire – then, happily, inexhaustibly, she would go about the business of love. Each evening at ten she would walk with him to the door, her black hair in disarray, her face pale without cosmetics, paler still under the whiteness of the moon. As a rule it would be bright and silver outside; now and then there was a slow warm rain, too indolent, almost, to reach the ground.

'Say you love me,' she would whisper.

'Why, of course, you sweet baby.'

'Am I a baby?' This almost wistfully.

'Just a little baby.'

She knew vaguely of Gloria. It gave her pain to think of it, so she imagined her to be haughty and proud and cold. She had decided that Gloria must be older than Anthony, and that there was no love between husband and wife. Sometimes she let herself dream that after the war Anthony would get a divorce and they would be married – but she never mentioned this to Anthony, she scarcely knew why. She shared his company's idea that he was a sort of bank clerk – she thought that he was respectable and poor. She would say: 'If I had some money, darlin', I'd give ev'y bit of it to you . . . I'd like to have about fifty thousand dollars.'

'I suppose that'd be plenty,' agreed Anthony.

– In her letter that day Gloria had written: 'I suppose if we *could* settle for a million it would be better to tell Mr Haight to go ahead and settle. But it'd seem a pity . . . '

. . . 'We could have an automobile,' exclaimed Dot, in a final burst of triumph.

AN IMPRESSIVE OCCASION

Captain Dunning prided himself on being a great reader of character. Half an hour after meeting a man he was accustomed to place him in one of a number of astonishing categories – fine man, good man, smart fellow, theoriser, poet and 'worthless'. One day early in February he caused Anthony to be summoned to his presence in the orderly tent.

'Patch,' he said sententiously, 'I've had my eye on you for several weeks.'

Anthony stood erect and motionless.

'And I think you've got the makings of a good soldier.'

He waited for the warm glow, which this would naturally arouse, to cool – and then continued: 'This is no child's play,' he said, narrowing his brows.

Anthony agreed with a melancholy 'No, sir.'

'It's a man's game – and we need leaders.' Then the climax, swift, sure and electric: 'Patch, I'm going to make you a corporal.'

At this point Anthony should have staggered slightly backward, overwhelmed. He was to be one of the quarter million selected for that consummate trust. He was going to be able to shout the technical phrase, 'Follow me!' to seven other frightened men.

'You seem to be a man of some education,' said Captain Dunning.

'Yes, sir.'

'That's good, that's good. Education's a great thing, but don't let it go to your head. Keep on the way you're doing and you'll be a good soldier.'

With these parting words lingering in his ears, Corporal Patch saluted, executed a right about face, and left the tent.

Though the conversation amused Anthony, it did generate the idea that life would be more amusing as a sergeant or, should he find a less exacting medical examiner, as an officer. He was little interested in the work, which seemed to belie the army's boasted gallantry. At the inspections one did not dress up to look well, one dressed up to keep from looking badly.

But as winter wore away – the short, snowless winter marked by damp nights and cool, rainy days – he marvelled at how quickly the system had grasped him. He was a soldier – all who were not soldiers were civilians. The world was divided primarily into those two classifications.

It occurred to him that all strongly accentuated classes, such as the military, divided men into two kinds: their own kind – and those without. To the clergyman there were clergy and laity, to the Catholic there were Catholics and non-Catholics, to the Negro there were blacks and whites, to the prisoner there were the imprisoned and the free, and to the sick man there were the sick and the well . . . So, without thinking of it once in his lifetime, he had been a civilian, a layman, a non-Catholic, a Gentile, white, free and well . . .

As the American troops were poured into the French and British trenches he began to find the names of many Harvard men among the casualties recorded in the *Army and Navy Journal*. But for all the sweat and blood the situation appeared unchanged, and he saw no prospect of the war's ending in the perceptible future. In the old chronicles the right wing of one army always defeated the left wing of the other, the left wing being, meanwhile, vanquished by the enemy's right. After that the mercenaries fled. It had been so simple, in those days, almost as if prearranged . . .

Gloria wrote that she was reading a great deal. What a mess they had made of their affairs, she said. She had so little to do now that she spent her time imagining how differently things might have turned out. Her whole environment appeared insecure – and a few years back she had seemed to hold all the strings in her own little hand . . .

In June her letters grew hurried and less frequent. She suddenly ceased to write about coming South.

DEFEAT

March in the country around was rare with jasmine and jonquils and patches of violets in the warming grass. Afterwards he remembered especially one afternoon of such a fresh and magic glamour that as he stood in the rifle-pit marking targets he recited 'Atalanta in Calydon' to an uncomprehending Pole, his voice mingling with the rip, sing, and splatter of the bullets overhead.

' "When the hounds of spring . . . " '

Spang!

' "Are on winter's traces . . . " '

Whirr-r-r-r! . . .

' "The mother of months . . . "

'*Hey!* Come to! Mark three-e-e! . . . '

In town the streets were in a sleepy dream again, and together Anthony and Dot idled in their own tracks of the previous autumn until he began to feel a drowsy attachment for this South – a South, it seemed, more of Algiers than of Italy, with faded aspirations pointing back over innumerable generations to some warm, primitive Nirvana, without hope or care. Here there was an inflection of cordiality, of comprehension, in every voice. 'Life plays the same lovely and agonising joke on all of us,' they seemed to say in their plaintive pleasant cadence, in the rising inflection terminating on an unresolved minor.

He liked his barbershop where he was 'Hi, corporal!' to a pale, emaciated young man, who shaved him and pushed a cool vibrating machine endlessly over his insatiable head. He liked 'Johnston's Gardens' where they danced, where a tragic Negro made yearning, aching music on a saxophone until the garish hall became an enchanted jungle of barbaric rhythms and smoky laughter, where to forget the uneventful passage of time upon Dorothy's soft sighs and tender whisperings was the consummation of all aspiration, of all content.

There was an undertone of sadness in her character, a conscious evasion of all except the pleasurable minutiae of life. Her violet eyes would remain for hours apparently insensate as, thoughtless and reckless, she basked like a cat in the sun. He wondered what the tired, spiritless mother thought of them, and whether in her moments of uttermost cynicism she ever guessed at their relationship.

On Sunday afternoons they walked along the countryside, resting at intervals on the dry moss in the outskirts of a wood. Here the birds had gathered and the clusters of violets and white dogwood; here the hoar trees shone crystalline and cool, oblivious to the intoxicating heat that waited outside; here he would talk, intermittently, in a sleepy monologue, in a conversation of no significance, of no replies.

July came scorching down. Captain Dunning was ordered to detail one of his men to learn blacksmithing. The regiment was filling up to war strength, and he needed most of his veterans for drill-masters, so he selected the little Italian, Baptiste, whom he could most easily spare. Little Baptiste had never had anything to do with horses. His fear made matters worse. He reappeared in the orderly room one day and told Captain Dunning that he wanted to die if he couldn't be relieved. The horses kicked at him, he said; he was no good at the work. Finally he fell on his knees and besought Captain Dunning, in a mixture of broken English and scriptural Italian, to get him out of it. He had not slept for three days; monstrous stallions reared and cavorted through his dreams.

Captain Dunning reproved the company clerk (who had burst out laughing), and told Baptiste he would do what he could. But when he thought it over he decided that he couldn't spare a better man. Little Baptiste went from bad to worse. The horses seemed to divine his fear and take every advantage of it. Two weeks later a great black mare crushed his skull in with her hoofs while he was trying to lead her from her stall.

In mid-July came rumours, and then orders, that concerned a change of camp. The brigade was to move to an empty cantonment, a hundred miles farther south, there to be expanded into a division. At first the men thought they were departing for the trenches, and all evening little groups jabbered in the company street, shouting to each other in swaggering exclamations: 'Su-u-ure we are!' When the truth leaked out, it was rejected indignantly as a blind to conceal their real destination. They revelled in their own importance. That night they told their girls in town that they were 'going to get the Germans'. Anthony circulated for a while among the groups – then, stopping a jitney, rode down to tell Dot that he was going away.

She was waiting on the dark veranda in a cheap white dress that accentuated the youth and softness of her face.

'Oh,' she whispered, 'I've wanted you so, honey. All this day.'

'I have something to tell you.'

She drew him down beside her on the swinging seat, not noticing his ominous tone.

'Tell me.'

'We're leaving next week.'

Her arms seeking his shoulders remained poised upon the dark air, her chin tipped up. When she spoke the softness was gone from her voice.

'Leaving for France?'

'No. Less luck than that. Leaving for some darn camp in Mississippi.'

She shut her eyes and he could see that the lids were trembling.

'Dear little Dot, life is so damned hard.'

She was crying upon his shoulder.

'So damned hard, so damned hard,' he repeated aimlessly; 'it just hurts people and hurts people, until finally it hurts them so that they can't be hurt ever any more. That's the last and worst thing it does.'

Frantic, wild with anguish, she strained him to her breast.

'Oh, God!' she whispered brokenly, 'you can't go way from me. I'd die.'

He was finding it impossible to pass off his departure as a common, impersonal blow. He was too near to her to do more than repeat, 'Poor little Dot. Poor little Dot.'

'And then what?' she demanded wearily.

'What do you mean?'

'You're my whole life, that's all. I'd die for you right now if you said so. I'd get a knife and kill myself. You can't leave me here.'

Her tone frightened him.

'These things happen,' he said evenly.

'Then I'm going with you.' Tears were streaming down her checks. Her mouth was trembling in an ecstasy of grief and fear.

'Sweet,' he muttered sentimentally, 'sweet little girl. Don't you see we'd just be putting off what's bound to happen? I'll be going to France in a few months – '

She leaned away from him and clenching her fists lifted her face towards the sky.

'I want to die,' she said, as if moulding each word carefully in her heart.

'Dot,' he whispered uncomfortably, 'you'll forget. Things are sweeter when they're lost. I know – because once I wanted something and got it. It was the only thing I ever wanted badly, Dot. And when I got it it turned to dust in my hands.'

'All right.'

Absorbed in himself, he continued: 'I've often thought that if I hadn't got what I wanted things might have been different with me. I might have found something in my mind and enjoyed putting it in circulation. I might have been content with the work of it, and had some sweet vanity out of the success. I suppose that at one time I could have had anything I wanted, within reason, but that was the only thing I ever wanted with any fervour. God! And that taught me you can't have *any*thing, you can't have anything at *all*. Because desire just cheats you. It's like a sunbeam skipping here and there about a room. It stops and gilds some inconsequential object, and we poor fools try to grasp it – but when we do the sunbeam moves on to something else, and you've got the inconsequential part, but the glitter that made you want it is gone – ' He broke off uneasily. She had risen and was standing, dry-eyed, picking little leaves from a dark vine.

'Dot – '

'Go way,' she said coldly.

'What? Why?'

'I don't want just words. If that's all you have for me you'd better go.'

'Why, Dot – '

'What's death to me is just a lot of words to you. You put 'em together so pretty.'

'I'm sorry. I was talking about you, Dot.'

'Go way from here.'

He approached her with arms outstretched, but she held him away.

'You don't want me to go with you,' she said evenly; 'maybe you're going to meet that – that girl – ' She could not bring herself to say wife. 'How do I know? Well, then, I reckon you're not my fellow any more. So go way.'

For a moment, while conflicting warnings and desires prompted Anthony, it seemed one of those rare times when he would take a step prompted from within. He hesitated. Then a wave of weariness broke against him. It was too late – everything was too late. For years now he had dreamed the world away, basing his decisions upon emotions unstable as water. The little girl in the white dress dominated him, as she approached beauty in the hard symmetry of her desire. The fire blazing in her dark and injured heart seemed to glow around her like a flame. With some profound and uncharted pride she had made herself remote and so achieved her purpose.

'I didn't – mean to seem so callous, Dot.'

'It don't matter.'

The fire rolled over Anthony. Something wrenched at his bowels, and he stood there helpless and beaten.

'Come with me, Dot – little loving Dot. Oh, come with me. I couldn't leave you now – '

With a sob she wound her arms around him and let him support her weight while the moon, at its perennial labour of covering the bad complexion of the world, showered its illicit honey over the drowsy street.

THE CATASTROPHE

Early September in Camp Boone, Mississippi. The darkness, alive with insects, beat in upon the mosquito-netting, beneath the shelter of which Anthony was trying to write a letter. An intermittent chatter over a poker game was going on in the next tent, and outside a man was strolling up the company street singing a current bit of doggerel about 'K-K-K-Katy'.

With an effort Anthony hoisted himself to his elbow and, pencil in hand, looked down at his blank sheet of paper. Then, omitting any heading, he began:

> I can't imagine what the matter is, Gloria. I haven't had a line from you for two weeks and it's only natural to be worried –

He threw this away with a disturbed grunt and began again:

> I don't know what to think, Gloria. Your last letter, short, cold, without a word of affection or even a decent account of what you've been doing, came two weeks ago. It's only natural that I should

wonder. If your love for me isn't absolutely dead it seems that you'd at least keep me from worry –

Again he crumpled the page and tossed it angrily through a tear in the tent wall, realising simultaneously that he would have to pick it up in the morning. He felt disinclined to try again. He could get no warmth into the lines – only a persistent jealousy and suspicion. Since midsummer these discrepancies in Gloria's correspondence had grown more and more noticeable. At first he had scarcely perceived them. He was so inured to the perfunctory 'dearests' and 'darlings' scattered through her letters that he was oblivious to their presence or absence. But in this last fortnight he had become increasingly aware that there was something amiss.

He had sent her a night-letter saying that he had passed his examinations for an officers' training-camp, and expected to leave for Georgia shortly. She had not answered. He had wired again – when he received no word he imagined that she might be out of town. But it occurred and recurred to him that she was not out of town, and a series of distraught imaginings began to plague him. Supposing Gloria, bored and restless, had found someone, even as he had. The thought terrified him with its possibility – it was chiefly because he had been so sure of her personal integrity that he had considered her so sparingly during the year. And now, as a doubt was born, the old angers, the rages of possession, swarmed back a thousandfold. What more natural than that she should be in love again?

He remembered the Gloria who promised that should she ever want anything, she would take it, insisting that since she would act entirely for her own satisfaction she could go through such an affair unsmirched – it was only the effect on a person's mind that counted, anyhow, she said, and her reaction would be the masculine one, of satiation and faint dislike.

But that had been when they were first married. Later, with the discovery that she could be jealous of Anthony, she had, outwardly at least, changed her mind. There were no other men in the world for her. This he had known only too surely. Perceiving that a certain fastidiousness would restrain her, he had grown lax in preserving the completeness of her love – which, after all, was the keystone of the entire structure.

Meanwhile all through the summer he had been maintaining Dot in a boarding-house downtown. To do this it had been necessary to write to his broker for money. Dot had covered her journey south by leaving her house a day before the brigade broke camp, informing her mother in a note that she had gone to New York. On the evening following Anthony had called as though to see her. Mrs Raycroft was in a state of collapse and there was a policeman in the parlour. A questionnaire had ensued, from which Anthony had extricated himself with some difficulty.

In September, with his suspicions of Gloria, the company of Dot had become tedious, then almost intolerable. He was nervous and irritable from lack of sleep; his heart was sick and afraid. Three days ago he had gone to Captain Dunning and asked for a furlough, only to be met with benignant procrastination. The division was starting overseas, while Anthony was going to an officers' training-camp; what furloughs could be given must go to the men who were leaving the country.

Upon this refusal Anthony had started to the telegraph office intending to wire Gloria to come South – he reached the door and receded despairingly, seeing the utter impracticability of such a move. Then he had spent the evening quarrelling irritably with Dot, and returned to camp morose and angry with the world. There had been a disagreeable scene, in the midst of which he had precipitately departed. What was to be done with her did not seem to concern him vitally at present – he was completely absorbed in the disheartening silence of his wife . . .

The flap of the tent made a sudden triangle back upon itself, and a dark head appeared against the night.

'Sergeant Patch?' The accent was Italian, and Anthony saw by the belt that the man was a headquarters orderly.

'Want me?'

'Lady call up headquarters ten minutes ago. Say she have speak with you. Ver' important.'

Anthony swept aside the mosquito-netting and stood up. It might be a wire from Gloria telephoned over.

'She say to get you. She call again ten o'clock.'

'All right, thanks.' He picked up his hat and in a moment was striding beside the orderly through the hot, almost suffocating, darkness. Over in the headquarters shack he saluted a dozing night-service officer.

'Sit down and wait,' suggested the lieutenant nonchalantly. 'Girl seemed awful anxious to speak to you.'

Anthony's hopes fell away.

'Thank you very much, sir.' And as the phone squeaked on the side-wall he knew who was calling.

'This is Dot,' came an unsteady voice, 'I've got to see you.'

'Dot, I told you I couldn't get down for several days.'

'I've got to see you tonight. It's important.'

'It's too late,' he said coldly; 'it's ten o'clock, and I have to be in camp at eleven.'

'All right.' There was so much wretchedness compressed into the two words that Anthony felt a measure of compunction.

'What's the matter?'

'I want to tell you goodbye.

'Oh, don't be a little idiot!' he exclaimed. But his spirits rose. What luck if she should leave town this very night! What a burden from his soul. But he said: 'You can't possibly leave before tomorrow.'

Out of the corner of his eye he saw the night-service officer regarding him quizzically. Then, startlingly, came Dot's next words: 'I don't mean "leave" that way.'

Anthony's hand clutched the receiver fiercely. He felt his nerves turning cold as if the heat was leaving his body.

'What?'

Then quickly in a wild broken voice he heard: 'Goodbye – oh, goodbye!'

Cul-*lup*! She had hung up the receiver. With a sound that was half a gasp, half a cry, Anthony hurried from the headquarters building. Outside, under the stars that dripped like silver tassels through the trees of the little grove, he stood motionless, hesitating. Had she meant to kill herself? – oh, the little fool! He was filled with bitter hate towards her. In this dénouement he found it impossible to realise that he had ever begun such an entanglement, such a mess, a sordid *mélange* of worry and pain.

He found himself walking slowly away, repeating over and over that it was futile to worry. He had best go back to his tent and sleep. He needed sleep. God! Would he ever sleep again? His mind was in a vast clamour and confusion; as he reached the road he turned around in a panic and began running, not towards his company but away from it. Men were returning now – he could find a taxicab. After a minute two yellow eyes appeared around a bend. Desperately he ran towards them.

'Jitney! Jitney!' . . . It was an empty Ford . . . 'I want to go to town.'

'Cost you a dollar.'

'All right. If you'll just hurry – '

After an interminable time, he ran up the steps of a dark ramshackle little house and through the door, almost knocking over an immense Negress who was walking, candle in hand, along the hall.

'Where's my wife?' he cried wildly.

'She gone to bed.'

Up the stairs three at a time, down the creaking passage. The room was dark and silent, and with trembling fingers he struck a match. Two wide eyes looked up at him from a wretched ball of clothes on the bed.

'Ah, I knew you'd come,' she murmured brokenly.

Anthony grew cold with anger.

'So it was just a plan to get me down here, get me in trouble!' he said. 'Goddamn it, you've shouted "wolf" once too often!'

She regarded him pitifully.

'I had to see you. I couldn't have lived. Oh, I had to see you – '

He sat down on the side of the bed and slowly shook his head.

'You're no good,' he said decisively, talking unconsciously as Gloria might have talked to him. 'This sort of thing isn't fair to me, you know.'

'Come closer.' Whatever he might say Dot was happy now. He cared for her. She had brought him to her side.

'Oh, God,' said Anthony hopelessly. As weariness rolled along its inevitable wave his anger subsided, receded, vanished. He collapsed suddenly, fell sobbing beside her on the bed.

'Oh, my darling,' she begged him, 'don't cry! Oh, don't cry!'

She took his head upon her breast and soothed him, mingled her happy tears with the bitterness of his. Her hand played gently with his dark hair.

'I'm such a little fool,' she murmured brokenly, 'but I love you, and when you're cold to me it seems as if it isn't worth while to go on livin'.'

After all, this was peace – the quiet room with the mingled scent of women's powder and perfume, Dot's hand soft as a warm wind upon his hair, the rise and fall of her bosom as she took breath – for a moment it was as though it were Gloria there, as though he were at rest in some sweeter and safer home than he had ever known.

An hour passed. A clock began to chime in the hall. He jumped to his feet and looked at the phosphorescent hands of his wristwatch. It was twelve o'clock.

He had trouble in finding a taxi that would take him out at that hour. As he urged the driver faster along the road he speculated on the best method of entering camp. He had been late several times recently, and he knew that were he caught again his name would probably be stricken from the list of officer candidates. He wondered if he had not better dismiss the taxi and take a chance on passing the sentry in the dark. Still, officers often rode past the sentries after midnight . . .

'Halt!' The monosyllable came from the yellow glare that the headlights dropped upon the changing road. The taxi-driver threw out his clutch and a sentry walked up, carrying his rifle at the port. With him, by an ill chance, was the officer of the guard.

'Out late, sergeant.'

'Yes, sir. Got delayed.'

'Too bad. Have to take your name.'

As the officer waited, notebook and pencil in hand, something not fully intended crowded to Anthony's lips, something born of panic, of muddle, of despair.

'Sergeant R. A. Foley,' he answered breathlessly.

'And the outfit?'

'Company Q, Eighty-Third Infantry.'

'All right. You'll have to walk from here, sergeant.'

Anthony saluted, quickly paid his taxi-driver, and set off at a run towards the regiment he had named. When he was out of sight he changed his course, and with his heart beating wildly, hurried to his company, feeling that he had made a fatal error of judgement.

Two days later the officer who had been in command of the guard recognised him in a barbershop downtown. In charge of a military policeman he was taken back to the camp, where he was reduced to the ranks without trial, and confined for a month to the limits of his company street.

With this blow a spell of utter depression overtook him, and within a week he was again caught downtown, wandering around in a drunken daze, with a pint of bootleg whiskey in his hip pocket. It was because of a sort of craziness in his behaviour at the trial that his sentence to the guardhouse was for only three weeks.

NIGHTMARE

Early in his confinement the conviction took root in him that he was going mad. It was as though there were a quantity of dark yet vivid personalities in his mind, some of them familiar, some of them strange and terrible, held in check by a little monitor, who sat aloft somewhere and looked on. The thing that worried him was that the monitor was sick, and holding out with difficulty. Should he give up, should he falter for a moment, out would rush these intolerable things – only Anthony could know what a state of blackness there would be if the worst of him could roam his consciousness unchecked.

The heat of the day had changed, somehow, until it was a burnished darkness crushing down upon a devastated land. Over his head the blue circles of ominous uncharted suns, of unnumbered centres of fire, revolved interminably before his eyes as though he were lying constantly exposed to the hot light and in a state of feverish coma. At seven in the morning something phantasmal, something almost absurdly unreal that he knew was his mortal body, went out with seven other prisoners and two guards to work on the camp roads. One day they loaded and unloaded quantities of gravel, spread it, raked it – the next day they worked with huge barrels of red-hot tar, flooding the gravel with black shining pools of molten heat. At night, locked up in the guardhouse, he would lie without thought, without courage to compass thought, staring at the irregular beams of the ceiling overhead until about three o'clock, when he would slip into a broken, troubled sleep.

During the work hours he laboured with uneasy haste, attempting, as the day bore towards the sultry Mississippi sunset, to tire himself physically so that in the evening he might sleep deeply from utter exhaustion . . . Then one afternoon in the second week he had a feeling that two eyes were watching him from a place a few feet beyond one of the guards. This aroused him to a sort of terror. He turned his back on the eyes and shovelled feverishly, until it became necessary for him to face about and go for more gravel. Then they entered his vision again, and his already taut nerves tightened up to the breaking-point. The eyes were leering at him. Out of a hot silence he heard his name called in a tragic voice, and the earth tipped absurdly back and forth to a babel of shouting and confusion.

When next he became conscious he was back in the guardhouse, and the other prisoners were throwing him curious glances. The eyes returned no more. It was many days before he realised that the voice must have been Dot's, that she had called out to him and made some sort of disturbance. He decided this just previous to the expiration of his sentence, when the cloud that oppressed him had lifted, leaving him in a deep, dispirited lethargy. As the conscious mediator, the monitor who kept that fearsome *ménage* of horror, grew stronger, Anthony became physically weaker. He was scarcely able to get through the last two days of toil, and when he was released, one rainy afternoon, and returned to his company, he reached his tent only to fall into a heavy doze, from which he awoke before dawn, aching and unrefreshed. Beside his cot were two letters that had been awaiting him in the orderly tent for some time. The first was from Gloria; it was short and cool:

> The case is coming to trial late in November. Can you possibly get leave?
>
> I've tried to write you again and again but it just seems to make things worse. I want to see you about several matters, but you know that you have once prevented me from coming and I am disinclined to try again. In view of a number of things it seems necessary that we have a conference. I'm very glad about your appointment.
>
> GLORIA

He was too tired to try to understand – or to care. Her phrases, her intentions, were all very far away in an incomprehensible past. At the second letter he scarcely glanced; it was from Dot – an incoherent, tear-swollen scrawl, a flood of protest, endearment and grief. After a page he let it slip from his inert hand and drowsed back into a nebulous hinterland of his own. At drill-call he awoke with a high fever and fainted when he tried to leave his tent – at noon he was sent to the base hospital with influenza.

He was aware that this sickness was providential. It saved him from a hysterical relapse – and he recovered in time to entrain on a damp November day for New York, and for the interminable massacre beyond.

When the regiment reached Camp Mills, Long Island, Anthony's single idea was to get into the city and see Gloria as soon as possible. It was now evident that an armistice would be signed within the week, but rumour had it that in any case troops would continue to be shipped to France until the last moment. Anthony was appalled at the notion of the long voyage, of a tedious debarkation at a French port, and of being kept abroad for a year, possibly, to replace the troops who had seen actual fighting.

His intention had been to obtain a two-day furlough, but Camp Mills proved to be under a strict influenza quarantine – it was impossible for even an officer to leave except on official business. For a private it was out of the question.

The camp itself was a dreary muddle, cold, windswept and filthy, with the accumulated dirt incidental to the passage through of many divisions. Their train came in at seven one night, and they waited in line until one while a military tangle was straightened out somewhere ahead. Officers ran up and down ceaselessly, calling orders and making a great uproar. It turned out that the trouble was due to the colonel, who was in a righteous temper because he was a West Pointer, and the war was going to stop before he could get overseas. Had the militant governments realised the number of broken hearts among the older West Pointers during that week, they would indubitably have prolonged the slaughter another month. The thing was pitiable!

Gazing out at the bleak expanse of tents extending for miles over a trodden welter of slush and snow, Anthony saw the impracticability of trudging to a telephone that night. He would call her at the first opportunity in the morning.

Aroused in the chill and bitter dawn, he stood at reveille and listened to a passionate harangue from Captain Dunning: 'You men may think the war is over. Well, let me tell you, it isn't! Those fellows aren't going to sign the armistice. It's another trick, and we'd be crazy to let anything slacken up here in the company, because, let me tell you, we're going to sail from here within a week, and when we do we're going to see some real fighting.'

He paused that they might get the full effect of his pronouncement. And then: 'If you think the war's over, just talk to anyone who's been in it and see if *they* think the Germans are all in. They don't. Nobody does. I've talked to the people that *know*, and they say there'll be, anyways, a year longer of war. *They* don't think it's over. So you men better not get any foolish ideas that it is.'

Doubly stressing this final admonition, he ordered the company dismissed.

At noon Anthony set off at a run for the nearest canteen telephone. As he approached what corresponded to the downtown of the camp, he noticed that many other soldiers were running also, that a man near him had suddenly leaped into the air and clicked his heels together. The tendency to run became general, and from little excited groups here and there came the sounds of cheering. He stopped and listened – over the cold country whistles were blowing and the chimes of the Garden City churches broke suddenly into reverberatory sound.

Anthony began to run again. The cries were clear and distinct now as they rose with clouds of frosted breath into the chilly air: 'Germany's surrendered! Germany's surrendered!'

That evening in the opaque gloom of six o'clock Anthony slipped between two freight-cars, and, once over the railroad, followed the track along to Garden City, where he caught an electric train for New York. He stood some chance of apprehension – he knew that the military police were often sent through the cars to ask for passes, but he imagined that tonight the vigilance would be relaxed. But, in any event, he would have tried to slip through, for he had been unable to locate Gloria by telephone, and another day of suspense would have been intolerable.

After inexplicable stops and waits that reminded him of the night he had left New York, over a year before, they drew into the Pennsylvania Station, and he followed the familiar way to the taxi-stand, finding it grotesque and oddly stimulating to give his own address.

Broadway was a riot of light, thronged as he had never seen it with a carnival crowd which swept its glittering way through scraps of paper, piled ankle-deep on the sidewalks. Here and there, elevated upon benches and boxes, soldiers addressed the heedless mass, each face in which was clear cut and distinct under the white glare overhead. Anthony picked out half a dozen figures – a drunken sailor, tipped backwards and supported by two other gobs, was waving his hat and emitting a wild series of roars; a wounded soldier, crutch in hand, was borne along in an eddy on the shoulders of some shrieking civilians; a dark-haired girl sat cross-legged and meditative on top of a parked taxicab. Here surely the victory had come in time, the climax had been scheduled with the uttermost celestial foresight. The great rich nation had made triumphant war, suffered enough for poignancy but not enough for bitterness – hence the carnival, the feasting, the triumph. Under these bright lights glittered the faces of peoples whose glory had long since passed away, whose very civilisations were dead – men whose ancestors had heard the news of victory in Babylon, in Nineveh, in Baghdad, in Tyre, a hundred generations before; men whose ancestors had seen a flower-decked, slave-adorned cortège drift with its wake of captives down the avenues of Imperial Rome . . .

Past the Rialto, the glittering front of the Astor, the jewelled magnificence of Times Square . . . a gorgeous alley of incandescence ahead . . . Then – was it years later? – he was paying the taxi-driver in front of a white building on Fifty-Seventh Street. He was in the hall – ah, there was the Negro boy from Martinique, lazy, indolent, unchanged.

'Is Mrs Patch in?'

'I have just came on, sah,' the man announced with his incongruous British accent.

'Take me up – '

Then the slow drone of the elevator, the three steps to the door, which swung open at the impetus of his knock.

'Gloria!' His voice was trembling. No answer. A faint string of smoke was rising from a cigarette-tray – a number of *Vanity Fair* sat astraddle on the table.

'Gloria!'

He ran into the bedroom, the bath. She was not there. A négligé of robin's-egg blue laid out upon the bed diffused a faint perfume, illusive and familiar. On a chair were a pair of stockings and a street dress; an open powder box yawned upon the bureau. She must just have gone out.

The telephone rang abruptly and he started – answered it with all the sensations of an impostor.

'Hello. Is Mrs Patch there?'

'No, I'm looking for her myself. Who is this?'

'This is Mr Crawford.'

'This is Mr Patch speaking. I've just arrived unexpectedly, and I don't know where to find her.'

'Oh.' Mr Crawford sounded a bit taken aback. 'Why, I imagine she's at the Armistice Ball. I know she intended going, but I didn't think she'd leave so early.'

'Where's the Armistice Ball?'

'At the Astor.'

'Thanks.'

Anthony hung up sharply and rose. Who was Mr Crawford? And who was it that was taking her to the ball? How long had this been going on? All these questions asked and answered themselves a dozen times, a dozen ways. His very proximity to her drove him half frantic.

In a frenzy of suspicion he rushed here and there about the apartment, hunting for some sign of masculine occupation, opening the bathroom cupboard, searching feverishly through the bureau drawers. Then he found something that made him stop suddenly and sit down on one of the twin beds, the corners of his mouth drooping as though he were about to weep. There in a corner of her drawer, tied with a frail blue ribbon, were all the letters and telegrams he had written her during the year past. He was suffused with happy and sentimental shame.

'I'm not fit to touch her,' he cried aloud to the four walls. 'I'm not fit to touch her little hand.'

Nevertheless, he went out to look for her.

In the Astor lobby he was engulfed immediately in a crowd so thick as to make progress almost impossible. He asked the direction of the ballroom from half a dozen people before he could get a sober and intelligible answer. Eventually, after a last long wait, he checked his military overcoat in the hall.

It was only nine but the dance was in full blast. The panorama was incredible. Women, women everywhere – girls gay with wine singing shrilly above the clamour of the dazzling confetti-covered throng; girls set off by the uniforms of a dozen nations; fat females collapsing without dignity upon the floor and retaining self-respect by shouting, 'Hurraw for the Allies!'; three women with white hair dancing hand in hand around a sailor, who revolved in a dizzying spin upon the floor, clasping to his heart an empty bottle of champagne.

Breathlessly Anthony scanned the dancers, scanned the muddled lines trailing in single file in and out among the tables, scanned the horn-blowing, kissing, coughing, laughing, drinking parties under the great full-bosomed flags which leaned in glowing colour over the pageantry and the sound.

Then he saw Gloria. She was sitting at a table for two directly across the room. Her dress was black, and above it her animated face, tinted with the most glamorous rose, made, he thought, a spot of poignant beauty in the room. His heart leaped as though to a new music. He jostled his way towards her and called her name just as the grey eyes looked up and found him. For that instant as their bodies met and melted, the world, the revel, the tumbling whimper of the music faded to an ecstatic monotone hushed as a song of bees.

'Oh, my Gloria!' he cried.

Her kiss was a cool rill flowing from her heart.

Chapter 2

A Matter of Aesthetics

On the night when Anthony had left for Camp Hooker one year before, all that was left of the beautiful Gloria Gilbert – her shell, her young and lovely body – moved up the broad marble steps of the Grand Central Station with the rhythm of the engine beating in her ears like a dream, and out on to Vanderbilt Avenue, where the huge bulk of the Biltmore overhung the street and, down at its low, gleaming entrance, sucked in the many-coloured opera-cloaks of gorgeously dressed girls. For a moment she paused by the taxi-stand and watched them – wondering that but a few years before she had been of their number, ever setting out for a radiant Somewhere, always just about to have that ultimate passionate adventure for which the girls' cloaks were delicate and beautifully furred, for which their cheeks were painted and their hearts higher than the transitory dome of pleasure that would engulf them, coiffure, cloak, and all.

It was growing colder and the men passing had flipped up the collars of their overcoats. This change was kind to her. It would have been kinder still had everything changed, weather, streets and people, and had she been whisked away, to wake in some high, fresh-scented room, alone and statuesque within and without, as in her virginal and colourful past.

Inside the taxicab she wept impotent tears. That she had not been happy with Anthony for over a year mattered little. Recently his presence had been no more than what it would awake in her of that memorable June. The Anthony of late, irritable, weak and poor, could do no less than make her irritable in turn – and bored with everything except the fact that in a highly imaginative and eloquent youth they had come together in an ecstatic revel of emotion. Because of this mutually vivid memory she would have done more for Anthony than for any other human – so when she got into the taxicab she wept passionately, and wanted to call his name aloud.

Miserable, lonesome as a forgotten child, she sat in the quiet apartment and wrote him a letter full of confused sentiment:

. . . I can almost look down the tracks and see you going but without you, dearest, dearest, I can't see or hear or feel or think. Being apart – whatever has happened or will happen to us – is like begging for mercy from a storm, Anthony; it's like growing old. I want to kiss you so – in the back of your neck where your old black hair starts. Because I love you and whatever we do or say to each other, or have done, or have said, you've got to feel how much I do, how inanimate I am when you're gone. I can't even hate the damnable presence of PEOPLE, those people in the station who haven't any right to live – I can't resent them even though they're dirtying up our world, because I'm engrossed in wanting you so.

If you hated me, if you were covered with sores like a leper, if you ran away with another woman or starved me or beat me – how absurd this sounds – I'd still want you, I'd still love you. I *know*, my darling.

It's late – I have all the windows open and the air outside is just as soft as spring, yet, somehow, much more young and frail than spring. Why do they make spring a young girl, why does that illusion dance and yodel its way for three months through the world's preposterous barrenness. Spring is a lean old plough horse with its ribs showing – it's a pile of refuse in a field, parched by the sun and the rain to an ominous cleanliness.

In a few hours you'll wake up, my darling – and you'll be miserable, and disgusted with life. You'll be in Delaware or Carolina or somewhere and so unimportant. I don't believe there's anyone alive who can contemplate themselves as an impermanent institution, as a luxury or an unnecessary evil. Very few of the people who accentuate the futility of life remark the futility of themselves. Perhaps they think that in proclaiming the evil of living they somehow salvage their own worth from the ruin – but they don't, even you and I . . .

. . . Still I can see you. There's blue haze about the trees where you'll be passing, too beautiful to be predominant. No, the fallow squares of earth will be most frequent – they'll be along beside the track like dirty coarse brown sheets drying in the sun, alive, mechanical, abominable. Nature, slovenly old hag, has been sleeping in them with every old farmer or Negro or immigrant who happened to covet her . . .

So you see that now you're gone I've written a letter all full of contempt and despair. And that just means that I love you, Anthony, with all there is to love within your

GLORIA

When she had addressed the letter she went to her twin bed and lay down upon it, clasping Anthony's pillow in her arms as though by sheer force of emotion she could metamorphose it into his warm and living body. Two o'clock saw her dry-eyed, staring with steady persistent grief into the darkness, remembering, remembering unmercifully, blaming herself for a hundred fancied unkindnesses, making a likeness of Anthony akin to some martyred and transfigured Christ. For a time she thought of him as he, in his more sentimental moments, probably thought of himself.

At five she was still awake. A mysterious grinding noise that went on every morning across the area-way told her the hour. She heard an alarm clock ring, and saw a light make a yellow square on an illusory blank wall opposite. With the half-formed resolution of following him South immediately, her sorrow grew remote and unreal, and moved off from her as the dark moved westward. She fell asleep.

When she awoke the sight of the empty bed beside her brought a renewal of misery, dispelled shortly, however, by the inevitable callousness of the bright morning. Though she was not conscious of it, there was relief in eating breakfast without Anthony's tired and worried face opposite her. Now that she was alone she lost all desire to complain about the food. She would change her breakfasts, she thought – have a lemonade and a tomato sandwich instead of the sempiternal bacon and eggs and toast.

Nevertheless, at noon, when she had called up several of her acquaintances, including the martial Muriel, and found each one engaged for lunch, she gave way to a quiet pity for herself and her loneliness. Curled on the bed with pencil and paper she wrote Anthony another letter.

Late in the afternoon arrived a special delivery, mailed from some small New Jersey town, and the familiarity of the phrasing, the almost audible undertone of worry and discontent, were so familiar that they comforted her. Who knew? Perhaps army discipline would harden Anthony and accustom him to the idea of work. She had immutable faith that the war would be over before he was called upon to fight, and meanwhile the suit would be won, and they could begin again, this time on a different basis. The first thing different would be that she would have a child. It was unbearable that she should be so utterly alone.

It was a week before she could stay in the apartment with the probability of remaining dry-eyed. There seemed little in the city that was amusing. Muriel had been shifted to a hospital in New Jersey, from which she took a metropolitan holiday only every other week, and with this defection Gloria grew to realise how few were the friends she had made in all these years of New York. The men she knew were in the army. 'Men she knew'? – she had conceded vaguely to herself that all the men who had ever been in love with her were her friends. Each one of them had at a certain considerable time professed to value her favour above anything in life. But now – where were they? At least two were dead, half a dozen or more were married, the rest scattered from France to the Philippines. She wondered whether any of them thought of her, and how often, and in what respect. Most of them must still picture the little girl of seventeen or so, the adolescent siren of nine years before.

The girls, too, were gone far afield. She had never been popular in school. She had been too beautiful, too lazy, not sufficiently conscious of being a Farmover girl and a 'FUTURE WIFE AND MOTHER' in perpetual capital letters. And girls who had never been kissed hinted, with shocked expressions on their plain but not particularly wholesome faces, that Gloria had. Then these girls had gone east or west or south, married and become 'people', prophesying, if they prophesied about Gloria, that she would come to a bad end – not knowing that no endings were bad, and that they, like her, were by no means the mistresses of their destinies.

Gloria told over to herself the people who had visited them in the grey house at Marietta. It had seemed at the time that they were always having company – she had indulged in an unspoken conviction that each guest was ever afterwards slightly indebted to her. They owed her a sort of moral ten dollars apiece, and should she ever be in need she might, so to speak, borrow from them this visionary currency. But they were gone, scattered like chaff, mysteriously and subtly vanished in essence or in fact.

By Christmas, Gloria's conviction that she should join Anthony had returned, no longer as a sudden emotion, but as a recurrent need. She decided to write him word of her coming, but postponed the announcement upon the advice of Mr Haight, who expected almost weekly that the case was coming up for trial.

One day, early in January, as she was walking on Fifth Avenue, bright now with uniforms and hung with the flags of the virtuous nations, she met Rachael Barnes, whom she had not seen for nearly a year. Even Rachael, whom she had grown to dislike, was a relief from ennui, and together they went to the Ritz for tea.

After a second cocktail they became enthusiastic. They liked each other. They talked about their husbands, Rachael in that tone of public vainglory, with private reservations, in which wives are wont to speak.

'Rodman's abroad in the Quartermaster Corps. He's a captain. He was determined to go, and he didn't think he could get into anything else.'

'Anthony's in the Infantry.' The words in their relation to the cocktail gave Gloria a sort of glow. With each sip she approached a warm and comforting patriotism.

'By the way,' said Rachael half an hour later, as they were leaving, 'can't you come up to dinner tomorrow night? I'm having two awfully sweet officers who are just going overseas. I think we ought to do all we can to make it attractive for them.'

Gloria accepted gladly. She took down the address – recognising by its number a fashionable apartment building on Park Avenue.

'It's been awfully good to have seen you, Rachael.'

'It's been wonderful. I've wanted to.'

With these three sentences a certain night in Marietta two summers before, when Anthony and Rachael had been unnecessarily attentive to each other, was forgiven – Gloria forgave Rachael, Rachael forgave Gloria. Also it was forgiven that Rachael had been witness to the greatest disaster in the lives of Mr and Mrs Anthony Patch –

Compromising with events time moves along.

THE WILES OF CAPTAIN COLLINS

The two officers were captains of the popular craft, machine-gunnery. At dinner they referred to themselves with conscious boredom as members of the 'Suicide Club' – in those days every recondite branch of the service referred to itself as the Suicide Club. One of the captains – Rachael's captain, Gloria observed – was a tall horsy man of thirty with a pleasant moustache and ugly teeth. The other, Captain Collins, was chubby, pink-faced, and inclined to laugh with abandon every time he caught Gloria's eye. He took an immediate fancy to her, and throughout dinner showered her with inane compliments. With her second glass of champagne Gloria decided that for the first time in months she was thoroughly enjoying herself.

After dinner it was suggested that they all go somewhere and dance. The two officers supplied themselves with bottles of liquor from Rachael's sideboard – a law forbade service to the military – and so equipped they went through innumerable foxtrots in several glittering caravanseries along Broadway, faithfully alternating partners – while Gloria became more and more uproarious and more and more amusing to the pink-faced captain, who seldom bothered to remove his genial smile at all.

At eleven o'clock to her great surprise she was in the minority for staying out. The others wanted to return to Rachael's apartment – to get some more liquor, they said. Gloria argued persistently that Captain Collins's flask was half full – she had just seen it – then catching Rachael's eye she received an unmistakable wink. She deduced, confusedly, that her hostess wanted to get rid of the officers and assented to being bundled into a taxicab outside.

Captain Wolf sat on the left with Rachael on his knees. Captain Collins sat in the middle, and as he settled himself he slipped his arm about Gloria's shoulder. It rested there lifelessly for a moment and then tightened like a vice. He leaned over her.

'You're awfully pretty,' he whispered.

'Thank you kindly, sir.' She was neither pleased nor annoyed. Before Anthony came so many arms had done likewise that it had become little more than a gesture, sentimental but without significance.

Up in Rachael's long front room a low fire and two lamps shaded with orange silk gave all the light, so that the corners were full of deep and somnolent shadows. The hostess, moving about in a dark-figured gown of loose chiffon, seemed to accentuate the already sensuous atmosphere. For a while they were all four together, tasting the sandwiches that waited on the tea table – then Gloria found herself alone with Captain Collins on the fireside lounge; Rachael and Captain Wolf had withdrawn to the other side of the room, where they were conversing in subdued voices.

'I wish you weren't married,' said Collins, his face a ludicrous travesty of 'in all seriousness'.

'Why?' She held out her glass to be filled with a highball.

'Don't drink any more,' he urged her, frowning.

'Why not?'

'You'd be nicer – if you didn't.'

Gloria caught suddenly the intended suggestion of the remark, the atmosphere he was attempting to create. She wanted to laugh – yet she realised that there was nothing to laugh at. She had been enjoying the evening, and she had no desire to go home – at the same time it hurt her pride to be flirted with on just that level.

'Pour me another drink,' she insisted.

'Please – '

'Oh, don't be ridiculous!' she cried in exasperation.

'Very well.' He yielded with ill grace.

Then his arm was about her again, and again she made no protest. But when his pink cheek came close she leaned away.

'You're awfully sweet,' he said with an aimless air.

She began to sing softly, wishing now that he would take down his arm. Suddenly her eye fell on an intimate scene across the room – Rachael and Captain Wolf were engrossed in a long kiss. Gloria shivered slightly – she knew not why . . . Pink face approached again.

'You shouldn't look at them,' he whispered.

Almost immediately his other arm was around her . . . his breath was on her cheek. Again absurdity triumphed over disgust, and her laugh was a weapon that needed no edge of words.

'Oh, I thought you were a sport,' he was saying.

'What's a sport?'

'Why, a person that likes to – to enjoy life.'

'Is kissing you generally considered a joyful affair?'

They were interrupted as Rachael and Captain Wolf appeared suddenly before them.

'It's late, Gloria,' said Rachael – she was flushed and her hair was dishevelled. 'You'd better stay here all night.'

For an instant Gloria thought the officers were being dismissed. Then she understood, and, understanding, got to her feet as casually as she was able.

Uncomprehendingly Rachael continued: 'You can have the room just off this one. I can lend you everything you need.'

Collins's eyes implored her like a dog's; Captain Wolf's arm had settled familiarly around Rachael's waist; they were waiting.

But the lure of promiscuity, colourful, various, labyrinthine, and ever a little odorous and stale, had no call or promise for Gloria. Had she so desired she would have remained, without hesitation, without regret; as it was she could face coolly the six hostile and offended eyes that followed her out into the hall with forced politeness and hollow words.

'*He* wasn't even sport enough to try to take me home,' she thought in the taxi, and then with a quick surge of resentment: 'How *utterly* common!'

GALLANTRY

In February she had an experience of quite a different sort. Tudor Baird, an ancient flame, a young man whom at one time she had fully intended to marry, came to New York by way of the Aviation Corps, and called upon her. They went several times to the theatre, and within a week, to her great enjoyment, he was as much in love with her as ever. Quite deliberately she brought it about, realising too late that she had done a mischief. He reached the point of sitting with her in miserable silence whenever they went out together.

A Scroll and Keys man at Yale, he possessed the correct reticences of a 'good egg', the correct notions of chivalry and *noblesse oblige* – and, of course but unfortunately, the correct biases and the correct lack of ideas – all those traits which Anthony had taught her to despise, but which, nevertheless, she rather admired. Unlike the majority of his type, she found that he was not a bore. He was handsome, witty in a light way, and when she was with him she felt that because of some quality he possessed – call it stupidity, loyalty, sentimentality, or something not quite as definite as any of the three – he would have done anything in his power to please her.

He told her this among other things, very correctly and with a ponderous manliness that masked a real suffering. Loving him not at all she grew sorry for him and kissed him sentimentally one night because he was so charming, a relic of a vanishing generation which lived a priggish and graceful illusion and was being replaced by less gallant fools. Afterwards she was glad she had kissed him, for next day when his plane fell fifteen hundred feet at Mineola a piece of a gasolene engine smashed through his heart.

GLORIA ALONE

When Mr Haight told her that the trial would not take place until autumn she decided that without telling Anthony she would go into the movies. When he saw her successful, both histrionically and financially, when he saw that she could have her will of Joseph Bloeckman, yielding nothing in return, he would lose his silly prejudices. She lay awake half one night planning her career and enjoying her successes in anticipation, and the next morning she called up 'Films Par Excellence'. Mr Bloeckman was in Europe.

But the idea had gripped her so strongly this time that she decided to go the rounds of the moving-picture employment agencies. As so often had been the case, her sense of smell worked against her good intentions. The employment agency smelt as though it had been dead a very long time. She waited five minutes inspecting her unprepossessing competitors – then she walked briskly out into the farthest recesses of Central Park and remained so long that she caught a cold. She was trying to air the employment agency out of her walking suit.

In the spring she began to gather from Anthony's letters – not from any one in particular but from their cumulative effect – that he did not want her to come South. Curiously repeated excuses that seemed to haunt him by their very insufficiency occurred with Freudian regularity. He set them down in each letter as though he feared he had forgotten them the last time, as though it were desperately necessary to impress her with them. And the dilutions of his letters with affectionate diminutives began to be mechanical and unspontaneous – almost as though, having completed the letter, he had looked it over and literally stuck them in, like epigrams in an Oscar Wilde play. She jumped to the solution, rejected it, was angry and depressed by turns – finally she shut her mind to it proudly, and allowed an increasing coolness to creep into her end of the correspondence.

Of late she had found a good deal to occupy her attention. Several aviators whom she had met through Tudor Baird came into New York to see her and two other ancient beaux turned up, stationed at Camp Dix. As these men were ordered overseas they, so to speak, handed her down to their friends. But after another rather disagreeable experience with a potential Captain Collins she made it plain that when anyone was introduced to her he should be under no misapprehensions as to her status and personal intentions.

When summer came she learned, like Anthony, to watch the officers' casualty list, taking a sort of melancholy pleasure in hearing of the death of someone with whom she had once danced a german and in identifying by name the younger brothers of former suitors – thinking, as the drive towards Paris progressed, that here at length went the world to inevitable and well-merited destruction.

She was twenty-seven. Her birthday fled by scarcely noticed. Years before it had frightened her when she became twenty, to some extent when she reached twenty-six – but now she looked in the glass with calm self-approval seeing the British freshness of her complexion and her figure boyish and slim as of old.

She tried not to think of Anthony. It was as though she were writing to a stranger. She told her friends that he had been made a corporal and was annoyed when they were politely unimpressed. One night she wept because she was sorry for him – had he been even slightly responsive she would have gone to him without hesitation on the first train – whatever he was doing he needed to be taken care of spiritually, and she felt that now she would be able to do even that. Recently, without his continual drain upon her moral strength she found herself wonderfully revived. Before he left she had been inclined through sheer association to brood on her wasted opportunities – now she returned to her normal state of mind, strong, disdainful, existing each day for each day's worth. She bought a doll and dressed it; one week she wept over *Ethan Frome*; the next she revelled in some novels of Galsworthy's, whom she liked for his power of recreating, by spring in darkness, that illusion of young romantic love to which women look forever forward and forever back.

In October Anthony's letters multiplied, became almost frantic – then suddenly ceased. For a worried month it needed all her powers of control to refrain from leaving immediately for Mississippi. Then a telegram told her that he had been in the hospital and that she could expect him in New York within ten days. Like a figure in a dream he came back into her life across the ballroom on that November evening – and all through long hours that held familiar gladness she took him close to her breast, nursing an illusion of happiness and security she had not thought that she would know again.

DISCOMFITURE OF THE GENERALS

After a week Anthony's regiment went back to the Mississippi camp to be discharged. The officers shut themselves up in the compartments on the Pullman cars and drank the whiskey they had bought in New York, and in the coaches the soldiers got as drunk as possible also – and pretended whenever the train stopped at a village that they were just returned from France, where they had practically put an end to the German army. As they all wore overseas caps and claimed that they had not had time to have their gold service stripes sewn on, the yokelry of the seaboard were much impressed and asked them how they liked the trenches – to which they replied, 'Oh, *boy*!' with great smacking of tongues and shaking of heads. Someone took a piece of chalk and scrawled on the side of the train, 'We won the war – now we're going home,' and the officers laughed and let it stay.

They were all getting what swagger they could out of this ignominious return.

As they rumbled on towards camp, Anthony was uneasy lest he should find Dot awaiting him patiently at the station. To his relief he neither saw nor heard anything of her and thinking that were she still in town she would certainly attempt to communicate with him, he concluded that she had gone – whither he neither knew nor cared. He wanted only to return to Gloria – Gloria reborn and wonderfully alive. When eventually he was discharged he left his company on the rear of a great truck with a crowd who had given tolerant, almost sentimental, cheers for their officers, especially for Captain Dunning. The captain, on his part, had addressed them with tears in his eyes as to the pleasure, etc., and the work, etc., and time not wasted, etc., and duty, etc. It was very dull and human; having given ear to it Anthony, whose mind was freshened by his week in New York, renewed his deep loathing for the military profession and all it connoted. In their childish hearts two out of every three professional officers considered that wars were made for armies and not armies for wars. He rejoiced to see general and field-officers riding desolately about the barren camp deprived of their commands. He rejoiced to hear the men in his company laugh scornfully at the inducements tendered them to remain in the army. They were to attend 'schools'. He knew what these 'schools' were.

Two days later he was with Gloria in New York.

ANOTHER WINTER

Late one February afternoon Anthony came into the apartment and groping through the little hall, pitch-dark in the winter dusk, found Gloria sitting by the window. She turned as he came in.

'What did Mr Haight have to say?' she asked listlessly.

'Nothing,' he answered, 'usual thing. Next month, perhaps.'

She looked at him closely; her ear attuned to his voice caught the slightest thickness in the dissyllable.

'You've been drinking,' she remarked dispassionately.

'Couple glasses.'

'Oh.'

He yawned in the armchair and there was a moment's silence between them. Then she demanded suddenly: 'Did you go to Mr Haight? Tell me the truth.'

'No.' He smiled weakly. 'As a matter of fact I didn't have time.'

'I thought you didn't go . . . He sent for you.'

'I don't give a damn. I'm sick of waiting around his office. You'd think he was doing *me* a favour.' He glanced at Gloria as though expecting moral support, but she had turned back to her contemplation of the dubious and unprepossessing out-of-doors.

'I feel rather weary of life today,' he offered tentatively. Still she was silent. 'I met a fellow and we talked in the Biltmore bar.'

The dusk had suddenly deepened but neither of them made any move to turn on the lights. Lost in heaven knew what contemplation, they sat there until a flurry of snow drew a languid sigh from Gloria.

'What've you been doing?' he asked, finding the silence oppressive.

'Reading a magazine – all full of idiotic articles by prosperous authors about how terrible it is for poor people to buy silk shirts. And while I was reading it I could think of nothing except how I wanted a grey squirrel coat – and how we can't afford one.'

'Yes, we can.'

'Oh, no.'

'Oh, yes! If you want a fur coat you can have one.'

Her voice coming through the dark held an implication of scorn.

'You mean we can sell another bond?'

'If necessary. I don't want to go without things. We have spent a lot, though, since I've been back.'

'Oh, shut up!' she said in irritation.

'Why?'

'Because I'm sick and tired of hearing you talk about what we've spent or what we've done. You came back two months ago and we've been on some sort of a party practically every night since. We've both wanted to go out, and we've gone. Well, you haven't heard me complain, have you? But all you do is whine, whine, whine. I don't care any more what we do or what becomes of us and at least I'm consistent. But I will *not* tolerate your complaining and calamity-howling – '

'You're not very pleasant yourself sometimes, you know.'

'I'm under no obligations to be. You're not making any attempt to make things different.'

'But I am – '

'Huh! Seems to me I've heard that before. This morning you weren't going to touch another thing to drink until you'd got a position. And you didn't even have the spunk to go to Mr Haight when he sent for you about the suit.'

Anthony got to his feet and switched on the lights.

'See here!' he cried, blinking, 'I'm getting sick of that sharp tongue of yours.'

'Well, what are you going to do about it?'

'Do you think *I'm* particularly happy?' he continued, ignoring her question. 'Do you think I don't know we're not living as we ought to?'

In an instant Gloria stood trembling beside him.

'I won't *stand* it!' she burst out. 'I won't be lectured to. You and your suffering! You're just a pitiful weakling and you always have been!'

They faced one another idiotically, each of them unable to impress the other, each of them tremendously, achingly, bored. Then she went into the bedroom and shut the door behind her.

His return had brought into the foreground all their pre-bellum exasperations. Prices had risen alarmingly and in perverse ratio their income had shrunk to a little over half of its original size. There had been the large retainer's fee to Mr Haight; there were stocks bought at one hundred now down to thirty and forty and other investments that were not paying at all. During the previous spring Gloria had been given the alternative of leaving the apartment or of signing a year's lease at two hundred and twenty-five a month. She had signed it. Inevitably as the necessity for economy had increased they found themselves as a pair quite unable to save. The old policy of prevarication was resorted to. Weary of their incapabilities they chattered of what they would do – oh – tomorrow, of how they would 'stop going on parties' and of how Anthony would go to work. But when dark came down Gloria, accustomed to an engagement every night, would feel the ancient restlessness creeping over her. She would stand in the doorway of the bedroom, chewing furiously at her fingers and sometimes meeting Anthony's eyes as he glanced up from his book. Then the telephone, and her nerves would relax, she would answer it with ill-concealed eagerness. Someone was coming up 'for just a few minutes' – and oh, the weariness of pretence, the appearance of the wine table, the revival of their jaded spirits – and the awakening, like the mid-point of a sleepless night in which they moved.

As the winter passed with the march of the returning troops along Fifth Avenue they became more and more aware that since Anthony's return their relations had entirely changed. After that reflowering of tenderness and passion each of them had returned into some solitary dream unshared by the other and what endearments passed between them passed, it seemed, from empty heart to empty heart, echoing hollowly the departure of what they knew at last was gone.

Anthony had again made the rounds of the metropolitan newspapers and had again been refused encouragement by a motley of office boys, telephone girls and city editors. The word was: 'We're keeping any vacancies open for our own men who are still in France.' Then, late in March, his eye fell on an advertisement in the morning paper and in consequence he found at last the semblance of an occupation.

YOU CAN SELL!!!

Why not earn while you learn?

Our salesmen make $50–$200 weekly.

There followed an address on Madison Avenue, and instructions to appear at one o'clock that afternoon. Gloria, glancing over his shoulder after one of their usual late breakfasts, saw him regarding it idly.

'Why don't you try it?' she suggested.

'Oh – it's one of these crazy schemes.'

'It might not be. At least it'd be experience.'

At her urging he went at one o'clock to the appointed address, where he found himself one of a dense miscellany of men waiting in front of the door. They ranged from a messenger-boy evidently misusing his company's time to an immemorial individual with a gnarled body and a gnarled cane. Some of the men were seedy, with sunken cheeks and puffy pink eyes – others were young, possibly still in high school. After a jostled fifteen minutes during which they all eyed one another with apathetic suspicion there appeared a smart young shepherd clad in a 'waistline' suit and wearing the manner of an assistant rector who herded them upstairs into a large room, which resembled a schoolroom and contained innumerable desks. Here the prospective salesmen sat down – and again waited. After an interval a platform at the end of the hall was clouded with half a dozen sober but sprightly men who, with one exception, took seats in a semicircle facing the audience.

The exception was the man who seemed the soberest, the most sprightly and the youngest of the lot, and who advanced to the front of the platform. The audience scrutinised him hopefully. He was rather small and rather pretty, with the commercial rather than the thespian sort of prettiness. He had straight blond bushy brows and eyes that were almost preposterously honest, and as he reached the edge of his rostrum he seemed to throw these eyes out into the audience, simultaneously extending his arm with two fingers outstretched. Then while he rocked himself to a state of balance an expectant silence settled over the hall. With perfect assurance the young man had taken his listeners in hand and his words when they came were steady and confident and of the school of 'straight from the shoulder'.

'Men!' – he began, and paused. The word died with a prolonged echo at the end of the hall, the faces regarding him, hopefully, cynically, wearily, were alike arrested, engrossed. Six hundred eyes were turned slightly upward. With an even graceless flow that reminded Anthony of the rolling of bowling balls he launched himself into the sea of exposition.

'This bright and sunny morning you picked up your favourite newspaper and you found an advertisement which made the plain, unadorned statement that *you* could sell. That was all it said – it didn't say "what", it didn't say "how", it didn't say "why". It just made one single solitary assertion that *you* and *you* and *you*' – business of pointing – 'could sell. Now my job isn't to make a success of you, because every man is born a success, he makes himself a failure; it's not to teach you how to talk, because each man is a natural orator and only makes himself a clam; my business is to tell you one thing in a way that will make you *know* it – it's to tell you that *you* and *you* and *you* have the heritage of money and prosperity waiting for you to come and claim it.'

At this point an Irishman of saturnine appearance rose from his desk near the rear of the hall and went out.

'That man thinks he'll go look for it in the beer parlour around the corner. [Laughter.] He won't find it there. Once upon a time I looked for it there myself [laughter], but that was before I did what every one of you men no matter how young or how old, how poor or how rich [a faint ripple of satirical laughter], can do. It was before I found – *myself*!

'Now I wonder if any of you men know what a "Heart Talk" is. A "Heart Talk" is a little book in which I started, about five years ago, to write down what I had discovered were the principal reasons for a man's failure and the principal reasons for a man's success – from John D. Rockerfeller back to John D. Napoleon [laughter], and before that, back in the days when Abel sold his birthright for a mess of pottage. There are now one hundred of these "Heart Talks". Those of you who are sincere, who are interested in our proposition, above all who are dissatisfied with the way things are breaking for you at present will be handed one to take home with you as you go out yonder door this afternoon.

'Now in my own pocket I have four letters just received concerning "Heart Talks". These letters have names signed to them that are familiar in every household in the USA. Listen to this one from Detroit:

DEAR MR CARELTON – I want to order three thousand more copies of "Heart Talks" for distribution among my salesmen. They have done more for getting work out of the men than any bonus proposition ever considered. I read them myself constantly, and I desire to heartily congratulate you on getting at the roots of the biggest problem that faces our generation today – the problem of salesmanship. The rock bottom on which the country is founded is the problem of salesmanship. With many felicitations I am

Yours very cordially,

HENRY W. TERRAL'

He brought the name out in three long booming triumphancies – pausing for it to produce its magical effect. Then he read two more letters, one from a manufacturer of vacuum cleaners and one from the president of the Great Northern Doily Company.

'And now,' he continued, 'I'm going to tell you in a few words what the proposition is that's going to *make* those of you who go into it in the right spirit. Simply put, it's this: "Heart Talks" have been incorporated as a company. We're going to put these little pamphlets into the hands of every big business organisation, every salesman, and every man who *knows* – I don't say "thinks", I say "*knows*" – that he can sell! We are offering some of the stock of the "Heart Talks" concern upon the market, and in order that the distribution may be as wide as possible, and in order also that we can furnish a living, concrete, flesh-and-blood example of what salesmanship is, or rather what it may be, we're going to give those of you who are the real thing a chance to sell that stock. Now, I don't care what you've tried to sell before or how you've tried to sell it. It don't matter how old you are or how young you are. I only want to know two things – first, do you *want* success, and, second, will you work for it?

'My name is Sammy Carleton. Not "Mr" Carleton, but just plain Sammy. I'm a regular no-nonsense man with no fancy frills about me. I want you to call me Sammy.

'Now this is all I'm going to say to you today. Tomorrow I want those of you who have thought it over and have read the copy of "Heart Talks" which will be given to you at the door, to come back to this same room at this same time, then we'll go into the proposition further and I'll explain to you what I've found the principles of success to be. I'm going to make you *feel* that *you* and *you* and *you* can sell!'

Mr Carleton's voice echoed for a moment through the hall and then died away. To the stamping of many feet Anthony was pushed and jostled with the crowd out of the room.

FURTHER ADVENTURES WITH 'HEART TALKS'

With an accompaniment of ironic laughter Anthony told Gloria the story of his commercial adventure. But she listened without amusement.

'You're going to give up again?' she demanded coldly.

'Why – you don't expect me to – '

'I never expected anything of you.'

He hesitated.

'Well – I can't see the slightest benefit in laughing myself sick over this sort of affair. If there's anything older than the old story, it's the new twist.'

It required an astonishing amount of moral energy on Gloria's part to intimidate him into returning, and when he reported next day, somewhat depressed from his perusal of the senile bromides skittishly set forth in 'Heart Talks on Ambition', he found only fifty of the original three hundred awaiting the appearance of the vital and compelling Sammy Carleton. Mr Carleton's powers of vitality and compulsion were this time exercised in elucidating that magnificent piece of speculation – how to sell. It seemed that the approved method was to state one's proposition and then to say not, 'And now, will you buy?' – this was not the way – oh, no! – the way was to state one's proposition and then, having reduced one's adversary to a state of exhaustion, to deliver oneself of the categorical imperative: 'Now see here! You've taken up my time explaining this matter to you. You've admitted my points – all I want to ask is how many do you want?'

As Mr Carleton piled assertion upon assertion Anthony began to feel a sort of disgusted confidence in him. The man appeared to know what he was talking about. Obviously prosperous, he had risen to the position of instructing others. It did not occur to Anthony that the type of man who attains commercial success seldom knows how or why, and, as in his grandfather's case, when he ascribes reasons, the reasons are generally inaccurate and absurd.

Anthony noted that of the numerous old men who had answered the original advertisement, only two had returned, and that among the thirty odd who assembled on the third day to get actual selling instructions from Mr Carleton, only one grey head was in evidence. These thirty were eager converts; with their mouths they followed the working of Mr Carleton's mouth; they swayed in their seats with enthusiasm, and in the intervals of his talk they spoke to each other in tense approving whispers. Yet of the chosen few who, in the words of Mr Carleton, 'were determined to get those deserts that rightly and truly belonged to them', less than half a dozen combined even a modicum of personal appearance with that great gift of being a 'pusher'. But they were told that they were all natural pushers – it was merely necessary that they should believe with a sort of savage passion in what they were selling. He even urged each one to buy some stock himself, if possible, in order to increase his own sincerity.

On the fifth day then, Anthony sallied into the street with all the sensations of a man wanted by the police. Acting according to instructions he selected a tall office building in order that he might ride to the top storey and work downward, stopping in every office that had a name on the door. But at the last minute he hesitated. Perhaps it would be more practicable to acclimate himself to the chilly atmosphere which he felt was awaiting him by trying a few offices on, say, Madison Avenue. He went into an arcade that seemed only semi-prosperous, and seeing a sign which read Percy B. Weatherbee, Architect, he opened the door heroically and entered. A starchy young woman looked up questioningly.

'Can I see Mr Weatherbee?' He wondered if his voice sounded tremulous.

She laid her hand tentatively on the telephone-receiver.

'What's the name, please?'

'He wouldn't – ah – know me. He wouldn't know my name.'

'What's your business with him? You an insurance agent?'

'Oh, no, nothing like that!' denied Anthony hurriedly. 'Oh, no. It's a – it's a personal matter.' He wondered if he should have said this. It had all sounded so simple when Mr Carleton had enjoined his flock: 'Don't allow yourself to be kept out! Show them you've made up your mind to talk to them, and they'll listen.'

The girl succumbed to Anthony's pleasant, melancholy face, and in a moment the door to the inner room opened and admitted a tall, splay-footed man with slicked hair. He approached Anthony with ill-concealed impatience.

'You wanted to see me on a personal matter?'

Anthony quailed.

'I wanted to talk to you,' he said defiantly.

'About what?'

'It'll take some time to explain.'

'Well, what's it about?' Mr Weatherbee's voice indicated rising irritation.

Then Anthony, straining at each word, each syllable, began: 'I don't know whether or not you've ever heard of a series of pamphlets called "Heart Talks" – '

'Good grief!' cried Percy B. Weatherbee, Architect, 'are you trying to touch my heart?'

'No, it's business. "Heart Talks" have been incorporated and we're putting some shares on the market – '

His voice faded slowly off, harassed by a fixed and contemptuous stare from his unwilling prey. For another minute he struggled on, increasingly sensitive, entangled in his own words. His confidence oozed from him in great retching emanations that seemed to be sections of his own body. Almost mercifully Percy B. Weatherbee, Architect, terminated the interview: 'Good grief!' he exploded in disgust, 'and you call that a *personal* matter!' He whipped about and strode into his private office, banging the door behind him. Not daring to look at the stenographer, Anthony in some shameful and mysterious way got himself from the room. Perspiring profusely he stood in the hall wondering why they didn't come and arrest him; in every hurried look he discerned infallibly a glance of scorn.

After an hour and with the help of two strong whiskies he brought himself up to another attempt. He walked into a plumber's shop, but when he mentioned his business the plumber began pulling on his coat in a great hurry, gruffly announcing that he had to go to lunch. Anthony remarked politely that it was futile to try to sell a man anything when he was hungry, and the plumber heartily agreed.

This episode encouraged Anthony; he tried to think that had the plumber not been bound for lunch he would at least have listened.

Passing by a few glittering and formidable bazaars he entered a grocery store. A talkative proprietor told him that before buying any stocks he was going to see how the armistice affected the market. To Anthony this seemed almost unfair. In Mr Carleton's salesman's Utopia the only reason prospective buyers ever gave for not purchasing stock was that they doubted it to be a promising investment. Obviously a man in that state was almost ludicrously easy game, to be brought down merely by the judicious application of the correct selling points. But these men – why, actually they weren't considering buying anything at all.

Anthony took several more drinks before he approached his fourth man, a real-estate agent; nevertheless, he was floored with a coup as decisive as a syllogism. The real-estate agent said that he had three brothers in the investment business. Viewing himself as a breaker-up of homes Anthony apologised and went out.

After another drink he conceived the brilliant plan of selling the stock to the bartenders along Lexington Avenue. This occupied several hours, for it was necessary to take a few drinks in each place in order to get the proprietor in the proper frame of mind to talk business. But the bartenders one and all contended that if they had any money to buy bonds they would not be bartenders. It was as though they had all convened and decided upon that rejoinder. As he approached a dark and soggy five o'clock he found that they were developing a still more annoying tendency to turn him off with a jest.

At five, then, with a tremendous effort at concentration he decided that he must put more variety into his canvassing. He selected a medium-sized delicatessen store, and went in. He felt, illuminatingly, that the thing to do was to cast a spell not only over the storekeeper but over all the customers as well – and perhaps through the psychology of the herd instinct they would buy as an astounded and immediately convinced whole.

'Af'ernoon,' he began in a loud thick voice. 'Ga l'il prop'sition.'

If he had wanted silence he obtained it. A sort of awe descended upon the half-dozen women marketing and upon the grey-haired ancient who in cap and apron was slicing chicken.

Anthony pulled a batch of papers from his flapping briefcase and waved them cheerfully.

'Buy a bon',' he suggested, 'good as liberty bon'!' The phrase pleased him and he elaborated upon it. 'Better'n liberty bon'. Every one these bon's worth *two* liberty bon's.' His mind made a hiatus and skipped to his peroration, which he delivered with appropriate gestures, these being somewhat marred by the necessity of clinging to the counter with one or both hands.

'Now see here. You taken up my time. I don't want know *why* you won't buy. I don't want you say *why*. Want you say *how many*!'

At this point they should have approached him with cheque-books and fountain-pens in hand. Realising that they must have missed a cue Anthony, with the instincts of an actor, went back and repeated his finale.

'Now see here! You taken up my time. You followed prop'sition.

You agreed 'th reasonin'? Now, all I want from *you* is, how many lib'ty bon's?'

'See here!' broke in a new voice. A portly man whose face was adorned with symmetrical scrolls of yellow hair had come out of a glass cage in the rear of the store and was bearing down upon Anthony. 'See here, you!'

'How many?' repeated the salesman sternly. 'You taken up my time – '

'Hey, you!' cried the proprietor, 'I'll have you taken up by the police.'

'You mos' cert'nly won't!' returned Anthony with fine defiance. 'All I want know is how many.'

From here and there in the store went up little clouds of comment and expostulation.

'How terrible!'

'He's a raving maniac.'

'He's disgracefully drunk.'

The proprietor grasped Anthony's arm sharply.

'Get out, or I'll call a policeman.'

Some relics of rationality moved Anthony to nod and replace his bonds clumsily in the case.

'How many?' he reiterated doubtfully.

'The whole force if necessary!' thundered his adversary, his yellow moustache trembling fiercely.

'Sell 'em all a bon'.'

With this Anthony turned, bowed gravely to his late auditors, and wobbled from the store. He found a taxicab at the corner and rode home to the apartment. There he fell sound asleep on the sofa, and so Gloria found him, his breath filling the air with an unpleasant pungency, his hand still clutching his open briefcase.

Except when Anthony was drinking, his range of sensation had become less than that of a healthy old man, and when Prohibition came in July he found that, among those who could afford it, there was more drinking than ever before. One's host now brought out a bottle upon the slightest pretext. The tendency to display liquor was a manifestation of the same instinct that led a man to deck his wife with jewels. To have liquor was a boast, almost a badge of respectability.

In the mornings Anthony awoke tired, nervous, and worried. Halcyon summer twilights and the purple chill of morning alike left him unresponsive. Only for a brief moment every day in the warmth and renewed life of a first highball did his mind turn to those opalescent dreams of future pleasure – the mutual heritage of the happy and the damned. But this was only for a little while. As he grew drunker the dreams faded and he became a confused spectre, moving in odd crannies of his own mind, full of unexpected devices, harshly contemptuous at best and reaching sodden and dispirited depths. One night in June he had quarrelled violently with Maury over a matter of the utmost triviality. He remembered dimly next morning that it had been about a broken pint bottle of champagne. Maury had told him to sober up and Anthony's feelings had been hurt, so with an attempted gesture of dignity he had risen from the table and seizing Gloria's arm half led, half shamed her into a taxicab outside, leaving Maury with three dinners ordered and tickets for the opera.

This sort of semi-tragic fiasco had become so usual that when they occurred he was no longer stirred into making amends. If Gloria protested – and of late she was more likely to sink into contemptuous silence – he would either engage in a bitter defence of himself or else stalk dismally from the apartment. Never since the incident on the station platform at Redgate had he laid his hands on her in anger – though he was withheld often only by some instinct that itself made him tremble with rage. Just as he still cared more for her than for any other creature, so did he more intensely and frequently hate her.

So far, the judges of the Appellate Division had failed to hand down a decision, but after another postponement they finally affirmed the decree of the lower court – two justices dissenting. A notice of appeal was served upon Edward Shuttleworth. The case was going to the Court of Last Resort, and they were in for another interminable wait. Six months, perhaps a year. It had grown enormously unreal to them, remote and uncertain as heaven.

Throughout the previous winter one small matter had been a subtle and omnipresent irritant – the question of Gloria's grey fur coat. At that time women enveloped in long squirrel wraps could be seen every few yards along Fifth Avenue. The women were converted to the shape of tops. They seemed porcine and obscene; they resembled kept women in the concealing richness, the feminine animality of the garment. Yet – Gloria wanted a grey squirrel coat.

Discussing the matter – or, rather, arguing it, for even more than in the first year of their marriage did every discussion take the form of bitter debate full of such phrases as 'most certainly', 'utterly outrageous', 'it's so, nevertheless', and the ultra-emphatic 'regardless' –

they concluded that they could not afford it. And so gradually it began to stand as a symbol of their growing financial anxiety.

To Gloria the shrinkage of their income was a remarkable phenomenon, without explanation or precedent – that it could happen all within the space of five years seemed almost an intended cruelty, conceived and executed by a sardonic God. When they were married seventy-five hundred a year had seemed ample for a young couple, especially when augmented by the expectation of many millions. Gloria had failed to realise that it was decreasing not only in amount but in purchasing power until the payment of Mr Haight's retaining fee of fifteen thousand dollars made the fact suddenly and startlingly obvious. When Anthony was drafted they had calculated their income at over four hundred a month, with the dollar even then decreasing in value, but on his return to New York they discovered an even more alarming condition of affairs. They were receiving only forty-five hundred a year from their investments. And though the suit over the will moved ahead of them like a persistent mirage and the financial danger-mark loomed up in the near distance they found, nevertheless, that living within their income was impossible.

So Gloria went without the squirrel coat and every day upon Fifth Avenue she was a little more conscious of her well-worn, half-length leopard skin, now hopelessly old-fashioned. Every other month they sold a bond, yet when the bills were paid it left only enough to be gulped down hungrily by their current expenses. Anthony's calculations showed that their capital would last about seven years longer. So Gloria's heart was very bitter, for in one week, on a prolonged hysterical party during which Anthony whimsically divested himself of coat, vest and shirt in a theatre and was assisted out by a posse of ushers, they spent twice what the grey squirrel coat would have cost.

It was November, Indian summer rather, and a warm, warm night – which was unnecessary, for the work of the summer was done. Babe Ruth had smashed the home-run record for the first time and Jack Dempsey had broken Jess Willard's cheekbone out in Ohio. Over in Europe the usual number of children had swollen stomachs from starvation, and the diplomats were at their customary business of making the world safe for new wars. In New York City the proletariat were being 'disciplined', and the odds on Harvard were generally quoted at five to three. Peace had come down in earnest, the beginning of new days.

Up in the bedroom of the apartment on Fifty-Seventh Street Gloria lay upon her bed and tossed from side to side, sitting up at intervals to throw off a superfluous cover and once asking Anthony, who was lying awake beside her, to bring her a glass of ice-water. 'Be sure and put ice in it,' she said with insistence; 'it isn't cold enough the way it comes from the faucet.'

Looking through the frail curtains she could see the rounded moon over the roofs and beyond it on the sky the yellow glow from Times Square – and watching the two incongruous lights, her mind worked over an emotion, or rather an interwoven complex of emotions, that had occupied it through the day, and the day before that and back to the last time when she could remember having thought clearly and consecutively about anything – which must have been while Anthony was in the army.

She would be twenty-nine in February. The month assumed an ominous and inescapable significance – making her wonder, through these nebulous half-fevered hours, whether after all she had not wasted her faintly tired beauty, whether there was such thing as a use for any quality bounded by a harsh and inevitable mortality.

Years before, when she was twenty-one, she had written in her diary: 'Beauty is only to be admired, only to be loved – to be harvested carefully and then flung at a chosen lover like a gift of roses. It seems to me, so far as I can judge clearly at all, that my beauty should be used like that . . . '

And now, all this November day, all this desolate day, under a sky dirty and white, Gloria had been thinking that perhaps she had been wrong. To preserve the integrity of her first gift she had looked no more for love. When the first flame and ecstasy had grown dim, sunk down, departed, she had begun preserving – what? It puzzled her that she no longer knew just what she was preserving – a sentimental memory or some profound and fundamental concept of honour. She was doubting now whether there had been any moral issue involved in her way of life – to walk unworried and unregretful along the gayest of all possible lanes and to keep her pride by being always herself and doing what it seemed beautiful that she should do. From the first little boy in an Eton collar whose 'girl' she had been, down to the latest casual man whose eyes had grown alert and appreciative as they rested upon her, there was needed only that matchless candour she could throw into a look or clothe with an inconsequent clause – for she had talked always in broken clauses – to weave about her immeasurable illusions, immeasurable distances, immeasurable light. To create souls in men, to create fine happiness and fine despair she must remain deeply proud – proud to be inviolate, proud also to be melting, to be passionate and possessed.

She knew that in her breast she had never wanted children. The reality, the earthiness, the intolerable sentiment of child-bearing, the menace to her beauty – had appalled her. She wanted to exist only as a conscious flower, prolonging and preserving itself. Her sentimentality could cling fiercely to her own illusions, but her ironic soul whispered that motherhood was also the privilege of the female baboon. So her dreams were of ghostly children only – the early, the perfect symbols of her early and perfect love for Anthony.

In the end then, her beauty was all that never failed her. She had never seen beauty like her own. What it meant ethically or aesthetically faded before the gorgeous concreteness of her pink-and-white feet, the clean perfectness of her body, and the baby mouth that was like the material symbol of a kiss.

She would be twenty-nine in February. As the long night waned she grew supremely conscious that she and beauty were going to make use of these next three months. At first she was not sure for what, but the problem resolved itself gradually into the old lure of the screen. She was in earnest now. No material want could have moved her as this fear moved her. No matter for Anthony, Anthony the poor in spirit, the weak and broken man with bloodshot eyes, for whom she still had moments of tenderness. No matter. She would be twenty-nine in February – a hundred days, so many days; she would go to Bloeckman tomorrow.

With the decision came relief. It cheered her that in some manner the illusion of beauty could be sustained, or preserved perhaps in celluloid after the reality had vanished. Well – tomorrow.

The next day she felt weak and ill. She tried to go out, and saved herself from collapse only by clinging to a mailbox near the front door. The Martinique elevator boy helped her upstairs, and she waited on the bed for Anthony's return without energy to unhook her brassiere.

For five days she was down with influenza, which, just as the month turned the corner into winter, ripened into double pneumonia. In the feverish perambulations of her mind she prowled through a house of bleak unlighted rooms hunting for her mother. All she wanted was to be a little girl, to be efficiently taken care of by some yielding yet superior power, stupider and steadier than herself. It seemed that the only lover she had ever wanted was a lover in a dream.

'ODI PROFANUM VULGUS'

One day in the midst of Gloria's illness there occurred a curious incident that puzzled Miss McGovern, the trained nurse, for some time afterwards. It was noon, but the room in which the patient lay was dark and quiet.

Miss McGovern was standing near the bed mixing some medicine when Mrs Patch, who had apparently been sound asleep, sat up and began to speak vehemently: 'Millions of people,' she said, 'swarming like rats, chattering like apes, smelling like all hell . . . monkeys! Or lice, I suppose. For one really exquisite palace . . . on Long Island, say – or even in Greenwich . . . for one palace full of pictures from the Old World and exquisite things – with avenues of trees and green lawns and a view of the blue sea, and lovely people about in slick dresses . . . I'd sacrifice a hundred thousand of them, a million of them.' She raised her hand feebly and snapped her fingers. 'I care nothing for them – understand me?'

The look she bent upon Miss McGovern at the conclusion of this speech was curiously elfin, curiously intent. Then she gave a short little laugh, polished with scorn, and tumbling backwards fell off again to sleep.

Miss McGovern was bewildered. She wondered what were the hundred thousand things that Mrs Patch would sacrifice for her palace. Dollars, she supposed – yet it had not sounded exactly like dollars.

THE MOVIES

It was February, seven days before her birthday, and the great snow that had filled up the cross-streets as dirt fills the cracks in a floor had turned to slush and was being escorted to the gutters by the hoses of the street-cleaning department. The wind, none the less bitter for being casual, whipped in through the open windows of the living-room bearing with it the dismal secrets of the area-way and clearing the Patch apartment of stale smoke in its cheerless circulation.

Gloria, wrapped in a warm kimona, came into the chilly room and taking up the telephone receiver called Joseph Bloeckman.

'Do you mean Mr Joseph *Black*?' demanded the telephone girl at 'Films Par Excellence'.

'Bloeckman, Joseph Bloeckman. B-l-o – '

'Mr Joseph Bloeckman has changed his name to Black. Do you want him?'

'Why – yes.' She remembered nervously that she had once called him 'Blockhead' to his face.

His office was reached by courtesy of two additional female voices; the last was a secretary who took her name. Only with the flow through the transmitter of his own familiar but faintly impersonal tone did she realise that it had been three years since they had met. And he had changed his name to Black.

'Can you see me?' she suggested lightly. 'It's on a business matter, really. I'm going into the movies at last – if I can.'

'I'm awfully glad. I've always thought you'd like it.'

'Do you think you can get me a trial?' she demanded with the arrogance peculiar to all beautiful women, to all women who have ever at any time considered themselves beautiful.

He assured her that it was merely a question of when she wanted the trial. Any time? Well, he'd phone later in the day and let her know a convenient hour. The conversation closed with conventional padding on both sides. Then from three o'clock to five she sat close to the telephone – with no result.

But next morning came a note that contented and excited her:

My dear Gloria – Just by luck a matter came to my attention that I think will be just suited to you. I would like to see you start with something that would bring you notice. At the same time if a very beautiful girl of your sort is put directly into a picture next to one of the rather shop-worn stars with which every company is afflicted, tongues would very likely wag. But there is a 'flapper' part in a Percy B. Debris production that I think would be just suited to you and would bring you notice. Willa Sable plays opposite Gaston Mears in a sort of character part and your part I believe would be her younger sister.

Anyway Percy B. Debris who is directing the picture says if you'll come to the studios day after tomorrow (Thursday) he will run off a test. If ten o'clock is suited to you I will meet you there at that time.

With all good wishes

Ever faithfully,

Joseph Black

Gloria had decided that Anthony was to know nothing of this until she had obtained a definite position, and accordingly she was dressed and out of the apartment next morning before he awoke. Her mirror had given her, she thought, much the same account as ever. She wondered if there were any lingering traces of her sickness. She was still slightly under weight, and she had fancied, a few days before, that her cheeks were a trifle thinner – but she felt that those were merely transitory conditions and that on this particular day she looked as fresh as ever. She had bought and charged a new hat, and as the day was warm she had left the leopard-skin coat at home.

At the 'Films Par Excellence' studios she was announced over the telephone and told that Mr Black would be down directly. She looked around her. Two girls were being shown about by a little fat man in a slash-pocket coat, and one of them had indicated a stack of thin parcels, piled breast-high against the wall, and extending along for twenty feet.

'That's studio mail,' explained the fat man. 'Pictures of the stars who are with "Films Par Excellence".'

'Oh.'

'Each one's autographed by Florence Kelley or Gaston Mears or Mack Dodge – ' He winked confidentially. 'At least, when Minnie McGlook out in Sauk Center gets the picture she wrote for, she *thinks* it's autographed.'

'Just a stamp?'

'Sure. It'd take 'em a good eight-hour day to autograph half of 'em. They say Mary Pickford's studio mail costs her fifty thousand a year.'

'Say!'

'Sure. Fifty thousand. But it's the best kinda advertising there is – '

They drifted out of earshot and almost immediately Bloeckman appeared – Bloeckman, a dark suave gentleman, gracefully engaged in the middle forties, who greeted her with courteous warmth and told her she had not changed a bit in three years. He led the way into a great hall, as large as an armoury and broken intermittently with busy sets and blinding rows of unfamiliar light. Each piece of scenery was marked in large white letters 'Gaston Mears Company', 'Mack Dodge Company', or simply 'Films Par Excellence'.

'Ever been in a studio before?'

'Never have.'

She liked it. There was no heavy closeness of greasepaint, no scent of soiled and tawdry costumes which years before had revolted her behind the scenes of a musical comedy. This work was done in the clean mornings; the appurtenances seemed rich and gorgeous and new. On a set that was joyous with Manchu hangings a perfect Chinaman was going through a scene according to megaphone directions as the great glittering machine ground out its ancient moral tale for the edification of the national mind.

A red-headed man approached them and spoke with familiar deference to Bloeckman, who answered: 'Hello, Debris. Want you to meet Mrs Patch . . . Mrs Patch wants to go into pictures, as I explained to you . . . All right, now, where do we go?'

Mr Debris – the great Percy B. Debris, thought Gloria – showed them to a set which represented the interior of an office. Some chairs were drawn up around the camera, which stood in front of it, and the three of them sat down.

'Ever been in a studio before?' asked Mr Debris, giving her a glance that was surely the quintessence of keenness. 'No? Well, I'll explain exactly what's going to happen. We're going to take what we call a test in order to see how your features photograph and whether you've got natural stage presence and how you respond to coaching. There's no need to be nervous over it. I'll just have the cameraman take a few hundred feet in an episode I've got marked here in the scenario. We can tell pretty much what we want to from that.'

He produced a typewritten continuity and explained to her the episode she was to enact. It developed that one Barbara Wainwright had been secretly married to the junior partner of the firm whose office was there represented. Entering the deserted office one day by accident she was naturally interested in seeing where her husband worked. The telephone rang and after some hesitation she answered it. She learned that her husband had been struck by an automobile and instantly killed. She was overcome. At first she was unable to realise the truth, but finally she succeeded in comprehending it, and went into a dead faint on the floor.

'Now that's all we want,' concluded Mr Debris. 'I'm going to stand here and tell you approximately what to do, and you're to act as though I wasn't here, and just go on, do it your own way. You needn't be afraid we're going to judge this too severely. We simply want to get a general idea of your screen personality.'

'I see.'

'You'll find make-up in the room in back of the set. Go light on it. Very little red.'

'I see,' repeated Gloria, nodding. She touched her lips nervously with the tip of her tongue.

As she came into the set through the real wooden door and closed it carefully behind her, she found herself inconveniently dissatisfied with her clothes. She should have bought a 'misses' dress for the occasion – she could still wear them, and it might have been a good investment if it had accentuated her airy youth.

Her mind snapped sharply into the momentous present as Mr Debris's voice came from the glare of the white lights in front.

'You look around for your husband . . . Now – you don't see him . . . you're curious about the office . . . '

She became conscious of the regular sound of the camera. It worried her. She glanced towards it involuntarily and wondered if she had made up her face correctly. Then, with a definite effort she forced herself to act – and she had never felt that the gestures of her body were so banal, so awkward, so bereft of grace or distinction. She strolled around the office, picking up articles here and there and looking at them inanely. Then she scrutinised the ceiling, the floor, and thoroughly inspected an inconsequential lead pencil on the desk. Finally, because she could think of nothing else to do, and less than nothing to express, she forced a smile.

'All right. Now the phone rings. Ting-a-ling-a-ling! Hesitate, and then answer it.'

She hesitated – and then, too quickly, she thought, picked up the receiver.

'Hello.'

Her voice was hollow and unreal. The words rang in the empty set like the ineffectualities of a ghost. The absurdities of their requirements appalled her – Did they expect that on an instant's notice she could put herself in the place of this preposterous and unexplained character?

' . . . No . . . no . . . Not yet! Now listen: "John Sumner has just been knocked over by an automobile and instantly killed!" '

Gloria let her baby mouth drop slowly open. Then: 'Now hang up! With a bang!'

She obeyed, clung to the table with her eyes wide and staring. At length she was feeling slightly encouraged and her confidence increased.

'My God!' she cried. Her voice was good, she thought. 'Oh, my God!'

'Now faint.'

She collapsed forward to her knees and throwing her body outwards on the ground lay without breathing.

'All right!' called Mr Debris. 'That's enough, thank you. That's plenty. Get up – that's enough.'

Gloria arose, mustering her dignity and brushing off her skirt.

'Awful!' she remarked with a cool laugh, though her heart was bumping tumultuously. 'Terrible, wasn't it?'

'Did you mind it?' said Mr Debris, smiling blandly. 'Did it seem hard? I can't tell anything about it until I have it run off.'

'Of course not,' she agreed, trying to attach some sort of meaning to his remark – and failing. It was just the sort of thing he would have said had he been trying not to encourage her.

A few moments later she left the studio. Bloeckman had promised that she should hear the result of the test within the next few days. Too proud to force any definite comment she felt a baffling uncertainty and only now when the step had at last been taken did she realise how the possibility of a successful screen career had played in the back of her mind for the past three years. That night she tried to tell over to herself the elements that might decide for or against her. Whether or not she had used enough make-up worried her, and as the part was that of a girl of twenty, she wondered if she had not been just a little too grave. About her acting she was least of all satisfied. Her entrance had been abominable – in fact not until she reached the phone had she displayed a shred of poise – and then the test had been over. If they had only realised! She wished that she could try it again. A mad plan to call up in the morning and ask for a new trial took possession of her, and as suddenly faded. It seemed neither politic nor polite to ask another favour of Bloeckman.

The third day of waiting found her in a highly nervous condition. She had bitten the insides of her mouth until they were raw and smarting, and burnt unbearably when she washed them with Listerine. She had quarrelled so persistently with Anthony that he had left the apartment in a cold fury. But because he was intimidated by her exceptional frigidity, he called up an hour afterwards, apologised and said he was having dinner at the Amsterdam Club, the only one in which he still retained membership.

It was after one o'clock and she had breakfasted at eleven, so, deciding to forgo luncheon, she started for a walk in the Park. At three there would be a mail. She would be back by three.

It was an afternoon of premature spring. Water was drying on the walks and in the Park little girls were gravely wheeling white doll-buggies up and down under the thin trees while behind them followed bored nursery-maids in twos, discussing with each other those tremendous secrets that are peculiar to nursery-maids.

Two o'clock by her little gold watch. She should have a new watch, one made in a platinum oblong and encrusted with diamonds – but those cost even more than squirrel coats and of course they were out of her reach now, like everything else – unless perhaps the right letter was awaiting her . . . in about an hour . . . fifty-eight minutes exactly. Ten to get there left forty-eight . . . forty-seven now . . .

Little girls soberly wheeling their buggies along the damp sunny walks. The nursery-maids chattering in pairs about their inscrutable secrets. Here and there a raggedy man seated upon newspapers spread on a drying bench, related not to the radiant and delightful afternoon but to the dirty snow that slept exhausted in obscure corners, waiting for extermination . . .

Ages later, coming into the dim hall she saw the Martinique elevator boy standing incongruously in the light of the stained-glass window.

'Is there any mail for us?' she asked.

'Up-stays, madame.'

The switchboard squawked abominably and Gloria waited while he ministered to the telephone. She sickened as the elevator groaned its way up – the floors passed like the slow lapse of centuries, each one ominous, accusing, significant. The letter, a white leprous spot, lay upon the dirty tiles of the hall . . .

> My dear Gloria – We had the test run off yesterday afternoon, and Mr Debris seemed to think that for the part he had in mind he needed a younger woman. He said that the acting was not bad, and that there was a small character part supposed to be a very haughty rich widow that he thought you might –

Desolately Gloria raised her glance until it fell out across the area-way. But she found she could not see the opposite wall, for her grey eyes were full of tears. She walked into the bedroom, the letter crinkled tightly in her hand, and sank down upon her knees before the long mirror on the wardrobe floor. This was her twenty-ninth birthday, and the world was melting away before her eyes. She tried to think that it had been the make-up, but her emotions were too profound, too overwhelming for any consolation that the thought conveyed.

She strained to see until she could feel the flesh on her temples pull forward. Yes – the cheeks were ever so faintly thin, the corners of the eyes were lined with tiny wrinkles. The eyes were different. Why, they were different! . . . And then suddenly she knew how tired her eyes were.

'Oh, my pretty face,' she whispered, passionately grieving. 'Oh, my pretty face! Oh, I don't want to live without my pretty face! Oh, what's *happened*?'

Then she slid towards the mirror and, as in the test, sprawled face downwards upon the floor – and lay there sobbing. It was the first awkward movement she had ever made.

Chapter 3

No Matter!

Within another year Anthony and Gloria had become like players who had lost their costumes, lacking the pride to continue on the note of tragedy – so that when Mrs and Miss Hulme of Kansas City cut them dead in the Plaza one evening, it was only that Mrs and Miss Hulme, like most people, abominated mirrors of their atavistic selves.

Their new apartment, for which they paid eighty-five dollars a month, was situated on Claremont Avenue, which is two blocks from the Hudson in the dim hundreds. They had lived there a month when Muriel Kane came to see them late one afternoon.

It was a reproachless twilight on the summer side of spring. Anthony lay upon the lounge looking up One Hundred and Twenty-Seventh Street towards the river, near which he could just see a single patch of vivid green trees that guaranteed the brummagem umbrageousness of Riverside Drive. Across the water were the Palisades, crowned by the ugly framework of the amusement park – yet soon it would be dusk and those same iron cobwebs would be a glory against the heavens, an enchanted palace set over the smooth radiance of a tropical canal.

The streets near the apartment, Anthony had found, were streets where children played – streets a little nicer than those he had been used to pass on his way to Marietta, but of the same general sort, with an occasional hand organ or hurdy-gurdy, and in the cool of the evening many pairs of young girls walking down to the corner drugstore for ice cream soda and dreaming unlimited dreams under the low heavens.

Dusk in the streets now, and children playing, shouting up incoherent ecstatic words that faded out close to the open window – and Muriel, who had come to find Gloria, chattering to him from an opaque gloom over across the room.

'Light the lamp, why don't we?' she suggested. 'It's getting *ghostly* in here.'

With a tired movement he arose and obeyed; the grey window-panes vanished. He stretched himself. He was heavier now, his stomach was a limp weight against his belt; his flesh had softened and expanded. He was thirty-two and his mind was a bleak and disordered wreck.

'Have a little drink, Muriel?'

'Not me, thanks. I don't use it any more. What're you doing these days, Anthony?' she asked curiously.

'Well, I've been pretty busy with this lawsuit,' he answered indifferently. 'It's gone to the Court of Appeals – ought to be settled up one way or another by autumn. There's been some objection as to whether the Court of Appeals has jurisdiction over the matter.'

Muriel made a clicking sound with her tongue and cocked her head on one side.

'Well, you tell 'em! I never heard of anything taking so long.'

'Oh, they all do,' he replied listlessly; 'all will cases. They say it's exceptional to have one settled under four or five years.'

'Oh . . . ' Muriel daringly changed her tack, 'why don't you go to work, you la-azy!'

'At what?' he demanded abruptly.

'Why, at anything, I suppose. You're still a young man.'

'If that's encouragement, I'm much obliged,' he answered dryly – and then with sudden weariness: 'Does it bother you particularly that I don't want to work?'

'It doesn't bother me – but, it does bother a lot of people who claim – '

'Oh, God!' he said brokenly, 'it seems to me that for three years I've heard nothing about myself but wild stories and virtuous admonitions. I'm tired of it. If you don't want to see us, let us alone. I don't bother my former "friends". But I need no charity calls, and no criticism disguised as good advice – ' Then he added apologetically: 'I'm sorry – but really, Muriel, you mustn't talk like a lady slum-worker even if you are visiting the lower middle classes.' He turned his bloodshot eyes on her reproachfully – eyes that had once been a deep, clear blue, that were weak now, strained, and half-ruined from reading when he was drunk.

'Why do you say such awful things?' she protested. 'You talk as if you and Gloria were in the middle classes.'

'Why pretend we're not? I hate people who claim to be great aristocrats when they can't even keep up the appearances of it.'

'Do you think a person has to have money to be aristocratic?'

Muriel . . . the horrified democrat . . . !

'Why, of course. Aristocracy's only an admission that certain traits which we call fine – courage and honour and beauty and all that sort of thing – can best be developed in a favourable environment, where you don't have the warpings of ignorance and necessity.'

Muriel bit her lower lip and waved her head from side to side.

'Well, all *I* say is that if a person comes from a good family they're always nice people. That's the trouble with you and Gloria. You think that just because things aren't going your way right now all your old friends are trying to avoid you. You're too sensitive – '

'As a matter of fact,' said Anthony, 'you know nothing at all about it. With me it's simply a matter of pride, and for once Gloria's reasonable enough to agree that we oughtn't go where we're not wanted. And people don't want us. We're too much the ideal bad examples.'

'Nonsense! You can't park your pessimism in my little sun-parlour. I think you ought to forget all those morbid speculations and go to work.'

'Here I am, thirty-two. Suppose I did start in at some idiotic business. Perhaps in two years I might rise to fifty dollars a week – with luck. That's *if* I could get a job at all; there's an awful lot of unemployment. Well, suppose I made fifty a week. Do you think I'd be any happier? Do you think that if I don't get this money of my grandfather's life will be *endurable*?'

Muriel smiled complacently.

'Well,' she said, 'that may be clever but it isn't common sense.'

A few minutes later Gloria came in seeming to bring with her into the room some dark colour, indeterminate and rare. In a taciturn way she was happy to see Muriel. She greeted Anthony with a casual 'Hi!'

'I've been talking philosophy with your husband,' cried the irrepressible Miss Kane.

'We took up some fundamental concepts,' said Anthony, a faint smile disturbing his pale cheeks, paler still under two days' growth of beard.

Oblivious to his irony Muriel rehashed her contention. When she had done, Gloria said quietly: 'Anthony's right. It's no fun to go around when you have the sense that people are looking at you in a certain way.'

He broke in plaintively: 'Don't you think that when even Maury Noble, who was my best friend, won't come to see us, it's high time to stop calling people up?' Tears were standing in his eyes.

'That was your fault about Maury Noble,' said Gloria coolly.

'It wasn't.'

'It most certainly was.'

Muriel intervened quickly: 'I met a girl who knew Maury, the other day, and she says he doesn't drink any more. He's getting pretty cagey.'

'Doesn't?'

'Practically not at all. He's making *piles* of money. He's sort of changed since the war. He's going to marry a girl in Philadelphia who has millions, Ceci Larrabee – anyhow, that's what *Town Tattle* said.'

'He's thirty-three,' said Anthony, thinking aloud. 'But it's odd to imagine his getting married. I used to think he was so brilliant.'

'He was,' murmured Gloria, 'in a way.'

'But brilliant people don't settle down in business – or do they? Or what do they do? Or what becomes of everybody you used to know and have so much in common with?'

'You drift apart,' suggested Muriel with the appropriate dreamy look.

'They change,' said Gloria. 'All the qualities that they don't use in their daily lives get cobwebbed up.'

'The last thing he said to me,' recollected Anthony, 'was that he was going to work so as to forget that there was nothing worth working for.'

Muriel caught at this quickly.

'That's what *you* ought to do,' she exclaimed triumphantly. 'Of course I shouldn't think anybody would want to work for nothing. But it'd give you something to do. What do you do with yourselves, anyway? Nobody ever sees you at Montmartre or – or anywhere. Are you economising?'

Gloria laughed scornfully, glancing at Anthony from the corners of her eyes.

'Well,' he demanded, 'what are you laughing at?'

'You know what I'm laughing at,' she answered coldly.

'At that case of whiskey?'

'Yes' – she turned to Muriel – 'he paid seventy-five dollars for a case of whiskey yesterday.'

'What if I did? It's cheaper that way than if you get it by the bottle. You needn't pretend that you won't drink any of it.'

'At least I don't drink in the daytime.'

'That's a fine distinction!' he cried, springing to his feet in a weak rage. 'What's more, I'll be damned if you can hurl that at me every few minutes!'

'It's true.'

'It is *not*! And I'm getting sick of this eternal business of criticising me before visitors!' He had worked himself up to such a state that his arms and shoulders were visibly trembling. 'You'd think everything was my fault. You'd think you hadn't encouraged me to spend money – and spent a lot more on yourself than I ever did by a long shot.'

Now Gloria rose to her feet.

'I *won't* let you talk to me that way!'

'All right, then; by heaven, you don't have to!'

In a sort of rush he left the room. The two women heard his steps in the hall and then the front door banged. Gloria sank back into her chair. Her face was lovely in the lamplight, composed, inscrutable.

'Oh – !' cried Muriel in distress. 'Oh, what *is* the matter?'

'Nothing particularly. He's just drunk.'

'Drunk? Why, he's perfectly sober. He talked – '

Gloria shook her head.

'Oh, no, he doesn't show it any more unless he can hardly stand up, and he talks all right until he gets excited. He talks much better than he does when he's sober. But he's been sitting here all day drinking – except for the time it took him to walk to the corner for a newspaper.'

'Oh, how terrible!' Muriel was sincerely moved. Her eyes filled with tears. 'Has this happened much?'

'Drinking, you mean?'

'No, this – leaving you?'

'Oh, yes. Frequently. He'll come in about midnight – and weep and ask me to forgive him.'

'And do you?'

'I don't know. We just go on.'

The two women sat there in the lamplight and looked at each other, each in a different way helpless before this thing. Gloria was still pretty, as pretty as she would ever be again – her cheeks were flushed and she was wearing a new dress that she had bought – imprudently – for fifty dollars. She had hoped she could persuade Anthony to take her out tonight, to a restaurant or even to one of the great, gorgeous moving-picture palaces where there would be a few people to look at her, at whom she could bear to look in turn. She wanted this because she knew her cheeks were flushed and because her dress was new and becomingly fragile. Only very occasionally, now, did they receive any invitations. But she did not tell these things to Muriel.

'Gloria, dear, I wish we could have dinner together, but I promised a man and it's seven-thirty already. I've got to *tear*.'

'Oh, I couldn't, anyway. In the first place I've been ill all day. I couldn't eat a thing.'

After she had walked with Muriel to the door, Gloria came back into the room, turned out the lamp, and leaning her elbows on the window sill looked out at Palisades Park, where the brilliant revolving circle of the Ferris wheel was like a trembling mirror catching the yellow reflection of the moon. The street was quiet now; the children had gone in – over the way she could see a family at dinner. Pointlessly, ridiculously, they rose and walked about the table; seen thus, all that they did appeared incongruous – it was as though they were being jiggled carelessly and to no purpose by invisible overhead wires.

She looked at her watch – it was eight o'clock. She had been pleased for a part of the day – the early afternoon – in walking along that Broadway of Harlem, One Hundred and Twenty-Fifth Street, with her nostrils alert to many odours, and her mind excited by the extraordinary beauty of some Italian children. It affected her curiously – as Fifth Avenue had affected her once, in the days when, with the placid confidence of beauty, she had known that it was all hers, every shop and all it held, every adult toy glittering in a window, all hers for the asking. Here on One Hundred and Twenty-Fifth Street there were Salvation Army bands and spectrum-shawled old ladies on doorsteps and sugary, sticky candy in the grimy hands of shiny-haired children – and the late sun striking down on the sides of the tall tenements. All very rich and racy and savoury, like a dish by a provident French chef that one could not help enjoying, even though one knew that the ingredients were probably leftovers . . .

Gloria shuddered suddenly as a river siren came moaning over the dusky roofs, and leaning back in till the ghostly curtains fell from her shoulder, she turned on the electric lamp. It was growing late. She knew there was some change in her purse, and she considered whether she would go down and have some coffee and rolls where the liberated subway made a roaring cave of Manhattan Street or eat the devilled ham and bread in the kitchen. Her purse decided for her. It contained a nickel and two pennies.

After an hour the silence of the room had grown unbearable, and she found that her eyes were wandering from her magazine to the ceiling, towards which she stared without thought. Suddenly she stood up, hesitated for a moment, biting at her finger – then she went to the pantry, took down a bottle of whiskey from the shelf and poured herself a drink. She filled up the glass with ginger ale, and returning to her chair finished an article in the magazine. It concerned the last revolutionary widow, who, when a young girl, had married an ancient veteran of the Continental Army and who had died in 1906. It seemed strange and oddly romantic to Gloria that she and this woman had been contemporaries.

She turned a page and learned that a candidate for Congress was being accused of atheism by an opponent. Gloria's surprise vanished when she found that the charges were false. The candidate had merely denied the miracle of the loaves and fishes. He admitted, under pressure, that he gave full credence to the stroll upon the water.

Finishing her first drink, Gloria got herself a second. After slipping on a négligé and making herself comfortable on the lounge, she became conscious that she was miserable and that the tears were rolling down her cheeks. She wondered if they were tears of self-pity, and tried resolutely not to cry, but this existence without hope, without happiness, oppressed her, and she kept shaking her head from side to side, her mouth drawn down tremulously in the corners, as though she were denying an assertion made by someone, somewhere. She did not know that this gesture of hers was years older than history, that, for a hundred generations of men, intolerable and persistent grief has offered that gesture, of denial, of protest, of bewilderment, to something more profound, more powerful than the God made in the image of man, and before which that God, did he exist, would be equally impotent. It is a truth set at the heart of tragedy that this force never explains, never answers – this force intangible as air, more definite than death.

RICHARD CARAMEL

Early in the summer Anthony resigned from his last club, the Amsterdam. He had come to visit it hardly twice a year, and the dues were a recurrent burden. He had joined it on his return from Italy because it had been his grandfather's club and his father's, and because it was a club that, given the opportunity, one indisputably joined – but as a matter of fact he had preferred the Harvard Club, largely because of Dick and Maury. However, with the decline of his fortunes, it had seemed an increasingly desirable bauble to cling to . . . It was relinquished, at the last, with some regret . . .

His companions numbered now a curious dozen. Several of them he had met in a place called 'Sammy's', on Forty-Third Street, where, if one knocked on the door and were favourably passed on from behind a grating, one could sit around a great round table drinking fairly good whiskey. It was here that he encountered a man named Parker Allison, who had been exactly the wrong sort of rounder at Harvard, and who was running through a large 'yeast' fortune as rapidly as possible.

Parker Allison's notion of distinction consisted in driving a noisy red-and-yellow racing-car up Broadway with two glittering, hard-eyed girls beside him. He was the sort who dined with two girls rather than with one – his imagination was almost incapable of sustaining a dialogue.

Besides Allison there was Pete Lytell, who wore a grey derby on the side of his head. He always had money and he was customarily cheerful, so Anthony held aimless, long-winded conversation with him through many afternoons of the summer and fall. Lytell, he found, not only talked but reasoned in phrases. His philosophy was a series of them, assimilated here and there through an active, thoughtless life. He had phrases about Socialism – the immemorial ones; he had phrases pertaining to the existence of a personal deity – something about one time when he had been in a railroad accident; and he had phrases about the Irish problem, the sort of woman he respected, and the futility of Prohibition. The only time his conversation ever rose superior to these muddled clauses, with which he interpreted the most rococo happenings in a life that had been more than usually eventful, was when he got down to the detailed discussion of his most animal existence: he knew, to a subtlety, the foods, the liquor, and the women that he preferred.

He was at once the commonest and the most remarkable product of civilisation. He was nine out of ten people that one passes on a city street – and he was a hairless ape with two dozen tricks. He was the hero of a thousand romances of life and art – and he was a virtual moron, performing staidly yet absurdly a series of complicated and infinitely astounding epics over a span of threescore years.

With such men as these two Anthony Patch drank and discussed and drank and argued. He liked them because they knew nothing about him, because they lived in the obvious and had not the faintest conception of the inevitable continuity of life. They sat not before a motion picture with consecutive reels, but at a musty old-fashioned travelogue with all values stark and hence all implications confused. Yet they themselves were not confused, because there was nothing in them to be confused – they changed phrases from month to month as they changed neckties.

Anthony, the courteous, the subtle, the perspicacious, was drunk each day – in Sammy's with these men, in the apartment over a book, some book he knew, and, very rarely, with Gloria, who, in his eyes, had begun to develop the unmistakable outlines of a quarrelsome and unreasonable woman. She was not the Gloria of old, certainly – the

Gloria who, had she been sick, would have preferred to inflict misery upon everyone around her, rather than confess that she needed sympathy or assistance. She was not above whining now; she was not above being sorry for herself. Each night when she prepared for bed she smeared her face with some new unguent which she hoped illogically would give back the glow and freshness to her vanishing beauty. When Anthony was drunk he taunted her about this. When he was sober he was polite to her, on occasions even tender; he seemed to show for short hours a trace of that old quality of understanding too well to blame – that quality which was the best of him and had worked swiftly and ceaselessly towards his ruin.

But he hated to be sober. It made him conscious of the people around him, of that air of struggle, of greedy ambition, of hope more sordid than despair, of incessant passage up or down, which in every metropolis is most in evidence through the unstable middle class. Unable to live with the rich he thought that his next choice would have been to live with the very poor. Anything was better than this cup of perspiration and tears.

The sense of the enormous panorama of life, never strong in Anthony, had become dim almost to extinction. At long intervals now some incident, some gesture of Gloria's, would take his fancy – but the grey veils had come down in earnest upon him. As he grew older those things faded – after that there was wine.

There was a kindliness about intoxication – there was that indescribable gloss and glamour it gave, like the memories of ephemeral and faded evenings. After a few highballs there was magic in the tall glowing Arabian night of the Bush Terminal Building – its summit a peak of sheer grandeur, gold and dreaming against the inaccessible sky. And Wall Street, the crass, the banal – again it was the triumph of gold, a gorgeous sentient spectacle; it was where the great kings kept the money for their wars . . .

. . . The fruit of youth or of the grape, the transitory magic of the brief passage from darkness to darkness – the old illusion that truth and beauty were in some way entwined.

As he stood in front of Delmonico's lighting a cigarette one night he saw two hansoms drawn up close to the curb, waiting for a chance drunken fare. The outmoded cabs were worn and dirty – the cracked patent leather wrinkled like an old man's face, the cushions faded to a brownish lavender; the very horses were ancient and weary, and so were the white-haired men who sat aloft, cracking their whips with a grotesque affectation of gallantry. A relic of vanished gaiety!

Anthony Patch walked away in a sudden fit of depression, pondering the bitterness of such survivals. There was nothing, it seemed, that grew stale so soon as pleasure.

On Forty-Second Street one afternoon he met Richard Caramel for the first time in many months, a prosperous, fattening Richard Caramel, whose face was filling out to match the Bostonian brow.

'Just got in this week from the Coast. Was going to call you up, but I didn't know your new address.'

'We've moved.'

Richard Caramel noticed that Anthony was wearing a soiled shirt, that his cuffs were slightly but perceptibly frayed, that his eyes were set in half-moons the colour of cigar smoke.

'So I gathered,' he said, fixing his friend with his bright-yellow eye. 'But where and how is Gloria? My God, Anthony, I've been hearing the dog-gonedest stories about you two even out in California – and when I get back to New York I find you've sunk absolutely out of sight. Why don't you pull yourself together?'

'Now, listen,' chattered Anthony unsteadily, 'I can't stand a long lecture. We've lost money in a dozen ways, and naturally people have talked – on account of the lawsuit, but the thing's coming to a final decision this winter, surely – '

'You're talking so fast that I can't understand you,' interrupted Dick calmly.

'Well, I've said all I'm going to say,' snapped Anthony. 'Come and see us if you like – or don't!'

With this he turned and started to walk off in the crowd, but Dick overtook him immediately and grasped his arm.

'Say, Anthony, don't fly off the handle so easily! You know Gloria's my cousin, and you're one of my oldest friends, so it's natural for me to be interested when I hear that you're going to the dogs – and taking her with you.'

'I don't want to be preached to.'

'Well, then, all right – How about coming up to my apartment and having a drink? I've just got settled. I've bought three cases of Gordon's gin from a revenue officer.'

As they walked along he continued in a burst of exasperation: 'And how about your grandfather's money – you going to get it?'

'Well,' answered Anthony resentfully, 'that old fool Haight seems hopeful, especially because people are tired of reformers right now – you know it might make a slight difference, for instance, if some judge thought that Adam Patch made it harder for him to get liquor.'

'You can't do without money,' said Dick sententiously. 'Have you tried to write any – lately?'

Anthony shook his head silently.

'That's funny,' said Dick. 'I always thought that you and Maury would write someday, and now he's grown to be a sort of tight-fisted aristocrat, and you're – '

'I'm the bad example.'

'I wonder why?'

'You probably think you know,' suggested Anthony, with an effort at concentration. 'The failure and the success both believe in their hearts that they have accurately balanced points of view, the success because he's succeeded, and the failure because he's failed. The successful man tells his son to profit by his father's good fortune, and the failure tells *his* son to profit by his father's mistakes.'

'I don't agree with you,' said the author of *A Shave-Tail in France*. 'I used to listen to you and Maury when we were young, and I used to be impressed because you were so consistently cynical, but now – well, after all, by God, which of us three has taken to the – to the intellectual life? I don't want to sound vainglorious, but – it's me, and I've always believed that moral values existed, and I always will.'

'Well,' objected Anthony, who was rather enjoying himself, 'even granting that, you know that in practice life never presents problems as clear cut, does it?'

'It does to me. There's nothing I'd violate certain principles for.'

'But how do you know when you're violating them? You have to guess at things just like most people do. You have to apportion the values when you look back. You finish up the portrait then – paint in the details and shadows.'

Dick shook his head with a lofty stubbornness. 'Same old futile cynic,' he said. 'It's just a mode of being sorry for yourself. You don't do anything – so nothing matters.'

'Oh, I'm quite capable of self-pity,' admitted Anthony, 'nor am I claiming that I'm getting as much fun out of life as you are.'

'You say – at least you used to – that happiness is the only thing worth while in life. Do you think you're any happier for being a pessimist?'

Anthony grunted savagely. His pleasure in the conversation began to wane. He was nervous and craving for a drink.

'My golly!' he cried, 'where do you live? I can't keep walking for ever.'

'Your endurance is all mental, eh?' returned Dick sharply. 'Well, I live right here.'

He turned in at the apartment house on Forty-Ninth Street, and a few minutes later they were in a large new room with an open fireplace and four walls lined with books. A coloured butler served them gin rickeys, and an hour vanished politely with the mellow shortening of their drinks and the glow of a light mid-autumn fire.

'The arts are very old,' said Anthony after a while. With a few glasses the tension of his nerves relaxed and he found that he could think again.

'Which art?'

'All of them. Poetry is dying first. It'll be absorbed into prose sooner or later. For instance, the beautiful word, the coloured and glittering word, and the beautiful simile belong in prose now. To get attention poetry has got to strain for the unusual word, the harsh, earthy word that's never been beautiful before. Beauty, as the sum of several beautiful parts, reached its apotheosis in Swinburne. It can't go any further – except in the novel, perhaps.'

Dick interrupted him impatiently: 'You know these new novels make me tired. My God! Everywhere I go some silly girl asks me if I've read *This Side of Paradise*. Are our girls really like that? If it's true to life, which I don't believe, the next generation is going to the dogs. I'm sick of all this shoddy realism. I think there's a place for the romanticist in literature.'

Anthony tried to remember what he had read lately of Richard Caramel's. There was *A Shave-Tail in France*, a novel called *The Land of Strong Men*, and several dozen short stories, which were even worse. It had become the custom among young and clever reviewers to mention Richard Caramel with a smile of scorn. 'Mr' Richard Caramel, they called him. His corpse was dragged obscenely through every literary supplement. He was accused of making a great fortune by writing trash for the movies. As the fashion in books shifted he was becoming almost a byword of contempt.

While Anthony was thinking this, Dick had got to his feet and seemed to be hesitating at an avowal.

'I've gathered quite a few books,' he said suddenly.

'So I see.'

'I've made an exhaustive collection of good American stuff, old and new. I don't mean the usual Longfellow–Whittier thing – in fact, most of it's modern.'

He stepped to one of the walls and, seeing that it was expected of him, Anthony arose and followed.

'Look!'

Under a printed tag *Americana* he displayed six long rows of books, beautifully bound and, obviously, carefully chosen.

'And here are the contemporary novelists.'

Then Anthony saw the joker. Wedged in between Mark Twain and Dreiser were eight strange and inappropriate volumes, the works of Richard Caramel – *The Demon Lover*, true enough . . . but also seven others that were execrably awful, without sincerity or grace.

Unwillingly Anthony glanced at Dick's face and caught a slight uncertainty there.

'I've put my own books in, of course,' said Richard Caramel hastily, 'though one or two of them are uneven – I'm afraid I wrote a little too fast when I had that magazine contract. But I don't believe in false modesty. Of course some of the critics haven't paid so much attention to me since I've been established – but, after all, it's not the critics that count. They're just sheep.'

For the first time in so long that he could scarcely remember, Anthony felt a touch of the old pleasant contempt for his friend. Richard Caramel continued: 'My publishers, you know, have been advertising me as the Thackeray of America – because of my New York novel.'

'Yes,' Anthony managed to muster, 'I suppose there's a good deal in what you say.'

He knew that his contempt was unreasonable. He knew that he would have changed places with Dick unhesitatingly. He himself had tried his best to write with his tongue in his cheek. Ah, well, then – can a man disparage his life-work so readily? . . .

– And that night while Richard Caramel was hard at toil, with great hittings of the wrong keys and screwings up of his weary, unmatched eyes, labouring over his trash far into those cheerless hours when the fire dies down and the head is swimming from the effect of prolonged concentration – Anthony, abominably drunk, was sprawled across the back seat of a taxi on his way to the flat on Claremont Avenue.

As winter approached it seemed that a sort of madness seized upon Anthony. He awoke in the morning so nervous that Gloria could feel him trembling in the bed before he could muster enough vitality to stumble into the pantry for a drink. He was intolerable now except under the influence of liquor, and as he seemed to decay and coarsen under her eyes, Gloria's soul and body shrank away from him; when he stayed out all night, as he did several times, she not only failed to be sorry but even felt a measure of relief. Next day he would be faintly repentant, and would remark in a gruff, hang-dog fashion that he guessed he was drinking a little too much.

For hours at a time he would sit in the great armchair that had been in his apartment, lost in a sort of stupor – even his interest in reading his favourite books seemed to have departed, and though an incessant bickering went on between husband and wife, the one subject upon which they ever really conversed was the progress of the will case. What Gloria hoped in the tenebrous depths of her soul, what she expected that great gift of money to bring about, is difficult to imagine. She was being bent by her environment into a grotesque similitude of a housewife. She who until three years before had never made coffee, prepared sometimes three meals a day. She walked a great deal in the afternoons, and in the evenings she read – books, magazines, anything she found at hand. If now she wished for a child, even a child of the Anthony who sought her bed blind drunk, she neither said so nor gave any show or sign of interest in children. It is doubtful if she could have made it clear to anyone what it was she wanted, or indeed what there was to want – a lonely, lovely woman, thirty now, retrenched behind some impregnable inhibition born and coexistent with her beauty.

One afternoon when the snow was dirty again along Riverside Drive, Gloria, who had been to the grocer's, entered the apartment to find Anthony pacing the floor in a state of aggravated nervousness. The feverish eyes he turned on her were traced with tiny pink lines that reminded her of rivers on a map. For a moment she received the impression that he was suddenly and definitely old.

'Have you any money?' he enquired of her precipitately.

'What? What do you mean?'

'Just what I said. Money! Money! Can't you speak English?'

She paid no attention but brushed by him and into the pantry to put the bacon and eggs in the ice-box. When his drinking had been unusually excessive he was invariably in a whining mood. This time he followed her and, standing in the pantry door, persisted in his question.

'You heard what I said. Have you any money?'

She turned about from the ice-box and faced him.

'Why, Anthony, you must be crazy! You know I haven't any money – except a dollar in change.'

He executed an abrupt about-face and returned to the living-room, where he renewed his pacing. It was evident that he had something portentous on his mind – he quite obviously wanted to be asked what was the matter. Joining him a moment later she sat upon the long lounge and began taking down her hair. It was no longer bobbed, and it had changed in the last year from a rich gold dusted with red to an unresplendent light brown. She had bought some shampoo soap and meant to wash it now; she had considered putting a bottle of peroxide into the rinsing water.

' – Well?' she implied silently.

'That darn bank!' he quavered. 'They've had my account for over ten years – ten *years*. Well, it seems they've got some autocratic rule that you have to keep over five hundred dollars there or they won't carry you. They wrote me a letter a few months ago and told me I'd been running too low. Once I gave out two bum cheques – remember? that night in Reisenweber's? – but I made them good the very next day. Well, I promised old Halloran – he's the manager, the greedy Mick – that I'd watch out. And I thought I was going all right; I kept up the stubs in my cheque-book pretty regular. Well, I went in there today to cash a cheque, and Halloran came up and told me they'd have to close my account. Too many bad cheques, he said, and I never had more than five hundred to my credit – and that only for a day or so at a time. And by God! What do you think he said then?'

'What?'

'He said this was a good time to do it because I didn't have a damn penny in there!'

'You didn't?'

'That's what he told me. Seems I'd given these Bedros people a cheque for sixty for that last case of liquor – and I only had forty-five dollars in the bank. Well, the Bedros people deposited fifteen dollars to my account and drew the whole thing out.'

In her ignorance Gloria conjured up a spectre of imprisonment and disgrace.

'Oh, they won't do anything,' he assured her. 'Bootlegging's too risky a business. They'll send me a bill for fifteen dollars and I'll pay it.'

'Oh.' She considered a moment. ' – Well, we can sell another bond.'

He laughed sarcastically.

'Oh, yes, that's always easy. When the few bonds we have that are paying any interest at all are only worth between fifty and eighty cents on the dollar. We lose about half the bond every time we sell.'

'What else can we do?'

'Oh, we'll sell something – as usual. We've got paper worth eighty thousand dollars at par.' Again he laughed unpleasantly. 'Bring about thirty thousand on the open market.'

'I distrusted those ten per cent investments.'

'The deuce you did!' he said. 'You pretended you did, so you could claw at me if they went to pieces, but you wanted to take a chance as much as I did.'

She was silent for a moment as if considering, then: 'Anthony,' she cried suddenly, 'two hundred a month is worse than nothing. Let's sell all the bonds and put the thirty thousand dollars in the bank – and if we lose the case we can live in Italy for three years, and then just die.' In her excitement as she talked she was aware of a faint flush of sentiment, the first she had felt in many days.

'Three years,' he said nervously, 'three years! You're crazy. Mr Haight'll take more than that if we lose. Do you think he's working for charity?'

'I forgot that.'

' – And here it is Saturday,' he continued, 'and I've only got a dollar and some change, and we've got to live till Monday, when I can get to my broker's . . . And not a drink in the house,' he added as a significant afterthought.

'Can't you call up Dick?'

'I did. His man says he's gone down to Princeton to address a literary club or some such thing. Won't be back till Monday.'

'Well, let's see – Don't you know some friend you might go to?'

'I tried a couple of fellows. Couldn't find anybody in. I wish I'd sold that Keats letter like I started to last week.'

'How about those men you play cards with in that Sammy place?'

'Do you think I'd ask *them*?' His voice rang with righteous horror. Gloria winced. He would rather contemplate her active discomfort than feel his own skin crawl at asking an inappropriate favour. 'I thought of Muriel,' he suggested.

'She's in California.'

'Well, how about some of those men who gave you such a good time while I was in the army? You'd think they might be glad to do a little favour for you.'

She looked at him contemptuously, but he took no notice.

'Or how about your old friend Rachael – or Constance Merriam?'

'Constance Merriam's been dead a year, and I wouldn't ask Rachael.'

'Well, how about that gentleman who was so anxious to help you once that he could hardly restrain himself, Bloeckman?'

'Oh – !' He had hurt her at last, and he was not too obtuse or too careless to perceive it.

'Why not him?' he insisted callously.

'Because – he doesn't like me any more,' she said with difficulty, and then as he did not answer but only regarded her cynically: 'If you want to know why, I'll tell you. A year ago I went to Bloeckman – he's changed his name to Black – and asked him to put me into pictures.'

'You went to Bloeckman?'

'Yes.'

'Why didn't you tell me?' he demanded incredulously, the smile fading from his face.

'Because you were probably off drinking somewhere. He had them give me a test, and they decided that I wasn't young enough for anything except a character part.'

'A character part?'

'The "woman of thirty" sort of thing. I wasn't thirty, and I didn't think I – looked thirty.'

'Why, damn him!' cried Anthony, championing her violently with a curious perverseness of emotion, 'why – '

'Well, that's why I can't go to him.'

'Why, the insolence!' insisted Anthony nervously, 'the insolence!'

'Anthony, that doesn't matter now; the thing is we've got to live over Sunday and there's nothing in the house but a loaf of bread and a half-pound of bacon and two eggs for breakfast.' She handed him the contents of her purse. 'There's seventy, eighty, a dollar fifteen. With what you have that makes about two and a half altogether, doesn't it? Anthony, we can get along on that. We can buy lots of food with that – more than we can possibly eat.'

Jingling the change in his hand he shook his head. 'No. I've got to have a drink. I'm so darn nervous that I'm shivering.' A thought struck him. 'Perhaps Sammy'd cash a check. And then Monday I could rush down to the bank with the money.'

'But they've closed your account.'

'That's right, that's right – I'd forgotten. I'll tell you what: I'll go down to Sammy's and I'll find somebody there who'll lend me something. I hate like the devil to ask them, though . . . ' He snapped his fingers suddenly. 'I know what I'll do. I'll hock my watch. I can get twenty dollars on it, and get it back Monday for sixty cents extra. It's been hocked before – when I was at Cambridge.'

He had put on his overcoat, and with a brief goodbye he started down the hall towards the outer door.

Gloria got to her feet. It had suddenly occurred to her where he would probably go first.

'Anthony!' she called after him, 'hadn't you better leave two dollars with me? You'll only need car-fare.'

The outer door slammed – he had pretended not to hear her. She stood for a moment looking after him; then she went into the bathroom among her tragic unguents and began preparations for washing her hair.

Down at Sammy's he found Parker Allison and Pete Lytell sitting alone at a table, drinking whiskey sours. It was just after six o'clock, and Sammy, or Samuele Bendiri, as he had been christened, was sweeping an accumulation of cigarette butts and broken glass into a corner.

'Hi, Tony!' called Parker Allison to Anthony. Sometimes he addressed him as Tony, at other times it was Dan. To him all Anthonys must sail under one of these diminutives.

'Sit down. What'll you have?'

On the subway Anthony had counted his money and found that he had almost four dollars. He could pay for two rounds at fifty cents a drink – which meant that he would have six drinks. Then he would go over to Sixth Avenue and get twenty dollars and a pawn ticket in exchange for his watch.

'Well, rough-necks,' he said jovially, 'how's the life of crime?'

'Pretty good,' said Allison. He winked at Pete Lytell. 'Too bad you're a married man. We've got some pretty good stuff lined up for about eleven o'clock, when the shows let out. Oh, boy! Yes, sir – too bad he's married – isn't it, Pete?'

‘ ’Sa shame.’

At half-past seven, when they had completed the six rounds, Anthony found that his intentions were giving audience to his desires. He was happy and cheerful now – thoroughly enjoying himself. It seemed to him that the story which Pete had just finished telling was unusually and profoundly humorous – and he decided, as he did every day at about this point, that they were ‘damn good fellows, by golly!’ who would do a lot more for him than anyone else he knew. The pawnshops would remain open until late Saturday nights, and he felt that if he took just one more drink he would attain a gorgeous rose-coloured exhilaration.

Artfully, he fished in his vest pockets, brought up his two quarters, and stared at them as though in surprise.

‘Well, I’ll be darned,’ he protested in an aggrieved tone, ‘here I’ve come out without my pocketbook.’

‘Need some cash?’ asked Lytell easily.

‘I left my money on the dresser at home. And I wanted to buy you another drink.’

‘Oh – knock it.’ Lytell waved the suggestion away disparagingly. ‘I guess we can blow a good fella to all the drinks he wants. What’ll you have – same?’

‘I tell you,’ suggested Parker Allison, ‘suppose we send Sammy across the street for some sandwiches and eat dinner here.’

The other two agreed.

‘Good idea.’

‘Hey, Sammy, wantcha do somep’m for us . . . ’

Just after nine o’clock Anthony staggered to his feet and, bidding them a thick good-night, walked unsteadily to the door, handing Sammy one of his two quarters as he passed out. Once in the street he hesitated uncertainly and then started in the direction of Sixth Avenue, where he remembered frequently to have passed several loan offices. He went by a news-stand and two drugstores – and then he realised that he was standing in front of the place which he sought, and that it was shut and barred. Unperturbed he continued; another one, half a block down, was also closed – so were two more across the street, and a fifth in the square below. Seeing a faint light in the last one, he began to knock on the glass door; he desisted only when a watchman appeared in the back of the shop and motioned him angrily to move on. With growing discouragement, with growing befuddlement, he crossed the street and walked back towards Forty-Third. On the corner near Sammy's he paused undecided – if he went back to the apartment, as he felt his body required, he would lay himself open to bitter reproach; yet, now that the pawnshops were closed, he had no notion where to get the money. He decided finally that he might ask Parker Allison, after all – but he approached Sammy's only to find the door locked and the lights out. He looked at his watch: nine-thirty. He began walking.

Ten minutes later he stopped aimlessly at the corner of Forty-Third Street and Madison Avenue, diagonally across from the bright but nearly deserted entrance to the Biltmore Hotel. Here he stood for a moment, and then sat down heavily on a damp board amid some débris of construction work. He rested there for almost half an hour, his mind a shifting pattern of surface thoughts, chiefest among which were that he must obtain some money and get home before he became too sodden to find his way.

Then, glancing over towards the Biltmore, he saw a man standing directly under the overhead glow of the porte-cochère lamps beside a woman in an ermine coat. As Anthony watched, the couple moved forward and signalled to a taxi. Anthony perceived by the infallible identification that lurks in the walk of a friend that it was Maury Noble.

He rose to his feet.

'Maury!' he shouted.

Maury looked in his direction, then turned back to the girl just as the taxi came up into place. With the chaotic idea of borrowing ten dollars, Anthony began to run as fast as he could across Madison Avenue and along Forty-Third Street.

As he came up Maury was standing beside the yawning door of the taxicab. His companion turned and looked curiously at Anthony.

'Hello, Maury!' he said, holding out his hand. 'How are you?'

'Fine, thank you.'

Their hands dropped and Anthony hesitated. Maury made no move to introduce him, but only stood there regarding him with an inscrutable feline silence.

'I wanted to see you – ' began Anthony uncertainly. He did not feel that he could ask for a loan with the girl not four feet away, so he broke off and made a perceptible motion of his head as if to beckon Maury to one side.

'I'm in rather a big hurry, Anthony.'

'I know – but can you, can you – ' Again he hesitated.

'I'll see you some other time,' said Maury.

'It's important.'

'I'm sorry, Anthony.'

Before Anthony could make up his mind to blurt out his request, Maury had turned coolly to the girl, helped her into the car and, with a polite 'good-evening', stepped in after her. As he nodded from the window it seemed to Anthony that his expression had not changed by a shade or a hair. Then with a fretful clatter the taxi moved off, and Anthony was left standing there alone under the lights.

Anthony went on into the Biltmore, for no reason in particular except that the entrance was at hand, and ascending the wide stair found a seat in an alcove. He was furiously aware that he had been snubbed; he was as hurt and angry as it was possible for him to be when in that condition. Nevertheless, he was stubbornly preoccupied with the necessity of obtaining some money before he went home, and once again he told over on his fingers the acquaintances he might conceivably call on in this emergency. He thought, eventually, that he might approach Mr Howland, his broker, at his home.

After a long wait he found that Mr Howland was out. He returned to the operator, leaning over her desk and fingering his quarter as though loath to leave unsatisfied.

'Call Mr Bloeckman,' he said suddenly. His own words surprised him. The name had come from some crossing of two suggestions in his mind.

'What's the number, please?'

Scarcely conscious of what he did, Anthony looked up Joseph Bloeckman in the telephone directory. He could find no such person, and was about to close the book when it flashed into his mind that Gloria had mentioned a change of name. It was the matter of a minute to find Joseph Black – then he waited in the booth while central called the number.

'Hello-o. Mr Bloeckman – I mean Mr Black in?'

'No, he's out this evening. Is there any message?' The intonation was cockney; it reminded him of the rich vocal deferences of Bounds.

'Where is he?'

'Why, ah, who is this, please, sir?'

'This Mr Patch. Matter of vi'al importance.'

'Why, he's with a party at the Boul' Mich', sir.'

'Thanks.'

Anthony got his five cents change and started for the Boul' Mich', a popular dancing resort on Forty-Fifth Street. It was nearly ten but the streets were dark and sparsely peopled until the theatres should eject their spawn an hour later. Anthony knew the Boul' Mich', for he had been there with Gloria during the year before, and he remembered the existence of a rule that patrons must be in evening dress. Well, he would not go upstairs – he would send a boy up for Bloeckman and wait for him in the lower hall. For a moment he did not doubt that the whole project was entirely natural and graceful. To his distorted imagination Bloeckman had become simply one of his old friends.

The entrance hall of the Boul' Mich' was warm. There were high yellow lights over a thick green carpet, from the centre of which a white stairway rose to the dancing floor.

Anthony spoke to the hallboy: 'I want to see Mr Bloeckman – Mr Black,' he said. 'He's upstairs – have him paged.'

The boy shook his head.

' 'Sagainsa rules to have him paged. You know what table he's at?'

'No. But I've got see him.'

'Wait an' I'll getcha waiter.'

After a short interval a head waiter appeared, bearing a card on which were charted the table reservations. He darted a cynical look at Anthony – which, however, failed of its target. Together they bent over the cardboard and found the table without difficulty – a party of eight, Mr Black's own.

'Tell him Mr Patch. Very, very important.'

Again he waited, leaning against the bannister and listening to the confused harmonies of 'Jazz-Mad' which came floating down the stairs. A check-girl near him was singing:

> 'Out in – the shimmee sanitarium
> The jazz-mad nuts reside.
> Out in – the shimmee sanitarium
> I left my blushing bride.
> She went and shook herself insane,
> So let her shiver back again – '

Then he saw Bloeckman descending the staircase, and took a step forward to meet him and shake hands.

'You wanted to see me?' said the older man coolly.

'Yes,' answered Anthony, nodding, 'personal matter. Can you jus' step over here?'

Regarding him narrowly Bloeckman followed Anthony to a half

bend made by the staircase where they were beyond observation or earshot of anyone entering or leaving the restaurant.

'Well?' he enquired.

'Wanted talk to you.'

'What about?'

Anthony only laughed – a silly laugh; he intended it to sound casual.

'What do you want to talk to me about?' repeated Bloeckman.

'Wha's hurry, old man?' He tried to lay his hand in a friendly gesture upon Bloeckman's shoulder, but the latter drew away slightly. 'How've been?'

'Very well, thanks . . . See here, Mr Patch, I've got a party upstairs. They'll think it's rude if I stay away too long. What was it you wanted to see me about?'

For the second time that evening Anthony's mind made an abrupt jump, and what he said was not at all what he had intended to say.

'Un'erstand you kep' my wife out of the movies.'

'What?' Bloeckman's ruddy face darkened in parallel planes of shadows.

'You heard me.'

'Look here, Mr Patch,' said Bloeckman, evenly and without changing his expression, 'you're drunk. You're disgustingly and insultingly drunk.'

'Not too drunk talk to you,' insisted Anthony with a leer. 'Firs' place, my wife wants nothin' whatever do with you. Never did. Un'erstand me?'

'Be quiet!' said the older man angrily. 'I should think you'd respect your wife enough not to bring her into the conversation under these circumstances.'

'Never you min' how I expect my wife. One thing – you leave her alone. You go to hell!'

'See here – I think you're a little crazy!' exclaimed Bloeckman. He took two paces forward as though to pass by, but Anthony stepped in his way.

'Not so fas', you goddam Jew.'

For a moment they stood regarding each other, Anthony swaying gently from side to side, Bloeckman almost trembling with fury.

'Be careful!' he cried in a strained voice.

Anthony might have remembered then a certain look Bloeckman had given him in the Biltmore Hotel years before. But he remembered nothing, nothing –

'I'll say it again, you god – '

Then Bloeckman struck out, with all the strength in the arm of a well-conditioned man of forty-five, struck out and caught Anthony squarely in the mouth. Anthony cracked up against the staircase, recovered himself and made a wild drunken swing at his opponent, but Bloeckman, who took exercise every day and knew something of sparring, blocked it with ease and struck him twice in the face with two swift smashing jabs. Anthony gave a little grunt and toppled over on to the green plush carpet, finding, as he fell, that his mouth was full of blood and seemed oddly loose in front. He struggled to his feet, panting and spitting, and then as he started towards Bloeckman, who stood a few feet away, his fists clenched but not up, two waiters who had appeared from nowhere seized his arms and held him, helpless. In back of them a dozen people had miraculously gathered.

'I'll kill him,' cried Anthony, pitching and straining from side to side. 'Let me kill – '

'Throw him out!' ordered Bloeckman excitedly, just as a small man with a pockmarked face pushed his way hurriedly through the spectators.

'Any trouble, Mr Black?'

'This bum tried to blackmail me!' said Bloeckman, and then, his voice rising to a faintly shrill note of pride: 'He got what was coming to him!'

The little man turned to a waiter.

'Call a policeman!' he commanded.

'Oh, no,' said Bloeckman quickly. 'I can't be bothered. Just throw him out in the street . . . Ugh! What an outrage!' He turned and with conscious dignity walked towards the washroom just as six brawny hands seized upon Anthony and dragged him towards the door. The 'bum' was propelled violently to the sidewalk, where he landed on his hands and knees with a grotesque slapping sound and rolled over slowly on to his side.

The shock stunned him. He lay there for a moment in acute distributed pain. Then his discomfort became centralised in his stomach, and he regained consciousness to discover that a large foot was prodding him.

'You've got to move on, y' bum! Move on!'

It was the bulky doorman speaking. A town car had stopped at the curb and its occupants had disembarked – that is, two of the women were standing on the running-board, waiting in offended delicacy until this obscene obstacle should be removed from their path.

'Move on! Or else I'll *throw* y'on!'

'Here – I'll get him.'

This was a new voice; Anthony imagined that it was somehow more tolerant, better disposed than the first. Again arms were about him, half lifting, half dragging him into a welcome shadow four doors up the street and propping him against the stone front of a millinery shop.

'Much obliged,' muttered Anthony feebly. Someone pushed his soft hat down upon his head and he winced.

'Just sit still, buddy, and you'll feel better. Those guys sure give you a bump.'

'I'm going back and kill that dirty – ' He tried to get to his feet but collapsed backwards against the wall.

'You can't do nothin' now,' came the voice. 'Get 'em some other time. I'm tellin' you straight, ain't I? I'm helpin' you.'

Anthony nodded.

'An' you better go home. You dropped a tooth tonight, buddy. You know that?'

Anthony explored his mouth with his tongue, verifying the statement. Then with an effort he raised his hand and located the gap.

'I'm agoin' to get you home, friend. Whereabouts do you live – '

'Oh, by God! By God!' interrupted Anthony, clenching his fists passionately. 'I'll show the dirty bunch. You help me show 'em and I'll fix it with you. My grandfather's Adam Patch, of Tarrytown – '

'Who?'

'Adam Patch, by God!'

'You wanna go all the way to Tarrytown?'

'No.'

'Well, you tell me where to go, friend, and I'll get a cab.'

Anthony made out that his Samaritan was a short, broad-shouldered individual, somewhat the worse for wear.

'Where d'you live, hey?'

Sodden and shaken as he was, Anthony felt that his address would be poor collateral for his wild boast about his grandfather.

'Get me a cab,' he commanded, feeling in his pockets.

A taxi drove up. Again Anthony essayed to rise, but his ankle swung loose, as though it were in two sections. The Samaritan must needs help him in – and climb in after him.

'See here, fella,' said he, 'you're soused and you're bunged up, and you won't be able to get in your house 'less somebody carries you in, so I'm going with you, and I know you'll make it all right with me. Where d'you live?'

With some reluctance Anthony gave his address. Then, as the cab moved off, he leaned his head against the man's shoulder and went into a shadowy, painful torpor. When he awoke, the man had lifted him from the cab in front of the apartment on Claremont Avenue and was trying to set him on his feet.

'Can y' walk?'

'Yes – sort of. You better not come in with me.' Again he felt helplessly in his pockets. 'Say,' he continued, apologetically, swaying dangerously on his feet, 'I'm afraid I haven't got a cent.'

'Huh?'

'I'm cleaned out.'

'Sa-a-ay! Didn't I hear you promise you'd fix it with me? Who's goin' to pay the taxi bill?' He turned to the driver for confirmation. 'Didn't you hear him say he'd fix it? All that about his grandfather?'

'Matter of fact,' muttered Anthony imprudently, 'it was you did all the talking; however, if you come round, tomorrow – '

At this point the taxi-driver leaned from his cab and said ferociously: 'Ah, poke him one, the dirty cheapskate. If he wasn't a bum they wouldn'ta throwed him out.'

In answer to this suggestion the fist of the Samaritan shot out like a battering-ram and sent Anthony crashing down against the stone steps of the apartment-house, where he lay without movement, while the tall buildings rocked to and fro above him . . .

After a long while he awoke and was conscious that it had grown much colder. He tried to move himself but his muscles refused to function. He was curiously anxious to know the time, but he reached for his watch only to find the pocket empty. Involuntarily his lips formed an immemorial phrase: 'What a night!'

Strangely enough, he was almost sober. Without moving his head he looked up to where the moon was anchored in mid-sky, shedding light down into Claremont Avenue as into the bottom of a deep and uncharted abyss. There was no sign or sound of life save for the continuous buzzing in his own ears, but after a moment Anthony himself broke the silence with a distinct and peculiar murmur. It was the sound that he had consistently attempted to make back there in the Boul' Mich', when he had been face to face with Bloeckman – the unmistakable sound of ironic laughter. And on his torn and bleeding lips it was like a pitiful retching of the soul.

Three weeks later the trial came to an end. The seemingly endless spool of legal red tape having unrolled over a period of four and a half years, suddenly snapped off. Anthony and Gloria and, on the other side, Edward Shuttleworth and a platoon of beneficiaries testified and lied and ill-behaved generally in varying degrees of greed and desperation. Anthony awoke one morning in March realising that the verdict was to be given at four that afternoon, and at the thought he got up out of his bed and began to dress. With his extreme nervousness there was mingled an unjustified optimism as to the outcome. He believed that the decision of the lower court would be reversed, if only because of the reaction, due to excessive Prohibition, that had recently set in against reforms and reformers. He counted more on the personal attacks that they had levelled at Shuttleworth than on the more sheerly legal aspects of the proceedings.

Dressed, he poured himself a drink of whiskey and then went into Gloria's room, where he found her already wide awake. She had been in bed for a week, humouring herself, Anthony fancied, though the doctor had said that she had best not be disturbed.

'Good-morning,' she murmured, without smiling. Her eyes seemed unusually large and dark.

'How do you feel?' he asked grudgingly. 'Better?'

'Yes.'

'Much?'

'Yes.'

'Do you feel well enough to go down to court with me this afternoon?'

She nodded.

'Yes. I want to. Dick said yesterday that if the weather was nice he was coming up in his car to take me for a ride in Central Park – and look, the room's all full of sunshine.'

Anthony glanced mechanically out of the window and then sat down upon the bed.

'God, I'm nervous!' he exclaimed.

'Please don't sit there,' she said quickly.

'Why not?'

'You smell of whiskey. I can't stand it.'

He got up absent-mindedly and left the room. A little later she called to him and he went out and brought her some potato salad and cold chicken from the delicatessen.

At two o'clock Richard Caramel's car arrived at the door and, when he phoned up, Anthony took Gloria down in the elevator and walked with her to the curb.

She told her cousin that it was sweet of him to take her riding. 'Don't be simple,' Dick replied disparagingly. 'It's nothing.'

But he did not mean that it was nothing and this was a curious thing. Richard Caramel had forgiven many people for many offences. But he had never forgiven his cousin, Gloria Gilbert, for a statement she had made just prior to her wedding, seven years before. She had said that she did not intend to read his book.

Richard Caramel remembered this – he had remembered it well for seven years.

'What time will I expect you back?' asked Anthony.

'We won't come back,' she answered, 'we'll meet you down there at four.'

'All right,' he muttered, 'I'll meet you.'

Upstairs he found a letter waiting for him. It was a mimeographed notice urging 'the boys' in condescendingly colloquial language to pay the dues of the American Legion. He threw it impatiently into the waste-basket and sat down with his elbows on the window sill, looking down blindly into the sunny street.

Italy – if the verdict was in their favour it meant Italy. The word had become a sort of talisman to him, a land where the intolerable anxieties of life would fall away like an old garment. They would go to the watering-places first and among the bright and colourful crowds forget the grey appendages of despair. Marvellously renewed, he would walk again in the Piazza di Spanga at twilight, moving in that drifting flotsam of dark women and ragged beggars, of austere, barefooted friars. The thought of Italian women stirred him faintly – when his purse hung heavy again even romance might fly back to perch upon it – the romance of blue canals in Venice, of the golden green hills of Fiesole after rain, and of women, women who changed, dissolved, melted into other women and receded from his life, but who were always beautiful and always young.

But it seemed to him that there should be a difference in his attitude. All the distress that he had ever known, the sorrow and the pain, had been because of women. It was something that in different ways they did to him, unconsciously, almost casually – perhaps finding him tender-minded and afraid, they killed the things in him that menaced their absolute sway.

Turning about from the window he faced his reflection in the mirror, contemplating dejectedly the wan, pasty face, the eyes with their criss-cross of lines like shreds of dried blood, the stooped and flabby figure whose very sag was a document in lethargy. He was thirty-three – he looked forty. Well, things would be different.

The doorbell rang abruptly and he started as though he had been dealt a blow. Recovering himself, he went into the hall and opened the outer door. It was Dot.

THE ENCOUNTER

He retreated before her into the living-room, comprehending only a word here and there in the slow flood of sentences that poured from her steadily, one after the other, in a persistent monotone. She was decently and shabbily dressed – a somehow pitiable little hat adorned with pink and blue flowers covered and hid her dark hair. He gathered from her words that several days before she had seen an item in the paper concerning the lawsuit, and had obtained his address from the clerk of the Appellate Division. She had called up the apartment and had been told that Anthony was out by a woman to whom she had refused to give her name.

In the living-room he stood by the door regarding her with a sort of stupefied horror as she rattled on . . . His predominant sensation was that all the civilisation and convention around him was curiously unreal . . . She was in a milliner's shop on Sixth Avenue, she said. It was a lonesome life. She had been sick for a long while after he left for Camp Mills; her mother had come down and taken her home again to Carolina . . . She had come to New York with the idea of finding Anthony.

She was appallingly in earnest. Her violet eyes were red with tears; her soft intonation was ragged with little gasping sobs.

That was all. She had never changed. She wanted him now, and if she couldn't have him she must die . . .

'You'll have to get out,' he said at length, speaking with tortuous intensity. 'Haven't I enough to worry me now without you coming here? My *God*! You'll have to get *out*!'

Sobbing, she sat down in a chair.

'I love you,' she cried; 'I don't care what you say to me! I love you.'

'I don't care!' he almost shrieked; 'get out – oh, get out! Haven't you done me harm enough? Haven't – you – done – *enough*?'

'Hit me!' she implored him – wildly, stupidly. 'Oh, hit me, and I'll kiss the hand you hit me with!'

His voice rose until it was pitched almost at a scream. 'I'll kill you!' he cried. 'If you don't get out I'll kill you, I'll kill you!'

There was madness in his eyes now, but, unintimidated, Dot rose and took a step towards him. 'Anthony! Anthony! – '

He made a little clicking sound with his teeth and drew back as though to spring at her – then, changing his purpose, he looked wildly about him on the floor and wall.

'I'll kill you!' he was muttering in short, broken gasps. 'I'll *kill* you!' He seemed to bite at the word as though to force it into materialisation. Alarmed at last she made no further movement forward, but meeting his frantic eyes took a step back towards the door. Anthony began to race here and there on his side of the room, still giving out his single cursing cry. Then he found what he had been seeking – a stiff oaken chair that stood beside the table. Uttering a harsh, broken shout, he seized it, swung it above his head and let it go with all his raging strength straight at the white, frightened face across the room . . . then a thick, impenetrable darkness came down upon him and blotted out thought, rage and madness together – with almost a tangible snapping sound the face of the world changed before his eyes . . .

Gloria and Dick came in at five and called his name. There was no answer – they went into the living-room and found a chair with its back smashed lying in the doorway, and they noticed that all about the room there was a sort of disorder – the rugs had slid, the pictures and bric-à-brac were upset upon the centre table. The air was sickly sweet with cheap perfume.

They found Anthony sitting in a patch of sunshine on the floor of his bedroom. Before him, open, were spread his three big stamp-books, and when they entered he was running his hands through a great pile of stamps that he had dumped from the back of one of them. Looking up and seeing Dick and Gloria he put his head critically on one side and motioned them back.

'Anthony!' cried Gloria tensely, 'we've won! They reversed the decision!'

'Don't come in,' he murmured wanly, 'you'll muss them. I'm sorting, and I know you'll step in them. Everything always gets mussed.'

'What are you doing?' demanded Dick in astonishment. 'Going back to childhood? Don't you realise you've won the suit? They've reversed the decision of the lower courts. You're worth thirty millions!'

Anthony only looked at him reproachfully.

'Shut the door when you go out.' He spoke like a pert child.

With a faint horror dawning in her eyes, Gloria gazed at him –

'Anthony!' she cried, 'what is it? What's the matter? Why didn't you come – why, what *is* it?'

'See here,' said Anthony softly, 'you two get out – now, both of you. Or else I'll tell my grandfather.'

He held up a handful of stamps and let them come drifting down about him like leaves, varicoloured and bright, turning and fluttering gaudily upon the sunny air: stamps of England and Ecuador, Venezuela and Spain – Italy . . .

TOGETHER WITH THE SPARROWS

That exquisite heavenly irony which has tabulated the demise of so many generations of sparrows doubtless records the subtlest verbal inflections of the passengers of such ships as the *Berengaria*. And doubtless it was listening when the young man in the plaid cap crossed the deck quickly and spoke to the pretty girl in yellow.

'That's him,' he said, pointing to a bundled figure seated in a wheelchair near the rail. 'That's Anthony Patch. First time he's been on deck.'

'Oh – that's him?'

'Yes. He's been a little crazy, they say, ever since he got his money, four or five months ago. You see, the other fellow, Shuttleworth, the religious fellow, the one that didn't get the money, he locked himself up in a room in a hotel and shot himself – '

'Oh, he *did* – '

'But I guess Anthony Patch don't care much. He got his thirty million. And he's got his private physician along in case he doesn't feel just right about it. Has *she* been on deck?' he asked.

The pretty girl in yellow looked around cautiously.

'She was here a minute ago. She had on a Russian-sable coat that must have cost a small fortune.' She frowned and then added decisively: 'I can't stand her, you know. She seems sort of – sort of dyed and *unclean*, if you know what I mean. Some people just have that look about them whether they are or not.'

'Sure, I know,' agreed the man with the plaid cap. 'She's not bad-looking, though.' He paused. 'Wonder what he's thinking about – his money, I guess, or maybe he's got remorse about that fellow Shuttleworth.'

'Probably . . . '

But the man in the plaid cap was quite wrong. Anthony Patch, sitting near the rail and looking out at the sea, was not thinking of his money, for he had seldom in his life been really preoccupied with material vainglory, nor of Edward Shuttleworth, for it is best to look on the sunny side of these things. No – he was concerned with a series of reminiscences, much as a general might look back upon a successful campaign and analyse his victories. He was thinking of the hardships, the insufferable tribulations he had gone through. They had tried to penalise him for the mistakes of his youth. He had been exposed to ruthless misery, his very craving for romance had been punished, his friends had deserted him – even Gloria had turned against him. He had been alone, alone – facing it all.

Only a few months before people had been urging him to give in, to submit to mediocrity, to go to work. But he had known that he was justified in his way of life – and he had stuck it out staunchly. Why, the very friends who had been most unkind had come to respect him, to know he had been right all along. Had not the Lacys and the Merediths and the Cartwright-Smiths called on Gloria and him at the Ritz-Carlton just a week before they sailed?

Great tears stood in his eyes, and his voice was tremulous as he whispered to himself.

'I showed them,' he was saying. 'It was a hard fight, but I didn't give up and I came through!'

THE GREAT GATSBY

The Great Gatsby

A novel first published in 1925

Then wear the golden hat, if that will move her;
If you can bounce high, bounce for her too,
Till she cry, 'Lover, gold-hatted, high-bouncing lover,
        I must have you!'

THOMAS PARKE D'INVILLIERS

Chapter 1

In my younger and more vulnerable years my father gave me some advice that I've been turning over in my mind ever since.

'Whenever you feel like criticising anyone,' he told me, 'just remember that all the people in this world haven't had the advantages that you've had.'

He didn't say any more, but we've always been unusually communicative in a reserved way, and I understood that he meant a great deal more than that. In consequence, I'm inclined to reserve all judgements, a habit that has opened up many curious natures to me and also made me the victim of not a few veteran bores. The abnormal mind is quick to detect and attach itself to this quality when it appears in a normal person, and so it came about that in college I was unjustly accused of being a politician, because I was privy to the secret griefs of wild, unknown men. Most of the confidences were unsought – frequently I have feigned sleep, preoccupation or a hostile levity when I realised by some unmistakable sign that an intimate revelation was quivering on the horizon; for the intimate revelations of young men, or at least the terms in which they express them, are usually plagiaristic and marred by obvious suppressions. Reserving judgements is a matter of infinite hope. I am still a little afraid of missing something if I forget that, as my father snobbishly suggested, and I snobbishly repeat, a sense of the fundamental decencies is parcelled out unequally at birth.

And, after boasting this way of my tolerance, I come to the admission that it has a limit. Conduct may be founded on the hard rock or the wet marshes, but after a certain point I don't care what it's founded on. When I came back from the East last autumn I felt that I wanted the world to be in uniform and at a sort of moral attention for ever; I wanted no more riotous excursions with privileged glimpses into the human heart. Only Gatsby, the man who gives his name to this book, was exempt from my reaction – Gatsby, who represented everything for which I have an unaffected scorn. If personality is an unbroken series of successful gestures, then there was something gorgeous about him, some heightened sensitivity to the promises of life, as if he were related to one of those intricate machines that register earthquakes ten thousand miles away. This responsiveness had nothing to do with that flabby impressionability which is dignified under the name of the 'creative temperament' – it was an extraordinary gift for hope, a romantic readiness such as I have never found in any other person and which it is not likely I shall ever find again. No – Gatsby turned out all right at the end; it is what preyed on Gatsby, what foul dust floated in the wake of his dreams that temporarily closed out my interest in the abortive sorrows and short-winded elations of men.

My family have been prominent, well-to-do people in this Middle Western city for three generations. The Carraways are something of a clan, and we have a tradition that we're descended from the Dukes of Buccleuch, but the actual founder of my line was my grandfather's brother, who came here in fifty-one, sent a substitute to the Civil War, and started the wholesale hardware business that my father carries on today.

I never saw this great-uncle, but I'm supposed to look like him – with special reference to the rather hard-boiled painting that hangs in father's office. I graduated from New Haven in 1915, just a quarter of a century after my father, and a little later I participated in that delayed Teutonic migration known as the Great War. I enjoyed the counter raid so thoroughly that I came back restless. Instead of being the warm centre of the world, the Middle West now seemed like the ragged edge of the universe – so I decided to go East and learn the bond business. Everybody I knew was in the bond business, so I supposed it could support one more single man. All my aunts and uncles talked it over as if they were choosing a prep school for me, and finally said, 'Why – ye-es,' with very grave, hesitant faces. Father agreed to finance me for a year, and after various delays I came East, permanently, I thought, in the spring of 'twenty-two.

The practical thing was to find rooms in the city, but it was a warm season, and I had just left a country of wide lawns and friendly trees, so when a young man at the office suggested that we take a house together in a commuting town, it sounded like a great idea. He found the house, a weather-beaten cardboard bungalow at eighty a month, but at the last minute the firm ordered him to Washington, and I went out to the country alone. I had a dog – at least I had him for a few days until he ran away – and an old Dodge and a Finnish woman, who made my bed and cooked breakfast and muttered Finnish wisdom to herself over the electric stove.

It was lonely for a day or so until one morning some man, more recently arrived than I, stopped me on the road.

'How do you get to West Egg village?' he asked helplessly.

I told him. And as I walked on I was lonely no longer. I was a guide, a pathfinder, an original settler. He had casually conferred on me the freedom of the neighbourhood.

And so with the sunshine and the great bursts of leaves growing on the trees, just as things grow in fast movies, I had that familiar conviction that life was beginning over again with the summer.

There was so much to read, for one thing, and so much fine health to be pulled down out of the young breath-giving air. I bought a dozen volumes on banking and credit and investment securities, and they stood on my shelf in red and gold like new money from the mint, promising to unfold the shining secrets that only Midas and Morgan and Maecenas knew. And I had the high intention of reading many other books besides. I was rather literary in college – one year I wrote a series of very solemn and obvious editorials for the *Yale News* – and now I was going to bring back all such things into my life and become again that most limited of all specialists, the 'well-rounded man'. This isn't just an epigram – life is much more successfully looked at from a single window, after all.

It was a matter of chance that I should have rented a house in one of the strangest communities in North America. It was on that slender riotous island which extends itself due east of New York – and where there are, among other natural curiosities, two unusual formations of land. Twenty miles from the city a pair of enormous eggs, identical in contour and separated only by a courtesy bay, jut out into the most domesticated body of salt water in the Western hemisphere, the great wet barnyard of Long Island Sound. They are not perfect ovals – like the egg in the Columbus story, they are both crushed flat at the contact end – but their physical resemblance must be a source of perpetual wonder to the gulls that fly overhead. To the wingless a more interesting phenomenon is their dissimilarity in every particular except shape and size.

I lived at West Egg, the – well, the less fashionable of the two, though this is a most superficial tag to express the bizarre and not a little sinister contrast between them. My house was at the very tip of the egg, only fifty yards from the Sound, and squeezed between two huge places that rented for twelve or fifteen thousand a season. The one on my right was a colossal affair by any standard – it was a factual imitation of some Hôtel de Ville in Normandy, with a tower on one side, spanking new under a thin beard of raw ivy, and a marble swimming pool, and more than forty acres of lawn and garden. It was Gatsby's mansion. Or, rather, as I didn't know Mr Gatsby, it was a mansion, inhabited by a gentleman of that name. My own house was an eyesore, but it was a small eyesore, and it had been overlooked, so I had a view of the water, a partial view of my neighbour's lawn, and the consoling proximity of millionaires – all for eighty dollars a month.

Across the courtesy bay the white palaces of fashionable East Egg glittered along the water, and the history of the summer really begins on the evening I drove over there to have dinner with the Tom Buchanans. Daisy was my second cousin once removed, and I'd known Tom in college. And just after the war I spent two days with them in Chicago.

Her husband, among various physical accomplishments, had been one of the most powerful ends that ever played football at New Haven – a national figure in a way, one of those men who reach such an acute limited excellence at twenty-one that everything afterwards savours of anticlimax. His family were enormously wealthy – even in college his freedom with money was a matter for reproach – but now he'd left Chicago and come East in a fashion that rather took your breath away; for instance, he'd brought down a string of polo ponies from Lake Forest. It was hard to realise that a man in my own generation was wealthy enough to do that.

Why they came East I don't know. They had spent a year in France for no particular reason, and then drifted here and there unrestfully wherever people played polo and were rich together. This was a permanent move, said Daisy over the telephone, but I didn't believe it – I had no sight into Daisy's heart, but I felt that Tom would drift on for ever, seeking, a little wistfully, for the dramatic turbulence of some irrecoverable football game.

And so it happened that on a warm windy evening I drove over to East Egg to see two old friends whom I scarcely knew at all. Their house was even more elaborate than I expected, a cheerful red-and-white Georgian colonial mansion, overlooking the bay. The lawn started at the beach and ran towards the front door for a quarter of a mile, jumping over sundials and brick walks and burning gardens – finally when it reached the house drifting up the side in bright vines as though from the momentum of its run. The front was broken by a line of French windows, glowing now with reflected gold and wide open to the warm windy afternoon, and Tom Buchanan in riding clothes was standing with his legs apart on the front porch.

He had changed since his New Haven years. Now he was a sturdy straw-haired man of thirty with a rather hard mouth and a supercilious manner. Two shining arrogant eyes had established dominance over his face and gave him the appearance of always leaning aggressively forward. Not even the effeminate swank of his riding clothes could hide the enormous power of that body – he seemed to fill those glistening boots until he strained the top lacing, and you could see a great pack of muscle shifting when his shoulder moved under his thin coat. It was a body capable of enormous leverage – a cruel body.

His speaking voice, a gruff husky tenor, added to the impression of fractiousness he conveyed. There was a touch of paternal contempt in it, even towards people he liked – and there were men at New Haven who had hated his guts.

'Now, don't think my opinion on these matters is final,' he seemed to say, 'just because I'm stronger and more of a man than you are.' We were in the same senior society, and while we were never intimate I always had the impression that he approved of me and wanted me to like him with some harsh, defiant wistfulness of his own.

We talked for a few minutes on the sunny porch.

'I've got a nice place here,' he said, his eyes flashing about restlessly.

Turning me around by one arm, he moved a broad flat hand along the front vista, including in its sweep a sunken Italian garden, a half-acre of deep, pungent roses, and a snub-nosed motorboat that bumped the tide offshore.

'It belonged to Demaine, the oil man.' He turned me around again, politely and abruptly. 'We'll go inside.'

We walked through a high hallway into a bright rose-coloured space, fragilely bound into the house by French windows at either end. The windows were ajar and gleaming white against the fresh grass outside that seemed to grow a little way into the house. A breeze blew through the room, blew curtains in at one end and out the other like pale flags, twisting them up towards the frosted wedding-cake of the ceiling, and then rippled over the wine-coloured rug, making a shadow on it as wind does on the sea.

The only completely stationary object in the room was an enormous couch on which two young women were buoyed up as though upon an anchored balloon. They were both in white, and their dresses were rippling and fluttering as if they had just been blown back in after a short flight around the house. I must have stood for a few moments listening to the whip and snap of the curtains and the groan of a picture on the wall. Then there was a boom as Tom Buchanan shut the rear windows and the caught wind died out about the room, and the curtains and the rugs and the two young women ballooned slowly to the floor.

The younger of the two was a stranger to me. She was extended full length at her end of the divan, completely motionless, and with her chin raised a little, as if she were balancing something on it which was quite likely to fall. If she saw me out of the corner of her eyes she gave no hint of it – indeed, I was almost surprised into murmuring an apology for having disturbed her by coming in.

The other girl, Daisy, made an attempt to rise – she leaned slightly forward with a conscientious expression – then she laughed, an absurd charming little laugh, and I laughed too and came forward into the room.

'I'm p-paralysed with happiness.'

She laughed again, as if she had said something very witty, and held my hand for a moment, looking up into my face, promising that there was no one in the world she so much wanted to see. That was a way she had. She hinted in a murmur that the surname of the balancing girl was Baker. (I've heard it said that Daisy's murmur was only to make people lean towards her; an irrelevant criticism that made it no less charming.)

At any rate, Miss Baker's lips fluttered, she nodded at me almost imperceptibly, and then quickly tipped her head back again – the object she was balancing had obviously tottered a little and given her something of a fright. Again a sort of apology arose to my lips. Almost any exhibition of complete self-sufficiency draws a stunned tribute from me.

I looked back at my cousin, who began to ask me questions in her low, thrilling voice. It was the kind of voice that the ear follows up and down, as if each speech is an arrangement of notes that will never be played again. Her face was sad and lovely with bright things in it, bright eyes and a bright passionate mouth, but there was an excitement in her voice that men who had cared for her found difficult to forget; a singing compulsion, a whispered 'Listen', a promise that she had done gay, exciting things just a while since and that there were gay, exciting things hovering in the next hour.

I told her how I had stopped off in Chicago for a day on my way East, and how a dozen people had sent their love through me.

'Do they miss me?' she cried ecstatically.

'The whole town is desolate. All the cars have the left rear wheel painted black as a mourning wreath, and there's a persistent wail all night along the north shore.'

'How gorgeous! Let's go back, Tom. Tomorrow!' Then she added irrelevantly: 'You ought to see the baby.'

'I'd like to.'

'She's asleep. She's three years old. Haven't you ever seen her?'

'Never.'

'Well, you ought to see her. She's – '

Tom Buchanan, who had been hovering restlessly about the room, stopped and rested his hand on my shoulder.

'What you doing, Nick?'

'I'm a bond man.'

'Who with?'

I told him.

'Never heard of them,' he remarked decisively.

This annoyed me.

'You will,' I answered shortly. 'You will if you stay in the East.'

'Oh, I'll stay in the East, don't you worry,' he said, glancing at Daisy and then back at me, as if he were alert for something more. 'I'd be a goddamned fool to live anywhere else.'

At this point Miss Baker said: 'Absolutely!' with such suddenness that I started – it was the first word she had uttered since I came into the room. Evidently it surprised her as much as it did me, for she yawned and with a series of rapid, deft movements stood up into the room.

'I'm stiff,' she complained. 'I've been lying on that sofa for as long as I can remember.'

'Don't look at me,' Daisy retorted, 'I've been trying to get you to New York all afternoon.'

'No, thanks,' said Miss Baker to the four cocktails just in from the pantry, 'I'm absolutely in training.'

Her host looked at her incredulously.

'You are!' He took down his drink as if it were a drop in the bottom of a glass. 'How you ever get anything done is beyond me.'

I looked at Miss Baker, wondering what it was she 'got done'. I enjoyed looking at her. She was a slender, small-breasted girl, with an erect carriage, which she accentuated by throwing her body backwards at the shoulders like a young cadet. Her grey sun-strained eyes looked back at me with polite reciprocal curiosity out of a wan, charming, discontented face. It occurred to me now that I had seen her, or a picture of her, somewhere before.

'You live in West Egg,' she remarked contemptuously. 'I know somebody there.'

'I don't know a single – '

'You must know Gatsby.'

'Gatsby?' demanded Daisy. 'What Gatsby?'

Before I could reply that he was my neighbour, dinner was announced; wedging his tense arm imperatively under mine, Tom Buchanan compelled me from the room as though he were moving a checker to another square.

Slenderly, languidly, their hands set lightly on their hips, the two young women preceded us out on to a rosy-coloured porch, open towards the sunset, where four candles flickered on the table in the diminished wind.

'Why *candles*?' objected Daisy, frowning. She snapped them out with her fingers. 'In two weeks it'll be the longest day in the year.' She looked at us all radiantly. 'Do you always watch for the longest day of the year and then miss it? I always watch for the longest day in the year and then miss it.'

'We ought to plan something,' yawned Miss Baker, sitting down at the table as if she were getting into bed.

'All right,' said Daisy. 'What'll we plan?' She turned to me helplessly: 'What do people plan?'

Before I could answer her eyes fastened with an awed expression on her little finger.

'Look!' she complained; 'I hurt it.'

We all looked – the knuckle was black and blue.

'You did it, Tom,' she said accusingly. 'I know you didn't mean to, but you *did* do it. That's what I get for marrying a brute of a man, a great, big, hulking physical specimen of a – '

'I hate that word hulking,' objected Tom crossly, 'even in kidding.'

'Hulking,' insisted Daisy.

Sometimes she and Miss Baker talked at once, unobtrusively and with a bantering inconsequence that was never quite chatter, that was as cool as their white dresses and their impersonal eyes in the absence of all desire. They were here, and they accepted Tom and me, making only a polite pleasant effort to entertain or to be entertained. They knew that presently dinner would be over and a little later the evening, too, would be over and casually put away. It was sharply different from the West, where an evening was hurried from phase to phase towards its close, in a continually disappointed anticipation or else in sheer nervous dread of the moment itself.

'You make me feel uncivilised, Daisy,' I confessed on my second glass of corky but rather impressive claret. 'Can't you talk about crops or something?'

I meant nothing in particular by this remark, but it was taken up in an unexpected way.

'Civilisation's going to pieces,' broke out Tom violently. 'I've gotten to be a terrible pessimist about things. Have you read *The Rise of the Coloured Empires* by this man Goddard?'

'Why, no,' I answered, rather surprised by his tone.

'Well, it's a fine book, and everybody ought to read it. The idea is if we don't look out the white race will be – will be utterly submerged. It's all scientific stuff; it's been proved.'

'Tom's getting very profound,' said Daisy, with an expression of unthoughtful sadness. 'He reads deep books with long words in them. What was that word we – '

'Well, these books are all scientific,' insisted Tom, glancing at her impatiently. 'This fellow has worked out the whole thing. It's up to us, who are the dominant race, to watch out or these other races will have control of things.'

'We've got to beat them down,' whispered Daisy, winking ferociously towards the fervent sun.

'You ought to live in California – ' began Miss Baker, but Tom interrupted her by shifting heavily in his chair.

'This idea is that we're Nordics. I am, and you are, and you are, and – ' After an infinitesimal hesitation he included Daisy with a slight nod, and she winked at me again. ' – And we've produced all the things that go to make civilisation – oh, science and art, and all that. Do you see?'

There was something pathetic in his concentration, as if his complacency, more acute than of old, was not enough to him any more. When, almost immediately, the telephone rang inside and the butler left the porch, Daisy seized upon the momentary interruption and leaned towards me.

'I'll tell you a family secret,' she whispered enthusiastically. 'It's about the butler's nose. Do you want to hear about the butler's nose?'

'That's why I came over tonight.'

'Well, he wasn't always a butler; he used to be the silver polisher for some people in New York that had a silver service for two hundred people. He had to polish it from morning till night, until finally it began to affect his nose – '

'Things went from bad to worse,' suggested Miss Baker.

'Yes. Things went from bad to worse, until finally he had to give up his position.'

For a moment the last sunshine fell with romantic affection upon her glowing face; her voice compelled me forward breathlessly as I listened – then the glow faded, each light deserting her with lingering regret, like children leaving a pleasant street at dusk.

The butler came back and murmured something close to Tom's ear, whereupon Tom frowned, pushed back his chair, and without a word went inside. As if his absence quickened something within her, Daisy leaned forward again, her voice glowing and singing.

'I love to see you at my table, Nick. You remind me of a – of a rose, an absolute rose. Doesn't he?' She turned to Miss Baker for confirmation: 'An absolute rose?'

This was untrue. I am not even faintly like a rose. She was only extemporising, but a stirring warmth flowed from her, as if her heart was trying to come out to you concealed in one of those breathless, thrilling words. Then suddenly she threw her napkin on the table and excused herself and went into the house.

Miss Baker and I exchanged a short glance consciously devoid of meaning. I was about to speak when she sat up alertly and said 'Sh!' in a warning voice. A subdued, impassioned murmur was audible in the room beyond, and Miss Baker leaned forward unashamed, trying to hear. The murmur trembled on the verge of coherence, sank down, mounted excitedly, and then ceased altogether.

'This Mr Gatsby you spoke of is my neighbour – ' I began.

'Don't talk. I want to hear what happens.'

'Is something happening?' I enquired innocently.

'You mean to say you don't know?' said Miss Baker, honestly surprised. 'I thought everybody knew.'

'I don't.'

'Why – ' she said hesitantly, 'Tom's got some woman in New York.'

'Got some woman?' I repeated blankly.

Miss Baker nodded.

'She might have the decency not to telephone him at dinner time. Don't you think?'

Almost before I had grasped her meaning there was the flutter of a dress and the crunch of leather boots, and Tom and Daisy were back at the table.

'It couldn't be helped!' cried Daisy with tense gaiety.

She sat down, glanced searchingly at Miss Baker and then at me, and continued: 'I looked outdoors for a minute, and it's very romantic outdoors. There's a bird on the lawn that I think must be a nightingale come over on the Cunard or White Star Line. He's singing away – ' Her voice sang: 'It's romantic, isn't it, Tom?'

'Very romantic,' he said, and then miserably to me: 'If it's light enough after dinner, I want to take you down to the stables.'

The telephone rang inside, startlingly, and as Daisy shook her head decisively at Tom the subject of the stables, in fact all subjects, vanished into air. Among the broken fragments of the last five minutes at table I remember the candles being lit again, pointlessly, and I was conscious of wanting to look squarely at everyone, and yet to avoid all eyes. I couldn't guess what Daisy and Tom were thinking, but I doubt if even Miss Baker, who seemed to have mastered a certain hardy scepticism, was able utterly to put this fifth guest's shrill metallic urgency out of mind. To a certain temperament the situation might have seemed intriguing – my own instinct was to telephone immediately for the police.

The horses, needless to say, were not mentioned again. Tom and Miss Baker, with several feet of twilight between them, strolled back into the library, as if to a vigil beside a perfectly tangible body, while, trying to look pleasantly interested and a little deaf, I followed Daisy around a chain of connecting verandas to the porch in front. In its deep gloom we sat down side by side on a wicker settee.

Daisy took her face in her hands as if feeling its lovely shape, and her eyes moved gradually out into the velvet dusk. I saw that turbulent emotions possessed her, so I asked what I thought would be some sedative questions about her little girl.

'We don't know each other very well, Nick,' she said suddenly. 'Even if we are cousins. You didn't come to my wedding.'

'I wasn't back from the war.'

'That's true.' She hesitated. 'Well, I've had a very bad time, Nick, and I'm pretty cynical about everything.'

Evidently she had reason to be. I waited but she didn't say any more, and after a moment I returned rather feebly to the subject of her daughter.

'I suppose she talks, and – eats, and everything.'

'Oh, yes.' She looked at me absently. 'Listen, Nick; let me tell you what I said when she was born. Would you like to hear?'

'Very much.'

'It'll show you how I've gotten to feel about – things. Well, she was less than an hour old and Tom was God knows where. I woke up out of the ether with an utterly abandoned feeling, and asked the nurse right away if it was a boy or a girl. She told me it was a girl, and so I turned my head away and wept. "All right," I said, "I'm glad it's a girl. And I hope she'll be a fool – that's the best thing a girl can be in this world, a beautiful little fool."

'You see I think everything's terrible anyhow,' she went on in a convinced way. 'Everybody thinks so – the most advanced people. And I *know*. I've been everywhere and seen everything and done everything.' Her eyes flashed around her in a defiant way, rather like Tom's, and she laughed with thrilling scorn. 'Sophisticated – God, I'm sophisticated!'

The instant her voice broke off, ceasing to compel my attention, my belief, I felt the basic insincerity of what she had said. It made me uneasy, as though the whole evening had been a trick of some sort to exact a contributory emotion from me. I waited, and sure enough, in a moment she looked at me with an absolute smirk on her lovely face, as if she had asserted her membership in a rather distinguished secret society to which she and Tom belonged.

Inside, the crimson room bloomed with light. Tom and Miss Baker sat at either end of the long couch and she read aloud to him from the *Saturday Evening Post* – the words, murmurous and uninflected, running together in a soothing tune. The lamplight, bright on his boots and dull on the autumn-leaf yellow of her hair, glinted along the paper as she turned a page with a flutter of slender muscles in her arms.

When we came in she held us silent for a moment with a lifted hand.

'To be continued,' she said, tossing the magazine on the table, 'in our very next issue.'

Her body asserted itself with a restless movement of her knee, and she stood up.

'Ten o'clock,' she remarked, apparently finding the time on the ceiling. 'Time for this good girl to go to bed.'

'Jordan's going to play in the tournament tomorrow,' explained Daisy, 'over at Westchester.'

'Oh – you're *Jor*dan Baker.'

I knew now why her face was familiar – its pleasing contemptuous expression had looked out at me from many rotogravure pictures of the sporting life at Asheville and Hot Springs and Palm Beach. I had heard some story of her too, a critical, unpleasant story, but what it was I had forgotten long ago.

'Good-night,' she said softly. 'Wake me at eight, won't you?'

'If you'll get up.'

'I will. Good-night, Mr Carraway. See you anon.'

'Of course you will,' confirmed Daisy. 'In fact, I think I'll arrange a marriage. Come over often Nick, and I'll sort of – oh – fling you together. You know – lock you up accidentally in linen closets and push you out to sea in a boat, and all that sort of thing – '

'Good-night,' called Miss Baker from the stairs. 'I haven't heard a word.'

'She's a nice girl,' said Tom after a moment. 'They oughtn't to let her run around the country this way.'

'Who oughtn't to?' enquired Daisy coldly.

'Her family.'

'Her family is one aunt about a thousand years old. Besides, Nick's going to look after her, aren't you, Nick? She's going to spend lots of weekends out here this summer. I think the home influence will be very good for her.'

Daisy and Tom looked at each other for a moment in silence.

'Is she from New York?' I asked quickly.

'From Louisville. Our white girlhood was passed together there. Our beautiful white – '

'Did you give Nick a little heart-to-heart talk on the veranda?' demanded Tom suddenly.

'Did I?' She looked at me. 'I can't seem to remember, but I think we talked about the Nordic race. Yes, I'm sure we did. It sort of crept up on us and first thing you know – '

'Don't believe everything you hear, Nick,' he advised me.

I said lightly that I had heard nothing at all, and a few minutes later I got up to go home. They came to the door with me and stood side by side in a cheerful square of light. As I started my motor Daisy peremptorily called: 'Wait! I forgot to ask you something, and it's important. We heard you were engaged to a girl out West.'

'That's right,' corroborated Tom kindly. 'We heard that you were engaged.'

'It's a libel. I'm too poor.'

'But we heard it,' insisted Daisy, surprising me by opening up again in a flower-like way. 'We heard it from three people, so it must be true.'

Of course I knew what they were referring to, but I wasn't even vaguely engaged. The fact that gossip had published the banns was one of the reasons I had come East. You can't stop going with an old friend on account of rumours, and on the other hand I had no intention of being rumoured into marriage.

Their interest rather touched me and made them less remotely rich – nevertheless, I was confused and a little disgusted as I drove away. It seemed to me that the thing for Daisy to do was to rush out of the house, child in arms – but apparently there were no such intentions in her head. As for Tom, the fact that he 'had some woman in New York' was really less surprising than that he had been depressed by a book. Something was making him nibble at the edge of stale ideas as if his sturdy physical egotism no longer nourished his peremptory heart.

Already it was deep summer on roadhouse roofs and in front of wayside garages, where new red gas-pumps sat out in pools of light, and when I reached my estate at West Egg I ran the car under its shed and sat for a while on an abandoned grass roller in the yard. The wind had blown off, leaving a loud, bright night, with wings beating in the trees and a persistent organ sound as the full bellows of the earth blew the frogs full of life. The silhouette of a moving cat wavered across the moonlight, and turning my head to watch it, I saw that I was not alone – fifty feet away a figure had emerged from the shadow of my neighbour's mansion and was standing with his hands in his pockets regarding the silver pepper of the stars. Something in his leisurely movements and the secure position of his feet upon the lawn suggested that it was Mr Gatsby himself, come out to determine what share was his of our local heavens.

I decided to call to him. Miss Baker had mentioned him at dinner, and that would do for an introduction. But I didn't call to him, for he gave a sudden intimation that he was content to be alone – he stretched out his arms towards the dark water in a curious way, and, far as I was from him, I could have sworn he was trembling. Involuntarily I glanced seaward – and distinguished nothing except a single green light, minute and far away, that might have been the end of a dock. When I looked once more for Gatsby he had vanished, and I was alone again in the unquiet darkness.

Chapter 2

About halfway between West Egg and New York the motor road hastily joins the railroad and runs beside it for a quarter of a mile, so as to shrink away from a certain desolate area of land. This is a valley of ashes – a fantastic farm where ashes grow like wheat into ridges and hills and grotesque gardens; where ashes take the forms of houses and chimneys and rising smoke and, finally, with a transcendent effort, of ash-grey men who move dimly and already crumbling through the powdery air. Occasionally a line of grey cars crawls along an invisible track, gives out a ghastly creak, and comes to rest, and immediately the ash-grey men swarm up with leaden spades and stir up an impenetrable cloud, which screens their obscure operations from your sight.

But above the grey land and the spasms of bleak dust which drift endlessly over it, you perceive, after a moment, the eyes of Dr T. J. Eckleburg. The eyes of Dr T. J. Eckleburg are blue and gigantic – their retinas are one yard high. They look out of no face, but, instead, from a pair of enormous yellow spectacles which pass over a non-existent nose. Evidently some wild wag of an oculist set them there to fatten his practice in the borough of Queens, and then sank down himself into eternal blindness, or forgot them and moved away. But his eyes, dimmed a little by many paintless days, under sun and rain, brood on over the solemn dumping ground.

The valley of ashes is bounded on one side by a small foul river, and, when the drawbridge is up to let barges through, the passengers on waiting trains can stare at the dismal scene for as long as half an hour. There is always a halt there of at least a minute, and it was because of this that I first met Tom Buchanan's mistress.

The fact that he had one was insisted upon wherever he was known. His acquaintances resented the fact that he turned up in popular cafés with her and, leaving her at a table, sauntered about, chatting with whomsoever he knew. Though I was curious to see her, I had no desire to meet her – but I did. I went up to New York with Tom on the train one afternoon, and when we stopped by the ash-heaps he jumped to his feet and, taking hold of my elbow, literally forced me from the car.

'We're getting off,' he insisted. 'I want you to meet my girl.'

I think he'd tanked up a good deal at luncheon, and his determination to have my company bordered on violence. The supercilious assumption was that on Sunday afternoon I had nothing better to do.

I followed him over a low whitewashed railroad fence, and we walked back a hundred yards along the road under Dr Eckleburg's persistent stare. The only building in sight was a small block of yellow brick sitting on the edge of the waste land, a sort of compact Main Street ministering to it, and contiguous to absolutely nothing. One of the three shops it contained was for rent and another was an all-night restaurant, approached by a trail of ashes; the third was a garage – *Repairs*. George B. Wilson. *Cars bought and sold*. – and I followed Tom inside.

The interior was unprosperous and bare; the only car visible was the dust-covered wreck of a Ford which crouched in a dim corner. It had occurred to me that this shadow of a garage must be a blind, and that sumptuous and romantic apartments were concealed overhead, when the proprietor himself appeared in the door of an office, wiping his hands on a piece of waste. He was a blond, spiritless man, anaemic, and faintly handsome. When he saw us a damp gleam of hope sprang into his light blue eyes.

'Hello, Wilson, old man,' said Tom, slapping him jovially on the shoulder. 'How's business?'

'I can't complain,' answered Wilson unconvincingly. 'When are you going to sell me that car?'

'Next week; I've got my man working on it now.'

'Works pretty slow, don't he?'

'No, he doesn't,' said Tom coldly. 'And if you feel that way about it, maybe I'd better sell it somewhere else after all.'

'I don't mean that,' explained Wilson quickly. 'I just meant – '

His voice faded off and Tom glanced impatiently around the garage. Then I heard footsteps on a stairs, and in a moment the thickish figure of a woman blocked out the light from the office door. She was in the middle thirties, and faintly stout, but she carried her flesh sensuously, as some women can. Her face, above a spotted dress of dark blue crêpe-de-chine, contained no facet or gleam of beauty, but there was an immediately perceptible vitality about her as if the nerves of her body were continually smouldering. She smiled slowly and, walking through her husband as if he were a ghost, shook hands with Tom, looking him flush in the eye. Then she wet her lips, and without turning around spoke to her husband in a soft, coarse, voice: 'Get some chairs, why don't you, so somebody can sit down.'

'Oh, sure,' agreed Wilson hurriedly, and went towards the little office, mingling immediately with the cement colour of the walls. A white ashen dust veiled his dark suit and his pale hair as it veiled everything in the vicinity – except his wife, who moved close to Tom.

'I want to see you,' said Tom intently. 'Get on the next train.'

'All right.'

'I'll meet you by the news-stand on the lower level.'

She nodded and moved away from him just as George Wilson emerged with two chairs from his office door.

We waited for her down the road and out of sight. It was a few days before the Fourth of July, and a grey, scrawny Italian child was setting torpedoes in a row along the railroad track.

'Terrible place, isn't it,' said Tom, exchanging a frown with Dr Eckleburg.

'Awful.'

'It does her good to get away.'

'Doesn't her husband object?'

'Wilson? He thinks she goes to see her sister in New York. He's so dumb he doesn't know he's alive.'

So Tom Buchanan and his girl and I went up together to New York – or not quite together, for Mrs Wilson sat discreetly in another car. Tom deferred that much to the sensibilities of those East Eggers who might be on the train.

She had changed her dress to a brown figured muslin, which stretched tight over her rather wide hips as Tom helped her to the platform in New York. At the news-stand she bought a copy of *Town Tattle* and a moving-picture magazine, and in the station drugstore some cold cream and a small flask of perfume. Upstairs, in the solemn echoing drive, she let four taxicabs drive away before she selected a new one, lavender-coloured with grey upholstery, and in this we slid out from the mass of the station into the glowing sunshine. But immediately she turned sharply from the window and, leaning forward, tapped on the front glass.

'I want to get one of those dogs,' she said earnestly. 'I want to get one for the apartment. They're nice to have – a dog.'

We backed up to a grey old man who bore an absurd resemblance to John D. Rockefeller. In a basket swung from his neck cowered a dozen very recent puppies of an indeterminate breed.

'What kind are they?' asked Mrs Wilson eagerly, as he came to the taxi-window.

'All kinds. What kind do you want, lady?'

'I'd like to get one of those police dogs; I don't suppose you got that kind?'

The man peered doubtfully into the basket, plunged in his hand and drew one up, wriggling, by the back of the neck.

'That's no police dog,' said Tom.

'No, it's not exactly a pol*ice* dog,' said the man with disappointment in his voice. 'It's more of an Airedale.' He passed his hand over the brown wash-rag of a back. 'Look at that coat. Some coat. That's a dog that'll never bother you with catching cold.'

'I think it's cute,' said Mrs Wilson enthusiastically. 'How much is it?'

'That dog?' He looked at it admiringly. 'That dog will cost you ten dollars.'

The Airedale – undoubtedly there was an Airedale concerned in it somewhere, though its feet were startlingly white – changed hands and settled down into Mrs Wilson's lap, where she fondled the weather-proof coat with rapture.

'Is it a boy or a girl?' she asked delicately.

'That dog? That dog's a boy.'

'It's a bitch,' said Tom decisively. 'Here's your money. Go and buy ten more dogs with it.'

We drove over to Fifth Avenue, warm and soft, almost pastoral, on the summer Sunday afternoon. I wouldn't have been surprised to see a great flock of white sheep turn the corner.

'Hold on,' I said, 'I have to leave you here.'

'No you don't,' interposed Tom quickly. 'Myrtle'll be hurt if you don't come up to the apartment. Won't you, Myrtle?'

'Come on,' she urged. 'I'll telephone my sister Catherine. She's said to be very beautiful by people who ought to know.'

'Well, I'd like to, but – '

We went on, cutting back again over the Park towards the West Hundreds. At 158th Street the cab stopped at one slice in a long white cake of apartment-houses. Throwing a regal homecoming glance around the neighbourhood, Mrs Wilson gathered up her dog and her other purchases, and went haughtily in.

'I'm going to have the McKees come up,' she announced as we rose in the elevator. 'And, of course, I got to call up my sister, too.'

The apartment was on the top floor – a small living-room, a small dining-room, a small bedroom, and a bath. The living-room was crowded to the doors with a set of tapestried furniture entirely too large for it, so that to move about was to stumble continually over scenes of ladies swinging in the gardens of Versailles. The only picture was an over-enlarged photograph, apparently a hen sitting on a blurred rock. Looked at from a distance, however, the hen resolved itself into a bonnet, and the countenance of a stout old lady beamed down into the room. Several old copies of *Town Tattle* lay on the table, together with a copy of *Simon Called Peter*, and some of the small scandal magazines of Broadway. Mrs Wilson was first concerned with the dog. A reluctant elevator-boy went for a box full of straw and some milk to which he added on his own initiative a tin of large, hard dog-biscuits – one of which decomposed apathetically in the saucer of milk all afternoon. Meanwhile Tom brought out a bottle of whiskey from a locked bureau drawer.

I have been drunk just twice in my life, and the second time was that afternoon; so everything that happened has a dim, hazy cast over it, although until after eight o'clock the apartment was full of cheerful sun. Sitting on Tom's lap Mrs Wilson called up several people on the telephone; then there were no cigarettes, and I went out to buy some at the drugstore on the corner. When I came back they had both disappeared, so I sat down discreetly in the living-room and read a chapter of *Simon Called Peter* – either it was terrible stuff or the whiskey distorted things, because it didn't make any sense to me.

Just as Tom and Myrtle (after the first drink Mrs Wilson and I called each other by our first names) reappeared, company commenced to arrive at the apartment door.

The sister, Catherine, was a slender, worldly girl of about thirty, with a solid, sticky bob of red hair, and a complexion powdered milky white. Her eyebrows had been plucked and then drawn on again at a more rakish angle but the efforts of nature towards the restoration of the old alignment gave a blurred air to her face. When she moved about there was an incessant clicking as innumerable pottery bracelets jingled up and down upon her arms. She came in with such a proprietary haste and looked around so possessively at the furniture that I wondered if she lived here. But when I asked her she laughed immoderately, repeated my question aloud, and told me she lived with a girl friend at a hotel.

Mr McKee was a pale, feminine man from the flat below. He had just shaved, for there was a white spot of lather on his cheekbone, and he was most respectful in his greeting to everyone in the room. He informed me that he was in the 'artistic game', and I gathered later that he was a photographer and had made the dim enlargement of Mrs Wilson's mother which hovered like an ectoplasm on the wall. His wife was shrill, languid, handsome, and horrible. She told me with pride that her husband had photographed her a hundred and twenty-seven times since they had been married.

Mrs Wilson had changed her costume sometime before, and was now attired in an elaborate afternoon dress of cream-coloured chiffon, which gave out a continual rustle as she swept about the room. With the influence of the dress her personality had also undergone a change. The intense vitality that had been so remarkable in the garage was converted into impressive hauteur. Her laughter, her gestures, her assertions became more violently affected moment by moment, and as she expanded the room grew smaller around her, until she seemed to be revolving on a noisy, creaking pivot through the smoky air.

'My dear,' she told her sister in a high, mincing shout, 'most of these fellas will cheat you every time. All they think of is money. I had a woman up here last week to look at my feet, and when she gave me the bill you'd of thought she'd had my appendicitis out.'

'What was the name of the woman?' asked Mrs McKee.

'Mrs Eberhardt. She goes around looking at people's feet in their own homes.'

'I like your dress,' remarked Mrs McKee, 'I think it's adorable.

Mrs Wilson rejected the compliment by raising her eyebrow in disdain.

'It's just a crazy old thing,' she said. 'I just slip it on sometimes when I don't care what I look like.'

'But it looks wonderful on you, if you know what I mean,' pursued Mrs McKee. 'If Chester could only get you in that pose I think he could make something of it.'

We all looked in silence at Mrs Wilson, who removed a strand of hair from over her eyes and looked back at us with a brilliant smile. Mr McKee regarded her intently with his head on one side, and then moved his hand back and forth slowly in front of his face.

'I should change the light,' he said after a moment. 'I'd like to bring out the modelling of the features. And I'd try to get hold of all the back hair.'

'I wouldn't think of changing the light,' cried Mrs McKee. 'I think it's – '

Her husband said '*Sh!*' and we all looked at the subject again, whereupon Tom Buchanan yawned audibly and got to his feet.

'You McKees have something to drink,' he said. 'Get some more ice and mineral water, Myrtle, before everybody goes to sleep.'

'I told that boy about the ice.' Myrtle raised her eyebrows in despair at the shiftlessness of the lower orders. 'These people! You have to keep after them all the time.'

She looked at me and laughed pointlessly. Then she flounced over to the dog, kissed it with ecstasy, and swept into the kitchen, implying that a dozen chefs awaited her orders there.

'I've done some nice things out on Long Island,' asserted Mr McKee.

Tom looked at him blankly.

'Two of them we have framed downstairs.'

'Two what?' demanded Tom.

'Two studies. One of them I call "Montauk Point – The Gulls", and the other I call "Montauk Point – The Sea".'

The sister Catherine sat down beside me on the couch.

'Do you live down on Long Island, too?' she enquired.

'I live at West Egg.'

'Really? I was down there at a party about a month ago. At a man named Gatsby's. Do you know him?'

'I live next door to him.'

'Well, they say he's a nephew or a cousin of Kaiser Wilhelm's. That's where all his money comes from.'

'Really?'

She nodded.

'I'm scared of him. I'd hate to have him get anything on me.'

This absorbing information about my neighbour was interrupted by Mrs McKee's pointing suddenly at Catherine: 'Chester, I think you could do something with *her*,' she broke out, but Mr McKee only nodded in a bored way, and turned his attention to Tom.

'I'd like to do more work on Long Island, if I could get the entry. All I ask is that they should give me a start.'

'Ask Myrtle,' said Tom, breaking into a short shout of laughter as Mrs Wilson entered with a tray. 'She'll give you a letter of introduction, won't you, Myrtle?'

'Do what?' she asked, startled.

'You'll give McKee a letter of introduction to your husband, so he can do some studies of him.' His lips moved silently for a moment as he invented. ' "George B. Wilson at the Gasoline Pump", or something like that.'

Catherine leaned close to me and whispered in my ear: 'Neither of them can stand the person they're married to.'

'Can't they?'

'Can't *stand* them.' She looked at Myrtle and then at Tom. 'What I say is, why go on living with them if they can't stand them? If I was them I'd get a divorce and get married to each other right away.'

'Doesn't she like Wilson either?'

The answer to this was unexpected. It came from Myrtle, who had overheard the question, and it was violent and obscene.

'You see,' cried Catherine triumphantly. She lowered her voice again. 'It's really his wife that's keeping them apart. She's a Catholic, and they don't believe in divorce.'

Daisy was not a Catholic, and I was a little shocked at the elaborateness of the lie.

'When they do get married,' continued Catherine, 'they're going West to live for a while until it blows over.'

'It'd be more discreet to go to Europe.'

'Oh, do you like Europe?' she exclaimed surprisingly. 'I just got back from Monte Carlo.'

'Really.'

'Just last year. I went over there with another girl.'

'Stay long?'

'No, we just went to Monte Carlo and back. We went by way of Marseilles. We had over twelve hundred dollars when we started, but we got gypped out of it all in two days in the private rooms. We had an awful time getting back, I can tell you. God, how I hated that town!'

The late afternoon sky bloomed in the window for a moment like the blue honey of the Mediterranean – then the shrill voice of Mrs McKee called me back into the room.

'I almost made a mistake, too,' she declared vigorously. 'I almost married a little kike who'd been after me for years. I knew he was below me. Everybody kept saying to me: "Lucille, that man's way below you!" But if I hadn't met Chester, he'd of got me sure.'

'Yes, but listen,' said Myrtle Wilson, nodding her head up and down, 'at least you didn't marry him.'

'I know I didn't.'

'Well, I married him,' said Myrtle, ambiguously. 'And that's the difference between your case and mine.'

'Why did you, Myrtle?' demanded Catherine. 'Nobody forced you to.'

Myrtle considered.

'I married him because I thought he was a gentleman,' she said finally. 'I thought he knew something about breeding, but he wasn't fit to lick my shoe.'

'You were crazy about him for a while,' said Catherine.

'Crazy about him!' cried Myrtle incredulously. 'Who said I was crazy about him? I never was any more crazy about him than I was about that man there.'

She pointed suddenly at me, and everyone looked at me accusingly. I tried to show by my expression that I expected no affection.

'The only *crazy* I was was when I married him. I knew right away I made a mistake. He borrowed somebody's best suit to get married in, and never even told me about it, and the man came after it one day when he was out: "Oh, is that your suit?" I said. "This is the first I ever heard about it." But I gave it to him and then I lay down and cried to beat the band all afternoon.'

'She really ought to get away from him,' resumed Catherine to me. 'They've been living over that garage for eleven years. And Tom's the first sweetie she ever had.'

The bottle of whiskey – a second one – was now in constant demand by all present, excepting Catherine, who 'felt just as good on nothing at all'. Tom rang for the janitor and sent him for some celebrated sandwiches, which were a complete supper in themselves. I wanted to get out and walk eastward towards the park through the soft twilight, but each time I tried to go I became entangled in some wild, strident argument which pulled me back, as if with ropes, into my chair. Yet high over the city our line of yellow windows must have contributed their share of human secrecy to the casual watcher in the darkening streets, and I saw him too, looking up and wondering. I was within and without, simultaneously enchanted and repelled by the inexhaustible variety of life.

Myrtle pulled her chair close to mine, and suddenly her warm breath poured over me the story of her first meeting with Tom.

'It was on the two little seats facing each other that are always the last ones left on the train. I was going up to New York to see my sister and spend the night. He had on a dress suit and patent-leather shoes, and I couldn't keep my eyes off him, but every time he looked at me I had to pretend to be looking at the advertisement over his head. When we came into the station he was next to me, and his white shirt-front pressed against my arm, and so I told him I'd have to call a policeman, but he knew I lied. I was so excited that when I got into a taxi with him I didn't hardly know I wasn't getting into a subway train. All I kept thinking about, over and over, was, "You can't live for ever; you can't live for ever." '

She turned to Mrs McKee and the room rang full of her artificial laughter. 'My dear,' she cried, 'I'm going to give you this dress as soon as I'm through with it. I've got to get another one tomorrow. I'm going to make a list of all the things I've got to get. A massage and a wave, and a collar for the dog, and one of those cute little ashtrays where you touch a spring, and a wreath with a black silk bow for mother's grave that'll last all summer. I got to write down a list so I won't forget all the things I got to do.'

It was nine o'clock – almost immediately afterwards I looked at my watch and found it was ten. Mr McKee was asleep on a chair with his fists clenched in his lap, like a photograph of a man of action. Taking out my handkerchief I wiped from his cheek the spot of dried lather that had worried me all the afternoon.

The little dog was sitting on the table looking with blind eyes through the smoke, and from time to time groaning faintly. People disappeared, reappeared, made plans to go somewhere, and then lost each other, searched for each other, found each other a few feet away. Sometime towards midnight Tom Buchanan and Mrs Wilson stood face to face discussing, in impassioned voices, whether Mrs Wilson had any right to mention Daisy's name.

'Daisy! Daisy! Daisy!' shouted Mrs Wilson. 'I'll say it whenever I want to! Daisy! Dai – '

Making a short deft movement, Tom Buchanan broke her nose with his open hand.

Then there were bloody towels upon the bathroom floor, and women's voices scolding, and high over the confusion a long broken wail of pain. Mr McKee awoke from his doze and started in a daze towards the door. When he had gone halfway he turned around and stared at the scene – his wife and Catherine scolding and consoling as they stumbled here and there among the crowded furniture with articles of aid, and the despairing figure on the couch, bleeding fluently, and trying to spread a copy of *Town Tattle* over the tapestry scenes of Versailles. Then Mr McKee turned and continued on out the door. Taking my hat from the chandelier, I followed.

'Come to lunch some day,' he suggested, as we groaned down in the elevator.

'Where?'

'Anywhere.'

'Keep your hands off the lever,' snapped the elevator boy.

'I beg your pardon,' said Mr McKee with dignity, 'I didn't know I was touching it.'

'All right,' I agreed, 'I'll be glad to.'

. . . I was standing beside his bed and he was sitting up between the sheets, clad in his underwear, with a great portfolio in his hands.

'Beauty and the Beast . . . Loneliness . . . Old Grocery Horse . . . Brook'n Bridge . . . '

Then I was lying half-asleep in the cold lower level of the Pennsylvania Station, staring at the morning *Tribune*, and waiting for the four o'clock train.

Chapter 3

There was music from my neighbour's house through the summer nights. In his blue gardens men and girls came and went like moths among the whisperings and the champagne and the stars. At high tide in the afternoon I watched his guests diving from the tower of his raft, or taking the sun on the hot sand of his beach while his two motorboats slit the waters of the Sound, drawing aquaplanes over cataracts of foam. On weekends his Rolls-Royce became an omnibus, bearing parties to and from the city between nine in the morning and long past midnight, while his station-wagon scampered like a brisk yellow bug to meet all trains. And on Mondays eight servants, including an extra gardener, toiled all day with mops and scrubbing-brushes and hammers and garden-shears, repairing the ravages of the night before.

Every Friday five crates of oranges and lemons arrived from a fruiterer in New York – every Monday these same oranges and lemons left his back door in a pyramid of pulpless halves. There was a machine in the kitchen which could extract the juice of two hundred oranges in half an hour if a little button was pressed two hundred times by a butler's thumb.

At least once a fortnight a corps of caterers came down with several hundred feet of canvas and enough coloured lights to make a Christmas tree of Gatsby's enormous garden. On buffet tables, garnished with glistening hors d'oeuvre, spiced baked hams crowded against salads of harlequin designs and pastry pigs and turkeys bewitched to a dark gold. In the main hall a bar with a real brass rail was set up, and stocked with gins and liquors and with cordials so long forgotten that most of his female guests were too young to know one from another.

By seven o'clock the orchestra has arrived, no thin five-piece affair, but a whole pitful of oboes and trombones and saxophones and viols and cornets and piccolos, and low and high drums. The last swimmers have come in from the beach now and are dressing upstairs; the cars from New York are parked five deep in the drive, and already the halls and salons and verandas are gaudy with primary colours, and hair bobbed in strange new ways, and shawls beyond the dreams of Castile. The bar is in full swing, and floating rounds of cocktails permeate the garden outside, until the air is alive with chatter and laughter, and casual innuendo and introductions forgotten on the spot, and enthusiastic meetings between women who never knew each other's names.

The lights grow brighter as the earth lurches away from the sun, and now the orchestra is playing yellow cocktail music, and the opera of voices pitches a key higher. Laughter is easier minute by minute, spilled with prodigality, tipped out at a cheerful word. The groups change more swiftly, swell with new arrivals, dissolve and form in the same breath; already there are wanderers, confident girls who weave here and there among the stouter and more stable, become for a sharp, joyous moment the centre of a group, and then, excited with triumph, glide on through the sea-change of faces and voices and colour under the constantly changing light.

Suddenly one of these gypsies, in trembling opal, seizes a cocktail out of the air, dumps it down for courage and, moving her hands like Frisco, dances out alone on the canvas platform. A momentary hush; the orchestra leader varies his rhythm obligingly for her, and there is a burst of chatter as the erroneous news goes around that she is Gilda Gray's understudy from the *Follies*. The party has begun.

I believe that on the first night I went to Gatsby's house I was one of the few guests who had actually been invited. People were not invited – they went there. They got into automobiles which bore them out to Long Island, and somehow they ended up at Gatsby's door. Once there they were introduced by somebody who knew Gatsby, and after that they conducted themselves according to the rules of behaviour associated with an amusement park. Sometimes they came and went without having met Gatsby at all, came for the party with a simplicity of heart that was its own ticket of admission.

I had been actually invited. A chauffeur in a uniform of robin's-egg blue crossed my lawn early that Saturday morning with a surprisingly formal note from his employer: the honour would be entirely Gatsby's, it said, if I would attend his 'little party' that night. He had seen me several times, and had intended to call on me long before, but a peculiar combination of circumstances had prevented it – signed Jay Gatsby, in a majestic hand.

Dressed up in white flannels I went over to his lawn a little while after seven, and wandered around rather ill at ease among swirls and eddies of people I didn't know – though here and there was a face I had noticed on the commuting train. I was immediately struck by the number of young Englishmen dotted about, all well dressed, all looking a little hungry, and all talking in low, earnest voices to solid and prosperous Americans. I was sure that they were selling something: bonds or insurance or automobiles. They were at least agonisingly aware of the easy money in the vicinity and convinced that it was theirs for a few words in the right key.

As soon as I arrived I made an attempt to find my host, but the two or three people of whom I asked his whereabouts stared at me in such an amazed way, and denied so vehemently any knowledge of his movements, that I slunk off in the direction of the cocktail table – the only place in the garden where a single man could linger without looking purposeless and alone.

I was on my way to getting roaring drunk from sheer embarrassment when Jordan Baker came out of the house and stood at the head of the marble steps, leaning a little backwards and looking with contemptuous interest down into the garden.

Welcome or not, I found it necessary to attach myself to someone before I could begin to address cordial remarks to the passers-by.

'Hello!' I roared, advancing towards her. My voice seemed unnaturally loud across the garden.

'I thought you might be here,' she responded absently as I came up. 'I remembered you lived next door to – '

She held my hand impersonally, as a promise that she'd take care of me in a minute, and gave ear to two girls in twin yellow dresses, who stopped at the foot of the steps.

'Hello!' they cried together. 'Sorry you didn't win.'

That was for the golf tournament she had lost in the finals the week before.

'You don't know who we are,' said one of the girls in yellow, 'but we met you here about a month ago.'

'You've dyed your hair since then,' remarked Jordan, and I started, but the girls had moved casually on and her remark was addressed to the premature moon, produced like the supper, no doubt, out of a caterer's basket. With Jordan's slender golden arm resting in mine, we descended the steps and sauntered about the garden. A tray of cocktails floated at us through the twilight, and we sat down at a table with the two girls in yellow and three men, each one introduced to us as Mr Mumble.

'Do you come to these parties often?' enquired Jordan of the girl beside her.

'The last one was the one I met you at,' answered the girl, in an alert confident voice. She turned to her companion: 'Wasn't it for you, Lucille?'

It was for Lucille, too.

'I like to come,' Lucille said. 'I never care what I do, so I always have a good time. When I was here last I tore my gown on a chair, and he asked me my name and address – inside of a week I got a package from Croirier's with a new evening gown in it.'

'Did you keep it?' asked Jordan.

'Sure I did. I was going to wear it tonight, but it was too big in the bust and had to be altered. It was gas blue with lavender beads. Two hundred and sixty-five dollars.'

'There's something funny about a fellow that'll do a thing like that,' said the other girl eagerly. 'He doesn't want any trouble with *any*body.'

'Who doesn't?' I enquired.

'Gatsby. Somebody told me – '

The two girls and Jordan leaned together confidentially.

'Somebody told me they thought he killed a man once.'

A thrill passed over all of us. The three Mr Mumbles bent forward and listened eagerly.

'I don't think it's so much *that*,' argued Lucille sceptically; 'it's more that he was a German spy during the war.'

One of the men nodded in confirmation.

'I heard that from a man who knew all about him, grew up with him in Germany,' he assured us positively.

'Oh, no,' said the first girl, 'it couldn't be that, because he was in the American army during the war.' As our credulity switched back to her she leaned forward with enthusiasm. 'You look at him sometimes when he thinks nobody's looking at him. I'll bet he killed a man.'

She narrowed her eyes and shivered. Lucille shivered. We all turned and looked around for Gatsby. It was testimony to the romantic speculation he inspired that there were whispers about him from those who had found little that it was necessary to whisper about in this world.

The first supper – there would be another one after midnight – was now being served, and Jordan invited me to join her own party, who were spread around a table on the other side of the garden. There were three married couples and Jordan's escort, a persistent undergraduate given to violent innuendo, and obviously under the impression that sooner or later Jordan was going to yield him up her person to a greater or lesser degree. Instead of rambling, this party had preserved a dignified homogeneity, and assumed to itself the function of representing the staid nobility of the countryside – East

Egg condescending to West Egg, and carefully on guard against its spectroscopic gaiety.

'Let's get out,' whispered Jordan, after a somehow wasteful and inappropriate half-hour; 'this is much too polite for me.'

We got up, and she explained that we were going to find the host: I had never met him, she said, and it was making me uneasy. The undergraduate nodded in a cynical, melancholy way.

The bar, where we glanced first, was crowded, but Gatsby was not there. She couldn't find him from the top of the steps, and he wasn't on the veranda. On a chance we tried an important-looking door, and walked into a high Gothic library, panelled with carved English oak, and probably transported complete from some ruin overseas.

A stout, middle-aged man, with enormous owl-eyed spectacles, was sitting somewhat drunk on the edge of a great table, staring with unsteady concentration at the shelves of books. As we entered he wheeled excitedly around and examined Jordan from head to foot.

'What do you think?' he demanded impetuously.

'About what?'

He waved his hand towards the bookshelves.

'About that. As a matter of fact you needn't bother to ascertain. I ascertained. They're real.'

'The books?'

He nodded.

'Absolutely real – have pages and everything. I thought they'd be a nice durable cardboard. Matter of fact, they're absolutely real. Pages and – Here! Lemme show you.'

Taking our scepticism for granted, he rushed to the bookcases and returned with Volume One of the *Stoddard Lectures*.

'See!' he cried triumphantly. 'It's a bona-fide piece of printed matter. It fooled me. This fella's a regular Belasco. It's a triumph. What thoroughness! What realism! Knew when to stop, too – didn't cut the pages. But what do you want? What do you expect?'

He snatched the book from me and replaced it hastily on its shelf, muttering that if one brick was removed the whole library was liable to collapse.

'Who brought you?' he demanded. 'Or did you just come? I was brought. Most people were brought.'

Jordan looked at him alertly, cheerfully, without answering.

'I was brought by a woman named Roosevelt,' he continued. 'Mrs Claude Roosevelt. Do you know her? I met her somewhere last night.

I've been drunk for about a week now, and I thought it might sober me up to sit in a library.'

'Has it?'

'A little bit, I think. I can't tell yet. I've only been here an hour. Did I tell you about the books? They're real. They're – '

'You told us.'

We shook hands with him gravely and went back outdoors.

There was dancing now on the canvas in the garden; old men pushing young girls backwards in eternal graceless circles, superior couples holding each other tortuously, fashionably, and keeping in the corners – and a great number of single girls dancing individualistically or relieving the orchestra for a moment of the burden of the banjo or the traps. By midnight the hilarity had increased. A celebrated tenor had sung in Italian, and a notorious contralto had sung in jazz, and between the numbers people were doing 'stunts' all over the garden, while happy, vacuous bursts of laughter rose towards the summer sky. A pair of stage twins, who turned out to be the girls in yellow, did a baby act in costume, and champagne was served in glasses bigger than finger-bowls. The moon had risen higher, and floating in the Sound was a triangle of silver scales, trembling a little to the stiff, tinny drip of the banjos on the lawn.

I was still with Jordan Baker. We were sitting at a table with a man of about my age and a rowdy little girl, who gave way upon the slightest provocation to uncontrollable laughter. I was enjoying myself now. I had taken two finger-bowls of champagne, and the scene had changed before my eyes into something significant, elemental and profound.

At a lull in the entertainment the man looked at me and smiled.

'Your face is familiar,' he said, politely. 'Weren't you in the First Division during the war?'

'Why, yes. I was in the Twenty-eighth Infantry.'

'I was in the Sixteenth until June 1918. I knew I'd seen you somewhere before.'

We talked for a moment about some wet, grey little villages in France. Evidently he lived in this vicinity, for he told me that he had just bought a hydroplane, and was going to try it out in the morning.

'Want to go with me, old sport? Just near the shore along the Sound.'

'What time?'

'Any time that suits you best.'

It was on the tip of my tongue to ask his name when Jordan looked around and smiled.

'Having a gay time now?' she enquired.

'Much better.' I turned again to my new acquaintance. 'This is an unusual party for me. I haven't even seen the host. I live over there – ' I waved my hand at the invisible hedge in the distance, 'and this man Gatsby sent over his chauffeur with an invitation.'

For a moment he looked at me as if he failed to understand.

'I'm Gatsby,' he said suddenly.

'What!' I exclaimed. 'Oh, I beg your pardon.'

'I thought you knew, old sport. I'm afraid I'm not a very good host.'

He smiled understandingly – much more than understandingly. It was one of those rare smiles with a quality of eternal reassurance in it, that you may come across four or five times in life. It faced – or seemed to face – the whole eternal world for an instant, and then concentrated on *you* with an irresistible prejudice in your favour. It understood you just as far as you wanted to be understood, believed in you as you would like to believe in yourself, and assured you that it had precisely the impression of you that, at your best, you hoped to convey. Precisely at that point it vanished – and I was looking at an elegant young roughneck, a year or two over thirty, whose elaborate formality of speech just missed being absurd. Sometime before he introduced himself I'd got a strong impression that he was picking his words with care.

Almost at the moment when Mr Gatsby identified himself, a butler hurried towards him with the information that Chicago was calling him on the wire. He excused himself with a small bow that included each of us in turn.

'If you want anything just ask for it, old sport,' he urged me. 'Excuse me. I will rejoin you later.'

When he was gone I turned immediately to Jordan – constrained to assure her of my surprise. I had expected that Mr Gatsby would be a florid and corpulent person in his middle years.

'Who is he?' I demanded. 'Do you know?'

'He's just a man named Gatsby.'

'Where is he from, I mean? And what does he do?'

'Now *you're* started on the subject,' she answered with a wan smile. 'Well, he told me once he was an Oxford man.'

A dim background started to take shape behind him, but at her next remark it faded away.

'However, I don't believe it.'

'Why not?'

'I don't know,' she insisted, 'I just don't think he went there.'

Something in her tone reminded me of the other girl's 'I think he killed a man', and had the effect of stimulating my curiosity. I would have accepted without question the information that Gatsby sprang from the swamps of Louisiana or from the lower East Side of New York. That was comprehensible. But young men didn't – at least in my provincial inexperience I believed they didn't – drift coolly out of nowhere and buy a palace on Long Island Sound.

'Anyhow, he gives large parties,' said Jordan, changing the subject with an urban taste for the concrete. 'And I like large parties. They're so intimate. At small parties there isn't any privacy.'

There was the boom of a bass drum, and the voice of the orchestra leader rang out suddenly above the echolalia of the garden.

'Ladies and gentlemen,' he cried. 'At the request of Mr Gatsby we are going to play for you Mr Vladimir Tostoff's latest work, which attracted so much attention at Carnegie Hall last May. If you read the papers, you know there was a big sensation.' He smiled with jovial condescension, and added: 'Some sensation!' Whereupon everybody laughed.

'The piece is known,' he concluded lustily, 'as Vladimir Tostoff's *Jazz History of the World*.'

The nature of Mr Tostoff's composition eluded me, because just as it began my eyes fell on Gatsby, standing alone on the marble steps and looking from one group to another with approving eyes. His tanned skin was drawn attractively tight on his face and his short hair looked as though it were trimmed every day. I could see nothing sinister about him. I wondered if the fact that he was not drinking helped to set him off from his guests, for it seemed to me that he grew more correct as the fraternal hilarity increased. When the *Jazz History of the World* was over, girls were putting their heads on men's shoulders in a puppyish, convivial way, girls were swooning backwards playfully into men's arms, even into groups, knowing that someone would arrest their falls – but no one swooned backwards on Gatsby, and no French bob touched Gatsby's shoulder, and no singing quartets were formed with Gatsby's head for one link.

'I beg your pardon.'

Gatsby's butler was suddenly standing beside us.

'Miss Baker?' he enquired. 'I beg your pardon, but Mr Gatsby would like to speak to you alone.'

'With me?' she exclaimed in surprise.

'Yes, madame.'

She got up slowly, raising her eyebrows at me in astonishment, and followed the butler towards the house. I noticed that she wore her evening-dress, all her dresses, like sports clothes – there was a jauntiness about her movements as if she had first learned to walk upon golf courses on clean, crisp mornings.

I was alone and it was almost two. For some time confused and intriguing sounds had issued from a long, many-windowed room which overhung the terrace. Eluding Jordan's undergraduate, who was now engaged in an obstetrical conversation with two chorus girls, and who implored me to join him, I went inside.

The large room was full of people. One of the girls in yellow was playing the piano, and beside her stood a tall, red-haired young lady from a famous chorus, engaged in song. She had drunk a quantity of champagne, and during the course of her song she had decided, ineptly, that everything was very, very sad – she was not only singing, she was weeping too. Whenever there was a pause in the song she filled it with gasping, broken sobs, and then took up the lyric again in a quavering soprano. The tears coursed down her cheeks – not freely, however, for when they came into contact with her heavily beaded eyelashes they assumed an inky colour, and pursued the rest of their way in slow black rivulets. A humorous suggestion was made that she sing the notes on her face, whereupon she threw up her hands, sank into a chair, and went off into a deep vinous sleep.

'She had a fight with a man who says he's her husband,' explained a girl at my elbow.

I looked around. Most of the remaining women were now having fights with men said to be their husbands. Even Jordan's party, the quartet from East Egg, were rent asunder by dissension. One of the men was talking with curious intensity to a young actress, and his wife, after attempting to laugh at the situation in a dignified and indifferent way, broke down entirely and resorted to flank attacks – at intervals she appeared suddenly at his side like an angry diamond, and hissed: 'You promised!' into his ear.

The reluctance to go home was not confined to wayward men. The hall was at present occupied by two deplorably sober men and their highly indignant wives. The wives were sympathising with each other in slightly raised voices.

'Whenever he sees I'm having a good time he wants to go home.'

'Never heard anything so selfish in my life.'

'We're always the first ones to leave.'

'So are we.'

'Well, we're almost the last tonight,' said one of the men sheepishly. 'The orchestra left half an hour ago.'

In spite of the wives' agreement that such malevolence was beyond credibility, the dispute ended in a short struggle, and both wives were lifted, kicking, into the night.

As I waited for my hat in the hall the door of the library opened and Jordan Baker and Gatsby came out together. He was saying some last word to her, but the eagerness in his manner tightened abruptly into formality as several people approached him to say goodbye.

Jordan's party were calling impatiently to her from the porch, but she lingered for a moment to shake hands.

'I've just heard the most amazing thing,' she whispered. 'How long were we in there?'

'Why, about an hour.'

'It was . . . simply amazing,' she repeated abstractedly. 'But I swore I wouldn't tell it and here I am tantalising you.' She yawned gracefully in my face. 'Please come and see me . . . Phone book . . . Under the name of Mrs Sigourney Howard . . . My aunt . . . ' She was hurrying off as she talked – her brown hand waved a jaunty salute as she melted into her party at the door.

Rather ashamed that on my first appearance I had stayed so late, I joined the last of Gatsby's guests, who were clustered around him. I wanted to explain that I'd hunted for him early in the evening and to apologise for not having known him in the garden.

'Don't mention it,' he enjoined me eagerly. 'Don't give it another thought, old sport.' The familiar expression held no more familiarity than the hand which reassuringly brushed my shoulder. 'And don't forget we're going up in the hydroplane tomorrow morning, at nine o'clock.'

Then the butler, behind his shoulder: 'Philadelphia wants you on the phone, sir.'

'All right, in a minute. Tell them I'll be right there . . . Good-night.'

'Good-night.'

'Good-night.' He smiled – and suddenly there seemed to be a pleasant significance in having been among the last to go, as if he had desired it all the time. 'Good-night, old sport . . . Good-night.'

But as I walked down the steps I saw that the evening was not quite over. Fifty feet from the door a dozen headlights illuminated a bizarre and tumultuous scene. In the ditch beside the road, right side up, but violently shorn of one wheel, rested a new coupé which had left Gatsby's drive not two minutes before. The sharp jut of a wall accounted for the detachment of the wheel, which was now getting considerable attention from half a dozen curious chauffeurs. However, as they had left their cars blocking the road, a harsh, discordant din from those in the rear had been audible for some time, and added to the already violent confusion of the scene.

A man in a long duster had dismounted from the wreck and now stood in the middle of the road, looking from the car to the tyre and from the tyre to the observers in a pleasant, puzzled way.

'See!' he explained. 'It went in the ditch.'

The fact was infinitely astonishing to him, and I recognised first the unusual quality of wonder, and then the man – it was the late patron of Gatsby's library.

'How'd it happen?'

He shrugged his shoulders.

'I know nothing whatever about mechanics,' he said decisively.

'But how did it happen? Did you run into the wall?'

'Don't ask me,' said Owl Eyes, washing his hands of the whole matter. 'I know very little about driving – next to nothing. It happened, and that's all I know.'

'Well, if you're a poor driver you oughtn't to try driving at night.'

'But I wasn't even trying,' he explained indignantly, 'I wasn't even trying.'

An awed hush fell upon the bystanders.

'Do you want to commit suicide?'

'You're lucky it was just a wheel! A bad driver and not even *try*ing!'

'You don't understand,' explained the criminal. 'I wasn't driving. There's another man in the car.'

The shock that followed this declaration found voice in a sustained 'Ah-h-h!' as the door of the coupé swung slowly open. The crowd – it was now a crowd – stepped back involuntarily, and when the door had opened wide there was a ghostly pause. Then, very gradually, part by part, a pale, dangling individual stepped out of the wreck, pawing tentatively at the ground with a large uncertain dancing shoe.

Blinded by the glare of the headlights and confused by the incessant groaning of the horns, the apparition stood swaying for a moment before he perceived the man in the duster.

'Wha's matter?' he enquired calmly. 'Did we run outa gas?'

'Look!'

Half a dozen fingers pointed at the amputated wheel – he stared at it for a moment, and then looked upward as though he suspected that it had dropped from the sky.

'It came off,' someone explained.

He nodded.

'At first I din' notice we'd stopped.'

A pause. Then, taking a long breath and straightening his shoulders, he remarked in a determined voice: 'Wonder'ff tell me where there's a gas'line station?'

At least a dozen men, some of them a little better off than he was, explained to him that wheel and car were no longer joined by any physical bond.

'Back out,' he suggested after a moment. 'Put her in reverse.'

'But the *wheel's* off!'

He hesitated.

'No harm in trying,' he said.

The caterwauling horns had reached a crescendo and I turned away and cut across the lawn towards home. I glanced back once. A wafer of a moon was shining over Gatsby's house, making the night fine as before, and surviving the laughter and the sound of his still glowing garden. A sudden emptiness seemed to flow now from the windows and the great doors, endowing with complete isolation the figure of the host, who stood on the porch, his hand up in a formal gesture of farewell.

Reading over what I have written so far, I see I have given the impression that the events of three nights several weeks apart were all that absorbed me. On the contrary, they were merely casual events in a crowded summer, and, until much later, they absorbed me infinitely less than my personal affairs.

Most of the time I worked. In the early morning the sun threw my shadow westward as I hurried down the white chasms of lower New York to the Probity Trust. I knew the other clerks and young bond-salesmen by their first names, and lunched with them in dark, crowded restaurants on little pig sausages and mashed potatoes and coffee. I even had a short affair with a girl who lived in Jersey City and worked in the accounting department, but her brother began throwing mean looks in my direction, so when she went on her vacation in July I let it blow quietly away.

I took dinner usually at the Yale Club – for some reason it was the gloomiest event of my day – and then I went upstairs to the library and studied investments and securities for a conscientious hour. There were generally a few rioters around, but they never came into the library, so it was a good place to work. After that, if the night was mellow, I strolled down Madison Avenue past the old Murray Hill Hotel, and over 33rd Street to the Pennsylvania Station.

I began to like New York, the racy, adventurous feel of it at night, and the satisfaction that the constant flicker of men and women and machines gives to the restless eye. I liked to walk up Fifth Avenue and pick out romantic women from the crowd and imagine that in a few minutes I was going to enter into their lives, and no one would ever know or disapprove. Sometimes, in my mind, I followed them to their apartments on the corners of hidden streets, and they turned and smiled back at me before they faded through a door into warm darkness. At the enchanted metropolitan twilight I felt a haunting loneliness sometimes, and felt it in others – poor young clerks who loitered in front of windows waiting until it was time for a solitary restaurant dinner – young clerks in the dusk, wasting the most poignant moments of night and life.

Again at eight o'clock, when the dark lanes of the Forties were lined five deep with throbbing taxicabs, bound for the theatre district, I felt a sinking in my heart. Forms leaned together in the taxis as they waited, and voices sang, and there was laughter from unheard jokes, and lighted cigarettes made unintelligible circles inside. Imagining that I, too, was hurrying towards gaiety and sharing their intimate excitement, I wished them well.

For a while I lost sight of Jordan Baker, and then in midsummer I found her again. At first I was flattered to go places with her, because she was a golf champion, and everyone knew her name. Then it was something more. I wasn't actually in love, but I felt a sort of tender curiosity. The bored haughty face that she turned to the world concealed something – most affectations conceal something eventually, even though they don't in the beginning – and one day I found what it was. When we were on a house-party together up in Warwick, she left a borrowed car out in the rain with the top down, and then lied about it – and suddenly I remembered the story about her that had eluded me that night at Daisy's. At her first big golf tournament there was a row that nearly reached the newspapers – a suggestion that she had moved her ball from a bad lie in the semi-final round. The thing approached the proportions of a scandal – then died away. A caddy retracted his statement, and the only other witness admitted that he might have been mistaken. The incident and the name had remained together in my mind.

Jordan Baker instinctively avoided clever, shrewd men, and now I saw that this was because she felt safer on a plane where any divergence from a code would be thought impossible. She was incurably dishonest. She wasn't able to endure being at a disadvantage and, given this unwillingness, I suppose she had begun dealing in subterfuges when she was very young in order to keep that cool, insolent smile turned to the world and yet satisfy the demands of her hard, jaunty body.

It made no difference to me. Dishonesty in a woman is a thing you never blame deeply – I was casually sorry, and then I forgot. It was on that same house-party that we had a curious conversation about driving a car. It started because she passed so close to some workmen that our fender flicked a button on one man's coat.

'You're a rotten driver,' I protested. 'Either you ought to be more careful, or you oughtn't to drive at all.'

'I am careful.'

'No, you're not.'

'Well, other people are,' she said lightly.

'What's that got to do with it?'

'They'll keep out of my way,' she insisted. 'It takes two to make an accident.'

'Suppose you met somebody just as careless as yourself.'

'I hope I never will,' she answered. 'I hate careless people. That's why I like you.'

Her grey, sun-strained eyes stared straight ahead, but she had deliberately shifted our relations, and for a moment I thought I loved her. But I am slow-thinking and full of interior rules that act as brakes on my desires, and I knew that first I had to get myself definitely out of that tangle back home. I'd been writing letters once a week and signing them: 'Love, Nick', and all I could think of was how, when that certain girl played tennis, a faint moustache of perspiration appeared on her upper lip. Nevertheless there was a vague understanding that had to be tactfully broken off before I was free.

Everyone suspects himself of at least one of the cardinal virtues, and this is mine: I am one of the few honest people that I have ever known.

Chapter 4

On Sunday morning while church bells rang in the villages alongshore, the world and its mistress returned to Gatsby's house and twinkled hilariously on his lawn.

'He's a bootlegger,' said the young ladies, moving somewhere between his cocktails and his flowers. 'One time he killed a man who had found out that he was nephew to Von Hindenburg and second cousin to the devil. Reach me a rose, honey, and pour me a last drop into that there crystal glass.'

Once I wrote down on the empty spaces of a timetable the names of those who came to Gatsby's house that summer. It is an old timetable now, disintegrating at its folds, and headed, 'This schedule in effect July 5th, 1922'. But I can still read the grey names, and they will give you a better impression than my generalities of those who accepted Gatsby's hospitality and paid him the subtle tribute of knowing nothing whatever about him.

From East Egg, then, came the Chester Beckers and the Leeches, and a man named Bunsen, whom I knew at Yale, and Dr Webster Civet, who was drowned last summer up in Maine. And the Hornbeams and the Willie Voltaires, and a whole clan named Blackbuck, who always gathered in a corner and flipped up their noses like goats at whomsoever came near. And the Ismays and the Chrysties (or rather Hubert Auerbach and Mr Chrystie's wife), and Edgar Beaver, whose hair, they say, turned cotton-white one winter afternoon for no good reason at all.

Clarence Endive was from East Egg, as I remember. He came only once, in white knickerbockers, and had a fight with a bum named Etty in the garden. From farther out on the Island came the Cheadles and the O. R. P. Schraeders, and the Stonewall Jackson Abrams of Georgia, and the Fishguards and the Ripley Snells. Snell was there three days before he went to the penitentiary, so drunk out on the gravel drive that Mrs Ulysses Swett's automobile ran over his right hand. The Dancies came, too, and S. B. Whitebait, who was well over sixty, and Maurice A. Flink, and the Hammerheads, and Beluga the tobacco importer, and Beluga's girls.

From West Egg came the Poles and the Mulreadys and Cecil Roebuck and Cecil Schoen and Gulick the state senator and Newton

Orchid, who controlled Films Par Excellence, and Eckhaust and Clyde Cohen and Don S. Schwartze (the son) and Arthur McCarty, all connected with the movies in one way or another. And the Catlips and the Bembergs and G. Earl Muldoon, brother to that Muldoon who afterwards strangled his wife. Da Fontano the promoter came there, and Ed Legros and James B. ('Rot-Gut') Ferret and the De Jongs and Ernest Lilly – they came to gamble, and when Ferret wandered into the garden it meant he was cleaned out and Associated Traction would have to fluctuate profitably next day.

A man named Klipspringer was there so often and so long that he became known as 'the boarder' – I doubt if he had any other home. Of theatrical people there were Gus Waize and Horace O'Donavan and Lester Myer and George Duckweed and Francis Bull. Also from New York were the Chromes and the Backhyssons and the Dennickers and Russell Betty and the Corrigans and the Kellehers and the Dewers and the Scullys and S. W. Belcher and the Smirkes and the young Quinns, divorced now, and Henry L. Palmetto, who killed himself by jumping in front of a subway train at Times Square.

Benny McClenahan arrived always with four girls. They were never quite the same ones in physical person, but they were so identical one with another that it inevitably seemed that they had been there before. I have forgotten their names – Jacqueline, I think, or else Consuela, or Gloria or Judy or June, and their last names were either the melodious names of flowers and months or the sterner ones of the great American capitalists whose cousins, if pressed, they would confess themselves to be.

In addition to all these I can remember that Faustina O'Brien came there at least once and the Baedeker girls and young Brewer, who had his nose shot off in the war, and Mr Albrucksburger and Miss Haag, his fiancée, and Ardita Fitz-Peters and Mr P. Jewett, once head of the American Legion, and Miss Claudia Hip, with a man reputed to be her chauffeur, and a prince of something, whom we called Duke, and whose name, if I ever knew it, I have forgotten.

All these people came to Gatsby's house in the summer.

At nine o'clock one morning late in July, Gatsby's gorgeous car lurched up the rocky drive to my door and gave out a burst of melody from its three-noted horn. It was the first time he had called on me, though I had gone to two of his parties, mounted in his hydroplane, and, at his urgent invitation, made frequent use of his beach.

'Good-morning, old sport. You're having lunch with me today and I thought we'd ride up together.'

He was balancing himself on the dashboard of his car with that resourcefulness of movement that is so peculiarly American – that comes, I suppose, with the absence of lifting work in youth and, even more, with the formless grace of our nervous, sporadic games. This quality was continually breaking through his punctilious manner in the shape of restlessness. He was never quite still; there was always a tapping foot somewhere or the impatient opening and closing of a hand.

He saw me looking with admiration at his car.

'It's pretty, isn't it, old sport?' He jumped off to give me a better view. 'Haven't you ever seen it before?'

I'd seen it. Everybody had seen it. It was a rich cream colour, bright with nickel, swollen here and there in its monstrous length with triumphant hatboxes and supper-boxes and tool-boxes, and terraced with a labyrinth of wind-shields that mirrored a dozen suns. Sitting down behind many layers of glass in a sort of green leather conservatory, we started to town.

I had talked with him perhaps half a dozen times in the past month and found, to my disappointment, that he had little to say. So my first impression, that he was a person of some undefined consequence, had gradually faded and he had become simply the proprietor of an elaborate roadhouse next door.

And then came that disconcerting ride. We hadn't reached West Egg Village before Gatsby began leaving his elegant sentences unfinished and slapping himself indecisively on the knee of his caramel-coloured suit.

'Look here, old sport,' he broke out surprisingly, 'what's your opinion of me, anyhow?'

A little overwhelmed, I began the generalised evasions which that question deserves.

'Well, I'm going to tell you something about my life,' he interrupted. 'I don't want you to get a wrong idea of me from all these stories you hear.'

So he was aware of the bizarre accusations that flavoured conversation in his halls.

'I'll tell you God's truth.' His right hand suddenly ordered divine retribution to stand by. 'I am the son of some wealthy people in the Middle West – all dead now. I was brought up in America but educated at Oxford, because all my ancestors have been educated there for many years. It is a family tradition.'

He looked at me sideways – and I knew why Jordan Baker had believed he was lying. He hurried the phrase 'educated at Oxford', or swallowed it, or choked on it, as though it had bothered him before. And with this doubt, his whole statement fell to pieces, and I wondered if there wasn't something a little sinister about him, after all.

'What part of the Middle West?' I enquired casually.

'San Francisco.'

'I see.'

'My family all died and I came into a good deal of money.'

His voice was solemn, as if the memory of that sudden extinction of a clan still haunted him. For a moment I suspected that he was pulling my leg, but a glance at him convinced me otherwise.

'After that I lived like a young rajah in all the capitals of Europe – Paris, Venice, Rome – collecting jewels, chiefly rubies, hunting big game, painting a little, things for myself only, and trying to forget something very sad that had happened to me long ago.'

With an effort I managed to restrain my incredulous laughter. The very phrases were worn so threadbare that they evoked no image except that of a turbaned 'character' leaking sawdust at every pore as he pursued a tiger through the Bois de Boulogne.

'Then came the war, old sport. It was a great relief, and I tried very hard to die, but I seemed to bear an enchanted life. I accepted a commission as first lieutenant when it began. In the Argonne Forest I took the remains of my machine-gun battalion so far forward that there was a half-mile gap on either side of us where the infantry couldn't advance. We stayed there two days and two nights, a hundred and thirty men with sixteen Lewis guns, and when the infantry came up at last they found the insignia of three German divisions among the piles of dead. I was promoted to be a major, and every Allied government gave me a decoration – even Montenegro, little Montenegro down on the Adriatic Sea!'

Little Montenegro! He lifted up the words and nodded at them – with his smile. The smile comprehended Montenegro's troubled history and sympathised with the brave struggles of the Montenegrin people. It appreciated fully the chain of national circumstances which had elicited this tribute from Montenegro's warm little heart. My incredulity was submerged in fascination now; it was like skimming hastily through a dozen magazines.

He reached in his pocket, and a piece of metal, slung on a ribbon, fell into my palm.

'That's the one from Montenegro.'

To my astonishment, the thing had an authentic look. 'Orderi di Danilo', ran the circular legend, 'Montenegro, Nicolas Rex'.

'Turn it.'

'Major Jay Gatsby,' I read, 'For Valour Extraordinary.'

'Here's another thing I always carry. A souvenir of Oxford days. It was taken in Trinity Quad – the man on my left is now the Earl of Doncaster.'

It was a photograph of half a dozen young men in blazers loafing in an archway through which was visible a host of spires. There was Gatsby, looking a little, not much, younger – with a cricket bat in his hand.

Then it was all true. I saw the skins of tigers flaming in his palace on the Grand Canal; I saw him opening a chest of rubies to ease, with their crimson-lighted depths, the gnawings of his broken heart.

'I'm going to make a big request of you today,' he said, pocketing his souvenirs with satisfaction, 'so I thought you ought to know something about me. I didn't want you to think I was just some nobody. You see, I usually find myself among strangers because I drift here and there trying to forget the sad thing that happened to me.' He hesitated. 'You'll hear about it this afternoon.'

'At lunch?'

'No, this afternoon. I happened to find out that you're taking Miss Baker to tea.'

'Do you mean you're in love with Miss Baker?'

'No, old sport, I'm not. But Miss Baker has kindly consented to speak to you about this matter.'

I hadn't the faintest idea what 'this matter' was, but I was more annoyed than interested. I hadn't asked Jordan to tea in order to discuss Mr Jay Gatsby. I was sure the request would be something utterly fantastic, and for a moment I was sorry I'd ever set foot upon his overpopulated lawn.

He wouldn't say another word. His correctness grew on him as we neared the city. We passed Port Roosevelt, where there was a glimpse of red-belted ocean-going ships, and sped along a cobbled slum lined with the dark, undeserted saloons of the faded-gilt nineteen-hundreds. Then the valley of ashes opened out on both sides of us, and I had a glimpse of Mrs Wilson straining at the garage pump with panting vitality as we went by.

With fenders spread like wings we scattered light through half Astoria – only half, for as we twisted among the pillars of the elevated I heard the familiar 'jug-jug-*spat*!' of a motorcycle, and a frantic policeman rode alongside.

'All right, old sport,' called Gatsby. We slowed down. Taking a white card from his wallet, he waved it before the man's eyes.

'Right you are,' agreed the policeman, tipping his cap. 'Know you next time, Mr Gatsby. Excuse *me*!'

'What was that?' I enquired. 'The picture of Oxford?'

'I was able to do the commissioner a favour once, and he sends me a Christmas card every year.'

Over the great bridge, with the sunlight through the girders making a constant flicker upon the moving cars, with the city rising up across the river in white heaps and sugar lumps all built with a wish out of non-olfactory money. The city seen from the Queensboro Bridge is always the city seen for the first time, in its first wild promise of all the mystery and the beauty in the world.

A dead man passed us in a hearse heaped with blooms, followed by two carriages with drawn blinds, and by more cheerful carriages for friends. The friends looked out at us with the tragic eyes and short upper lips of south-eastern Europe, and I was glad that the sight of Gatsby's splendid car was included in their sombre holiday. As we crossed Blackwell's Island a limousine passed us, driven by a white chauffeur, in which sat three modish Negroes, two bucks and a girl. I laughed aloud as the yolks of their eyeballs rolled towards us in haughty rivalry.

'Anything can happen now that we've slid over this bridge,' I thought; 'anything at all . . .'

Even Gatsby could happen, without any particular wonder.

Roaring noon. In a well-fanned Forty-second Street cellar I met Gatsby for lunch. Blinking away the brightness of the street outside, my eyes picked him out obscurely in the ante-room, talking to another man.

'Mr Carraway, this is my friend Mr Wolfsheim.'

A small, flat-nosed Jew raised his large head and regarded me with two fine growths of hair which luxuriated in either nostril. After a moment I discovered his tiny eyes in the half-darkness.

' – So I took one look at him,' said Mr Wolfsheim, shaking my hand earnestly, 'and what do you think I did?'

'What?' I enquired politely.

But evidently he was not addressing me, for he dropped my hand and covered Gatsby with his expressive nose.

'I handed the money to Katspaugh and I said: "All right, Katspaugh, don't pay him a penny till he shuts his mouth." He shut it then and there.'

Gatsby took an arm of each of us and moved forward into the restaurant, whereupon Mr Wolfsheim swallowed a new sentence he was starting and lapsed into a somnambulatory abstraction.

'Highballs?' asked the head waiter.

'This is a nice restaurant here,' said Mr Wolfsheim, looking at the Presbyterian nymphs on the ceiling. 'But I like across the street better!'

'Yes, highballs,' agreed Gatsby, and then to Mr Wolfsheim: 'It's too hot over there.'

'Hot and small – yes,' said Mr Wolfsheim, 'but full of memories.'

'What place is that?' I asked.

'The old Metropole.'

'The old Metropole,' brooded Mr Wolfsheim gloomily. 'Filled with faces dead and gone. Filled with friends gone now for ever. I can't forget so long as I live the night they shot Rosy Rosenthal there. It was six of us at the table, and Rosy had ate and drunk a lot all evening. When it was almost morning the waiter came up to him with a funny look and says somebody wants to speak to him outside. "All right," says Rosy, and begins to get up, and I pulled him down in his chair.

' "Let the bastards come in here if they want you, Rosy, but don't you, so help me, move outside this room."

'It was four o'clock in the morning then, and if we'd of raised the blinds we'd of seen daylight.'

'Did he go?' I asked innocently.

'Sure he went.' Mr Wolfsheim's nose flashed at me indignantly. 'He turned around in the door and says: "Don't let that waiter take away my coffee!" Then he went out on the sidewalk, and they shot him three times in his full belly and drove away.'

'Four of them were electrocuted,' I said, remembering.

'Five, with Becker.' His nostrils turned to me in an interested way. 'I understand you're looking for a business gonnegtion.'

The juxtaposition of these two remarks was startling.

Gatsby answered for me: 'Oh, no,' he exclaimed, 'this isn't the man.'

'No?' Mr Wolfsheim seemed disappointed.

'This is just a friend. I told you we'd talk about that some other time.'

'I beg your pardon,' said Mr Wolfsheim, 'I had a wrong man.'

A succulent hash arrived, and Mr Wolfsheim, forgetting the more sentimental atmosphere of the old Metropole, began to eat with ferocious delicacy. His eyes, meanwhile, roved very slowly all around the room – he completed the arc by turning to inspect the people directly behind. I think that, except for my presence, he would have taken one short glance beneath our own table.

'Look here, old sport,' said Gatsby leaning towards me, 'I'm afraid I made you a little angry this morning in the car.'

There was the smile again, but this time I held out against it.

'I don't like mysteries,' I answered, 'and I don't understand why you won't come out frankly and tell me what you want. Why has it all got to come through Miss Baker?'

'Oh, it's nothing underhand,' he assured me. 'Miss Baker's a great sportswoman, you know, and she'd never do anything that wasn't all right.'

Suddenly he looked at his watch, jumped up, and hurried from the room, leaving me with Mr Wolfsheim at the table.

'He has to telephone,' said Mr Wolfsheim, following him with his eyes. 'Fine fellow, isn't he? Handsome to look at and a perfect gentleman.'

'Yes.'

'He's an Oggsford man.'

'Oh!'

'He went to Oggsford College in England. You know Oggsford College?'

'I've heard of it.'

'It's one of the most famous colleges in the world.'

'Have you known Gatsby for a long time?' I enquired.

'Several years,' he answered in a gratified way. 'I made the pleasure of his acquaintance just after the war. But I knew I had discovered a man of fine breeding after I talked with him an hour. I said to myself: "There's the kind of man you'd like to take home and introduce to your mother and sister." ' He paused. 'I see you're looking at my cuff buttons.'

I hadn't been looking at them, but I did now. They were composed of oddly familiar pieces of ivory.

'Finest specimens of human molars,' he informed me.

'Well!' I inspected them. 'That's a very interesting idea.'

'Yeah.' He flipped his sleeves up under his coat. 'Yeah, Gatsby's very careful about women. He would never so much as look at a friend's wife.'

When the subject of this instinctive trust returned to the table and sat down, Mr Wolfsheim drank his coffee with a jerk and got to his feet.

'I have enjoyed my lunch,' he said, 'and I'm going to run off from you two young men before I outstay my welcome.'

'Don't hurry, Meyer,' said Gatsby, without enthusiasm. Mr Wolfsheim raised his hand in a sort of benediction.

'You're very polite, but I belong to another generation,' he announced solemnly. 'You sit here and discuss your sports and your young ladies and your – ' He supplied an imaginary noun with another wave of his hand. 'As for me, I am fifty years old, and I won't impose myself on you any longer.'

As he shook hands and turned away his tragic nose was trembling. I wondered if I had said anything to offend him.

'He becomes very sentimental sometimes,' explained Gatsby. 'This is one of his sentimental days. He's quite a character around New York – a denizen of Broadway.'

'Who is he, anyhow, an actor?'

'No.'

'A dentist?'

'Meyer Wolfsheim? No, he's a gambler.' Gatsby hesitated, then added coolly: 'He's the man who fixed the World's Series back in 1919.'

'Fixed the World's Series?' I repeated.

The idea staggered me. I remembered, of course, that the World's Series had been fixed in 1919, but if I had thought of it at all I would have thought of it as a thing that merely *happened*, the end of some inevitable chain. It never occurred to me that one man could start to play with the faith of fifty million people – with the single-mindedness of a burglar blowing a safe.

'How did he happen to do that?' I asked after a minute.

'He just saw the opportunity.'

'Why isn't he in jail?'

'They can't get him, old sport. He's a smart man.'

I insisted on paying the check. As the waiter brought my change I caught sight of Tom Buchanan across the crowded room.

'Come along with me for a minute,' I said; 'I've got to say hello to someone.'

When he saw us Tom jumped up and took half a dozen steps in our direction.

'Where've you been?' he demanded eagerly. 'Daisy's furious because you haven't called up.'

'This is Mr Gatsby, Mr Buchanan.'

They shook hands briefly, and a strained, unfamiliar look of embarrassment came over Gatsby's face.

'How've you been, anyhow?' demanded Tom of me. 'How'd you happen to come up this far to eat?'

'I've been having lunch with Mr Gatsby.'

I turned towards Mr Gatsby, but he was no longer there.

One October day in 1917 – (said Jordan Baker that afternoon, sitting up very straight on a straight chair in the tea-garden at the Plaza Hotel) – I was walking along from one place to another, half on the sidewalks and half on the lawns. I was happier on the lawns because I had on shoes from England with rubber nobs on the soles that bit into the soft ground. I had on a new plaid skirt also that blew a little in the wind, and whenever this happened the red-white-and-blue banners in front of all the houses stretched out stiff and said *tut-tut-tut-tut*, in a disapproving way.

The largest of the banners and the largest of the lawns belonged to Daisy Fay's house. She was just eighteen, two years older than me, and by far the most popular of all the young girls in Louisville. She dressed in white, and had a little white roadster, and all day long the telephone rang in her house and excited young officers from Camp Taylor demanded the privilege of monopolising her that night. 'Anyways, for an hour!'

When I came opposite her house that morning her white roadster was beside the curb, and she was sitting in it with a lieutenant I had never seen before. They were so engrossed in each other that she didn't see me until I was five feet away.

'Hello, Jordan,' she called unexpectedly. 'Please come here.'

I was flattered that she wanted to speak to me, because of all the older girls I admired her most. She asked me if I was going to the Red Cross and make bandages. I was. Well, then, would I tell them that she couldn't come that day? The officer looked at Daisy while she was speaking, in a way that every young girl wants to be looked at sometime, and because it seemed romantic to me I have remembered the incident ever since. His name was Jay Gatsby, and I didn't lay eyes on him again for over four years – even after I'd met him on Long Island I didn't realise it was the same man.

That was 1917. By the next year I had a few beaux myself, and I began to play in tournaments, so I didn't see Daisy very often. She went with a slightly older crowd – when she went with anyone at all. Wild rumours were circulating about her – how her mother had found her packing her bag one winter night to go to New York and say goodbye to a soldier who was going overseas. She was effectually prevented, but she wasn't on speaking terms with her family for several weeks. After that she didn't play around with the soldiers any more, but only with a few flat-footed, short-sighted young men in town, who couldn't get into the army at all.

By the next autumn she was gay again, gay as ever. She had a début after the Armistice, and in February she was presumably engaged to a man from New Orleans. In June she married Tom Buchanan of Chicago, with more pomp and circumstance than Louisville ever knew before. He came down with a hundred people in four private cars, and hired a whole floor of the Muhlbach Hotel, and the day before the wedding he gave her a string of pearls valued at three hundred and fifty thousand dollars.

I was a bridesmaid. I came into her room half an hour before the bridal dinner, and found her lying on her bed as lovely as the June night in her flowered dress – and as drunk as a monkey. She had a bottle of Sauterne in one hand and a letter in the other.

' 'Gratulate me,' she muttered. 'Never had a drink before, but oh how I do enjoy it.'

'What's the matter, Daisy?'

I was scared, I can tell you; I'd never seen a girl like that before.

'Here, deares'.' She groped around in a waste-basket she had with her on the bed and pulled out the string of pearls. 'Take 'em downstairs and give 'em back to whoever they belong to. Tell 'em all Daisy's change' her mine. Say: "Daisy's change' her mine!" '

She began to cry – she cried and cried. I rushed out and found her mother's maid, and we locked the door and got her into a cold bath. She wouldn't let go of the letter. She took it into the tub with her and squeezed it up into a wet ball, and only let me leave it in the soap-dish when she saw that it was coming to pieces like snow.

But she didn't say another word. We gave her spirits of ammonia and put ice on her forehead and hooked her back into her dress, and half an hour later, when we walked out of the room, the pearls were around her neck and the incident was over. Next day at five o'clock she married Tom Buchanan without so much as a shiver, and started off on a three months' trip to the South Seas.

I saw them in Santa Barbara when they came back, and I thought I'd never seen a girl so mad about her husband. If he left the room for a minute she'd look around uneasily, and say: 'Where's Tom gone?' and wear the most abstracted expression until she saw him coming in the door. She used to sit on the sand with his head in her lap by the hour, rubbing her fingers over his eyes and looking at him with unfathomable delight. It was touching to see them together – it made you laugh in a hushed, fascinated way. That was in August. A week after I left Santa Barbara, Tom ran into a wagon on the Ventura road one night, and ripped a front wheel off his car. The girl who was with him got into the papers, too, because her arm was broken – she was one of the chambermaids in the Santa Barbara Hotel.

The next April Daisy had her little girl, and they went to France for a year. I saw them one spring in Cannes, and later in Deauville, and then they came back to Chicago to settle down. Daisy was popular in Chicago, as you know. They moved with a fast crowd, all of them young and rich and wild, but she came out with an absolutely perfect reputation. Perhaps because she doesn't drink. It's a great advantage not to drink among hard-drinking people. You can hold your tongue, and, moreover, you can time any little irregularity of your own so that everybody else is so blind that they don't see or care. Perhaps Daisy never went in for amour at all – and yet there's something in that voice of hers . . .

Well, about six weeks ago, she heard the name Gatsby for the first time in years. It was when I asked you – do you remember? – if you knew Gatsby in West Egg. After you had gone home she came into my room and woke me up, and said: 'What Gatsby?' and when I described him – I was half-asleep – she said in the strangest voice that it must be the man she used to know. It wasn't until then that I connected this Gatsby with the officer in her white car.

When Jordan Baker had finished telling all this we had left the Plaza for half an hour and were driving in a victoria through Central Park. The sun had gone down behind the tall apartments of the movie stars in the West Fifties, and the clear voices of children, already gathered like crickets on the grass, rose through the hot twilight:

> 'I'm the Sheik of Araby.
> Your love belongs to me.
> At night when you're asleep
> Into your tent I'll creep – '

'It was a strange coincidence,' I said.

'But it wasn't a coincidence at all.'

'Why not?'

'Gatsby bought that house so that Daisy would be just across the bay.'

Then it had not been merely the stars to which he had aspired on that June night. He came alive to me, delivered suddenly from the womb of his purposeless splendour.

'He wants to know,' continued Jordan, 'if you'll invite Daisy to your house some afternoon and then let him come over.'

The modesty of the demand shook me. He had waited five years and bought a mansion where he dispensed starlight to casual moths – so that he could 'come over' some afternoon to a stranger's garden.

'Did I have to know all this before he could ask such a little thing?'

'He's afraid, he's waited so long. He thought you might be offended. You see, he's regular tough underneath it all.'

Something worried me.

'Why didn't he ask you to arrange a meeting?'

'He wants her to see his house,' she explained. 'And your house is right next door.'

'Oh!'

'I think he half expected her to wander into one of his parties, some night,' went on Jordan, 'but she never did. Then he began asking people casually if they knew her, and I was the first one he found. It was that night he sent for me at his dance, and you should have heard the elaborate way he worked up to it. Of course, I immediately suggested a luncheon in New York – and I thought he'd go mad: ' "I don't want to do anything out of the way!" he kept saying. "I want to see her right next door."

'When I said you were a particular friend of Tom's, he started to abandon the whole idea. He doesn't know very much about Tom, though he says he's read a Chicago paper for years just on the chance of catching a glimpse of Daisy's name.'

It was dark now, and as we dipped under a little bridge I put my arm around Jordan's golden shoulder and drew her towards me and asked her to dinner. Suddenly I wasn't thinking of Daisy and Gatsby any more, but of this clean, hard, limited person, who dealt in universal scepticism, and who leaned back jauntily just within the circle of my arm. A phrase began to beat in my ears with a sort of heady excitement: 'There are only the pursued, the pursuing, the busy and the tired.'

'And Daisy ought to have something in her life,' murmured Jordan to me.

'Does she want to see Gatsby?'

'She's not to know about it. Gatsby doesn't want her to know. You're just supposed to invite her to tea.'

We passed a barrier of dark trees, and then the façade of Fifty-ninth Street, a block of delicate pale light, beamed down into the park. Unlike Gatsby and Tom Buchanan, I had no girl whose disembodied face floated along the dark cornices and blinding signs, and so I drew up the girl beside me, tightening my arms. Her wan, scornful mouth smiled, and so I drew her up again closer, this time to my face.

Chapter 5

When I came home to West Egg that night I was afraid for a moment that my house was on fire. Two o'clock and the whole corner of the peninsula was blazing with light, which fell unreal on the shrubbery and made thin elongating glints upon the roadside wires. Turning a corner, I saw that it was Gatsby's house, lit from tower to cellar.

At first I thought it was another party, a wild rout that had resolved itself into 'hide-and-seek' or 'sardines-in-the-box', with all the house thrown open to the game. But there wasn't a sound. Only wind in the trees, which blew the wires and made the lights go off and on again as if the house had winked into the darkness. As my taxi groaned away I saw Gatsby walking towards me across his lawn.

'Your place looks like the World's Fair,' I said.

'Does it?' He turned his eyes towards it absently. 'I have been glancing into some of the rooms. Let's go to Coney Island, old sport. In my car.'

'It's too late.'

'Well, suppose we take a plunge in the swimming-pool? I haven't made use of it all summer.'

'I've got to go to bed.'

'All right.'

He waited, looking at me with suppressed eagerness.

'I talked with Miss Baker,' I said after a moment. 'I'm going to call up Daisy tomorrow and invite her over here to tea.'

'Oh, that's all right,' he said carelessly. 'I don't want to put you to any trouble.'

'What day would suit you?'

'What day would suit *you*?' he corrected me quickly. 'I don't want to put you to any trouble, you see.'

'How about the day after tomorrow?'

He considered for a moment. Then, with reluctance: 'I want to get the grass cut,' he said.

We both looked down at the grass – there was a sharp line where my ragged lawn ended and the darker, well-kept expanse of his began. I suspected that he meant my grass.

'There's another little thing,' he said uncertainly, and hesitated.

'Would you rather put it off for a few days?' I asked.

'Oh, it isn't about that. At least – ' He fumbled with a series of beginnings. 'Why, I thought – why, look here, old sport, you don't make much money, do you?'

'Not very much.'

This seemed to reassure him and he continued more confidently.

'I thought you didn't, if you'll pardon my – you see, I carry on a little business on the side, a sort of sideline, you understand. And I thought that if you don't make very much – You're selling bonds, aren't you, old sport?'

'Trying to.'

'Well, this would interest you. It wouldn't take up much of your time and you might pick up a nice bit of money. It happens to be a rather confidential sort of thing.'

I realise now that under different circumstances that conversation might have been one of the crises of my life. But, because the offer was obviously and tactlessly for a service to be rendered, I had no choice except to cut him off there.

'I've got my hands full,' I said. 'I'm much obliged but I couldn't take on any more work.'

'You wouldn't have to do any business with Wolfsheim.' Evidently he thought that I was shying away from the 'gonnegtion' mentioned at lunch, but I assured him he was wrong. He waited a moment longer, hoping I'd begin a conversation, but I was too absorbed to be responsive, so he went unwillingly home.

The evening had made me light-headed and happy; I think I walked into a deep sleep as I entered my front door. So I don't know whether or not Gatsby went to Coney Island, or for how many hours he 'glanced into rooms' while his house blazed gaudily on. I called up Daisy from the office next morning, and invited her to come to tea.

'Don't bring Tom,' I warned her.

'What?'

'Don't bring Tom.'

'Who is "Tom"?' she asked innocently.

The day agreed upon was pouring rain. At eleven o'clock a man in a raincoat, dragging a lawn-mower, tapped at my front door and said that Mr Gatsby had sent him over to cut my grass. This reminded me that I had forgotten to tell my Finn to come back, so I drove into West Egg Village to search for her among soggy whitewashed alleys and to buy some cups and lemons and flowers.

The flowers were unnecessary, for at two o'clock a greenhouse arrived from Gatsby's, with innumerable receptacles to contain it. An hour later the front door opened nervously, and Gatsby, in a white flannel suit, silver shirt and gold-coloured tie, hurried in. He was pale, and there were dark signs of sleeplessness beneath his eyes.

'Is everything all right?' he asked immediately.

'The grass looks fine, if that's what you mean.'

'What grass?' he enquired blankly. 'Oh, the grass in the yard.' He looked out the window at it, but, judging from his expression, I don't believe he saw a thing.

'Looks very good,' he remarked vaguely. 'One of the papers said they thought the rain would stop about four. I think it was the *Journal*. Have you got everything you need in the shape of – of tea?'

I took him into the pantry, where he looked a little reproachfully at the Finn. Together we scrutinised the twelve lemon cakes from the delicatessen shop.

'Will they do?' I asked.

'Of course, of course! They're fine!' and he added hollowly, '. . . old sport.'

The rain cooled about half-past three to a damp mist, through which occasional thin drops swam like dew. Gatsby looked with vacant eyes through a copy of Clay's *Economics*, starting at the Finnish tread that shook the kitchen floor and peering towards the bleared windows from time to time as if a series of invisible but alarming happenings were taking place outside. Finally he got up and informed me, in an uncertain voice, that he was going home.

'Why's that?'

'Nobody's coming to tea. It's too late!' He looked at his watch as if there was some pressing demand on his time elsewhere. 'I can't wait all day.'

'Don't be silly; it's just two minutes to four.'

He sat down miserably, as if I had pushed him, and simultaneously there was the sound of a motor turning into my lane. We both jumped up, and, a little harrowed myself, I went out into the yard.

Under the dripping bare lilac trees a large open car was coming up the drive. It stopped. Daisy's face, tipped sideways beneath a three-cornered lavender hat, looked at me with a bright ecstatic smile.

'Is this absolutely where you live, my dearest one?'

The exhilarating ripple of her voice was a wild tonic in the rain. I had to follow the sound of it for a moment, up and down, with my ear alone, before any words came through. A damp streak of hair lay like a dash of blue paint across her cheek, and her hand was wet with glistening drops as I took it to help her from the car.

'Are you in love with me,' she said low in my ear, 'or why did I have to come alone?'

'That's the secret of Castle Rackrent. Tell your chauffeur to go far away and spend an hour.'

'Come back in an hour, Ferdie.' Then in a grave murmur: 'His name is Ferdie.'

'Does the gasoline affect his nose?'

'I don't think so,' she said innocently. 'Why?'

We went in. To my overwhelming surprise the living-room was deserted. 'Well, that's funny,' I exclaimed.

'What's funny?'

She turned her head as there was a light dignified knocking at the front door. I went out and opened it. Gatsby, pale as death, with his hands plunged like weights in his coat pockets, was standing in a puddle of water glaring tragically into my eyes.

With his hands still in his coat pockets he stalked by me into the hall, turned sharply as if he were on a wire, and disappeared into the living-room. It wasn't a bit funny. Aware of the loud beating of my own heart I pulled the door to against the increasing rain.

For half a minute there wasn't a sound. Then from the living-room I heard a sort of choking murmur and part of a laugh, followed by Daisy's voice on a clear artificial note: 'I certainly am awfully glad to see you again.'

A pause; it endured horribly. I had nothing to do in the hall, so I went into the room.

Gatsby, his hands still in his pockets, was reclining against the mantelpiece in a strained counterfeit of perfect ease, even of boredom. His head leaned back so far that it rested against the face of a defunct mantelpiece clock, and from this position his distraught eyes stared down at Daisy, who was sitting, frightened but graceful, on the edge of a stiff chair.

'We've met before,' muttered Gatsby. His eyes glanced momentarily at me, and his lips parted with an abortive attempt at a laugh. Luckily the clock took this moment to tilt dangerously at the pressure of his head, whereupon he turned and caught it with trembling fingers and set it back in place. Then he sat down, rigidly, his elbow on the arm of the sofa and his chin in his hand.

'I'm sorry about the clock,' he said.

My own face had now assumed a deep tropical burn. I couldn't muster up a single commonplace out of the thousand in my head.

'It's an old clock,' I told them idiotically.

I think we all believed for a moment that it had smashed in pieces on the floor.

'We haven't met for many years,' said Daisy, her voice as matter-of-fact as it could ever be.

'Five years next November.'

The automatic quality of Gatsby's answer set us all back at least another minute. I had them both on their feet with the desperate suggestion that they help me make tea in the kitchen when the demoniac Finn brought it in on a tray.

Amid the welcome confusion of cups and cakes a certain physical decency established itself. Gatsby got himself into a shadow and, while Daisy and I talked, looked conscientiously from one to the other of us with tense, unhappy eyes. However, as calmness wasn't an end in itself, I made an excuse at the first possible moment, and got to my feet.

'Where are you going?' demanded Gatsby in immediate alarm.

'I'll be back.'

'I've got to speak to you about something before you go.'

He followed me wildly into the kitchen, closed the door, and whispered: 'Oh, God!' in a miserable way.

'What's the matter?'

'This is a terrible mistake,' he said, shaking his head from side to side, 'a terrible, terrible mistake.'

'You're just embarrassed, that's all,' and luckily I added: 'Daisy's embarrassed too.'

'She's embarrassed?' he repeated incredulously.

'Just as much as you are.'

'Don't talk so loud.'

'You're acting like a little boy,' I broke out impatiently. 'Not only that, but you're rude. Daisy's sitting in there all alone.'

He raised his hand to stop my words, looked at me with unforgettable reproach, and, opening the door cautiously, went back into the other room.

I walked out the back way – just as Gatsby had when he had made his nervous circuit of the house half an hour before – and ran for a huge black knotted tree, whose massed leaves made a fabric against the rain. Once more it was pouring, and my irregular lawn, well shaved by Gatsby's gardener, abounded in small muddy swamps and prehistoric marshes. There was nothing to look at from under the tree except Gatsby's enormous house, so I stared at it, like Kant at his church steeple, for half an hour. A brewer had built it early in the 'period' craze a decade before, and there was a story that he'd agreed to pay five years' taxes on all the neighbouring cottages if the owners would have their roofs thatched with straw. Perhaps their refusal took the heart out of his plan to Found a Family – he went into an immediate decline. His children sold his house with the black wreath still on the door. Americans, while willing, even eager, to be serfs, have always been obstinate about being peasantry.

After half an hour, the sun shone again, and the grocer's automobile rounded Gatsby's drive with the raw material for his servants' dinner – I felt sure he wouldn't eat a spoonful. A maid began opening the upper windows of his house, appeared momentarily in each, and, leaning from the large central bay, spat meditatively into the garden. It was time I went back. While the rain continued it had seemed like the murmur of their voices, rising and swelling a little now and then with gusts of emotion. But in the new silence I felt that silence had fallen within the house too.

I went in – after making every possible noise in the kitchen, short of pushing over the stove – but I don't believe they heard a sound. They were sitting at either end of the couch, looking at each other as if some question had been asked, or was in the air, and every vestige of embarrassment was gone. Daisy's face was smeared with tears, and when I came in she jumped up and began wiping at it with her handkerchief before a mirror. But there was a change in Gatsby that was simply confounding. He literally glowed; without a word or a gesture of exultation a new well-being radiated from him and filled the little room.

'Oh hello, old sport,' he said, as if he hadn't seen me for years. I thought for a moment he was going to shake hands.

'It's stopped raining.'

'Has it?' When he realised what I was talking about, that there were twinkle-bells of sunshine in the room, he smiled like a weather man, like an ecstatic patron of recurrent light, and repeated the news to Daisy. 'What do you think of that? It's stopped raining.'

'I'm glad, Jay.' Her throat, full of aching, grieving beauty, told only of her unexpected joy.

'I want you and Daisy to come over to my house,' he said, 'I'd like to show her around.'

'You're sure you want me to come?'

'Absolutely, old sport.'

Daisy went upstairs to wash her face – too late, I thought with humiliation of my towels – while Gatsby and I waited on the lawn.

'My house looks well, doesn't it?' he demanded. 'See how the whole front of it catches the light.'

I agreed that it was splendid.

'Yes.' His eyes went over it, every arched door and square tower. 'It took me just three years to earn the money that bought it.'

'I thought you inherited your money.'

'I did, old sport,' he said automatically, 'but I lost most of it in the big panic – the panic of the war.'

I think he hardly knew what he was saying, for when I asked him what business he was in he answered: 'That's my affair,' before he realised that it wasn't an appropriate reply.

'Oh, I've been in several things,' he corrected himself. 'I was in the drug business and then I was in the oil business. But I'm not in either one now.' He looked at me with more attention. 'Do you mean you've been thinking over what I proposed the other night?'

Before I could answer, Daisy came out of the house and two rows of brass buttons on her dress gleamed in the sunlight.

'That huge place *there*?' she cried pointing.

'Do you like it?'

'I love it, but I don't see how you live there all alone.'

'I keep it always full of interesting people, night and day. People who do interesting things. Celebrated people.'

Instead of taking the short cut along the Sound we went down to the road and entered by the big postern. With enchanting murmurs, Daisy admired this aspect or that of the feudal silhouette against the sky, admired the gardens, the sparking odour of jonquils and the frothy odour of hawthorn and plum blossoms and the pale gold odour of kiss-me-at-the-gate. It was strange to reach the marble steps and find no stir of bright dresses in and out of the door, and hear no sound but bird voices in the trees.

And inside, as we wandered through Marie Antoinette music-rooms and Restoration salons, I felt that there were guests concealed behind every couch and table, under orders to be breathlessly silent until we had passed through. As Gatsby closed the door of 'the Merton College

Library' I could have sworn I heard the owl-eyed man break into ghostly laughter.

We went upstairs, through period bedrooms swathed in rose and lavender silk and vivid with new flowers, through dressing-rooms and poolrooms and bathrooms with sunken baths – intruding into one chamber where a dishevelled man in pyjamas was doing liver exercises on the floor. It was Mr Klipspringer, the 'boarder'. I had seen him wandering hungrily about the beach that morning. Finally we came to Gatsby's own apartment, a bedroom and a bath, and an Adam study, where we sat down and drank a glass of some Chartreuse he took from a cupboard in the wall.

He hadn't once ceased looking at Daisy, and I think he revalued everything in his house according to the measure of response it drew from her well-loved eyes. Sometimes, too, he stared around at his possessions in a dazed way, as though in her actual and astounding presence none of it was any longer real. Once he nearly toppled down a flight of stairs.

His bedroom was the simplest room of all – except where the dresser was garnished with a toilet set of pure dull gold. Daisy took the brush with delight, and smoothed her hair, whereupon Gatsby sat down and shaded his eyes and began to laugh.

'It's the funniest thing, old sport,' he said hilariously. 'I can't – When I try to – '

He had passed visibly through two states and was entering upon a third. After his embarrassment and his unreasoning joy he was consumed with wonder at her presence. He had been full of the idea so long, dreamed it right through to the end, waited with his teeth set, so to speak, at an inconceivable pitch of intensity. Now, in the reaction, he was running down like an overwound clock.

Recovering himself in a minute he opened for us two hulking patent cabinets which held his massed suits and dressing-gowns and ties, and his shirts, piled like bricks in stacks a dozen high.

'I've got a man in England who buys me clothes. He sends over a selection of things at the beginning of each season, spring and fall.'

He took out a pile of shirts and began throwing them, one by one, before us, shirts of sheer linen and thick silk and fine flannel, which lost their folds as they fell and covered the table in many-coloured disarray. While we admired he brought more and the soft rich heap mounted higher – shirts with stripes and scrolls and plaids in coral and apple-green and lavender and faint orange, with monograms of

Indian blue. Suddenly, with a strained sound, Daisy bent her head into the shirts and began to cry stormily.

'They're such beautiful shirts,' she sobbed, her voice muffled in the thick folds. 'It makes me sad because I've never seen such – such beautiful shirts before.'

After the house, we were to see the grounds and the swimming-pool, and the hydroplane and the midsummer flowers – but outside Gatsby's window it began to rain again, so we stood in a row looking at the corrugated surface of the Sound.

'If it wasn't for the mist we could see your home across the bay,' said Gatsby. 'You always have a green light that burns all night at the end of your dock.'

Daisy put her arm through his abruptly, but he seemed absorbed in what he had just said. Possibly it had occurred to him that the colossal significance of that light had now vanished for ever. Compared to the great distance that had separated him from Daisy it had seemed very near to her, almost touching her. It had seemed as close as a star to the moon. Now it was again a green light on a dock. His count of enchanted objects had diminished by one.

I began to walk about the room, examining various indefinite objects in the half darkness. A large photograph of an elderly man in yachting costume attracted me, hung on the wall over his desk.

'Who's this?'

'That? That's Mr Dan Cody, old sport.'

The name sounded faintly familiar.

'He's dead now. He used to be my best friend years ago.'

There was a small picture of Gatsby, also in yachting costume, on the bureau – Gatsby with his head thrown back defiantly – taken apparently when he was about eighteen.

'I adore it,' exclaimed Daisy. 'The pompadour. You never told me you had a pompadour – or a yacht.'

'Look at this,' said Gatsby quickly. 'Here's a lot of clippings – about you.'

They stood side by side examining them. I was going to ask to see the rubies when the phone rang, and Gatsby took up the receiver.

'Yes . . . Well, I can't talk now . . . I can't talk now, old sport . . . I said a *small* town . . . He must know what a *small* town is . . . Well, he's no use to us if Detroit is his idea of a small town . . . '

He rang off.

'Come here *quick*!' cried Daisy at the window.

The rain was still falling, but the darkness had parted in the west, and there was a pink and golden billow of foamy clouds above the sea.

'Look at that,' she whispered, and then after a moment: 'I'd like to just get one of those pink clouds and put you in it and push you around.'

I tried to go then, but they wouldn't hear of it; perhaps my presence made them feel more satisfactorily alone.

'I know what we'll do,' said Gatsby, 'we'll have Klipspringer play the piano.'

He went out of the room calling, 'Ewing!' and returned in a few minutes accompanied by an embarrassed, slightly worn young man, with shell-rimmed glasses and scanty blond hair. He was now decently clothed, in a 'sport shirt', open at the neck, sneakers and duck trousers of a nebulous hue.

'Did we interrupt your exercises?' enquired Daisy politely.

'I was asleep,' cried Mr Klipspringer, in a spasm of embarrassment. 'That is, I'd *been* asleep. Then I got up . . . '

'Klipspringer plays the piano,' said Gatsby, cutting him off. 'Don't you, Ewing, old sport?'

'I don't play well. I don't – I hardly play at all, I'm all out of prac – '

'We'll go downstairs,' interrupted Gatsby. He flipped a switch. The grey windows disappeared as the house glowed full of light.

In the music-room Gatsby turned on a solitary lamp beside the piano. He lit Daisy's cigarette from a trembling match, and sat down with her on a couch far across the room, where there was no light save what the gleaming floor bounced in from the hall.

When Klipspringer had played *The Love Nest* he turned around on the bench and searched unhappily for Gatsby in the gloom.

'I'm all out of practice, you see. I told you I couldn't play. I'm all out of prac – '

'Don't talk so much, old sport,' commanded Gatsby. 'Play!'

In the morning,
In the evening,
Ain't we got fun –

Outside the wind was loud and there was a faint flow of thunder along the Sound. All the lights were going on in West Egg now; the electric trains, men-carrying, were plunging home through the rain from New York. It was the hour of a profound human change, and excitement was generating on the air.

> One thing's sure and nothing's surer
> The rich get richer and the poor get – children.
> In the meantime,
> In between time –

As I went over to say goodbye I saw that the expression of bewilderment had come back into Gatsby's face, as though a faint doubt had occurred to him as to the quality of his present happiness. Almost five years! There must have been moments even that afternoon when Daisy tumbled short of his dreams – not through her own fault, but because of the colossal vitality of his illusion. It had gone beyond her, beyond everything. He had thrown himself into it with a creative passion, adding to it all the time, decking it out with every bright feather that drifted his way. No amount of fire or freshness can challenge what a man can store up in his ghostly heart.

As I watched him he adjusted himself a little, visibly. His hand took hold of hers, and as she said something low in his ear he turned towards her with a rush of emotion. I think that voice held him most, with its fluctuating, feverish warmth, because it couldn't be over-dreamed – that voice was a deathless song.

They had forgotten me, but Daisy glanced up and held out her hand; Gatsby didn't know me now at all. I looked once more at them and they looked back at me, remotely, possessed by intense life. Then I went out of the room and down the marble steps into the rain, leaving them there together.

Chapter 6

About this time an ambitious young reporter from New York arrived one morning at Gatsby's door and asked him if he had anything to say.

'Anything to say about what?' enquired Gatsby politely.

'Why – any statement to give out.'

It transpired after a confused five minutes that the man had heard Gatsby's name around his office in a connection which he either wouldn't reveal or didn't fully understand. This was his day off and with laudable initiative he had hurried out 'to see'.

It was a random shot, and yet the reporter's instinct was right. Gatsby's notoriety, spread about by the hundreds who had accepted his hospitality and so become authorities upon his past, had increased all summer until he fell just short of being news. Contemporary legends such as the 'underground pipeline to Canada' attached themselves to him, and there was one persistent story that he didn't live in a house at all, but in a boat that looked like a house and was moved secretly up and down the Long Island shore. Just why these inventions were a source of satisfaction to James Gatz of North Dakota isn't easy to say.

James Gatz – that was really, or at least legally, his name. He had changed it at the age of seventeen and at the specific moment that witnessed the beginning of his career – when he saw Dan Cody's yacht drop anchor over the most insidious flat on Lake Superior. It was James Gatz who had been loafing along the beach that afternoon in a torn green jersey and a pair of canvas pants, but it was already Jay Gatsby who borrowed a rowboat, pulled out to the *Tuolomee* and informed Cody that a wind might catch him and break him up in half an hour.

I suppose he'd had the name ready for a long time, even then. His parents were shiftless and unsuccessful farm people – his imagination had never really accepted them as his parents at all. The truth was that Jay Gatsby of West Egg, Long Island, sprang from his Platonic conception of himself. He was a son of God – a phrase which, if it means anything, means just that – and he must be about His Father's business, the service of a vast, vulgar and meretricious beauty. So he invented just the sort of Jay Gatsby that a seventeen-year-old boy would be likely to invent, and to this conception he was faithful to the end.

For over a year he had been beating his way along the south shore of Lake Superior as a clam-digger and a salmon-fisher or in any other capacity that brought him food and bed. His brown, hardening body lived naturally through the half-fierce, half-lazy work of the bracing days. He knew women early, and since they spoiled him he became contemptuous of them, of young virgins because they were ignorant, of the others because they were hysterical about things which in his overwhelming self-absorption he took for granted.

But his heart was in a constant, turbulent riot. The most grotesque and fantastic conceits haunted him in his bed at night. A universe of ineffable gaudiness spun itself out in his brain while the clock ticked on the washstand and the moon soaked with wet light his tangled clothes upon the floor. Each night he added to the pattern of his fancies until drowsiness closed down upon some vivid scene with an oblivious embrace. For a while these reveries provided an outlet for his imagination; they were a satisfactory hint of the unreality of reality, a promise that the rock of the world was founded securely on a fairy's wing.

An instinct towards his future glory had led him, some months before, to the small Lutheran College of St Olaf's in southern Minnesota. He stayed there two weeks, dismayed at its ferocious indifference to the drums of his destiny, to destiny itself, and despising the janitor's work with which he was to pay his way through. Then he drifted back to Lake Superior, and he was still searching for something to do on the day that Dan Cody's yacht dropped anchor in the shallows alongshore.

Cody was fifty years old then, a product of the Nevada silver fields, of the Yukon, of every rush for metal since 1875. The transactions in Montana copper that made him many times a millionaire found him physically robust but on the verge of soft-mindedness, and, suspecting this, an infinite number of women tried to separate him from his money. The none too savoury ramifications by which Ella Kaye, the newspaper woman, played Madame de Maintenon to his weakness and sent him to sea in a yacht, were common property of the turgid journalism of 1902. He had been coasting along all too hospitable shores for five years when he turned up as James Gatz's destiny in Little Girl Bay.

To young Gatz, resting on his oars and looking up at the railed deck, that yacht represented all the beauty and glamour in the world. I suppose he smiled at Cody – he had probably discovered that people liked him when he smiled. At any rate Cody asked him a few questions (one of them elicited the brand new name) and found that he was quick and extravagantly ambitious. A few days later he took him to Duluth and bought him a blue coat, six pairs of white duck trousers, and a yachting cap. And when the *Tuolomee* left for the West Indies and the Barbary Coast, Gatsby left too.

He was employed in a vague personal capacity – while he remained with Cody he was in turn steward, mate, skipper, secretary and even jailor, for Dan Cody sober knew what lavish doings Dan Cody drunk might soon be about, and he provided for such contingencies by reposing more and more trust in Gatsby. The arrangement lasted five years, during which the boat went three times around the Continent. It might have lasted indefinitely except for the fact that Ella Kaye came on board one night in Boston and a week later Dan Cody inhospitably died.

I remember the portrait of him up in Gatsby's bedroom, a grey, florid man with a hard, empty face – the pioneer debauchée, who during one phase of American life brought back to the Eastern seaboard the savage violence of the frontier brothel and saloon. It was indirectly due to Cody that Gatsby drank so little. Sometimes in the course of gay parties women used to rub champagne into his hair; for himself he formed the habit of letting liquor alone.

And it was from Cody that he inherited money – a legacy of twenty-five thousand dollars. He didn't get it. He never understood the legal device that was used against him, but what remained of the millions went intact to Ella Kaye. He was left with his singularly appropriate education; the vague contour of Jay Gatsby had filled out to the substantiality of a man.

He told me all this very much later, but I've put it down here with the idea of exploding those first wild rumours about his antecedents, which weren't even faintly true. Moreover he told it to me at a time of confusion, when I had reached the point of believing everything and nothing about him. So I take advantage of this short halt, while Gatsby, so to speak, caught his breath, to clear this set of misconceptions away.

It was a halt, too, in my association with his affairs. For several weeks I didn't see him or hear his voice on the phone – mostly I was in New York, trotting around with Jordan and trying to ingratiate myself with her senile aunt – but finally I went over to his house one Sunday afternoon. I hadn't been there two minutes when somebody brought Tom Buchanan in for a drink. I was startled, naturally, but the really surprising thing was that it hadn't happened before.

They were a party of three on horseback – Tom and a man named Sloane and a pretty woman in a brown riding-habit, who had been there previously.

'I'm delighted to see you,' said Gatsby, standing on his porch. 'I'm delighted that you dropped in.'

As though they cared!

'Sit right down. Have a cigarette or a cigar.' He walked around the room quickly, ringing bells. 'I'll have something to drink for you in just a minute.'

He was profoundly affected by the fact that Tom was there. But he would be uneasy anyhow until he had given them something, realising in a vague way that that was all they came for. Mr Sloane wanted nothing. A lemonade? No, thanks. A little champagne? Nothing at all, thanks . . . I'm sorry –

'Did you have a nice ride?'

'Very good roads around here.'

'I suppose the automobiles – '

'Yeah.'

Moved by an irresistible impulse, Gatsby turned to Tom, who had accepted the introduction as a stranger.

'I believe we've met somewhere before, Mr Buchanan.'

'Oh, yes,' said Tom, gruffly polite, but obviously not remembering. 'So we did. I remember very well.'

'About two weeks ago.'

'That's right. You were with Nick here.'

'I know your wife,' continued Gatsby, almost aggressively.

'That so?'

Tom turned to me.

'You live near here, Nick?'

'Next door.'

'That so?'

Mr Sloane didn't enter into the conversation, but lounged back haughtily in his chair; the woman said nothing either – until unexpectedly, after two highballs, she became cordial.

'We'll all come over to your next party, Mr Gatsby,' she suggested. 'What do you say?'

'Certainly; I'd be delighted to have you.'

'Be ver' nice,' said Mr Sloane, without gratitude. 'Well – think ought to be starting home.'

'Please don't hurry,' Gatsby urged them. He had control of himself now, and he wanted to see more of Tom. 'Why don't you – why don't you stay for supper? I wouldn't be surprised if some other people dropped in from New York.'

'You come to supper with *me*,' said the lady enthusiastically. 'Both of you.'

This included me. Mr Sloane got to his feet.

'Come along,' he said – but to her only.

'I mean it,' she insisted. 'I'd love to have you. Lots of room.'

Gatsby looked at me questioningly. He wanted to go, and he didn't see that Mr Sloane had determined he shouldn't.

'I'm afraid I won't be able to,' I said.

'Well, you come,' she urged, concentrating on Gatsby.

Mr Sloane murmured something close to her ear.

'We won't be late if we start now,' she insisted aloud.

'I haven't got a horse,' said Gatsby. 'I used to ride in the army, but I've never bought a horse. I'll have to follow you in my car. Excuse me for just a minute.'

The rest of us walked out on the porch, where Sloane and the lady began an impassioned conversation aside.

'My God, I believe the man's coming,' said Tom. 'Doesn't he know she doesn't want him?'

'She says she does want him.'

'She has a big dinner party and he won't know a soul there.' He frowned. 'I wonder where in the devil he met Daisy. By God, I may be old-fashioned in my ideas, but women run around too much these days to suit me. They meet all kinds of crazy fish.'

Suddenly Mr Sloane and the lady walked down the steps and mounted their horses.

'Come on,' said Mr Sloane to Tom, 'we're late. We've got to go.' And then to me: 'Tell him we couldn't wait, will you?'

Tom and I shook hands, the rest of us exchanged a cool nod, and they trotted quickly down the drive, disappearing under the August foliage just as Gatsby, with hat and light overcoat in hand, came out the front door.

Tom was evidently perturbed at Daisy's running around alone, for on the following Saturday night he came with her to Gatsby's party. Perhaps his presence gave the evening its peculiar quality of oppressiveness – it stands out in my memory from Gatsby's other parties that summer. There were the same people, or at least the same sort of people, the same profusion of champagne, the same many-coloured, many-keyed commotion, but I felt an unpleasantness in the air, a pervading harshness that hadn't been there before. Or perhaps I had merely grown used to it, grown to accept West Egg as a world complete in itself, with its own standards and its own great figures, second to nothing because it had no consciousness of being so, and now I was looking at it again, through Daisy's eyes. It is invariably saddening to look through new eyes at things upon which you have expended your own powers of adjustment.

They arrived at twilight, and, as we strolled out among the sparkling hundreds, Daisy's voice was playing murmurous tricks in her throat.

'These things excite me *so*,' she whispered. 'If you want to kiss me any time during the evening, Nick, just let me know and I'll be glad to arrange it for you. Just mention my name. Or present a green card. I'm giving out green – '

'Look around,' suggested Gatsby.

'I'm looking around. I'm having a marvellous – '

'You must see the faces of many people you've heard about.'

Tom's arrogant eyes roamed the crowd.

'We don't go around very much,' he said; 'in fact, I was just thinking I don't know a soul here.'

'Perhaps you know that lady,' Gatsby indicated a gorgeous, scarcely human orchid of a woman who sat in state under a white-plum tree. Tom and Daisy stared, with that particularly unreal feeling that accompanies the recognition of a hitherto ghostly celebrity of the movies.

'She's lovely,' said Daisy.

'The man bending over her is her director.'

He took them ceremoniously from group to group: 'Mrs Buchanan . . . and Mr Buchanan – ' After an instant's hesitation he added: 'the polo player.'

'Oh, no,' objected Tom quickly, 'not me.'

But evidently the sound of it pleased Gatsby, for Tom remained 'the polo player' for the rest of the evening.

'I've never met so many celebrities,' Daisy exclaimed. 'I liked that man – what was his name? – with the sort of blue nose.'

Gatsby identified him, adding that he was a small producer.

'Well, I liked him anyhow.'

'I'd a little rather not be the polo player,' said Tom pleasantly. 'I'd rather look at all these famous people in – in oblivion.'

Daisy and Gatsby danced. I remember being surprised by his graceful, conservative foxtrot – I had never seen him dance before. Then they sauntered over to my house and sat on the steps for half an hour, while, at her request, I remained watchfully in the garden. 'In case there's a fire, or a flood,' she explained, 'or any act of God.'

Tom appeared from his oblivion as we were sitting down to supper together. 'Do you mind if I eat with some people over here?' he said. 'A fellow's getting off some funny stuff.'

'Go ahead,' answered Daisy genially, 'and if you want to take down any addresses here's my little gold pencil.' . . . She looked around after a moment and told me the girl was 'common but pretty', and I knew that except for the half-hour she'd been alone with Gatsby she wasn't having a good time.

We were at a particularly tipsy table. That was my fault – Gatsby had been called to the phone, and I'd enjoyed these same people only two weeks before. But what had amused me then turned septic on the air now.

'How do you feel, Miss Baedeker?'

The girl addressed was trying, unsuccessfully, to slump against my shoulder. At this enquiry she sat up and opened her eyes.

'Wha'?'

A massive and lethargic woman, who had been urging Daisy to play golf with her at the local club tomorrow, spoke in Miss Baedeker's defence: 'Oh, she's all right now. When she's had five or six cocktails she always starts screaming like that. I tell her she ought to leave it alone.'

'I do leave it alone,' affirmed the accused hollowly.

'We heard you yelling, so I said to Doc Civet here: "There's somebody that needs your help, Doc." '

'She's much obliged, I'm sure,' said another friend, without gratitude, 'but you got her dress all wet when you stuck her head in the pool.'

'Anything I hate is to get my head stuck in a pool,' mumbled Miss Baedeker. 'They almost drowned me once over in New Jersey.'

'Then you ought to leave it alone,' countered Dr Civet.

'Speak for yourself!' cried Miss Baedeker violently. 'Your hand shakes. I wouldn't let you operate on me!'

It was like that. Almost the last thing I remember was standing with Daisy and watching the moving-picture director and his Star. They were still under the white-plum tree and their faces were touching except for a pale, thin ray of moonlight between. It occurred to me that he had been very slowly bending towards her all evening to attain this proximity, and even while I watched I saw him stoop one ultimate degree and kiss at her cheek.

'I like her,' said Daisy, 'I think she's lovely.'

But the rest offended her – and inarguably, because it wasn't a gesture but an emotion. She was appalled by West Egg, this unprecedented 'place' that Broadway had begotten upon a Long Island fishing village – appalled by its raw vigour that chafed under the old euphemisms and by the too obtrusive fate that herded its inhabitants along a short-cut from nothing to nothing. She saw something awful in the very simplicity she failed to understand.

I sat on the front steps with them while they waited for their car. It was dark here; only the bright door sent ten square feet of light volleying out into the soft black morning. Sometimes a shadow moved against a dressing-room blind above, gave way to another shadow, an indefinite procession of shadows, that rouged and powdered in an invisible glass.

'Who is this Gatsby anyhow?' demanded Tom suddenly. 'Some big bootlegger?'

'Where'd you hear that?' I enquired.

'I didn't hear it. I imagined it. A lot of these newly rich people are just big bootleggers, you know.'

'Not Gatsby,' I said shortly.

He was silent for a moment. The pebbles of the drive crunched under his feet.

'Well, he certainly must have strained himself to get this menagerie together.'

A breeze stirred the grey haze of Daisy's fur collar.

'At least they are more interesting than the people we know,' she said with an effort.

'You didn't look so interested.'

'Well, I was.'

Tom laughed and turned to me.

'Did you notice Daisy's face when that girl asked her to put her under a cold shower?'

Daisy began to sing with the music in a husky, rhythmic whisper, bringing out a meaning in each word that it had never had before and would never have again. When the melody rose, her voice broke up sweetly, following it, in a way contralto voices have, and each change tipped out a little of her warm human magic upon the air.

'Lots of people come who haven't been invited,' she said suddenly.

'That girl hadn't been invited. They simply force their way in and he's too polite to object.'

'I'd like to know who he is and what he does,' insisted Tom. 'And I think I'll make a point of finding out.'

'I can tell you right now,' she answered. 'He owned some drugstores, a lot of drugstores. He built them up himself.'

The dilatory limousine came rolling up the drive.

'Good-night, Nick,' said Daisy.

Her glance left me and sought the lighted top of the steps, where 'Three O'Clock in the Morning', a neat, sad little waltz of that year, was drifting out the open door. After all, in the very casualness of Gatsby's party there were romantic possibilities totally absent from her world. What was it up there in the song that seemed to be calling her back inside? What would happen now in the dim, incalculable hours? Perhaps some unbelievable guest would arrive, a person infinitely rare and to be marvelled at, some authentically radiant young girl who with one fresh glance at Gatsby, one moment of magical encounter, would blot out those five years of unwavering devotion.

I stayed late that night. Gatsby asked me to wait until he was free, and I lingered in the garden until the inevitable swimming party had run up, chilled and exalted, from the black beach, until the lights were extinguished in the guest-rooms overhead. When he came down the steps at last the tanned skin was drawn unusually tight on his face, and his eyes were bright and tired.

'She didn't like it,' he said immediately.

'Of course she did.'

'She didn't like it,' he insisted. 'She didn't have a good time.'

He was silent, and I guessed at his unutterable depression. 'I feel far away from her,' he said. 'It's hard to make her understand.'

'You mean about the dance?'

'The dance?' He dismissed all the dances he had given with a snap of his fingers. 'Old sport, the dance is unimportant.'

He wanted nothing less of Daisy than that she should go to Tom and say: 'I never loved you.' After she had obliterated four years with that sentence they could decide upon the more practical measures to be taken. One of them was that, after she was free, they were to go back to Louisville and be married from her house – just as if it were five years ago.

'And she doesn't understand,' he said. 'She used to be able to understand. We'd sit for hours – '

He broke off and began to walk up and down a desolate path of fruit rinds and discarded favours and crushed flowers.

'I wouldn't ask too much of her,' I ventured. 'You can't repeat the past.'

'Can't repeat the past?' he cried incredulously. 'Why of course you can!'

He looked around him wildly, as if the past were lurking here in the shadow of his house, just out of reach of his hand.

'I'm going to fix everything just the way it was before,' he said, nodding determinedly. 'She'll see.'

He talked a lot about the past, and I gathered that he wanted to recover something, some idea of himself perhaps, that had gone into loving Daisy. His life had been confused and disordered since then, but if he could once return to a certain starting place and go over it all slowly, he could find out what that thing was . . .

. . . One autumn night, five years before, they had been walking down the street when the leaves were falling, and they came to a place where there were no trees and the sidewalk was white with moonlight. They stopped here and turned towards each other. Now it was a cool night with that mysterious excitement in it which comes at the two changes of the year. The quiet lights in the houses were burning out into the darkness and there was a stir and bustle among the stars. Out of the corner of his eye Gatsby saw that the blocks of the sidewalks really formed a ladder and mounted to a secret place above the trees – he could climb to it, if he climbed alone, and once there he could suck on the pap of life, gulp down the incomparable milk of wonder.

His heart beat faster and faster as Daisy's white face came up to his own. He knew that when he kissed this girl, and forever wed his unutterable visions to her perishable breath, his mind would never romp again like the mind of God. So he waited, listening for a moment longer to the tuning-fork that had been struck upon a star. Then he kissed her. At his lips' touch she blossomed for him like a flower and the incarnation was complete.

Through all he said, even through his appalling sentimentality, I was reminded of something – an elusive rhythm, a fragment of lost words, that I had heard somewhere a long time ago. For a moment a phrase tried to take shape in my mouth and my lips parted like a dumb man's, as though there was more struggling upon them than a wisp of startled air. But they made no sound, and what I had almost remembered was uncommunicable for ever.

Chapter 7

It was when curiosity about Gatsby was at its highest that the lights in his house failed to go on one Saturday night – and, as obscurely as it had begun, his career as Trimalchio was over. Only gradually did I become aware that the automobiles which turned expectantly into his drive stayed for just a minute and then drove sulkily away. Wondering if he were sick I went over to find out – an unfamiliar butler with a villainous face squinted at me suspiciously from the door.

'Is Mr Gatsby sick?'

'Nope.' After a pause he added 'sir' in a dilatory, grudging way.

'I hadn't seen him around, and I was rather worried. Tell him Mr Carraway came over.'

'Who?' he demanded rudely.

'Carraway.'

'Carraway. All right, I'll tell him.'

Abruptly he slammed the door.

My Finn informed me that Gatsby had dismissed every servant in his house a week ago and replaced them with half a dozen others, who never went into West Egg Village to be bribed by the tradesmen, but ordered moderate supplies over the telephone. The grocery boy reported that the kitchen looked like a pigsty, and the general opinion in the village was that the new people weren't servants at all.

Next day Gatsby called me on the phone.

'Going away?' I enquired.

'No, old sport.'

'I hear you fired all your servants.'

'I wanted somebody who wouldn't gossip. Daisy comes over quite often – in the afternoons.'

So the whole caravansarai had fallen in like a card house at the disapproval in her eyes.

'They're some people Wolfsheim wanted to do something for. They're all brothers and sisters. They used to run a small hotel.'

'I see.'

He was calling up at Daisy's request – would I come to lunch at her house tomorrow? Miss Baker would be there. Half an hour later Daisy herself telephoned and seemed relieved to find that I was coming.

Something was up. And yet I couldn't believe that they would choose this occasion for a scene – especially for the rather harrowing scene that Gatsby had outlined in the garden.

The next day was broiling, almost the last, certainly the warmest, of the summer. As my train emerged from the tunnel into sunlight, only the hot whistles of the National Biscuit Company broke the simmering hush at noon. The straw seats of the car hovered on the edge of combustion; the woman next to me perspired delicately for a while into her white shirtwaist, and then, as her newspaper dampened under her fingers, lapsed despairingly into deep heat with a desolate cry. Her pocketbook slapped to the floor.

'Oh, my!' she gasped.

I picked it up with a weary bend and handed it back to her, holding it at arm's length and by the extreme tip of the corners to indicate that I had no designs upon it – but everyone near by, including the woman, suspected me just the same.

'Hot!' said the conductor to familiar faces. 'Some weather . . . Hot! . . . Hot! . . . Hot! . . . Is it hot enough for you? Is it hot? Is it . . . ?'

My commutation ticket came back to me with a dark stain from his hand. That anyone should care in this heat whose flushed lips he kissed, whose head made damp the pyjama pocket over his heart!

. . . Through the hall of the Buchanans' house blew a faint wind, carrying the sound of the telephone bell out to Gatsby and me as we waited at the door.

'The master's body!' roared the butler into the mouthpiece. 'I'm sorry, madame, but we can't furnish it – it's far too hot to touch this noon!'

What he really said was: 'Yes . . . Yes . . . I'll see.'

He set down the receiver and came towards us, glistening slightly, to take our stiff straw hats.

'Madame expects you in the salon!' he cried, needlessly indicating the direction. In this heat every extra gesture was an affront to the common store of life.

The room, shadowed well with awnings, was dark and cool. Daisy and Jordan lay upon an enormous couch, like silver idols weighing down their own white dresses against the singing breeze of the fans.

'We can't move,' they said together.

Jordan's fingers, powdered white over their tan, rested for a moment in mine.

'And Mr Thomas Buchanan, the athlete?' I enquired.

Simultaneously I heard his voice, gruff, muffled, husky, at the hall telephone.

Gatsby stood in the centre of the crimson carpet and gazed around with fascinated eyes. Daisy watched him and laughed her sweet, exciting laugh; a tiny gust of powder rose from her bosom into the air.

'The rumour is,' whispered Jordan, 'that that's Tom's girl on the telephone.'

We were silent. The voice in the hall rose high with annoyance: 'Very well, then, I won't sell you the car at all . . . I'm under no obligations to you at all . . . and as for your bothering me about it at lunchtime, I won't stand that at all!'

'Holding down the receiver,' said Daisy cynically.

'No, he's not,' I assured her. 'It's a bona-fide deal. I happen to know about it.'

Tom flung open the door, blocked out its space for a moment with his thick body, and hurried into the room.

'Mr Gatsby!' He put out his broad, flat hand with well-concealed dislike. 'I'm glad to see you, sir . . . Nick . . . '

'Make us a cold drink,' cried Daisy.

As he left the room again she got up and went over to Gatsby and pulled his face down, kissing him on the mouth.

'You know I love you,' she murmured.

'You forget there's a lady present,' said Jordan.

Daisy looked around doubtfully.

'You kiss Nick too.'

'What a low, vulgar girl!'

'I don't care!' cried Daisy, and began to clog on the brick fireplace. Then she remembered the heat and sat down guiltily on the couch just as a freshly laundered nurse leading a little girl came into the room.

'Bles-sed pre-cious,' she crooned, holding out her arms. 'Come to your own mother that loves you.'

The child, relinquished by the nurse, rushed across the room and rooted shyly into her mother's dress.

'The bles-sed pre-cious! Did mother get powder on your old yellowy hair? Stand up now, and say – How-de-do.'

Gatsby and I in turn leaned down and took the small reluctant hand. Afterwards he kept looking at the child with surprise. I don't think he had ever really believed in its existence before.

'I got dressed before luncheon,' said the child, turning eagerly to Daisy.

'That's because your mother wanted to show you off.' Her face bent into the single wrinkle of the small white neck. 'You dream, you. You absolute little dream.'

'Yes,' admitted the child calmly. 'Aunt Jordan's got on a white dress, too.'

'How do you like mother's friends?' Daisy turned her around so that she faced Gatsby. 'Do you think they're pretty?'

'Where's daddy?'

'She doesn't look like her father,' explained Daisy. 'She looks like me. She's got my hair and shape of the face.'

Daisy sat back upon the couch. The nurse took a step forward and held out her hand.

'Come, Pammy.'

'Goodbye, sweetheart!'

With a reluctant backward glance the well-disciplined child held to her nurse's hand and was pulled out of the door, just as Tom came back, preceding four gin rickeys that clicked full of ice.

Gatsby took up his drink.

'They certainly look cool,' he said, with visible tension.

We drank in long, greedy swallows.

'I read somewhere that the sun's getting hotter every year,' said Tom genially. 'It seems that pretty soon the earth's going to fall into the sun – or wait a minute – it's just the opposite – the sun's getting colder every year.

'Come outside,' he suggested to Gatsby, 'I'd like you to have a look at the place.'

I went with them out to the veranda. On the green Sound, stagnant in the heat, one small sail crawled slowly towards the fresher sea. Gatsby's eyes followed it momentarily; he raised his hand and pointed across the bay.

'I'm right across from you.'

'So you are.'

Our eyes lifted over the rose-beds and the hot lawn and the weedy refuse of the dog-days alongshore. Slowly the white wings of the boat moved against the blue cool limit of the sky. Ahead lay the scalloped ocean and the abounding blessed isles.

'There's sport for you,' said Tom, nodding. 'I'd like to be out there with him for about an hour.'

We had luncheon in the dining-room, darkened too against the heat, and drank down nervous gaiety with the cold ale.

'What'll we do with ourselves this afternoon?' cried Daisy, 'and the day after that, and the next thirty years?'

'Don't be morbid,' Jordan said. 'Life starts all over again when it gets crisp in the fall.'

'But it's so hot,' insisted Daisy, on the verge of tears, 'and everything's so confused. Let's all go to town!'

Her voice struggled on through the heat, beating against it, moulding its senselessness into forms.

'I've heard of making a garage out of a stable,' Tom was saying to Gatsby, 'but I'm the first man who ever made a stable out of a garage.'

'Who wants to go to town?' demanded Daisy insistently. Gatsby's eyes floated towards her. 'Ah,' she cried, 'you look so cool.'

Their eyes met, and they stared together at each other, alone in space. With an effort she glanced down at the table.

'You always look so cool,' she repeated.

She had told him that she loved him, and Tom Buchanan saw. He was astounded. His mouth opened a little, and he looked at Gatsby, and then back at Daisy as if he had just recognised her as someone he knew a long time ago.

'You resemble the advertisement of the man,' she went on innocently. 'You know the advertisement of the man – '

'All right,' broke in Tom quickly, 'I'm perfectly willing to go to town. Come on – we're all going to town.'

He got up, his eyes still flashing between Gatsby and his wife. No one moved.

'Come on!' His temper cracked a little. 'What's the matter, anyhow? If we're going to town, let's start.'

His hand, trembling with his effort at self-control, bore to his lips the last of his glass of ale. Daisy's voice got us to our feet and out on to the blazing gravel drive.

'Are we just going to go?' she objected. 'Like this? Aren't we going to let anyone smoke a cigarette first?'

'Everybody smoked all through lunch.'

'Oh, let's have fun,' she begged him. 'It's too hot to fuss.'

He didn't answer.

'Have it your own way,' she said. 'Come on, Jordan.'

They went upstairs to get ready while we three men stood there shuffling the hot pebbles with our feet. A silver curve of the moon hovered already in the western sky. Gatsby started to speak, changed his mind, but not before Tom wheeled and faced him expectantly.

'Have you got your stables here?' asked Gatsby with an effort.

'About a quarter of a mile down the road.'

'Oh.'

A pause.

'I don't see the idea of going to town,' broke out Tom savagely. 'Women get these notions in their heads – '

'Shall we take anything to drink?' called Daisy from an upper window.

'I'll get some whiskey,' answered Tom. He went inside.

Gatsby turned to me rigidly: 'I can't say anything in his house, old sport.'

'She's got an indiscreet voice,' I remarked. 'It's full of – ' I hesitated.

'Her voice is full of money,' he said suddenly.

That was it. I'd never understood before. It was full of money – that was the inexhaustible charm that rose and fell in it, the jingle of it, the cymbals' song of it . . . High in a white palace the king's daughter, the golden girl . . .

Tom came out of the house wrapping a quart bottle in a towel, followed by Daisy and Jordan wearing small tight hats of metallic cloth and carrying light capes over their arms.

'Shall we all go in my car?' suggested Gatsby. He felt the hot, green leather of the seat. 'I ought to have left it in the shade.'

'Is it standard shift?' demanded Tom.

'Yes.'

'Well, you take my coupé and let me drive your car to town.'

The suggestion was distasteful to Gatsby.

'I don't think there's much gas,' he objected.

'Plenty of gas,' said Tom boisterously. He looked at the gauge. 'And if it runs out I can stop at a drugstore. You can buy anything at a drugstore nowadays.'

A pause followed this apparently pointless remark. Daisy looked at Tom frowning, and an indefinable expression, at once definitely unfamiliar and vaguely recognisable, as if I had only heard it described in words, passed over Gatsby's face.

'Come on, Daisy,' said Tom, pressing her with his hand towards Gatsby's car. 'I'll take you in this circus wagon.'

He opened the door, but she moved out from the circle of his arm.

'You take Nick and Jordan. We'll follow you in the coupé.'

She walked close to Gatsby, touching his coat with her hand. Jordan and Tom and I got into the front seat of Gatsby's car, Tom pushed the unfamiliar gears tentatively, and we shot off into the oppressive heat, leaving them out of sight behind.

'Did you see that?' demanded Tom.

'See what?'

He looked at me keenly, realising that Jordan and I must have known all along.

'You think I'm pretty dumb, don't you?' he suggested. 'Perhaps I am, but I have a – almost a second sight, sometimes, that tells me what to do. Maybe you don't believe that, but science – '

He paused. The immediate contingency overtook him, pulled him back from the edge of the theoretical abyss.

'I've made a small investigation of this fellow,' he continued. 'I could have gone deeper if I'd known – '

'Do you mean you've been to a medium?' enquired Jordan humorously.

'What?' Confused, he stared at us as we laughed. 'A medium?'

'About Gatsby.'

'About Gatsby! No, I haven't. I said I'd been making a small investigation of his past.'

'And you found he was an Oxford man,' said Jordan helpfully.

'An Oxford man!' He was incredulous. 'Like hell he is! He wears a pink suit.'

'Nevertheless he's an Oxford man.'

'Oxford, New Mexico,' snorted Tom contemptuously, 'or something like that.'

'Listen, Tom. If you're such a snob, why did you invite him to lunch?' demanded Jordan crossly.

'Daisy invited him; she knew him before we were married – God knows where!'

We were all irritable now with the fading ale, and aware of it we drove for a while in silence. Then as Dr T. J. Eckleburg's faded eyes came into sight down the road, I remembered Gatsby's caution about gasoline.

'We've got enough to get us to town,' said Tom.

'But there's a garage right here,' objected Jordan. 'I don't want to get stalled in this baking heat.'

Tom threw on both brakes impatiently, and we slid to an abrupt dusty stop under Wilson's sign. After a moment the proprietor emerged from the interior of his establishment and gazed hollow-eyed at the car.

'Let's have some gas!' cried Tom roughly. 'What do you think we stopped for – to admire the view?'

'I'm sick,' said Wilson without moving. 'Been sick all day.'

'What's the matter?'

'I'm all run down.'

'Well, shall I help myself?' Tom demanded. 'You sounded well enough on the phone.'

With an effort Wilson left the shade and support of the doorway and, breathing hard, unscrewed the cap of the tank. In the sunlight his face was green.

'I didn't mean to interrupt your lunch,' he said. 'But I need money pretty bad, and I was wondering what you were going to do with your old car.'

'How do you like this one?' enquired Tom. 'I bought it last week.'

'It's a nice yellow one,' said Wilson, as he strained at the handle.

'Like to buy it?'

'Big chance,' Wilson smiled faintly. 'No, but I could make some money on the other.'

'What do you want money for, all of a sudden?'

'I've been here too long. I want to get away. My wife and I want to go West.'

'Your wife does?' exclaimed Tom, startled.

'She's been talking about it for ten years.' He rested for a moment against the pump, shading his eyes. 'And now she's going whether she wants to or not. I'm going to get her away.'

The coupé flashed by us with a flurry of dust and the flash of a waving hand.

'What do I owe you?' demanded Tom harshly.

'I just got wised up to something funny the last two days,' remarked Wilson. 'That's why I want to get away. That's why I been bothering you about the car.'

'What do I owe you?'

'Dollar twenty.'

The relentless beating heat was beginning to confuse me and I had a bad moment there before I realised that so far his suspicions hadn't alighted on Tom. He had discovered that Myrtle had some sort of life apart from him in another world, and the shock had made him physically sick. I stared at him and then at Tom, who had made a parallel discovery less than an hour before – and it occurred to me that there was no difference between men, in intelligence or race, so profound as the difference between the sick and the well. Wilson was so sick that he looked guilty, unforgivably guilty – as if he had just got some poor girl with child.

'I'll let you have that car,' said Tom. 'I'll send it over tomorrow afternoon.'

That locality was always vaguely disquieting, even in the broad glare of afternoon, and now I turned my head as though I had been warned of something behind. Over the ash heaps the giant eyes of Dr T. J. Eckleburg kept their vigil, but I perceived, after a moment, that other eyes were regarding us less than twenty feet away.

In one of the windows over the garage the curtains had been moved aside a little, and Myrtle Wilson was peering down at the car. So engrossed was she that she had no consciousness of being observed, and one emotion after another crept into her face like objects into a slowly developing picture. Her expression was curiously familiar – it was an expression I had often seen on women's faces, but on Myrtle Wilson's face it seemed purposeless and inexplicable until I realised that her eyes, wide with jealous terror, were fixed not on Tom, but on Jordan Baker, whom she took to be his wife.

There is no confusion like the confusion of a simple mind, and as we drove away Tom was feeling the hot whips of panic. His wife and his mistress, until an hour ago secure and inviolate, were slipping precipitately from his control. Instinct made him step on the accelerator with the double purpose of overtaking Daisy and leaving Wilson behind, and we sped along towards Astoria at fifty miles an hour, until, among the spidery girders of the elevated, we came in sight of the easy-going blue coupé.

'Those big movies around Fiftieth Street are cool,' suggested Jordan. 'I love New York on summer afternoons when everyone's away. There's something very sensuous about it – overripe, as if all sorts of funny fruits were going to fall into your hands.'

The word 'sensuous' had the effect of further disquieting Tom, but before he could invent a protest the coupé came to a stop, and Daisy signalled us to draw up alongside.

'Where are we going?' she cried.

'How about the movies?'

'It's so hot,' she complained. 'You go. We'll ride around and meet you after.' With an effort her wit rose faintly, 'We'll meet you on some corner. I'll be the man smoking two cigarettes.'

'We can't argue about it here,' Tom said impatiently, as a truck gave out a cursing whistle behind us. 'You follow me to the south side of Central Park, in front of the Plaza.'

Several times he turned his head and looked back for their car, and if the traffic delayed them he slowed up until they came into sight. I think he was afraid they would dart down a side street and out of his life for ever.

But they didn't. And we all took the less explicable step of engaging the parlour of a suite in the Plaza Hotel.

The prolonged and tumultuous argument that ended by herding us into that room eludes me, though I have a sharp physical memory that, in the course of it, my underwear kept climbing like a damp snake around my legs and intermittent beads of sweat raced cool across my back. The notion originated with Daisy's suggestion that we hire five bathrooms and take cold baths, and then assumed more tangible form as 'a place to have a mint julep'. Each of us said over and over that it was a 'crazy idea' – we all talked at once to a baffled clerk and thought, or pretended to think, that we were being very funny . . .

The room was large and stifling, and, though it was already four o'clock, opening the windows admitted only a gust of hot shrubbery from the Park. Daisy went to the mirror and stood with her back to us, fixing her hair.

'It's a swell suite,' whispered Jordan respectfully, and everyone laughed.

'Open another window,' commanded Daisy, without turning around.

'There aren't any more.'

'Well, we'd better telephone for an axe – '

'The thing to do is to forget about the heat,' said Tom impatiently. 'You make it ten times worse by crabbing about it.'

He unrolled the bottle of whiskey from the towel and put it on the table.

'Why not let her alone, old sport?' remarked Gatsby. 'You're the one that wanted to come to town.'

There was a moment of silence. The telephone book slipped from its nail and splashed to the floor, whereupon Jordan whispered, 'Excuse me' – but this time no one laughed.

'I'll pick it up,' I offered.

'I've got it.' Gatsby examined the parted string, muttered, 'Hum!' in an interested way, and tossed the book on a chair.

'That's a great expression of yours, isn't it?' said Tom sharply.

'What is?'

'All this "old sport" business. Where'd you pick that up?'

'Now see here, Tom,' said Daisy, turning around from the mirror, 'if you're going to make personal remarks I won't stay here a minute. Call up and order some ice for the mint julep.'

As Tom took up the receiver the compressed heat exploded into sound and we were listening to the portentous chords of Mendelssohn's Wedding March from the ballroom below.

'Imagine marrying anybody in this heat!' cried Jordan dismally.

'Still – I was married in the middle of June,' Daisy remembered. 'Louisville in June! Somebody fainted. Who was it fainted, Tom?'

'Biloxi,' he answered shortly.

'A man named Biloxi. "Blocks" Biloxi, and he made boxes – that's a fact – and he was from Biloxi, Tennessee.'

'They carried him into my house,' appended Jordan, 'because we lived just two doors from the church. And he stayed three weeks, until daddy told him he had to get out. The day after he left daddy died.' After a moment she added, 'There wasn't any connection.'

'I used to know a Bill Biloxi from Memphis,' I remarked.

'That was his cousin. I knew his whole family history before he left. He gave me an aluminium putter that I use today.'

The music had died down as the ceremony began and now a long cheer floated in at the window, followed by intermittent cries of 'Yea-ea-ea!' and finally by a burst of jazz as the dancing began.

'We're getting old,' said Daisy. 'If we were young we'd rise and dance.'

'Remember Biloxi,' Jordan warned her. 'Where'd you know him, Tom?'

'Biloxi?' He concentrated with an effort. 'I didn't know him. He was a friend of Daisy's.'

'He was not,' she denied. 'I'd never seen him before. He came down in the private car.'

'Well, he said he knew you. He said he was raised in Louisville. Asa Bird brought him around at the last minute and asked if we had room for him.'

Jordan smiled.

'He was probably bumming his way home. He told me he was president of your class at Yale.'

Tom and I looked at each other blankly.

'Bil*oxi*?'

'First place, we didn't have any president – '

Gatsby's foot beat a short, restless tattoo and Tom eyed him suddenly.

'By the way, Mr Gatsby, I understand you're an Oxford man.'

'Not exactly.'

'Oh, yes, I understand you went to Oxford.'

'Yes – I went there.'

A pause. Then Tom's voice incredulous and insulting: 'You must have gone there about the time Biloxi went to New Haven.'

Another pause. A waiter knocked and came in with crushed mint and ice, but the silence was unbroken by his 'thank you' and the soft closing of the door. This tremendous detail was to be cleared up at last.

'I told you I went there,' said Gatsby.

'I heard you, but I'd like to know when.'

'It was in 1919. I only stayed five months. That's why I can't really call myself an Oxford man.'

Tom glanced around to see if we mirrored his unbelief. But we were all looking at Gatsby.

'It was an opportunity they gave to some of the officers after the Armistice,' he continued. 'We could go to any of the universities in England or France.'

I wanted to get up and slap him on the back. I had one of those renewals of complete faith in him that I'd experienced before.

Daisy rose, smiling faintly, and went to the table.

'Open the whiskey, Tom,' she ordered, 'and I'll make you a mint julep. Then you won't seem so stupid to yourself . . . Look at the mint!'

'Wait a minute,' snapped Tom, 'I want to ask Mr Gatsby one more question.'

'Go on,' Gatsby said politely.

'What kind of a row are you trying to cause in my house anyhow?'

They were out in the open at last and Gatsby was content.

'He isn't causing a row,' Daisy looked desperately from one to the other. 'You're causing a row. Please have a little self-control.'

'Self-control!' repeated Tom incredulously. 'I suppose the latest thing is to sit back and let Mr Nobody from Nowhere make love to your wife. Well, if that's the idea you can count me out . . . Nowadays people begin by sneering at family life and family institutions, and next they'll throw everything overboard and have intermarriage between black and white.'

Flushed with his impassioned gibberish, he saw himself standing alone on the last barrier of civilisation.

'We're all white here,' murmured Jordan.

'I know I'm not very popular. I don't give big parties. I suppose you've got to make your house into a pigsty in order to have any friends – in the modern world.'

Angry as I was, as we all were, I was tempted to laugh whenever he opened his mouth. The transition from libertine to prig was so complete.

'I've got something to tell *you*, old sport – ' began Gatsby. But Daisy guessed at his intention.

'Please don't!' she interrupted helplessly. 'Please let's all go home. Why don't we all go home?'

'That's a good idea.' I got up. 'Come on, Tom. Nobody wants a drink.'

'I want to know what Mr Gatsby has to tell me.'

'Your wife doesn't love you,' said Gatsby. 'She's never loved you. She loves me.'

'You must be crazy!' exclaimed Tom automatically.

Gatsby sprang to his feet, vivid with excitement.

'She never loved you, do you hear?' he cried. 'She only married you because I was poor and she was tired of waiting for me. It was a terrible mistake, but in her heart she never loved anyone except me!'

At this point Jordan and I tried to go, but Tom and Gatsby insisted with competitive firmness that we remain – as though neither of them had anything to conceal and it would be a privilege to partake vicariously of their emotions.

'Sit down, Daisy,' Tom's voice groped unsuccessfully for the paternal note. 'What's been going on? I want to hear all about it.'

'I told you what's been going on,' said Gatsby. 'Going on for five years – and you didn't know.'

Tom turned to Daisy sharply.

'You've been seeing this fellow for five years?'

'Not seeing,' said Gatsby. 'No, we couldn't meet. But both of us loved each other all that time, old sport, and you didn't know. I used to laugh sometimes' – but there was no laughter in his eyes – 'to think that you didn't know.'

'Oh – that's all.' Tom tapped his thick fingers together like a clergyman and leaned back in his chair. 'You're crazy!' he exploded. 'I can't speak about what happened five years ago because I didn't know Daisy then – and I'll be damned if I see how you got within a mile of her unless you brought the groceries to the back door. But all the rest of that's a goddamned lie. Daisy loved me when she married me and she loves me now.'

'No,' said Gatsby, shaking his head.

'She does, though. The trouble is that sometimes she gets foolish ideas in her head and doesn't know what she's doing.' He nodded sagely. 'And what's more I love Daisy too. Once in a while I go off on a spree and make a fool of myself, but I always come back, and in my heart I love her all the time.'

'You're revolting,' said Daisy. She turned to me, and her voice, dropping an octave lower, filled the room with thrilling scorn: 'Do you know why we left Chicago? I'm surprised that they didn't treat you to the story of that little spree.'

Gatsby walked over and stood beside her.

'Daisy, that's all over now,' he said earnestly. 'It doesn't matter any more. Just tell him the truth – that you never loved him – and it's all wiped out for ever.'

She looked at him blindly. 'Why – how could I love him – possibly?'

'You never loved him.'

She hesitated. Her eyes fell on Jordan and me with a sort of appeal, as though she realised at last what she was doing – and as though she had never, all along, intended doing anything at all. But it was done now. It was too late.

'I never loved him,' she said, with perceptible reluctance.

'Not at Kapiolani?' demanded Tom suddenly.

'No.'

From the ballroom beneath, muffled and suffocating chords were drifting up on hot waves of air.

'Not that day I carried you down from the Punch Bowl to keep your shoes dry?' There was a husky tenderness in his tone . . . 'Daisy?'

'Please don't.' Her voice was cold, but the rancour was gone from it. She looked at Gatsby. 'There, Jay,' she said – but her hand as she tried to light a cigarette was trembling. Suddenly she threw the cigarette and the burning match on the carpet.

'Oh, you want too much!' she cried to Gatsby. 'I love you now – isn't that enough? I can't help what's past.' She began to sob helplessly. 'I did love him once – but I loved you too.'

Gatsby's eyes opened and closed.

'You loved me *too*?' he repeated.

'Even that's a lie,' said Tom savagely. 'She didn't know you were alive. Why – there're things between Daisy and me that you'll never know, things that neither of us can ever forget.'

The words seemed to bite physically into Gatsby.

'I want to speak to Daisy alone,' he insisted. 'She's all excited now – '

'Even alone I can't say I never loved Tom,' she admitted in a pitiful voice. 'It wouldn't be true.'

'Of course it wouldn't,' agreed Tom.

She turned to her husband. 'As if it mattered to you,' she said.

'Of course it matters. I'm going to take better care of you from now on.'

'You don't understand,' said Gatsby, with a touch of panic. 'You're not going to take care of her any more.'

'I'm not?' Tom opened his eyes wide and laughed. He could afford to control himself now. 'Why's that?'

'Daisy's leaving you.'

'Nonsense.'

'I am, though,' she said with a visible effort.

'She's not leaving me!' Tom's words suddenly leaned down over Gatsby. 'Certainly not for a common swindler who'd have to steal the ring he put on her finger.'

'I won't stand this!' cried Daisy. 'Oh, please let's get out.'

'Who are you, anyhow?' broke out Tom. 'You're one of that bunch that hangs around with Meyer Wolfsheim – that much I happen to know. I've made a little investigation into your affairs – and I'll carry it further tomorrow.'

'You can suit yourself about that, old sport,' said Gatsby steadily.

'I found out what your "drugstores" were.' He turned to us and spoke rapidly. 'He and this Wolfsheim bought up a lot of side-street drugstores here and in Chicago and sold grain alcohol over the counter. That's one of his little stunts. I picked him for a bootlegger the first time I saw him, and I wasn't far wrong.'

'What about it?' said Gatsby politely. 'I guess your friend Walter Chase wasn't too proud to come in on it.'

'And you left him in the lurch, didn't you? You let him go to jail for a month over in New Jersey. God! You ought to hear Walter on the subject of *you*.'

'He came to us dead broke. He was very glad to pick up some money, old sport.'

'Don't you call me "old sport"!' cried Tom. Gatsby said nothing.

'Walter could have you up on the betting laws too, but Wolfsheim scared him into shutting his mouth.'

That unfamiliar yet recognisable look was back again in Gatsby's face.

'That drugstore business was just small change,' continued Tom slowly, 'but you've got something on now that Walter's afraid to tell me about.'

I glanced at Daisy, who was staring terrified between Gatsby and her husband, and at Jordan, who had begun to balance an invisible but absorbing object on the tip of her chin. Then I turned back to Gatsby – and was startled at his expression. He looked – and this is said in all contempt for the babbled slander of his garden – as if he had 'killed a man'. For a moment the set of his face could be described in just that fantastic way.

It passed, and he began to talk excitedly to Daisy, denying everything, defending his name against accusations that had not been made. But with every word she was drawing further and further into herself, so he gave that up, and only the dead dream fought on as the afternoon slipped away, trying to touch what was no longer tangible, struggling unhappily, undespairingly, towards that lost voice across the room.

The voice begged again to go.

'*Please*, Tom! I can't stand this any more.'

Her frightened eyes told that whatever intentions, whatever courage she had had, were definitely gone.

'You two start on home, Daisy,' said Tom. 'In Mr Gatsby's car.'

She looked at Tom, alarmed now, but he insisted with magnanimous scorn.

'Go on. He won't annoy you. I think he realises that his presumptuous little flirtation is over.'

They were gone, without a word, snapped out, made accidental, isolated, like ghosts, even from our pity.

After a moment Tom got up and began wrapping the unopened bottle of whiskey in the towel.

'Want any of this stuff? Jordan? . . . Nick?'

I didn't answer.

'Nick?' He asked again.

'What?'

'Want any?'

'No . . . I just remembered that today's my birthday.'

I was thirty. Before me stretched the portentous, menacing road of a new decade.

It was seven o'clock when we got into the coupé with him and started for Long Island. Tom talked incessantly, exulting and laughing, but his voice was as remote from Jordan and me as the foreign clamour on the sidewalk or the tumult of the elevated overhead. Human sympathy has its limits, and we were content to let all their tragic arguments fade with the city lights behind. Thirty – the promise of a decade of loneliness, a thinning list of single men to know, a thinning briefcase of enthusiasm, thinning hair. But there was Jordan beside me, who, unlike Daisy, was too wise ever to carry well-forgotten dreams from age to age. As we passed over the dark bridge her wan face fell lazily against my coat's shoulder and the formidable stroke of thirty died away with the reassuring pressure of her hand.

So we drove on towards death through the cooling twilight.

The young Greek, Michaelis, who ran the coffee joint beside the ash heaps was the principal witness at the inquest. He had slept through the heat until after five, when he strolled over to the garage, and found George Wilson sick in his office – really sick, pale as his own pale hair and shaking all over. Michaelis advised him to go to bed, but Wilson refused, saying that he'd miss a lot of business if he did. While his neighbour was trying to persuade him a violent racket broke out overhead.

'I've got my wife locked in up there,' explained Wilson calmly. 'She's going to stay there till the day after tomorrow, and then we're going to move away.'

Michaelis was astonished; they had been neighbours for four years, and Wilson had never seemed faintly capable of such a statement. Generally he was one of these worn-out men: when he wasn't working, he sat on a chair in the doorway and stared at the people and the cars that passed along the road. When anyone spoke to him he invariably laughed in an agreeable, colourless way. He was his wife's man and not his own.

So naturally Michaelis tried to find out what had happened, but Wilson wouldn't say a word – instead he began to throw curious suspicious glances at his visitor and ask him what he'd been doing at certain times on certain days. Just as the latter was getting uneasy, some workmen came past the door bound for his restaurant, and Michaelis took the opportunity to get away, intending to come back later. But he didn't. He supposed he forgot to, that's all. When he came outside again, a little after seven, he was reminded of the conversation because he heard Mrs Wilson's voice, loud and scolding, downstairs in the garage.

'Beat me!' he heard her cry. 'Throw me down and beat me, you dirty little coward!'

A moment later she rushed out into the dusk, waving her hands and shouting – before he could move from his door the business was over.

The 'death car' as the newspapers called it, didn't stop; it came out of the gathering darkness, wavered tragically for a moment, and then disappeared around the next bend. Mavromichaelis wasn't even sure of its colour – he told the first policeman that it was light green. The other car, the one going towards New York, came to rest a hundred yards beyond, and its driver hurried back to where Myrtle Wilson, her life violently extinguished, knelt in the road and mingled her thick dark blood with the dust.

Michaelis and this man reached her first, but when they had torn open her shirtwaist, still damp with perspiration, they saw that her left breast was swinging loose like a flap, and there was no need to listen for the heart beneath. The mouth was wide open and ripped a little at the corners, as though she had choked a little in giving up the tremendous vitality she had stored so long.

We saw the three or four automobiles and the crowd when we were still some distance away.

'Wreck!' said Tom. 'That's good. Wilson'll have a little business at last.'

He slowed down, but still without any intention of stopping, until, as we came nearer, the hushed, intent faces of the people at the garage door made him automatically put on his brakes.

'We'll take a look,' he said doubtfully, 'just a look.'

I became aware now of a hollow, wailing sound which issued incessantly from the garage, a sound which as we got out of the coupé and walked towards the door resolved itself into the words, 'Oh, my God!' uttered over and over in a gasping moan.

'There's some bad trouble here,' said Tom excitedly.

He reached up on tiptoes and peered over a circle of heads into the garage, which was lit only by a yellow light in a swinging metal basket overhead. Then he made a harsh sound in his throat, and with a violent thrusting movement of his powerful arms pushed his way through.

The circle closed up again with a running murmur of expostulation;

it was a minute before I could see anything at all. Then new arrivals deranged the line, and Jordan and I were pushed suddenly inside.

Myrtle Wilson's body, wrapped in a blanket, and then in another blanket, as though she suffered from a chill in the hot night, lay on a work-table by the wall, and Tom, with his back to us, was bending over it, motionless. Next to him stood a motorcycle policeman taking down names with much sweat and correction in a little book. At first I couldn't find the source of the high, groaning words that echoed clamorously through the bare garage – then I saw Wilson standing on the raised threshold of his office, swaying back and forth and holding to the doorposts with both hands. Some man was talking to him in a low voice and attempting, from time to time, to lay a hand on his shoulder, but Wilson neither heard nor saw. His eyes would drop slowly from the swinging light to the laden table by the wall, and then jerk back to the light again, and he gave out incessantly his high, horrible call: 'Oh, my Ga-od! Oh, my Ga-od! Oh, Ga-od! Oh, my Ga-od!'

Presently Tom lifted his head with a jerk and, after staring around the garage with glazed eyes, addressed a mumbled incoherent remark to the policeman.

'M, a, v – ' the policeman was saying, 'o – '

'No, r,' corrected the man, 'M, a, v, r, o – '

'Listen to me!' muttered Tom fiercely.

'r,' said the policeman, 'o – '

'g.'

'g – ' He looked up as Tom's broad hand fell sharply on his shoulder. 'What you want, fella?'

'What happened? – that's what I want to know.'

'Auto hit her. Ins'antly killed.'

'Instantly killed,' repeated Tom, staring.

'She ran out ina road. Son-of-a-bitch didn't even stopus car.'

'There was two cars,' said Michaelis, 'one comin', one goin', see?'

'Going where?' asked the policeman keenly.

'One goin' each way. Well, she' – his hand rose towards the blankets but stopped halfway and fell to his side – 'she ran out there an' the one comin' from N'York knock right into her, goin' thirty or forty miles an hour.'

'What's the name of this place here?' demanded the officer.

'Hasn't got any name.'

A pale well-dressed Negro stepped near.

'It was a yellow car,' he said, 'big yellow car. New.'

'See the accident?' asked the policeman.

'No, but the car passed me down the road, going faster'n forty. Going fifty, sixty.'

'Come here and let's have your name. Look out now. I want to get his name.'

Some words of this conversation must have reached Wilson, swaying in the office door, for suddenly a new theme found voice among his gasping cries: 'You don't have to tell me what kind of car it was! I know what kind of car it was!'

Watching Tom, I saw the wad of muscle back of his shoulder tighten under his coat. He walked quickly over to Wilson and, standing in front of him, seized him firmly by the upper arms.

'You've got to pull yourself together,' he said with soothing gruffness.

Wilson's eyes fell upon Tom; he started up on his tiptoes and then would have collapsed to his knees had not Tom held him upright.

'Listen,' said Tom, shaking him a little. 'I just got here a minute ago, from New York. I was bringing you that coupé we've been talking about. That yellow car I was driving this afternoon wasn't mine – do you hear? I haven't seen it all afternoon.'

Only the Negro and I were near enough to hear what he said, but the policeman caught something in the tone and looked over with truculent eyes.

'What's all that?' he demanded.

'I'm a friend of his.' Tom turned his head but kept his hands firm on Wilson's body. 'He says he knows the car that did it . . . It was a yellow car.'

Some dim impulse moved the policeman to look suspiciously at Tom.

'And what colour's your car?'

'It's a blue car, a coupé.'

'We've come straight from New York,' I said.

Someone who had been driving a little behind us confirmed this, and the policeman turned away.

'Now, if you'll let me have that name again correct – '

Picking up Wilson like a doll, Tom carried him into the office, set him down in a chair, and came back.

'If somebody'll come here and sit with him – ' he snapped authoritatively. He watched while the two men standing closest glanced at each other and went unwillingly into the room. Then Tom shut the door on them and came down the single step, his eyes avoiding the table. As he passed close to me he whispered: 'Let's get out.'

Self-consciously, with his authoritative arms breaking the way, we pushed through the still-gathering crowd, passing a hurried doctor, case in hand, who had been sent for in wild hope half an hour ago.

Tom drove slowly until we were beyond the bend – then his foot came down hard, and the coupé raced along through the night. In a little while I heard a low husky sob, and saw that the tears were overflowing down his face.

'The goddamned coward!' he whimpered. 'He didn't even stop his car.'

The Buchanans' house floated suddenly towards us through the dark rustling trees. Tom stopped beside the porch and looked up at the second floor, where two windows bloomed with light among the vines.

'Daisy's home,' he said. As we got out of the car he glanced at me and frowned slightly.

'I ought to have dropped you in West Egg, Nick. There's nothing we can do tonight.'

A change had come over him, and he spoke gravely, and with decision. As we walked across the moonlight gravel to the porch he disposed of the situation in a few brisk phrases.

'I'll telephone for a taxi to take you home, and while you're waiting you and Jordan better go in the kitchen and have them get you some supper – if you want any.' He opened the door. 'Come in.'

'No, thanks. But I'd be glad if you'd order me the taxi. I'll wait outside.'

Jordan put her hand on my arm.

'Won't you come in, Nick?'

'No, thanks.'

I was feeling a little sick and I wanted to be alone. But Jordan lingered for a moment more.

'It's only half-past nine,' she said.

I'd be damned if I'd go in; I'd had enough of all of them for one day, and suddenly that included Jordan too. She must have seen something of this in my expression, for she turned abruptly away and ran up the porch steps into the house. I sat down for a few minutes with my head in my hands, until I heard the phone taken up inside and the butler's voice calling a taxi. Then I walked slowly down the drive away from the house, intending to wait by the gate.

I hadn't gone twenty yards when I heard my name and Gatsby stepped from between two bushes into the path. I must have felt pretty weird by that time, because I could think of nothing except the luminosity of his pink suit under the moon.

'What are you doing?' I enquired.

'Just standing here, old sport.'

Somehow, that seemed a despicable occupation. For all I knew he was going to rob the house in a moment; I wouldn't have been surprised to see sinister faces, the faces of 'Wolfsheim's people', behind him in the dark shrubbery.

'Did you see any trouble on the road?' he asked after a minute.

'Yes.'

He hesitated.'Was she killed?'

'Yes.'

'I thought so; I told Daisy I thought so. It's better that the shock should all come at once. She stood it pretty well.'

He spoke as if Daisy's reaction was the only thing that mattered.

'I got to West Egg by a side road,' he went on, 'and left the car in my garage. I don't think anybody saw us, but of course I can't be sure.'

I disliked him so much by this time that I didn't find it necessary to tell him he was wrong.

'Who was the woman?' he enquired.

'Her name was Wilson. Her husband owns the garage. How the devil did it happen?'

'Well, I tried to swing the wheel – ' He broke off, and suddenly I guessed at the truth.

'Was Daisy driving?'

'Yes,' he said after a moment, 'but of course I'll say I was. You see, when we left New York she was very nervous and she thought it would steady her to drive – and this woman rushed out at us just as we were passing a car coming the other way. It all happened in a minute, but it seemed to me that she wanted to speak to us, thought we were somebody she knew. Well, first Daisy turned away from the woman towards the other car, and then she lost her nerve and turned back. The second my hand reached the wheel I felt the shock – it must have killed her instantly.'

'It ripped her open – '

'Don't tell me, old sport.' He winced. 'Anyhow – Daisy stepped on it. I tried to make her stop, but she couldn't, so I pulled on the emergency brake. Then she fell over into my lap and I drove on.

'She'll be all right tomorrow,' he said presently. 'I'm just going to wait here and see if he tries to bother her about that unpleasantness this afternoon. She's locked herself into her room, and if he tries any brutality she's going to turn the light out and on again.'

'He won't touch her,' I said. 'He's not thinking about her.'

'I don't trust him, old sport.'

'How long are you going to wait?'

'All night, if necessary. Anyhow, till they all go to bed.'

A new point of view occurred to me. Suppose Tom found out that Daisy had been driving. He might think he saw a connection in it – he might think anything. I looked at the house; there were two or three bright windows downstairs and the pink glow from Daisy's room on the second floor.

'You wait here,' I said. 'I'll see if there's any sign of a commotion.'

I walked back along the border of the lawn, traversed the gravel softly, and tiptoed up the veranda steps. The drawing-room curtains were open, and I saw that the room was empty. Crossing the porch where we had dined that June night three months before, I came to a small rectangle of light which I guessed was the pantry window. The blind was drawn, but I found a rift at the sill.

Daisy and Tom were sitting opposite each other at the kitchen table, with a plate of cold fried chicken between them, and two bottles of ale. He was talking intently across the table at her, and in his earnestness his hand had fallen upon and covered her own. Once in a while she looked up at him and nodded in agreement.

They weren't happy, and neither of them had touched the chicken or the ale – and yet they weren't unhappy either. There was an unmistakable air of natural intimacy about the picture, and anybody would have said that they were conspiring together.

As I tiptoed from the porch I heard my taxi feeling its way along the dark drive towards the house. Gatsby was waiting where I had left him in the drive.

'Is it all quiet up there?' he asked anxiously.

'Yes, it's all quiet.' I hesitated. 'You'd better come home and get some sleep.'

He shook his head.

'I want to wait here till Daisy goes to bed. Good-night, old sport.'

He put his hands in his coat pockets and turned back eagerly to his scrutiny of the house, as though my presence marred the sacredness of the vigil. So I walked away and left him standing there in the moonlight – watching over nothing.

Chapter 8

I couldn't sleep all night; a foghorn was groaning incessantly on the Sound, and I tossed half-sick between grotesque reality and savage, frightening dreams. Towards dawn I heard a taxi go up Gatsby's drive, and immediately I jumped out of bed and began to dress – I felt that I had something to tell him, something to warn him about, and morning would be too late.

Crossing his lawn, I saw that his front door was still open and he was leaning against a table in the hall, heavy with dejection or sleep.

'Nothing happened,' he said wanly. 'I waited, and about four o'clock she came to the window and stood there for a minute and then turned out the light.'

His house had never seemed so enormous to me as it did that night when we hunted through the great rooms for cigarettes. We pushed aside curtains that were like pavilions, and felt over innumerable feet of dark wall for electric-light switches – once I tumbled with a sort of splash upon the keys of a ghostly piano. There was an inexplicable amount of dust everywhere, and the rooms were musty, as though they hadn't been aired for many days. I found the humidor on an unfamiliar table, with two stale, dry cigarettes inside. Throwing open the French windows of the drawing-room, we sat smoking out into the darkness.

'You ought to go away,' I said. 'It's pretty certain they'll trace your car.'

'Go away *now*, old sport?'

'Go to Atlantic City for a week, or up to Montreal.'

He wouldn't consider it. He couldn't possibly leave Daisy until he knew what she was going to do. He was clutching at some last hope and I couldn't bear to shake him free.

It was this night that he told me the strange story of his youth with Dan Cody – told it to me because 'Jay Gatsby' had broken up like glass against Tom's hard malice, and the long secret extravaganza was played out. I think that he would have acknowledged anything now, without reserve, but he wanted to talk about Daisy.

She was the first 'nice girl' he had ever known. In various unrevealed capacities he had come in contact with such people, but always with indiscernible barbed wire between. He found her excitingly desirable. He went to her house, at first with other officers from Camp Taylor, then alone. It amazed him – he had never been in such a beautiful house before. But what gave it an air of breathless intensity was that Daisy lived there – it was as casual a thing to her as his tent out at camp was to him. There was a ripe mystery about it, a hint of bedrooms upstairs more beautiful and cool than other bedrooms, of gay and radiant activities taking place through its corridors, and of romances that were not musty and laid away already in lavender but fresh and breathing and redolent of this year's shining motor cars and of dances whose flowers were scarcely withered. It excited him, too, that many men had already loved Daisy – it increased her value in his eyes. He felt their presence all about the house, pervading the air with the shades and echoes of still vibrant emotions.

But he knew that he was in Daisy's house by a colossal accident. However glorious might be his future as Jay Gatsby, he was at present a penniless young man without a past, and at any moment the invisible cloak of his uniform might slip from his shoulders. So he made the most of his time. He took what he could get, ravenously and unscrupulously – eventually he took Daisy one still October night, took her because he had no real right to touch her hand.

He might have despised himself, for he had certainly taken her under false pretences. I don't mean that he had traded on his phantom millions, but he had deliberately given Daisy a sense of security; he let her believe that he was a person from much the same strata as herself – that he was fully able to take care of her. As a matter of fact, he had no such facilities – he had no comfortable family standing behind him, and he was liable at the whim of an impersonal government to be blown anywhere about the world.

But he didn't despise himself and it didn't turn out as he had imagined. He had intended, probably, to take what he could and go – but now he found that he had committed himself to the following of a grail. He knew that Daisy was extraordinary, but he didn't realise just how extraordinary a 'nice' girl could be. She vanished into her rich house, into her rich, full life, leaving Gatsby – nothing. He felt married to her, that was all.

When they met again, two days later, it was Gatsby who was breathless, who was, somehow, betrayed. Her porch was bright with the bought luxury of star-shine; the wicker of the settee squeaked fashionably as she turned towards him and he kissed her curious and lovely mouth. She had caught a cold, and it made her voice huskier and more charming than ever, and Gatsby was overwhelmingly aware of the youth and mystery that wealth imprisons and preserves, of the freshness of many clothes, and of Daisy, gleaming like silver, safe and proud above the hot struggles of the poor.

'I can't describe to you how surprised I was to find out I loved her, old sport. I even hoped for a while that she'd throw me over, but she didn't, because she was in love with me too. She thought I knew a lot because I knew different things from her . . . Well, there I was, 'way off my ambitions, getting deeper in love every minute, and all of a sudden I didn't care. What was the use of doing great things if I could have a better time telling her what I was going to do?'

On the last afternoon before he went abroad, he sat with Daisy in his arms for a long, silent time. It was a cold fall day, with fire in the room and her cheeks flushed. Now and then she moved and he changed his arm a little, and once he kissed her dark shining hair. The afternoon had made them tranquil for a while, as if to give them a deep memory for the long parting the next day promised. They had never been closer in their month of love, nor communicated more profoundly one with another, than when she brushed silent lips against his coat's shoulder or when he touched the end of her fingers, gently, as though she were asleep.

He did extraordinarily well in the war. He was a captain before he went to the front, and following the Argonne battles he got his majority and the command of the divisional machine-guns. After the Armistice he tried frantically to get home, but some complication or misunderstanding sent him to Oxford instead. He was worried now – there was a quality of nervous despair in Daisy's letters. She didn't see why he couldn't come. She was feeling the pressure of the world outside, and she wanted to see him and feel his presence beside her and be reassured that she was doing the right thing after all.

For Daisy was young and her artificial world was redolent of orchids and pleasant, cheerful snobbery and orchestras which set the rhythm of the year, summing up the sadness and suggestiveness of life in new tunes. All night the saxophones wailed the hopeless comment of the 'Beale Street Blues' while a hundred pairs of golden and silver slippers shuffled the shining dust. At the grey tea hour there were always rooms that throbbed incessantly with this low, sweet fever, while fresh faces drifted here and there like rose petals blown by the sad horns around the floor.

Through this twilight universe Daisy began to move again with the season; suddenly she was again keeping half a dozen dates a day with half a dozen men, and drowsing asleep at dawn with the beads and chiffon of an evening dress tangled among dying orchids on the floor beside her bed. And all the time something within her was crying for a decision. She wanted her life shaped now, immediately – and the decision must be made by some force – of love, of money, of unquestionable practicality – that was close at hand.

That force took shape in the middle of spring with the arrival of Tom Buchanan. There was a wholesome bulkiness about his person and his position, and Daisy was flattered. Doubtless there was a certain struggle and a certain relief. The letter reached Gatsby while he was still at Oxford.

It was dawn now on Long Island and we went about opening the rest of the windows downstairs, filling the house with grey-turning, gold-turning light. The shadow of a tree fell abruptly across the dew and ghostly birds began to sing among the blue leaves. There was a slow, pleasant movement in the air, scarcely a wind, promising a cool, lovely day.

'I don't think she ever loved him,' Gatsby turned around from a window and looked at me challengingly. 'You must remember, old sport, she was very excited this afternoon. He told her those things in a way that frightened her – that made it look as if I was some kind of cheap sharper. And the result was she hardly knew what she was saying.'

He sat down gloomily.

'Of course she might have loved him just for a minute, when they were first married – and loved me more even then, do you see?'

Suddenly he came out with a curious remark.

'In any case,' he said, 'it was just personal.'

What could you make of that, except to suspect some intensity in his conception of the affair that couldn't be measured?

He came back from France when Tom and Daisy were still on their wedding trip, and made a miserable but irresistible journey to Louisville on the last of his army pay. He stayed there a week, walking the streets where their footsteps had clicked together through the November night and revisiting the out-of-the-way places to which they had driven in her white car. Just as Daisy's house had always seemed to him more mysterious and gay than other houses, so his idea of the city itself, even though she was gone from it, was pervaded with a melancholy beauty.

He left, feeling that if he had searched harder, he might have found her – that he was leaving her behind. The day-coach – he was penniless now – was hot. He went out to the open vestibule and sat down on a folding-chair, and the station slid away and the backs of unfamiliar buildings moved by. Then out into the spring fields, where a yellow trolley raced them for a minute with people in it who might once have seen the pale magic of her face along the casual street.

The track curved and now it was going away from the sun, which, as it sank lower, seemed to spread itself in benediction over the vanishing city where she had drawn her breath. He stretched out his hand desperately as if to snatch only a wisp of air, to save a fragment of the spot that she had made lovely for him. But it was all going by too fast now for his blurred eyes and he knew that he had lost that part of it, the freshest and the best, for ever.

It was nine o'clock when we finished breakfast and went out on the porch. The night had made a sharp difference in the weather and there was an autumn flavour in the air. The gardener, the last one of Gatsby's former servants, came to the foot of the steps.

'I'm going to drain the pool today, Mr Gatsby. Leaves'll start falling pretty soon, and then there's always trouble with the pipes.'

'Don't do it today,' Gatsby answered. He turned to me apologetically. 'You know, old sport, I've never used that pool all summer.'

I looked at my watch and stood up.

'Twelve minutes to my train.'

I didn't want to go to the city. I wasn't worth a decent stroke of work, but it was more than that – I didn't want to leave Gatsby. I missed that train, and then another, before I could get myself away.

'I'll call you up,' I said finally.

'Do, old sport.'

'I'll call you about noon.'

We walked slowly down the steps.

'I suppose Daisy'll call too.' He looked at me anxiously, as if he hoped I'd corroborate this.

'I suppose so.'

'Well, goodbye.'

We shook hands and I started away. Just before I reached the hedge I remembered something and turned around.

'They're a rotten crowd,' I shouted across the lawn. 'You're worth the whole damn bunch put together.'

I've always been glad I said that. It was the only compliment I ever gave him, because I disapproved of him from beginning to end. First he nodded politely, and then his face broke into that radiant and understanding smile, as if we'd been in ecstatic cahoots on that fact all the time. His gorgeous pink rag of a suit made a bright spot of colour against the white steps, and I thought of the night when I first came to his ancestral home, three months before. The lawn and drive had been crowded with the faces of those who guessed at his corruption – and he had stood on those steps, concealing his incorruptible dream, as he waved them goodbye.

I thanked him for his hospitality. We were always thanking him for that – I and the others.

'Goodbye,' I called. 'I enjoyed breakfast, Gatsby.'

Up in the city, I tried for a while to list the quotations on an interminable amount of stock, then I fell asleep in my swivel-chair. Just before noon the phone woke me, and I started up with sweat breaking out on my forehead. It was Jordan Baker; she often called me up at this hour because the uncertainty of her own movements between hotels and clubs and private houses made her hard to find in any other way. Usually her voice came over the wire as something fresh and cool, as if a divot from a green golf-links had come sailing in at the office window, but this morning it seemed harsh and dry.

'I've left Daisy's house,' she said. 'I'm at Hempstead, and I'm going down to Southampton this afternoon.'

Probably it had been tactful to leave Daisy's house, but the act annoyed me, and her next remark made me rigid.

'You weren't so nice to me last night.'

'How could it have mattered then?'

Silence for a moment. Then: 'However – I want to see you.'

'I want to see you, too.'

'Suppose I don't go to Southampton, and come into town this afternoon?'

'No – I don't think this afternoon.'

'Very well.'

'It's impossible this afternoon. Various – '

We talked like that for a while, and then abruptly we weren't talking any longer. I don't know which of us hung up with a sharp click, but I know I didn't care. I couldn't have talked to her across a tea-table that day if I never talked to her again in this world.

I called Gatsby's house a few minutes later, but the line was busy. I tried four times; finally an exasperated central told me the wire was being kept open for long distance from Detroit. Taking out my time-table, I drew a small circle around the three-fifty train. Then I leaned back in my chair and tried to think. It was just noon.

When I passed the ash heaps on the train that morning I had crossed deliberately to the other side of the car. I supposed there'd be a curious crowd around there all day, with little boys searching for dark spots in the dust and some garrulous man telling over and over what had happened, until it became less and less real even to him and he could tell it no longer, and Myrtle Wilson's tragic achievement was forgotten. Now I want to go back a little and tell what happened at the garage after we left there the night before.

They had difficulty in locating the sister, Catherine. She must have broken her rule against drinking that night, for when she arrived she was stupid with liquor and unable to understand that the ambulance had already gone to Flushing. When they convinced her of this, she immediately fainted, as if that was the intolerable part of the affair. Someone, kind or curious, took her in his car and drove her in the wake of her sister's body.

Until long after midnight a changing crowd lapped up against the front of the garage, while George Wilson rocked himself back and forth on the couch inside. For a while the door of the office was open, and everyone who came into the garage glanced irresistibly through it. Finally someone said it was a shame, and closed the door. Michaelis and several other men were with him; first, four or five men, later two or three men. Still later Michaelis had to ask the last stranger to wait there fifteen minutes longer while he went back to his own place and made a pot of coffee. After that, he stayed there alone with Wilson until dawn.

About three o'clock the quality of Wilson's incoherent muttering changed – he grew quieter and began to talk about the yellow car. He announced that he had a way of finding out whom the yellow car belonged to, and then he blurted out that a couple of months ago his wife had come from the city with her face bruised and her nose swollen.

But when he heard himself say this, he flinched and began to cry,

'Oh, my God!' again in his groaning voice. Michaelis made a clumsy attempt to distract him.

'How long have you been married, George? Come on there, try and sit still a minute and answer my question. How long have you been married?'

'Twelve years.'

'Ever had any children? Come on, George, sit still – I asked you a question. Did you ever have any children?'

The hard brown beetles kept thudding against the dull light, and whenever Michaelis heard a car go tearing along the road outside it sounded to him like the car that hadn't stopped a few hours before. He didn't like to go into the garage, because the work bench was stained where the body had been lying, so he moved uncomfortably around the office – he knew every object in it before morning – and from time to time sat down beside Wilson, trying to keep him more quiet.

'Have you got a church you go to sometimes, George? Maybe even if you haven't been there for a long time? Maybe I could call up the church and get a priest to come over and he could talk to you, see?'

'Don't belong to any.'

'You ought to have a church, George, for times like this. You must have gone to church once. Didn't you get married in a church? Listen, George, listen to me. Didn't you get married in a church?'

'That was a long time ago.'

The effort of answering broke the rhythm of his rocking – for a moment he was silent. Then the same half-knowing, half-bewildered look came back into his faded eyes.

'Look in the drawer there,' he said, pointing at the desk.

'Which drawer?'

'That drawer – that one.'

Michaelis opened the drawer nearest his hand. There was nothing in it but a small, expensive dog-leash, made of leather and braided silver. It was apparently new.

'This?' he enquired, holding it up.

Wilson stared and nodded. 'I found it yesterday afternoon. She tried to tell me about it, but I knew it was something funny.'

'You mean your wife bought it?'

'She had it wrapped in tissue paper on her bureau.'

Michaelis didn't see anything odd in that, and he gave Wilson a dozen reasons why his wife might have bought the dog-leash. But conceivably Wilson had heard some of these same explanations before, from Myrtle, because he began saying, 'Oh, my God!' again in a whisper – his comforter left several explanations in the air.

'Then he killed her,' said Wilson. His mouth dropped open suddenly.

'Who did?'

'I have a way of finding out.'

'You're morbid, George,' said his friend. 'This has been a strain to you and you don't know what you're saying. You'd better try and sit quiet till morning.'

'He murdered her.'

'It was an accident, George.'

Wilson shook his head. His eyes narrowed and his mouth widened slightly with the ghost of a superior, 'Hm!'

'I know,' he said definitely. 'I'm one of these trusting fellas and I don't think any harm to *no*body, but when I get to know a thing I know it. It was the man in that car. She ran out to speak to him and he wouldn't stop.'

Michaelis had seen this too, but it hadn't occurred to him that there was any special significance in it. He believed that Mrs Wilson had been running away from her husband, rather than trying to stop any particular car.

'How could she of been like that?'

'She's a deep one,' said Wilson, as if that answered the question. 'Ah-h-h – '

He began to rock again, and Michaelis stood twisting the leash in his hand.

'Maybe you got some friend that I could telephone for, George?'

This was a forlorn hope – he was almost sure that Wilson had no friend: there was not enough of him for his wife. He was glad a little later when he noticed a change in the room, a blue quickening by the window, and realised that dawn wasn't far off. About five o'clock it was blue enough outside to snap off the light.

Wilson's glazed eyes turned out to the ash heaps, where small grey clouds took on fantastic shapes and scurried here and there in the faint dawn wind.

'I spoke to her,' he muttered, after a long silence. 'I told her she might fool me but she couldn't fool God. I took her to the window' – with an effort he got up and walked to the rear window and leaned with his face pressed against it – 'and I said, "God knows what you've been doing, everything you've been doing. You may fool me, but you can't fool God!" '

Standing behind him, Michaelis saw with a shock that he was looking at the eyes of Dr T. J. Eckleburg, which had just emerged, pale and enormous, from the dissolving night.

'God sees everything,' repeated Wilson.

'That's an advertisement,' Michaelis assured him. Something made him turn away from the window and look back into the room. But Wilson stood there a long time, his face close to the window pane, nodding into the twilight.

By six o'clock Michaelis was worn out, and grateful for the sound of a car stopping outside. It was one of the watchers of the night before who had promised to come back, so he cooked breakfast for three, which he and the other man ate together. Wilson was quieter now, and Michaelis went home to sleep; when he awoke four hours later and hurried back to the garage, Wilson was gone.

His movements – he was on foot all the time – were afterwards traced to Port Roosevelt and then to Gad's Hill, where he bought a sandwich, that he didn't eat, and a cup of coffee. He must have been tired and walking slowly, for he didn't reach Gad's Hill until noon. Thus far there was no difficulty in accounting for his time – there were boys who had seen a man 'acting sort of crazy', and motorists at whom he stared oddly from the side of the road. Then for three hours he disappeared from view. The police, on the strength of what he had said to Michaelis, that he 'had a way of finding out', supposed that he spent that time going from garage to garage thereabouts, enquiring for a yellow car. On the other hand, no garage man who had seen him ever came forward, and perhaps he had an easier, surer way of finding out what he wanted to know. By half-past two he was in West Egg, where he asked someone the way to Gatsby's house. So by that time he knew Gatsby's name.

At two o'clock Gatsby put on his bathing-suit and left word with the butler that if anyone phoned word was to be brought to him at the pool. He stopped at the garage for a pneumatic mattress that had amused his guests during the summer, and the chauffeur helped him pump it up. Then he gave instructions that the open car wasn't to be taken out under any circumstances – and this was strange, because the front right fender needed repair.

Gatsby shouldered the mattress and started for the pool. Once he stopped and shifted it a little, and the chauffeur asked him if he needed help, but he shook his head and in a moment disappeared among the yellowing trees.

No telephone message arrived, but the butler went without his sleep and waited for it until four o'clock – until long after there was anyone to give it to if it came. I have an idea that Gatsby himself didn't believe it would come, and perhaps he no longer cared. If that was true he must have felt that he had lost the old warm world, paid a high price for living too long with a single dream. He must have looked up at an unfamiliar sky through frightening leaves and shivered as he found what a grotesque thing a rose is and how raw the sunlight was upon the scarcely created grass. A new world, material without being real, where poor ghosts, breathing dreams like air, drifted fortuitously about . . . like that ashen, fantastic figure gliding towards him through the amorphous trees.

The chauffeur – he was one of Wolfsheim's protégés – heard the shots – afterwards he could only say that he hadn't thought anything much about them. I drove from the station directly to Gatsby's house and my rushing anxiously up the front steps was the first thing that alarmed anyone. But they knew then, I firmly believe. With scarcely a word said, four of us, the chauffeur, butler, gardener and I, hurried down to the pool.

There was a faint, barely perceptible movement of the water as the fresh flow from one end urged its way towards the drain at the other. With little ripples that were hardly the shadows of waves, the laden mattress moved irregularly down the pool. A small gust of wind that scarcely corrugated the surface was enough to disturb its accidental course with its accidental burden. The touch of a cluster of leaves revolved it slowly, tracing, like the leg of transit, a thin red circle in the water.

It was after we started with Gatsby towards the house that the gardener saw Wilson's body a little way off in the grass, and the holocaust was complete.

Chapter 9

After two years I remember the rest of that day, and that night and the next day, only as an endless drill of police and photographers and newspaper men in and out of Gatsby's front door. A rope stretched across the main gate and a policeman by it kept out the curious, but little boys soon discovered that they could enter through my yard, and there were always a few of them clustered open-mouthed about the pool. Someone with a positive manner, perhaps a detective, used the expression 'madman' as he bent over Wilson's body that afternoon, and the adventitious authority of his voice set the key for the newspaper reports next morning.

Most of those reports were a nightmare – grotesque, circumstantial, eager and untrue. When Michaelis's testimony at the inquest brought to light Wilson's suspicions of his wife I thought the whole tale would shortly be served up in racy pasquinade – but Catherine, who might have said anything, didn't say a word. She showed a surprising amount of character about it too – looked at the coroner with determined eyes under that corrected brow of hers, and swore that her sister had never seen Gatsby, that her sister was completely happy with her husband, that her sister had been into no mischief whatever. She convinced herself of it, and cried into her handkerchief, as if the very suggestion was more than she could endure. So Wilson was reduced to a man 'deranged by grief' in order that the case might remain in its simplest form. And it rested there.

But all this part of it seemed remote and unessential. I found myself on Gatsby's side, and alone. From the moment I telephoned news of the catastrophe to West Egg village, every surmise about him, and every practical question, was referred to me. At first I was surprised and confused; then, as he lay in his house and didn't move or breathe or speak, hour upon hour, it grew upon me that I was responsible, because no one else was interested – interested, I mean, with that intense personal interest to which everyone has some vague right at the end.

I called up Daisy half an hour after we found him, called her instinctively and without hesitation. But she and Tom had gone away early that afternoon, and taken baggage with them.

'Left no address?'

'No.'

'Say when they'd be back?'

'No.'

'Any idea where they are? How I could reach them?'

'I don't know. Can't say.'

I wanted to get somebody for him. I wanted to go into the room where he lay and reassure him: 'I'll get somebody for you, Gatsby. Don't worry. Just trust me and I'll get somebody for you – '

Meyer Wolfsheim's name wasn't in the phone book. The butler gave me his once address on Broadway, and I called Information, but by the time I had the number it was long after five, and no one answered the phone.

'Will you ring again?'

'I've rung them three times.'

'It's very important.'

'Sorry. I'm afraid no one's there.'

I went back to the drawing-room and thought for an instant that they were chance visitors, all these official people who suddenly filled it. But, though they drew back the sheet and looked at Gatsby with shocked eyes, his protest continued in my brain: 'Look here, old sport, you've got to get somebody for me. You've got to try hard. I can't go through this alone.'

Someone started to ask me questions, but I broke away and going upstairs looked hastily through the unlocked parts of his desk – he'd never told me definitely that his parents were dead. But there was nothing – only the picture of Dan Cody, a token of forgotten violence, staring down from the wall.

Next morning I sent the butler to New York with a letter to Wolfsheim, which asked for information and urged him to come out on the next train. That request seemed superfluous when I wrote it. I was sure he'd start when he saw the newspapers, just as I was sure there'd be a wire from Daisy before noon – but neither a wire nor Mr Wolfsheim arrived; no one arrived except more police and photographers and newspaper men. When the butler brought back Wolfsheim's answer I began to have a feeling of defiance, of scornful solidarity between Gatsby and me against them all.

Dear Mr Carraway – This has been one of the most terrible shocks of my life to me I hardly can believe it that it is true at all.

Such a mad act as that man did should make us all think. I cannot come down now as I am tied up in some very important business and cannot get mixed up in this thing now. If there is anything I can do a little later let me know in a letter by Edgar. I hardly know where I am when I hear about a thing like this and am completely knocked down and out.

Yours truly

MEYER WOLFSHEIM

and then hasty addenda beneath:

Let me know about the funeral etc. Do not know his family at all.

When the phone rang that afternoon and Long Distance said Chicago was calling I thought this would be Daisy at last. But the connection came through as a man's voice, very thin and far away.

'This is Slagle speaking . . . '

'Yes?' The name was unfamiliar.

'Hell of a note, isn't it? Get my wire?'

'There haven't been any wires.'

'Young Parke's in trouble,' he said rapidly. 'They picked him up when he handed the bonds over the counter. They got a circular from New York giving 'em the numbers just five minutes before. What d'you know about that, hey? You never can tell in these hick towns – '

'Hello!' I interrupted breathlessly. 'Look here – this isn't Mr Gatsby. Mr Gatsby's dead.'

There was a long silence on the other end of the wire, followed by an exclamation . . . then a quick squawk as the connection was broken.

I think it was on the third day that a telegram signed Henry C. Gatz arrived from a town in Minnesota. It said only that the sender was leaving immediately and to postpone the funeral until he came.

It was Gatsby's father, a solemn old man, very helpless and dismayed, bundled up in a long cheap ulster against the warm September day. His eyes leaked continuously with excitement, and when I took the bag and umbrella from his hands he began to pull so incessantly at his sparse grey beard that I had difficulty in getting off his coat. He was on the point of collapse, so I took him into the music-room and made him sit down while I sent for something to eat. But he wouldn't eat, and the glass of milk spilled from his trembling hand.

'I saw it in the Chicago newspaper,' he said. 'It was all in the Chicago newspaper. I started right away.'

'I didn't know how to reach you.'

His eyes, seeing nothing, moved ceaselessly about the room.

'It was a madman,' he said. 'He must have been mad.'

'Wouldn't you like some coffee?' I urged him.

'I don't want anything. I'm all right now, Mr — '

'Carraway.'

'Well, I'm all right now. Where have they got Jimmy?'

I took him into the drawing-room, where his son lay, and left him there. Some little boys had come up on the steps and were looking into the hall; when I told them who had arrived, they went reluctantly away.

After a little while Mr Gatz opened the door and came out, his mouth ajar, his face flushed slightly, his eyes leaking isolated and unpunctual tears. He had reached an age where death no longer has the quality of ghastly surprise, and when he looked around him now for the first time and saw the height and splendour of the hall and the great rooms opening out from it into other rooms, his grief began to be mixed with an awed pride. I helped him to a bedroom upstairs; while he took off his coat and vest I told him that all arrangements had been deferred until he came.

'I didn't know what you'd want, Mr Gatsby – '

'Gatz is my name.'

' – Mr Gatz. I thought you might want to take the body West.'

He shook his head.

'Jimmy always liked it better down East. He rose up to his position in the East. Were you a friend of my boy's, Mr – ?'

'We were close friends.'

'He had a big future before him, you know. He was only a young man, but he had a lot of brain power here.'

He touched his head impressively, and I nodded.

'If he'd of lived, he'd of been a great man. A man like James J. Hill. He'd of helped build up the country.'

'That's true,' I said, uncomfortably.

He fumbled at the embroidered coverlet, trying to take it from the bed, and lay down stiffly – and was instantly asleep.

That night an obviously frightened person called up, and demanded to know who I was before he would give his name.

'This is Mr Carraway,' I said.

'Oh!' He sounded relieved. 'This is Klipspringer.'

I was relieved too, for that seemed to promise another friend at Gatsby's grave. I didn't want it to be in the papers and draw a sightseeing crowd, so I'd been calling up a few people myself. They were hard to find.

'The funeral's tomorrow,' I said. 'Three o'clock, here at the house. I wish you'd tell anybody who'd be interested.'

'Oh, I will,' he broke out hastily. 'Of course I'm not likely to see anybody, but if I do – '

His tone made me suspicious.

'Of course you'll be there yourself.'

'Well, I'll certainly try. What I called up about is – '

'Wait a minute,' I interrupted. 'How about saying you'll come?'

'Well, the fact is – the truth of the matter is that I'm staying with some people up here in Greenwich, and they rather expect me to be with them tomorrow. In fact, there's a sort of picnic or something. Of course I'll do my very best to get away.'

I ejaculated an unrestrained 'Huh' and he must have heard me, for he went on nervously: 'What I called up about was a pair of shoes I left there. I wonder if it'd be too much trouble to have the butler send them on. You see, they're tennis shoes, and I'm sort of helpless without them. My address is care of B. F. – '

I didn't hear the rest of the name, because I hung up the receiver.

After that I felt a certain shame for Gatsby – one gentleman to whom I telephoned implied that he had got what he deserved. However, that was my fault, for he was one of those who used to sneer most bitterly at Gatsby on the courage of Gatsby's liquor, and I should have known better than to call him.

The morning of the funeral I went up to New York to see Meyer Wolfsheim; I couldn't seem to reach him any other way. The door that I pushed open, on the advice of an elevator boy, was marked 'The Swastika Holding Company', and at first there didn't seem to be anyone inside. But when I'd shouted, 'Hello,' several times in vain, an argument broke out behind a partition, and presently a lovely Jewess appeared at an interior door and scrutinised me with black hostile eyes.

'Nobody's in,' she said. 'Mr Wolfsheim's gone to Chicago.'

The first part of this was obviously untrue, for someone had begun to whistle 'The Rosary', tunelessly, inside.

'Please say that Mr Carraway wants to see him.'

'I can't get him back from Chicago, can I?'

At this moment a voice, unmistakably Wolfsheim's, called 'Stella!' from the other side of the door.

'Leave your name on the desk,' she said quickly. 'I'll give it to him when he gets back.'

'But I know he's there.'

She took a step towards me and began to slide her hands indignantly up and down her hips.

'You young men think you can force your way in here any time,' she scolded. 'We're getting sickantired of it. When I say he's in Chicago, he's in Chi*ca*go.'

I mentioned Gatsby.

'Oh-h!' She looked at me over again. 'Will you just – What was your name?'

She vanished. In a moment Meyer Wolfsheim stood solemnly in the doorway, holding out both hands. He drew me into his office, remarking in a reverent voice that it was a sad time for all of us, and offered me a cigar.

'My memory goes back to when first I met him,' he said. 'A young major just out of the army and covered over with medals he got in the war. He was so hard up he had to keep on wearing his uniform because he couldn't buy some regular clothes. First time I saw him was when he come into Winebrenner's poolroom at Forty-third Street and asked for a job. He hadn't ate anything for a couple of days. "Come on have some lunch with me," I said. He ate more than four dollars' worth of food in half an hour.'

'Did you start him in business?' I enquired.

'Start him! I made him.'

'Oh.'

'I raised him up out of nothing, right out of the gutter. I saw right away he was a fine-appearing, gentlemanly young man, and when he told me he was an Oggsford I knew I could use him good. I got him to join up in the American Legion and he used to stand high there. Right off he did some work for a client of mine up to Albany. We were so thick like that in everything' – he held up two bulbous fingers – 'always together.'

I wondered if this partnership had included the World's Series transaction in 1919.

'Now he's dead,' I said after a moment. 'You were his closest friend, so I know you'll want to come to his funeral this afternoon.'

'I'd like to come.'

'Well, come then.'

The hair in his nostrils quivered slightly, and as he shook his head his eyes filled with tears.

'I can't do it – I can't get mixed up in it,' he said.

'There's nothing to get mixed up in. It's all over now.'

'When a man gets killed I never like to get mixed up in it in any way. I keep out. When I was a young man it was different – if a friend of mine died, no matter how, I stuck with them to the end. You may think that's sentimental, but I mean it – to the bitter end.'

I saw that for some reason of his own he was determined not to come, so I stood up.

'Are you a college man?' he enquired suddenly.

For a moment I thought he was going to suggest a 'gonnegtion', but he only nodded and shook my hand.

'Let us learn to show our friendship for a man when he is alive and not after he is dead,' he suggested. 'After that, my own rule is to let everything alone.'

When I left his office the sky had turned dark and I got back to West Egg in a drizzle. After changing my clothes I went next door and found Mr Gatz walking up and down excitedly in the hall. His pride in his son and in his son's possessions was continually increasing and now he had something to show me.

'Jimmy sent me this picture.' He took out his wallet with trembling fingers. 'Look there.'

It was a photograph of the house, cracked in the corners and dirty with many hands. He pointed out every detail to me eagerly. 'Look there!' and then sought admiration from my eyes. He had shown it so often that I think it was more real to him now than the house itself.

'Jimmy sent it to me. I think it's a very pretty picture. It shows up well.'

'Very well. Had you seen him lately?'

'He came out to see me two years ago and bought me the house I live in now. Of course we was broke up when he run off from home, but I see now there was a reason for it. He knew he had a big future in front of him. And ever since he made a success he was very generous with me.'

He seemed reluctant to put away the picture, held it for another minute, lingeringly, before my eyes. Then he returned the wallet and pulled from his pocket a ragged old copy of a book called *Hopalong Cassidy*.

'Look here, this is a book he had when he was a boy. It just shows you.'

He opened it at the back cover and turned it around for me to see. On the last flyleaf was printed the word Schedule, and the date September 12, 1906. And underneath:

Rise from bed	6.00	a.m.
Dumb-bell exercise and wall-scaling	6.15–6.30	"
Study electricity, etc.	7.15–8.15	"
Work	8.30–4.30	p.m.
Baseball and sports	4.30–5.00	"
Practise elocution, poise and how to attain it	5.00–6.00	"
Study needed inventions	7.00–9.00	"

GENERAL RESOLVES

No wasting time at Shafters or [a name, indecipherable]
No more smoking or chewing
Bath every other day
Read one improving book or magazine per week
Save $5.00 [crossed out] $3.00 per week
Be better to parents

'I come across this book by accident,' said the old man. 'It just shows you, don't it?

'Jimmy was bound to get ahead. He always had some resolves like this or something. Do you notice what he's got about improving his mind? He was always great for that. He told me I et like a hog once, and I beat him for it.'

He was reluctant to close the book, reading each item aloud and then looking eagerly at me. I think he rather expected me to copy down the list for my own use.

A little before three the Lutheran minister arrived from Flushing, and I began to look involuntarily out the windows for other cars. So did Gatsby's father. And as the time passed and the servants came in and stood waiting in the hall, his eyes began to blink anxiously, and he spoke of the rain in a worried, uncertain way. The minister glanced several times at his watch, so I took him aside and asked him to wait for half an hour. But it wasn't any use. Nobody came.

About five o'clock our procession of three cars reached the cemetery and stopped in a thick drizzle beside the gate – first a motor hearse, horribly black and wet, then Mr Gatz and the minister and I in the limousine, and a little later four or five servants and the postman from West Egg, in Gatsby's station-wagon, all wet to the skin. As we started through the gate into the cemetery I heard a car stop and then the sound of someone splashing after us over the soggy ground. I looked around. It was the man with owl-eyed glasses whom I had found marvelling over Gatsby's books in the library one night three months before.

I'd never seen him since then. I don't know how he knew about the funeral, or even his name. The rain poured down his thick glasses, and he took them off and wiped them to see the protecting canvas unrolled from Gatsby's grave.

I tried to think about Gatsby then for a moment, but he was already too far away, and I could only remember, without resentment, that Daisy hadn't sent a message or a flower. Dimly I heard someone murmur, 'Blessed are the dead that the rain falls on,' and then the owl-eyed man said, 'Amen to that,' in a brave voice.

We straggled down quickly through the rain to the cars. Owl-eyes spoke to me by the gate.

'I couldn't get to the house,' he remarked.

'Neither could anybody else.'

'Go on!' He started. 'Why, my God! they used to go there by the hundreds.' He took off his glasses and wiped them again, outside and in. 'The poor son-of-a-bitch,' he said.

One of my most vivid memories is of coming back West from prep school and later from college at Christmastime. Those who went farther than Chicago would gather in the old dim Union Station at six o'clock of a December evening, with a few Chicago friends, already caught up into their own holiday gaieties, to bid them a hasty good-bye. I remember the fur coats of the girls returning from Miss This-or-That's and the chatter of frozen breath and the hands waving overhead as we caught sight of old acquaintances, and the matchings of invitations: 'Are you going to the Ordways'? the Herseys'? the Schultzes'?' and the long green tickets clasped tight in our gloved hands. And last the murky yellow cars of the Chicago, Milwaukee & St Paul Railroad looking cheerful as Christmas itself on the tracks beside the gate.

When we pulled out into the winter night and the real snow, our snow, began to stretch out beside us and twinkle against the windows, and the dim lights of small Wisconsin stations moved by, a sharp wild brace came suddenly into the air. We drew in deep breaths of it as we walked back from dinner through the cold vestibules, unutterably aware of our identity with this country for one strange hour, before we melted indistinguishably into it again.

That's my Middle West – not the wheat or the prairies or the lost Swede towns, but the thrilling returning trains of my youth, and the street lamps and sleigh bells in the frosty dark and the shadows of holly wreaths thrown by lighted windows on the snow. I am part of that, a little solemn with the feel of those long winters, a little complacent from growing up in the Carraway house in a city where dwellings are still called through decades by a family's name. I see now that this has been a story of the West, after all – Tom and Gatsby, Daisy and Jordan and I were all Westerners, and perhaps we possessed some deficiency in common which made us subtly unadaptable to Eastern life.

Even when the East excited me most, even when I was most keenly aware of its superiority to the bored, sprawling, swollen towns beyond the Ohio, with their interminable inquisitions which spared only the children and the very old – even then it had always for me a quality of distortion. West Egg, especially, still figures in my more fantastic dreams. I see it as a night scene by El Greco: a hundred houses, at once conventional and grotesque, crouching under a sullen, overhanging sky and a lustreless moon. In the foreground four solemn men in dress suits are walking long the sidewalk with a stretcher on which lies a drunken woman in a white evening dress. Her hand, which dangles over the side, sparkles cold with jewels. Gravely the men turn in at a house – the wrong house. But no one knows the woman's name, and no one cares.

After Gatsby's death the East was haunted for me like that, distorted beyond my eyes' power of correction. So when the blue smoke of brittle leaves was in the air and the wind blew the wet laundry stiff on the line I decided to come back home.

There was one thing to be done before I left, an awkward, unpleasant thing that perhaps had better have been let alone. But I wanted to leave things in order and not just trust that obliging and indifferent sea to sweep my refuse away. I saw Jordan Baker and talked over and around what had happened to us together, and what had happened afterwards to me, and she lay perfectly still, listening, in a big chair.

She was dressed to play golf, and I remember thinking she looked like a good illustration, her chin raised a little jauntily, her hair the colour of an autumn leaf, her face the same brown tint as the fingerless glove on her knee. When I had finished she told me without comment that she was engaged to another man. I doubted that, though there were several she could have married at a nod of her head, but I pretended to be surprised. For just a minute I wondered if I wasn't making a mistake, then I thought it all over again quickly and got up to say goodbye.

'Nevertheless you did throw me over,' said Jordan suddenly. 'You threw me over on the telephone. I don't give a damn about you now, but it was a new experience for me, and I felt a little dizzy for a while.'

We shook hands.

'Oh, and do you remember' – she added – 'a conversation we had once about driving a car?'

'Why – not exactly.'

'You said a bad driver was only safe until she met another bad driver? Well, I met another bad driver, didn't I? I mean it was careless of me to make such a wrong guess. I thought you were rather an honest, straightforward person. I thought it was your secret pride.'

'I'm thirty,' I said. 'I'm five years too old to lie to myself and call it honour.'

She didn't answer. Angry, and half in love with her, and tremendously sorry, I turned away.

One afternoon late in October I saw Tom Buchanan. He was walking ahead of me along Fifth Avenue in his alert, aggressive way, his hands out a little from his body as if to fight off interference, his head moving sharply here and there, adapting itself to his restless eyes. Just as I slowed up to avoid overtaking him he stopped and began frowning into the windows of a jewellery store. Suddenly he saw me and walked back, holding out his hand.

'What's the matter, Nick? Do you object to shaking hands with me?'

'Yes. You know what I think of you.'

'You're crazy, Nick,' he said quickly. 'Crazy as hell. I don't know what's the matter with you.'

'Tom,' I enquired, 'what did you say to Wilson that afternoon?'

He stared at me without a word, and I knew I had guessed right about those missing hours. I started to turn away, but he took a step after me and grabbed my arm.

'I told him the truth,' he said. 'He came to the door while we were getting ready to leave, and when I sent down word that we weren't in he tried to force his way upstairs. He was crazy enough to kill me if I hadn't told him who owned the car. His hand was on a revolver in his pocket every minute he was in the house – ' He broke off defiantly. 'What if I did tell him? That fellow had it coming to him. He threw dust into your eyes just like he did in Daisy's, but he was a tough one. He ran over Myrtle like you'd run over a dog and never even stopped his car.'

There was nothing I could say, except the one unutterable fact that it wasn't true.

'And if you think I didn't have my share of suffering – look here, when I went to give up that flat and saw that damn box of dog biscuits sitting there on the sideboard, I sat down and cried like a baby. By God, it was awful – '

I couldn't forgive him or like him, but I saw that what he had done was, to him, entirely justified. It was all very careless and confused. They were careless people, Tom and Daisy – they smashed up things and creatures and then retreated back into their money or their vast carelessness, or whatever it was that kept them together, and let other people clean up the mess they had made . . .

I shook hands with him; it seemed silly not to for I felt suddenly as though I were talking to a child. Then he went into the jewellery store to buy a pearl necklace – or perhaps only a pair of cuff buttons – rid of my provincial squeamishness for ever.

Gatsby's house was still empty when I left – the grass on his lawn had grown as long as mine. One of the taxi drivers in the village never took a fare past the entrance gate without stopping for a minute and pointing inside; perhaps it was he who drove Daisy and Gatsby over to East Egg the night of the accident, and perhaps he had made a story about it all his own. I didn't want to hear it and I avoided him when I got off the train.

I spent my Saturday nights in New York, because those gleaming, dazzling parties of his were with me so vividly that I could still hear the music and the laughter, faint and incessant, from his garden, and the cars going up and down his drive. One night I did hear a material car there, and saw its lights stop at his front steps. But I didn't investigate. Probably it was some final guest who had been away at the ends of the earth and didn't know that the party was over.

On the last night, with my trunk packed and my car sold to the grocer, I went over and looked at that huge incoherent failure of a house once more. On the white steps an obscene word, scrawled by some boy with a piece of brick, stood out clearly in the moonlight, and I erased it, drawing my shoe raspingly along the stone. Then I wandered down to the beach and sprawled out on the sand.

Most of the big shore places were closed now and there were hardly any lights except the shadowy, moving glow of a ferryboat across the Sound. And as the moon rose higher the inessential houses began to melt away until gradually I became aware of the old island here that flowered once for Dutch sailors' eyes – a fresh, green breast of the new world. Its vanished trees, the trees that had made way for Gatsby's house, had once pandered in whispers to the last and greatest of all human dreams; for a transitory enchanted moment man must have held his breath in the presence of this continent, compelled into an aesthetic contemplation he neither understood nor desired, face to face for the last time in history with something commensurate to his capacity for wonder.

And as I sat there brooding on the old, unknown world, I thought of Gatsby's wonder when he first picked out the green light at the end of Daisy's dock. He had come a long way to this blue lawn, and his dream must have seemed so close that he could hardly fail to grasp it. He did not know that it was already behind him, somewhere back in that vast obscurity beyond the city, where the dark fields of the republic rolled on under the night.

Gatsby believed in the green light, the orgastic future that year by year recedes before us. It eluded us then, but that's no matter – tomorrow we will run faster, stretch out our arms farther . . . And one fine morning –

So we beat on, boats against the current, borne back ceaselessly into the past.

TENDER IS THE NIGHT

Tender is the Night

A novel first published in 1934

TO

GERALD AND SARA

many fêtes

BOOK ONE

Chapter 1

On the pleasant shore of the French Riviera, about halfway between Marseilles and the Italian border, stands a large, proud, rose-coloured hotel. Deferential palms cool its flushed façade, and before it stretches a short dazzling beach. Lately it has become a summer resort of notable and fashionable people; a decade ago it was almost deserted after its English clientele went north in April. Now, many bungalows cluster near it, but when this story begins only the cupolas of a dozen old villas rotted like water-lilies among the massed pines between Gausse's Hôtel des Étrangers and Cannes, five miles away.

The hotel and its bright tan prayer rug of a beach were one. In the early morning the distant image of Cannes, the pink and cream of old fortifications, the purple Alps that bounded Italy, were cast across the water and lay quavering in the ripples and rings sent up by sea-plants through the clear shallows. Before eight a man came down to the beach in a blue bathrobe and with much preliminary application to his person of the chilly water, and much grunting and loud breathing, floundered a minute in the sea. When he had gone, beach and bay were quiet for an hour. Merchantmen crawled westward on the horizon; bus boys shouted in the hotel court; the dew dried upon the pines. In another hour the horns of motors began to blow down from the winding road along the low range of the Maures, which separates the littoral from true Provençal France.

A mile from the sea, where pines give way to dusty poplars, is an isolated railroad stop, whence one June morning in 1925 a victoria brought a woman and her daughter down to Gausse's Hôtel. The mother's face was of a fading prettiness that would soon be patted with broken veins; her expression was both tranquil and aware in a pleasant way. However, one's eyes moved on quickly to her daughter, who had magic in her pink palms and her cheeks lit to a lovely flame, like the thrilling flush of children after their cold bath in the evening. Her fine high forehead sloped gently up to where her hair, bordering it like an armorial shield, burst into lovelocks and waves and curlicues of ash blonde and gold. Her eyes were bright, big, clear, wet, and shining, the colour of her cheeks was real, breaking close to the surface from the strong young pump of her heart. Her body hovered delicately on the last edge of childhood – she was almost eighteen, nearly complete, but the dew was still on her.

As sea and sky appeared below them in a thin, hot line the mother said: 'Something tells me we're not going to like this place.'

'I want to go home anyhow,' the girl answered.

They both spoke cheerfully but were obviously without direction and bored by the fact – moreover, just any direction would not do. They wanted high excitement, not from the necessity of stimulating jaded nerves but with the avidity of prize-winning schoolchildren who deserved their vacations.

'We'll stay three days and then go home. I'll wire right away for steamer tickets.'

At the hotel the girl made the reservation in idiomatic but rather flat French, like something remembered. When they were installed on the ground floor she walked into the glare of the French windows and out a few steps on to the stone veranda that ran the length of the hotel. When she walked she carried herself like a ballet-dancer, not slumped down on her hips but held up in the small of her back. Out there the hot light clipped close her shadow and she retreated – it was too bright to see. Fifty yards away the Mediterranean yielded up its pigments, moment by moment, to the brutal sunshine; below the balustrade a faded Buick cooked on the hotel drive.

Indeed, of all the region only the beach stirred with activity. Three British nannies sat knitting the slow pattern of Victorian England, the pattern of the forties, the sixties, and the eighties, into sweaters and socks, to the tune of gossip as formalised as incantation; closer to the sea a dozen persons kept house under striped umbrellas, while their dozen children pursued unintimidated fish through the shallows or lay naked and glistening with coconut oil out in the sun.

As Rosemary came on to the beach a boy of twelve ran past her and dashed into the sea with exultant cries. Feeling the impactive scrutiny of strange faces, she took off her bathrobe and followed. She floated face down for a few yards and finding it shallow staggered to her feet and plodded forward, dragging slim legs like weights against the resistance of the water. When it was about breast high, she glanced back towards shore: a bald man in a monocle and a pair of tights, his tufted chest thrown out, his brash navel sucked in, was regarding her attentively. As Rosemary returned the gaze the man dislodged the monocle, which went into hiding amid the facetious whiskers of his chest, and poured himself a glass of something from a bottle in his hand.

Rosemary laid her face on the water and swam a choppy little four-beat crawl out to the raft. The water reached up for her, pulled her down tenderly out of the heat, seeped in her hair and ran into the corners of her body. She turned round and round in it, embracing it, wallowing in it. Reaching the raft she was out of breath, but a tanned woman with very white teeth looked down at her, and Rosemary, suddenly conscious of the raw whiteness of her own body, turned on her back and drifted towards shore. The hairy man holding the bottle spoke to her as she came out.

'I say – they have sharks out behind the raft.' He was of indeterminate nationality, but spoke English with a slow Oxford drawl. 'Yesterday they devoured two British sailors from the *flotte* at Golfe Juan.'

'Heavens!' exclaimed Rosemary.

'They come in for the refuse from the *flotte*.'

Glazing his eyes to indicate that he had only spoken in order to warn her, he minced off two steps and poured himself another drink.

Not unpleasantly self-conscious, since there had been a slight sway of attention towards her during this conversation, Rosemary looked for a place to sit. Obviously each family possessed the strip of sand immediately in front of its umbrella; besides there was much visiting and talking back and forth – the atmosphere of a community upon which it would be presumptuous to intrude. Farther up, where the beach was strewn with pebbles and dead seaweed, sat a group with flesh as white as her own. They lay under small hand-parasols instead of beach umbrellas and were obviously less indigenous to the place. Between the dark people and the light, Rosemary found room and spread out her peignoir on the sand.

Lying so, she first heard their voices and felt their feet skirt her body and their shapes pass between the sun and herself. The breath of an inquisitive dog blew warm and nervous on her neck; she could feel her skin broiling a little in the heat and hear the small exhausted wa-waa of the expiring waves. Presently her ear distinguished individual voices and she became aware that someone referred to scornfully as 'that North guy' had kidnapped a waiter from a café in Cannes last night in order to saw him in two. The sponsor of the story was a white-haired woman in full evening dress, obviously a relic of the previous evening, for a tiara still clung to her head and a discouraged orchid expired from her shoulder. Rosemary, forming a vague antipathy to her and her companions, turned away.

Nearest her, on the other side, a young woman lay under a roof of umbrellas making out a list of things from a book open on the sand. Her bathing-suit was pulled off her shoulders, and her back, a ruddy, orange brown, set off by a string of creamy pearls, shone in the sun. Her face was hard and lovely and pitiful. Her eyes met Rosemary's but did not see her. Beyond her was a fine man in a jockey cap and red-striped tights; then the woman Rosemary had seen on the raft, and who looked back at her, seeing her; then a man with a long face and a golden, leonine head, with blue tights and no hat, talking very seriously to an unmistakably Latin young man in black tights, both of them picking at little pieces of seaweed in the sand. She thought they were mostly Americans, but something made them unlike the Americans she had known of late.

After a while she realised that the man in the jockey cap was giving a quiet little performance for this group; he moved gravely about with a rake, ostensibly removing gravel and meanwhile developing some esoteric burlesque held in suspension by his grave face. Its faintest ramification had become hilarious, until whatever he said released a burst of laughter. Even those who, like herself, were too far away to hear, sent out antennae of attention until the only person on the beach not caught up in it was the young woman with the string of pearls. Perhaps from modesty of possession she responded to each salvo of amusement by bending closer over her list.

The man of the monocle and bottle spoke suddenly out of the sky above Rosemary.

'You are a ripping swimmer.'

She demurred.

'Jolly good. My name is Campion. Here is a lady who says she saw you in Sorrento last week and knows who you are and would so like to meet you.'

Glancing around with concealed annoyance Rosemary saw the untanned people were waiting. Reluctantly she got up and went over to them.

'Mrs Abrams – Mrs McKisco – Mr McKisco – Mr Dumphry – '

'We know who you are,' spoke up the woman in evening dress. 'You're Rosemary Hoyt and I recognised you in Sorrento and asked the hotel clerk and we all think you're perfectly marvellous and we want to know why you're not back in America making another marvellous moving picture.'

They made a superfluous gesture of moving over for her. The woman who had recognised her was not a Jewess, despite her name. She was one of those elderly 'good sports' preserved by an imperviousness to experience and a good digestion into another generation.

'We wanted to warn you about getting burned the first day,' she continued cheerily, 'because *your* skin is important, but there seems to be so darn much formality on this beach that we didn't know whether you'd mind.'

Chapter 2

'We thought maybe you were in the plot,' said Mrs McKisco. She was a shabby-eyed, pretty young woman with a disheartening intensity. 'We don't know who's in the plot and who isn't. One man my husband had been particularly nice to turned out to be a chief character – practically the assistant hero.'

'The plot?' enquired Rosemary, half understanding. 'Is there a plot?'

'My dear, we don't *know*,' said Mrs Abrams, with a convulsive, stout woman's chuckle. 'We're not in it. We're the gallery.'

Mr Dumphry, a tow-headed, effeminate young man, remarked: 'Mama Abrams is a plot in herself,' and Campion shook his monocle at him, saying: 'Now, Royal, don't be too ghastly for words.' Rosemary looked at them all uncomfortably, wishing her mother had come down here with her. She did not like these people, especially in her immediate comparison of them with those who had interested her at the other end of the beach. Her mother's modest but compact social gift got them out of unwelcome situations swiftly and firmly. But Rosemary had been a celebrity for only six months, and sometimes the French manners of her early adolescence and the democratic manners of America, these latter superimposed, made a certain confusion and let her in for just such things.

Mr McKisco, a scrawny, freckle-and-red man of thirty, did not find the topic of the 'plot' amusing. He had been staring at the sea – now after a swift glance at his wife he turned to Rosemary and demanded aggressively: 'Been here long?'

'Only a day.'

'Oh.'

Evidently feeling that the subject had been thoroughly changed, he looked in turn at the others.

'Going to stay all summer?' asked Mrs McKisco, innocently. 'If you do you can watch the plot unfold.'

'For God's sake, Violet, drop the subject!' exploded her husband. 'Get a new joke, for God's sake!'

Mrs McKisco swayed towards Mrs Abrams and breathed audibly: 'He's nervous.'

'I'm not nervous,' disagreed McKisco. 'It just happens I'm not nervous at all.'

He was burning visibly – a greyish flush had spread over his face, dissolving all his expressions into a vast ineffectuality. Suddenly remotely conscious of his condition he got up to go in the water, followed by his wife, and seizing the opportunity Rosemary followed.

Mr McKisco drew a long breath, flung himself into the shallows and began a stiff-armed batting of the Mediterranean, obviously intended to suggest a crawl – his breath exhausted he rose and looked around with an expression of surprise that he was still in sight of shore.

'I haven't learned to breathe yet. I never quite understood how they breathed.' He looked at Rosemary enquiringly.

'I think you breathe out under water,' she explained. 'And every fourth beat you roll your head over for air.'

'The breathing's the hardest part for me. Shall we go to the raft?'

The man with the leonine head lay stretched out upon the raft, which tipped back and forth with the motion of the water. As Mrs McKisco reached for it a sudden tilt struck her arm up roughly, whereupon the man started up and pulled her on board.

'I was afraid it hit you.' His voice was slow and shy; he had one of the saddest faces Rosemary had ever seen, the high cheekbones of an Indian, a longer upper lip, and enormous deep-set dark golden eyes. He had spoken out of the side of his mouth, as if he hoped his words would reach Mrs McKisco by a circuitous and unobtrusive route; in a minute he had shoved off into the water and his long body lay motionless towards shore.

Rosemary and Mrs McKisco watched him. When he had exhausted his momentum he abruptly bent double, his thin thighs rose above the surface, and he disappeared totally, leaving scarcely a fleck of foam behind.

'He's a good swimmer,' Rosemary said.

Mrs McKisco's answer came with surprising violence.

'Well, he's a rotten musician.' She turned to her husband, who after two unsuccessful attempts had managed to climb on the raft, and having attained his balance was trying to make some kind of compensatory flourish, achieving only an extra stagger. 'I was just saying that Abe North may be a good swimmer but he's a rotten musician.'

'Yes,' agreed McKisco, grudgingly. Obviously he had created his wife's world, and allowed her few liberties in it.

'Antheil's my man.' Mrs McKisco turned challengingly to Rosemary, 'Antheil and Joyce. I don't suppose you ever hear much about those sort of people in Hollywood, but my husband wrote the first criticism of *Ulysses* that ever appeared in America.'

'I wish I had a cigarette,' said McKisco calmly. 'That's more important to me just now.'

'He's got insides – don't you think so, Albert?'

Her voice faded off suddenly. The woman of the pearls had joined her two children in the water, and now Abe North came up under one of them like a volcanic island, raising him on his shoulders. The child yelled with fear and delight and the woman watched with a lovely peace, without a smile.

'Is that his wife?' Rosemary asked.

'No, that's Mrs Diver. They're not at the hotel.' Her eyes, photographic, did not move from the woman's face. After a moment she turned vehemently to Rosemary.

'Have you been abroad before?'

'Yes – I went to school in Paris.'

'Oh! Well then you probably know that if you want to enjoy yourself here the thing is to get to know some real French families. What do these people get out of it?' She pointed her left shoulder towards shore. 'They just stick around with each other in little cliques. Of course, we had letters of introduction and met all the best French artists and writers in Paris. That made it very nice.'

'I should think so.'

'My husband is finishing his first novel, you see.'

Rosemary said: 'Oh, he is?' She was not thinking anything special, except wondering whether her mother had got to sleep in this heat.

'It's on the idea of *Ulysses*,' continued Mrs McKisco. 'Only instead of taking twenty-four hours my husband takes a hundred years. He takes a decayed old French aristocrat and puts him in contrast with the mechanical age – '

'Oh, for God's sake, Violet, don't go telling everybody the idea,' protested McKisco. 'I don't want it to get all around before the book's published.'

Rosemary swam back to the shore, where she threw her peignoir over her already sore shoulders and lay down again in the sun. The man with the jockey cap was now going from umbrella to umbrella carrying a bottle and little glasses in his hands; presently he and his friends grew livelier and closer together and now they were all under a single assemblage of umbrellas – she gathered that someone was leaving and that this was a last drink on the beach. Even the children knew that excitement was generating under that umbrella and turned towards it – and it seemed to Rosemary that it all came from the man in the jockey cap.

Noon dominated sea and sky – even the white line of Cannes, five miles off, had faded to a mirage of what was fresh and cool; a robin-breasted sailing-boat pulled in behind it a strand from the outer, darker sea. It seemed that there was no life anywhere in all this expanse of coast except under the filtered sunlight of those umbrellas, where something went on amid the colour and the murmur.

Campion walked near her, stood a few feet away and Rosemary closed her eyes, pretending to be asleep; then she half-opened them and watched two dim, blurred pillars that were legs. The man tried to edge his way into a sand-coloured cloud, but the cloud floated off into the vast hot sky. Rosemary fell really asleep.

She awoke drenched with sweat to find the beach deserted save for the man in the jockey cap, who was folding a last umbrella. As Rosemary lay blinking, he walked nearer and said: 'I was going to wake you before I left. It's not good to get too burned right away.'

'Thank you.' Rosemary looked down at her crimson legs. 'Heavens!'

She laughed cheerfully, inviting him to talk, but Dick Diver was already carrying a tent and a beach umbrella up to a waiting car, so she went into the water to wash off the sweat. He came back and gathering up a rake, a shovel, and a sieve, stowed them in a crevice of a rock. He glanced up and down the beach to see if he had left anything.

'Do you know what time it is?' Rosemary asked.

'It's about half-past one.'

They faced the seascape together momentarily.

'It's not a bad time,' said Dick Diver, 'it's not one of the worst times of the day.'

He looked at her and for a moment she lived in the bright blue worlds of his eyes, eagerly and confidently. Then he shouldered his last piece of junk and went up to his car, and Rosemary came out of the water, shook out her peignoir and walked up to the hotel.

Chapter 3

It was almost two when they went into the dining-rooms. Back and forth over the deserted tables a heavy pattern of beams and shadows swayed with the motion of the pines outside. Two waiters, piling plates and talking loud Italian, fell silent when they came in and brought them a tired version of the table d'hôte luncheon.

'I fell in love on the beach,' said Rosemary.

'Who with?'

'First with a whole lot of people who looked nice. Then with one man.'

'Did you talk to him?'

'Just a little. Very handsome. With reddish hair.' She was eating, ravenously. 'He's married though – it's usually the way.'

Her mother was her best friend and had put every last possibility into the guiding of her, not so rare a thing in the theatrical profession, but rather special in that Mrs Elsie Speers was not recompensing herself for a defeat of her own. She had no personal bitterness or resentments about life – twice satisfactorily married and twice widowed, her cheerful stoicism had each time deepened. One of her husbands had been a cavalry officer and one an army doctor, and they both left something to her that she tried to present intact to Rosemary. By not sparing Rosemary she had made her hard – by not sparing her own labour and devotion she had cultivated an idealism in Rosemary, which at present was directed towards herself and saw the world through her eyes. So that while Rosemary was a 'simple' child she was protected by a double sheath of her mother's armour and her own – she had a mature distrust of the trivial, the facile and the vulgar. However, with Rosemary's sudden success in pictures Mrs Speers felt that it was time she were spiritually weaned; it would please rather than pain her if this somewhat bouncing, breathless and exigent idealism would focus on something except herself.

'Then you like it here?' she asked.

'It might be fun if we knew those people. There were some other people, but they weren't nice. They recognised me – no matter where we go everybody's seen *Daddy's Girl*.'

Mrs Speers waited for the glow of egotism to subside; then she said in a matter-of-fact way: 'That reminds me, when are you going to see Earl Brady?'

'I thought we might go this afternoon – if you're rested.'

'You go – I'm not going.'

'We'll wait till tomorrow then.'

'I want you to go alone. It's only a short way – it isn't as if you didn't speak French.'

'Mother – aren't there some things I don't have to do?'

'Oh, well, then go later – but some day before we leave.'

'All right, mother.'

After lunch they were both overwhelmed by the sudden flatness that comes over American travellers in quiet foreign places. No stimuli worked upon them, no voices called them from without, no fragments of their own thoughts came suddenly from the minds of others, and missing the clamour of Empire they felt that life was not continuing here.

'Let's only stay three days, mother,' Rosemary said when they were back in their rooms. Outside a light wind blew the heat around, straining it through the trees and sending little hot gusts through the shutters.

'How about the man you fell in love with on the beach?'

'I don't love anybody but you, mother, darling.'

Rosemary stopped in the lobby and spoke to Gausse *père* about trains. The concierge, lounging in light-brown khaki by the desk, stared at her rigidly, then suddenly remembered the manners of his *métier*. She took the bus and rode with a pair of obsequious waiters to the station, embarrassed by their deferential silence, waiting to urge them: 'Go on, talk, enjoy yourselves. It doesn't bother me.'

The first-class compartment was stifling; the vivid advertising cards of the railroad companies – the Pont du Gard at Arles, the Amphitheatre at Orange, winter sports at Chamonix – were fresher than the long motionless sea outside. Unlike American trains that were absorbed in an intense destiny of their own, and scornful of people on another world less swift and breathless, this train was part of the country through which it passed. Its breath stirred the dust from the palm leaves, the cinders mingled with the dry dung in the gardens. Rosemary was sure she could lean from the window and pull flowers with her hand.

A dozen cabbies slept in their hacks outside the Cannes station. Over on the promenade the Casino, the smart shops, and the great hotels turned blank iron masks to the summer sea. It was unbelievable that there could ever have been a 'season', and Rosemary, half in the grip of fashion, became a little self-conscious, as though she were displaying an unhealthy taste for the moribund; as though people were wondering why she was here in the lull between the gaiety of last winter and next winter, while up north the true world thundered by.

As she came out of a drugstore with a bottle of coconut oil, a woman, whom she recognised as Mrs Diver, crossed her path with arms full of sofa cushions, and went to a car parked down the street. A long, low black dog barked at her, a dozing chauffeur woke with a start. She sat in the car, her lovely face set, controlled, her eyes brave and watchful, looking straight ahead towards nothing. Her dress was bright red and her brown legs were bare. She had thick, dark, gold hair like a chow's.

With half an hour to wait for her train Rosemary sat down in the Café des Alliés on the Croisette, where the trees made a green twilight over the tables and an orchestra wooed an imaginary public of cosmopolites with the Nice Carnival Song and last year's American tune. She had bought *Le Temps* and the *Saturday Evening Post* for her mother, and as she drank her citronade she opened the latter at the memoirs of a Russian princess, finding the dim conventions of the nineties realer and nearer than the headlines of the French paper. It was the same feeling that had oppressed her at the hotel – accustomed to seeing the starkest grotesqueries of a continent heavily underlined as comedy or tragedy, untrained to the task of separating out the essential for herself, she now began to feel that French life was empty and stale. This feeling was surcharged by listening to the sad tunes of the orchestra, reminiscent of the melancholy music played for acrobats in vaudeville. She was glad to go back to Gausse's Hôtel.

Her shoulders were too burned to swim with the next day, so she and her mother hired a car – after much haggling, for Rosemary had formed her valuation of money in France – and drove along the Riviera, the delta of many rivers. The chauffeur, a Russian Czar of the period of Ivan the Terrible, was a self-appointed guide, and the resplendent names – Cannes, Nice, Monte Carlo – began to glow through their torpid camouflage, whispering of old kings come here to dine or die, of rajahs tossing Buddha's eyes to English ballerinas, of Russian princes turning the weeks into Baltic twilights in the lost caviare days. Most of all, there was the scent of the Russians along the coast – their closed bookshops and grocery stores. Ten years ago, when the season ended in April, the doors of the Orthodox Church were locked, and the sweet champagnes they favoured were put away until their return. 'We'll be back next season,' they said, but this was premature, for they were never coming back any more.

It was pleasant to drive back to the hotel in the late afternoon, above a sea as mysteriously coloured as the agates and cornelian of childhood, green as green milk, blue as laundry water, wine dark. It was pleasant to pass people eating outside their doors, and to hear the fierce mechanical pianos behind the vines of country estaminets. When they turned off the Corniche d'Or and down to Gausse's Hôtel through the darkening banks of trees, set one behind another in many greens, the moon already hovered over the ruins of the aqueducts . . .

Somewhere in the hills behind the hotel there was a dance, and Rosemary listened to the music through the ghostly moonshine of her mosquito net, realising that there was gaiety too somewhere about, and she thought of the nice people on the beach. She thought she might meet them in the morning, but they obviously formed a self-sufficient little group, and once their umbrellas, bamboo rugs, dogs, and children were set out in place that part of the plage was literally fenced in. She resolved in any case not to spend her last two mornings with the other ones.

Chapter 4

The matter was solved for her. The McKiscos were not yet there and she had scarcely spread her peignoir when two men – the man with the jockey cap and the tall blond man, given to sawing waiters in two – left the group and came down towards her.

'Good-morning,' said Dick Diver. He broke down. 'Look – sunburn or no sunburn, why did you stay away yesterday? We worried about you.'

She sat up and her happy little laugh welcomed their intrusion.

'We wondered,' Dick Diver said, 'if you wouldn't come over this morning. We go in, we take food and drink, so it's a substantial invitation.'

He seemed kind and charming – his voice promised that he would take care of her, and that a little later he would open up whole new worlds for her, unroll an endless succession of magnificent possibilities. He managed the introduction so that her name wasn't mentioned and then let her know easily that everyone knew who she was but was respecting the completeness of her private life – a courtesy that Rosemary had not met with save from professional people since her success.

Nicole Diver, her brown back hanging from her pearls, was looking through a recipe book for chicken Maryland. She was about twenty-four, Rosemary guessed – her face could have been described in terms of conventional prettiness, but the effect was that it had been made first on the heroic scale with strong structure and marking, as if the features and vividness of brow and colouring, everything we associate with temperament and character, had been moulded with a Rodinesque intention, and then chiselled away in the direction of prettiness to a point where a single slip would have irreparably diminished its force and quality. With the mouth the sculptor had taken desperate chances – it was the cupid's bow of a magazine cover, yet it shared the distinction of the rest.

'Are you here for a long time?' Nicole asked. Her voice was low, almost harsh.

Suddenly Rosemary let the possibility enter her mind that they might stay another week.

'Not very long,' she answered vaguely. 'We've been abroad a long time – we landed in Sicily in March and we've been slowly working our way north. I got pneumonia making a picture last January and I've been recuperating.'

'Mercy! How did that happen?'

'Well, it was from swimming.' Rosemary was rather reluctant at embarking upon personal revelations. 'One day I happened to have the grippe and didn't know it, and they were taking a scene where I dove into a canal in Venice. It was a very expensive set, so I had to dive and dive and dive all morning. Mother had a doctor right there, but it was no use – I got pneumonia.' She changed the subject determinedly before they could speak. 'Do you like it here – this place?'

'They have to like it,' said Abe North slowly. 'They invented it.' He turned his noble head slowly so that his eyes rested with tenderness and affection on the two Divers.

'Oh, did you?'

'This is only the second season that the hotel's been open in summer,' Nicole explained. 'We persuaded Gausse to keep on a cook and a *garçon* and a *chasseur* – it paid its way and this year it's doing even better.'

'But you're not in the hotel.'

'We built a house, up at Tarmes.'

'The theory is,' said Dick, arranging an umbrella to clip a square of sunlight off Rosemary's shoulder, 'that all the northern places, like Deauville, were picked out by Russians and English who don't mind the cold, while half of us Americans come from tropical climates – that's why we're beginning to come here.'

The young man of Latin aspect had been turning the pages of the *New York Herald.*

'Well, what nationality are these people?' he demanded, suddenly, and read with a slight French intonation, ' "Registered at the Hôtel Palace at Vevey are Mr Pandely Vlasco, Mme Bonneasse" – I don't exaggerate – "Corinna Medonca, Mme Pasche, Seraphim Tullio, Maria Amalia Roto Mais, Moises Teubel, Mme Paragoris, Apostle Alexandre, Yolanda Yosfuglu and Geneveva de Momus!" She attracts me most – Geneveva de Momus. Almost worth running up to Vevey to take a look at Geneveva de Momus.'

He stood up with sudden restlessness, stretching himself with one sharp movement. He was a few years younger than Diver or North. He was tall and his body was hard but overspare save for the bunched force gathered in his shoulders and upper arms. At first glance he seemed conventionally handsome – but there was a faint disgust always in his face which marred the full fierce lustre of his brown eyes. Yet one remembered them afterwards, when one had forgotten the inability of the mouth to endure boredom and the young forehead with its furrows of fretful and unprofitable pain.

'We found some fine ones in the news of Americans last week,' said Nicole. 'Mrs Evelyn Oyster and – what were the others?'

'There was Mr S. Flesh,' said Diver, getting up also. He took his rake and began to work seriously at getting small stones out of the sand.

'Oh, yes – S. Flesh – doesn't he give you the creeps?'

It was quiet alone with Nicole – Rosemary found it even quieter than with her mother. Abe North and Barban, the Frenchman, were talking about Morocco, and Nicole having copied her recipe picked up a piece of sewing. Rosemary examined their appurtenances – four large parasols that made a canopy of shade, a portable bath-house for dressing, a pneumatic rubber horse, new things that Rosemary had never seen, from the first burst of luxury manufacturing after the war, and probably in the hands of the first of purchasers. She had gathered that they were fashionable people, but though her mother had brought her up to beware such people as drones, she did not feel that way here. Even in their absolute immobility, complete as that of the morning, she felt a purpose, a working over something, a direction, an act of creation different from any she had known. Her immature mind made no speculations upon the nature of their relation to each other, she was only concerned with their attitude towards herself – but she perceived the web of some pleasant interrelation, which she expressed with the thought that they seemed to have a very good time.

She looked in turn at the three men, temporarily expropriating them. All three were personable in different ways; all were of a special gentleness that she felt was part of their lives, past and future, not circumstanced by events, not at all like the company manners of actors, and she detected also a far-reaching delicacy that was different from the rough and ready good fellowship of directors, who represented the intellectuals in her life. Actors and directors – those were the only men she had ever known, those and the heterogeneous, indistinguishable mass of college boys, interested only in love at first sight, whom she had met at the Yale prom last fall.

These three were different. Barban was less civilised, more sceptical and scoffing, his manners were formal, even perfunctory. Abe North had, under his shyness, a desperate humour that amused but puzzled her. Her serious nature distrusted its ability to make a supreme impression on him.

But Dick Diver – he was all complete there. Silently she admired him. His complexion was reddish and weather-burned, so was his short hair – a light growth of it rolled down his arms and hands. His eyes were of a bright, hard blue. His nose was somewhat pointed and there was never any doubt at whom he was looking or talking – and this is a flattering attention, for who looks at us? – glances fall upon us, curious or disinterested, nothing more. His voice, with some faint Irish melody running through it, wooed the world, yet she felt the layer of hardness in him, of self-control and of self-discipline, her own virtues. Oh, she chose him, and Nicole, lifting her head, saw her choose him, heard the little sigh at the fact that he was already possessed.

Towards noon the McKiscos, Mrs Abrams, Mr Dumphry, and Señor Campion came on the beach. They had brought a new umbrella that they set up with side glances towards the Divers, and crept under with satisfied expressions – all save Mr McKisco, who remained derisively without. In his raking Dick had passed near them and now he returned to the umbrellas.

'The two young men are reading the Book of Etiquette together,' he said in a low voice.

'Planning to mix wit' de quality,' said Abe.

Mary North, the very tanned young woman whom Rosemary had encountered the first day on the raft, came in from swimming and said with a smile that was a rakish gleam: 'So Mr and Mrs Neverquiver have arrived.'

'They're this man's friends,' Nicole reminded her, indicating Abe. 'Why doesn't he go and speak to them? Don't you think they're attractive?'

'I think they're very attractive,' Abe agreed. 'I just don't think they're attractive, that's all.'

'Well, I *have* felt there were too many people on the beach this summer,' Nicole admitted. '*Our* beach that Dick made out of a pebble pile.' She considered, and then lowering her voice out of the range of the trio of nannies who sat back under another umbrella, 'Still they're preferable to those British last summer who kept shouting about: "Isn't the sea blue? Isn't the sky white? Isn't little Nellie's nose red?" '

Rosemary thought she would not like to have Nicole for an enemy.

'But you didn't see the fight,' Nicole continued. 'The day before you came, the married man, the one with the name that sounds like a substitute for gasoline or butter – '

'McKisco?'

'Yes – well they were having words and she tossed some sand in his face. So naturally he sat on top of her and rubbed her face in the sand. We were – electrified. I wanted Dick to interfere.'

'I think,' said Dick Diver, staring down abstractedly at the straw mat, 'that I'll go over and invite them to dinner.'

'No, you won't,' Nicole told him quickly.

'I think it would be a very good thing. They're here – let's adjust ourselves.'

'We're very well adjusted,' she insisted, laughing. 'I'm not going to have *my* nose rubbed in the sand. I'm a mean, hard woman,' she explained to Rosemary, and then raising her voice: 'Children, put on your bathing-suits!'

Rosemary felt that this swim would become the typical one of her life, the one that would always pop up in her memory at the mention of swimming. Simultaneously the whole party moved towards the water, super-ready from the long, forced inaction, passing from the heat to the cool with the *gourmandise* of a tingling curry eaten with chilled white wine. The Divers' day was spaced like the day of the older civilisations to yield the utmost from the materials at hand, and to give all the transitions their full value, and she did not know that there would be another transition presently from the utter absorption of the swim to the garrulity of the Provençal lunch hour. But again she had the sense that Dick was taking care of her, and she delighted in responding to the eventual movement as if it had been an order.

Nicole handed her husband the curious garment on which she had been working. He went into the dressing tent and inspired a commotion by appearing in a moment clad in transparent black lace drawers. Close inspection revealed that actually they were lined with flesh-coloured cloth.

'Well, if that isn't a pansy's trick!' exclaimed Mr McKisco contemptuously – then turning quickly to Mr Dumphry and Mr Campion, he added, 'oh, I beg your pardon.'

Rosemary bubbled with delight at the trunks. Her naïvety responded wholeheartedly to the expensive simplicity of the Divers, unaware of its complexity and its lack of innocence, unaware that it was all a selection of quality rather than quantity from the run of the world's bazaar; and that the simplicity of behaviour also, the nursery-like peace and goodwill, the emphasis on the simpler virtues, was part of a desperate bargain with the gods and had been attained through struggles she could not have guessed at. At that moment the Divers represented externally the exact furthermost evolution of a class, so that most people seemed awkward beside them – in reality a qualitative change had already set in that was not at all apparent to Rosemary.

She stood with them as they took sherry and ate crackers. Dick Diver looked at her with cold blue eyes; his kind, strong mouth said thoughtfully and deliberately: 'You're the only girl I've seen for a long time that actually did look like something blooming.'

* * *

In her mother's lap afterwards Rosemary cried and cried.

'I love him, mother, I'm desperately in love with him – I never knew I could feel that way about anybody. And he's married and I like her too – it's just hopeless. Oh, I love him so!'

'I'm curious to meet him.'

'She invited us to dinner Friday.'

'If you're in love it ought to make you happy. You ought to laugh.'

Rosemary looked up and gave a beautiful little shiver of her face and laughed. Her mother always had a great influence on her.

Chapter 5

Rosemary went to Monte Carlo feeling nearly as sulky as it was possible for her to be. She rode up the rugged hill to La Turbie, to an old Gaumont lot in process of reconstruction, and as she stood by the grilled entrance waiting for an answer to the message on her card, she might have been looking into Hollywood. The bizarre débris of some recent picture, a decayed street scene in India, a great cardboard whale, a monstrous tree bearing cherries large as basketballs, bloomed there by exotic dispensation, autochthonous as the pale amaranth, mimosa, cork oak or dwarfed pine. There were a quick-lunch shack and two barnlike stages, and everywhere about the lot, groups of waiting, hopeful, painted faces.

After ten minutes a young man with hair the colour of canary feathers hurried down to the gate.

'Come in, Miss Hoyt, Mr Brady's on the set, but he's very anxious to see you. I'm sorry you were kept waiting, but you know some of these French dames are worse about pushing themselves in – '

The studio manager opened a small door in the blank wall of stage building and with sudden glad familiarity Rosemary followed him into half-darkness. Here and there figures spotted the twilight, turning up ashen faces to her like souls in purgatory watching the passage of a mortal through. There were whispers and soft voices and, apparently from afar, the gentle tremolo of a small organ. Turning the corner made by some flats, they came upon the white crackling glow of a stage, where a French actor – his shirt-front, collar, and cuffs tinted a brilliant pink – and an American actress stood motionless face to face. They stared at each other with dogged eyes, as though they had been in the same position for hours; and still for a long time nothing happened, no one moved. A bank of lights went off with a savage hiss, went on again; the plaintive tap of a hammer begged admission to nowhere in the distance; a blue face appeared among the blinding lights above, called something unintelligible into the upper blackness. Then the silence was broken by a voice in front of Rosemary.

'Baby, you don't take off the stockings, you can spoil ten more pairs. That dress is fifteen pounds.'

Stepping backward the speaker ran against Rosemary, whereupon the studio manager said, 'Hey, Earl – Miss Hoyt.'

They were meeting for the first time. Brady was quick and strenuous. As he took her hand she saw him look her over from head to foot, a gesture she recognised and that made her feel at home, but gave her always a faint feeling of superiority to whoever made it. If her person was property she could exercise whatever advantage was inherent in its ownership.

'I thought you'd be along any day now,' Brady said, in a voice that was just a little too compelling for private life, and that trailed with it a faintly defiant cockney accent. 'Have a good trip?'

'Yes, but we're glad to be going home.'

'No-o-o!' he protested. 'Stay awhile – I want to talk to you. Let me tell you that was some picture of yours – that *Daddy's Girl*. I saw it in Paris. I wired the coast right away to see if you were signed.'

'I just had – I'm sorry.'

'God, what a picture!'

Not wanting to smile in silly agreement Rosemary frowned.

'Nobody wants to be thought of forever for just one picture,' she said.

'Sure – that's right. What're your plans?'

'Mother thought I needed a rest. When I get back we'll probably either sign up with First National or keep on with Famous.'

'Who's we?'

'My mother. She decides business matters. I couldn't do without her.'

Again he looked her over completely, and, as he did, something in Rosemary went out to him. It was not liking, not at all the spontaneous admiration she had felt for the man on the beach this morning. It was a click. He desired her and, so far as her virginal emotions went, she contemplated a surrender with equanimity. Yet she knew she would forget him half an hour after she left him – like an actor kissed in a picture.

'Where are you staying?' Brady asked. 'Oh, yes, at Gausse's. Well, my plans are made for this year, too, but that letter I wrote you still stands. Rather make a picture with you than any girl since Connie Talmadge was a kid.'

'I feel the same way. Why don't you come back to Hollywood?'

'I can't stand the damn place. I'm fine here. Wait till after this shot and I'll show you around.'

Walking on to the set he began to talk to the French actor in a low, quiet voice.

Five minutes passed – Brady talked on, while from time to time the Frenchman shifted his feet and nodded. Abruptly, Brady broke off, calling something to the lights that startled them into a humming glare. Los Angeles was loud about Rosemary now. Unappalled she moved once more through the city of thin partitions, wanting to be back there. But she did not want to see Brady in the mood she sensed he would be in after he had finished and she left the lot with a spell still upon her. The Mediterranean world was less silent now that she knew the studio was there. She liked the people on the streets and bought herself a pair of espadrilles on the way to the train.

Her mother was pleased that she had done so accurately what she was told to do, but she still wanted to launch her out and away. Mrs Speers was fresh in appearance but she was tired; deathbeds make people tired indeed and she had watched beside a couple.

Chapter 6

Feeling good from the rosy wine at lunch, Nicole Diver folded her arms high enough for the artificial camellia on her shoulder to touch her cheek, and went out into her lovely grassless garden. The garden was bounded on one side by the house, from which it flowed and into which it ran, on two sides by the old village, and on the last by the cliff falling by ledges to the sea.

Along the walls on the village side all was dusty, the wriggling vines, the lemon and eucalyptus trees, the casual wheelbarrow, left only a moment since, but already grown into the path, atrophied and faintly rotten. Nicole was invariably somewhat surprised that by turning in the other direction past a bed of peonies she walked into an area so green and cool that the leaves and petals were curled with tender damp.

Knotted at her throat she wore a lilac scarf that even in the achromatic sunshine cast its colour up to her face and down around her moving feet in a lilac shadow. Her face was hard, almost stern, save for the soft gleam of piteous doubt that looked from her green eyes. Her once fair hair had darkened, but she was lovelier now at twenty-four than she had been at eighteen, when her hair was brighter than she.

Following a walk marked by an intangible mist of bloom that followed the white border stones she came to a space overlooking the sea where there were lanterns asleep in the fig trees and a big table and wicker chairs and a great market umbrella from Sienna, all gathered about an enormous pine, the biggest tree in the garden. She paused there a moment, looking absently at a growth of nasturtiums and iris tangled at its foot, as though sprung from a careless handful of seeds, listening to the plaints and accusations of some nursery squabble in the house. When this died away on the summer air, she walked on, between kaleidoscopic peonies massed in pink clouds, black and brown tulips and fragile mauve-stemmed roses, transparent like sugar flowers in a confectioner's window – until, as if the scherzo of colour could reach no further intensity, it broke off suddenly in mid-air, and moist steps went down to a level five feet below.

Here there was a well with the boarding around it dank and slippery even on the brightest days. She went up the stairs on the other side and into the vegetable garden; she walked rather quickly; she liked to be active, though at times she gave an impression of repose that was at once static and evocative. This was because she knew few words and believed in none, and in the world she was rather silent, contributing just her share of urbane humour with a precision that approached meagreness. But at the moment when strangers tended to grow uncomfortable in the presence of this economy she would seize the topic and rush off with it, feverishly surprised with herself – then bring it back and relinquish it abruptly, almost timidly, like an obedient retriever, having been adequate and something more.

As she stood in the fuzzy green light of the vegetable garden, Dick crossed the path ahead of her going to his work house. Nicole waited silently till he had passed; then she went on through lines of prospective salads to a little menagerie where pigeons and rabbits and a parrot made a medley of insolent noises at her. Descending to another ledge she reached a low, curved wall and looked down seven hundred feet to the Mediterranean Sea.

She stood in the ancient hill village of Tarmes. The villa and its grounds were made out of a row of peasant dwellings that abutted on the cliff – five small houses had been combined to make the house and four destroyed to make the garden. The exterior walls were untouched so that from the road far below it was indistinguishable from the violet grey mass of the town.

For a moment Nicole stood looking down at the Mediterranean but there was nothing to do with that, even with her tireless hands. Presently Dick came out of his one-room house carrying a telescope and looked east towards Cannes. In a moment Nicole swam into his field of vision, whereupon he disappeared into his house and came out with a megaphone. He had many light mechanical devices.

'Nicole,' he shouted, 'I forgot to tell you that as a final apostolic gesture I invited Mrs Abrams, the woman with the white hair.'

'I suspected it. It's an outrage.'

The ease with which her reply reached him seemed to belittle his megaphone, so she raised her voice and called, 'Can you hear me?'

'Yes.' He lowered the megaphone and then raised it stubbornly. 'I'm going to invite some more people too. I'm going to invite the two young men.'

'All right,' she agreed placidly.

'I want to give a really *bad* party. I mean it. I want to give a party where there's a brawl and seductions and people going home with their feelings hurt and women passed out in the *cabinet de toilette*. You wait and see.'

He went back into his house and Nicole saw that one of his most characteristic moods was upon him, the excitement that swept everyone up into it and was inevitably followed by his own form of melancholy, which he never displayed but at which she guessed. This excitement about things reached an intensity out of proportion to their importance, generating a really extraordinary virtuosity with people. Save among a few of the tough-minded and perennially suspicious, he had the power of arousing a fascinated and uncritical love. The reaction came when he realised the waste and extravagance involved. He sometimes looked back with awe at the carnivals of affection he had given, as a general might gaze upon a massacre he had ordered to satisfy an impersonal blood-lust.

But to be included in Dick Diver's world for a while was a remarkable experience: people believed he made special reservations about them, recognising the proud uniqueness of their destinies, buried under the compromises of how many years. He won everyone quickly with an exquisite consideration and a politeness that moved so fast and intuitively that it could be examined only in its effect. Then, without caution, lest the first bloom of the relation wither, he opened the gate to his amusing world. So long as they subscribed to it completely, their happiness was his preoccupation, but at the first flicker of doubt as to its all-inclusiveness he evaporated before their eyes, leaving little communicable memory of what he had said or done.

At eight-thirty that evening he came out to meet his first guests, his coat carried rather ceremoniously, rather promisingly, in his hand, like a toreador's cape. It was characteristic that after greeting Rosemary and her mother he waited for them to speak first, as if to allow them the reassurance of their own voices in the new surroundings.

To resume Rosemary's point of view it should be said that, under the spell of the climb to Tarmes and the fresher air, she and her mother looked about appreciatively. Just as the personal qualities of extraordinary people can make themselves plain in an unaccustomed change of expression, so the intensely calculated perfection of Villa Diana transpired all at once through such minute failures as the chance apparition of a maid in the background or the perversity of a cook. While the first guests arrived bringing with them the excitement of the night, the domestic activity of the day receded past them gently, symbolised by the Diver children and their governess still at supper on the terrace.

'What a beautiful garden!' Mrs Speers exclaimed.

'Nicole's garden,' said Dick. 'She won't let it alone – she nags it all the time, worries about its diseases. Any day now I expect to have her come down with Powdery Mildew or Fly Speck, or Late Blight.' He pointed his forefinger decisively at Rosemary, saying with a lightness seeming to conceal a paternal interest, 'I'm going to save your reason – I'm going to give you a hat to wear on the beach.'

He turned them from the garden to the terrace, where he poured a cocktail. Earl Brady arrived, discovering Rosemary with surprise. His manner was softer than at the studio, as if his differentness had been put on at the gate, and Rosemary, comparing him instantly with Dick Diver, swung sharply towards the latter. In comparison Earl Brady seemed faintly gross, faintly ill-bred; once more, though, she felt an electric response to his person.

He spoke familiarly to the children, who were getting up from their outdoor supper.

'Hello, Lanier, how about a song? Will you and Topsy sing me a song?'

'What shall we sing?' agreed the little boy, with the odd chanting accent of American children brought up in France.

'That song about "*Mon ami Pierrot*".'

Brother and sister stood side by side without self-consciousness and their voices soared sweet and shrill upon the evening air.

'Au clair de la lune,
Mon ami Pierrot,
Prête-moi ta plume
Pour écrire un mot.
Ma chandelle est morte,
Je n'ai plus de feu,
Ouvre-moi ta porte,
Pour l'amour de Dieu.'

The singing ceased and the children, their faces aglow with the late sunshine, stood smiling calmly at their success. Rosemary was thinking that the Villa Diana was the centre of the world. On such a stage some memorable thing was sure to happen. She lighted up higher as the gate tinkled open and the rest of the guests arrived in a body – the McKiscos, Mrs Abrams, Mr Dumphry, and Mr Campion came up to the terrace.

Rosemary had a sharp feeling of disappointment – she looked quickly at Dick, as though to ask an explanation of this incongruous mingling. But there was nothing unusual in his expression. He greeted his new guests with a proud bearing and an obvious deference to their infinite and unknown possibilities. She believed in him so much that presently she accepted the rightness of the McKiscos' presence as if she had expected to meet them all along.

'I've met you in Paris,' McKisco said to Abe North, who with his wife had arrived on their heels, 'in fact I've met you twice.'

'Yes, I remember,' Abe said.

'Then where was it?' demanded McKisco, not content to let well enough alone.

'Why, I think – ' Abe got tired of the game, 'I can't remember.'

The interchange filled a pause and Rosemary's instinct was that something tactful should be said by somebody, but Dick made no attempt to break up the grouping formed by these late arrivals, not even to disarm Mrs McKisco of her air of supercilious amusement. He did not solve this social problem because he knew it was not of importance at the moment and would solve itself. He was saving his newness for a larger effort, waiting a more significant moment for his guests to be conscious of a good time.

Rosemary stood beside Tommy Barban – he was in a particularly scornful mood and there seemed to be some special stimulus working upon him. He was leaving in the morning.

'Going home?'

'Home? I have no home. I am going to a war.'

'What war?'

'What war? Any war. I haven't seen a paper lately but I suppose there's a war – there always is.'

'Don't you care what you fight for?'

'Not at all – so long as I'm well treated. When I'm in a rut I come to see the Divers, because then I know that in a few weeks I'll want to go to war.'

Rosemary stiffened.

'You like the Divers,' she reminded him.

'Of course – especially her – but they make me want to go to war.'

She considered this, to no avail. The Divers made her want to stay near them for ever.

'You're half American,' she said, as if that should solve the problem.

'Also I'm half French, and I was educated in England and since I was eighteen I've worn the uniforms of eight countries. But I hope I did not give you the impression that I am not fond of the Divers – I am, especially of Nicole.'

'How could anyone help it?' she said simply.

She felt far from him. The undertone of his words repelled her and she withdrew her adoration for the Divers from the profanity of his bitterness. She was glad he was not next to her at dinner and she was still thinking of his words 'especially her' as they moved towards the table in the garden.

For a moment now she was beside Dick Diver on the path. Alongside his hard, neat brightness everything faded into the surety that he knew everything. For a year, which was for ever, she had had money and a certain celebrity and contact with the celebrated, and these latter had presented themselves merely as powerful enlargements of the people with whom the doctor's widow and her daughter had associated in a hotel-pension in Paris. Rosemary was a romantic and her career had not provided many satisfactory opportunities on that score. Her mother, with the idea of a career for Rosemary, would not tolerate any such spurious substitutes as the excitations available on all sides, and indeed Rosemary was already beyond that – she was In the movies but not at all At them. So when she had seen approval of Dick Diver in her mother's face it meant that he was 'the real thing'; it meant permission to go as far as she could.

'I was watching you,' he said, and she knew he meant it. 'We've grown very fond of you.'

'I fell in love with you the first time I saw you,' she said quietly.

He pretended not to have heard, as if the compliment were purely formal.

'New friends,' he said, as if it were an important point, 'can often have a better time together than old friends.'

With that remark, which she did not understand precisely, she found herself at the table, picked out by slowly emerging lights against the dark dust. A chord of delight struck inside her when she saw that Dick had taken her mother on his right hand; for herself she was between Luis Campion and Brady.

Surcharged with her emotion she turned to Brady with the intention of confiding in him, but at her first mention of Dick a hard-boiled sparkle in his eyes gave her to understand that he refused the fatherly office. In turn she was equally firm when he tried to monopolise her hand, so they talked shop or rather she listened while he talked shop, her polite eyes never leaving his face, but her mind was so definitely elsewhere that she felt he must guess the fact. Intermittently she caught the gist of his sentences and supplied the rest from her subconscious, as one picks up the striking of a clock in the middle with only the rhythm of the first uncounted strokes lingering in the mind.

Chapter 7

In a pause Rosemary looked away and up the table where Nicole sat between Tommy Barban and Abe North, her chow's hair foaming and frothing in the candlelight. Rosemary listened, caught sharply by the rich clipped voice in infrequent speech: 'The poor man,' Nicole exclaimed. 'Why did you want to saw him in two?'

'Naturally I wanted to see what was inside a waiter. Wouldn't you like to know what was inside a waiter?'

'Old menus,' suggested Nicole with a short laugh. 'Pieces of broken china and tips and pencil stubs.'

'Exactly – but the thing was to prove it scientifically. And of course doing it with that musical saw would have eliminated any sordidness.'

'Did you intend to play the saw while you performed the operation?' Tommy enquired.

'We didn't get quite that far. We were alarmed by the screams. We thought he might rupture something.'

'All sounds very peculiar to me,' said Nicole. 'Any musician that'll use another musician's saw to – '

They had been at table half an hour and a perceptible change had set in – person by person had given up something, a preoccupation, an anxiety, a suspicion, and now they were only their best selves and the Divers' guests. Not to have been friendly and interested would have seemed to reflect on the Divers, so now they were all trying, and seeing this, Rosemary liked everyone – except McKisco, who had contrived to be the unassimilated member of the party. This was less from ill will than from his determination to sustain with wine the good spirit he had enjoyed on his arrival. Lying back in his place between Earl Brady, to whom he had addressed several withering remarks about the movies, and Mrs Abrams, to whom he said nothing, he stared at Dick Diver with an expression of devastating irony, the effect being occasionally interrupted by his attempts to engage Dick in a cater-cornered conversation across the table.

'Aren't you a friend of Van Buren Denby?' he would say.

'I don't believe I know him.'

'I thought you were a friend of his,' he persisted irritably.

When the subject of Mr Denby fell of its own weight, he essayed other equally irrelevant themes, but each time the very deference of Dick's attention seemed to paralyse him, and after a moment's stark pause the conversation that he had interrupted would go on without him. He tried breaking into other dialogues, but it was like continually shaking hands with a glove from which the hand had been withdrawn – so finally, with a resigned air of being among children, he devoted his attention entirely to the champagne. Rosemary's glance moved at intervals around the table, eager for the others' enjoyment, as if they were her future stepchildren. A gracious table light, emanating from a bowl of spicy pinks, fell upon Mrs Abrams' face, cooked to a turn in Veuve Cliquot, full of vigour, tolerance, adolescent goodwill; next to her sat Mr Royal Dumphry, his girl's comeliness less startling in the pleasure world of evening. Then Violet McKisco, whose prettiness had been piped to the surface of her, so that she ceased her struggle to make tangible to herself her shadowy position as the wife of an arriviste who had not arrived.

Then came Dick, with his arms full of the slack he had taken up from others, deeply merged in his own party.

Then her mother, for ever perfect.

Then Barban talking to her mother with an urbane fluency that made Rosemary like him again. Then Nicole. Rosemary saw her suddenly in a new way and found her one of the most beautiful people she had ever known. Her face, the face of a saint, a viking Madonna, shone through the faint motes that snowed across the candlelight, drew down its flush from the wine-coloured lanterns in the pine. She was still as still.

Abe North was talking to her about his moral code: 'Of course I've got one,' he insisted, ' – a man can't live without a moral code. Mine is that I'm against the burning of witches. Whenever they burn a witch I get all hot under the collar.' Rosemary knew from Brady that he was a musician who after a brilliant and precocious start had composed nothing for seven years.

Next was Campion, managing somehow to restrain his most blatant effeminacy, and even to visit upon those near him a certain disinterested motherliness. Then Mary North with a face so merry that it was impossible not to smile back into the white mirrors of her teeth – the whole area around her parted lips was a lovely little circle of delight.

Finally Brady, whose heartiness became, moment by moment, a social thing instead of a crude assertion and reassertion of his own mental health, and his preservation of it by a detachment from the frailties of others.

Rosemary, as dewy with belief as a child from one of Mrs Burnett's vicious tracts, had a conviction of homecoming, of a return from the derisive and salacious improvisations of the frontier. There were fireflies riding on the dark air and a dog baying on some low and faraway ledge of the cliff. The table seemed to have risen a little towards the sky like a mechanical dancing platform, giving the people around it a sense of being alone with each other in the dark universe, nourished by its only good, warmed by its only lights. And, as if a curious hushed laugh from Mrs McKisco were a signal that such a detachment from the world had been attained, the two Divers began suddenly to warm and glow and expand, as if to make up to their guests, already so subtly assured of their importance, so flattered with politeness, for anything they might still miss from that country well left behind. Just for a moment they seemed to speak to everyone at the table, singly and together, assuring them of their friendliness, their affection. And for a moment the faces turned up towards them were like the faces of poor children at a Christmas tree. Then abruptly the table broke up – the moment when the guests had been daringly lifted above conviviality into the rarer atmosphere of sentiment was over before it could be irreverently breathed, before they had half realised it was there.

But the diffused magic of the hot sweet South had withdrawn into them – the soft-pawed night and the ghostly wash of the Mediterranean far below – the magic left these things and melted into the two Divers and became part of them. Rosemary watched Nicole pressing upon her mother a yellow evening bag she had admired, saying, 'I think things ought to belong to the people that like them' – and then sweeping into it all the yellow articles she could find, a pencil, a lipstick, a little notebook, 'because they all go together.'

Nicole disappeared and presently Rosemary noticed that Dick was no longer there; the guests distributed themselves in the garden or drifted in towards the terrace.

'Do you want,' Violet McKisco asked Rosemary, 'to go to the bathroom?'

Not at that precise moment.

'I want,' insisted Mrs McKisco, 'to go to the bathroom.' As a frank outspoken woman she walked towards the house, dragging her secret after her, while Rosemary looked after with reprobation. Earl Brady proposed that they walk down to the sea wall but she felt that this was her time to have a share of Dick Diver when he reappeared, so she stalled, listening to McKisco quarrel with Barban.

'Why do you want to fight the Soviets?' McKisco said. 'The greatest experiment ever made by humanity? And the Riff? It seems to me it would be more heroic to fight on the just side.'

'How do you find out which it is?' asked Barban dryly.

'Why – usually everybody intelligent knows.'

'Are you a Communist?'

'I'm a Socialist,' said McKisco, 'I sympathise with Russia.'

'Well, I'm a soldier,' Barban answered pleasantly. 'My business is to kill people. I fought against the Riff because I am a European, and I have fought the Communists because they want to take my property from me.'

'Of all the narrow-minded excuses.' McKisco looked around to establish a derisive liaison with someone else, but without success. He had no idea what he was up against in Barban, neither of the simplicity of the other man's bag of ideas nor the complexity of his training. McKisco knew what ideas were, and as his mind grew he was able to recognise and sort an increasing number of them – but faced by a man whom he considered 'dumb', one in whom he found no ideas he could recognise as such, and yet to whom he could not feel personally superior, he jumped at the conclusion that Barban was the end product of an archaic world, and as such, worthless. McKisco's contacts with the princely classes in America had impressed upon him their uncertain and fumbling snobbery, their delight in ignorance and their deliberate rudeness, all lifted from the English with no regard paid to factors that make English philistinism and rudeness purposeful, and applied in a land where a little knowledge and civility buy more than they do anywhere else – an attitude which reached its apogee in the 'Harvard manner' of about 1900. He thought that this Barban was of that type, and being drunk rashly forgot that he was in awe of him – this led up to the trouble in which he presently found himself.

Feeling vaguely ashamed for McKisco, Rosemary waited, placid but inwardly on fire, for Dick Diver's return. From her chair at the deserted table with Barban, McKisco, and Abe she looked up along the path edged with shadowy myrtle and fern to the stone terrace, and falling in love with her mother's profile against a lighted door, was about to go there when Mrs McKisco came hurrying down from the house.

She exuded excitement. In the very silence with which she pulled out a chair and sat down, her eyes staring, her mouth working a little, they all recognised a person crop-full of news, and her husband's 'What's the matter, Vi?' came naturally, as all eyes turned towards her.

'My dear – ' she said at large, and then addressed Rosemary, 'my dear – it's nothing. I really can't say a word.'

'You are among friends,' said Abe.

'Well, upstairs I came upon a scene, my dears – '

Shaking her head cryptically she broke off just in time, for Tommy arose and addressed her politely but sharply: 'It's inadvisable to comment on what goes on in this house.'

Chapter 8

Violet breathed loud and hard once and with an effort brought another expression into her face.

Dick came finally and with a sure instinct he separated Barban and the McKiscos and became excessively ignorant and inquisitive about literature with McKisco – thus giving the latter the moment of superiority which he required. The others helped him carry lamps up – who would not be pleased at carrying lamps helpfully through the darkness? Rosemary helped, meanwhile responding patiently to Royal Dumphry's inexhaustible curiosity about Hollywood.

Now – she was thinking – I've earned a time alone with him. He must know that because his laws are like the laws mother taught me.

Rosemary was right – presently he detached her from the company on the terrace, and they were alone together, borne away from the house towards the seaside wall with what were less steps than irregularly spaced intervals through some of which she was pulled, through others blown.

They looked out over the Mediterranean. Far below, the last excursion boat from the Îles des Lérins floated across the bay like a Fourth-of-July balloon footloose in the heavens. Between the black isles it floated, softly parting the dark tide.

'I understand why you speak as you do of your mother,' he said. 'Her attitude towards you is very fine, I think. She has a sort of wisdom that's rare in America.'

'Mother is perfect,' she prayed.

'I was talking to her about a plan I have – she told me that how long you both stayed in France depended on you.'

On *you*, Rosemary all but said aloud.

'So since things are over down here –'

'Over?' she enquired.

'Well, this is over – this part of the summer is over. Last week Nicole's sister left, tomorrow Tommy Barban leaves, Monday Abe and Mary North are leaving. Maybe we'll have more fun this summer but this particular fun is over. I want it to die violently instead of fading out sentimentally – that's why I gave this party. What I'm coming to is – Nicole and I are going up to Paris to see Abe North off for America – I wonder if you'd like to go with us.'

'What did mother say?'

'She seemed to think it would be fine. She doesn't want to go herself. She wants you to go alone.'

'I haven't seen Paris since I've been grown,' said Rosemary. 'I'd love to see it with you.'

'That's nice of you.' Did she imagine that his voice was suddenly metallic? 'Of course we've been excited about you from the moment you came on the beach. That vitality, we were sure it was professional – especially Nicole was. It'd never use itself up on any one person or group.'

Her instinct cried out to her that he was passing her along slowly towards Nicole and she put her own brakes on, saying with an equal hardness: 'I wanted to know all of you too – especially you. I told you I fell in love with you the first time I saw you.'

She was right going at it that way. But the space between heaven and earth had cooled his mind, destroyed the impulsiveness that had led him to bring her here, and made him aware of the too obvious appeal, the struggle with an unrehearsed scene and unfamiliar words.

He tried now to make her want to go back to the house and it was difficult, and he did not quite want to lose her. She felt only the draught blowing as he joked with her good-humouredly.

'You don't know what you want. You go and ask your mother what you want.'

She was stricken. She touched him, feeling the smooth cloth of his dark coat like a chasuble. She seemed about to fall to her knees – from that position she delivered her last shot.

'I think you're the most wonderful person I ever met – except my mother.'

'You have romantic eyes.'

His laughter swept them on up towards the terrace where he delivered her to Nicole . . .

Too soon it had become time to go and the Divers helped them all to go quickly. In the Divers' big Isotta there would be Tommy Barban and his baggage – he was spending the night at the hotel to catch an early train – with Mrs Abrams, the McKiscos and Campion. Earl Brady was going to drop Rosemary and her mother on his way to Monte Carlo, and Royal Dumphry rode with them because the Divers' car was crowded. Down in the garden lanterns still glowed over the table where they had dined, as the Divers stood side by side in the gate, Nicole blooming away and filling the night with graciousness, and

Dick bidding goodbye to everyone by name. To Rosemary it seemed very poignant to drive away and leave them in their house. Again she wondered what Mrs McKisco had seen in the bathroom.

Chapter 9

It was a limpid black night, hung as in a basket from a single dull star. The horn of the car ahead was muffled by the resistance of the thick air. Brady's chauffeur drove slowly; the tail-light of the other car appeared from time to time at turnings – then not at all. But after ten minutes it came into sight again, drawn up at the side of the road. Brady's chauffeur slowed up behind but immediately it began to roll forward slowly and they passed it. In the instant they passed it they heard a blur of voices from behind the reticence of the limousine and saw that the Divers' chauffeur was grinning. Then they went on, going fast through the alternating banks of darkness and thin night, descending at last in a series of roller-coaster swoops, to the great bulk of Gausse's Hôtel.

Rosemary dozed for three hours and then lay awake, suspended in the moonshine. Cloaked by the erotic darkness she exhausted the future quickly, with all the eventualities that might lead up to a kiss, but with the kiss itself as blurred as a kiss in pictures. She changed position in bed, deliberately, the first sign of insomnia she had ever had, and tried to think with her mother's mind about the question. In this process she was often acute beyond her experience, with remembered things from old conversations that had gone into her half-heard.

Rosemary had been brought up with the idea of work. Mrs Speers had spent the slim leavings of the men who had widowed her on her daughter's education, and when she blossomed out at sixteen with that extraordinary hair, rushed her to Aix-les-Bains and marched her unannounced into the suite of an American producer who was recuperating there. When the producer went to New York they went too. Thus Rosemary had passed her entrance examinations. With the ensuing success and the promise of comparative stability that followed, Mrs Speers had felt free to tacitly imply tonight: 'You were brought up to work – not especially to marry. Now you've found your first nut to crack and it's a good nut – go ahead and put whatever happens down to experience. Wound yourself or him – whatever happens it can't spoil you because economically you're a boy, not a girl.'

Rosemary had never done much thinking, save about the illimitability of her mother's perfections, so this final severance of the umbilical cord disturbed her sleep. A false dawn sent the sky passing through the tall French windows, and getting up she walked out on the terrace, warm to her bare feet. There were secret noises in the air, an insistent bird achieved an ill-natured triumph with regularity in the trees above the tennis court; footfalls followed a round drive in the rear of the hotel, taking their tone in turn from the dust road, the crushed-stone walk, the cement steps, and then reversing the process in going away. Beyond the inky sea and far up that high, black shadow of a hill lived the Divers. She thought of them both together, heard them still singing faintly a song like rising smoke, like a hymn, very remote in time and far away. Their children slept, their gate was shut for the night.

She went inside and dressing in a light gown and espadrilles went out her window again and along the continuous terrace towards the front door, going fast since she found that other private rooms, exuding sleep, gave upon it. She stopped at the sight of a figure seated on the wide white stairway of the formal entrance – then she saw that it was Luis Campion and that he was weeping.

He was weeping hard and quietly and shaking in the same parts as a weeping woman. A scene in a role she had played last year swept over her irresistibly and advancing she touched him on the shoulder. He gave a little yelp before he recognised her.

'What is it?' Her eyes were level and kind and not slanted into him with hard curiosity. 'Can I help you?'

'Nobody can help me. I knew it. I have only myself to blame. It's always the same.'

'What is it – do you want to tell me?'

He looked at her to see.

'No,' he decided. 'When you're older you'll know what people who love suffer. The agony. It's better to be cold and young than to love. It's happened to me before but never like this – so accidental – just when everything was going well.'

His face was repulsive in the quickening light. Not by a flicker of her personality, a movement of the smallest muscle, did she betray her sudden disgust with whatever it was. But Campion's sensitivity realised it and he changed the subject rather suddenly.

'Abe North is around here somewhere.'

'Why, he's staying at the Divers'!'

'Yes, but he's up – don't you know what happened?'

A shutter opened suddenly in a room two storeys above and an English voice spat distinctly: 'Will you kaindlay stup tucking!'

Rosemary and Luis Campion went humbly down the steps and to a bench beside the road to the beach.

'Then you have no idea what's happened? My dear, the most extraordinary thing – ' He was warming up now, hanging on to his revelation. 'I've never seen a thing come so suddenly – I have always avoided violent people – they upset me so I sometimes have to go to bed for days.'

He looked at her triumphantly. She had no idea what he was talking about.

'My dear,' he burst forth, leaning towards her with his whole body as he touched her on the upper leg, to show it was no mere irresponsible venture of his hand – he was so sure of himself. 'There's going to be a duel.'

'Wh-at?'

'A duel with – we don't know what yet.'

'Who's going to duel?'

'I'll tell you from the beginning.' He drew a long breath and then said, as if it were rather to her discredit but he wouldn't hold it against her, 'Of course, you were in the other automobile. Well, in a way you were lucky – I lost at least two years of my life, it came so suddenly.'

'What came?' she demanded.

'I don't know what began it. First she began to talk – '

'Who?'

'Violet McKisco.' He lowered his voice as if there were people under the bench. 'But don't mention the Divers because he made threats against anybody who mentioned it.'

'Who did?'

'Tommy Barban, so don't you say I so much as mentioned them. None of us ever found out anyhow what it was Violet had to say because he kept interrupting her, and then her husband got into it and now, my dear, we have the duel. This morning – at five o'clock – in an hour.' He sighed, suddenly thinking of his own griefs. 'I almost wish it were I. I might as well be killed now I have nothing to live for.' He broke off and rocked to and fro with sorrow.

Again the iron shutter parted above and the same British voice said: 'Rilly, this must stup immejetely.'

Simultaneously Abe North, looking somewhat distracted, came out of the hotel, perceived them against the sky, white over the sea. Rosemary shook her head warningly before he could speak and they moved to another bench further down the road. Rosemary saw that Abe was a little tight.

'What are *you* doing up?' he demanded.

'I just got up.' She started to laugh, but remembering the voice above, she restrained herself.

'Plagued by the nightingale,' Abe suggested, and repeated, 'probably plagued by the nightingale. Has this sewing-circle member told you what happened?'

Campion said with dignity: 'I only know what I heard with my own ears.'

He got up and walked swiftly away; Abe sat down beside Rosemary.

'Why did you treat him so badly?'

'Did I?' he asked surprised. 'He's been weeping around here all morning.'

'Well, maybe he's sad about something.'

'Maybe he is.'

'What about a duel? Who's going to duel? I thought there was something strange in that car. Is it true?'

'It certainly is cuckoo but it seems to be true.'

Chapter 10

The trouble began at the time Earl Brady's car passed the Divers' car stopped on the road – Abe's account melted impersonally into the thronged night – Violet McKisco was telling Mrs Abrams something she had found out about the Divers – she had gone upstairs in their house and she had come upon something there which had made a great impression on her. But Tommy is a watch-dog about the Divers. As a matter of fact she is inspiring and formidable – but it's a mutual thing, and the fact of The Divers together is more important to their friends than many of them realise. Of course it's done at a certain sacrifice – sometimes they seem just rather charming figures in a ballet, and worth just the attention you give a ballet, but it's more than that – you'd have to know the story. Anyhow Tommy is one of those men that Dick's passed along to Nicole and when Mrs McKisco kept hinting at her story, he called them on it. He said: 'Mrs McKisco, please don't talk further about Mrs Diver.'

'I wasn't talking to you,' she objected.

'I think it's better to leave them out.'

'Are they so sacred?'

'Leave them out. Talk about something else.'

He was sitting on one of the two little seats beside Campion. Campion told me the story.

'Well, you're pretty high-handed,' Violet came back.

You know how conversations are in cars late at night, some people murmuring and some not caring, giving up after the party, or bored or asleep. Well, none of them knew just what happened until the car stopped and Barban cried in a voice that shook everybody, a voice for cavalry.

'Do you want to step out here – we're only a mile from the hotel and you can walk it or I'll drag you there. *You've got to shut up and shut your wife up!*'

'You're a bully,' said McKisco. 'You know you're stronger muscularly than I am. But I'm not afraid of you – what they ought to have is the code duello – '

There's where he made his mistake because Tommy, being French, leaned over and clapped him one, and then the chauffeur drove on. That was where you passed them. Then the women began. That was still the state of things when the car got to the hotel.

Tommy telephoned some man in Cannes to act as second and McKisco said he wasn't going to be seconded by Campion, who wasn't crazy for the job anyhow, so he telephoned me not to say anything but to come right down. Violet McKisco collapsed and Mrs Abrams took her to her room and gave her a bromide whereupon she fell comfortably asleep on the bed. When I got there I tried to argue with Tommy but the latter wouldn't accept anything short of an apology and McKisco rather spunkily wouldn't give it.

When Abe had finished, Rosemary asked thoughtfully: 'Do the Divers know it was about them?'

'No – and they're not ever going to know they had anything to do with it. That damn Campion had no business talking to you about it, but since he did – I told the chauffeur I'd get out the old musical saw if he opened his mouth about it. This fight's between two men – what Tommy needs is a good war.'

'I hope the Divers don't find out,' Rosemary said.

Abe peered at his watch.

'I've got to go up and see McKisco – do you want to come? – he feels sort of friendless – I bet he hasn't slept.'

Rosemary had a vision of the desperate vigil that high-strung, badly organised man had probably kept. After a moment balanced between pity and repugnance she agreed, and full of morning energy, bounced upstairs beside Abe.

McKisco was sitting on his bed with his alcoholic combativeness vanished, in spite of the glass of champagne in his hand. He seemed very puny and cross and white. Evidently he had been writing and drinking all night. He stared confusedly at Abe and Rosemary and asked: 'Is it time?'

'No, not for half an hour.'

The table was covered with papers which he assembled with some difficulty into a long letter; the writing on the last pages was very large and illegible. In the delicate light of electric lamps fading, he scrawled his name at the bottom, crammed it into an envelope and handed it to Abe. 'For my wife.'

'You better souse your head in cold water,' Abe suggested.

'You think I'd better?' enquired McKisco doubtfully. 'I don't want to get too sober.'

'Well, you look terrible now.'

Obediently McKisco went into the bathroom.

'I'm leaving everything in an awful mess,' he called. 'I don't know how Violet will get back to America. I don't carry any insurance. I never got around to it.'

'Don't talk nonsense, you'll be right here eating breakfast in an hour.'

'Sure, I know.' He came back with his hair wet and looked at Rosemary as if he saw her for the first time. Suddenly tears stood in his eyes. 'I never have finished my novel. That's what makes me so sore. You don't like me,' he said to Rosemary, 'but that can't be helped. I'm primarily a literary man.' He made a vague discouraged sound and shook his head helplessly. 'I've made lots of mistakes in my life – many of them. But I've been one of the most prominent – in some ways – '

He gave this up and puffed at a dead cigarette.

'I do like you,' said Rosemary, 'but I don't think you ought to fight a duel.'

'Yeah, I should have tried to beat him up, but it's done now. I've let myself be drawn into something that I had no right to be. I have a very violent temper – ' He looked closely at Abe as if he expected the statement to be challenged. Then with an aghast laugh he raised the cold cigarette butt towards his mouth. His breathing quickened.

'The trouble was I suggested the duel – if Violet had only kept her mouth shut I could have fixed it. Of course even now I can just leave, or sit back and laugh at the whole thing – but I don't think Violet would ever respect me again.'

'Yes, she would,' said Rosemary. 'She'd respect you more.'

'No – you don't know Violet. She's very hard when she gets an advantage over you. We've been married twelve years, we had a little girl seven years old and she died and after that you know how it is. We both played around on the side a little, nothing serious but drifting apart – she called me a coward out there tonight.'

Troubled, Rosemary didn't answer.

'Well, we'll see there's as little damage done as possible,' said Abe. He opened the leather case. 'These are Barban's duelling pistols – I borrowed them so you could get familiar with them. He carries them in his suitcase.' He weighed one of the archaic weapons in his hand. Rosemary gave an exclamation of uneasiness and McKisco looked at the pistols anxiously.

'Well – it isn't as if we were going to stand up and pot each other with forty-fives,' he said.

'I don't know,' said Abe cruelly; 'the idea is you can sight better along a long barrel.'

'How about distance?' asked McKisco.

'I've enquired about that. If one or the other parties has to be definitely eliminated they make it eight paces, if they're just good and sore it's twenty paces, and if it's only to vindicate their honour it's forty paces. His second agreed with me to make it forty.'

'That's good.'

'There's a wonderful duel in a novel of Pushkin's,' recollected Abe. 'Each man stood on the edge of a precipice, so if he was hit at all he was done for.'

This seemed very remote and academic to McKisco, who stared at him and said, 'What?'

'Do you want to take a quick dip and freshen up?'

'No – no, I couldn't swim.' He sighed. 'I don't see what it's all about,' he said helplessly. 'I don't see why I'm doing it.'

It was the first thing he had ever done in his life. Actually he was one of those for whom the sensual world does not exist, and faced with a concrete fact he brought to it a vast surprise.

'We might as well be going,' said Abe, seeing him fail a little.

'All right.' He drank off a stiff drink of brandy, put the flask in his pocket, and said with almost a savage air: 'What'll happen if I kill him – will they throw me in jail?'

'I'll run you over the Italian border.'

He glanced at Rosemary – and then said apologetically to Abe: 'Before we start there's one thing I'd like to see you about alone.'

'I hope neither of you gets hurt,' Rosemary said. 'I think it's very foolish and you ought to try to stop it.'

Chapter 11

She found Campion downstairs in the deserted lobby. 'I saw you go upstairs,' he said excitedly. 'Is he all right? When is the duel going to be?'

'I don't know.' She resented his speaking of it as a circus, with McKisco as the tragic clown.

'Will you go with me?' he demanded, with the air of having seats. 'I've hired the hotel car.'

'I don't want to go.'

'Why not? I imagine it'll take years off my life but I wouldn't miss it for worlds. We could watch it from quite far away.'

'Why don't you get Mr Dumphry to go with you?'

His monocle fell out, with no whiskers to hide in – he drew himself up.

'I never want to see him again.'

'Well, I'm afraid I can't go. Mother wouldn't like it.'

As Rosemary entered her room Mrs Speers stirred sleepily and called to her: 'Where've you been?'

'I just couldn't sleep. You go back to sleep, mother.'

'Come in my room.' Hearing her sit up in bed, Rosemary went in and told her what had happened.

'Why don't you go and see it?' Mrs Speers suggested. 'You needn't go up close and you might be able to help afterwards.'

Rosemary did not like the picture of herself looking on and she demurred, but Mrs Speers' consciousness was still clogged with sleep and she was reminded of night calls to death and calamity when she was the wife of a doctor. 'I like you to go places and do things on your own initiative without me – you did much harder things for Rainy's publicity stunts.'

Still Rosemary did not see why she should go, but she obeyed the sure, clear voice that had sent her into the stage entrance of the Odéon in Paris when she was twelve and greeted her when she came out again.

She thought she was reprieved when from the steps she saw Abe and McKisco drive away – but after a moment the hotel car came around the corner. Squealing delightedly Luis Campion pulled her in beside him.

'I hid there because they might not let us come. I've got my movie camera, you see.'

She laughed helplessly. He was so terrible that he was no longer terrible, only dehumanised.

'I wonder why Mrs McKisco didn't like the Divers?' she said. 'They were very nice to her.'

'Oh, it wasn't that. It was something she saw. We never did find exactly what it was because of Barban.'

'Then that wasn't what made you so sad.'

'Oh, no,' he said, his voice breaking, 'that was something else that happened when we got back to the hotel. But now I don't care – I wash my hands of it completely.'

They followed the other car east along the shore past Juan les Pins, where the skeleton of the new Casino was rising. It was past four and under a blue-grey sky the first fishing-boats were creaking out into a glaucous sea. Then they turned off the main road and into the back country.

'It's the golf course,' cried Campion. 'I'm sure that's where it's going to be.'

He was right. When Abe's car pulled up ahead of them the east was crayoned red and yellow, promising a sultry day. Ordering the hotel car into a grove of pines Rosemary and Campion kept in the shadow of a wood and skirted the bleached fairway where Abe and McKisco were walking up and down, the latter raising his head at intervals like a rabbit scenting. Presently there were moving figures over by a farther tree and the watchers made out Barban and his French second – the latter carried the box of pistols under his arm.

Somewhat appalled, McKisco slipped behind Abe and took a long swallow of brandy. He walked on choking and would have marched directly up into the other party, but Abe stopped him and went forward to talk to the Frenchman. The sun was over the horizon.

Campion grabbed Rosemary's arm.

'I can't stand it,' he squeaked, almost voiceless. 'It's too much. This will cost me – '

'Let go,' Rosemary said peremptorily. She breathed a frantic prayer in French.

The principals faced each other, Barban with the sleeve rolled up from his arm. His eyes gleamed restlessly in the sun, but his motion was deliberate as he wiped his palm on the seam of his trousers. McKisco, reckless with brandy, pursed his lips in a whistle and pointed his long nose about nonchalantly, until Abe stepped forward with a handkerchief in his hand. The French second stood with his face turned away. Rosemary caught her breath in terrible pity and gritted her teeth with hatred for Barban; then: 'One – two – three!' Abe counted in a strained voice.

They fired at the same moment. McKisco swayed but recovered himself. Both shots had missed.

'Now, that's enough!' cried Abe.

The duellists walked in, and everyone looked at Barban enquiringly.

'I declare myself unsatisfied.'

'What? Sure you're satisfied,' said Abe impatiently. 'You just don't know it.'

'Your man refuses another shot?'

'You're damn right, Tommy. You insisted on this and my client went through with it.'

Tommy laughed scornfully.

'The distance was ridiculous,' he said. 'I'm not accustomed to such farces – your man must remember he's not now in America.'

'No use cracking at America,' said Abe rather sharply. And then, in a more conciliatory tone, 'This has gone far enough, Tommy.' They parleyed briskly for a moment – then Barban nodded and bowed coldly to his late antagonist.

'No shake hand?' suggested the French doctor.

'They already know each other,' said Abe.

He turned to McKisco.

'Come on, let's get out.'

As they strode off, McKisco, in exultation, gripped his arm.

'Wait a minute!' Abe said. 'Tommy wants his pistol back. He might need it again.'

McKisco handed it over.

'To hell with him,' he said in a tough voice. 'Tell him he can – '

'Shall I tell him you want another shot?'

'Well, I did it,' cried McKisco, as they went along. 'And I did it pretty well, didn't I? I wasn't yellow.'

'You were pretty drunk,' said Abe bluntly.

'No, I wasn't.'

'All right, then, you weren't.'

'Why would it make any difference if I had a drink or so?'

As his confidence mounted he looked resentfully at Abe.

'What difference does that make?' he repeated.

'If you can't see it, there's no use going into it.'

'Don't you know everybody was drunk all the time during the war?'

'Well, let's forget it.'

But the episode was not quite over. There were urgent footsteps in the heather behind them and the doctor drew up alongside.

'Pardon, messieurs,' he panted. 'Voulez-vous régler mes honoraires? Naturellement c'est pour soins médicaux seulement. M. Barban n'a qu'un billet de mille et ne peut pas les régler et l'autre a laissé son porte-monnaie chez lui.'

'Trust a Frenchman to think of that,' said Abe, and then to the doctor. 'Combien?'

'Let me pay this,' said McKisco.

'No, I've got it. We were all in about the same danger.'

Abe paid the doctor while McKisco suddenly turned into the bushes and was sick there. Then paler than before he strutted on with Abe towards the car through the now rosy morning.

Campion lay gasping on his back in the shrubbery, the only casualty of the duel, while Rosemary suddenly hysterical with laughter kept kicking at him with her espadrille. She did this persistently until she roused him – the only matter of importance to her now was that on the beach in a few hours she would see the person whom she still referred to in her mind as 'the Divers'.

Chapter 12

They were at Voisins waiting for Nicole, six of them, Rosemary, the Norths, Dick Diver and two young French musicians. They were looking over the other patrons of the restaurant to see if they had repose – Dick said no American men had any repose, except himself, and they were seeking an example to confront him with. Things looked black for them – not a man had come into the restaurant for ten minutes without raising his hand to his face.

'We ought never to have given up waxed moustaches,' said Abe. 'Nevertheless Dick isn't the *only* man with repose – '

'Oh, yes, I am.'

' – but he may be the only sober man with repose.'

A well-dressed American had come in with two women who swooped and fluttered unself-consciously around a table. Suddenly, he perceived that he was being watched – whereupon his hand rose spasmodically and arranged a phantom bulge in his necktie. In another unseated party a man endlessly patted his shaven cheek with his palm, and his companion mechanically raised and lowered the stub of a cold cigar. The luckier ones fingered eyeglasses and facial hair, the unequipped stroked blank mouths, or even pulled desperately at the lobes of their ears.

A well-known general came in, and Abe, counting on the man's first year at West Point – that year during which no cadet can resign and from which none ever recovers – made a bet with Dick of five dollars.

His hands hanging naturally at his sides, the general waited to be seated. Once his arms swung suddenly backward like a jumper's and Dick said, 'Ah!' supposing he had lost control, but the general recovered and they breathed again – the agony was nearly over, the *garçon* was pulling out his chair . . .

With a touch of fury the conqueror shot up his hand and scratched his grey immaculate head.

'You see,' said Dick smugly, 'I'm the only one.'

Rosemary was quite sure of it, and Dick, realising that he never had a better audience, made the group into so bright a unit that Rosemary felt an impatient disregard for all who were not at their table. They had been two days in Paris but actually they were still under the beach umbrella. When, as at the ball of the Corps des Pages the night before, the surroundings seemed formidable to Rosemary, who had yet to attend a Mayfair party in Hollywood, Dick would bring the scene within range by greeting a few people, a sort of selection – the Divers seemed to have a large acquaintance, but it was always as if the person had not seen them for a long, long time, and was utterly bowled over, 'Why, where do you *keep* yourselves?' – and then recreate the unity of his own party by destroying the outsiders softly but permanently with an ironic *coup de grâce*. Presently Rosemary seemed to have known those people herself in some deplorable past, and then got on to them, rejected them, discarded them.

Their own party was overwhelmingly American and sometimes scarcely American at all. It was themselves he gave back to them, blurred by the compromises of how many years.

Into the dark, smoky restaurant, smelling of the rich raw foods on the buffet, slid Nicole's sky-blue suit like a stray segment of the weather outside. Seeing from their eyes how beautiful she was, she thanked them with a smile of radiant appreciation. They were all very nice people for a while, very courteous and all that. Then they grew tired of it and they were funny and bitter, and finally they made a lot of plans. They laughed at things that they would not remember clearly afterwards – laughed a lot and the men drank three bottles of wine. The trio of women at the table were representative of the enormous flux of American life. Nicole was the granddaughter of a self-made American capitalist and the granddaughter of a Count of the House of Lippe Weissenfeld. Mary North was the daughter of a journeyman paperhanger and a descendant of President Tyler. Rosemary was from the middle of the middle class, catapulted by her mother on to the uncharted heights of Hollywood. Their point of resemblance to each other and their difference from so many American women, lay in the fact that they were all happy to exist in a man's world – they preserved their individuality through men and not by opposition to them. They would all three have made alternatively good courtesans or good wives not by the accident of birth but through the greater accident of finding their man or not finding him.

So Rosemary found it a pleasant party, that luncheon, nicer in that there were only seven people, about the limit of a good party. Perhaps, too, the fact that she was new to their world acted as a sort of catalytic agent to precipitate out all their old reservations about one another. After the table broke up, a waiter directed Rosemary back into the dark hinterland of all French restaurants, where she looked up a phone number by a dim orange bulb, and called Franco-American Films. Sure, they had a print of *Daddy's Girl* – it was out for the moment but they would run it off later in the week for her at 341 Rue des Saintes Anges – ask for Mr Crowder.

The semi-booth gave on the *vestiaire* and as Rosemary hung up the receiver she heard two low voices not five feet from her on the other side of a row of coats.

'– So you love me?'

'Oh, *do* I!'

It was Nicole – Rosemary hesitated in the door of the booth – then she heard Dick say: 'I want you terribly – let's go to the hotel now.' Nicole gave a little gasping sigh. For a moment the words conveyed nothing at all to Rosemary – but the tone did. The vast secretiveness of it vibrated to herself.

'I want you.'

'I'll be at the hotel at four.'

Rosemary stood breathless as the voices moved away. She was at first astonished – she had seen them in their relation to each other as people without personal exigencies – as something cooler. Now a strong current of emotion flowed through her, profound and unidentified. She did not know whether she was attracted or repelled, but only that she was deeply moved. It made her feel very alone as she went back into the restaurant, but it was touching to look in upon, and the passionate gratitude of Nicole's 'Oh, *do I*!' echoed in her mind. The particular mood of the passage she had witnessed lay ahead of her; but however far she was from it her stomach told her it was all right – she had none of the aversion she had felt in the playing of certain love scenes in pictures.

Being far away from it she nevertheless irrevocably participated in it now, and shopping with Nicole she was much more conscious of the assignation than Nicole herself. She looked at Nicole in a new way, estimating her attractions. Certainly she was the most attractive woman Rosemary had ever met – with her hardness, her devotions and loyalties, and a certain elusiveness, which Rosemary, thinking now through her mother's middle-class mind, associated with her attitude about money. Rosemary spent money she had earned – she was here in Europe due to the fact that she had gone in the pool six times that January day with her temperature roving from ninety-nine degrees in the early morning to a hundred and three degrees, when her mother stopped it.

With Nicole's help Rosemary bought two dresses and two hats and four pairs of shoes with her money. Nicole bought from a great list that ran to two pages, and bought the things in the windows besides. Everything she liked that she couldn't possibly use herself, she bought as a present for a friend. She bought coloured beads, folding beach cushions, artificial flowers, honey, a guest bed, bags, scarfs, love-birds, miniatures for a doll's house, and three yards of some new cloth the colour of prawns. She bought a dozen bathing-suits, a rubber alligator, a travelling chess set of gold and ivory, big linen handkerchiefs for Abe, two chamois leather jackets of kingfisher blue and burning bush from Hermès – bought all these things not a bit like a high-class courtesan buying underwear and jewels, which were after all professional equipment and insurance – but with an entirely different point of view. Nicole was the product of much ingenuity and toil. For her sake trains began their run at Chicago and traversed the round belly of the continent to California; chicle factories fumed and link belts grew link by link in factories; men mixed toothpaste in vats and drew mouthwash out of copper hogsheads; girls canned tomatoes quickly in August or worked rudely at the Five-and-Tens on Christmas Eve; half-breed Indians toiled on Brazilian coffee plantations and dreamers were muscled out of patent rights in new tractors – these were some of the people who gave a tithe to Nicole, and as the whole system swayed and thundered onward it lent a feverish bloom to such processes of hers as wholesale buying, like the flush of a fireman's face holding his post before a spreading blaze. She illustrated very simple principles, containing in herself her own doom, but illustrated them so accurately that there was grace in the procedure, and presently Rosemary would try to imitate it.

It was almost four. Nicole stood in a shop with a love-bird on her shoulder, and had one of her infrequent outbursts of speech.

'Well, what if you hadn't gone in that pool that day – I sometimes wonder about such things. Just before the war we were in Berlin – I was thirteen, it was just before mother died. My sister was going to a court ball and she had three of the royal princes on her dance card, all arranged by a chamberlain and everything. Half an hour before she was going to start she had a side ache and high fever. The doctor said it was appendicitis and she ought to be operated on. But mother had her plans made, so Baby went to the ball and danced till two with an ice pack strapped on under her evening dress. She was operated on at seven o'clock next morning.'

It was good to be hard, then; all nice people were hard on themselves. But it was four o'clock and Rosemary kept thinking of Dick waiting for Nicole now at the hotel. She must go there, she must not make him wait for her. She kept thinking, 'Why don't you go?' and then suddenly, 'or let me go if you don't want to.' But Nicole went to one more place to buy corsages for them both and sent one to Mary North. Only then she seemed to remember and with sudden abstraction she signalled for a taxi.

'Goodbye,' said Nicole. 'We had fun, didn't we?'

'Loads of fun,' said Rosemary. It was more difficult than she thought and her whole self protested as Nicole drove away.

Chapter 13

Dick turned the corner of the traverse and continued along the trench walking on the duckboard. He came to a periscope, looked through it a moment, then he got up on the step and peered over the parapet. In front of him beneath a dingy sky was Beaumont-Hamel; to his left the tragic hill of Thiepval. Dick stared at them through his field-glasses, his throat straining with sadness.

He went on along the trench, and found the others waiting for him in the next traverse. He was full of excitement and he wanted to communicate it to them, to make them understand about this, though actually Abe North had seen battle service and he had not.

'This land here cost twenty lives a foot that summer,' he said to Rosemary. He looked out obediently at the rather bare green plain with its low trees of six years' growth. If Dick had added that they were now being shelled she would have believed him that afternoon. Her love had reached a point where now at last she was beginning to be unhappy, to be desperate. She didn't know what to do – she wanted to talk to her mother.

'There are lots of people dead since and we'll all be dead soon,' said Abe consolingly.

Rosemary waited tensely for Dick to continue.

'See that little stream – we could walk to it in two minutes. It took the British a month to walk to it – a whole empire walking very slowly, dying in front and pushing forward behind. And another empire walked very slowly backward a few inches a day, leaving the dead like a million bloody rugs. No Europeans will ever do that again in this generation.'

'Why, they've only just quit over in Turkey,' said Abe. 'And in Morocco – '

'That's different. This western-front business couldn't be done again, not for a long time. The young men think they could do it but they couldn't. They could fight the first Marne again but not this. This took religion and years of plenty and tremendous sureties and the exact relation that existed between the classes. The Russians and

Italians weren't any good on this front. You had to have a whole-souled sentimental equipment going back further than you could remember. You had to remember Christmas, and postcards of the Crown Prince and his fiancée, and little cafés in Valence and beer gardens in Unter den Linden and weddings at the *mairie*, and going to the Derby, and your grandfather's whiskers.'

'General Grant invented this kind of battle at Petersburg in sixty-five.'

'No, he didn't – he just invented mass butchery. This kind of battle was invented by Lewis Carroll and Jules Verne and whoever wrote *Undine*, and country deacons bowling and *marraines* in Marseilles and girls seduced in the back lanes of Württemberg and Westphalia. Why, this was a love battle – there was a century of middle-class love spent here. This was the last love battle.'

'You want to hand over this battle to D. H. Lawrence,' said Abe.

'All my beautiful lovely safe world blew itself up here with a great gust of high explosive love,' Dick mourned persistently. 'Isn't that true, Rosemary?'

'I don't know,' she answered with a grave face. 'You know everything.'

They dropped behind the others. Suddenly a shower of earth gobs and pebbles came down on them and Abe yelled from the next traverse: 'The war spirit's getting into me again. I have a hundred years of Ohio love behind me and I'm going to bomb out this trench.' His head popped up over the embankment. 'You're dead – don't you know the rules? That was a grenade.'

Rosemary laughed and Dick picked up a retaliatory handful of stones and then put them down.

'I couldn't kid here,' he said rather apologetically. 'The silver cord is cut and the golden bowl is broken and all that, but an old romantic like me can't do anything about it.'

'I'm romantic too.'

They came out of the neat restored trench, and faced a memorial to the Newfoundland dead. Reading the inscription Rosemary burst into sudden tears. Like most women, she liked to be told how she should feel, and she liked Dick's telling her which things were ludicrous and which things were sad. But most of all she wanted him to know how she loved him, now that the fact was upsetting everything, now that she was walking over the battlefield in a thrilling dream.

After that they got in their car and started back towards Amiens. A thin warm rain was falling on the new scrubby woods and underbrush and they passed great funeral pyres of sorted duds, shells, bombs, grenades, and equipment, helmets, bayonets, gun stocks and rotten leather, abandoned six years in the ground. And suddenly around a bend the white caps of a great sea of graves. Dick asked the chauffeur to stop.

'There's that girl – and she still has her wreath.'

They watched as he got out and went over to the girl, who stood uncertainly by the gate with a wreath in her hand. Her taxi waited. She was a red-haired girl from Tennessee whom they had met on the train this morning, come from Knoxville to lay a memorial on her brother's grave. There were tears of vexation on her face.

'The War Department must have given me the wrong number,' she whimpered. 'It had another name on it. I been lookin' for it since two o'clock, and there's so many graves.'

'Then if I were you I'd just lay it on any grave without looking at the name,' Dick advised her.

'You reckon that's what I ought to do?'

'I think that's what he'd have wanted you to do.'

It was growing dark and the rain was coming down harder. She left the wreath on the first grave inside the gate, and accepted Dick's suggestion that she dismiss her taxi-cab and ride back to Amiens with them.

Rosemary shed tears again when she heard of the mishap – altogether it had been a watery day, but she felt that she had learned something, though exactly what it was she did not know. Later she remembered all the hours of the afternoon as happy – one of those uneventful times that seem at the moment only a link between past and future pleasure but turn out to have been the pleasure itself.

Amiens was an echoing purple town, still sad with the war, as some railroad stations were: the Gare du Nord and Waterloo Station in London. In the daytime one is deflated by such towns, with their little trolley cars of twenty years ago crossing the great grey cobblestoned squares in front of the cathedral, and the very weather seems to have a quality of the past, faded weather like that of old photographs. But after dark all that is most satisfactory in French life swims back into the picture – the sprightly tarts, the men arguing with a hundred *voilàs* in the cafés, the couples drifting, head to head, towards the satisfactory inexpensiveness of nowhere. Waiting for the train they sat in a big arcade, tall enough to release the smoke and chatter and music upwards, and obligingly the orchestra launched into 'Yes, We Have No Bananas' – they clapped, because the leader looked so pleased with himself. The Tennessee girl forgot her sorrow and enjoyed herself, even began flirtations of tropical eye-rollings and pawings, with Dick and Abe. They teased her gently.

Then, leaving infinitesimal sections of Württembergers, Prussian Guards, Chasseurs Alpins, Manchester mill-hands and old Etonians to pursue their eternal dissolution under the warm rain, they took the train for Paris. They ate sandwiches of mortadella sausage and bel paese cheese made up in the station restaurant, and drank Beaujolais. Nicole was abstracted, biting her lip restlessly and reading over the guidebooks to the battlefield that Dick had brought along – indeed, he had made a quick study of the whole affair, simplifying it always until it bore a faint resemblance to one of his own parties.

Chapter 14

When they reached Paris Nicole was too tired to go on to the grand illumination at the Decorative Arts Exposition as they had planned. They left her at the Hôtel Roi George, and as she disappeared between the intersecting planes made by lobby lights of the glass doors, Rosemary's oppression lifted. Nicole was a force – not necessarily well disposed or predictable like her mother – an incalculable force. Rosemary was somewhat afraid of her.

At eleven she sat with Dick and the Norths at a houseboat café just opened on the Seine. The river shimmered with lights from the bridges and cradled many cold moons. On Sundays sometimes when Rosemary and her mother had lived in Paris they had taken the little steamer up to Suresnes and talked about plans for the future. They had little money, but Mrs Speers was so sure of Rosemary's beauty and had implanted in her so much ambition, that she was willing to gamble the money on 'advantages'; Rosemary in turn was to repay her mother when she got her start . . .

Since reaching Paris Abe North had had a thin vinous fur over him; his eyes were bloodshot from sun and wine. Rosemary realised for the first time that he was always stopping in places to get a drink, and she wondered how Mary North liked it. Mary was quiet, so quiet save for her frequent laughter that Rosemary had learned little about her. She liked the straight dark hair brushed back until it met some sort of natural cascade that took care of it – from time to time it eased with a jaunty slant over the corner of her temple, until it was almost in her eye when she tossed her head and caused it to fall sleek into place once more.

'We'll turn in early tonight, Abe, after this drink.' Mary's voice was light but it held a little flicker of anxiety. 'You don't want to be poured on the boat.'

'It's pretty late now,' Dick said. 'We'd all better go.'

The noble dignity of Abe's face took on a certain stubbornness, and he remarked with determination: 'Oh, no.' He paused gravely. 'Oh, no, not yet. We'll have another bottle of champagne.'

'No more for me,' said Dick.

'It's Rosemary I'm thinking of. She's a natural alcoholic – keeps a bottle of gin in the bathroom and all that – her mother told me.'

He emptied what was left of the first bottle into Rosemary's glass. She had made herself quite sick the first day in Paris with quarts of lemonade; after that she had taken nothing with them, but now she raised the champagne and drank at it.

'But what's this?' exclaimed Dick. 'You told me you didn't drink.'

'I didn't say I was never going to.'

'What about your mother?'

'I'm just going to drink this one glass.' She felt some necessity for it. Dick drank, not too much, but he drank, and perhaps it would bring her closer to him, be a part of the equipment for what she had to do. She drank it quickly, choked and then said, 'Besides, yesterday was my birthday – I was eighteen.'

'Why didn't you tell us?' they said indignantly.

'I knew you'd make a fuss over it and go to a lot of trouble.' She finished the champagne. 'So this is the celebration.'

'It most certainly is not,' Dick assured her. 'The dinner tomorrow night is your birthday party and don't forget it. Eighteen – why that's a terribly important age.'

'I used to think until you're eighteen nothing matters,' said Mary.

'That's right,' Abe agreed. 'And afterwards it's the same way.'

'Abe feels that nothing matters till he gets on the boat,' said Mary. 'This time he really has got everything planned out when he gets to New York.' She spoke as though she were tired of saying things that no longer had a meaning for her, as if in reality the course that she and her husband followed, or failed to follow, had become merely an intention.

'He'll be writing music in America and I'll be working at singing in Munich, so when we get together again there'll be nothing we can't do.'

'That's wonderful,' agreed Rosemary, feeling the champagne.

'Meanwhile, another touch of champagne for Rosemary. Then she'll be more able to rationalise the acts of her lymphatic glands. They only begin to function at eighteen.'

Dick laughed indulgently at Abe, whom he loved, and in whom he had long lost hope: 'That's medically incorrect and we're going.' Catching the faint patronage Abe said lightly: 'Something tells me I'll have a new score on Broadway long before you've finished your scientific treatise.'

'I hope so,' said Dick evenly. 'I hope so. I may even abandon what you call my "scientific treatise".'

'Oh, Dick!' Mary's voice was startled, was shocked. Rosemary had never before seen Dick's face utterly expressionless; she felt that this announcement was something momentous and she was inclined to exclaim with Mary, 'Oh, Dick!'

But suddenly Dick laughed again, added to his remark ' – abandon it for another one,' and got up from the table.

'But Dick, sit down. I want to know – '

'I'll tell you sometime. Good-night, Abe. Good-night, Mary.'

'Good-night, dear Dick.' Mary smiled as if she were going to be perfectly happy sitting there on the almost deserted boat. She was a brave, hopeful woman and she was following her husband somewhere, changing herself to this kind of person or that, without being able to lead him a step out of his path, and sometimes realising with discouragement how deep in him the guarded secret of her direction lay. And yet an air of luck clung about her, as if she were a sort of token.

Chapter 15

'What is it you are giving up?' demanded Rosemary, facing Dick earnestly in the taxi.

'Nothing of importance.'

'Are you a scientist?'

'I'm a doctor of medicine.'

'Oh-h!' she smiled delightedly. 'My father was a doctor too. Then why don't you – ' she stopped.

'There's no mystery. I didn't disgrace myself at the height of my career, and hide away on the Riviera. I'm just not practising. You can't tell, I'll probably practise again someday.'

Rosemary put up her face quietly to be kissed. He looked at her for a moment as if he didn't understand. Then holding her in the hollow of his arm he rubbed his cheek against her cheek's softness, and then looked down at her for another long moment.

'Such a lovely child,' he said gravely.

She smiled up at him; her hands playing conventionally with the lapels of his coat. 'I'm in love with you and Nicole. Actually that's my secret – I can't even talk about you to anybody because I don't want any more people to know how wonderful you are. Honestly – I love you and Nicole – I do.'

So many times he had heard this – even the formula was the same.

Suddenly she came towards him, her youth vanishing as she passed inside the focus of his eyes and he had kissed her breathlessly as if she were any age at all. Then she lay back against his arm and sighed.

'I've decided to give you up,' she said.

Dick started – had he said anything to imply that she possessed any part of him?

'But that's very mean,' he managed to say lightly, 'just when I was getting interested.'

'I've loved you so – ' As if it had been for years. She was weeping a little now. 'I've loved you s-o-o.'

Then he should have laughed, but he heard himself saying, 'Not only are you beautiful but you are somehow on the grand scale. Everything you do, like pretending to be in love or pretending to be shy, gets across.'

In the dark cave of the taxi, fragrant with the perfume Rosemary had bought with Nicole, she came close again, clinging to him. He kissed her without enjoying it. He knew that there was passion there, but there was no shadow of it in her eyes or on her mouth; there was a faint spray of champagne on her breath. She clung nearer desperately and once more he kissed her and was chilled by the innocence of her kiss, by the glance that at the moment of contact looked beyond him out into the darkness of the night, the darkness of the world. She did not know yet that splendour is something in the heart; at the moment when she realised that and melted into the passion of the universe he could take her without question or regret.

Her room in the hotel was diagonally across from theirs and nearer the elevator. When they reached the door she said suddenly: 'I know you don't love me – I don't expect it. But you said I should have told you about my birthday. Well, I did, and now for my birthday present I want you to come into my room a minute while I tell you something. Just one minute.'

They went in and he closed the door, and Rosemary stood close to him, not touching him. The night had drawn the colour from her face – she was pale as pale now, she was a white carnation left after a dance.

'When you smile – ' he had recovered his paternal attitude, perhaps because of Nicole's silent proximity – 'I always think I'll see a gap where you've lost some baby teeth.'

But he was too late – she came close up against him with a forlorn whisper.

'Take me.'

'Take you where?'

Astonishment froze him rigid.

'Go on,' she whispered. 'Oh, please go on, whatever they do. I don't care if I don't like it – I never expected to – I've always hated to think about it but now I don't. I want you to.'

She was astonished at herself – she had never imagined she could talk like that. She was calling on things she had read, seen, dreamed through a decade of convent hours. Suddenly she knew too that it was one of her greatest roles and she flung herself into it more passionately.

'This is not as it should be,' Dick deliberated. 'Isn't it just the champagne? Let's more or less forget it.'

'Oh, no, *now*. I want you to do it now, take me, show me, I'm absolutely yours and I want to be.'

'For one thing, have you thought how much it would hurt Nicole?'

'She won't know – this won't have anything to do with her.'

He continued kindly.

'Then there's the fact that I love Nicole.'

'But you can love more than just one person, can't you? Like I love mother and I love you – more. I love you more now.'

' – the fourth place you're not in love with me but you might be afterwards, and that would begin your life with a terrible mess.'

'No, I promise I'll never see you again. I'll get mother and go to America right away.'

He dismissed this. He was remembering too vividly the youth and freshness of her lips. He took another tone.

'You're just in that mood.'

'Oh, please, I don't care even if I had a baby. I could go into Mexico like a girl at the studio. Oh, this is so different from anything I ever thought – I used to hate it when they kissed me seriously.' He saw she was still under the impression that it must happen. 'Some of them had great big teeth, but you're all different and beautiful. I want you to do it.'

'I believe you think people just kiss some way and you want me to kiss you.'

'Oh, don't tease me – I'm not a baby. I know you're not in love with me.' She was suddenly humble and quiet. 'I didn't expect that much. I know I must seem just nothing to you.'

'Nonsense. But you seem young to me.' His thoughts added, ' – there'd be so much to teach you.'

Rosemary waited, breathing eagerly till Dick said: 'And lastly things aren't arranged so that this could be as you want.'

Her face drooped with dismay and disappointment and Dick said automatically, 'We'll have to simply – ' He stopped himself, followed her to the bed, sat down beside her while she wept. He was suddenly confused, not about the ethics of the matter, for the impossibility of it was sheerly indicated from all angles, but simply confused, and for a moment his usual grace, the tensile strength of his balance, was absent.

'I knew you wouldn't,' she sobbed. 'It was just a forlorn hope.'

He stood up.

'Good-night, child. This is a damn shame. Let's drop it out of the picture.' He gave her two lines of hospital patter to go to sleep on. 'So many people are going to love you and it might be nice to meet your first love all intact, emotionally too. That's an old-fashioned idea, isn't it?' She looked up at him as he took a step towards the door; she looked at him without the slightest idea as to what was in his head, she saw him take another step in slow motion, turn and look at her again, and she wanted for a moment to hold him and devour him, wanted his mouth, his ears, his coat collar, wanted to surround him and engulf him; she saw his hand fall on the doorknob. Then she gave up and sank back on the bed. When the door closed she got up and went to the mirror, where she began brushing her hair, sniffling a little. One hundred and fifty strokes Rosemary gave it, as usual, then a hundred and fifty more. She brushed it until her arm ached, then she changed arms and went on brushing.

Chapter 16

She woke up cooled and shamed. The sight of her beauty in the mirror did not reassure her but only awakened the ache of yesterday, and a letter, forwarded by her mother, from the boy who had taken her to the Yale prom last fall, which announced his presence in Paris, was no help – all that seemed far away. She emerged from her room for the ordeal of meeting the Divers weighted with a double trouble. But it was hidden by a sheath as impermeable as Nicole's when they met and went together to a series of fittings. It was consoling, though, when Nicole remarked, apropos of a distraught saleswoman: 'Most people think everybody feels about them much more violently than they actually do – they think other people's opinions of them swing through great arcs of approval or disapproval.' Yesterday in her expansiveness Rosemary would have resented that remark – today in her desire to minimise what had happened she welcomed it eagerly. She admired Nicole for her beauty and her wisdom, and also for the first time in her life she was jealous. Just before leaving Gausse's Hôtel her mother had said in that casual tone, which Rosemary knew concealed her most significant opinions, that Nicole was a great beauty, with the frank implication that Rosemary was not. This did not bother Rosemary, who had only recently been allowed to learn that she was even personable; so that her prettiness never seemed exactly her own but rather an acquirement, like her French. Nevertheless, in the taxi she looked at Nicole, matching herself against her. There were all the potentialities for romantic love in that lovely body and in the delicate mouth, sometimes tight, sometimes expectantly half open to the world. Nicole had been a beauty as a young girl and she would be a beauty later when her skin stretched tight over her high cheekbones – the essential structure was there. She had been white-Saxon-blonde but she was more beautiful now that her hair had darkened than when it had been like a cloud and more beautiful than she.

'We lived there,' Rosemary suddenly pointed to a building in the Rue des Saints-Pères.

'That's strange. Because, when I was twelve, mother and Baby and I once spent a winter there,' and she pointed to a hotel directly across the street. The two dingy fronts stared at them, grey echoes of girlhood.

'We'd just built our Lake Forest house and we were economising,'

Nicole continued. 'At least Baby and I and the governess economised and mother travelled.'

'We were economising too,' said Rosemary, realising that the word meant different things to them.

'Mother always spoke of it very carefully as a small hotel – ' Nicole gave her quick magnetic little laugh ' – I mean instead of saying a "cheap" hotel. If any swanky friends asked us our address we'd never say, "We're in a dingy little hole over in the apache quarter where we're glad of running water," – we'd say "We're in a small hotel." As if all the big ones were too noisy and vulgar for us. Of course the friends always saw through us and told everyone about it, but mother always said it showed we knew our way around Europe. She did, of course: she was born a German citizen. But her mother was American, and she was brought up in Chicago, and she was more American than European.'

They were meeting the others in two minutes, and Rosemary reconstructed herself once more as they got out of the taxi in the Rue Guynemer, across from the Luxembourg Gardens. They were lunching in the Norths' already dismantled apartment high above the green mass of leaves. The day seemed different to Rosemary from the day before. When she saw him face to face their eyes met and brushed like birds' wings. After that everything was all right, everything was wonderful, she knew that he was beginning to fall in love with her. She felt wildly happy, felt the warm sap of emotion being pumped through her body. A cool, clear confidence deepened and sang in her. She scarcely looked at Dick but she knew everything was all right.

After luncheon the Divers and the Norths and Rosemary went to the Franco-American Films, to be joined by Collis Clay, her young man from New Haven, to whom she had telephoned. He was a Georgian, with the peculiarly regular, even stencilled ideas of Southerners who are educated in the North. Last winter she had thought him attractive – once they held hands in an automobile going from New Haven to New York; now he no longer existed for her.

In the projection room she sat between Collis Clay and Dick while the mechanic mounted the reels of *Daddy's Girl* and a French executive fluttered about her trying to talk American slang. 'Yes, boy,' he said when there was trouble with the projector, 'I have not any benenas.' Then the lights went out, there was a sudden click and a flickering noise and she was alone with Dick at last. They looked at each other in the half-darkness.

'Dear Rosemary,' he murmured. Their shoulders touched. Nicole stirred restlessly at the end of the row and Abe coughed convulsively and blew his nose; then they all settled down and the picture ran.

There she was – the schoolgirl of a year ago, hair down her back and rippling out stiffly like the solid hair of a Tanagra figure; there she was – *so* young and innocent – the product of her mother's loving care; there she was – embodying all the immaturity of the race, cutting a new cardboard paper doll to pass before its empty harlot's mind. She remembered how she had felt in that dress, especially fresh and new under the fresh young silk.

Daddy's girl. Was it a 'itty-bitty bravekins and did it suffer? Ooo-ooo-tweet, de tweetest thing, wasn't she dest too tweet?' Before her tiny fist the forces of lust and corruption rolled away; nay, the very march of destiny stopped; inevitably became evitable, syllogism, dialectic, all rationality fell away. Women would forget the dirty dishes at home and weep, even within the picture one woman wept so long that she almost stole the film away from Rosemary. She wept all over a set that cost a fortune, in a Duncan Phyfe dining-room, in an aviation port, and during a yacht race that was only used in two flashes, in a subway and finally in a bathroom. But Rosemary triumphed. Her fineness of character, her courage and steadfastness intruded upon by the vulgarity of the world, and Rosemary showing what it took with a face that had not yet become mask-like – yet it was actually so moving that the emotions of the whole row of people went out to her at intervals during the picture. There was a break once and the light went on and after the chatter of applause Dick said to her sincerely: 'I'm simply astounded. You're going to be one of the best actresses on the stage.'

Then back to *Daddy's Girl*: happier days now, and a lovely shot of Rosemary and her parent united at the last in a father complex so apparent that Dick winced for all psychologists at the vicious sentimentality. The screen vanished, the lights went on, the moment had come.

'I've arranged one other thing,' announced Rosemary to the company at large, 'I've arranged a test for Dick.'

'A what?'

'A screen-test, they'll take one now.'

There was an awful silence – then an irrepressible chortle from the Norths. Rosemary watched Dick comprehend what she meant, his face moving first in an Irish way; simultaneously she realised that she had made some mistake in the playing of her trump and still she did not suspect that the card was at fault.

'I don't want a test,' said Dick firmly; then, seeing the situation as a whole, he continued lightly, 'Rosemary, I'm disappointed. The pictures make a fine career for a woman – but my God, they can't photograph me. I'm an old scientist all wrapped up in his private life.'

Nicole and Mary urged him ironically to seize the opportunity; they teased him, both faintly annoyed at not having been asked for a sitting. But Dick closed the subject with a somewhat tart discussion of actors: 'The strongest guard is placed at the gateway to nothing,' he said. 'Maybe because the condition of emptiness is too shameful to be divulged.'

In the taxi with Dick and Collis Clay – they were dropping Collis, and Dick was taking Rosemary to a tea from which Nicole and the Norths had resigned in order to do the things Abe had left undone till the last – in the taxi Rosemary reproached him.

'I thought if the test turned out to be good I could take it to California with me. And then maybe if they liked it you'd come out and be my leading man in a picture.'

He was overwhelmed. 'It was a darn sweet thought, but I'd rather look at you. You were about the nicest sight I ever looked at.'

'That's a great picture,' said Collis. 'I've seen it four times. I know one boy at New Haven who's seen it a dozen times – he went all the way to Hartford to see it one time. And when I brought Rosemary up to New Haven he was so shy he wouldn't meet her. Can you beat that? This girl knocks them cold.'

Dick and Rosemary looked at each other, wanting to be alone, but Collis failed to understand.

'I'll drop you where you're going,' he suggested. 'I'm staying at the Lutetia.'

'We'll drop you,' said Dick.

'It'll be easier for me to drop you. No trouble at all.'

'I think it will be better if we drop you.'

'But – ' began Collis; he grasped the situation at last and began discussing with Rosemary when he would see her again.

Finally, he was gone, with a shadowy unimportance but the offensive bulk of the third party. The car stopped unexpectedly, unsatisfactorily, at the address Dick had given. He drew a long breath.

'Shall we go in?'

'I don't care.' Rosemary said. 'I'll do anything you want.'

He considered.

'I almost have to go in – she wants to buy some pictures from a friend of mine who needs the money.'

Rosemary smoothed the brief expressive disarray of her hair.

'We'll stay just five minutes,' he decided. 'You're not going to like these people.'

She assumed that they were dull and stereotyped people, or gross and drunken people, or tiresome, insistent people, or any of the sorts of people that the Divers avoided. She was entirely unprepared for the impression that the scene made on her.

Chapter 17

It was a house hewn from the frame of Cardinal de Retz's palace in the Rue Monsieur, but once inside the door there was nothing of the past, nor of any present that Rosemary knew. The outer shell, the masonry, seemed rather to enclose the future so that it was an electric-like shock, a definite nervous experience, perverted as a breakfast of oatmeal and hashish, to cross that threshold, if it could be so called, into the long hall of blue steel, silver-gilt, and the myriad facets of many oddly bevelled mirrors. The effect was unlike that of any part of the Decorative Arts Exhibition – for there were people in it, not in front of it. Rosemary had the detached false-and-exalted feeling of being on a set and she guessed that everyone else present had that feeling too.

There were about thirty people, mostly women, and all fashioned by Louisa M. Alcott or Madame de Ségur; and they functioned on this set as cautiously, as precisely, as does a human hand picking up jagged broken glass. Neither individually nor as a crowd could they be said to dominate the environment, as one comes to dominate a work of art he may possess, no matter how esoteric. No one knew what this room meant because it was evolving into something else, becoming everything a room was not; to exist in it was as difficult as walking on a highly polished moving stairway, and no one could succeed at all save with the aforementioned qualities of a hand moving among broken glass – which qualities limited and defined the majority of those present.

These were of two sorts. There were the Americans and English who had been dissipating all spring and summer, so that now everything they did had a purely nervous inspiration. They were very quiet and lethargic at certain hours and then they exploded into sudden quarrels and breakdowns and seductions. The other class, who might be called the exploiters, was formed by the spongers, who were sober, serious people by comparison, with a purpose in life and no time for fooling. These kept their balance best in that environment, and what tone there was beyond the apartment's novel organisation of light values came from them.

The Frankenstein took down Dick and Rosemary at a gulp – it separated them immediately and Rosemary suddenly discovered herself to be an insincere little person, living all in the upper registers of her throat and wishing the director would come. There was however such a wild beating of wings in the room that she did not feel her position was more incongruous than anyone else's. In addition, her training told and after a series of semi-military turns, shifts, and marches she found herself presumably talking to a neat, slick girl with a lovely boy's face, but actually absorbed by a conversation taking place on a sort of gun-metal ladder diagonally opposite her and four feet away.

There was a trio of young women sitting on the bench. They were all tall and slender with small heads groomed like mannequins' heads, and as they talked the heads waved gracefully about above their dark tailored suits, rather like long-stemmed flowers and rather like cobras' hoods.

'Oh, they give a good show,' said one of them, in a deep rich voice. 'Practically the best show in Paris – I'd be the last one to deny that. But after all – ' She sighed. 'Those phrases he uses over and over – "Oldest inhabitant gnawed by rodents." You laugh once.'

'I prefer people whose lives have more corrugated surfaces,' said the second, 'and I don't like her.'

'I've never really been able to get very excited about them, or their entourage either. Why, for example, the entirely liquid Mr North?'

'He's out,' said the first girl. 'But you must admit that the party in question can be one of the most charming human beings you have ever met.'

It was the first hint Rosemary had had that they were talking about the Divers, and her body grew tense with indignation. But the girl talking to her, in the starched blue shirt with the bright blue eyes and the red cheeks and the very grey suit, a poster of a girl, had begun to play up. Desperately she kept sweeping things from between them, afraid that Rosemary couldn't see her, sweeping them away until presently there was not so much as a veil of brittle humour hiding the girl, and with distaste Rosemary saw her plain.

'Couldn't you have lunch, or maybe dinner, or lunch the day after?' begged the girl. Rosemary looked about for Dick, finding him with the hostess, to whom he had been talking since they came in. Their eyes met and he nodded slightly, and simultaneously the three cobra women noticed her; their long necks darted towards her and they fixed finely critical glances upon her. She looked back at them defiantly, acknowledging that she had heard what they said. Then she threw off her exigent vis-à-vis with a polite but clipped parting that she had just learned from Dick, and went over to join him. The hostess – she was another tall rich American girl, promenading insouciantly upon the national prosperity – was asking Dick innumerable questions about Gausse's Hôtel, whither she evidently wanted to come, and battering persistently against his reluctance. Rosemary's presence reminded her that she had been recalcitrant as a hostess and glancing about she said: 'Have you met anyone amusing, have you met Mr – ' Her eyes groped for a male who might interest Rosemary, but Dick said they must go. They left immediately, moving over the brief threshold of the future to the sudden past of the stone façade without.

'Wasn't it terrible?' he said.

'Terrible,' she echoed obediently.

'Rosemary?'

She murmured, 'What?' in an awed voice.

'I feel terribly about this.'

She was shaken with audibly painful sobs. 'Have you got a handkerchief?' she faltered. But there was little time to cry, and lovers now they fell ravenously on the quick seconds, while outside the taxi windows the green and cream twilight faded, and the fire-red, gas-blue, ghost-green signs began to shine smokily through the tranquil rain. It was nearly six, the streets were in movement, the bistros gleamed, the Place de la Concorde moved by in pink majesty as the cab turned north.

They looked at each other at last, murmuring names that were a spell. Softly the two names lingered on the air, died away more slowly than other words, other names, slower than music in the mind.

'I don't know what came over me last night,' Rosemary said. 'That glass of champagne? I've never done anything like that before.'

'You simply said you loved me.'

'I do love you – I can't change that.' It was time for Rosemary to cry, so she cried a little in her handkerchief.

'I'm afraid I'm in love with you,' said Dick, 'and that's not the best thing that could happen.'

Again the names – then they lurched together as if the taxi had swung them. Her breasts crushed flat against him, her mouth was all new and warm, owned in common. They stopped thinking with an almost painful relief, stopped seeing; they only breathed and sought each other. They were both in the grey gentle world of a mild hangover of fatigue when the nerves relax in bunches like piano strings, and crackle suddenly like wicker chairs. Nerves so raw and tender must surely join other nerves, lips to lips, breast to breast . . .

They were still in the happier stage of love. They were full of brave illusions about each other, tremendous illusions, so that the communion of self with self seemed to be on a plane where no other human relations mattered. They both seemed to have arrived there with an extraordinary innocence as though a series of pure accidents had driven them together, so many accidents that at last they were forced to conclude that they were for each other. They had arrived with clean hands, or so it seemed, after no traffic with the merely curious and clandestine.

But for Dick that portion of the road was short; the turning came before they reached the hotel.

'There's nothing to do about it,' he said, with a feeling of panic. 'I'm in love with you but it doesn't change what I said last night.'

'That doesn't matter now. I just wanted to make you love me – if you love me everything's all right.'

'Unfortunately I do. But Nicole mustn't know – she mustn't suspect even faintly. Nicole and I have got to go on together. In a way that's more important than just wanting to go on.'

'Kiss me once more.'

He kissed her, but momentarily he had left her.

'Nicole mustn't suffer – she loves me and I love her – you understand that.'

She did understand – it was the sort of thing she understood well, not hurting people. She knew the Divers loved each other because it had been her primary assumption. She had thought however that it was a rather cooled relation, and actually rather like the love of herself and her mother. When people have so much for outsiders didn't it indicate a lack of inner intensity?

'And I mean love,' he said, guessing her thoughts. 'Active love – it's more complicated than I can tell you. It was responsible for that crazy duel.'

'How did you know about the duel? I thought we were to keep it from you.'

'Do you think Abe can keep a secret?' He spoke with incisive irony. 'Tell a secret over the radio, publish it in a tabloid, but never tell it to a man who drinks more than three or four a day.'

She laughed in agreement, staying close to him.

'So you understand my relations with Nicole are complicated. She's not very strong – she looks strong but she isn't. And this makes rather a mess.'

'Oh, say that later! But kiss me now – love me now. I'll love you and never let Nicole see.'

'You darling.'

They reached the hotel and Rosemary walked a little behind him, to admire him, to adore him. His step was alert as if he had just come from some great doings and was hurrying on towards others. Organiser of private gaiety, curator of a richly incrusted happiness. His hat was a perfect hat and he carried a heavy stick and yellow gloves. She thought what a good time they would all have being with him tonight.

They walked upstairs – five flights. At the first landing they stopped and kissed; she was careful on the next landing, on the third more careful still. On the next – there were two more – she stopped halfway and kissed him fleetingly goodbye. At his urgency she walked down with him to the one below for a minute – and then up and up. Finally it was goodbye with their hands stretching to touch along the diagonal of the banister and then the fingers slipping apart. Dick went back downstairs to make some arrangements for the evening – Rosemary ran to her room and wrote a letter to her mother; she was conscience-stricken because she did not miss her mother at all.

Chapter 18

Although the Divers were honestly apathetic to organised fashion, they were nevertheless too acute to abandon its contemporaneous rhythm and beat – Dick's parties were all concerned with excitement, and a chance breath of fresh night air was the more precious for being experienced in the intervals of the excitement.

The party that night moved with the speed of a slapstick comedy. They were twelve, they were sixteen, they were quartets in separate motors bound on a quick odyssey over Paris. Everything had been foreseen. People joined them as if by magic, accompanied them as specialists, almost guides, through a phase of the evening, dropped out and were succeeded by other people, so that it appeared as if the freshness of each one had been husbanded for them all day. Rosemary appreciated how different it was from any party in Hollywood, no matter how splendid in scale. There was, among many diversions, the car of the Shah of Persia. Where Dick had commandeered this vehicle, what bribery was employed, these were facts of irrelevance. Rosemary accepted it as merely a new facet of the fabulous, which for two years had filled her life. The car had been built on a special chassis in America. Its wheels were of silver, so was the radiator. The inside of the body was inlaid with innumerable brilliants which would be replaced with true gems by the court jeweller when the car arrived in Teheran the following week. There was only one real seat in back, because the Shah must ride alone, so they took turns riding in it and sitting on the marten fur that covered the floor.

But always there was Dick. Rosemary assured the image of her mother, ever carried with her, that never, never had she known anyone so nice, so thoroughly nice as Dick was that night. She compared him with the two Englishmen, whom Abe addressed conscientiously as 'Major Hengist and Mr Horsa', and with the heir to a Scandinavian throne and the novelist just back from Russia, and with Abe, who was desperate and witty, and with Collis Clay, who joined them somewhere and stayed along – and felt there was no comparison. The enthusiasm, the selflessness behind the whole performance ravished her, the technique of moving many varied types, each as immobile, as dependent on supplies of attention as an infantry battalion is dependent on rations, appeared so effortless that he still had pieces of his own most personal self for everyone.

Afterwards she remembered the times when she had felt the happiest. The first time was when she and Dick danced together and she felt her beauty sparkling bright against his tall, strong form as they floated, hovering like people in an amusing dream – he turned her here and there with such a delicacy of suggestion that she was like a bright bouquet, a piece of precious cloth being displayed before fifty eyes. There was a moment when they were not dancing at all, simply clinging together. Some time in the early morning they were alone, and her damp powdery young body came up close to him in a crush of tired cloth, and stayed there, crushed against a background of other people's hats and wraps . . .

The time she laughed most was later, when six of them, the best of them, noblest relics of the evening, stood in the dusky front lobby of the Ritz telling the night concierge that General Pershing was outside and wanted caviare and champagne. 'He brooks no delay. Every man, every gun is at his service.' Frantic waiters emerged from nowhere, a table was set in the lobby, and Abe came in representing General Pershing while they stood up and mumbled remembered fragments of war songs at him. In the waiter's injured reaction to this anticlimax they found themselves neglected, so they built a waiter trap – a huge and fantastic device constructed of all the furniture in the lobby and functioning like one of the bizarre machines of a Goldberg cartoon. Abe shook his head doubtfully at it.

'Perhaps it would be better to steal a musical saw and – '

'That's enough,' Mary interrupted. 'When Abe begins bringing up that it's time to go home.' Anxiously she confided to Rosemary: 'I've got to get Abe home. His boat train leaves at eleven. It's so important – I feel the whole future depends on his catching it, but whenever I argue with him he does the exact opposite.'

'I'll try and persuade him,' offered Rosemary.

'Would you?' Mary said doubtfully. 'Maybe you could.'

Then Dick came up to Rosemary: 'Nicole and I are going home and we thought you'd want to go with us.'

Her face was pale with fatigue in the false dawn. Two wan dark spots in her cheek marked where the colour was by day.

'I can't,' she said. 'I promised Mary North to stay along with them – or Abe'll never go to bed. Maybe you could do something.'

'Don't you know you can't do anything about people?' he advised her. 'If Abe was my room-mate in college, tight for the first time, it'd be different. Now there's nothing to do.'

'Well, I've got to stay. He says he'll go to bed if we only come to the Halles with him,' she said, almost defiantly.

He kissed the inside of her elbow quickly.

'Don't let Rosemary go home alone,' Nicole called to Mary as they left. 'We feel responsible to her mother.'

Later Rosemary and the Norths and a manufacturer of dolls' voices from Newark and ubiquitous Collis and a big splendidly dressed oil Indian named George T. Horse-protection were riding along on top of thousands of carrots in a market wagon. The earth in the carrot beards was fragrant and sweet in the darkness, and Rosemary was so high up in the load that she could hardly see the others in the long shadow between infrequent street lamps. Their voices came from far off, as if they were having experiences different from hers, different and far away, for she was with Dick in her heart, sorry she had come with the Norths, wishing she was at the hotel and him asleep across the hall, or that he was here beside her with the warm darkness streaming down.

'Don't come up,' she called to Collis, 'the carrots will all roll.' She threw one at Abe, who was sitting beside the driver, stiffly like an old man . . .

Later she was homeward bound at last in broad daylight, with the pigeons already breaking over Saint-Sulpice. All of them began to laugh spontaneously because they knew it was still last night while the people in the streets had the delusion that it was bright hot morning.

'At last I've been on a wild party,' thought Rosemary, 'but it's no fun when Dick isn't there.'

She felt a little betrayed and sad, but presently a moving object came into sight. It was a huge horse-chestnut tree in full bloom bound for the Champs-Élysées, strapped now into a long truck and simply shaking with laughter – like a lovely person in an undignified position yet confident none the less of being lovely. Looking at it with fascination Rosemary identified herself with it, and laughed cheerfully with it, and everything all at once seemed gorgeous.

Chapter 19

Abe left from the Gare Saint-Lazare at eleven – he stood alone under the fouled glass dome, relic of the seventies, era of the Crystal Palace; his hands, of that vague grey colour that only twenty-four hours can produce, were in his coat pockets to conceal the trembling fingers. With his hat removed it was plain that only the top layer of his hair was brushed back – the lower levels were pointed resolutely sidewise. He was scarcely recognisable as the man who had swum upon Gausse's beach a fortnight ago.

He was early; he looked from left to right with his eyes only; it would have taken nervous forces out of his control to use any other part of his body. New-looking baggage went past him; presently prospective passengers, with dark little bodies, were calling: 'Jew-uls-*Hoo-oo*!' in dark piercing voices.

At the minute when he wondered whether or not he had time for a drink at the buffet, and began clutching at the soggy wad of thousand-franc notes in his pocket, one end of his pendulous glance came to rest upon the apparition of Nicole at the stairhead. He watched her – she was self-revelatory in her little expressions as people seem to someone waiting for them, who as yet is himself unobserved. She was frowning, thinking of her children, less gloating over them than merely animally counting them – a cat checking her cubs with a paw.

When she saw Abe, the mood passed out of her face; the glow of the morning skylight was sad, and Abe made a gloomy figure with dark circles that showed through the crimson tan under his eyes. They sat down on a bench.

'I came because you asked me,' said Nicole defensively. Abe seemed to have forgotten why he asked her and Nicole was quite content to look at the travellers passing by.

'That's going to be the belle of your boat – that one with all the men to say goodbye – you see why she bought that dress?' Nicole talked faster and faster. 'You see why nobody else would buy it except the belle of the world cruise? See? No? Wake up! That's a story dress – that extra material tells a story and somebody on a world cruise would be lonesome enough to want to hear it.'

She bit close her last words; she had talked too much for her; and Abe found it difficult to gather from her serious set face that she had spoken at all. With an effort he drew himself up to a posture that looked as if he were standing up while he was sitting down.

'The afternoon you took me to that funny ball – you know, St Genevieve's – ' he began.

'I remember. It was fun, wasn't it?'

'No fun for me. I haven't had fun seeing you this time. I'm tired of you both, but it doesn't show because you're even more tired of me – you know what I mean. If I had any enthusiasm, I'd go on to new people.'

There was a rough nap on Nicole's velvet gloves as she slapped him back: 'Seems rather foolish to be unpleasant, Abe. Anyhow you don't mean that. I can't see why you've given up about everything.'

Abe considered, trying hard not to cough or blow his nose.

'I suppose I got bored; and then it was such a long way to go back in order to get anywhere.'

Often a man can play the helpless child in front of a woman, but he can almost never bring it off when he feels most like a helpless child.

'No excuse for it,' Nicole said crisply.

Abe was feeling worse every minute – he could think of nothing but disagreeable and sheerly nervous remarks. Nicole thought that the correct attitude for her was to sit staring straight ahead, hands in her lap. For a while there was no communication between them – each was racing away from the other, breathing only insofar as there was blue space ahead, a sky not seen by the other. Unlike lovers, they possessed no past; unlike man and wife, they possessed no future; yet up to this morning Nicole had liked Abe better than anyone except Dick – and he had been heavy, belly-frightened, with love for her for years.

'Tired of women's worlds,' he spoke up suddenly.

'Then why don't you make a world of your own?'

'Tired of friends. The thing is to have sycophants.'

Nicole tried to force the minute hand around on the station clock, but, 'You agree?' he demanded.

'I am a woman and my business is to hold things together.'

'My business is to tear them apart.'

'When you get drunk you don't tear anything apart except yourself,' she said, cold now, and frightened and unconfident. The station was filling but no one she knew came. After a moment her eyes fell gratefully on a tall girl with straw hair like a helmet, who was dropping letters in the mail slot.

'A girl I have to speak to, Abe. Abe, wake up! You fool!'

Patiently Abe followed her with his eyes. The woman turned in a startled way to greet Nicole, and Abe recognised her as someone he had seen around Paris. He took advantage of Nicole's absence to cough hard and retchingly into his handkerchief, and to blow his nose loud. The morning was warmer and his underwear was soaked with sweat. His fingers trembled so violently that it took four matches to light a cigarette; it seemed absolutely necessary to make his way into the buffet for a drink, but immediately Nicole returned.

'That was a mistake,' she said with frosty humour. 'After begging me to come and see her, she gave me a good snubbing. She looked at me as if I were rotted.' Excited she did a little laugh, as with two fingers high in the scales. 'Let people come to you.'

Abe recovered from a cigarette cough and remarked: 'Trouble is when you're sober you don't want to see anybody, and when you're tight nobody wants to see you.'

'Who, me?' Nicole laughed again, for some reason the late encounter had cheered her.

'No – me.'

'Speak for yourself. I like people, a lot of people – I like – '

Rosemary and Mary North came in sight, walking slowly and searching for Abe, and Nicole burst forth grossly with 'Hey! Hi! Hey!' and laughed and waved the package of handkerchiefs she had bought for Abe.

They stood in an uncomfortable little group weighted down by Abe's gigantic presence: he lay athwart them like the wreck of a galleon, dominating with his presence his own weakness and self-indulgence, his narrowness and bitterness. All of them were conscious of the solemn dignity that flowed from him, of his achievement, fragmentary, suggestive and surpassed. But they were frightened at his survivant will, once a will to live, now become a will to die.

Dick Diver came and brought with him a fine glowing surface on which the three women sprang like monkeys with cries of relief, perching on his shoulders, on the beautiful crown of his hat or the gold head of his cane. Now, for a moment, they could disregard the spectacle of Abe's gigantic obscenity. Dick saw the situation quickly and grasped it quietly. He pulled them out of themselves into the station, making plain its wonders. Nearby, some Americans were saying goodbye in voices that mimicked the cadence of water running into a large old bathtub. Standing in the station, with Paris in back of them, it seemed as if they were vicariously leaning a little over the ocean, already undergoing a sea-change, a shifting about of atoms to form the essential molecule of a new people.

So the well-to-do Americans poured through the station on to the platforms with frank new faces, intelligent, considerate, thoughtless, thought-for. An occasional English face among them seemed sharp and emergent. When there were enough Americans on the platform the first impression of their immaculacy and their money began to fade into a vague racial dusk that hindered and blinded both them and their observers.

Nicole seized Dick's arm crying, 'Look!' Dick turned in time to see what took place in half a minute. At a Pullman entrance two cars off, a vivid scene detached itself from the tenor of many farewells. The young woman with the helmet-like hair to whom Nicole had spoken made an odd dodging little run away from the man to whom she was talking and plunged a frantic hand into her purse; then the sound of two revolver shots cracked the narrow air of the platform. Simultaneously the engine whistled sharply and the train began to move, momentarily dwarfing the shots in significance. Abe waved again from his window, oblivious to what had happened. But before the crowd closed in, the others had seen the shots take effect, seen the target sit down upon the platform.

Only after a hundred years did the train stop; Nicole, Mary, and Rosemary waited on the outskirts while Dick fought his way through. It was five minutes before he found them again – by this time the crowd had split into two sections, following, respectively, the man on a stretcher and the girl walking pale and firm between distraught gendarmes.

'It was Maria Wallis,' Dick said hurriedly. 'The man she shot was an Englishman – they had an awful time finding out who, because she shot him through his identification card.' They were walking quickly from the train, swayed along with the crowd. 'I found out what *poste de police* they're taking her to so I'll go there – '

'But her sister lives in Paris,' Nicole objected. 'Why not phone her? Seems very peculiar nobody thought of that. She's married to a Frenchman, and he can do more than we can.'

Dick hesitated, shook his head and started off.

'Wait!' Nicole cried after him. 'That's foolish – how can you do any good – with your French?'

'At least I'll see they don't do anything outrageous to her.'

'They're certainly going to hold on to her,' Nicole assured him briskly. 'She *did* shoot the man. The best thing is to phone right away to Laura – she can do more than we can.'

Dick was unconvinced – also he was showing off for Rosemary.

'You wait,' said Nicole firmly, and hurried off to a telephone booth.

'When Nicole takes things into her hands,' he said with affectionate irony, 'there is nothing more to be done.'

He saw Rosemary for the first time that morning. They exchanged glances, trying to recognise the emotions of the day before. For a moment each seemed unreal to the other – then the slow warm hum of love began again.

'You like to help everybody, don't you?' Rosemary said.

'I only pretend to.'

'Mother likes to help everybody – of course she can't help as many people as you do.' She sighed. 'Sometimes I think I'm the most selfish person in the world.'

For the first time the mention of her mother annoyed rather than amused Dick. He wanted to sweep away her mother, remove the whole affair from the nursery footing upon which Rosemary persistently established it. But he realised that this impulse was a loss of control – what would become of Rosemary's urge towards him if, for even a moment, he relaxed. He saw, not without panic, that the affair was sliding to rest; it could not stand still, it must go on or go back; for the first time it occurred to him that Rosemary had her hand on the lever more authoritatively than he.

Before he had thought out a course of procedure, Nicole returned. 'I found Laura. It was the first news she had and her voice kept fading away and then getting loud again – as if she was fainting and then pulling herself together. She said she knew something was going to happen this morning.'

'Maria ought to be with Diaghilev,' said Dick in a gentle tone, in order to bring them back to quietude. 'She has a nice sense of décor – not to say rhythm. Will any of us ever see a train out without hearing a few shots?'

They bumped down the wide steel steps. 'I'm sorry for the poor man,' Nicole said. 'Course that's why she talked so strange to me – she was getting ready to open fire.'

She laughed, Rosemary laughed too, but they were both horrified, and both of them deeply wanted Dick to make a moral comment on the matter and not leave it to them. This wish was not entirely conscious, especially on the part of Rosemary, who was accustomed to having shell fragments of such events shriek past her head. But a totality of shock had piled up in her too. For the moment, Dick was too shaken by the impetus of his newly recognised emotion to resolve things into the pattern of the holiday, so the women, missing something, lapsed into a vague unhappiness.

Then, as if nothing had happened, the lives of the Divers and their friends flowed out into the street.

However, everything had happened – Abe's departure and Mary's impending departure for Salzburg this afternoon had ended the time in Paris. Or perhaps the shots, the concussions that had finished God knew what dark matter, had terminated it. The shots had entered into all their lives: echoes of violence followed them out on to the pavement where two porters held a post-mortem beside them as they waited for a taxi.

'Tu as vu le revolver? Il était très petit, vrai perle – *un jouet*.'

'Mais assez puissant!' said the other porter sagely. 'Tu as vu sa chemise? Assez de sang pour se croire à la guerre.'

Chapter 20

In the square, as they came out, a suspended mass of gasoline exhaust cooked slowly in the July sun. It was a terrible thing – unlike pure heat it held no promise of rural escape but suggested only roads choked with the same foul asthma. During their luncheon, outdoors, across from the Luxembourg Gardens, Rosemary had cramps and felt fretful and full of impatient lassitude – it was the foretaste of this that had inspired her self-accusation of selfishness in the station.

Dick had no suspicion of the sharpness of the change; he was profoundly unhappy and the subsequent increase of egotism tended momentarily to blind him to what was going on round about him, and deprive him of the long ground-swell of imagination that he counted on for his judgements.

After Mary North left them, accompanied by the Italian singing teacher who had joined them for coffee and was taking her to her train, Rosemary, too, stood up, bound for an engagement at her studio: 'meet some officials.'

'And oh – ' she proposed ' – if Collis Clay, that Southern boy – if he comes while you are still sitting here, just tell him I couldn't wait; tell him to call me tomorrow.'

Too insouciant, in reaction from the late disturbance, she had assumed the privileges of a child – the result being to remind the Divers of their exclusive love for their own children; Rosemary was sharply rebuked in a short passage between the women: 'You'd better leave the message with a waiter,' Nicole's voice was stern and unmodulated, 'we're leaving immediately.'

Rosemary got it, took it without resentment.

'I'll let it go then. Goodbye, you darlings.'

Dick asked for the check; the Divers relaxed, chewing tentatively on toothpicks.

'Well – ' they said together.

He saw a flash of unhappiness on her mouth, so brief that only he would have noticed, and he could pretend not to have seen. What did Nicole think? Rosemary was one of a dozen people he had 'worked over' in the past years: these had included a French circus clown, Abe and Mary North, a pair of dancers, a writer, a painter, a comedienne from the Grand Guignol, a half-crazy pederast from the Russian

Ballet, a promising tenor they had staked to a year in Milan. Nicole well knew how seriously those people interpreted his interest and enthusiasm; but she realised also that, except while their children were being born, Dick had not spent a night apart from her since their marriage. On the other hand, there was a pleasingness about him that simply had to be used – those who possessed that pleasingness had to keep their hands in, and go along attaching people that they had no use to make of.

Now Dick hardened himself and let minutes pass without making any gestures of confidence, any representation of constantly renewed surprise that they were one together.

Collis Clay out of the South edged a passage between the closely packed tables and greeted the Divers cavalierly. Such salutations always astonished Dick – acquaintances saying 'Hi!' to them, or speaking only to one of them. He felt so intensely about people that in moments of apathy he preferred to remain concealed; that one could parade a casualness into his presence was a challenge to the key on which he lived.

Collis, unaware that he was without a wedding garment, heralded his arrival with: 'I reckon I'm late – the beyed has flown.' Dick had to wrench something out of himself before he could forgive him for not having first complimented Nicole.

She left almost immediately and he sat with Collis, finishing the last of his wine. He rather like Collis – he was 'post-war'; less difficult than most of the Southerners he had known at New Haven a decade previously. Dick listened with amusement to the conversation that accompanied the slow, profound stuffing of a pipe. In the early afternoon children and nurses were trekking into the Luxembourg Gardens; it was the first time in months that Dick had let this part of the day out of his hands.

Suddenly his blood ran cold as he realised the content of Collis's confidential monologue.

' – she's not so cold as you'd probably think. I admit I thought she was cold for a long time. But she got into a jam with a friend of mine going from New York to Chicago at Easter – a boy named Hillis she thought was pretty nutsey at New Haven – she had a compartment with a cousin of mine but she and Hillis wanted to be alone, so in the afternoon my cousin came and played cards in our compartment. Well, after about two hours we went back and there was Rosemary and Bill Hillis standing in the vestibule arguing with the conductor – Rosemary white as a sheet. Seems they locked the door and pulled down the blinds and I guess there was some heavy stuff going on when the conductor came for the tickets and knocked on the door. They thought it was us kidding them and wouldn't let him in at first, and when they did, he was plenty sore. He asked Hillis if that was his compartment and whether he and Rosemary were married that they locked the door, and Hillis lost his temper trying to explain there was nothing wrong. He said the conductor had insulted Rosemary and he wanted him to fight, but that conductor could have made trouble – and believe me I had an awful time smoothing it over.'

With every detail imagined, with even envy for the pair's community of misfortune in the vestibule, Dick felt a change taking place within him. Only the image of a third person, even a vanished one, entering into his relation with Rosemary was needed to throw him off his balance and send through him waves of pain, misery, desires, desperation. The vividly pictured hand on Rosemary's cheek, the quicker breath, the white excitement of the event viewed from outside, the inviolable secret warmth within.

– Do you mind if I pull down the curtain?

– Please do. It's too light in here.

Collis Clay was now speaking about fraternity politics at New Haven, in the same tone, with the same emphasis. Dick had gathered that he was in love with Rosemary in some curious way Dick could not have understood. The affair with Hillis seemed to have made no emotional impression on Collis save to give him a joyful conviction that Rosemary was 'human'.

'Bones got a wonderful crowd,' he said. 'We all did, as a matter of fact. New Haven's so big now the sad thing is the men we have to leave out.'

– Do you mind if I pull down the curtain?

– Please do. It's too light in here.

. . . Dick went over Paris to his bank. Writing a cheque, he looked along the row of men at the desks deciding to which one he would present it for an OK. As he wrote he engrossed himself in the material act, examining meticulously the pen, writing laboriously upon the high glass-topped desk. Once he raised glazed eyes to look towards the mail department, then glazed his spirit again by concentration upon the objects he dealt with.

Still he failed to decide to whom the cheque should be presented, which man in the line would guess least of the unhappy predicament in which he found himself and, also, which one would be least likely to talk. There was Perrin, the suave New Yorker, who had asked him to luncheons at the American Club, there was Casasus, the Spaniard, with whom he usually discussed a mutual friend in spite of the fact that the friend had passed out of his life a dozen years before; there was Muchhause, who always asked him whether he wanted to draw upon his wife's money or his own.

As he entered the amount on the stub, and drew two lines under it, he decided to go to Pierce, who was young and for whom he would have to put on only a small show. It was often easier to give a show than to watch one.

He went to the mail desk first – as the woman who served him pushed up with her bosom a piece of paper that had nearly escaped the desk, he thought how differently women use their bodies from men. He took his letters aside to open. There was a bill for seventeen psychiatric books from a German concern, a bill from Brentano's, a letter from Buffalo from his father, in a handwriting that year by year became more indecipherable; there was a card from Tommy Barban postmarked Fez and bearing a facetious communication; there were letters from doctors in Zurich, both in German; a disputed bill from a plasterer in Cannes; a bill from a furniture maker; a letter from the publisher of a medical journal in Baltimore, miscellaneous announcements, and an invitation to a showing of pictures by an incipient artist; also there were three letters for Nicole, and a letter for Rosemary sent in his care.

– Do you mind if I pull down the curtain?

He went towards Pierce but he was engaged with a woman, and Dick saw with his heels that he would have to present his cheque to Casasus at the next desk, who was free.

'How are you, Diver?' Casasus was genial. He stood up, his moustache spreading with his smile. 'We were talking about Featherstone the other day and I thought of you – he's out in California now.'

Dick widened his eyes and bent forward a little.

'In Cali*for*nia?'

'That's what I heard.'

Dick held the cheque poised; to focus the attention of Casasus upon it he looked towards Pierce's desk, holding the latter for a moment in a friendly eye-play conditioned by an old joke of three years before when Pierce had been involved with a Lithuanian countess. Pierce played up with a grin until Casasus had authorised the cheque and had no further recourse to detain Dick, whom he liked, than to stand up holding his pince-nez and repeat, 'Yes, he's in California.'

Meanwhile Dick had seen that Perrin, at the head of the line of desks, was in conversation with the heavyweight champion of the world; from a sidesweep of Perrin's eye Dick saw that he was considering calling him over and introducing him, but that he finally decided against it.

Cutting across the social mood of Casasus with the intensity he had accumulated at the glass desk – which is to say he looked hard at the cheque, studying it, and then fixed his eyes on grave problems beyond the first marble pillar to the right of the banker's head and made a business of shifting the cane, hat, and letters he carried – he said goodbye and went out. He had long ago purchased the doorman; his taxi sprang to the curb.

'I want to go to the Films Par Excellence Studio – it's on a little street in Passy. Go to the Muette. I'll direct you from there.'

He was rendered so uncertain by the events of the last forty-eight hours that he was not even sure of what he wanted to do; he paid off the taxi at the Muette and walked, in the direction of the studio, crossing to the opposite side of the street before he came to the building. Dignified in his fine clothes, with their fine accessories, he was yet swayed and driven as an animal. Dignity could come only with an overthrowing of his past, of the effort of the last six years. He went briskly around the block with the fatuousness of one of Tarkington's adolescents, hurrying at the blind places lest he miss Rosemary's coming out of the studio. It was a melancholy neighbourhood. Next door to the place he saw a sign: '1000 Chemises'. The shirts filled the window, piled, cravated, stuffed, or draped with shoddy grace on the showcase floor: '1000 Chemises' – count them! on either side he read: 'Papeterie', 'Pâtisserie', 'Solde', 'Réclame' – and Constance Talmadge in 'Déjeuner de Soleil', and farther away there were more sombre announcements: 'Vêtements Ecclésiastiques', 'Déclaration de Décès' and 'Pompes Funèbres'. Life and death.

He knew that what he was now doing marked a turning point in his life – it was out of line with everything that had preceded it – even out of line with what effect he might hope to produce upon Rosemary. Rosemary saw him always as a model of correctness – his presence walking around this block was an intrusion. But Dick's necessity of behaving as he did was a projection of some submerged reality: he was compelled to walk there, or stand there, his shirt-sleeve fitting his wrist and his coat sleeve encasing his shirt-sleeve like a sleeve valve, his collar moulded plastically to his neck, his red hair cut exactly, his hand holding his briefcase like a dandy – just as another man once found it necessary to stand in front of a church in Ferrara, in sackcloth and ashes. Dick was paying some tribute to things unforgotten, unshriven, unexpurgated.

Chapter 21

After three-quarters of an hour of standing around, he became suddenly involved in a human contact. It was just the sort of thing that was likely to happen to him when he was in the mood of not wanting to see anyone. So rigidly did he sometimes guard his exposed self-consciousness that frequently he defeated his own purposes; as an actor who underplays a part sets up a craning forward, a stimulated emotional attention in an audience, and seems to create in others an ability to bridge the gap he has left open. Similarly we are seldom sorry for those who need and crave our pity – we reserve this for those who, by other means, make us exercise the abstract function of pity.

So Dick might, himself, have analysed the incident that ensued. As he paced the Rue des Saints-Anges he was spoken to by a thin-faced American, perhaps thirty, with an air of being scarred and a slight but sinister smile. As Dick gave him the light he requested, he placed him as one of a type of which he had been conscious since early youth – a type that loafed about tobacco stores with one elbow on the counter and watched, through heaven knew what small chink of the mind, the people who came in and out. Intimate to garages, where he had vague business conducted in undertones, to barbershops, to the lobbies of theatres – in such places, at any rate, Dick placed him. Sometimes the face bobbed up in one of Tad's more savage cartoons – in boyhood Dick had often thrown an uneasy glance at the dim borderland of crime on which he stood.

'How do you like Paris, Buddy?'

Not waiting for an answer the man tried to fit in his footsteps with Dick's: 'Where you from?' he asked encouragingly.

'From Buffalo.'

'I'm from San Antone – but I been over here since the war.'

'You in the army?'

'*I'll* say I was. Eighty-fourth Division – ever heard of that outfit?'

The man walked a little ahead of him and fixed him with eyes that were practically menacing.

'Staying in Paris awhile, Buddy? or just passing through.'

'Passing through.'

'What hotel you staying at?'

Dick had begun laughing to himself – the party had the intention of rifling his room that night. His thoughts were read apparently without self-consciousness.

'With a build like yours you oughtn't to be afraid of me, Buddy. There's a lot of bums around just laying for American tourists, but you needn't be afraid of me.'

Becoming bored, Dick stopped walking: 'I just wonder why you've got so much time to waste.'

'I'm in business here in Paris.'

'In what line?'

'Selling papers.'

The contrast between the formidable manner and the mild profession was absurd – but the man amended it with: 'Don't worry; I made plenty money last year – ten or twenty francs for a *Sunny Times* that cost six.'

He produced a newspaper clipping from a rusty wallet and passed it over to one who had become a fellow stroller – the cartoon showed a stream of Americans pouring from the gangplank of a liner freighted with gold.

'Two hundred thousand – spending ten million a summer.'

'What you doing out here in Passy?'

His companion looked around cautiously. 'Movies,' he said darkly. 'They got an American studio over there. And they need guys can speak English. I'm waiting for a break.'

Dick shook him off quickly and firmly.

It had become apparent that Rosemary either had escaped on one of his early circuits of the block or else had left before he came into the neighbourhood; he went into the bistro on the corner, bought a lead disc and, squeezed in an alcove between the kitchen and the foul toilet, he called the Roi George. He recognised Cheyne-Stokes tendencies in his respiration – but like everything the symptom served only to turn him in towards his emotion. He gave the number of the hotel; then stood holding the phone and staring into the café; after a long while a strange little voice said hello.

'This is Dick – I had to call you.'

A pause from her – then bravely, and in key with his emotion: 'I'm glad you did.'

'I came to meet you at your studio – I'm out in Passy across the way from it. I thought maybe we'd ride around through the Bois.'

'Oh, I only stayed there a minute! I'm so sorry.' A silence.

'Rosemary.'

'Yes, Dick.'

'Look, I'm in an extraordinary condition about you. When a child can disturb a middle-aged gent – things get difficult.'

'You're not middle-aged, Dick – you're the youngest person in the world.'

'Rosemary?' Silence while he stared at a shelf that held the humbler poisons of France – bottles of Otard, Rhum St James, Marie Brizard, Punch orangeade, André Fernet Blanca, Cherry Rocher, and Armagnac.

'Are you alone?'

– Do you mind if I pull down the curtain?

'Who do you think I'd be with?'

'That's the state I'm in. I'd like to be with you now.'

Silence, then a sigh and an answer. 'I wish you were with me now.'

There was the hotel room where she lay behind a telephone number, and little gusts of music wailed around her –

And two – for tea.
And me for you,
And you for me
Alow-own.

There was the remembered dust of powder over her tan – when he kissed her face it was damp around the corners of her hair; there was the flash of a white face under his own, the arc of a shoulder.

'It's impossible,' he said to himself. In a minute he was out in the street marching along towards the Muette, or away from it, his small briefcase still in his hand, his gold-headed stick held at a sword-like angle.

Rosemary returned to her desk and finished a letter to her mother.

' – I only saw him for a little while but I thought he was wonderful looking. I fell in love with him (of course I Do Love Dick Best but you know what I mean). He really is going to direct the picture and is leaving immediately for Hollywood, and I think we ought to leave, too. Collis Clay has been here. I like him all right but have not seen much of him because of the Divers, who really are divine, about the

Nicest People I ever Knew. I am feeling not very well today and am taking the Medicine, though see No need for it. I'm not even Going to Try to tell you All that's Happened until I see You!!! So when you get this letter *wire, wire, wire!* Are you coming north or shall I come south with the Divers?'

At six Dick called Nicole.

'Have you any special plans?' he asked. 'Would you like to do something quiet – dinner at the hotel and then a play?'

'Would you? I'll do whatever you want. I phoned Rosemary a while ago and she's having dinner in her room. I think this upset all of us, don't you?'

'It didn't upset me,' he objected. 'Darling, unless you're physically tired let's do something. Otherwise we'll get south and spend a week wondering why we didn't see Boucher. It's better than brooding – '

That was a blunder and Nicole took him up sharply.

'Brooding about what?'

'About Maria Wallis.'

She agreed to go to a play. It was a tradition between them that they should never be too tired for anything, and they found it made the days better on the whole and put the evenings more in order. When, inevitably, their spirits flagged they shifted the blame to the weariness and fatigue of others. Before they went out, as fine-looking a couple as could be found in Paris, they knocked softly at Rosemary's door. There was no answer; judging that she was asleep they walked into a warm strident Paris night, snatching a vermouth and bitters in the shadow by Fouquet's bar.

Chapter 22

Nicole awoke late, murmuring something back into her dream before she parted her long lashes tangled with sleep. Dick's bed was empty – only after a minute did she realise that she had been awakened by a knock at their salon door.

'*Entrez!*' she called, but there was no answer, and after a moment she slipped on a dressing-gown and went to open it. A *sergent de ville* confronted her courteously and stepped inside the door.

'Mr Afghan North – he is here?'

'What? No – he's gone to America.'

'When did he leave, madame?'

'Yesterday morning.'

He shook his head and waved his forefinger at her in a quicker rhythm.

'He was in Paris last night. He is registered here but his room is not occupied. They told me I had better ask at this room.'

'Sounds very peculiar to me – we saw him off yesterday morning on the boat train.'

'Be that as it may, he has been seen here this morning. Even his *carte d'identité* has been seen. And there you are.'

'We know nothing about it,' she proclaimed in amazement.

He considered. He was an ill-smelling, handsome man.

'You were not with him at all last night?'

'But no.'

'We have arrested a Negro. We are convinced we have at last arrested the correct Negro.'

'I assure you that I haven't an idea what you're talking about. If it's the Mr Abraham North, the one we know, well, if he was in Paris last night we weren't aware of it.'

The man nodded, sucked his upper lip, convinced but disappointed.

'What happened?' Nicole demanded.

He showed his palms, puffing out his closed mouth. He had begun to find her attractive and his eyes flickered at her.

'What do you wish, madame? A summer affair. Mr Afghan North was robbed and he made a complaint. We have arrested the miscreant. Mr Afghan should come to identify him and make the proper charges.'

Nicole pulled her dressing-gown closer around her and dismissed him briskly. Mystified she took a bath and dressed. By this time it was after ten and she called Rosemary but got no answer – then she phoned the hotel office and found that Abe had indeed registered, at six-thirty this morning. His room, however, was still unoccupied. Hoping for a word from Dick she waited in the parlour of the suite; just as she had given up and decided to go out, the office called and announced: 'Meestaire Crawshow, *un nègre*.'

'On what business?' she demanded.

'He says he knows you and the doctaire. He says there is a Meestaire Freeman into prison that is a friend of all the world. He says there is injustice and he wishes to see Meestaire North before he himself is arrested.'

'We know nothing about it.' Nicole disclaimed the whole business with a vehement clap on the receiver. Abe's bizarre reappearance made it plain to her how fatigued she was with his dissipation. Dismissing him from her mind she went out, ran into Rosemary at the dressmaker's, and shopped with her for artificial flowers and all-coloured strings of coloured beads on the Rue de Rivoli. She helped Rosemary choose a diamond for her mother, and some scarfs and novel cigarette cases to take home to business associates in California. For her son she bought Greek and Roman soldiers, a whole army of them, costing over a thousand francs. Once again they spent their money in different ways, and again Rosemary admired Nicole's method of spending. Nicole was sure that the money she spent was hers – Rosemary still thought her money was miraculously lent to her and she must consequently be very careful of it.

It was fun spending money in the sunlight of the foreign city, with healthy bodies under them that sent streams of colour up to their faces; with arms and hands, legs and ankles that they stretched out confidently, reaching or stepping with the confidence of women lovely to men.

When they got back to the hotel and found Dick, all bright and new in the morning, both of them had a moment of complete childish joy.

He had just received a garbled telephone call from Abe, who, so it appeared, had spent the forenoon in hiding.

'It was one of the most extraordinary telephone conversations I've ever held.'

Dick had talked not only to Abe but to a dozen others. On the phone these supernumeraries had been typically introduced as: ' – man wants to talk to you is in the teput dome, well he says he was in it – what is it?

'Hey, somebody, shut up – anyhow, he was in some shandel-scandal and he kaa *poss*ibly go home. My own *per*sonal is that – my personal is he's had a – ' Gulps sounded and thereafter what the party had, rested with the unknown.

The phone yielded up a supplementary offer: 'I thought it would appeal to you anyhow as a psychologist.' The vague personality who corresponded to this statement was eventually hung on to the phone; in the sequence he failed to appeal to Dick, as a psychologist, or indeed as anything else. Abe's conversation flowed on as follows: 'Hello.'

'Well?'

'Well, hello.'

'Who are you?'

'Well.' There were interpolated snorts of laughter.

'Well, I'll put somebody else on the line.'

Sometimes Dick could hear Abe's voice, accompanied by scufflings, droppings of the receiver, far-away fragments such as, 'No, I don't, Mr North . . . ' Then a pert decided voice had said: 'If you are a friend of Mr North you will come down and take him away.'

Abe cut in, solemn and ponderous, beating it all down with an overtone of earth-bound determination.

'Dick, I've launched a race riot in Montmartre. I'm going over and get Freeman out of jail. If a Negro from Copenhagen that makes shoe polish – hello, can you hear me – well, look, if anybody comes there – ' once again the receiver was a chorus of innumerable melodies.

'Why are you back in Paris?' Dick demanded.

'I got as far as Evreux, and I decided to take a plane back so I could compare it with St Sulpice. I mean I don't intend to bring St Sulpice back to Paris. I don't even mean Baroque! I mean St Germain. For God's sake, wait a minute and I'll put the *chasseur* on the wire.'

'For God's sake, don't.'

'Listen – did Mary get off all right?'

'Yes.'

'Dick, I want you to talk with a man I met here this morning, the son of a naval officer that's been to every doctor in Europe. Let me tell you about him – '

Dick had rung off at this point – perhaps that was a piece of ingratitude, for he needed grist for the grinding activity of his mind.

'Abe used to be so nice,' Nicole told Rosemary. 'So nice. Long ago – when Dick and I were first married. If you had known him then. He'd come to stay with us for weeks and weeks and we scarcely knew he was in the house. Sometimes he'd play – sometimes he'd be in the library with a muted piano, making love to it by the hour – Dick, do you remember that maid? She thought he was a ghost and sometimes Abe used to meet her in the hall and moo at her, and it cost us a whole tea service once – but we didn't care.'

So much fun – so long ago. Rosemary envied them their fun, imagining a life of leisure unlike her own. She knew little of leisure but she had the respect for it of those who have never had it. She thought of it as a resting, without realising that the Divers were as far from relaxing as she was herself.

'What did this to him?' she asked. 'Why does he have to drink?'

Nicole shook her head right and left, disclaiming responsibility for the matter: 'So many smart men go to pieces nowadays.'

'And when haven't they?' Dick asked. 'Smart men play close to the line because they have to – some of them can't stand it, so they quit.'

'It must lie deeper than that.' Nicole clung to her conversation; also she was irritated that Dick should contradict her before Rosemary. 'Artists like – well, like Fernand don't seem to have to wallow in alcohol. Why is it just Americans who dissipate?'

There were so many answers to this question that Dick decided to leave it in the air, to buzz victoriously in Nicole's ears. He had become intensely critical of her. Though he thought she was the most attractive human creature he had ever seen, though he got from her everything he needed, he scented battle from afar, and subconsciously he had been hardening and arming himself, hour by hour. He was not given to self-indulgence and he felt comparatively graceless at this moment of indulging himself, blinding his eyes with the hope that Nicole guessed at only an emotional excitement about Rosemary. He was not sure – last night at the theatre she had referred pointedly to Rosemary as a child.

The trio lunched downstairs in an atmosphere of carpets and padded waiters, who did not march at the stomping quickstep of those men who brought good food to the tables whereon they had recently dined. Here there were families of Americans staring around at families of Americans, and trying to make conversation with one another.

There was a party at the next table that they could not account for. It consisted of an expansive, somewhat secretarial, would-you-mind-repeating young man, and a score of women. The women were neither young nor old nor of any particular social class; yet the party gave the impression of a unit, held more closely together for example than a group of wives stalling through a professional congress of their husbands. Certainly it was more of a unit than any conceivable tourist party.

An instinct made Dick suck back the grave derision that formed on his tongue; he asked the waiter to find out who they were.

'Those are the gold-star muzzers,' explained the waiter.

Aloud and in low voices they exclaimed. Rosemary's eyes filled with tears.

'Probably the young ones are the wives,' said Nicole.

Over his wine Dick looked at them again; in their happy faces, the dignity that surrounded and pervaded the party, he perceived all the maturity of an older America. For a while the sobered women who had come to mourn for their dead, for something they could not repair, made the room beautiful. Momentarily, he sat again on his father's knee, riding with Mosby while the old loyalties and devotions fought on around him. Almost with an effort he turned back to his two women at the table and faced the whole new world in which he believed.

– Do you mind if I pull down the curtain?

Chapter 23

Abe North was still in the Ritz bar, where he had been since nine in the morning. When he arrived seeking sanctuary the windows were open and great beams were busy at pulling up the dust from smoky carpets and cushions. *Chasseurs* tore through the corridors, liberated and disembodied, moving for the moment in pure space. The sit-down bar for women, across from the bar proper, seemed very small – it was hard to imagine what throngs it could accommodate in the afternoon.

The famous Paul, the concessionaire, had not arrived, but Claude, who was checking stock, broke off his work with no improper surprise to make Abe a pick-me-up. Abe sat on a bench against a wall. After two drinks he began to feel better – so much better that he mounted to the barbershop and was shaved. When he returned to the bar Paul had arrived – in his custom-built motor, from which he had disembarked correctly at the Boulevard des Capucines. Paul liked Abe and came over to talk.

'I was supposed to ship home this morning,' Abe said. 'I mean yesterday morning, or whatever this is.'

'Why din you?' asked Paul.

Abe considered, and happened finally to a reason: 'I was reading a serial in *Liberty* and the next instalment was due here in Paris – so if I'd sailed I'd have missed it – then I never would have read it.'

'It must be a very good story.'

'It's a terr-r-rible story.'

Paul arose chuckling and paused, leaning on the back of a chair: 'If you really want to get off, Mr North, there are friends of yours going tomorrow on the *France* – Mister what is his name – and Slim Pearson. Mister – I'll think of it – tall with a new beard.'

'Yardly,' Abe supplied.

'Mr Yardly. They're both going on the *France*.'

He was on his way to his duties but Abe tried to detain him: 'If I didn't have to go by way of Cherbourg. The baggage went that way.'

'Get your baggage in New York,' said Paul, receding.

The logic of the suggestion fitted gradually into Abe's pitch – he grew rather enthusiastic about being cared for, or rather of prolonging his state of irresponsibility.

Other clients had meanwhile drifted into the bar: first came a huge Dane whom Abe had somewhere encountered. The Dane took a seat across the room, and Abe guessed he would be there all the day, drinking, lunching, talking or reading newspapers. He felt a desire to outstay him. At eleven the college boys began to step in, stepping gingerly lest they tear one another bag from bag. It was about then he had the *chasseur* telephone to the Divers; by the time he was in touch with them he was in touch also with other friends – and his hunch was to put them all on different phones at once – the result was somewhat general. From time to time his mind reverted to the fact that he ought to go over and get Freeman out of jail, but he shook off all facts as parts of the nightmare.

By one o'clock the bar was jammed; amidst the consequent mixture of voices the staff of waiters functioned, pinning down their clients to the facts of drink and money.

'That makes two stingers . . . and one more . . . two martinis and one . . . nothing for you, Mr Quarterly . . . that makes three rounds. That makes seventy-five francs, Mr Quarterly. Mr Schaeffer said he had this – you had the last . . . I can only do what you say . . . thanks veramuch.'

In the confusion Abe had lost his seat; now he stood gently swaying and talking to some of the people with whom he had involved himself. A terrier ran a leash around his legs but Abe managed to extricate himself without upsetting and became the recipient of profuse apologies. Presently he was invited to lunch, but declined. It was almost Briglith, he explained, and there was something he had to do at Briglith. A little later, with the exquisite manners of the alcoholic that are like the manners of a prisoner or a family servant, he said goodbye to an acquaintance, and turning around discovered that the bar's great moment was over as precipitately as it had begun.

Across from him the Dane and his companions had ordered luncheon. Abe did likewise but scarcely touched it. Afterwards, he just sat, happy to live in the past. The drink made past happy things contemporary with the present, as if they were still going on, contemporary even with the future as if they were about to happen again.

At four the *chasseur* approached him: 'You wish to see a coloured fellow of the name Jules Peterson?'

'God! How did he find me?'

'I didn't tell him you were present.'

'Who did?' Abe fell over his glasses but recovered himself.

'Says he's already been around to all the American bars and hotels.'

'Tell him I'm not here – ' As the *chasseur* turned away Abe asked: 'Can he come in here?'

'I'll find out.'

Receiving the question Paul glanced over his shoulder; he shook his head, then seeing Abe he came over.

'I'm sorry; I can't allow it.'

Abe got himself up with an effort and went out to the Rue Cambon.

Chapter 24

With his miniature leather briefcase in his hand Richard Diver walked from the seventh *arrondissement* – where he left a note for Maria Wallis signed 'Dicole', the word with which he and Nicole had signed communications in the first days of love – to his shirt-makers where the clerks made a fuss over him out of proportion to the money he spent. Ashamed at promising so much to these poor Englishmen, with his fine manners, his air of having the key to security, ashamed of making a tailor shift an inch of silk on his arm. Afterwards he went to the bar of the Crillon and drank a small coffee and two fingers of gin.

As he entered the hotel the halls had seemed unnaturally bright; when he left he realised that it was because it had already turned dark outside. It was a windy four-o'clock night with the leaves on the Champs-Élysées singing and falling, thin and wild. Dick turned down the Rue de Rivoli, walking two squares under the arcades to his bank where there was mail. Then he took a taxi and started up the Champs-Élysées through the first patter of rain, sitting alone with his love.

Back at two o'clock in the Roi George corridor the beauty of Nicole had been to the beauty of Rosemary as the beauty of Leonardo's girl was to that of the girl of an illustrator. Dick moved on through the rain, demoniac and frightened, the passions of many men inside him and nothing simple that he could see.

Rosemary opened her door full of emotions no one else knew of. She was now what is sometimes called a 'little wild thing' – by twenty-four full hours she was not yet unified and she was absorbed in playing around with chaos; as if her destiny were a picture puzzle – counting benefits, counting hopes, telling off Dick, Nicole, her mother, the director she met yesterday, like stops on a string of beads.

When Dick knocked she had just dressed and had been watching the rain, thinking of some poem, and of full gutters in Beverly Hills. When she opened the door she saw him as something fixed and godlike as he had always been, as older people are to younger, rigid and unmalleable. Dick saw her with an inevitable sense of disappointment. It took him a moment to respond to the unguarded sweetness of her smile, her body calculated to a millimetre to suggest a bud yet guarantee a flower. He was conscious of the print of her wet foot on a rug through the bathroom door.

'Miss Television,' he said with a lightness he did not feel. He put his gloves, his briefcase on the dressing-table, his stick against the wall. His chin dominated the lines of pain around his mouth, forcing them up into his forehead and the corner of his eyes, like fear that cannot be shown in public.

'Come and sit on my lap close to me,' he said softly, 'and let me see about your lovely mouth.'

She came over and sat there and while the dripping slowed down outside – drip-dri-i-p, she laid her lips to the beautiful cold image she had created.

Presently she kissed him several times in the mouth, her face getting big as it came up to him; he had never seen anything so dazzling as the quality of her skin, and since sometimes beauty gives back the images of one's best thoughts he thought of his responsibility about Nicole, and of the responsibility of her being two doors down across the corridor.

'The rain's over,' he said. 'Do you see the sun on the slate?'

Rosemary stood up and leaned down and said her most sincere thing to him.

'Oh, we're such *actors* – you and I.'

She went to her dresser and the moment that she laid her comb flat against her hair there was a slow persistent knocking at the door.

They were shocked motionless; the knock was repeated insistently, and in the sudden realisation that the door was not locked Rosemary finished her hair with one stroke, nodded at Dick who had quickly jerked the wrinkles out of the bed where they had been sitting, and started for the door. Dick said in quite a natural voice, not too loud:

' – so if you don't feel up to going out, I'll tell Nicole and we'll have a very quiet last evening.'

The precautions were needless for the situation of the parties outside the door was so harassed as to preclude any but the most fleeting judgements on matters not pertinent to themselves. Standing there was Abe, aged by several months in the last twenty-four hours, and a very frightened, concerned coloured man whom Abe introduced as Mr Peterson of Stockholm.

'He's in a terrible situation and it's my fault,' said Abe. 'We need some good advice.'

'Come in our rooms,' said Dick.

Abe insisted that Rosemary come too and they crossed the hall to the Divers' suite. Jules Peterson, a small, respectable Negro, on the suave model that heels the Republican party in the border states, followed.

It appeared that the latter had been a legal witness to the early-morning dispute in Montparnasse; he had accompanied Abe to the police station and supported his assertion that a thousand-franc note had been seized out of his hand by a Negro, whose identification was one of the points of the case. Abe and Jules Peterson, accompanied by an agent of police, returned to the bistro and too hastily identified as the criminal a Negro who, so it was established after an hour, had only entered the place after Abe left. The police had further complicated the situation by arresting the prominent Negro restaurateur, Freeman, who had only drifted through the alcoholic fog at a very early stage and then vanished. The true culprit, whose case, as reported by his friends, was that he had merely commandeered a fifty-franc note to pay for drinks that Abe had ordered, had only recently and in a somewhat sinister role, reappeared upon the scene.

In brief, Abe had succeeded in the space of an hour in entangling himself with the personal lives, consciences, and emotions of one Afro-European and three Afro-Americans inhabiting the French Latin quarter. The disentanglement was not even faintly in sight and the day had passed in an atmosphere of unfamiliar Negro faces bobbing up in unexpected places and around unexpected corners, and insistent Negro voices on the phone.

In person, Abe had succeeded in evading all of them, save Jules Peterson. Peterson was rather in the position of the friendly Indian who had helped a white. The Negroes who suffered from the betrayal were not so much after Abe as after Peterson, and Peterson was very much after what protection he might get from Abe.

Up in Stockholm Peterson had failed as a small manufacturer of shoe polish and now possessed only his formula and sufficient trade tools to fill a small box; however, his new protector had promised in the early hours to set him up in business in Versailles. Abe's former chauffeur was a shoemaker there and Abe had handed Peterson two hundred francs on account.

Rosemary listened with distaste to this rigmarole; to appreciate its grotesquerie required a more robust sense of humour than hers. The little man with his portable manufactory, his insincere eyes that, from time to time, rolled white semicircles of panic into view; the figure of Abe, his face as blurred as the gaunt fine lines of it would permit – all this was as remote from her as sickness.

'I ask only a chance in life,' said Peterson with the sort of precise yet distorted intonation peculiar to colonial countries. 'My methods are simple, my formula is so good that I was drove away from Stockholm, ruined, because I did not care to dispose of it.'

Dick regarded him politely – interest formed, dissolved, he turned to Abe: 'You go to some hotel and go to bed. After you're all straight Mr Peterson will come and see you.'

'But don't you appreciate the mess that Peterson's in?' Abe protested.

'I shall wait in the hall,' said Mr Peterson with delicacy. 'It is perhaps hard to discuss my problems in front of me.'

He withdrew after a short travesty of a French bow; Abe pulled himself to his feet with the deliberation of a locomotive.

'I don't seem highly popular today.'

'Popular but not probable,' Dick advised him. 'My advice is to leave this hotel – by way of the bar, if you want. Go to the Chambord, or if you'll need a lot of service, go over to the Majestic.'

'Could I annoy you for a drink?'

'There's not a thing up here,' Dick lied.

Resignedly Abe shook hands with Rosemary; he composed his face slowly, holding her hand a long time and forming sentences that did not emerge.

'You are the most – one of the most – '

She was sorry, and rather revolted at his dirty hands, but she laughed in a well-bred way, as though it were nothing unusual to her to watch a man walking in a slow dream. Often people display a curious respect for a man drunk, rather like the respect of simple races for the insane. Respect rather than fear. There is something awe-inspiring in one who has lost all inhibitions, who will do anything. Of course we make him pay afterwards for his moment of superiority, his moment of impressiveness. Abe turned to Dick with a last appeal.

'If I go to a hotel and get all steamed and curry-combed, and sleep awhile, and fight off these Senegalese – could I come and spend the evening by the fireside?'

Dick nodded at him, less in agreement than in mockery and said: 'You have a high opinion of your current capacities.'

'I bet if Nicole was here she'd let me come back.'

'All right.' Dick went to a trunk tray and brought a box to the central table; inside were innumerable cardboard letters.

'You can come if you want to play anagrams.'

Abe eyed the contents of the box with physical revulsion as though he had been asked to eat them like oats.

'What are anagrams? Haven't I had enough strange – '

'It's a quiet game. You spell words with them – any word except alcohol.'

'I bet you can spell alcohol,' Abe plunged his hand among the counters. 'Can I come back if I can spell alcohol?'

'You can come back if you want to play anagrams.'

Abe shook his head resignedly.

'If you're in that frame of mind there's no use – I'd just be in the way.' He waved his finger reproachfully at Dick. 'But remember what George the Third said, that if Grant was drunk he wished he would bite the other generals.'

With a last desperate glance at Rosemary from the golden corners of his eyes, he went out. To his relief Peterson was no longer in the corridor. Feeling lost and homeless he went back to ask Paul the name of that boat.

Chapter 25

When he had tottered out, Dick and Rosemary embraced fleetingly. There was a dust of Paris over both of them through which they scented each other: the rubber guard on Dick's fountain pen, the faintest odour of warmth from Rosemary's neck and shoulders. For another half-minute Dick clung to the situation; Rosemary was first to return to reality.

'I must go, youngster,' she said.

They blinked at each other across a widening space, and Rosemary made an exit that she had learned young, and on which no director had ever tried to improve.

She opened the door of her room and went directly to her desk where she had suddenly remembered leaving her wristwatch. It was there; slipping it on she glanced down at the daily letter to her mother; finishing the last sentence in her mind. Then, rather gradually, she realised without turning about that she was not alone in the room.

In an inhabited room there are refracting objects only half noticed: varnished wood, more or less polished brass, silver and ivory, and beyond these a thousand conveyors of light and shadow so mild that one scarcely thinks of them as that, the tops of picture-frames, the edges of pencils or ashtrays, of crystal or china ornaments; the totality of this refraction – appealing to equally subtle reflexes of the vision as well as to those associational fragments in the subconscious that we seem to hang on to, as a glass-fitter keeps the irregularly shaped pieces that may do sometime – this fact might account for what Rosemary afterwards mystically described as realising that there was someone in the room, before she could determine it. But when she did realise it she turned swift in a sort of ballet step and saw that a dead Negro was stretched upon her bed.

As she cried 'Aaouu!' and her still unfastened wristwatch banged against the desk she had the preposterous idea that it was Abe North. Then she dashed for the door and across the hall.

Dick was straightening up; he had examined the gloves worn that day and thrown them into a pile of soiled gloves in a corner of a trunk. He had hung up coat and vest and spread his shirt on another hanger – a trick of his own. 'You'll wear a shirt that's a little dirty where you won't wear a mussed shirt.' Nicole had come in and was dumping one of Abe's extraordinary ashtrays into the waste-basket when Rosemary tore into the room.

'*Dick! Dick!* Come and see!'

Dick jogged across the hall into her room. He knelt to Peterson's heart, and felt the pulse – the body was warm, the face, harassed and indirect in life, was gross and bitter in death; the box of materials was held under one arm but the shoe that dangled over the bedside was bare of polish and its sole was worn through. By French law Dick had no right to touch the body but he moved the arm a little to see something – there was a stain on the green coverlet, there would be faint blood on the blanket beneath.

Dick closed the door and stood thinking; he heard cautious steps in the corridor and then Nicole calling him by name. Opening the door he whispered: 'Bring the *couverture* and top blanket from one of our beds – don't let anyone see you.' Then, noticing the strained look on her face, he added quickly, 'Look here, you mustn't get upset over this – it's only some nigger scrap.'

'I want it to be over.'

The body, as Dick lifted it, was light and ill-nourished. He held it so that further haemorrhages from the wound would flow into the man's clothes. Laying it beside the bed he stripped off the coverlet and top blanket and then opening the door an inch, listened – there was a clank of dishes down the hall followed by a loud patronising '*Merci, madame*,' but the waiter went in the other direction, towards the service stairway. Quickly Dick and Nicole exchanged bundles across the corridor; after spreading this covering on Rosemary's bed, Dick stood sweating in the warm twilight, considering. Certain points had become apparent to him in the moment following his examination of the body; first, that Abe's first hostile Indian had tracked the friendly Indian and discovered him in the corridor, and when the latter had taken desperate refuge in Rosemary's room, had hunted down and slain him; second, that if the situation were allowed to develop naturally, no power on earth could keep the smear off Rosemary – the paint was scarcely dry on the Arbuckle case. Her contract was contingent upon an obligation to continue rigidly and unexceptionally as *Daddy's Girl*.

Automatically Dick made the old motion of turning up his sleeves though he wore a sleeveless undershirt, and bent over the body. Getting a purchase on the shoulders of the coat he kicked open the door with his heel, and dragged the body quickly into a plausible position in the corridor. He came back into Rosemary's room and smoothed back the grain of the plush floor rug. Then he went to the phone in his suite and called the manager-owner of the hotel.

'McBeth? – it's Dr Diver speaking – something very important. Are we on a more or less private line?'

It was good that he had made the extra effort which had firmly entrenched him with Mr McBeth. Here was one use for all the pleasingness that Dick had expended over a large area he would never retrace . . .

'Going out of the suite we came on a dead Negro . . . in the hall . . . no, no, he's a civilian. Wait a minute now – I knew you didn't want any guests to blunder on the body so I'm phoning you. Of course I must ask you to keep my name out of it. I don't want any French red tape just because I discovered the man.'

What exquisite consideration for the hotel! only because Mr McBeth, with his own eyes, had seen these traits in Dr Diver two nights before, could he credit the story without question.

In a minute Mr McBeth arrived and in another minute he was joined by a gendarme. In the interval he found time to whisper to Dick, 'You can be sure the name of any guest will be protected. I'm only too grateful to you for your pains.'

Mr McBeth took an immediate step that may only be imagined, but that influenced the gendarme so as to make him pull his moustaches in a frenzy of uneasiness and greed. He made perfunctory notes and sent a telephone call to his post. Meanwhile, with a celerity that Jules Peterson, as a businessman, would have quite understood, the remains were carried into another apartment of one of the most fashionable hotels in the world.

Dick went back to his salon.

'What *hap*pened?' cried Rosemary. 'Do all the Americans in Paris just shoot at each other all the time?'

'This seems to be the open season,' he answered. 'Where's Nicole?'

'I think she's in the bathroom.'

She adored him for saving her – disasters that could have attended upon the event had passed in prophecy through her mind; and she had listened in wild worship to his strong, sure, polite voice making it all right. But before she reached him in a sway of soul and body his attention focused on something else: he went into the bedroom and towards the bathroom. And now Rosemary, too, could hear, louder and louder, a verbal inhumanity that penetrated the keyholes and the cracks in the doors, swept into the suite and in the shape of horror took form again.

With the idea that Nicole had fallen in the bathroom and hurt herself, Rosemary followed Dick. That was not the condition of affairs at which she stared before Dick shouldered her back and brusquely blocked her view.

Nicole knelt beside the tub swaying sideways and sideways. 'It's you!' she cried, ' – it's you come to intrude on the only privacy I have in the world – with your spread with red blood on it. I'll wear it for you – I'm not ashamed, though it was such a pity. On All Fools' Day we had a party on the Zurichsee, and all the fools were there, and I wanted to come dressed in a spread but they wouldn't let me – '

'Control yourself!'

' – so I sat in the bathroom and they brought me a domino and said wear that. I did. What else could I do?'

'Control yourself, Nicole!'

'I never expected you to love me – it was too late – only don't come in the bathroom, the only place I can go for privacy, dragging spreads with red blood on them and asking me to fix them.'

'Control yourself. Get up – '

Rosemary, back in the salon, heard the bathroom door bang, and stood trembling: now she knew what Violet McKisco had seen in the bathroom at Villa Diana. She answered the ringing phone and almost cried with relief when she found it was Collis Clay, who had traced her to the Divers' apartment. She asked him to come up while she got her hat, because she was afraid to go into her room alone.

BOOK TWO

Chapter 1

In the spring of 1917, when Dr Richard Diver first arrived in Zurich, he was twenty-six years old, a fine age for a man, indeed the very acme of bachelorhood. Even in war-time days, it was a fine age for Dick, who was already too valuable, to much of a capital investment to be shot off in a gun. Years later it seemed to him that even in this sanctuary he did not escape lightly, but about that he never made up his mind – in 1917 he laughed at the idea, saying apologetically that the war didn't touch him at all. Instructions from his local board were that he was to complete his studies in Zurich and take a degree as he had planned.

Switzerland was an island, washed on one side by the waves of thunder around Gorizia and on another by the cataracts along the Somme and the Aisne. For once there seemed more intriguing strangers than sick ones in the cantons, but that had to be guessed at – the men who whispered in the little cafés of Berne and Geneva were as likely to be diamond salesmen or commercial travellers. However, no one had missed the long trains of blinded or one-legged men, or dying trunks, that crossed each other between the bright lakes of Constance and Neuchâtel. In the beer-halls and shop windows were bright posters presenting the Swiss defending their frontiers in 1914 – with inspiring ferocity young men and old men glared down from the mountains at phantom French and Germans; the purpose was to assure the Swiss heart that it had shared the contagious glory of those days. As the massacre continued the posters withered away, and no country was more surprised than its sister republic when the United States bungled its way into the war.

Dr Diver had seen around the edges of the war by that time: he was an Oxford Rhodes Scholar from Connecticut in 1914. He returned home for a final year at Johns Hopkins, and took his degree. In 1916 he managed to get to Vienna under the impression that, if he did not make haste, the great Freud would eventually succumb to an airplane bomb. Even then Vienna was old with death but Dick managed to get enough coal and oil to sit in his room in the Damenstiftgasse and write the pamphlets that he later destroyed, but that, rewritten, were the backbone of the book he published in Zurich in 1920.

Most of us have a favourite, a heroic period, in our lives and that was Dick Diver's. For one thing he had no idea that he was charming, that the affection he gave and inspired was anything unusual among healthy people. In his last year at New Haven someone referred to him as 'lucky Dick' – the name lingered in his head.

'Lucky Dick, you big stiff,' he would whisper to himself, walking around the last sticks of flame in his room. 'You hit it, my boy. Nobody knew it was there before you came along.'

At the beginning of 1917, when it was becoming difficult to find coal, Dick burned for fuel almost a hundred textbooks that he had accumulated; but only, as he laid each one on the fire, with an assurance chuckling inside him that he was himself a digest of what was within the book, that he could brief it five years from now, if it deserved to be briefed. This went on at any odd hour, if necessary, with a floor rug over his shoulders, with the fine quiet of the scholar which is nearest of all things to heavenly peace – but which, as will presently be told, had to end.

For its temporary continuance he thanked his body that had done the flying rings at New Haven, and now swam in the winter Danube. With Elkins, second secretary at the Embassy, he shared an apartment, and there were two nice girl visitors – which was that and not too much of it, nor too much of the Embassy either. His contact with Ed Elkins aroused in him a first faint doubt as to the quality of his mental processes; he could not feel that they were profoundly different from the thinking of Elkins – Elkins, who would name you all the quarter-backs in New Haven for thirty years.

' – And Lucky Dick can't be one of these clever men; he must be less intact, even faintly destroyed. If life won't do it for him it's not a substitute to get a disease, or a broken heart, or an inferiority complex, though it'd be nice to build out some broken side till it was better than the original structure.'

He mocked at his reasoning, calling it specious and 'American' – his criteria of uncerebral phrase-making was that it was American. He knew, though, that the price of his intactness was incompleteness.

'The best I can wish you, my child,' so said the Fairy Blackstick in Thackeray's *The Rose and the Ring*, 'is a little misfortune.'

In some moods he griped at his own reasoning: Could I help it that

Pete Livingstone sat in the locker-room Tap Day when everybody looked all over hell for him? And I got an election when otherwise I wouldn't have got Elihu, knowing so few men. He was good and right and I ought to have sat in the locker-room instead. Maybe I would, if I'd thought I had a chance at an election. But Mercer kept coming to my room all those weeks. I guess I knew I had a chance all right, all right. But it would have served me right if I'd swallowed my pin in the shower and set up a conflict.

After the lectures at the university he used to argue this point with a young Rumanian intellectual who reassured him: 'There's no evidence that Goethe ever had a "conflict" in a modern sense, or a man like Jung, for instance. You're not a romantic philosopher – you're a scientist. Memory, force, character – especially good sense. That's going to be your trouble – judgement about yourself – once I knew a man who worked two years on the brain of an armadillo, with the idea that he would sooner or later know more about the brain of an armadillo than anyone. I kept arguing with him that he was not really pushing out the extension of the human range – it was too arbitrary. And sure enough, when he sent his work to the medical journal they refused it – they had just accepted a thesis by another man on the same subject.'

Dick got up to Zurich on fewer Achilles' heels than would be required to equip a centipede, but with plenty – the illusion of eternal strength and health, and of the essential goodness of people; illusions of a nation, the lies of generations of frontier mothers who had to croon falsely that there were no wolves outside the cabin door. After he took his degree, he received his orders to join a neurological unit forming in Bar-sur-Aube.

In France, to his disgust, the work was executive rather than practical. In compensation he found time to complete the short textbook and assemble the material for his next venture. He returned to Zurich in the spring of 1919 discharged.

The foregoing has the ring of a biography, without the satisfaction of knowing that the hero, like Grant, lolling in his general store in Galena, is ready to be called to an intricate destiny. Moreover it is confusing to come across a youthful photograph of someone known in a rounded maturity and gaze with a shock upon a fiery, wiry, eagle-eyed stranger. Best to be reassuring – Dick Diver's moment now began.

Chapter 2

It was a damp April day, with long diagonal clouds over the Albishorn and water inert in the low places. Zurich is not unlike an American city. Missing something ever since his arrival two days before, Dick perceived that it was the sense he had had in finite French lanes that there was nothing more. In Zurich there was a lot besides Zurich – the roofs up-led the eyes to tinkling cow pastures, which in turn modified hilltops farther up – so life was a perpendicular starting off to a post-card heaven. The Alpine lands, home of the toy and the funicular, the merry-go-round and the thin chime, were not a being *here*, as in France, with French vines growing over one's feet on the ground.

In Salzburg once Dick had felt the superimposed quality of a bought and borrowed century of music; once in the laboratories of the university in Zurich, delicately poking at the cervical of a brain, he had felt like a toy-maker rather than like the tornado who had hurried through the old red buildings of Hopkins, two years before, unstayed by the irony of the gigantic Christ in the entrance hall.

Yet he had decided to remain another two years in Zurich, for he did not underestimate the value of toy-making, of infinite precision, of infinite patience.

Today he went out to see Franz Gregorovious at Dohmler's clinic on the Zurichsee. Franz, resident pathologist at the clinic, a Vaudois by birth, a few years older than Dick, met him at the tram stop. He had a dark and magnificent aspect of Cagliostro about him, contrasted with holy eyes; he was the third of the Gregoroviouses – his grandfather had instructed Kraepelin when psychiatry was just emerging from the darkness of all time. In personality he was proud, fiery, and sheep-like – he fancied himself as a hypnotist. If the original genius of the family had grown a little tired, Franz would without doubt become a fine clinician.

On the way to the clinic he said: 'Tell me of your experiences in the war. Are you changed like the rest? You have the same stupid and unageing American face, except I know you're not stupid, Dick.'

'I didn't see any of the war – you must have gathered that from my letters, Franz.'

'That doesn't matter – we have some shell-shocks who merely heard an air raid from a distance. We have a few who merely read newspapers.'

'It sounds like nonsense to me.'

'Maybe it is, Dick. But, we're a rich person's clinic – we don't use the word nonsense. Frankly, did you come down to see me or to see that girl?'

They looked sideways at each other; Franz smiled enigmatically.

'Naturally I saw all the first letters,' he said in his official basso. 'When the change began, delicacy prevented me from opening any more. Really it had become your case.'

'Then she's well?' Dick demanded.

'Perfectly well, I have charge of her, in fact I have charge of the majority of the English and American patients. They call me Dr Gregory.'

'Let me explain about that girl,' Dick said. 'I only saw her one time, that's a fact. When I came out to say goodbye to you just before I went over to France. It was the first time I put on my uniform and I felt very bogus in it – went around saluting private soldiers and all that.'

'Why didn't you wear it today?'

'Hey! I've been discharged three weeks. Here's the way I happened to see that girl. When I left you I walked down towards that building of yours on the lake to get my bicycle.'

' – towards the "Cedars"?'

' – a wonderful night, you know – moon over that mountain – '

'The Krenzegg.'

' – I caught up with a nurse and a young girl. I didn't think the girl was a patient; I asked the nurse about tram times and we walked along. The girl was about the prettiest thing I ever saw.'

'She still is.'

'She'd never seen an American uniform and we talked, and I didn't think anything about it.' He broke off, recognising a familiar perspective, and then resumed: ' – except, Franz, I'm not as hard-boiled as you are yet; when I see a beautiful shell like that I can't help feeling a regret about what's inside it. That was absolutely all – till the letters began to come.'

'It was the best thing that could have happened to her,' said Franz dramatically, 'transference of the most fortuitous kind. That's why I came down to meet you on a very busy day. I want you to come into my office and talk a long time before you see her. In fact, I sent her into Zurich to do errands.' His voice was tense with enthusiasm. 'In fact, I sent her without a nurse, with a less stable patient. I'm intensely proud of this case, which I handled, with your accidental assistance.'

The car had followed the shore of the Zurichsee into a fertile region of pasture farms and low hills, steepled with châlets. The sun swam out into a blue sea of sky and suddenly it was a Swiss valley at its best – pleasant sounds and murmurs and a good fresh smell of health and cheer.

Professor Dohmler's plant consisted of three old buildings and a pair of new ones, between a slight eminence and the shore of the lake. At its founding, ten years before, it had been the first modern clinic for mental illness; at a casual glance no layman would recognise it as a refuge for the broken, the incomplete, the menacing, of this world, though two buildings were surrounded with vine-softened walls of a deceptive height. Some men raked straw in the sunshine; here and there, as they rode into the grounds, the car passed the white flag of a nurse waving beside a patient on a path.

After conducting Dick to his office, Franz excused himself for half an hour. Left alone Dick wandered about the room and tried to reconstruct Franz from the litter of his desk, from his books and the books of and by his father and grandfather; from the Swiss piety of a huge claret-coloured photo of the former on the wall. There was smoke in the room; pushing open a French window, Dick let in a cone of sunshine. Suddenly his thoughts swung to the patient, the girl.

He had received about fifty letters from her written over a period of eight months. The first one was apologetic, explaining that she had heard from America how girls wrote to soldiers whom they did not know. She had obtained the name and address from Dr Gregory and she hoped he would not mind if she sometimes sent word to wish him well, etc., etc.

So far it was easy to recognise the tone – from *Daddy-Long-Legs* and *Molly-Make-Believe*, sprightly and sentimental epistolary collections enjoying a vogue in the States. But there the resemblance ended.

The letters were divided into two classes, of which the first class, up to about the time of the armistice, was of marked pathological turn, and of which the second class, running from thence up to the present, was entirely normal, and displayed a richly maturing nature. For these latter letters Dick had come to wait eagerly in the last dull months at Bar-sur-Aube – yet even from the first letters he had pieced together more than Franz would have guessed of the story.

> MON CAPITAINE – I thought when I saw you in your uniform you were so handsome. Then I thought Je m'en fiche French too and German. You thought I was pretty too but I've had that before and a long time I've stood it. If you come here again with that

attitude base and criminal and not even faintly what I had been taught to associate with the role of gentleman then heaven help

(2)

you. However, you seem quieter than the others, all soft like a big cat. I have only gotten to like boys who are rather sissies. Are you a sissy? There were some somewhere.

Excuse all this, it is the third letter I have written you and will send immediately or will never send. I've thought a lot about moonlight too and there are many witnesses I could find if I could only be out of here.

(3)

They said you were a doctor, but so long as you are a cat it is different. My head aches so, so excuse this walking there like an ordinary with a white cat will explain, I think. I can speak three languages, four with English, and am sure I could be useful interpreting if you arrange such thing in France I'm sure I could control everything with the belts all bound around everybody like

(4)

it was Wednesday. It is now Saturday and you are far away, perhaps killed.

Come back to me someday, for I will be here always on this green hill. Unless they will let me write my father, whom I loved dearly.

Excuse this. I am not myself today. I will write when I feel better.

Cheerio

NICOLE WARREN

Excuse all this.

CAPTAIN DIVER – I know introspection is not good for a highly nervous state like mine, but I would like you to know where I stand. Last year or whenever it was in Chicago when I got so I couldn't speak to servants or walk in the street I kept waiting for someone to tell me. It was the duty of someone who understood. The blind must be led. Only no one would tell me everything – they would just tell me half and I was already too muddled to put two and two together. One man was nice – he was a French officer and he understood. He gave me a flower and said it was 'plus petite et moins entendue.' We were friends. Then he took it away. I grew sicker and there was no one to explain to me. They had a song

(2)

about Joan of Arc that they used to sing at me that was just mean – it would just make me cry, for there was nothing the matter with my head then. They kept making reference to sports, too, but I didn't care by that time. So there was that day I went walking on Michigan Boulevard on and on for miles and finally they followed me in an

(3)

automobile, but I wouldn't get in. Finally they pulled me in and there were nurses. After that time I began to realise it all, because I could feel what was happening in others. So you see how I stand. And what good can it be for me to stay here with the doctors harping constantly in the things I was here to get over. So today I have written my father to come and take me away. I am glad you are

(4)

so interested in examining people and sending them back. It must be so much fun.

And again, from another letter:

You might pass up your next examination and write me a letter. They just sent me some phonograph records in case I should forget my lesson and I broke them all so the nurse won't speak to me. They were in English, so that the nurses would not understand. One doctor in Chicago said I was bluffing, but what he really meant was that I was a twin six and he had never seen one before. But I was very busy being mad then, so I didn't care what he said, when I am very busy being mad I don't usually care what they say, not if I were a million girls.

You told me that night you'd teach me to play. Well, I think love

(2)

is all there is or should be. Anyhow I am glad your interest in examinations keeps you busy.

Tout à vous,

NICOLE WARREN

There were other letters among whose helpless caesuras lurked darker rhythms.

DEAR CAPTAIN DIVER – I write to you because there is no one else to whom I can turn and it seems to me if this farcical situation is apparent to one as sick as me it should be apparent to you. The mental trouble is all over and besides that I am completely broken and humiliated if that was what they wanted. My family have shamefully neglected me, there's no use asking them for help or pity. I have had enough and it is simply ruining my health and wasting my time pretending that what is the matter with my head is curable.

(2)

Here I am in what appears to be semi-insane-asylum, all because nobody saw fit to tell me the truth about anything. If I had only known what was going on like I know now I could have stood it I guess for I am pretty strong, but those who should have, did not see fit to enlighten me. And now, when I know and have paid such a price for knowing, they sit there with their dogs' lives and say I

(3)

should believe what I did believe. Especially one does but I know now. I am lonesome all the time far away from friends and family across the Atlantic I roam all over the place in a half daze. If you could get me a position as interpreter (I know French and German like a native, fair Italian and a little Spanish) or in the Red Cross

(4)

Ambulance or as a train nurse, though I would have to train you would prove a great blessing.

And again:

Since you will not accept my explanation of what is the matter you could at least explain to me what you think, because you have a kind cat's face, and not that funny look that seems to be so fashionable here. Dr Gregory gave me a snapshot of you, not as handsome as you are in your uniform, but younger looking.

Mon Capitaine – It was fine to have your postcard. I am so glad you take such interest in disqualifying nurses – oh, I understood your note very well indeed. Only I thought from the moment I met you that you were different.

Dear Capitaine – I think one thing today and another tomorrow. That is really all that's the matter with me, except a crazy defiance and a lack of proportion. I would gladly welcome any alienist you might suggest. Here they lie in their bathtubs and sing 'Play in Your Own Backyard' as if I had my backyard to play in or any hope which I can find by looking either backwards or forwards. They tried

(2)

it again in the candy store again and I almost hit the man with the weight, but they held me.

I am not going to write you any more. I am too unstable.

And then a month with no letters. And then suddenly the change.

– I am slowly coming back to life . . .
– Today the flowers and the clouds . . .
– The war is over and I scarcely knew there was a war . . .
– How kind you have been! You must be very wise behind your face like a white cat, except you don't look like that in the picture Dr Gregory gave me . . .
– Today I went to Zurich, how strange a feeling to see a city again.
– Today we went to Berne, it was so nice with the clocks.
– Today we climbed high enough to find asphodel and edelweiss . . .

After that the letters were fewer, but he answered them all. There was one:

I wish someone were in love with me like boys were ages ago before I was sick. I suppose it will be years, though, before I could think of anything like that.

But when Dick's answer was delayed for any reason, there was a fluttering burst of worry – like a worry of a lover: 'Perhaps I have bored you,' and: 'Afraid I have presumed,' and: 'I keep thinking at night you have been sick.'

In actuality Dick was sick with the flu. When he recovered, all except the formal part of his correspondence was sacrificed to the consequent fatigue, and shortly afterwards the memory of her became overlaid by the vivid presence of a Wisconsin telephone girl at headquarters in Bar-sur-Aube. She was red-lipped like a poster, and known obscenely in the messes as 'The Switchboard'.

Franz came back into his office feeling self-important. Dick thought he would probably be a fine clinician, for the sonorous or staccato cadences by which he disciplined nurse or patient came not from his nervous system but from a tremendous and harmless vanity. His true emotions were more ordered and kept to himself.

'Now about the girl, Dick,' he said. 'Of course, I want to find out about you and tell you about myself, but first about the girl, because I have been waiting to tell you about it so long.'

He searched for and found a sheaf of papers in a filing cabinet, but after shuffling through them he found they were in his way and put them on his desk. Instead he told Dick the story.

Chapter 3

About a year and a half before, Dr Dohmler had some vague correspondence with an American gentleman living in Lausanne, a Mr Devereux Warren, of the Warren family of Chicago. A meeting was arranged and one day Mr Warren arrived at the clinic with his daughter Nicole, a girl of sixteen. She was obviously not well and the nurse who was with her took her to walk about the grounds while Mr Warren had his consultation.

Warren was a strikingly handsome man looking less than forty. He was a fine American type in every way, tall, broad, well made – '*un homme très chic*', as Dr Dohmler described him to Franz. His large grey eyes were sun-veined from rowing on Lake Geneva, and he had that special air about him of having known the best of this world. The conversation was in German, for it developed that he had been educated at Göttingen. He was nervous and obviously very moved by his errand.

'Dr Dohmler, my daughter isn't right in the head. I've had lots of specialists and nurses for her and she's taken a couple of rest cures but the thing has grown too big for me and I've been strongly recommended to come to you.'

'Very well,' said Dr Dohmler. 'Suppose you start at the beginning and tell me everything.'

'There isn't any beginning, at least there isn't any insanity in the family that I know of, on either side. Nicole's mother died when she was eleven and I've sort of been father and mother both to her, with the help of governesses – father and mother both to her.'

He was very moved as he said this. Dr Dohmler saw that there were tears in the corners of his eyes and noticed for the first time that there was whisky on his breath.

'As a child she was a darling thing – everybody was crazy about her, everybody that came in contact with her. She was smart as a whip and happy as the day is long. She liked to read or draw or dance or play the piano – anything. I used to hear my wife say she was the only one of our children who never cried at night. I've got an older girl, too, and there was a boy that died, but Nicole was – Nicole was – Nicole – '

He broke off and Dr Dohmler helped him.

'She was a perfectly normal, bright, happy child.'

'Perfectly.'

Dr Dohmler waited. Mr Warren shook his head, blew a long sigh, glanced quickly at Dr Dohmler and then at the floor again.

'About eight months ago, or maybe it was six months ago or maybe ten – I try to figure but I can't remember exactly where we were when she began to do funny things – crazy things. Her sister was the first one to say anything to me about it – because Nicole was always the same to me,' he added rather hastily, as if someone had accused him of being to blame, ' – the same loving little girl. The first thing was about a valet.'

'Oh, yes,' said Dr Dohmler, nodding his venerable head, as if, like Sherlock Holmes, he had expected a valet and only a valet to be introduced at this point.

'I had a valet – been with me for years – Swiss, by the way.' He looked up for Dr Dohmler's patriotic approval. 'And she got some crazy idea about him. She thought he was making up to her – of course, at the time I believed her and I let him go, but I know now it was all nonsense.'

'What did she claim he had done?'

'That was the first thing – the doctors couldn't pin her down. She just looked at them as if they ought to know what he'd done. But she certainly meant he'd made some kind of indecent advances to her – she didn't leave us in any doubt of that.'

'I see.'

'Of course, I've read about women getting lonesome and thinking there's a man under the bed and all that, but why should Nicole get such an idea? She could have all the young men she wanted. We were in Lake Forest – that's a summer place near Chicago where we have a place – and she was out all day playing golf or tennis with boys. And some of them pretty gone on her at that.'

All the time Warren was talking to the dried old package of Dr Dohmler, one section of the latter's mind kept thinking intermittently of Chicago. Once in his youth he could have gone to Chicago as fellow and docent at the university, and perhaps become rich there and owned his own clinic instead of being only a minor shareholder in a clinic. But when he had thought of what he considered his own thin knowledge spread over that whole area, over all those wheat-fields, those endless prairies, he had decided against it. But he had heard about Chicago in those days, about the great feudal families of Armour, Palmer, Field, Crane, Warren, Swift, and McCormick and many others, and since that time not a few patients had come to him from that stratum of Chicago and New York.

'She got worse,' continued Warren. 'She had a fit or something – the things she said got crazier and crazier. Her sister wrote some of them down – ' He handed a much-folded piece of paper to the doctor. 'Almost always about men going to attack her, men she knew or men on the street – anybody – '

He told of their alarm and distress, of the horrors families go through under such circumstances, of the ineffectual efforts they had made in America, finally of the faith in a change of scene that had made him run the submarine blockade and bring his daughter to Switzerland.

' – on a United States cruiser,' he specified with a touch of hauteur. 'It was possible for me to arrange that, by a stroke of luck. And, may I add,' he smiled apologetically, 'that as they say: money is no object.'

'Certainly not,' agreed Dohmler dryly.

He was wondering why and about what the man was lying to him. Or, if he was wrong about that, what was the falsity that pervaded the whole room, the handsome figure in tweeds sprawling in his chair with a sportsman's ease? That was a tragedy out there, in the February day, the young bird with wings crushed somehow, and inside here it was all too thin, thin and wrong.

'I would like – to talk to her – a few minutes now,' said Dr Dohmler, going into English as if it would bring him closer to Warren.

Afterwards when Warren had left his daughter and returned to Lausanne, and several days had passed, the doctor and Franz entered upon Nicole's card:

> Diagnostic: Schizophrénie. Phase aiguë en décroissance. La peur des hommes est un symptôme de la maladie, et n'est point constitutionelle . . . Le pronostic doit rester réservé.*

And then they waited with increasing interest as the days passed for Mr Warren's promised second visit.

It was slow in coming. After a fortnight Dr Dohmler wrote. Confronted with further silence he committed what was for those days *une folie*, and telephoned to the Grand Hôtel at Vevey. He learned from

* Diagnosis: Divided Personality. Acute and downhill phase of the illness. The fear of men is a symptom of the illness and is not at all constitutional . . . The prognosis must be reserved.

Mr Warren's valet that he was at the moment packing to sail for America. But reminded that the forty francs Swiss for the call would show up on the clinic books, the blood of the Tuileries Guard rose to Dr Dohmler's aid and Mr Warren was got to the phone.

'It is – absolutely necessary – that you come. Your daughter's health – all depends. I can take no responsibility.'

'But look here, doctor, that's just what you're for. I have a hurry call to go home!'

Dr Dohmler had never yet spoken to anyone so far away but he dispatched his ultimatum so firmly into the phone that the agonised American at the other end yielded. Half an hour after this second arrival on the Zurichsee, Warren had broken down, his fine shoulders shaking with awful sobs inside his easy-fitting coat, his eyes redder than the very sun on Lake Geneva, and they had the awful story.

'It just happened,' he said hoarsely. 'I don't know – I don't know.

'After her mother died when she was little she used to come into my bed every morning, sometimes she'd sleep in my bed. I was sorry for the little thing. Oh, after that, whenever we went places in an automobile or a train we used to hold hands. She used to sing to me. We used to say, "Now let's not pay any attention to anybody else this afternoon – let's just have each other – for this morning you're mine." ' A broken sarcasm came into his voice. 'People used to say what a wonderful father and daughter we were – they used to wipe their eyes. We were just like lovers – and then all at once we were lovers – and ten minutes after it happened I could have shot myself – except I guess I'm such a goddamned degenerate I didn't have the nerve to do it.'

'Then what?' said Dr Dohmler, thinking again of Chicago and of a mild pale gentleman with a pince-nez who had looked him over in Zurich thirty years before. 'Did this thing go on?'

'Oh, no! She almost – she seemed to freeze up right away. She'd just say, "Never mind, never mind, daddy. It doesn't matter, never mind." '

'There were no consequences?'

'No.' He gave one short convulsive sob and blew his nose several times. 'Except now there're plenty of consequences.'

As the story concluded, Dohmler sat back in the focal armchair of the middle class and said to himself sharply, 'Peasant!' – it was one of the few absolute worldly judgements that he had permitted himself for twenty years. Then he said: 'I would like for you to go to a hotel in Zurich and spend the night and come see me in the morning.'

'And then what?'

Dr Dohmler spread his hands wide enough to carry a young pig. 'Chicago,' he suggested.

Chapter 4

'Then we knew where we stood,' said Franz. 'Dohmler told Warren we would take the case if he would agree to keep away from his daughter indefinitely, with an absolute minimum of five years. After Warren's first collapse, he seemed chiefly concerned as to whether the story would ever leak back to America.

'We mapped out a routine for her and waited. The prognosis was bad – as you know, the percentage of cures, even so-called social cures, is very low at that age.'

'These first letters looked bad,' agreed Dick.

'Very bad – very typical. I hesitated about letting the first one get out of the clinic. Then I thought it will be good for Dick to know we're carrying on here. It was generous of you to answer them.'

Dick sighed. 'She was such a pretty thing – she enclosed a lot of snapshots of herself. And for a month there I didn't have anything to do. All I said in my letters was "Be a good girl and mind the doctors." '

'That was enough – it gave her somebody to think of outside. For a while she didn't have anybody – only one sister that she doesn't seem very close to. Besides, reading her letters helped us here – they were a measure of her condition.'

'I'm glad.'

'You see now what happened? She felt complicity – that's neither here nor there, except as we want to revalue her ultimate stability and strength of character. First came this shock. Then she went off to a boarding-school and heard the girls talking – so from sheer self-protection she developed the idea that she had had no complicity – and from there it was easy to slide into a phantom world where all men, the more you liked them and trusted them, the more evil – '

'Did she ever go into the – horror directly?'

'No, and as a matter of fact when she began to seem normal, about October, we were in a predicament. If she had been thirty years old we would have let her make her own adjustment, but she was so young we were afraid she might harden with it all twisted inside her. So Dr Dohmler said to her frankly, "Your duty now is to yourself. This doesn't by any account mean the end of anything for you – your life is just at its beginning," and so forth and so forth. She really has an excellent mind, so he gave her a little Freud to read, not too much, and she was very interested. In fact, we've made rather a pet of her around here. But she is reticent,' he added; he hesitated: 'We have wondered if in her recent letter to you which she mailed herself from Zurich, she has said anything that would be illuminating about her state of mind and her plans for the future.'

Dick considered.

'Yes and no – I'll bring the letters out here if you want. She seems hopeful and normally hungry for life – even rather romantic. Sometimes she speaks of "the past" as people speak who have been in prison. But you never know whether they refer to the crime or the imprisonment or the whole experience. After all I'm only a sort of stuffed figure in her life.'

'Of course, I understand your position exactly, and I express our gratitude once again. That was why I wanted to see you before you see her.'

Dick laughed.

'You think she's going to make a flying leap at my person?'

'No, not that. But I want to ask you to go very gently. You are attractive to women, Dick.'

'Then God help me! Well, I'll be gentle and repulsive – I'll chew garlic whenever I'm going to see her and wear a stubble beard. I'll drive her to cover.'

'Not garlic!' said Franz, taking him seriously. 'You don't want to compromise your career. But you're partly joking.'

' – and I can limp a little. And there's no real bathtub where I'm living, anyhow.'

'You're entirely joking.' Franz relaxed – or rather assumed the posture of one relaxed. 'Now tell me about yourself and your plans?'

'I've only got one, Franz, and that's to be a good psychologist – maybe to be the greatest one that ever lived.'

Franz laughed pleasantly, but he saw that this time Dick wasn't joking.

'That's very good – and very American,' he said. 'It's more difficult for us.' He got up and went to the French window. 'I stand here and I see Zurich – there is the steeple of the Gross-Münster. In its vault my grandfather is buried. Across the bridge from it lies my ancestor Lavater, who would not be buried in any church. Nearby is the statue of another ancestor, Heinrich Pestalozzi, and one of Dr Alfred Escher. And over everything there is always Zwingli – I am continually confronted with a pantheon of heroes.'

'Yes, I see.' Dick got up. 'I was only talking big. Everything's just starting over. Most of the Americans in France are frantic to get home, but not me – I draw military pay all the rest of the year if I only attend lectures at the university. How's that for a government on the grand scale that knows its future great men? Then I'm going home for a month and see my father. Then I'm coming back – I've been offered a job.'

'Where?'

'Your rivals – Gisler's Clinic at Interlaken.'

'Don't touch it,' Franz advised him. 'They've had a dozen young men there in a year. Gisler's a manic-depressive himself, his wife and her lover run the clinic – of course, you understand that's confidential.'

'How about your old scheme for America?' asked Dick lightly. 'We were going to New York and start an up-to-date establishment for billionaires.'

'That was students' talk.'

Dick dined with Franz and his bride and a small dog with a smell of burning rubber, in the cottage on the edge of the grounds. He felt vaguely oppressed, not by the atmosphere of modest retrenchment, nor by Frau Gregorovious, who might have been prophesied, but by the sudden contracting of horizons to which Franz seemed so reconciled. For him the boundaries of asceticism were differently marked – he could see it as a means to an end, even as a carrying on with a glory it would itself supply, but it was hard to think of deliberately cutting life down to the scale of an inherited suit. The domestic gestures of Franz and his wife as they turned in a cramped space lacked grace and advantage. The post-war months in France, and the lavish liquidations taking place under the aegis of American splendour, had affected Dick's outlook. Also, men and women had made much of him, and perhaps what had brought him back to the centre of the great Swiss watch was an intuition that this was not too good for a serious man.

He made Kaethe Gregorovious feel charming, meanwhile becoming increasingly restless at the all-pervading cauliflower – simultaneously hating himself too for this incipience of he knew not what superficiality.

'God, am I like the rest after all?' – so he used to think starting awake at night – 'Am I like the rest?'

This was poor material for a socialist but good material for those who do much of the world's rarest work. The truth was that for some months he had been going through that partitioning of the things of youth wherein it is decided whether or not to die for what one no longer believes. In the dead white hours in Zurich staring into a stranger's pantry across the upshine of a street lamp, he used to think that he wanted to be good, he wanted to be kind, he wanted to be brave and wise, but it was all pretty difficult. He wanted to be loved, too, if he could fit it in.

Chapter 5

The veranda of the central building was illuminated from open French windows, save where the black shadows of stripling walls and the fantastic shadows of iron chairs slithered down into a gladiolus bed. From the figures that shuffled between the rooms Miss Warren emerged first in glimpses and then sharply when she saw him; as she crossed the threshold her face caught the room's last light and brought it outside with her. She walked to a rhythm – all that week there had been singing in her ears, summer songs of ardent skies and wild shade, and with his arrival the singing had become so loud she could have joined in with it.

'How do you do, Captain,' she said, unfastening her eyes from his with difficulty, as though they had become entangled. 'Shall we sit out here?' She stood still, her glance moving about for a moment. 'It's summer practically.'

A woman had followed her out, a dumpy woman in a shawl, and Nicole presented Dick: 'Señora – '

Franz excused himself and Dick grouped three chairs together.

'The lovely night,' the señora said.

'*Muy bella*,' agreed Nicole; then to Dick, 'Are you here for a long time?'

'I'm in Zurich for a long time, if that's what you mean.'

'This is really the first night of real spring,' the señora suggested.

'To stay?'

'At least till July.'

'I'm leaving in June.'

'June is a lovely month here,' the señora commented. 'You should stay for June and then leave in July when it gets really too hot.'

'You're going where?' Dick asked Nicole.

'Somewhere with my sister – somewhere exciting, I hope, because I've lost so much time. But perhaps they'll think I ought to go to a quiet place at first – perhaps Como. Why don't you come to Como?'

'Ah, Como – ' began the señora.

Within the building a trio broke into Suppé's 'Light Cavalry'. Nicole took advantage of this to stand up and the impression of her youth and beauty grew on Dick until it welled up inside him in a compact paroxysm of emotion. She smiled, a moving childish smile that was like all the lost youth in the world.

'The music's too loud to talk against – suppose we walk around. *Buenas noches, señora*.'

'G't night – g't night.'

They went down two steps to the path where in a moment a shadow cut across it. She took his arm.

'I have some phonograph records my sister sent me from America,' she said. 'Next time you come here I'll play them for you – I know a place to put the phonograph where no one can hear.'

'That'll be nice.'

'Do you know "Hindustan"?' she asked wistfully. 'I'd never heard it before, but I like it. And I've got "Why Do They Call Them Babies?" and "I'm Glad I Can Make You Cry". I suppose you've danced to all those tunes in Paris?'

'I haven't been to Paris.'

Her cream-coloured dress, alternately blue or grey as they walked, and her very blonde hair, dazzled Dick – whenever he turned towards her she was smiling a little, her face lighting up like an angel's when they came into the range of a roadside arc. She thanked him for everything rather as if he had taken her to some party, and as Dick became less and less certain of his relation to her, her confidence increased – there was that excitement about her that seemed to reflect all the excitement of the world.

'I'm not under any restraint at all,' she said. 'I'll play you two good tunes called "Wait Till the Cows Come Home" and "Goodbye, Alexander".'

He was late the next time, a week later, and Nicole was waiting for him at a point in the path which he would pass walking from Franz's house. Her hair, drawn back behind her ears, brushed her shoulders in such a way that the face seemed to have just emerged from it, as if this were the exact moment when she was coming from a wood into clear moonlight. The unknown yielded her up: Dick wished she had no background, that she was just a girl lost with no address save the night from which she had come. They went to the cache where she had left the phonograph, turned a corner by the workshop, climbed a rock, and sat down behind a low wall, facing miles and miles of rolling night.

They were in America now; even Franz with his conception of Dick as an irresistible Lothario would never have guessed that they had gone so far away. They were so sorry, dear; they went down to meet each other in a taxi, honey; they had preferences in smiles and had met in Hindustan, and shortly afterwards they must have quarrelled, for nobody knew and nobody seemed to care – yet finally one of them had gone and left the other crying, only to feel blue, to feel sad.

The thin tunes, holding lost times and future hopes in liaison, twisted upon the Valais night. In the lulls of the phonograph a cricket held the scene together with a single note. By and by Nicole stopped playing the machine and sang to him.

'Lay a silver dollar
 On the ground
And watch it roll
 Because it's round – '

On the pure parting of her lips no breath hovered. Dick stood up suddenly.

'What's the matter, you don't like it?'

'Of course I do.'

'Our cook at home taught it to me:

A woman never knows
 What a good man she's got
Till after she turns him down . . .

You like it?'

She smiled at him, making sure that the smile gathered up everything inside her and directed it towards him, making him a profound promise of herself for so little, for the beat of a response, the assurance of a complementary vibration in him. Minute by minute the sweetness drained down into her out of the willow trees, out of the dark world.

She stood up too, and stumbling over the phonograph, was momentarily against him, leaning into the hollow of his rounded shoulder.

'I've got one more record,' she said. 'Have you heard "So Long, Letty"? I suppose you have.'

'Honestly, you don't understand – I haven't heard a thing.'

Nor known, nor smelt, nor tasted, he might have added; only hot-cheeked girls in hot secret rooms. The young maidens he had known at New Haven in 1914 kissed men, saying 'There!' hands at the man's chest to push him away. Now there was this scarcely saved waif of disaster bringing him the essence of a continent . . .

Chapter 6

It was May when he next found her. The luncheon in Zurich was a council of caution; obviously the logic of his life tended away from the girl; yet when a stranger stared at her from a nearby table, eyes burning disturbingly like an uncharted light, he turned to the man with an urbane version of intimidation and broke the regard.

'He was just a peeper,' he explained cheerfully. 'He was just looking at your clothes. Why do you have so many different clothes?'

'Sister says we're very rich,' she offered humbly. 'Since Grandmother is dead.'

'I forgive you.'

He was enough older than Nicole to take pleasure in her youthful vanities and delights, the way she paused fractionally in front of the hall mirror on leaving the restaurant, so that the incorruptible quicksilver could give her back to herself. He delighted in her stretching out her hands to new octaves now that she found herself beautiful and rich. He tried honestly to divorce her from any obsession that he had stitched her together – glad to see her build up happiness and confidence apart from him; the difficulty was that, eventually, Nicole brought everything to his feet, gifts of sacrificial ambrosia, of worshipping myrtle.

The first week of summer found Dick re-established in Zurich. He had arranged his pamphlets and what work he had done in the army into a pattern from which he intended to make his revise of *A Psychology for Psychiatrists*. He thought he had a publisher; he had established contact with a poor student who would iron out his errors in German. Franz considered it a rash business, but Dick pointed out the disarming modesty of the theme.

'This is stuff I'll never know so well again,' he insisted. 'I have a hunch it's a thing that only fails to be basic because it's never had material recognition. The weakness of this profession is its attraction for the man a little crippled and broken. Within the walls of the profession he compensates by tending towards the clinical, the "practical" – he has won his battle without a struggle.

'On the contrary, you are a good man, Franz, because fate selected you for your profession before you were born. You'd better thank God you had no "bent" – I got to be a psychiatrist because there was a girl at St Hilda's in Oxford that went to the same lectures. Maybe I'm getting trite but I don't want to let my current ideas slide away with a few dozen glasses of beer.'

'All right,' Franz answered. 'You are an American. You can do this without professional harm. I do not like these generalities. Soon you will be writing little books called "Deep Thoughts for the Layman", so simplified that they are positively guaranteed not to cause thinking. If my father were alive he would look at you and grunt, Dick. He would take his napkin and fold it so, and hold his napkin ring, this very one – ' he held it up, a boar's head was carved in the brown wood – 'and he would say, "Well, my impression is – " then he would look at you and think suddenly, "What is the use?" then he would stop and grunt again; then we would be at the end of dinner.'

'I am alone today,' said Dick testily. 'But I may not be alone tomorrow. After that I'll fold up my napkin like your father and grunt.'

Franz waited a moment.

'How about our patient?' he asked.

'I don't know.'

'Well you should know about her by now.'

'I like her. She's attractive. What do you want me to do – take her up in the edelweiss?'

'No, I thought since you go in for scientific books you might have an idea.'

' – devote my life to her?'

Franz called his wife in the kitchen: 'Du lieber Gott! Bitte, bringe Dick noch ein Glas-Bier.'

'I don't want any more if I've got to see Dohmler.'

'We think it's best to have a programme. Four weeks have passed away – apparently the girl is in love with you. That's not our business if we were in the world, but here in the clinic we have a stake in the matter.'

'I'll do whatever Dr Dohmler says,' Dick agreed.

But he had little faith that Dohmler would throw much light on the matter; he himself was the incalculable element involved. By no conscious volition of his own, the thing had drifted into his hands. It reminded him of a scene in his childhood when everyone in the house was looking for the lost key to the silver closet, Dick knowing he had hidden it under the handkerchiefs in his mother's top drawer; at that time he had experienced a philosophical detachment, and this was repeated now when he and Franz went together to Professor Dohmler's office.

The professor, his face beautiful under straight whiskers, like a vine-overgrown veranda of some fine old house, disarmed him. Dick knew some individuals with more talent, but no person of a class qualitatively superior to Dohmler.

Six months later he thought the same way when he saw Dohmler dead, the light out on the veranda, the vines of his whiskers tickling his stiff white collar, the many battles that had swayed before the chink-like eyes stilled for ever under the frail delicate lids –

' . . . Good-morning, sir.' He stood formally, thrown back to the army.

Professor Dohmler interlaced his tranquil fingers. Franz spoke in terms half of liaison officer, half of secretary, till his senior cut through him in mid-sentence.

'We have gone a certain way,' he said mildly. 'It's you, Dr Diver, who can best help us now.'

Routed out, Dick confessed: 'I'm not so straight on it myself.'

'I have nothing to do with your personal reactions,' said Dohmler. 'But I have much to with the fact that this so-called "transference",' he darted a short ironic look at Franz which the latter returned in kind, 'must be terminated. Miss Nicole does well indeed, but she is in no condition to survive what she might interpret as a tragedy.'

Again Franz began to speak, but Dr Dohmler motioned him silent.

'I realise that your position has been difficult.'

'Yes, it has.'

Now the professor sat back and laughed, saying on the last syllable of his laughter, with his sharp little grey eyes shining through: 'Perhaps you have got sentimentally involved yourself.'

Aware that he was being drawn on, Dick, too, laughed.

'She's a pretty girl – anybody responds to that to a certain extent. I have no intention – '

Again Franz tried to speak – again Dohmler stopped him with a question directed pointedly at Dick. 'Have you thought of going away?'

'I can't go away.'

Dr Dohmler turned to Franz: 'Then we can send Miss Warren away.'

'As you think best, Professor Dohmler,' Dick conceded. 'It's certainly a situation.'

Professor Dohmler raised himself like a legless man mounting a pair of crutches.

'But it is a professional situation,' he cried quietly.

He sighed himself back into his chair, waiting for the reverberating thunder to die out about the room. Dick saw that Dohmler had reached his climax, and he was not sure that he himself had survived it. When the thunder had diminished Franz managed to get his word in.

'Dr Diver is a man of fine character,' he said. 'I feel he only has to appreciate the situation in order to deal correctly with it. In my opinion Dick can co-operate right here, without anyone going away.'

'How do you feel about that?' Professor Dohmler asked Dick.

Dick felt churlish in the face of the situation; at the same time he realised in the silence after Dohmler's pronouncement that the state of inanimation could not be indefinitely prolonged; suddenly he spilled everything.

'I'm half in love with her – the question of marrying her has passed through my mind.'

'Tch! Tch!' uttered Franz.

'Wait.' Dohmler warned him. Franz refused to wait: 'What! And devote half your life to being doctor and nurse and all – never! I know what these cases are. One time in twenty it's finished in the first push – better never see her again!'

'What do you think?' Dohmler asked Dick.

'Of course Franz is right.'

Chapter 7

It was late afternoon when they wound up the discussion as to what Dick should do: he must be most kind and yet eliminate himself. When the doctors stood up at last, Dick's eyes fell outside the window to where a light rain was falling – Nicole was waiting, expectant, somewhere in that rain. When, presently, he went out buttoning his oilskin at the throat, pulling down the brim of his hat, he came upon her immediately under the roof of the main entrance.

'I know a new place we can go,' she said. 'When I was ill I didn't mind sitting inside with the others in the evening – what they said seemed like everything else. Naturally now I see them as ill and it's – it's – '

'You'll be leaving soon.'

'Oh, soon. My sister, Beth, but she's always been called Baby, she's coming in a few weeks to take me somewhere; after that I'll be back here for a last month.'

'The older sister?'

'Oh, quite a bit older. She's twenty-four – she's very English. She lives in London with my father's sister. She was engaged to an Englishman but he was killed – I never saw him.'

Her face, ivory gold against the blurred sunset that strove through the rain, had a promise Dick had never seen before: the high cheekbones, the faintly wan quality, cool rather than feverish, was reminiscent of the frame of a promising colt – a creature whose life did not promise to be only a projection of youth upon a greyer screen, but instead, a true growing; the face would be handsome in middle life; it would be handsome in old age: the essential structure and the economy were there.

'What are you looking at?'

'I was just thinking that you're going to be rather happy.'

Nicole was frightened: 'Am I? All right – things couldn't be worse than they have been.'

In the covered woodshed to which she had led him, she sat cross-legged upon her golf shoes, her burberry wound about her and her cheeks stung alive by the damp air. Gravely she returned his gaze, taking in his somewhat proud carriage that never quite yielded to the wooden post against which he leaned; she looked into his face that always tried to discipline itself into moulds of attentive seriousness, after excursions into joys and mockeries of its own. That part of him which seemed to fit his reddish Irish colouring she knew least; she was afraid of it, yet more anxious to explore – this was his more masculine side: the other part, the trained part, the consideration in the polite eyes, she expropriated without question, as most women did.

'At least this institution has been good for languages,' said Nicole. 'I've spoken French with two doctors, and German with the nurses, and Italian, or something like it, with a couple of scrub-women and one of the patients, and I've picked up a lot of Spanish from another.'

'That's fine.'

He tried to arrange an attitude but no logic seemed forthcoming.

' – Music too. Hope you didn't think I was only interested in ragtime. I practise every day – the last few months I've been taking a course in Zurich on the history of music. In fact it was all that kept me going at times – music and the drawing.' She leaned suddenly and twisted a loose strip from the sole of her shoe, and then looked up. 'I'd like to draw you just the way you are now.'

It made him sad when she brought out her accomplishments for his approval.

'I envy you. At present I don't seem to be interested in anything except my work.'

'Oh, I think that's fine for a man,' she said quickly. 'But for a girl I think she ought to have lots of minor accomplishments and pass them on to her children.'

'I suppose so,' said Dick with deliberated indifference.

Nicole sat quiet. Dick wished she would speak so that he could play the easy role of wet blanket, but now she sat quiet.

'You're all well,' he said. 'Try to forget the past; don't overdo things for a year or so. Go back to America and be a débutante and fall in love – and be happy.'

'I couldn't fall in love.' Her injured shoe scraped a cocoon of dust from the log on which she sat.

'Sure you can,' Dick insisted. 'Not for a year maybe, but sooner or later.' Then he added brutally: 'You can have a perfectly normal life with a houseful of beautiful descendants. The very fact that you could make a complete comeback at your age proves that the precipitating factors were pretty near everything. Young woman, you'll be pulling your weight long after your friends are carried off screaming.'

– But there was a look of pain in her eyes as she took the rough dose, the harsh reminder.

'I know I wouldn't be fit to marry anyone for a long time,' she said humbly.

Dick was too upset to say any more. He looked out into the grain field trying to recover his hard brassy attitude.

'You'll be all right – everybody here believes in you. Why, Dr Gregory is so proud of you that he'll probably – '

'I hate Dr Gregory.'

'Well, you shouldn't.'

Nicole's world had fallen to pieces, but it was only a flimsy and scarcely created world; beneath it her emotions and instincts fought on. Was it an hour ago she had waited by the entrance, wearing her hope like a corsage at her belt?

. . . Dresses stay crisp for him, button stay put, bloom narcissus – air stay still and sweet.

'It will be nice to have fun again,' she fumbled on. For a moment she entertained a desperate idea of telling him how rich she was, what big houses she lived in, that really she was a valuable property – for a moment she made herself into her grandfather, Sid Warren, the horse-trader. But she survived the temptation to confuse all values and shut these matters into the Victorian side-chambers – even though there was no home left to her, save emptiness and pain.

'I have to go back to the clinic. It's not raining now.'

Dick walked beside her, feeling her unhappiness, and wanting to drink the rain that touched her cheek.

'I have some new records,' she said. 'I can hardly wait to play them. Do you know – '

After supper that evening, Dick thought, he would finish the break; also he wanted to kick Franz's bottom for having partially introduced him to such a sordid business. He waited in the hall. His eyes followed a beret, not wet with waiting like Nicole's beret, but covering a skull recently operated on. Beneath it human eyes peered, found him and came over: 'Bonjour, docteur.'

'Bonjour, monsieur.'

'Il fait beau temps.'

'Oui, merveilleux.'

'Vous êtes ici maintenant?'

'Non, pour la journée seulement.'

'Ah, bon. Alors – au revoir, monsieur.'

Glad at having survived another contact, the wretch in the beret moved away. Dick waited. Presently a nurse came downstairs and delivered him a message.

'Miss Warren asks to be excused, doctor. She wants to lie down. She wants to have dinner upstairs tonight.'

The nurse hung on his response, half expecting him to imply that Miss Warren's attitude was pathological.

'Oh, I see. Well – ' He rearranged the flow of his own saliva, the pulse of his heart. 'I hope she feels better. Thanks.'

He was puzzled and discontent. At any rate it freed him.

Leaving a note for Franz begging off from supper, he walked

through the countryside to the tram station. As he reached the platform, with spring twilight gilding the rails and the glass in the slot machines, he began to feel that the station, the hospital, was hovering between being centripetal and centrifugal. He felt frightened. He was glad when the substantial cobblestones of Zurich clicked once more under his shoes.

He expected to hear from Nicole next day but there was no word. Wondering if she was ill, he called the clinic and talked to Franz.

'She came downstairs to luncheon yesterday and today,' said Franz. 'She seemed a little abstracted and in the clouds. How did it go off?'

Dick tried to plunge over the Alpine crevasse between the sexes.

'We didn't get to it – at least I didn't think we did. I tried to be distant, but I didn't think enough happened to change her attitude if it ever went deep.'

Perhaps his vanity had been hurt that there was no *coup de grâce* to administer.

'From some things she said to her nurse I'm inclined to think she understood.'

'All right.'

'It was the best thing that could have happened. She doesn't seem over-agitated – only a little in the clouds.'

'All right, then.'

'Dick, come soon and see me.'

Chapter 8

During the next weeks Dick experienced a vast dissatisfaction. The pathological origin and mechanistic defeat of the affair left a flat and metallic taste. Nicole's emotions had been used unfairly – what if they turned out to have been his own? Necessarily he must absent himself from felicity a while – in dreams he saw her walking on the clinic path swinging her wide straw hat . . .

One time he saw her in person; as he walked past the Palace Hôtel, a magnificent Rolls curved into the half-moon entrance. Small within its gigantic proportions, and buoyed up by the power of a hundred superfluous horses, sat Nicole and a young woman whom he assumed was her sister. Nicole saw him and momentarily her lips parted in an expression of fright. Dick shifted his hat and passed, yet for a moment the air around him was loud with the circlings of all the goblins on the

Gross-Münster. He tried to write the matter out of his mind in a memorandum that went into detail as to the solemn regime before her; the possibilities of another 'push' of the malady under the stresses which the world would inevitably supply – in all a memorandum that would have been convincing to anyone save to him who had written it.

The total value of this effort was to make him realise once more how far his emotions were involved; thenceforth he resolutely provided antidotes. One was the telephone girl from Bar-sur-Aube, now touring Europe from Nice to Coblenz, in a desperate round-up of the men she had known in her never-to-be-equalled holiday; another was the making of arrangements to get home on a government transport in August; a third was a consequent intensification of work on his proofs for the book that this autumn was to be presented to the German-speaking world of psychiatry.

Dick had outgrown the book; he wanted now to do more spade-work; if he got an exchange fellowship he could count on plenty of routine.

Meanwhile he had projected a new work: 'An attempt at a uniform and pragmatic classification of the neuroses and psychoses, based on an examination of fifteen hundred pre-Krapaelin and post-Krapaelin cases as they would be diagnosed in the terminology of the different contemporary schools' and another sonorous paragraph 'Together with a chronology of such subdivisions of opinion as have arisen independently'.

This title would look monumental in German.*

Going into Montreux Dick pedalled slowly, gaping at the Jugenhorn whenever possible, and blinded by glimpses of the lake through the alleys of the shore hotels. He was conscious of the groups of English, emergent after four years and walking with detective-story suspicion in their eyes, as though they were about to be assaulted in this questionable country by German train-bands. There was building and awakening everywhere on this mound of débris formed by a mountain torrent. At Berne and at Lausanne on the way south, Dick had been

* Ein Versuch die Neurosen und Psychosen gleichmässig und pragmatisch zu klassifizieren auf Grund der Untersuchung von fünfzehn hundert pre-Krapaelin und post-Krapaelin Fällen wie sie diagnostiziert sein würden in der Terminologie von den verschiedenen Schulen der Gegenwart, Zusammen mit einer Chronologie solcher Subdivisionen der Meinung welche unabhängig entstanden sind.

eagerly asked if there would be Americans this year. 'By August, if not in June?'

He wore leather shorts, an army shirt, mountain shoes. In his knapsack were a cotton suit and a change of underwear. At the Glion funicular he checked his bicycle and took a small beer on the terrace of the station buffet, meanwhile watching the little bug crawl down the eighty-degree slope of the hill. His ear was full of dried blood from La Tour de Pelz, where he had sprinted under the impression that he was a spoiled athlete. He asked for alcohol and cleared up the exterior while the funicular slid down into port. He saw his bicycle embarked, slung his knapsack into the lower compartment of the car, and followed it in.

Mountain-climbing cars are built on a slant similar to the angle of a hat-brim of a man who doesn't want to be recognised. As water gushed from the chamber under the car, Dick was impressed with the ingenuity of the whole idea – a complementary car was now taking on mountain water at the top and would pull the lightened car up by gravity, as soon as the brakes were released. It must have been a great inspiration. In the seat across, a couple of British were discussing the cable itself.

'The ones made in England always last five or six years. Two years ago the Germans underbid us, and how long do you think their cable lasted?'

'How long?'

'A year and ten months. Then the Swiss sold it to the Italians. They don't have rigid inspections of cables.'

'I can see it would be a terrible thing for Switzerland if a cable broke.'

The conductor shut a door; he telephoned his confrère among the undulati, and with a jerk the car was pulled upward, heading for a pinpoint on an emerald hill above. After it cleared the low roofs, the skies of Vaud, Valais, Swiss Savoy, and Geneva spread around the passengers in cyclorama. On the centre of the lake, cooled by the piercing current of the Rhône, lay the true centre of the Western world. Upon it floated swans like boats and boats like swans, both lost in the nothingness of the heartless beauty. It was a bright day, with sun glittering on the grass beach below and the white courts of the Kursaal. The figures on the courts threw no shadows.

When Chillon and the island palace of Salagnon came into view Dick turned his eyes inward. The funicular was above the highest houses of the shore; on both sides a tangle of foliage and flowers culminated at intervals in masses of colour. It was a rail-side garden, and in the car was a sign: 'Défense de cueillir les fleurs.'

Though one must not pick flowers on the way up, the blossoms trailed in as they passed – Dorothy Perkins roses dragged patiently through each compartment slowly waggling with the motion of the funicular, letting go at the last to swing back to their rosy cluster. Again and again these branches went through the car.

In the compartment above and in front of Dick's, a group of English were standing up and exclaiming upon the backdrop of sky, when suddenly there was a confusion among them – they parted to give passage to a couple of young people who made apologies and scrambled over into the rear compartment of the funicular – Dick's compartment. The young man was a Latin with the eyes of a stuffed deer; the girl was Nicole.

The two climbers gasped momentarily from their efforts; as they settled into seats, laughing and crowding the English to the corners, Nicole said, 'Hel*lo*.' She was lovely to look at; immediately Dick saw that something was different; in a second he realised it was her fine-spun hair, bobbed like Irene Castle's and fluffed into curls. She wore a sweater of powder blue and white tennis skirt – she was the first morning in May and every taint of the clinic was departed.

'Plunk!' she gasped. 'Whoo-oo, that guard. They'll arrest us at the next stop. Dr Diver, the Conte de Marmora.'

'Gee-imminy!' She felt her new hair, panting. 'Sister bought first-class tickets – it's a matter of principle with her.' She and Marmora exchanged glances and shouted: 'Then we found that first-class is the hearse part behind the chauffeur – shut in with curtains for a rainy day, so you can't see anything. But Sister's very dignified – ' Again Nicole and Marmora laughed with young intimacy.

'Where you bound?' asked Dick.

'Caux. You, too?' Nicole looked at his costume. 'That your bicycle they got up in front?'

'Yes. I'm going to coast down Monday.'

'With me on your handlebars? I mean, really – will you? I can't think of more fun.'

'But I will carry you down in my arms,' Marmora protested intensely. 'I will roller-skate you – or I will throw you and you will fall slowly like a feather.'

The delight in Nicole's face – to be a feather again instead of a plummet, to float not to drag. She was a carnival to watch – at times primly coy, posing, grimacing and gesturing – sometimes the shadow fell and the dignity of old suffering flowed down into her fingertips. Dick wished himself away from her, fearing that he was a reminder of a world well left behind. He resolved to go to the other hotel.

When the funicular came to rest, those new to it stirred in suspension between the blues of two heavens. It was merely for a mysterious exchange between the conductor of the car going up and the conductor of the car coming down. Then up and up over a forest path and a gorge – then again up a hill that became solid with narcissus, from passengers to sky. The people in Montreux playing tennis in the lakeside courts were pinpoints now. Something new was in the air; freshness – freshness embodying itself in music as the car slid into Glion and they heard the orchestra in the hotel garden.

When they changed to the mountain train the music was drowned by the rushing water released from the hydraulic chamber. Almost overhead was Caux, where the thousand windows of a hotel burned in the late sun.

But the approach was different – a leather-lunged engine pushed the passengers round and round in a corkscrew, mounting, rising; they chugged through low-level clouds and for a moment Dick lost Nicole's face in the spray of the slanting donkey-engine; they skirted a lost streak of wind with the hotel growing in size at each spiral, until with a vast surprise they were there, on top of the sunshine.

In the confusion of arrival, as Dick slung his knapsack and started forward on the platform to get his bicycle, Nicole was beside him.

'Aren't you at our hotel?' she asked.

'I'm economising.'

'Will you come down and have dinner?' Some confusion with baggage ensued. 'This is my sister – Dr Diver from Zurich.'

Dick bowed to a young woman of twenty-five, tall and confident. She was both formidable and vulnerable, he decided, remembering other women with flower-like mouths grooved for bits.

'I'll drop in after dinner,' Dick promised. 'First I must get acclimated.'

He wheeled off his bicycle, feeling Nicole's eyes following him, feeling her helpless first love, feeling it twist around inside him. He went three hundred yards up the slope to the other hotel, he engaged a room and found himself washing without a memory of the intervening ten minutes, only a sort of drunken flush pierced with voices, unimportant voices that did not know how much he was loved.

Chapter 9

They were waiting for him and incomplete without him. He was still the incalculable element; Miss Warren and the young Italian wore their anticipation as obviously as Nicole. The salon of the hotel, a room of fabled acoustics, was stripped for dancing, but there was a small gallery of Englishwomen of a certain age, with neckbands, dyed hair, and faces powdered pinkish grey; and of American women of a certain age, with snowy-white transformations, black dresses, and lips of cherry red. Miss Warren and Marmora were at a corner table – Nicole was diagonally across from them forty yards away, and as Dick arrived he heard her voice: 'Can you hear me? I'm speaking naturally.'

'Perfectly.'

'Hello, Dr Diver.'

'What's this?'

'You realise the people in the centre of the floor can't hear what I say, but you can?'

'A waiter told us about it,' said Miss Warren. 'Corner to corner – it's like wireless.'

It was exciting up on the mountain, like a ship at sea. Presently Marmora's parents joined them. They treated the Warrens with respect – Dick gathered that their fortunes had something to do with a bank in Milan that had something to do with the Warren fortunes. But Baby Warren wanted to talk to Dick, wanted to talk to him with the impetus that sent her out vagrantly towards all new men, as though she were on an inelastic tether and considered that she might as well get to the end of it as soon as possible. She crossed and recrossed her knees frequently in the manner of tall restless virgins.

' – Nicole told me that you took part care of her, and had a lot to do with her getting well. What I can't understand is what *we're* supposed to do – they were so indefinite at the sanatorium; they only told me she ought to be natural and gay. I knew the Marmoras were up here so I asked Tino to meet us at the funicular. And you see what happens – the very first thing Nicole has him crawling over the sides of the car as if they were both insane – '

'That was absolutely normal,' Dick laughed. 'I'd call it a good sign. They were showing off for each other.'

'But how can I tell? Before I knew it, almost in front of my eyes, she had her hair cut off, in Zurich, because of a picture in *Vanity Fair*.'

'That's all right. She's a schizoid – a permanent eccentric. You can't change that.'

'What is it?'

'Just what I said – an eccentric.'

'Well, how can anyone tell what's eccentric and what's crazy?'

'Nothing is going to be crazy – Nicole is all fresh and happy, you needn't be afraid.'

Baby shifted her knees about – she was a compendium of all the discontented women who had loved Byron a hundred years before, yet, in spite of the tragic affair with the Guards officer, there was something wooden and onanistic about her.

'I don't mind the responsibility,' she declared, 'but I'm in the air. We've never had anything like this in the family before – we know Nicole had some shock and my opinion is it was about a boy, but we don't really know. Father says he would have shot him if he could have found out.'

The orchestra was playing 'Poor Butterfly'; young Marmora was dancing with his mother. It was a tune new enough to them all. Listening, and watching Nicole's shoulders as she chattered to the elder Marmora, whose hair was dashed with white like a piano keyboard, Dick thought of the shoulders of a violin, and then he thought of the dishonour, the secret. Oh, butterfly – the moments pass into hours –

'Actually *I* have a plan,' Baby continued with apologetic hardness. 'It may seem absolutely impractical to you but they say Nicole will need to be looked after for a few years. I don't know whether you know Chicago or not – '

'I don't.'

'Well, there's a North Side and a South Side and they're very much separated. The North Side is chic and all that, and we've always lived over there, at least for many years, but lots of old families, old Chicago families, if you know what I mean, still live on the South Side. The University is there. I mean it's stuffy to some people, but anyhow it's different from the North Side. I don't know whether you understand.'

He nodded. With some concentration he had been able to follow her.

'Now of course we have lots of connections there – father controls certain chairs and fellowships and so forth at the University, and I thought if we took Nicole home and threw her with that crowd – you see she's quite musical and speaks all these languages – what could be better in her condition than if she fell in love with some good doctor – '

A burst of hilarity surged up in Dick, the Warrens were going to buy Nicole a doctor – You got a nice doctor you can let us use? There was no use worrying about Nicole when they were in the position of being able to buy her a nice young doctor, the paint scarcely dry on him.

'But how about the doctor?' he said automatically.

'There must be many who'd jump at the chance.'

The dancers were back, but Baby whispered quickly: 'This is the sort of thing I mean. Now where is Nicole – she's gone off somewhere. Is she upstairs in her room? What am I supposed to do? I never know whether it's something innocent or whether I ought to go find her.'

'Perhaps she just wants to be by herself – people living alone get used to loneliness.' Seeing that Miss Warren was not listening he stopped. 'I'll take a look around.'

For a moment all the outdoors shut in with mist was like spring with the curtains drawn. Life was gathered near the hotel. Dick passed some cellar windows where bus boys sat on bunks and played cards over a litre of Spanish wine. As he approached the promenade, the stars began to come through the white crests of the high Alps. On the horseshoe walk overlooking the lake Nicole was the figure motionless between two lampstands, and he approached silently across the grass. She turned to him with an expression of: 'Here you are,' and for a moment he was sorry he had come.

'Your sister wondered.'

'Oh!' She was accustomed to being watched. With an effort she explained herself: 'Sometimes I get a little – it gets a little too much. I've lived so quietly. Tonight that music was too much. It made me want to cry – '

'I understand.'

'This has been an awfully exciting day.'

'I know.'

'I don't want to do anything antisocial – I've caused everybody enough trouble. But tonight I wanted to get away.'

It occurred to Dick suddenly, as it might occur to a dying man that he had forgotten to tell where his will was, that Nicole had been 're-educated' by Dohmler and the ghostly generations behind him; it occurred to him also that there would be so much she would have to be told. But having recorded this wisdom within himself, he yielded to the insistent face-value of the situation and said: 'You're a nice person – just keep using your own judgement about yourself.'

'You like me?'

'Of course.'

'Would you – ' They were strolling along towards the dim end of the horseshoe, two hundred yards ahead. 'If I hadn't been sick would you – I mean, would I have been the sort of girl you might have – oh, slush, you know what I mean.'

He was in for it now, possessed by a vast irrationality. She was so near that he felt his breathing change but again his training came to his aid in a boy's laugh and a trite remark.

'You're teasing yourself, my dear. Once I knew a man who fell in love with his nurse – ' The anecdote rambled on, punctuated by their footsteps. Suddenly Nicole interrupted in succinct Chicagoese: 'Bull!'

'That's a very vulgar expression.'

'What about it?' she flared up. 'You don't think I've got any common sense – before I was sick I didn't have any, but I have now. And if I don't know you're the most attractive man I ever met you must think I'm still crazy. It's my hard luck, all right – don't pretend I don't *know* – I know everything about you and me.'

Dick was at an additional disadvantage. He remembered the statement of the elder Miss Warren as to the young doctors that could be purchased in the intellectual stockyards of the South Side of Chicago, and he hardened for a moment. 'You're a fetching kid, but I couldn't fall in love.'

'You won't give me a chance.'

'What!'

The impertinence, the right to invade implied, astounded him. Short of anarchy he could not think of any chance that Nicole Warren deserved.

'Give me a chance now.'

The voice fell low, sank into her breast and stretched the tight bodice over her heart as she came up close. He felt the young lips, her body sighing in relief against the arm growing stronger to hold her. There were now no more plans than if Dick had arbitrarily made some indissoluble mixture, with atoms joined and inseparable; you could throw it all out but never again could they fit back into atomic scale. As he held her and tasted her, and as she curved in further and further towards him, with her own lips, new to herself, drowned and engulfed in love, yet solaced and triumphant, he was thankful to have an existence at all, if only as a reflection in her wet eyes.

'My God,' he gasped, 'you're fun to kiss.'

That was talk, but Nicole had a better hold on him now and she held it; she turned coquette and walked away, leaving him as suspended as in the funicular of the afternoon. She felt: There, that'll show him, how conceited; how he could do with me; oh, wasn't it wonderful! I've got him, he's mine. Now in the sequence came flight, but it was all so sweet and new that she dawdled, wanting to draw all of it in.

She shivered suddenly. Two thousand feet below she saw the necklace and bracelet of lights that were Montreux and Vevey, beyond them a dim pendant of Lausanne. From down there somewhere ascended a faint sound of dance music. Nicole was up in her head now, cool as cool, trying to collate the sentimentalities of her childhood, as deliberate as a man getting drunk after battle. But she was still afraid of Dick, who stood near her, leaning, characteristically, against the iron fence that rimmed the horseshoe; and this prompted her to say: 'I can remember how I stood waiting for you in the garden – holding all my self in my arms like a basket of flowers. It was that to me anyhow – I thought I was sweet – waiting to hand that basket to you.'

He breathed over her shoulder and turned her insistently about; she kissed him several times, her face getting big every time she came close, her hands holding him by the shoulders.

'It's raining hard.'

Suddenly there was a booming from the wine slopes across the lake; cannons were shooting at hail-bearing clouds in order to break them. The lights of the promenade went off, went on again. Then the storm came swiftly, first falling from the heavens, then doubly falling in torrents from the mountains and washing loud down the roads and stone ditches; with it came a dark, frightening sky and savage filaments of lightning and world-splitting thunder, while ragged, destroying clouds fled along past the hotel. Mountains and lake disappeared – the hotel crouched amid tumult, chaos and darkness.

By this time Dick and Nicole had reached the vestibule, where Baby Warren and the three Marmoras were anxiously awaiting them. It was exciting coming out of the wet fog – with the doors banging, to stand and laugh and quiver with emotion, wind in their ears and rain on their clothes. Now in the ballroom the orchestra was playing a Strauss waltz, high and confusing.

. . . For Dr Diver to marry a mental patient? How did it happen? Where did it begin?

'Won't you come back after you've changed?' Baby Warren asked after a close scrutiny.

'I haven't got any change, except some shorts.'

As he trudged up to his hotel in a borrowed raincoat he kept laughing derisively in his throat.

'Big chance – oh, yes. My God! – they decided to buy a doctor? Well, they better stick to whoever they've got in Chicago.' Revolted by his harshness he made amends to Nicole, remembering that nothing had ever felt so young as her lips, remembering rain like tears shed for him that lay upon her softly shining porcelain cheeks . . . the silence of the storm ceasing woke him about three o'clock and he went to the window. Her beauty climbed the rolling slope, it came into the room, rustling ghost-like through the curtains . . .

. . . He climbed two thousand metres to Rocher de Naye the following morning, amused by the fact that his conductor of the day before was using his day off to climb also.

Then Dick descended all the way to Montreux for a swim, got back to his hotel in time for dinner. Two notes awaited him.

> I'm not ashamed about last night – it was the nicest thing that ever happened to me and even if I never saw you again, Mon Capitaine, I would be glad it happened.

That was disarming enough – the heavy shade of Dohmler retreated as Dick opened the second envelope:

> Dear Dr Diver – I phoned but you were out. I wonder if I may ask you a great big favour. Unforeseen circumstances call me back to Paris, and I find I can make better time by way of Lausanne. Can you let Nicole ride as far as Zurich with you, since you are going back Monday? and drop her at the sanatorium? Is this too much to ask?
>
> Sincerely,
>
> Beth Evan Warren

Dick was furious – Miss Warren had known he had a bicycle with him; yet she had so phrased her note that it was impossible to refuse. Throw us together! Sweet propinquity and the Warren money!

He was wrong; Baby Warren had no such intentions. She had looked Dick over with worldly eyes; she had measured him with the warped rule of an Anglophile and found him wanting – in spite of the fact that she found him toothsome. But for her he was too 'intellectual' and she pigeon-holed him with a shabby-snobby crowd she had once known in London – he put himself out too much to be really of the correct stuff. She could not see how he could be made into her idea of an aristocrat.

In addition to that he was stubborn – she had seen him leave her conversation and get down behind his eyes in that odd way that people did, half a dozen times. She had not liked Nicole's free and easy manner as a child and now she was sensibly habituated to thinking of her as a 'gone coon'; and anyhow Dr Diver was not the sort of medical man she could envisage in the family.

She only wanted to use him innocently as a convenience.

But her request had the effect that Dick assumed she desired. A ride in a train can be a terrible, heavy-hearted or comic thing; it can be a trial flight; it can be a prefiguration of another journey just as a given day with a friend can be long, from the taste of hurry in the morning up to the realisation of both being hungry and taking food together. Then comes the afternoon with the journey fading and dying, but quickening again at the end. Dick was sad to see Nicole's meagre joy; yet it was a relief for her, going back to the only home she knew. They made no love that day, but when he left her outside the sad door on the Zurichsee and she turned and looked at him he knew her problem was one they had together for good now.

Chapter 10

In Zurich in September Dr Diver had tea with Baby Warren.

'I think it's ill advised,' she said, 'I'm not sure I truly understand your motives.'

'Don't let's be unpleasant.'

'After all I'm Nicole's sister.'

'That doesn't give you the right to be unpleasant.' It irritated Dick that he knew so much that he could not tell her. 'Nicole's rich, but that doesn't make me an adventurer.'

'That's just it,' complained Baby stubbornly. 'Nicole's rich.'

'Just how much money has she got?' he asked.

She started; and with a silent laugh he continued, 'You see how silly this is? I'd rather talk to some man in your family – '

'Everything's been left to me,' she persisted. 'It isn't we think you're an adventurer. We don't know who you are.'

'I'm a doctor of medicine,' he said. 'My father is a clergyman, now retired. We lived in Buffalo and my past is open to investigation. I went to New Haven; afterwards I was a Rhodes scholar. My great-grandfather was Governor of North Carolina and I'm a direct descendant of Mad Anthony Wayne.'

'Who was Mad Anthony Wayne?' Baby asked suspiciously.

'Mad Anthony Wayne?'

'I think there's enough madness in this affair.'

He shook his head hopelessly, just as Nicole came out on the hotel terrace and looked around for them.

'He was too mad to leave as much money as Marshall Field,' he said.

'That's all very well –'

Baby was right and she knew it. Face to face, her father would have it on almost any clergyman. They were an American ducal family without a title – the very name written in a hotel register, signed to an introduction, used in a difficult situation, caused a psychological metamorphosis in people, and in return this change had crystallised her own sense of position. She knew these facts from the English, who had known them for over two hundred years. But she did not know that twice Dick had come close to flinging the marriage in her face. All that saved it this time was Nicole finding their table and glowing away, white and fresh and new in the September afternoon.

How do you do, lawyer. We're going to Como tomorrow for a week and then back to Zurich. That's why I wanted you and sister to settle this, because it doesn't matter to us how much I'm allowed. We're going to live very quietly in Zurich for two years and Dick has enough to take care of us. No, Baby, I'm more practical than you think – It's only for clothes and things I'll need it . . . Why, that's more than – can the estate really afford to give me all that? I know I'll never manage to spend it. Do you have that much? Why do you have more – is it because I'm supposed to be incompetent? All right, let my share pile up then . . . No, Dick refuses to have anything whatever to do with it. I'll have to feel bloated for us both . . . Baby, you have no more idea of what Dick is like than, than – Now where do I sign? oh, I'm sorry.

. . . Isn't it funny and lovely being together, Dick? No place to go except close. Shall we just love and love? Ah, but I love the most, and I can tell when you're away from me, even a little. I think it's wonderful to be just like everybody else, to reach out and find you all warm beside me in the bed.

. . . If you will kindly call my husband at the hospital. Yes, the little book is selling everywhere – they want it published in six languages. I was to do the French translation but I'm tired these days – I'm afraid of falling, I'm so heavy and clumsy – like a broken roly-poly that can't stand up straight. The cold stethoscope against my heart and my strongest feeling '*Je m'en fiche de tout*' – oh, that poor woman in the hospital with the blue baby, much better dead. Isn't it fine there are three of us now?

. . . That seems unreasonable, Dick – we have every reason for taking the bigger apartment. Why should we penalise ourselves just because there's more Warren money than Diver money? Oh, thank you, *camérière*, but we've changed our minds. This English clergyman tells us that your wine here in Orvieto is excellent. It doesn't travel? That must be why we have never heard of it, because we love wine.

The lakes are sunk in the brown clay and the slopes have all the creases of a belly. The photographer gave us the picture of me, my hair limp over the rail on the boat to Capri. 'Goodbye, Blue Grotto,' sang the boatman, 'come again soo-oon.' And afterwards tracing down the hot sinister shin of the Italian boot with the wind soughing around those eerie castles, the dead watching from up on those hills.

. . . This ship is nice, with our heels hitting the deck together. This is the blowy corner and each time we turn it I slant forwards against the wind and pull my coat together without losing step with Dick. We are chanting nonsense:

'Oh-oh-oh-oh
Other flamingoes than me,
Oh-oh-oh-oh
Other flamingoes than me – '

Life is fun with Dick – the people in deck-chairs look at us, and a woman is trying to hear what we are singing. Dick is tired of singing it, so go on alone, Dick. You will walk differently alone, dear, through a thicker atmosphere, forcing your way through the shadows of chairs, through the dripping smoke of the funnels. You will feel your own reflection sliding along the eyes of those who look at you. You are no longer insulated; but I suppose you must touch life in order to spring from it.

Sitting on the stanchion of this lifeboat I look seaward and let my hair blow and shine. I am motionless against the sky and the boat is made to carry my form onward into the blue obscurity of the future, I am Pallas Athene carved reverently on the front of a galley. The waters are lapping in the public toilets and the agate green foliage of spray changes and complains about the stern.

. . . We travelled a lot that year – from Woolloomooloo Bay to Biskra. On the edge of the Sahara we ran into a plague of locusts and the chauffeur explained kindly that they were bumble-bees. The sky was low at night, full of the presence of a strange and watchful God. Oh, the poor little naked Ouled Naïl: the night was noisy with drums from Senegal and flutes and whining camels, and the natives pattering about in shoes made of old automobile tyres.

But I was gone again by that time – trains and beaches they were all one. That was why he took me travelling, but after my second child, my little girl Topsy, was born everything got dark again.

. . . If I could get word to my husband who has seen fit to desert me here, to leave me in the hands of incompetents. You tell me my baby is black – that's farcical, that's very cheap. We went to Africa merely to see Timgad, since my principal interest in life is archaeology. I am tired of knowing nothing and being reminded of it all the time.

. . . When I get well I want to be a fine person like you, Dick – I would study medicine except it's too late. We must spend my money and have a house – I'm tired of apartments and waiting for you. You're bored with Zurich and you can't find time for writing here and you say that it's a confession of weakness for a scientist not to write. And I'll look over the whole field of knowledge and pick out something and really know about it, so I'll have it to hang on to if I go to pieces again. You'll help me, Dick, so I won't feel so guilty. We'll live near a warm beach where we can be brown and young together.

. . . This is going to be Dick's work house. Oh, the idea came to us both at the same moment. We had passed Tarmes a dozen times and we rode up here and found the houses empty, except two stables. When we bought we acted through a Frenchman, but the navy sent spies up here in no time when they found that Americans had bought part of a hill village. They looked for cannons all through the building material, and finally Baby had to twitch wires for us at the Affaires Étrangères in Paris.

No one comes to the Riviera in summer, so we expect to have a few guests and to work. There are some French people here – Mistinguett last week, surprised to find the hotel open, and Picasso and the man who wrote *Pas sur la Bouche*.

. . . Dick, why did you register Mr and Mrs Diver instead of Dr and Mrs Diver? I just wondered – it just floated through my mind. – You've taught me that work is everything and I believe you. You used to say a man knows things and when he stops knowing things he's like anybody else, and the thing is to get power before he stops knowing things. If you want to turn things topsy-turvy, all right, but must your Nicole follow you walking on her hands, darling?

. . . Tommy says I am silent. Since I was well the first time I talked a lot to Dick late at night, both of us sitting up in bed and lighting cigarettes, then diving down afterwards out of the blue dawn and into the pillows, to keep the light from our eyes. Sometimes I sing, and play with the animals, and I have a few friends too – Mary, for instance. When Mary and I talk neither of us listens to the other. Talk is men. When I talk I say to myself that I am probably Dick. Already I have even been my son, remembering how wise and slow he is. Sometimes I am Dr Dohmler and one time I may even be an aspect of you, Tommy Barban. Tommy is in love with me, I think, but gently, reassuringly. Enough, though, so that he and Dick have begun to disapprove of each other. All in all, everything has never gone better. I am among friends who like me. I am here on this tranquil beach with my husband and two children. Everything is all right – if I can finish translating this damn recipe for chicken à la Maryland into French. My toes feel warm in the sand.

'Yes, I'll look. More new people – oh, that girl – yes. Who did you say she looked like . . . No, I haven't, we don't get much chance to see the new American pictures over here. Rosemary who? Well, we're getting very fashionable for July – seems very peculiar to me. Yes, she's lovely, but there can be too many people.'

Chapter 11

Dr Richard Diver and Mrs Elsie Speers sat in the Café des Alliés in August, under cool and dusty trees. The sparkle of the mica was dulled by the baked ground, and a few gusts of mistral from down the coast seeped through the Esterel and rocked the fishing-boats in the harbour, pointing the masts here and there at a featureless sky.

'I had a letter this morning,' said Mrs Speers. 'What a terrible time you all must have had with those Negroes! But Rosemary said you were perfectly wonderful to her.'

'Rosemary ought to have a service stripe. It was pretty harrowing – the only person it didn't disturb was Abe North – he flew off to Havre – he probably doesn't know about it yet.'

'I'm sorry Mrs Diver was upset,' she said carefully.

Rosemary had written:

> Nicole seemed out of her mind. I didn't want to come South with them because I felt Dick had enough on his hands.

'She's all right now.' He spoke almost impatiently. 'So you're leaving tomorrow. When will you sail?'

'Right away.'

'My God, it's awful to have you go.'

'We're glad we came here. We've had a good time, thanks to you. You're the first man Rosemary ever cared for.'

Another gust of wind strained around the porphyry hills of la Napoule. There was a hint in the air that the earth was hurrying on towards other weather; the lush midsummer moment outside of time was already over.

'Rosemary's had crushes, but sooner or later she always turned the man over to me – ' Mrs Speers laughed, ' – for dissection.'

'So I was spared.'

'There was nothing I could have done. She was in love with you before I ever saw you. I told her to go ahead.'

He saw that no provision had been made for him, or for Nicole, in Mrs Speers' plans – and he saw that her amorality sprang from the conditions of her own withdrawal. It was her right, the pension on which her own emotions had retired. Women are necessarily capable of almost anything in their struggle for survival and can scarcely be convicted of such man-made crimes as 'cruelty'. So long as the shuffle of love and pain went on within proper walls Mrs Speers could view it with as much detachment and humour as a eunuch. She had not even allowed for the possibility of Rosemary's being damaged – or was she certain that she couldn't be?

'If what you say is true I don't think it did her any harm.' He was keeping up to the end the pretence that he could still think objectively about Rosemary. 'She's over it already. Still – so many of the important times in life begin by seeming incidental.'

'This wasn't incidental,' Mrs Speers insisted. 'You were the first man – you're an ideal to her. In every letter she says that.'

'She's so polite.'

'You and Rosemary are the politest people I've ever known, but she means this.'

'My politeness is a trick of the heart.'

This was partly true. From his father Dick had learned the somewhat conscious good manners of the young Southerner coming north after the Civil War. Often he used them and just as often he despised them because they were not a protest against how unpleasant selfishness was but against how unpleasant it looked.

'I'm in love with Rosemary,' he told her suddenly. 'It's a kind of self-indulgence saying that to you.'

It seemed very strange and official to him, as if the very tables and chairs in the Café des Alliés would remember it for ever. Already he felt her absence from these skies: on the beach he could only remember the sun-torn flesh of her shoulders; at Tarmes he crushed out her footprints as he crossed the garden; and now the orchestra launching into the 'Nice Carnival Song', an echo of last year's vanished gaieties, started the little dance that went on all about her. In a hundred hours she had come to possess all the world's dark magic; the blinding belladonna, the caffeine converting physical into nervous energy, the mandragora that imposes harmony.

With an effort he once more accepted the fiction that he shared Mrs Speers' detachment.

'You and Rosemary aren't really alike,' he said. 'The wisdom she got from you is all moulded up into her persona, into the mask she faces the world with. She doesn't think; her real depths are Irish and romantic and illogical.'

Mrs Speers knew too that Rosemary, for all her delicate surface, was a young mustang, perceptibly by Captain Dr Hoyt, USA Cross-sectioned, Rosemary would have displayed an enormous heart, liver and soul, all crammed close together under the lovely shell.

Saying goodbye, Dick was aware of Elsie Speers' full charm, aware that she meant rather more to him than merely a last unwillingly relinquished fragment of Rosemary. He could possibly have made up Rosemary – he could never have made up her mother. If the cloak, spurs, and brilliants in which Rosemary had walked off were things with which he had endowed her, it was nice in contrast to watch her mother's grace knowing it was surely something he had not evoked.

She had an air of seeming to wait, as if for a man to get through with something more important than herself, a battle or an operation, during which he must not be hurried or interfered with. When the man had finished she would be waiting, without fret or impatience, somewhere on a high stool, turning the pages of a newspaper.

'Goodbye – and I want you both to remember always how fond of you Nicole and I have grown.'

Back at the Villa Diana, he went to his workroom, and opened the shutters, closed against the midday glare. On his two long tables, in ordered confusion, lay the materials of his book. Volume I, concerned with Classification, had achieved some success in a small subsidised edition. He was negotiating for its reissue. Volume II was to be a great amplification of his first little book, *A Psychology for Psychiatrists*. Like so many men he had found that he had only one or two ideas – that his little collection of pamphlets now in its fiftieth German edition contained the germ of all he would ever think or know.

But he was currently uneasy about the whole thing. He resented the wasted years at New Haven, but mostly he felt a discrepancy between the growing luxury in which the Divers lived, and the need for display which apparently went along with it. Remembering his Rumanian friend's story, about the man who had worked for years on the brain of an armadillo, he suspected that patient Germans were sitting close to the libraries of Berlin and Vienna callously anticipating him. He had about decided to brief the work in its present condition and publish it in an undocumented volume of a hundred thousand words as an introduction to more scholarly volumes to follow.

He confirmed this decision walking around the rays of late afternoon in his workroom. With the new plan he could be through by spring. It seemed to him that when a man with his energy was pursued for a year by increasing doubts, it indicated some fault in the plan.

He laid the bars of gilded metal that he used as paperweights along the sheaves of notes. He swept up, for no servant was allowed in here, treated his washroom sketchily with Bon Ami, repaired a screen, and sent off an order to a publishing house in Zurich. Then he drank an ounce of gin with twice as much water.

He saw Nicole in the garden. Presently he must encounter her and the prospect gave him a leaden feeling. Before her he must keep up a perfect front, now and tomorrow, next week and next year. All night in Paris he had held her in his arms while she slept light under the luminal; in the early morning he broke in upon her confusion before it could form, with words of tenderness and protection, and she slept again with his face against the warm scent of her hair. Before she woke he had arranged everything at the phone in the next room. Rosemary was to move to another hotel. She was to be 'Daddy's Girl' and even to give up saying goodbye to them. The proprietor of the hotel, Mr McBeth, was to be the three Chinese monkeys. Packing amid the piled boxes and tissue paper of many purchases, Dick and Nicole left for the Riviera at noon.

Then there was a reaction. As they settled down in the *wagon-lit* Dick saw that Nicole was waiting for it, and it came quickly and desperately, before the train was out of the *ceinture* – his only instinct was to step off while the train was still going slow, rush back and see where Rosemary was, what she was doing. He opened a book and bent his pince-nez upon it, aware that Nicole was watching him from her pillow across the compartment. Unable to read, he pretended to be tired and shut his eyes, but she was still watching him, and though still she was half-asleep from the hangover of the drug, she was relieved and almost happy that he was hers again.

It was worse with his eyes shut for it gave a rhythm of finding and losing, finding and losing; but so as not to appear restless he lay like that until noon. At luncheon things were better – it was always a fine meal; a thousand lunches in inns and restaurants, *wagon-lits*, buffets, and aeroplanes were a mighty collation to have taken together. The familiar hurry of the train waiters, the little bottles of wine and mineral water, the excellent food of the Paris–Lyons–Méditerranée gave them the illusion that everything was the same as before, but it was almost the first trip he had ever taken with Nicole that was a going away rather than a going towards. He drank a whole bottle of wine save for Nicole's single glass; they talked about the house and the children. But once back in the compartment a silence fell over them like the silence in the restaurant across from the Luxembourg. Receding from a grief, it seems necessary to retrace the same steps that brought us there. An unfamiliar impatience settled on Dick; suddenly Nicole said: 'It seemed too bad to leave Rosemary like that – do you suppose she'll be all right?'

'Of course. She could take care of herself anywhere – ' Lest this belittle Nicole's ability to do likewise, he added, 'After all, she's an actress, and even though her mother's in the background she *has* to look out for herself.'

'She's very attractive.'

'She's an infant.'

'She's attractive though.'

They talked aimlessly back and forth, each speaking for the other.

'She's not as intelligent as I thought,' Dick offered.

'She's quite smart.'

'Not very, though – there's a persistent aroma of the nursery.'

'She's very – very pretty,' Nicole said in a detached, emphatic way, 'and I thought she was very good in the picture.'

'She was well directed. Thinking it over, it wasn't very individual.'

'I thought it was. I can see how she'd be very attractive to men.'

His heart twisted. To what men? How many men?

– Do you mind if I pull down the curtain?

– Please do, it's too light in here.

Where now? And with whom?

'In a few years she'll look ten years older than you.'

'On the contrary. I sketched her one night on a theatre programme, I think she'll last.'

They were both restless in the night. In a day or two Dick would try to banish the ghost of Rosemary before it became walled up with them, but for the moment he had no force to do it. Sometimes it is harder to deprive oneself of a pain than of a pleasure, and the memory so possessed him that for the moment there was nothing to do but to pretend. This was more difficult because he was currently annoyed with Nicole, who, after all these years, should recognise symptoms of strain in herself and guard against them. Twice within a fortnight she had broken up: there had been the night of the dinner at Tarmes when he had found her in her bedroom dissolved in crazy laughter telling Mrs McKisco she could not go in the bathroom because the key was thrown down the well. Mrs McKisco was astonished and resentful, baffled and yet in a way comprehending. Dick had not been particularly alarmed then, for afterwards Nicole was repentant. She called at Gausse's Hôtel but the McKiscos were gone.

The collapse in Paris was another matter, adding significance to the first one. It prophesied possibly a new cycle, a new *pousse* of the malady. Having gone through unprofessional agonies during her long relapse following Topsy's birth, he had, perforce, hardened himself about her, making a cleavage between Nicole sick and Nicole well. This made it difficult now to distinguish between his self-protective professional detachment and some new coldness in his heart. As an indifference cherished, or left to atrophy, becomes an emptiness, to this extent he had learned to become empty of Nicole, serving her against his will with negations and emotional neglect. One writes of scars healed, a loose parallel to the pathology of the skin, but there is no such thing in the life of an individual. There are open wounds, shrunk sometimes to the size of a pin-prick, but wounds still. The marks of suffering are more comparable to the loss of a finger, or of the sight of an eye. We may not miss them, either, for one minute in a year, but if we should there is nothing to be done about it.

Chapter 12

He found Nicole in the garden with her arms folded high on her shoulders. She looked at him with straight grey eyes, with a child's searching wonder.

'I went to Cannes,' he said. 'I ran into Mrs Speers. She's leaving tomorrow. She wanted to come up and say goodbye to you, but I slew the idea.'

'I'm sorry. I'd like to have seen her. I like her.'

'Who else do you think I saw – Bartholomew Tailor.'

'You didn't.'

'I couldn't have missed that face of his, the old experienced weasel. He was looking over the ground for Ciro's Menagerie – they'll all be down next year. I suspected Mrs Abrams was a sort of outpost.'

'And Baby was outraged the first summer we came here.'

'They don't really give a damn where they are, so I don't see why they don't stay and freeze in Deauville.'

'Can't we start rumours about cholera or something?'

'I told Bartholomew that some categories died off like flies here – I told him the life of a suck was as short as the life of a machine-gunner in the war.'

'You didn't.'

'No, I didn't,' he admitted. 'He was very pleasant. It was a beautiful sight, he and I shaking hands there on the boulevard. The meeting of Sigmund Freud and Ward McAllister.'

Dick didn't want to talk – he wanted to be alone so that his thoughts about work and the future would overpower his thoughts of love and today. Nicole knew about it but only darkly and tragically, hating him a little in an animal way, yet wanting to rub against his shoulder.

'The darling,' Dick said lightly.

He went into the house, forgetting something he wanted to do there, and then remembering it was the piano. He sat down whistling and played by ear:

'Just picture you upon my knee
With tea for two and two for tea
And me for you and you for me – '

Through the melody flowed a sudden realisation that Nicole, hearing it, would guess quickly at a nostalgia for the past fortnight. He broke off with a casual chord and left the piano.

It was hard to know where to go. He glanced about the house that Nicole had made, that Nicole's grandfather had paid for. He owned only his work house and the ground on which it stood. Out of three thousand a year and what dribbled in from his publications he paid for his clothes and personal expenses, for cellar charges, and for Lanier's education, so far confined to a nurse's wage. Never had a move been contemplated without Dick's figuring his share. Living rather ascetically, travelling third-class when he was alone, with the cheapest wine, and good care of his clothes, and penalising himself for any extravagances, he maintained a qualified financial independence. After a certain point, though, it was difficult – again and again it was necessary to decide together as to the uses to which Nicole's money should be put. Naturally Nicole, wanting to own him, wanting him to stand still for ever, encouraged any slackness on his part, and in multiplying ways he was constantly inundated by a trickling of goods and money. The inception of the idea of the cliff villa which they had elaborated as a fantasy one day was a typical example of the forces divorcing them from the first simple arrangements in Zurich.

'Wouldn't it be fun if – ' it had been; and then, 'Won't it be fun when – '

It was not so much fun. His work became confused with Nicole's problems; in addition, her income had increased so fast of late that it seemed to belittle his work. Also, for the purpose of her cure, he had for many years pretended to a rigid domesticity from which he was drifting away, and this pretence became more arduous in this effortless immobility, in which he was inevitably subjected to microscopic examination. When Dick could no longer play what he wanted to play on the piano, it was an indication that life was being refined down to a point. He stayed in the big room a long time listening to the buzz of the electric clock, listening to time.

In November the waves grew black and dashed over the sea wall on to the shore road – such summer life as had survived disappeared and the beaches were melancholy and desolate under the mistral and rain. Gausse's Hôtel was closed for repairs and enlargement and the scaffolding of the summer Casino at Juan les Pins grew larger and more formidable. Going into Cannes or Nice, Dick and Nicole met new people – members of orchestras, restaurateurs, horticultural enthusiasts, shipbuilders – for Dick had bought an old dinghy – and members of the *Syndicat d'Initiative*. They knew their servants well and gave thought to the children's education. In December, Nicole seemed well-knit again; when a month had passed without tension, without the tight mouth, the unmotivated smile, the unfathomable remark, they went to the Swiss Alps for the Christmas holidays.

Chapter 13

With his cap, Dick slapped the snow from his dark blue ski-suit before going inside. The great hall, its floor pockmarked by two decades of hobnails, was cleared for the tea dance, and fourscore young Americans, domiciled in schools near Gstaad, bounced about to the frolic of 'Don't Bring Lulu', or exploded violently with the first percussions of the Charleston. It was a colony of the young, simple, and expensive – the *Sturmtruppen* of the rich were at St Moritz. Baby Warren felt that she had made a gesture of renunciation in joining the Divers here.

Dick picked out the two sisters easily across the delicately haunted, soft-swaying room – they were poster-like, formidable in their snow costumes, Nicole's of cerulean blue, Baby's of brick red. The young Englishman was talking to them; but they were paying no attention, lulled to the staring point by the adolescent dance.

Nicole's snow-warm face lighted up further as she saw Dick. 'Where is he?'

'He missed the train – I'm meeting him later.' Dick sat down, swinging a heavy boot over his knee. 'You two look very striking together. Every once in a while I forget we're in the same party and get a big shock at seeing you.'

Baby was a tall, fine-looking woman, deeply engaged in being almost thirty. Symptomatically she had pulled two men with her from London, one scarcely down from Cambridge, one old and hard with Victorian lecheries. Baby had certain spinster's characteristics – she was alien from touch, she started if she was touched suddenly, and such lingering touches as kisses and embraces slipped directly through the flesh into the forefront of her consciousness. She made few gestures with her trunk, her body proper – instead, she stamped her foot and tossed her head in almost an old-fashioned way. She relished the foretaste of death, prefigured by the catastrophes of friends – persistently she clung to the idea of Nicole's tragic destiny.

Baby's younger Englishman had been chaperoning the women down appropriate inclines and harrowing them on the bob-run. Dick, having turned an ankle in a too ambitious telemark, loafed gratefully about the 'nursery slope' with the children or drank kvass with a Russian doctor at the hotel.

'Please be happy, Dick,' Nicole urged him. 'Why don't you meet some of these ickle durls and dance with them in the afternoon?'

'What would I say to them?'

Her low almost harsh voice rose a few notes, simulating a plaintive coquetry: 'Say: "Ickle durl, oo is de pwettiest sing." What do you think you say?'

'I don't like ickle durls. They smell of Castile soap and peppermint. When I dance with them, I feel as if I'm pushing a baby carriage.'

It was a dangerous subject – he was careful, to the point of self-consciousness, to stare far over the heads of young maidens.

'There's a lot of business,' said Baby. 'First place, there's news from home – the property we used to call the station property. The railroads only bought the centre of it at first. Now they've bought the rest, and it belonged to mother. It's a question of investing the money.'

Pretending to be repelled by this gross turn in the conversation, the Englishman made for a girl on the floor. Following him for an instant with the uncertain eyes of an American girl in the grip of a lifelong Anglophilia, Baby continued defiantly: 'It's a lot of money. It's three hundred thousand apiece. I keep an eye on my own investments but Nicole doesn't know anything about securities, and I don't suppose you do either.'

'I've got to meet the train,' Dick said evasively.

Outside he inhaled damp snowflakes that he could no longer see against the darkening sky. Three children sledding past shouted a warning in some strange language; he heard them yell at the next bend and a little farther on he heard sleighbells coming up the hill in the dark. The holiday station glittered with expectancy, boys and girls waiting for new boys and girls, and by the time the train arrived, Dick had caught the rhythm and pretended to Franz Gregorovious that he was clipping off a half-hour from an endless roll of pleasures. But Franz had some intensity of purpose at the moment that fought through any superimposition of mood on Dick's part. 'I may get up to Zurich for a day,' Dick had written, 'or you can manage to come to Lausanne.' Franz had managed to come all the way to Gstaad.

He was forty. Upon his healthy maturity reposed a set of pleasant official manners, but he was most at home in a somewhat stuffy safety from which he could despise the broken rich whom he re-educated. His scientific heredity might have bequeathed him a wider world but he seemed to have deliberately chosen the standpoint of a humbler class, a choice typified by his selection of a wife. At the hotel Baby Warren made a quick examination of him, and failing to find any of the hallmarks she respected, the subtler virtues or courtesies by which the privileged classes recognised one another, treated him thereafter with her second manner. Nicole was always a little afraid of him. Dick liked him, as he liked his friends, without reservations.

For the evening they were sliding down the hill into the village, on those little sleds which serve the same purpose as gondolas do in Venice. Their destination was a hotel with an old-fashioned Swiss taproom, wooden and resounding, a room of clocks, kegs, steins, and antlers. Many parties at long tables blurred into one great party and ate fondue – a peculiarly indigestible form of Welsh rarebit, mitigated by hot spiced wine.

It was jolly in the big room; the younger Englishman remarked it and Dick conceded that there was no other word. With the pert heady wine he relaxed and pretended that the world was all put together again by the grey-haired men of the golden nineties who shouted old glees at the piano, by the young voices and the bright costumes toned into the room by the swirling smoke. For a moment he felt that they were in a ship with landfall just ahead; in the faces of all the girls was the same innocent expectation of the possibilities inherent in the situation and the night. He looked to see if that special girl was there and got an impression that she was at the table behind them – then he forgot her and invented a rigmarole and tried to make his party have a good time.

'I must talk to you,' said Franz in English. 'I have only twenty-four hours to spend here.'

'I suspected you had something on your mind.'

'I have a plan that is – so marvellous.' His hand fell upon Dick's knee. 'I have a plan that will be the making of us two.'

'Well?'

'Dick – there is a clinic we could have together – the old clinic of Braun on the Zugersee. The plant is all modern except for a few points. He is sick – he wants to go up in Austria, to die probably. It is a chance that is just insuperable. You and me – what a pair! Now don't say anything yet until I finish.'

From the yellow glint in Baby's eyes, Dick saw she was listening.

'We must undertake it together. It would not bind you too tight – it would give you a base, a laboratory, a centre. You could stay in residence say no more than half the year, when the weather is fine. In winter you could go to France or America and write your texts fresh from clinical experience.' He lowered his voice. 'And for the convalescence of your family, there are the atmosphere and regularity of the clinic at hand.' Dick's expression did not encourage this note so Franz dropped it with the punctuation of his tongue leaving his lip quickly. 'We could be partners. I the executive manager, you the theoretician, the brilliant consultant and all that. I know myself – I know I have no genius and you have. But, in my way, I am thought very capable; I am utterly competent at the most modern clinical methods. Sometimes for months I have served as the practical head of the old clinic. The professor says this plan is excellent, he advises me to go ahead. He says he is going to live for ever, and work up to the last minute.'

Dick formed imaginary pictures of the prospect as a preliminary to any exercise of judgement.

'What's the financial angle?' he asked.

Franz threw up his chin, his eyebrows, the transient wrinkles of his forehead, his hands, his elbows, his shoulders; he strained up the muscles of his legs, so that the cloth of his trousers bulged, pushed up his heart into his throat and his voice into the roof of his mouth.

'There we have it! Money!' he bewailed. 'I have little money. The price in American money is two hundred thousand dollars. The innovation-ary – ' he tasted the coinage doubtfully, ' – steps, that you will agree are necessary, will cost twenty thousand dollars American. But the clinic is a gold-mine – I tell you, I have seen the books. For an investment of two hundred and twenty thousand dollars we have an assured income of – '

Baby's curiosity was such that Dick brought her into the conversation.

'In your experience, Baby,' he demanded, 'have you found that when a European wants to see an American very pressingly it is invariably something concerned with money?'

'What is it?' she said innocently.

'This young *Privatdozent* thinks that he and I ought to launch into big business and try to attract nervous breakdowns from America.'

Worried, Franz stared at Baby as Dick continued: 'But who are we, Franz? You bear a big name and I've written two textbooks. Is that enough to attract anybody? And I haven't got that much money – I haven't got a tenth of it.' Franz smiled cynically. 'Honestly I haven't. Nicole and Baby are rich as Croesus but I haven't managed to get my hands on any of it yet.'

They were all listening now – Dick wondered if the girl at the table behind was listening too. The idea attracted him. He decided to let Baby speak for him, as one often lets women raise their voices over issues that are not in their hands. Baby became suddenly her grandfather, cool and experimental.

'I think it's a suggestion you ought to consider, Dick. I don't know what Dr Gregory was saying – but it seems to me – '

Behind him the girl had leaned forward into a smoke ring and was picking up something from the floor. Nicole's face, fitted into his own across the table – her beauty, tentatively nesting and posing, flowed into his love, ever braced to protect it.

'Consider it, Dick,' Franz urged excitedly. 'When one writes on psychiatry, one should have actual clinical contacts. Jung writes, Bleuler writes, Freud writes, Forel writes, Adler writes – also they are in constant contact with mental disorder.'

'Dick has me,' laughed Nicole. 'I should think that'd be enough mental disorder for one man.'

'That's different,' said Franz cautiously.

Baby was thinking that if Nicole lived beside a clinic she would always feel quite safe about her.

'We must think it over carefully,' she said.

Though amused at her insolence, Dick did not encourage it.

'The decision concerns me, Baby,' he said gently. 'It's nice of you to want to buy me a clinic.'

Realising she had meddled, Baby withdrew hurriedly: 'Of course, it's entirely your affair.'

'A thing as important as this will take weeks to decide. I wonder how I like the picture of Nicole and me anchored to Zurich – ' He turned to Franz, anticipating: ' – I know. Zurich has a gashouse and running water and electric light – I lived there three years.'

'I will leave you to think it over,' said Franz. 'I am confident – '

One hundred pairs of five-pound boots had begun to clump towards the door, and they joined the press. Outside in the crisp moonlight, Dick saw the girl tying her sled to one of the sleighs ahead. They piled into their own sleigh and at the crisp-cracking whips the horses strained, breasting the dark air. Past them figures ran and scrambled, the younger ones shoving each other from sleds and runners, landing in the soft snow, then panting after the horses to drop exhausted on a sled or wail that they were abandoned. On either side the fields were beneficently tranquil; the space through which the cavalcade moved was high and limitless. In the country there was less noise as though they were all listening atavistically for wolves in the wide snow.

In Saanen, they poured into the municipal dance, crowded with cow herders, hotel servants, shopkeepers, ski teachers, guides, tourists, peasants. To come into the warm enclosed place after the pantheistic animal feeling without, was to reassume some absurd and impressive knightly name, as thunderous as spurred boots in war, as football cleats on the cement of a locker-room floor. There was conventional yodelling, and the familiar rhythm of it separated Dick from what he had first found romantic in the scene. At first he thought it was because he had hounded the girl out of his consciousness; then it came to him under the form of what Baby had said: 'We must think it over carefully – ' and the unsaid lines back of that: 'We own you, and you'll admit it sooner or later. It is absurd to keep up the pretence of independence.'

It had been years since Dick had bottled up malice against a creature – since freshman year at New Haven when he had come upon a popular essay about 'mental hygiene'. Now he lost his temper at Baby and simultaneously tried to coop it up within him, resenting her cold rich insolence. It would be hundreds of years before any emergent Amazons would ever grasp the fact that a man is vulnerable only in his pride, but delicate as Humpty-Dumpty once that is meddled with – though some of them paid the fact a cautious lip-service. Dr Diver's profession of sorting the broken shells of another sort of egg had given him a dread of breakage. But: 'There's too much good manners,' he said on the way back to Gstaad in the smooth sleigh.

'Well, I think that's nice,' said Baby.

'No, it isn't,' he insisted to the anonymous bundle of fur. 'Good manners are an admission that everybody is so tender that they have to be handled with gloves. Now, human respect – you don't call a man a coward or a liar lightly, but if you spend your life sparing people's feelings and feeding their vanity, you get so you can't distinguish what *should* be respected in them.'

'I think Americans take their manners rather seriously,' said the elder Englishman.

'I guess so,' said Dick. 'My father had the kind of manners he inherited from the days when you shot first and apologised afterwards. Men armed – why, you Europeans haven't carried arms in civil life since the beginning of the eighteenth century – '

'Not actually, perhaps – '

'Not *act*ually. Not really.'

'Dick, you've always had such beautiful manners,' said Baby conciliatingly.

The women were regarding him across the zoo of robes with some alarm. The younger Englishman did not understand – he was one of the kind who were always jumping around cornices and balconies, as if they thought they were in the rigging of a ship – and filled the ride to the hotel with a preposterous story about a boxing match with his best friend in which they loved and bruised each other for an hour, always with great reserve. Dick became facetious.

'So every time he hit you you considered him an even better friend?'

'I respected him more.'

'It's the premise I don't understand. You and your best friend scrap about a trivial matter – '

'If you don't understand, I can't explain it to you,' said the young Englishman coldly.

– This is what I'll get if I begin saying what I think, Dick said to himself.

He was ashamed at baiting the man, realising that the absurdity of the story rested in the immaturity of the attitude combined with the sophisticated method of its narration.

The carnival spirit was strong and they went with the crowd into the grill, where a Tunisian barman manipulated the illumination in a counterpoint, whose other melody was the moon off the ice rink staring in the big windows. In that light, Dick found the girl devitalised, and uninteresting – he turned from her to enjoy the darkness, the cigarette points going green and silver when the lights shone red, the band of white that fell across the dancers as the door to the bar was opened and closed.

'Now, tell me, Franz,' he demanded, 'do you think after sitting up all night drinking beer, you can go back and convince your patients that you have any character? Don't you think they'll see you're a gastropath?'

'I'm going to bed,' Nicole announced. Dick accompanied her to the door of the elevator.

'I'd come with you but I must show Franz that I'm not intended for a clinician.'

Nicole walked into the elevator.

'Baby has lots of common sense,' she said meditatively.

'Baby is one of – '

The door slashed shut – facing a mechanical hum, Dick finished the sentence in his mind, ' – Baby is a trivial, selfish woman.'

But two days later, sleighing to the station with Franz, Dick admitted that he thought favourably upon the matter.

'We're beginning to turn in a circle,' he admitted. 'Living on this scale, there's an unavoidable series of strains, and Nicole doesn't survive them. The pastoral quality down on the summer Riviera is all changing anyhow – next year they'll have a Season.'

They passed the crisp green rinks where Wiener waltzes blared and the colours of many mountain schools flashed against the pale-blue skies.

' – I hope we'll be able to do it, Franz. There's nobody I'd rather try it with than you – '

Goodbye, Gstaad! Goodbye, fresh faces, cold sweet flowers, flakes in the darkness. Goodbye, Gstaad, goodbye!

Chapter 14

Dick awoke at five after a long dream of war, walked to the window and stared out at the Zugersee. His dream had begun in sombre majesty; navy-blue uniforms crossed a dark plaza behind bands playing the second movement of Prokofieff's 'Love of Three Oranges'. Presently there were fire-engines, symbols of disaster, and a ghastly uprising of the mutilated in dressing-station. He turned on his bed-lamp light and made a thorough note of it ending with the half-ironic phrase: 'non-combatant's shell-shock'.

As he sat on the side of his bed, he felt the room, the house and the night as empty. In the next room Nicole muttered something desolate and he felt sorry for whatever loneliness she was feeling in her sleep. For him time stood still and then every few years accelerated in a rush, like the quick rewind of a film, but for Nicole the years slipped away by clock and calendar and birthday, with the added poignance of her perishable beauty.

Even this past year and a half on the Zugersee seemed wasted time for her, the seasons marked only by the workmen on the road turning pink in May, brown in July, black in September, white again in spring. She had come out of her first illness alive with new hopes, expecting so much, yet deprived of any subsistence except Dick, bringing up children she could only pretend gently to love, guided orphans. The people she liked, rebels mostly, disturbed her and were bad for her – she sought in them the vitality that had made them independent or creative or rugged, sought in vain – for their secrets were buried deep in childhood struggles they had forgotten. They were more interested in Nicole's exterior harmony and charm, the other face of her illness. She led a lonely life owning Dick, who did not want to be owned.

Many times he had tried unsuccessfully to let go his hold on her. They had many fine times together, fine talks between the loves of the white nights, but always when he turned away from her into himself he left her holding Nothing in her hands and staring at it, calling it many names, but knowing it was only the hope that he would come back soon.

He scrunched his pillow hard, lay down, and put the back of his neck against it as a Japanese does to slow the circulation, and slept again for a time. Later, while he shaved, Nicole awoke and marched around, giving abrupt, succinct orders to children and servants. Lanier came in to watch his father shave – living beside a psychiatric clinic he had developed an extraordinary confidence in and admiration for his father, together with an exaggerated indifference towards most other adults; the patients appeared to him either in their odd aspects, or else as devitalised, over-correct creatures without personality. He was a handsome, promising boy and Dick devoted much time to him, in the relationship of a sympathetic but exacting officer and a respectful enlisted man.

'Why,' Lanier asked, 'do you always leave a little lather on the top of your hair when you shave?'

Cautiously Dick parted soapy lips: 'I have never been able to find out. I've often wondered. I think it's because I get the first finger soapy when I make the line of my sideburn, but how it gets up on top of my head I don't know.'

'I'm going to watch it all tomorrow.'

'That's your only question before breakfast.'

'I don't really call it a question.'

'That's one on you.'

Half an hour later Dick started up to the administration building. He was thirty-eight – still declining a beard, he yet had a more medical aura about him than he had worn upon the Riviera. For eighteen months now he had lived at the clinic – certainly one of the best-appointed in Europe. Like Dohmler's it was of the modern type – no longer a single dark and sinister building but a small, scattered, yet deceitfully integrated village – Dick and Nicole had added much in the domain of taste, so that the plant was a thing of beauty, visited by every psychologist passing through Zurich. With the addition of a caddy-house it might very well have been a country club. The Eglantine and the Beeches, houses for those sunk into eternal darkness, were screened by little copses from the main building, camouflaged strong-points. Behind was a large truck farm, worked partly by the patients. The workshops for ego-therapy were three, placed under a single roof, and there Dr Diver began his morning's inspection. The carpentry shop, full of sunlight, exuded the sweetness of sawdust, of a lost age of wood; always half a dozen men were there, hammering, planing, buzzing – silent men, who lifted solemn eyes from their work as he passed through. Himself a good carpenter, he discussed with them the efficiency of some tools for a moment in a quiet, personal, interested voice. Adjoining was the bookbindery, adapted to the most mobile of patients, who were not always, however, those who had the greatest chance for recovery. The last chamber was devoted to bead-work, weaving, and work in brass. The faces of the patients here wore the expression of one who has just sighed profoundly, dismissing something insoluble – but their sighs only marked the beginning of another ceaseless round of ratiocination, not in a line as with normal people but in the same circle. Round, round, and round. Around for ever. But the bright colours of the stuffs they worked with gave strangers a momentary illusion that all was well, as in a kindergarten. These patients brightened as Dr Diver came in. Most of them liked him better than they liked Dr Gregorovious. Those who had once lived in the great world invariably liked him better. There were a few who thought he neglected them, or that he was not simple, or that he posed. Their responses were not dissimilar to those that Dick evoked in non-professional life, but here they were warped and distorted.

One Englishwoman spoke to him always about a subject which she considered her own.

'Have we got music tonight?'

'I don't know,' he answered. 'I haven't seen Dr Lladislau. How did you enjoy the music that Mrs Sachs and Mr Longstreet gave us last night?'

'It was so-so.'

'I thought it was fine – especially the Chopin.'

'I thought it was so-so.'

'When are you going to play for us yourself?'

She shrugged her shoulders, as pleased at this question as she had been for several years.

'Sometime. But I only play so-so.'

They knew that she did not play at all – she had had two sisters who were brilliant musicians, but she had never been able to learn the notes when they had been young together.

From the workshop Dick went to visit the Eglantine and the Beeches. Exteriorly these houses were as cheerful as the others; Nicole had designed the decoration and the furniture on a necessary base of concealed grilles and bars and immovable furniture. She had worked with so much imagination – the inventive quality, which she lacked, being supplied by the problem itself – that no instructed visitor would have dreamed that the light, graceful filigree work at a window was a strong unyielding end of a tether, that the pieces reflecting modern tubular tendencies were stauncher than the massive creations of the Edwardians – even the flowers lay in iron fingers and every casual ornament and fixture was as necessary as a girder in a skyscraper. Her tireless eyes had made each room yield up its greatest usefulness. Complimented, she referred to herself brusquely as a master plumber.

For those whose compasses were not depolarised there seemed many odd things in these houses. Dr Diver was often amused in the Eglantine, the men's building – here there was a strange little exhibitionist who thought that if he could walk unclothed and unmolested from the Étoile to the Place de la Concorde he would solve many things – and, perhaps, Dick thought, he was quite right.

His most interesting case was in the main building. The patient was a woman of thirty who had been in the clinic six months; she was an American painter who had lived long in Paris. They had no very satisfactory history of her. A cousin had happened upon her all mad and gone and after an unsatisfactory interlude at one of the whoopee cures that fringed the city, dedicated largely to tourist victims of drug and drink, he had managed to get her to Switzerland. On her admittance she had been exceptionally pretty – now she was a living agonising sore. All blood tests had failed to give a positive reaction and the trouble was unsatisfactorily catalogued as nervous eczema. For two months she had lain under it, as if imprisoned in the Iron Maiden. She was coherent, even brilliant, within the limits of her special hallucinations.

She was particularly his patient. During spells of over-excitement he was the only doctor who could 'do anything with her'. Several weeks ago, on one of many nights that she had passed in sleepless torture, Franz had succeeded in hypnotising her into a few hours of needed rest, but he had never again succeeded. Hypnosis was a tool that Dick distrusted and seldom used, for he knew that he could not always summon up the mood in himself – he had once tried it on Nicole and she had scornfully laughed at him.

The woman in room twenty could not see him when he came in – the area about her eyes was too tightly swollen. She spoke in a strong, rich, deep, thrilling voice.

'How long will this last? Is it going to be for ever?'

'It's not going to be very long now. Dr Lladislau tells me there are whole areas cleared up.'

'If I knew what I had done to deserve this I could accept it with equanimity.'

'It isn't wise to be mystical about it – we recognise it as a nervous phenomenon. It's related to the blush – when you were a girl, did you blush easily?'

She lay with her face turned to the ceiling.

'I have found nothing to blush for since I cut my wisdom teeth.'

'Haven't you committed your share of petty sins and mistakes?'

'I have nothing to reproach myself with.'

'You're very fortunate.'

The woman thought a moment; her voice came up through her

bandaged face afflicted with subterranean melodies: 'I'm sharing the fate of the women of my time who challenged men to battle.'

'To your vast surprise it was just like all battles,' he answered adopting her formal diction.

'Just like all battles.' She thought this over. 'You pick a set-up, or else win a Pyrrhic victory, or you're wrecked and ruined – you're a ghostly echo from a broken wall.'

'You are neither wrecked nor ruined,' he told her. 'Are you quite sure you've been in a real battle?'

'Look at me!' she cried furiously.

'You've suffered, but many women suffered before they mistook themselves for men.' It was becoming an argument and he retreated. 'In any case you mustn't confuse single failure with a final defeat.'

She sneered. 'Beautiful words,' and the phrase transpiring up through the crust of pain humbled him.

'We would like to go into the true reasons that brought you here –' he began but she interrupted.

'I am here as a symbol of something. I thought perhaps you would know what it was.'

'You are sick,' he said mechanically.

'Then what was it I had almost found?'

'A greater sickness.'

'That's all?'

'That's all.' With disgust he heard himself lying, but here and now the vastness of the subject could only be compressed into a lie. 'Outside of that there's only confusion and chaos. I won't lecture to you – we have too acute a realisation of your physical suffering. But it's only by meeting the problems of every day, no matter how trifling and boring they seem, that you can make things drop back into place again. After that – perhaps you'll be able again to examine –'

He had slowed up to avoid the inevitable end of his thought: ' – the frontiers of consciousness.' The frontiers that artists must explore were not for her, ever. She was fine-spun, inbred – eventually she might find rest in some quiet mysticism. Exploration was for those with a measure of peasant blood, those with big thighs and thick ankles who could take punishment as they took bread and salt, on every inch of flesh and spirit.

– Not for you, he almost said. It's too tough a game for you.

Yet in the awful majesty of her pain he went out to her unreservedly, almost sexually. He wanted to gather her up in his arms, as he so often had Nicole, and cherish even her mistakes, so deeply were they part of her. The orange light through the drawn blind, the sarcophagus of her figure on the bed, the spot of face, the voice searching the vacuity of her illness and finding only remote abstractions.

As he arose the tears fled lava-like into her bandages.

'That is for something,' she whispered. 'Something must come out of it.'

He stooped and kissed her forehead.

'We must all try to be good,' he said.

Leaving her room he sent the nurse in to her. There were other patients to see: an American girl of fifteen who had been brought up on the basis that childhood was intended to be all fun – his visit was provoked by the fact that she had just hacked off all her hair with nail scissors. There was nothing much to be done for her – a family history of neurosis and nothing stable in her past to build on. The father, normal and conscientious himself, had tried to protect a nervous brood from life's troubles and had succeeded merely in preventing them from developing powers of adjustment to life's inevitable surprises. There was little that Dick could say: 'Helen, when you're in doubt you must ask a nurse, you must learn to take advice. Promise me you will.'

What was a promise with the head sick? He looked in upon a frail exile from the Caucasus buckled securely in a sort of hammock which in turn was submerged in a warm medical bath, and upon the three daughters of a Portuguese general who slid almost imperceptibly towards paresis. He went into the room next to them and told a collapsed psychiatrist that he was better, always better, and the man tried to read his face for conviction, since he hung on the real world only through such reassurance as he could find in the resonance, or lack of it, in Dr Diver's voice. After that Dick discharged a shiftless orderly and by then it was the lunch hour.

Chapter 15

Meals with the patients were a chore he approached with apathy. The gathering, which of course did not include residents at the Eglantine or the Beeches, was conventional enough at first sight, but over it brooded always a heavy melancholy. Such doctors as were present kept up a conversation, but most of the patients, as if exhausted by their morning's endeavour, or depressed by the company, spoke little, and ate looking into their plates.

Luncheon over, Dick returned to his villa. Nicole was in the salon wearing a strange expression.

'Read that,' she said.

He opened the letter. It was from a woman recently discharged, though with scepticism on the part of the faculty. It accused him in no uncertain terms of having seduced her daughter, who had been at her mother's side during the crucial stage of the illness. It presumed that Mrs Diver would be glad to have this information and learn what her husband was 'really like'.

Dick read the letter again. Couched in clear and concise English he yet recognised it as the letter of a maniac. Upon a single occasion he had let the girl, a flirtatious little brunette, ride into Zurich with him, upon her request, and in the evening had brought her back to the clinic. In an idle, almost indulgent way, he kissed her. Later, she tried to carry the affair further, but he was not interested and subsequently, probably consequently, the girl had come to dislike him, and taken her mother away.

'This letter is deranged,' he said. 'I had no relations of any kind with that girl. I didn't even like her.'

'Yes, I've tried thinking that,' said Nicole.

'Surely you don't believe it?'

'I've been sitting here.'

He sank his voice to a reproachful note and sat beside her.

'This is absurd. This is a letter from a mental patient.'

'I was a mental patient.'

He stood up and spoke more authoritatively.

'Suppose we don't have any nonsense, Nicole. Go and round up the children and we'll start.'

In the car, with Dick driving, they followed the little promontories of the lake, catching the burn of light and water in the windshield, tunnelling through cascades of evergreen. It was Dick's car, a Renault so dwarfish that they all stuck out of it except the children, between whom Mademoiselle towered mast-like in the rear seat. They knew every kilometre of the road – where they would smell the pine needles and the black stove smoke. A high sun with a face traced on it beat fierce on the straw hats of the children.

Nicole was silent; Dick was uneasy at her straight hard gaze. Often he felt lonely with her, and frequently she tired him with the short floods of personal revelations that she reserved exclusively for him. 'I'm like this – I'm more like that,' but this afternoon he would have been glad had she rattled on in staccato for a while and given him glimpses of her thoughts. The situation was always most threatening when she backed up into herself and closed the doors behind her.

At Zug Mademoiselle got out and left them. The Divers approached the Agiri Fair through a menagerie of mammoth steamrollers that made way for them. Dick parked the car, and as Nicole looked at him without moving, he said: 'Come on, darl.' Her lips drew apart into a sudden awful smile, and his belly quailed, but as if he hadn't seen it he repeated: 'Come on. So the children can get out.'

'Oh, I'll come all right,' she answered, tearing the words from some story spinning itself out inside her, too fast for him to grasp. 'Don't worry about that. I'll come – '

'Then come.'

She turned from him as he walked beside her but the smile still flickered across her face, derisive and remote. Only when Lanier spoke to her several times did she manage to fix her attention upon an object, a Punch-and-Judy show, and to orient herself by anchoring to it.

Dick tried to think what to do. The dualism in his views of her – that of the husband, that of the psychiatrist – was increasingly paralysing his faculties. In these six years she had several times carried him over the line with her, disarming him by exciting emotional pity or by a flow of wit, fantastic and disassociated, so that only after the episode did he realise with the consciousness of his own relaxation from tension, that she had succeeded in getting a point against his better judgement.

A discussion with Topsy about the guignol – as to whether the Punch was the same Punch they had seen last year in Cannes – having been settled, the family walked along again between the booths under the open sky. The women's bonnets, perching over velvet vests, the bright, spreading skirts of many cantons, seemed demure against the blue and orange paint of the wagons and displays. There was the sound of a whining, tinkling hootchy-kootchy show.

Nicole began to run very suddenly, so suddenly that for a moment Dick did not miss her. Far ahead he saw her yellow dress twisting through the crowd, an ochre stitch along the edge of reality and unreality, and started after her. Secretly she ran and secretly he followed. As the hot afternoon went shrill and terrible with her flight he had forgotten the children; then he wheeled and ran back to them, drawing them this way and that by their arms, his eyes jumping from booth to booth.

'Madame,' he cried to a young woman behind a white lottery wheel, 'est-ce que je peux laisser ces petits avec vous deux minutes? C'est très urgent – je vous donnerai dix francs.'

'Mais oui.'

He headed the children into the booth. 'Alors – restez avec cette gentille dame.'

'Oui, Dick.'

He darted off again but he had lost her; he circled the merry-go-round, keeping up with it till he realised he was running beside it, staring always at the same horse. He elbowed through the crowd in the *buvette*; then remembering a predilection of Nicole's he snatched up an edge of a fortune-teller's tent and peered within. A droning voice greeted him: 'La septième fille d'une septième fille née sur les rives de Nil – entrez, monsieur – '

Dropping the flap he ran along towards where the *Plaisance* terminated at the lake and a small ferris wheel revolved slowly against the sky. There he found her.

She was alone in what was momentarily the top boat of the wheel, and as it descended he saw that she was laughing hilariously; he slunk back in the crowd, a crowd which, at the wheel's next revolution, spotted the intensity of Nicole's hysteria.

'Regardez-moi ça!'

'Regarde donc cette Anglaise!'

Down she dropped again – this time the wheel and its music were slowing and a dozen people were around her car, all of them impelled by the quality of her laughter to smile in sympathetic idiocy. But when Nicole saw Dick her laughter died – she made a gesture of slipping by and away from him but he caught her arm and held it as they walked away.

'Why did you lose control of yourself like that?'

'You know very well why.'

'No, I don't.'

'That's just preposterous – let me loose – that's an insult to my intelligence. Don't you think I saw that girl look at you – that little dark girl. Oh, this is farcical – a child, not more than fifteen. Don't you think I saw?'

'Stop here a minute and quiet down.'

They sat at a table, her eyes in a profundity of suspicion, her hand moving across her line of light as if it were obstructed. 'I want a drink – I want a brandy.'

'You can't have brandy – you can have a bock if you want it.'

'Why can't I have a brandy?'

'We won't go into that. Listen to me – this business about a girl is a delusion, do you understand that word?'

'It's always a delusion when I see what you don't want me to see.'

He had a sense of guilt as in one of those nightmares where we are accused of a crime which we recognise as something undeniably experienced, but which upon waking we realise we have not committed. His eyes wavered from hers.

'I left the children with a gypsy woman in a booth. We ought to get them.'

'Who do you think you are?' she demanded. 'Svengali?'

Fifteen minutes ago they had been a family. Now as she was crushed into a corner by his unwilling shoulder, he saw them all, child and man, as a perilous accident.

'We're going home.'

'Home!' she roared in a voice so abandoned that its louder tones wavered and cracked. 'And sit and think that we're all rotting and the children's ashes are rotting in every box I open? That filth!'

Almost with relief he saw that her words sterilised her, and Nicole, sensitised down to the corium of the skin, saw the withdrawal in his face. Her own face softened and she begged, 'Help me, help me, Dick!'

A wave of agony went over him. It was awful that such a fine tower should not be erected, only suspended, suspended from him. Up to a point that was right; men were for that, beam and idea, girder and logarithm; but somehow Dick and Nicole had become one and equal, not opposite and complementary; she was Dick too, the drought in the marrow of his bones. He could not watch her disintegrations without participating in them. His intuition rilled out of him as tenderness and compassion – he could only take the characteristically modern course, to interpose – he would get a nurse from Zurich, to take her over tonight.

'You *can* help me.'

Her sweet bullying pulled him forward off his feet. 'You've helped me before – you can help me now.'

'I can only help you the same old way.'

'Someone can help me.'

'Maybe so. You can help yourself most. Let's find the children.'

There were numerous lottery booths with white wheels – Dick was startled when he enquired at the first and encountered blank disavowals. Evil-eyed, Nicole stood apart, denying the children, resenting them as part of a downright world she sought to make amorphous. Presently Dick found them, surrounded by women who were examining them with delight like fine goods, and by peasant children staring.

'Merci, monsieur, ah monsieur est trop généreux. C'était un plaisir, m'sieur, madame. Au revoir, mes petits.'

They started back with a hot sorrow streaming down upon them; the car was weighted with their mutual apprehension and anguish, and the children's mouths were grave with disappointment. Grief presented itself in its terrible, dark unfamiliar colour. Somewhere around Zug, Nicole, with a convulsive effort, reiterated a remark she had made before about a misty yellow house set back from the road that looked like a painting not yet dry, but it was just an attempt to catch at a rope that was paying out too swiftly. Dick tried to rest – the struggle would come presently at home and he might have to sit a long time, restating the universe for her. A 'schizophrenic' is well named as a split personality – Nicole was alternately a person to whom nothing need be explained and one to whom nothing *could* be explained. It was necessary to treat her with active and affirmative insistence, keeping the road to reality always open, making the road to escape harder going. But the brilliance, the versatility of madness is akin to the resourcefulness of water seeping through, over and around a dyke. It requires the united front of many people to work against it. He felt it necessary that this time Nicole cure herself; he wanted to wait until she remembered the other times, and revolted from them. In a tired way, he planned that they would again resume the regime relaxed a year before.

He had turned up a hill that made a short cut to the clinic, and now as he stepped on the accelerator for a short straightaway run parallel to the hillside the car swerved violently left, swerved right, tipped on two wheels and, as Dick, with Nicole's voice screaming in his ear, crushed down the mad hand clutching the steering wheel, righted itself, swerved once more and shot off the road; it tore through low underbrush, tipped again and settled slowly at an angle of ninety degrees against a tree.

The children were screaming and Nicole was screaming and cursing and trying to tear at Dick's face. Thinking first of the list of the car and unable to estimate it, Dick bent away Nicole's arm, climbed over the top side and lifted out the children; then he saw the car was in a stable position. Before doing anything else he stood there shaking and panting.

'You – ' he cried.

She was laughing hilariously, unashamed, unafraid, unconcerned. No one coming on the scene would have imagined that she had caused it; she laughed as after some mild escape of childhood.

'You were scared, weren't you?' she accused him. 'You wanted to live!'

She spoke with such force that in his shocked state Dick wondered if he had been frightened for himself – but the strained faces of the children, looking from parent to parent, made him want to grind her grinning mask into jelly.

Directly above them, half a kilometre by the winding road but only a hundred yards climbing, was an inn; one of its wings showed through the wooded hill.

'Take Topsy's hand,' he said to Lanier, 'like that, tight, and climb up that hill – see the little path? When you get to the inn tell them "La voiture Divare est cassée." Someone must come right down.'

Lanier, not sure what had happened, but suspecting the dark and unprecedented, asked: 'What will you do, Dick?'

'We'll stay here with the car.'

Neither of them looked at their mother as they started off. 'Be careful crossing the road up there! Look both ways!' Dick shouted after them.

He and Nicole looked at each other directly, their eyes like blazing windows across a court of the same house. Then she took out a compact, looked in its mirror, and smoothed back the temple hair. Dick watched the children climbing for a moment until they disappeared among the pines halfway up; then he walked around the car to see the damage and plan how to get it back on the road. In the dirt he could trace the rocking course they had pursued for over a hundred feet; he was filled with a violent disgust that was not like anger.

In a few minutes the proprietor of the inn came running down.

'My God!' he exclaimed. 'How did it happen, were you going fast? What luck! Except for that tree you'd have rolled downhill!'

Taking advantage of Émile's reality, the wide black apron, the sweat upon the rolls of his face, Dick signalled to Nicole in a matter-of-fact way to let him help her from the car; whereupon she jumped over the lower side, lost her balance on the slope, fell to her knees and got up again. As she watched the men trying to move the car her expression became defiant. Welcoming even that mood Dick said: 'Go and wait with the children, Nicole.'

Only after she had gone did he remember that she had wanted cognac, and that there was cognac available up there – he told Émile never mind about the car; they would wait for the chauffeur and the big car to pull it up on the road. Together they hurried up to the inn.

Chapter 16

'I want to go away,' he told Franz. 'For a month or so, as long as I can.'

'Why not, Dick? That was our original arrangement – it was you who insisted on staying. If you and Nicole – '

'I don't want to go away with Nicole. I want to go away alone. This last thing knocked me sideways – if I get two hours' sleep in twenty-four, it's one of Zwingli's miracles.'

'You wish a real leave of abstinence.'

'The word is "absence". Look here: if I go to Berlin to the Psychiatric Congress could you manage to keep the peace? For three months she's been all right and she likes her nurse. My God, you're the only human being in this world I can ask this of.'

Franz grunted, considering whether or not he could be trusted to think always of his partner's interest.

In Zurich the next week Dick drove to the airport and took the big plane for Munich. Soaring and roaring into the blue he felt numb, realising how tired he was. A vast persuasive quiet stole over him, and he abandoned sickness to the sick, sound to the motors, direction to the pilot. He had no intention of attending so much as a single session of the congress – he could imagine it well enough, new pamphlets by Bleuler and the elder Forel that he could much better digest at home, the paper by the American who cured dementia praecox by pulling out his patients' teeth or cauterising their tonsils, the half-derisive respect with which this idea would be greeted, for no more reason than that America was such a rich and powerful country. The other delegates from America – red-headed Schwartz with his saint's face and his infinite patience in straddling two worlds, as well as dozens of commercial alienists with hangdog faces, who would be present partly to increase their standing, and hence their reach for the big plums of the criminal practice, partly to master novel sophistries that they could weave into their stock-in-trade, to the infinite confusion of all values.

There would be cynical Latins, and some man of Freud's from Vienna. Articulate among them would be the great Jung, bland, super-vigorous, on his rounds between the forests of anthropology and the neuroses of schoolboys. At first there would be an American cast to the congress, almost Rotarian in its forms and ceremonies, then the closer-knit European vitality would fight through, and finally the Americans would play their trump card, the announcement of colossal gifts and endowments, of great new plants and training schools, and in the presence of the figures the Europeans would blanch and walk timidly. But he would not be there to see.

They skirted the Vorarlberg Alps, and Dick felt a pastoral delight in watching the villages. There were always four or five in sight, each one gathered around a church. It was simple looking at the earth from far off, simple as playing grim games with dolls and soldiers. This was the way statesmen and commanders and all retired people looked at things. Anyhow, it was a good draught of relief.

An Englishman spoke to him from across the aisle but he found something antipathetic in the English lately. England was like a rich man after a disastrous orgy who makes up to the household by chatting with them individually, when it is obvious to them that he is only trying to get back his self-respect in order to usurp his former power.

Dick had with him what magazines were available on the station quays: *The Century*, *The Motion Picture*, *L'Illustration*, and the *Fliegende Blätter*, but it was more fun to descend in his imagination into the villages and shake hands with the rural characters. He sat in the churches as he sat in his father's church in Buffalo, amid the starchy must of Sunday clothes. He listened to the wisdom of the Near East, was Crucified, Died, and was Buried in the cheerful church, and once more worried between five or ten cents for the collection plate, because of the girl who sat in the pew behind.

The Englishman suddenly borrowed his magazines with a little small change of conversation, and Dick, glad to see them go, thought of the voyage ahead of him. Wolf-like under his sheep's clothing of long-staple Australian wool, he considered the world of pleasure – the incorruptible Mediterranean with sweet old dirt caked in the olive trees, the peasant girl near Savona with a face as green and rose as the colour of an illuminated missal. He would take her in his hands and snatch her across the border . . .

. . . But there he deserted her – he must press on towards the Isles of Greece, the cloudy waters of unfamiliar ports, the lost girl on shore, the moon of popular songs. A part of Dick's mind was made up of the tawdry souvenirs of his boyhood. Yet in that somewhat littered Five-and-Ten, he had managed to keep alive the low painful fire of intelligence.

Chapter 17

Tommy Barban was a ruler, Tommy was a hero – Dick happened upon him in the Marienplatz in Munich, in one of those cafés where small gamblers diced on 'tapestry' mats. The air was full of politics, and the slap of cards.

Tommy was at a table laughing his martial laugh: 'Um-buh-ha-ha! Um-buh-ha-ha!' As a rule, he drank little; courage was his game and his companions were always a little afraid of him. Recently an eighth of the area of his skull had been removed by a Warsaw surgeon and was knitting under his hair, and the weakest person in the café could have killed him with a flip of a knotted napkin.

' – This is Prince Chillicheff – ' a battered, powder-grey Russian of fifty ' – and Mr McKibben – and Mr Hannan – ' the latter was a lively ball of black eyes and hair, a clown; and he said immediately to Dick: 'The first thing before we shake hands – what do you mean by fooling around with my aunt?'

'Why, I – '

'You heard me. What are you doing here in Munich anyhow?'

'Um-bah-ha-ha!' laughed Tommy.

'Haven't you got aunts of your own? Why don't you fool with them?'

Dick laughed, whereupon the man shifted his attack: 'Now let's not have any more talk about aunts. How do I know you didn't make up the whole thing? Here you are a complete stranger with an acquaintance of less than half an hour, and you come up to me with a cock-and-bull story about your aunts. How do I know what you have concealed about you?'

Tommy laughed again, then he said good-naturedly, but firmly, 'That's enough, Carly. Sit down, Dick – how're you? How's Nicole?'

He did not like any man very much nor feel their presence with much intensity – he was all relaxed for combat; as a fine athlete playing secondary defence in any sport is really resting much of the time, while a lesser man only pretends to rest and is at a continual and self-destroying nervous tension.

Hannan, not entirely suppressed, moved to an adjoining piano, and with recurring resentment on his face whenever he looked at Dick, played chords, from time to time muttering, 'Your aunts,' and, in a dying cadence, 'I didn't say aunts anyhow. I said pants.'

'Well, how're you?' repeated Tommy. 'You don't look so – ' he fought for a word, ' – so jaunty as you used to, so spruce, you know what I mean.'

The remark sounded too much like one of those irritating accusations of waning vitality and Dick was about to retort by commenting on the extraordinary suits worn by Tommy and Prince Chillicheff, suits of a cut and pattern fantastic enough to have sauntered down Beale Street on a Sunday – when an explanation was forthcoming.

'I see you are regarding our clothes,' said the Prince. 'We have just come out of Russia.'

'These were made in Poland by the court tailor,' said Tommy. 'That's a fact – Pilsudski's own tailor.'

'You've been touring?' Dick asked.

They laughed, the Prince inordinately meanwhile clapping Tommy on the back.

'Yes, we have been touring. That's it, touring. We have made the Grand Tour of all the Russias. In state.'

Dick waited for an explanation. It came from Mr McKibben in two words.

'They escaped.'

'Have you been prisoners in Russia?'

'It was I,' explained Prince Chillicheff, his dead yellow eyes staring at Dick. 'Not a prisoner but in hiding.'

'Did you have much trouble getting out?'

'Some trouble. We left three Red Guards dead at the border. Tommy left two – ' He held up two fingers like a Frenchman – 'I left one.'

'That's the part I don't understand,' said Mr McKibben. 'Why they should have objected to your leaving.'

Hannan turned from the piano and said, winking at the others: 'Mac thinks a Marxian is somebody who went to St Mark's school.'

It was an escape story in the best tradition – an aristocrat hiding nine years with a former servant and working in a government bakery; the eighteen-year-old daughter in Paris who knew Tommy Barban . . . During the narrative Dick decided that this parched papier-mâché relic of the past was scarcely worth the lives of three young men. The question arose as to whether Tommy and Chillicheff had been frightened.

'When I was cold,' Tommy said. 'I always get scared when I'm cold. During the war I was always frightened when I was cold.'

McKibben stood up.

'I must leave. Tomorrow morning I'm going to Innsbruck by car with my wife and children – and the governess.'

'I'm going there tomorrow, too,' said Dick.

'Oh, are you?' exclaimed McKibben. 'Why not come with us? It's a big Packard and there's only my wife and my children and myself – and the governess – '

'I can't possibly – '

'Of course she's not really a governess,' McKibben concluded, looking rather pathetically at Dick. 'As a matter of fact my wife knows your sister-in-law, Baby Warren.'

But Dick was not to be drawn in a blind contract.

'I've promised to travel with two men.'

'Oh,' McKibben's face fell. 'Well, I'll say goodbye.' He unscrewed two blooded wire-hairs from a nearby table and departed; Dick pictured the jammed Packard pounding towards Innsbruck with the McKibbens and their children and their baggage and yapping dogs – and the governess.

'The paper says they know the man who killed him,' said Tommy. 'But his cousins did not want it in the paper because it happened in a speakeasy. What do you think of that?'

'It's what's known as family pride.'

Hannan played a loud chord on the piano to attract attention to himself.

'I don't believe his first stuff holds up,' he said. 'Even barring the Europeans there are a dozen Americans can do what North did.'

It was the first indication Dick had had that they were talking about Abe North.

'The only difference is that Abe did it first,' said Tommy.

'I don't agree,' persisted Hannan. 'He got the reputation for being a good musician because he drank so much that his friends had to explain him away somehow – '

'What's this about Abe North? What about him? Is he in a jam?'

'Didn't you read the *Herald* this morning?'

'No.'

'He's dead. He was beaten to death in a speakeasy in New York. He just managed to crawl home to the Racquet Club to die – '

'*Abe North?*'

'Yes, sure, they – '

'*Abe North?*' Dick stood up. 'Are you sure he's dead?'

Hannan turned around to McKibben: 'It wasn't the Racquet Club he crawled to – it was the Harvard Club. I'm sure he didn't belong to the Racquet.'

'The paper said so,' McKibben insisted.

'It must have been a mistake. I'm quite sure.'

'*Beaten to death in a speakeasy.*'

'But I happen to know most of the members of the Racquet Club,' said Hannan. 'It *must* have been the Harvard Club.'

Dick got up, Tommy too. Prince Chillicheff started out of a wan study of nothing, perhaps of his chances of ever getting out of Russia, a study that had occupied him so long that it was doubtful if he could give it up immediately, and joined them in leaving.

'*Abe North beaten to death.*'

On the way to the hotel, a journey of which Dick was scarcely aware, Tommy said: 'We're waiting for a tailor to finish some suits so we can get to Paris. I'm going into stockbroking and they wouldn't take me if I showed up like this. Everybody in your country is making millions. Are you really leaving tomorrow? We can't even have dinner with you. It seems the Prince had an old girl in Munich. He called her up but she'd been dead five years and we're having dinner with the two daughters.'

The Prince nodded.

'Perhaps I could have arranged for Dr Diver.'

'No, no,' said Dick hastily.

He slept deep and awoke to a slow mournful march passing his window. It was a long column of men in uniform, wearing the familiar helmets of 1914, thick men in frock coats and silk hats, burghers, aristocrats, plain men. It was a society of veterans going to lay wreaths on the tombs of the dead. The column marched slowly with a sort of swagger for a lost magnificence, a past effort, a forgotten sorrow. The faces were only formally sad but Dick's lungs burst for a moment with regret for Abe's death, and his own youth of ten years ago.

Chapter 18

He reached Innsbruck at dusk, sent his bags up to a hotel and walked into town. In the sunset the Emperor Maximilian knelt in prayer above his bronze mourners; a quartet of Jesuit novices paced and read in the university garden. The marble souvenirs of old sieges, marriages, anniversaries, faded quickly when the sun was down, and he had *Erbsen-suppe* with *Würstchen* cut up in it, drank four seidels of Pilsner and refused a formidable dessert known as '*Kaiserschmarren*'.

Despite the overhanging mountains Switzerland was far away, Nicole was far away. Walking in the garden later when it was dark he thought about her with detachment, loving her for her best self. He remembered once when the grass was damp and she came to him on hurried feet, her thin slippers drenched with dew. She stood upon his shoes nestling close and held up her face, showing it as a book open at a page.

'Think how you love me,' she whispered. 'I don't ask you to love me always like this, but I ask you to remember. Somewhere inside me there'll always be the person I am tonight.'

But Dick had come away for his soul's sake, and he began thinking about that. He had lost himself – he could not tell the hour when, or the day or the week, the month or the year. Once he had cut through things, solving the most complicated equations as the simplest problems of his simplest patients. Between the time he found Nicole flowering under a stone on the Zürichsee and the moment of his meeting with Rosemary the spear had been blunted.

Watching his father's struggles in poor parishes had wedded a desire for money to an essentially unacquisitive nature. It was not a healthy necessity for security – he had never felt more sure of himself, more thoroughly his own man, than at the time of his marriage to Nicole. Yet he had been swallowed up like a gigolo, and somehow permitted his arsenal to be locked up in the Warren safety-deposit vaults.

'There should have been a settlement in the Continental style; but it isn't over yet. I've wasted eight years teaching the rich the ABC's of human decency, but I'm not done. I've got too many unplayed trumps in my hand.'

He loitered among the fallow rose bushes and the beds of damp sweet indistinguishable fern. It was warm for October but cool enough to wear a heavy tweed coat buttoned by a little elastic tape at the neck. A figure detached itself from the black shape of a tree and he knew it was the woman whom he had passed in the lobby coming out. He was in love with every pretty woman he saw now, their forms at a distance, their shadows on a wall.

Her back was towards him as she faced the lights of the town. He scratched a match that she must have heard, but she remained motionless.

– Was it an invitation? or an indication of obliviousness? He had long been outside of the world of simple desires and their fulfilments, and he was inept and uncertain. For all he knew there might be some code among the wanderers of obscure spas by which they found each other quickly.

– Perhaps the next gesture was his. Strange children should smile at each other and say, 'Let's play.'

He moved closer, the shadow moved sideways. Possibly he would be snubbed like the scapegrace drummers he had heard of in youth. His heart beat loud in contact with the unprobed, undissected, unanalysed, unacccounted for. Suddenly he turned away, and, as he did, the girl, too, broke the black frieze she made with the foliage, rounded a bench at a moderate but determined pace and took the path back to the hotel.

With a guide and two other men, Dick started up the Birkkarspitze next morning. It was a fine feeling once they were above the cowbells of the highest pastures – Dick looked forward to the night in the shack, enjoying his own fatigue, enjoying the captaincy of the guide, feeling a delight in his own anonymity. But at midday the weather changed to black sleet and hail and mountain thunder. Dick and one of the other climbers wanted to go on but the guide refused. Regretfully they struggled back to Innsbruck to start again tomorrow.

After dinner and a bottle of heavy local wine in the deserted dining-room, he felt excited, without knowing why, until he began thinking of the garden. He had passed the girl in the lobby before supper and this time she had looked at him and approved of him, but it kept worrying him: Why? When I could have had a good share of the pretty women of my time for the asking, why start that now? With a wraith, with a fragment of my desire? Why?

His imagination pushed ahead – the old asceticism, the actual unfamiliarity, triumphed: God, I might as well go back to the Riviera and sleep with Janice Caricamento or the Wilburhazy girl. To belittle all these years with something cheap and easy?

He was still excited, though, and he turned from the veranda and went up to his room to think. Being alone in body and spirit begets loneliness, and loneliness begets more loneliness.

Upstairs he walked around thinking of the matter and laying out his climbing clothes advantageously on the faint heater; he again encountered Nicole's telegram, still unopened, with which diurnally she accompanied his itinerary. He had delayed opening it before supper – perhaps because of the garden. It was a cablegram from Buffalo, forwarded through Zurich.

Your father died peacefully tonight.

HOLMES

He felt a sharp wince at the shock, a gathering of the forces of resistance; then it rolled up through his loins and stomach and throat.

He read the message again. He sat down on the bed, breathing and staring; thinking first the old selfish child's thought that comes with the death of a parent, how will it affect me now that this earliest and strongest of protections is gone?

The atavism passed and he walked the room still, stopping from time to time to look at the telegram. Holmes was formally his father's curate but actually, and for a decade, rector of the church. How did he die? Of old age – he was seventy-five. He had lived a long time.

Dick felt sad that he had died alone – he had survived his wife, and his brothers and sisters; there were cousins in Virginia but they were poor and not able to come north, and Holmes had had to sign the telegram. Dick loved his father – again and again he referred judgements to what his father would probably have thought or done. Dick was born several months after the death of two young sisters, and his father, guessing what would be the effect on Dick's mother, had saved him from a spoiling by becoming his moral guide. He was of tired stock yet he raised himself to that effort.

In the summer father and son walked downtown together to have their shoes shined – Dick in his starched duck sailor suit, his father always in beautifully cut clerical clothes – and the father was very proud of his handsome little boy. He told Dick all he knew about life, not much but most of it true, simple things, matters of behaviour that came within his clergyman's range. 'Once in a strange town when I was first ordained, I went into a crowded room and was confused as to who was my hostess. Several people I knew came towards me, but I disregarded them because I had seen a grey-haired woman sitting by a window far across the room. I went over to her and introduced myself. After that I made many friends in that town.'

His father had done that from a good heart – his father had been sure of what he was, with a deep pride of the two proud widows who had raised him to believe that nothing could be superior to 'good instincts', honour, courtesy, and courage.

The father always considered that his wife's small fortune belonged to his son, and in college and in medical school sent him a cheque for all of it four times a year. He was one of those about whom it was said with smug finality in the gilded age: 'Very much the gentleman, but not much get-up-and-go about him.'

. . . Dick sent down for a newspaper. Still pacing to and from the telegram open on his bureau, he chose a ship to go to America. Then he put in a call for Nicole in Zurich, remembering so many things as he waited, and wishing he had always been as good as he had intended to be.

Chapter 19

For an hour, tied up with his profound reaction to his father's death, the magnificent façade of the homeland, the harbour of New York, seemed all sad and glorious to Dick, but once ashore the feeling vanished, nor did he find it again in the streets or the hotels or the trains that bore him first to Buffalo, and then south to Virginia with his father's body. Only as the local train shambled into the low-forested clayland of Westmoreland County, did he feel once more identified with his surroundings; at the station he saw a star he knew, and a cold moon bright over Chesapeake Bay; he heard the rasping wheels of buckboards turning, the lovely fatuous voices, the sound of sluggish primeval rivers flowing softly under soft Indian names.

Next day at the churchyard his father was laid among a hundred Divers, Dorseys, and Hunters. It was very friendly leaving him there with all his relations around him. Flowers were scattered on the brown unsettled earth. Dick had no more ties here now and did not believe he would come back. He knelt on the hard soil. These dead, he knew them all, their weather-beaten faces with blue flashing eyes, the spare violent bodies, the souls made of new earth in the forest – heavy darkness of the seventeenth century.

'Goodbye, my father – goodbye, all my fathers.'

* * *

On the long-roofed steamship piers one is in a country that is no longer here and not yet there. The hazy yellow vault is full of echoing shouts. There are the rumble of trucks and the clump of trunks, the strident chatter of cranes, the first salt smell of the sea. One hurries through, even though there's time; the past, the continent, is behind; the future is the glowing mouth in the side of the ship; the dim, turbulent alley is too confusedly the present.

Up the gangplank and the vision of the world adjusts itself, narrows. One is a citizen of a commonwealth smaller than Andorra, no longer sure of anything. The men at the purser's desk are as oddly shaped as the cabins; disdainful are the eyes of voyagers and their friends. Next the loud mournful whistles, the portentous vibration, and the boat, the human idea, is in motion. The pier and its faces slide by and for a moment the boat is a piece accidentally split off from them; the faces become remote, voiceless, the pier is one of many blurs along the waterfront. The harbour flows swiftly towards the sea.

With it flowed Albert McKisco, labelled by the newspapers as its most precious cargo. McKisco was having a vogue. His novels were pastiches of the work of the best people of his time, a feat not to be disparaged, and in addition he possessed a gift for softening and debasing what he borrowed, so that many readers were charmed by the ease with which they could follow him. Success had improved him and humbled him. He was no fool about his capacities – he realised that he possessed more vitality than many men of superior talent, and he was resolved to enjoy the success he had earned. 'I've done nothing yet,' he would say. 'I don't think I've got any real genius. But if I keep trying I may write a good book.' Fine dives have been made from flimsier springboards. The innumerable snubs of the past were forgotten. Indeed, his success was founded psychologically upon his duel with Tommy Barban, upon the basis of which, as it withered in his memory, he had created, afresh, a new self-respect.

Spotting Dick Diver the second day out, he eyed him tentatively, then introduced himself in a friendly way and sat down. Dick laid aside his reading and, after the few minutes that it took to realise the change in McKisco, the disappearance of the man's annoying sense of inferiority, found himself pleased to talk to him. McKisco was 'well-informed' on a range of subjects wider than Goethe's – it was interesting to listen to the innumerable facile combinations that he referred to as his opinions. They struck up an acquaintance, and Dick had several meals with them. The McKiscos had been invited to sit at the captain's table but with nascent snobbery they told Dick that they 'couldn't stand that bunch'.

Violet was very grand now, decked out by the grand couturiers, charmed about the little discoveries that well-bred girls make in their teens. She could, indeed, have learned them from her mother in Boise but her soul was born dismally in the small movie houses of Idaho, and she had had no time for her mother. Now she 'belonged' – together with several million other people – and she was happy, though her husband still shushed her when she grew violently naïve.

The McKiscos got off at Gibraltar. Next evening in Naples Dick picked up a lost and miserable family of two girls and their mother in the bus from the hotel to the station. He had seen them on the ship. An overwhelming desire to help, or to be admired, came over him: he showed them fragments of gaiety; tentatively he bought them wine, with pleasure saw them begin to regain their proper egotism. He pretended they were this and that, and falling in with his own plot, and drinking too much to sustain the illusion, and all this time the women thought only that this was a windfall from heaven. He withdrew from them as the night waned and the train rocked and snorted at Cassino and Frosinone. After weird American partings in the station at Rome, Dick went to the Hotel Quirinal, somewhat exhausted.

At the desk he suddenly stared and upped his head. As if a drink were acting on him, warming the lining of his stomach, throwing a flush up into his brain, he saw the person he had come to see, the person for whom he had made the Mediterranean crossing.

Simultaneously Rosemary saw him, acknowledging him before placing him; she looked back startled, and, leaving the girl she was with, she hurried over. Holding himself erect, holding his breath, Dick turned to her. As she came across the lobby, her beauty all groomed, like a young horse dosed with Black-seed oil, and hoofs varnished, shocked him awake; but it all came too quick for him to do anything except conceal his fatigue as best he could. To meet her starry-eyed confidence he mustered an insincere pantomime implying, 'You *would* turn up here – of all the people in the world.'

Her gloved hands closed over his on the desk; 'Dick – we're making *The Grandeur that was Rome* – at least we think we are; we may quit any day.'

He looked at her hard, trying to make her a little self-conscious, so that she would observe less closely his unshaven face, his crumpled and slept-in collar. Fortunately, she was in a hurry.

'We begin early because the mists rise at eleven – phone me at two.'

In his room Dick collected his faculties. He left a call for noon, stripped off his clothes and dived literally into a heavy sleep.

He slept over the phone call but awoke at two, refreshed. Unpacking his bag, he sent out suits and laundry. He shaved, lay for half an hour in a warm bath and had breakfast. The sun had dipped into the Via Nazionale and he let it through the portières with a jingling of old brass rings. Waiting for a suit to be pressed, he discovered from the *Corriere della Sera* that 'una novella di Sainclair Lewis *Wall Street* nella quale l'autore analizza la vita sociale di una piccola città Americana'. Then he tried to think about Rosemary.

At first he thought nothing. She was young and magnetic, but so was Topsy. He guessed that she had had lovers and had loved them in the last four years. Well, you never knew exactly how much space you occupied in people's lives. Yet from this fog his affection emerged – the best contacts are when one knows the obstacles and still wants to preserve a relation. The past drifted back and he wanted to hold her eloquent giving-of-herself in its precious shell, till he enclosed it, till it no longer existed outside him. He tried to collect all that might attract her – it was less than it had been four years ago. Eighteen might look at thirty-four through a rising mist of adolescence, but twenty-two would see thirty-eight with discerning clarity. Moreover, Dick had been at an emotional peak at the time of the previous encounter; since then there had been a lesion of enthusiasm.

When the valet returned he put on a white shirt and collar and a black tie with a pearl; the cords of his reading-glasses passed through another pearl of the same size that swung a casual inch below. After sleep, his face had resumed the ruddy brown of many Riviera summers, and to limber himself up he stood on his hands on a chair until his fountain pen and coins fell out. At three he called Rosemary and was bidden to come up. Momentarily dizzy from his acrobatics, he stopped in the bar for a gin-and-tonic.

'Hi, Dr Diver!'

Only because of Rosemary's presence in the hotel did Dick place the man immediately as Collis Clay. He had his old confidence and an air of prosperity and big sudden jowls.

'Do you know Rosemary's here?' Collis asked.

'I ran into her.'

'I was in Florence and I heard she was here so I came down last week. You'd never know mama's little girl.' He modified the remark, 'I mean she was so carefully brought up and now she's a woman of the world – if you know what I mean. Believe me, has she got some of these Roman boys tied up in bags! And how!'

'You studying in Florence?'

'Me? Sure, I'm studying architecture there. I go back Sunday – I'm staying for the races.'

With difficulty Dick restrained him from adding the drink to the account he carried in the bar, like a stock-market report.

Chapter 20

When Dick got out of the elevator he followed a tortuous corridor and turned at length towards a distant voice outside a lighted door. Rosemary was in black pyjamas; a luncheon table was still in the room; she was having coffee.

'You're still beautiful,' he said. 'A little more beautiful than ever.'

'Do you want coffee, youngster?'

'I'm sorry I was so unpresentable this morning.'

'You didn't look well – you all right now? Want coffee?'

'No, thanks.'

'You're fine again, I was scared this morning. Mother's coming over next month, if the company stays. She always asks me if I've seen you over here, as if she thought we were living next door. Mother always liked you – she always felt you were someone I ought to know.'

'Well, I'm glad she still thinks of me.'

'Oh, she does,' Rosemary reassured him. 'A very great deal.'

'I've seen you here and there in pictures,' said Dick. 'Once I had *Daddy's Girl* run off just for myself.'

'I have a good part in this one if it isn't cut.'

She crossed behind him, touching his shoulder as she passed. She phoned for the table to be taken away and settled in a big chair.

'I was just a little girl when I met you, Dick. Now I'm a woman.'

'I want to hear everything about you.'

'How is Nicole – and Lanier and Topsy?'

'They're fine. They often speak of you – '

The phone rang. While she answered it Dick examined two novels – one by Edna Ferber, one by Albert McKisco. The waiter came for the table; bereft of its presence Rosemary seemed more alone in her black pyjamas.

' . . . I have a caller . . . No, not very well. I've got to go to the costumer's for a long fitting . . . No, not now . . .'

As though with the disappearance of the table she felt released, Rosemary smiled at Dick – that smile as if they two together had managed to get rid of all the trouble in the world and were now at peace in their own heaven . . .

'That's done,' she said. 'Do you realise I've spent the last hour getting ready for you?'

But again the phone called her. Dick got up to change his hat from the bed to the luggage stand, and in alarm Rosemary put her hand over the mouthpiece of the phone. 'You're not going!'

'No.'

When the communication was over he tried to drag the afternoon together, saying: 'I expect some nourishment from people now.'

'Me too,' Rosemary agreed. 'The man that just phoned me once knew a second cousin of mine. Imagine calling anybody up for a reason like that!'

Now she lowered the lights for love. Why else should she want to shut off his view of her? He sent his words to her like letters, as though they left him some time before they reached her.

'Hard to sit here and be close to you, and not kiss you.' Then they kissed passionately in the centre of the floor. She pressed against him, and went back to her chair.

It could not go on being merely pleasant in the room. Forward or backward; when the phone rang once more he strolled into the bed-chamber and lay down on her bed, opening Albert McKisco's novel. Presently Rosemary came in and sat beside him.

'You have the longest eyelashes,' she remarked.

'We are now back at the Junior Prom. Among those present are Miss Rosemary Hoyt, the eyelash fancier – '

She kissed him and he pulled her down so that they lay side by side, and then they kissed till they were both breathless. Her breathing was young and eager and exciting. Her lips were faintly chapped but soft in the corners.

When they were still limbs and feet and clothes, struggles of his arms and back, and her throat and breasts, she whispered, 'No, not now – those things are rhythmic.'

Disciplined he crushed his passion into a corner of his mind, but bearing up her fragility on his arm until she was poised half a foot above him, he said lightly: 'Darling – that doesn't matter.'

Her face had changed with his looking up at it; there was the eternal moonlight in it.

'That would be poetic justice if it should be you,' she said. She twisted away from him, walked to the mirror, and boxed her disarranged hair with her hands. Presently she drew a chair close to the bed and stroked his cheek.

'Tell me the truth about you,' he demanded.

'I always have.'

'In a way – but nothing hangs together.'

They both laughed but he pursued.

'Are you actually a virgin?'

'No-o-!' she sang. 'I've slept with six hundred and forty men – if that's the answer you want.'

'It's none of my business.'

'Do you want me for a case in psychology?'

'Looking at you as a perfectly normal girl of twenty-two, living in the year nineteen twenty-eight, I guess you've taken a few shots at love.'

'It's all been – abortive,' she said.

Dick couldn't believe her. He could not decide whether she was deliberately building a barrier between them or whether this was intended to make an eventual surrender more significant.

'Let's go walk in the Pincio,' he suggested.

He shook himself straight in his clothes and smoothed his hair. A moment had come and somehow passed. For three years Dick had been the ideal by which Rosemary measured other men and inevitably his stature had increased to heroic size. She did not want him to be like other men, yet here were the same exigent demands, as if he wanted to take some of herself away, carry it off in his pocket.

Walking on the greensward between cherubs and philosophers, fauns and falling water, she took his arm smugly, settling into it with a series of little readjustments, as if she wanted it to be right because it was going to be there forever. She plucked a twig and broke it, but she found no spring in it. Suddenly seeing what she wanted in Dick's face she took his gloved hand and kissed it. Then she cavorted childishly for him until he smiled and she laughed and they began having a good time.

'I can't go out with you tonight, darling, because I promised some people a long time ago. But if you'll get up early I'll take you out to the set tomorrow.'

He dined alone at the hotel, went to bed early, and met Rosemary in the lobby at half-past six. Beside him in the car she glowed away fresh and new in the morning sunshine. They went out through the Porta San Sebastiano and along the Appian Way until they came to the huge set of the forum, larger than the forum itself. Rosemary turned him over to a man who led him about the great props; the arches and tiers of seats and the sanded arena. She was working on a stage which represented a guardroom for Christian prisoners, and presently they went there and watched Nicotera, one of many hopeful Valentinos, strut and pose before a dozen female 'captives', their eyes melancholy and startling with mascara.

Rosemary appeared in a knee-length tunic.

'Watch this,' she whispered to Dick. 'I want your opinion. Everybody that's seen the rushes says – '

'What are the rushes?'

'When they run off what they took the day before. They say it's the first thing I've had sex appeal in.'

'I don't notice it.'

'You wouldn't! But I have.'

Nicotera in his leopard skin talked attentively to Rosemary while the electrician discussed something with the director, meanwhile leaning on him. Finally the director pushed his hand off roughly and wiped a sweating forehead, and Dick's guide remarked: 'He's on the hop again, and how!'

'Who?' asked Dick, but before the man could answer the director walked swiftly over to them.

'Who's on the hop – you're on the hop yourself.' He spoke vehemently to Dick, as if to a jury. 'When he's on the hop he always thinks everybody else is, and how!' He glared at the guide a moment longer, then he clapped his hands: 'All right – everybody on the set.'

It was like visiting a great turbulent family. An actress approached Dick and talked to him for five minutes under the impression that he was an actor recently arrived from London. Discovering her mistake she scuttled away in panic. The majority of the company felt either sharply superior or sharply inferior to the world outside, but the former feeling prevailed. They were people of bravery and industry; they were risen to a position of prominence in a nation that for a decade had wanted only to be entertained.

The session ended as the light grew misty – a fine light for painters, but, for the camera, not to be compared with the clear California air. Nicotera followed Rosemary to the car and whispered something to her – she looked at him without smiling as she said goodbye.

Dick and Rosemary had luncheon at the Castelli dei Caesari, a splendid restaurant in a high-terraced villa overlooking the ruined forum of an undetermined period of the decadence. Rosemary took a cocktail and a little wine, and Dick took enough so that his feeling of dissatisfaction left him. Afterwards they drove back to the hotel, all flushed and happy, in a sort of exalted quiet. She wanted to be taken and she was, and what had begun with a childish infatuation on a beach was accomplished at last.

Chapter 21

Rosemary had another date, a birthday party for a member of the company. Dick ran into Collis Clay in the lobby, but he wanted to dine alone, and pretended an engagement at the Excelsior. He drank a cocktail with Collis and his vague dissatisfaction crystallised as impatience – he no longer had an excuse for playing truant to the clinic. This was less an infatuation than a romantic memory. Nicole was his girl – too often he was sick at heart about her, yet she was his girl. Time with Rosemary was self-indulgence – time with Collis was nothing plus nothing.

In the doorway of the Excelsior he ran into Baby Warren. Her large beautiful eyes, looking precisely like marbles, stared at him with surprise and curiosity. 'I thought you were in America, Dick! Is Nicole with you?'

'I came back by way of Naples.'

The black band on his arm reminded her to say: 'I'm so sorry to hear of your trouble.'

Inevitably they dined together.

'Tell me about everything,' she demanded.

Dick gave her a version of the facts, and Baby frowned. She found it necessary to blame someone for the catastrophe in her sister's life.

'Do you think Dr Dohmler took the right course with her from the first?'

'There's not much variety in treatment any more – of course you try to find the right personality to handle a particular case.'

'Dick, I don't pretend to advise you or to know much about it but don't you think a change might be good for her – to get out of that atmosphere of sickness and live in the world like other people?'

'But you were keen for the clinic,' he reminded her. 'You told me you'd never feel really safe about her – '

'That was when you were leading that hermit's life on the Riviera, up on a hill way off from anybody. I didn't mean to go back to that life. I meant, for instance, London. The English are the best-balanced race in the world.'

'They are not,' he disagreed.

'They are. I know them, you see. I mean it might be nice for you to take a house in London for the spring season – I know a dove of a house in Talbot Square you could get, furnished. I mean, living with sane, well-balanced English people.'

She would have gone on to tell him all the old propaganda stories of 1914 if he had not laughed and said: 'I've been reading a book by Michael Arlen and if that's – '

She ruined Michael Arlen with a wave of her salad spoon.

'He only writes about degenerates. I mean the worthwhile English.'

As she thus dismissed her friends they were replaced in Dick's mind only by a picture of the alien, unresponsive faces that peopled the small hotels of Europe.

'Of course it's none of my business,' Baby repeated, as a preliminary to a further plunge, 'but to leave her alone in an atmosphere like that – '

'I went to America because my father died.'

'I understand that, I told you how sorry I was.' She fiddled with the glass grapes on her necklace. 'But there's *so much* money now. Plenty for everything, and it ought to be used to get Nicole well.'

'For one thing I can't see myself in London.'

'Why not? I should think you could work there as well as anywhere else.'

He sat back and looked at her. If she had ever suspected the rotted old truth, the real reason for Nicole's illness, she had certainly determined to deny it to herself, shoving it back in a dusty closet like one of the paintings she bought by mistake.

They continued the conversation in the Ulpia, where Collis Clay came over to their table and sat down, and a gifted guitar player thrummed and rumbled 'Suona Fanfara Mia' in the cellar piled with wine casks.

'It's possible that I was the wrong person for Nicole,' Dick said. 'Still she would probably have married someone of my type, someone she thought she could rely on – indefinitely.'

'You think she'd be happier with somebody else?' Baby thought aloud suddenly. 'Of course it could be arranged.'

Only as she saw Dick bend forward with helpless laughter did she realise the preposterousness of her remark.

'Oh, you understand,' she assured him. 'Don't think for a moment that we're not grateful for all you've done. And we know you've had a hard time – '

'For God's sake,' he protested. 'If I didn't love Nicole it might be different.'

'But you do love Nicole?' she demanded in alarm.

Collis was catching up with the conversation now and Dick switched it quickly: 'Suppose we talk about something else – about you, for instance. Why don't you get married? We heard you were engaged to Lord Paley, the cousin of the – '

'Oh, no.' She became coy and elusive. 'That was last year.'

'Why don't you marry?' Dick insisted stubbornly.

'I don't know. One of the men I loved was killed in the war, and the other one threw me over.'

'Tell me about it. Tell me about your private life, Baby, and your opinions. You never do – we always talk about Nicole.'

'Both of them were Englishmen. I don't think there's any higher type in the world than a first-rate Englishman, do you? If there is I haven't met him. This man – oh, it's a long story. I hate long stories, don't you?'

'And how!' said Collis.

'Why, no – I like them if they're good.'

'That's something you do so well, Dick. You can keep a party moving by just a little sentence or a saying here and there. I think that's a wonderful talent.'

'It's a trick,' he said gently. That made three of her opinions he disagreed with.

'Of course I like formality – I like things to be just so, and on the grand scale. I know you probably don't but you must admit it's a sign of solidity in me.'

Dick did not even bother to dissent from this.

'Of course I know people say Baby Warren is racing around over Europe, chasing one novelty after another, and missing the best things in life, but I think on the contrary that I'm one of the few people who really go after the best things. I've known the most interesting people of my time.' Her voice blurred with the tinny drumming of another guitar number, but she called over it, 'I've made very few big mistakes – '

' – Only the very big ones, Baby.'

She had caught something facetious in his eyes and she changed the subject. It seemed impossible for them to hold anything in common. But he admired something in her, and he deposited her at the Excelsior with a series of compliments that left her shimmering.

Rosemary insisted on treating Dick to lunch next day. They went to a little *trattoria* kept by an Italian who had worked in America, and ate ham and eggs and waffles. Afterwards, they went to the hotel. Dick's discovery that he was not in love with her, nor she with him, had added to rather than diminished his passion for her. Now that he knew he would not enter further into her life, she became the strange woman for him. He supposed many men meant no more than that when they said they were in love – not a wild submergence of soul, a dipping of all colours into an obscuring dye, such as his love for Nicole had been. Certain thoughts about Nicole, that she should die, sink into mental darkness, love another man, made him physically sick.

Nicotera was in Rosemary's sitting-room, chattering about a professional matter. When Rosemary gave him his cue to go, he left with humorous protests and a rather insolent wink at Dick. As usual the phone clamoured and Rosemary was engaged at it for ten minutes to Dick's increasing impatience.

'Let's go up to my room,' he suggested, and she agreed.

She lay across his knees on a big sofa; he ran his fingers through the lovely forelocks of her hair.

'Let me be curious about you again?' he asked.

'What do you want to know?'

'About men. I'm curious, not to say prurient.'

'You mean how long after I met you?'

'Or before.'

'Oh, no.' She was shocked. 'There was nothing before. You were the first man I cared about. You're still the only man I really care about.' She considered. 'It was about a year, I think.'

'Who was it?'

'Oh, a man.'

He closed in on her evasion.

'I'll bet I can tell you about it: the first affair was unsatisfactory and after that there was a long gap. The second was better, but you hadn't been in love with the man in the first place. The third was all right – '

Torturing himself he ran on. 'Then you had one real affair that fell of its own weight, and by that time you were getting afraid that you wouldn't have anything to give to the man you finally loved.' He felt increasingly Victorian. 'Afterwards there were half a dozen just episodic affairs, right up to the present. Is that close?'

She laughed between amusement and tears.

'It's about as wrong as it could be,' she said, to Dick's relief. 'But someday I'm going to find somebody and love him and love him and never let him go.'

Now his phone rang and Dick recognised Nicotera's voice, asking for Rosemary. He put his palm over the transmitter.

'Do you want to talk to him?'

She went to the phone and jabbered in a rapid Italian Dick could not understand.

'This telephoning takes time,' he said. 'It's after four and I have an engagement at five. You better go play with Signor Nicotera.'

'Don't be silly.'

'Then I think that while I'm here you ought to count him out.'

'It's difficult.' She was suddenly crying. 'Dick, I do love you, never anybody like you. But what have you got for me?'

'What has Nicotera got for anybody?'

'That's different.'

Because youth called to youth.

'He's a spic!' he said. He was frantic with jealousy, he didn't want to be hurt again.

'He's only a baby,' she said, sniffling. 'You know I'm yours first.'

In reaction he put his arms about her but she relaxed wearily backwards; he held her like that for a moment as in the end of an adagio, her eyes closed, her hair falling straight back like that of a girl drowned.

'Dick, let me go. I never felt so mixed up in my life.'

He was a gruff red bird and instinctively she drew away from him as his unjustified jealousy began to snow over the qualities of consideration and understanding with which she felt at home.

'I want to know the truth,' he said.

'Yes, then. We're a lot together, he wants to marry me, but I don't want to. What of it? What do you expect me to do? You never asked me to marry you. Do you want me to play around for ever with half-wits like Collis Clay?'

'You were with Nicotera last night?'

'That's none of your business,' she sobbed. 'Excuse me, Dick, it is your business. You and mother are the only two people in the world I care about.'

'How about Nicotera?'

'How do I know?'

She had achieved the elusiveness that gives hidden significance to the least significant remarks.

'Is it like you felt towards me in Paris?'

'I feel comfortable and happy when I'm with you. In Paris it was different. But you never know how you once felt. Do you?'

He got up and began collecting his evening clothes – if he had to bring all the bitterness and hatred of the world into his heart, he was not going to be in love with her again.

'I don't care about Nicotera!' she declared. 'But I've got to go to Livorno with the company tomorrow. Oh, why did this have to happen?' There was a new flood of tears. 'It's such a shame. Why did you come here? Why couldn't we just have the memory anyhow? I feel as if I'd quarrelled with mother.'

As he began to dress, she got up and went to the door.

'I won't go to the party tonight.' It was her last effort. 'I'll stay with you. I don't want to go anyhow.'

The tide began to flow again, but he retreated from it.

'I'll be in my room,' she said. 'Goodbye, Dick.'

'Goodbye.'

'Oh, such a shame, such a shame. Oh, such a shame. What's it all about anyhow?'

'I've wondered for a long time.'

'But why bring it to me?'

'I guess I'm the Black Death,' he said slowly. 'I don't seem to bring people happiness any more.'

Chapter 22

There were five people in the Quirinal bar after dinner, a high-class Italian frail who sat on a stool making persistent conversation against the bartender's bored: 'Si . . . Si . . . Si', a light, snobbish Egyptian who was lonely but chary of the woman, and the two Americans.

Dick was always vividly conscious of his surroundings, while Collis Clay lived vaguely, the sharpest impressions dissolving upon a recording apparatus that had early atrophied, so the former talked and the latter listened, like a man sitting in a breeze.

Dick, worn away by the events of the afternoon, was taking it out on the inhabitants of Italy. He looked around the bar as if he hoped an Italian had heard him and would resent his words.

'This afternoon I had tea with my sister-in-law at the Excelsior. We got the last table and two men came up and looked around for a table and couldn't find one. So one of them came up to us and said, "Isn't this table reserved for the Princess Orsini?" and I said: "There was no sign on it," and he said: "But I think it's reserved for the Princess Orsini." I couldn't even answer him.'

'What'd he do?'

'He retired.' Dick switched around in his chair. 'I don't like these people. The other day I left Rosemary for two minutes in front of a store and an officer started walking up and down in front of her, tipping his hat.'

'I don't know,' said Collis after a moment. 'I'd rather be here than up in Paris with somebody picking your pocket every minute.'

He had been enjoying himself, and he held out against anything that threatened to dull his pleasure.

'I don't know,' he persisted. 'I don't mind it here.'

Dick evoked the picture that the few days had imprinted on his mind, and stared at it. The walk towards the American Express past the odorous confectioneries of the Via Nationale, through the foul tunnel up to the Spanish Steps, where his spirit soared before the flower stalls and the house where Keats had died. He cared only about people; he was scarcely conscious of places except for their weather, until they had been invested with colour by tangible events. Rome was the end of his dream of Rosemary.

A bellboy came in and gave him a note.

'I did not go to the party,' it said. 'I am in my room. We leave for Livorno early in the morning.'

Dick handed the note and a tip to the boy.

'Tell Miss Hoyt you couldn't find me.' Turning to Collis he suggested the Bonbonieri.

They inspected the tart at the bar, granting her the minimum of interest exacted by her profession, and she stared back with bright boldness; they went through the deserted lobby oppressed by draperies holding Victorian dust in stuffy folds, and they nodded at the night concierge, who returned the gesture with the bitter servility peculiar to night servants. Then in a taxi they rode along cheerless streets through a dank November night. There were no women in the streets, only pale men with dark coats buttoned to the neck, who stood in groups beside shoulders of cold stone.

'My God!' Dick sighed.

'What's a matter?'

'I was thinking of that man this afternoon: "This table is reserved for the Princess Orsini." Do you know what these old Roman families are? They're bandits, they're the ones who got possession of the temples and palaces after Rome went to pieces and preyed on the people.'

'I like Rome,' insisted Collis. 'Why won't you try the races?'

'I don't like races.'

'But all the women turn out – '

'I know I wouldn't like anything here. I like France, where everybody thinks he's Napoleon – down here everybody thinks he's Christ.'

At the Bonbonieri they descended to a panelled cabaret, hopelessly impermanent amid the cold stone. A listless band played a tango and a dozen couples covered the wide floor with those elaborate and dainty steps so offensive to the American eye. A surplus of waiters precluded the stir and bustle that even a few busy men can create; over the scene as its form of animation brooded an air of waiting for something, for the dance, the night, the balance of forces which kept it stable, to cease. It assured the impressionable guest that whatever he was seeking he would not find it here.

This was plain as plain to Dick. He looked around, hoping his eye would catch on something, so that spirit instead of imagination could carry on for an hour. But there was nothing and after a moment he turned back to Collis. He had told Collis some of his current notions, and he was bored with his audience's short memory and lack of response. After half an hour of Collis he felt a distinct lesion of his own vitality.

They drank a bottle of Italian mousseux, and Dick became pale and somewhat noisy. He called the orchestra leader over to their table; this was a Bahama Negro, conceited and unpleasant, and in a few minutes there was a row.

'You asked me to sit down.'

'All right. And I gave you fifty lire, didn't I?'

'All right. All right. All right.'

'All right, I gave you fifty lire, didn't I? Then you came up and asked me to put some more in the horn!'

'You asked me to sit down, didn't you? Didn't you?'

'I asked you to sit down but I gave you fifty lire, didn't I?'

'All right. All right.'

The Negro got up sourly and went away, leaving Dick in a still more evil humour. But he saw a girl smiling at him from across the room and immediately the pale Roman shapes around him receded into decent, humble perspective. She was a young English girl, with blonde hair and a healthy, pretty English face, and she smiled at him again with an invitation he understood, that denied the flesh even in the act of tendering it.

'There's a quick trick or else I don't know bridge,' said Collis.

Dick got up and walked to her across the room.

'Won't you dance?'

The middle-aged Englishman with whom she was sitting said, almost apologetically: 'I'm going out soon.'

Sobered by excitement, Dick danced. He found in the girl a suggestion of all the pleasanter English things; the story of safe gardens ringed around by the sea was implicit in her bright voice, and as he leaned back to look at her, he meant what he said to her so sincerely that his voice trembled. When her current escort should leave, she promised to come and sit with them. The Englishman accepted her return with repeated apologies and smiles.

Back at his table Dick ordered another bottle of spumante.

'She looks like somebody in the movies,' he said. 'I can't think who.' He glanced impatiently over his shoulder. 'Wonder what's keeping her?'

'I'd like to get in the movies,' said Collis thoughtfully. 'I'm supposed to go into my father's business but it doesn't appeal to me much. Sit in an office in Birmingham for twenty years – '

His voice resisted the pressure of materialistic civilisation.

'Too good for it?' suggested Dick.

'No, I don't mean that.'

'Yes, you do.'

'How do you know what I mean? Why don't you practise as a doctor, if you like to work so much?'

Dick had made them both wretched by this time, but simultaneously they had become vague with drink and in a moment they forgot; Collis left, and they shook hands warmly.

'Think it over,' said Dick sagely.

'Think what over?'

'You know.' It had been something about Collis going into his father's business – good sound advice.

Clay walked off into space. Dick finished his bottle and then danced with the English girl again, conquering his unwilling body with bold revolutions and stern determined marches down the floor. The most remarkable thing suddenly happened. He was dancing with the girl, the music stopped – and she had disappeared.

'Have you seen her?'

'Seen who?'

'The girl I was dancing with. Su'nly disappeared. Must be in the building.'

'No! No! That's the ladies' room.'

He stood up by the bar. There were two other men there, but he could think of no way of starting a conversation. He could have told them all about Rome and the violent origins of the Colonna and Gaetani families, but he realised that as a beginning that would be somewhat abrupt. A row of Yenci dolls on the cigar counter fell suddenly to the floor; there was a subsequent confusion and he had a sense of having been the cause of it, so he went back to the cabaret and drank a cup of black coffee. Collis was gone and the English girl was gone and there seemed nothing to do but go back to the hotel and lie down with his black heart. He paid his check and got his hat and coat.

There was dirty water in the gutters and between the rough cobblestones; a marshy vapour from the Campagna, a sweat of exhausted cultures tainted the morning air. A quartet of taxi-drivers, their little eyes bobbing in dark pouches, surrounded him. One who leaned insistently in his face he pushed harshly away.

'Quanto a Hotel Quirinal?'

'Cento lire.'

Six dollars. He shook his head and offered thirty lire which was twice the daytime fare, but they shrugged their shoulders as one pair, and moved off.

'Trenta-cinque lire e mancie,' he said firmly.

'Cento lire.'

He broke into English.

'To go half a mile? You'll take me for forty lire.'

'Oh, no.'

He was very tired. He pulled open the door of a cab and got in.

'Hotel Quirinal!' he said to the driver who stood obstinately outside the window. 'Wipe that sneer off your face and take me to the Quirinal.'

'Ah, no.'

Dick got out. By the door of the Bonbonieri someone was arguing with the taxi-drivers, someone who now tried to explain their attitude to Dick; again one of the men pressed close, insisting and gesticulating, and Dick shoved him away.

'I want to go the Quirinal Hotel.'

'He says wan huner lire,' explained the interpreter.

'I understand. I'll give him fifty lire. Go on away.' This last to the insistent man who had edged up once more. The man looked at him and spat contemptuously.

The passionate impatience of the week leaped up in Dick and clothed itself like a flash in violence, the honourable, the traditional resource of his land; he stepped forward and clapped the man's face.

They surged about him, threatening, waving their arms, trying ineffectually to close in on him – with his back against the wall Dick hit out clumsily, laughing a little, and for a few minutes the mock fight, an affair of foiled rushes and padded, glancing blows, swayed back and forth in front of the door. Then Dick tripped and fell; he was hurt somewhere but he struggled up again wrestling in arms that suddenly broke apart. There was a new voice and a new argument, but he leaned against the wall, panting, and furious at the indignity of his position. He saw there was no sympathy for him but he was unable to believe that he was wrong.

They were going to the police station and settle it there. His hat was retrieved and handed to him, and with someone holding his arm lightly he strode around the corner with the taxi-men and entered a bare barrack where *carabinieri* lounged under a single dim light.

At a desk sat a captain, to whom the officious individual who had stopped the battle spoke at length in Italian, at times pointing at Dick, and letting himself be interrupted by the taxi-men who delivered short bursts of invective and denunciation. The captain began to nod impatiently. He held up his hand and the hydra-headed address, with a few parting exclamations, died away. Then he turned to Dick.

'Spick Italiano?' he asked.

'No.'

'Spick Français?'

'Oui,' said Dick glowering.

'Alors. Écoute. Va au Quirinal. Espèce d'endormi. Écoute: vous êtes saoul. Payez ce que le chauffeur demande. Comprenez-vous?'

Diver shook his head.

'Non, je ne veux pas.'

'Comment?'

'Je paierai quarante lires. C'est bien assez.'

The captain stood up.

'Écoute!' he cried portentously, 'Vous êtes saoul. Vous avez battu le chauffeur. Comme ci, comme ça.' He struck the air excitedly with right hand and left. 'C'est bon que je vous donne la liberté. Payez ce qu'il a dit – cento lire. Va au Quirinal.'

Raging with humiliation, Dick stared back at him.

'All right.' He turned blindly to the door – before him, leering and nodding, was the man who had brought him to the police station. 'I'll go home,' he shouted, 'but first I'll fix this baby.'

He walked past the staring *carabinieri* and up to the grinning face, hit it with a smashing left beside the jaw. The man dropped to the floor.

For a moment he stood over him in savage triumph – but even as a first pang of doubt shot through him the world reeled; he was clubbed down, and fists and boots beat on him in a savage tattoo. He felt his nose break like a shingle and his eyes jerk as if they had snapped back on a rubber band into his head. A rib splintered under a stamping heel. Momentarily he lost consciousness, regained it as he was raised to a sitting position and his wrists jerked together with handcuffs. He struggled automatically. The plainclothes lieutenant whom he had knocked down stood dabbing his jaw with a handkerchief and looking into it for blood; he came over to Dick, poised himself, drew back his arm and smashed him to the floor.

When Dr Diver lay quite still a pail of water was sloshed over him. One of his eyes opened dimly as he was being dragged along by the wrists through a bloody haze, and he made out the human and ghastly face of one of the taxi-drivers.

'Go to the Excelsior Hotel,' he cried faintly. 'Tell Miss Warren.

Two hundred lire! Miss Warren. *Due centi lire!* Oh, you dirty – you god –'

Still he was dragged along through the bloody haze, choking and sobbing, over vague irregular surfaces into some small place where he was dropped upon a stone floor. The men went out, a door clanged, he was alone.

Chapter 23

Until one o'clock Baby Warren lay in bed, reading one of Marion Crawford's curiously inanimate Roman stories; then she went to a window and looked down into the street. Across from the hotel two *carabinieri*, grotesque in swaddling capes and harlequin hats, swung voluminously from this side to that, like mains'ls coming about, and watching them she thought of the Guards officer who had stared at her so intensely at lunch. He had possessed the arrogance of a tall member of a short race, with no obligation save to be tall. Had he come up to her and said: 'Let's go along, you and I,' she would have answered: 'Why not?' – at least it seemed so now, for she was still disembodied by an unfamiliar background.

Her thoughts drifted back slowly through the guardsman to the two *carabinieri*, to Dick – she got into bed and turned out the light.

A little before four she was awakened by a brusque knocking.

'Yes – what is it?'

'It's the concierge, madame.'

She pulled on her kimono and faced him sleepily.

'You friend named Deever he's in a trouble. He had trouble with the police, and they have him in the jail. He sent a taxi up to tell, the driver says that he promised him two hundred lire.' He paused cautiously for this to be approved. 'The driver says Mr Deever in the bad trouble. He had a fight with the police and is terribly bad hurt.'

'I'll be right down.'

She dressed to an accompaniment of anxious heartbeats and ten minutes later stepped out of the elevator into the dark lobby. The chauffeur who brought the message was gone; the concierge hailed another one and told him the location of the jail. As they rode, the darkness lifted and thinned outside and Baby's nerves, scarcely awake, cringed faintly at the unstable balance between night and day. She began to race against the day; sometimes on the broad avenues she gained but whenever the thing that was pushing up paused for a moment, gusts of wind blew here and there impatiently and the slow creep of light began once more. The cab went past a loud fountain splashing in a voluminous shadow, turned into an alley so curved that the buildings were warped and strained following it, bumped and rattled over cobblestones, and stopped with a jerk where two sentry-boxes were bright against a wall of green damp. Suddenly from the violet darkness of an archway came Dick's voice, shouting and screaming.

'Are there any English? Are there any Americans? Are there any English? Are there any – oh, my God! You dirty Wops!'

His voice died away and she heard a dull sound of beating on the door. Then the voice began again.

'Are there any Americans? Are there any English?'

Following the voice she ran through the arch into a court, whirled about in momentary confusion and located the small guardroom whence the cries came. Two *carabinieri* started to their feet, but Baby brushed past them to the door of the cell.

'Dick!' she called. 'What's the trouble?'

'They've put out my eye,' he cried. 'They handcuffed me and then they beat me, the goddamn – the – '

Flashing around Baby took a step towards the two *carabinieri*.

'What have you done to him?' she whispered so fiercely that they flinched before her gathering fury.

'Non capisco inglese.'

In French she execrated them; her wild, confident rage filled the room, enveloped them until they shrank and wriggled from the garments of blame with which she invested them. 'Do something! Do something!'

'We can do nothing until we are ordered.'

'Bene. Bay-nay! Bene!'

Once more Baby let her passion scorch around them until they sweated out apologies for their impotence, looking at each other with the sense that something had after all gone terribly wrong. Baby went to the cell door, leaned against it, almost caressing it, as if that could make Dick feel her presence and power, and cried: 'I'm going to the Embassy, I'll be back.' Throwing a last glance of infinite menace at the *carabinieri* she ran out.

She drove to the American Embassy where she paid off the taxi-driver upon his insistence. It was still dark when she ran up the steps and pressed the bell. She had pressed it three times before a sleepy English porter opened the door to her.

'I want to see someone,' she said. 'Anyone – but right away.'

'No one's awake, madame. We don't open until nine o'clock.'

Impatiently she waved the hour away.

'This is important. A man – an American has been terribly beaten. He's in an Italian jail.'

'No one's awake now. At nine o'clock – '

'I can't wait. They've put out a man's eye – my brother-in-law, and they won't let him out of jail. I must talk to someone – can't you see? Are you crazy? Are you an idiot, you stand there with that look in your face?'

'Hime unable to do anything, madame.'

'You've got to wake someone up!' She seized him by the shoulders and jerked him violently. 'It's a matter of life and death. If you won't wake someone a terrible thing will happen to you – '

'Kindly don't lay hands on me, madame.'

From above and behind the porter floated down a weary Groton voice.

'What is it there?'

The porter answered with relief.

'It's a lady, sir, and she has shaken me.' He had stepped back to speak and Baby pushed forward into the hall. On an upper landing, just aroused from sleep and wrapped in a white embroidered Persian robe, stood a singular young man. His face was of a monstrous and unnatural pink, vivid yet dead, and over his mouth was fastened what appeared to be a gag. When he saw Baby he moved his head back into a shadow.

'What is it?' he repeated.

Baby told him, in her agitation edging forward to the stairs. In the course of her story she realised that the gag was in reality a moustache bandage and that the man's face was covered with pink cold cream, but the fact fitted quietly into the nightmare. The thing to do, she cried passionately, was for him to come to the jail with her at once to get Dick out.

'It's a bad business,' he said.

'Yes,' she agreed conciliatingly. 'Yes?'

'This trying to fight the police.' A note of personal affront crept into his voice. 'I'm afraid there's nothing to be done until nine o'clock.'

'Till nine o'clock,' she repeated aghast. 'But you can do something, certainly! You can come to the jail with me and see that they don't hurt him any more.'

'We aren't permitted to do anything like that. The Consulate handles these things. The Consulate will be open at nine.'

His face, constrained to impassivity by the binding strap, infuriated Baby.

'I can't wait until nine. My brother-in-law says they've put his eye out – he's seriously hurt! I have to get to him. I have to find a doctor.' She let herself go and began to cry angrily as she talked, for she knew that he would respond to her agitation rather than her words. 'You've got to do something about this. It's your business to protect American citizens in trouble.'

But he was of the Eastern seaboard and too hard for her. Shaking his head patiently at her failure to understand his position he drew the Persian robe closer about him and came down a few steps.

'Write down the address of the Consulate for this lady,' he said to the porter, 'and look up Dr Colazzo's address and telephone number and write that down too.' He turned to Baby, with the expression of an exasperated Christ. 'My dear lady, the diplomatic corps represents the Government of the United States to the Government of Italy. It has nothing to do with the protection of citizens, except under specific instructions from the State Department. Your brother-in-law has broken the laws of this country and been put in jail, just as an Italian might be put in jail in New York. The only people who can let him go are the Italian courts and if your brother-in-law has a case you can get aid and advice from the Consulate, which protects the rights of American citizens. The Consulate does not open until nine o'clock. Even if it were my brother I couldn't do anything – '

'Can you phone the Consulate?' she broke in.

'We can't interfere with the Consulate. When the Consul gets there at nine – '

'Can you give me his home address?'

After a fractional pause the man shook his head. He took the memorandum from the porter and gave it to her.

'Now I'll ask you to excuse me.'

He had manoeuvred her to the door: for an instant the violet dawn fell shrilly upon his pink mask and upon the linen sack that supported his moustache; then Baby was standing on the front steps alone. She had been in the Embassy ten minutes.

The piazza whereon it faced was empty save for an old man gathering cigarette butts with a spiked stick. Baby caught a taxi presently and went to the Consulate but there was no one there save a trio of wretched women scrubbing the stairs. She could not make them understand that she wanted the Consul's home address – in a sudden resurgence of anxiety she rushed out and told the chauffeur to take her to the jail. He did not know where it was, but by the use of words *semper diretto*, *dextra* and *sinestra* she manoeuvred him to its approximate locality, where she dismounted and explored a labyrinth of familiar alleys. But the buildings and the alleys all looked alike. Emerging from one trail into the Piazza di Spagna she saw the American Express Company and her heart lifted at the word 'American' on the sign. There was a light in the window and hurrying across the square she tried the door, but it was locked, and inside the clock stood at seven. Then she thought of Collis Clay.

She remembered the name of his hotel, a stuffy villa sealed in red plush across from the Excelsior. The woman on duty at the office was not disposed to help her – she had no authority to disturb Mr Clay, and refused to let Miss Warren go up to his room alone; convinced finally that this was not an affair of passion she accompanied her.

Collis lay naked upon his bed. He had come in tight and, awakening, it took him some moments to realise his nudity. He atoned for it by an excess of modesty. Taking his clothes into the bathroom he dressed in haste, muttering to himself, 'Gosh. She certainly musta got a good look at me.' After some telephoning, he and Baby found the jail and went to it.

The cell door was open and Dick was slumped on a chair in the guardroom. The *carabinieri* had washed some of the blood from his face, brushed him and set his hat concealingly upon his head. Baby stood in the doorway trembling.

'Mr Clay will stay with you,' she said. 'I want to get the Consul and a doctor.'

'All right.'

'Just stay quiet.'

'All right.'

'I'll be back.'

She drove to the Consulate; it was after eight now, and she was permitted to sit in the ante-room. Towards nine the Consul came in and Baby, hysterical with impotence and exhaustion, repeated her story. The Consul was disturbed. He warned her against getting into brawls in strange cities, but he was chiefly concerned that she should wait outside – with despair she read in his elderly eye that he wanted to be mixed up as little as possible in this catastrophe. Waiting on his action, she passed the minutes by phoning a doctor to go to Dick. There were other people in the ante-room and several were admitted to the Consul's office. After half an hour she chose the moment of someone's coming out and pushed past the secretary into the room.

'This is outrageous! An American has been beaten half to death and thrown into prison and you make no move to help.'

'Just a minute, Mrs – '

'I've waited long enough. You come right down to the jail and get him out!'

'Mrs – '

'We're people of considerable standing in America – ' Her mouth hardened as she continued. 'If it wasn't for the scandal we can – I shall see that your indifference to this matter is reported in the proper quarter. If my brother-in-law were a British citizen he'd have been free hours ago, but you're more concerned with what the police will think than about what you're here for.'

'Mrs – '

'You put on your hat and come with me right away.'

The mention of his hat alarmed the Consul, who began to clean his spectacles hurriedly and to ruffle his papers. This proved of no avail: the American Woman, aroused, stood over him; the clean-sweeping irrational temper that had broken the moral back of a race and made a nursery out of a continent, was too much for him. He rang for a vice-consul – Baby had won.

Dick sat in the sunshine that fell profusely through the guardroom window. Collis was with him and two *carabinieri*, and they were waiting for something to happen. With the narrowed vision of his one eye Dick could see the *carabinieri*; they were Tuscan peasants with short upper lips, and he found it difficult to associate them with the brutality of last night. He sent one of them to fetch him a glass of beer.

The beer made him light-headed and the episode was momentarily illuminated by a ray of sardonic humour. Collis was under the impression that the English girl had something to do with the catastrophe, but Dick was sure she had disappeared long before it happened. Collis was still absorbed by the fact that Miss Warren had found him naked on his bed.

Dick's rage had retreated into him a little and he felt a vast criminal irresponsibility. What had happened to him was so awful that nothing could make any difference unless he could choke it to death, and, as this was unlikely, he was hopeless. He would be a different person henceforward, and in his raw state he had bizarre feelings of what the new self would be. The matter had about it the impersonal quality of an act of God. No mature Aryan is able to profit by a humiliation; when he forgives, it has become part of his life, he has identified himself with the thing which has humiliated him – an upshot that in this case was impossible.

When Collis spoke of retribution, Dick shook his head and was silent. A lieutenant of *carabinieri*, pressed, burnished, vital, came into the room like three men and the guards jumped to attention. He seized the empty beer bottle and directed a stream of scolding at his men. The new spirit was in him, and the first thing was to get the beer bottle out of the guardroom. Dick looked at Collis and laughed.

The vice-consul, an overworked young man named Swanson, arrived, and they started to the court; Collis and Swanson on either side of Dick and the two *carabinieri* close behind. It was a yellow, hazy morning; the squares and arcades were crowded and Dick, pulling his hat low over his head, walked fast, setting the pace, until one of the short-legged *carabinieri* ran alongside and protested. Swanson arranged matters.

'I've disgraced you, haven't I?' said Dick jovially.

'You're liable to get killed fighting Italians,' replied Swanson sheepishly. 'They'll probably let you go this time, but if you were an Italian you'd get a couple of months in prison. And how!'

'Have you ever been in prison?'

Swanson laughed.

'I like him,' announced Dick to Clay. 'He's a very likeable young man and he gives people excellent advice, but I'll bet he's been to jail himself. Probably spent weeks at a time in jail.'

Swanson laughed.

'I mean you want to be careful. You don't know how these people are.'

'Oh, I know how they are,' broke out Dick, irritably. 'They're god-damn stinkers.' He turned around to the *carabinieri*: 'Did you get that?'

'I'm leaving you here,' Swanson said quickly. 'I told your sister-in-law I would – our lawyer will meet you upstairs in the court-room. You want to be careful.'

'Goodbye.' Dick shook hands politely. 'Thank you very much. I feel you have a future – '

With another smile Swanson hurried away, resuming his official expression of disapproval.

Now they came into a courtyard on all four sides of which outer stairways mounted to the chambers above. As they crossed the flags a groaning, hissing, booing sound went up from the loiterers in the courtyard, voices full of fury and scorn. Dick stared about.

'What's that?' he demanded, aghast.

One of the *carabinieri* spoke to a group of men and the sound died away.

They came into the court-room. A shabby Italian lawyer from the Consulate spoke at length to the judge while Dick and Collis waited aside. Someone who knew English turned from the window that gave on the yard and explained the sound that had accompanied their passage through. A native of Frascati had raped and slain a five-year-old child and was to be brought in that morning – the crowd had assumed it was Dick.

In a few minutes the lawyer told Dick that he was freed – the court considered him punished enough.

'Enough!' Dick cried. 'Punished for what?'

'Come along,' said Collis. 'You can't do anything now.'

'But what did I do, except get into a fight with some taxi-men?'

'They claim you went up to a detective as if you were going to shake hands with him and hit him – '

'That's not true! I told him I was going to hit him – I didn't know he was a detective.'

'You better go along,' urged the lawyer.

'Come along.' Collis took his arm and they descended the steps.

'I want to make a speech,' Dick cried. 'I want to explain to these people how I raped a five-year-old girl. Maybe I did – '

'Come along.'

Baby was waiting with a doctor in a taxi-cab. Dick did not want to look at her and he disliked the doctor, whose stern manner revealed him as one of the least palatable of European types, the Latin moralist. Dick summed up his conception of the disaster, but no one had much to say. In his room in the Quirinal the doctor washed off the rest of the blood and the oily sweat, set his nose, his fractured ribs and fingers, disinfected the smaller wounds and put a hopeful dressing on the eye. Dick asked for a quarter of a grain of morphine, for he was still wide awake and full of nervous energy. With the morphine he fell asleep; the doctor and Collis left and Baby waited with him until a woman could arrive from the English nursing home. It had been a hard night but she had the satisfaction of feeling that, whatever Dick's previous record was, they now possessed a moral superiority over him for as long as he proved of any use.

BOOK THREE

Chapter 1

Frau Kaethe Gregorovious overtook her husband on the path of their villa. 'How was Nicole?' she asked mildly; but she spoke out of breath, giving away the fact that she had held the question in her mind during her run.

Franz looked at her in surprise.

'Nicole's not sick. What makes you ask, dearest one?'

'You see her so much – I thought she must be sick.'

'We will talk of this in the house.'

Kaethe agreed meekly. His study was over in the administration building and the children were with their tutor in the living-room; they went up to the bedroom.

'Excuse me, Franz,' said Kaethe before he could speak. 'Excuse me, dear, I had no right to say that. I know my obligations and I am proud of them. But there is a bad feeling between Nicole and me.'

'Birds in their little nests agree,' Franz thundered. Finding the tone inappropriate to the sentiment, he repeated his command in the spaced and considered rhythm with which his old master, Dr Dohmler, could cast significance on the tritest platitude. 'Birds-in-their-nests-*agree*!'

'I realise that. You haven't seen me fail in courtesy towards Nicole.'

'I see you failing in common sense. Nicole is half a patient – she will possibly remain something of a patient all her life. In the absence of Dick I am responsible.' He hesitated; sometimes as a quiet joke he tried to keep news from Kaethe. 'There was a cable from Rome this morning. Dick has had grippe and is starting home tomorrow.'

Relieved, Kaethe pursued her course in a less personal tone: 'I think Nicole is less sick than anyone thinks – she only cherishes her illness as an instrument of power. She ought to be in the cinema, like your Norma Talmadge – that's where all American women would be happy.'

'Are you jealous of Norma Talmadge, on a film?'

'I don't like Americans. They're selfish, *self*ish!'

'You like Dick?'

'I like him,' she admitted. 'He's different, he thinks of others.'

– And so does Norma Talmadge, Franz said to himself. Norma Talmadge must be a fine, noble woman beyond her loveliness. They must compel her to play foolish roles; Norma Talmadge must be a woman whom it would be a great privilege to know.

Kaethe had forgotten about Norma Talmadge, a vivid shadow that she had fretted bitterly upon one night as they were driving home from the movies in Zurich.

' – Dick married Nicole for her money,' she said. 'That was his weakness – you hinted as much yourself one night.'

'You're being malicious.'

'I shouldn't have said that,' she retracted. 'We must all live together like birds, as you say. But it's difficult when Nicole acts as – when Nicole pulls herself back a little, as if she were holding her breath – as if I *smelt* bad!'

Kaethe had touched a material truth. She did most of her work herself, and, frugal, she bought few clothes. An American shop-girl, laundering two changes of underwear every night, would have noticed a hint of yesterday's reawakened sweat about Kaethe's person, less a smell than an ammoniacal reminder of the eternity of toil and decay. To Franz this was as natural as the thick dark scent of Kaethe's hair, and he would have missed it equally; but to Nicole, born hating the smell of a nurse's fingers dressing her, it was an offence only to be endured.

'And the children,' Kaethe continued. 'She doesn't like them to play with our children – ' but Franz had heard enough: 'Hold your tongue – that kind of talk can hurt me professionally, since we owe this clinic to Nicole's money. Let us have lunch.'

Kaethe realised that her outburst had been ill-advised, but Franz's last remark reminded her that other Americans had money, and a week later she put her dislike of Nicole into new words.

The occasion was the dinner they tendered the Divers upon Dick's return. Hardly had their footfalls ceased on the path when she shut the door and said to Franz: 'Did you see around his eyes? He's been on a debauch!'

'Go gently,' Franz requested. 'Dick told me about that as soon as he came home. He was boxing on the trans-Atlantic ship. The American passengers box a lot on these trans-Atlantic ships.'

'I believe that?' she scoffed. 'It hurts him to move one of his arms and he has an unhealed scar on his temple – you can see where the hair's been cut away.'

Franz had not noticed these details.

'But what?' Kaethe demanded. 'Do you think that sort of thing does the clinic any good? The liquor I smelt on him tonight, and several other times since he's been back.'

She slowed her voice to fit the gravity of what she was about to say: 'Dick is no longer a serious man.'

Franz rocked his shoulders up the stairs, shaking off her persistence. In their bedroom he turned on her.

'He is most certainly a serious man and a brilliant man. Of all the men who have recently taken their degrees in neuro-pathology in Zurich, Dick has been regarded as the most brilliant – more brilliant than I could ever be.'

'For shame!'

'It's the truth – the shame would be not to admit it. I turn to Dick when cases are highly involved. His publications are still standard in their line – go into any medical library and ask. Most students think he's an Englishman – they don't believe that such thoroughness could come out of America.' He groaned domestically, taking his pyjamas from under the pillow, 'I can't understand why you talk this way, Kaethe – I thought you liked him.'

'For shame!' Kaethe said. 'You're the solid one, you do the work. It's a case of hare and tortoise – and in my opinion the hare's race is almost done.'

'Tch! Tch!'

'Very well, then. It's true.'

With his open hand he pushed down air briskly.

'Stop!'

The upshot was that they had exchanged viewpoints like debaters. Kaethe admitted to herself she had been too hard on Dick, whom she admired and of whom she stood in awe, who had been so appreciative and understanding of herself. As for Franz, once Kaethe's idea had had time to sink in, he never after believed that Dick was a serious person. And as time went on he convinced himself that he had never thought so.

Chapter 2

Dick told Nicole an expurgated version of the catastrophe in Rome – in his version he had gone philanthropically to the rescue of a drunken friend. He could trust Baby Warren to hold her tongue, since he had painted the disastrous effect of the truth upon Nicole. All this, however, was a low hurdle compared to the lingering effect of the episode upon him.

In reaction he took himself for an intensified beating in his work, so that Franz, trying to break with him, could find no basis on which to begin a disagreement. No friendship worth the name was ever destroyed in an hour without some painful flesh being torn – so Franz let himself believe with ever-increasing conviction that Dick travelled intellectually and emotionally at such a rate of speed that the vibrations jarred him – this was a contrast that had previously been considered a virtue in their relation. So, for the shoddiness of needs, are shoes made out of last year's hide.

Yet it was May before Franz found an opportunity to insert the first wedge. Dick came into his office white and tired one noon and sat down, saying: 'Well, she's gone.'

'She's dead?'

'The heart quit.'

Dick sat exhausted in the chair nearest the door. During three nights he had remained with the scabbed anonymous woman-artist he had come to love, formally to portion out the adrenalin, but really to throw as much wan light as he could into the darkness ahead.

Half appreciating his feeling, Franz travelled quickly over an opinion: 'It was neuro-syphilis. All the Wassermanns we took won't tell me differently. The spinal fluid –'

'Never mind,' said Dick. 'Oh, God, never mind! If she cared enough about her secret to take it away with her, let it go at that.'

'You better lay off for a day.'

'Don't worry, I'm going to.'

Franz had his wedge; looking up from the telegram that he was writing to the woman's brother he enquired: 'Or do you want to take a little trip?'

'Not now.'

'I don't mean a vacation. There's a case in Lausanne. I've been on the phone with a Chilean all morning – '

'She was so damn brave,' said Dick. 'And it took her so long.' Franz shook his head sympathetically and Dick got himself together. 'Excuse me for interrupting you.'

'This is just a change – the situation is a father's problem with his son – the father can't get the son up here. He wants somebody to come down there.'

'What is it? Alcoholism? Homosexuality? When you say Lausanne – '

'A little of everything.'

'I'll go down. Is there any money in it?'

'Quite a lot, I'd say. Count on staying two or three days, and get the boy up here if he needs to be watched. In any case take your time, take your ease; combine business with pleasure.'

After two hours' train sleep Dick felt renewed, and he approached the interview with Señor Pardo y Ciudad Real in good spirits.

These interviews were much of a type. Often the sheer hysteria of the family representative was as interesting psychologically as the condition of the patient. This one was no exception: Señor Pardo y Ciudad Real, a handsome iron-grey Spaniard, noble of carriage, with all the appurtenances of wealth and power, raged up and down his suite in the Hôtel des Trois Mondes and told the story of his son with no more self-control than a drunken woman.

'I am at the end of my invention. My son is corrupt. He was corrupt at Harrow, he was corrupt at King's College, Cambridge. He's incorrigibly corrupt. Now that there is this drinking it is more and more obvious how he is, and there is continual scandal. I have tried everything – I worked out a plan with a doctor friend of mine, sent them together for a tour of Spain. Every evening Francisco had an injection of cantharides and then the two went together to a reputable bordello – for a week or so it seemed to work but the result was nothing. Finally last week in this very room, rather in that bathroom' – he pointed at it – 'I made Francisco strip to the waist and lashed him with a whip – '

Exhausted with his emotion he sat down and Dick spoke: 'That was foolish – the trip to Spain was futile also – ' He struggled against an upsurging hilarity – that any reputable medical man should have lent himself to such an amateurish experiment! '– Señor, I must tell you that in these cases we can promise nothing. In the case of the drinking we can often accomplish something – with proper co-operation. The first thing is to see the boy, get enough of his confidence to find whether he has any insight into the matter.'

– The boy, with whom he sat on the terrace, was about twenty, handsome and alert.

'I'd like to know your attitude,' Dick said. 'Do you feel that the situation is getting worse? And do you want to do anything about it?'

'I suppose I do,' said Francisco, 'I am very unhappy.'

'Do you think it's from the drinking or from the abnormality?'

'I think the drinking is caused by the other.' He was serious for a while – suddenly an irrepressible facetiousness broke through and he laughed, saying, 'It's hopeless. At King's I was known as the Queen of Chile. That trip to Spain – all it did was to make me nauseated by the sight of a woman.'

Dick caught him up sharply.

'If you're happy in this mess, then I can't help you and I'm wasting my time.'

'No, let's talk – I despise most of the others so.' There was some manliness in the boy, perverted now into an active resistance to his father. But he had that typically roguish look in his eyes that homosexuals assume in discussing the subject.

'It's a hole-and-corner business at best,' Dick told him. 'You'll spend your life on it, and its consequences, and you won't have time or energy for any other decent or social act. If you want to face the world you'll have to begin by controlling your sensuality – and, first of all, the drinking that provokes it – '

He talked automatically, having abandoned the case ten minutes before. They talked pleasantly through another hour about the boy's home in Chile and about his ambitions. It was as close as Dick had ever come to comprehending such a character from any but the pathological angle – he gathered that this very charm made it possible for Francisco to perpetrate his outrages, and, for Dick, charm always had an independent existence, whether it was the mad gallantry of the wretch who had died in the clinic this morning, or the courageous grace which this lost young man brought to a drab old story. Dick tried to dissect it into pieces small enough to store away – realising that the totality of a life may be different in quality from its segments, and also that life during the forties seemed capable of being observed only in segments. His love for Nicole and Rosemary, his friendship with Abe North, with Tommy Barban in the broken universe of the war's ending – in such contacts the personalities had seemed to press up so close to him that he became the personality itself – there seemed some necessity of taking all or nothing; it was as if for the remainder of his life he was condemned to carry with him the egos of certain people, early met and early loved, and to be only as complete as they were complete themselves. There was some element of loneliness involved – so easy to be loved – so hard to love.

As he sat on the veranda with young Francisco, a ghost of the past swam into his ken. A tall, singularly swaying male detached himself from the shrubbery and approached Dick and Francisco with feeble resolution. For a moment he formed such an apologetic part of the vibrant landscape that Dick scarcely remarked him – then Dick was on his feet, shaking hands with an abstracted air, thinking, 'My God, I've stirred up a nest!' and trying to recollect the man's name.

'This is Dr Diver, isn't it?'

'Well, well – Mr Dumphry, isn't it?'

'Royal Dumphry. I had the pleasure of having dinner one night in that lovely garden of yours.'

'Of course.' Trying to dampen Mr Dumphry's enthusiasm, Dick went into impersonal chronology. 'It was in nineteen – twenty-four – or twenty-five – '

He had remained standing, but Royal Dumphry, shy as he had seemed at first, was no laggard with his pick and spade; he spoke to Francisco in a flip, intimate manner, but the latter, ashamed of him, joined Dick in trying to freeze him away.

'Dr Diver – one thing I want to say before you go. I've never forgotten that evening in your garden – how nice you and your wife were. To me it's one of the finest memories in my life, one of the happiest ones. I've always thought of it as the most civilised gathering of people that I have ever known.'

Dick continued a crab-like retreat towards the nearest door of the hotel.

'I'm glad you remembered it so pleasantly. Now I've got to see – '

'I understand,' Royal Dumphry pursued sympathetically. 'I hear he's dying.'

'Who's dying?'

'Perhaps I shouldn't have said that – but we have the same physician.'

Dick paused, regarding him in astonishment. 'Who're you talking about?'

'Why, your wife's father – perhaps I – '

'My *what*?'

'I suppose – you mean I'm the first person – '

'You mean my wife's father is here, in Lausanne?'

'Why, I thought you knew – I thought that was why you were here.'

'What doctor is taking care of him?'

Dick scrawled the name in a notebook, excused himself, and hurried to a telephone booth.

It was convenient for Dr Dangeu to see Dr Diver at his house immediately.

Dr Dangeu was a young *genevois*; for a moment he was afraid that he was going to lose a profitable patient, but when Dick reassured him, he divulged the fact that Mr Warren was indeed dying.

'He is only fifty but the liver has stopped restoring itself; the precipitating factor is alcoholism.'

'Doesn't respond?'

'The man can take nothing except liquids – I give him three days, or at most, a week.'

'Does his elder daughter, Miss Warren, know his condition?'

'By his own wish no one knows except the manservant. It was only this morning I felt I had to tell him – he took it excitedly, although he has been in a very religious and resigned mood from the beginning of his illness.'

Dick considered: 'Well – ' he decided slowly, 'in any case I'll take care of the family angle. But I imagine they would want a consultation.'

'As you like.'

'I know I speak for them when I ask you to call in one of the best-known medical men around the lake – Herbrugge, from Geneva.'

'I was thinking of Herbrugge.'

'Meanwhile I'm here for a day at least and I'll keep in touch with you.'

That evening Dick went to Señor Pardo y Ciudad Real and they talked.

'We have large estates in Chile – ' said the old man. 'My son could well be taking care of them. Or I can get him in any one of a dozen enterprises in Paris – ' He shook his head and paced across the windows against a spring rain so cheerful that it didn't even drive the swans to cover. 'My only son! Can't you take him with you?'

The Spaniard knelt suddenly at Dick's feet.

'Can't you cure my only son? I believe in you – you can take him with you, cure him.'

'It's impossible to commit a person on such grounds. I wouldn't if I could.'

The Spaniard got up from his knees.

'I have been hasty – I have been driven – '

Descending to the lobby Dick met Dr Dangeu in the elevator.

'I was about to call your room,' the latter said. 'Can we speak out on the terrace?'

'Is Mr Warren dead?' Dick demanded.

'He is the same – the consultation is in the morning. Meanwhile he wants to see his daughter – your wife – with the greatest fervour. It seems there was some quarrel – '

'I know all about that.'

The doctors looked at each other, thinking.

'Why don't you talk to him before you make up your mind?' Dangeu suggested. 'His death will be graceful – merely a weakening and sinking.'

With an effort Dick consented.

'All right.'

The suite in which Charles Warren was gracefully weakening and sinking was of the same size as that of the Señor Pardo y Ciudad Real – throughout this hotel there were many chambers wherein rich ruins, fugitives from justice, claimants to the thrones of mediatised principalities, lived on the derivatives of opium or barbital, listening eternally, as to an inescapable radio, to the coarse melodies of old sins. This corner of Europe does not so much draw people as accept them without inconvenient questions. Routes cross here – people bound for private sanatoriums or tuberculosis resorts in the mountains, people who are no longer *persona grata* in France or Italy.

The suite was darkened. A nun with a holy face was nursing the man whose emaciated fingers stirred a rosary on the white sheet. He was still handsome and his voice summoned up a thick burr of individuality as he spoke to Dick, after Dangeu had left them together.

'We get a lot of understanding at the end of life. Only now, Dr Diver, do I realise what it was all about.'

Dick waited.

'I've been a bad man. You must know how little right I have to see Nicole again, yet a Bigger Man than either of us says to forgive and to pity.' The rosary slipped from his weak hands and slid off the smooth bed-covers. Dick picked it up for him. 'If I could see Nicole for ten minutes I would go happy out of the world.'

'It's not a decision I can make for myself,' said Dick. 'Nicole is not strong.' He made his decision but pretended to hesitate. 'I can put it up to my professional associate.'

'What your associate says goes with me – very well, doctor. Let me tell you my debt to you is so large – '

Dick stood up quickly.

'I'll let you know the result through Dr Dangeu.'

In his room he called the clinic on the Zugersee. After a long time Kaethe answered from her own house.

'I want to get in touch with Franz.'

'Franz is up on the mountain. I'm going up myself – is it something I can tell him, Dick?'

'It's about Nicole – her father is dying here in Lausanne. Tell Franz that, to show him it's important; and ask him to phone me from up there.'

'I will.'

'Tell him I'll be in my room here at the hotel from three to five, and again from seven to eight, and after that to page me in the dining-room.'

In plotting these hours he forgot to add that Nicole was not to be told; when he remembered it he was talking into a dead telephone. Certainly Kaethe should realise.

. . . Kaethe had no exact intention of telling Nicole about the call when she rode up the deserted hill of mountain wild-flowers and secret winds, where the patients were taken to ski in winter and to climb in spring. Getting off the train she saw Nicole shepherding the children through some organised romp. Approaching, she drew her arm gently along Nicole's shoulder, saying: 'You are clever with children – you must teach them more about swimming in the summer.'

In the play they had grown hot, and Nicole's reflex in drawing away from Kaethe's arm was automatic to the point of rudeness. Kaethe's hand fell awkwardly into space, and then she too reacted, verbally and deplorably.

'Did you think I was going to embrace you?' she demanded sharply. 'It was only about Dick. I talked on the phone to him and I was sorry – '

'Is anything the matter with Dick?'

Kaethe suddenly realised her error, but she had taken a tactless course and there was no choice but to answer as Nicole pursued her with reiterated questions: '. . . then *why* were you sorry?'

'Nothing about Dick. I must talk to Franz.'

'It *is* about Dick.'

There was terror in her face and collaborating alarm in the faces of the Diver children, near at hand. Kaethe collapsed with: 'Your father is ill in Lausanne – Dick wants to talk to Franz about it.'

'Is he very sick?' Nicole demanded – just as Franz came up with his hearty hospital manner. Gratefully Kaethe passed the remnant of the buck to him – but the damage was done.

'I'm going to Lausanne,' announced Nicole.

'One minute,' said Franz. 'I'm not sure it's advisable. I must first talk on the phone to Dick.'

'Then I'll miss the train down,' Nicole protested, 'and then I'll miss the three o'clock from Zurich! If my father is dying I must – ' She left this in the air, afraid to formulate it. 'I *must* go. I'll have to run for the train.' She was running even as she spoke towards the sequence of flat cars that crowned the bare hill with bursting steam and sound. Over her shoulder she called back, 'If you phone Dick tell him I'm coming, Franz!'

. . . Dick was in his own room in the hotel reading the *New York Herald* when the swallow-like nun rushed in – simultaneously the phone rang.

'Is he dead?' Dick demanded of the nun, hopefully.

'Monsieur, il est parti – he has gone away.'

'Comment?'

'Il est parti – his man and his baggage have gone away too!'

It was incredible. A man in that condition to arise and depart.

Dick answered the phone call from Franz. 'You shouldn't have told Nicole,' he protested.

'Kaethe told her, very unwisely.'

'I suppose it was my fault. Never tell a thing to a woman till it's done. However, I'll meet Nicole . . . say, Franz, the craziest thing has happened down here – the old boy took up his bed and walked . . .'

'At what? What did you say?'

'I say he walked, old Warren – he walked!'

'But why not?'

'He was supposed to be dying of general collapse . . . He got up and walked away, back to Chicago, I guess . . . I don't know, the nurse is here now . . . I don't know, Franz – I've just heard about it . . . Call me later.'

He spent the better part of two hours tracing Warren's movements. The patient had found an opportunity between the change of day and night nurses to resort to the bar where he had gulped down four whiskies; he paid his hotel bill with a thousand-dollar note, instructing the desk that the change should be sent after him, and departed, presumably for America. A last-minute dash by Dick and

Dangeu to overtake him at the station resulted only in Dick's failing to meet Nicole; when they did meet in the lobby of the hotel she seemed suddenly tired, and there was a tight purse to her lips that disquieted him.

'How's father?' she demanded.

'He's much better. He seemed to have a good deal of reserve energy after all.' He hesitated, breaking it to her easy. 'In fact, he got up and went away.'

Wanting a drink, for the chase had occupied the dinner hour, he led her, puzzled, towards the grill, and continued as they occupied two leather easy-chairs and ordered a highball and a glass of beer: 'The man who was taking care of him made a wrong prognosis or something – wait a minute, I've hardly had time to think the thing out myself.'

'He's *gone*?'

'He got the evening train for Paris.'

They sat silent. From Nicole flowed a vast tragic apathy.

'It was instinct,' Dick said, finally. 'He was really dying, but he tried to get a resumption of rhythm – he's not the first person that ever walked off his deathbed – like an old clock – you know, you shake it and somehow from sheer habit it gets going again. Now your father – '

'Oh, don't tell me,' she said.

'His principal fuel was fear,' he continued. 'He got afraid, and off he went. He'll probably live till ninety – '

'Please don't tell me any more,' she said. 'Please don't – I couldn't stand any more.'

'All right. The little devil I came down to see is hopeless. We may as well go back tomorrow.'

'I don't see why you have to – come in contact with all this,' she burst forth.

'Oh, don't you? Sometimes I don't either.'

She put her hand on his.

'Oh, I'm sorry I said that, Dick.'

Someone had brought a phonograph into the bar and they sat listening to 'The Wedding of the Painted Doll'.

Chapter 3

One morning a week later, stopping at the desk for his mail, Dick became aware of some extra commotion outside: Patient Von Cohn Morris was going away. His parents, Australians, were putting his baggage vehemently into a large limousine, and beside them stood Dr Lladislau protesting with ineffectual attitudes against the violent gesturings of Morris, senior.

The young man was regarding his embarkation with aloof cynicism as Dr Diver approached.

'Isn't this a little sudden, Mr Morris?'

Mr Morris started as he saw Dick – his florid face and the large checks on his suit seemed to turn off and on like electric lights. He approached Dick as though to strike him.

'High time we left, we and those who have come with us,' he began, and paused for breath. 'It is high time, Dr Diver. High time.'

'Will you come in my office?' Dick suggested.

'Not I! I'll talk to you, but I'm washing my hands of you and your place.'

'I'm sorry about that.'

He shook his finger at Dick. 'I was just telling this doctor here. We've wasted our time and our money.'

Dr Lladislau stirred in a feeble negative, signalling up a vague Slavic evasiveness. Dick had never liked Lladislau. He managed to walk the excited Australian along the path in the direction of his office, trying to persuade him to enter; but the man shook his head.

'It's you, Dr Diver, *you*, the very man. I went to Dr Lladislau because you were not to be found, Dr Diver, and because Dr Gregorovious is not expected until the nightfall, and I would not wait. No, sir! I would not wait a minute after my son told me the truth.'

He came up menacingly to Dick, who kept his hands loose enough to drop him if it seemed necessary. 'My son is here for alcoholism, and he told us he smelt liquor on your breath. Yes, sir!' He made a quick, apparently unsuccessful sniff. 'Not once, but twice Von Cohn says he has smelt liquor on your breath. I and my lady have never touched a drop of it in our lives. We hand Von Cohn to you to be cured, and within a month he twice smells liquor on your breath! What kind of cure is that there?'

Dick hesitated; Mr Morris was quite capable of making a scene on the clinic drive.

'After all, Mr Morris, some people are not going to give up what they regard as food because of your son – '

'But you're a doctor, man!' cried Morris furiously. 'When the workmen drink their beer that's bad 'cess to them – but you're here supposing to cure – '

'This has gone too far. Your son came to us because of kleptomania.'

'What was behind it?' The man was almost shrieking. 'Drink – black drink. Do you know what colour black is? It's black! My own uncle was hung by the neck because of it, you hear! My son comes to a sanatorium, and a doctor reeks of it!'

'I must ask you to leave.'

'You *ask* me! We *are* leaving!'

'If you could be a little temperate we could tell you the results of the treatment to date. Naturally, since you feel as you do, we would not want your son as a patient – '

'You dare to use the word temperate to me?'

Dick called to Dr Lladislau and as he approached, said: 'Will you represent us in saying goodbye to the patient and to his family?'

He bowed slightly to Morris and went into his office, and stood rigid for a moment just inside the door. He watched until they drove away, the gross parents, the bland, degenerate offspring; it was easy to prophesy the family's swing around Europe, bullying their betters with hard ignorance and hard money. But what absorbed Dick after the disappearance of the caravan was the question as to what extent he had provoked this. He drank claret with each meal, took a nightcap, generally in the form of hot rum, and sometimes he tippled with gin in the afternoons – gin was the most difficult to detect on the breath. He was averaging a half-pint of alcohol a day, too much for his system to burn up.

Dismissing a tendency to justify himself, he sat down at his desk and wrote out, like a prescription, a regime that would cut his liquor in half. Doctors, chauffeurs, and Protestant clergymen could never smell of liquor, as could painters, brokers, cavalry leaders; Dick blamed himself only for indiscretion. But the matter was by no means clarified half an hour later when Franz, revivified by an Alpine fortnight, rolled up the drive, so eager to resume work that he was plunged in it before he reached his office. Dick met him there.

'How was Mount Everest?'

'We could very well have done Mount Everest the rate we were doing. We thought of it. How goes it all? How is my Kaethe, how is your Nicole?'

'All goes smooth domestically. But my God, Franz, we had a rotten scene this morning.'

'How? What was it?'

Dick walked around the room while Franz got in touch with his villa by telephone. After the family exchange was over, Dick said: 'The Morris boy was taken away – there was a row.'

Franz's buoyant face fell.

'I knew he'd left. I met Lladislau on the veranda.'

'What did Lladislau say?'

'Just that young Morris had gone – that you'd tell me about it. What about it?'

'The usual incoherent reasons.'

'He was a devil, that boy.'

'He was a case for anaesthesia,' Dick agreed. 'Anyhow, the father had beaten Lladislau into a colonial subject by the time I came along. What about Lladislau? Do we keep him? I say no – he's not much of a man, he can't seem to cope with anything.' Dick hesitated on the verge of the truth, swung away to give himself space within which to recapitulate. Franz perched on the edge of a desk, still in his linen duster and travelling gloves. Dick said: 'One of the remarks the boy made to his father was that your distinguished collaborator was a drunkard. The man is a fanatic, and the descendant seems to have caught traces of *vin du pays* on me.'

Franz sat down, musing on his lower lip. 'You can tell me at length,' he said finally.

'Why not now?' Dick suggested. 'You must know I'm the last man to abuse liquor.' His eyes and Franz's glinted on each other, pair on pair. 'Lladislau let the man get so worked up that I was on the defensive. It might have happened in front of patients, and you can imagine how hard it could be to defend yourself in a situation like that!'

Franz took off his gloves and coat. He went to the door and told the secretary, 'Don't disturb us.' Coming back into the room he flung himself at the long table and fooled with his mail, reasoning as little as is characteristic of people in such postures, rather summoning up a suitable mask for what he had to say.

'Dick, I know well that you are a temperate, well-balanced man, even though we do not entirely agree on the subject of alcohol. But a time has come – Dick, I must say frankly that I have been aware several times that you have had a drink when it was not the moment to have one. There is some reason. Why not try another leave of abstinence?'

'Absence,' Dick corrected him automatically. 'It's no solution for me to go away.'

They were both chafed, Franz at having his return marred and blurred.

'Sometimes you don't use your common sense, Dick.'

'I never understood what common sense meant applied to complicated problems – unless it means that a general practitioner can perform a better operation than a specialist.'

He was seized by an overwhelming disgust for the situation. To explain, to patch – these were not natural functions at their age – better to continue with the cracked echo of an old truth in the ears.

'This is no go,' he said suddenly.

'Well, that's occurred to me,' Franz admitted. 'Your heart isn't in this project any more, Dick.'

'I know. I want to leave – we could strike some arrangement about taking Nicole's money out gradually.'

'I have thought about that too, Dick – I have seen this coming. I am able to arrange other backing, and it will be possible to take all your money out by the end of the year.'

Dick had not intended to come to a decision so quickly, nor was he prepared for Franz's so ready acquiescence in the break, yet he was relieved. Not without desperation he had long felt the ethics of his profession dissolving into a lifeless mass.

Chapter 4

The Divers would return to the Riviera, which was home. The Villa Diana had been rented again for the summer, so they divided the intervening time between German spas and French cathedral towns where they were always happy for a few days. Dick wrote a little with no particular method; it was one of those parts of life that is an awaiting; not upon Nicole's health, which seemed to thrive on travel, nor upon work, but simply an awaiting. The factor that gave purposefulness to the period was the children.

Dick's interest in them increased with their ages, now eleven and nine. He managed to reach them over the heads of employees on the principle that both the forcing of children and the fear of forcing them were inadequate substitutes for the long, careful watchfulness, the checking and balancing and reckoning of accounts, to the end that there should be no slip below a certain level of duty. He came to know them much better than Nicole did, and in expansive moods over the wines of several countries he talked and played with them at length. They had that wistful charm, almost sadness, peculiar to children who have learned early not to cry or laugh with abandon; they were apparently moved to no extremes of emotion, but content with a simple regimen and the simple pleasures allowed them. They lived on the even tenor found advisable in the experience of old families of the Western world, brought up rather than brought out. Dick thought, for example, that nothing was more conducive to the development of observation than compulsory silence.

Lanier was an unpredictable boy with an inhuman curiosity. 'Well, how many Pomeranians would it take to lick a lion, father?' was typical of the questions with which he harassed Dick. Topsy was easier. She was nine and very fair and exquisitely made like Nicole, and in the past Dick had worried about that. Lately she had become as robust as any American child. He was satisfied with them both, but conveyed the fact to them only in a tacit way. They were not let off breaches of good conduct – 'Either one learns politeness at home,' Dick said, 'or the world teaches it to you with a whip and you may get hurt in the process. What do I care whether Topsy "adores" me or not? I'm not bringing her up to be my wife.'

Another element that distinguished this summer and autumn for the Divers was a plentitude of money. Due to the sale of their interest in the clinic, and to developments in America, there was now so much that the mere spending of it, the care of goods, was an absorption in itself. The style in which they travelled seemed fabulous.

Regard them, for example, as the train slows up at Boyen, where they are to spend a fortnight visiting. The shifting from the *wagon-lit* has begun at the Italian frontier. The governess's maid and Madame Diver's maid have come up from second class to help with the baggage and the dogs. Mlle Bellois will superintend the hand-luggage, leaving the Sealyhams to one maid and the pair of Pekinese to the other. It is not necessarily poverty of spirit that makes a woman surround herself with life – it can be a superabundance of interest, and, except during her flashes of illness, Nicole was capable of being curator of it all. For example with the great quantity of heavy baggage – presently from the van would be unloaded four wardrobe trunks, a shoe trunk, three hat trunks, and two hat boxes, a chest of servants' trunks, a portable filing-cabinet, a medicine case, a spirit-lamp container, a picnic set, four tennis rackets in presses and cases, a phonograph, a typewriter. Distributed among the spaces reserved for family and entourage were two dozen supplementary grips, satchels and packages, each one numbered, down to the tag on the cane case. Thus all of it could be checked up in two minutes on any station platform, some for storage, some for accompaniment from the 'light trip list' or the 'heavy trip list', constantly revised, and carried on metal-edged plaques in Nicole's purse. She had devised the system as a child when travelling with her failing mother. It was equivalent to the system of a regimental supply officer who must think of the bellies and equipment of three thousand men.

The Divers flocked from the train into the early gathered twilight of the valley. The village people watched the debarkation with an awe akin to that which followed the Italian pilgrimages of Lord Byron a century before. Their hostess was the Contessa di Minghetti, lately Mary North. The journey that had begun in a room over the shop of a paperhanger in Newark had ended in an extraordinary marriage.

'Conte di Minghetti' was merely a papal title – the wealth of Mary's husband flowed from his being ruler-owner of manganese deposits in south-western Asia. He was not quite light enough to travel in a Pullman south of Mason-Dixon; he was of the Kabyle-Berber-Sabaean-Hindu strain that belts across North Africa and Asia, more sympathetic to the European than the mongrel faces of the ports.

When these princely households, one of the East, one of the West, faced each other on the station platform, the splendour of the Divers seemed pioneer simplicity by comparison. Their hosts were accompanied by an Italian major-domo carrying a staff, by a quartet of turbaned retainers on motorcycles, and by two half-veiled females who stood respectfully a little behind Mary and salaamed at Nicole, making her jump with the gesture.

To Mary as well as to the Divers the greeting was faintly comic; Mary gave an apologetic, belittling giggle; yet her voice, as she introduced her husband by his Asiatic title, flew proud and high.

In their rooms as they dressed for dinner, Dick and Nicole grimaced at each other in an awed way: such rich as want to be thought democratic pretend in private to be swept off their feet by swank.

'Little Mary North knows what she wants,' Dick muttered through his shaving cream. 'Abe educated her, and now she's married to a Buddha. If Europe ever goes Bolshevik she'll turn up as the bride of Stalin.'

Nicole looked around from her dressing-case. 'Watch your tongue, Dick, will you?' But she laughed. 'They're very swell. The warships all fire at them or salute them or something. Mary rides in the royal bus in London.'

'All right,' he agreed. As he heard Nicole at the door asking for pins, he called, 'I wonder if I could have some whisky; I feel the mountain air!'

'She'll see to it,' presently Nicole called through the bathroom door. 'It was one of those women who were at the station. She has her veil off.'

'What did Mary tell you about life?' he asked.

'She didn't say so much – she was interested in high life – she asked me a lot of questions about my genealogy and all that sort of thing, as if I knew anything about it. But it seems the bridegroom has two very tan children by another marriage – one of them ill with some Asiatic thing they can't diagnose. I've got to warn the children. Sounds very peculiar to me. Mary will see how we'd feel about it.' She stood worrying a minute.

'She'll understand,' Dick reassured her. 'Probably the child's in bed.'

At dinner Dick talked to Hosain, who had been at an English public school. Hosain wanted to know about stocks and about Hollywood, and Dick, whipping up his imagination with champagne told him preposterous tales.

'Billions?' Hosain demanded.

'Trillions,' Dick assured him.

'I didn't truly realise – '

'Well, perhaps millions,' Dick conceded. 'Every hotel guest is assigned a harem – or what amounts to a harem.'

'Other than the actors and directors?'

'Every hotel guest – even travelling salesmen. Why, they tried to send me up a dozen candidates, but Nicole wouldn't stand for it.'

Nicole reproved him when they were in their room alone. 'Why so many highballs? Why did you use your word spic in front of him?'

'Excuse me, I meant smoke. The tongue slipped.'

'Dick, this isn't faintly like you.'

'Excuse me again. I'm not much like myself any more.'

That night Dick opened a bathroom window, giving on a narrow and tubular court of the château, grey as rats but echoing at the moment to plaintive and peculiar music, sad as a flute. Two men were chanting in an Eastern language or dialect full of k's and l's – he leaned out but he could not see them; there was obviously a religious significance in the sounds, and tired and emotionless he let them pray for him too, but what for, save that he should not lose himself in his increasing melancholy, he did not know.

Next day, over a thinly wooded hillside, they shot scrawny birds, distant poor relations to the partridge. It was done in a vague imitation of the English manner, with a corps of inexperienced beaters whom Dick managed to miss by firing only directly overhead.

On their return Lanier was waiting in their suite.

'Father, you said tell you immediately if we were near the sick boy.'

Nicole whirled about, immediately on guard.

' – so, mother,' Lanier continued, turning to her, 'the boy takes a bath every evening and tonight he took his bath just before mine and I had to take mine in his water, and it was dirty.'

'What? Now what?'

'I saw them take Tony out of it, and then they called me into it and the water was dirty.'

'But – did you take it?'

'Yes, mother.'

'Heavens!' she exclaimed to Dick.

He demanded: 'Why didn't Lucienne draw your bath?'

'Lucienne can't. It's a funny heater – it reached out and burned her arm last night and she's afraid of it, so one of those two women – '

'You go in this bathroom and take a bath now.'

'Don't say *I* told you,' said Lanier from the doorway.

Dick went in and sprinkled the tub with sulphur; closing the door he said to Nicole: 'Either we speak to Mary or we'd better get out.'

She agreed and he continued: 'People think their children are constitutionally cleaner than other people's, and their diseases are less contagious.'

Dick came in and helped himself from the decanter, chewing a biscuit savagely in the rhythm of the pouring water in the bathroom.

'Tell Lucienne that she's got to learn about the heater – ' he suggested. At that moment the Asiatic woman came in person to the door.

'El Contessa – '

Dick beckoned her inside and closed the door.

'Is the little sick boy better?' he enquired pleasantly.

'Better, yes, but he still has the eruptions frequently.'

'That's too bad – I'm very sorry. But you see our children mustn't be bathed in his water. That's out of the question – I'm sure your mistress would be furious if she had known you had done a thing like that.'

'I?' She seemed thunderstruck. 'Why, I merely saw your maid had difficulty with the heater – I told her about it and started the water.'

'But with a sick person you must empty the bathwater entirely out, and clean the tub.'

'I?'

Chokingly the woman drew a long breath, uttered a convulsed sob and rushed from the room.

'She mustn't get up on western civilisation at our expense,' he said grimly.

At dinner that night he decided that it must inevitably be a truncated visit: about his own country Hosain seemed to have observed only that there were many mountains and some goats and herders of goats. He was a reserved young man – to draw him out would have required the sincere effort that Dick now reserved for his family. Soon after dinner Hosain left Mary and the Divers to themselves, but the old unity was split – between them lay the restless social fields that Mary was about to conquer. Dick was relieved when, at nine-thirty, Mary received and read a note and got up.

'You'll have to excuse me. My husband is leaving on a short trip – and I must be with him.'

Next morning, hard on the heels of the servant bringing coffee, Mary entered their room. She was dressed and they were not dressed, and she had the air of having been up for some time. Her face was toughened with quiet jerky fury.

'What is this story about Lanier having been bathed in a dirty bath?'

Dick began to protest, but she cut through: '*What* is this story that you commanded my husband's sister to clean Lanier's tub?'

She remained on her feet staring at them, as they sat impotent as idols in their beds, weighted by their trays. Together they exclaimed: 'His *sister!*'

'That you ordered one of his sisters to clean out a tub!'

'We didn't – ' their voices rang together saying the same thing, ' – I spoke to the native servant – '

'You spoke to Hosain's sister.'

Dick could only say: 'I supposed they were two maids.'

'You were told they were Himadoun.'

'What?' Dick got out of bed and into a robe.

'I explained it to you at the piano night before last. Don't tell me you were too merry to understand.'

'Was that what you said? I didn't hear the beginning. I didn't connect the – we didn't make any connection, Mary. Well, all we can do is see her and apologise.'

'See her and apologise! I explained to you that when the oldest member of the family – when the oldest one marries, well, the two oldest sisters consecrate themselves to being Himadoun, to being his wife's ladies-in-waiting.'

'Was that why Hosain left the house last night?'

Mary hesitated; then nodded.

'He had to – they all left. His honour makes it necessary.'

Now both the Divers were up and dressing; Mary went on: 'And what's all that about the bathwater. As if a thing like that could happen in this house! We'll ask Lanier about it.'

Dick sat on the bedside indicating in a private gesture to Nicole that she should take over. Meanwhile, Mary went to the door and spoke to an attendant in Italian.

'Wait a minute,' Nicole said. 'I won't have that.'

'You accused us,' answered Mary, in a tone she had never used to Nicole before. 'Now I have a right to see.'

'I won't have the child brought in.' Nicole threw on her clothes as though they were chain mail.

'That's all right,' said Dick. 'Bring Lanier in. We'll settle this bathtub matter – fact or myth.'

Lanier, half clothed mentally and physically, gazed at the angered faces of the adults.

'Listen, Lanier,' Mary demanded, 'how did you come to think you were bathed in water that had been used before?'

'Speak up,' Dick added.

'It was just dirty, that was all.'

'Couldn't you hear the new water running, from your room next door?'

Lanier admitted the possibility but reiterated his point – the water was dirty. He was a little awed; he tried to see ahead: 'It couldn't have been running, because – '

They pinned him down.

'Why not?'

He stood in his little kimono arousing the sympathy of his parents and further arousing Mary's impatience – then he said: 'The water was dirty, it was full of soapsuds.'

'When you're not sure what you're saying – ' Mary began, but Nicole interrupted.

'Stop it, Mary. If there were dirty suds in the water it was logical to think it was dirty. His father told him to come – '

'There couldn't have been dirty suds in the water.'

Lanier looked reproachfully at his father, who had betrayed him. Nicole turned him about by the shoulders and sent him out of the room; Dick broke the tenseness with a laugh.

Then, as if the sound recalled the past, the old friendship, Mary guessed how far away from them she had gone and said in a mollifying tone: 'It's always like that with children.'

Her uneasiness grew as she remembered the past. 'You'd be silly to go – Hosain wanted to make this trip anyhow. After all, you're my guests and you just blundered into the thing.' But Dick, made more angry by this obliqueness and the use of the word blunder, turned away and began arranging his effects, saying: 'It's too bad about the young women. I'd like to apologise to the one who came in here.'

'If you'd only listened on the piano seat!'

'But you've gotten so damned dull, Mary. I listened as long as I could.'

'Be quiet!' Nicole advised him.

'I return his compliment,' said Mary bitterly. 'Goodbye, Nicole.' She went out.

After all that there was no question of her coming to see them off; the major-domo arranged the departure. Dick left formal notes for Hosain and the sisters. There was nothing to do except to go, but all of them, especially Lanier, felt bad about it.

'I insist,' insisted Lanier on the train, 'that it was dirty bathwater.'

'That'll do,' his father said. 'You better forget it – unless you want me to divorce you. Did you know there was a new law in France that you can divorce a child?'

Lanier roared with delight and the Divers were unified again – Dick wondered how many more times it could be done.

Chapter 5

Nicole went to the window and bent over the sill to take a look at the rising altercation on the terrace; the April sun shone pink on the saintly face of Augustine, the cook, and blue on the butcher's knife she waved in her drunken hand. She had been with them since their return to Villa Diana in February.

Because of an obstruction of an awning she could see only Dick's head and his hand holding one of his heavy canes with a bronze knob on it. The knife and the cane, menacing each other, were like tripod and short sword in a gladiatorial combat. Dick's words reached her first: ' – care how much kitchen wine you drink but when I find you digging into a bottle of Chablis Mouton – '

'You talk about drinking!' Augustine cried, flourishing her sabre. 'You drink – all the time!'

Nicole called over the awning: 'What's the matter, Dick?' and he answered in English: 'The old girl has been polishing off the vintage wines. I'm firing her – at least I'm trying to.'

'Heavens! Well, don't let her reach you with that knife.'

Augustine shook her knife up at Nicole. Her old mouth was made of two small intersecting cherries.

'I would like to say, madame, if you knew that your husband drinks over at his Bastide comparatively as a day labourer – '

'Shut up and get out!' interrupted Nicole. 'We'll get the gendarmes.'

'*You'll* get the gendarmes! With my brother in the corps! You – a disgusting American?'

In English Dick called up to Nicole: 'Get the children away from the house till I settle this.'

' – disgusting Americans who come here and drink up our finest wines,' screamed Augustine with the voice of the commune.

Dick mastered a firmer tone.

'You must leave now! I'll pay you what we owe you.'

'Very sure you'll pay me! And let me tell you – ' she came close and waved the knife so furiously that Dick raised his stick, whereupon she rushed into the kitchen and returned with the carving knife reinforced by a hatchet.

The situation was not prepossessing – Augustine was a strong woman and could be disarmed only at the risk of serious results to herself – and severe legal complications which were the lot of one who molested a French citizen. Trying a bluff Dick called up to Nicole: 'Phone the *poste de police*.' Then to Augustine, indicating her armament, 'This means arrest for you.'

'Ha-*ha!*' she laughed demoniacally; nevertheless she came no nearer. Nicole phoned the police but was answered with what was almost an echo of Augustine's laugh. She heard mumbles and passings of the word around – the connection was suddenly broken.

Returning to the window she called down to Dick: 'Give her something extra!'

'If I could get to that phone!' As this seemed impracticable, Dick capitulated. For fifty francs, increased to a hundred as he succumbed to the idea of getting her out hastily, Augustine yielded her fortress, covering the retreat with stormy grenades of '*Salaud!*' She would leave only when her nephew could come for her baggage. Waiting cautiously in the neighbourhood of the kitchen Dick heard a cork pop, but he yielded the point. There was no further trouble – when the nephew arrived, all apologetic, Augustine bade Dick a cheerful, convivial goodbye, and called up 'Au revoir, madame! Bonne chance!' to Nicole's window.

The Divers went to Nice and dined on a bouillabaisse, which is a stew of rock fish and small lobsters, highly seasoned with saffron, and a bottle of cold Chablis. He expressed pity for Augustine.

'I'm not sorry a bit,' said Nicole.

'I'm sorry – and yet I wish I'd shoved her over the cliff.'

There was little they dared talk about in these days; seldom did they find the right word when it counted, it arrived always a moment too late when one could not reach the other any more. Tonight Augustine's outburst had shaken them from their separate reveries; with the burn and chill of the spiced broth and the parching wine they talked.

'We can't go on like this,' Nicole suggested. 'Or can we? – what do you think?' Startled that for the moment Dick did not deny it, she continued, 'Some of the time I think it's my fault – I've ruined you.'

'So I'm ruined, am I?' he enquired pleasantly.

'I didn't mean that. But you used to want to create things – now you seem to want to smash them up.'

She trembled at criticising him in these broad terms – but his enlarging silence frightened her even more. She guessed that something was developing behind the silence, behind the hard, blue eyes, the almost unnatural interest in the children. Uncharacteristic bursts of temper surprised her – he would suddenly unroll a long scroll of contempt for some person, race, class, way of life, way of thinking. It was as though an incalculable story was telling itself inside him, about which she could only guess in the moments when it broke through the surface.

'After all, what do you get out of this?' she demanded.

'Knowing you're stronger every day. Knowing that your illness follows the law of diminishing returns.'

His voice came to her from far off, as though he were speaking of something remote and academic; her alarm made her exclaim, 'Dick!' and she thrust her hand forward to his across the table. A reflex pulled Dick's hand back and he added: 'There's the whole situation to think of, isn't there? There's not just you.' He covered her hand with his and said in the old pleasant voice of a conspirator for pleasure, mischief, profit, and delight: 'See that boat out there?'

It was the motor yacht of T. F. Golding lying placid among the little swells of the Nicean Bay, constantly bound upon a romantic voyage that was not dependent upon actual motion. 'We'll go out there now and ask the people on board what's the matter with them. We'll find out if they're happy.'

'We hardly know him,' Nicole objected.

'He urged us. Besides, Baby knows him – she practically married him, doesn't she – didn't she?'

When they put out from the port in a hired launch it was already summer dusk and lights were breaking out in spasms along the rigging of the *Margin*. As they drew up alongside, Nicole's doubts reasserted themselves.

'He's having a party – '

'It's only a radio,' he guessed.

They were hailed – a huge white-haired man in a white suit looked down at them, calling: 'Do I recognise the Divers?'

'Boat ahoy, *Margin*!'

Their boat moved under the companionway; as they mounted, Golding doubled his huge frame to give Nicole a hand.

'Just in time for dinner.'

A small orchestra was playing astern.

> I'm yours for the asking –
> But till then you can't ask me to behave –

And as Golding's cyclonic arms blew them aft without touching them, Nicole was sorrier they had come, and more impatient at Dick.

Having taken up an attitude of aloofness from the gay people here, at the time when Dick's work and her health were incompatible with going about, they had a reputation as refusers. Riviera replacements during the ensuing years interpreted this as a vague unpopularity. Nevertheless, having taken such a stand, Nicole felt it should not be cheaply compromised for a momentary self-indulgence.

As they passed through the principal salon they saw ahead of them figures that seemed to dance in the half-light of the circular stern. This was an illusion made by the enchantment of the music, the unfamiliar lighting, and the surrounding presence of water. Actually, save for some busy stewards, the guests loafed on a wide divan that followed the curve of the deck. There were a white, a red, a blurred dress, the laundered chests of several men, of whom one, detaching and identifying himself, brought from Nicole a rare little cry of delight.

'Tommy!'

Brushing aside the Gallicism of his formal dip at her hand, Nicole pressed her face against his. They sat, or rather lay down together on the Antoninian bench. His handsome face was so dark as to have lost the pleasantness of deep tan, without attaining the blue beauty of Negroes – it was just worn leather. The foreignness of his pigmentation by unknown suns, his nourishment by strange soils, his tongue awkward with the curl of many dialects, his reactions attuned to odd alarms – these things fascinated and rested Nicole – in the moment of meeting she lay on his bosom, spiritually, going out and out . . . Then self-preservation reasserted itself and retiring to her own world she spoke lightly.

'You look just like all the adventurers in the movies – but why do you have to stay away so long?'

Tommy Barban looked at her, uncomprehending but alert; the pupils of his eyes flashed.

'Five years,' she continued, in throaty mimicry of nothing. '*Much* too long. Couldn't you only slaughter a certain number of creatures and then come back, and breathe air for a while?'

In her cherished presence Tommy Europeanised himself quickly.

'Mais pour nous héros,' he said, 'il nous faut de temps, Nicole. Nous ne pouvons pas faire de petits exercises d'héroisme – il faut faire les grandes compositions.'

'Talk English to me, Tommy.'

'Parlez français avec moi, Nicole.'

'But the meanings are different – in French you can be heroic and gallant with dignity, and you know it. But in English you can't be heroic and gallant without being a little absurd, and you know that too. That gives me an advantage.'

'But after all – ' He chuckled suddenly. 'Even in English I'm brave, heroic and all that.'

She pretended to be groggy with wonderment but he was not abashed.

'I only know what I see in the cinema,' he said.

'Is it all like the movies?'

'The movies aren't so bad – now this Ronald Colman – have you seen his pictures about the Corps d'Afrique du Nord? They're not bad at all.'

'Very well, whenever I go to the movies I'll know you're going through just that sort of thing at that moment.'

As she spoke, Nicole was aware of a small, pale, pretty young woman with lovely metallic hair, almost green in the deck lights, who had been sitting on the other side of Tommy and might have been part either of their conversation or of the one next to them. She had obviously had a monopoly of Tommy, for now she abandoned hope of his attention with what was once called ill grace, and petulantly crossed the crescent of the deck.

'After all, I am a hero,' Tommy said calmly, only half joking. 'I have ferocious courage, *us*ually, something like a lion, something like a drunken man.'

Nicole waited until the echo of his boast had died away in his mind – she knew he had probably never made such a statement before. Then she looked among the strangers, and found, as usual, the fierce neurotics, pretending calm, liking the country only in horror of the city, of the sound of their own voices which had set the tone and pitch . . . She asked: 'Who is the woman in white?'

'The one who was beside me? Lady Caroline Sibley-Biers.' – They listened for a moment to her voice across the way: 'The man's a scoundrel, but he's a cat of the stripe. We sat up all night playing two-handed chemin-de-fer, and he owes me a mille Swiss.'

Tommy laughed and said: 'She is now the wickedest woman in London – whenever I come back to Europe there is a new crop of the wickedest women from London. She's the very latest – though I believe there is now one other who's considered almost as wicked.'

Nicole glanced again at the woman across the deck – she was fragile, tubercular – it was incredible that such narrow shoulders, such puny arms could bear aloft the pennon of decadence, last ensign of the fading empire. Her resemblance was rather to one of John Held's flat-chested flappers than to the hierarchy of tall languid blondes who had posed for painters and novelists since before the war.

Golding approached, fighting down the resonance of his huge bulk, which transmitted his will as through a gargantuan amplifier, and Nicole, still reluctant, yielded to his reiterated points: that the *Margin* was starting for Cannes immediately after dinner; that they could always pack in some caviare and champagne, even though they had dined; that in any case Dick was now on the phone, telling their chauffeur in Nice to drive their car back to Cannes and leave it in front of the Café des Alliés, where the Divers could retrieve it.

They moved into the dining salon and Dick was placed next to Lady Sibley-Biers. Nicole saw that his usually ruddy face was drained of blood; he talked in a dogmatic voice, of which only snatches reached Nicole: '. . . It's all right for you English, you're doing a dance of death . . . Sepoys in the ruined fort, I mean Sepoys at the gate and gaiety in the fort and all that. The green hat, the crushed hat, no future.'

Lady Caroline answered him in short sentences spotted with the terminal 'What?' the double-edged 'Quite!' the depressing 'Cheerio!' that always had a connotation of imminent peril, but Dick appeared oblivious to the warning signals. Suddenly he made a particularly vehement pronouncement, the purport of which eluded Nicole, but she saw the young woman turn dark and sinewy, and heard her answer sharply: 'After all a chep's a chep and a chum's a chum.'

Again he had offended someone – couldn't he hold his tongue a little longer? How long? To death then.

At the piano, a fair-haired young Scotsman from the orchestra (entitled by its drum 'The Ragtime College Jazzes of Edinboro') had begun singing in a Danny Deever monotone, accompanying himself with low chords on the piano. He pronounced his words with great precision, as though they impressed him almost intolerably.

'There was a young lady from hell,
Who jumped at the sound of a bell,
Because she was bad – bad – bad,
She jumped at the sound of a bell,
    From hell (*Boomboom*)
    From hell (*Toottoot*)
    There was a young lady from hell – '

'What is all this?' whispered Tommy to Nicole.

The girl on the other side of him supplied the answer: 'Caroline Sibley-Biers wrote the words. He wrote the music.'

'Quelle enfantillage!' Tommy murmured as the next verse began, hinting at the jumpy lady's further predilections. 'On dirait qu'il récite Racine!'

On the surface at least, Lady Caroline was paying no attention to the performance of her work. Glancing at her again Nicole found herself impressed, neither with the character nor the personality, but with the sheer strength derived from an attitude; Nicole thought that she was formidable, and she was confirmed in this point of view as the party rose from table. Dick remained in his seat wearing an odd expression; then he crashed into words with a harsh ineptness.

'I don't like innuendo in these deafening English whispers.'

Already halfway out of the room Lady Caroline turned and walked back to him; she spoke in a low clipped voice purposely audible to the whole company.

'You came to me asking for it – disparaging my countrymen, disparaging my friend, Mary Minghetti. I simply said you were observed associating with a questionable crowd in Lausanne. Is that a deafening whisper? or does it simply deafen *you*?'

'It's still all not loud enough,' said Dick, a little too late. 'So I am actually a notorious – '

Golding crushed out the phrase with his voice saying: 'What! What!' and moved his guests on out, with the threat of his powerful body. Turning the corner of the door Nicole saw that Dick was still sitting at the table. She was furious at the woman for her preposterous statement, equally furious at Dick for having brought them here, for having become fuddled, for having untipped the capped barbs of his irony, for having come off humiliated – she was a little more annoyed because she knew that her taking possession of Tommy Barban on their arrival had first irritated the Englishwoman.

A moment later she saw Dick standing in the gangway, apparently in complete control of himself as he talked with Golding; then for half an hour she did not see him anywhere about the deck and she broke out of an intricate Malay game, played with string and coffee beans, and said to Tommy: 'I've got to find Dick.'

Since dinner the yacht had been in motion westward. The fine night streamed away on either side, the diesel engines pounded softly, there was a spring wind that blew Nicole's hair abruptly when she reached the bow, and she had a sharp lesion of anxiety at seeing Dick standing in the angle by the flagstaff. His voice was serene as he recognised her.

'It's a nice night.'

'I was worried.'

'Oh, you were worried?'

'Oh, don't talk that way. It would give me so much pleasure to think of a little something I could do for you, Dick.'

He turned away from her, towards the veil of starlight over Africa.

'I believe that's true, Nicole. And sometimes I believe that the littler it was, the more pleasure it would give you.'

'Don't talk like that – don't say such things.'

His face, wan in the light that the white spray caught and tossed back to the brilliant sky, had none of the lines of annoyance she had expected. It was even detached; his eyes focused upon her gradually as upon a chessman to be moved; in the same slow manner he caught her wrist and drew her near.

'You ruined me, did you?' he enquired blandly. 'Then we're both ruined. So – '

Cold with terror she put her other wrist into his grip. All right, she would go with him – again she felt the beauty of the night vividly in one moment of complete response and abnegation – all right, then –

– But now she was unexpectedly free and Dick turned his back sighing, 'Tch! tch!'

Tears streamed down Nicole's face – in a moment she heard someone approaching; it was Tommy.

'You found him! Nicole thought maybe you jumped overboard, Dick,' he said, 'because that little English *poule* slanged you.'

'It'd be a good setting to jump overboard,' said Dick mildly.

'Wouldn't it?' agreed Nicole hastily. 'Let's borrow life-preservers and jump over. I think we should do something spectacular. I feel that all our lives have been too restrained.'

Tommy sniffed from one to the other, trying to breathe in the situation with the night. 'We'll go ask the Lady Beer-and-Ale what to do – she should know the latest things. And we should memorise her song "There was a young lady from *l'enfer*". I shall translate it, and make a fortune from its success at the Casino.'

'Are you rich, Tommy?' Dick asked him, as they retraced the length of the boat.

'Not as things go now. I got tired of the brokerage business and went away. But I have good stocks in the hands of friends who are holding it for me. All goes well.'

'Dick's getting rich,' Nicole said. In reaction her voice had begun to tremble.

On the after-deck Golding had fanned three pairs of dancers into action with his colossal paws. Nicole and Tommy joined them and Tommy remarked: 'Dick seems to be drinking.'

'Only moderately,' she said loyally.

'There are those who can drink and those who can't. Obviously Dick can't. You ought to tell him not to.'

'I!' she exclaimed in amazement. '*I* tell Dick what he should do or shouldn't do!'

But in a reticent way Dick was still vague and sleepy when they reached the pier at Cannes. Golding buoyed him down into the launch of the *Margin*, whereupon Lady Caroline shifted her place conspicuously. On the dock he bowed goodbye with exaggerated formality, and for a moment he seemed about to speed her with a salty epigram, but the bone of Tommy's arm went into the soft part of his and they walked to the attendant car.

'I'll drive you home,' Tommy suggested.

'Don't bother – we can get a cab.'

'I'd like to, if you can put me up.'

On the back seat of the car Dick remained quiescent until the yellow monolith of Golfe Juan was passed, and then the constant carnival at Juan les Pins, where the night was musical and strident in many languages. When the car turned up the hill towards Tarmes, he sat up suddenly, prompted by the tilt of the vehicle, and delivered a peroration: 'A charming representative of the – ' he stumbled momentarily, ' – a firm of – bring me Brains addled *à l'Anglaise*.' Then he went into an appeased sleep, belching now and then contentedly into the soft warm darkness.

Chapter 6

Next morning Dick came early into Nicole's room. 'I waited till I heard you up. Needless to say I feel badly about the evening – but how about no post-mortems?'

'I'm agreed,' she answered coolly, carrying her face to the mirror.

'Tommy drove us home? Or did I dream it?'

'You know he did.'

'Seems probable,' he admitted, 'since I just heard him coughing. I think I'll call on him.'

She was glad when he left her, for almost the first time in her life – his awful faculty of being right seemed to have deserted him at last.

Tommy was stirring in his bed, waking for *café au lait*.

'Feel all right?' Dick asked.

When Tommy complained of a sore throat he seized at a professional attitude.

'Better have a gargle or something.'

'You have one?'

'Oddly enough I haven't – probably Nicole has.'

'Don't disturb her.'

'She's up.'

'How is she?'

Dick turned around slowly. 'Did you expect her to be dead because I was tight?' His tone was pleasant. 'Nicole is now made of – of Georgia pine, which is the hardest wood known, except lignum vitae from New Zealand – '

Nicole, going downstairs, heard the end of the conversation. She knew, as she had always known, that Tommy loved her; she knew he had come to dislike Dick, and that Dick had realised it before he did, and would react in some positive way to the man's lonely passion. This thought was succeeded by a moment of sheerly feminine satisfaction. She leaned over her children's breakfast table and told off instructions to the governess, while upstairs two men were concerned about her.

Later in the garden she was happy; she did not want anything to happen, but only for the situation to remain in suspension as the two men tossed her from one mind to another; she had not existed for a long time, even as a ball.

'Nice, Rabbits, isn't it – Or is it? Hey, Rabbit – hey you! Is it nice? – hey? – Or does it sound very peculiar to you?'

The rabbit, after an experience of practically nothing else and cabbage leaves, agreed after a few tentative shiftings of the nose.

Nicole went on through her garden routine. She left the flowers she cut in designated spots to be brought to the house later by the gardener. Reaching the sea wall she fell into a communicative mood and no one to communicate with; so she stopped and deliberated. She was somewhat shocked at the idea of being interested in another man – but other women have lovers – why not me? In the fine spring morning the inhibitions of the male world disappeared and she reasoned as gaily as a flower, while the wind blew her hair until her head moved with it. Other women have had lovers – the same forces that last night had made her yield to Dick up to the point of death, now kept her head nodding to the wind, content and happy with the logic of, Why shouldn't I?

She sat upon the low wall and looked down upon the sea. But from another sea, the wide swell of fantasy, she had fished out something tangible to lay beside the rest of her loot. If she need not, in her spirit, be for ever one with Dick as he had appeared last night, she must be something in addition, not just an image on his mind, condemned to endless parades around the circumference of a medal.

Nicole had chosen this part of the wall on which to sit, because the cliff shaded to a slanting meadow with a cultivated vegetable garden. Through a cluster of boughs she saw two men carrying rakes and spades and talking in a counterpoint of Niçois and Provençal. Attracted by their words and gestures she caught the sense: 'I laid her down here.'

'I took her behind the vines there.'

'She doesn't care – neither does he. It was that sacred dog. Well, I laid her down here – '

'You got the rake?'

'You got it yourself, you clown.'

'Well, I don't care where you laid her down. Until that night I never even felt a woman's breast against my chest since I married – twelve years ago. And now you tell me – '

'But listen about the dog – '

Nicole watched them through the boughs; it seemed all right what they were saying – one thing was good for one person, another for another. Yet it was a man's world she had overheard; going back to the house she became doubtful again.

Dick and Tommy were on the terrace. She walked through them and into the house, brought out a sketch pad and began a head of Tommy.

'Hands never idle – distaff flying,' Dick said lightly. How could he talk so trivially with the blood still drained down from his cheeks so that the auburn lather of beard showed red as his eyes? She turned to Tommy saying: 'I can always do something. I used to have a nice active little Polynesian ape and juggle him around for hours till people began to make the most dismal rough jokes – '

She kept her eyes resolutely away from Dick. Presently he excused himself and went inside – she saw him pour himself two glasses of water, and she hardened further.

'Nicole – ' Tommy began, but interrupted himself to clear the harshness from his throat.

'I'm going to get you some special camphor rub,' she suggested. 'It's American – Dick believes in it. I'll be just a minute.'

'I must go, really.'

Dick came out and sat down. 'Believes in what?'

When she returned with the jar neither of them had moved, though she gathered they had had some sort of excited conversation about nothing.

The chauffeur was at the door, with a bag containing Tommy's clothes of the night before. The sight of Tommy in clothes borrowed from Dick moved her sadly, falsely, as though Tommy were not able to afford such clothes.

'When you get to the hotel rub this into your throat and chest and then inhale it,' she said.

'Say, there,' Dick murmured as Tommy went down the steps, 'don't give Tommy the whole jar – it has to be ordered from Paris – it's out of stock down here.'

Tommy came back within hearing and the three of them stood in the sunshine, Tommy squarely before the car so that it seemed by leaning forward he would tip it upon his back.

Nicole stepped down to the path.

'Now catch it,' she advised him. 'It's extremely rare.'

She heard Dick grow silent at her side; she took a step off from him and waved as the car drove off with Tommy and the special camphor rub. Then she turned to take her own medicine.

'There was no necessity for that gesture,' Dick said. 'There are four of us here – and for years whenever there's a cough – '

They looked at each other.

'We can always get another jar – ' then she lost her nerve and presently followed him upstairs where he lay down on his own bed and said nothing.

'Do you want lunch to be brought up to you?' she asked.

He nodded and continued to lie quiescent, staring at the ceiling. Doubtfully she went to give the order. Upstairs again she looked into his room – the blue eyes, like searchlights, played on a dark sky. She stood a minute in the doorway, aware of the sin she had committed against him, half afraid to come in . . . She put out her hand as if to rub his head, but he turned away like a suspicious animal. Nicole could stand the situation no longer; in a kitchen-maid's panic she ran downstairs, afraid of what the stricken man above would feed on while she must still continue dry suckling at his lean chest.

In a week Nicole forgot her flash about Tommy – she had not much memory for people and forgot them easily. But in the first hot blast of June she heard he was in Nice. He wrote a little note to them both – and she opened it under the parasol, together with other mail they had brought from the house. After reading it she tossed it over to Dick, and in exchange he threw a telegram into the lap of her beach pyjamas:

> Dears will be at Gausses tomorrow unfortunately without mother am counting on seeing you. ROSEMARY

'I'll be glad to see her,' said Nicole, grimly.

Chapter 7

But she went to the beach with Dick next morning with a renewal of her apprehension that Dick was contriving at some desperate solution. Since the evening on Golding's yacht she had sensed what was going on. So delicately balanced was she between an old foothold that had always guaranteed her security, and the imminence of a leap from which she must alight changed in the very chemistry of blood and muscle, that she did not dare bring the matter into the true forefront of consciousness. The figures of Dick and herself, mutating, undefined, appeared as spooks caught up into a fantastic dance. For months every word had seemed to have an overtone of some other meaning, soon to be resolved under circumstances that Dick would determine. Though this state of mind was perhaps more hopeful – the long years of sheer being had had an enlivening effect on the parts of her nature that early illness had killed, that Dick had not reached – through no fault of his but simply because no one nature can extend entirely inside another – it was still disquieting. The most unhappy aspect of their relations was Dick's growing indifference, at present personified by too much drink; Nicole did not know whether she was to be crushed or spared – Dick's voice, throbbing with insincerity, confused the issue; she couldn't guess how he was going to behave next upon the tortuously slow unrolling of the carpet, nor what would happen at the end, at the moment of the leap.

For what might occur thereafter she had no anxiety – she suspected that that would be the lifting of a burden, an unblinding of eyes. Nicole had been designed for change, for flight, with money as fins and wings. The new state of things would be no more than if a racing chassis, concealed for years under the body of a family limousine, should be stripped to its original self. Nicole could feel the fresh breeze already – the wrench it was she feared, and the dark manner of its coming.

The Divers went out on the beach with her white suit and his white trunks very white against the colour of their bodies. Nicole saw Dick peer about for the children among the confused shapes and shadows of many umbrellas, and as his mind temporarily left her, ceasing to grip her, she looked at him with detachment, and decided that he was seeking his children, not protectively but for protection. Probably it was the beach he feared, like a deposed ruler secretly visiting an old court. She had come to hate his world with its delicate jokes and politenesses, forgetting that for many years it was the only world open to her. Let him look at it – his beach, perverted now to the tastes of the tasteless; he could search it for a day and find no stone of the Chinese wall he had once erected around it, no footprint of an old friend.

For a moment Nicole was sorry it was so; remembering the glass he had raked out of the old trash heap, remembering the sailor trunks and sweaters they had bought in a Nice back-street – garments that afterwards ran through a vogue in silk among the Paris couturiers, remembering the simple little French girls climbing on the break-waters crying, 'Dites donc! Dites donc!' like birds, and the ritual of the morning time, the quiet restful extraversion towards sea and sun – many inventions of his, buried deeper than the sand under the span of so few years . . .

Now the swimming place was a 'club', though, like the international society it represented, it would be hard to say who was not admitted.

Nicole hardened again as Dick knelt on the straw mat and looked about for Rosemary. Her eyes followed his, searching among the new paraphernalia, the trapezes over the water, the swinging rings, the portable bath-houses, the floating towers, the searchlights from last night's fêtes, the modernistic buffet, white with a hackneyed motif of endless handlebars.

The water was almost the last place he looked for Rosemary, because few people swam any more in that blue paradise, children and one exhibitionistic valet who punctuated the morning with spectacular dives from a fifty-foot rock – most of Gausse's guests stripped the concealing pyjamas from their flabbiness for only a short hangover dip at one o'clock.

'There she is,' Nicole remarked.

She watched Dick's eyes following Rosemary's track from raft to raft; but the sigh that rocked out of her bosom was something left over from five years ago.

'Let's swim out and speak to Rosemary,' he suggested.

'You go.'

'We'll both go.' She struggled a moment against his pronouncement, but eventually they swam out together, tracing Rosemary by the school of little fish who followed her, taking their dazzle from her, the shining spoon of a trout hook.

Nicole stayed in the water while Dick hoisted himself up beside Rosemary, and the two sat dripping and talking, exactly as if they had never loved or touched each other. Rosemary was beautiful – her youth was a shock to Nicole, who rejoiced, however, that the young girl was less slender by a hairline than herself. Nicole swam around in little rings, listening to Rosemary, who was acting amusement, joy, and expectation – more confident than she had been five years ago.

'I miss mother so, but she's meeting me in Paris, Monday.'

'Five years ago you came here,' said Dick. 'And what a funny little thing you were, in one of those hotel peignoirs!'

'How you remember things! You always did – and always the nice things.'

Nicole saw the old game of flattery beginning again and she dove under water, coming up again to hear: 'I'm going to pretend it's five years ago and I'm a girl of eighteen again. You could always make me feel some you know, kind of, you know, kind of happy way – you and Nicole. I feel as if you're still on the beach there, under one of those umbrellas – the nicest people I'd ever known, maybe ever will.'

Swimming away, Nicole saw that the cloud of Dick's heartsickness had lifted a little as he began to play with Rosemary, bringing out his old expertness with people, a tarnished object of art; she guessed that with a drink or so he would have done his stunts on the swinging rings for her, fumbling through stunts he had once done with ease. She noticed that this summer, for the first time, he avoided high diving.

Later, as she dodged her way from raft to raft, Dick overtook her.

'Some of Rosemary's friends have a speedboat, the one out there. Do you want to aquaplane? I think it would be amusing.'

Remembering that once he could stand on his hands on a chair at the end of a board, she indulged him as she might have indulged Lanier. Last summer on the Zugersee they had played at that pleasant water game, and Dick had lifted a two-hundred-pound man from the board on to his shoulders and stood up. But women marry all their husbands' talents and naturally, afterwards, are not so impressed with them as they may keep up the pretence of being. Nicole had not even pretended to be impressed, though she had said 'Yes' to him, and 'Yes, I think so too.'

She knew, though, that he was somewhat tired, that it was only the closeness of Rosemary's exciting youth that prompted the impending effort – she had seen him draw the same inspiration from the new bodies of her children and she wondered coldly if he would make a spectacle of himself. The Divers were older than the others in the boat – the young people were polite, deferential, but Nicole felt an undercurrent of 'Who are these Numbers anyhow?' and she missed Dick's easy talent of taking control of situations and making them all right – he had concentrated on what he was going to try to do.

The motor throttled down two hundred yards from shore and one of the young men dove flat over the edge. He swam at the aimless twisting board, steadied it, climbed slowly to his knees on it – then got on his feet as the boat accelerated. Leaning back he swung his light vehicle ponderously from side to side in slow, breathless arcs that rode the trailing side-swell at the end of each swing. In the direct wake of the boat he let go his rope, balanced for a moment, then back-flipped into the water, disappearing like a statue of glory, and reappearing as an insignificant head while the boat made the circle back to him.

Nicole refused her turn; then Rosemary rode the board neatly and conservatively, with facetious cheers from her admirers. Three of them scrambled egotistically for the honour of pulling her into the boat, managing, among them, to bruise her knee and hip against the side.

'Now you, doctor,' said the Mexican at the wheel.

Dick and the last young man dove over the side and swam to the board. Dick was going to try his lifting trick and Nicole began to watch with smiling scorn. This physical showing-off for Rosemary irritated her most of all.

When the men had ridden long enough to find their balance, Dick knelt, and putting the back of his neck in the other man's crotch, found the rope through his legs, and slowly began to rise.

The people in the boat, watching closely, saw that he was having difficulties. He was on one knee; the trick was to straighten all the way up in the same motion with which he left his kneeling position. He rested for a moment, then his face contracted as he put his heart into the strain, and lifted.

The board was narrow, the man, though weighing less than a hundred and fifty, was awkward with his weight and grabbed clumsily at Dick's head. When, with a last wrenching effort of his back, Dick stood upright, the board slid sidewise and the pair toppled into the sea.

In the boat Rosemary exclaimed: 'Wonderful! They almost had it.'

But as they came back to the swimmers Nicole watched for a sight of Dick's face. It was full of annoyance as she expected, because he had done the thing with ease only two years ago.

The second time he was more careful. He rose a little, testing the balance of his burden, settled down again on his knee; then, grunting 'Alley oop!' began to rise – but before he could really straighten out, his legs suddenly buckled and he shoved the board away with his feet to avoid being struck as they fell off.

This time when the *Baby Gar* came back it was apparent to all the passengers that he was angry.

'Do you mind if I try that once more?' he called, treading water. 'We almost had it then.'

'Sure. Go ahead.'

To Nicole he looked white-around-the-gills, and she cautioned him: 'Don't you think that's enough for now?'

He didn't answer. The first partner had had plenty and was hauled over the side, the Mexican driving the motorboat obligingly took his place.

He was heavier than the first man. As the boat gathered motion, Dick rested for a moment, belly-down on the board. Then he got beneath the man and took the rope, and his muscles flexed as he tried to rise.

He could not rise. Nicole saw him shift his position and strain upward again, but at the instant when the weight of his partner was full upon his shoulders he became immovable. He tried again – lifting an inch, two inches – Nicole felt the sweat glands of her forehead open as she strained with him – then he was simply holding his ground, then he collapsed back down on his knees with a smack, and they went over, Dick's head barely missing a kick of the board.

'Hurry back!' Nicole called to the driver; even as she spoke she saw him slide under water and she gave a little cry; but he came up again and turned on his back, and the Mexican swam near to help. It seemed for ever till the boat reached them, but when they came alongside at last and Nicole saw Dick floating exhausted and expressionless, alone with the water and the sky, her panic changed suddenly to contempt.

'We'll help you up, doctor . . . Get his foot . . . all right . . . now all together . . . '

Dick sat panting and looking at nothing.

'I knew you shouldn't have tried it,' Nicole could not help saying.

'He'd tired himself the first two times,' said the Mexican.

'It was a foolish thing,' Nicole insisted. Rosemary tactfully said nothing.

After a minute Dick got his breath, panting, 'I couldn't have lifted a paper doll that time.'

An explosive little laugh relieved the tension caused by his failure. They were all attentive to Dick as he disembarked at the dock. But Nicole was annoyed – everything he did annoyed her now.

She sat with Rosemary under an umbrella while Dick went to the buffet for a drink – he returned presently with some sherry for them.

'The first drink I ever had was with you,' Rosemary said, and with a spurt of enthusiasm she added, 'Oh, I'm so glad to see you and *know* you're all right. I was worried – ' Her sentence broke as she changed direction, ' – that maybe you wouldn't be.'

'Did you hear I'd gone into a process of deterioration?'

'Oh, no. I simply – just heard you'd changed. And I'm glad to see with my own eyes it isn't true.'

'It is true,' Dick answered, sitting down with them. 'The change came a long way back – but at first it didn't show. The manner remains intact for some time after the morale cracks.'

'Do you practise on the Riviera?' Rosemary demanded hastily.

'It'd be a good ground to find likely specimens.' He nodded here and there at the people milling about in the golden sand. 'Great candidates. Notice our old friend, Mrs Abrams, playing duchess to Mary North's queen? Don't get jealous about it – think of Mrs Abrams' long climb up the back stairs of the Ritz on her hands and knees and all the carpet dust she had to inhale.'

Rosemary interrupted him. 'But is that really Mary North?' She was regarding a woman sauntering in their direction followed by a small group who behaved as if they were accustomed to being looked at. When they were ten feet away, Mary's glance flickered fractionally over the Divers, one of those unfortunate glances that indicate to the glanced-upon that they have been observed but are to be overlooked, the sort of glance that neither the Divers nor Rosemary Hoyt had ever permitted themselves to throw at anyone in their lives. Dick was amused when Mary perceived Rosemary, changed her plans and came over. She spoke to Nicole with pleasant heartiness, nodded unsmilingly to Dick as if he were somewhat contagious – whereupon he bowed in ironic respect – as she greeted Rosemary.

'I heard you were here. For how long?'

'Until tomorrow,' Rosemary answered.

She, too, saw how Mary had walked through the Divers to talk to her, and a sense of obligation kept her unenthusiastic. No, she could not dine tonight.

Mary turned to Nicole, her manner indicating affection blended with pity.

'How are the children?' she asked.

They came up at the moment, and Nicole gave ear to a request that she overrule the governess on a swimming point.

'No,' Dick answered for her. 'What Mademoiselle says must go.'

Agreeing that one must support delegated authority, Nicole refused their request, whereupon Mary – who in the manner of an Anita Loos heroine had dealings only with *faits accomplis*, who indeed could not have housebroken a French poodle puppy – regarded Dick as though he were guilty of a most flagrant bullying. Dick, chafed by the tiresome performance, enquired with mock solicitude: 'How are your children – and their aunts?'

Mary did not answer; she left them, first draping a sympathetic hand over Lanier's reluctant head. After she had gone Dick said: 'When I think of the time I spent working over her.'

'I like her,' said Nicole.

Dick's bitterness had surprised Rosemary, who had thought of him as all-forgiving, all-comprehending. Suddenly she recalled what it was she had heard about him. In conversation with some State Department people on the boat – Europeanised Americans who had reached a position where they could scarcely have been said to belong to any nation at all, at least not to any great power though perhaps to a Balkan-like state composed of similar citizens – the name of the ubiquitously renowned Baby Warren had occurred and it was remarked that Baby's younger sister had thrown herself away on a dissipated doctor. 'He's not received anywhere any more,' the woman said.

The phrase disturbed Rosemary, though she could not place the Divers as living in any relation to society where such a fact, if fact it was, could have any meaning, yet the hint of a hostile and organised public opinion rang in her ears. 'He's not received anywhere any more.' She pictured Dick climbing the steps of a mansion, presenting cards and being told by a butler: 'We're not receiving you any more'; then proceeding down an avenue only to be told the same thing by the countless other butlers of countless Ambassadors, Ministers, Chargés d'Affaires . . .

Nicole wondered how she could get away. She guessed that Dick, stung into alertness, would grow charming and would make Rosemary respond to him. Sure enough, in a moment his voice managed to qualify everything unpleasant he had said: 'Mary's all right – she's done very well. But it's hard to go on liking people who don't like you.'

Rosemary, falling into line, swayed towards Dick and crooned: 'Oh, you're so nice. I can't imagine anybody not forgiving you anything, no matter what you did to them.' Then feeling that her exuberance had transgressed on Nicole's rights, she looked at the sand exactly between them: 'I wanted to ask you both what you thought of my latest pictures – if you saw them.'

Nicole said nothing, having seen one of them and thought little about it.

'It'll take a few minutes to tell you,' Dick said. 'Let's suppose that Nicole says to you that Lanier is ill. What do you do in life? What does anyone do? They *act* – face, voice, words – the face shows sorrow, the voice shows shock, the words show sympathy.'

'Yes – I understand.'

'But, in the theatre, no. In the theatre all the best comédiennes have built up their reputation by burlesquing the correct emotional responses – fear and love and sympathy.'

'I see.' Yet she did not quite see.

Losing the thread of it, Nicole's impatience increased as Dick continued: 'The danger to an actress is in responding. Again, let's suppose that somebody told you, "Your lover is dead." In life you'd probably go to pieces. But on the stage you're trying to entertain – the audience can do the "responding" for themselves. First the actress has lines to follow, then she has to get the audience's attention back on herself, away from the murdered Chinese or whatever the thing is. So she must do something unexpected. If the audience thinks the character is hard she goes soft on them – if they think she's soft she goes hard. You go all *out* of character – you understand?'

'I don't quite,' admitted Rosemary. 'How do you mean out of character?'

'You do the unexpected thing until you've manoeuvred the audience back from the objective fact to yourself. *Then* you slide into character again.'

Nicole could stand no more. She stood up sharply, making no attempt to conceal her impatience. Rosemary, who had been for a few minutes half-conscious of this, turned in a conciliatory way to Topsy.

'Would you like to be an actress when you grow up? I think you'd make a fine actress.'

Nicole stared at her deliberately and in her grandfather's voice said, slow and distinct: 'It's absolutely *out* to put such ideas in the heads of other people's children. Remember, we may have quite different plans for them.' She turned sharply to Dick. 'I'm going to take the car home. I'll send Michelle for you and the children.'

'You haven't driven for months,' he protested.

'I haven't forgotten how.'

Without a glance at Rosemary, whose face was responding violently, Nicole left the umbrella.

In the bath-house, she changed to pyjamas, her expression still hard as a plaque. But she turned into the road of arched pines and the atmosphere changed – with a squirrel's flight on a branch, a wind nudging at the leaves, a cock splitting distant air, with a creep of sunlight transpiring through the immobility, then the voice of the beach receded – Nicole relaxed and felt new and happy; her thoughts were clear as good bells – she had a sense of being cured and in a new way. Her ego began blooming like a great rich rose as she scrambled back along the labyrinths in which she had wandered for years. She hated the beach, resented the places where she had played planet to Dick's sun.

'Why, I'm almost complete,' she thought. 'I'm practically standing alone, without him.' And like a happy child, wanting the completion as soon as possible, and knowing vaguely that Dick had planned for her to have it, she lay on her bed as soon as she got home and wrote Tommy Barban in Nice a short provocative letter.

But that was for the daytime – towards evening with the inevitable diminution of nervous energy, her spirits flagged, and the arrows flew a little in the twilight. She was afraid of what was in Dick's mind; again she felt that a plan underlay his current actions and she was afraid of his plans – they worked well and they had an all-inclusive logic about them which Nicole was not able to command. She had somehow given over the thinking to him, and in his absences her every action seemed automatically governed by what he would like, so that now she felt inadequate to match her intentions against his. Yet think she must; she knew at last the number on the dreadful door of fantasy, the threshold to the escape that was no escape; she knew that for her the greatest sin now and in the future was to delude herself. It had been a long lesson but she had learned it. Either you think – or else others have to think for you and take power from you, pervert and discipline your natural tastes, civilise and sterilise you.

They had a tranquil supper, with Dick drinking much beer and being cheerful with the children in the dusky room. Afterwards he played some Schubert songs and some new jazz from America that Nicole hummed in her harsh, sweet contralto over his shoulder.

'Thank y' father-r
Thank y' mother-r
Thanks for meeting up with one another – '

'I don't like that one,' Dick said, starting to turn the page.

'Oh, play it!' she exclaimed. 'Am I going through the rest of life flinching at the word "father"?'

' – Thank the horse that pulled the buggy that night!
Thank you both for being justabit tight – '

Later they sat with the children on the Moorish roof and watched the fireworks of two casinos, far apart, far down on the shore. It was lonely and sad to be so empty-hearted towards each other.

Next morning, back from shopping in Cannes, Nicole found a note saying that Dick had taken the small car and gone up into Provence for a few days by himself. Even as she read it the phone rang – it was Tommy Barban from Monte Carlo, saying that he had received her letter and was driving over. She felt her lips' warmth in the receiver as she welcomed his coming.

Chapter 8

She bathed and anointed herself and covered her body with a layer of powder, while her toes crunched another pile on a bath towel. She looked microscopically at the lines of her flanks, wondering how soon the fine, slim edifice would begin to sink squat and earthward. In about six years, but now I'll do – in fact I'll do as well as anyone I know.

She was not exaggerating. The only physical disparity between Nicole at present and the Nicole of five years before was simply that she was no longer a young girl. But she was enough ridden by the current youth worship, the moving pictures with their myriad faces of girl-children, blandly represented as carrying on the work and wisdom of the world, to feel a jealousy of youth.

She put on the first ankle-length day dress that she had owned for many years, and crossed herself reverently with Chanel Sixteen. When Tommy drove up at one o'clock she had made her person into the trimmest of gardens.

How good to have things like this, to be worshipped again, to pretend to have a mystery! She had lost two of the great arrogant years in the life of a pretty girl – now she felt like making up for them; she greeted Tommy as if he were one of many men at her feet, walking ahead of him instead of beside him as they crossed the garden towards the market umbrella. Attractive women of nineteen and of twenty-nine are alike in their breezy confidence; on the contrary, the exigent womb of the twenties does not pull the outside world centripetally around itself. The former are ages of insolence, comparable the one to a young cadet, the other to a fighter strutting after combat.

But whereas a girl of nineteen draws her confidence from a surfeit of attention, a woman of twenty-nine is nourished on subtler stuff. Desirous, she chooses her *apéritifs* wisely, or, content, she enjoys the caviare of potential power. Happily she does not seem, in either case, to anticipate the subsequent years when her insight will often be blurred by panic, by the fear of stopping or the fear of going on. But on the landings of nineteen or twenty-nine she is pretty sure that there are no bears in the hall.

Nicole did not want any vague spiritual romance – she wanted an 'affair'; she wanted a change. She realised, thinking with Dick's thoughts, that from a superficial view it was a vulgar business to enter, without emotion, into an indulgence that menaced all of them. On the other hand, she blamed Dick for the immediate situation, and honestly thought that such an experiment might have therapeutic value. All summer she had been stimulated by watching people do exactly what they were tempted to do and pay no penalty for it – moreover, in spite of her intention of no longer lying to herself, she preferred to consider that she was merely feeling her way and that at any moment she could withdraw . . .

In the light shade Tommy caught her up in his white-duck arms and pulled her around to him, looking at her eyes.

'Don't move,' he said. 'I'm going to look at you a great deal from now on.'

There was some scent on his hair, a faint aura of soap from his white clothes. Her lips were tight, not smiling, and they both simply looked for a moment.

'Do you like what you see?' she murmured.

'Parle français.'

'Very well,' and she asked again in French. 'Do you like what you see?'

He pulled her closer.

'I like whatever I see about you.' He hesitated. 'I thought I knew your face but it seems there are some things I didn't know about it. When did you begin to have white crook's eyes?'

She broke away, shocked and indignant, and cried in English: 'Is that why you wanted to talk French?' Her voice quieted as the butler came with sherry. 'So you could be offensive more accurately?'

She parked her small seat violently on the cloth-of-silver chair cushion.

'I have no mirror here,' she said, again in French, but decisively, 'but if my eyes have changed it's because I'm well again. And being well perhaps I've gone back to my true self – I suppose my grandfather was a crook and I'm a crook by heritage, so there we are. Does that satisfy your logical mind?'

He scarcely seemed to know what she was talking about.

'Where's Dick – is he lunching with us?'

Seeing that his remark had meant comparatively little to him she suddenly laughed away its effect.

'Dick's on a tour,' she said. 'Rosemary Hoyt turned up, and either they're together or she upset him so much that he wants to go away and dream about her.'

'You know, you're a little complicated after all.'

'Oh no,' she assured him hastily. 'No, I'm not really – I'm just a – I'm just a whole lot of different simple people.'

Marius brought out melon and an ice pail, and Nicole, thinking irresistibly about her crook's eyes, did not answer; he gave one an entire nut to crack, this man, instead of giving it in fragments to pick at for meat.

'Why didn't they leave you in your natural state?' Tommy demanded presently. 'You are the most dramatic person I have known.'

She had no answer.

'All this taming of women!' he scoffed.

'In any society there are certain – ' She felt Dick's ghost prompting at her elbow but she subsided at Tommy's overtone: 'I've brutalised many men into shape but I wouldn't take a chance on half the number of women. Especially this "kind" bullying – what good does it do anybody? – you or him or anybody?'

Her heart leaped and then sank faintly with a sense of what she owed Dick.

'I suppose I've got – '

'You've got too much money,' he said impatiently 'That's the crux of the matter. Dick can't beat that.'

She considered while the melons were removed.

'What do you think I ought to do?'

For the first time in ten years she was under the sway of a personality other than her husband's. Everything Tommy said to her became part of her for ever.

They drank the bottle of wine while a faint wind rocked the pine needles and the sensuous heat of early afternoon made blinding freckles on the chequered luncheon cloth. Tommy came over behind her and laid his arms along hers, clasping her hands. Their cheeks touched and then their lips and she gasped, half with passion for him, half with the sudden surprise of its force . . .

'Can't you send the governess and the children away for the afternoon?'

'They have a piano lesson. Anyhow I don't want to stay here.'

'Kiss me again.'

A little later, riding towards Nice, she thought: So I have white crook's eyes, have I? Very well then, better a sane crook than a mad puritan.

His assertion seemed to absolve her from all blame or responsibility and she had a thrill of delight in thinking of herself in a new way. New vistas appeared ahead, peopled with the faces of many men, none of whom she need obey or even love. She drew in her breath, hunched her shoulders with a wriggle and turned to Tommy.

'Have we got to go all the way to your hotel at Monte Carlo?'

He brought the car to a stop with a squeak of tyres.

'No!' he answered. 'And my God, I have never been so happy as I am this minute.'

They had passed through Nice following the blue coast and begun to mount to the middling-high Corniche. Now Tommy turned sharply down to the shore, ran out a blunt peninsula, and stopped in the rear of a small shore hotel.

Its tangibility frightened Nicole for a moment. At the desk an American was arguing interminably with the clerk about the rate of exchange. She hovered, outwardly tranquil but inwardly miserable, as Tommy filled out the police blanks – his real, hers false. Their room was a Mediterranean room, almost ascetic, almost clean, darkened to the glare of the sea. Simplest of pleasures – simplest of places. Tommy ordered two cognacs, and when the door closed behind the waiter, he sat in the only chair, dark, scarred and handsome, his eyebrows arched and upcurling, a fighting Puck, an earnest Satan.

Before they had finished the brandy they suddenly moved together and met standing up; then they were sitting on the bed and he kissed her hardy knees. Struggling a little still, like a decapitated animal, she forgot about Dick and her new white eyes, forgot Tommy himself and sank deeper into the minutes and the moment.

. . . When he got up to open a shutter and find out what caused the increasing clamour below their windows, his figure was darker and stronger than Dick's, with high lights along the rope-twists of muscle. Momentarily he had forgotten her too – almost in the second of his flesh breaking from hers she had a foretaste that things were going to be different than she had expected. She felt the nameless fear which precedes all emotions, joyous or sorrowful, inevitably as a hum of thunder precedes a storm.

Tommy peered cautiously from the balcony and reported.

'All I can see is two women on the balcony below this. They're talking about weather and tipping back and forth in American rocking-chairs.'

'Making all that noise?'

'The noise is coming from somewhere below them. Listen.'

'Oh, way down South in the land of cotton
Hotels bum and business rotten
Look away – '

'It's Americans.'

Nicole flung her arms wide on the bed and stared at the ceiling; the powder had dampened on her to make a milky surface. She liked the bareness of the room, the sound of the single fly navigating overhead. Tommy brought the chair over to the bed and swept the clothes off it to sit down; she liked the economy of the weightless dress and espadrilles that mingled with his ducks upon the floor.

He inspected the oblong white torso joined abruptly to the brown limb and head, and said, laughing gravely: 'You are all new like a baby.'

'With white eyes.'

'I'll take care of that.'

'It's very hard taking care of white eyes – especially the ones made in Chicago.'

'I know all the old Languedoc peasant remedies.'

'Kiss me, on the lips, Tommy.'

'That's so American,' he said, kissing her nevertheless. 'When I was in America last there were girls who would tear you apart with their lips, tear themselves too, until their faces were scarlet with the blood around the lips all brought out in a patch – but nothing further.'

Nicole leaned up on one elbow.

'I like this room,' she said.

He looked around.

'I find it somewhat meagre. Darling, I'm glad you wouldn't wait until we got to Monte Carlo.'

'Why only meagre? Why, this is a wonderful room, Tommy – like the bare tables in so many Cézannes and Picassos.'

'I don't know.' He did not try to understand her. 'There's that noise again. My God, has there been a murder?'

He went to the window and reported once more: 'It seems to be two American sailors fighting and a lot more cheering them on. They are from your battleship offshore.' He wrapped a towel around himself and went farther out on the balcony. 'They have *poules* with them. I have heard about this now – the women follow them from place to place wherever the ship goes. But what women! one would think with their pay they could find better women! Why the women who followed Korniloff! Why, we never looked at anything less than a ballerina!'

Nicole was glad he had known so many women, so that the word itself meant nothing to him; she would be able to hold him so long as the person in her transcended the universals of her body.

'Hit him where it hurts!'

'Yah-h-h-!'

'Hey, what I tell you get inside that right!'

'Come on, Dulschmit, you son!'

'Yaa-Yaa!'

'YAA-YEH-YAH!'

Tommy turned away.

'This place seems to have outlived its usefulness, you agree?'

She agreed, but they clung together for a moment before dressing, and then for a while longer it seemed as good enough a place as any . . .

Dressing at last Tommy exclaimed: '*My God*, those two women in the rocking-chairs on the balcony below us haven't moved. They're trying to talk this matter out of existence. They're here on an economical holiday, and all the American navy and all the whores in Europe couldn't spoil it.'

He came over gently and surrounded her, pulling the shoulder strap of her slip into place with his teeth; then a sound split the air outside: Cr-ACK-BOOM-m-*m*! It was the battleship sounding a recall.

Now, down below their window, it was pandemonium indeed – for the boat was moving to shores as yet unannounced. Waiters called accounts and demanded settlements in impassioned voices, there were oaths and denials; the tossing of bills too large and change too small; pass-outs were assisted to the boats, and the voices of the naval police chopped with quick commands through all voices. There were cries, tears, shrieks, promises as the first launch shoved off and the women crowded forward on the wharf, screaming and waving.

Tommy saw a girl rush out upon the balcony below waving a napkin, and before he could see whether or not the rocking Englishwomen gave in at last and acknowledged her presence, there was a knock at their own door. Outside, excited female voices made them agree to unlock it, disclosing two girls, young, thin and barbaric, unfound rather than lost, in the hall. One of them wept chokingly.

'Kwee wave off your porch?' implored the other in passionate American. 'Kwee please? Wave at the boy friends? Kwee, please. The other rooms is all locked.'

'With pleasure,' Tommy said.

The girls rushed out on the balcony and presently their voices struck a loud treble over the din.

' 'By, Charlie! Charlie, look *up!'*

'Send a wire gen'al alivery Nice!'

'Charlie! He don't see me.'

One of the girls hoisted her skirt suddenly, pulled and ripped at her pink step-ins and tore them to a sizable flag; then, screaming 'Ben! Ben!' she waved it wildly. As Tommy and Nicole left the room it still fluttered against the blue sky. Oh, say, can you see the tender colour of remembered flesh? – while at the stern of the battleship rose in rivalry the Star-Spangled Banner.

They dined at the new Beach Casino at Monte Carlo . . . much later they swam in Beaulieu in a roofless cavern of white moonlight formed by a circlet of pale boulders about a cup of phosphorescent water, facing Monaco and the blur of Menton. She liked his bringing her there to the eastward vision and the novel tricks of wind and water; it was all as new as they were to each other. Symbolically she lay across his saddle-bow as surely as if he had wolfed her away from Damascus and they had come out upon the Mongolian plain. Moment by moment all that Dick had taught her fell away and she was ever nearer to what she had been in the beginning, prototype of that obscure yielding up of swords that was going on in the world about her. Tangled with love in the moonlight she welcomed the anarchy of her lover.

They awoke together finding the moon gone down and the air cool. She struggled up demanding the time and Tommy called it roughly at three.

'I've got to go home then.'

'I thought we'd sleep in Monte Carlo.'

'No. There's a governess and the children. I've got to roll in before daylight.'

'As you like.'

They dipped for a second, and when he saw her shivering he rubbed her briskly with a towel. As they got into the car with their heads still damp, their skins fresh and glowing, they were loath to start back. It was very bright where they were and as Tommy kissed her she felt him losing himself in the whiteness of her cheeks and her white teeth and her cool brow and the hand that touched his face. Still attuned to Dick, she waited for interpretation or qualification; but none was forthcoming. Reassured sleepily and happily that none would be, she sank low in the seat and drowsed until the sound of the motor changed and she felt them climbing towards Villa Diana. At the gate she kissed him an almost automatic goodbye. The sound of her feet on the walk was changed, the night noises of the garden were suddenly in the past but she was glad, none the less, to be back. The day had progressed at a staccato rate, and in spite of its satisfactions she was not habituated to such strain.

Chapter 9

At four o'clock next afternoon a station taxi stopped at the gate and Dick got out. Suddenly off-balance, Nicole ran from the terrace to meet him, breathless with her effort at self-control.

'Where's the car?' she asked.

'I left it in Arles. I didn't feel like driving any more.'

'I thought from your note that you'd be several days.'

'I ran into a mistral and some rain.'

'Did you have fun?'

'Just as much fun as anybody has running away from things. I drove Rosemary as far as Avignon and put her on her train there.' They walked towards the terrace together, where he deposited his bag. 'I didn't tell you in the note because I thought you'd imagine a lot of things.'

'That was very considerate of you.' Nicole felt surer of herself now.

'I wanted to find out if she had anything to offer – the only way was to see her alone.'

'Did she have – anything to offer?'

'Rosemary didn't grow up,' he answered. 'It's probably better that way. What have you been doing?'

She felt her face quiver like a rabbit's.

'I went dancing last night – with Tommy Barban. We went –'

He winced, interrupting her.

'Don't tell me about it. It doesn't matter what you do, only I don't want to know anything definitely.'

'There isn't anything to know.'

'All right, all right.' Then as if he had been away a week: 'How are the children?'

The phone rang in the house.

'If it's for me I'm not home,' said Dick turning away quickly. 'I've got some things to do over in the workroom.'

Nicole waited till he was out of sight behind the well; then she went into the house and took up the phone.

'Nicole, comment vas-tu?'

'Dick's home.'

He groaned.

'Meet me here in Cannes,' he suggested. 'I've got to talk to you.'

'I can't.'

'Tell me you love me.' Without speaking she nodded at the receiver; he repeated, 'Tell me you love me.'

'Oh, I do,' she assured him. 'But there's nothing to be done right now.'

'Of course there is,' he said impatiently. 'Dick sees it's over between you two – it's obvious he has quit. What does he expect you to do?'

'I don't know. I'll have to – ' She stopped herself from saying ' – to wait until I can ask Dick,' and instead finished with: 'I'll write and I'll phone you tomorrow.'

She wandered about the house rather contentedly, resting on her achievement. She was a mischief, and that was a satisfaction; no longer was she a huntress of corralled game. Yesterday came back to her now in innumerable detail – detail that began to overlay her memory of similar moments when her love for Dick was fresh and intact. She began to slight that love, so that it seemed to have been tinged with sentimental habit from the first. With the opportunistic memory of women she scarcely recalled how she had felt when she and Dick had possessed each other in secret places around the corners of the world, during the month before they were married. Just so had she lied to Tommy last night, swearing to him that never before had she so entirely, so completely, so utterly . . .

. . . then remorse for this moment of betrayal, which so cavalierly belittled a decade of her life, turned her walk towards Dick's sanctuary.

Approaching noiselessly she saw him behind his cottage, sitting in a steamer chair by the cliff wall, and for a moment she regarded him silently. He was thinking, he was living a world completely his own and in the small motions of his face, the brow raised or lowered, the eyes narrowed or widened, the lips set and reset, the play of his hands, she saw him progress from phase to phase of his own story spinning out inside him, his own, not hers. Once he clenched his fists and leaned forward, once it brought into his face an expression of torment and despair – when this passed its stamp lingered in his eyes. For almost the first time in her life she was sorry for him – it is hard for those who have once been mentally afflicted to be sorry for those who are well, and though Nicole often paid lip-service to the fact that he had led her back to the world she had forfeited, she had thought of him really as an inexhaustible energy, incapable of fatigue – she forgot the troubles she caused him at the moment when she forgot the troubles of her own that had prompted her. That he no longer controlled her – did he know that? Had he willed it all? – she felt as sorry for him as she had sometimes felt for Abe North and his ignoble destiny, sorry as for the helplessness of infants and the old.

She went up to him and, putting her arm around his shoulder and touching their heads together, said: 'Don't be sad.'

He looked at her coldly.

'Don't touch me!' he said.

Confused she moved a few feet away.

'Excuse me,' he continued abstractedly. 'I was just thinking what I thought of you – '

'Why not add the new classification to your book?'

'I have thought of it – "Furthermore and beyond the psychoses and neuroses – " '

'I didn't come over here to be disagreeable.'

'Then why *did* you come, Nicole? I can't do anything for you any more. I'm trying to save myself.'

'From my contamination?'

'My profession throws me in contact with questionable company sometimes.'

She wept with anger at the abuse.

'You're a coward! You've made a failure of your life, and you want to blame it on me.'

While he did not answer she began to feel the old hypnotism of his intelligence, sometimes exercised without power but always with substrata of truth under truth which she could not break or even crack. Again she struggled with it, fighting him with her small, fine eyes, with the plush arrogance of a top dog, with her nascent transference to another man, with the accumulated resentment of years; she fought him with her money and her faith that her sister disliked him and was behind her now; with the thought of the new enemies he was making with his bitterness, with her quick guile against his wining and dining slowness, her health and beauty against his physical deterioration, her unscrupulousness against his moralities – for this inner battle she used even her weaknesses – fighting bravely and courageously with the old cans and crockery and bottles, empty receptacles of her expiated sins, outrages, mistakes. And suddenly, in the space of two minutes, she achieved her victory and justified herself to herself without lie or subterfuge, cut the cord for ever. Then she walked, weak in the legs, and sobbing coolly, towards the household that was hers at last.

Dick waited until she was out of sight. Then he leaned his head forward on the parapet. The case was finished. Dr Diver was at liberty.

Chapter 10

At two o'clock that night the phone woke Nicole and she heard Dick answer it from what they called the restless bed, in the next room.

'Oui, oui . . . mais à qui est-ce-que je parle? . . . Oui . . .' His voice woke up with surprise. 'But can I speak to one of the ladies, Sir the Officer? They are both ladies of the very highest prominence, ladies of connections that might cause political complications of the most serious . . . It is a fact, I swear to you . . . Very well, you will see.'

He got up and, as he absorbed the situation, his self-knowledge assured him that he would undertake to deal with it – the old fatal pleasingness, the old forceful charm, swept back with its cry of 'Use me!' He would have to go fix this thing that he didn't care a damn about, because it had early become a habit to be loved, perhaps from the moment when he had realised that he was the last hope of a decaying clan. On an almost parallel occasion, back in Dohmler's clinic on the Zürichsee, realising this power, he had made his choice, chosen Ophelia, chosen the sweet poison and drunk it. Wanting above all to be brave and kind, he had wanted, even more than that, to be loved. So it had been. So it would ever be, he saw, simultaneously with the slow archaic tinkle from the phone box as he rang off.

There was a long pause. Nicole called, 'What is it? Who is it?'

Dick had begun to dress even as he hung up the phone.

'It's the *poste de police* in Antibes – they're holding Mary North and that Sibley-Biers. It's something serious – the agent wouldn't tell me; he kept saying "pas de mortes – pas d'automobiles", but he implied it was just about everything else.'

'Why on earth did they call on you? It sounds very peculiar to me.'

'They've got to get out on bail to save their faces; and only some property owner in the Alpes Maritimes can give bail.'

'They had their nerve.'

'I don't mind. However, I'll pick up Gausse at the hotel – '

Nicole stayed awake after he had departed, wondering what offence they could have committed; then she slept. A little after three when Dick came in she sat up stark awake saying, 'What?' as if to a character in her dream.

'It was an extraordinary story – ' Dick said. He sat on the foot of her bed, telling her how he had roused old Gausse from an Alsatian coma, told him to clean out his cash drawer, and driven him to the police station.

'I don't like to do something for that *Anglaise*,' Gausse grumbled.

Mary North and Lady Caroline, dressed in the costume of French sailors, lounged on a bench outside the two dingy cells. The latter had the outraged air of a Briton who momentarily expected the Mediterranean fleet to steam up to her assistance. Mary Minghetti was in a condition of panic and collapse – she literally flung herself at Dick's stomach as though that were the point of greatest association, imploring him to do something. Meanwhile the chief of police explained the matter to Gausse, who listened to each word with reluctance, divided between being properly appreciative of the officer's narrative gift and showing that, as the perfect servant, the story had no shocking effect on him.

'It was merely a lark,' said Lady Caroline with scorn. 'We were pretending to be sailors on leave, and we picked up two silly girls. They got the wind up and made a rotten scene in a lodging-house.'

Dick nodded gravely, looking at the stone floor, like a priest in the confessional – he was torn between a tendency to ironic laughter and another tendency to order fifty stripes of the cat and a fortnight of bread and water. The lack, in Lady Caroline's face, of any sense of evil, except the evil wrought by cowardly Provençal girls and stupid police, confounded him; yet he had long concluded that certain classes of English people lived upon a concentrated essence of the antisocial that, in comparison, reduced the gorgings of New York to something like a child contracting indigestion from ice cream.

'I've got to get out before Hosain hears about this,' Mary pleaded. 'Dick, you can always arrange things – you always could. Tell 'em we'll go right home, tell 'em we'll pay anything.'

'I shall not,' said Lady Caroline disdainfully. 'Not a shilling. But I shall jolly well find out what the Consulate in Cannes has to say about this.'

'No, no!' insisted Mary. 'We've got to get out tonight.'

'I'll see what I can do,' said Dick, and added, 'but money will certainly have to change hands.' Looking at them as though they were the innocents that he knew they were not, he shook his head: 'Of all the crazy stunts!'

Lady Caroline smiled complacently.

'You're an insanity doctor, aren't you? You ought to be able to help us – and Gausse has *got* to!'

At this point Dick went aside with Gausse and talked over the old man's findings. The affair was more serious than had been indicated – one of the girls whom they had picked up was of a respectable family. The family were furious, or pretended to be; a settlement would have to be made with them. The other girl, a girl of the port, could be more easily dealt with. There were French statutes that would make conviction punishable by imprisonment or, at the very least, public expulsion from the country. In addition to the difficulties, there was a growing difference in tolerance between such townspeople as benefited by the foreign colony and the ones who were annoyed by the consequent rise of prices. Gausse, having summarised the situation, turned it over to Dick. Dick called the chief of police into conference.

'Now you know that the French government wants to encourage American touring – so much so that in Paris this summer there's an order that Americans can't be arrested except for the most serious offences.'

'This is serious enough, my God.'

'But look now – you have their *cartes d'identité*?'

'They had none. They had nothing – two hundred francs and some rings. Not even shoe-laces that they could have hung themselves with!'

Relieved that there had been no *cartes d'identité* Dick continued.

'The Italian Countess is still an American citizen. She is the granddaughter – ' he told a string of lies slowly and portentously, 'of John D. Rockefeller Mellon. You have heard of him?'

'Yes, oh heavens, yes. You mistake me for a nobody?'

'In addition she is the niece of Lord Henry Ford and so connected with the Renault and Citroën companies – ' He thought he had better stop here. However, the sincerity of his voice had begun to affect the officer, so he continued: 'To arrest her is just as if you arrested a great royalty of England. It might mean – War!'

'But how about the Englishwoman?'

'I'm coming to that. She is affianced to the brother of the Prince of Wales – the Duke of Buckingham.'

'She will be an exquisite bride for him.'

'Now we are prepared to give – ' Dick calculated quickly, 'one thousand francs to each of the girls – and an additional thousand to the father of the "serious" one. Also two thousand in addition, for you to distribute as you think best – ' he shrugged his shoulders, ' – among the men who made the arrest, the lodging-house keeper and so forth. I shall hand you the five thousand and expect you to do the negotiating immediately. Then they can be released on bail on some charge like disturbing the peace, and whatever fine there is will be paid before the magistrate tomorrow – by messenger.'

Before the officer spoke Dick saw by his expression that it would be all right. The man said hesitantly, 'I have made no entry because they have no *cartes d'identité*. I must see – give me the money.'

An hour later Dick and M. Gausse dropped the women by the Majestic Hotel, where Lady Caroline's chauffeur slept in her landaulet.

'Remember,' said Dick, 'you owe Monsieur Gausse a hundred dollars apiece.'

'All right,' Mary agreed, 'I'll give him a cheque tomorrow – and something more.'

'Not I!' Startled, they all turned to Lady Caroline, who, now entirely recovered, was swollen with righteousness. 'The whole thing was an outrage. By no means did I authorise you to give a hundred dollars to those people.'

Little Gausse stood beside the car, his eyes blazing suddenly.

'You won't pay me?'

'Of course she will,' said Dick.

Suddenly the abuse that Gausse had once endured as a bus boy in London flamed up and he walked through the moonlight up to Lady Caroline.

He whipped a string of condemnatory words about her, and as she turned away with a frozen laugh, he took a step after her and swiftly planted his little foot in the most celebrated of targets. Lady Caroline, taken by surprise, flung up her hands like a person shot as her sailor-clad form sprawled forward on the sidewalk.

Dick's voice cut across her raging: 'Mary, you quiet her down! or you'll both be in leg-irons in ten minutes!'

On the way back to the hotel old Gausse said not a word, until they passed the Juan-les-Pins Casino, still sobbing and coughing with jazz; then he sighed forth, 'I have never seen women like this sort of women. I have known many of the great courtesans of the world, and for them I have much respect often, but women like these women I have never seen before.'

Chapter 11

Dick and Nicole were accustomed to go together to the barber, and have haircuts and shampoos in adjoining rooms. From Dick's side Nicole could hear the snip of shears, the count of change, the *voilàs* and *pardons*. The day after his return they went down to be shorn and washed in the perfumed breeze of the fans.

In front of the Carleton Hotel, its windows as stubbornly blank to the summer as so many cellar doors, a car passed them and Tommy Barban was in it. Nicole's momentary glimpse of his expression, taciturn and thoughtful and, in the second of seeing her, wide-eyed and alert, disturbed her. She wanted to be going where he was going. The hour with the hairdresser seemed one of the wasteful intervals that composed her life, another little prison. The *coiffeuse* in her white uniform, faintly sweating lip-rouge and cologne, reminded her of many nurses.

In the next room Dick dozed under an apron and a lather of soap. The mirror in front of Nicole reflected the passage between the men's side and the women's, and Nicole started up at the sight of Tommy entering and wheeling sharply into the men's shop. She knew with a flush of joy that there was going to be some sort of showdown.

She heard fragments of its beginning.

'Hello, I want to see you.'

'. . . serious.'

'. . . serious.'

'. . . perfectly agreeable.'

In a minute Dick came into Nicole's booth, his expression emerging annoyed from behind the towel of his hastily rinsed face.

'Your friend has worked himself up into a state. He wants to see us together, so I agreed to have it over with. Come along!'

'But my hair – it's half-cut.'

'Never mind – come along!'

Resentfully she had the staring *coiffeuse* remove the towels.

Feeling messy and unadorned she followed Dick from the hotel. Outside Tommy bent over her hand.

'We'll go to the Café des Alliés,' said Dick.

'Where we can be alone,' Tommy agreed.

Under the arching trees, central in summer, Dick asked: 'Will you take anything, Nicole?'

'A *citron pressé*.'

'For me a *demi*,' said Tommy.

'The Blackenwite with siphon,' said Dick.

'Il n'y a plus de Blackenwite. Nous n'avons que la Johnny Walkair.'

'Ça va.'

> 'She's – not – wired for sound
> but on the quiet
> you ought to try it –'

'Your wife does not love you,' said Tommy suddenly. 'She loves me.'

The two men regarded each other with a curious impotence of expression. There can be little communication between men in that position, for their relation is indirect, and consists of how much each of them has possessed or will possess of the woman in question, so that their emotions pass through her divided self as through a bad telephone connection.

'Wait a minute,' Dick said. 'Donnez-moi du gin et du siphon.'

'Bien, monsieur.'

'All right, go on, Tommy.'

'It's very plain to me that your marriage to Nicole has run its course. She is through. I've waited five years for that to be so.'

'What does Nicole say?'

They both looked at her.

'I've gotten very fond of Tommy, Dick.'

He nodded.

'You don't care for me any more,' she continued. 'It's all just habit. Things were never the same after Rosemary.'

Unattracted to this angle, Tommy broke in sharply with: 'You don't understand Nicole. You treat her always like a patient because she was once sick.'

They were suddenly interrupted by an insistent American, of sinister aspect, vending copies of the *Herald* and of the *Times* fresh from New York.

'Got everything here, buddies,' he announced. 'Been here long?'

'Cessez cela! Allez ouste!' Tommy cried, and then to Dick, 'Now no woman would stand such –'

'Buddies,' interrupted the American again. 'You think I'm wasting my time – but lots of others don't.' He brought a grey clipping from his purse – and Dick recognised it as he saw it. It cartooned millions of Americans pouring from liners with bags of gold. 'You think I'm not going to get part of that? Well, I am. I'm just over from Nice for the Tour de France.'

As Tommy got him off with a fierce 'allez-vous-en', Dick identified him as the man who had once hailed him in the Rue des Saints-Anges, five years before.

'When does the Tour de France get here?' he called after him.

'Any minute now, buddy.'

He departed at last with a cheery wave and Tommy returned to Dick.

'Elle doit avoir plus avec moi qu'avec vous.'

'Speak English! What do you mean "*doit avoir*"?'

' "Doit avoir"? Would have more happiness with me.'

'You'd be new to each other. But Nicole and I have had much happiness together, Tommy.'

'L'amour de famille,' Tommy said, scoffing.

'If you and Nicole married won't that be "l'amour de famille"?' The increasing commotion made him break off; presently it came to a serpentine head on the promenade and a group, presently a crowd, of people sprung from hidden siestas, lined the curbstone.

Boys sprinted past on bicycles, automobiles jammed with elaborate betasselled sportsmen slid up the street, high horns tooted to announce the approach of the race, and unsuspected cooks in undershirts appeared at restaurant doors as around a bend a procession came into sight. First was a lone cyclist in a red jersey, toiling intent and confident out of the westering sun, passing to the melody of a high chattering cheer. Then three together in a harlequinade of faded colour, legs caked yellow with dust and sweat, faces expressionless, eyes heavy and endlessly tired.

Tommy faced Dick, saying: 'I think Nicole wants a divorce – I suppose you'll make no obstacles?'

A troupe of fifty more swarmed after the first bicycle racers, strung out over two hundred yards; a few were smiling and self-conscious, a few obviously exhausted, most of them indifferent and weary. A retinue of small boys passed, a few defiant stragglers, a light truck carried the dupes of accident and defeat. They were back at the table. Nicole wanted Dick to take the initiative, but he seemed content to sit with his face half-shaved matching her hair half-cut.

'Isn't it true you're not happy with me any more?' Nicole continued. 'Without me you could get to your work again – you could work better if you didn't worry about me.'

Tommy moved impatiently.

'That is so useless. Nicole and I love each other, that's all there is to it.'

'Well, then,' said the doctor, 'since it's all settled, suppose we go back to the barbershop.'

Tommy wanted a row: 'There are several points – '

'Nicole and I will talk things over,' said Dick equitably. 'Don't worry – I agree in principal, and Nicole and I understand each other. There's less chance of unpleasantness if we avoid a three-cornered discussion.'

Unwillingly acknowledging Dick's logic, Tommy was moved by an irresistible racial tendency to chisel for an advantage.

'Let it be understood that from this moment,' he said, 'I stand in the position of Nicole's protector until details can be arranged. And I shall hold you strictly accountable for any abuse of the fact that you continue to inhabit the same house.'

'I never did go in for making love to dry loins,' said Dick.

He nodded, and walked off towards the hotel with Nicole's whitest eyes following him.

'He was fair enough,' Tommy conceded. 'Darling, will we be together tonight?'

'I suppose so.'

So it had happened – and with a minimum of drama; Nicole felt outguessed, realising that from the episode of the camphor-rub, Dick had anticipated everything. But also she felt happy and excited, and the odd little wish that she could tell Dick all about it faded quickly. But her eyes followed his figure until it became a dot and mingled with the other dots in the summer crowd.

Chapter 12

The day before Dr Diver left the Riviera he spent all his time with his children. He was not young any more with a lot of nice thoughts and dreams to have about himself, so he wanted to remember them well. The children had been told that this winter they would be with their aunt in London and that soon they were going to come and see him in America. Fräulein was not to be discharged without his consent.

He was glad he had given so much to the little girl – about the boy he was more uncertain – always he had been uneasy about what he had to give to the ever-climbing, ever-clinging, breast-searching young.

But, when he said goodbye to them, he wanted to lift their beautiful heads off their necks and hold them close for hours.

He embraced the old gardener who had made the first garden at Villa Diana six years ago; he kissed the Provençal girl who helped with the children. She had been with them for almost a decade and she fell on her knees and cried until Dick jerked her to her feet and gave her three hundred francs. Nicole was sleeping late, as had been agreed upon – he left a note for her, and one for Baby Warren, who was just back from Sardinia and staying at the house. Dick took a big drink from a bottle of brandy three feet high, holding ten quarts, that someone had presented them with.

Then he decided to leave his bags by the station in Cannes and take a last look at Gausse's beach.

The beach was peopled with only an advance guard of children when Nicole and her sister arrived that morning. A white sun, chivied of outline by a white sky, boomed over a windless day. Waiters were putting extra ice into the bar; an American photographer from the AP worked with his equipment in a precarious shade and looked up quickly at every footfall descending the stone steps. At the hotel his prospective subjects slept late in darkened rooms upon their recent opiate of dawn.

When Nicole started out on the beach she saw Dick, not dressed for swimming, sitting on a rock above. She shrank back in the shadow of her dressing-tent. In a minute Baby joined her, saying: 'Dick's still there.'

'I saw him.'

'I think he might have the delicacy to go.'

'This is his place – in a way, he discovered it. Old Gausse always says he owes everything to Dick.'

Baby looked calmly at her sister.

'We should have let him confine himself to his bicycle excursions,' she remarked. 'When people are taken out of their depths they lose their heads, no matter how charming a bluff they put up.'

'Dick was a good husband to me for six years,' Nicole said. 'All that time I never suffered a minute's pain because of him, and he always did his best never to let anything hurt me.'

Baby's lower jaw projected slightly as she said: 'That's what he was educated for.'

The sisters sat in silence; Nicole wondering in a tired way about things; Baby considering whether or not to marry the latest candidate for her hand and money, an authenticated Hapsburg. She was not quite *thinking* about it. Her affairs had long shared such a sameness, that, as she dried out, they were more important for their conversational value than for themselves. Her emotions had their truest existence in the telling of them.

'Is he gone?' Nicole asked after a while, 'I think his train leaves at noon.'

Baby looked.

'No. He's moved up higher on the terrace and he's talking to some women. Anyhow there are so many people now that he doesn't *have* to see us.'

He had seen them though, as they left their pavilion, and he followed them with his eyes until they disappeared again. He sat with Mary Minghetti, drinking anisette.

'You were like you used to be the night you helped us,' she was saying, 'except at the end, when you were horrid about Caroline. Why aren't you nice like that always? You can be.'

It seemed fantastic to Dick to be in a position where Mary North could tell him about things.

'Your friends still like you, Dick. But you say awful things to people when you've been drinking. I've spent most of my time defending you this summer.'

'That remark is one of Dr Eliot's classics.'

'It's true. Nobody cares whether you drink or not – ' She hesitated. 'Even when Abe drank hardest, he never offended people like you do.'

'You're all so dull,' he said.

'But we're all there is!' cried Mary. 'If you don't like nice people, try the ones who aren't nice, and see how you like that! All people want is to have a good time and if you make them unhappy you cut yourself off from nourishment.'

'Have I been nourished?' he asked.

Mary was having a good time, though she did not know it, as she had sat down with him only out of fear. Again she refused a drink and said: 'Self-indulgence is back of it. Of course, after Abe you can imagine how I feel about it – since I watched the progress of a good man towards alcoholism – '

Down the steps tripped Lady Caroline Sibley-Biers with blithe theatricality.

Dick felt fine – he was already well in advance of the day; arrived at where a man should be at the end of a good dinner, yet he showed only a fine, considered, restrained interest in Mary. His eyes, for the moment clear as a child's, asked her sympathy and stealing over him he felt the old necessity of convincing her that he was the last man in the world and she was the last woman.

. . . Then he would not have to look at those two other figures, a man and a woman, black and white and metallic against the sky . . .

'You once liked me, didn't you?' he asked.

'*Liked* you – I *loved* you. Everybody loved you. You could've had anybody you wanted for the asking – '

'There has always been something between you and me.'

She bit eagerly. 'Has there, Dick?'

'Always – I knew your troubles and how brave you were about them.' But the old interior laughter had begun inside him and he knew he couldn't keep it up much longer.

'I always thought you knew a lot,' Mary said enthusiastically. 'More about me than anyone has ever known. Perhaps that's why I was so afraid of you when we didn't get along so well.'

His glance fell soft and kind upon hers, suggesting an emotion underneath; their glances married suddenly, bedded, strained together. Then as the laughter inside of him became so loud that it seemed as if Mary must hear it, Dick switched off the light and they were back in the Riviera sun.

'I must go,' he said. As he stood up he swayed a little; he did not feel well any more – his blood raced slow. He raised his right hand and with a papal cross he blessed the beach from the high terrace. Faces turned upward from several umbrellas.

'I'm going to him.' Nicole got to her knees.

'No, you're not,' said Tommy, pulling her down firmly. 'Let well enough alone.'

Chapter 13

Nicole kept in touch with Dick after her new marriage; there were letters on business matters, and about the children. When she said, as she often did, 'I loved Dick and I'll never forget him,' Tommy answered, 'Of course not – why should you?'

Dick opened an office in Buffalo, but evidently without success. Nicole did not find what the trouble was, but she heard a few months later that he was in a little town named Batavia, New York, practising general medicine, and later that he was in Lockport, doing the same thing. By accident she heard more about his life there than anywhere: that he bicycled a lot, was much admired by the ladies, and always had a big stack of papers on his desk that were known to be an important treatise on some medical subject, almost in process of completion. He was considered to have fine manners and once made a good speech at a public health meeting on the subject of drugs; but he became entangled with a girl who worked in a grocery store, and he was also involved in a lawsuit about some medical question; so he left Lockport.

After that he didn't ask for the children to be sent to America and didn't answer when Nicole wrote asking him if he needed money. In the last letter she had from him he told her that he was practising in Geneva, New York, and she got the impression that he had settled down with someone to keep house for him. She looked up Geneva in an atlas and found it was in the heart of the Finger Lakes Section and considered a pleasant place. Perhaps, so she liked to think, his career was biding its time, again like Grant's in Galena; his latest note was postmarked from Hornell, New York, which is some distance from Geneva and a very small town; in any case he is almost certainly in that section of the country, in one town or another.

[illegible] was in a little out-of-the-way [illegible] New York, practising general medicine, and later that he was in Lockport doing the same thing. He [illegible] I heard more about his life there than anywhere, but [illegible] was much admired by [illegible] and [illegible] [illegible] to [illegible] own [illegible] [illegible] medical [illegible] of complete [illegible] [illegible] and [illegible] made [illegible] good [illegible] [illegible] not [illegible] but [illegible] [illegible] and [illegible] in a [illegible] some [illegible].

[illegible] look up the [illegible] [illegible] when [illegible] and [illegible] she had [illegible] that he was [illegible] in the [illegible] and the [illegible] that he had [illegible] him. [illegible] was [illegible] the [illegible] [illegible] Perhaps [illegible] was [illegible] again [illegible] Oregon [illegible] from [illegible] New York, which [illegible] distance [illegible] and [illegible] current [illegible] section of the country, [illegible]

THE LAST TYCOON

The Last Tycoon

A novel, unfinished at the author's death and first published in 1941

Chapter 1

Though I haven't ever been on the screen I was brought up in pictures. Rudolph Valentino came to my fifth birthday party – or so I was told. I put this down only to indicate that even before the age of reason I was in a position to watch the wheels go round.

I was going to write my memoirs once, *The Producer's Daughter*, but at eighteen you never quite get around to anything like that. It's just as well – it would have been as flat as an old column of Lolly Parsons'. My father was in the picture business as another man might be in cotton or steel, and I took it tranquilly. At the worst I accepted Hollywood with the resignation of a ghost assigned to a haunted house. I knew what you were supposed to think about it but I was obstinately unhorrified.

This is easy to say, but harder to make people understand. When I was at Bennington some of the English teachers who pretended an indifference to Hollywood or its products, really *hated* it. Hated it way down deep as a threat to their existence. Even before that, when I was in a convent, a sweet little nun asked me to get her a script of a screenplay so she could 'teach her class about movie writing' as she had taught them about the essay and the short story. I got the script for her, and I suppose she puzzled over it and puzzled over it, but it was never mentioned in class, and she gave it back to me with an air of offended surprise and not a single comment. That's what I half expect to happen to this story.

You can take Hollywood for granted like I did, or you can dismiss it with the contempt we reserve for what we don't understand. It can be understood too, but only dimly and in flashes. Not half a dozen men have ever been able to keep the whole equation of pictures in their heads. And perhaps the closest a woman can come to the set-up is to try and understand one of those men.

The world from an aeroplane I knew. Father always had us travel back and forth that way from school and college. After my sister died when I was a junior, I travelled to and fro alone, and the journey always made me think of her, made me somewhat solemn and subdued. Sometimes there were picture people I knew on board the plane, and occasionally there was an attractive college boy – but not often during the Depression. I seldom really fell asleep during the trip, what with thoughts of Eleanor and the sense of that sharp rip between coast and coast – at least not till we had left those lonely little airports in Tennessee.

This trip was so rough that the passengers divided early into those who turned in right away and those who didn't want to turn in at all. There were two of these latter right across from me, and I was pretty sure from their fragmentary conversation that they were from Hollywood – one of them because he looked like it: a middle-aged Jew, who alternately talked with nervous excitement or else crouched as if ready to spring, in a harrowing silence; the other a pale, plain, stocky man of thirty, whom I was sure I had seen before. He had been to the house or something. But it might have been when I was a little girl, and so I wasn't offended that he didn't recognise me.

The stewardess – she was tall, handsome and flashing dark, a type that they seemed to run to – asked me if she could make up my berth.

' – and, dear, do you want an aspirin?' She perched on the side of the seat and rocked precariously to and fro with the June hurricane. ' – or nembutal?'

'No.'

'I've been so busy with everyone else that I've had no time to ask you.' She sat down beside me and buckled us both in. 'Do you want some gum?'

This reminded me to get rid of the piece that had been boring me for hours. I wrapped it in a piece of magazine and put it into the automatic ash-holder.

'I can always tell people are nice,' the stewardess said approvingly, 'if they wrap their gum in paper before they put it in there.'

We sat for a while in the half-light of the swaying car. It was vaguely like a swanky restaurant at that twilight time between meals. We were all lingering – and not quite on purpose. Even the stewardess, I think, had to keep reminding herself why she was there.

She and I talked about a young actress I knew, whom she had flown West with two years before. It was in the very lowest time of the Depression, and the young actress kept staring out the window in such an intent way that the stewardess was afraid she was contemplating a leap. It appeared though that she was not afraid of poverty, but only of revolution.

'I know what mother and *I* are going to do,' she confided to the stewardess. 'We're coming out to the Yellowstone and we're just going to live simply till it all blows over. Then we'll come back. They don't kill artists – you know?'

The proposition pleased me. It conjured up a pretty picture of the actress and her mother being fed by kind Tory bears who brought them honey, and by gentle fawns who fetched extra milk from the does and then lingered near to make pillows for their heads at night. In turn I told the stewardess about the lawyer and the director who told their plans to father one night in those brave days. If the bonus army conquered Washington, the lawyer had a boat hidden in the Sacramento River, and he was going to row upstream for a few months and then come back 'because they always needed lawyers after a revolution to straighten out the legal side'.

The director had tended more toward defeatism. He had an old suit, shirt and shoes in waiting – he never did say whether they were his own or whether he got them from the prop department – and he was going to Disappear into the Crowd. I remember father saying: 'But they'll look at your hands! They'll know you haven't done manual work for years. And they'll ask for your union card.' And I remember how the director's face fell, and how gloomy he was while he ate his dessert, and how funny and puny they sounded to me.

'Is your father an actor, Miss Brady?' asked the stewardess. 'I've certainly heard the name.'

At the name Brady, both the men across the aisle looked up. Sideways – that Hollywood look, that always seems thrown over one shoulder. Then the young, pale, stocky man unbuttoned his safety strap and stood in the aisle beside us.

'Are you Cecilia *Bra*dy?' he demanded accusingly, as if I'd been holding out on him. 'I *thought* I recognised you. I'm Wylie White.'

He could have omitted this – for at the same moment a new voice said, 'Watch your step, Wylie!', and another man brushed by him in the aisle and went forward in the direction of the cockpit. Wylie White started, and a little too late called after him defiantly: 'I only take orders from the pilot.'

I recognised the kind of pleasantry that goes on between the powers in Hollywood and their satellites.

The stewardess reproved him: 'Not so loud, please – some of the passengers are asleep.'

I saw now that the other man across the aisle, the middle-aged Jew, was on his feet also, staring with shameless economic lechery, after the man who had just gone by. Or rather at the back of the man, who gestured sideways with his hand in a sort of farewell, as he went out of my sight.

I asked the stewardess: 'Is he the as*sis*tant pilot?'

She was unbuckling our belt, about to abandon me to Wylie White.

'No. That's Mr Smith. He has the private compartment, the "bridal suite" – only he has it alone. The assistant pilot is always in uniform.' She stood up: 'I want to find out if we're going to be grounded in Nashville.'

Wylie White was aghast.

'Why?'

'It's a storm coming up in the Mississippi Valley.'

'Does that mean we'll have to stay here all *night*?'

'If this keeps up!'

A sudden dip indicated that it would. It tipped Wylie White into the seat opposite me, shunted the stewardess precipitately down in the direction of the cockpit, and plunked the Jewish man into a sitting position. After the studied, unruffled exclamations of distaste that befitted the air-minded, we settled down. There was an introduction.

'Miss Brady – Mr Schwartz,' said Wylie White. 'He's a great friend of your father's, too.'

Mr Schwartz nodded so vehemently that I could almost hear him saying: 'It's true. As God is my judge, it's true!'

He might have said this right out loud at one time in his life – but he was obviously a man to whom something had happened. Meeting him was like encountering a friend who has been in a fist fight or collision, and got flattened. You stare at your friend and say: 'What happened to you?' And he answers something unintelligible through broken teeth and swollen lips. He can't even tell you about it.

Mr Schwartz was physically unmarked; the exaggerated Persian nose and oblique eye-shadow were as congenital as the tip-tilted Irish redness around my father's nostrils.

'Nashville!' cried Wylie White. 'That means we go to an hotel. We don't get to the coast till tomorrow night – if then. My God! I was born in Nashville.'

'I should think you'd like to see it again.'

'Never – I've kept away for fifteen years. I hope I'll *never* see it again.'

But he would – for the plane was unmistakably going down, down, down, like Alice in the rabbit hole. Cupping my hand against the window I saw the blur of the city far away on the left. The green sign

'Fasten your belts – No smoking' had been on since we first rode into the storm.

'Did you hear what he said?' said Schwartz from one of his fiery silences across the aisle.

'Hear what?' asked Wylie.

'Hear what he's calling himself,' said Schwartz. 'Mr *Smith*!'

'Why not?' asked Wylie.

'Oh, nothing,' said Schwartz quickly. 'I just thought it was funny. Smith.' I never heard a laugh with less mirth in it: 'Smith!'

I suppose there has been nothing like the airports since the days of the stage-stops – nothing quite as lonely, as sombre-silent. The old red-brick depots were built right into the towns they marked – people didn't get off at those isolated stations unless they lived there. But airports lead you way back in history like oases, like the stops on the great trade routes. The sight of air travellers strolling in ones and twos into midnight airports will draw a small crowd any night up to two. The young people look at the planes, the older ones look at the passengers with a watchful incredulity. In the big transcontinental planes we were the coastal rich, who casually alighted from our cloud in mid-America. High adventure might be among us, disguised as a movie star. But mostly it wasn't. And I always wished fervently that we looked more interesting than we did – just as I often have at premières, when the fans look at you with scornful reproach because you're not a star.

On the ground Wylie and I were suddenly friends because he held out his arm to steady me when I got out of the plane. From then on, he made a dead set for me – and I didn't mind. From the moment we walked into the airport it had become plain that if we were stranded here we were stranded here together. (It wasn't like the time I lost my boy – the time my boy played the piano with that girl Reina in a little New England farmhouse near Bennington, and I realised at last I wasn't wanted. Guy Lombardo was on the air playing 'Top Hat' and 'Cheek to Cheek', and she taught him the melodies. The keys falling like leaves and her hands splayed over his as she showed him a black chord. I was a freshman then.)

When we went into the airport Mr Schwartz was along with us, too, but he seemed in a sort of dream. All the time we were trying to get accurate information at the desk, he kept staring at the door that led out to the landing field, as if he were afraid the plane would leave without him. Then I excused myself for a few minutes and something happened that I didn't see, but when I came back he and White were standing close together, White talking and Schwartz looking twice as much as if a great truck had just backed up over him. He didn't stare at the door to the landing field any more. I heard the end of Wylie White's remark . . .

' – I told you to shut up. It serves you right.'

'I only said – '

He broke off as I came up and asked if there was any news. It was then half-past two in the morning.

'A little,' said Wylie White. 'They don't think we'll be able to start for three hours anyhow, so some of the softies are going to an hotel. But I'd like to take you out to the Hermitage, Home of Andrew Jackson.'

'How could we see it in the dark?' demanded Schwartz.

'Hell, it'll be sunrise in two hours.'

'You two go,' said Schwartz.

'All right – you take the bus to the hotel. It's still waiting – *he*'s in there.' Wylie's voice had a taunt in it. 'Maybe it'd be a good thing.'

'No, I'll go along with you,' said Schwartz hastily.

We took a taxi in the sudden country dark outside, and he seemed to cheer up. He patted my kneecap encouragingly.

'I should go along,' he said, 'I should be chaperone. Once upon a time when I was in the big money, I had a daughter – a beautiful daughter.'

He spoke as if she had been sold to creditors as a tangible asset.

'You'll have another,' Wylie assured him. 'You'll get it all back. Another turn of the wheel and you'll be where Cecilia's papa is, won't he Cecilia?'

'Where is this Hermitage?' asked Schwartz presently. 'Far away at the end of nowhere? We will miss the plane?'

'Skip it,' said Wylie. 'We ought to've brought the stewardess along for you. Didn't you admire the stewardess? *I* thought she was pretty cute.'

We drove for a long time over a bright level countryside, just a road and a tree and a shack and a tree, and then suddenly along a winding twist of woodland. I could feel even in the darkness that the trees of the woodland were green – that it was all different from the dusty olive-tint of California. Somewhere we passed a Negro driving three cows ahead of him, and they mooed as he scattered them to the side of the road. They were real cows, with warm, fresh, silky flanks, and the

Negro grew gradually real out of the darkness with his big brown eyes staring at us close to the car, as Wylie gave him a quarter. He said '*Thank* you – thank you,' and stood there, and the cows mooed again into the night as we drove off.

I thought of the first sheep I ever remember seeing – hundreds of them, and how our car drove suddenly into them on the back lot of the old Laemmle studio. They were unhappy about being in pictures, but the men in the car with us kept saying: 'Swell!'

'Is that what you wanted, Dick?'

'Isn't that swell?' And the man named Dick kept standing up in the car as if he were Cortez or Balboa, looking over that grey fleecy undulation. If I ever knew what picture they were in, I have long forgotten.

We had driven an hour. We crossed a brook over an old rattly iron bridge laid with planks. Now there were roosters crowing and blue-green shadows stirring every time we passed a farmhouse.

'I told you it'd be morning soon,' said Wylie. 'I was born near here – the son of impoverished southern paupers. The family mansion is now used as an outhouse. We had four servants – my father, my mother and my two sisters. I refused to join the guild, and so I went to Memphis to start my career, which has now reached a dead end.' He put his arm around me: 'Cecilia, will you marry me, so I can share the Brady fortune?'

He was disarming enough, so I let my head lie on his shoulder.

'What do you do, Cecilia. Go to school?'

'I go to Bennington. I'm a junior.'

'Oh, I beg your pardon. I should have known, but I never had the advantage of college training. But a *ju*nior – why I read in *Esquire* that juniors have nothing to learn, Cecilia.'

'Why do people think that college girls – '

'Don't apologise – knowledge is power.'

'You'd know from the way you talk that we were on our way to Hollywood,' I said. 'It's always years and years behind the times.'

He pretended to be shocked.

'You mean girls in the East have no private lives?'

'That's the point. They *have* got private lives. You're bothering me, let go.'

'I can't. It might wake Schwartz, and I think this is the first sleep he's had for weeks. Listen, Cecilia: I once had an affair with the wife of a producer. A very short affair. When it was over she said to me in no uncertain terms, she said: "Don't you ever tell about this or I'll have you thrown out of Hollywood. My husband's a much more important man than you!" '

I liked him again now, and presently the taxi turned down a long lane fragrant with honeysuckle and narcissus, and stopped beside the great grey hulk of the Andrew Jackson house. The driver turned around to tell us something about it, but Wylie shushed him, pointing at Schwartz, and we tiptoed out of the car.

'You can't get into the Mansion now,' the taxi man told us politely.

Wylie and I went and sat against the wide pillars of the steps.

'What about Mr Schwartz?' I asked. 'Who is he?'

'To hell with Schwartz. He was the head of some combine once – First National? Paramount? United Artists? Now he's down and out. But he'll be back. You can't flunk out of pictures unless you're a dope or a drunk.'

'You don't like Hollywood,' I suggested.

'Yes I do. Sure I do. Say! This isn't anything to talk about on the steps of Andrew Jackson's house – at dawn.'

'I *like* Hollywood,' I persisted.

'It's all right. It's a mining town in lotus land. Who said that? I did. It's a good place for toughies, but I went there from Savannah, Georgia. I went to a garden party the first day. My host shook hands and left me. It was all there – that swimming pool, green moss at two dollars an inch, beautiful felines having drinks and fun –

' – And nobody spoke to me. Not a soul. I spoke to half a dozen people but they didn't answer. That continued for an hour, two hours – then I got up from where I was sitting and ran out at a dog trot like a crazy man. I didn't feel I had any rightful identity until I got back to the hotel and the clerk handed me a letter addressed to me in my name.'

Naturally I hadn't ever had such an experience, but looking back on parties I'd been to, I realised that such things could happen. We don't go for strangers in Hollywood unless they wear a sign saying that their axe has been thoroughly ground elsewhere, and that in any case it's not going to fall on our necks – in other words, unless they're a celebrity. And they'd better look out even then.

'You should have risen above it,' I said smugly. 'It's not a slam at *you* when people are rude – it's a slam at the people they've met before.'

'Such a pretty girl – to say such wise things.'

There was an eager to-do in the eastern sky, and Wylie could see me plain – thin with good features and lots of style, and the kicking foetus of a mind. I wonder what I looked like in that dawn, five years ago. A little rumpled and pale, I suppose, but at that age, when one has the young illusion that most adventures are good, I needed only a bath and a change to go on for hours.

Wylie stared at me with really flattering appreciation – and then suddenly we were not alone. Mr Schwartz wandered apologetically into the pretty scene.

'I fell upon a large metal handle,' he said, touching the corner of his eye.

Wylie jumped up.

'Just in time, Mr Schwartz,' he said. 'The tour is just starting. Home of Old Hickory – America's tenth president. The victor of New Orleans, opponent of the National Bank, and inventor of the Spoils System.'

Schwartz looked towards me as towards a jury.

'There's a writer for you,' he said. 'Knows everything and at the same time he knows nothing.'

'What's that?' said Wylie, indignant.

It was my first inkling that he was a writer. And while I like writers – because if you ask a writer anything, you usually get an answer – still it belittled him in my eyes. Writers aren't people exactly. Or, if they're any good, they're a whole *lot* of people trying so hard to be one person. It's like actors, who try so pathetically not to look in mirrors, who lean *back*ward trying – only to see their faces in the reflecting chandeliers.

'Ain't writers like that, Cecilia?' demanded Schwartz. 'I have no words for them. I only know it's true.'

Wylie looked at him with slowly gathering indignation. 'I've heard that before,' he said. 'Look, Manny, I'm a more practical man than you any day! I've sat in an office and listened to some mystic stalk up and down for hours spouting tripe that'd land him on a nut-farm anywhere outside of California – and then at the end tell me how *practical* he was, and I was a dreamer – and would I kindly go away and make sense out of what he'd said.'

Mr Schwartz's face fell into its more disintegrated alignments. One eye looked upwards through the tall elms. He raised his hand and bit without interest at the cuticle on his second finger. There was a bird flying about the chimney of the house, and his glance followed it. It perched on the chimney pot like a raven, and Mr Schwartz's eyes remained fixed upon it as he said: 'We can't get in, and it's time for you two to go back to the plane.'

It was still not quite dawn. The Hermitage looked like a nice big white box, but a little lonely and vacated still after a hundred years. We walked back to the car. Only after we had gotten in, and Mr Schwartz had surprisingly shut the taxi door on us, did we realise he didn't intend to come along.

'I'm not going to the Coast – I decided that when I woke up. So I'll stay here, and afterwards the driver could come back for me.'

'Going back East?' said Wylie with surprise. 'Just because – '

'I have decided,' said Schwartz, faintly smiling. 'Once I used to be a regular man of decision – you'd be surprised.' He felt in his pocket, as the taxi driver warmed up the engine. 'Will you give this note to Mr Smith?'

'Shall I come in two hours?' the driver asked Schwartz.

'Yes . . . sure. I shall be glad to entertain myself looking around.'

I kept thinking of him all the way back to the airport – trying to fit him into that early hour and into that landscape. He had come a long way from some Ghetto to present himself at that raw shrine. Manny Schwartz and Andrew Jackson – it was hard to say them in the same sentence. It was doubtful if he knew who Andrew Jackson was as he wandered around, but perhaps he figured that if people had preserved his house Andrew Jackson must have been someone who was large and merciful, able to understand. At both ends of life man needed nourishment: a breast – a shrine. Something to lay himself beside when no one wanted him further, and shoot a bullet into his head.

Of course we did not know this for twenty hours. When we got to the airport we told the purser that Mr Schwartz was not continuing, and then forgot about him. The storm had wandered away into Eastern Tennessee and broken against the mountains, and we were taking off in less than an hour. Sleepy-eyed travellers appeared from the hotel, and I dozed a few minutes on one of those Iron Maidens they use for couches. Slowly the idea of a perilous journey was recreated out of the débris of our failure: a new stewardess, tall, handsome, flashing dark, exactly like the other except she wore seersucker instead of French red-and-blue, went briskly past us with a suitcase. Wylie sat beside me as we waited.

'Did you give the note to Mr Smith?' I asked, half asleep.

'Yeah.'

'Who is Mr Smith? I suspect he spoiled Mr Schwartz's trip.'

'It was Schwartz's fault.'

'I'm prejudiced against steamrollers,' I said. 'My father tries to be a steamroller around the house, and I tell him to save it for the studio.'

I wondered if I was being fair; words are the palest counters at that time in the morning. 'Still, he steamrollered me into Bennington and I've always been grateful for that.'

'There would be quite a crash,' Wylie said, 'if steamroller Brady met steamroller Smith.'

'Is Mr Smith a competitor of father's?'

'Not exactly. I should say no. But if he was a competitor I know where my money would be.'

'On father?'

'I'm afraid not.'

It was too early in the morning for family patriotism. The pilot was at the desk with the purser and he shook his head as they regarded a prospective passenger who had put two nickels in the electric phonograph and lay alcoholically on a bench fighting off sleep. The first song he had chosen, 'Lost', thundered through the room, followed, after a slight interval, by his other choice, 'Gone', which was equally dogmatic and final. The pilot shook his head emphatically and walked over to the passenger.

'Afraid we're not going to be able to carry you this time, old man.'

'Wha'?'

The drunk sat up, awful-looking, yet discernibly attractive, and I was sorry for him in spite of his passionately ill-chosen music.

'Go back to the hotel and get some sleep. There'll be another plane tonight.'

'Only going up in ee *air*.'

'Not this time, old man.'

In his disappointment the drunk fell off the bench – and above the phonograph, a loudspeaker summoned us respectable people outside. In the corridor of the plane I ran into Monroe Stahr and fell all over him, or wanted to. There was a man any girl would go for, with or without encouragement. I was emphatically with*out* it, but he liked me and sat down opposite till the plane took off.

'Let's all ask for our money back,' he suggested. His dark eyes took me in, and I wondered what they would look like if he fell in love. They were kind, aloof, and, though they often reasoned with you gently, somewhat superior. It was no fault of theirs if they saw so much. He darted in and out of the role of 'one of the boys' with dexterity – but on the whole I should say he wasn't one of them. But he knew how to shut up, how to draw into the background, how to listen. From where he stood (and though he was not a tall man, it always seemed high up) he watched the multitudinous practicalities of his world like a proud young shepherd to whom night and day had never mattered. He was born sleepless, without a talent for rest or the desire for it.

We sat in unembarrassed silence – I had known him since he became father's partner a dozen years ago, when I was seven and Stahr was twenty-two. Wylie was across the aisle and I didn't know whether or not to introduce them, but Stahr kept turning his ring so abstractedly that he made me feel young and invisible, and I didn't care. I never dared look quite away from him or quite *at* him, unless I had something important to say – and I knew he affected many other people in the same manner.

'I'll *give* you this ring, Cecilia.'

'I beg your pardon. I didn't realise that I was – '

'I've got half a dozen like it.'

He handed it to me, a gold nugget with the letter S in bold relief. I had been thinking how oddly its bulk contrasted with his fingers, which were delicate and slender like the rest of his body, and like his slender face with the arched eyebrows and the dark curly hair. He looked spiritual at times, but he was a fighter – somebody out of his past knew him when he was one of a gang of kids in the Bronx, and gave me a description of how he walked always at the head of his gang, this rather frail boy, occasionally throwing a command backward out of the corner of his mouth.

Stahr folded my hand over the ring, stood up, and addressed Wylie.

'Come up to the bridal suite,' he said. 'See you later, Cecilia.'

Before they went out of hearing, I heard Wylie's question: 'Did you open Schwartz's note?' And Stahr: 'Not yet.'

I must be slow, for only then did I realise that Stahr was Mr Smith.

Afterwards Wylie told me what was in the note. Written by the headlights of the taxi, it was almost illegible.

> Dear Monroe – You are the best of them all I have always admired your mentality so when you turn against me I know it's no use! I must be no good and am not going to continue the journey let me warn you once again look out! I know.
>
> Your friend
>
> Manny

Stahr read it twice, and raised his hand to the morning stubble on his chin.

'He's a nervous wreck,' he said. 'There's nothing to be done –

absolutely nothing. I'm sorry I was short with him – but I don't like a man to approach me telling me it's for *my* sake.'

'Maybe it was,' said Wylie.

'It's poor technique.'

'I'd fall for it,' said Wylie. 'I'm vain as a woman. If anybody pretends to be interested in me, I'll ask for more. I like advice.'

Stahr shook his head distastefully. Wylie kept on ribbing him – he was one of those to whom this privilege was permitted.

'You fall for some kinds of flattery,' he said. 'This "little Napoleon stuff".'

'It makes me sick,' said Stahr, 'but it's not as bad as some man trying to help you.'

'If you don't like advice, why do you pay *me*?'

'That's a question of merchandise,' said Stahr. 'I'm a merchant. I want to buy what's in your mind.'

'You're no merchant,' said Wylie. 'I knew a lot of them when I was a publicity man, and I agree with Charles Francis Adams.'

'What did he say?'

'He knew them all – Gould, Vanderbilt, Carnegie, Astor – and he said there wasn't one he'd care to meet again in the hereafter. Well – they haven't improved since then, and that's why I say you're no merchant.'

'Adams was probably a sourbelly,' said Stahr. 'He wanted to be head man himself, but he didn't have the judgement or else the character.'

'He had brains,' said Wylie rather tartly.

'It takes more than brains. You writers and artists poop out and get all mixed up, and somebody has to come in and straighten you out.' He shrugged his shoulders. 'You seem to take things so personally, hating people and worshipping them – always thinking people are so important – especially yourselves. You just ask to be kicked around. I like people and I like them to like me, but I wear my heart where God put it – on the inside.'

He broke off.

'What did I say to Schwartz in the airport? Do you remember – exactly?'

'You said, "Whatever you're after, the answer is No!" ' Stahr was silent.

'He was sunk,' said Wylie, 'but I laughed him out of it. We took Billy Brady's daughter for a ride.'

Stahr rang for the stewardess.

'That pilot,' he said, 'would he mind if I sat up in front with him a while?'

'That's against the rules, Mr Smith.'

'Ask him to step in here a minute when he's free.'

Stahr sat up front all afternoon. While we slid off the endless desert and over the tablelands, dyed with many colours like the white sands we dyed with colours when I was a child. Then in the late afternoon, the peaks themselves – the Mountains of the Frozen Saw – slid under our propellers and we were close to home.

When I wasn't dozing I was thinking that I wanted to marry Stahr, that I wanted to make him love me. Oh, the conceit! What on earth did I have to offer? But I didn't think like that then. I had the pride of young women, which draws its strength from such sublime thoughts as 'I'm as good as *she* is.' For my purposes I was just as beautiful as the great beauties who must have inevitably thrown themselves at his head. My little spurt of intellectual interest was of course making me fit to be a brilliant ornament of any salon.

I know now it was absurd. Though Stahr's education was founded on nothing more than a night-school course in stenography, he had a long time ago run ahead through trackless wastes of perception into fields where very few men were able to follow him. But in my reckless conceit I matched my grey eyes against his brown ones for guile, my young golf-and-tennis heart-beats against his, which must be slowing a little after years of overwork. And I planned and I contrived and I plotted – any women can tell you – but it never came to anything, as you will see. I still like to think that if he'd been a poor boy and nearer my age I could have managed it, but of course the real truth was that I had nothing to offer that he didn't have; some of my more romantic ideas actually stemmed from pictures – *42nd Street*, for example, had a great influence on me. It's more than possible that some of the pictures which Stahr himself conceived had shaped me into what I was.

So it was rather hopeless. Emotionally, at least, people can't live by taking in each other's washing.

But at that time it was different: father might help, the stewardess might help. She might go up in the cockpit and say to Stahr: 'If I ever saw love, it's in that girl's eyes.'

The pilot might help: 'Man, are you blind? Why don't you go back there?'

Wylie White might help – instead of standing in the aisle looking at me doubtfully, wondering whether I was awake or asleep.

'Sit down,' I said. 'What's new? – where are we?'

'Up in the air.'

'Oh, so that's it. Sit down.' I tried to show a cheerful interest: 'What are you writing?'

'Heaven help me, I am writing about a Boy Scout – *The* Boy Scout.'

'Is it Stahr's idea?'

'I don't know – he told me to look into it. He may have ten writers working ahead of me or behind me, a system which he so thoughtfully invented. So you're in love with him?'

'I should say not,' I said indignantly. 'I've known him all my life.'

'Desperate, eh? Well, I'll arrange it if you'll use all your influence to advance me. I want a unit of my own.'

I closed my eyes and drifted off. When I woke up, the stewardess was putting a blanket over me.

'Almost there,' she said.

Out the window I could see by the sunset that we were in a greener land.

'I just heard something funny,' she volunteered, 'up in the cockpit – that Mr Smith – or Mr Stahr – I never remember seeing his name – '

'It's never on any pictures,' I said.

'Oh. Well, he's been asking the pilots a lot about flying – I mean he's interested? You *know*?'

'I know.'

'I mean one of them told me he bet he could teach Mr Stahr solo flying in ten minutes. He has such a fine mentality, that's what he said.'

I was getting impatient.

'Well, what was so funny?'

'Well, finally one of the pilots asked Mr Smith if he liked his business, and Mr Smith said, "Sure. Sure I like it. It's nice being the only sound nut in a hatful of cracked ones." '

The stewardess doubled up with laughter – and I could have spat at her.

'I mean calling all those people a hatful of nuts. I mean *cracked* nuts.' Her laughter stopped with unexpected suddenness, and her face was grave as she stood up. 'Well, I've got to finish my chart.'

'Goodbye.'

Obviously Stahr had put the pilots right up on the throne with him and let them rule with him for a while. Years later I travelled with one of those same pilots and he told me one thing Stahr had said.

He was looking down at the mountains.

'Suppose you were a railroad man,' he said. 'You have to send a train through there somewhere. Well, you get your surveyors' reports, and you find there's three or four or half a dozen gaps, and not one is better than the other. You've got to decide – on what basis? you can't test the best way – except by doing it. So you just do it.'

The pilot thought he had missed something.

'How do you mean?'

'You choose some one way for no reason at all – because that mountain's pink or the blueprint is a better blue. You see?'

The pilot considered that this was very valuable advice. But he doubted if he'd ever be in a position to apply it.

'What I wanted to know,' he told me ruefully, 'is how he ever got to be Mr Stahr.'

I'm afraid Stahr could never have answered that one; for the embryo is not equipped with a memory. But I could answer a little. He had flown up very high to see, on strong wings, when he was young. And while he was up there he had looked on all the kingdoms, with the kind of eyes that can stare straight into the sun. Beating his wings tenaciously – finally frantically – and keeping on beating them, he had stayed up there longer than most of us, and then, remembering all he had seen from his great height of how things were, he had settled gradually to earth.

The motors were off, and all our five senses began to readjust themselves for landing. I could see a line of lights for the Long Beach Naval Station ahead and to the left, and on the right a twinkling blur for Santa Monica. The California moon was out, huge and orange over the Pacific. However I happened to feel about these things – and they were home, after all – I know that Stahr must have felt much more. These were the things I had first opened my eyes on, like the sheep on the back lot of the old Laemmle studio; but this was where Stahr had come to earth after that extraordinary illuminating flight where he saw which way we were going, and how we looked doing it, and how much of it mattered. You could say that this was where an accidental wind blew him, but I don't think so. I would rather think that in a 'long shot' he saw a new way of measuring our jerky hopes and graceful rogueries and awkward sorrows, and that he came here from choice to be with us to the end. Like the plane coming down into the Glendale airport, into the warm darkness.

Chapter 2

It was nine o'clock of a July night and there were still some extras in the drugstore across from the studio – I could see them bent over the pin-games inside – as I parked my car. 'Old' Johnny Swanson stood on the corner in his semi-cowboy clothes, staring gloomily past the moon. Once he had been as big in pictures as Tom Mix or Bill Hart – now it was too sad to speak to him, and I hurried across the street and through the front gate.

There is never a time when a studio is absolutely quiet. There is always a night shift of technicians in the laboratories and dubbing-rooms and people on the maintenance staff dropping in at the commissary. But the sounds are all different – the padded hush of tyres, the quiet tick of a motor running idle, the naked cry of a soprano singing into a nightbound microphone. Around a corner I came upon a man in rubber boots washing down a car in a wonderful white light – a fountain among the dead industrial shadows. I slowed up as I saw Mr Marcus being hoisted into his car in front of the administration building, because he took so long to say anything, even good-night – and while I waited I realised that the soprano was singing, *Come, come, I love you only* over and over; I remember this because she kept singing the same line during the earthquake. That didn't come for five minutes yet.

Father's offices were in the old building with the long balconies and iron rails with their suggestion of a perpetual tightrope. Father was on the second floor, with Stahr on one side and Mr Marcus on the other – this evening there were lights all along the row. My stomach dipped a little at the proximity to Stahr, but that was in pretty good control now – I'd seen him only once in the month I'd been home.

There were a lot of strange things about father's office, but I'll make it brief. In the outer part were three poker-faced secretaries who had sat there like witches ever since I could remember – Birdy Peters, Maude something, and Rosemary Schmiel; I don't know whether this was her name, but she was the dean of the trio, so to speak, and under her desk was the kick-lock that admitted you to father's throne room. All three of the secretaries were passionate capitalists, and Birdy had invented the rule that if typists were seen eating together more than once in a single week, they were hauled up on the carpet. At that time the studios feared mob rule.

I went on in. Nowadays all chief executives have huge drawing-rooms, but my father's was the first. It was also the first to have one-way glass in the big French windows, and I've heard a story about a trap in the floor that would drop unpleasant visitors to an oubliette below, but believe it to be an invention. There was a big painting of Will Rogers, hung conspicuously and intended, I think, to suggest father's essential kinship with Hollywood's St Francis; there was a signed photograph of Minna Davis, Stahr's dead wife, and photos of other studio celebrities and big chalk drawings of mother and me. Tonight the one-way French windows were open and a big moon, rosy-gold with a haze around, was wedged helpless in one of them. Father and Jacques La Borwitz and Rosemary Schmiel were down at the end around a big circular desk.

What did father look like? I couldn't describe him except for once in New York when I met him where I didn't expect to; I was aware of a bulky, middle-aged man who looked a little ashamed of himself, and I wished he'd move on – and then I saw he was father. Afterwards I was shocked at my impression. Father can be very magnetic – he had a tough jaw and an Irish smile.

But as for Jacques La Borwitz, I shall spare you. Let me just say he was an assistant producer, which is something like a commissar, and let it go at that. Where Stahr picked up such mental cadavers or had them forced upon him – or especially how he got any use out of them – has always amazed me, as it amazed everyone fresh from the East who slapped up against them. Jacques La Borwitz had his points, no doubt, but so have the sub-microscopic protozoa, so has a dog prowling for a bitch and a bone. Jacques La – oh my!

From their expressions I was sure they had been talking about Stahr. Stahr had ordered something or forbidden something, or defied father or junked one of La Borwitz's pictures or something catastrophic, and they were sitting there in protest at night in a community of rebellion and helplessness. Rosemary Schmiel sat pad in hand, as if ready to write down their dejection.

'I'm to drive you home dead or alive,' I told father. 'All those birthday presents rotting away in their packages!'

'A birthday!' cried Jacques in a flurry of apology. 'How old? I didn't know.'

'Forty-three,' said father distinctly.

He was older than that – four years – and Jacques knew it; I saw him note it down in his account book to use sometime. Out here these account books are carried open in the hand. One can see the entries being made without recourse to lip-reading, and Rosemary Schmiel was compelled in emulation to make a mark on her pad. As she rubbed it out, the earth quaked under us.

We didn't get the full shock like at Long Beach, where the upper storeys of shops were spewed into the streets and small hotels drifted out to sea – but for a full minute our bowels were one with the bowels of the earth – like some nightmare attempt to attach our navel cords again and jerk us back to the womb of creation.

Mother's picture fell off the wall, revealing a small safe – Rosemary and I grabbed frantically for each other and did a strange screaming waltz across the room. Jacques fainted or at least disappeared, and father clung to his desk and shouted, 'Are you all right?' Outside the window the singer came to the climax of 'I Love You Only', held it a moment and then, I swear, started it all over. Or maybe they were playing it back to her from the recording machine.

The room stood still, shimmying a little. We made our way to the door, suddenly including Jacques, who had reappeared, and tottered out dizzily through the ante-room on to the iron balcony. Almost all the lights were out, and from here and there we could hear cries and calls. Momentarily we stood waiting for a second shock – then, as with a common impulse, we went into Stahr's entry and through to his office.

The office was big, but not as big as father's. Stahr sat on the side of his couch rubbing his eyes. When the quake came he had been asleep, and he wasn't sure yet whether he had dreamed it. When we convinced him he thought it was all rather funny – until the telephones began to ring. I watched him as unobtrusively as possible. He was grey with fatigue while he listened to the phone and dictagraph; but as the reports came in, his eyes began to pick up shine.

'A couple of water mains have burst,' he said to father, ' – they're heading into the back lot.'

'Gray's shooting in the French Village,' said father.

'It's flooded around the Station, too, and in the Jungle and the City Corner. What the hell – nobody seems to be hurt.' In passing, he shook my hands gravely: 'Where've you been, Cecilia?'

'You going out there, Monroe?' father asked.

'When all the news is in. One of the power lines is off, too – I've sent for Robinson.'

He made me sit down with him on the couch and tell about the quake again.

'You look tired,' I said, cute and motherly.

'Yes,' he agreed, 'I've got no place to go in the evenings, so I just work.'

'I'll arrange some evenings for you.'

'I used to play poker with a gang,' he said thoughtfully, 'before I was married. But they all drank themselves to death.'

Miss Doolan, his secretary, came in with fresh bad news.

'Robby'll take care of everything when he comes,' Stahr assured father. He turned to me. 'Now there's a man – that Robinson. He was a trouble-shooter – fixed the telephone wires in Minnesota blizzards – nothing stumps him. He'll be here in a minute – you'll like Robby.' He said it as if it had been his life-long intention to bring us together, and he had arranged the whole earthquake with just that in mind. 'Yes, you'll like Robby,' he repeated. 'When do you go back to college?'

'I've just come home.'

'You get the whole summer?'

'I'm sorry,' I said. 'I'll go back as soon as I can.'

I was in a mist. It hadn't failed to cross my mind that he might have some intention about me, but if it was so, it was in an exasperatingly early stage – I was merely 'a good property'. And the idea didn't seem so attractive at that moment – like marrying a doctor. He seldom left the studio before eleven.

'How long,' he asked my father, 'before she graduates from college. That's what I was trying to say.'

And I think I was about to sing out eagerly that I needn't go back at all, that I was quite educated already – when the totally admirable Robinson came in. He was a bow-legged young redhead, all ready to go.

'This is Robby, Cecilia,' said Stahr. 'Come on, Robby.'

So I met Robby. I can't say it seemed like fate – but it was. For it was Robby who later told me how Stahr found his love that night.

* * *

Under the moon the back lot was thirty acres of fairyland – not because the locations really looked like African jungles and French châteaux and schooners at anchor and Broadway at night, but because they looked like the torn picture books of childhood, like fragments of stories dancing in an open fire. I never lived in a house with an attic, but a back lot must be something like that, and at night of course in an enchanted distorted way, it all comes true.

When Stahr and Robby arrived, clusters of lights had already picked out the danger spots in the flood.

'We'll pump it out into the swamp on Thirty-Sixth Street,' said Robby after a moment. 'It's city property – but isn't this an act of God? Say – look there!'

On top of a huge head of the Goddess Siva, two women were floating down the current of an impromptu river. The idol had come unloosed from a set of Burma, and it meandered earnestly on its way, stopping sometimes to waddle and bump in the shallows with the other débris of the tide. The two refugees had found sanctuary along a scroll of curls on its bald forehead and seemed at first glance to be sightseers on an interesting bus-ride through the scene of the flood.

'Will you look at that, Monroe!' said Robby. 'Look at those dames!'

Dragging their legs through sudden bogs, they made their way to the bank of the stream. Now they could see the women, looking a little scared but brightening at the prospect of rescue.

'We ought to let 'em drift out to the waste pipe,' said Robby gallantly, 'but DeMille needs that head next week.'

He wouldn't have hurt a fly, though, and presently he was hip deep in the water, fishing for them with a pole and succeeding only in spinning it in a dizzy circle. Help arrived, and the impression quickly got around that one of them was very pretty, and then that they were people of importance. But they were just strays, and Robby waited disgustedly to give them hell while the thing was brought finally into control and beached.

'Put that head back!' he called up to them. 'You think it's a souvenir?'

One of the women came sliding smoothly down the cheek of the idol, and Robby caught her and set her on solid ground; the other one hesitated and then followed. Robby turned to Stahr for judgement.

'What'll we do with them, chief?'

Stahr did not answer. Smiling faintly at him from not four feet away was the face of his dead wife, identical even to the expression. Across the four feet of moonlight, the eyes he knew looked back at him, a curl blew a little on a familiar forehead; the smile lingered, changed a little according to pattern; the lips parted – the same. An awful fear went over him, and he wanted to cry aloud. Back from the still sour room, the muffled glide of the limousine hearse, the falling concealing flowers, from out there in the dark – here now warm and glowing. The river passed him in a rush, the great spotlights swooped and blinked – and then he heard another voice speak that was not Minna's voice.

'We're sorry,' said the voice. 'We followed a truck in through a gate.'

A little crowd had gathered – electricians, grips, truckers, and Robby began to nip at them like a sheep dog.

'. . . get the big pumps on the tanks on Stage 4 . . . put a cable around this head . . . raft it up on a couple of two by fours . . . get the water out of the jungle first, for Christ's sake . . . that big "A" pipe, lay it down . . . all that stuff is plastic . . .'

Stahr stood watching the two women as they threaded their way after a policeman towards an exit gate. Then he took a tentative step to see if the weakness had gone out of his knees. A loud tractor came bumping through the slush, and men began streaming by him – every second one glancing at him, smiling, speaking: 'Hello, Monroe . . . Hello, Mr Stahr . . . wet night, Mr Stahr . . . Monroe . . . Monroe . . . Stahr . . . Stahr . . . Stahr.'

He spoke and waved back as the people streamed by in the darkness, looking, I suppose, a little like the Emperor and the Old Guard. There is no world so but it has its heroes, and Stahr was the hero. Most of these men had been here a long time – through the beginnings and the great upset, when sound came, and the three years of Depression, he had seen that no harm came to them. The old loyalties were trembling now, there were clay feet everywhere; but still he was their man, the last of the princes. And their greeting was a sort of low cheer as they went by.

Chapter 3

Between the night I got back and the quake, I'd made many observations.

About father, for example. I loved father – in a sort of irregular graph with many low swoops – but I began to see that his strong will didn't fill him out as a passable man. Most of what he accomplished boiled down to shrewd. He had acquired with luck and shrewdness a quarter interest in a booming circus – together with young Stahr. That was his life's effort – all the rest was an instinct to hang on. Of course, he talked that double talk to Wall Street about how mysterious it was to make a picture, but father didn't know the ABCs of dubbing or even cutting. Nor had he learned much about the feel of America as a bar boy in Ballyhegan, nor did he have any more than a drummer's sense of a story. On the other hand, he didn't have concealed paresis like – ; he came to the studio before noon, and, with a suspiciousness developed like a muscle, it was hard to put anything over on him.

Stahr had been his luck – and Stahr was something else again. He was a marker in industry like Edison and Lumière and Griffith and Chaplin. He led pictures way up past the range and power of the theatre, reaching a sort of golden age, before the censorship.

Proof of his leadership was the spying that went on around him – not just for inside information or patented process secrets – but spying on his scent for a trend in taste, his guess as to how things were going to be. Too much of his vitality was taken by the mere parrying of these attempts. It made his work secret in part, often devious, slow – and hard to describe as the plans of a general, where the psychological factors become too tenuous and we end by merely adding up the successes and failures. But I have determined to give you a glimpse of him functioning, which is my excuse for what follows. It is drawn partly from a paper I wrote in college on *A Producer's Day* and partly from my imagination. More often I have blocked in the ordinary events myself, while the stranger ones are true.

* * *

In the early morning after the flood, a man walked up to the outside balcony of the Administration Building. He lingered there some time, according to an eyewitness, then mounted to the iron railing and dove head first to the pavement below. Breakage – one arm.

Miss Doolan, Stahr's secretary, told him about it when he buzzed for her at nine. He had slept in his office without hearing the small commotion.

'Pete Zavras!' Stahr exclaimed, ' – the cameraman?'

'They took him to a doctor's office. It won't be in the paper.'

'Hell of a thing,' he said. 'I knew he'd gone to pot – but I don't know why. He was all right when we used him two years ago – why should he come here? How did he get in?'

'He bluffed it with his old studio pass,' said Catherine Doolan. She was a dry hawk, the wife of an assistant director. 'Perhaps the quake had something to do with it.'

'He was the best cameraman in town,' Stahr said. When he had heard of the hundreds dead at Long Beach, he was still haunted by the abortive suicide at dawn. He told Catherine Doolan to trace the matter down.

The first dictagraph messages blew in through the warm morning. While he shaved and had coffee, he talked and listened. Robby had left a message: 'If Mr Stahr wants me tell him to hell with it I'm in bed.' An actor was sick or thought so; the Governor of California was bringing a party out; a supervisor had beaten up his wife for the prints and must be 'reduced to a writer' – these three affairs were father's job – unless the actor was under personal contract to Stahr. There was early snow on a location in Canada with the company already there – Stahr raced over the possibilities of salvage, reviewing the story of the picture. Nothing. Stahr called Catherine Doolan.

'I want to speak to the cop who put two women off the back lot last night. I think his name's Malone.'

'Yes, Mr Stahr. I've got Joe Wyman – about the trousers.'

'Hello, Joe,' said Stahr. 'Listen – two people at the sneak preview complained that Morgan's fly was open for half the picture . . . of course they're exaggerating, but even if it's only ten feet . . . no, we can't find the people, but I want that picture run over and over until you find that footage. Get a lot of people in the projection room – somebody'll spot it.'

'Tout passe – L'art robuste
Seul a l'éternité.'

'And there's the Prince from Denmark,' said Catherine Doolan. 'He's very handsome.' She was impelled to add pointlessly, ' – for a tall man.'

'Thanks,' Stahr said. 'Thank you, Catherine, I appreciate it that I am now the handsomest small man on the lot. Send the Prince out on the sets and tell him we'll lunch at one.'

'And Mr George Boxley – looking very angry in a British way.'

'I'll see him for ten minutes.'

As she went out, he asked: 'Did Robby phone in?'

'No.'

'Call sound, and if he's been heard from, call him and ask him this. Ask him this – did he hear that woman's name last night? Either of those women. Or anything so they could be traced.'

'Anything else?'

'No, but tell him it's important while he still remembers. What were they? I mean what kind of people – ask him that, too. I mean were they – '

She waited, scratching his words on her pad without looking.

' – oh, were they – questionable? Were they theatrical? Never mind – skip that. Just ask if he knows how they can be traced.'

The policeman, Malone, had known nothing. Two dames, and he had hustled 'em, you betcha. One of them was sore. Which one? One of them. They had a car, a Chevvy – he thought of taking the licence. Was it – the good looker who was sore? It was one of them.

Not which one – he had noticed nothing. Even on the lot here Minna was forgotten. In three years. So much for that, then.

Stahr smiled at Mr George Boxley. It was a kindly fatherly smile Stahr had developed inversely when he was a young man pushed into high places. Originally it had been a smile of respect towards his elders, then as his own decisions grew rapidly to displace theirs, a smile so that they should not feel it – finally emerging as what it was: a smile of kindness – sometimes a little hurried and tired, but always there – towards anyone who had not angered him within the hour. Or anyone he did not intend to insult, aggressive and outright.

Mr Boxley did not smile back. He came in with the air of being violently dragged, though no one apparently had a hand on him. He stood in front of a chair, and again it was as if two invisible attendants seized his arms and set him down forcibly into it. He sat there morosely. Even when he lit a cigarette on Stahr's invitation, one felt that the match was held to it by exterior forces he disdained to control.

Stahr looked at him courteously.

'Something not going well, Mr Boxley?'

The novelist looked back at him in thunderous silence.

'I read your letter,' said Stahr. The tone of the pleasant young headmaster was gone. He spoke as to an equal, with a faint two-edged deference.

'I can't get what I write on paper,' broke out Boxley. 'You've all been very decent, but it's a sort of conspiracy. Those two hacks you've teamed me with listen to what I say, but they spoil it – they seem to have a vocabulary of about a hundred words.'

'Why don't you write it yourself?' asked Stahr.

'I have. I sent you some.'

'But it was just talk, back and forth,' said Stahr mildly. 'Interesting talk but nothing more.'

Now it was all the two ghostly attendants could do to hold Boxley in the deep chair. He struggled to get up; he uttered a single quiet bark which had some relation to laughter but none to amusement, and said: 'I don't think you people read things. The men are duelling when the conversation takes place. At the end one of them falls into a well and has to be hauled up in a bucket.'

He barked again and subsided.

'Would you write that in a book of your own, Mr Boxley?'

'What? Naturally not.'

'You'd consider it too cheap.'

'Movie standards are different,' said Boxley, hedging.

'Do you ever go to them?'

'No – almost never.'

'Isn't it because people are always duelling and falling down wells?'

'Yes – and wearing strained facial expressions and talking incredible and unnatural dialogue.'

'Skip the dialogue for a minute,' said Stahr. 'Granted your dialogue is more graceful than what these hacks can write – that's why we brought you out here. But let's imagine something that isn't either bad dialogue or jumping down a well. Has your office got a stove in it that lights with a match?'

'I think it has,' said Boxley stiffly, ' – but I never use it.'

'Suppose you're in your office. You've been fighting duels or writing all day and you're too tired to fight or write any more. You're sitting there staring – dull, like we all get sometimes. A pretty stenographer that you've seen before comes into the room and you watch her – idly.

She doesn't see you, though you're very close to her. She takes off her gloves, opens her purse and dumps it out on a table –'

Stahr stood up, tossing his key-ring on his desk.

'She has two dimes and a nickel – and a cardboard matchbox. She leaves the nickel on the desk, puts the two dimes back into her purse and takes her black gloves to the stove, opens it and puts them inside. There is one match in the matchbox and she starts to light it kneeling by the stove. You notice that there's a stiff wind blowing in the window – but just then your telephone rings. The girl picks it up, says hello – listens – and says deliberately into the phone, "I've never owned a pair of black gloves in my life." She hangs up, kneels by the stove again, and just as she lights the match, you glance around very suddenly and see that there's another man in the office, watching every move the girl makes – '

Stahr paused. He picked up his keys and put them in his pocket.

'Go on,' said Boxley, smiling. 'What happens?'

'I don't know,' said Stahr. 'I was just making pictures.'

Boxley felt he was being put in the wrong.

'It's just melodrama,' he said.

'Not necessarily,' said Stahr. 'In any case, nobody has moved violently or talked cheap dialogue or had any facial expression at all. There was only one bad line, and a writer like you could improve it. But you were interested.'

'What was the nickel for?' asked Boxley evasively.

'I don't know,' said Stahr. Suddenly he laughed. 'Oh, yes – the nickel was for the movies.'

The two invisible attendants seemed to release Boxley. He relaxed, leaned back in his chair and laughed.

'What in hell do you pay me for?' he demanded. 'I don't understand the damn stuff.'

'You will,' said Stahr grinning, 'or you wouldn't have asked about the nickel.'

* * *

A dark saucer-eyed man was waiting in the outer office as they came out.

'Mr Boxley, this is Mr Mike Van Dyke,' Stahr said. 'What is it, Mike?'

'Nothing,' Mike said. 'I just came up to see if you were real.'

'Why don't you go to work?' Stahr said. 'I haven't had a laugh in the rushes for days.'

'I'm afraid of a nervous breakdown.'

'You ought to keep in form,' Stahr said. 'Let's see you peddle your stuff.' He turned to Boxley: 'Mike's a gag man – he was out here when I was in the cradle. Mike, show Mr Boxley a double wing, clutch, kick and scram.'

'Here?' asked Mike.

'Here.'

'There isn't much room. I wanted to ask you about – '

'There's lots of room.'

'Well,' he looked around tentatively. 'You shoot the gun.'

Miss Doolan's assistant, Katy, took a paper bag, blew it open.

'It was a routine,' Mike said to Boxley, ' – back in the Keystone days.' He turned to Stahr: 'Does he know what a routine is?'

'It means an act,' Stahr explained. 'Georgie Jessel talks about "Lincoln's Gettysburg routine".'

Katy poised the neck of the blown-up bag in her mouth. Mike stood with his back to her.

'Ready?' Katy asked. She brought her hands down on the side. Immediately Mike grabbed his bottom with both hands, jumped in the air, slid his feet out on the floor one after the other, remaining in place and flapping his arms twice like a bird –

'Double wing,' said Stahr.

– and then ran out the screen-door which the office boy held open for him and disappeared past the window of the balcony.

'Mr Stahr,' said Miss Doolan, 'Mr Hanson is on the phone from New York.'

Ten minutes later he clicked his dictagraph, and Miss Doolan came in. There was a male star waiting to see him in the outer office, Miss Doolan said.

'Tell him I went out by the balcony,' Stahr advised her.

'All right. He's been in four times this week. He seems very anxious.'

'Did he give you any hint of what he wanted? Isn't it something he can see Mr Brady about?'

'He didn't say. You have a conference coming up. Miss Meloney and Mr White are outside. Mr Broaca is next door in Mr Reinmund's office.'

'Send Mr Roderiguez in,' said Stahr. 'Tell him I can see him only for a minute.'

When the handsome actor came in, Stahr remained standing.

'What is it that can't wait?' he asked pleasantly.

The actor waited carefully till Miss Doolan had gone out.

'Monroe, I'm through,' he said. 'I had to see you.'

'Through!' said Stahr. 'Have you seen *Variety*? Your picture's held over at Roxy's and did thirty-seven thousand in Chicago last week.'

'That's the worst of it. That's the tragedy. I get everything I want, and now it means nothing.'

'Well, go on, explain.'

'There's nothing between Esther and me any more. There never can be again.'

'A row.'

'Oh, no – worse – I can't bear to mention it. My head's in a daze. I wander around like a madman. I go through my part as if I was asleep.'

'I haven't noticed it,' said Stahr. 'You were great in your rushes yesterday.'

'Was I? That just shows you nobody ever guesses.'

'Are you trying to tell me that you and Esther are separating?'

'I suppose it'll come to that. Yes – inevitably – it will.'

'What was it?' demanded Stahr impatiently. 'Did she come in without knocking?'

'Oh, there's nobody else. It's just – me. I'm through.'

Stahr got it suddenly.

'How do you know?'

'It's been true for six weeks.'

'It's your imagination,' said Stahr. 'Have you been to a doctor?'

The actor nodded.

'I've tried everything. I even – one day in desperation I went down to – to Claris. But it was hopeless. I'm washed up.'

Stahr had an impish temptation to tell him to go to Brady about it. Brady handled all matters of public relations. Or was this private relations. He turned away for a moment, got his face in control, turned back.

'I've been to Pat Brady,' said the star, as if guessing the thought. 'He gave me a lot of phoney advice and I tried it all, but nothing doing. Esther and I sit opposite each other at dinner, and I'm ashamed to look at her. She's been a good sport about it, but I'm ashamed. I'm ashamed all day long. I think *Rainy Day* grossed twenty-five thousand in Des Moines and broke all records in St Louis and did twenty-seven thousand in Kansas City. My fan mail's way up, and there I am afraid to go home at night, afraid to go to bed.'

Stahr began to be faintly oppressed. When the actor first came in,

Stahr had intended to invite him to a cocktail party, but now it scarcely seemed appropriate. What would he want with a cocktail party with this hanging over him? In his mind's eye he saw him wandering haunted from guest to guest with a cocktail in his hand and his grosses up twenty-seven thousand.

'So I came to you, Monroe. I never saw a situation where you didn't know a way out. I said to myself: even if he advises me to kill myself, I'll ask Monroe.'

The buzzer sounded on Stahr's desk – he switched on the dictagraph and heard Miss Doolan's voice.

'Five minutes, Mr Stahr.'

'I'm sorry,' said Stahr. 'I'll need a few minutes more.'

'Five hundred girls marched to my house from the high school,' the actor said gloomily, 'and I stood behind the curtains and watched them. I couldn't go out.'

'You sit down,' said Stahr. 'We'll take plenty of time and talk this over.'

In the outer office, two members of the conference group had already waited ten minutes – Wylie White and Jane Meloney. The latter was a dried-up little blonde of fifty about whom one could hear the fifty assorted opinions of Hollywood – 'a sentimental dope', 'the best writer on construction in Hollywood', 'a veteran', 'that old hack', 'the smartest woman on the lot', 'the cleverest plagiarist in the biz'; and, of course, in addition she was variously described as a nymphomaniac, a virgin, a pushover, a Lesbian, and a faithful wife. Without being an old maid, she was, like most self-made women, rather old maidish. She had ulcers of the stomach, and her salary was over a hundred thousand a year. A complicated treatise could be written on whether she was 'worth it' or more than that or nothing at all. Her value lay in such ordinary assets as the bare fact that she was a woman and adaptable, quick and trustworthy, 'knew the game', and was without egotism. She had been a great friend of Minna's, and over a period of years Stahr had managed to stifle what amounted to a sharp physical revulsion.

She and Wylie waited in silence – occasionally addressing a remark to Miss Doolan. Every few minutes Reinmund, the supervisor, called up from his office, where he and Broaca, the director, were waiting. After ten minutes Stahr's button went on, and Miss Doolan called Reinmund and Broaca; simultaneously Stahr and the actor came out of Stahr's office with Stahr holding the man's arm. He was so wound up now that when Wylie White asked him how he was he opened his mouth and began to tell him then and there.

'Oh, I've had an awful time,' he said, but Stahr interrupted sharply.

'No, you haven't. Now you go along and do the role the way I said.'

'Thank you, Monroe.'

Jane Meloney looked after him without speaking.

'Somebody been catching flies on him?' she asked – a phrase for stealing scenes.

'I'm sorry I kept you waiting,' Stahr said. 'Come on in.'

* * *

It was noon already and the conferees were entitled to exactly an hour of Stahr's time. No less, for such a conference could only be interrupted by a director who was held up in his shooting; seldom much more, because every eight days the company must release a production as complex and costly as Reinhardt's *Miracle*.

Occasionally, less often than five years ago, Stahr would work all through the night on a single picture. But after such a spree he felt badly for days. If he could go from problem to problem, there was a certain rebirth of vitality with each change. And like those sleepers who can wake whenever they wish, he had set his psychological clock to run one hour.

The cast assembled included, besides the writers, Reinmund, one of the most favoured of the supervisors, and John Broaca, the picture's director.

Broaca, on the surface, was all engineer – large and without nerves, quietly resolute, popular. He was an ignoramus, and Stahr often caught him making the same scenes over and over – one scene about a rich young girl occurred in all his pictures with the same action, the same business. A bunch of large dogs entered the room and jumped around the girl. Later the girl went to a stable and slapped a horse on the rump. The explanation was probably not Freudian; more likely that at a drab moment in youth he had looked through a fence and seen a beautiful girl with dogs and horses. As a trademark for glamour it was stamped on his brain forever.

Reinmund was a handsome young opportunist, with a fairly good education. Originally a man of some character, he was being daily forced by his anomalous position into devious ways of acting and thinking. He was a bad man now, as men go. At thirty he had none of the virtues which either gentile Americans or Jews are taught to think admirable.

But he got his pictures out in time, and by manifesting an almost homosexual fixation on Stahr, seemed to have dulled Stahr's usual acuteness. Stahr liked him – considered him a good all-round man.

Wylie White, of course, in any country would have been recognisable as an intellectual of the second order. He was civilised and voluble, both simple and acute, half dazed and half saturnine. His jealousy of Stahr showed only in unguarded flashes, and was mingled with admiration and even affection.

'The production date for this picture is two weeks from Saturday,' said Stahr. 'I think basically it's all right – much improved.'

Reinmund and the two writers exchanged a glance of congratulation.

'Except for one thing,' said Stahr, thoughtfully. 'I don't see why it should be produced at all, and I've decided to put it away.'

There was a moment of shocked silence – and then murmurs of protest, stricken queries.

'It's not your fault,' Stahr said. 'I thought there was something there that wasn't there – that was all.' He hesitated, looking regretfully at Reinmund: 'It's too bad – it was a good play. We paid fifty thousand for it.'

'What's the matter with it, Monroe?' asked Broaca bluntly.

'Well, it hardly seems worth while to go into it,' said Stahr.

Reinmund and Wylie White were both thinking of the professional effect on them. Reinmund had two pictures to his account this year – but Wylie White needed a credit to start his comeback to the scene. Jane Meloney was watching Stahr closely from little skull-like eyes.

'Couldn't you give us some clue,' Reinmund asked. 'This is a good deal of a blow, Monroe.'

'I just wouldn't put Margaret Sullavan in it,' said Stahr. 'Or Colman either. I wouldn't advise them to play it –'

'Specifically, Monroe,' begged Wylie White. 'What didn't you like? The scenes? the dialogue? the humour? construction?'

Stahr picked up the script from his desk, let it fall as if it were, physically, too heavy to handle.

'I don't like the people,' he said. 'I wouldn't like to meet them – if I knew they were going to be somewhere, I'd go somewhere else.'

Reinmund smiled, but there was worry in his eyes.

'Well, that's a damning criticism,' he said. 'I thought the people were rather interesting.'

'So did I,' said Broaca. 'I thought Em was very sympathetic.'

'Did you?' asked Stahr sharply. 'I could just barely believe she was alive. And when I came to the end, I said to myself, "So what?" '

'There must be something to do,' Reinmund said. 'Naturally we feel bad about this. This is the structure we agreed on – '

'But it's not the story,' said Stahr. 'I've told you many times that the first thing I decide is the *kind* of story I want. We change in every other regard, but once that is set we've got to work towards it with every line and movement. This is not the kind of story I want. The story we bought had shine and glow – it was a happy story. This is all full of doubt and hesitation. The hero and heroine stop loving each other over trifles – then they start up again over trifles. After the first sequence, you don't care if she never sees him again or he her.'

'That's my fault,' said Wylie suddenly. 'You see, Monroe, I don't think stenographers have the same dumb admiration for their bosses they had in 1929. They've been laid off – they've seen their bosses jittery. The world has moved on, that's all.'

Stahr looked at him impatiently, gave a short nod.

'That's not under discussion,' he said. 'The premise of this story is that the girl did have a dumb admiration for her boss, if you want to call it that. And there wasn't any evidence that he'd ever been jittery. When you make her doubt him in any way, you have a different kind of story. Or rather you haven't anything at all. These people are extraverts – get that straight – and I want them to extravert all over the lot. When I want to do a Eugene O'Neill play, I'll buy one.'

Jane Meloney, who had never taken her eyes off Stahr, knew it was going to be all right now. If he had really been going to abandon the picture, he wouldn't have gone at it like this. She had been in this game longer than any of them except Broaca, with whom she had had a three-day affair twenty years ago.

Stahr turned to Reinmund.

'You ought to have understood from the casting, Reiny, what kind of a picture I wanted. I started marking the lines that Corliss and McKelway couldn't say and got tired of it. Remember this in the future – if I order a limousine, I want that kind of car. And the fastest midget racer you ever saw wouldn't do. Now – ' He looked around. ' – shall we go any further? Now that I've told you I don't even like the kind of picture this is? Shall we go on? We've got two weeks. At the end of that time I'm going to put Corliss and McKelway into this or something else – is it worth while?'

'Well, naturally,' said Reinmund, 'I think it is. I feel bad about this. I should have warned Wylie. I thought he had some good ideas.'

'Monroe's right,' said Broaca bluntly. 'I felt this was wrong all the time, but I couldn't put my finger on it.'

Wylie and Rose looked at him contemptuously and exchanged a glance.

'Do you writers think you can get hot on it again?' asked Stahr, not unkindly. 'Or shall I try somebody fresh?'

'I'd like another shot,' said Wylie.

'How about you, Jane?'

She nodded briefly.

'What do you think of the girl?' asked Stahr.

'Well – naturally I'm prejudiced in her favour.'

'You better forget it,' said Stahr warningly. 'Ten million Americans would put thumbs down on that girl if she walked on the screen. We've got an hour and twenty-five minutes on the screen – you show a woman being unfaithful to a man for one-third of that time and you've given the impression that she's one-third whore.'

'Is that a big proportion?' asked Jane slyly, and they laughed.

'It is for me,' said Stahr thoughtfully, 'even if it wasn't for the Hays office. If you want to paint a scarlet letter on her back, it's all right, but that's another story. Not this story. This is a future wife and mother. However – *however* – '

He pointed his pencil at Wylie White.

' – this has as much passion as that Oscar on my desk.'

'What the hell!' said Wylie. 'She's full of it. Why she goes to – '

'She's loose enough,' said Stahr, ' – but that's all. There's one scene in the play better than all this you cooked up, and you've left it out. When she's trying to make the time pass by changing her watch.'

'It didn't seem to fit,' Wylie apologised.

'Now,' said Stahr, 'I've got about fifty ideas. I'm going to call Miss Doolan.' He pressed a button. ' – And if there's anything you don't understand, speak up – '

Miss Doolan slid in almost imperceptibly. Pacing the floor swiftly, Stahr began. In the first place he wanted to tell them what kind of girl she was – what kind of a girl he approved of here. She was a perfect girl with a few small faults as in the play, but a perfect girl not because the public wanted her that way but because it was the kind of girl that he, Stahr, liked to see in this sort of picture. Was that clear? It was no character role. She stood for health, vitality, ambition, and love. What gave the play its importance was entirely a situation in which she found herself. She became possessed of a secret that affected a great many lives. There was a right thing and a wrong thing to do – at first it was not plain which was which, but when it was, she went right away and did it. That was the kind of story this was – thin, clean, and shining. No doubts.

'She has never heard the word labour troubles,' he said with a sigh. 'She might be living in 1929. Is it plain what kind of girl I want?'

'It's very plain, Monroe.'

'Now about the things she does,' said Stahr. 'At all times, at all moments when she is on the screen in our sight, she wants to sleep with Ken Willard. Is that plain, Wylie?'

'Passionately plain.'

'Whatever she does, it is in place of sleeping with Ken Willard. If she walks down the street she is walking to sleep with Ken Willard, if she eats her food it is to give her strength to sleep with Ken Willard. *But* at no time do you give the impression that she would even consider sleeping with Ken Willard unless they were properly sanctified. I'm ashamed of having to tell you these kindergarten facts, but they have somehow leaked out of the story.'

He opened the script and began to go through it page by page. Miss Doolan's notes would be typed in quintuplicate and given to them, but Jane Meloney made notes of her own. Broaca put his hand up to his half-closed eyes – he could remember 'when a director was something out here', when writers were gag-men or eager and ashamed young reporters full of whiskey – a director was all there was then. No supervisor – no Stahr.

He started wide-awake as he heard his name.

'It would be nice, John, if you could put the boy on a pointed roof and let him walk around and keep the camera on him. You might get a nice feeling – not danger, not suspense, not pointing for anything – a kid on the roof in the morning.'

Broaca brought himself back in the room.

'All right,' he said, ' – just an element of danger.'

'Not exactly,' said Stahr. 'He doesn't start to fall off the roof. Break into the next scene with it.'

'Through the window,' suggested Jane Meloney. 'He could climb in his sister's window.'

'That's a good transition,' said Stahr. 'Right into the diary scene.'

Broaca was wide-awake now.

'I'll shoot up at him,' he said. 'Let him go away from the camera. Just a fixed shot from quite a distance – let him go away from the camera. Don't follow him. Pick him up in a close shot and let him go away again. No attention on him except against the whole roof and the sky.' He liked the shot – it was a director's shot that didn't come up on every page any more. He might use a crane – it would be cheaper in the end than building the roof on the ground with a process sky. That was one thing about Stahr – the literal sky was the limit. He had worked with Jews too long to believe legends that they were small with money.

'In the third sequence have him hit the priest,' Stahr said.

'What!' Wylie cried, ' – and have the Catholics on our neck.'

'I've talked to Joe Breen. Priests have been hit. It doesn't reflect on them.'

His quiet voice ran on – stopped abruptly as Miss Doolan glanced at the clock.

'Is that too much to do before Monday?' he asked Wylie.

Wylie looked at Jane and she looked back, not even bothering to nod. He saw their weekend melting away, but he was a different man from when he entered the room. When you were paid fifteen hundred a week, emergency work was one thing you did not skimp, not when your picture was threatened. As a 'free lance' writer Wylie had failed from lack of caring, but here was Stahr to care, for all of them. The effect would not wear off when he left the office – nor anywhere within the walls of the lot. He felt a great purposefulness. The mixture of common sense, wise sensibility, theatrical ingenuity, and a certain half-naïve conception of the common weal which Stahr had just stated aloud, inspired him to do his part, to get his block of stone in place, even if the effort were foredoomed, the result as dull as a pyramid.

Out of the window Jane Meloney watched the trickle streaming towards the commissary. She would have her lunch in her office and knit a few rows while it came. The man was coming at one-fifteen with the French perfume smuggled over the Mexican border. That was no sin – it was like Prohibition.

Broaca watched as Reinmund fawned upon Stahr. He sensed that Reinmund was on his way up. He received seven hundred and fifty a week for his partial authority over directors, writers, and stars who got much more. He wore a pair of cheap English shoes he had bought near the Beverly Wilshire, and Broaca hoped they hurt his feet, but soon now he would order his shoes from Peel's and put away his little green Alpine hat with a feather. Broaca was years ahead of him. He had a fine record in the war, but he had never felt quite the same with himself since he had let Ike Franklin strike him in the face with his open hand.

There was smoke in the room, and behind it, behind his great desk, Stahr was withdrawing further and further, in all courtesy, still giving Reinmund an ear and Miss Doolan an ear. The conference was over.

* * *

[*Stahr was to have received the Danish Prince Agge, who wanted 'to learn about pictures from the beginning' and who in the author's cast of characters is described as an 'early Fascist'.*]

'Mr Marcus calling from New York,' said Miss Doolan.

'What do you mean?' demanded Stahr. 'Why, I saw him here last night.'

'Well, he's on the phone – it's a New York call and Miss Jacobs' voice. It's his office.'

Stahr laughed.

'I'm seeing him at lunch,' he said. 'There's no aeroplane fast enough to take him there.'

Miss Doolan returned to the phone. Stahr lingered to hear the outcome.

'It's all right,' said Miss Doolan presently. 'It was a mistake. Mr Marcus called East this morning to tell them about the quake and the flood on the back lot, and it seems he asked them to ask you about it. It was a new secretary who didn't understand Mr Marcus. I think she got mixed up.'

'I think she did,' said Stahr grimly.

Prince Agge did not understand either of them, but, looking for the fabulous, he felt it was something triumphantly American. Mr Marcus, whose quarters could be seen across the way, had called his New York office to ask Stahr about the flood. The Prince imagined some intricate relationship without realising that the transaction had taken place entirely within the once brilliant steel-trap mind of Mr Marcus, which was intermittently slipping.

'I think she was a very new secretary,' repeated Stahr. 'Any other messages?'

'Mr Robinson called in,' Miss Doolan said, as she started for the commissary. 'One of the women told him her name, but he's forgotten it – he thinks it was Smith or Brown or Jones.'

'That's a great help.'

'And he remembers she says she just moved to Los Angeles.'

'I remember she had a silver belt,' Stahr said, 'with stars cut out of it.'

'I'm still trying to find out more about Pete Zavras. I talked to his wife.'

'What did she say?'

'Oh, they've had an awful time – given up their house – she's been sick – '

'Is the eye-trouble hopeless?'

'She didn't seem to know anything about the state of his eyes. She didn't even know he was going blind.'

'That's funny.'

He thought about it on the way to luncheon, but it was as confusing as the actor's trouble this morning. Troubles about people's health didn't seem within his range – he gave no thought to his own. In the lane beside the commissary he stepped back as an open electric truck crammed with girls in the bright costumes of the Regency came rolling in from the back lot. The dresses were fluttering in the wind, the young painted faces looked at him curiously, and he smiled as it went by.

* * *

Eleven men and their guest, Prince Agge, sat at lunch in the private dining-room of the studio commissary. They were the money men – they were the rulers; and unless there was a guest, they ate in broken silence, sometimes asking questions about each other's wives and children, sometimes discharging a single absorption from the forefront of their consciousness. Eight out of the ten were Jews – five of the ten were foreign-born, including a Greek and an Englishman; and they had all known each other for a long time: there was a rating in the group, from old Marcus down to old Leanbaum, who had bought the most fortunate block of stock in the business and never was allowed to spend over a million a year producing.

Old Marcus still managed to function with disquieting resilience. Some never-atrophying instinct warned him of danger, of gangings up against him – he was never so dangerous himself as when others considered him surrounded. His grey face had attained such immobility that even those who were accustomed to watch the reflex of the inner corner of his eye could no longer see it. Nature had grown a little white whisker there to conceal it; his armour was complete.

As he was the oldest, Stahr was the youngest of the group – not by many years at this date, though he had first sat with most of these men when he was a boy wonder of twenty-two. Then, more than now, he had been a money man among money men. Then he had been able to figure costs in his head with a speed and accuracy that dazzled them – for they were not wizards or even experts in that regard, despite the popular conception of Jews in finance. Most of them owed their success to different and incompatible qualities. But in a group a tradition carries along the less adept, and they were content to look at Stahr for the sublimated auditing, and experience a sort of glow as if they had done it themselves, like rooters at a football game.

Stahr, as will presently be seen, had grown away from that particular gift, though it was always there.

Prince Agge sat between Stahr and Mort Fleishacker, the company lawyer, and across from Joe Popolos the theatre owner. He was hostile to Jews in a vague general way that he tried to cure himself of. As a turbulent man, serving his time in the Foreign Legion, he thought that Jews were too fond of their own skins. But he was willing to concede that they might be different in America under different circumstances, and certainly he found Stahr was much of a man in every way. For the rest – he thought most business men were dull dogs – for final reference he reverted always to the blood of Bernadotte in his veins.

My father – I will call him Mr Brady, as Prince Agge did when he told me of this luncheon – was worried about a picture, and when Leanbaum went out early, he came up and took his chair opposite.

'How about the South America picture idea, Monroe?' he asked.

Prince Agge noticed a blink of attention towards them as distinct as if a dozen pairs of eyelashes had made the sound of batting wings. Then silence again.

'We're going ahead with it,' said Stahr.

'With that same budget?' Brady asked.

Stahr nodded.

'It's out of proportion,' said Brady. 'There won't be any miracle in these bad times – no *Hell's Angels* or *Ben Hur*, when you throw it away and get it back.'

Probably the attack was planned, for Popolos, the Greek, took up the matter in a sort of double talk.

'It's not adoptable, Monroe, in as we wish adopt to this times in as it changes. It what could be done as we run the gamut of prosperity is scarcely conceptuable now.'

'What do you think, Mr Marcus?' asked Stahr.

All eyes followed his down the table, but, as if forewarned, Mr

Marcus had already signalled his private waiter behind him that he wished to rise, and was even now in a basket-like position in the waiter's arms. He looked at them with such helplessness that it was hard to realise that in the evenings he sometimes went dancing with his young Canadian girl.

'Monroe is our production genius,' he said. 'I count upon Monroe and lean heavily upon him. I have not seen the flood myself.'

There was a moment of silence as he moved from the room.

'There's not a two million dollar gross in the country now,' said Brady.

'Is not,' agreed Popolos. 'Even as if so you could grab them by the head and push them by and in, is not.'

'Probably not,' agreed Stahr. He paused as if to make sure that all were listening. 'I think we can count on a million and a quarter from the road-show. Perhaps a million and a half altogether. And a quarter of a million abroad.'

Again there was silence – this time puzzled, a little confused. Over his shoulder Stahr asked the waiter to be connected with his office on the phone.

'But your budget?' said Fleishacker. 'Your budget is seventeen hundred and fifty thousand, I understand. And your expectations only add up to that without profits.'

'Those aren't my expectations,' said Stahr. 'We're not sure of more than a million and a half.'

The room had grown so motionless that Prince Agge could hear a grey chunk of ash fall from a cigar in mid-air. Fleishacker started to speak, his face fixed with amazement, but a phone had been handed over Stahr's shoulder.

'Your office, Mr Stahr.'

'Oh, yes – oh, hello, Miss Doolan. I've figured it out about Zavras. It's one of those lousy rumours – I'll bet my shirt on it . . . Oh, you did. Good . . . good. Now here's what to do: send him to my oculist this afternoon – Dr John Kennedy – and have him get a report and have it photostatted – you understand?'

He hung up – turned with a touch of passion to the table at large.

'Did any of you ever hear a story that Pete Zavras was going blind?'

There were a couple of nods. But most of those present were poised breathlessly on whether Stahr had slipped on his figures a minute before.

'It's pure bunk. He says he's never even been to an oculist – never knew why the studios turned against him,' said Stahr. 'Somebody didn't like him or somebody talked too much, and he's been out of work for a year.'

There was a conventional murmur of sympathy. Stahr signed the check and made as though to get up.

'Excuse me, Monroe,' said Fleishacker persistently, while Brady and Popolos watched. 'I'm fairly new here, and perhaps I fail to comprehend implicitly and explicitly.' He was talking fast, but the veins on his forehead bulged with pride at the big words from NYU. 'Do I understand you to say you expect to gross a quarter million short of your budget?'

'It's a quality picture,' said Stahr with assumed innocence.

It had dawned on them all now, but they still felt there was a trick in it. Stahr really thought it would make money. No one in his senses –

'For two years we've played safe,' said Stahr. 'It's time we made a picture that'll lose some money. Write it off as goodwill – this'll bring in new customers.'

Some of them still thought he meant it was a flyer and a favourable one, but he left them in no doubt.

'It'll lose money,' he said as he stood up, his jaw just slightly out and his eyes smiling and shining. 'It would be a bigger miracle than *Hell's Angels* if it broke even. But we have a certain duty to the public, as Pat Brady has said at Academy dinners. It's a good thing for the production schedule to slip in a picture that'll lose money.'

He nodded at Prince Agge. As the latter made his bows quickly, he tried to take in with a last glance the general effect of what Stahr had said, but he could tell nothing. The eyes, not so much downcast as fixed upon an indefinite distance just above the table, were all blinking quickly now, but there was not a whisper in the room.

* * *

Coming out of the private dining-room they passed through a corner of the commissary proper. Prince Agge drank it in – eagerly. It was gay with gypsies and with citizens and soldiers, with the sideburns and braided coats of the First Empire. From a little distance they were men who lived and walked a hundred years ago, and Agge wondered how he and the men of his time would look as extras in some future costume picture.

Then he saw Abraham Lincoln, and his whole feeling suddenly changed. He had been brought up in the dawn of Scandinavian socialism when Nicolay's biography was much read. He had been told Lincoln was a great man whom he should admire, and he hated him instead, because he was forced upon him. But now seeing him sitting here, his legs crossed, his kindly face fixed on a forty-cent dinner, including dessert, his shawl wrapped around him as if to protect himself from the erratic air-cooling – now Prince Agge, who was in America at last, stared as a tourist at the mummy of Lenin in the Kremlin. This, then, was Lincoln. Stahr had walked on far ahead of him, turned waiting for him – but still Agge stared.

This, then, he thought, was what they all meant to be.

Lincoln suddenly raised a triangle of pie and jammed it in his mouth, and, a little frightened, Prince Agge hurried to join Stahr.

'I hope you're getting what you want,' said Stahr, feeling he had neglected him. 'We'll have some rushes in half an hour and then you can go on to as many sets as you want.'

'I should rather stay with you,' said Prince Agge.

'I'll see what there is for me,' said Stahr. 'Then we'll go on together.'

There was the Japanese consul on the release of a spy story which might offend the national sensibilities of Japan. There were phone calls and telegrams. There was some further information from Robby.

'Now he remembers the name of the woman. He's sure it was Smith,' said Miss Doolan. 'He asked her if she wanted to come on the lot and get some dry shoes, and she said no – so she can't sue.'

'That's pretty bad for a total recall – "Smith". That's a great help.' He thought a moment: 'Ask the phone company for a list of Smiths that have taken new phones here in the last month. Call them all.'

'All right.'

Chapter 4

'How are you, Monroe,' said Red Ridingwood. 'I'm glad you came down.'

Stahr walked past him, heading across the great stage towards the set of a brilliant room that would be used tomorrow. Director Ridingwood followed, realising after a moment that, however fast he walked Stahr managed to be a step or two ahead. He recognised the indication of displeasure – he had used it himself. He had had his own studio once and he had used everything. There was no stop Stahr could pull that would surprise him. His task was the delivery of situations, and Stahr by effective business could not outplay him on his own grounds. Goldwyn had once interfered with him, and Ridingwood had led Goldwyn into trying to act out a part in front of fifty people – with the result that he had anticipated: his own authority had been restored.

Stahr reached the brilliant set and stopped.

'It's no good,' said Ridingwood. 'No imagination. I don't care how you light it – '

'Why did you call me about it?' Stahr asked, standing close to him. 'Why didn't you take it up with Art?'

'I didn't ask you to come down, Monroe.'

'You wanted to be your own supervisor.'

'I'm sorry, Monroe,' said Ridingwood patiently, 'but I didn't ask you to come down.'

Stahr turned suddenly and walked back towards the camera set-up. The eyes and open mouths of a group of visitors moved momentarily off the heroine of the picture, took in Stahr, and then moved vacantly back to the heroine again. They were Knights of Columbus. They had seen the host carried in procession, but this was the dream made flesh.

Stahr stopped beside her chair. She wore a low gown which displayed the bright eczema of her chest and back. Before each take, the blemished surface was plastered over with an emollient, which was removed immediately after the take. Her hair was of the colour and viscosity of drying blood, but there was starlight that actually photographed in her eyes.

Before Stahr could speak, he heard a helpful voice behind him: 'She's radiunt. Absolutely radiunt.'

It was an assistant director, and the intention was delicate compliment. The actress was being complimented so that she did not have to strain her poor skin to bend and hear. Stahr was being complimented for having her under contract. Ridingwood was being remotely complimented.

'Everything all right?' Stahr asked her pleasantly.

'Oh, it's fine,' she agreed, ' – except for the —ing publicity men.'

He winked at her gently.

'We'll keep them away,' he said.

Her name had become currently synonymous with the expression 'bitch'. Presumably she had modelled herself after one of those queens in the Tarzan comics who rule mysteriously over a nation of blacks. She regarded the rest of the world as black. She was a necessary evil, borrowed for a single picture.

Ridingwood walked with Stahr towards the door of the stage.

'Everything's all right,' the director said. 'She's as good as she can be.'

They were out of hearing range, and Stahr stopped suddenly and looked at Red with blazing eyes.

'You've been photographing crap,' he said. 'Do you know what she reminds me of in the rushes – "Miss Foodstuffs".'

'I'm trying to get the best performance – '

'Come along with me,' said Stahr abruptly.

'With you? Shall I tell them to rest?'

'Leave it as it is,' said Stahr, pushing the padded outer door.

His car and chauffeur waited outside. Minutes were precious most days.

'Get in,' said Stahr.

Red knew now it was serious. He even knew all at once what was the matter. The girl had got the whip hand on him the first day with her cold lashing tongue. He was a peace-loving man and he had let her walk through her part cold rather than cause trouble.

Stahr spoke into his thoughts.

'You can't handle her,' he said. 'I told you what I wanted. I wanted her *mean* – and she comes out bored. I'm afraid we'll have to call it off, Red.'

'The picture?'

'No. I'm putting Harley on it.'

'All right, Monroe.'

'I'm sorry, Red. We'll try something else another time.'

The car drew up in front of Stahr's office.

'Shall I finish this take?' said Red.

'It's being done now,' said Stahr grimly. 'Harley's in there.'

'What the hell – '

'He went in when we came out. I had him read the script last night.'

'Now listen, Monroe – '

'It's my busy day, Red,' said Stahr, tersely. 'You lost interest about three days ago.'

It was a sorry mess, Ridingwood thought. It meant he would have slight, very slight loss of position – it probably meant that he could not have a third wife just now as he had planned. There wasn't even the satisfaction of raising a row about it – if you disagreed with Stahr, you did not advertise it. Stahr was his world's great customer, who was always – almost always – right.

'How about my coat?' he asked suddenly. 'I left it over a chair on the set.'

'I know you did,' said Stahr. 'Here it is.'

He was trying so hard to be charitable about Ridingwood's lapse that he had forgotten that he had it in his hand.

* * *

'Mr Stahr's Projection Room' was a miniature picture theatre with four rows of over-stuffed chairs. In front of the front row ran long tables with dim lamps, buzzers, and telephones. Against the wall was an upright piano, left there since the early days of sound. The room had been redecorated and reupholstered only a year before, but already it was ragged again with work and hours.

Here Stahr sat at two-thirty and again at six-thirty watching the lengths of film taken during the day. There was often a savage tensity about the occasion – he was dealing with *faits accomplis* – the net results of months of buying, planning, writing and rewriting, casting, constructing, lighting, rehearsing, and shooting – the fruit of brilliant hunches or of counsels of despair, of lethargy, conspiracy, and sweat. At this point the tortuous manoeuvre was staged and in suspension – there were reports from the battle-line.

Besides Stahr, there were present the representatives of all technical departments, together with the supervisors and unit managers of the pictures concerned. The directors did not appear at these showings – officially because their work was considered done, actually because few punches were pulled here as money ran out in silver spools. There had evolved a delicate staying away.

The staff was already assembled. Stahr came in and took his place quickly, and the murmur of conversation died away. As he sat back and drew his thin knee up beside him in the chair, the lights in the room went out. There was the flare of a match in the back row – then silence.

On the screen a troop of French Canadians pushed their canoes up a rapids. The scene had been photographed in a studio tank, and at the end of each take, after the director's voice could be heard saying 'Cut,' the actors on the screen relaxed and wiped their brows and sometimes laughed hilariously – and the water in the tank stopped flowing and the illusion ceased. Except to name his choice from each set of takes and to remark that it was 'a good process', Stahr made no comment.

The next scene, still in the rapids, called for dialogue between the Canadian girl (Claudette Colbert) and the *courrier du bois* (Ronald Colman), with her looking down at him from a canoe. After a few strips had run through, Stahr spoke up suddenly.

'Has the tank been dismantled?'

'Yes, sir.'

'Monroe – they needed it for – '

Stahr cut in peremptorily.

'Have it set up again right away. Let's have that second take again.'

The lights went on momentarily. One of the unit managers left his chair and came and stood in front of Stahr.

'A beautifully acted scene thrown away,' raged Stahr quietly. 'It wasn't centred. The camera was set up so it caught the beautiful top of Claudette's head all the time she was talking. That's just what we want, isn't it? That's just what people go to see – the top of a beautiful girl's head. Tell Tim he could have saved wear and tear by using her stand-in.'

The lights went out again. The unit manager squatted by Stahr's chair to be out of the way. The take was run again.

'Do you see now?' asked Stahr. 'And there's a hair in the picture – there on the right, see it? Find out if it's in the projector or the film.'

At the very end of the take, Claudette Colbert slowly lifted her head, revealing her great liquid eyes.

'That's what we should have had all the way,' said Stahr. 'She gave a fine performance too. See if you can fit it in tomorrow or late this afternoon.'

Pete Zavras would not have made a slip like that. There were not six cameramen in the industry you could entirely trust.

The lights went on; the supervisor and unit manager for that picture went out.

'Monroe, this stuff was shot yesterday – it came through late last night.'

The room darkened. On the screen appeared the head of Siva, immense and imperturbable, oblivious to the fact that in a few hours it was to be washed away in a flood. Around it milled a crowd of the faithful.

'When you take that scene again,' said Stahr suddenly, 'put a couple of little kids up on top. You better check about whether it's reverent or not, but I think it's all right. Kids'll do anything.'

'Yes, Monroe.'

A silver belt with stars cut out of it . . . Smith, Jones, or Brown . . . Personal – will the woman with the silver belt who –?

With another picture the scene shifted to New York, a gangster story, and suddenly Stahr became restive.

'That scene's trash,' he called suddenly in the darkness. 'It's badly written, it's miscast, it accomplishes nothing. Those types aren't tough. They look like a lot of dressed-up lollipops – what the hell is the matter, Lee?'

'The scene was written on the set this morning,' said Lee Kapper. 'Burton wanted to get all the stuff on Stage 6.'

'Well – it's trash. And so is this one. There's no use printing stuff like that. She doesn't believe what she's saying – neither does Cary. "I love you" in a close-up – they'll cluck you out of the house! And the girl's overdressed.'

In the darkness a signal was given, the projector stopped, the lights went on. The room waited in utter silence. Stahr's face was expressionless.

'Who wrote the scene?' he asked after a minute.

'Wylie White.'

'Is he sober?'

'Sure he is.'

Stahr considered.

'Put about four writers on that scene tonight,' he said. 'See who we've got. Is Sidney Howard here yet?'

'He got in this morning.'

'Talk to him about it. Explain to him what I want there. The girl is in deadly terror – she's stalling. It's as simple as that. People don't have three emotions at once. And Kapper – '

The art director leaned forward out of the second row.

'Yeah.'

'There's something the matter with that set.'

There were little glances exchanged all over the room.

'What is it, Monroe?'

'You tell *me*,' said Stahr. 'It's crowded. It doesn't carry your eye out. It looks cheap.'

'It wasn't.'

'I know it wasn't. There's not much the matter, but there's something. Go over and take a look tonight. It may be too much furniture – or the wrong kind. Perhaps a window would help. Couldn't you force the perspective in that hall a little more?'

'I'll see what I can do.' Kapper edged his way out of the row, looking at his watch.

'I'll have to get at it right away,' he said. 'I'll work tonight and we'll put it up in the morning.'

'All right. Lee, you can shoot around those scenes, can't you?'

'I think so, Monroe.'

'I take the blame for this. Have you got the fight stuff?'

'Coming up now.'

Stahr nodded. Kapper hurried out, and the room went dark again. On the screen four men staged a terrific socking match in a cellar. Stahr laughed.

'Look at Tracy,' he said. 'Look at him go down after that guy. I bet he's been in a few.'

The men fought over and over. Always the same fight. Always at the end they faced each other smiling, sometimes touching the opponent in a friendly gesture on the shoulder. The only one in danger was the stunt man, a pug who could have murdered the other three. He was in danger only if they swung wild and didn't follow the blows he had taught them. Even so, the youngest actor was afraid for his face and the director had covered his flinches with ingenious angles and interpositions.

And then two men met endlessly in a door, recognised each other, and went on. They met, they started, they went on.

Then a little girl read underneath a tree with a boy reading on a limb of the tree above. The little girl was bored and wanted to talk to the boy. He would pay no attention. The core of the apple he was eating fell on the little girl's head.

A voice spoke up out of the darkness: 'It's pretty long, isn't it, Monroe?'

'Not a bit,' said Stahr. 'It's nice. It has nice feeling.'

'I just thought it was long.'

'Sometimes ten feet can be too long – sometimes a scene two hundred feet long can be too short. I want to speak to the cutter before he touches this scene – this is something that'll be remembered in the picture.'

The oracle had spoken. There was nothing to question or argue. Stahr must be right always, not most of the time, but always – or the structure would melt down like gradual butter.

Another hour passed. Dreams hung in fragments at the far end of the room, suffered analysis, passed – to be dreamed in crowds, or else discarded. The end was signalled by two tests, a character man and a girl. After the rushes, which had a tense rhythm of their own, the tests were smooth and finished; the observers settled in their chairs; Stahr's foot slipped to the floor. Opinions were welcome. One of the technical men let it be known that he would willingly cohabit with the girl; the rest were indifferent.

'Somebody sent up a test of that girl two years ago. She must be getting around – but she isn't getting any better. But the man's good. Can't we use him as the old Russian Prince in *Steppes*?'

'He *is* an old Russian Prince,' said the casting director, 'but he's ashamed of it. He's a Red. And that's one part he says he wouldn't play.'

'It's the only part he could play,' said Stahr.

The lights went on. Stahr rolled his gum into its wrapper and put it in an ashtray. He turned questioningly to his secretary.

'The processes on Stage 2,' she said.

He looked in briefly at the processes, moving pictures taken against a background of other moving pictures by an ingenious device. There was a meeting in Marcus' office on the subject of *Manon* with a happy ending, and Stahr had his say on that as he had had before – it had been making money without a happy ending for a century and a half. He was obdurate – at this time in the afternoon he was at his most fluent and the opposition faded into another subject: they would lend a dozen stars to the benefit for those the quake had made homeless at Long Beach. In a sudden burst of giving, five of them all at once made up a purse of twenty-five thousand dollars. They gave well, but not as poor men give. It was not charity.

At his office there was word from the oculist to whom he had sent Pete Zavras that the cameraman's eyes were 19–20: approximately perfect. He had written a letter that Zavras was having photostated. Stahr walked around his office cockily while Miss Doolan admired him. Prince Agge had dropped in to thank him for his afternoon on the sets, and while they talked, a cryptic word came from a supervisor that some writers named Tarleton had 'found out' and were about to quit.

'These are good writers,' Stahr explained to Prince Agge, 'and we don't have good writers out here.'

'Why, you can hire anyone!' exclaimed his visitor in surprise.

'Oh, we hire them, but when they get out here, they're not good writers – so we have to work with the material we have.'

'Such as what?'

'Anybody that'll accept the system and stay decently sober – we have all sorts of people – disappointed poets, one-hit playwrights – college girls – we put them on an idea in pairs, and if it slows down, we put two more writers working behind them. I've had as many as three pairs working independently on the same idea.'

'Do they like that?'

'Not if they know about it. They're not geniuses – none of them could make as much any other way. But these Tarletons are a husband and wife team from the East – pretty good playwrights. They've just found out they're not alone on the story and it shocks them – shocks their sense of unity – that's the word they'll use.'

'But what does make the – the unity?'

Stahr hesitated – his face was grim except that his eyes twinkled.

'I'm the unity,' he said. 'Come and see us again.'

He saw the Tarletons. He told them he liked their work, looking at Mrs Tarleton as if he could read her handwriting through the typescript. He told them kindly that he was taking them from the picture and putting them on another, where there was less pressure, more time. As he had half expected, they begged to stay on the first picture, seeing a quicker credit, even though it was shared with others. The system was a shame, he admitted – gross, commercial, to be deplored. He had originated it – a fact that he did not mention.

When they had gone, Miss Doolan came in triumphant.

'Mr Stahr, the lady with the belt is on the phone.'

Stahr walked into his office alone and sat down behind his desk and picked up the phone with a great sinking of his stomach. He did not know what he wanted. He had not thought about the matter as he had thought about the matter of Pete Zavras. At first he had only wanted to know if they were 'professional' people, if the woman was an actress who had got herself up to look like Minna, as he had once had a young actress made up like Claudette Colbert and photographed her from the same angles.

'Hello,' he said.

'Hello.'

As he searched the short, rather surprised word for a vibration of last night, the feeling of terror began to steal over him, and he choked it off with an effort of will.

'Well – you were hard to find,' he said. '*Smith* – and you moved here recently. That was all we had. And a silver belt.'

'Oh, yes,' the voice said, still uneasy, unpoised, 'I had on a silver belt last night.'

Now, where from here?

'Who *are* you?' the voice said, with a touch of flurried bourgeois dignity.

'My name is Monroe Stahr,' he said.

A pause. It was a name that never appeared on the screen, and she seemed to have trouble placing it.

'Oh, yes – yes. You were the husband of Minna Davis.'

'Yes.'

Was it a trick? As the whole vision of last night came back to him – the very skin with that peculiar radiance as if phosphorus had touched it – he thought whether it might not be a trick to reach him from somewhere. Not Minna and yet Minna. The curtains blew suddenly into the room, the papers whispered on his desk, and his heart cringed faintly at the intense reality of the day outside his window. If he could go out now this way, what would happen if he saw her again – the starry veiled expression, the mouth strongly formed for poor brave human laughter.

'I'd like to see you. Would you like to come to the studio?'

Again the hesitancy – then a blank refusal.

'Oh, I don't think I ought to. I'm awfully sorry.'

This last was purely formal, a brush-off, a final axe. Ordinary skin-deep vanity came to Stahr's aid, adding persuasion to his urgency.

'I'd like to see you,' he said. 'There's a reason.'

'Well – I'm afraid that – '

'Could I come and see you?'

A pause again, not from hesitation, he felt, but to assemble her answer.

'There's something you don't know,' she said finally.

'Oh, you're probably married,' he was impatient. 'It has nothing to do with that. I asked you to come here openly, bring your husband if you have one.'

'It's – it's quite impossible.'

'Why?'

'I feel silly even talking to you, but your secretary insisted – I thought I'd dropped something in the flood last night and you'd found it.'

'I want very much to see you for five minutes.'

'To put me in the movies?'

'That wasn't my idea.'

There was such a long pause that he thought he had offended her.

'Where could I meet you?' she asked unexpectedly.

'Here? At your house?'

'No – somewhere outside.'

Suddenly Stahr could think of no place. His own house – a restaurant. Where did people meet? – a house of assignation, a cocktail bar?

'I'll meet you somewhere at nine o'clock,' she said.

'That's impossible, I'm afraid.'

'Then never mind.'

'All right, then, nine o'clock, but can we make it near here? There's a drugstore on Wilshire – '

* * *

It was a quarter to six. There were two men outside who had come every day at this time only to be postponed. This was an hour of fatigue – the men's business was not so important that it must be seen to, nor so insignificant that it could be ignored. So he postponed it again and sat motionless at his desk for a moment, thinking about Russia. Not so much about Russia as about the picture about Russia which would consume a hopeless half-hour presently. He knew there were many stories about Russia, not to mention The Story, and he had employed a squad of writers and research men for over a year, but all the stories involved had the wrong feel. He felt it could be told in terms of the American thirteen states, but it kept coming out different, in new terms that opened unpleasant possibilities and problems. He considered he was very fair to Russia – he had no desire to make anything but a sympathetic picture, but it kept turning into a headache.

'Mr Stahr – Mr Drummon's outside, and Mr Kirstoff and Mrs Cornhill, about the Russian picture.'

'All right – send them in.'

Afterwards from six-thirty to seven-thirty he watched the afternoon rushes. Except for his engagement with the girl, he would ordinarily have spent the early evening in the projection room or the dubbing-room, but it had been a late night with the earthquake, and he decided to go to dinner. Coming in through his front office, he found Pete Zavras waiting, his arm in a sling.

'You are the Aeschylus and the Euripides of the moving picture,' said Zavras simply. 'Also the Aristophanes and the Menander.'

He bowed.

'Who are they?' asked Stahr smiling.

'They are my countrymen.'

'I didn't know you made pictures in Greece.'

'You're joking with me, Monroe,' said Zavras. 'I want to say you are as dandy a fellow as they come. You have saved me one hundred per cent.'

'You feel all right now?'

'My arm is nothing. It feels like someone kisses me there. It was worth doing what I did, if this is the outcome.'

'How did you happen to do it here?' Stahr asked curiously.

'Before the Delphic oracle,' said Zavras. 'The Oedipus who solved the riddle. I wish I had my hands on the son-of-a-bitch who started the story.'

'You make me sorry I didn't get an education,' said Stahr.

'It isn't worth a damn,' said Pete. 'I took my baccalaureate in Salonika and look how I ended up.'

'Not quite,' said Stahr.

'If you want anybody's throat cut any time day or night,' said Zavras, 'my number is in the book.'

Stahr closed his eyes and opened them again. Zavras's silhouette had blurred a little against the sun. He hung on to the table behind him and said in an ordinary voice, 'Good luck, Pete.'

The room was almost black, but he made his feet move, following a pattern, into his office and waited till the door clicked shut before he felt for the pills. The water decanter clattered against the table; the glass clacked. He sat down in a big chair, waiting for the benzedrine to take effect before he went to dinner.

* * *

As Stahr walked back from the commissary, a hand waved at him from an open roadster. From the heads showing over the back he recognised a young actor and his girl, and watched them disappear through the gate, already part of the summer twilight. Little by little he was losing the feel of such things, until it seemed that Minna had taken their poignancy with her; his appreciation of splendour was fading so that presently the luxury of eternal mourning would depart. A childish association of Minna with the material heavens made him, when he reached his office, order out his roadster for the first time this year. The big limousine seemed heavy with remembered conferences or exhausted sleep.

Leaving the studio, he was still tense, but the open car pulled the summer evening up close, and he looked at it. There was a moon down at the end of the boulevard, and it was a good illusion that it was a different moon every evening, every year. Other lights shone in Hollywood since Minna's death: in the open markets lemons and grapefruit and green apples slanted a misty glare into the street. Ahead of him the stop-signal of a car winked violet and at another crossing he watched it wink again. Everywhere floodlights raked the sky. On an empty corner two mysterious men moved a gleaming drum in pointless arcs over the heavens.

In the drugstore a woman stood by the candy counter. She was tall, almost as tall as Stahr, and embarrassed. Obviously it was a situation for her, and if Stahr had not looked as he did – most considerate and polite – she would not have gone through with it. They said hello, and walked out without another word, scarcely a glance – yet before they reached the curb Stahr knew: this was just exactly a pretty American woman and nothing more – no beauty like Minna.

'Where are we going?' she asked. 'I thought there'd be a chauffeur. Never mind – I'm a good boxer.'

'Boxer?'

'That didn't sound very polite.' She forced a smile. 'But you people are supposed to be such *horrors*.'

The conception of himself as sinister amused Stahr – then suddenly it failed to amuse him.

'Why did you want to see me?' she asked as she got in.

He stood motionless, wanting to tell her to get out immediately. But she had relaxed in the car, and he knew the unfortunate situation was of his own making – he shut his teeth and walked round to get in. The street lamp fell full upon her face, and it was difficult to believe that this was the girl of last night. He saw no resemblance to Minna at all.

'I'll run you home,' he said. 'Where do you live?'

'Run me home?' She was startled. 'There's no hurry – I'm sorry if I offended you.'

'No. It was nice of you to come. I've been stupid. Last night I had an idea that you were an exact double for someone I knew. It was dark and the light was in my eyes.'

She was offended – he had reproached her for not looking like someone else.

'It was just that!' she said. 'That's funny.'

They rode in silence for a minute.

'You were married to Minna Davis, weren't you?' she said with a flash of intuition. 'Excuse me for referring to it.'

He was driving as fast as he could without making it conspicuous.

'I'm quite a different type from Minna Davis,' she said, '– if that's who you meant. You might have referred to the girl who was with me. She looks more like Minna Davis than I do.'

That was of no interest now. The thing was to get this over quick and forget it.

'Could it have been her?' she asked. 'She lives next door.'

'Not possibly,' he said. 'I remember the silver belt you wore.'

'That was me all right.'

They were northwest of Sunset, climbing one of the canyons through the hills. Lighted bungalows rose along the winding road, and the electric current that animated them sweated into the evening air as radio sound.

'You see that last highest light – Kathleen lives there. I live just over the top of the hill.'

A moment later she said, 'Stop here.'

'I thought you said over the top.'

'I want to stop at Kathleen's.'

'I'm afraid I'm – '

'I want to get out here myself,' she said impatiently.

Stahr slid out after her. She started towards a new little house almost roofed over by a single willow tree, and automatically he followed her to the steps. She rang a bell and turned to say good-night.

'I'm sorry you were disappointed,' she said.

He was sorry for her now – sorry for them both.

'It was my fault. Good-night.'

A wedge of light came out the opening door, and as a girl's voice enquired, 'Who is it?' Stahr looked up.

There she was – face and form and smile against the light from inside. It was Minna's face – the skin with its peculiar radiance as if phosphorus had touched it, the mouth with its warm line that never counted costs – and over all the haunting jollity that had fascinated a generation.

With a leap his heart went out of him as it had the night before, only this time it stayed out there with a vast beneficence.

'Oh, Edna, you can't come in,' the girl said. 'I've been cleaning and the house is full of ammonia smell.'

Edna began to laugh, bold and loud. 'I believe it was you he wanted to see, Kathleen,' she said.

Stahr's eyes and Kathleen's met and tangled. For an instant they made love as no one ever dares to do after. Their glance was slower than an embrace, more urgent than a call.

'He telephoned me,' said Edna. 'It seems he thought – '

Stahr interrupted, stepping forward into the light.

'I was afraid we were rude at the studio, yesterday evening.'

But there were no words for what he really said. She listened closely without shame. Life flared high in them both – Edna seemed at a distance and in darkness.

'You weren't rude,' said Kathleen. A cool wind blew the brown curls around her forehead. 'We had no business there.'

'I hope you'll both,' Stahr said, 'come and make a tour of the studio.'

'Who are you? Somebody important?'

'He was Minna Davis's husband, he's a producer,' said Edna, as if it were a rare joke, ' – and this isn't at all what he just told me. I think he has a crush on you.'

'Shut up, Edna,' said Kathleen sharply.

As if suddenly realising her offensiveness, Edna said, 'Phone me, will you?' and stalked away towards the road. But she carried their secret with her – she had seen a spark pass between them in the darkness.

'I remember you,' Kathleen said to Stahr. 'You got us out of the flood.'

Now what? The other woman was more missed in her absence. They were alone and on too slim a basis for what had passed already. They existed nowhere. His world seemed far away – she had no world at all except the idol's head, the half-open door.

'You're Irish,' he said, trying to build one for her.

She nodded.

'I've lived in London a long time – I didn't think you could tell.'

The wild green eyes of a bus sped up the road in the darkness. They were silent until it went by.

'Your friend Edna didn't like me,' he said. 'I think it was the word Producer.'

'She's just come out here, too. She's a silly creature who means no harm. *I* shouldn't be afraid of you.'

She searched his face. She thought, like everyone, that he seemed tired – then she forgot it at the impression he gave of a brazier out of doors on a cool night.

'I suppose the girls are all after you to put them on the screen.'

'They've given up,' he said.

This was an understatement – they were all there, he knew, just over the threshold, but they had been there so long that their clamouring voices were no more than the sound of the traffic in the street. But his position remained more than royal: a king could make only one queen; Stahr, at least so they supposed, could make many.

'I'm thinking that it would turn you into a cynic,' she said. 'You didn't want to put me in pictures?'

'No.'

'That's good. I'm no actress. Once in London a man came up to me in the Carlton and asked me to make a test, but I thought a while and finally I didn't go.'

They had been standing nearly motionless, as if in a moment he would leave and she would go in. Stahr laughed suddenly.

'I feel as if I had my foot in the door – like a collector.'

She laughed, too.

'I'm sorry I can't ask you in. Shall I get my reefer and sit outside?'

'No.' He scarcely knew why he felt it was time to go. He might see her again – he might not. It was just as well this way.

'You'll come to the studio?' he said. 'I can't promise to go around with you, but if you come, you must be sure to send word to my office.'

A frown, the shadow of a hair in breadth, appeared between her eyes.

'I'm not sure,' she said. 'But I'm very much obliged.'

He knew that, for some reason, she would not come – in an instant she had slipped away from him. They both sensed that the moment was played out. He must go, even though he went nowhere, and it left him with nothing. Practically, vulgarly, he did not have her telephone number – or even her name; but it seemed impossible to ask for them now.

She walked with him to the car, her glowing beauty and her unexplored novelty pressing up against him; but there was a foot of moonlight between them when they came out of the shadow.

'Is this all?' he said spontaneously.

He saw regret in her face – but there was a flick of the lip, also, a bending of the smile towards some indirection, a momentary dropping and lifting of a curtain over a forbidden passage.

'I do hope we'll meet again,' she said almost formally.

'I'd be sorry if we didn't.'

They were distant for a moment. But as he turned his car in the next drive, and came back with her still waiting, and waved and drove on, he felt exalted and happy. He was glad that there was beauty in the world that would not be weighed in the scales of the casting department.

But at home he felt a curious loneliness as his butler made him tea in the samovar. It was the old hurt come back, heavy and delightful. When he took up the first of two scripts that were his evening stint, that presently he would visualise line by line on the screen, he waited a moment, thinking of Minna. He explained to her that it was really nothing, that no one could ever be like she was, that he was sorry.

* * *

That was substantially a day of Stahr's. I don't know about the illness, when it started, etc., because he was secretive, but I know he fainted a couple of times that month because father told me. Prince Agge is my authority for the luncheon in the commissary where he told them he was going to make a picture that would lose money – which was something, considering the men he had to deal with and that he held a big block of stock and had a profit-sharing contract.

And Wylie White told me a lot, which I believed because he felt Stahr intensely with a mixture of jealousy and admiration. As for me, I was head over heels in love with him then, and you can take what I say for what it's worth.

Chapter 5

Fresh as the morning, I went up to see him a week later. Or so I thought; when Wylie called for me, I had gotten into riding clothes to give the impression I'd been out in the dew since early morning.

'I'm going to throw myself under the wheel of Stahr's car, this morning,' I said.

'How about this car?' he suggested. 'It's one of the best cars Mort Fleishacker ever sold second-hand.'

'Not on your flowing veil,' I answered like a book. 'You have a wife in the East.'

'She's the past,' he said. 'You've got one great card, Celia – your valuation of yourself. Do you think anybody would look at you if you weren't Pat Brady's daughter?'

We don't take abuse like our mothers would have. Nothing – no remark from a contemporary means much. They tell you to be smart, they're marrying you for your money, or you tell them. Everything's simpler. Or is it? as we used to say.

But as I turned on the radio and the car raced up Laurel Canyon to 'The Thundering Beat of My Heart', I didn't believe he was right. I had good features except my face was too round, and a skin they seemed to love to touch, and good legs, and I didn't have to wear a brassière. I haven't a sweet nature, but who was Wylie to reproach me for that?

'Don't you think I'm smart to go in the morning?' I asked.

'Yeah. To the busiest man in California. He'll appreciate it. Why didn't you wake him up at four?'

'That's just it. At night he's tired. He's been looking at people all day, and some of them not bad. I come in in the morning and start a train of thought.'

'I don't like it. It's brazen.'

'What have you got to offer? And don't be rough.'

'I love you,' he said without much conviction. 'I love you more than I love your money, and that's plenty. Maybe your father would make me a supervisor.'

'I could marry the last man tapped for Bones this year and live in Southampton.'

I turned the dial and got either 'Gone' or 'Lost' – there were good songs that year. The music was getting better again. When I was young during the Depression, it wasn't so hot, and the best numbers were from the twenties, like Benny Goodman playing 'Blue Heaven' or Paul Whiteman with 'When Day Is Done'. There were only the bands to listen to. But now I liked almost everything except father singing 'Little Girl, You've Had A Busy Day' to try to create a sentimental father-and-daughter feeling.

'Lost' and 'Gone' were the wrong mood, so I turned again and got 'Lovely To Look At', which was my kind of poetry. I looked back as we crossed the crest of the foothills – with the air so clear you could see the leaves on Sunset Mountain two miles away. It's startling to you sometimes – just air, unobstructed, uncomplicated air.

'*Lovely to look at – de-lightful to know-w*,' I sang.

'Are you going to sing for Stahr?' Wylie said. 'If you do, get in a line about my being a good supervisor.'

'Oh, this'll be only Stahr and me,' I said. 'He's going to look at me and think, "I've never really seen her before".'

'We don't use that line this year,' he said.

' – Then he'll say "Little Cecilia", like he did the night of the earthquake. He'll say he never noticed I have become a woman.'

'You won't have to do a thing.'

'I'll stand there and bloom. After he kisses me as you would a child – '

'That's all in my script,' complained Wylie, 'and I've got to show it to him tomorrow.'

' – he'll sit down and put his face in his hands and say he never thought of me like that.'

'You mean you get in a little fast work during the kiss?'

'I bloom, I told you. How often do I have to tell you I bloom.'

'It's beginning to sound pretty randy to me,' said Wylie. 'How about laying off – I've got to work this morning.'

'Then he says it seems as if he was always meant to be this way.'

'Right in the industry. Producer's blood.' He pretended to shiver. 'I'd hate to have a transfusion of that.'

'Then he says – '

'I know all his lines,' said Wylie. 'What I want to know is what you say.'

'Somebody comes in,' I went on.

'And you jump up quickly off the casting couch, smoothing your skirts.'

'Do you want me to walk out and get home?'

We were in Beverly Hills, getting very beautiful now with the tall Hawaiian pines. Hollywood is a perfectly zoned city, so you know exactly what kind of people economically live in each section, from executives and directors, through technicians in their bungalows, right down to extras. This was the executive section and a very fancy lot of pastry. It wasn't as romantic as the dingiest village of Virginia or New Hampshire, but it looked nice this morning.

'They asked me how I knew,' sang the radio, *' – my true love was true.'*

My heart was fire, and smoke was in my eyes and everything, but I figured my chance at about fifty-fifty. I would walk right up on him as if I was either going to walk through him or kiss him on the mouth – and stop a bare foot away and say 'Hello' with disarming understatement.

And I did – though of course it wasn't like I expected: Stahr's beautiful dark eyes looking back into mine, knowing, I am dead sure, everything I was thinking – and not a bit embarrassed. I stood there an hour, I think, without moving, and all he did was twitch the side of his mouth and put his hands in his pockets.

'Will you go with me to the ball tonight?' I asked.

'What ball?'

'The screenwriters' ball down at the Ambassador.'

'Oh, yes.' He considered. 'I can't go with you. I might just come in late. We've got a sneak preview in Glendale.'

How different it all was from what you'd planned. When he sat down, I went over and put my head among his telephones, like a sort of desk appendage, and looked at him; and his dark eyes looked back so kind and nothing. Men don't often know those times when a girl could be had for nothing. All I succeeded in putting into his head was: 'Why don't you get married, Celia?'

Maybe he'd bring up Robby again, try to make a match there.

'What could I do to interest an interesting man?' I asked him.

'Tell him you're in love with him.'

'Should I chase him?'

'Yes,' he said smiling.

'I don't know. If it isn't there, it isn't there.'

'I'd marry you,' he said unexpectedly. 'I'm lonesome as hell. But I'm too old and tired to undertake anything.'

I went around the desk and stood beside him.

'Undertake me.'

He looked up in surprise, understanding for the first time that I was in deadly earnest.

'Oh, no,' he said. He looked almost miserable for a minute. 'Pictures are my girl. I haven't got much time – ' He corrected himself quickly, 'I mean any time.'

'You couldn't love me.'

'It's not that,' he said and – right out of my dream but with a difference: 'I never thought of you that way, Celia. I've known you so long. Somebody told me you were going to marry Wylie White.'

'And you had – no reaction.'

'Yes, I did. I was going to speak to you about it. Wait till he's been sober for two years.'

'I'm not even considering it, Monroe.'

We were way off the track, and just as in my daydream, somebody came in – only I was quite sure Stahr had pressed a concealed button.

I'll always think of that moment, when I felt Miss Doolan behind me with her pad, as the end of childhood, the end of the time when you cut out pictures. What I was looking at wasn't Stahr but a picture of him I cut out over and over: the eyes that flashed a sophisticated understanding at you and then darted up too soon into his wide brow with its ten thousand plots and plans; the face that was ageing from within, so that there were no casual furrows of worry and vexation but a drawn asceticism as if from a silent self-set struggle – or a long illness. It was handsomer to me than all the rosy tan from Coronado to Del Monte. He was my picture, as sure as if he had been pasted on the inside of my old locker in school. That's what I told Wylie White, and when a girl tells the man she likes second best about the other one – then she's in love.

* * *

I noticed the girl long before Stahr arrived at the dance. Not a pretty girl, for there are none of those in Los Angeles – one girl can be pretty, but a dozen are only a chorus. Nor yet a professional beauty – they do all the breathing for everyone, and finally even the men have to go outside for air. Just a girl, with the skin of one of Raphael's corner angels and a style that made you look back twice to see if it were something she had on.

I noticed her and forgot her. She was sitting back behind the pillars at a table whose ornament was a faded semi-star, who, in hopes of being noticed and getting a bit, rose and danced regularly with some scarecrow males. It reminded me shamefully of my first party, where mother made me dance over and over with the same boy to keep in the spotlight. The semi-star spoke to several people at our table, but we were busy being Café Society and she got nowhere at all.

From our angle it appeared that they all wanted something.

'You're expected to fling it around,' said Wylie, ' – like in the old days. When they find out you're hanging on to it, they get discouraged. That's what all this brave gloom is about – the only way to keep their self-respect is to be Hemingway characters. But underneath they hate you in a mournful way, and you know it.'

He was right – I knew that since 1933 the rich could only be happy alone together.

I saw Stahr come into the half-light at the top of the wide steps and stand there with his hands in his pockets, looking around. It was late and the lights seemed to have burned a little lower, though they were the same. The floor show was finished, except for a man who still wore a placard which said that at midnight in the Hollywood Bowl Sonja Henie was going to skate on hot soup. You could see the sign as he danced becoming less funny on his back. A few years before there would have been drunks around. The faded actress seemed to be looking for them hopefully over her partner's shoulder. I followed her with my eyes when she went back to her table –

– and there, to my surprise, was Stahr talking to the other girl. They were smiling at each other as if this was the beginning of the world.

* * *

Stahr had expected nothing like this when he stood at the head of the steps a few minutes earlier. The 'sneak preview' had disappointed him, and afterwards he had had a scene with Jacques La Borwitz right in front of the theatre, for which he was now sorry. He had started towards the Brady party when he saw Kathleen sitting in the middle of a long white table alone.

Immediately things changed. As he walked towards her, the people shrank back against the walls till they were only murals; the white table lengthened and became an altar where the priestess sat alone. Vitality swelled up in him, and he could have stood a long time across the table from her, looking and smiling.

The incumbents of the table were crawling back – Stahr and Kathleen danced.

When she came close, his several visions of her blurred; she was momentarily unreal. Usually a girl's skull made her real, but not this time – Stahr continued to be dazzled as they danced out along the floor – to the last edge, where they stepped through a mirror into another dance with new dancers whose faces were familiar but nothing more. In this new region he talked, fast and urgently.

'What's your name?'

'Kathleen Moore.'

'Kathleen Moore,' he repeated.

'I have no telephone, if that's what you're thinking.'

'When will you come to the studio?'

'It's not possible. Truly.'

'Why isn't it? Are you married?'

'No.'

'You're not married?'

'No, nor never have been. But then I may be.'

'Someone there at the table.'

'No.' She laughed. 'What curiosity!'

But she was deep in it with him, no matter what the words were. Her eyes invited him to a romantic communion of unbelievable intensity. As if she realised this, she said, frightened: 'I must go back now. I promised this dance.'

'I don't want to lose you. Couldn't we have lunch or dinner?'

'It's impossible.' But her expression helplessly amended the words to, 'It's just possible. The door is still open by a chink, if you could squeeze past. But quickly – so little time.'

'I must go back,' she repeated aloud. Then she dropped her arms, stopped dancing, and looked at him, a laughing wanton.

'When I'm with you, I don't breathe quite right,' she said.

She turned, picked up her long dress, and stepped back through the mirror. Stahr followed until she stopped near her table.

'Thank you for the dance,' she said, 'and now really, good-night.'

Then she nearly ran.

Stahr went to the table where he was expected and sat down with the Café Society group – from Wall Street, Grand Street, Loudon County, Virginia, and Odessa, Russia. They were all talking with enthusiasm about a horse that had run very fast, and Mr Marcus was the most enthusiastic of all. Stahr guessed that the Jews had taken over the worship of horses as a symbol – for years it had been the Cossacks mounted and the Jews on foot. Now the Jews had horses, and it gave them a sense of extraordinary well-being and power.

Stahr sat pretending to listen and even nodding when something was referred to him, but all the time watching the table behind the pillars. If everything had not happened as it had, even to his connecting the silver belt with the wrong girl, he might have thought it was some elaborate frame-up. But the elusiveness was beyond suspicion. For there in a moment he saw that she was escaping again – the pantomime at the table indicated goodbye. She was leaving, she was gone.

'There,' said Wylie White with malice, 'goes Cinderella. Simply bring the slipper to the Regal Shoe Company, 812 South Broadway.'

Stahr overtook her in the long upper lobby, where middle-aged women sat behind a roped-off space, watching the ballroom entrance.

'Am I responsible for this?' he asked.

'I was going, anyhow.' But she added almost resentfully, 'They talked as if I'd been dancing with the Prince of Wales. They all stared at me. One of the men wanted to draw my picture, and another one wanted to see me tomorrow.'

'That's just what I want,' said Stahr gently, 'but I want to see you much more than he does.'

'You insist so,' she said wearily. 'One reason I left England was that men always wanted their own way. I thought it was different here. Isn't it enough that I don't want to see you?'

'Ordinarily,' agreed Stahr. 'Please believe me, I'm way out of my depth already. I feel like a fool. But I must see you again and talk to you.'

She hesitated.

'There's no reason for feeling like a fool,' she said. 'You're too good a man to feel like a fool. But you should see this for what it is.'

'What is it?'

'You've fallen for me – completely. You've got me in your dreams.'

'I'd forgotten you,' he declared, '– till the moment I walked in that door.'

'Forgotten me with your head perhaps. But I knew the first time I saw you that you were the kind that likes me – '

She stopped herself. Near them a man and woman from the party were saying goodbye: 'Tell her hello – tell her I love her dearly,' said the woman, ' – you both – all of you – the children.' Stahr could not talk like that, the way everyone talked now. He could think of nothing further to say as they walked towards the elevator except: 'I suppose you're perfectly right.'

'Oh, you admit it?'

'No, I don't,' he retracted. 'It's just the whole way you're made. What you say – how you walk – the way you look right this minute – ' He saw she had melted a little, and his hopes rose. 'Tomorrow is Sunday, and usually I work on Sunday, but if there's anything you're curious about in Hollywood, any person you want to meet or see, please let me arrange it.'

They were standing by the elevator. It opened, but she let it go.

'You're very modest,' she said. 'You always talk about showing me the studio and taking me around. Don't you ever stay alone?'

'Tomorrow I'll feel very much alone.'

'Oh, the poor man – I could weep for him. He could have all the stars jumping around him and he chooses me.'

He smiled – he had laid himself open to that one.

The elevator came again. She signalled for it to wait.

'I'm a weak woman,' she said. 'If I meet you tomorrow, will you leave me in peace? No, you won't. You'll make it worse. It wouldn't do any good but harm, so I'll say no and thank you.'

She got into the elevator. Stahr got in too, and they smiled as they dropped two floors to the hall, cross-sectioned with small shops. Down at the end, held back by police, was the crowd, their heads and shoulders leaning forward to look down the alley. Kathleen shivered.

'They looked so strange when I came in,' she said, ' – as if they were furious at me for not being someone famous.'

'I know another way out,' said Stahr.

They went through a drugstore, down an alley, and came out into the clear cool California night beside the car park. He felt detached from the dance now, and she did, too.

'A lot of picture people used to live down here,' he said. 'John Barrymore and Pola Negri in those bungalows. And Connie Talmadge lived in that tall thin apartment house over the way.'

'Doesn't anybody live here now?'

'The studios moved out into the country,' he said, ' – what used to be the country. I had some good times around here, though.'

He did not mention that ten years ago Minna and her mother had lived in another apartment over the way.

'How old are you?' she asked suddenly.

'I've lost track – almost thirty-five, I think.'

'They said at the table you were the boy wonder.'

'I'll be that when I'm sixty,' he said grimly. 'You will meet me tomorrow, won't you?'

'I'll meet you,' she said. 'Where?'

Suddenly there was no place to meet. She would not go to a party at anyone's house, nor to the country, nor swimming, though she hesitated, nor to a well-known restaurant. She seemed hard to please, but he knew there was some reason. He would find out in time. It occurred to him that she might be the sister or daughter of someone well-known who was pledged to keep in the background. He suggested that he come for her and they could decide.

'That wouldn't do,' she said. 'What about right here? – the same spot.'

He nodded – pointing up at the arch under which they stood.

He put her into her car, which would have brought eighty dollars from any kindly dealer, and watched it rasp away. Down by the entrance a cheer went up as a favourite emerged, and Stahr wondered whether to show himself and say good-night.

* * *

This is Celia taking up the narrative in person. Stahr came back finally – it was about half-past three – and asked me to dance.

'How are you?' he asked me, just as if he hadn't seen me that morning. 'I got involved in a long conversation with a man.'

It was secret, too – he cared that much about it.

'I took him for a drive,' he went on innocently. 'I didn't realise how much this part of Hollywood had changed.'

'Has it changed?'

'Oh, yes,' he said, ' – changed completely. Unrecognisable. I couldn't tell you exactly, but it's all changed – everything. It's like a new city.' After a moment he amplified: 'I had no idea how much it had changed.'

'Who was the man?' I ventured.

'An old friend,' he said vaguely, ' – someone I knew a long time ago.'

I had made Wylie try to find out quietly who she was. He had gone over and the ex-star had asked him excitedly to sit down. No: she didn't know who the girl was – a friend of a friend of someone – even the man who had brought her didn't know.

So Stahr and I danced to the beautiful music of Glenn Miller playing 'I'm On A See-Saw'. It was good dancing now, with plenty of room. But it was lonely – lonelier than before the girl had gone. For me, as well as for Stahr, she took the evening with her, took along the stabbing pain I had felt – left the great ballroom empty and without emotion. Now it was nothing, and I was dancing with an absent-minded man who told me how much Los Angeles had changed.

* * *

They met, next afternoon, as strangers in an unfamiliar country. Last night was gone, the girl he had danced with was gone. A misty rose-and-blue hat with a trifling veil came along the terrace to him, and paused, searching his face. Stahr was strange, too, in a brown suit and a black tie that blocked him out more tangibly than a formal dinner coat, or when he was simply a face and voice in the darkness the night they had first met.

He was the first to be sure it was the same person as before: the upper part of the face that was Minna's, luminous, with creamy temples and opalescent brown – the cool-coloured curly hair. He could have put his arm around her and pulled her close with an almost family familiarity – already he knew the down on her neck, the very set of her backbone, the corners of her eyes, and how she breathed – the very texture of the clothes that she would wear.

'Did you wait here all night,' she said, in a voice that was like a whisper.

'I didn't move – didn't stir.'

Still the problem remained, the same one – there was no special place to go.

'I'd like tea,' she suggested, ' – if it's some place you're not known.'

'That sounds as if one of us had a bad reputation.'

'Doesn't it?' she laughed.

'We'll go to the shore,' Stahr suggested. 'There's a place there where I got out once and was chased by a trained seal.'

'Do you think the seal could make tea?'

'Well – he's trained. And I don't think he'll talk – I don't think his training got that far. What in *hell* are you trying to hide?'

After a moment she said lightly: 'Perhaps the future,' in a way that might mean anything or nothing at all.

As they drove away, she pointed at her jalopy in the parking lot.

'Do you think it's safe?'

'I doubt it. I noticed some black-bearded foreigners snooping around.'

Kathleen looked at him alarmed.

'Really?' She saw he was smiling. 'I believe everything you say,' she said. 'You've got such a gentle way about you that I don't see why they're all so afraid of you.' She examined him with approval – fretting a little about his pallor, which was accentuated by the bright afternoon. 'Do you work very hard? Do you really always work on Sundays?'

He responded to her interest – impersonal yet not perfunctory.

'Not always. Once we had – we had a house with a pool and all – and people came on Sunday. I played tennis and swam. I don't swim any more.'

'Why not? It's good for you. I thought all Americans swam.'

'My legs got very thin – a few years ago, and it embarrassed me. There were other things I used to do – lots of things: I used to play handball when I was a kid, and sometimes out here – I had a court that was washed away in a storm.'

'You have a good build,' she said in formal compliment, meaning only that he was made with thin grace.

He rejected this with a shake of his head.

'I enjoy working most,' he said. 'My work is very congenial.'

'Did you always want to be in movies?'

'No. When I was young I wanted to be a chief clerk – the one who knew where everything was.'

She smiled.

'That's odd. And now you're much more than that.'

'No, I'm still a chief clerk,' Stahr said. 'That's my gift, if I have one. Only when I got to be it, I found out that no one knew where anything was. And I found out that you had to know why it was where it was, and whether it should be left there. They began throwing it all at me, and it was a very complex office. Pretty soon I had all the keys. And they wouldn't have remembered what locks they fitted if I'd given them back.'

They stopped for a red light, and a newsboy bleated at him: 'Mickey Mouse Murdered! Randolph Hearst declares war on China!'

'We'll have to buy this paper,' she said.

As they drove on, she straightened her hat and preened herself. Seeing him looking at her, she smiled.

She was alert and calm – qualities that were currently at a premium. There was lassitude in plenty – California was filling up with weary desperados. And there were tense young men and women who lived back East in spirit while they carried on a losing battle against the climate. But it was everyone's secret that sustained effort was difficult here – a secret that Stahr scarcely admitted to himself. But he knew that people from other places spurted a pure rill of new energy for a while.

They were very friendly now. She had not made a move or a gesture that was out of keeping with her beauty, that pressed it out of its contour one way or another. It was all proper to itself. He judged her as he would a shot in a picture. She was not trash, she was not confused but clear – in his special meaning of the word, which implied balance, delicacy and proportion, she was 'nice'.

They reached Santa Monica, where there were the stately houses of a dozen picture stars, penned in the middle of a crawling Coney Island. They turned downhill into the wide blue sky and sea and went on along the sea till the beach slid out again from under the bathers in a widening and narrowing yellow strand.

'I'm building a house out here,' Stahr said, ' – much farther on. I don't know why I'm building it.'

'Perhaps it's for me,' she said.

'Maybe it is.'

'I think it's splendid for you to build a big house for me without even knowing what I looked like.'

'It isn't too big. And it hasn't any roof. I didn't know what kind of roof you wanted.'

'We don't want a roof. They told me it never rained here. It – '

She stopped so suddenly that he knew she was reminded of something.

'Just something that's past,' she said.

'What was it?' he demanded, ' – another house without a roof?'

'Yes. Another house without a roof.'

'Were you happy there?'

'I lived with a man,' she said, 'a long, long time – too long. It was one of those awful mistakes people make. I lived with him a long time after I wanted to get out, but he couldn't let me go. He'd try, but he couldn't. So finally I ran away.'

He was listening, weighing but not judging. Nothing changed under the rose and blue hat. She was twenty-five or so. It would have been a waste if she had not loved and been loved.

'We were too close,' she said. 'We should probably have had children – to stand between us. But you can't have children when there's no roof to the house.'

All right, he knew something of her. It would not be like last night when something kept saying, as in a story conference: 'We know nothing about the girl. We don't have to know much – but we have to know something.' A vague background spread behind her, something more tangible than the head of Siva in the moonlight.

They came to the restaurant, forbidding with many Sunday automobiles. When they got out, the trained seal growled reminiscently at Stahr. The man who owned it said that the seal would never ride in the back seat of his car but always climbed over the back and up in front. It was plain that the man was in bondage to the seal, though he had not yet acknowledged it to himself.

'I'd like to see the house you're building,' said Kathleen. 'I don't want tea – tea is the past.'

Kathleen drank a coke instead and they drove on ten miles into a sun so bright that he took out two pairs of cheaters from a compartment. Five miles further on they turned down a small promontory and came to the fuselage of Stahr's house.

A headwind blowing out of the sun threw spray up the rocks and over the car. Concrete mixer, raw yellow wood and builders' rubble waited, an open wound in the seascape for Sunday to be over. They walked around front, where great boulders rose to what would be the terrace.

She looked at the feeble hills behind and winced faintly at the barren glitter, and Stahr saw –

'No use looking for what's not here,' he said cheerfully. 'Think of it as if you were standing on one of those globes with a map on it – I always wanted one when I was a boy.'

'I understand,' she said after a minute. 'When you do that, you can feel the earth turn, can't you?'

He nodded.

'Yes. Otherwise it's all just *mañana* – waiting for the morning or the moon.'

They went in under the scaffolding. One room, which was to be the chief salon, was completed even to the built-in book shelves and the curtain rods and the trap in the floor for the motion picture projection machine. And to her surprise, this opened out to a porch with cushioned chairs in place and a ping-pong table. There was another ping-pong table on the newly laid sod beyond.

'Last week I gave a premature luncheon,' he admitted, 'I had some props brought out – some grass and things. I wanted to see how the place felt.'

She laughed suddenly.

'Isn't that real grass?'

'Oh yes – it's grass.'

Beyond the strip of anticipatory lawn was the excavation for a swimming pool, patronised now by a crowd of seagulls, which saw them and took flight.

'Are you going to live here all alone?' she asked him, ' – not even dancing girls?'

'Probably. I used to make plans, but not any more. I thought this would be a nice place to read scripts. The studio is really home.'

'That's what I've heard about American business men.'

He caught a tilt of criticism in her voice.

'You do what you're born to do,' he said gently. 'About once a month somebody tries to reform me, tells me what a barren old age I'll have when I can't work any more. But it's not so simple.'

The wind was rising. It was time to go, and he had his car keys out of his pocket, absent-mindedly jingling them in his hand. There was the silvery 'hey!' of a telephone, coming from somewhere across the sunshine.

It was not from the house, and they hurried here and there around the garden, like children playing warmer and colder – closing in finally on a tool shack by the tennis court. The phone, irked with delay, barked at them suspiciously from the wall. Stahr hesitated.

'Shall I let the damn thing ring?'

'I couldn't. Unless I was sure who it was.'

'Either it's for somebody else or they've made a wild guess.'

He picked up the receiver.

'Hello . . . Long distance from where? Yes, this is Mr Stahr.'

His manner changed perceptibly. She saw what few people had seen for a decade: Stahr impressed. It was not discordant, because he often pretended to be impressed, but it made him momentarily a little younger.

'It's the President,' he said to her, almost stiffly.

'Of your company?'

'No, of the United States.'

He was trying to be casual for her benefit, but his voice was eager.

'All right, I'll wait,' he said into the phone, and then to Kathleen: 'I've talked to him before.'

She watched. He smiled at her and winked, as an evidence that while he must give this his best attention, he had not forgotten her.

'Hello,' he said presently. He listened. Then he said 'Hello' again. He frowned.

'Can you talk a little louder,' he said politely, and then: 'Who? . . . What's that?'

She saw a disgusted look come into his face.

'I don't want to talk to him,' he said. 'No!'

He turned to Kathleen: 'Believe it or not, it's an orang-utan.'

He waited while something was explained to him at length; then he repeated: 'I don't want to talk to it, Lew. I haven't got anything to say that would interest an orang-utan.'

He beckoned to Kathleen, and when she came close to the phone, he held the receiver so that she heard odd breathing and a gruff growl. Then a voice: 'This is no phoney, Monroe. It can talk and it's a dead ringer for McKinley. Mr Horace Wickersham is with me here with a picture of McKinley in his hand – '

Stahr listened patiently.

'We've got a chimp,' he said, after a minute. 'He bit a chunk out of John Gilbert last year . . . All right, put him on again.'

He spoke formally as if to a child.

'Hello, orang-utan.'

His face changed, and he turned to Kathleen.

'He said "Hello".'

'Ask him his name,' suggested Kathleen.

'Hello, orang-utan – God, what a thing to be! – Do you know your name? . . . He doesn't seem to know his name . . . Listen, Lew. We're not making anything like *King Kong*, and there is no monkey in *The Hairy Ape* . . . Of course I'm sure. I'm sorry, Lew, goodbye.'

He was annoyed with Lew because he had thought it was the President and had changed his manner, acting as if it were. He felt a little ridiculous, but Kathleen felt sorry and liked him better because it had been an orang-utan.

* * *

They started back along the shore with the sun behind them. The house seemed kindlier when they left it, as if warmed by their visit – the hard glitter of the place was more endurable if they were not bound there like people on the shiny surface of a moon. Looking back from a curve of the shore, they saw the sky growing pink behind the indecisive structure, and the point of land seemed a friendly island, not without promise of fine hours on a further day.

Past Malibu with its gaudy shacks and fishing barges they came into the range of human kind again, the cars stacked and piled along the road, the beaches like ant hills without a pattern, save for the dark drowned heads that sprinkled the sea.

Goods from the city were increasing in sight – blankets, matting, umbrellas, cook stoves, reticules full of clothing – the prisoners had laid out their shackles beside them on this sand. It was Stahr's sea if he wanted it, or knew what to do with it – only by sufferance did these others wet their feet and fingers in the wild cool reservoirs of man's world.

Stahr turned off the road by the sea and up a canyon and along a hill road, and the people dropped away. The hill became the outskirts of the city. Stopping for gasoline, he stood beside the car.

'We could have dinner,' he said almost anxiously.

'You have work you could do.'

'No – I haven't planned anything. Couldn't we have dinner?'

He knew that she had nothing to do either – no planned evening or special place to go.

She compromised.

'Do you want to get something in that drugstore across the street?'

He looked at it tentatively.

'Is that really what you want?'

'I like to eat in American drugstores. It seems so queer and strange.'

They sat on high stools and had tomato broth and hot sandwiches. It was more intimate than anything they had done, and they both felt a dangerous sort of loneliness, and felt it in each other. They shared in varied scents of the drugstore, bitter and sweet and sour, and the mystery of the waitress, with only the outer part of her hair dyed and black beneath, and, when it was over, the still life of their empty plates – a sliver of potato, a sliced pickle, and an olive stone.

* * *

It was dusk in the street, it seemed nothing to smile at him now when they got into the car.

'Thank you so much. It's been a nice afternoon.'

It was not far from her house. They felt the beginning of the hill, and the louder sound of the car in second was the beginning of the end. Lights were on in the climbing bungalows – he turned on the headlights of the car. Stahr felt heavy in the pit of his stomach.

'We'll go out again.'

'No,' she said quickly, as if she had been expecting this. 'I'll write you a letter. I'm sorry I've been so mysterious – it was really a compliment because I like you so much. You should try not to work so hard. You ought to marry again.'

'Oh, that isn't what you should say,' he broke out protestingly. 'This has been you and me today. It may have meant nothing to you – it meant a lot to me. I'd like time to tell you about it.'

But if he were to take time it must be in her house, for they were there and she was shaking her head as the car drew up to the door.

'I must go now. I do have an engagement. I didn't tell you.'

'That's not true. But it's all right.'

He walked to the door with her and stood in his own footsteps of that other night, while she felt in her bag for the key.

'Have you got it?'

'I've got it,' she said.

That was the moment to go in, but she wanted to see him once more and she leaned her head to the left, then to the right, trying to catch his face against the last twilight. She leaned too far and too long, and it was natural when his hand touched the back of her upper arm and shoulder and pressed her forward into the darkness of his throat. She shut her eyes, feeling the bevel of the key in her tight-clutched hand. She said 'Oh' in an expiring sigh, and then 'Oh' again, as he pulled her in close and his chin pushed her cheek around gently. They were both smiling just faintly, and she was frowning, too, as the inch between them melted into darkness.

When they were apart, she shook her head still, but more in wonder than in denial. It came like this then, it was your own fault, now far back, when was the moment? It came like this, and every instant the burden of tearing herself away from them together, from it, was heavier and more unimaginable. He was exultant; she resented and could not blame him, but she would not be part of his exultation, for it was a defeat. So far it was a defeat. And then she thought that if she stopped it being a defeat, broke off and went inside, it was still not a victory. Then it was just nothing.

'This was not my idea,' she said, 'not at all my idea.'

'Can I come in?'

'Oh, no – no.'

'Then let's jump in the car and drive somewhere.'

With relief, she caught at the exact phrasing – to get away from here immediately, that was accomplishment or sounded like it – as if she were fleeing from the spot of a crime. Then they were in the car, going down hill with the breeze cool in their faces, and she came slowly to herself. Now it was all clear in black and white.

'We'll go back to your house on the beach,' she said.

'Back there?'

'Yes – we'll go back to your house. Don't let's talk. I just want to ride.'

* * *

When they got to the coast again the sky was grey, and at Santa Monica a sudden gust of rain bounced over them. Stahr halted beside the road, put on a raincoat, and lifted the canvas top. 'We've got a roof,' he said.

The windshield wiper ticked domestically as a grandfather's clock. Sullen cars were leaving the wet beaches and starting back into the city. Further on they ran into fog – the road lost its boundaries on either side, and the lights of cars coming towards them were stationary until just before they flared past.

They had left a part of themselves behind, and they felt light and free in the car. Fog fizzed in at a chink, and Kathleen took off the rose-and-blue hat in a calm, slow way that made him watch tensely, and put it under a strip of canvas in the back seat. She shook out her hair and, when she saw Stahr was looking at her, she smiled.

The trained seal's restaurant was only a sheen of light off towards the ocean. Stahr cranked down a window and looked for landmarks, but after a few more miles the fog fell away, and just ahead of them the road turned off that led to his house. Out here a moon showed behind the clouds. There was still a shifting light over the sea.

The house had dissolved a little back into its elements. They found the dripping beams of a doorway and groped over mysterious waist-high obstacles to the single finished room, odorous of sawdust and wet wood. When he took her in his arms, they could just see each other's eyes in the half darkness. Presently his raincoat dropped to the floor.

'Wait,' she said.

She needed a minute. She did not see how any good could come from this, and though this did not prevent her from being happy and desirous, she needed a minute to think how it was, to go back an hour and know how it had happened. She waited in his arms, moving her head a little from side to side as she had before, only more slowly, and never taking her eyes from his. Then she discovered that he was trembling.

He discovered it at the same time, and his arms relaxed. Immediately she spoke to him coarsely and provocatively, and pulled his face down to hers. Then, with her knees she struggled out of something, still standing up and holding him with one arm, and kicked it off beside the coat. He was not trembling now and he held her again, as they knelt down together and slid to the raincoat on the floor.

* * *

Afterwards they lay without speaking, and then he was full of such tender love for her that he held her tight till a stitch tore in her dress. The small sound brought them to reality.

'I'll help you up,' he said, taking her hands.

'Not just yet. I was thinking of something.'

She lay in the darkness, thinking irrationally that it would be such a bright indefatigable baby, but presently she let him help her up . . . When she came back into the room, it was lit from a single electric fixture.

'A one-bulb lighting system,' he said. 'Shall I turn it off?'

'No. It's very nice. I want to see you.'

They sat in the wooden frame of the window seat, with the soles of their shoes touching.

'You seem far away,' she said.

'So do you.'

'Are you surprised?'

'At what?'

'That we're two people again. Don't you always think – hope that you'll be one person, and then find you're still two?'

'I feel very close to you.'

'So do I to you,' she said.

'Thank you.'

'Thank *you*.'

They laughed.

'Is this what you wanted?' she asked. 'I mean last night.'

'Not consciously.'

'I wonder when it was settled,' she brooded. 'There's a moment when you needn't, and then there's another moment when you know nothing in the world could keep it from happening.'

This had an experienced ring, and to his surprise he liked her even more. In his mood, which was passionately to repeat yet not recapitulate the past, it was right that it should be that way.

'I *am* rather a trollop,' she said, following his thoughts. 'I suppose that's why I didn't get on to Edna.'

'Who is Edna?'

'The girl you thought was me. The one you phoned to – who lived across the road. She's moved to Santa Barbara.'

'You mean she was a tart?'

'So it seems. She went to what you call call-houses.'

'That's funny.'

'If she had been English, I'd have known right away. But she seemed like everyone else. She only told me just before she went away.'

He saw her shiver and got up, putting the raincoat around her shoulders. He opened a closet and a pile of pillows and beach mattress fell out on the floor. There was a box of candles, and he lit them around the room, attaching the electric heater where the bulb had been.

'Why was Edna afraid of me?' he asked suddenly.

'Because you were a producer. She had some awful experience or a friend of hers did. Also, I think she was extremely stupid.'

'How did you happen to know her?'

'She came over. Maybe she thought I was a fallen sister. She seemed quite pleasant. She said "Call me Edna" all the time – "Please call me Edna," so finally I called her Edna and we were friends.'

She got off the window seat so he could lay pillows along it and behind her.

'What can I do?' she said. 'I'm a parasite.'

'No, you're not.' He put his arms around her. 'Be still. Get warm.'

They sat for a while quiet.

'I know why you liked me at first,' she said. 'Edna told me.'

'What did she tell you?'

'That I looked like – Minna Davis. Several people have told me that.'

He leaned away from her and nodded.

'It's here,' she said, putting her hands on her cheekbones and distorting her cheeks slightly. 'Here and here.'

'Yes,' said Stahr. 'It was very strange. You look more like she actually *looked* than how she was on the screen.'

She got up, changing the subject with her gesture as if she were afraid of it.

'I'm warm now,' she said. She went to the closet and peered in, came back wearing a little apron with a crystalline pattern like a snowfall. She stared around critically.

'Of course we've just moved in,' she said, ' – and there's a sort of echo.'

She opened the door of the veranda and pulled in two wicker chairs, drying them off. He watched her move, intently, yet half afraid that her body would fail somewhere and break the spell. He had watched women in screen-tests and seen their beauty vanish second by second, as if a lovely statue had begun to walk with the meagre joints of a paper doll. But Kathleen was ruggedly set on the balls of her feet – the fragility was, as it should be, an illusion.

'It's stopped raining,' she said. 'It rained the day I came. Such an awful rain – so loud – like horses weeing.'

He laughed.

'You'll like it. Especially if you've got to stay here. Are you going to stay here? Can't you tell me now? What's the mystery?'

She shook her head.

'Not now – it's not worth telling.'

'Come here then.'

She came over and stood near him, and he pressed his cheek against the cool fabric of the apron.

'You're a tired man,' she said, putting her hand in his hair.

'Not that way.'

'I didn't mean that way,' she said hastily. 'I meant you'll work yourself sick.'

'Don't be a mother,' he said.

Be a trollop, he thought. He wanted the pattern of his life broken. If he was going to die soon, like the two doctors said, he wanted to stop being Stahr for a while and hunt for love like men who had no gifts to give, like young nameless men who looked along the streets in the dark.

'You've taken off my apron,' she said gently.

'Yes.'

'Would anyone be passing along the beach? Shall we put out the candles?'

'No, don't put out the candles.'

Afterwards she lay half on a white cushion and smiled up at him.

'I feel like Venus on the half shell,' she said.

'What made you think of that?'

'Look at me – isn't it Botticelli?'

'I don't know,' he said smiling. 'It is if you say so.'

She yawned.

'I've had such a good time. And I'm very fond of you.'

'You know a lot, don't you?'

'What do you mean?'

'Oh, from little things you've said. Or perhaps the way you say them.'

She deliberated.

'Not much,' she said. 'I never went to a university, if that's what you mean. But the man I told you about knew everything and he had a passion for educating me. He made out schedules and made me take courses at the Sorbonne and go to museums. I picked up a little.'

'What was he?'

'He was a painter of sorts and a hell-cat. And a lot besides. He wanted me to read Spengler – everything was for that. All the history and philosophy and harmony was all so I could read Spengler, and then I left him before we got to Spengler. At the end I think that was the chief reason he didn't want me to go.'

'Who was Spengler?'

'I tell you we didn't get to him,' she laughed, 'and now I'm forgetting everything very patiently, because it isn't likely I'll ever meet anyone like him again.'

'Oh, but you shouldn't forget,' said Stahr, shocked. He had an intense respect for learning, a racial memory of the old *schules*. 'You shouldn't forget.'

'It was just in place of babies.'

'You could teach your babies,' he said.

'Could I?'

'Sure you could. You could give it to them while they were young. When I want to know anything, I've got to ask some drunken writer. Don't throw it away.'

'All right,' she said, getting up. 'I'll tell it to my children. But it's so endless – the more you know, the more there is just beyond, and it keeps on coming. This man could have been anything if he hadn't been a coward and a fool.'

'But you were in love with him.'

'Oh, yes – with all my heart.' She looked through the window, shading her eyes. 'It's light out there. Let's go down to the beach.'

He jumped up, exclaiming: 'Why, I think it's the grunion!'

'What?'

'It's tonight. It's in all the papers.' He hurried out the door, and she heard him open the door of the car. Presently he returned with a newspaper.

'It's at ten-sixteen. That's five minutes.'

'An eclipse or something?'

'Very punctual fish,' he said. 'Leave your shoes and stockings and come with me.'

It was a fine blue night. The tide was at the turn, and the little silver fish rocked off shore waiting for 10.16. A few seconds after the time they came swarming in with the tide, and Stahr and Kathleen stepped over them barefoot as they flicked slip-slop on the sand. A Negro man came along the shore towards them, collecting the grunion quickly, like twigs, into two pails. They came in twos and threes and platoons and companies, relentless and exalted and scornful, round the great bare feet of the intruders, as they had come before Sir Francis Drake had nailed his plaque to the boulder on the shore.

'I wish for another pail,' the Negro man said, resting a moment.

'You've come a long way out,' said Stahr.

'I used to go to Malibu, but they don't like it, those moving picture people.'

A wave came in and forced them back, receded swiftly, leaving the sand alive again.

'Is it worth the trip?' Stahr asked.

'I don't figure it that way. I really come out to read some Emerson. Have you ever read him?'

'I have,' said Kathleen. 'Some.'

'I've got him inside my shirt. I got some Rosicrucian literature with me, too, but I'm fed up with them.'

The wind had changed a little – the waves were stronger further down, and they walked along the foaming edge of the water.

'What's your work?' the Negro asked Stahr.

'I work for the pictures.'

'Oh.' After a moment he added, 'I never go to movies.'

'Why not?' asked Stahr sharply.

'There's no profit. I never let my children go.'

Stahr watched him, and Kathleen watched Stahr protectively.

'Some of them are good,' she said, against a wave of spray; but he did not hear her. She felt she could contradict him and said it again, and this time he looked at her indifferently.

'Are the Rosicrucian brotherhood against pictures?' asked Stahr.

'Seems as if they don't know what they *are* for. One week they for one thing and next week for another.'

Only the little fish were certain. Half an hour had gone, and still they came. The Negro's two pails were full, and finally he went off over the beach towards the road, unaware that he had rocked an industry.

Stahr and Kathleen walked back to the house, and she thought how to drive his momentary blues away.

'Poor old Sambo,' she said.

'What?'

'Don't you call them poor old Sambo?'

'We don't call them anything especially.' After a moment, he said, 'They have pictures of their own.'

In the house she drew on her shoes and stockings before the heater.

'I like California better,' she said deliberately. 'I think I was a bit sex-starved.'

'That wasn't quite all, was it?'

'You know it wasn't.'

'It's nice to be near you.'

She gave a little sigh as she stood up, so small that he did not notice it.

'I don't want to lose you now,' he said. 'I don't know what you think of me or whether you think of me at all. As you've probably guessed, my heart's in the grave – ' He hesitated, wondering if this was quite true. ' – but you're the most attractive woman I've met since I don't know when. I can't stop looking at you. I don't know now exactly the colour of your eyes, but they make me sorry for everyone in the world – '

'Stop it, stop it!' she cried laughing. 'You'll have me looking in the mirror for weeks. My eyes aren't any colour – they're just eyes to see with, and I'm just as ordinary as I can be. I have nice teeth for an English girl – '

'You have beautiful teeth.'

' – but I couldn't hold a candle to these girls I see here – '

'*You* stop it,' he said. 'What I said is true, and I'm a cautious man.'

She stood motionless a moment – thinking. She looked at him, then she looked back into herself, then at him again – then she gave up her thought.

'We must go,' she said.

* * *

Now they were different people as they started back. Four times they had driven along the shore road today, each time a different pair.

Curiosity, sadness, and desire were behind them now; this was a true returning – to themselves and all their past and future and the encroaching presence of tomorrow. He asked her to sit close in the car, and she did, but they did not seem close, because for that you have to seem to be growing closer. Nothing stands still. It was on his tongue to ask her to come to the house he rented and sleep there tonight – but he felt that it would make him sound lonely. As the car climbed the hill to her house, Kathleen looked for something behind the seat cushion.

'What have you lost?'

'It might have fallen out,' she said, feeling through her purse in the darkness.

'What was it?'

'An envelope.'

'Was it important?'

'No.'

But when they got to her house and Stahr turned on the dashboard light, she helped take the cushions out and look again.

'It doesn't matter,' she said, as they walked to the door. 'What's your address where you really live?'

'Just Bel Air. There's no number.'

'Where is Bel Air?'

'It's a sort of development, near Santa Monica. But you'd better call me at the studio.'

'All right . . . good-night, Mr Stahr.'

'*Mister* Stahr,' he repeated, astonished.

She corrected herself gently.

'Well, then, good-night, Stahr. Is that better?'

He felt as though he had been pushed away a little.

'As you like,' he said. He refused to let the aloofness communicate itself. He kept looking at her and moved his head from side to side in her own gesture, saying without words: 'You know what's happened to me.' She sighed. Then she came into his arms and for a moment was his again completely. Before anything could change, Stahr whispered good-night and turned away and went to his car.

Winding down the hill, he listened inside himself as if something by an unknown composer, powerful and strange and strong, was about to be played for the first time. The theme would be stated presently, but because the composer was always new, he would not recognise it as the theme right away. It would come in some such guise as the auto horns from the technicolor boulevards below, or be barely audible, a tattoo on the muffled drum of the moon. He strained to hear it, knowing only that music was beginning, new music that he liked and did not understand. It was hard to react to what one could entirely compass – this was new and confusing, nothing one could shut off in the middle and supply the rest from an old score.

Also, and persistently, and bound up with the other, there was the Negro on the sand. He was waiting at home for Stahr, with his pails of silver fish, and he would be waiting at the studio in the morning. He had said that he did not allow his children to listen to Stahr's story. He was prejudiced and wrong, and he must be shown somehow, some way. A picture, many pictures, a decade of pictures, must be made to show him he was wrong. Since he had spoken, Stahr had thrown four pictures out of his plans – one that was going into production this week. They were borderline pictures in point of interest, but at least he submitted the borderline pictures to the Negro and found them trash. And he put back on his list a difficult picture that he had tossed to the wolves, to Brady and Marcus and the rest, to get his way on something else. He rescued it for the Negro man.

When he drove up to his door, the porch lights went on, and his Filipino came down the steps to put away the car. In the library, Stahr found a list of phone calls:

La Borwitz
Marcus
Harlow
Reinmund
Fairbanks
Brady
Colman
Skouras
Fleishacker, *etc.*

The Filipino came into the room with a letter.

'This fell out of the car,' he said.

'Thanks,' said Stahr. 'I was looking for it.'

'Will you be running a picture tonight, Mr Stahr?'

'No, thanks – you can go to bed.'

The letter, to his surprise, was addressed to Monroe Stahr, Esq. He started to open it – then it occurred to him that she had wanted to recapture it, and possibly to withdraw it. If she had had a phone, he would have called her for permission before opening it. He held it for a moment. It had been written before they met – it was odd to think that whatever it said was now invalidated; it possessed the interest of a souvenir by representing a mood that was gone.

Still he did not like to read it without asking her. He put it down beside a pile of scripts and sat down with the top script in his lap. He was proud of resisting his first impulse to open the letter. It seemed to prove that he was not 'losing his head'. He had never lost his head about Minna, even in the beginning – it had been the most appropriate and regal match imaginable. She had loved him always and just before she died, all unwilling and surprised, his tenderness had burst and surged forward and he had been in love with her. In love with Minna and death together – with the world in which she looked so alone that he wanted to go with her there.

But 'falling for dames' had never been an obsession – his brother had gone to pieces over a dame, or rather over dame after dame after dame. But Stahr, in his younger days, had them once and never more than once – like one drink. He had quite another sort of adventure reserved for his mind – something better than a series of emotional sprees. Like many brilliant men, he had grown up dead cold. Beginning at about twelve, probably, with the total rejection common to those of extraordinary mental powers, the 'See here: this is all wrong – a mess – all a lie – and a sham – ', he swept it all away, everything, as men of his type do; and then instead of being a son-of-a-bitch as most of them are, he looked around at the barrenness that was left and said to himself, '*This* will never do.' And so he had learned tolerance, kindness, forbearance, and even affection like lessons.

The Filipino boy brought in a carafe of water and bowls of nuts and fruit, and said good-night. Stahr opened the first script and began to read.

He read for three hours – stopping from time to time, editing without a pencil. Sometimes he looked up, warm from some very vague happy thought that was not in the script, and it took him a minute each time to remember what it was. Then he knew it was Kathleen, and he looked at the letter – it was nice to have a letter.

It was three o'clock when a vein began to bump in the back of his hand, signalling that it was time to quit. Kathleen was really far away now with the waning night – the different aspects of her telescoped into the memory of a single thrilling stranger, bound to him only by a few slender hours. It seemed perfectly all right to open the letter.

DEAR MR STAHR – In half an hour I will be keeping my date with you. When we say goodbye I will hand you this letter. It is to tell you that I am to be married soon and that I won't be able to see you after today.

I should have told you last night but it didn't seem to concern you. And it would seem silly to spend this beautiful afternoon telling you about it and watching your interest fade. Let it fade all at once – now. I will have told you enough to convince you that I am Nobody's Prize Potato. (I have just learned that expression – from my hostess of last night, who called and stayed an hour. She seems to believe that everyone is Nobody's Prize Potato – except you. I think I am supposed to tell you she thinks this, so give her a job if you can.)

I am very flattered that anyone who sees so many lovely women – I can't finish this sentence but you know what I mean. And I will be late if I don't go to meet you right now.

With all good wishes

KATHLEEN MOORE

Stahr's first feeling was like fear; his second thought was that the letter was invalidated – she had even tried to retrieve it. But then he remembered 'Mr Stahr' just at the end, and that she had asked him his address – she had probably already written another letter which would also say goodbye. Illogically he was shocked by the letter's indifference to what had happened later. He read it again, realising that it foresaw nothing. Yet in front of the house she had decided to let it stand, belittling everything that had happened, curving her mind away from the fact that there had been no other man in her consciousness that afternoon. But he could not even believe this now, and the whole adventure began to peel away even as he recapitulated it searchingly to himself. The car, the hill, the hat, the music, the letter itself, blew off like the scraps of tar paper from the rubble of his house. And Kathleen departed, packing up her remembered gestures, her softly moving head, her sturdy eager body, her bare feet in the wet swirling sand. The skies paled and faded – the wind and rain turned dreary, washing the silver fish back to sea. It was only one more day, and nothing was left except the pile of scripts upon the table.

He went upstairs. Minna died again on the first landing, and he forgot her lingeringly and miserably again, step by step to the top. The empty floor stretched around him – the doors with no one sleeping behind. In his room, Stahr took off his tie, untied his shoes, and sat on the side of his bed. It was all closed out, except for something that he could not remember; then he remembered: her car was still down in the parking lot of the hotel. He set his clock to give him six hours' sleep.

* * *

This is Cecilia taking up the story. I think it would be most interesting to follow my own movements at this point, as this is a time in my life that I am ashamed of. What people are ashamed of usually makes a good story.

When I sent Wylie over to Martha Dodd's table, he had no success in finding out who the girl was, but it had suddenly become my chief interest in life. Also, I guessed – correctly – that it would be Martha Dodd's. To have had at your table a girl who is admired by royalty, who may be tagged for a coronet in our little feudal system – and not even know her name!

I had only a speaking acquaintance with Martha, and it would be too obvious to approach her directly, but I went out to the studio Monday and dropped in on Jane Meloney.

Jane Meloney was quite a friend of mine. I thought of her rather as a child thinks of a family dependant. I knew she was a writer, but I grew up thinking that writer and secretary were the same, except that a writer usually smelled of cocktails and came more often to meals. They were spoken of the same way when they were not around – except for a species called playwrights, who came from the East. These were treated with respect if they did not stay long – if they did, they sank with the others into the white collar class.

Jane's office was in the 'old writers' building'. There was one on every lot, a row of iron maidens left over from silent days and still resounding with the dull moans of cloistered hacks and bums. There was the story of the new producer who had gone down the line one day and then reported excitedly to the head office.

'Who are those men?'

'They're supposed to be writers.'

'I thought so. Well, I watched them for ten minutes and there were two of them that didn't write a line.'

Jane was at her typewriter, about to break off for lunch. I told her frankly that I had a rival.

'It's a dark horse,' I said. 'I can't even find out her name.'

'Oh,' said Jane. 'Well, maybe I know something about that. I heard something from somebody.'

The somebody, of course, was her nephew, Ned Sollinger, Stahr's office boy. He had been her pride and hope. She had sent him through New York University, where he played on the football team. Then in his first year at medical school, after a girl turned him down, he dissected out the least publicised section of a lady corpse and sent it to the girl. Don't ask me why. In disgrace with fortune and men's eyes, he had begun life at the bottom again, and was still there.

'What do you know?' I asked.

'It was the night of the earthquake. She fell into the lake on the back lot, and he dove in and saved her life. Someone else told me it was his balcony she jumped off of and broke her arm.'

'Who was she?'

'Well, that's funny, too – '

Her phone rang, and I waited restlessly during a long conversation she had with Joe Reinmund. He seemed to be trying to find out over the phone how good she was or whether she had ever written any pictures at all. And she was reputed to have been on the set the day Griffith invented the close-up! While he talked she groaned silently, writhed, made faces into the receiver, held it all in her lap so that the voice reached her faintly – and kept up a side chatter to me.

'What is *he* doing – killing time between appointments? . . . He's asked me every one of these questions ten times . . . that's all on a memorandum I sent him . . .'

And into the phone: 'If this goes up to Monroe, it won't be my doing. I want to go right through to the end.'

She shut her eyes in agony again.

'Now he's casting it . . . he's casting the minor characters . . . he's going to have Buddy Ebson . . . My God, he just hasn't anything to do . . . now he's on Walter Davenport – he means Donald Crisp . . . he's got a big casting directory open in his lap and I can hear him turn the pages . . . he's a big important man this morning, a second Stahr, and for Christ sake I've got two scenes to do before lunch.'

Reinmund quit finally or was interrupted at his end. A waiter came in from the commissary with Jane's luncheon and a Coca-Cola for me – I wasn't lunching that summer. Jane wrote down one sentence on her typewriter before she ate. It interested me the way she wrote. One day I was there when she and a young man had just lifted a story out of *The Saturday Evening Post* – changing the characters and all. Then they began to write it, making each line answer the line before it, and of course it sounded just like people do in life when they're straining to be anything – funny or gentle or brave. I always wanted to see that one on the screen, but I missed it somehow.

I found her as lovable as a cheap old toy. She made three thousand a week, and her husbands all drank and beat her nearly to death. But today I had an axe to grind.

'You don't know her name?' I persisted.

'Oh – ' said Jane, 'that. Well, he kept calling her up afterwards, and he told Katy Doolan it was the wrong name after all.'

'I think he found her,' I said. 'Do you know Martha Dodd?'

'Hasn't that little girl had a tough break, though!' she exclaimed with ready theatrical sympathy.

'Could you possibly invite her to lunch tomorrow?'

'Oh, I think she gets enough to eat all right. There's a Mexican – '

I explained that my motives were not charitable. Jane agreed to co-operate. She called Martha Dodd.

We had lunch next day at the Bev Brown Derby, a languid restaurant, patronised for its food by clients who always look as if they'd like to lie down. There is some animation at lunch, where the women put on a show for the first five minutes after they eat, but we were a tepid threesome. I should have come right out with my curiosity. Martha Dodd was an agricultural girl, who had never quite understood what had happened to her and had nothing to show for it except a washed-out look about the eyes. She still believed that the life she had tasted was reality and this was only a long waiting.

'I had a beautiful place in 1928,' she told us, ' – thirty acres, with a miniature golf course and a pool and a gorgeous view. All spring I was up to my ass in daisies.'

I ended by asking her to come over and meet father. This was pure penance for having had 'a mixed motive' and being ashamed of it. One doesn't mix motives in Hollywood – it is confusing. Everybody understands, and the climate wears you down. A mixed motive is conspicuous waste.

Jane left us at the studio gate, disgusted by my cowardice. Martha had worked up inside to a pitch about her career – not a very high pitch, because of seven years of neglect, but a sort of nervous acquiescence, and I was going to speak strongly to father. They never did anything for people like Martha, who had made them so much money at one time. They let them slip away into misery eked out with extra work – it would have been kinder to ship them out of town. And father was being so proud of me this summer. I had to keep him from telling everybody just how I had been brought up so as to produce such a perfect jewel. And Bennington – oh, what an exclusive – dear God, my heart. I assured him there was the usual proportion of natural-born skivvies and biddies tastefully concealed by throw-overs from sex Fifth Avenue; but father had worked himself up to practically an alumnus. 'You've had everything,' he used to say happily. Everything included roughly the two years in Florence, where I managed against heavy odds to be the only virgin in school, and the courtesy début in Boston, Massachusetts. I was a veritable flower of the fine old cost-and-gross aristocracy.

So I knew he would do something for Martha Dodd, and as he went into his office, I had great dreams of doing something for Johnny Swanson, the cowboy, too, and Evelyn Brent, and all sorts of discarded flowers. Father was a charming and sympathetic man – except for that time I had seen him unexpectedly in New York – and there was something touching about his being my father. After all, he was *my* father – he would do anything in the world for me.

Only Rosemary Schmiel was in the outer office, and she was on Birdy Peters's phone. She waved for me to sit down, but I was full of my plans and, telling Martha to take it easy, I pressed the clicker under Rosemary's desk and went towards the opened door.

'Your father's in conference,' Rosemary called. 'Not in conference, but I ought to –'

By this time I was through the door and a little vestibule and another door, and caught father in his shirtsleeves, very sweaty and trying to open a window. It was a hot day, but I hadn't realised it was that hot, and thought he was ill.

'No, I'm all right,' he said. 'What is it?'

I told him. I told him the whole theory of people like Martha Dodd, walking up and down his office. How could he use them and guarantee them regular employment? He seemed to take me up excitedly and kept nodding and agreeing, and I felt closer to him than I had for a long time. I came close and kissed him on his cheek. He was trembling and his shirt was soaked through.

'You're not well,' I said, 'or you're in some sort of stew.'

'No, I'm not at all.'

'What is it?'

'Oh, it's Monroe,' he said. 'That goddam little Vine Street Jesus! He's in my hair night and day!'

'What's happened?' I asked, very much cooler.

'Oh, he sits like a little goddam priest or rabbi and says what he'll do and he won't do. I can't tell you now – I'm half crazy. Why don't you go along?'

'I won't have you like this.'

'Go along, I tell you!' I sniffed, but he never drank.

'Go and brush your hair,' I said. 'I want you to see Martha Dodd.'

'In here! I'd never get rid of her.'

'Out there then. Go wash up first. Put on another shirt.'

With an exaggerated gesture of despair, he went into the little bathroom adjoining. It was hot in the office as if it had been closed for hours, and maybe that was making him sick, so I opened two more windows.

'You go along,' father called from behind the closed door of the bathroom. 'I'll be there presently.'

'Be awfully nice to her,' I said. 'No charity.'

As if it were Martha speaking for herself, a long low moan came from somewhere in the room. I was startled – then transfixed, as it came again, not from the bathroom where father was, not from outside, but from a closet in the wall across from me. How I was brave enough I don't know, but I ran across to it and opened it, and father's secretary, Birdy Peters, tumbled out stark naked – just like a corpse in the movies. With her came a gust of stifling, stuffy air. She flopped sideways on the floor, with the one hand still clutching some clothes, and lay on the floor bathed in sweat – just as father came in from the bathroom. I could feel him standing behind me, and without turning I knew exactly how he looked, for I had surprised him before.

'Cover her up,' I said, covering her up myself with a rug from the couch. 'Cover her *up*!'

I left the office. Rosemary Schmiel saw my face as I came out and responded with a terrified expression. I never saw her again or Birdy Peters either. As Martha and I went out, Martha asked: 'What's the matter, dear?' – and when I didn't say anything: 'You did your best. Probably it was the wrong time. I'll tell you what I'll do. I'll take you to see a very nice English girl. Did you see the girl that Stahr danced with at our table the other night?'

So at the price of a little immersion in the family drains I had what I wanted.

* * *

I don't remember much about our call. She wasn't at home was one reason. The screen-door of her house was unlocked, and Martha went in calling 'Kathleen' with bright familiarity. The room we saw was bare and formal as an hotel; there were flowers about, but they did not look like sent flowers. Also, Martha found a note on the table, which said: 'Leave the dress. Have gone looking for a job. Will drop by tomorrow.'

Martha read it twice but it didn't seem to be for Stahr, and we waited five minutes. People's houses are very still when they are gone. Not that I expect them to be jumping around, but I leave the observation for what it's worth. Very still. Prim almost, with just a fly holding down the place and paying no attention to you, and the corner of a curtain blowing.

'I wonder what kind of a job,' said Martha. 'Last Sunday she went somewhere with Stahr.'

But I was no longer interested. It seemed awful to be here – producer's blood, I thought in horror. And in quick panic I pulled her out into the placid sunshine. It was no use – I felt just black and awful. I had always been proud of my body – I had a way of thinking of it as geometric which made everything it did seem all right. And there was probably not any kind of place, including churches and office and shrines, where people had not embraced – but no one had ever stuffed me naked into a hole in the wall in the middle of a business day.

* * *

'If you were in a drugstore,' said Stahr, ' – having a prescription filled – '

'You mean a chemist's?' Boxley asked.

'If you were in a chemist's,' conceded Stahr, 'and you were getting a prescription for some member of your family who was very sick – '

' – Very ill?' queried Boxley.

'Very ill. *Then* whatever caught your attention through the window, whatever distracted you and held you would probably be material for pictures.'

'A murder outside the window, you mean.'

'There you go,' said Stahr, smiling. 'It might be a spider working on the pane.'

'Of course – I see.'

'I'm afraid you don't, Mr Boxley. You see it for *your* medium, but not for ours. You keep the spiders for yourself and you try to pin the murders on us.'

'I might as well leave,' said Boxley. 'I'm no good to you. I've been here three weeks and I've accomplished nothing. I make suggestions, but no one writes them down.'

'I want you to stay. Something in you doesn't like pictures, doesn't like telling a story this way – '

'It's such a damned bother,' exploded Boxley. 'You can't let yourself go – '

He checked himself. He knew that Stahr, the helmsman, was finding time for him in the middle of a constant stiff blow – that they were talking in the always creaking rigging of a ship sailing in great awkward tacks along an open sea. Or else – it seemed at times – they were in a huge quarry – where even the newly-cut marble bore the tracery of old pediments, half-obliterated inscriptions of the past.

'I keep wishing you could start over,' Boxley said. 'It's this mass production.'

'That's the condition,' said Stahr. 'There's always some lousy condition. We're making a life of Rubens – suppose I asked you to do portraits of rich dopes like Bill Brady and me and Gary Cooper and Marcus when you wanted to paint Jesus Christ? Wouldn't you feel you had a condition? Our condition is that we have to take people's own favourite folklore and dress it up and give it back to them. Anything beyond that is sugar. So won't you give us some sugar, Mr Boxley?'

Boxley knew he could sit with Wylie White tonight at the Troc raging at Stahr, but he had been reading Lord Charnwood and he recognised that Stahr like Lincoln was a leader carrying on a long war on many fronts; almost single-handed he had moved pictures sharply forward through a decade, to a point where the content of the 'A productions' was wider and richer than that of the stage. Stahr was an artist only, as Mr Lincoln was a general, perforce and as a layman.

'Come down to La Borwitz's office with me,' said Stahr. 'They sure need some sugar there.'

In La Borwitz's office, two writers, a shorthand secretary and a hushed supervisor, sat in a tense smoky stalemate, where Stahr had left them three hours before. He looked at the faces one after another and found nothing. La Borwitz spoke with awed reverence for his defeat.

'We've just got too many characters, Monroe.'

Stahr snorted affably.

'That's the principal idea of the picture.'

He took some change out of his pocket, looked up at the suspended light and tossed up half a dollar, which clanked into the bowl. He looked at the coins in his hands and selected a quarter.

La Borwitz watched miserably; he knew this was a favourite trick of Stahr's and he saw the sands running out. At the moment everyone's back was towards him. Suddenly he brought up his hands from their placid position under the desk and threw them high in the air, so high that they seemed to leave his wrist – and then he caught them neatly as they were descending. After that he felt better. He was in control.

One of the writers had taken out some coins, also, and presently rules were defined. 'You have to toss your coin through the chains without hitting them. Whatever falls into the light is the kitty.'

They played for half an hour – all except Boxley, who sat aside and dug into the script, and the secretary, who kept tally. She calculated the cost of the four men's time, arriving at a figure of sixteen hundred dollars. At the end, La Borwitz was winner by $5.50, and a janitor brought in a stepladder to take the money out of the light.

Boxley spoke up suddenly.

'You have the stuffings of a turkey here,' he said.

'What!'

'It's not pictures.'

They looked at him in astonishment. Stahr concealed a smile.

'So we've got a real picture man here!' exclaimed La Borwitz.

'A lot of beautiful speeches,' said Boxley boldly, 'but no situations. After all, you know, it's not going to be a novel. And it's too long. I can't exactly describe how I feel, but it's not quite right. And it leaves me cold.'

He was giving them back what had been handed him for three weeks. Stahr turned away, watching the others out of the corner of his eye.

'We don't need *less* characters,' said Boxley. 'We need *more*. As I see it, that's the idea.'

'That's the idea,' said the writers.

'Yes – that's the idea,' said La Borwitz.

Boxley was inspired by the attention he had created.

'Let each character see himself in the other's place,' he said. 'The policeman is about to arrest the thief when he sees that the thief actually has *his* face. I mean, show it that way. You could almost call the thing *Put Yourself in My Place*.'

Suddenly they were at work again – taking up this new theme in turn like hepcats in a swing band and going to town with it. They might throw it out again tomorrow, but life had come back for a moment. Pitching the coins had done it as much as Boxley. Stahr had recreated the proper atmosphere – never consenting to be a driver of the driven, but feeling like and acting like and even sometimes looking like a small boy getting up a show.

He left them, touching Boxley on the shoulder in passing – a deliberate accolade – he didn't want them to gang up on him and break his spirit in an hour.

* * *

Dr Baer was waiting in his inner office. With him was a coloured man with a portable cardiograph like a huge suitcase. Stahr called it the lie detector. Stahr stripped to the waist, and the weekly examination began.

'How've you been feeling?'

'Oh – the usual,' said Stahr.

'Been hard at it? Getting any sleep?'

'No – about five hours. If I go to bed early, I just lie there.'

'Take the sleeping pills.'

'The yellow one gives me a hangover.'

'Take two red ones, then.'

'That's a nightmare.'

'Take one of each – the yellow first.'

'All right – I'll try. How've *you* been?'

'Say – I take care of myself, Monroe, I save myself.'

'The hell you do – you're up all night sometimes.'

'Then I sleep all next day.'

After ten minutes, Baer said: 'Seems OK. The blood pressure's up five points.'

'Good,' said Stahr. 'That's good, isn't it?'

'That's good. I'll develop the cardiographs tonight. When are you coming away with me?'

'Oh, sometime,' said Stahr lightly. 'In about six weeks things'll ease up.'

Baer looked at him with a genuine liking that had grown over three years.

'You got better in thirty-three when you laid up,' he said. 'Even for three weeks.'

'I will again.'

No he wouldn't, Baer thought. With Minna's help he had enforced a few short rests years ago and lately he had hinted around, trying to find who Stahr considered his closest friends. Who could take him away and keep him away? It would almost surely be useless. He was due to die very soon now. Within six months one could say definitely. What was the use of developing the cardiograms? You couldn't persuade a man like Stahr to stop and lie down and look at the sky for six months. He would much rather die. He said differently, but what it added up to was the definite urge towards total exhaustion that he had run into before. Fatigue was a drug as well as a poison, and Stahr apparently derived some rare almost physical pleasure from working light-headed with weariness. It was a perversion of the life force he had seen before, but he had almost stopped trying to interfere with it. He had cured a man or so – a hollow triumph of killing and preserving the shell.

'You hold your own,' he said.

They exchanged a glance. Did Stahr know? Probably. But he did not know when – he did not know how soon now.

'If I hold my own, I can't ask more,' said Stahr.

The coloured man had finished packing the apparatus.

'Next week same time?'

'OK, Bill,' said Stahr. 'Goodbye.'

As the door closed, Stahr switched open the dictagraph. Miss Doolan's voice came through immediately.

'Do you know a Miss Kathleen Moore?'

'What do you mean?' he asked startled.

'A Miss Kathleen Moore is on the line. She said you asked her to call.'

'Well, my God!' he exclaimed. He was swept with indignant rapture. It had been five days – this would never do at all.

'She's on now?'

'Yes.'

'Well, all right then.'

In a moment he heard the voice up close to him.

'Are you married?' he asked, low and surly.

'No, not yet.'

His memory blocked out her face and form – as he sat down, she seemed to lean down to his desk, keeping level with his eyes.

'What's on your mind?' he asked in the same surly voice. It was hard to talk that way.

'You did find the letter?' she asked.

'Yes. It turned up that night.'

'That's what I want to speak to you about.'

He found an attitude at length – he was outraged.

'What is there to talk about?' he demanded.

'I tried to write you another letter, but it wouldn't write.'

'I know that, too.'

There was a pause.

'Oh, cheer up!' she said surprisingly. 'This doesn't sound like you. It *is* Stahr, isn't it? That very nice Mr Stahr?'

'I feel a little outraged,' he said almost pompously. 'I don't see the use of this. I had at least a pleasant memory of you.'

'I don't believe it's you,' she said. 'Next thing you'll wish me luck.' Suddenly she laughed: 'Is this what you planned to say? I know how awful it gets when you plan to say anything – '

'I never expected to hear from you again,' he said with dignity; but it was no use, she laughed again – a woman's laugh that is like a child's, just one syllable, a crow and a cry of delight.

'Do you know how you make me feel?' she demanded. 'Like a day in London during a caterpillar plague when a hot furry thing dropped in my mouth.'

'I'm sorry.'

'Oh, please wake up,' she begged. 'I want to see you. I can't explain things on the phone. It was no fun for me either, you understand.'

'I'm very busy. There's a sneak preview in Glendale tonight.'

'Is that an invitation?'

'George Boxley, the English writer, is going with me.' He surprised himself. 'Do you want to come along?'

'How could we talk?'

She considered. 'Why don't you call for me afterwards,' she suggested. 'We could ride around.'

Miss Doolan on the huge dictagraph was trying to cut in on the line with a shooting director – the only interruption ever permitted. He flipped the button and called 'Wait' impatiently into the machine.

'About eleven?' Kathleen was saying confidentially.

The idea of 'riding around' seemed so unwise that if he could have thought of the words to refuse her he would have spoken them, but he did not want to be the caterpillar. Suddenly he had no attitude left except the sense that the day, at least, was complete. He had an evening – a beginning, a middle, and an end.

* * *

He rapped on the screen-door, heard her call from inside, and stood waiting where the level fell away. From below came the whir of a lawn mower – a man was cutting his grass at midnight. The moon was so bright that Stahr could see him plainly, a hundred feet off and down, as he stopped and rested on the handle before pushing it back across his garden. There was a midsummer restlessness abroad – early August with imprudent loves and impulsive crimes. With little more to expect from summer, one tried anxiously to live in the present – or, if there was no present, to invent one.

She came at last. She was all different and delighted. She wore a suit with a skirt that she kept hitching up as they walked down to the car with a brave, gay, stimulating, reckless air of 'Tighten up your belt, baby. Let's get going.' Stahr had brought his limousine with the chauffeur, and the intimacy of the four walls whisking them along a new curve in the dark took away any strangeness at once. In its way, the little trip they made was one of the best times he had ever had in his life. It was certainly one of the times when, if he knew he was going to die, it was not tonight.

She told him her story. She sat beside him cool and gleaming for a while, spinning on excitedly, carrying him to far places with her, meeting and knowing the people she had known. The story was vague at first. 'This Man' was the one she had loved and lived with. 'This American' was the one who had rescued her when she was sinking into a quicksand.

'Who is he – the American?'

Oh, names – what did they matter? No one important like Stahr, not rich. He had lived in London and now they would live out here. She was going to be a good wife, a real person. He was getting a divorce – not just on account of her – but that was the delay.

'But the first man?' asked Stahr. 'How did you get into that?'

Oh, that was a blessing at first. From sixteen to twenty-one the thing was to eat. The day her stepmother presented her at Court they had one shilling to eat with so as not to feel faint. Sixpence apiece, but the stepmother watched while she ate. After a few months the stepmother died, and she would have sold out for that shilling but she was too weak to go into the streets. London can be harsh – oh, quite.

Was there nobody?

There were friends in Ireland who sent butter. There was a soup kitchen. There was a visit to an uncle, who made advances to her when she had a full stomach, and she held out and got fifty pounds out of him for not telling his wife.

'Couldn't you work?' Stahr asked.

'I worked. I sold cars. Once I sold a car.'

'But couldn't you get a regular job?'

'It's hard – it's different. There was a feeling that people like me forced other people out of jobs. A woman struck me when I tried to get a job as chambermaid in an hotel.'

'But you were presented at Court?'

'That was my stepmother who did that – on an off-chance. I was nobody. My father was shot by the Black-and-Tans in twenty-two when I was a child. He wrote a book called *Last Blessing*. Did you ever read it?'

'I don't read.'

'I wish you'd buy it for the movies. It's a good little book. I still get a royalty from it – ten shillings a year.'

Then she met 'The Man' and they travelled the world around. She had been to all the places that Stahr made movies of, and lived in cities whose name he had never heard. Then The Man went to seed, drinking and sleeping with the housemaids and trying to force her off on his friends. They all tried to make her stick with him. They said she had saved him and should cleave to him longer now, indefinitely, to the end. It was her duty. They brought enormous pressure to bear. But she had met The American, and so finally she ran away.

'You should have run away before.'

'Well, you see, it was difficult.' She hesitated, and plunged. 'You see, I ran away from a king.'

His moralities somehow collapsed – she had managed to top him. A confusion of thoughts raced through his head – one of them a faint old credo that all royalty was diseased.

'It wasn't the King of England,' she said. 'My king was out of a job as he used to say. There are lots of kings in London.' She laughed – then added almost defiantly, 'He was very attractive until he began drinking and raising hell.'

'What was he king of?'

She told him – and Stahr visualised the face out of old newsreels.

'He was a very learned man,' she said. 'He could have taught all sorts of subjects. But he wasn't much like a king. Not nearly as much as you. None of them were.'

This time Stahr laughed.

'You know what I mean. They all felt old-fashioned. Most of them tried so hard to keep up with things. They were always advised to keep up with things. One was a syndicalist, for instance. And one used to carry around a couple of clippings about a tennis tournament when he was in the semi-finals. I saw those clippings a dozen times.'

They rode through Griffith Park and out past the dark studios of Burbank, past the airports, and along the way to Pasadena past the neon signs of roadside cabarets. Up in his head he wanted her, but it was late and just the ride was an overwhelming joy. They held hands and once she came close into his arms saying, 'Oh, you're *so* nice. I *do* like to be with you.' But her mind was divided – this was not his night as the Sunday afternoon had been his. She was absorbed in herself, stung into excitement by telling of her own adventures; he could not help wondering if he was getting the story she had saved up for The American.

'How long have you known The American?' he asked.

'Oh, I knew him for several months. We used to meet. We understood each other. He used to say, "It looks like a cinch from now on." '

'Then why did you call me up?'

She hesitated.

'I wanted to see you once more. Then, *too* – he was supposed to arrive today, but last night he wired that he'd be another week. I wanted to talk to a friend – after all, you *are* my friend.'

He wanted her very much now, but one part of his mind was cold and kept saying: She wants to see if I'm in love with her, if I want to marry her. Then she'd consider whether or not to throw this man over. She won't consider it till I've committed myself.

'Are you in love with The American?' he asked.

'Oh, yes. It's absolutely arranged. He saved my life and my reason. He's moving halfway round the world for me. I insisted on that.'

'But are you in love with him?'

'Oh, yes. I'm in love with him.'

The 'Oh, yes,' told him she was not – told him to speak for himself – that she would see. He took her in his arms and kissed her deliberately on the mouth and held her for a long time. It was so warm.

'Not tonight,' she whispered.

'All right.'

They passed over suicide bridge with the high new wire.

'I know what it is,' she said, 'but how stupid. English people don't kill themselves when they don't get what they want.'

They turned around in the driveway of an hotel and started back. It was a dark night with no moon. The wave of desire had passed and neither spoke for a while. Her talk of kings had carried him oddly back in flashes to the pearly White Way of Main Street in Erie, Pennsylvania, when he was fifteen. There was a restaurant with lobsters in the window and green weeds and bright lights on a shell cavern, and beyond behind a red curtain the terribly strange brooding mystery of people and violin music. That was just before he left for New York. This girl reminded him of the fresh iced fishes and lobsters in the window. She was Beautiful Doll. Minna had never been Beautiful Doll.

They looked at each other and her eyes asked, 'Shall I marry The American?' He did not answer. After a while he said: 'Let's go somewhere for the weekend.'

She considered.

'Are you talking about tomorrow?'

'I'm afraid I am.'

'Well, I'll tell you tomorrow,' she said.

'Tell me tonight. I'd be afraid – '

' – find a note in the car?' she laughed. 'No there's no note in the car. You know almost everything now.'

'Almost everything.'

'Yes – almost. A few little things.'

He would have to know what they were. She would tell him tomorrow. He doubted – he wanted to doubt – if there had been a maze of philandering: a fixation had held her to The Man, the king, firmly and long. Three years of a highly anomalous position – one foot in the palace and one in the background. 'You had to laugh a lot,' she said. 'I learned to laugh a lot.'

'He could have married you – like Mrs Simpson,' Stahr said in protest.

'Oh, he was married. And he wasn't a romantic.' She stopped herself.

'Am I?'

'Yes,' she said, unwillingly, as if she were laying down a trump. 'Part of you is. You're three or four different men but each of them out in the open. Like all Americans.'

'Don't start trusting Americans too implicitly,' he said smiling. 'They may be out in the open, but they change very fast.'

She looked concerned.

'Do they?'

'Very fast and all at once,' he said, 'and nothing ever changes them back.'

'You frighten me. I always had a great sense of security with Americans.'

She seemed suddenly so alone that he took her hand.

'Where will we go tomorrow?' he said. 'Maybe up in the mountains. I've got everything to do tomorrow, but I won't do any of it. We can start at four and get there by afternoon.'

'I'm not sure. I seem to be a little mixed up. This doesn't seem to be quite the girl who came out to California for a new life.'

He could have said it then, said, 'It *is* a new life,' for he knew it was, he knew he could not let her go now; but something else said to sleep on it as an adult, no romantic. And not to tell her till tomorrow. Still she was looking at him, her eyes wandering from his forehead to his chin and back again, and then up and down once more, with that odd slowly-waving motion of her head.

. . . It is your chance, Stahr. Better take it now. This is your girl. She can save you, she can worry you back to life. She will take looking after and you will grow strong to do it. But take her now – tell her and take her away. Neither of you knows it, but far away over the night The American has changed his plans. At this moment his train is speeding through Albuquerque; the schedule is accurate. The engineer is on time. In the morning he will be here.

. . . The chauffeur turned up the hill to Kathleen's house. It seemed warm even in darkness – wherever he had been near here was by way of being an enchanted place for Stahr: this limousine, the rising house at the beach, the very distances they had already covered together over the sprawled city. The hill they climbed now gave forth a sort of glow, a sustained sound that struck his soul alert with delight.

As he said goodbye he felt again that it was impossible to leave her, even for a few hours. There were only ten years between them, but he felt that madness about it akin to the love of an ageing man for a young girl. It was a deep and desperate time-need, a clock ticking with his heart, and it urged him, against the whole logic of his life, to walk past her into the house now and say, 'This is forever.'

Kathleen waited, irresolute herself – pink and silver frost waiting to melt with spring. She was a European, humble in the face of power, but there was a fierce self-respect that would only let her go so far. She had no illusions about the considerations that swayed princes.

'We'll go to the mountains tomorrow,' said Stahr. Many thousands of people depended on his balanced judgement – you can suddenly blunt a quality you have lived by for twenty years.

He was very busy the next morning, Saturday. At two o'clock when he came from luncheon, there was a stack of telegrams – a company ship was lost in the Arctic; a star was in disgrace; a writer was suing for one million dollars. Jews were dead miserably beyond the sea. The last telegram stared up at him: 'I was married at noon today. Goodbye'; and on a sticker attached, 'Send your answer by Western Union Telegram'.

Chapter 6

I knew nothing about any of this. I went up to Lake Louise, and when I came back didn't go near the studio. I think I would have started East in mid-August – if Stahr hadn't called me up one day at home.

'I want you to arrange something, Celia – I want to meet a Communist Party member.'

'Which one?' I asked, somewhat startled.

'Any one.'

'Haven't you got plenty out there?'

'I mean one of their organisers – from New York.'

The summer before I had been all politics – I could probably have arranged a meeting with Harry Bridges. But my boy had been killed in an auto accident after I went back to college, and I was out of touch with such things. I had heard there was a man from *The New Masses* around somewhere.

'Will you promise him immunity?' I asked, joking.

'Oh, yes,' Stahr answered seriously. 'I won't hurt him. Get one that can talk – tell him to bring one of his books along.'

He spoke as if he wanted to meet a member of the 'I am' cult.

'Do you want a blonde or a brunette?'

'Oh, get a man,' he said hastily.

Hearing Stahr's voice cheered me up – since I had barged in on father it had all seemed a paddling about in thin spittle. Stahr changed everything about it – changed the angle from which I saw it, changed the very air.

'I don't think your father ought to know,' he said. 'Can we pretend the man is a Bulgarian musician or something?'

'Oh, they don't dress up any more,' I said.

It was harder to arrange than I thought – Stahr's negotiations with the Writers' Guild, which had continued over a year, were approaching a dead end. Perhaps they were afraid of being corrupted, and I was asked what Stahr's 'proposition' was. Afterwards Stahr told me that he prepared for the meeting by running off the Russian Revolutionary films that he had in his film library at home. He also ran off *Dr Caligari* and Salvador Dali's *Le Chien Andalou*, possibly suspecting that they had a bearing on the matter. He had been startled by the Russian films back in the twenties, and on Wylie White's suggestion he had had the script department get him up a two-page 'treatment' of the *Communist Manifesto*.

But his mind was closed on the subject. He was a rationalist who did his own reasoning without benefit of books – and he had just managed to climb out of a thousand years of Jewry into the late eighteenth century. He could not bear to see it melt away – he cherished the parvenu's passionate loyalty to an imaginary past.

The meeting took place in what I called the 'processed leather room' – it was one of six done for us by a decorator from Sloane's years ago, and the term stuck in my head. It was *the* most decorator's room: an angora wool carpet the colour of dawn, the most delicate grey imaginable – you hardly dared walk on it; and the silver panelling and leather tables and creamy pictures and slim fragilities looked so easy to stain that we could not breathe hard in there, though it was wonderful to look into from the door when the windows were open and the curtains whimpered querulously against the breeze. It was a lineal descendant of the old American parlour that used to be closed except on Sundays. But it was exactly the room for the occasion, and I hoped that whatever happened would give it character and make it henceforth part of our house.

Stahr arrived first. He was white and nervous and troubled – except for his voice, which was always quiet and full of consideration. There was a brave personal quality in the way he would meet you – he would walk right up to you and put aside something that was in the way, and grow to know you all over as if he couldn't help himself. I kissed him for some reason, and took him into the processed leather room.

'When do you go back to college?' he asked.

We had been over this fascinating ground before.

'Would you like me if I were a little shorter?' I asked, 'I could wear low heels and plaster down my hair.'

'Let's have dinner tonight,' he suggested. 'People will think I'm your father but I don't mind.'

'I *love* old men,' I assured him. 'Unless the man has a crutch, I feel it's just a boy and girl affair.'

'Have you had many of those?'

'Enough.'

'People fall in and out of love all the time, don't they?'

'Every three years or so, Fanny Brice says. I just read it in the paper.'

'I wonder how they manage it,' he said. 'I know it's true because I see them. But they look so con*vinced* every time. And then suddenly they don't look convinced. But they get convinced all over.'

'You've been making too many movies.'

'I wonder if they're as convinced the second time or the third time or the fourth time,' he persisted.

'More each time,' I said. 'Most of all the last time.'

He thought this over and seemed to agree.

'I suppose so. Most of all the last time.'

I didn't like the way he said this, and I suddenly saw that under the surface he was miserable.

'It's a great nuisance,' he said. 'It'll be better when it's over.'

'Wait a *min*ute! Perhaps pictures are in the wrong hands.'

Brimmer, the Party Member, was announced, and going to meet him I slid over to the door on one of those gossamer throw-rugs and practically into his arms.

He was a nice-looking man, this Brimmer – a little on the order of Spencer Tracy, but with a stronger face and a wider range of reactions written up in it. I couldn't help thinking as he and Stahr smiled and shook hands and squared off, that they were two of the most alert men I had ever seen. They were very conscious of each other immediately – both as polite to me as you please, but with a softening of the ends of their sentences when they turned in my direction.

'What are you people trying to do?' demanded Stahr. 'You've got my young men all upset.'

'That keeps them awake, doesn't it?' said Brimmer.

'First we let half a dozen Russians study the plant,' said Stahr. 'As a model plant, you understand. And then you try to break up the unity that makes it a model plant.'

'The unity?' Brimmer repeated. 'Do you mean what's known as The Company Spirit?'

'Oh, not that,' said Stahr, impatiently. 'It seems to be *me* you're after. Last week a writer came into my office – a drunk – a man who's been floating around for years just two steps out of the bughouse – and began telling me my business.'

Brimmer smiled.

'You don't look to me like a man who could be told his business, Mr Stahr.'

They would both have tea. When I came back, Stahr was telling a story about the Warner Brothers and Brimmer was laughing with him.

'I'll tell you another one,' Stahr said. 'Balanchine the Russian dancer had them mixed up with the Ritz Brothers. He didn't know which ones he was training and which ones he was working for. He used to go around saying, "I cannot train these Warner Brothers to dance."'

It looked like a quiet afternoon. Brimmer asked him why the producers didn't back the anti-Nazi League.

'Because of you people,' said Stahr. 'It's your way of getting at the writers. In the long view you're wasting your time. Writers are children – even in normal times they can't keep their minds on their work.'

'They're the farmers in this business,' said Brimmer pleasantly. 'They grow the grain but they're not in at the feast. Their feeling towards the producer is like the farmers' resentment of the city fellow.'

I was wondering about Stahr's girl – whether it was all over between them. Later, when I heard the whole thing from Kathleen, standing in the rain in a wretched road called Goldwyn Avenue, I figured out that this must have been a week after she sent him the telegram. She couldn't help the telegram. The man got off the train unexpectedly and walked her to the registry office without a flicker of doubt that this was what she wanted. It was eight in the morning, and Kathleen was in such a daze that she was chiefly concerned about how to get the telegram to Stahr. In theory you could stop and say, 'Listen, I forgot to tell you but I met a man.' But this track had been laid down so thoroughly, with such confidence, such struggle, such relief, that when it came along, suddenly cutting across the other, she found herself on it like a car on a closed switch. He watched her write the telegram, looking directly at it across the table, and she hoped he couldn't read it upside down . . .

When my mind came back into the room, they had destroyed the poor writers – Brimmer had gone so far as to admit they were 'unstable'.

'They are not equipped for authority,' said Stahr. 'There is no substitute for will. Sometimes you have to fake will when you don't feel it at all.'

'I've had that experience.'

'You have to say, "It's got to be like this – no other way" – even if you're not sure. A dozen times a week that happens to me. Situations where there is no real reason for anything. You pretend there is.'

'All leaders have felt that,' said Brimmer. 'Labour leaders, and certainly military leaders.'

'So I've had to take an attitude in this Guild matter. It looks to me like a try for power, and all I am going to give the writers is money.'

'You give some of them very little money. Thirty dollars a week.'

'Who gets that?' asked Stahr, surprised.

'The ones that are commodities and easy to replace.'

'Not on my lot,' said Stahr.

'Oh, yes,' said Brimmer. 'Two men in your shorts department get thirty dollars a week.'

'Who?'

'Man named Ransome – man named O'Brien.'

Stahr and I smiled together.

'Those are not writers,' said Stahr. 'Those are cousins of Cecilia's father.'

'There are some in other studios,' said Brimmer.

Stahr took his teaspoon and poured himself some medicine from a little bottle.

'What's a fink?' he asked suddenly.

'A fink? That's a strike-breaker or a company tec.'

'I thought so,' said Stahr. 'I've got a fifteen-hundred-dollar writer that every time he walks through the commissary keeps saying "Fink!" behind other writers' chairs. If he didn't scare hell out of them, it'd be funny.'

Brimmer laughed.

'I'd like to see that,' he said.

'You wouldn't like to spend a day with me over there?' suggested Stahr.

Brimmer laughed with genuine amusement.

'No, Mr Stahr. But I don't doubt but that I'd be impressed. I've heard you're one of the hardest working and most efficient men in the entire West. It'd be a privilege to watch you, but I'm afraid I'll have to deny myself.'

Stahr looked at me.

'I like your friend,' he said. 'He's crazy, but I like him.' He looked closely at Brimmer: 'Born on this side?'

'Oh, yes. Several generations.'

'Many of them like you?'

'My father was a Baptist minister.'

'I mean are many of them Reds. I'd like to meet this big Jew that tried to blow over the Ford factory. What's his name – '

'Frankensteen?'

'That's the man. I guess some of you believe in it.'

'Quite a few,' said Brimmer dryly.

'Not you,' said Stahr.

A shade of annoyance floated across Brimmer's face.

'Oh, yes,' he said.

'Oh, no,' said Stahr. 'Maybe you did once.'

Brimmer shrugged his shoulders.

'Perhaps the boot's on the other foot,' he said. 'At the bottom of your heart, Mr Stahr, you know I'm right.'

'No,' said Stahr, 'I think it's a bunch of tripe.'

' – you think to yourself, "He's right," but you think the system will last out your time.'

'You don't really think you're going to overthrow the government.'

'No, Mr Stahr. But we think perhaps you are.'

They were nicking at each other – little pricking strokes like men do sometimes. Women do it, too; but it is a joined battle then with no quarter. But it is not pleasant to watch men do it, because you never know what's next. Certainly it wasn't improving the tonal associations of the room for me, and I moved them out the french window into our golden-yellow California garden.

It was midsummer, but fresh water from the gasping sprinklers made the lawn glitter like spring. I could see Brimmer look at it with a sigh in his glance – a way they have. He opened up big outside – inches taller than I thought and broad-shouldered. He reminded me a little of Superman when he takes off his spectacles. I thought he was as attractive as men can be who don't really care about women as such. We played a round robin game of ping-pong, and he handled his bat well. I heard father come into the house singing that damned 'Little Girl, You've Had A Busy Day', and then breaking off, as if he remembered we weren't speaking any more. It was half-past six – my car was standing in the drive, and I suggested we go down to the Trocadero for dinner.

Brimmer had that look that Father O'Ney had that time in New York when he turned his collar around and went with father and me to the Russian Ballet. He hadn't quite ought to be here. When Bernie, the photographer, who was waiting there for some big game or other, came up to our table, he looked trapped – Stahr made Bernie go away, and I would like to have had the picture.

Then, to my astonishment, Stahr had three cocktails, one after the other.

'Now I know you've been disappointed in love,' I said.

'What makes you think that, Cecilia?'

'Cocktails.'

'Oh, I never drink, Cecilia. I get dyspepsia – I've never been tight.'

I counted them: ' – two – *three*.'

'I didn't realise. I couldn't taste them. I thought there was something the matter.'

A silly glassy look darted into his eye – then passed away.

'This is my first drink in a week,' said Brimmer. 'I did my drinking in the Navy.'

The look was back in Stahr's eye – he winked fatuously at me and said: 'This soap-box son-of-a-bitch has been working on the Navy.'

Brimmer didn't know quite how to take this. Evidently he decided to include it with the evening, for he smiled faintly, and I saw Stahr was smiling, too. I was relieved when I saw it was safely in the great American tradition, and I tried to take hold of the conversation, but Stahr seemed suddenly all right.

'Here's my typical experience,' he said very succinctly and clearly to Brimmer. 'The best director in Hollywood – a man I never interfere with – has some streak in him that wants to slip a pansy into every picture, or something on that order. Something offensive. He stamps it in deep like a watermark so I can't get it out. Every time he does it the Legion of Decency moves a step forward, and something has to be sacrificed out of some honest film.'

'Typical organisational trouble,' agreed Brimmer.

'Typical,' said Stahr. 'It's an endless battle. So now this director tells me it's all right because he's got a Directors' Guild and I can't oppress the poor. That's how you add to my troubles.'

'It's a little remote from us,' said Brimmer smiling. 'I don't think we'd make much headway with the directors.'

'The directors used to be my pals,' said Stahr proudly.

It was like Edward VII's boast that he had moved in the best society in Europe.

'But some of them have never forgiven me,' he continued, 'for bringing out stage directors when sound came in. It put them on their toes and made them learn their jobs all over, but they never did really forgive me. That time we imported a whole new hogshead full of writers, and I thought they were great fellows till they all went red.'

Gary Cooper came in and sat down in a corner with a bunch of men who breathed whenever he did and looked as if they lived off him and weren't budging. A woman across the room looked around and turned out to be Carole Lombard – I was glad that Brimmer was at least getting an eyeful.

Stahr ordered a whiskey-and-soda and, almost immediately, another. He ate nothing but a few spoonfuls of soup and he said all the awful things about everybody being lazy so-and-so's and none of it mattered to *him* because he had lots of money – it was the kind of talk you heard whenever father and his friends were together. I think Stahr realised that it sounded pretty ugly outside of the proper company – maybe he had never heard how it sounded before. Anyhow he shut up and drank off a cup of black coffee. I loved him, and what he said didn't change that, but I hated Brimmer to carry off this impression. I wanted him to see Stahr as a sort of technological virtuoso, and here Stahr had been playing the wicked overseer to a point he would have called trash if he had watched it on the screen.

'I'm a production man,' he said, as if to modify his previous attitude. 'I like writers – I think I understand them. I don't want to kick anybody out if they do their work.'

'We don't want you to,' said Brimmer pleasantly. 'We'd like to take you over as a going concern.'

Stahr nodded grimly.

'I'd like to put you in a roomful of my partners. They've all got a dozen reasons for having Fitts run you fellows out of town.'

'We appreciate your protection,' said Brimmer with a certain irony. 'Frankly we *do* find you difficult, Mr Stahr – precisely because you are a paternalistic employer and your influence is very great.'

Stahr was only half listening.

'I never thought,' he said, 'that I had more brains than a writer has. But I always thought that his brains *belonged* to me – because I knew how to use them. Like the Romans – I've heard that they never invented things but they knew what to do with them. Do you see? I don't say it's right. But it's the way I've always felt – since I was a boy.'

This interested Brimmer – the first thing that had interested him for an hour.

'You know yourself very well, Mr Stahr,' he said.

I think he wanted to get away. He had been curious to see what kind of man Stahr was, and now he thought he knew. Still hoping things would be different, I rashly urged him to ride home with us, but when Stahr stopped by the bar for another drink I knew I'd made a mistake.

It was a gentle, harmless, motionless evening with a lot of Saturday cars. Stahr's hand lay along the back of the seat touching my hair. Suddenly I wished it had been about ten years ago – I would have been nine, Brimmer about eighteen and working his way through some mid-western college, and Stahr twenty-five, just having inherited the world and full of confidence and joy. We would both have looked up to Stahr so, without question. And here we were in an adult conflict, to which there was no peaceable solution, complicated now with the exhaustion and drink.

We turned in at our drive, and I drove around to the garden again.

'I must go along now,' said Brimmer. 'I've got to meet some people.'

'No, stay,' said Stahr. 'I never have said what I wanted. We'll play ping-pong and have another drink, and then we'll tear into each other.'

Brimmer hesitated. Stahr turned on the floodlight and picked up his ping-pong bat, and I went into the house for some whiskey – I wouldn't have dared disobey him.

When I came back, they were not playing, but Stahr was batting a whole box of new balls across to Brimmer, who turned them aside. When I arrived, he quit and took the bottle and retired to a chair just out of the floodlight, watching in dark dangerous majesty. He was pale – he was so transparent that you could almost watch the alcohol mingle with the poison of his exhaustion.

'Time to relax on Saturday night,' he said.

'You're not relaxing,' I said.

He was carrying on a losing battle with his instinct towards schizophrenia.

'I'm going to beat up Brimmer,' he announced after a moment. 'I'm going to handle this thing personally.'

'Can't you pay somebody to do it?' asked Brimmer.

I signalled him to keep quiet.

'I do my own dirty work,' said Stahr. 'I'm going to beat hell out of you and put you on a train.'

He got up and came forward, and I put my arms around him, gripping him.

'Please *stop* this!' I said. 'Oh, you're being so bad.'

'This fellow has an influence over you,' he said darkly. 'Over all you young people. You don't know what you're doing.'

'Please go home,' I said to Brimmer.

Stahr's suit was made of slippery cloth and suddenly he slipped away from me and went for Brimmer. Brimmer retreated backwards around the table. There was an odd expression in his face, and afterwards I thought it looked as if he were saying, 'Is *this* all? This frail half-sick person holding up the whole thing.'

Then Stahr came close, his hands going up. It seemed to me that Brimmer held him off with his left arm a minute, and then I looked away – I couldn't bear to watch.

When I looked back, Stahr was out of sight below the level of the table, and Brimmer was looking down at him.

'Please go home,' I said to Brimmer.

'All right.' He stood looking down at Stahr as I came around the table. 'I always wanted to hit ten million dollars, but I didn't know it would be like this.'

Stahr lay motionless.

'Please go,' I said.

'I'm sorry. Can I help – '

'No. Please go. I understand.'

He looked again, a little awed at the depths of Stahr's repose, which he had created in a split second. Then he went quickly away over the grass, and I knelt down and shook Stahr. After a moment he came awake with a terrific convulsion and bounced up on his feet.

'Where is he?' he shouted.

'Who?' I asked innocently.

'That American. Why in hell did you have to marry him, you damn fool?'

'Monroe – he's gone. I didn't marry anybody.'

I pushed him down in a chair.

'He's been gone half an hour,' I lied.

The ping-pong balls lay around in the grass like a constellation of stars. I turned on a sprinkler and came back with a wet handkerchief, but there was no mark on Stahr – he must have been hit in the side of the head. He went off behind some trees and was sick, and I heard him kicking up some earth over it. After that he seemed all right, but he wouldn't go into the house till I got him some mouthwash, so I took back the whiskey bottle and got a mouthwash bottle. His wretched essay at getting drunk was over. I've been out with college freshmen, but for sheer ineptitude and absence of the Bacchic spirit it unquestionably took the cake. Every bad thing happened to him, but that was all.

* * *

We went in the house; the cook said father and Mr Marcus and Fleishacker were on the veranda, so we stayed in the 'processed leather room'. We both sat down in a couple of places and seemed to slide off, and finally I sat on a fur rug and Stahr on a footstool beside me.

'Did I hit him?' he asked.

'Oh, yes,' I said. 'Quite badly.'

'I don't believe it.' After a minute he added: 'I didn't want to hurt him. I just wanted to chase him out. I guess he got scared and hit me.'

If this was his interpretation of what had happened, it was all right with me.

'Do you hold it against him?'

'Oh, no,' he said. 'I was drunk.' He looked around. 'I've never been in here before – who did this room? – somebody from the studio?

'Well, I'll have to get out of here,' he said in his old pleasant way. 'How would you like to go out to Doug Fairbanks' ranch and spend the night?' he asked me. 'I know he'd love to have you.'

That's how the two weeks started that he and I went around together. It only took one of them for Louella to have us married.

The manuscript stops at this point. The following synopsis of the rest of the story has been put together from Fitzgerald's notes and outlines and from the reports of persons with whom he discussed his work:

Soon after his interview with Brimmer, Stahr makes a trip East. A wage-cut has been threatened in the studio, and Stahr has gone to talk to the stockholders – presumably with the idea of inducing them to retrench in some other way. He and Brady have long been working at cross-purposes, and the struggle between them for the control of the company is rapidly coming to a climax. We do not know about the results of this trip from the business point of view, but, whether or not on a business errand, Stahr for the first time visits Washington with the intention of seeing the city; and it is to be presumed that the author had meant to return here to the motif introduced in the first chapter with the visit of the Hollywood people to the home of Andrew Jackson and their failure to gain admittance or even to see the place clearly: the relation of the moving-picture industry to the American ideals and tradition. It is midsummer; Washington is stifling; Stahr comes down with summer grippe and goes around the city in a daze of fever and heat. He never succeeds in becoming acquainted with it as he had hoped to.

When he recovers and gets back to Hollywood, he finds that Brady has taken advantage of his absence to put through a fifty per cent pay-cut. Brady had called a meeting of writers and told them in a tearful speech that he and the other executives would take a cut themselves if the writers would consent to take one. If they would agree, it would not be necessary to reduce the salaries of the stenographers and the other low-paid employees. The writers had accepted this arrangement, but had then been double-crossed by Brady, who had proceeded to slash the stenographers just the same. Stahr is revolted by this; and he and Brady have a violent falling-out. Stahr, though opposed to the unions, believing that any enterprising office-boy can make his way to the top as he has done, is an old-fashioned paternalistic employer, who likes to feel that the people who work for him are contented, and that he and they are on friendly terms. On the other hand, he quarrels also with Wylie White, who he finds has become truculently hostile to him, in spite of the fact that Stahr was not personally responsible for the pay-cut. Stahr has been patient in the past with White's drinking and his practical jokes, and he is hurt that the writer should not feel towards him the same kind of personal loyalty – which is the only solidarity that Stahr understands in the field of business relations. 'The Reds see him now as a conservative – Wall Street as a Red.' But he finds himself driven by the logic of the situation to fall in with the idea which has been proposed and is heartily approved by Brady, of setting up a company union.

As for his own position in the studio, he had in Washington already thought of quitting; but, intimately involved in the struggle, ill, unhappy, and embittered though he is, it is difficult for him to surrender to Brady. In the meantime, he has been going around with Cecilia. The girl, in a conversation with her father about the attentions Stahr has apparently been paying her, has carelessly let Brady know that Stahr is in love with someone else. Brady finds out about Kathleen, whom Stahr has been seeing again, and attempts to blackmail Stahr. Stahr in disgust with the Bradys abruptly drops Cecilia. He on his side has known for years – having learned it by way of his wife's trained nurse – that Brady had had a hand in the death of the husband of a woman with whom he (Brady) had been in love. The two men threaten one another with no really conclusive evidence on either side.

But Brady has an instrument ready to his hand. The man whom Kathleen has married – whose name is W. Bronson Smith – is a technician working in the studios, who has been taking an active part in his union. It is impossible to tell precisely how Scott Fitzgerald imagined the labour situation in Hollywood for the purposes of his story. At the time of which he is writing, the various kinds of technicians had already been organised in the International Alliance of Theatrical Stage Employees; and it is obvious that he intended to exploit the element of racketeering and gangsterism revealed in this organisation by the case of William Bioff. Brady was to go to Kathleen's husband and play upon his jealousy of his wife. We do not know what Fitzgerald intended that these two should try to do to Stahr. Robinson, the cutter (there are notes on this character), was originally to have undertaken to murder him; but it seems more probable from the author's outline that Stahr was to be caught in some trap which would supply Kathleen's husband with grounds for bringing a suit against Stahr for alienation of his wife's affection. In Fitzgerald's story outline, the theme of Chapter 8 is indicated by the words, 'The suit and the price'. This is evidently partly explained by the following note of material which Fitzgerald intended to make use of, though it is impossible to tell how it was to be modified to meet the demands of the story: 'One of the — brothers is accused by an employee of seducing his wife. Sued for alienation. They try to settle it out of court, but the man bringing suit is a labour leader and won't be bought. Neither will he divorce his wife. He considers rougher measures. His price is that — shall go away for a year. —'s instinct is to stay and fight it, but the other brothers get to a doctor and pronounce death sentence on him and retire him. He tries to get the girl to go with him, but is afraid of the Mann Act. She is to follow him and they'll go abroad.'

In any case, Stahr is to be saved by the intervention of the cameraman, Pete Zavras, whom he has befriended at the beginning of the story, when Zavras had lost his standing with the studios.

In the meantime, Stahr is now seriously ill. He and Kathleen have been 'taking breathless chances'. They have succeeded in having 'one last fling', which has taken place during an overpowering heatwave in the early part of September. But their meetings have proved unsatisfactory. The author has indicated in an early sketch that Kathleen was to 'come of very humble parents' – her father was to have been the captain of a Newfoundland fishing smack; and in another place he says that Stahr has found it difficult to accept her as a permanent part of his life because she is 'poor, unfortunate and tagged with a middle-class exterior which doesn't fit in with the grandeur Stahr demands of life'. It is possible that the labour conflict in which her husband has become involved was intended to alienate her and Stahr. Stahr is now being pushed into the past by Brady and by the unions alike. The split between the controllers of the movie industry, on the one hand, and the various groups of employees, on the other, is widening and leaving no place for real individualists of business like Stahr, whose successes are personal achievements and whose career has always been invested with a certain personal glamour. He has held himself directly responsible to everyone with whom he has worked; he has even wanted to beat up his enemies himself. In Hollywood he is 'the last tycoon'.

Stahr has not been afraid, as we have seen in the conference in Chapter 3, to risk money on unpopular films which would afford him some artistic satisfaction. He has had a craftsman's interest in the pictures, and it has been natural for him to want to make them better. But he has been 'lying low' since the wage-cut and has ceased to make pictures altogether. There was to have been a second series of scenes showing him at a story conference, at the rushes, and on the sets, which was to have contrasted with the similar series in Chapters 3 and 4, and to have shown the change that has taken place in his attitude and status.

He must, however, stand up to Brady, who he knows will stop at nothing. He evidently fears Brady will murder him, for he now decides to resort to Brady's own methods and get his partner murdered. For this he apparently goes straight to the gangsters. It is not clear how the murder is to be accomplished; but in order to be away at the time, Stahr arranges a trip to New York. He sees Kathleen for the last time at the airport, and also meets Cecilia, who is going back to college on a different plane. On the plane he has a reaction of disgust against the course he has taken; he realises that he has let himself be degraded to the same plane of brutality as Brady. He decides to call off the murder and intends to wire orders as soon as the plane descends at the next airport. But the plane has an accident and crashes before they reach the next stop. Stahr is killed, and the murder goes through. The ominous suicide of Schwartz in the opening chapter of the story is thus balanced by the death of Stahr. In the note that Schwartz had sent him, he had been trying to warn him against Brady, who had long wanted to get Stahr out of the company.

* * *

Stahr's funeral, which was to have been described in detail, is an orgy of Hollywood servility and hypocrisy. Everybody is weeping copiously or conspicuously stifling emotion with an eye on the right people. Cecilia imagines Stahr present and can hear him saying, 'Trash!' The old cowboy actor, Johnny Swanson, who has been mentioned at the beginning of Chapter 2 and for whom in his forlorn situation Cecilia has later had the idea of trying to do something at the time of her visit to her father's office, has been invited to the funeral by mistake – through the confusion of his name with someone else's – and asked to officiate as pallbearer along with the most intimate and important of the dead producer's friends. Johnny goes through with the ceremony, rather dazed; and then finds out, to his astonishment, that his fortunes have been gloriously restored. From this time on, he is deluged with offers of jobs.

In the meantime, a final glimpse of Fleishacker, the ambitious company lawyer, a man totally without conscience or creative brains, was to have shown him as prefiguring the immediate future of the moving-picture business. There was also to have been a passage towards the end between Fleishacker and Cecilia, in which the former, who has been to New York University and who was perhaps to have tried to marry Cecilia, was to have attempted a conversation with her on an 'intellectual' plane.

Cecilia, on the rebound from Stahr, has had an affair with a man she does not love – probably Wylie White, who has been after her from the first and who represents the opposition to Stahr. As a result of the death of Stahr and the murder of her father, she now breaks down completely. She develops tuberculosis, and we were to learn for the first time at the end that she has been putting together her story in a tuberculosis sanatorium.

We were to have had a final picture of Kathleen standing outside the studio. She has presumably separated from her husband as a result of the plot against Stahr. It had been one of her chief attractions for Stahr that she did not belong to the Hollywood world; and now she knows that she is never to be part of it. She is always to remain on the outside of things – a situation which also has its tragedy.

SELECTED SHORT STORIES

Selected Short Stories

CONTENTS OF THE SELECTED SHORT STORIES

Winter Dreams

Metropolitan Magazine (December 1922)

1

Some of the caddies were poor as sin and lived in one-room houses with a neurasthenic cow in the front yard, but Dexter Green's father owned the second best grocery-store in Black Bear – the best one was the Hub, patronised by the wealthy people from Sherry Island – and Dexter caddied only for pocket-money.

In the fall when the days became crisp and grey, and the long Minnesota winter shut down like the white lid of a box, Dexter's skis moved over the snow that hid the fairways of the golf course. At these times the country gave him a feeling of profound melancholy – it offended him that the links should lie in enforced fallowness, haunted by ragged sparrows for the long season. It was dreary, too, that on the tees where the gay colours fluttered in summer there were now only the desolate sand-boxes knee-deep in crusted ice. When he crossed the hills the wind blew cold as misery, and if the sun was out he tramped with his eyes squinted up against the hard dimensionless glare.

In April the winter ceased abruptly. The snow ran down into Black Bear Lake scarcely tarrying for the early golfers to brave the season with red and black balls. Without elation, without an interval of moist glory, the cold was gone.

Dexter knew that there was something dismal about this Northern spring, just as he knew there was something gorgeous about the fall. Fall made him clench his hands and tremble and repeat idiotic sentences to himself, and make brisk abrupt gestures of command to imaginary audiences and armies. October filled him with hope which November raised to a sort of ecstatic triumph, and in this mood the fleeting brilliant impressions of the summer at Sherry Island were ready grist to his mill. He became a golf champion and defeated Mr T. A. Hedrick in a marvellous match played a hundred times over the fairways of his imagination, a match each detail of which he changed about untiringly – sometimes he won with almost laughable ease, sometimes he came up magnificently from behind. Again, stepping from a Pierce-Arrow automobile, like Mr Mortimer Jones, he strolled frigidly into the lounge of the Sherry Island Golf Club – or perhaps, surrounded by an admiring crowd, he gave an exhibition of fancy diving from the springboard of the club raft . . . Among those who watched him in open-mouthed wonder was Mr Mortimer Jones.

And one day it came to pass that Mr Jones – himself and not his ghost – came up to Dexter with tears in his eyes and said that Dexter was the darned best caddy in the club, and wouldn't he decide not to quit if Mr Jones made it worth his while, because every other darned caddy in the club lost one ball a hole for him – regularly –

'No, sir,' said Dexter decisively, 'I don't want to caddy any more.' Then, after a pause: 'I'm too old.'

'You're not more than fourteen. Why the devil did you decide just this morning that you wanted to quit? You promised that next week you'd go over to the state tournament with me.'

'I decided I was too old.'

Dexter handed in his 'A Class' badge, collected what money was due to him from the caddy-master, and walked home to Black Bear Village.

'The best darned caddy I ever saw,' shouted Mr Mortimer Jones over a drink that afternoon. 'Never lost a ball! Willing! Intelligent! Quiet! Honest! Grateful!'

The little girl who had done this was eleven – beautifully ugly as little girls are apt to be who are destined after a few years to be inexpressibly lovely and bring no end of misery to a great number of men. The spark, however, was perceptible. There was a general ungodliness in the way her lips twisted down at the corners when she smiled, and in the – heaven help us! – in the almost passionate quality of her eyes. Vitality is born early in such women. It was utterly in evidence now, shining through her thin frame in a sort of glow.

She had come eagerly out on to the course at nine o'clock with a white-linen nurse and five small new golf-clubs in a white canvas bag which the nurse was carrying. When Dexter first saw her she was standing by the caddy-house rather ill at ease and trying to conceal the fact by engaging her nurse in an obviously unnatural conversation, graced by startling and irrelevant grimaces from herself.

'Well, it's certainly a nice day, Hilda,' Dexter heard her say. She drew down the corners of her mouth, smiled, and glanced furtively around, her eyes in transit falling for an instant on Dexter.

Then to the nurse: 'Well, I guess there aren't very many people out here this morning, are there?'

The smile again – radiant, blatantly artificial – convincing.

'I don't know what we're supposed to do now,' said the nurse, looking nowhere in particular.

'Oh, that's all right. I'll fix it up.'

Dexter stood perfectly still, his mouth slightly ajar. He knew that if he moved forward a step his stare would be in her line of vision – if he moved backwards he would lose his full view of her face. For a moment he had not realised how young she was. Now he remembered having seen her several times the year before – in bloomers.

Suddenly, involuntarily, he laughed, a short abrupt laugh – then, startled by himself, he turned and began to walk quickly away.

'Boy!'

Dexter stopped.

'Boy – '

Beyond question he was addressed. Not only that, but he was treated to that absurd smile, that preposterous smile – the memory of which at least a dozen men were to carry into middle age.

'Boy, do you know where the golf teacher is?'

'He's giving a lesson.'

'Well, do you know where the caddy-master is?'

'He isn't here yet this morning.'

'Oh.' For a moment this baffled her. She stood alternately on her right and left foot.

'We'd like to get a caddy,' said the nurse. 'Mrs Mortimer Jones sent us out to play golf, and we don't know how without we get a caddy.'

Here she was stopped by an ominous glance from Miss Jones, followed immediately by the smile.

'There aren't any caddies here except me,' said Dexter to the nurse, 'and I got to stay here in charge until the caddy-master gets here.'

'Oh.'

Miss Jones and her retinue now withdrew, and at a proper distance from Dexter became involved in a heated conversation, which was concluded by Miss Jones taking one of the clubs and hitting it on the ground with violence. For further emphasis she raised it again and was about to bring it down smartly upon the nurse's bosom, when the nurse seized the club and twisted it from her hands.

'You damn little mean old *thing*!' cried Miss Jones wildly.

Another argument ensued. Realising that the elements of the comedy were implied in the scene, Dexter several times began to laugh, but each time restrained the laugh before it reached audibility. He could not resist the monstrous conviction that the little girl was justified in beating the nurse.

The situation was resolved by the fortuitous appearance of the caddy-master, who was appealed to immediately by the nurse.

'Miss Jones is to have a little caddy, and this one says he can't go.'

'Mr McKenna said I was to wait here till you came,' said Dexter quickly.

'Well, he's here now.' Miss Jones smiled cheerfully at the caddy-master. Then she dropped her bag and set off at a haughty mince towards the first tee.

'Well?' The caddy-master turned to Dexter. 'What you standing there like a dummy for? Go pick up the young lady's clubs.'

'I don't think I'll go out today,' said Dexter.

'You don't – '

'I think I'll quit.'

The enormity of his decision frightened him. He was a favourite caddy, and the thirty dollars a month he earned through the summer were not to be made elsewhere around the lake. But he had received a strong emotional shock, and his perturbation required a violent and immediate outlet.

It was not so simple as that, either. As so frequently would be the case in the future, Dexter was unconsciously dictated to by his winter dreams.

2

Now, of course, the quality and the seasonability of these winter dreams varied, but the stuff of them remained. They persuaded Dexter several years later to pass up a business course at the state university – his father, prospering now, would have paid his way – for the precarious advantage of attending an older and more famous university in the East, where he was bothered by his scanty funds. But do not get the impression, because his winter dreams happened to be concerned at first with musings on the rich, that there was anything merely snobbish in the boy. He wanted not association with glittering things and glittering people – he wanted the glittering things themselves. Often he reached out for the best without knowing why he wanted it – and sometimes he ran up against the mysterious denials and prohibitions in which life indulges. It is with one of those denials and not with his career as a whole that this story deals.

He made money. It was rather amazing. After college he went to the city from which Black Bear Lake draws its wealthy patrons. When he was only twenty-three and had been there not quite two years, there were already people who liked to say: 'Now *there's* a boy – ' All about him rich men's sons were peddling bonds precariously, or investing patrimonies precariously, or plodding through the two dozen volumes of the 'George Washington Commercial Course', but Dexter borrowed a thousand dollars on his college degree and his confident mouth, and bought a partnership in a laundry.

It was a small laundry when he went into it but Dexter made a specialty of learning how the English washed fine woollen golf-stockings without shrinking them, and within a year he was catering to the trade that wore knickerbockers. Men were insisting that their Shetland hose and sweaters go to his laundry just as they had insisted on a caddy who could find golf-balls. A little later he was doing their wives' lingerie as well – and running five branches in different parts of the city. Before he was twenty-seven he owned the largest string of laundries in his section of the country. It was then that he sold out and went to New York. But the part of his story that concerns us goes back to the days when he was making his first big success.

When he was twenty-three Mr Hart – one of the grey-haired men who liked to say: 'Now there's a boy' – gave him a guest card to the Sherry Island Golf Club for a weekend. So he signed his name one day on the register, and that afternoon played golf in a foursome with Mr Hart and Mr Sandwood and Mr T. A. Hedrick. He did not consider it necessary to remark that he had once carried Mr Hart's bag over this same links, and that he knew every trap and gully with his eyes shut – but he found himself glancing at the four caddies who trailed them, trying to catch a gleam or gesture that would remind him of himself, that would lessen the gap which lay between his present and his past.

It was a curious day, slashed abruptly with fleeting, familiar impressions. One minute he had the sense of being a trespasser – in the next he was impressed by the tremendous superiority he felt towards Mr T. A. Hedrick, who was a bore and not even a good golfer any more.

Then, because of a ball Mr Hart lost near the fifteenth green, an enormous thing happened. While they were searching the stiff grasses of the rough there was a clear call of 'Fore!' from behind a hill in their rear. And as they all turned abruptly from their search a bright new ball sliced abruptly over the hill and caught Mr T. A. Hedrick in the abdomen.

'By Gad!' cried Mr T. A. Hedrick, 'they ought to put some of these crazy women off the course. It's getting to be outrageous.'

A head and a voice came up together over the hill: 'Do you mind if we go through?'

'You hit me in the stomach!' declared Mr Hedrick wildly.

'Did I?' The girl approached the group of men. 'I'm sorry. I yelled "Fore!" '

Her glance fell casually on each of the men – then scanned the fairway for her ball.

'Did I bounce into the rough?'

It was impossible to determine whether this question was ingenuous or malicious. In a moment, however, she left no doubt, for as her partner came up over the hill she called cheerfully: 'Here I am! I'd have gone on the green except that I hit something.'

As she took her stance for a short mashie shot, Dexter looked at her closely. She wore a blue gingham dress, rimmed at throat and shoulders with a white edging that accentuated her tan. The quality of exaggeration, of thinness, which had made her passionate eyes and down-turning mouth absurd at eleven, was gone now. She was arrestingly beautiful. The colour in her cheeks was centred like the colour in a picture – it was not a 'high' colour, but a sort of fluctuating and feverish warmth, so shaded that it seemed at any moment it would recede and disappear. This colour and the mobility of her mouth gave a continual impression of flux, of intense life, of passionate vitality – balanced only partially by the sad luxury of her eyes.

She swung her mashie impatiently and without interest, pitching the ball into a sand-pit on the other side of the green. With a quick, insincere smile and a careless 'Thank you!' she went on after it.

'That Judy Jones!' remarked Mr Hedrick on the next tee, as they waited – some moments – for her to play on ahead. 'All she needs is to be turned up and spanked for six months and then to be married off to an old-fashioned cavalry captain.'

'My God, she's good-looking!' said Mr Sandwood, who was just over thirty.

'Good-looking!' cried Mr Hedrick contemptuously, 'she always looks as if she wants to be kissed! Turning those big cow-eyes on every calf in town!'

It was doubtful if Mr Hedrick intended a reference to the maternal instinct.

'She'd play pretty good golf if she'd try,' said Mr Sandwood.

'She has no form,' said Mr Hedrick solemnly.

'She has a nice figure,' said Mr Sandwood.

'Better thank the Lord she doesn't drive a swifter ball,' said Mr Hart, winking at Dexter.

Later in the afternoon the sun went down with a riotous swirl of gold and varying blues and scarlets, and left the dry, rustling night of Western summer. Dexter watched from the veranda of the Golf Club, watched the even overlap of the waters in the little wind, silver molasses under the harvest-moon. Then the moon held a finger to her lips and the lake became a clear pool, pale and quiet. Dexter put on his bathing-suit and swam out to the farthest raft, where he stretched dripping on the wet canvas of the springboard.

There was a fish jumping and a star shining and the lights around the lake were gleaming. Over on a dark peninsula a piano was playing the songs of last summer and of summers before that – songs from *Chin-Chin* and *The Count of Luxembourg* and *The Chocolate Soldier* – and because the sound of a piano over a stretch of water had always seemed beautiful to Dexter he lay perfectly quiet and listened.

The tune the piano was playing at that moment had been gay and new five years before when Dexter was a sophomore at college. They had played it at a prom once when he could not afford the luxury of proms, and he had stood outside the gymnasium and listened. The sound of the tune precipitated in him a sort of ecstasy and it was with that ecstasy he viewed what happened to him now. It was a mood of intense appreciation, a sense that, for once, he was magnificently attuned to life and that everything about him was radiating a brightness and a glamour he might never know again.

A low, pale oblong detached itself suddenly from the darkness of the Island, spitting forth the reverberate sound of a racing motorboat. Two white streamers of cleft water rolled themselves out behind it and almost immediately the boat was beside him, drowning out the hot tinkle of the piano in the drone of its spray. Dexter raising himself on his arms was aware of a figure standing at the wheel, of two dark eyes regarding him over the lengthening space of water – then the boat had gone by and was sweeping in an immense and purposeless circle of spray round and round in the middle of the lake. With equal eccentricity one of the circles flattened out and headed back towards the raft.

'Who's that?' she called, shutting off her motor. She was so near now that Dexter could see her bathing-suit, which consisted apparently of pink rompers.

The nose of the boat bumped the raft, and as the latter tilted rakishly he was precipitated towards her. With different degrees of interest they recognised each other.

'Aren't you one of those men we played through this afternoon?' she demanded.

He was.

'Well, do you know how to drive a motorboat? Because if you do I wish you'd drive this one so I can ride on the surfboard behind. My name is Judy Jones' – she favoured him with an absurd smirk – rather, what tried to be a smirk, for, twist her mouth as she might, it was not grotesque, it was merely beautiful – 'and I live in a house over there on the Island, and in that house there is a man waiting for me. When he drove up at the door I drove out of the dock because he says I'm his ideal.'

There was a fish jumping and a star shining and the lights around the lake were gleaming. Dexter sat beside Judy Jones and she explained how her boat was driven. Then she was in the water, swimming to the floating surfboard with a sinuous crawl. Watching her was without effort to the eye, like watching a branch waving or a seagull flying. Her arms, burned to butternut, moved sinuously among the dull platinum ripples, elbow appearing first, casting the forearm back with a cadence of falling water, then reaching out and down, stabbing a path ahead.

They moved out into the lake; turning, Dexter saw that she was kneeling on the low rear of the now uptilted surfboard.

'Go faster,' she called, 'fast as it'll go.'

Obediently he jammed the lever forward and the white spray mounted at the bow. When he looked around again the girl was standing up on the rushing board, her arms spread wide, her eyes lifted towards the moon.

'It's awful cold,' she shouted. 'What's your name?'

He told her.

'Well, why don't you come to dinner tomorrow night?'

His heart turned over like the flywheel of the boat, and, for the second time, her casual whim gave a new direction to his life.

3

Next evening, while he waited for her to come downstairs, Dexter peopled the soft deep summer room and the sun-porch that opened from it with the men who had already loved Judy Jones. He knew the sort of men they were – the men who when he first went to college had entered from the great prep schools with graceful clothes and the deep tan of healthy summers. He had seen that, in one sense, he was better than these men. He was newer and stronger. Yet in acknowledging to himself that he wished his children to be like them he was admitting that he was but the rough, strong stuff from which they eternally sprang.

When the time had come for him to wear good clothes, he had known who were the best tailors in America, and the best tailors in America had made him the suit he wore this evening. He had acquired that particular reserve peculiar to his university, that set it off from other universities. He recognised the value to him of such a mannerism and he had adopted it; he knew that to be careless in dress and manner required more confidence than to be careful. But carelessness was for his children. His mother's name had been Krimslich. She was a Bohemian of the peasant class and she had talked broken English to the end of her days. Her son must keep to the set patterns.

At a little after seven Judy Jones came downstairs. She wore a blue silk afternoon dress, and he was disappointed at first that she had not put on something more elaborate. This feeling was accentuated when, after a brief greeting, she went to the door of a butler's pantry and pushing it open called: 'You can serve dinner, Martha.' He had rather expected that a butler would announce dinner, that there would be a cocktail. Then he put these thoughts behind him as they sat down side by side on a lounge and looked at each other.

'Father and mother won't be here,' she said thoughtfully.

He remembered the last time he had seen her father, and he was glad the parents were not to be here tonight – they might wonder who he was. He had been born in Keeble, a Minnesota village fifty miles farther north, and he always gave Keeble as his home instead of Black Bear Village. Country towns were well enough to come from if they weren't inconveniently in sight and used as footstools by fashionable lakes.

They talked of his university, which she had visited frequently during the past two years, and of the nearby city which supplied Sherry Island with its patrons, and whither Dexter would return next day to his prospering laundries.

During dinner she slipped into a moody depression which gave Dexter a feeling of uneasiness. Whatever petulance she uttered in her throaty voice worried him. Whatever she smiled at – at him, at a chicken liver, at nothing – it disturbed him that her smile could have no root in mirth, or even in amusement. When the scarlet corners of her lips curved down, it was less a smile than an invitation to a kiss.

Then, after dinner, she led him out on the dark sun-porch and deliberately changed the atmosphere.

'Do you mind if I weep a little?' she said.

'I'm afraid I'm boring you,' he responded quickly.

'You're not. I like you. But I've just had a terrible afternoon. There was a man I cared about, and this afternoon he told me out of a clear sky that he was poor as a church-mouse. He'd never even hinted it before. Does this sound horribly mundane?'

'Perhaps he was afraid to tell you.'

'Suppose he was,' she answered. 'He didn't start right. You see, if I'd thought of him as poor – well, I've been mad about loads of poor men, and fully intended to marry them all. But in this case, I hadn't thought of him that way, and my interest in him wasn't strong enough to survive the shock. As if a girl calmly informed her fiancé that she was a widow. He might not object to widows, but –

'Let's start right,' she interrupted herself suddenly. 'Who are you, anyhow?'

For a moment Dexter hesitated.

Then: 'I'm nobody,' he announced. 'My career is largely a matter of futures.'

'Are you poor?'

'No,' he said frankly, 'I'm probably making more money than any man my age in the Northwest. I know that's an obnoxious remark, but you advised me to start right.'

There was a pause. Then she smiled and the corners of her mouth drooped and an almost imperceptible sway brought her closer to him, looking up into his eyes. A lump rose in Dexter's throat, and he waited breathless for the experiment, facing the unpredictable compound that would form mysteriously from the elements of their lips. Then he saw – she communicated her excitement to him, lavishly, deeply, with kisses that were not a promise but a fulfilment. They aroused in him not hunger demanding renewal but surfeit that would demand more surfeit . . . kisses that were like charity, creating want by holding back nothing at all.

It did not take him many hours to decide that he had wanted Judy Jones ever since he was a proud, desirous little boy.

4

It began like that – and continued, with varying shades of intensity, on such a note right up to the dénouement. Dexter surrendered a part of himself to the most direct and unprincipled personality with which he had ever come in contact. Whatever Judy wanted, she went after with the full pressure of her charm. There was no divergence of method, no jockeying for position or premeditation of effects – there was very little mental side to any of her affairs. She simply made men conscious to the highest degree of her physical loveliness. Dexter had no desire to change her. Her deficiencies were knit up with a passionate energy that transcended and justified them.

When, as Judy's head lay against his shoulder that first night, she whispered, 'I don't know what's the matter with me. Last night I thought I was in love with a man and tonight I think I'm in love with you – ', it seemed to him a beautiful and romantic thing to say. It was the exquisite excitability that for the moment he controlled and owned. But a week later he was compelled to view this same quality in a different light. She took him in her roadster to a picnic supper, and after supper she disappeared, likewise in her roadster, with another man. Dexter became enormously upset and was scarcely able to be decently civil to the other people present. When she assured him that she had not kissed the other man, he knew she was lying – yet he was glad that she had taken the trouble to lie to him.

He was, as he found before the summer ended, one of a varying dozen who circulated about her. Each of them had at one time been favoured above all others – about half of them still basked in the solace of occasional sentimental revivals. Whenever one showed signs of dropping out through long neglect, she granted him a brief honeyed hour, which encouraged him to tag along for a year or so longer. Judy made these forays upon the helpless and defeated without malice, indeed half unconscious that there was anything mischievous in what she did.

When a new man came to town everyone dropped out – dates were automatically cancelled.

The helpless part of trying to do anything about it was that she did it all herself. She was not a girl who could be 'won' in the kinetic sense – she was proof against cleverness, she was proof against charm;

if any of these assailed her too strongly she would immediately resolve the affair to a physical basis, and under the magic of her physical splendour the strong as well as the brilliant played her game and not their own. She was entertained only by the gratification of her desires and by the direct exercise of her own charm. Perhaps from so much youthful love, so many youthful lovers, she had come, in self-defence, to nourish herself wholly from within.

Succeeding Dexter's first exhilaration came restlessness and dissatisfaction. The helpless ecstasy of losing himself in her was opiate rather than tonic. It was fortunate for his work during the winter that those moments of ecstasy came infrequently. Early in their acquaintance it had seemed for a while that there was a deep and spontaneous mutual attraction – that first August, for example – three days of long evenings on her dusky veranda, of strange wan kisses through the late afternoon, in shadowy alcoves or behind the protecting trellises of the garden arbours, of mornings when she was fresh as a dream and almost shy at meeting him in the clarity of the rising day. There was all the ecstasy of an engagement about it, sharpened by his realisation that there was no engagement. It was during those three days that, for the first time, he had asked her to marry him. She said 'maybe some day', she said 'kiss me', she said 'I'd like to marry you', she said 'I love you' – she said – nothing.

The three days were interrupted by the arrival of a New York man who visited at her house for half September. To Dexter's agony, rumour engaged them. The man was the son of the president of a great trust company. But at the end of a month it was reported that Judy was yawning. At a dance one night she sat all evening in a motorboat with a local beau, while the New Yorker searched the club for her frantically. She told the local beau that she was bored with her visitor, and two days later he left. She was seen with him at the station, and it was reported that he looked very mournful indeed.

On this note the summer ended. Dexter was twenty-four, and he found himself increasingly in a position to do as he wished. He joined two clubs in the city and lived at one of them. Though he was by no means an integral part of the stag-lines at these clubs, he managed to be on hand at dances where Judy Jones was likely to appear. He could have gone out socially as much as he liked – he was an eligible young man, now, and popular with downtown fathers. His confessed devotion to Judy Jones had rather solidified his position. But he had no social aspirations and rather despised the dancing men who were always on tap for the Thursday or Saturday parties and who filled in at dinners with the younger married set. Already he was playing with the idea of going East to New York. He wanted to take Judy Jones with him. No disillusion as to the world in which she had grown up could cure his illusion as to her desirability.

Remember that – for only in the light of it can what he did for her be understood.

Eighteen months after he first met Judy Jones he became engaged to another girl. Her name was Irene Scheerer, and her father was one of the men who had always believed in Dexter. Irene was light-haired and sweet and honourable, and a little stout, and she had two suitors whom she pleasantly relinquished when Dexter formally asked her to marry him.

Summer, fall, winter, spring, another summer, another fall – so much he had given of his active life to the incorrigible lips of Judy Jones. She had treated him with interest, with encouragement, with malice, with indifference, with contempt. She had inflicted on him the innumerable little slights and indignities possible in such a case – as if in revenge for having ever cared for him at all. She had beckoned him and yawned at him and beckoned him again and he had responded often with bitterness and narrowed eyes. She had brought him ecstatic happiness and intolerable agony of spirit. She had caused him untold inconvenience and not a little trouble. She had insulted him, and she had ridden over him, and she had played his interest in her against his interest in his work – for fun. She had done everything to him except to criticise him – this she had not done – it seemed to him only because it might have sullied the utter indifference she manifested and sincerely felt towards him.

When autumn had come and gone again it occurred to him that he could not have Judy Jones. He had to beat this into his mind but he convinced himself at last. He lay awake at night for a while and argued it over. He told himself the trouble and the pain she had caused him, he enumerated her glaring deficiencies as a wife. Then he said to himself that he loved her, and after a while he fell asleep. For a week, lest he imagined her husky voice over the telephone or her eyes opposite him at lunch, he worked hard and late, and at night he went to his office and plotted out his years.

At the end of a week he went to a dance and cut in on her once. For almost the first time since they had met he did not ask her to sit out with him or tell her that she was lovely. It hurt him that she did not miss these things – that was all. He was not jealous when he saw that there was a new man tonight. He had been hardened against jealousy long before.

He stayed late at the dance. He sat for an hour with Irene Scheerer and talked about books and about music. He knew very little about either. But he was beginning to be master of his own time now, and he had a rather priggish notion that he – the young and already fabulously successful Dexter Green – should know more about such things.

That was in October, when he was twenty-five. In January, Dexter and Irene became engaged. It was to be announced in June, and they were to be married three months later.

The Minnesota winter prolonged itself interminably, and it was almost May when the winds came soft and the snow ran down into Black Bear Lake at last. For the first time in over a year Dexter was enjoying a certain tranquillity of spirit. Judy Jones had been in Florida, and afterwards in Hot Springs, and somewhere she had been engaged, and somewhere she had broken it off. At first, when Dexter had definitely given her up, it had made him sad that people still linked them together and asked for news of her, but when he began to be placed at dinner next to Irene Scheerer people didn't ask him about her any more – they told him about her. He ceased to be an authority on her.

May at last. Dexter walked the streets at night when the darkness was damp as rain, wondering that so soon, with so little done, so much of ecstasy had gone from him. May one year back had been marked by Judy's poignant, unforgivable, yet forgiven turbulence – it had been one of those rare times when he fancied she had grown to care for him. That old penny's worth of happiness he had spent for this bushel of content. He knew that Irene would be no more than a curtain spread behind him, a hand moving among gleaming teacups, a voice calling to children . . . fire and loveliness were gone, the magic of nights and the wonder of the varying hours and seasons . . . slender lips, down-turning, dropping to his lips and bearing him up into a heaven of eyes . . . The thing was deep in him. He was too strong and alive for it to die lightly.

In the middle of May when the weather balanced for a few days on the thin bridge that led to deep summer he turned in one night at Irene's house. Their engagement was to be announced in a week now – no one would be surprised at it. And tonight they would sit together on the lounge at the University Club and look on for an hour at the dancers. It gave him a sense of solidity to go with her – she was so sturdily popular, so intensely 'great'.

He mounted the steps of the brownstone house and stepped inside.

'Irene,' he called.

Mrs Scheerer came out of the living-room to meet him.

'Dexter,' she said, 'Irene's gone upstairs with a splitting headache. She wanted to go with you but I made her go to bed.'

'Nothing serious, I—'

'Oh, no. She's going to play golf with you in the morning. You can spare her for just one night, can't you, Dexter?'

Her smile was kind. She and Dexter liked each other. In the living-room he talked for a moment before he said good-night.

Returning to the University Club, where he had rooms, he stood in the doorway for a moment and watched the dancers. He leaned against the doorpost, nodded at a man or two – yawned.

'Hello, darling.'

The familiar voice at his elbow startled him. Judy Jones had left a man and crossed the room to him – Judy Jones, a slender enamelled doll in cloth of gold: gold in a band at her head, gold in two slipper points at her dress's hem. The fragile glow of her face seemed to blossom as she smiled at him. A breeze of warmth and light blew through the room. His hands in the pockets of his dinner-jacket tightened spasmodically. He was filled with a sudden excitement.

'When did you get back?' he asked casually.

'Come here and I'll tell you about it.'

She turned and he followed her. She had been away – he could have wept at the wonder of her return. She had passed through enchanted streets, doing things that were like provocative music. All mysterious happenings, all fresh and quickening hopes, had gone away with her, had come back with her now.

She turned in the doorway.

'Have you a car here? If you haven't, I have.'

'I have a coupé.'

In then, with a rustle of golden cloth. He slammed the door. Into so many cars she had stepped – like this – like that – her back against the leather, so – her elbow resting on the door – waiting. She would have been soiled long since had there been anything to soil her – except herself – but this was her own self-outpouring.

With an effort he forced himself to start the car and back into the street. This was nothing, he must remember. She had done this before, and he had put her behind him, as he would have crossed a bad account from his books.

He drove slowly downtown and, affecting abstraction, traversed the deserted streets of the business section, peopled here and there where a movie was giving out its crowd or where consumptive or pugilistic youth lounged in front of pool halls. The clink of glasses and the slap of hands on the bars issued from saloons, cloisters of glazed glass and dirty yellow light.

She was watching him closely and the silence was embarrassing, yet in this crisis he could find no casual word with which to profane the hour. At a convenient turning he began to zigzag back towards the University Club.

'Have you missed me?' she asked suddenly.

'Everybody missed you.'

He wondered if she knew of Irene Scheerer. She had been back only a day – her absence had been almost contemporaneous with his engagement.

'What a remark!' Judy laughed sadly – without sadness. She looked at him searchingly. He became absorbed in the dashboard.

'You're handsomer than you used to be,' she said thoughtfully. 'Dexter, you have the most rememberable eyes.'

He could have laughed at this, but he did not laugh. It was the sort of thing that was said to sophomores. Yet it stabbed at him.

'I'm awfully tired of everything, darling.' She called everyone darling, endowing the endearment with careless, individual comraderie. 'I wish you'd marry me.'

The directness of this confused him. He should have told her now that he was going to marry another girl, but he could not tell her. He could as easily have sworn that he had never loved her.

'I think we'd get along,' she continued, on the same note, 'unless probably you've forgotten me and fallen in love with another girl.'

Her confidence was obviously enormous. She had said, in effect, that she found such a thing impossible to believe, that if it were true he had merely committed a childish indiscretion – and probably to show off. She would forgive him, because it was not a matter of any moment but rather something to be brushed aside lightly.

'Of course you could never love anybody but me,' she continued. 'I like the way you love me. Oh, Dexter, have you forgotten last year?'

'No, I haven't forgotten.'

'Neither have I!'

Was she sincerely moved – or was she carried along by the wave of her own acting?

'I wish we could be like that again,' she said, and he forced himself to answer: 'I don't think we can.'

'I suppose not . . . I hear you're giving Irene Scheerer a violent rush.'

There was not the faintest emphasis on the name, yet Dexter was suddenly ashamed.

'Oh, take me home,' cried Judy suddenly; 'I don't want to go back to that idiotic dance – with those children.'

Then, as he turned up the street that led to the residence district, Judy began to cry quietly to herself. He had never seen her cry before.

The dark street lightened, the dwellings of the rich loomed up around them, he stopped his coupé in front of the great white bulk of the Mortimer Joneses' house, somnolent, gorgeous, drenched with the splendour of the damp moonlight. Its solidity startled him. The strong walls, the steel of the girders, the breadth and beam and pomp of it were there only to bring out the contrast with the young beauty beside him. It was sturdy to accentuate her slightness – as if to show what a breeze could be generated by a butterfly's wing.

He sat perfectly quiet, his nerves in wild clamour, afraid that if he moved he would find her irresistibly in his arms. Two tears had rolled down her wet face and trembled on her upper lip.

'I'm more beautiful than anybody else,' she said brokenly, 'why can't I be happy?' Her moist eyes tore at his stability – her mouth turned slowly downward with an exquisite sadness: 'I'd like to marry you if you'll have me, Dexter. I suppose you think I'm not worth having, but I'll be so beautiful for you, Dexter.'

A million phrases of anger, pride, passion, hatred, tenderness fought on his lips. Then a perfect wave of emotion washed over him, carrying off with it a sediment of wisdom, of convention, of doubt, of honour. This was his girl who was speaking, his own, his beautiful, his pride.

'Won't you come in?' He heard her draw in her breath sharply.

Waiting.

'All right,' his voice was trembling, 'I'll come in.'

5

It was strange that neither when it was over nor a long time afterwards did he regret that night. Looking at it from the perspective of ten years, the fact that Judy's flare for him endured just one month seemed of little importance. Nor did it matter that by his yielding he subjected himself to a deeper agony in the end and gave serious hurt to Irene Scheerer and to Irene's parents, who had befriended him. There was nothing sufficiently pictorial about Irene's grief to stamp itself on his mind.

Dexter was at bottom hard-minded. The attitude of the city on his action was of no importance to him, not because he was going to leave the city, but because any outside attitude on the situation seemed superficial. He was completely indifferent to popular opinion. Nor, when he had seen that it was no use, that he did not possess in himself the power to move fundamentally or to hold Judy Jones, did he bear any malice towards her. He loved her, and he would love her until the day he was too old for loving – but he could not have her. So he tasted the deep pain that is reserved only for the strong, just as he had tasted for a little while the deep happiness.

Even the ultimate falsity of the grounds upon which Judy terminated the engagement – that she did not want to 'take him away' from Irene – Judy, who had wanted nothing else – did not revolt him. He was beyond any revulsion or any amusement.

He went East in February with the intention of selling out his laundries and settling in New York – but the war came to America in March and changed his plans. He returned to the West, handed over the management of the business to his partner, and went into the first officers' training-camp in late April. He was one of those young thousands who greeted the war with a certain amount of relief, welcoming the liberation from webs of tangled emotion.

6

This story is not his biography, remember, although things creep into it which have nothing to do with those dreams he had when he was young. We are almost done with them and with him now. There is only one more incident to be related here, and it happens seven years further on.

It took place in New York, where he had done well – so well that there were no barriers too high for him. He was thirty-two years old, and, except for one flying trip immediately after the war, he had not been West in seven years. A man named Devlin from Detroit came into his office to see him in a business way, and then and there this incident occurred, and closed out, so to speak, this particular side of his life.

'So you're from the Middle West,' said the man Devlin with careless curiosity. 'That's funny – I thought men like you were probably born and raised on Wall Street. You know – wife of one of my best friends in Detroit came from your city. I was an usher at the wedding.'

Dexter waited with no apprehension of what was coming.

'Judy Simms,' said Devlin with no particular interest; 'Judy Jones she was once.'

'Yes, I knew her.' A dull impatience spread over him. He had heard, of course, that she was married – perhaps deliberately he had heard no more.

'Awfully nice girl,' brooded Devlin meaninglessly, 'I'm sort of sorry for her.'

'Why?' Something in Dexter was alert, receptive, at once.

'Oh, Lud Simms has gone to pieces in a way. I don't mean he ill-uses her, but he drinks and runs around – '

'Doesn't she run around?'

'No. Stays at home with her kids.'

'Oh.'

'She's a little too old for him,' said Devlin.

'Too old!' cried Dexter. 'Why, man, she's only twenty-seven.'

He was possessed with a wild notion of rushing out into the streets and taking a train to Detroit. He rose to his feet spasmodically.

'I guess you're busy,' Devlin apologised quickly. 'I didn't realise'

'No, I'm not busy,' said Dexter, steadying his voice. 'I'm not busy at all. Not busy at all. Did you say she was – twenty-seven? No, I said she was twenty-seven.'

'Yes, you did,' agreed Devlin dryly.

'Go on, then. Go on.'

'What do you mean?'

'About Judy Jones.'

Devlin looked at him helplessly.

'Well, that's – I told you all there is to it. He treats her like the devil. Oh, they're not going to get divorced or anything. When he's particularly outrageous she forgives him. In fact, I'm inclined to think she loves him. She was a pretty girl when she first came to Detroit.'

A pretty girl! The phrase struck Dexter as ludicrous.

'Isn't she – a pretty girl, any more?'

'Oh, she's all right.'

'Look here,' said Dexter, sitting down suddenly, 'I don't understand. You say she was a "pretty girl" and now you say she's "all right". I don't understand what you mean – Judy Jones wasn't a pretty girl, at all. She was a great beauty. Why, I knew her, I knew her. She was – '

Devlin laughed pleasantly.

'I'm not trying to start a row,' he said. 'I think Judy's a nice girl and I like her. I can't understand how a man like Lud Simms could fall madly in love with her, but he did.' Then he added: 'Most of the women like her.'

Dexter looked closely at Devlin, thinking wildly that there must be a reason for this, some insensitivity in the man or some private malice.

'Lots of women fade just like *that*,' Devlin snapped his fingers. 'You must have seen it happen. Perhaps I've forgotten how pretty she was at her wedding. I've seen her so much since then, you see. She has nice eyes.'

A sort of dullness settled down upon Dexter. For the first time in his life he felt like getting very drunk. He knew that he was laughing loudly at something Devlin had said, but he did not know what it was or why it was funny. When, in a few minutes, Devlin went he lay down on his lounge and looked out the window at the New York skyline into which the sun was sinking in dull lovely shades of pink and gold.

He had thought that having nothing else to lose he was invulnerable at last – but he knew that he had just lost something more, as surely as if he had married Judy Jones and seen her fade away before his eyes.

The dream was gone. Something had been taken from him. In a sort of panic he pushed the palms of his hands into his eyes and tried to bring up a picture of the waters lapping on Sherry Island and the moonlit veranda, and gingham on the golf-links and the dry sun and the gold colour of her neck's soft down. And her mouth damp to his kisses and her eyes plaintive with melancholy and her freshness like new fine linen in the morning. Why, these things were no longer in the world! They had existed and they existed no longer.

For the first time in years the tears were streaming down his face. But they were for himself now. He did not care about mouth and eyes and moving hands. He wanted to care, and he could not care. For he had gone away and he could never go back any more. The gates were closed, the sun was gone down, and there was no beauty but the grey beauty of steel that withstands all time. Even the grief he could have borne was left behind in the country of illusion, of youth, of the richness of life, where his winter dreams had flourished.

'Long ago,' he said, 'long ago, there was something in me, but now that thing is gone. Now that thing is gone, that thing is gone. I cannot cry. I cannot care. That thing will come back no more.'

Gretchen's Forty Winks

Saturday Evening Post (15 March 1924)

1

The sidewalks were scratched with brittle leaves, and the bad little boy next door froze his tongue to the iron mail-box. Snow before night, sure. Autumn was over. This, of course, raised the coal question and the Christmas question; but Roger Halsey, standing on his own front porch, assured the dead suburban sky that he hadn't time for worrying about the weather. Then he let himself hurriedly into the house, and shut the subject out into the cold twilight.

The hall was dark, but from above he heard the voices of his wife and the nursemaid and the baby in one of their interminable conversations, which consisted chiefly of, 'Don't!' and, 'Look out, Maxy!' and, 'Oh, there he *goes*!' punctuated by wild threats and vague bumpings and the recurrent sound of small, venturing feet.

Roger turned on the hall-light and walked into the living-room and turned on the red silk lamp. He put his bulging portfolio on the table, and sitting down rested his intense young face in his hand for a few minutes, shading his eyes carefully from the light. Then he lit a cigarette, squashed it out, and going to the foot of the stairs called for his wife.

'Gretchen!'

'Hello, dear.' Her voice was full of laughter. 'Come see baby.'

He swore softly.

'I can't see baby now,' he said aloud. 'How long 'fore you'll be down?'

There was a mysterious pause, and then a succession of 'Don't's and 'Look out, Maxy's evidently meant to avert some threatened catastrophe.

'How long 'fore you'll be down?' repeated Roger, slightly irritated.

'Oh, I'll be right down.'

'How soon?' he shouted.

He had trouble every day at this hour in adapting his voice from the urgent key of the city to the proper casualness for a model home. But tonight he was deliberately impatient. It almost disappointed him when Gretchen came running down the stairs, three at a time, crying, 'What is it?' in a rather surprised voice.

They kissed – lingered over it some moments. They had been married three years, and they were much more in love than that implies. It was seldom that they hated each other with that violent hate of which only young couples are capable, for Roger was still actively sensitive to her beauty.

'Come in here,' he said abruptly. 'I want to talk to you.'

His wife, a bright-coloured, Titian-haired girl, vivid as a French rag doll, followed him into the living-room.

'Listen, Gretchen' – he sat down at the end of the sofa – 'beginning with tonight I'm going to – What's the matter?'

'Nothing. I'm just looking for a cigarette. Go on.'

She tiptoed breathlessly back to the sofa and settled at the other end.

'Gretchen – ' Again he broke off. Her hand, palm upwards, was extended towards him. 'Well, what is it?' he asked wildly.

'Matches.'

'What?'

In his impatience it seemed incredible that she should ask for matches, but he fumbled automatically in his pocket.

'Thank you,' she whispered. 'I didn't mean to interrupt you. Go on.'

'Gretch – '

Scratch! The match flared. They exchanged a tense look.

Her fawn's eyes apologised mutely this time, and he laughed. After all, she had done no more than light a cigarette; but when he was in this mood her slightest positive action irritated him beyond measure.

'When you've got time to listen,' he said crossly, 'you might be interested in discussing the poorhouse question with me.'

'What poorhouse?' Her eyes were wide, startled; she sat quiet as a mouse.

'That was just to get your attention. But, beginning tonight, I start on what'll probably be the most important six weeks of my life – the six weeks that'll decide whether we're going on for ever in this rotten little house in this rotten little suburban town.'

Boredom replaced alarm in Gretchen's black eyes. She was a Southern girl, and any question that had to do with getting ahead in the world always tended to give her a headache.

'Six months ago I left the New York Lithographic Company,' announced Roger, 'and went into the advertising business for myself.'

'I know,' interrupted Gretchen resentfully; 'and now instead of getting six hundred a month sure, we're living on a risky five hundred.'

'Gretchen,' said Roger sharply, 'if you'll just believe in me as hard an you can for six weeks more we'll be rich. I've got a chance now to get some of the biggest accounts in the country.' He hesitated. 'And for these six weeks we won't go out at all, and we won't have anyone here. I'm going to bring home work every night, and we'll pull down all the blinds and if anyone rings the doorbell we won't answer.'

He smiled airily as if it were a new game they were going to play. Then, as Gretchen was silent, his smile faded, and he looked at her uncertainly.

'Well, what's the matter?' she broke out finally. 'Do you expect me to jump up and sing? You do enough work as it is. If you try to do any more you'll end up with a nervous breakdown. I read about a – '

'Don't worry about me,' he interrupted; 'I'm all right. But you're going to be bored to death sitting here every evening.'

'No, I won't,' she said without conviction – 'except tonight.'

'What about tonight?'

'George Tompkins asked us to dinner.'

'Did you accept?'

'Of course I did,' she said impatiently. 'Why not? You're always talking about what a terrible neighbourhood this is, and I thought maybe you'd like to go to a nicer one for a change.'

'When I go to a nicer neighbourhood I want to go for good,' he said grimly.

'Well, can we go?'

'I suppose we'll have to if you've accepted.'

Somewhat to his annoyance the conversation abruptly ended. Gretchen jumped up and kissed him sketchily and rushed into the kitchen to light the hot water for a bath. With a sigh he carefully deposited his portfolio behind the bookcase – it contained only sketches and layouts for display advertising, but it seemed to him the first thing a burglar would look for. Then he went abstractedly upstairs, dropping into the baby's room for a casual moist kiss, and began dressing for dinner.

They had no automobile, so George Tompkins called for them at half-past six. Tompkins was a successful interior decorator, a broad, rosy man with a handsome moustache and a strong odour of jasmine. He and Roger had once roomed side by side in a boarding-house in New York, but they had met only intermittently in the past five years.

'We ought to see each other more,' he told Roger tonight. 'You ought to go out more often, old boy. Cocktail?'

'No, thanks.'

'No? Well, your fair wife will – won't you, Gretchen?'

'I love this house,' she exclaimed, taking the glass and looking admiringly at ship models, colonial whiskey bottles and other fashionable débris of 1925.

'I like it,' said Tompkins with satisfaction. 'I did it to please myself, and I succeeded.'

Roger stared moodily around the stiff, plain room, wondering if they could have blundered into the kitchen by mistake.

'You look like the devil, Roger,' said his host. 'Have a cocktail and cheer up.'

'Have one,' urged Gretchen.

'What?' Roger turned around absently. 'Oh, no, thanks. I've got to work after I get home.'

'Work!' Tompkins smiled. 'Listen, Roger, you'll kill yourself with work. Why don't you bring a little balance into your life – work a little, then play a little?'

'That's what I tell him,' said Gretchen.

'Do you know an average businessman's day?' demanded Tompkins as they went in to dinner. 'Coffee in the morning, eight hours' work interrupted by a bolted luncheon, and then home again with dyspepsia and a bad temper to give the wife a pleasant evening.'

Roger laughed shortly.

'You've been going to the movies too much,' he said dryly.

'What?' Tompkins looked at him with some irritation. 'Movies? I've hardly ever been to the movies in my life. I think the movies are atrocious. My opinions on life are drawn from my own observations. I believe in a balanced life.'

'What's that?' demanded Roger.

'Well' – he hesitated – 'probably the best way to tell you would be to describe my own day. Would that seem horribly egotistic?'

'Oh, no!' Gretchen looked at him with interest. 'I'd love to hear about it.'

'Well, in the morning I get up and go through a series of exercises. I've got one room fitted up as a little gymnasium, and I punch the bag and do shadow-boxing and weight-pulling for an hour. Then after a cold bath – There's a thing now! Do you take a daily cold bath?'

'No,' admitted Roger, 'I take a hot bath in the evening three or four times a week.'

A horrified silence fell. Tompkins and Gretchen exchanged a glance as if something obscene had been said.

'What's the matter?' broke out Roger, glancing from one to the other in some irritation. 'You know I don't take a bath every day – I haven't got the time.'

Tompkins gave a prolonged sigh.

'After my bath,' he continued, drawing a merciful veil of silence over the matter, 'I have breakfast and drive to my office in New York, where I work until four. Then I lay off, and if it's summer I hurry out here for nine holes of golf, or if it's winter I play squash for an hour at my club. Then a good snappy game of bridge until dinner. Dinner is liable to have something to do with business, but in a pleasant way. Perhaps I've just finished a house for some customer, and he wants me to be on hand for his first party to see that the lighting is soft enough and all that sort of thing. Or maybe I sit down with a good book of poetry and spend the evening alone. At any rate, I do something every night to get me out of myself.'

'It must be wonderful,' said Gretchen enthusiastically. 'I wish we lived like that.'

Tompkins bent forward earnestly over the table.

'You can,' he said impressively. 'There's no reason why you shouldn't. Look here, if Roger'll play nine holes of golf every day it'll do wonders for him. He won't know himself. He'll do his work better, never get that tired, nervous feeling – What's the matter?'

He broke off. Roger had perceptibly yawned.

'Roger,' cried Gretchen sharply, 'there's no need to be so rude. If you did what George said, you'd be a lot better off.' She turned indignantly to their host. 'The latest is that he's going to work at night for the next six weeks. He says he's going to pull down the blinds and shut us up like hermits in a cave. He's been doing it every Sunday for the last year; now he's going to do it every night for six weeks.'

Tompkins shook his head sadly.

'At the end of six weeks,' he remarked, 'he'll be starting for the sanatorium. Let me tell you, every private hospital in New York is full of cases like yours. You just strain the human nervous system a little too far, and bang! – you've broken something. And in order to save sixty hours you're laid up sixty weeks for repairs.' He broke off, changed his tone, and turned to Gretchen with a smile. 'Not to mention what happens to you. It seems to me it's the wife rather than the husband who bears the brunt of these insane periods of overwork.'

'I don't mind,' protested Gretchen loyally.

'Yes, she does,' said Roger grimly; 'she minds like the devil. She's a short-sighted little egg, and she thinks it's going to be for ever until I get started and she can have some new clothes. But it can't be helped. The saddest thing about women is that, after all, their best trick is to sit down and fold their hands.'

'Your ideas on women are about twenty years out of date,' said Tompkins pityingly. 'Women won't sit down and wait any more.'

'Then they'd better marry men of forty,' insisted Roger stubbornly. 'If a girl marries a young man for love she ought to be willing to make any sacrifice within reason, so long as her husband keeps going ahead.'

'Let's not talk about it,' said Gretchen impatiently. 'Please, Roger, let's have a good time just this once.'

When Tompkins dropped them in front of their house at eleven Roger and Gretchen stood for a moment on the sidewalk looking at the winter moon. There was a fine, damp, dusty snow in the air, and Roger drew a long breath of it and put his arm around Gretchen exultantly.

'I can make more money than he can,' he said tensely. 'And I'll be doing it in just forty days.'

'Forty days,' she sighed. 'It seems such a long time – when everybody else is always having fun. If I could only sleep for forty days.'

'Why don't you, honey? Just take forty winks, and when you wake up everything'll be fine.'

She was silent for a moment.

'Roger,' she asked thoughtfully, 'do you think George meant what he said about taking me horseback-riding on Sunday?'

Roger frowned.

'I don't know. Probably not – I hope to heaven he didn't.' He hesitated. 'As a matter of fact, he made me sort of sore tonight – all that junk about his cold bath.'

With their arms about each other, they started up the walk to the house.

'I'll bet he doesn't take a cold bath every morning,' continued Roger ruminatively; 'or three times a week, either.' He fumbled in his pocket for the key and inserted it in the lock with savage precision. Then he turned around defiantly. 'I'll bet he hasn't had a bath for a month.'

2

After a fortnight of intensive work, Roger Halsey's days blurred into each other and passed by in blocks of twos and threes and fours. From eight until half-past five he was in his office. Then a half-hour on the commuting train, where he scrawled notes on the backs of envelopes under the dull yellow light. By half-past seven his crayons, shears and sheets of white cardboard were spread over the living-room table, and he laboured there with much grunting and sighing until midnight, while Gretchen lay on the sofa with a book, and the doorbell tinkled occasionally behind the drawn blinds. At twelve there was always an argument as to whether he would come to bed. He would agree to come after he had cleared up everything; but as he was invariably sidetracked by half a dozen new ideas, he usually found Gretchen sound asleep when he tiptoed upstairs.

Sometimes it was three o'clock before Roger squashed his last cigarette into the overloaded ashtray, and he would undress in the dark, disembodied with fatigue, but with a sense of triumph that he had lasted out another day.

Christmas came and went and he scarcely noticed that it was gone. He remembered it afterwards as the day he completed the window-cards for Garrod's shoes. This was one of the eight large accounts for which he was pointing in January – if he got half of them he was assured a quarter of a million dollars' worth of business during the year.

But the world outside his business became a chaotic dream. He was aware that on two cool December Sundays George Tompkins had taken Gretchen horseback-riding, and that another time she had gone out with him in his automobile to spend the afternoon skiing on the country-club hill. A picture of Tompkins, in an expensive frame, had appeared one morning on their bedroom wall. And one night he was shocked into a startled protest when Gretchen went to the theatre with Tompkins in town.

But his work was almost done. Daily now his layouts arrived from the printers until seven of them were piled and docketed in his office safe. He knew how good they were. Money alone couldn't buy such work; more than he realised himself, it had been a labour of love.

December tumbled like a dead leaf from the calendar. There was an agonising week when he had to give up coffee because it made his heart pound so. If he could hold on now for four days – three days –

On Thursday afternoon H. G. Garrod was to arrive in New York. On Wednesday evening Roger came home at seven to find Gretchen poring over the December bills with a strange expression in her eyes.

'What's the matter?'

She nodded at the bills. He ran through them, his brow wrinkling in a frown.

'Gosh!'

'I can't help it,' she burst out suddenly. 'They're terrible.'

'Well, I didn't marry you because you were a wonderful housekeeper. I'll manage about the bills some way. Don't worry your little head over it.'

She regarded him coldly.

'You talk as if I were a child.'

'I have to,' he said with sudden irritation.

'Well, at least I'm not a piece of bric-à-brac that you can just put somewhere and forget.'

He knelt down by her quickly, and took her arms in his hands.

'Gretchen, listen!' he said breathlessly. 'For God's sake, don't go to pieces now! We're both all stored up with malice and reproach, and if we had a quarrel it'd be terrible. I love you, Gretchen. Say you love me – quick!'

'You know I love you.'

The quarrel was averted, but there was an unnatural tenseness all through dinner. It came to a climax afterwards when he began to spread his working materials on the table.

'Oh, Roger,' she protested, 'I thought you didn't have to work tonight.'

'I didn't think I'd have to, but something came up.'

'I've invited George Tompkins over.'

'Oh, gosh!' he exclaimed. 'Well, I'm sorry, honey, but you'll have to phone him not to come.'

'He's left,' she said. 'He's coming straight from town. He'll be here any minute now.'

Roger groaned. It occurred to him to send them both to the movies, but somehow the suggestion stuck on his lips. He did not want her at the movies; he wanted her here, where he could look up and know she was by his side.

George Tompkins arrived breezily at eight o'clock. 'Aha!' he cried reprovingly, coming into the room. 'Still at it.'

Roger agreed coolly that he was.

'Better quit – better quit before you have to.' He sat down with a long sigh of physical comfort and lit a cigarette. 'Take it from a fellow who's looked into the question scientifically. We can stand so much, and then – bang!'

'If you'll excuse me' – Roger made his voice as polite as possible – 'I'm going upstairs to finish this work.'

'Just as you like, Roger.' George waved his hand carelessly. 'It isn't that I mind. I'm the friend of the family and I'd just as soon see the missus as the mister.' He smiled playfully. 'But if I were you, old boy, I'd put away my work and get a good-night's sleep.'

When Roger had spread out his materials on the bed upstairs he found that he could still hear the rumble and murmur of their voices through the thin floor. He began wondering what they found to talk about. As he plunged deeper into his work his mind had a tendency to revert sharply to this question, and several times he arose and paced nervously up and down the room.

The bed was ill adapted to his work. Several times the paper slipped from the board on which it rested, and the pencil punched through. Everything was wrong tonight. Letters and figures blurred before his eyes, and as an accompaniment to the beating of his temples came those persistent murmuring voices.

At ten he realised that he had done nothing for more than an hour, and with a sudden exclamation he gathered together his papers, replaced them in his portfolio, and went downstairs. They were sitting together on the sofa when he came in.

'Oh, hello!' cried Gretchen, rather unnecessarily, he thought. 'We were just discussing you.'

'Thank you,' he answered ironically. 'What particular part of my anatomy was under the scalpel?'

'Your health,' said Tompkins jovially.

'My health's all right,' answered Roger shortly.

'But you look at it so selfishly, old fella,' cried Tompkins. 'You only consider yourself in the matter. Don't you think Gretchen has any rights? If you were working on a wonderful sonnet or a – a portrait of some madonna or something' – he glanced at Gretchen's Titian hair – 'why, then I'd say go ahead. But you're not. It's just some silly advertisement about how to sell Nobald's hair tonic, and if all the hair tonic ever made was dumped into the ocean tomorrow the world wouldn't be one bit the worse for it.'

'Wait a minute,' said Roger angrily, 'that's not quite fair. I'm not kidding myself about the importance of my work – it's just as useless as the stuff you do. But to Gretchen and me it's just about the most important thing in the world.'

'Are you implying that my work is useless?' demanded Tompkins incredulously.

'No; not if it brings happiness to some poor sucker of a pants manufacturer who doesn't know how to spend his money.'

Tompkins and Gretchen exchanged a glance.

'Oh-h-h!' exclaimed Tompkins ironically. 'I didn't realise that all these years I've just been wasting my time.'

'You're a loafer,' said Roger rudely.

'Me?' cried Tompkins angrily. 'You call me a loafer because I have a little balance in my life and find time to do interesting things? Because I play hard as well as work hard and don't let myself get to be a dull, tiresome drudge?'

Both men were angry now, and their voices had risen, though on Tompkins's face there still remained the semblance of a smile.

'What I object to,' said Roger steadily, 'is that for the last six weeks you seem to have done all your playing around here.'

'Roger!' cried Gretchen. 'What do you mean by talking like that?'

'Just what I said.'

'You've just lost your temper.' Tompkins lit a cigarette with ostentatious coolness. 'You're so nervous from overwork you don't know what you're saying. You're on the verge of a nervous break – '

'You get out of here!' cried Roger fiercely. 'You get out of here right now – before I throw you out!'

Tompkins got angrily to his feet.

'You – you throw me out?' he cried incredulously.

They were actually moving towards each other when Gretchen stepped between them, and grabbing Tompkins's arm urged him towards the door.

'He's acting like a fool, George, but you better get out,' she cried, groping in the hall for his hat.

'He insulted me!' shouted Tompkins. 'He threatened to throw me out!'

'Never mind, George,' pleaded Gretchen. 'He doesn't know what he's saying. Please go! I'll see you at ten o'clock tomorrow.'

She opened the door.

'You won't see him at ten o'clock tomorrow,' said Roger steadily. 'He's not coming to this house any more.'

Tompkins turned to Gretchen.

'It's his house,' he suggested. 'Perhaps we'd better meet at mine.'

Then he was gone, and Gretchen had shut the door behind him. Her eyes were full of angry tears.

'See what you've done!' she sobbed. 'The only friend I had, the only person in the world who liked me enough to treat me decently, is insulted by my husband in my own house.'

She threw herself on the sofa and began to cry passionately into the pillows.

'He brought it on himself,' said Roger stubbornly. 'I've stood as much as my self-respect will allow. I don't want you going out with him any more.'

'I will go out with him!' cried Gretchen wildly. 'I'll go out with him all I want! Do you think it's any fun living here with you?'

'Gretchen,' he said coldly, 'get up and put on your hat and coat and go out that door and never come back!'

Her mouth fell slightly ajar.

'But I don't want to get out,' she said dazedly.

'Well, then, behave yourself.' And he added in a gentler voice: 'I thought you were going to sleep for this forty days.'

'Oh, yes,' she cried bitterly, 'easy enough to say! But I'm tired of sleeping.' She got up, faced him defiantly. 'And what's more, I'm going riding with George Tompkins tomorrow.'

'You won't go out with him if I have to take you to New York and sit you down in my office until I get through.'

She looked at him with rage in her eyes.

'I hate you,' she said slowly. 'And I'd like to take all the work you've done and tear it up and throw it in the fire. And just to give you something to worry about tomorrow, I probably won't be here when you get back.'

She got up from the sofa, and very deliberately looked at her flushed, tear-stained face in the mirror. Then she ran upstairs and slammed herself into the bedroom.

Automatically Roger spread out his work on the living-room table. The bright colours of the designs, the vivid ladies – Gretchen had posed for one of them – holding orange ginger ale or glistening silk hosiery, dazzled his mind into a sort of coma. His restless crayon moved here and there over the pictures, shifting a block of letters half an inch to the right, trying a dozen blues for a cool blue, and eliminating the word that made a phrase anaemic and pale. Half an hour passed – he was deep in the work now; there was no sound in the room but the velvety scratch of the crayon over the glossy board.

After a long while he looked at his watch – it was after three. The wind had come up outside and was rushing by the house corners in loud, alarming swoops, like a heavy body falling through space. He stopped his work and listened. He was not tired now, but his head felt as if it was covered with bulging veins like those pictures that hang in doctors' offices showing a body stripped of decent skin. He put his hands to his head and felt it all over. It seemed to him that on his temple the veins were knotty and brittle around an old scar.

Suddenly he began to be afraid. A hundred warnings he had heard swept into his mind. People did wreck themselves with overwork, and his body and brain were of the same vulnerable and perishable stuff. For the first time he found himself envying George Tompkins's calm nerves and healthy routine. He arose and began pacing the room in a panic.

'I've got to sleep,' he whispered to himself tensely. 'Otherwise I'm going crazy.'

He rubbed his hand over his eyes, and returned to the table to put up his work, but his fingers were shaking so that he could scarcely grasp the board. The sway of a bare branch against the window made him start and cry out. He sat down on the sofa and tried to think.

'Stop! Stop! Stop!' the clock said. 'Stop! Stop! Stop!'

'I can't stop,' he answered aloud. 'I can't afford to stop.'

Listen! Why, there was the wolf at the door now! He could hear its sharp claws scrape along the varnished woodwork. He jumped up, and running to the front door flung it open; then started back with a ghastly cry. An enormous wolf was standing on the porch, glaring at him with red, malignant eyes. As he watched it the hair bristled on its neck; it gave a low growl and disappeared in the darkness. Then Roger realised with a silent, mirthless laugh that it was the police dog from over the way.

Dragging his limbs wearily into the kitchen, he brought the alarm-clock into the living-room and set it for seven. Then he wrapped himself in his overcoat, lay down on the sofa and fell immediately into a heavy, dreamless sleep.

When he awoke the light was still shining feebly, but the room was the grey colour of a winter morning. He got up, and looking anxiously at his hands found to his relief that they no longer trembled. He felt much better. Then he began to remember in detail the events of the night before, and his brow drew up again in three shallow wrinkles. There was work ahead of him, twenty-four hours of work; and Gretchen, whether she wanted to or not, must sleep for one more day.

Roger's mind glowed suddenly as if he had just thought of a new advertising idea. A few minutes later he was hurrying through the sharp morning air to Kingsley's drugstore.

'Is Mr Kingsley down yet?'

The druggist's head appeared around the corner of the prescription-room.

'I wonder if I can talk to you alone.'

At half-past seven, back home again, Roger walked into his own kitchen. The general housework girl had just arrived and was taking off her hat.

'Bebé' – he was not on familiar terms with her; this was her name – 'I want you to cook Mrs Halsey's breakfast right away. I'll take it up myself.'

It struck Bebé that this was an unusual service for so busy a man to render his wife, but if she had seen his conduct when he had carried the tray from the kitchen she would have been even more surprised. For he set it down on the dining-room table and put into the coffee half a teaspoonful of a white substance that was not powdered sugar. Then he mounted the stairs and opened the door of the bedroom.

Gretchen woke up with a start, glanced at the twin bed which had not been slept in, and bent on Roger a glance of astonishment, which changed to contempt when she saw the breakfast in his hand. She thought he was bringing it as a capitulation.

'I don't want any breakfast,' she said coldly, and his heart sank, 'except some coffee.'

'No breakfast?' Roger's voice expressed disappointment

'I said I'd take some coffee.'

Roger discreetly deposited the tray on a table beside the bed and returned quickly to the kitchen.

'We're going away until tomorrow afternoon,' he told Bebé, 'and I want to close up the house right now. So you just put on your hat and go home.'

He looked at his watch. It was ten minutes to eight, and he wanted to catch the 8.10 train. He waited five minutes and then tiptoed softly upstairs and into Gretchen's room. She was sound asleep. The coffee cup was empty save for black dregs and a film of thin brown paste on the bottom. He looked at her rather anxiously, but her breathing was regular and clear.

From the closet he took a suitcase and very quickly began filling it with her shoes – street shoes, evening slippers, rubber-soled oxfords – he had not realised that she owned so many pairs. When he closed the suitcase it was bulging.

He hesitated a minute, took a pair of sewing scissors from a box, and following the telephone-wire until it went out of sight behind the dresser, severed it in one neat clip. He jumped as there was a soft knock at the door. It was the nursemaid. He had forgotten her existence.

'Mrs Halsey and I are going up to the city till tomorrow,' he said glibly. 'Take Maxy to the beach and have lunch there. Stay all day.'

Back in the room, a wave of pity passed over him. Gretchen seemed suddenly lovely and helpless, sleeping there. It was somehow terrible to rob her young life of a day. He touched her hair with his fingers, and as she murmured something in her dream he leaned over and kissed her bright cheek. Then he picked up the suitcase full of shoes, locked the door, and ran briskly down the stairs.

3

By five o'clock that afternoon the last package of cards for Garrod's shoes had been sent by messenger to H. G. Garrod at the Biltmore Hotel. He was to give a decision next morning. At half-past five Roger's stenographer tapped him on the shoulder.

'Mr Golden, the superintendent of the building, to see you.'

Roger turned around dazedly.

'Oh, how do?'

Mr Golden came directly to the point. If Mr Halsey intended to keep the office any longer, the little oversight about the rent had better be remedied right away.

'Mr Golden,' said Roger wearily, 'everything'll be all right tomorrow. If you worry me now maybe you'll never get your money. After tomorrow nothing'll matter.'

Mr Golden looked at the tenant uneasily. Young men sometimes did away with themselves when business went wrong. Then his eye fell unpleasantly on the initialled suitcase beside the desk.

'Going on a trip?' he asked pointedly.

'What? Oh, no. That's just some clothes.'

'Clothes, eh? Well, Mr Halsey, just to prove that you mean what you say, suppose you let me keep that suitcase until tomorrow noon.'

'Help yourself.'

Mr Golden picked it up with a deprecatory gesture.

'Just a matter of form,' he remarked.

'I understand,' said Roger, swinging around to his desk. 'Good-afternoon.'

Mr Golden seemed to feel that the conversation should close on a softer key.

'And don't work too hard, Mr Halsey. You don't want to have a nervous break – '

'No,' shouted Roger, 'I don't. But I will if you don't leave me alone.'

As the door closed behind Mr Golden, Roger's stenographer turned sympathetically around.

'You shouldn't have let him get away with that,' she said. 'What's in there? Clothes?'

'No,' answered Roger absently. 'Just all my wife's shoes.'

He slept in the office that night on a sofa beside his desk. At dawn he awoke with a nervous start, rushed out into the street for coffee, and returned in ten minutes in a panic – afraid that he might have missed Mr Garrod's telephone call. It was then six-thirty.

By eight o'clock his whole body seemed to be on fire. When his two artists arrived he was stretched on the couch in almost physical pain. The phone rang imperatively at nine-thirty, and he picked up the receiver with trembling hands.

'Hello.'

'Is this the Halsey agency?'

'Yes, this is Mr Halsey speaking.'

'This is Mr H. G. Garrod.'

Roger's heart stopped beating.

'I called up, young fellow, to say that this is wonderful work you've given us here. We want all of it and as much more as your office can do.'

'Oh, God!' cried Roger into the transmitter.

'What?' Mr H. G. Garrod was considerably startled. 'Say, wait a minute there!'

But he was talking to nobody. The phone had clattered to the floor, and Roger, stretched full length on the couch, was sobbing as if his heart would break.

4

Three hours later, his face somewhat pale, but his eyes calm as a child's, Roger opened the door of his wife's bedroom with the morning paper under his arm. At the sound of his footsteps she started awake.

'What time is it?' she demanded.

He looked at his watch.

'Twelve o'clock.'

Suddenly she began to cry.

'Roger,' she said brokenly, 'I'm sorry I was so bad last night.'

He nodded coolly.

'Everything's all right now,' he answered. Then, after a pause: 'I've got the account – the biggest one.'

She turned towards him quickly.

'You have?' Then, after a minute's silence: 'Can I get a new dress?'

'Dress?' He laughed shortly. 'You can get a dozen. This account alone will bring us in forty thousand a year. It's one of the biggest in the West.'

She looked at him, startled.

'Forty thousand a year!'

'Yes.'

'Gosh' – and then faintly – 'I didn't know it'd really be anything like that.' Again she thought a minute. 'We can have a house like George Tompkins'.'

'I don't want an interior-decoration shop.'

'Forty thousand a year!' she repeated again, and then added softly: 'Oh, Roger – '

'Yes?'

'I'm not going out with George Tompkins.'

'I wouldn't let you, even if you wanted to,' he said shortly.

She made a show of indignation.

'Why, I've had a date with him for this Thursday for weeks.'

'It isn't Thursday.'

'It is.'

'It's Friday.'

'Why, Roger, you must be crazy! Don't you think I know what day it is?'

'It isn't Thursday,' he said stubbornly. 'Look!' And he held out the morning paper.

'Friday!' she exclaimed. 'Why, this is a mistake! This must be last week's paper. Today's Thursday.'

She closed her eyes and thought for a moment.

'Yesterday was Wednesday,' she said decisively. 'The laundress came yesterday. I guess I know.'

'Well,' he said smugly, 'look at the paper. There isn't any question about it.'

With a bewildered look on her face she got out of bed and began searching for her clothes. Roger went into the bathroom to shave. A minute later he heard the springs creak again. Gretchen was getting back into bed.

'What's the matter?' he enquired, putting his head around the corner of the bathroom.

'I'm scared,' she said in a trembling voice. 'I think my nerves are giving way. I can't find any of my shoes.'

'Your shoes? Why, the closet's full of them.'

'I know, but I can't see one.' Her face was pale with fear. 'Oh, Roger!'

Roger came to her bedside and put his arm around her.

'Oh, Roger,' she cried, 'what's the matter with me? First that newspaper, and now all my shoes. Take care of me, Roger.'

'I'll get the doctor,' he said.

He walked remorselessly to the telephone and took up the receiver.

'Phone seems to be out of order,' he remarked after a minute; 'I'll send Bebé.'

The doctor arrived in ten minutes.

'I think I'm on the verge of a collapse,' Gretchen told him in a strained voice.

Dr Gregory sat down on the edge of the bed and took her wrist in his hand.

'It seems to be in the air this morning.'

'I got up,' said Gretchen in an awed voice, 'and I found that I'd lost a whole day. I had an engagement to go riding with George Tompkins – '

'What?' exclaimed the doctor in surprise. Then he laughed. 'George Tompkins won't go riding with anyone for many days to come.'

'Has he gone away?' asked Gretchen curiously.

'He's going West.'

'Why?' demanded Roger. 'Is he running away with somebody's wife?'

'No,' said Dr Gregory. 'He's had a nervous breakdown.'

'What?' they exclaimed in unison.

'He just collapsed like an opera-hat in his cold shower.'

'But he was always talking about his – his balanced life,' gasped Gretchen. 'He had it on his mind.'

'I know,' said the doctor. 'He's been babbling about it all morning. I think it's driven him a little mad. He worked pretty hard at it, you know.'

'At what?' demanded Roger in bewilderment.

'At keeping his life balanced.' He turned to Gretchen. 'Now all I'll prescribe for this lady here is a good rest. If she'll just stay around the house for a few days and take forty winks of sleep she'll be as fit as ever. She's been under some strain.'

'Doctor,' exclaimed Roger hoarsely, 'don't you think I'd better have a rest or something? I've been working pretty hard lately.'

'You!' Dr Gregory laughed, slapping him violently on the back. 'My boy, I never saw you looking better in your life.'

Roger turned away quickly to conceal his smile – and to wink forty times, or almost forty times, at the autographed picture of Mr George Tompkins, which hung slightly askew on the bedroom wall.

Absolution

The American Mercury, June 1924

1

There was once a priest with cold, watery eyes, who, in the still of the night, wept cold tears. He wept because the afternoons were warm and long, and he was unable to attain a complete mystical union with our Lord. Sometimes, near four o'clock, there was a rustle of Swede girls along the path by his window, and in their shrill laughter he found a terrible dissonance that made him pray aloud for the twilight to come. At twilight the laughter and the voices were quieter, but several times he had walked past Romberg's Drugstore when it was dusk and the yellow lights shone inside and the nickel taps of the soda-fountain were gleaming, and he had found the scent of cheap toilet soap desperately sweet upon the air. He passed that way when he returned from hearing confessions on Saturday nights, and he grew careful to walk on the other side of the street so that the smell of the soap would float upwards before it reached his nostrils as it drifted, rather like incense, towards the summer moon.

But there was no escape from the hot madness of four o'clock. From his window, as far as he could see, the Dakota wheat thronged the valley of the Red River. The wheat was terrible to look upon and the carpet pattern to which in agony he bent his eyes sent his thoughts brooding through grotesque labyrinths, open always to the unavoidable sun.

One afternoon when he had reached the point where the mind runs down like an old clock, his housekeeper brought into his study a beautiful, intense little boy of eleven named Rudolph Miller. The little boy sat down in a patch of sunshine, and the priest, at his walnut desk, pretended to be very busy. This was to conceal his relief that someone had come into his haunted room.

Presently he turned around and found himself staring into two enormous, staccato eyes, lit with gleaming points of cobalt light. For a moment their expression startled him – then he saw that his visitor was in a state of abject fear.

'Your mouth is trembling,' said Father Schwartz, in a haggard voice.

The little boy covered his quivering mouth with his hand.

'Are you in trouble?' asked Father Schwartz, sharply. 'Take your hand away from your mouth and tell me what's the matter.'

The boy – Father Schwartz recognised him now as the son of a parishioner, Mr Miller the freight-agent – moved his hand reluctantly off his mouth and became articulate in a despairing whisper.

'Father Schwartz – I've committed a terrible sin.'

'A sin against purity?'

'No, father . . . worse.'

Father Schwartz's body jerked sharply.

'Have you killed somebody?'

'No – but I'm afraid – ' the voice rose to a shrill whimper.

'Do you want to go to confession?'

The little boy shook his head miserably. Father Schwartz cleared his throat so that he could make his voice soft and say some quiet, kind thing. In this moment he should forget his own agony, and try to act like God. He repeated to himself a devotional phrase, hoping that in return God would help him to act correctly.

'Tell me what you've done,' said his new soft voice.

The little boy looked at him through his tears, and was reassured by the impression of moral resiliency which the distraught priest had created. Abandoning as much of himself as he was able to this man, Rudolph Miller began to tell his story.

'On Saturday, three days ago, my father he said I had to go to confession, because I hadn't been for a month, and the family they go every week, and I hadn't been. So I knew I had to go, I didn't care. But I put it off till after supper because I was playing with a bunch of kids and father asked me if I went, and I said, "No," and he took me by the neck and he said, "You go now," so I said, "All right," so I went over to church. And he yelled after me: "Don't come back till you go" . . . '

2

'On Saturday, Three Days Ago . . . '

The plush curtain of the confessional rearranged its dismal creases, leaving exposed only the bottom of an old man's old shoe. Behind the curtain an immortal soul was alone with God and the Revd Adolphus Schwartz, priest of the parish. Sound began, a laboured whispering, sibilant and discreet, broken at intervals by the voice of the priest in audible question.

Rudolph Miller knelt in the pew beside the confessional and waited, straining nervously to hear and yet not to hear what was being said within. The fact that the priest was audible alarmed him. His own turn came next, and the three or four others who waited might listen unscrupulously while he admitted his violations of the Sixth and Ninth Commandments.

Rudolph had never committed adultery, nor even coveted his neighbour's wife – but it was the confession of the associate sins that was particularly hard to contemplate. In comparison he relished the less shameful fallings away – they formed a greyish background which relieved the ebony mark of sexual offences upon his soul.

He had been covering his ears with his hands, hoping that his refusal to hear would be noticed, and a like courtesy rendered to him in turn, when a sharp movement of the penitent in the confessional made him sink his face precipitately into the crook of his elbow. Fear assumed solid form, and pressed out a lodging between his heart and his lungs. He must try now with all his might to be sorry for his sins – not because he was afraid, but because he had offended God. He must convince God that he was sorry and to do so he must first convince himself. After a tense emotional struggle he achieved a tremulous self-pity, and decided that he was now ready. If, by allowing no other thought to enter his head, he could preserve this state of emotion unimpaired until he went into that large coffin set on end, he would have survived another crisis in his religious life.

For some time, however, a demoniac notion had partially possessed him. He could go home now, before his turn came, and tell his mother that he had arrived too late, and found the priest gone. This, unfortunately, involved the risk of being caught in a lie. As an alternative he could say that he *had* gone to confession, but this meant that he must avoid communion next day, for communion taken upon an uncleansed soul would turn to poison in his mouth, and he would crumple limp and damned from the altar-rail.

Again Father Schwartz's voice became audible.

'And for your – '

The words blurred to a husky mumble, and Rudolph got excitedly to his feet. He felt that it was impossible for him to go to confession this afternoon. He hesitated tensely. Then from the confessional came a tap, a creak and a sustained rustle. The slide had fallen and the plush curtain trembled. Temptation had come to him too late . . .

'Bless me, father, for I have sinned . . . I confess to Almighty God and to you, father, that I have sinned . . . Since my last confession it has been one month and three days . . . I accuse myself of – taking the Name of the Lord in vain . . . '

This was an easy sin. His curses had been but bravado – telling of them was little less than a brag.

' . . . of being mean to an old lady.'

The wan shadow moved a little on the latticed slat.

'How, my child?'

'Old lady Swenson,' Rudolph's murmur soared jubilantly. 'She got our baseball that we knocked in her window, and she wouldn't give it back, so we yelled, "Twenty-three, Skidoo," at her all afternoon. Then about five o'clock she had a fit, and they had to have the doctor.'

'Go on, my child.'

'Of – of not believing I was the son of my parents.'

'What?' The interrogator was distinctly startled.

'Of not believing that I was the son of my parents.'

'Why not?'

'Oh, just pride,' answered the penitent airily.

'You mean you thought you were too good to be the son of your parents?'

'Yes, father.' On a less jubilant note.

'Go on.'

'Of being disobedient and calling my mother names. Of slandering people behind their back. Of smoking – '

Rudolph had now exhausted the minor offences, and was approaching the sins it was agony to tell. He held his fingers against his face like bars as if to press out between them the shame in his heart.

'Of dirty words and immodest thoughts and desires,' he whispered very low.

'How often?'

'I don't know.'

'Once a week? Twice a week?'

'Twice a week.'

'Did you yield to these desires?'

'No, father.'

'Were you alone when you had them?'

'No, father. I was with two boys and a girl.'

'Don't you know, my child, that you should avoid the occasions of sin as well as the sin itself? Evil companionship leads to evil desires and evil desires to evil actions. Where were you when this happened?'

'In a barn in back of – '

'I don't want to hear any names,' interrupted the priest sharply.

'Well, it was up in the loft of this barn and this girl and – a fella, they were saying things – saying immodest things, and I stayed.'

'You should have gone – you should have told the girl to go.'

He should have gone! He could not tell Father Schwartz how his pulse had bumped in his wrist, how a strange, romantic excitement had possessed him when those curious things had been said. Perhaps in the houses of delinquency among the dull and hard-eyed incorrigible girls can be found those for whom has burned the whitest fire.

'Have you anything else to tell me?'

'I don't think so, father.'

Rudolph felt a great relief. Perspiration had broken out under his tight-pressed fingers.

'Have you told any lies?'

The question startled him. Like all those who habitually and instinctively lie, he had an enormous respect and awe for the truth. Something almost exterior to himself dictated a quick, hurt answer.

'Oh, no, father, I never tell lies.'

For a moment, like the commoner in the king's chair, he tasted the pride of the situation. Then as the priest began to murmur conventional admonitions he realised that in heroically denying he had told lies, he had committed a terrible sin – he had told a lie in confession.

In automatic response to Father Schwartz's, 'Make an act of contrition,' he began to repeat aloud meaninglessly: 'Oh, my God, I am heartily sorry for having offended Thee . . . '

He must fix this now – it was a bad mistake – but as his teeth shut on the last words of his prayer there was a sharp sound, and the slat was closed.

A minute later when he emerged into the twilight the relief in coming from the muggy church into an open world of wheat and sky postponed the full realisation of what he had done. Instead of worrying he took a deep breath of the crisp air and began to say over and over to himself the words 'Blatchford Sarnemington, Blatchford Sarnemington!'

Blatchford Sarnemington was himself, and these words were in effect a lyric. When he became Blatchford Sarnemington a suave nobility flowed from him. Blatchford Sarnemington lived in great sweeping triumphs. When Rudolph half closed his eyes it meant that Blatchford had established dominance over him and, as he went by, there were envious mutters in the air: 'Blatchford Sarnemington! There goes Blatchford Sarnemington.'

He was Blatchford now for a while as he strutted homewards along the staggering road, but when the road braced itself in macadam in order to become the main street of Ludwig, Rudolph's exhilaration faded out and his mind cooled, and he felt the horror of his lie. God, of course, already knew of it – but Rudolph reserved a corner of his mind where he was safe from God, where he prepared the subterfuges with which he often tricked God. Hiding now in this corner he considered how he could best avoid the consequences of his misstatement.

At all costs he must avoid communion next day. The risk of angering God to such an extent was too great. He would have to drink water 'by accident' in the morning, and thus, in accordance with a church law, render himself unfit to receive communion that day. In spite of its flimsiness, this subterfuge was the most feasible that occurred to him. He accepted its risks, and was concentrating on how best to put it into effect as he turned the corner by Romberg's Drugstore and came in sight of his father's house.

3

Rudolph's father, the local freight-agent, had floated with the second wave of German and Irish stock to the Minnesota-Dakota country. Theoretically, great opportunities lay ahead of a young man of energy in that day and place, but Carl Miller had been incapable of establishing either with his superiors or his subordinates the reputation for approximate immutability which is essential to success in a hierarchic industry. Somewhat gross, he was, nevertheless, insufficiently hard-headed and unable to take fundamental relationships for granted, and this inability made him suspicious, unrestful, and continually dismayed.

His two bonds with the colourful life were his faith in the Roman Catholic Church and his mystical worship of the Empire Builder, James J. Hill. Hill was the apotheosis of that quality in which Miller himself was deficient – the sense of things, the feel of things, the hint of rain in the wind on the cheek. Miller's mind worked late on the old decisions of other men, and he had never in his life felt the balance of any single thing in his hands. His weary, sprightly, undersized body was growing old in Hill's gigantic shadow. For twenty years he had lived alone with Hill's name and God.

On Sunday morning Carl Miller awoke in the dustless quiet of six o'clock. Kneeling by the side of the bed he bent his yellow-grey hair and the full dapple bangs of his moustache into the pillow, and prayed for several minutes. Then he drew off his nightshirt – like the rest of his generation he had never been able to endure pyjamas – and clothed his thin, white, hairless body in woollen underwear.

He shaved. Silence in the other bedroom where his wife lay nervously asleep. Silence from the screened-off corner of the hall where his son's cot stood, and his son slept among his Alger books, his collection of cigar-bands, his mothy pennants – 'Cornell', 'Hamlin', and 'Greetings from Pueblo, New Mexico' – and the other possessions of his private life. From outside Miller could hear the shrill birds and the whirring movement of the poultry, and, as an undertone, the low, swelling click-a-tick of the six-fifteen through-train for Montana and the green coast beyond. Then as the cold water dripped from the wash-rag in his hand he raised his head suddenly – he had heard a furtive sound from the kitchen below.

He dried his razor hastily, slipped his dangling suspenders to his shoulder, and listened. Someone was walking in the kitchen, and he knew by the light footfall that it was not his wife. With his mouth faintly ajar he ran quickly down the stairs and opened the kitchen door.

Standing by the sink, with one hand on the still dripping faucet and the other clutching a full glass of water, stood his son. The boy's eyes, still heavy with sleep, met his father's with a frightened, reproachful beauty. He was barefooted, and his pyjamas were rolled up at the knees and sleeves.

For a moment they both remained motionless – Carl Miller's brow went down and his son's went up, as though they were striking a balance between the extremes of emotion which filled them. Then the bangs of the parent's moustache descended portentously until they obscured his mouth, and he gave a short glance around to see if anything had been disturbed.

The kitchen was garnished with sunlight which beat on the pans and made the smooth boards of the floor and table yellow and clean as wheat. It was the centre of the house where the fire burned and the tins fitted into tins like toys, and the steam whistled all day on a thin pastel note. Nothing was moved, nothing touched – except the faucet where beads of water still formed and dripped with a white flash into the sink below.

'What are you doing?'

'I got awful thirsty, so I thought I'd just come down and get – '

'I thought you were going to communion.'

A look of vehement astonishment spread over his son's face.

'I forgot all about it.'

'Have you drunk any water?'

'No – '

As the word left his mouth Rudolph knew it was the wrong answer, but the faded indignant eyes facing him had signalled up the truth before the boy's will could act. He realised, too, that he should never have come downstairs; some vague necessity for verisimilitude had made him want to leave a wet glass as evidence by the sink; the honesty of his imagination had betrayed him.

'Pour it out,' commanded his father, 'that water!'

Rudolph despairingly inverted the tumbler.

'What's the matter with you, anyways?' demanded Miller angrily.

'Nothing.'

'Did you go to confession yesterday?'

'Yes.'

'Then why were you going to drink water?'

'I don't know – I forgot.'

'Maybe you care more about being a little bit thirsty than you do about your religion.'

'I forgot.' Rudolph could feel the tears straining in his eyes.

'That's no answer.'

'Well, I did.'

'You better look out!' His father held to a high, persistent, inquisitory note: 'If you're so forgetful that you can't remember your religion something better be done about it.'

Rudolph filled a sharp pause with: 'I can remember it all right.'

'First you begin to neglect your religion,' cried his father, fanning his own fierceness, 'the next thing you'll begin to lie and steal, and the *next* thing is the *reform* school!'

Not even this familiar threat could deepen the abyss that Rudolph saw before him. He must either tell all now, offering his body for what he knew would be a ferocious beating, or else tempt the thunderbolts by receiving the Body and Blood of Christ with sacrilege upon his soul. And of the two the former seemed more terrible – it was not so much the beating he dreaded as the savage ferocity, outlet of the ineffectual man, which would lie behind it.

'Put down that glass and go upstairs and dress!' his father ordered, 'and when we get to church, before you go to communion, you better kneel down and ask God to forgive you for your carelessness.'

Some accidental emphasis in the phrasing of this command acted like a catalytic agent on the confusion and terror of Rudolph's mind. A wild, proud anger rose in him, and he dashed the tumbler passionately into the sink.

His father uttered a strained, husky sound, and sprang for him. Rudolph dodged to the side, tipped over a chair, and tried to get beyond the kitchen table. He cried out sharply when a hand grasped his pajama shoulder, then he felt the dull impact of a fist against the side of his head, and glancing blows on the upper part of his body. As he slipped here and there in his father's grasp, dragged or lifted when he clung instinctively to an arm, aware of sharp smarts and strains, he made no sound except that he laughed hysterically several times. Then in less than a minute the blows abruptly ceased. After a lull during which Rudolph was tightly held, and during which they both trembled violently and uttered strange, truncated words, Carl Miller half dragged, half threatened his son upstairs.

'Put on your clothes!'

Rudolph was now both hysterical and cold. His head hurt him, and there was a long, shallow scratch on his neck from his father's fingernail, and he sobbed and trembled as he dressed. He was aware of his mother standing at the doorway in a wrapper, her wrinkled face compressing and squeezing and opening out into new series of wrinkles which floated and eddied from neck to brow. Despising her nervous ineffectuality and avoiding her rudely when she tried to touch his neck with witch-hazel, he made a hasty, choking toilet. Then he followed his father out of the house and along the road towards the Catholic church.

4

They walked without speaking except when Carl Miller acknowledged automatically the existence of passers-by. Rudolph's uneven breathing alone ruffled the hot Sunday silence.

His father stopped decisively at the door of the church.

'I've decided you'd better go to confession again. Go in and tell Father Schwartz what you did and ask God's pardon.'

'You lost your temper, too!' said Rudolph quickly.

Carl Miller took a step towards his son, who moved cautiously backwards.

'All right, I'll go.'

'Are you going to do what I say?' cried his father in a hoarse whisper.

'All right.'

Rudolph walked into the church, and for the second time in two days entered the confessional and knelt down. The slat went up almost at once.

'I accuse myself of missing my morning prayers.'

'Is that all?'

'That's all.'

A maudlin exultation filled him. Not easily ever again would he be able to put an abstraction before the necessities of his ease and pride. An invisible line had been crossed, and he had become aware of his isolation – aware that it applied not only to those moments when he was Blatchford Sarnemington but that it applied to all his inner life. Hitherto such phenomena as 'crazy' ambitions and petty shames and fears had been but private reservations, unacknowledged before the throne of his official soul. Now he realised unconsciously that his private reservations were himself – and all the rest a garnished front and a conventional flag. The pressure of his environment had driven him into the lonely secret road of adolescence.

He knelt in the pew beside his father. Mass began. Rudolph knelt up – when he was alone he slumped his posterior back against the seat – and tasted the consciousness of a sharp, subtle revenge. Beside him his father prayed that God would forgive Rudolph, and asked also that his own outbreak of temper would be pardoned. He glanced sidewise at his son, and was relieved to see that the strained, wild look had gone from his face and that he had ceased sobbing. The Grace of God, inherent in the Sacrament, would do the rest, and perhaps after Mass everything would be better. He was proud of Rudolph in his heart, and beginning to be truly as well as formally sorry for what he had done.

Usually, the passing of the collection box was a significant point for Rudolph in the services. If, as was often the case, he had no money to drop in he would be furiously ashamed and bow his head and pretend not to see the box, lest Jeanne Brady in the pew behind should take notice and suspect an acute family poverty. But today he glanced coldly into it as it skimmed under his eyes, noting with casual interest the large number of pennies it contained.

When the bell rang for communion, however, he quivered. There was no reason why God should not stop his heart. During the past twelve hours he had committed a series of mortal sins increasing in gravity, and he was now to crown them all with a blasphemous sacrilege.

'Domine, non sum dignus; ut interes sub tectum meum; sed tantum dic verbo, et sanabitur anima mea . . . '

There was a rustle in the pews, and the communicants worked their ways into the aisle with downcast eyes and joined hands. Those of larger piety pressed together their fingertips to form steeples. Among these latter was Carl Miller. Rudolph followed him towards the altar-rail and knelt down, automatically taking up the napkin under his chin. The bell rang sharply, and the priest turned from the altar with the white Host held above the chalice: 'Corpus Domini nostri Jesu Christi custodiat animam meam in vitam aeternam.'

A cold sweat broke out on Rudolph's forehead as the communion began. Along the line Father Schwartz moved, and with gathering nausea Rudolph felt his heart-valves weakening at the will of God. It seemed to him that the church was darker and that a great quiet had fallen, broken only by the inarticulate mumble which announced the approach of the Creator of Heaven and Earth. He dropped his head down between his shoulders and waited for the blow.

Then he felt a sharp nudge in his side. His father was poking him to sit up, not to slump against the rail; the priest was only two places away.

'Corpus Domini nostri Jesu Christi custodiat animam meam in vitam aeternam.'

Rudolph opened his mouth. He felt the sticky wax taste of the wafer on his tongue. He remained motionless for what seemed an interminable period of time, his head still raised, the wafer undissolved in his mouth. Then again he started at the pressure of his father's elbow, and saw that the people were falling away from the altar like leaves and turning with blind downcast eyes to their pews, alone with God.

Rudolph was alone with himself, drenched with perspiration and deep in mortal sin. As he walked back to his pew the sharp taps of his cloven hoofs were loud upon the floor, and he knew that it was a dark poison he carried in his heart.

5

'Sagitta Volante in Dei'

The beautiful little boy with eyes like blue stones, and lashes that sprayed open from them like flower-petals had finished telling his sin to Father Schwartz – and the square of sunshine in which he sat had moved forward half an hour into the room. Rudolph had become less frightened now; once eased of the story a reaction had set in. He knew that as long as he was in the room with this priest God would not stop his heart, so he sighed and sat quietly, waiting for the priest to speak.

Father Schwartz's cold watery eyes were fixed upon the carpet pattern on which the sun had brought out the swastikas and the flat bloomless vines and the pale echoes of flowers. The hall-clock ticked insistently towards sunset, and from the ugly room and from the afternoon outside the window arose a stiff monotony, shattered now and then by the reverberate clapping of a faraway hammer on the dry air. The priest's nerves were strung thin and the beads of his rosary were crawling and squirming like snakes upon the green felt of his table top. He could not remember now what it was he should say.

Of all the things in this lost Swede town he was most aware of this little boy's eyes – the beautiful eyes, with lashes that left them reluctantly and curved back as though to meet them once more.

For a moment longer the silence persisted while Rudolph waited, and the priest struggled to remember something that was slipping further and further away from him, and the clock ticked in the broken house. Then Father Schwartz stared hard at the little boy and remarked in a peculiar voice: 'When a lot of people get together in the best places things go glimmering.'

Rudolph started and looked quickly at Father Schwartz's face.

'I said – ' began the priest, and paused, listening. 'Do you hear the hammer and the clock ticking and the bees? Well, that's no good. The thing is to have a lot of people in the centre of the world, wherever that happens to be. Then' – his watery eyes widened knowingly – 'things go glimmering.'

'Yes, father,' agreed Rudolph, feeling a little frightened.

'What are you going to be when you grow up?'

'Well, I was going to be a baseball-player for a while,' answered Rudolph nervously, 'but I don't think that's a very good ambition, so I think I'll be an actor or a navy officer.'

Again the priest stared at him.

'I see *exactly* what you mean,' he said, with a fierce air.

Rudolph had not meant anything in particular, and at the implication that he had, he became more uneasy.

'This man is crazy,' he thought, 'and I'm scared of him. He wants me to help him out some way, and I don't want to.'

'You look as if things went glimmering,' cried Father Schwartz wildly. 'Did you ever go to a party?'

'Yes, father.'

'And did you notice that everybody was properly dressed? That's what I mean. Just as you went into the party there was a moment when everybody was properly dressed. Maybe two little girls were standing by the door and some boys were leaning over the banisters, and there were bowls around full of flowers.'

'I've been to a lot of parties,' said Rudolph, rather relieved that the conversation had taken this turn.

'Of course,' continued Father Schwartz triumphantly, 'I knew you'd agree with me. But my theory is that when a whole lot of people get together in the best places things go glimmering all the time.'

Rudolph found himself thinking of Blatchford Sarnemington.

'Please listen to me!' commanded the priest impatiently. 'Stop worrying about last Saturday. Apostasy implies an absolute damnation only on the supposition of a previous perfect faith. Does that fix it?'

Rudolph had not the faintest idea what Father Schwartz was talking about, but he nodded and the priest nodded back at him and returned to his mysterious preoccupation.

'Why,' he cried, 'they have lights now as big as stars – do you realise that? I heard of one light they had in Paris or somewhere that was as big as a star. A lot of people had it – a lot of gay people. They have all sorts of things now that you never dreamed of.

'Look here – ' He came nearer to Rudolph, but the boy drew away, so Father Schwartz went back and sat down in his chair, his eyes dried out and hot. 'Did you ever see an amusement park?'

'No, father.'

'Well, go and see an amusement park.' The priest waved his hand vaguely. 'It's a thing like a fair, only much more glittering. Go to one at night and stand a little way off from it in a dark place – under dark trees. You'll see a big wheel made of lights turning in the air, and a long slide shooting boats down into the water. A band playing somewhere, and a smell of peanuts – and everything will twinkle. But it won't remind you of anything, you see. It will all just hang out there in the night like a coloured balloon – like a big yellow lantern on a pole.'

Father Schwartz frowned as he suddenly thought of something.

'But don't get up close,' he warned Rudolph, 'because if you do you'll only feel the heat and the sweat and the life.'

All this talking seemed particularly strange and awful to Rudolph because this man was a priest. He sat there, half terrified, his beautiful eyes open wide and staring at Father Schwartz. But underneath his terror he felt that his own inner convictions were confirmed. There was something ineffably gorgeous somewhere that had nothing to do with God. He no longer thought that God was angry at him about the original lie, because He must have understood that Rudolph had done it to make things finer in the confessional, brightening up the dinginess of his admissions by saying a thing radiant and proud. At the moment when he had affirmed immaculate honour a silver pennon had flapped out into the breeze somewhere and there had been the crunch of leather and the shine of silver spurs and a troop of horsemen waiting for dawn on a low green hill. The sun had made stars of light on their breastplates like the picture at home of the German cuirassiers at Sedan.

But now the priest was muttering inarticulate and heart-broken words, and the boy became wildly afraid. Horror entered suddenly in at the open window, and the atmosphere of the room changed. Father Schwartz collapsed precipitously down on his knees, and let his body settle back against a chair.

'Oh, my God!' he cried out, in a strange voice, and wilted to the floor.

Then a human oppression rose from the priest's worn clothes, and mingled with the faint smell of old food in the corners. Rudolph gave a sharp cry and ran in a panic from the house – while the collapsed man lay there quite still, filling his room, filling it with voices and faces until it was crowded with echolalia, and rang loud with a steady, shrill note of laughter.

Outside the window the blue sirocco trembled over the wheat, and girls with yellow hair walked sensuously along roads that bounded the fields, calling innocent, exciting things to the young men who were working in the lines between the grain. Legs were shaped under starchless gingham, and rims of the necks of dresses were warm and damp. For five hours now hot fertile life had burned in the afternoon. It would be night in three hours, and all along the land there would be these blonde Northern girls and the tall young men from the farms lying out beside the wheat, under the moon.

'The Sensible Thing'

Liberty, 15 July 1924

1

At the Great American Lunch Hour young George O'Kelly straightened his desk deliberately and with an assumed air of interest. No one in the office must know that he was in a hurry, for success is a matter of atmosphere, and it is not well to advertise the fact that your mind is separated from your work by a distance of seven hundred miles.

But once out of the building he set his teeth and began to run, glancing now and then at the gay noon of early spring which filled Times Square and loitered less than twenty feet over the heads of the crowd. The crowd all looked slightly upwards and took deep March breaths, and the sun dazzled their eyes so that scarcely anyone saw anyone else but only their own reflection on the sky.

George O'Kelly, whose mind was over seven hundred miles away, thought that all outdoors was horrible. He rushed into the subway, and for ninety-five blocks bent a frenzied glance on a car-card which showed vividly how he had only one chance in five of keeping his teeth for ten years. At 137th Street he broke off his study of commercial art, left the subway, and began to run again, a tireless, anxious run that brought him this time to his home – one room in a high, horrible apartment-house in the middle of nowhere.

There it was on the bureau, the letter – in sacred ink, on blessed paper – all over the city, people, if they listened, could hear the beating of George O'Kelly's heart. He read the commas, the blots and the thumb-smudge on the margin – then he threw himself hopelessly upon his bed.

He was in a mess, one of those terrific messes which are ordinary incidents in the life of the poor, which follow poverty like birds of prey. The poor go under or go up or go wrong or even go on, somehow, in a way the poor have – but George O'Kelly was so new to poverty that had anyone denied the uniqueness of his case he would have been astounded.

Less than two years ago he had been graduated with honours from the Massachusetts Institute of Technology and had taken a position with a firm of construction engineers in southern Tennessee. All his life he had thought in terms of tunnels and skyscrapers and great squat dams and tall, three-towered bridges that were like dancers holding hands in a row, with heads as tall as cities and skirts of cable strand. It had seemed romantic to George O'Kelly to change the sweep of rivers and the shape of mountains so that life could flourish in the old bad lands of the world where it had never taken root before. He loved steel, and there was always steel near him in his dreams, liquid steel, steel in bars and blocks and beams and formless plastic masses, waiting for him, as paint and canvas to his hand. Steel inexhaustible, to be made lovely and austere in his imaginative fire . . .

At present he was an insurance clerk at forty dollars a week with his dream slipping fast behind him. The dark little girl who had made this mess, this terrible and intolerable mess, was waiting to be sent for in a town in Tennessee.

In fifteen minutes the woman from whom he sublet his room knocked and asked him with maddening kindness if, since he was home, he would have some lunch. He shook his head, but the interruption aroused him, and getting up from the bed he wrote a telegram.

> Letter depressed me have you lost your nerve you are foolish and just upset to think of breaking off why not marry me immediately sure we can make it all right –

He hesitated for a wild minute, and then added in a hand that could scarcely be recognised as his own:

> In any case I will arrive tomorrow at six o'clock.

When he finished he ran out of the apartment and down to the telegraph office near the subway stop. He possessed in this world not quite one hundred dollars, but the letter showed that she was 'nervous' and this left him no choice. He knew what 'nervous' meant – that she was emotionally depressed, that the prospect of marrying into a life of poverty and struggle was putting too much strain upon her love.

George O'Kelly reached the insurance company at his usual run, the run that had become almost second nature to him, that seemed best to express the tension under which he lived. He went straight to the manager's office.

'I want to see you, Mr Chambers,' he announced breathlessly.

'Well?' Two eyes, eyes like winter windows, glared at him with ruthless impersonality.

'I want to get four days' vacation.'

'Why, you had a vacation just two weeks ago!' said Mr Chambers in surprise.

'That's true,' admitted the distraught young man, 'but now I've got to have another.'

'Where'd you go last time? To your home?'

'No, I went to – a place in Tennessee.'

'Well, where do you want to go this time?'

'Well, this time I want to go to – a place in Tennessee.'

'You're consistent, anyhow,' said the manager dryly. 'But I didn't realise you were employed here as a travelling salesman.'

'I'm not,' cried George desperately, 'but I've got to go.'

'All right,' agreed Mr Chambers, 'but you don't have to come back. So don't!'

'I won't.' And to his own astonishment as well as Mr Chambers's George's face grew pink with pleasure. He felt happy, exultant – for the first time in six months he was absolutely free. Tears of gratitude stood in his eyes, and he seized Mr Chambers warmly by the hand.

'I want to thank you,' he said with a rush of emotion. 'I don't want to come back. I think I'd have gone crazy if you'd said that I could come back. Only I couldn't quit myself, you see, and I want to thank you for – for quitting for me.'

He waved his hand magnanimously, shouted aloud, 'You owe me three days' salary but you can keep it!' and rushed from the office. Mr Chambers rang for his stenographer to ask if O'Kelly had seemed queer lately. He had fired many men in the course of his career, and they had taken it in many different ways, but none of them had thanked him – ever before.

2

Jonquil Cary was her name, and to George O'Kelly nothing had ever looked so fresh and pale as her face when she saw him and fled to him eagerly along the station platform. Her arms were raised to him, her mouth was half parted for his kiss, when she held him off suddenly and lightly and, with a touch of embarrassment, looked around. Two boys, somewhat younger than George, were standing in the background.

'This is Mr Craddock and Mr Holt,' she announced cheerfully. 'You met them when you were here before.'

Disturbed by the transition of a kiss into an introduction and suspecting some hidden significance, George was more confused when he found that the automobile which was to carry them to Jonquil's house belonged to one of the two young men. It seemed to put him at a disadvantage. On the way Jonquil chattered between the front and back seats, and when he tried to slip his arm around her under cover of the twilight she compelled him with a quick movement to take her hand instead.

'Is this street on the way to your house?' he whispered. 'I don't recognise it.'

'It's the new boulevard. Jerry just got this car today, and he wants to show it to me before he takes us home.'

When, after twenty minutes, they were deposited at Jonquil's house, George felt that the first happiness of the meeting, the joy he had recognised so surely in her eyes back in the station, had been dissipated by the intrusion of the ride. Something that he had looked forward to had been rather casually lost, and he was brooding on this as he said good-night stiffly to the two young men. Then his ill-humour faded as Jonquil drew him into a familiar embrace under the dim light of the front hall and told him in a dozen ways, of which the best was without words, how she had missed him. Her emotion reassured him, promised his anxious heart that everything would be all right.

They sat together on the sofa, overcome by each other's presence, beyond all except fragmentary endearments. At the supper hour Jonquil's father and mother appeared and were glad to see George. They liked him, and had been interested in his engineering career when he had first come to Tennessee over a year before. They had been sorry when he had given it up and gone to New York to look for something more immediately profitable, but while they deplored the curtailment of his career they sympathised with him and were ready to recognise the engagement. During dinner they asked about his progress in New York.

'Everything's going fine,' he told them with enthusiasm. 'I've been promoted – better salary.'

He was miserable as he said this – but they were all *so* glad.

'They must like you,' said Mrs Cary, 'that's certain – or they wouldn't let you off twice in three weeks to come down here.'

'I told them they had to,' explained George hastily; 'I told them if they didn't I wouldn't work for them any more.'

'But you ought to save your money,' Mrs Cary reproached him gently. 'Not spend it all on this expensive trip.'

Dinner was over – he and Jonquil were alone and she came back into his arms.

'So glad you're here,' she sighed. 'Wish you never were going away again, darling.'

'Do you miss me?'

'Oh, so much, so much.'

'Do you – do other men come to see you often? Like those two kids?'

The question surprised her. The dark velvet eyes stared at him.

'Why, of course they do. All the time. Why – I've told you in letters that they did, dearest.'

This was true – when he had first come to the city there had been already a dozen boys around her, responding to her picturesque fragility with adolescent worship, and a few of them perceiving that her beautiful eyes were also sane and kind.

'Do you expect me never to go anywhere' – Jonquil demanded, leaning back against the sofa-pillows until she seemed to look at him from many miles away – 'and just fold my hands and sit still – for ever?'

'What do you mean?' he blurted out in a panic. 'Do you mean you think I'll never have enough money to marry you?'

'Oh, don't jump at conclusions so, George.'

'I'm not jumping at conclusions. That's what you said.'

George decided suddenly that he was on dangerous ground. He had not intended to let anything spoil this night. He tried to take her again in his arms, but she resisted unexpectedly, saying: 'It's hot. I'm going to get the electric fan.'

When the fan was adjusted they sat down again, but he was in a super-sensitive mood and involuntarily he plunged into the specific world he had intended to avoid.

'When will you marry me?'

'Are you ready for me to marry you?'

All at once his nerves gave way, and he sprang to his feet.

'Let's shut off that damned fan,' he cried, 'it drives me wild. It's like a clock ticking away all the time I'll be with you. I came here to be happy and forget everything about New York and time – '

He sank down on the sofa as suddenly as he had risen. Jonquil turned off the fan, and drawing his head down into her lap began stroking his hair.

'Let's sit like this,' she said softly, 'just sit quiet like this, and I'll put you to sleep. You're all tired and nervous and your sweetheart'll take care of you.'

'But I don't want to sit like this,' he complained, jerking up suddenly, 'I don't want to sit like this at all. I want you to kiss me. That's the only thing that makes me rest. And anyways I'm not nervous – it's you that's nervous. I'm not nervous at all.'

To prove that he wasn't nervous he left the couch and plumped himself into a rocking-chair across the room.

'Just when I'm ready to marry you you write me the most nervous letters, as if you're going to back out, and I have to come rushing down here – '

'You don't have to come if you don't want to.'

'But I *do* want to!' insisted George.

It seemed to him that he was being very cool and logical and that she was putting him deliberately in the wrong. With every word they were drawing further and further apart – and he was unable to stop himself or to keep worry and pain out of his voice.

But in a minute Jonquil began to cry sorrowfully and he came back to the sofa and put his arm around her. He was the comforter now, drawing her head close to his shoulder, murmuring old familiar things until she grew calmer and only trembled a little, spasmodically, in his arms. For over an hour they sat there, while the evening pianos thumped their last cadences into the street outside. George did not move, or think, or hope, lulled into numbness by the premonition of disaster. The clock would tick on, past eleven, past twelve, and then Mrs Cary would call down gently over the bannister – beyond that he saw only tomorrow and despair.

3

In the heat of the next day the breaking-point came. They had each guessed the truth about the other, but of the two she was the more ready to admit the situation.

'There's no use going on,' she said miserably, 'you know you hate the insurance business, and you'll never do well in it.'

'That's not it,' he insisted stubbornly; 'I hate going on alone. If you'll marry me and come with me and take a chance with me, I can make good at anything, but not while I'm worrying about you down here.'

She was silent a long time before she answered, not thinking – for she had seen the end – but only waiting, because she knew that every word would seem more cruel than the last. Finally she spoke: 'George, I love you with all my heart, and I don't see how I can ever love anyone else but you. If you'd been ready for me two months ago I'd have married you – now I can't because it doesn't seem to be the sensible thing.'

He made wild accusations – there was someone else – she was keeping something from him!

'No, there's no one else.'

This was true. But reacting from the strain of this affair she had found relief in the company of young boys like Jerry Holt, who had the merit of meaning absolutely nothing in her life.

George didn't take the situation well, at all. He seized her in his arms and tried literally to kiss her into marrying him at once. When this failed, he broke into a long monologue of self-pity, and ceased only when he saw that he was making himself despicable in her sight. He threatened to leave when he had no intention of leaving, and refused to go when she told him that, after all, it was best that he should.

For a while she was sorry, then for another while she was merely kind.

'You'd better go now,' she cried at last, so loud that Mrs Cary came downstairs in alarm.

'Is something the matter?'

'I'm going away, Mrs Cary,' said George brokenly. Jonquil had left the room.

'Don't feel so badly, George.' Mrs Cary blinked at him in helpless sympathy – sorry and, in the same breath, glad that the little tragedy was almost done. 'If I were you I'd go home to your mother for a week or so. Perhaps after all this is the sensible thing – '

'Please don't talk,' he cried. 'Please don't say anything to me now!'

Jonquil came into the room again, her sorrow and her nervousness alike tucked under powder and rouge and hat.

'I've ordered a taxicab,' she said impersonally. 'We can drive around until your train leaves.'

She walked out on the front porch. George put on his coat and hat and stood for a minute exhausted in the hall – he had eaten scarcely a bite since he had left New York. Mrs Cary came over, drew his head down and kissed him on the cheek, and he felt very ridiculous and weak in his knowledge that the scene had been ridiculous and weak at the end. If he had only gone the night before – left her for the last time with a decent pride.

The taxi had come, and for an hour these two that had been lovers rode along the less-frequented streets. He held her hand and grew calmer in the sunshine, seeing too late that there had been nothing all along to do or say.

'I'll come back,' he told her.

'I know you will,' she answered, trying to put a cheery faith into her voice. 'And we'll write each other – sometimes.'

'No,' he said, 'we won't write. I couldn't stand that. Someday I'll come back.'

'I'll never forget you, George.'

They reached the station, and she went with him while he bought his ticket . . .

'Why, George O'Kelly and Jonquil Cary!'

It was a man and a girl whom George had known when he had worked in town, and Jonquil seemed to greet their presence with relief. For an interminable five minutes they all stood there talking; then the train roared into the station, and with ill-concealed agony in his face George held out his arms towards Jonquil. She took an uncertain step towards him, faltered, and then pressed his hand quickly as if she were taking leave of a chance friend.

'Goodbye, George,' she was saying, 'I hope you have a pleasant trip.

'Goodbye, George. Come back and see us all again.'

Dumb, almost blind with pain, he seized his suitcase, and in some dazed way got himself aboard the train.

Past clanging street-crossings, gathering speed through wide suburban spaces towards the sunset. Perhaps she too would see the sunset and pause for a moment, turning, remembering, before he faded with her sleep into the past. This night's dusk would cover up for ever the sun and the trees and the flowers and the laughter of his young world.

4

On a damp afternoon in September of the following year a young man with his face burned to a deep copper glow got off a train at a city in Tennessee. He looked around anxiously, and seemed relieved when he found that there was no one at the station to meet him. He taxied to the best hotel in the city where he registered with some satisfaction as George O'Kelly, Cuzco, Peru.

Up in his room he sat for a few minutes at the window looking down into the familiar street below. Then with his hand trembling faintly he took off the telephone receiver and called a number.

'Is Miss Jonquil in?'

'This is she.'

'Oh – ' His voice, after overcoming a faint tendency to waver, went on with friendly formality.

'This is George O'Kelly. Did you get my letter?'

'Yes. I thought you'd be in today.'

Her voice, cool and unmoved, disturbed him, but not as he had expected. This was the voice of a stranger, unexcited, pleasantly glad to see him – that was all. He wanted to put down the telephone and catch his breath.

'I haven't seen you for – a long time.' He succeeded in making this sound offhand. 'Over a year.'

He knew how long it had been – to the day.

'It'll be awfully nice to talk to you again.'

'I'll be there in about an hour.'

He hung up. For four long seasons every minute of his leisure had been crowded with anticipation of this hour, and now this hour was here. He had thought of finding her married, engaged, in love – he had not thought she would be unstirred at his return.

There would never again in his life, he felt, be another ten months like these he had just gone through. He had made an admittedly remarkable showing for a young engineer – stumbled into two unusual opportunities, one in Peru, whence he had just returned, and another, consequent upon it, in New York, whither he was bound. In this short time he had risen from poverty into a position of unlimited opportunity.

He looked at himself in the dressing-table mirror. He was almost black with tan, but it was a romantic black, and in the last week, since he had had time to think about it, it had given him considerable pleasure. The hardiness of his frame, too, he appraised with a sort of fascination. He had lost part of an eyebrow somewhere, and he still wore an elastic bandage on his knee, but he was too young not to realise that on the steamer many women had looked at him with unusual tributary interest.

His clothes, of course, were frightful. They had been made for him by a Greek tailor in Lima – in two days. He was young enough, too, to have explained this sartorial deficiency to Jonquil in his otherwise laconic note. The only further detail it contained was a request that he should *not* be met at the station.

George O'Kelly, of Cuzco, Peru, waited an hour and a half in the hotel, until, to be exact, the sun had reached a midway position in the sky. Then, freshly shaven and talcum-powdered towards a somewhat more Caucasian hue, for vanity at the last minute had overcome romance, he engaged a taxicab and set out for the house he knew so well.

He was breathing hard – he noticed this but he told himself that it was excitement, not emotion. He was here; she was not married – that was enough. He was not even sure what he had to say to her. But this was the moment of his life that he felt he could least easily have dispensed with. There was no triumph, after all, without a girl concerned, and if he did not lay his spoils at her feet he could at least hold them for a passing moment before her eyes.

The house loomed up suddenly beside him, and his first thought was that it had assumed a strange unreality. There was nothing changed – only everything was changed. It was smaller and it seemed shabbier than before – there was no cloud of magic hovering over its roof and issuing from the windows of the upper floor. He rang the doorbell and an unfamiliar coloured maid appeared. Miss Jonquil would be down in a moment. He wet his lips nervously and walked into the sitting-room – and the feeling of unreality increased. After all, he saw, this was only a room, and not the enchanted chamber where he had passed those poignant hours. He sat in a chair, amazed to find it a chair, realising that his imagination had distorted and coloured all these simple familiar things.

Then the door opened and Jonquil came into the room – and it was as though everything in it suddenly blurred before his eyes. He had not remembered how beautiful she was, and he felt his face grow pale and his voice diminish to a poor sigh in his throat.

She was dressed in pale green, and a gold ribbon bound back her dark, straight hair like a crown. The familiar velvet eyes caught his as she came through the door, and a spasm of fright went through him at her beauty's power of inflicting pain.

He said, 'Hello,' and they each took a few steps forward and shook hands. Then they sat in chairs quite far apart and gazed at each other across the room.

'You've come back,' she said, and he answered just as tritely: 'I wanted to stop in and see you as I came through.'

He tried to neutralise the tremor in his voice by looking anywhere but at her face. The obligation to speak was on him, but, unless he immediately began to boast, it seemed that there was nothing to say. There had never been anything casual in their previous relations – it didn't seem possible that people in this position would talk about the weather.

'This is ridiculous,' he broke out in sudden embarrassment. 'I don't know exactly what to do. Does my being here bother you?'

'No.' The answer was both reticent and impersonally sad. It depressed him.

'Are you engaged?' he demanded.

'No.'

'Are you in love with someone?'

She shook her head.

'Oh.' He leaned back in his chair. Another subject seemed exhausted – the interview was not taking the course he had intended.

'Jonquil,' he began, this time on a softer key, 'after all that's happened between us, I wanted to come back and see you. Whatever I do in the future I'll never love another girl as I've loved you.'

This was one of the speeches he had rehearsed. On the steamer it had seemed to have just the right note – a reference to the tenderness he would always feel for her combined with a non-committal attitude towards his present state of mind. Here with the past around him, beside him, growing minute by minute more heavy on the air, it seemed theatrical and stale.

She made no comment, sat without moving, her eyes fixed on him with an expression that might have meant everything or nothing.

'You don't love me any more, do you?' he asked her in a level voice.

'No.'

When Mrs Cary came in a minute later, and spoke to him about his success – there had been a half column about him in the local paper – he was a mixture of emotions. He knew now that he still wanted this girl, and he knew that the past sometimes comes back – that was all. For the rest he must be strong and watchful and he would see.

'And now,' Mrs Cary was saying, 'I want you two to go and see the lady who has the chrysanthemums. She particularly told me she wanted to see you because she'd read about you in the paper.'

They went to see the lady with the chrysanthemums. They walked along the street, and he recognised with a sort of excitement just how her shorter footsteps always fell in between his own. The lady turned out to be nice, and the chrysanthemums were enormous and extraordinarily beautiful. The lady's gardens were full of them, white and pink and yellow, so that to be among them was a trip back into the heart of summer. There were two gardens full, and a gate between them; when they strolled towards the second garden the lady went first through the gate.

And then a curious thing happened. George stepped aside to let Jonquil pass, but instead of going through she stood still and stared at him for a minute. It was not so much the look, which was not a smile, as it was the moment of silence. They saw each other's eyes, and both took a short, faintly accelerated breath, and then they went on into the second garden. That was all.

The afternoon waned. They thanked the lady and walked home slowly, thoughtfully, side by side. Through dinner too they were silent. George told Mr Cary something of what had happened in South America, and managed to let it be known that everything would be plain sailing for him in the future.

Then dinner was over, and he and Jonquil were alone in the room which had seen the beginning of their love affair and the end. It seemed to him long ago and inexpressibly sad. On that sofa he had felt agony and grief such as he would never feel again. He would never be so weak or so tired and miserable and poor. Yet he knew that that boy of fifteen months before had had something, a trust, a warmth that was gone for ever. The sensible thing – they had done the sensible thing. He had traded his first youth for strength and carved success out of despair. But with his youth, life had carried away the freshness of his love.

'You won't marry me, will you?' he said quietly.

Jonquil shook her dark head.

'I'm never going to marry,' she answered.

He nodded.

'I'm going on to Washington in the morning,' he said.

'Oh – '

'I have to go. I've got to be in New York by the first, and meanwhile I want to stop off in Washington.'

'Business!'

'No-o,' he said as if reluctantly. 'There's someone there I must see who was very kind to me when I was so – down and out.'

This was invented. There was no one in Washington for him to see – but he was watching Jonquil narrowly, and he was sure that she winced a little, that her eyes closed and then opened wide again.

'But before I go I want to tell you the things that happened to me since I saw you, and, as maybe we won't meet again, I wonder if – if just this once you'd sit in my lap like you used to. I wouldn't ask except since there's no one else – yet – perhaps it doesn't matter.'

She nodded, and in a moment was sitting in his lap as she had sat so often in that vanished spring. The feel of her head against his shoulder, of her familiar body, sent a shock of emotion over him. His arms holding her had a tendency to tighten around her, so he leaned back and began to talk thoughtfully into the air.

He told her of a despairing two weeks in New York which had terminated with an attractive if not very profitable job in a construction plant in Jersey City. When the Peru business had first presented itself it had not seemed an extraordinary opportunity. He was to be third assistant engineer on the expedition, but only ten of the American party, including eight rodmen and surveyors, had ever reached Cuzco. Ten days later the chief of the expedition was dead of yellow fever. That had been his chance, a chance for anybody but a fool, a marvellous chance –

'A chance for anybody but a fool?' she interrupted innocently.

'Even for a fool,' he continued. 'It was wonderful. Well, I wired New York – '

'And so,' she interrupted again, 'they wired that you ought to take a chance?'

'Ought to!' he exclaimed, still leaning back. 'That I *had* to. There was no time to lose – '

'Not a minute?'

'Not a minute.'

'Not even time for – ' she paused.

'For what?'

'Look.'

He bent his head forward suddenly, and she drew herself to him in the same moment, her lips half open like a flower.

'Yes,' he whispered into her lips. 'There's all the time in the world . . . '

All the time in the world – his life and hers. But for an instant as he kissed her he knew that though he search through eternity he could never recapture those lost April hours. He might press her close now till the muscles knotted on his arms – she was something desirable and rare that he had fought for and made his own – but never again an intangible whisper in the dusk, or on the breeze of night . . .

Well, let it pass, he thought; April is over, April is over. There are all kinds of love in the world, but never the same love twice.

Love in the Night

Saturday Evening Post (14 March 1925)

1

The words thrilled Val. They had come into his mind sometime during the fresh gold April afternoon and he kept repeating them to himself over and over: 'Love in the night; love in the night.' He tried them in three languages – Russian, French and English – and decided that they were best in English. In each language they meant a different sort of love and a different sort of night – the English night seemed the warmest and softest with the thinnest and most crystalline sprinkling of stars. The English love seemed the most fragile and romantic – a white dress and a dim face above it and eyes that were pools of light. And when I add that it was a French night he was thinking about, after all, I see I must go back and begin over.

Val was half Russian and half American. His mother was the daughter of that Morris Hasylton who helped finance the Chicago World's Fair in 1892, and his father was – see the *Almanach de Gotha*, issue of 1910 – Prince Paul Serge Boris Rostoff, son of Prince Vladimir Rostoff, grandson of a grand duke – 'Jimber-Jawed Serge' – and third-cousin-once-removed to the Tsar. It was all very impressive, you see, on that side – house in St Petersburg, shooting lodge near Riga, and swollen villa, more like a palace, overlooking the Mediterranean. It was at this villa in Cannes that the Rostoffs passed the winter – and it wasn't at all the thing to remind Princess Rostoff that this Riviera villa, from the marble fountain – after Bernini – to the gold cordial glasses – after dinner – was paid for with American gold.

The Russians, of course, were gay people on the Continent in the gala days before the war. Of the three races that used Southern France for a pleasure ground they were easily the most adept at the grand manner. The English were too practical, and the Americans, though they spent freely, had no tradition of romantic conduct. But the Russians – there was a people as gallant as the Latins, and rich besides! When the Rostoffs arrived at Cannes late in January the restaurateurs telegraphed north for the prince's favourite labels to paste on their champagne, and the jewellers put incredibly gorgeous articles aside to show to him – but not to the princess – and the Russian Church was swept and garnished for the season that the prince might beg Orthodox forgiveness for his sins. Even the Mediterranean turned obligingly to a deep wine colour in the spring evenings, and fishing boats with robin-breasted sails loitered exquisitely offshore.

In a vague way young Val realised that this was all for the benefit of him and his family. It was a privileged paradise, this white little city on the water, in which he was free to do what he liked because he was rich and young and the blood of Peter the Great ran indigo in his veins. He was only seventeen in 1914, when this history begins, but he had already fought a duel with a young man four years his senior, and he had a small hairless scar to show for it on top of his handsome head.

But the question of love in the night was the thing nearest his heart. It was a vague pleasant dream he had, something that was going to happen to him someday that would be unique and incomparable. He could have told no more about it than that there was a lovely unknown girl concerned in it, and that it ought to take place beneath the Riviera moon.

The odd thing about all this was not that he had this excited and yet almost spiritual hope of romance, for all boys of any imagination have just such hopes, but that it actually came true. And when it happened, it happened so unexpectedly; it was such a jumble of impressions and emotions, of curious phrases that sprang to his lips, of sights and sounds and moments that were here, were lost, were past, that he scarcely understood it at all. Perhaps its very vagueness preserved it in his heart and made him for ever unable to forget.

There was an atmosphere of love all about him that spring – his father's loves, for instance, which were many and indiscreet, and which Val became aware of gradually from overhearing the gossip of servants, and definitely from coming on his American mother unexpectedly one afternoon, to find her storming hysterically at his father's picture on the salon wall. In the picture his father wore a white uniform with a furred dolman and looked back impassively at his wife as if to say, 'Were you under the impression, my dear, that you were marrying into a family of clergymen?'

Val tiptoed away, surprised, confused – and excited. It didn't shock him as it would have shocked an American boy of his age. He had known for years what life was among the Continental rich, and he condemned his father only for making his mother cry.

Love went on around him – reproachless love and illicit love alike. As he strolled along the seaside promenade at nine o'clock, when the stars were bright enough to compete with the bright lamps, he was aware of love on every side. From the open-air cafés, vivid with dresses just down from Paris, came a sweet pungent odour of flowers and chartreuse and fresh black coffee and cigarettes – and mingled with them all he caught another scent, the mysterious thrilling scent of love. Hands touched jewel-sparkling hands upon the white tables. Gay dresses and white shirt-fronts swayed together, and matches were held, trembling a little, for slow-lighting cigarettes. On the other side of the boulevard lovers less fashionable, young Frenchmen who worked in the stores of Cannes, sauntered with their fiancées under the dim trees, but Val's young eyes seldom turned that way. The luxury of music and bright colours and low voices – they were all part of his dream. They were the essential trappings of love in the night.

But assume as he might the rather fierce expression that was expected from a young Russian gentleman who walked the streets alone, Val was beginning to be unhappy. April twilight had succeeded March twilight, the season was almost over, and he had found no use to make of the warm spring evenings. The girls of sixteen and seventeen whom he knew, were chaperoned with care between dusk and bedtime – this, remember, was before the war – and the others who might gladly have walked beside him were an affront to his romantic desire. So April passed by – one week, two weeks, three weeks –

He had played tennis until seven and loitered at the courts for another hour, so it was half-past eight when a tired cab horse accomplished the hill on which gleamed the façade of the Rostoff villa. The lights of his mother's limousine were yellow in the drive, and the princess, buttoning her gloves, was just coming out of the glowing door. Val tossed two francs to the cabman and went to kiss her on the cheek.

'Don't touch me,' she said quickly. 'You've been handling money.'

'But not in my mouth, mother,' he protested humorously.

The princess looked at him impatiently.

'I'm angry,' she said. 'Why must you be so late tonight? We're dining on a yacht and you were to have come along too.'

'What yacht?'

'Americans.' There was always a faint irony in her voice when she mentioned the land of her nativity. Her America was the Chicago of the nineties which she still thought of as the vast upstairs of a butcher's shop. Even the irregularities of Prince Paul were not too high a price to have paid for her escape.

'Two yachts,' she continued; 'in fact we don't know which one. The note was very indefinite. Very careless indeed.'

Americans. Val's mother had taught him to look down on Americans, but she hadn't succeeded in making him dislike them. American men noticed you, even if you were seventeen. He liked Americans. Although he was thoroughly Russian he wasn't immaculately so – the exact proportion, like that of a celebrated soap, was about ninety-nine and three-quarters per cent.

'I want to come,' he said. 'I'll hurry up, mother. I'll – '

'We're late now.' The princess turned as her husband appeared in the door. 'Now Val says he wants to come.'

'He can't,' said Prince Paul shortly. 'He's too outrageously late.'

Val nodded. Russian aristocrats, however indulgent about themselves, were always admirably Spartan with their children. There were no arguments.

'I'm sorry,' he said.

Prince Paul grunted. The footman, in red and silver livery, opened the limousine door. But the grunt decided the matter for Val, because Princess Rostoff at that day and hour had certain grievances against her husband which gave her command of the domestic situation.

'On second thoughts you'd better come, Val,' she announced coolly. 'It's too late now, but come after dinner. The yacht is either the *Minnehaha* or the *Privateer*.' She got into the limousine. 'The one to come to will be the gayer one, I suppose – the Jacksons' yacht – '

'Find got sense,' muttered the Prince cryptically, conveying that Val would find it if he had any sense. 'Have my man take a look at you 'fore you start. Wear tie of mine 'stead of that outrageous string you affected in Vienna. Grow up. High time.'

As the limousine crawled crackling down the pebbled drive Val's face was burning.

2

It was dark in Cannes harbour, rather it seemed dark after the brightness of the promenade that Val had just left behind. Three frail dock lights glittered dimly upon innumerable fishing boats heaped like shells along the beach. Farther out in the water there were other lights where a fleet of slender yachts rode the tide with slow dignity, and farther still a full ripe moon made the water bosom into a polished dancing floor. Occasionally there was a swish! creak! drip! as a rowboat moved about in the shallows, and its blurred shape threaded the labyrinth of hobbled fishing skiffs and launches. Val, descending the velvet slope of sand, stumbled over a sleeping boatman and caught the rank savour of garlic and plain wine. Taking the man by the shoulders he shook open his startled eyes.

'Do you know where the *Minnehaha* is anchored, and the *Privateer*?'

As they slid out into the bay he lay back in the stern and stared with vague discontent at the Riviera moon. That was the right moon, all right. Frequently, five nights out of seven, there was the right moon. And here was the soft air, aching with enchantment, and here was the music, many strains of music from many orchestras, drifting out from the shore. Eastward lay the dark Cape of Antibes, and then Nice, and beyond that Monte Carlo, where the night rang chinking full of gold. Someday he would enjoy all that, too, know its every pleasure and success – when he was too old and wise to care.

But tonight – tonight, that stream of silver that waved like a wide strand of curly hair towards the moon; those soft romantic lights of Cannes behind him, the irresistible ineffable love in this air – that was to be wasted for ever.

'Which one?' asked the boatman suddenly.

'Which what?' demanded Val, sitting up.

'Which boat?'

He pointed. Val turned; above hovered the grey, sword-like prow of a yacht. During the sustained longing of his wish they had covered half a mile.

He read the brass letters over his head. It was the *Privateer*, but there were only dim lights on board, and no music and no voices, only a murmurous k-plash at intervals as the small waves leaped at the sides.

'The other one,' said Val; 'the *Minnehaha*.'

'Don't go yet.'

Val started. The voice, low and soft, had dropped down from the darkness overhead.

'What's the hurry?' said the soft voice. 'Thought maybe somebody was coming to see me, and have suffered terrible disappointment.'

The boatman lifted his oars and looked hesitatingly at Val. But Val was silent, so the man let the blades fall into the water and swept the boat out into the moonlight.

'Wait a minute!' cried Val sharply.

'Goodbye,' said the voice. 'Come again when you can stay longer.'

'But I am going to stay now,' he answered breathlessly.

He gave the necessary order and the rowboat swung back to the foot of the small companionway. Someone young, someone in a misty white dress, someone with a lovely low voice, had actually called to him out of the velvet dark. 'If she has eyes!' Val murmured to himself. He liked the romantic sound of it and repeated it under his breath – 'If she has eyes.'

'What are you?' She was directly above him now; she was looking down and he was looking up as he climbed the ladder, and as their eyes met they both began to laugh.

She was very young, slim, almost frail, with a dress that accentuated her youth by its blanched simplicity. Two wan dark spots on her cheeks marked where the colour was by day.

'What are you?' she repeated, moving back and laughing again as his head appeared on the level of the deck. 'I'm frightened now and I want to know.'

'I am a gentleman,' said Val, bowing.

'What sort of a gentleman? There are all sorts of gentlemen. There was a – there was a coloured gentleman at the table next to ours in Paris, and so – ' She broke off. 'You're not American, are you?'

'I'm Russian,' he said, as he might have announced himself to be an archangel. He thought quickly and then added, 'And I am the most fortunate of Russians. All this day, all this spring I have dreamed of falling in love on such a night, and now I see that heaven has sent me to you.'

'Just one moment!' she said, with a little gasp. 'I'm sure now that this visit is a mistake. I don't go in for anything like that. Please!'

'I beg your pardon.' He looked at her in bewilderment, unaware that he had taken too much for granted. Then he drew himself up formally.

'I have made an error. If you will excuse me I will say good-night.'

He turned away. His hand was on the rail.

'Don't go,' she said, pushing a strand of indefinite hair out of her eyes. 'On second thoughts you can talk any nonsense you like if you'll only not go. I'm miserable and I don't want to be left alone.'

Val hesitated; there was some element in this that he failed to understand. He had taken it for granted that a girl who called to a strange man at night, even from the deck of a yacht, was certainly in a mood for romance. And he wanted intensely to stay. Then he remembered that this was one of the two yachts he had been seeking.

'I imagine that the dinner's on the other boat,' he said.

'The dinner? Oh, yes, it's on the *Minnehaha*. Were you going there?'

'I was going there – a long time ago.'

'What's your name?'

He was on the point of telling her when something made him ask a question instead.

'And you? Why are you not at the party?'

'Because I preferred to stay here. Mrs Jackson said there would be some Russians there – I suppose that's you.' She looked at him with interest. 'You're a very young man, aren't you?'

'I am much older than I look,' said Val stiffly. 'People always comment on it. It's considered rather a remarkable thing.'

'How old are you?'

'Twenty-one,' he lied.

She laughed.

'What nonsense! You're not more than nineteen.'

His annoyance was so perceptible that she hastened to reassure him. 'Cheer up! I'm only seventeen myself. I might have gone to the party if I'd thought there'd be anyone under fifty there.'

He welcomed the change of subject.

'You preferred to sit and dream here beneath the moon.'

'I've been thinking of mistakes.' They sat down side by side in two canvas deckchairs. 'It's a most engrossing subject – the subject of mistakes. Women very seldom brood about mistakes – they're much more willing to forget than men are. But when they do brood –'

'You have made a mistake?' enquired Val.

She nodded.

'Is it something that cannot be repaired?'

'I think so,' she answered. 'I can't be sure. That's what I was considering when you came along.'

'Perhaps I can help in some way,' said Val. 'Perhaps your mistake is not irreparable, after all.'

'You can't,' she said unhappily. 'So let's not think about it. I'm very tired of my mistake and I'd much rather you'd tell me about all the gay, cheerful things that are going on in Cannes tonight.'

They glanced shoreward at the line of mysterious and alluring lights, the big toy banks with candles inside that were really the great fashionable hotels, the lighted clock in the old town, the blurred glow of the Café de Paris, the pricked-out points of villa windows rising on slow hills towards the dark sky.

'What is everyone doing there?' she whispered. 'It looks as though something gorgeous was going on, but what it is I can't quite tell.'

'Everyone there is making love,' said Val quietly.

'Is that it?' She looked for a long time, with a strange expression in her eyes. 'Then I want to go home to America,' she said. 'There is too much love here. I want to go home tomorrow.'

'You are afraid of being in love then?'

She shook her head.

'It isn't that. It's just because – there is no love here for me.'

'Or for me either,' added Val quietly. 'It is sad that we two should be at such a lovely place on such a lovely night and have – nothing.'

He was leaning towards her intently, with a sort of inspired and chaste romance in his eyes – and she drew back.

'Tell me more about yourself,' she enquired quickly. 'If you are Russian where did you learn to speak such excellent English?'

'My mother is American,' he admitted. 'My grandfather was American also, so she had no choice in the matter.'

'Then you're American too!'

'I am Russian,' said Val with dignity.

She looked at him closely, smiled and decided not to argue. 'Well then,' she said diplomatically, 'I suppose you must have a Russian name.'

But he had no intention now of telling her his name. A name, even the Rostoff name, would be a desecration of the night. They were their own low voices, their two white faces – and that was enough. He was sure, without any reason for being sure but with a sort of instinct that sang triumphantly through his mind, that in a little while, a minute or an hour, he was going to undergo an initiation into the life of romance. His name had no reality beside what was stirring in his heart.

'You are beautiful,' he said suddenly.

'How do you know?'

'Because for women moonlight is the hardest light of all.'

'Am I nice in the moonlight?'

'You are the loveliest thing that I have ever known.'

'Oh.' She thought this over. 'Of course I had no business to let you come on board. I might have known what we'd talk about – in this moon. But I can't sit here and look at the shore – for ever. I'm too young for that. Don't you think I'm too young for that?'

'Much too young,' he agreed solemnly.

Suddenly they both became aware of new music that was close at hand, music that seemed to come out of the water not a hundred yards away.

'Listen!' she cried. 'It's from the *Minnehaha*. They've finished dinner.'

For a moment they listened in silence.

'Thank you,' said Val suddenly.

'For what?'

He hardly knew he had spoken. He was thanking the deep low horns for singing in the breeze, the sea for its warm murmurous complaint against the bow, the milk of the stars for washing over them until he felt buoyed up in a substance more taut than air.

'So lovely,' she whispered.

'What are we going to do about it?'

'Do we have to do something about it? I thought we could just sit and enjoy – '

'You didn't think that,' he interrupted quietly. 'You know that we must do something about it. I am going to make love to you – and you are going to be glad.'

'I can't,' she said very low. She wanted to laugh now, to make some light cool remark that would bring the situation back into the safe waters of a casual flirtation. But it was too late now. Val knew that the music had completed what the moon had begun.

'I will tell you the truth,' he said. 'You are my first love. I am seventeen – the same age as you, no more.'

There was something utterly disarming about the fact that they were the same age. It made her helpless before the fate that had thrown them together. The deckchairs creaked and he was conscious of a faint illusive perfume as they swayed suddenly and childishly together.

3

Whether he kissed her once or several times he could not afterwards remember, though it must have been an hour that they sat there close together and he held her hand. What surprised him most about making love was that it seemed to have no element of wild passion – regret, desire, despair – but a delirious promise of such happiness in the world, in living, as he had never known. First love – this was only first love! What must love itself in its fullness, its perfection be. He did not know that what he was experiencing then, that unreal, undesirous medley of ecstasy and peace, would be unrecapturable for ever.

The music had ceased for some time when presently the murmurous silence was broken by the sound of a rowboat disturbing the quiet waves. She sprang suddenly to her feet and her eyes strained out over the bay.

'Listen!' she said quickly. 'I want you to tell me your name.'

'No.'

'Please,' she begged him. 'I'm going away tomorrow.'

He didn't answer.

'I don't want you to forget me,' she said. 'My name is – '

'I won't forget you. I will promise to remember you always. Whoever I may love I will always compare her to you, my first love. So long as I live you will always have that much freshness in my heart.'

'I want you to remember,' she murmured brokenly. 'Oh, this has meant more to me than it has to you – much more.'

She was standing so close to him that he felt her warm young breath on his face. Once again they swayed together. He pressed her hands and wrists between his as it seemed right to do, and kissed her lips. It was the right kiss, he thought, the romantic kiss – not too little or too much. Yet there was a sort of promise in it of other kisses he might have had, and it was with a slight sinking of his heart that he heard the rowboat close to the yacht and realised that her family had returned. The evening was over.

'And this is only the beginning,' he told himself. 'All my life will be like this night.'

She was saying something in a low quick voice and he was listening tensely.

'You must know one thing – I am married. Three months ago. That was the mistake that I was thinking about when the moon brought you out here. In a moment you will understand.'

She broke off as the boat swung against the companionway and a man's voice floated up out of the darkness.

'Is that you, my dear?'

'Yes.'

'What is this other rowboat waiting?'

'One of Mrs Jackson's guests came here by mistake and I made him stay and amuse me for an hour.'

A moment later the thin white hair and weary face of a man of sixty appeared above the level of the deck. And then Val saw and realised too late how much he cared.

4

When the Riviera season ended in May the Rostoffs and all the other Russians closed their villas and went north for the summer. The Russian Orthodox Church was locked up and so were the bins of rarer wine, and the fashionable spring moonlight was put away, so to speak, to wait for their return.

'We'll be back next season,' they said as a matter of course.

But this was premature, for they were never coming back any more. Those few who straggled south again after five tragic years were glad to get work as chambermaids or *valets de chambre* in the great hotels where they had once dined. Many of them, of course, were killed in the war or in the revolution; many of them faded out as spongers and small cheats in the big capitals, and not a few ended their lives in a sort of stupefied despair.

When the Kerensky government collapsed in 1917, Val was a lieutenant on the eastern front, trying desperately to enforce authority in his company long after any vestige of it remained. He was still trying when Prince Paul Rostoff and his wife gave up their lives one rainy morning to atone for the blunders of the Romanoffs – and the enviable career of Morris Hasylton's daughter ended in a city that bore even more resemblance to a butcher shop's than had Chicago in 1892.

After that Val fought with Denikin's army for a while until he realised that he was participating in a hollow farce and the glory of Imperial Russia was over. Then he went to France and was suddenly confronted with the astounding problem of keeping his body and soul together.

It was, of course, natural that he should think of going to America. Two vague aunts with whom his mother had quarrelled many years ago still lived there in comparative affluence. But the idea was repugnant to the prejudices his mother had implanted in him, and besides he hadn't sufficient money left to pay for his passage over. Until a possible counter-revolution should restore to him the Rostoff properties in Russia he must somehow keep alive in France.

So he went to the little city he knew best of all. He went to Cannes. His last two hundred francs bought him a third-class ticket and when he arrived he gave his dress suit to an obliging party who dealt in such things and received in return money for food and bed. He was sorry afterwards that he had sold the dress suit, because it might have helped him to a position as a waiter. But he obtained work as a taxi driver instead and was quite as happy, or rather quite as miserable, at that.

Sometimes he carried Americans to look at villas for rent, and when the front glass of the automobile was up, curious fragments of conversation drifted out to him from within.

'– heard this fellow was a Russian prince.' . . . 'Sh!' . . . 'No, this one right here.' . . . 'Be quiet, Esther!' – followed by subdued laughter.

When the car stopped, his passengers would edge around to have a look at him. At first he was desperately unhappy when girls did this; after a while he didn't mind any more. Once a cheerfully intoxicated American asked him if it were true and invited him to lunch, and another time an elderly woman seized his hand as she got out of the taxi, shook it violently and then pressed a hundred-franc note into his palm.

'Well, Florence, now I can tell 'em back home I shook hands with a Russian prince.'

The inebriated American who had invited him to lunch thought at first that Val was a son of the czar, and it had to be explained to him that a prince in Russia was simply the equivalent of a British courtesy lord. But he was puzzled that a man of Val's personality didn't go out and make some real money.

'This is Europe,' said Val gravely. 'Here money is not made. It is inherited or else it is slowly saved over a period of many years and maybe in three generations a family moves up into a higher class.'

'Think of something people want – like we do.'

'That is because there is more money to want with in America. Everything that people want here has been thought of long ago.'

But after a year and with the help of a young Englishman he had played tennis with before the war, Val managed to get into the Cannes branch of an English bank. He forwarded mail and bought railroad tickets and arranged tours for impatient sightseers. Sometimes a familiar face came to his window; if Val was recognised he shook hands; if not he kept silence. After two years he was no longer pointed out as a former prince, for the Russians were an old story now – the splendour of the Rostoffs and their friends was forgotten.

He mixed with people very little. In the evenings he walked for a while on the promenade, took a slow glass of beer in a café, and went early to bed. He was seldom invited anywhere because people thought that his sad, intent face was depressing – and he never accepted anyhow. He wore cheap French clothes now instead of the rich tweeds and flannels that had been ordered with his father's from England. As for women, he knew none at all. Of the many things he had been certain about at seventeen, he had been most certain about this – that his life would be full of romance. Now after eight years he knew that it was not to be. Somehow he had never had time for love – the war, the revolution, and now his poverty had conspired against his expectant heart. The springs of his emotion which had first poured forth one April night had dried up immediately and only a faint trickle remained.

His happy youth had ended almost before it began. He saw himself growing older and more shabby, and living always more and more in the memories of his gorgeous boyhood. Eventually he would become absurd, pulling out an old heirloom of a watch and showing it to amused young fellow clerks who would listen with winks to his tales of the Rostoff name.

He was thinking these gloomy thoughts one April evening in 1922 as he walked beside the sea and watched the never-changing magic of the awakening lights. It was no longer for his benefit, that magic, but it went on, and he was somehow glad. Tomorrow he was going away on his vacation, to a cheap hotel farther down the shore where he could bathe and rest and read; then he would come back and work some more. Every year for three years he had taken his vacation during the last two weeks in April, perhaps because it was then that he felt the most need for remembering. It was in April that what was destined to be the best part of his life had come to a culmination under a romantic moonlight. It was sacred to him – for what he had thought of as an initiation and a beginning had turned out to be the end.

He paused now in front of the Café des Étrangers and after a moment crossed the street on impulse and sauntered down to the shore. A dozen yachts, already turned to a beautiful silver colour, rode at anchor in the bay. He had seen them that afternoon, and read the names painted on their bows – but only from habit. He had done it for three years now, and it was almost a natural function of his eye.

'Un beau soir,' remarked a French voice at his elbow. It was a boatman who had often seen Val here before. 'Monsieur finds the sea beautiful?'

'Very beautiful.'

'I too. But a bad living except in the season. Next week, though, I earn something special. I am paid well for simply waiting here and doing nothing more from eight o'clock until midnight.'

'That's very nice,' said Val politely.

'A widowed lady, very beautiful, from America, whose yacht always anchors in the harbour for the last two weeks in April. If the *Privateer* comes tomorrow it will make three years.'

5

All night Val didn't sleep – not because there was any question in his mind as to what he should do, but because his long stupefied emotions were suddenly awake and alive. Of course he must not see her – not he, a poor failure with a name that was now only a shadow – but it would make him a little happier always to know that she remembered. It gave his own memory another dimension, raised it like those stereopticon glasses that bring out a picture from the flat paper. It made him sure that he had not deceived himself – he had been charming once upon a time to a lovely woman, and she did not forget.

An hour before train time next day he was at the railway station with his grip, so as to avoid any chance encounter in the street. He found himself a place in a third-class carriage of the waiting train.

Somehow as he sat there he felt differently about life – a sort of hope, faint and illusory, that he hadn't felt twenty-four hours before. Perhaps there was some way in those next few years in which he could make it possible to meet her once again – if he worked hard, threw himself passionately into whatever was at hand. He knew of at least two Russians in Cannes who had started over again with nothing except good manners and ingenuity and were now doing surprisingly well. The blood of Morris Hasylton began to throb a little in Val's temples and made him remember something he had never before cared to remember – that Morris Hasylton, who had built his daughter a palace in St Petersburg, had also started from nothing at all.

Simultaneously another emotion possessed him, less strange, less dynamic but equally American – the emotion of curiosity. In case he did – well, in case life should ever make it possible for him to seek her out, he should at least know her name.

He jumped to his feet, fumbled excitedly at the carriage handle and jumped from the train. Tossing his valise into the check room he started at a run for the American consulate.

'A yacht came in this morning,' he said hurriedly to a clerk, 'an American yacht – the *Privateer*. I want to know who owns it.'

'Just a minute,' said the clerk, looking at him oddly. 'I'll try to find out.'

After what seemed to Val an interminable time he returned.

'Why, just a minute,' he repeated hesitantly. 'We're – it seems we're finding out.'

'Did the yacht come?'

'Oh, yes – it's here all right. At least I think so. If you'll just wait in that chair.'

After another ten minutes Val looked impatiently at his watch. If they didn't hurry he'd probably miss his train. He made a nervous movement as if to get up from his chair.

'Please sit still,' said the clerk, glancing at him quickly from his desk. 'I ask you. Just sit down in that chair.'

Val stared at him. How could it possibly matter to the clerk whether or not he waited?

'I'll miss my train,' he said impatiently. 'I'm sorry to have given you all this bother – '

'Please sit still! We're glad to get it off our hands. You see, we've been waiting for your enquiry for – ah – three years.'

Val jumped to his feet and jammed his hat on his head.

'Why didn't you tell me that?' he demanded angrily.

'Because we had to get word to our – our client. Please don't go! It's – ah, it's too late.'

Val turned. Someone slim and radiant with dark frightened eyes was standing behind him, framed against the sunshine of the doorway.

'Why – '

Val's lips parted, but no words came through. She took a step towards him.

'I – ' She looked at him helplessly, her eyes filling with tears. 'I just wanted to say hello,' she murmured. 'I've come back for three years just because I wanted to say hello.'

Still Val was silent.

'You might answer,' she said impatiently. 'You might answer when I'd – when I'd just about begun to think you'd been killed in the war.' She turned to the clerk. 'Please introduce us!' she cried. 'You see, I can't say hello to him when we don't even know each other's names.'

It's the thing to distrust these international marriages, of course. It's an American tradition that they always turn out badly, and we are accustomed to such headlines as: ' "Would Trade Coronet for True American Love," says Duchess', and 'Claims Count Mendicant Tortured Toledo Wife'. The other sort of headlines are never printed, for who would want to read: ' "Castle is Love Nest," Asserts Former Georgia Belle', or 'Duke and Packer's Daughter Celebrate Golden Honeymoon'.

So far there have been no headlines at all about the young Rostoffs. Prince Val is much too absorbed in that string of moonlight-blue taxicabs which he manipulates with such unusual efficiency, to give out interviews. He and his wife only leave New York once a year – but there is still a boatman who rejoices when the *Privateer* steams into Cannes harbour on a mid-April night.

A Short Trip Home

Saturday Evening Post (17 December 1927)

1

Author's Note: In a moment of hasty misjudgement a whole paragraph of description was lifted out of this tale where it originated, and properly belongs, and applied to quite a different character in a novel of mine. I have ventured none the less to leave it here, even at the risk of seeming to serve warmed-over fare.

I was near her, for I had lingered behind in order to get the short walk with her from the living-room to the front door. That was a lot, for she had flowered suddenly and I, being a man and only a year older, hadn't flowered at all, had scarcely dared to come near her in the week we'd been home. Nor was I going to say anything in that walk of ten feet, or touch her; but I had a vague hope she'd do something, give a gay little performance of some sort, personal only in so far as we were alone together.

She had bewitchment suddenly in the twinkle of short hairs on her neck, in the sure, clear confidence that at about eighteen begins to deepen and sing in attractive American girls. The lamplight shopped in the yellow strands of her hair.

Already she was sliding into another world – the world of Joe Jelke and Jim Cathcart waiting for us now in the car. In another year she would pass beyond me for ever.

As I waited, feeling the others outside in the snowy night, feeling the excitement of Christmas week and the excitement of Ellen here, blooming away, filling the room with 'sex appeal' – a wretched phrase to express a quality that isn't like that at all – a maid came in from the dining-room, spoke to Ellen quietly and handed her a note. Ellen read it and her eyes faded down, as when the current grows weak on rural circuits, and smouldered off into space. Then she gave me an odd look – in which I probably didn't show – and without a word, followed the maid into the dining-room and beyond. I sat turning over the pages of a magazine for a quarter of an hour.

Joe Jelke came in, red-faced from the cold, his white silk muffler gleaming at the neck of his fur coat. He was a senior at New Haven, I was a sophomore. He was prominent, a member of Scroll and Keys, and, in my eyes, very distinguished and handsome.

'Isn't Ellen coming?'

'I don't know,' I answered discreetly. 'She was all ready.'

'Ellen!' he called. 'Ellen!'

He had left the front door open behind him and a great cloud of frosty air rolled in from outside. He went halfway up the stairs – he was a familiar in the house – and called again, till Mrs Baker came to the bannister and said that Ellen was below. Then the maid, a little excited, appeared in the dining-room door.

'Mr Jelke,' she called in a low voice.

Joe's face fell as he turned towards her, sensing bad news.

'Miss Ellen says for you to go on to the party. She'll come later.'

'What's the matter?'

'She can't come now. She'll come later.'

He hesitated, confused. It was the last big dance of vacation, and he was mad about Ellen. He had tried to give her a ring for Christmas, and failing that, got her to accept a gold mesh bag that must have cost two hundred dollars. He wasn't the only one – there were three or four in the same wild condition, and all in the ten days she'd been home – but his chance came first, for he was rich and gracious and at that moment the 'desirable' boy of St Paul. To me it seemed impossible that she could prefer another, but the rumour was she'd described Joe as much too perfect. I suppose he lacked mystery for her, and when a man is up against that with a young girl who isn't thinking of the practical side of marriage yet – well –

'She's in the kitchen,' Joe said angrily.

'No, she's not.' The maid was defiant and a little scared.

'She is.'

'She went out the back way, Mr Jelke.'

'I'm going to see.'

I followed him. The Swedish servants washing dishes looked up sideways at our approach and an interested crashing of pans marked our passage through. The storm door, unbolted, was flapping in the wind and as we walked out into the snowy yard we saw the tail light of a car turn the corner at the end of the back alley.

'I'm going after her,' Joe said slowly. 'I don't understand this at all.'

I was too awed by the calamity to argue. We hurried to his car and drove in a fruitless, despairing zigzag all over the residence section, peering into every machine on the streets. It was half an hour before the futility of the affair began to dawn upon him – St Paul is a city of almost three hundred thousand people – and Jim Cathcart reminded him that we had another girl to stop for. Like a wounded animal he sank into a melancholy mass of fur in the corner, from which position he jerked upright every few minutes and waved himself backwards and forwards a little in protest and despair.

Jim's girl was ready and impatient, but after what had happened her impatience didn't seem important. She looked lovely though. That's one thing about Christmas vacation – the excitement of growth and change and adventure in foreign parts transforming the people you've known all your life. Joe Jelke was polite to her in a daze – he indulged in one burst of short, loud, harsh laughter by way of conversation – and we drove to the hotel.

The chauffeur approached it on the wrong side – the side on which the line of cars was not putting forth guests – and because of that we came suddenly upon Ellen Baker just getting out of a small coupé. Even before we came to a stop, Joe Jelke had jumped excitedly from the car.

Ellen turned towards us, a faintly distracted look – perhaps of surprise, but certainly not of alarm – in her face; in fact, she didn't seem very aware of us. Joe approached her with a stern, dignified, injured and, I thought, just exactly correct reproof in his expression. I followed.

Seated in the coupé – he had not dismounted to help Ellen out – was a hard thin-faced man of about thirty-five with an air of being scarred, and a slight sinister smile. His eyes were a sort of taunt to the whole human family – they were the eyes of an animal, sleepy and quiescent in the presence of another species. They were helpless yet brutal, unhopeful yet confident. It was as if they felt themselves powerless to originate activity, but infinitely capable of profiting by a single gesture of weakness in another.

Vaguely I placed him as one of the sort of men whom I had been conscious of from my earliest youth as 'hanging around' – leaning with one elbow on the counters of tobacco stores, watching, through heaven knows what small chink of the mind, the people who hurried in and out. Intimate to garages, where he had vague business conducted in undertones, to barbershops and to the lobbies of theatres – in such places, anyhow, I placed the type, if type it was, that he reminded me of. Sometimes his face bobbed up in one of Tad's more savage cartoons, and I had always from earliest boyhood thrown a nervous glance towards the dim borderland where he stood, and seen him watching me and despising me. Once, in a dream, he had taken a few steps towards me, jerking his head back and muttering: 'Say, kid,' in what was intended to be a reassuring voice, and I had broken for the door in terror. This was that sort of man.

Joe and Ellen faced each other silently; she seemed, as I have said, to be in a daze. It was cold, but she didn't notice that her coat had blown open; Joe reached out and pulled it together, and automatically she clutched it with her hand.

Suddenly the man in the coupé, who had been watching them silently, laughed. It was a bare laugh, done with the breath – just a noisy jerk of the head – but it was an insult if I had ever heard one; definite and not to be passed over. I wasn't surprised when Joe, who was quick tempered, turned to him angrily and said: 'What's your trouble?'

The man waited a moment, his eyes shifting and yet staring, and always seeing. Then he laughed again in the same way. Ellen stirred uneasily.

'Who is this – this – ' Joe's voice trembled with annoyance.

'Look out now,' said the man slowly.

Joe turned to me. 'Eddie, take Ellen and Catherine in, will you?' he said quickly . . . 'Ellen, go with Eddie.'

'Look out now,' the man repeated.

Ellen made a little sound with her tongue and teeth, but she didn't resist when I took her arm and moved her towards the side door of the hotel. It struck me as odd that she should be so helpless, even to the point of acquiescing by her silence in this imminent trouble.

'Let it go, Joe!' I called back over my shoulder. 'Come inside!'

Ellen, pulling against my arm, hurried us on. As we were caught up into the swinging doors I had the impression that the man was getting out of his coupé.

Ten minutes later, as I waited for the girls outside the women's dressing-room, Joe Jelke and Jim Cathcart stepped out of the elevator. Joe was very white, his eyes were heavy and glazed, there was a trickle of dark blood on his forehead and on his white muffler. Jim had both their hats in his hand.

'He hit Joe with brass knuckles,' Jim said in a low voice. 'Joe was out cold for a minute or so. I wish you'd send a bellboy for some witch-hazel and court-plaster.'

It was late and the hall was deserted; brassy fragments of the dance below reached us as if heavy curtains were being blown aside and dropping back into place. When Ellen came out I took her directly downstairs. We avoided the receiving line and went into a dim room set with scraggly hotel palms where couples sometimes sat out during the dance; there I told her what had happened.

'It was Joe's own fault,' she said, surprisingly. 'I told him not to interfere.'

This wasn't true. She had said nothing, only uttered one curious little click of impatience.

'You ran out the back door and disappeared for almost an hour,' I protested. 'Then you turned up with a hard-looking customer who laughed in Joe's face.'

'A hard-looking customer,' she repeated, as if tasting the sound of the words.

'Well, wasn't he? Where on earth did you get hold of him, Ellen?'

'On the train,' she answered. Immediately she seemed to regret this admission. 'You'd better stay out of things that aren't your business, Eddie. You see what happened to Joe.'

Literally I gasped. To watch her, seated beside me, immaculately glowing, her body giving off wave after wave of freshness and delicacy – and to hear her talk like that.

'But that man's a thug!' I cried. 'No girl could be safe with him. He used brass knuckles on Joe – brass knuckles!'

'Is that pretty bad?'

She asked this as she might have asked such a question a few years ago. She looked at me at last and really wanted an answer; for a moment it was as if she were trying to recapture an attitude that had almost departed; then she hardened again. I say 'hardened', for I began to notice that when she was concerned with this man her eyelids fell a little, shutting other things – everything else – out of view.

That was a moment I might have said something, I suppose, but in spite of everything, I couldn't light into her. I was too much under the spell of her beauty and its success. I even began to find excuses for her – perhaps that man wasn't what he appeared to be; or perhaps – more romantically – she was involved with him against her will to shield someone else. At this point people began to drift into the room and come up to speak to us. We couldn't talk any more, so we went in and bowed to the chaperones. Then I gave her up to the bright restless sea of the dance, where she moved in an eddy of her own among the pleasant islands of coloured favours set out on tables and the south winds from the brasses moaning across the hall. After a while I saw Joe Jelke sitting in a corner with a strip of court-plaster on his forehead watching Ellen as if she herself had struck him down, but I didn't go up to him. I felt queer myself – like I feel when I wake up after sleeping through an afternoon, strange and portentous, as if something had gone on in the interval that changed the values of everything and that I didn't see.

The night slipped on through successive phases of cardboard horns, amateur tableaux and flashlights for the morning papers. Then was the grand march and supper, and about two o'clock some of the committee dressed up as revenue agents pinched the party, and a facetious newspaper was distributed, burlesquing the events of the evening. And all the time out of the corner of my eye I watched the shining orchid on Ellen's shoulder as it moved like Stuart's plume about the room. I watched it with a definite foreboding until the last sleepy groups had crowded into the elevators, and then, bundled to the eyes in great shapeless fur coats, drifted out into the clear dry Minnesota night.

2

There is a sloping mid-section of our city which lies between the residence quarter on the hill and the business district on the level of the river. It is a vague part of town, broken by its climb into triangles and odd shapes – there are names like Seven Corners – and I don't believe a dozen people could draw an accurate map of it, though everyone traversed it by trolley, auto or shoe leather twice a day. And though it was a busy section, it would be hard for me to name the business that comprised its activity. There were always long lines of trolley cars waiting to start somewhere; there was a big movie theatre and many small ones with posters of Hoot Gibson and Wonder Dogs and Wonder Horses outside; there were small stores with 'Old King Brady' and 'The Liberty Boys of '76' in the windows, and marbles, cigarettes and candy inside; and – one definite place at least – a fancy costumier whom we all visited at least once a year. Sometime during boyhood I became aware that one side of a certain obscure street there were bawdy houses, and all through the district were pawnshops, cheap jewellers, small athletic clubs and gymnasiums and somewhat too blatantly run-down saloons.

The morning after the Cotillion Club party, I woke up late and lazy, with the happy feeling that for a day or two more there was no chapel, no classes – nothing to do but wait for another party tonight. It was crisp and bright – one of those days when you forget how cold it is until your cheek freezes – and the events of the evening before seemed dim and far away. After luncheon I started downtown on foot through a light, pleasant snow of small flakes that would probably fall all afternoon, and I was about half through that halfway section of town – so far as I know, there's no inclusive name for it – when suddenly whatever idle thought was in my head blew away like a hat and I began thinking hard of Ellen Baker. I began worrying about her as I'd never worried about anything outside myself before. I began to loiter, with an instinct to go up on the hill again and find her and talk to her; then I remembered that she was at a tea, and I went on again, but still thinking of her, and harder than ever. Right then the affair opened up again.

It was snowing, I said, and it was four o'clock on a December afternoon, when there is a promise of darkness in the air and the street lamps are just going on. I passed a combination pool-parlour and restaurant, with a stove loaded with hot-dogs in the window, and a few loungers hanging around the door. The lights were on inside – not bright lights but just a few pale yellow ones high up on the ceiling – and the glow they threw out into the frosty dusk wasn't bright enough to tempt you to stare inside. As I went past, thinking hard of Ellen all this time, I took in the quartet of loafers out of the corner of my eye. I hadn't gone half a dozen steps down the street when one of them called to me, not by name but in a way clearly intended for my ear. I thought it was a tribute to my raccoon coat and paid no attention, but a moment later whoever it was called to me again in a peremptory voice. I was annoyed and turned around. There, standing in the group not ten feet away and looking at me with the half sneer on his face with which he'd looked at Joe Jelke was the scarred, thin-faced man of the night before.

He had on a black fancy-cut coat, buttoned up to his neck as if he were cold. His hands were deep in his pockets and he wore a derby and high button shoes. I was startled, and for a moment I hesitated, but I was most of all angry, and knowing that I was quicker with my hands than Joe Jelke, I took a tentative step back towards him. The other men weren't looking at me – I don't think they saw me at all – but I knew that this one recognised me; there was nothing casual about his look, no mistake.

'Here I am. What are you going to do about it?' his eyes seemed to say.

I took another step towards him and he laughed soundlessly, but with active contempt, and drew back into the group. I followed. I was going to speak to him – I wasn't sure what I was going to say – but when I came up he had either changed his mind and backed off, or else he wanted me to follow him inside, for he had slipped off and the three men watched my intent approach without curiosity. They were the same kind – sporty, but, unlike him, smooth rather than truculent; I didn't find any personal malice in their collective glance.

'Did he go inside?' I asked.

They looked at one another in that cagey way; a wink passed between them, and after a perceptible pause, one said: 'Who go inside?'

'I don't know his name.'

There was another wink. Annoyed and determined, I walked past them and into the pool-room. There were a few people at a lunch counter along one side and a few more playing billiards, but he was not among them.

Again I hesitated. If his idea was to lead me into any blind part of the establishment – there were some half-open doors farther back – I wanted more support. I went up to the man at the desk.

'What became of the fellow who just walked in here?'

Was he on his guard immediately, or was that my imagination?

'What fellow?'

'Thin face – derby hat.'

'How long ago?'

'Oh – a minute.'

He shook his head again. 'Didn't see him,' he said.

I waited. The three men from outside had come in and were lined up beside me at the counter. I felt that all of them were looking at me in a peculiar way. Feeling helpless and increasingly uneasy, I turned suddenly and went out. A little way down the street I turned again and took a good look at the place, so I'd know it and could find it again. On the next corner I broke impulsively into a run, found a taxicab in front of the hotel and drove back up the hill.

Ellen wasn't home. Mrs Baker came downstairs and talked to me. She seemed entirely cheerful and proud of Ellen's beauty, and ignorant of anything being amiss or of anything unusual having taken place the night before. She was glad that vacation was almost over – it was a strain and Ellen wasn't very strong. Then she said something that relieved my mind enormously. She was glad that I had come in, for of course Ellen would want to see me, and the time was so short. She was going back at half-past eight tonight.

'Tonight!' I exclaimed. 'I thought it was the day after tomorrow.'

'She's going to visit the Brokaws in Chicago,' Mrs Baker said. 'They want her for some party. We just decided it today. She's leaving with the Ingersoll girls tonight.'

I was so glad I could barely restrain myself from shaking her hand. Ellen was safe. It had been nothing all along but a moment of the most casual adventure. I felt like an idiot, but I realised how much I cared about Ellen and how little I could endure anything terrible happening to her.

'She'll be in soon?'

'Any minute now. She just phoned from the University Club.'

I said I'd be over later – I lived almost next door and I wanted to be alone. Outside I remembered I didn't have a key, so I started up the Bakers' driveway to take the old cut we used in childhood through the intervening yard. It was still snowing, but the flakes were bigger now against the darkness, and trying to locate the buried walk I noticed that the Bakers' back door was ajar.

I scarcely know why I turned and walked into that kitchen. There was a time when I would have known the Bakers' servants by name. That wasn't true now, but they knew me, and I was aware of a sudden suspension as I came in – not only a suspension of talk but of some mood or expectation that had filled them. They began to go to work too quickly; they made unnecessary movements and clamour – those three. The parlour maid looked at me in a frightened way and I suddenly guessed she was waiting to deliver another message. I beckoned her into the pantry.

'I know all about this,' I said. 'It's a very serious business. Shall I go to Mrs Baker now, or will you shut and lock that back door?'

'Don't tell Mrs Baker, Mr Stinson!'

'Then I don't want Miss Ellen disturbed. If she is – and if she is I'll know of it – ' I delivered some outrageous threat about going to all the employment agencies and seeing she never got another job in the city. She was thoroughly intimidated when I went out; it wasn't a minute before the back door was locked and bolted behind me.

Simultaneously I heard a big car drive up in front, chains crunching on the soft snow; it was bringing Ellen home, and I went in to say goodbye.

Joe Jelke and two other boys were along, and none of the three could manage to take their eyes off her, even to say hello to me. She had one of those exquisite rose skins frequent in our part of the country, and beautiful until the little veins begin to break at about forty; now, flushed with the cold, it was a riot of lovely delicate pinks like many carnations. She and Joe had reached some sort of reconciliation, or at least he was too far gone in love to remember last night; but I saw that though she laughed a lot she wasn't really paying any attention to him or any of them. She wanted them to go, so that there'd be a message from the kitchen, but I knew that the message wasn't coming – that she was safe. There was talk of the Pump and Slipper dance at New Haven and of the Princeton Prom, and then, in various moods, we four left and separated quickly outside. I walked home with a certain depression of spirit and lay for an hour in a hot bath thinking that vacation was all over for me now that she was gone; feeling, even more deeply than I had yesterday, that she was out of my life.

And something eluded me, some one more thing to do, something that I had lost amid the events of the afternoon, promising myself to go back and pick it up, only to find that it had escaped me. I associated it vaguely with Mrs Baker, and now I seemed to recall that it had poked up its head somewhere in the stream of conversation with her. In my relief about Ellen I had forgotten to ask her a question regarding something she had said.

The Brokaws – that was it – where Ellen was to visit. I knew Bill Brokaw well; he was in my class at Yale. Then I remembered and sat bolt upright in the tub – the Brokaws weren't in Chicago this Christmas; they were at Palm Beach!

Dripping, I sprang out of the tub, threw an insufficient union suit around my shoulders and sprang for the phone in my room. I got the connection quick, but Miss Ellen had already started for the train.

Luckily our car was in, and while I squirmed, still damp, into my clothes, the chauffeur brought it around to the door. The night was cold and dry, and we made good time to the station through the hard, crusty snow. I felt queer and insecure starting out this way, but somehow more confident as the station loomed up bright and new against the dark, cold air. For fifty years my family had owned the land on which it was built and that made my temerity seem all right somehow. There was always a possibility that I was rushing in where angels feared to tread, but that sense of having a solid foothold in the past made me willing to make a fool of myself. This business was all wrong – terribly wrong. Any idea I had entertained that it was harmless dropped away now; between Ellen and some vague overwhelming catastrophe there stood me, or else the police and a scandal. I'm no moralist – there was another element here, dark and frightening, and I didn't want Ellen to go through it alone.

There are three competing trains from St Paul to Chicago that all leave within a few minutes of half-past eight. Hers was the Burlington, and as I ran across the station I saw the grating being pulled over and the light above it go out. I knew, though, that she had a drawing-room with the Ingersoll girls, because her mother had mentioned buying the ticket, so she was, literally speaking, tucked in until tomorrow.

The C M & St P gate was down at the other end and I raced for it and made it. I had forgotten one thing, though, and that was enough to keep me awake and worried half the night. This train got into Chicago ten minutes after the other. Ellen had that much time to disappear into one of the largest cities in the world.

I gave the porter a wire to my family to send from Milwaukee, and at eight o'clock next morning I pushed violently by a whole line of passengers, clambering over their bags parked in the vestibule, and shot out of the door with a sort of scramble over the porter's back. For a moment the confusion of a great station, the voluminous sounds and echoes and cross-currents of bells and smoke struck me helpless. Then I dashed for the exit and towards the only chance I knew of finding her.

I had guessed right. She was standing at the telegraph counter, sending off heaven knows what black lie to her mother, and her expression when she saw me had a sort of terror mixed up with its surprise. There was cunning in it too. She was thinking quickly – she would have liked to walk away from me as if I weren't there, and go about her own business, but she couldn't. I was too matter-of-fact a thing in her life. So we stood silently watching each other and each thinking hard.

'The Brokaws are in Florida,' I said after a minute.

'It was nice of you to take such a long trip to tell me that.'

'Since you've found it out, don't you think you'd better go on to school?'

'Please let me alone, Eddie,' she said.

'I'll go as far as New York with you. I've decided to go back early myself.'

'You'd better let me alone.' Her lovely eyes narrowed and her face took on a look of dumb-animal-like resistance. She made a visible effort, the cunning flickered back into it, then both were gone, and in their stead was a cheerful reassuring smile that all but convinced me.

'Eddie, you silly child, don't you think I'm old enough to take care of myself?' I didn't answer. 'I'm going to meet a man, you understand. I just want to see him today. I've got my ticket East on the five o'clock train. If you don't believe it, here it is in my bag.'

'I believe you.'

'The man isn't anybody that you know and – frankly, I think you're being awfully fresh and impossible.'

'I know who the man is.'

Again she lost control of her face. That terrible expression came back into it and she spoke with almost a snarl: 'You'd better let me alone.'

I took the blank out of her hand and wrote out an explanatory telegram to her mother. Then I turned to Ellen and said a little roughly: 'We'll take the five o'clock train East together. Meanwhile you're going to spend the day with me.'

The mere sound of my own voice saying this so emphatically encouraged me, and I think it impressed her too; at any rate, she submitted – at least temporarily – and came along without protest while I bought my ticket.

When I start to piece together the fragments of that day a sort of confusion begins, as if my memory didn't want to yield up any of it, or my consciousness let any of it pass through. There was a bright, fierce morning during which we rode about in a taxicab and went to a department store where Ellen said she wanted to buy something and then tried to slip away from me by a back way. I had the feeling, for an hour, that someone was following us along Lake Shore Drive in a taxicab, and I would try to catch them by turning quickly or looking suddenly into the chauffeur's mirror; but I could find no one, and when I turned back I could see that Ellen's face was contorted with mirthless, unnatural laughter.

All morning there was a raw, bleak wind off the lake, but when we went to the Blackstone for lunch a light snow came down past the windows and we talked almost naturally about our friends, and about casual things. Suddenly her tone changed; she grew serious and looked me in the eye, straight and sincere.

'Eddie, you're the oldest friend I have,' she said, 'and you oughtn't to find it too hard to trust me. If I promise you faithfully on my word of honour to catch that five o'clock train, will you let me alone a few hours this afternoon?'

'Why?'

'Well' – she hesitated and hung her head a little – 'I guess everybody has a right to say – goodbye.'

'You want to say goodbye to that – '

'Yes, yes,' she said hastily; 'just a few hours, Eddie, and I promise faithfully that I'll be on that train.'

'Well, I suppose no great harm could be done in two hours. If you really want to say goodbye – '

I looked up suddenly, and surprised a look of such tense cunning in her face that I winced before it. Her lip was curled up and her eyes were slits again; there wasn't the faintest touch of fairness and sincerity in her whole face.

We argued. The argument was vague on her part and somewhat hard and reticent on mine. I wasn't going to be cajoled again into any weakness or be infected with any – and there was a contagion of evil in the air. She kept trying to imply, without any convincing evidence to bring forward, that everything was all right. Yet she was too full of the thing itself – whatever it was – to build up a real story, and she wanted to catch at any credulous and acquiescent train of thought that might start in my head, and work that for all it was worth. After every reassuring suggestion she threw out, she stared at me eagerly, as if she hoped I'd launch into a comfortable moral lecture with the customary sweet at the end – which in this case would be her liberty. But I was wearing her away a little. Two or three times it needed just a touch of pressure to bring her to the point of tears – which, of course, was what I wanted – but I couldn't seem to manage it. Almost I had her – almost possessed her interior attention – then she would slip away.

I bullied her remorselessly into a taxi about four o'clock and started for the station. The wind was raw again, with a sting of snow in it, and the people in the streets, waiting for buses and street cars too small to take them all in, looked cold and disturbed and unhappy. I tried to think how lucky we were to be comfortably off and taken care of, but all the warm, respectable world I had been part of yesterday had dropped away from me. There was something we carried with us now that was the enemy and the opposite of all that; it was in the cabs beside us, the streets we passed through. With a touch of panic, I wondered if I wasn't slipping almost imperceptibly into Ellen's attitude of mind. The column of passengers waiting to go aboard the train were as remote from me as people from another world, but it was I that was drifting away and leaving them behind.

My lower was in the same car with her compartment. It was an old-fashioned car, its lights somewhat dim, its carpets and upholstery full of the dust of another generation. There were half a dozen other travellers, but they made no special impression on me, except that they shared the unreality that I was beginning to feel everywhere around me. We went into Ellen's compartment, shut the door and sat down.

Suddenly I put my arms around her and drew her over to me, just as tenderly as I knew how – as if she were a little girl – as she was. She resisted a little, but after a moment she submitted and lay tense and rigid in my arms.

'Ellen,' I said helplessly, 'you asked me to trust you. You have much more reason to trust me. Wouldn't it help to get rid of all this, if you told me a little?'

'I can't,' she said, very low – 'I mean, there's nothing to tell.'

'You met this man on the train coming home and you fell in love with him, isn't that true?'

'I don't know.'

'Tell me, Ellen. You fell in love with him?'

'I don't know. Please let me alone.'

'Call it anything you want,' I went on, 'he has some sort of hold over you. He's trying to use you; he's trying to get something from you. He's not in love with you.'

'What does that matter?' she said in a weak voice.

'It does matter. Instead of trying to fight this – this thing – you're trying to fight me. And I love you, Ellen. Do you hear? I'm telling you all of a sudden, but it isn't new with me. I love you.'

She looked at me with a sneer on her gentle face; it was an expression I had seen on men who were tight and didn't want to be taken home. But it was human. I was reaching her, faintly and from far away, but more than before.

'Ellen, I want you to answer me one question. Is he going to be on this train?'

She hesitated; then, an instant too late, she shook her head.

'Be careful, Ellen. Now I'm going to ask you one thing more, and I wish you'd try very hard to answer. Coming West, when did this man get on the train?'

'I don't know,' she said with an effort.

Just at that moment I became aware, with the unquestionable knowledge reserved for facts, that he was just outside the door. She knew it, too; the blood left her face and that expression of low-animal perspicacity came creeping back. I lowered my face into my hands and tried to think.

We must have sat there, with scarcely a word, for well over an hour. I was conscious that the lights of Chicago, then of Englewood and of endless suburbs, were moving by, and then there were no more lights and we were out on the dark flatness of Illinois. The train seemed to draw in upon itself; it took on an air of being alone. The porter knocked at the door and asked if he could make up the berth, but I said no and he went away.

After a while I convinced myself that the struggle inevitably coming wasn't beyond what remained of my sanity, my faith in the essential all-rightness of things and people. That this person's purpose was what we call 'criminal', I took for granted, but there was no need of ascribing to him an intelligence that belonged to a higher plane of human, or inhuman, endeavour. It was still as a man that I considered him, and tried to get at his essence, his self-interest – what took the place in him of a comprehensible heart – but I suppose I more than half knew what I would find when I opened the door.

When I stood up Ellen didn't seem to see me at all. She was hunched into the corner staring straight ahead with a sort of film over her eyes, as if she were in a state of suspended animation of body and mind. I lifted her and put two pillows under her head and threw my fur coat over her knees. Then I knelt beside her and kissed her two hands, opened the door and went out into the hall.

I closed the door behind me and stood with my back against it for a minute. The car was dark save for the corridor lights at each end. There was no sound except the groaning of the couplers, the even click-a-click of the rails and someone's loud sleeping breath farther down the car. I became aware after a moment that the figure of a man was standing by the water cooler just outside the men's smoking room, his derby hat on his head, his coat collar turned up around his neck as if he were cold, his hands in his coat pockets. When I saw him, he turned and went into the smoking room, and I followed. He was sitting in the far corner of the long leather bench; I took the single armchair beside the door.

As I went in I nodded to him and he acknowledged my presence with one of those terrible soundless laughs of his. But this time it was prolonged, it seemed to go on for ever, and mostly to cut it short, I asked: 'Where are you from?' in a voice I tried to make casual.

He stopped laughing and looked at me narrowly, wondering what my game was. When he decided to answer, his voice was muffled as though he were speaking through a silk scarf, and it seemed to come from a long way off.

'I'm from St Paul, Jack.'

'Been making a trip home?'

He nodded. Then he took a long breath and spoke in a hard, menacing voice: 'You better get off at Fort Wayne, Jack.'

He was dead. He was dead as hell – he had been dead all along, but what force had flowed through him, like blood in his veins, out to St Paul and back, was leaving him now. A new outline – the outline of him dead – was coming through the palpable figure that had knocked down Joe Jelke.

He spoke again, with a sort of jerking effort: 'You get off at Fort Wayne, Jack, or I'm going to wipe you out.' He moved his hand in his coat pocket and showed me the outline of a revolver.

I shook my head. 'You can't touch me,' I answered. 'You see, I know.'

His terrible eyes shifted over me quickly, trying to determine whether or not I did know. Then he gave a snarl and made as though he were going to jump to his feet. 'You climb off here or else I'm going to get you, Jack!' he cried hoarsely.

The train was slowing up for Fort Wayne and his voice rang loud in the comparative quiet, but he didn't move from his chair – he was too weak, I think – and we sat staring at each other while workmen passed up and down outside the window banging the brakes and wheels, and the engine gave out loud mournful pants up ahead. No one got into our car. After a while the porter closed the vestibule door and passed back along the corridor, and we slid out of the murky yellow station light and into the long darkness.

What I remember next must have extended over a space of five or six hours, though it comes back to me as something without any existence in time – something that might have taken five minutes or a year. There began a slow, calculated assault on me, wordless and terrible. I felt what I can only call a strangeness stealing over me – akin to the strangeness I had felt all afternoon, but deeper and more intensified. It was like nothing so much as the sensation of drifting away, and I gripped the arms of the chair convulsively, as if to hang on to a piece of the living world. Sometimes I felt myself going out with a rush. There would be almost a warm relief about it, a sense of not caring; then, with a violent wrench of the will, I'd pull myself back into the room.

Suddenly I realised that from a while back I had stopped hating him, stopped feeling violently alien to him, and with the realisation, I went cold and sweat broke out all over my head. He was getting around my abhorrence, as he had got around Ellen coming West on the train; and it was just that strength he drew from preying on people that had brought him up to the point of concrete violence in St Paul, and that, fading and flickering out, still kept him fighting now.

He must have seen that faltering in my heart, for he spoke at once, in a low, even, almost gentle voice: 'You better go now.'

'Oh, I'm not going,' I forced myself to say.

'Suit yourself, Jack.'

He was my friend, he implied. He knew how it was with me and he wanted to help. He pitied me. I'd better go away before it was too late. The rhythm of his attack was soothing as a song: I'd better go away – *and let him get at Ellen.* With a little cry I sat bolt upright.

'What do you want of this girl?' I said, my voice shaking. 'To make a sort of walking hell of her.'

His glance held a quality of dumb surprise, as if I were punishing an animal for a fault of which he was not conscious. For an instant I faltered; then I went on blindly: 'You've lost her; she's put her trust in me.'

His countenance went suddenly black with evil, and he cried: 'You're a liar!' in a voice that was like cold hands.

'She trusts me,' I said. 'You can't touch her. She's safe!'

He controlled himself. His face grew bland, and I felt that curious weakness and indifference begin again inside me. What was the use of all this? What was the use?

'You haven't got much time left,' I forced myself to say, and then, in a flash of intuition, I jumped at the truth. 'You died, or you were killed, not far from here!' – Then I saw what I had not seen before – that his forehead was drilled with a small round hole like a large picture nail leaves when it's pulled from a plaster wall. 'And now you're sinking. You've only got a few hours. The trip home is over!'

His face contorted, lost all semblance of humanity, living or dead. Simultaneously the room was full of cold air and with a noise that was something between a paroxysm of coughing and a burst of horrible laughter, he was on his feet, reeking of shame and blasphemy.

'Come and look!' he cried. 'I'll show you – '

He took a step towards me, then another and it was exactly as if a door stood open behind him, a door yawning out to an inconceivable abyss of darkness and corruption. There was a scream of mortal agony, from him or from somewhere behind, and abruptly the strength went out of him in a long husky sigh and he wilted to the floor . . .

How long I sat there, dazed with terror and exhaustion, I don't know. The next thing I remember is the sleepy porter shining shoes across the room from me, and outside the window the steel fires of Pittsburgh breaking the flat perspective – also something too faint for a man, too heavy for a shadow, of the night. There was something extended on the bench. Even as I perceived it it faded off and away.

Some minutes later I opened the door of Ellen's compartment. She was asleep where I had left her. Her lovely cheeks were white and wan, but she lay naturally – her hands relaxed and her breathing regular and clear. What had possessed her had gone out of her, leaving her exhausted but her own dear self again.

I made her a little more comfortable, tucked a blanket around her, extinguished the light and went out.

3

When I came home for Easter vacation, almost my first act was to go down to the billiard parlour near Seven Corners. The man at the cash register quite naturally didn't remember my hurried visit of three months before.

'I'm trying to locate a certain party who, I think, came here a lot some time ago.'

I described the man rather accurately, and when I had finished, the cashier called to a little jockey-like fellow who was sitting near with an air of having something very important to do that he couldn't quite remember.

'Hey, Shorty, talk to this guy, will you? I think he's looking for Joe Varland.'

The little man gave me a tribal look of suspicion. I went and sat near him.

'Joe Varland's dead, fella,' he said grudgingly. 'He died last winter.'

I described him again – his overcoat, his laugh, the habitual expression of his eyes.

'That's Joe Varland you're looking for all right, but he's dead.'

'I want to find out something about him.'

'What you want to find out?'

'What did he do, for instance?'

'How should I know?'

'Look here! I'm not a policeman. I just want some kind of information about his habits. He's dead now and it can't hurt him. And it won't go beyond me.'

'Well' – he hesitated, looking me over – 'he was a great one for travelling. He got in a row in the station in Pittsburgh and a dick got him.'

I nodded. Broken pieces of the puzzle began to assemble in my head.

'Why was he a lot on trains?'

'How should I know, fella?'

'If you can use ten dollars, I'd like to know anything you may have heard on the subject.'

'Well,' said Shorty reluctantly, 'all I know is they used to say he worked the trains.'

'Worked the trains?'

'He had some racket of his own he'd never loosen up about. He used to work the girls travelling alone on the trains. Nobody ever knew much about it – he was a pretty smooth guy – but sometimes he'd turn up here with a lot of dough and he let 'em know it was the janes he got it off of.'

I thanked him and gave him the ten dollars and went out, very thoughtful, without mentioning that part of Joe Varland had made a last trip home.

Ellen wasn't West for Easter, and even if she had been I wouldn't have gone to her with the information, either – at least I've seen her almost every day this summer and we've managed to talk about everything else. Sometimes, though, she gets silent about nothing and wants to be very close to me, and I know what's in her mind.

Of course she's coming out this fall, and I have two more years at New Haven; still, things don't look so impossible as they did a few months ago. She belongs to me in a way – even if I lose her she belongs to me. Who knows? Anyhow, I'll always be there.

Magnetism

Saturday Evening Post (3 March 1928)

1

The pleasant, ostentatious boulevard was lined at prosperous intervals with New England colonial houses – without ship models in the hall. When the inhabitants moved out here the ship models had at last been given to the children. The next street was a complete exhibit of the Spanish-bungalow phase of West Coast architecture; while two streets over, the cylindrical windows and round towers of 1897 – melancholy antiques which sheltered swamis, yogis, fortune-tellers, dressmakers, dancing teachers, art academies and chiropractors – looked down now upon brisk buses and trolley cars. A little walk around the block could, if you were feeling old that day, be a discouraging affair.

On the green flanks of the modern boulevard children, with their knees marked by the red stains of the mercurochrome era, played with toys with a purpose – beams that taught engineering, soldiers that taught manliness, and dolls that taught motherhood. When the dolls were so banged up that they stopped looking like real babies and began to look like dolls, the children developed affection for them. Everything in the vicinity – even the March sunlight – was new, fresh, hopeful and thin, as you would expect in a city that had tripled its population in fifteen years.

Among the very few domestics in sight that morning was a handsome young maid sweeping the steps of the biggest house on the street. She was a large, simple Mexican girl with the large, simple ambitions of the time and the locality, and she was already conscious of being a luxury – she received one hundred dollars a month in return for her personal liberty. Sweeping, Dolores kept an eye on the stairs inside, for Mr Hannaford's car was waiting and he would soon be coming down to breakfast. The problem came first this morning, however – the problem as to whether it was a duty or a favour when she helped the English nurse down the steps with the perambulator. The English nurse always said, 'Please,' and 'Thanks very much,' but Dolores hated her and would have liked, without any special excitement, to beat her insensible. Like most Latins under the stimulus of American life, she had irresistible impulses towards violence.

The nurse escaped, however. Her blue cape faded haughtily into the distance just as Mr Hannaford, who had come quietly downstairs, stepped into the space of the front door.

'Good-morning.' He smiled at Dolores; he was young and extraordinarily handsome. Dolores tripped on the broom and fell off the stoop. George Hannaford hurried down the steps, reached her as she was getting to her feet cursing volubly in Mexican, just touched her arm with a helpful gesture and said, 'I hope you didn't hurt yourself.'

'Oh, no.'

'I'm afraid it was my fault; I'm afraid I startled you, coming out like that.'

His voice had real regret in it; his brow was knit with solicitude.

'Are you sure you're all right?'

'Aw, sure.'

'Didn't turn your ankle?'

'Aw, no.'

'I'm terribly sorry about it.'

'Aw, it wasn't your fault.'

He was still frowning as she went inside, and Dolores, who was not hurt and thought quickly, suddenly contemplated having a love affair with him. She looked at herself several times in the pantry mirror and stood close to him as she poured his coffee, but he read the paper and she saw that that was all for the morning.

Hannaford entered his car and drove to Jules Rennard's house. Jules was a French Canadian by birth, and George Hannaford's best friend; they were fond of each other and spent much time together. Both of them were simple and dignified in their tastes and in their way of thinking, instinctively gentle, and in a world of the volatile and the bizarre found in each other a certain quiet solidity.

He found Jules at breakfast.

'I want to fish for barracuda,' said George abruptly. 'When will you be free? I want to take the boat and go down to Lower California.'

Jules had dark circles under his eyes. Yesterday he had closed out the greatest problem of his life by settling with his ex-wife for two hundred thousand dollars. He had married too young, and the former slavey from the Quebec slums had taken to drugs upon her failure to rise with him. Yesterday, in the presence of lawyers, her final gesture had been to smash his finger with the base of a telephone. He was tired of women for a while and welcomed the suggestion of a fishing trip.

'How's the baby?' he asked.

'The baby's fine.'

'And Kay?'

'Kay's not herself, but I don't pay any attention. What did you do to your hand?'

'I'll tell you another time. What's the matter with Kay, George?'

'Jealous.'

'Of who?'

'Helen Avery. It's nothing. She's not herself, that's all.' He got up. 'I'm late,' he said. 'Let me know as soon as you're free. Any time after Monday will suit me.'

George left and drove out by an interminable boulevard which narrowed into a long, winding concrete road and rose into the hilly country behind. Somewhere in the vast emptiness a group of buildings appeared, a barn-like structure, a row of offices, a large but quick restaurant and half a dozen small bungalows. The chauffeur dropped Hannaford at the main entrance. He went in and passed through various enclosures, each marked off by swinging gates and inhabited by a stenographer.

'Is anybody with Mr Schroeder?' he asked, in front of a door lettered with that name.

'No, Mr Hannaford.'

Simultaneously his eye fell on a young lady who was writing at a desk aside, and he lingered a moment.

'Hello, Margaret,' he said. 'How are you, darling?'

A delicate, pale beauty looked up, frowning a little, still abstracted in her work. It was Miss Donovan, the script girl, a friend of many years.

'Hello. Oh, George, I didn't see you come in. Mr Douglas wants to work on the book sequence this afternoon.'

'All right.'

'These are the changes we decided on Thursday night.' She smiled up at him and George wondered for the thousandth time why she had never gone into pictures.

'All right,' he said. 'Will initials do?'

'Your initials look like George Harris's.'

'Very well, darling.'

As he finished, Pete Schroeder opened his door and beckoned him.

'George, come here!' he said with an air of excitement. 'I want you to listen to someone on the phone.'

Hannaford went in.

'Pick up the phone and say hello,' directed Schroeder. 'Don't say who you are.'

'Hello,' said Hannaford obediently.

'Who is this?' asked a girl's voice.

Hannaford put his hand over the mouthpiece. 'What am I supposed to do?'

Schroeder snickered and Hannaford hesitated, smiling and suspicious.

'Who do you want to speak to?' he temporised into the phone.

'To George Hannaford, I want to speak to. Is this him?'

'Yes.'

'Oh, George; it's me.'

'Who?'

'Me – Gwen. I had an awful time finding you. They told me –'

'Gwen who?'

'Gwen – can't you hear? From San Francisco – last Thursday night.'

'I'm sorry,' objected George. 'Must be some mistake.'

'Is this George Hannaford?'

'Yes.'

The voice grew slightly tart: 'Well, this is Gwen Becker you spent last Thursday evening with in San Francisco. There's no use pretending you don't know who I am, because you do.'

Schroeder took the apparatus from George and hung up the receiver.

'Somebody has been doubling for me up in Frisco,' said Hannaford.

'So that's where you were Thursday night!'

'Those things aren't funny to me – not since that crazy Zeller girl. You can never convince them they've been sold because the man always looks something like you. What's new, Pete?'

'Let's go over to the stage and see.'

Together they walked out a back entrance, along a muddy walk, and opening a little door in the big blank wall of the studio building entered into its half darkness.

Here and there figures spotted the dim twilight, figures that turned up white faces to George Hannaford, like souls in purgatory watching the passage of a half-god. Here and there were whispers and soft voices and, apparently from afar, the gentle tremolo of a small organ. Turning the corner made by some flats, they came upon the white crackling glow of a stage with two people motionless upon it.

An actor in evening clothes, his shirt-front, collar and cuffs tinted a brilliant pink, made as though to get chairs for them, but they shook their heads and stood watching. For a long while nothing happened on the stage – no one moved. A row of lights went off with a savage hiss, went on again. The plaintive tap of a hammer begged admission to nowhere in the distance; a blue face appeared among the blinding lights above and called something unintelligible into the upper blackness. Then the silence was broken by a low clear voice from the stage: 'If you want to know why I haven't got stockings on, look in my dressing-room. I spoiled four pairs yesterday and two already this morning . . . This dress weighs six pounds.'

A man stepped out of the group of observers and regarded the girl's brown legs; their lack of covering was scarcely distinguishable, but, in any event, her expression implied that she would do nothing about it. The lady was annoyed, and so intense was her personality that it had taken only a fractional flexing of her eyes to indicate the fact. She was a dark, pretty girl with a figure that would be full-blown sooner than she wished. She was just eighteen.

Had this been the week before, George Hannaford's heart would have stood still. Their relationship had been in just that stage. He hadn't said a word to Helen Avery that Kay could have objected to, but something had begun between them on the second day of this picture that Kay had felt in the air. Perhaps it had begun even earlier, for he had determined, when he saw Helen Avery's first release, that she should play opposite him. Helen Avery's voice and the dropping of her eyes when she finished speaking, like a sort of exercise in control, fascinated him. He had felt that they both tolerated something, that each knew half of some secret about people and life, and that if they rushed towards each other there would be a romantic communion of almost unbelievable intensity. It was this element of promise and possibility that had haunted him for a fortnight and was now dying away.

Hannaford was thirty, and he was a moving-picture actor only through a series of accidents. After a year in a small technical college he had taken a summer job with an electric company, and his first appearance in a studio was in the role of repairing a bank of Klieg lights. In an emergency he played a small part and made good, but for fully a year after that he thought of it as a purely transitory episode in his life. At first much of it had offended him – the almost hysterical egotism and excitability hidden under an extremely thin veil of elaborate good-fellowship. It was only recently, with the advent of such men as

Jules Rennard into pictures, that he began to see the possibilities of a decent and secure private life, much as his would have been as a successful engineer. At last his success felt solid beneath his feet.

He met Kay Tomkins at the old Griffith Studios at Mamaroneck and their marriage was a fresh, personal affair, removed from most stage marriages. Afterwards they had possessed each other completely, had been pointed to: 'Look, there's one couple in pictures who manage to stay together.' It would have taken something out of many people's lives – people who enjoyed a vicarious security in the contemplation of their marriage – if they hadn't stayed together, and their love was fortified by a certain effort to live up to that.

He held women off by a polite simplicity that underneath was hard and watchful; when he felt a certain current being turned on he became emotionally stupid. Kay expected and took much more from men, but she, too, had a careful thermometer against her heart. Until the other night, when she reproached him for being interested in Helen Avery, there had been an absolute minimum of jealousy between them.

George Hannaford was still absorbed in the thought of Helen Avery as he left the studio and walked towards his bungalow over the way. There was in his mind, first, a horror that anyone should come between him and Kay, and second, a regret that he no longer carried that possibility in the forefront of his mind. It had given him a tremendous pleasure, like the things that had happened to him during his first big success, before he was so 'made' that there was scarcely anything better ahead; it was something to take out and look at – a new and still mysterious joy. It hadn't been love, for he was critical of Helen Avery as he had never been critical of Kay. But his feeling of last week had been sharply significant and memorable, and he was restless, now that it had passed.

Working that afternoon, they were seldom together, but he was conscious of her and he knew that she was conscious of him.

She stood a long time with her back to him at one point, and when she turned at length, their eyes swept past each other's, brushing like bird wings. Simultaneously he saw they had gone far, in their way; it was well that he had drawn back. He was glad that someone came for her when the work was almost over.

Dressed, he returned to the office wing, stopping in for a moment to see Schroeder. No one answered his knock, and, turning the knob, he went in. Helen Avery was there alone.

Hannaford shut the door and they stared at each other. Her face was young, frightened. In a moment, in which neither of them spoke, it was decided that they would have some of this out now. Almost thankfully he felt the warm sap of emotion flow out of his heart and course through his body.

'Helen!'

She murmured, 'What?' in an awed voice.

'I feel terribly about this.' His voice was shaking.

Suddenly she began to cry; painful, audible sobs shook her. 'Have you got a handkerchief?' she said.

He gave her a handkerchief. At that moment there were steps outside. George opened the door halfway just in time to keep Schroeder from entering on the spectacle of her tears.

'Nobody's in,' he said facetiously. For a moment longer he kept his shoulder against the door. Then he let it open slowly.

Outside in his limousine, he wondered how soon Jules would be ready to go fishing.

2

From the age of twelve Kay Tompkins had worn men like rings on every finger. Her face was round, young, pretty and strong; a strength accentuated by the responsive play of brows and lashes around her clear, glossy, hazel eyes. She was the daughter of a senator from a Western state and she hunted unsuccessfully for glamour through a small Western city until she was seventeen, when she ran away from home and went on the stage. She was one of those people who are famous far beyond their actual achievement.

There was that excitement about her that seemed to reflect the excitement of the world. While she was playing small parts in Ziegfeld shows she attended proms at Yale, and during a temporary venture into pictures she met George Hannaford, already a star of the new 'natural' type then just coming into vogue. In him she found what she had been seeking.

She was at present in what is known as a dangerous state. For six months she had been helpless and dependent entirely upon George, and now that her son was the property of a strict and possessive English nurse, Kay, free again, suddenly felt the need of proving herself attractive. She wanted things to be as they had been before the baby was thought of. Also she felt that lately George had taken her too much for granted; she had a strong instinct that he was interested in Helen Avery.

When George Hannaford came home that night he had minimised to himself their quarrel of the previous evening and was honestly surprised at her perfunctory greeting.

'What's the matter, Kay?' he asked after a minute. 'Is this going to be another night like last night?'

'Do you know we're going out tonight?' she said, avoiding an answer.

'Where?'

'To Katherine Davis's. I didn't know whether you'd want to go – '

'I'd like to go.'

'I didn't know whether you'd want to go. Arthur Busch said he'd stop for me.'

They dined in silence. Without any secret thoughts to dip into like a child into a jam jar, George felt restless, and at the same time was aware that the atmosphere was full of jealousy, suspicion and anger. Until recently they had preserved between them something precious that made their house one of the pleasantest in Hollywood to enter. Now suddenly it might be any house; he felt common and he felt unstable. He had come near to making something bright and precious into something cheap and unkind. With a sudden surge of emotion, he crossed the room and was about to put his arm around her when the doorbell rang. A moment later Dolores announced Mr Arthur Busch.

Busch was an ugly, popular little man, a continuity writer and lately a director. A few years ago they had been hero and heroine to him, and even now, when he was a person of some consequence in the picture world, he accepted with equanimity Kay's use of him for such purposes as tonight's. He had been in love with her for years, but, because his love seemed hopeless, it had never caused him much distress.

They went on to the party. It was a housewarming, with Hawaiian musicians in attendance, and the guests were largely of the old crowd. People who had been in the early Griffith pictures, even though they were scarcely thirty, were considered to be of the old crowd; they were different from those coming along now, and they were conscious of it. They had a dignity and straightforwardness about them from the fact that they had worked in pictures before pictures were bathed in a golden haze of success. They were still rather humble before their amazing triumph, and thus, unlike the new generation, who took it all for granted, they were constantly in touch with reality. Half a dozen or so of the women were especially aware of being unique. No one had come along to fill their places; here and there a pretty face had caught the public imagination for a year, but those of the old crowd were already legends, ageless and disembodied. With all this, they were still young enough to believe that they would go on for ever.

George and Kay were greeted affectionately: people moved over and made place for them. The Hawaiians performed and the Duncan sisters sang at the piano. From the moment George saw who was here he guessed that Helen Avery would be here, too, and the fact annoyed him. It was not appropriate that she should be part of this gathering through which he and Kay had moved familiarly and tranquilly for years.

He saw her first when someone opened the swinging door to the kitchen, and when, a little later, she came out and their eyes met, he knew absolutely that he didn't love her. He went up to speak to her, and at her first words he saw something had happened to her, too, that had dissipated the mood of the afternoon. She had got a big part.

'And I'm in a daze!' she cried happily. 'I didn't think there was a chance and I've thought of nothing else since I read the book a year ago.'

'It's wonderful. I'm awfully glad.'

He had the feeling, though, that he should look at her with a certain regret; one couldn't jump from such a scene as this afternoon to a plane of casual friendly interest. Suddenly she began to laugh.

'Oh, we're such actors, George – you and I.'

'What do you mean?'

'You know what I mean.'

'I don't.'

'Oh, yes, you do. You did this afternoon. It was a pity we didn't have a camera.'

Short of declaring then and there that he loved her, there was absolutely nothing more to say. He grinned acquiescently. A group formed around them and absorbed them, and George, feeling that the evening had settled something, began to think about going home. An excited and sentimental elderly lady – someone's mother – came up and began telling him how much she believed in him, and he was polite and charming to her, as only he could be, for half an hour. Then he went to Kay, who had been sitting with Arthur Busch all evening, and suggested that they go.

She looked up unwillingly. She had had several highballs and the fact was mildly apparent. She did not want to go, but she got up after a mild argument and George went upstairs for his coat. When he came down Katherine Davis told him that Kay had already gone out to the car.

The crowd had increased; to avoid a general good-night he went out through the sun-parlour door to the lawn; less than twenty feet away from him he saw the figures of Kay and Arthur Busch against a bright street lamp; they were standing close together and staring into each other's eyes. He saw that they were holding hands.

After the first start of surprise George instinctively turned about, retraced his steps, hurried through the room he had just left, and came noisily out the front door. But Kay and Arthur Busch were still standing close together, and it was lingeringly and with abstracted eyes that they turned around finally and saw him. Then both of them seemed to make an effort; they drew apart as if it was a physical ordeal. George said goodbye to Arthur Busch with special cordiality, and in a moment he and Kay were driving homeward through the clear California night.

He said nothing, Kay said nothing. He was incredulous. He suspected that Kay had kissed a man here and there, but he had never seen it happen or given it any thought. This was different; there had been an element of tenderness in it and there was something veiled and remote in Kay's eyes that he had never seen there before.

Without having spoken, they entered the house; Kay stopped by the library door and looked in.

'There's someone there,' she said, and she added without interest: 'I'm going upstairs. Good-night.'

As she ran up the stairs the person in the library stepped out into the hall.

'Mr Hannaford – '

He was a pale and hard young man; his face was vaguely familiar, but George didn't remember where he had seen it before.

'Mr Hannaford?' said the young man. 'I recognise you from your pictures.' He looked at George, obviously a little awed.

'What can I do for you?'

'Well, will you come in here?'

'What is it? I don't know who you are.'

'My name is Donovan. I'm Margaret Donovan's brother.' His face toughened a little.

'Is anything the matter?'

Donovan made a motion towards the door. 'Come in here.' His voice was confident now, almost threatening.

George hesitated, then he walked into the library. Donovan followed and stood across the table from him, his legs apart, his hands in his pockets.

'Hannaford,' he said, in the tone of a man trying to whip himself up to anger, 'Margaret wants fifty thousand dollars.'

'What the devil are you talking about?' exclaimed George incredulously.

'Margaret wants fifty thousand dollars,' repeated Donovan.

'You're Margaret Donovan's brother?'

'I am.'

'I don't believe it.' But he saw the resemblance now. 'Does Margaret know you're here?'

'She sent me here. She'll hand over those two letters for fifty thousand, and no questions asked.'

'What letters?' George chuckled irresistibly. 'This is some joke of Schroeder's, isn't it?'

'This ain't a joke, Hannaford. I mean the letters you signed your name to this afternoon.'

3

An hour later George went upstairs in a daze. The clumsiness of the affair was at once outrageous and astounding. That a friend of seven years should suddenly request his signature on papers that were not what they purported to be made all his surroundings seem diaphanous and insecure. Even now the design engrossed him more than a defence against it, and he tried to recreate the steps by which Margaret had arrived at this act of recklessness or despair.

She had served as a script girl in various studios and for various directors for ten years, earning first twenty, now a hundred dollars a week. She was lovely-looking and she was intelligent; at any moment in those years she might have asked for a screen-test, but some quality of initiative or ambition had been lacking. Not a few times had her opinion made or broken incipient careers. Still she waited at directors' elbows, increasingly aware that the years were slipping away.

That she had picked George as a victim amazed him most of all. Once, during the year before his marriage, there had been a momentary warmth; he had taken her to a Mayfair ball, and he remembered that he had kissed her going home that night in the car. The flirtation trailed along hesitatingly for a week. Before it could develop into anything serious he had gone East and met Kay.

Young Donovan had shown him a carbon of the letters he had signed.

They were written on the typewriter that he kept in his bungalow at the studio, and they were carefully and convincingly worded. They purported to be love letters, asserting that he was Margaret Donovan's lover, that he wanted to marry her, and that for that reason he was about to arrange a divorce. It was incredible. Someone must have seen him sign them that morning; someone must have heard her say: 'Your initials are like Mr Harris's.'

George was tired. He was training for a screen football game to be played next week, with the Southern California varsity as extras, and he was used to regular hours. In the middle of a confused and despairing sequence of thought about Margaret Donovan and Kay, he suddenly yawned. Mechanically he went upstairs, undressed and got into bed.

Just before dawn Kay came to him in the garden. There was a river that flowed past it now, and boats faintly lit with green and yellow lights moved slowly, remotely by. A gentle starlight fell like rain upon the dark, sleeping face of the world, upon the black mysterious bosoms of the trees, the tranquil gleaming water and the farther shore.

The grass was damp, and Kay came to him on hurried feet; her thin slippers were drenched with dew. She stood upon his shoes, nestling close to him, and held up her face as one shows a book open at a page.

'Think how you love me,' she whispered. 'I don't ask you to love me always like this, but I ask you to remember.'

'You'll always be like this to me.'

'Oh no; but promise me you'll remember.' Her tears were falling. 'I'll be different, but somewhere lost inside me there'll always be the person I am tonight.'

The scene dissolved slowly but George struggled into consciousness. He sat up in bed; it was morning. In the yard outside he heard the nurse instructing his son in the niceties of behaviour for two-month-old babies. From the yard next door a small boy shouted mysteriously: 'Who let that barrier through on me?'

Still in his pyjamas, George went to the phone and called his lawyers. Then he rang for his man, and while he was being shaved a certain order evolved from the chaos of the night before. First, he must deal with Margaret Donovan; second, he must keep the matter from Kay, who in her present state might believe anything; and third, he must fix things up with Kay. The last seemed the most important of all.

As he finished dressing he heard the phone ring downstairs and, with an instinct of danger, picked up the receiver.

'Hello . . . Oh, yes.' Looking up, he saw that both his doors were closed. 'Good-morning, Helen . . . It's all right, Dolores. I'm taking it up here.' He waited till he heard the receiver click downstairs.

'How are you this morning, Helen?'

'George, I called up about last night. I can't tell you how sorry I am.'

'Sorry? Why are you sorry?'

'For treating you like that. I don't know what was in me, George. I didn't sleep all night thinking how terrible I'd been.'

A new disorder established itself in George's already littered mind.

'Don't be silly,' he said. To his despair he heard his own voice run on: 'For a minute I didn't understand, Helen. Then I thought it was better so.'

'Oh, George,' came her voice after a moment, very low.

Another silence. He began to put in a cuff button.

'I had to call up,' she said after a moment. 'I couldn't leave things like that.'

The cuff button dropped to the floor; he stooped to pick it up, and then said 'Helen!' urgently into the mouthpiece to cover the fact that he had momentarily been away.

'What, George?'

At this moment the hall door opened and Kay, radiating a faint distaste, came into the room. She hesitated.

'Are you busy?'

'It's all right.' He stared into the mouthpiece for a moment.

'Well, goodbye,' he muttered abruptly and hung up the receiver. He turned to Kay: 'Good-morning.'

'I didn't mean to disturb you,' she said distantly.

'You didn't disturb me.' He hesitated. 'That was Helen Avery.'

'It doesn't concern me who it was. I came to ask you if we're going to the Coconut Grove tonight.'

'Sit down, Kay.'

'I don't want to talk.'

'Sit down a minute,' he said impatiently. She sat down. 'How long are you going to keep this up?' he demanded.

'I'm not keeping up anything. We're simply through, George, and you know it as well as I do.'

'That's absurd,' he said. 'Why, a week ago – '

'It doesn't matter. We've been getting nearer to this for months, and now it's over.'

'You mean you don't love me?' He was not particularly alarmed. They had been through scenes like this before.

'I don't know. I suppose I'll always love you in a way.' Suddenly she began to sob. 'Oh, it's all so sad. He's cared for me so long.'

George stared at her. Face to face with what was apparently a real emotion, he had no words of any kind. She was not angry, not threatening or pretending, not thinking about him at all, but concerned entirely with her emotions towards another man.

'What is it?' he cried. 'Are you trying to tell me you're in love with this man?'

'I don't know,' she said helplessly.

He took a step towards her, then went to the bed and lay down on it, staring in misery at the ceiling. After a while a maid knocked to say that Mr Busch and Mr Castle, George's lawyer, were below. The fact carried no meaning to him. Kay went into her room and he got up and followed her.

'Let's send word we're out,' he said. 'We can go away somewhere and talk this over.'

'I don't want to go away.'

She was already away, growing more mysterious and remote with every minute. The things on her dressing-table were the property of a stranger.

He began to speak in a dry, hurried voice. 'If you're still thinking about Helen Avery, it's nonsense. I've never given a damn for anybody but you.'

They went downstairs and into the living-room. It was nearly noon – another bright emotionless California day. George saw that Arthur Busch's ugly face in the sunshine was wan and white; he took a step towards George and then stopped, as if he were waiting for something – a challenge, a reproach, a blow.

In a flash the scene that would presently take place ran itself off in George's mind. He saw himself moving through the scene, saw his part, an infinite choice of parts, but in every one of them Kay would be against him and with Arthur Busch. And suddenly he rejected them all.

'I hope you'll excuse me,' he said quickly to Mr Castle. 'I called you up because a script girl named Margaret Donovan wants fifty thousand dollars for some letters she claims I wrote her. Of course the whole thing is – ' He broke off. It didn't matter. 'I'll come to see you tomorrow.' He walked up to Kay and Arthur, so that only they could hear.

'I don't know about you two – what you want to do. But leave me out of it; you haven't any right to inflict any of it on me, for after all it's not my fault. I'm not going to be mixed up in your emotions.'

He turned and went out. His car was before the door and he said, 'Go to Santa Monica,' because it was the first name that popped into his head. The car drove off into the everlasting hazeless sunlight.

He rode for three hours, past Santa Monica and then along towards Long Beach by another road. As if it were something he saw out of the corner of his eye and with but a fragment of his attention, he imagined Kay and Arthur Busch progressing through the afternoon. Kay would cry a great deal and the situation would seem harsh and unexpected to them at first, but the tender closing of the day would draw them together. They would turn inevitably towards each other and he would slip more and more into the position of the enemy outside.

Kay had wanted him to get down in the dirt and dust of a scene and scramble for her. Not he; he hated scenes. Once he stooped to compete with Arthur Busch in pulling at Kay's heart, he would never be the same to himself. He would always be a little like Arthur Busch; they would always have that in common, like a shameful secret. There was little of the theatre about George; the millions before whose eyes the moods and changes of his face had flickered during ten years had not been deceived about that. From the moment when, as a boy of twenty, his handsome eyes had gazed off into the imaginary distance of a Griffith Western, his audience had been really watching the progress of a straightforward, slow-thinking, romantic man through an accidentally glamorous life.

His fault was that he had felt safe too soon. He realised suddenly that the two Fairbankses, in sitting side by side at table, were not keeping up a pose. They were giving hostages to fate. This was perhaps the most bizarre community in the rich, wild, bored empire, and for a marriage to succeed here, you must expect nothing or you must be always together. For a moment his glance had wavered from Kay and he stumbled blindly into disaster.

As he was thinking this and wondering where he would go and what he should do, he passed an apartment house that jolted his memory. It was on the outskirts of town, a pink horror built to represent something, somewhere, so cheaply and sketchily that whatever it copied the architect must have long since forgotten. And suddenly George remembered that he had once called for Margaret Donovan here the night of a Mayfair dance.

'Stop at this apartment!' he called through the speaking-tube.

He went in. The Negro elevator boy stared open-mouthed at him as they rose in the cage. Margaret Donovan herself opened the door.

When she saw him she shrank away with a little cry. As he entered and closed the door she retreated before him into the front room. George followed.

It was twilight outside and the apartment was dusky and sad. The last light fell softly on the standardised furniture and the great gallery of signed photographs of moving-picture people that covered one wall. Her face was white, and as she stared at him she began nervously wringing her hands.

'What's this nonsense, Margaret?' George said, trying to keep any reproach out of his voice. 'Do you need money that bad?'

She shook her head vaguely. Her eyes were still fixed on him with a sort of terror; George looked at the floor.

'I suppose this was your brother's idea. At least I can't believe you'd be so stupid.' He looked up, trying to preserve the brusque masterly attitude of one talking to a naughty child, but at the sight of her face every emotion except pity left him. 'I'm a little tired. Do you mind if I sit down?'

'No.'

'I'm a little confused today,' said George after a minute. 'People seem to have it in for me today.'

'Why, I thought' – her voice became ironic in mid-sentence – 'I thought everybody loved you, George.'

'They don't.'

'Only me?'

'Yes,' he said abstractedly.

'I wish it had been only me. But then, of course, you wouldn't have been you.'

Suddenly he realised that she meant what she was saying.

'That's just nonsense.'

'At least you're here,' Margaret went on. 'I suppose I ought to be glad of that. And I am. I most decidedly am. I've often thought of you sitting in that chair, just at this time when it was almost dark. I used to make up little one-act plays about what would happen then. Would you like to hear one of them? I'll have to begin by coming over and sitting on the floor at your feet.'

Annoyed and yet spellbound, George kept trying desperately to seize upon a word or mood that would turn the subject.

'I've seen you sitting there so often that you don't look a bit more real than your ghost. Except that your hat has squashed your beautiful hair down on one side and you've got dark circles or dirt under your eyes. You look white, too, George. Probably you were at a party last night.'

'I was. And I found your brother waiting for me when I got home.'

'He's a good waiter, George. He's just out of San Quentin prison, where he's been waiting the last six years.'

'Then it was his idea?'

'We cooked it up together. I was going to China on my share.'

'Why was I the victim?'

'That seemed to make it realer. Once I thought you were going to fall in love with me five years ago.'

The bravado suddenly melted out of her voice and it was still light enough to see that her mouth was quivering.

'I've loved you for years,' she said – 'since the first day you came West and walked into the old Realart Studio. You were so brave about people, George. Whoever it was, you walked right up to them and tore something aside as if it was in your way and began to know them. I tried to make love to you, just like the rest, but it was difficult. You drew people right up close to you and held them there, not able to move either way.'

'This is all entirely imaginary,' said George, frowning uncomfortably, 'and I can't control – '

'No, I know. You can't control charm. It's simply got to be used. You've got to keep your hand in if you have it, and go through life attaching people to you that you don't want. I don't blame you. If you only hadn't kissed me the night of the Mayfair dance. I suppose it was the champagne.'

George felt as if a band which had been playing for a long time in the distance had suddenly moved up and taken a station beneath his window. He had always been conscious that things like this were going on around him. Now that he thought of it, he had always been conscious that Margaret loved him, but the faint music of these emotions in his ear had seemed to bear no relation to actual life. They were phantoms that he had conjured up out of nothing; he had never imagined their actual incarnations. At his wish they should die inconsequently away.

'You can't imagine what it's been like,' Margaret continued after a minute. 'Things you've just said and forgotten, I've put myself asleep night after night remembering – trying to squeeze something more out of them. After that night you took me to the Mayfair other men didn't exist for me any more. And there were others, you know – lots of them. But I'd see you walking along somewhere about the lot, looking at the ground and smiling a little, as if something very amusing had just happened to you, the way you do. And I'd pass you and you'd look up and really smile: "Hello, darling!" "Hello, darling," and my heart would turn over. That would happen four times a day.'

George stood up and she, too, jumped up quickly.

'Oh, I've bored you,' she cried softly. 'I might have known I'd bore you. You want to go home. Let's see – is there anything else? Oh, yes; you might as well have those letters.'

Taking them out of a desk, she took them to a window and identified them by a rift of lamplight.

'They're really beautiful letters. They'd do you credit. I suppose it was pretty stupid, as you say, but it ought to teach you a lesson about – about signing things, or something.' She tore the letters small and threw them in the waste-basket: 'Now go on,' she said.

'Why must I go now?'

For the third time in twenty-four hours sad and uncontrollable tears confronted him.

'Please go!' she cried angrily – 'or stay if you like. I'm yours for the asking. You know it. You can have any woman you want in the world by just raising your hand. Would I amuse you?'

'Margaret – '

'Oh, go on then.' She sat down and turned her face away. 'After all you'll begin to look silly in a minute. You wouldn't like that, would you? So get out.'

George stood there helpless, trying to put himself in her place and say something that wouldn't be priggish, but nothing came.

He tried to force down his personal distress, his discomfort, his vague feeling of scorn, ignorant of the fact that she was watching him and understanding it all and loving the struggle in his face. Suddenly his own nerves gave way under the strain of the past twenty-four hours and he felt his eyes grow dim and his throat tighten. He shook his head helplessly. Then he turned away – still not knowing that she was watching him and loving him until she thought her heart would burst with it – and went out to the door.

4

The car stopped before his house, dark save for small lights in the nursery and the lower hall. He heard the telephone ringing but when he answered it, inside, there was no one on the line. For a few minutes he wandered about in the darkness, moving from chair to chair and going to the window to stare out into the opposite emptiness of the night.

It was strange to be alone, to feel alone. In his overwrought condition the fact was not unpleasant. As the trouble of last night had made Helen Avery infinitely remote, so his talk with Margaret had acted as a catharsis to his own personal misery. It would swing back upon him presently, he knew, but for a moment his mind was too tired to remember, to imagine or to care.

Half an hour passed. He saw Dolores issue from the kitchen, take the paper from the front steps and carry it back to the kitchen for a preliminary inspection. With a vague idea of packing his grip, he went upstairs. He opened the door of Kay's room and found her lying down.

For a moment he didn't speak, but moved around the bathroom between. Then he went into her room and switched on the lights.

'What's the matter?' he asked casually. 'Aren't you feeling well?'

'I've been trying to get some sleep,' she said. 'George, do you think that girl's gone crazy?'

'What girl?'

'Margaret Donovan. I've never heard of anything so terrible in my life.'

For a moment he thought that there had been some new development.

'Fifty thousand dollars!' she cried indignantly. 'Why, I wouldn't give it to her even if it were true. She ought to be sent to jail.'

'Oh, it's not so terrible as that,' he said. 'She has a brother who's a pretty bad egg and it was his idea.'

'She's capable of anything,' Kay said solemnly. 'And you're just a fool if you don't see it. I've never liked her. She has dirty hair.'

'Well, what of it?' he demanded impatiently, and added: 'Where's Arthur Busch?'

'He went home right after lunch. Or rather I sent him home.'

'You decided you were not in love with him?'

She looked up almost in surprise. 'In love with him? Oh, you mean this morning. I was just mad at you; you ought to have known that. I was a little sorry for him last night, but I guess it was the highballs.'

'Well, what did you mean when you – ' He broke off. Wherever he turned he found a muddle, and he resolutely determined not to think.

'My heavens!' exclaimed Kay. 'Fifty thousand dollars!'

'Oh, drop it. She tore up the letters – she wrote them herself – and everything's all right.'

'George.'

'Yes.'

'Of course Douglas will fire her right away.'

'Of course he won't. He won't know anything about it.'

'You mean to say you're not going to let her go? After this?'

He jumped up. 'Do you suppose she thought that?' he cried.

'Thought what?'

'That I'd have them let her go?'

'You certainly ought to.'

He looked hastily through the phone book for her name.

'Oxford — ' he called.

After an unusually long time the switchboard operator answered: 'Bourbon Apartments.'

'Miss Margaret Donovan, please.'

'Why – ' The operator's voice broke off. 'If you'll just wait a minute, please.' He held the line; the minute passed, then another. Then the operator's voice: 'I couldn't talk to you then. Miss Donovan has had an accident. She's shot herself. When you called they were taking her through the lobby to St Catherine's Hospital.'

'Is she – is it serious?' George demanded frantically.

'They thought so at first, but now they think she'll be all right. They're going to probe for the bullet.'

'Thank you.'

He got up and turned to Kay.

'She's tried to kill herself,' he said in a strained voice. 'I'll have to go around to the hospital. I was pretty clumsy this afternoon and I think I'm partly responsible for this.'

'George,' said Kay suddenly.

'What?'

'Don't you think it's sort of unwise to get mixed up in this? People might say – '

'I don't give a damn what they say,' he answered roughly.

He went to his room and automatically began to prepare for going out. Catching sight of his face in the mirror, he closed his eyes with a sudden exclamation of distaste, and abandoned the intention of brushing his hair.

'George,' Kay called from the next room, 'I love you.'

'I love you too.'

'Jules Rennard called up. Something about barracuda fishing. Don't you think it would be fun to get up a party? Men and girls both?'

'Somehow the idea doesn't appeal to me. The whole idea of barracuda fishing – '

The phone rang below and he started. Dolores was answering it.

It was a lady who had already called twice today.

'Is Mr Hannaford in?'

'No,' said Dolores promptly. She stuck out her tongue and hung up the phone just as George Hannaford came downstairs. She helped him into his coat, standing as close as she could to him, opened the door and followed a little way out on the porch.

'Meester Hannaford,' she said suddenly, 'that Miss Avery she call up five-six times today. I tell her you out and say nothing to missus.'

'What?' He stared at her, wondering how much she knew about his affairs.

'She call up just now and I say you out.'

'All right,' he said absently.

'Meester Hannaford.'

'Yes, Dolores.'

'I deedn't hurt myself thees morning when I fell off the porch.'

'That's fine. Good-night, Dolores.'

'Good-night, Meester Hannaford.'

George smiled at her, faintly, fleetingly, tearing a veil from between them, unconsciously promising her a possible admission to the thousand delights and wonders that only he knew and could command. Then he went to his waiting car and Dolores, sitting down on the stoop, rubbed her hands together in a gesture that might have expressed either ecstasy or strangulation and watched the rising of the thin, pale California moon.

A Night at the Fair

Saturday Evening Post (21 July 1928)

The two cities were separated only by a thin well-bridged river; their tails curling over the banks met and mingled, and at the juncture, under the jealous eye of each, lay, every fall, the State Fair. Because of this advantageous position, and because of the agricultural eminence of the state, the fair was one of the most magnificent in America. There were immense exhibits of grain, livestock and farming machinery; there were horse races and automobile races and, lately, aeroplanes that really left the ground; there was a tumultuous Midway with Coney Island thrillers to whirl you through space, and a whining, tinkling hoochie-coochie show. As a compromise between the serious and the trivial, a grand exhibition of fireworks, culminating in a representation of the Battle of Gettysburg, took place in the Grand Concourse every night.

On the late afternoon of a hot September day two boys of fifteen, somewhat replete with food and pop, and fatigued by eight hours of constant motion, issued from the Penny Arcade. The one with dark, handsome, eager eyes was, according to the cosmic inscription in his last year's *Ancient History*, 'Basil Duke Lee, Holly Avenue, St Paul, Minnesota, United States, North America, Western Hemisphere, the World, the Universe'. Though slightly shorter than his companion, he appeared taller, for he projected, so to speak, from short trousers, while Riply Buckner Jr had graduated into long ones the week before. This event, so simple and natural, was having a disrupting influence on the intimate friendship between them that had endured for several years.

During that time Basil, the imaginative member of the firm, had been the dominating partner, and the displacement effected by two feet of blue serge filled him with puzzled dismay – in fact, Riply Buckner had become noticeably indifferent to the pleasure of Basil's company in public. His own assumption of long trousers had seemed to promise a liberation from the restraints and inferiorities of boyhood, and the companionship of one who was, in token of his short pants, still a boy was an unwelcome reminder of how recent was his own metamorphosis. He scarcely admitted this to himself, but a certain shortness of temper with Basil, a certain tendency to belittle him with superior laughter, had been in evidence all afternoon. Basil felt the new difference keenly. In August a family conference had decided that even though he was going East to school, he was too small for long trousers. He had countered by growing an inch and a half in a fortnight, which added to his reputation for unreliability, but led him to hope that his mother might be persuaded, after all.

Coming out of the stuffy tent into the glow of sunset, the two boys hesitated, glancing up and down the crowded highway with expressions compounded of a certain ennui and a certain inarticulate yearning. They were unwilling to go home before it became necessary, yet they knew they had temporarily glutted their appetite for sights; they wanted a change in the tone, the motif, of the day. Near them was the parking space, as yet a modest yard; and as they lingered indecisively, their eyes were caught and held by a small car, red in colour and slung at that proximity to the ground which indicated both speed of motion and speed of life. It was a Blatz Wildcat, and for the next five years it represented the ambition of several million American boys. Occupying it, in the posture of aloof exhaustion exacted by the sloping seat, was a blonde, gay, baby-faced girl.

The two boys stared. She bent upon them a single cool glance and then returned to her avocation of reclining in a Blatz Wildcat and looking haughtily at the sky. The two boys exchanged a glance, but made no move to go. They watched the girl – when they felt that their stares were noticeable they dropped their eyes and gazed at the car.

After several minutes a young man with a very pink face and pink hair, wearing a yellow suit and hat and drawing on yellow gloves, appeared and got into the car. There was a series of frightful explosions; then, with a measured tup-tup-tup from the open cut-out, insolent, percussive and thrilling as a drum, the car and the girl and the young man, whom they had recognised as Speed Paxton, slid smoothly away.

Basil and Riply turned and strolled back thoughtfully towards the Midway. They knew that Speed Paxton was dimly terrible – the wild and pampered son of a local brewer – but they envied him – to ride off into the sunset in such a chariot, into the very hush and mystery of night, beside him the mystery of that baby-faced girl. It was probably this envy that made them begin to shout when they perceived a tall youth of their own age issuing from a shooting gallery.

'Oh, El! Hey, El! Wait a minute!'

Elwood Leaming turned around and waited. He was the dissipated one among the nice boys of the town – he had drunk beer, he had learned from chauffeurs, he was already thin from too many cigarettes. As they greeted him eagerly, the hard, wise expression of a man of the world met them in his half-closed eyes.

'Hello, Rip. Put it there, Rip. Hello, Basil, old boy. Put it there.'

'What you doing, El?' Riply asked.

'Nothing. What are you doing?'

'Nothing.'

Elwood Leaming narrowed his eyes still further, seemed to give thought, and then made a decisive clicking sound with his teeth.

'Well, what do you say we pick something up?' he suggested. 'I saw some pretty good stuff around here this afternoon.'

Riply and Basil drew tense, secret breaths. A year before they had been shocked because Elwood went to the burlesque shows at the Star – now here he was holding the door open to his own speedy life.

The responsibility of his new maturity impelled Riply to appear most eager. 'All right with me,' he said heartily.

He looked at Basil.

'All right with me,' mumbled Basil.

Riply laughed, more from nervousness than from derision. 'Maybe you better grow up first, Basil.' He looked at Elwood, seeking approval. 'You better stick around till you get to be a man.'

'Oh, dry up!' retorted Basil. 'How long have you had yours? Just a week!'

But he realised that there was a gap separating him from these two, and it was with a sense of tagging them that he walked along beside.

Glancing from right to left with the expression of a keen and experienced frontiersman, Elwood Leaming led the way. Several pairs of strolling girls met his mature glance and smiled encouragingly, but he found them unsatisfactory – too fat, too plain or too hard. All at once their eyes fell upon two who sauntered along a little ahead of them, and they increased their pace, Elwood with confidence, Riply with its nervous counterfeit and Basil suddenly in the grip of wild excitement.

They were abreast of them. Basil's heart was in his throat. He looked away as he heard Elwood's voice.

'Hello, girls! How are you this evening?'

Would they call for the police? Would his mother and Riply's suddenly turn the corner?

'Hello, yourself, kiddo!'

'Where you going, girls?'

'Nowhere.'

'Well, let's all go together.'

Then all of them were standing in a group and Basil was relieved to find that they were only girls his own age, after all. They were pretty, with clear skins and red lips and maturely piled-up hair. One he immediately liked better than the other – her voice was quieter and she was shy. Basil was glad when Elwood walked on with the bolder one, leaving him and Riply to follow with the other, behind.

The first lights of the evening were springing into pale existence; the afternoon crowd had thinned a little, and the lanes, empty of people, were heavy with the rich various smells of popcorn and peanuts, molasses and dust and cooking Wienerwurst and a not-unpleasant overtone of animals and hay. The Ferris wheel, pricked out now in lights, revolved leisurely through the dusk; a few empty cars of the roller coaster rattled overhead. The heat had blown off and there was the crisp stimulating excitement of Northern autumn in the air.

They walked. Basil felt that there was some way of talking to this girl, but he could manage nothing in the key of Elwood Leaming's intense and confidential manner to the girl ahead – as if he had inadvertently discovered a kinship of tastes and of hearts. So to save the progression from absolute silence – for Riply's contribution amounted only to an occasional burst of silly laughter – Basil pretended an interest in the sights they passed and kept up a sort of comment thereon.

'There's the six-legged calf. Have you seen it?'

'No, I haven't.'

'There's where the man rides the motorcycle around. Did you go there?'

'No, I didn't.'

'Look! They're beginning to fill the balloon. I wonder what time they start the fireworks.'

'Have you been to the fireworks?'

'No, I'm going tomorrow night. Have you?'

'Yes, I been every night. My brother works there. He's one of them that helps set them off.'

'Oh!'

He wondered if her brother cared that she had been picked up by strangers. He wondered even more if she felt as silly as he. It must be getting late, and he had promised to be home by half-past seven on pain of not being allowed out tomorrow night. He walked up beside Elwood.

'Hey, El,' he asked, 'where we going?'

Elwood turned to him and winked. 'We're going around the Old Mill.'

'Oh!'

Basil dropped back again – became aware that in his temporary absence Ripley and the girl had linked arms. A twinge of jealousy went through him and he inspected the girl again and with more appreciation, finding her prettier than he had thought. Her eyes, dark and intimate, seemed to have wakened at the growing brilliance of the illumination overhead; there was the promise of excitement in them now, like the promise of the cooling night.

He considered taking her other arm, but it was too late; she and Riply were laughing together at something – rather, at nothing. She had asked him what he laughed at all the time and he had laughed again for an answer. Then they both laughed hilariously and sporadically together.

Basil looked disgustedly at Riply. 'I never heard such a silly laugh in my life,' he said indignantly.

'Didn't you?' chuckled Riply Buckner. 'Didn't you, little boy?'

He bent double with laughter and the girl joined in. The words 'little boy' had fallen on Basil like a jet of cold water. In his excitement he had forgotten something, as a cripple might forget his limp only to discover it when he began to run.

'You think you're so big!' he exclaimed. 'Where'd you get the pants? Where'd you get the pants?' He tried to work this up with gusto and was about to add: 'They're your father's pants,' when he remembered that Riply's father, like his own, was dead.

The couple ahead reached the entrance to the Old Mill and waited for them. It was an off hour, and half a dozen scows bumped in the wooden offing, swayed by the mild tide of the artificial river. Elwood and his girl got into the front seat and he promptly put his arm around her. Basil helped the other girl into the rear seat, but, dispirited, he offered no resistance when Riply wedged in and sat down between.

They floated off, immediately entering upon a long echoing darkness. Somewhere far ahead a group in another boat were singing, their voices now remote and romantic, now nearer and yet more mysterious as the canal doubled back and the boats passed close to each other with an invisible veil between.

The three boys yelled and called, Basil attempting by his

vociferousness and variety to outdo Riply in the girl's eyes, but after a few moments there was no sound except his own voice and the continual bump-bump of the boat against the wooden sides, and he knew without looking that Riply had put his arm about the girl's shoulder.

They slid into a red glow – a stage set of hell, with grinning demons and lurid paper fires – he made out that Elwood and his girl sat cheek to cheek – then again into the darkness, with the gently lapping water and the passing of the singing boat now near, now far away. For a while Basil pretended that he was interested in this other boat, calling to them, commenting on their proximity. Then he discovered that the scow could be rocked and took to this poor amusement until Elwood Leaming turned around indignantly and cried: 'Hey! What are you trying to do?'

They came back finally to the entrance and the two couples broke apart. Basil jumped miserably ashore.

'Give us some more tickets,' Riply cried. 'We want to go around again.'

'Not me,' said Basil with elaborate indifference. 'I have to go home.'

Riply began to laugh in derision and triumph. The girl laughed too.

'Well, so long, little boy,' Riply cried hilariously.

'Oh, shut up! So long, Elwood.'

'So long, Basil.'

The boat was already starting off; arms settled again about the girls' shoulders.

'So long, little boy!'

'So long, you big cow!' Basil cried. 'Where'd you get the pants? Where'd you get the pants?'

But the boat had already disappeared into the dark mouth of the tunnel, leaving the echo of Riply's taunting laughter behind.

It is an ancient tradition that all boys are obsessed with the idea of being grown. This is because they occasionally give voice to their impatience with the restraints of youth, while those great stretches of time when they are more than content to be boys find expression in action and not in words. Sometimes Basil wanted to be just a little bit older, but no more. The question of long pants had not seemed vital to him – he wanted them, but as a costume they had no such romantic significance as, for example, a football suit or an officer's uniform, or even the silk hat and opera cape in which gentlemen burglars were wont to prowl the streets of New York by night.

But when he awoke next morning they were the most important necessity in his life. Without them he was cut off from his contemporaries, laughed at by a boy whom he had hitherto led. The actual fact that last night some chicken had preferred Riply to himself was of no importance in itself, but he was fiercely competitive and he resented being required to fight with one hand tied behind his back. He felt that parallel situations would occur at school, and that was unbearable. He approached his mother at breakfast in a state of wild excitement.

'Why, Basil,' she protested in surprise, 'I thought when we talked it over you didn't especially care.'

'I've got to have them,' he declared. 'I'd rather be dead than go away to school without them.'

'Well, there's no need of being silly.'

'It's true – I'd rather be dead. If I can't have long trousers I don't see any use in my going away to school.'

His emotion was such that the vision of his demise began actually to disturb his mother.

'Now stop that silly talk and come and eat your breakfast. You can go down and buy some at Barton Leigh's this morning.'

Mollified, but still torn by the urgency of his desire, Basil strode up and down the room.

'A boy is simply helpless without them,' he declared vehemently. The phrase pleased him and he amplified it. 'A boy is simply and utterly helpless without them. I'd rather be dead than go away to school – '

'Basil, stop talking like that. Somebody has been teasing you about it.'

'Nobody's been teasing me,' he denied indignantly – 'nobody at all.'

After breakfast, the maid called him to the phone.

'This is Riply,' said a tentative voice. Basil acknowledged the fact coldly. 'You're not sore about last night, are you?' Riply asked.

'Me? No. Who said I was sore?'

'Nobody. Well, listen, you know about us going to the fireworks together tonight.'

'Yes.' Basil's voice was still cold.

'Well, one of those girls – the one Elwood had – has got a sister that's even nicer than she is, and she can come out tonight and you could have her. And we thought we could meet about eight, because the fireworks don't start till nine.'

'What to do?'

'Well, we could go on the Old Mill again. We went around three times more last night.'

There was a moment's silence. Basil looked to see if his mother's door was closed.

'Did you kiss yours?' he demanded into the transmitter.

'Sure I did!' Over the wire came the ghost of a silly laugh. 'Listen, El thinks he can get his auto. We could call for you at seven.'

'All right,' agreed Basil gruffly, and he added, 'I'm going down and get some long pants this morning.'

'Are you?' Again Basil detected ghostly laughter. 'Well, you be ready at seven tonight.'

Basil's uncle met him at Barton Leigh's clothing store at ten, and Basil felt a touch of guilt at having put his family to all this trouble and expense. On his uncle's advice, he decided finally on two suits – a heavy chocolate brown for every day and a dark blue for formal wear. There were certain alterations to be made but it was agreed that one of the suits was to be delivered without fail that afternoon.

His momentary contriteness at having been so expensive made him save car-fare by walking home from downtown. Passing along Crest Avenue, he paused speculatively to vault the high hydrant in front of the Van Schellinger house, wondering if one did such things in long trousers and if he would ever do it again. He was impelled to leap it two or three times as a sort of ceremonial farewell, and was so engaged when the Van Schellinger limousine turned into the drive and stopped at the front door.

'Oh, Basil,' a voice called.

A fresh delicate face, half buried under a mass of almost white curls, was turned towards him from the granite portico of the city's second largest mansion.

'Hello, Gladys.'

'Come here a minute, Basil.'

He obeyed. Gladys Van Schellinger was a year younger than Basil – a tranquil, carefully nurtured girl who, so local tradition had it, was being brought up to marry in the East. She had a governess and always played with a certain few girls at her house or theirs, and was not allowed the casual freedom of children in a Midwestern city. She was never present at such rendezvous as the Whartons' yard, where the others played games in the afternoons.

'Basil, I wanted to ask you something – are you going to the State Fair tonight?'

'Why, yes, I am.'

'Well, wouldn't you like to come and sit in our box and watch the fireworks?'

Momentarily he considered the matter. He wanted to accept, but he was mysteriously impelled to refuse – to forgo a pleasure in order to pursue a quest that in cold logic did not interest him at all.

'I can't. I'm awfully sorry.'

A shadow of discontent crossed Gladys's face. 'Oh? Well, come and see me sometime soon, Basil. In a few weeks I'm going East to school.'

He walked on up the street in a state of dissatisfaction. Gladys Van Schellinger had never been his girl, nor indeed anyone's girl, but the fact that they were starting away to school at the same time gave him a feeling of kinship with her – as if they had been selected for the glamorous adventure of the East, chosen together for a high destiny that transcended the fact that she was rich and he was only comfortable. He was sorry that he could not sit with her in her box tonight.

By three o'clock, Basil, reading *The Crimson Sweater* up in his room, began giving attentive ear to every ring at the bell. He would go to the head of the stairs, lean over and call, 'Hilda, was that a package for me?' And at four, dissatisfied with her indifference, her lack of feeling for important things, her slowness in going to and returning from the door, he moved downstairs and began attending to it himself. But nothing came. He phoned Barton Leigh's and was told by a busy clerk: 'You'll get that suit. I'll guarantee that you'll get that suit.' But he did not believe in the clerk's honour and he moved out on the porch and watched for Barton Leigh's delivery wagon.

His mother came home at five. 'There were probably more alterations than they thought,' she suggested helpfully. 'You'll probably get it tomorrow morning.'

'Tomorrow morning!' he exclaimed incredulously. 'I've got to have that suit tonight.'

'Well, I wouldn't be too disappointed if I were you, Basil. The stores all close at half-past five.'

Basil took one agitated look up and down Holly Avenue. Then he got his cap and started on a run for the street car at the corner. A moment later a cautious afterthought caused him to retrace his steps with equal rapidity.

'If they get here, keep them for me,' he instructed his mother – a man who thought of everything.

'All right,' she promised dryly, 'I will.'

It was later than he thought. He had to wait for a trolley, and when he reached Barton Leigh's he saw with horror that the doors were locked and the blinds drawn. He intercepted a last clerk coming out and explained vehemently that he had to have his suit tonight. The clerk knew nothing about the matter . . . Was Basil Mr Schwartze?

No, Basil was not Mr Schwartze. After a vague argument wherein he tried to convince the clerk that whoever promised him the suit should be fired, Basil went dispiritedly home.

He would not go to the fair without his suit – he would not go at all. He would sit at home and luckier boys would go adventuring along its Great White Way. Mysterious girls, young and reckless, would glide with them through the enchanted darkness of the Old Mill, but because of the stupidity, selfishness and dishonesty of a clerk in a clothing store he would not be there. In a day or so the fair would be over – for ever – those girls, of all living girls the most intangible, the most desirable, that sister, said to be nicest of all – would be lost out of his life. They would ride off in Blatz Wildcats into the moonlight without Basil having kissed them. No, all his life – though he would lose the clerk his position: 'You see now what your act did to me' – he would look back with infinite regret upon that irretrievable hour. Like most of us, he was unable to perceive that he would have any desires in the future equivalent to those that possessed him now.

He reached home; the package had not arrived. He moped dismally about the house, consenting at half-past six to sit silently at dinner with his mother, his elbows on the table.

'Haven't you any appetite, Basil?'

'No, thanks,' he said absently, under the impression he had been offered something.

'You're not going away to school for two more weeks. Why should it matter – '

'Oh, that isn't the reason I can't eat. I had a sort of headache all afternoon.'

Towards the end of the meal his eye focused abstractedly on some slices of angel cake; with the air of a somnambulist, he ate three.

At seven he heard the sounds that should have ushered in a night of romantic excitement.

The Leaming car stopped outside, and a moment later Riply Buckner rang the bell. Basil rose gloomily.

'I'll go,' he said to Hilda. And then to his mother, with vague impersonal reproach, 'Excuse me a minute. I just want to tell them I can't go to the fair tonight.'

'But of course you can go, Basil. Don't be silly. Just because – '

He scarcely heard her. Opening the door, he faced Riply on the steps. Beyond was the Leaming limousine, an old high car, quivering in silhouette against the harvest moon.

Clop-clop-clop! Up the street came the Barton Leigh delivery wagon. Clop-clop! A man jumped out, dumped an iron anchor to the pavement, hurried along the street, turned away, turned back again, came towards them with a long square box in his hand.

'You'll have to wait a minute,' Basil was calling wildly. 'It can't make any difference. I'll dress in the library. Look here, if you're a friend of mine, you'll wait a minute.' He stepped out on the porch. 'Hey, El, I've just got my – got to change my clothes. You can wait a minute, can't you?'

The spark of a cigarette flushed in the darkness as El spoke to the chauffeur; the quivering car came to rest with a sigh and the skies filled suddenly with stars.

Once again the fair – but differing from the fair of the afternoon as a girl in the daytime differs from her radiant presentation of herself at night. The substance of the cardboard booths and plaster palaces was gone, the forms remained. Outlined in lights, these forms suggested things more mysterious and entrancing than themselves, and the people strolling along the network of little Broadways shared this quality, as their pale faces singly and in clusters broke the half darkness.

The boys hurried to their rendezvous, finding the girls in the deep shadow of the Temple of Wheat. Their forms had scarcely merged into a group when Basil became aware that something was wrong. In growing apprehension, he glanced from face to face and, as the introductions were made, he realised the appalling truth – the younger sister was, in point of fact, a fright, squat and dingy, with a bad complexion brooding behind a mask of cheap pink powder and a shapeless mouth that tried ceaselessly to torture itself into the mould of charm.

In a daze he heard Riply's girl say, 'I don't know whether I ought to go with you. I had a sort of date with another fellow I met this afternoon.'

Fidgeting, she looked up and down the street, while Riply, in astonishment and dismay, tried to take her arm.

'Come on,' he urged. 'Didn't I have a date with you first?'

'But I didn't know whether you'd come or not,' she said perversely.

Elwood and the two sisters added their entreaties.

'Maybe I could go on the Ferris wheel,' she said grudgingly, 'but not the Old Mill. This fellow would be sore.'

Riply's confidence reeled with the blow; his mouth fell ajar, his hand desperately pawed her arm. Basil stood glancing now with agonised politeness at his own girl, now at the others, with an expression of infinite reproach. Elwood alone was successful and content.

'Let's go on the Ferris wheel,' he said impatiently. 'We can't stand here all night.'

At the ticket booth the recalcitrant Olive hesitated once more, frowning and glancing about as if she still hoped Riply's rival would appear.

But when the swooping cars came to rest she let herself be persuaded in, and the three couples, with their troubles, were hoisted slowly into the air.

As the car rose, following the imagined curve of the sky, it occurred to Basil how much he would have enjoyed it in other company, or even alone, the fair twinkling beneath him with new variety, the velvet quality of the darkness that is on the edge of light and is barely permeated by its last attenuations. But he was unable to hurt anyone whom he thought of as an inferior. After a minute he turned to the girl beside him.

'Do you live in St Paul or Minneapolis?' he enquired formally.

'St Paul. I go to Number 7 School.' Suddenly she moved closer. 'I bet you're not so slow,' she encouraged him.

He put his arm around her shoulder and found it warm. Again they reached the top of the wheel and the sky stretched out overhead, again they lapsed down through gusts of music from remote calliopes. Keeping his eyes turned carefully away, Basil pressed her to him, and as they rose again into darkness, leaned and kissed her cheek.

The significance of the contact stirred him, but out of the corner of his eye he saw her face – he was thankful when a gong struck below and the machine settled slowly to rest.

The three couples were scarcely reunited outside when Olive uttered a yelp of excitement.

'There he is!' she cried. 'That Bill Jones I met this afternoon – that I had the date with.'

A youth of their own age was approaching, stepping like a circus pony and twirling, with the deftness of a drum major, a small rattan cane. Under the cautious alias, the three boys recognised a friend and contemporary – none other than the fascinating Hubert Blair.

He came nearer. He greeted them all with a friendly chuckle. He took off his cap, spun it, dropped it, caught it, set it jauntily on the side of his head.

'You're a nice one,' he said to Olive. 'I waited here fifteen minutes this evening.'

He pretended to belabour her with the cane; she giggled with delight. Hubert Blair possessed the exact tone that all girls of fourteen, and a somewhat cruder type of grown women, find irresistible. He was a gymnastic virtuoso and his figure was in constant graceful motion; he had a jaunty piquant nose, a disarming laugh and a shrewd talent for flattery. When he took a piece of toffee from his pocket, placed it on his forehead, shook it off and caught it in his mouth, it was obvious to any disinterested observer that Riply was destined to see no more of Olive that night.

So fascinated were the group that they failed to see Basil's eyes brighten with a ray of hope, his feet take four quick steps backwards with all the guile of a gentleman burglar, his torso writhe through the parting of a tent wall into the deserted premises of the Harvester and Tractor Show. Once safe, Basil's tensity relaxed, and as he considered Riply's unconsciousness of the responsibilities presently to devolve upon him, he bent double with hilarious laughter in the darkness.

Ten minutes later, in a remote part of the fairgrounds, a youth made his way briskly and cautiously towards the fireworks exhibit, swinging as he walked a recently purchased rattan cane. Several girls eyed him with interest, but he passed them haughtily; he was weary of people for a brief moment – a moment which he had almost mislaid in the bustle of life – he was enjoying his long pants.

He bought a bleacher seat and followed the crowd around the race track, seeking his section. A few Union troops were moving cannon about in preparation for the Battle of Gettysburg, and, stopping to watch them, he was hailed by Gladys Van Schellinger from the box behind.

'Oh, Basil, don't you want to come and sit with us?'

He turned about and was absorbed. Basil exchanged courtesies with Mr and Mrs Van Schellinger and he was affably introduced to several other people as 'Alice Riley's boy', and a chair was placed for him beside Gladys in front.

'Oh, Basil,' she whispered, glowing at him, 'isn't this fun?'

Distinctly, it was. He felt a vast wave of virtue surge through him. How anyone could have preferred the society of those common girls was at this moment incomprehensible.

'Basil, won't it be fun to go East? Maybe we'll be on the same train.'

'I can hardly wait,' he agreed gravely. 'I've got on long pants. I had to have them to go away to school.'

One of the ladies in the box leaned towards him. 'I know your mother very well,' she said. 'And I know another friend of yours. I'm Riply Buckner's aunt.'

'Oh, yes!'

'Riply's such a nice boy,' beamed Mrs Van Schillinger.

And then, as if the mention of his name had evoked him, Riply Buckner came suddenly into sight. Along the now empty and brightly illuminated race track came a short but monstrous procession, a sort of Lilliputian burlesque of the wild gay life. At its head marched Hubert Blair and Olive, Hubert prancing and twirling his cane like a drum major to the accompaniment of her appreciative screams of laughter. Next followed Elwood Leaming and his young lady, leaning so close together that they walked with difficulty, apparently wrapped in each other's arms. And bringing up the rear without glory were Riply Buckner and Basil's late companion, rivalling Olive in exhibitionist sound.

Fascinated, Basil stared at Riply, the expression of whose face was curiously mixed. At moments he would join in the general tone of the parade with silly guffaw, at others a pained expression would flit across his face, as if he doubted that, after all, the evening was a success.

The procession was attracting considerable notice – so much that not even Riply was aware of the particular attention focused upon him from this box, though he passed by it four feet away. He was out of hearing when a curious rustling sigh passed over its inhabitants and a series of discreet whispers began.

'What funny girls,' Gladys said. 'Was that first boy Hubert Blair?'

'Yes.' Basil was listening to a fragment of conversation behind: 'His mother will certainly hear of this in the morning.'

As long as Riply had been in sight, Basil had been in an agony of shame for him, but now a new wave of virtue, even stronger than the first, swept over him. His memory of the incident would have reached actual happiness, save for the fact that Riply's mother might not let him go away to school. And a few minutes later, even that seemed endurable. Yet Basil was not a mean boy. The natural cruelty of his species towards the doomed was not yet disguised by hypocrisy – that was all.

In a burst of glory, to the alternate strains of Dixie and The Star-Spangled Banner, the Battle of Gettysburg ended. Outside by the waiting cars, Basil, on a sudden impulse, went up to Riply's aunt.

'I think it would be sort of a – a mistake to tell Riply's mother. He didn't do any harm. He – '

Annoyed by the event of the evening, she turned on him cool, patronising eyes.

'I shall do as I think best,' she said briefly.

He frowned. Then he turned and got into the Van Schellinger limousine.

Sitting beside Gladys in the little seats, he loved her suddenly. His hand swung gently against hers from time to time and he felt the warm bond that they were both going away to school tightened around them and pulling them together.

'Can't you come and see me tomorrow?' she urged him. 'Mother's going to be away and she says I can have anybody I like.'

'All right.'

As the car slowed up for Basil's house, she leaned towards him swiftly. 'Basil – '

He waited. Her breath was warm on his cheek. He wanted her to hurry, or, when the engine stopped, her parents, dozing in back, might hear what she said. She seemed beautiful to him then; that vague unexciting quality about her was more than compensated for by her exquisite delicacy, the fine luxury of her life.

'Basil – Basil, when you come tomorrow, will you bring that Hubert Blair?'

The chauffeur opened the door and Mr and Mrs Van Schellinger woke up with a start. When the car had driven off, Basil stood looking after it thoughtfully until it turned the corner of the street.

Basil: The Freshest Boy

Saturday Evening Post (28 July 1928)

1

It was a hidden Broadway restaurant in the dead of the night, and a brilliant and mysterious group of society people, diplomats and members of the underworld were there. A few minutes ago the sparkling wine had been flowing and a girl had been dancing gaily upon a table, but now the whole crowd was hushed and breathless. All eyes were fixed upon the masked but well-groomed man in the dress suit and opera hat who stood nonchalantly in the door.

'Don't move, please,' he said, in a well-bred, cultivated voice that had, nevertheless, a ring of steel in it. 'This thing in my hand might – go off.'

His glance roved from table to table – fell upon the malignant man higher up with his pale saturnine face; upon Heatherly, the suave secret agent from a foreign power; then rested a little longer, a little more softly perhaps, upon the table where the girl with dark hair and dark tragic eyes sat alone.

'Now that my purpose is accomplished, it might interest you to know who I am.' There was a gleam of expectation in every eye. The breast of the dark-eyed girl heaved faintly and a tiny burst of subtle French perfume rose into the air. 'I am none other than that elusive gentleman, Basil Lee, better known as The Shadow.'

Taking off his well-fitting opera hat, he bowed ironically from the waist. Then, like a flash, he turned and was gone into the night.

'You get up to New York only once a month,' Lewis Crum was saying, 'and then you have to take a master along.'

Slowly, Basil Lee's glazed eyes turned from the barns and billboards of the Indiana countryside to the interior of the Broadway Limited. The hypnosis of the swift telegraph poles faded and Lewis Crum's stolid face took shape against the white slip-cover of the opposite bench.

'I'd just duck the master when I got to New York,' said Basil.

'Yes, you would!'

'I bet I would.'

'You try it and you'll see.'

'What do you mean saying I'll see, all the time, Lewis? What'll I see?'

His very bright dark-blue eyes were at this moment fixed upon his companion with boredom and impatience. The two had nothing in common except their age, which was fifteen, and the lifelong friendship of their fathers – which is less than nothing. Also they were bound from the same Middle-Western city for Basil's first and Lewis's second year at the same Eastern school.

But, contrary to all the best traditions, Lewis the veteran was miserable and Basil the neophyte was happy. Lewis hated school. He had grown entirely dependent on the stimulus of a hearty, vital mother, and as he felt her slipping farther and farther away from him, he plunged deeper into misery and homesickness. Basil, on the other hand, had lived with such intensity on so many stories of boarding-school life that, far from being homesick, he had a glad feeling of recognition and familiarity. Indeed, it was with some sense of doing the appropriate thing, having the traditional rough-house, that he had thrown Lewis's comb off the train at Milwaukee last night for no reason at all.

To Lewis, Basil's ignorant enthusiasm was distasteful – his instinctive attempt to dampen it had contributed to the mutual irritation.

'I'll tell you what you'll see,' he said ominously. 'They'll catch you smoking and put you on bounds.'

'No, they won't, because I won't be smoking. I'll be in training for football.'

'Football! Yeah! Football!'

'Honestly, Lewis, you don't like anything, do you?'

'I don't like football. I don't like to go out and get a crack in the eye.' Lewis spoke aggressively, for his mother had canonised all his timidities as common sense. Basil's answer, made with what he considered kindly intent, was the sort of remark that creates lifelong enmities.

'You'd probably be a lot more popular in school if you played football,' he suggested patronisingly.

Lewis did not consider himself unpopular. He did not think of it in that way at all. He was astounded.

'You wait!' he cried furiously. 'They'll take all that freshness out of you.'

'Clam yourself,' said Basil, coolly plucking at the creases of his first long trousers. 'Just clam yourself.'

'I guess everybody knows you were the freshest boy at the Country Day!'

'Clam yourself,' repeated Basil, but with less assurance. 'Kindly clam yourself.'

'I guess I know what they had in the school paper about you –'

Basil's own coolness was no longer perceptible.

'If you don't clam yourself,' he said darkly, 'I'm going to throw your brushes off the train too.'

The enormity of this threat was effective. Lewis sank back in his seat, snorting and muttering, but undoubtedly calmer. His reference had been to one of the most shameful passages in his companion's life. In a periodical issued by the boys of Basil's late school there had appeared under the heading PERSONALS:

> If someone will please poison young Basil, or find some other means to stop his mouth, the school at large and myself will be much obliged.

The two boys sat there fuming wordlessly at each other. Then, resolutely, Basil tried to reinter this unfortunate souvenir of the past. All that was behind him now. Perhaps he had been a little fresh, but he was making a new start. After a moment, the memory passed and with it the train and Lewis's dismal presence – the breath of the East came sweeping over him again with a vast nostalgia. A voice called him out of the fabled world; a man stood beside him with a hand on his sweater-clad shoulder.

'Lee!'

'Yes, sir.'

'It all depends on you now. Understand?'

'Yes, sir.'

'All right,' the coach said, 'go in and win.'

Basil tore the sweater from his stripling form and dashed out on the field. There were two minutes to play and the score was 3 to 0 for the enemy, but at the sight of young Lee, kept out of the game all year by a malicious plan of Dan Haskins, the school bully, and Weasel Weems, his toady, a thrill of hope went over the St Regis stand.

'33-12-16-22!' barked Midget Brown, the diminutive little quarter-back.

It was his signal –

'Oh, gosh!' Basil spoke aloud, forgetting the late unpleasantness. 'I wish we'd get there before tomorrow.'

2

St Regis School, Eastchester
November 18, 19—

Dear Mother – There is not much to say today, but I thought I would write you about my allowance. All the boys have a bigger allowance than me, because there are a lot of little things I have to get, such as shoe laces, etc. School is still very nice and am having a fine time, but football is over and there is not much to do. I am going to New York this week to see a show. I do not know yet what it will be, but probably the Quacker Girl or little boy Blue as they are both very good. Dr Bacon is very nice and there's a good phycission in the village. No more now as I have to study Algebra.

Your affectionate Son,

Basil D. Lee

As he put the letter in its envelope, a wizened little boy came into the deserted study hall where he sat and stood staring at him.

'Hello,' said Basil, frowning.

'I been looking for you,' said the little boy, slowly and judicially. 'I looked all over – up in your room and out in the gym, and they said you probably might of sneaked off in here.'

'What do you want?' Basil demanded.

'Hold your horses, Bossy.'

Basil jumped to his feet. The little boy retreated a step.

'Go on, hit me!' he chirped nervously. 'Go on, hit me, 'cause I'm just half your size – Bossy.'

Basil winced. 'You call me that again and I'll spank you.'

'No, you won't spank me. Brick Wales said if you ever touched any of us – '

'But I never did touch any of you.'

'Didn't you chase a lot of us one day and didn't Brick Wales – '

'Oh, what do you want?' Basil cried in desperation.

'Dr Bacon wants you. They sent me after you and somebody said maybe you sneaked in here.'

Basil dropped his letter in his pocket and walked out – the little boy and his invective following him through the door. He traversed a long corridor, muggy with that odour best described as the smell of stale caramels that is so peculiar to boys' schools, ascended a stairs and knocked at an unexceptional but formidable door.

Dr Bacon was at his desk. He was a handsome, red-headed Episcopal clergyman of fifty whose original real interest in boys was now tempered by the flustered cynicism which is the fate of all headmasters and settles on them like green mould. There were certain preliminaries before Basil was asked to sit down – gold-rimmed glasses had to be hoisted up from nowhere by a black cord and fixed on Basil to be sure that he was not an impostor; great masses of paper on the desk had to be shuffled through, not in search of anything but as a man nervously shuffles a pack of cards.

'I had a letter from your mother this morning – ah – Basil.' The use of his first name had come to startle Basil. No one else in school had yet called him anything but Bossy or Lee. 'She feels that your marks have been poor. I believe you have been sent here at a certain amount of – ah – sacrifice and she expects – '

Basil's spirit writhed with shame, not at his poor marks but that his financial inadequacy should be so bluntly stated. He knew that he was one of the poorest boys in a rich boys' school.

Perhaps some dormant sensibility in Dr Bacon became aware of his discomfort; he shuffled through the papers once more and began on a new note.

'However, that was not what I sent for you about this afternoon. You applied last week for permission to go to New York on Saturday, to a matinée. Mr Davis tells me that for almost the first time since school opened you will be off bounds tomorrow.'

'Yes, sir.'

'That is not a good record. However, I would allow you to go to New York if it could be arranged. Unfortunately, no masters are available this Saturday.'

Basil's mouth dropped ajar. 'Why, I – why, Dr Bacon, I know two parties that are going. Couldn't I go with one of them?'

Dr Bacon ran through all his papers very quickly. 'Unfortunately, one is composed of slightly older boys and the other group made arrangements some weeks ago.'

'How about the party that's going to the *Quaker Girl* with Mr Dunn?'

'It's that party I speak of. They feel that the arrangements are complete and they have purchased seats together.'

Suddenly Basil understood.

At the look in his eye Dr Bacon went on hurriedly. 'There's perhaps one thing I can do. Of course there must be several boys in the party so that the expenses of the master can be divided up among all. If you can find two other boys who would like to make up a party, and let me have their names by five o'clock, I'll send Mr Rooney with you.'

'Thank you,' Basil said.

Dr Bacon hesitated. Beneath the cynical encrustations of many years an instinct stirred to look into the unusual case of this boy and find out what made him the most detested boy in school. Among boys and masters there seemed to exist an extraordinary hostility towards him, and though Dr Bacon had dealt with many sorts of schoolboy crimes, he had neither by himself nor with the aid of trusted sixth-formers been able to lay his hands on its underlying cause. It was probably no single thing, but a combination of things; it was most probably one of those intangible questions of personality. Yet he remembered that when he first saw Basil he had considered him unusually prepossessing.

He sighed. Sometimes these things worked themselves out. He wasn't one to rush in clumsily. 'Let us have a better report to send home next month, Basil.'

'Yes, sir.'

Basil ran quickly downstairs to the recreation room. It was Wednesday and most of the boys had already gone into the village of Eastchester, whither Basil, who was still on bounds, was forbidden to follow. When he looked at those still scattered about the pool tables and piano, he saw that it was going to be difficult to get anyone to go with him at all. For Basil was quite conscious that he was the most unpopular boy at school.

It had begun almost immediately. One day, less than a fortnight after he came, a crowd of the smaller boys, perhaps urged on to it, gathered suddenly around him and began calling him Bossy. Within the next week he had two fights, and both times the crowd was vehemently and eloquently with the other boy. Soon after, when he was merely shoving indiscriminately, like everyone else, to get into the dining-room, Carver, the captain of the football team, turned about and, seizing him by the back of the neck, held him and dressed him down savagely. He joined a group innocently at the piano and was told, 'Go on away. We don't want you around.'

After a month he began to realise the full extent of his unpopularity. It shocked him. One day after a particularly bitter humiliation he went up to his room and cried. He tried to keep out of the way for a while, but it didn't help. He was accused of sneaking off here and there, as if bent on a series of nefarious errands. Puzzled and wretched, he looked at his face in the glass, trying to discover there the secret of their dislike – in the expression of his eyes, his smile.

He saw now that in certain ways he had erred at the outset – he had boasted, he had been considered yellow at football, he had pointed out people's mistakes to them, he had showed off his rather extraordinary fund of general information in class. But he had tried to do better and couldn't understand his failure to atone. It must be too late. He was queered for ever.

He had, indeed, become the scapegoat, the immediate villain, the sponge which absorbed all malice and irritability abroad – just as the most frightened person in a party seems to absorb all the others' fear, seems to be afraid for them all. His situation was not helped by the fact, obvious to all, that the supreme self-confidence with which he had come to St Regis's in September was thoroughly broken. Boys taunted him with impunity who would not have dared raise their voices to him several months before.

This trip to New York had come to mean everything to him – surcease from the misery of his daily life as well as a glimpse into the long-waited heaven of romance. Its postponement for week after week due to his sins – he was constantly caught reading after lights, for example, driven by his wretchedness into such vicarious escapes from reality – had deepened his longing until it was a burning hunger. It was unbearable that he should not go, and he told over the short list of those whom he might get to accompany him. The possibilities were Fat Gaspar, Treadway and Bugs Brown. A quick journey to their rooms showed that they had all availed themselves of the Wednesday permission to go into Eastchester for the afternoon.

Basil did not hesitate. He had until five o'clock and his only chance was to go after them. It was not the first time he had broken bounds, though the last attempt had ended in disaster and an extension of his confinement. In his room, he put on a heavy sweater – an overcoat was a betrayal of intent – replaced his jacket over it and hid a cap in his back pocket. Then he went downstairs and with an elaborate careless whistle struck out across the lawn for the gymnasium. Once there, he stood for a while as if looking in the windows, first the one close to the walk, then one near the corner of the building. From here he moved quickly, but not too quickly, into a grove of lilacs. Then he dashed around the corner, down a long stretch of lawn that was blind from all windows and, parting the strands of a wire fence, crawled through and stood upon the grounds of a neighbouring estate. For the moment he was free. He put on his cap against the chilly November wind, and set out along the half-mile of road to town.

Eastchester was a suburban farming community, with a small shoe factory. The institutions which pandered to the factory workers were the ones patronised by the boys – a movie house, a quick-lunch wagon on wheels known as the Dog and the Bostonian Candy Kitchen. Basil tried the Dog first and happened immediately upon a prospect.

This was Bugs Brown, a hysterical boy, subject to fits and strenuously avoided. Years later he became a brilliant lawyer, but at that time he was considered by the boys of St Regis's to be a typical lunatic because of the peculiar series of sounds with which he assuaged his nervousness all day long.

He consorted with boys younger than himself, who were without the prejudices of their elders, and was in the company of several when Basil came in.

'Who-ee!' he cried. 'Ee-ee-ee!' He put his hand over his mouth and bounced it quickly, making a wah-wah-wah sound. 'It's Bossy Lee! It's Bossy Lee! It's Boss-Boss-Boss-Boss-Bossy Lee!'

'Wait a minute, Bugs,' said Basil anxiously, half afraid that Bugs would go finally crazy before he could persuade him to come to town. 'Say, Bugs, listen. Don't, Bugs – wait a minute. Can you come up to New York Saturday afternoon?'

'Whe-ee-ee!' cried Bugs to Basil's distress. 'Wee-ee-ee!'

'Honestly, Bugs, tell me, can you? We could go up together if you could go.'

'I've got to see a doctor,' said Bugs, suddenly calm. 'He wants to see how crazy I am.'

'Can't you have him see about it some other day?' said Basil without humour.

'Whee-ee-ee!' cried Bugs.

'All right then,' said Basil hastily. 'Have you seen Fat Gaspar in town?'

Bugs was lost in shrill noise, but someone had seen Fat: Basil was directed to the Bostonian Candy Kitchen.

This was a gaudy paradise of cheap sugar. Its odour, heavy and sickly and calculated to bring out a sticky sweat upon an adult's palms, hung suffocatingly over the whole vicinity and met one like a strong moral dissuasion at the door. Inside, beneath a pattern of flies, material as black point lace, a line of boys sat eating heavy dinners of banana splits, maple nut, and chocolate marshmallow nut sundaes. Basil found Fat Gaspar at a table on the side.

Fat Gaspar was at once Basil's most unlikely and most ambitious quest. He was considered a nice fellow – in fact he was so pleasant that he had been courteous to Basil and had spoken to him politely all fall. Basil realised that he was like that to everyone, yet it was just possible that Fat liked him, as people used to in the past, and he was driven desperately to take a chance. But it was undoubtedly a presumption, and as he approached the table and saw the stiffened faces which the other two boys turned towards him, Basil's hope diminished.

'Say, Fat –' he said, and hesitated. Then he burst forth suddenly. 'I'm on bounds, but I ran off because I had to see you. Dr Bacon told me I could go to New York Saturday if I could get two other boys to go. I asked Bugs Brown and he couldn't go, and I thought I'd ask you.'

He broke off, furiously embarrassed, and waited. Suddenly the two boys with Fat burst into a shout of laughter.

'Bugs wasn't crazy enough!'

Fat Gaspar hesitated. He couldn't go to New York Saturday and ordinarily he would have refused without offending. He had nothing against Basil; nor, indeed, against anybody; but boys have only a certain resistance to public opinion and he was influenced by the contemptuous laughter of the others.

'I don't want to go,' he said indifferently. 'Why do you want to ask *me*?' Then, half in shame, he gave a deprecatory little laugh and bent over his ice cream.

'I just thought I'd ask you,' said Basil.

Turning quickly away, he went to the counter and in a hollow and unfamiliar voice ordered a strawberry sundae. He ate it mechanically, hearing occasional whispers and snickers from the table behind. Still in a daze, he started to walk out without paying his check, but the clerk called him back and he was conscious of more derisive laughter.

For a moment he hesitated whether to go back to the table and hit one of those boys in the face, but he saw nothing to be gained. They would say the truth – that he had done it because he couldn't get anybody to go to New York. Clenching his fists with impotent rage, he walked from the store.

He came immediately upon his third prospect, Treadway. Treadway had entered St Regis's late in the year and had been put in to room with Basil the week before. The fact that Treadway hadn't witnessed his humiliations of the autumn encouraged Basil to behave naturally towards him, and their relations had been, if not intimate, at least tranquil.

'Hey, Treadway,' he called, still excited from the affair in the Bostonian, 'can you come up to New York to a show Saturday afternoon?'

He stopped, realising that Treadway was in the company of Brick Wales, a boy he had had a fight with and one of his bitterest enemies. Looking from one to the other, Basil saw a look of impatience in Treadway's face and a faraway expression in Brick Wales's, and he realised what must have been happening. Treadway, making his way into the life of the school, had just been enlightened as to the status of his roommate. Like Fat Gaspar, rather than acknowledge himself eligible to such an intimate request, he preferred to cut their friendly relations short.

'Not on your life,' he said briefly. 'So long.' The two walked past him into the Candy Kitchen.

Had these slights, so much the bitterer for their lack of passion, been visited upon Basil in September, they would have been unbearable. But since then he had developed a shell of hardness which, while it did not add to his attractiveness, spared him certain delicacies of torture. In misery enough, and despair and self-pity, he went the other way along the street for a little distance until he could control the violent contortions of his face. Then, taking a roundabout route, he started back to school.

He reached the adjoining estate, intending to go back the way he had come. Halfway through a hedge, he heard footsteps approaching along the sidewalk and stood motionless, fearing the proximity of masters. Their voices grew nearer and louder; before he knew it he was listening with horrified fascination:

' – so, after he tried Bugs Brown, the poor nut asked Fat Gaspar to go with him and Fat said, 'What do you ask me for?' It serves him right if he couldn't get anybody at all.'

It was the dismal but triumphant voice of Lewis Crum.

3

Up in his room, Basil found a package lying on his bed. He knew its contents and for a long time he had been eagerly expecting it, but such was his depression that he opened it listlessly. It was a series of eight colour reproductions of Harrison Fisher girls 'on glossy paper, without printing or advertising matter and suitable for framing'.

The pictures were named Dora, Marguerite, Babette, Lucille, Gretchen, Rose, Katherine and Mina. Two of them – Marguerite and Rose – Basil looked at, slowly tore up, and dropped in the waste-basket, as one who disposes of the inferior pups from a litter. The other six he pinned at intervals around the room. Then he lay down on his bed and regarded them.

Dora, Lucille and Katherine were blonde; Gretchen was medium; Babette and Mina were dark. After a few minutes, he found that he was looking oftenest at Dora and Babette and, to a lesser extent, at Gretchen, though the latter's Dutch cap seemed unromantic and precluded the element of mystery. Babette, a dark little violet-eyed beauty in a tight-fitting hat, attracted him most; his eyes came to rest on her at last.

'Babette,' he whispered to himself – 'beautiful Babette.'

The sound of the word, so melancholy and suggestive, like 'Vilia' or 'I'm happy at Maxim's' on the phonograph, softened him and, turning over on his face, he sobbed into the pillow. He took hold of the bed rails over his head and, sobbing and straining, began to talk to himself brokenly – how he hated them and whom he hated – he listed a dozen – and what he would do to them when he was great and powerful. In previous moments like these he had always rewarded Fat Gaspar for his kindness, but now he was like the rest. Basil set upon him, pummelling him unmercifully, or laughed sneeringly when he passed him blind and begging on the street.

He controlled himself as he heard Treadway come in, but did not move or speak. He listened as the other moved about the room, and after a while became conscious that there was an unusual opening of closets and bureau drawers. Basil turned over, his arm concealing his tear-stained face. Treadway had an armful of shirts in his hand.

'What are you doing?' Basil demanded.

His roommate looked at him stonily. 'I'm moving in with Wales,' he said.

'Oh!'

Treadway went on with his packing. He carried out a suitcase full, then another, took down some pennants and dragged his trunk into the hall. Basil watched him bundle his toilet things into a towel and take one last survey about the room's new barrenness to see if there was anything forgotten.

'Goodbye,' he said to Basil, without a ripple of expression on his face.

'Goodbye.'

Treadway went out. Basil turned over once more and choked into the pillow.

'Oh, poor Babette!' he cried huskily. 'Poor little Babette! Poor little Babette!' Babette, svelte and piquante, looked down at him coquettishly from the wall.

4

Dr Bacon, sensing Basil's predicament and perhaps the extremity of his misery, arranged it that he should go into New York, after all. He went in the company of Mr Rooney, the football coach and history teacher. At twenty Mr Rooney had hesitated for some time between joining the police force and having his way paid through a small New England college; in fact he was a hard specimen and Dr Bacon was planning to get rid of him at Christmas. Mr Rooney's contempt for Basil was founded on the latter's ambiguous and unreliable conduct on the football field during the past season – he had consented to take him to New York for reasons of his own.

Basil sat meekly beside him on the train, glancing past Mr Rooney's bulky body at the Sound and the fallow fields of Westchester County. Mr Rooney finished his newspaper, folded it up and sank into a moody silence. He had eaten a large breakfast and the exigencies of time had not allowed him to work it off with exercise. He remembered that Basil was a fresh boy, and it was time he did something fresh and could be called to account. This reproachless silence annoyed him.

'Lee,' he said suddenly, with a thinly assumed air of friendly interest, 'why don't you get wise to yourself?'

'What, sir?' Basil was startled from his excited trance of this morning.

'I said why don't you get wise to yourself?' said Mr Rooney in a somewhat violent tone. 'Do you want to be the butt of the school all your time here?'

'No, I don't.' Basil was chilled. Couldn't all this be left behind for just one day?

'You oughtn't to get so fresh all the time. A couple of times in history class I could just about have broken your neck.' Basil could think of no appropriate answer. 'Then out playing football,' continued Mr Rooney, ' – you didn't have any nerve. You could play better than a lot of 'em when you wanted, like that day against the Pomfret seconds, but you lost your nerve.'

'I shouldn't have tried for the second team,' said Basil. 'I was too light. I should have stayed on the third.'

'You were yellow, that was all the trouble. You ought to get wise to yourself. In class, you're always thinking of something else. If you don't study, you'll never get to college.'

'I'm the youngest boy in the fifth form,' Basil said rashly.

'You think you're pretty bright, don't you?' He eyed Basil ferociously. Then something seemed to occur to him that changed his attitude and they rode for a while in silence. When the train began to run through the thickly clustered communities near New York, he spoke again in a milder voice and with an air of having considered the matter for a long time: 'Lee, I'm going to trust you.'

'Yes, sir.'

'You go and get some lunch and then go on to your show. I've got some business of my own I got to attend to, and when I've finished I'll try to get to the show. If I can't, I'll anyhow meet you outside.'

Basil's heart leaped up. 'Yes, sir.'

'I don't want you to open your mouth about this at school – I mean, about me doing some business of my own.'

'No, sir.'

'We'll see if you can keep your mouth shut for once,' he said, making it fun. Then he added, on a note of moral sternness, 'And no drinks, you understand that?'

'Oh, no, sir!' The idea shocked Basil. He had never tasted a drink, nor even contemplated the possibility, save the intangible and non-alcoholic champagne of his café dreams.

On the advice of Mr Rooney he went for luncheon to the Manhattan Hotel, near the station, where he ordered a club sandwich, French fried potatoes, and a chocolate parfait. Out of the corner of his eye he watched the nonchalant, debonair, blasé New Yorkers at neighbouring tables, investing them with a romance by which these possible fellow citizens of his from the Middle West lost nothing. School had fallen from him like a burden; it was no more than an unheeded clamour, faint and far away. He even delayed opening the letter from the morning's mail which he found in his pocket, because it was addressed to him at school.

He wanted another chocolate parfait, but being reluctant to bother the busy waiter any more, he opened the letter and spread it before him instead. It was from his mother:

Dear Basil – This is written in great haste, as I didn't want to frighten you by telegraphing. Grandfather is going abroad to take the waters and he wants you and me to come too. The idea is that you'll go to school at Grenoble or Montreux for the rest of the year and learn the language and we'll be close by. That is, if you want to. I know how you like St Regis's and playing football and baseball, and of course there would be none of that; but on the other hand, it would be a nice change, even if it postponed your entering Yale by an extra year. So, as usual, I want you to do just as you like. We will be leaving home almost as soon as you get this and will come to the Waldorf in New York, where you can come in and see us for a few days, even if you decide to stay. Think it over, dear.

With love to my dearest boy,

Mother

Basil got up from his chair with a dim idea of walking over to the Waldorf and having himself locked up safely until his mother came. Then, impelled to some gesture, he raised his voice and in one of his first basso notes called boomingly and without reticence for the waiter. No more St Regis's! No more St Regis's! He was almost strangling with happiness.

'Oh, gosh!' he cried to himself. 'Oh, golly! Oh, gosh! Oh, gosh!' No more Dr Bacon and Mr Rooney and Brick Wales and Fat Gaspar. No more Bugs Brown and on bounds and being called Bossy. He need no longer hate them, for they were impotent shadows in the stationary world that he was sliding away from, sliding past, waving his hand. 'Goodbye!' he pitied them. 'Goodbye!'

It required the din of Forty-Second Street to sober his maudlin joy. With his hand on his purse to guard against the omnipresent pick-pocket, he moved cautiously towards Broadway. What a day! He would tell Mr Rooney – Why, he needn't ever go back! Or perhaps it would be better to go back and let them know what he was going to do, while they went on and on in the dismal, dreary round of school.

He found the theatre and entered the lobby with its powdery feminine atmosphere of a matinée. As he took out his ticket, his gaze was caught and held by a sculptured profile a few feet away. It was that of a well-built blond young man of about twenty with a strong chin and direct grey eyes. Basil's brain spun wildly for a moment and then came to rest upon a name – more than a name – upon a legend, a sign in the sky. What a day! He had never seen the young man before, but from a thousand pictures he knew beyond the possibility of a doubt that it was Ted Fay, the Yale football captain, who had almost single-handed beaten Harvard and Princeton last fall. Basil felt a sort of exquisite pain. The profile turned away; the crowd revolved; the hero disappeared. But Basil would know all through the next hours that Ted Fay was here too.

In the rustling, whispering, sweet-smelling darkness of the theatre he read the programme. It was the show of all shows that he wanted to see, and until the curtain actually rose the programme itself had a curious sacredness – a prototype of the thing itself. But when the curtain rose it became waste paper to be dropped carelessly to the floor.

Act I. The Village Green of a Small Town near New York

It was too bright and blinding to comprehend all at once, and it went so fast that from the very first Basil felt he had missed things; he would make his mother take him again when she came – next week – tomorrow.

An hour passed. It was very sad at this point – a sort of gay sadness, but sad. The girl – the man. What kept them apart even now? Oh, those tragic errors and misconceptions. So sad. Couldn't they look into each other's eyes and *see*?

In a blaze of light and sound, of resolution, anticipation and imminent trouble, the act was over.

He went out. He looked for Ted Fay and thought he saw him leaning rather moodily on the plush wall at the rear of the theatre, but he could not be sure. He bought cigarettes and lit one, but fancying at the first puff he heard a blare of music he rushed back inside.

Act 2. The Foyer of the Hotel Astor

Yes, she was, indeed, like a song – a Beautiful Rose of the Night. The waltz buoyed her up, brought her with it to a point of aching beauty and then let her slide back to life across its last bars as a leaf slants to earth across the air. The high life of New York! Who could blame her if she was carried away by the glitter of it all, vanishing into the bright morning of the amber window borders or into distant and entrancing music as the door opened and closed that led to the ballroom? The toast of the shining town.

Half an hour passed. Her true love brought her roses like herself and she threw them scornfully at his feet. She laughed and turned to the other, and danced – danced madly, wildly. Wait! That delicate treble among the thin horns, the low curving note from the great strings. There it was again, poignant and aching, sweeping like a great gust of emotion across the stage, catching her again like a leaf helpless in the wind:

> 'Rose – Rose – Rose of the night
> When the spring moon is bright you'll be fair – '

A few minutes later, feeling oddly shaken and exalted, Basil drifted outside with the crowd. The first thing upon which his eyes fell was the almost forgotten and now curiously metamorphosed spectre of Mr Rooney.

Mr Rooney had, in fact, gone a little to pieces. He was, to begin with, wearing a different and much smaller hat than when he left Basil at noon. Secondly, his face had lost its somewhat gross aspect and turned a pure and even delicate white, and he was wearing his necktie and even portions of his shirt on the outside of his unaccountably wringing-wet overcoat. How, in the short space of four hours, Mr Rooney had got himself in such shape is explicable only by the pressure of confinement in a boys' school upon a fiery outdoor spirit. Mr Rooney was born to toil under the clear light of heaven and, perhaps half-consciously, he was headed towards his inevitable destiny.

'Lee,' he said dimly, 'you ought to get wise to y'self. I'm going to put you wise y'self.'

To avoid the ominous possibility of being put wise to himself in the lobby, Basil uneasily changed the subject.

'Aren't you coming to the show?' he asked, flattering Mr Rooney by implying that he was in any condition to come to the show. 'It's a wonderful show.'

Mr Rooney took off his hat, displaying wringing-wet matted hair. A picture of reality momentarily struggled for development in the back of his brain.

'We got to get back to school,' he said in a sombre and unconvinced voice.

'But there's another act,' protested Basil in horror. 'I've got to stay for the last act.'

Swaying, Mr Rooney looked at Basil, dimly realising that he had put himself in the hollow of this boy's hand.

'All righ',' he admitted. 'I'm going to get somethin' to eat. I'll wait for you next door.'

He turned abruptly, reeled a dozen steps, and curved dizzily into a bar adjoining the theatre. Considerably shaken, Basil went back inside.

Act 3. The Roof Garden of Mr Van Astor's House. Night.

Half an hour passed. Everything was going to be all right, after all. The comedian was at his best now, with the glad appropriateness of laughter after tears, and there was a promise of felicity in the bright tropical sky. One lovely plaintive duet, and then abruptly the long moment of incomparable beauty was over.

Basil went into the lobby and stood in thought while the crowd passed out. His mother's letter and the show had cleared his mind of bitterness and vindictiveness – he was his old self and he wanted to do the right thing. He wondered if it was the right thing to get Mr Rooney back to school. He walked towards the saloon, slowed up as he came to it and, gingerly opening the swinging door, took a quick peer inside. He saw only that Mr Rooney was not one of those drinking at the bar. He walked down the street a little way, came back and tried again. It was as if he thought the doors were teeth to bite him, for he had the old-fashioned Middle-Western boy's horror of the saloon. The third time he was successful. Mr Rooney was sound asleep at a table in the back of the room.

Outside again Basil walked up and down, considering. He would give Mr Rooney half an hour. If, at the end of that time, he had not come out, he would go back to school. After all, Mr Rooney had laid for him ever since football season – Basil was simply washing his hands of the whole affair, as in a day or so he would wash his hands of school.

He had made several turns up and down, when glancing up an alley that ran beside the theatre his eye was caught by the sign, Stage Entrance. He could watch the actors come forth.

He waited. Women streamed by him, but those were the days before Glorification and he took these drab people for wardrobe women or something. Then suddenly a girl came out and with her a man, and Basil turned and ran a few steps up the street as if afraid they would recognise him – and ran back, breathing as if with a heart attack – for the girl, a radiant little beauty of nineteen, was Her, and the young man by her side was Ted Fay.

Arm in arm, they walked past him, and irresistibly Basil followed. As they walked, she leaned towards Ted Fay in a way that gave them a fascinating air of intimacy. They crossed Broadway and turned into the Knickerbocker Hotel, and twenty feet behind them Basil followed, in time to see them go into a long room set for afternoon tea. They sat at a table for two, spoke vaguely to a waiter, and then, alone at last, bent eagerly towards each other. Basil saw that Ted Fay was holding her gloved hand.

The tea room was separated only by a hedge of potted firs from the main corridor. Basil went along this to a lounge which was almost up against their table and sat down.

Her voice was low and faltering, less certain than it had been in the play, and very sad: 'Of course I do, Ted.' For a long time, as their conversation continued, she repeated, 'Of course I do,' or, 'But I do, Ted.' Ted Fay's remarks were too low for Basil to hear.

' – says next month, and he won't be put off any more . . . I do in a way, Ted. It's hard to explain, but he's done everything for mother and me . . . There's no use kidding myself. It was a foolproof part and any girl he gave it to was made right then and there . . . He's been awfully thoughtful. He's done everything for me.'

Basil's ears were sharpened by the intensity of his emotion; now he could hear Ted Fay's voice too: 'And you say you love me.'

'But don't you see I promised to marry him more than a year ago.'

'Tell him the truth – that you love me. Ask him to let you off.'

'This isn't musical comedy, Ted.'

'That was a mean one,' he said bitterly.

'I'm sorry, Ted darling, but you're driving me crazy going on this way. You're making it so hard for me.'

'I'm going to leave New Haven, anyhow.'

'No, you're not. You're going to stay and play baseball this spring. Why, you're an ideal to all those boys! Why, if you – '

He laughed shortly. 'You're a fine one to talk about ideals.'

'Why not? I'm living up to my responsibility to Beltzman; you've got to make up your mind just like I have – that we can't have each other.'

'Jerry! Think what you're doing! All my life, whenever I hear that waltz – '

Basil got to his feet and hurried down the corridor, through the lobby and out of the hotel. He was in a state of wild emotional confusion. He did not understand all he had heard, but from his clandestine glimpse into the privacy of these two, with all the world that his short experience could conceive of at their feet, he had gathered that life for everybody was a struggle, sometimes magnificent from a distance, but always difficult and surprisingly simple and a little sad.

They would go on. Ted Fay would go back to Yale, put her picture in his bureau drawer and knock out home runs with the bases full this spring – at half-past eight the curtain would go up and She would miss something warm and young out of her life, something she had had this afternoon.

It was dark outside and Broadway was a blazing forest fire as Basil walked slowly along towards the point of brightest light. He looked up at the great intersecting planes of radiance with a vague sense of approval and possession. He would see it a lot now, lay his restless heart upon this greater restlessness of a nation – he would come whenever he could get off from school.

But that was all changed – he was going to Europe. Suddenly Basil realised that he wasn't going to Europe. He could not forgo the moulding of his own destiny just to alleviate a few months of pain. The conquest of the successive worlds of school, college and New York – why, that was his true dream that he had carried from boyhood into adolescence, and because of the jeers of a few boys he had been about to abandon it and run ignominiously up a back alley! He shivered violently, like a dog coming out of the water, and simultaneously he was reminded of Mr Rooney.

A few minutes later he walked into the bar, past the quizzical eyes of the bartender and up to the table where Mr Rooney still sat asleep. Basil shook him gently, then firmly. Mr Rooney stirred and perceived Basil.

'G'wise to yourself,' he muttered drowsily. 'G'wise to yourself an' let me alone.'

'I am wise to myself,' said Basil. 'Honest, I am wise to myself, Mr Rooney. You got to come with me into the washroom and get cleaned up, and then you can sleep on the train again, Mr Rooney. Come on, Mr Rooney, please – '

5

It was a long hard time. Basil got on bounds again in December and wasn't free again until March. An indulgent mother had given him no habits of work and this was almost beyond the power of anything but life itself to remedy, but he made numberless new starts and failed and tried again.

He made friends with a new boy named Maplewood after Christmas, but they had a silly quarrel; and through the winter term, when a boys' school is shut in with itself and only partly assuaged from its natural savagery by indoor sports, Basil was snubbed and slighted a good deal for his real and imaginary sins, and he was much alone. But on the other hand, there was Ted Fay, and Rose of the Night on the phonograph – 'All my life whenever I hear that waltz' – and the remembered lights of New York, and the thought of what he was going to do in football next autumn and the glamorous image of Yale and the hope of spring in the air.

Fat Gaspar and a few others were nice to him now. Once when he and Fat walked home together by accident from downtown they had a long talk about actresses – a talk that Basil was wise enough not to presume upon afterwards. The smaller boys suddenly decided that they approved of him, and a master who had hitherto disliked him put his hand on his shoulder walking to a class one day. They would all forget eventually – maybe during the summer. There would be new fresh boys in September; he would have a clean start next year.

One afternoon in February, playing basketball, a great thing happened. He and Brick Wales were at forward on the second team and in the fury of the scrimmage the gymnasium echoed with sharp slapping contacts and shrill cries.

'Here yar!'

'Bill! Bill!'

Basil had dribbled the ball down the court and Brick Wales, free, was crying for it.

'Here yar! Lee! Hey! Lee-y!'

Lee-y! Basil flushed and made a poor pass. He had been called by a nickname. It was a poor makeshift, but it was something more than the stark bareness of his surname or a term of derision. Brick Wales went on playing, unconscious that he had done anything in particular or that he had contributed to the events by which another boy was saved from the army of the bitter, the selfish, the neurasthenic and the unhappy. It isn't given to us to know those rare moments when people are wide open and the lightest touch can wither or heal. A moment too late and we can never reach them any more in this world. They will not be cured by our most efficacious drugs or slain with our sharpest swords.

Lee-y! it could scarcely be pronounced. But Basil took it to bed with him that night, and thinking of it, holding it to him happily to the last, fell easily to sleep.

Forging Ahead

Saturday Evening Post (30 March 1929)

Basil Duke Lee and Riply Buckner Jr sat on the Lees' front steps in the regretful gold of a late summer afternoon. Inside the house the telephone sang out with mysterious promise.

'I thought you were going home,' Basil said.

'I thought you were.'

'I am.'

'So am I.'

'Well, why don't you go, then?'

'Why don't you, then?'

'I am.'

They laughed, ending with yawning gurgles that were not laughed out but sucked in. As the telephone rang again, Basil got to his feet.

'I've got to study trig before dinner.'

'Are you honestly going to Yale this fall?' demanded Riply sceptically.

'Yes.'

'Everybody says you're foolish to go at sixteen.'

'I'll be seventeen in September. So long. I'll call you up tonight.'

Basil heard his mother at the upstairs telephone and he was immediately aware of distress in her voice.

'Yes . . . Isn't that awful, Everett! . . . Yes . . . Oh-h my!' After a minute he gathered that it was only the usual worry about business and went on into the kitchen for refreshments. Returning, he met his mother hurrying downstairs. She was blinking rapidly and her hat was on backwards – characteristic testimony to her excitement.

'I've got to go over to your grandfather's.'

'What's the matter, mother?'

'Uncle Everett thinks we've lost a lot of money.'

'How much?' he asked, startled.

'Twenty-two thousand dollars apiece. But we're not sure.'

She went out.

'Twenty-two thousand dollars!' he repeated in an awed whisper.

His ideas of money were vague and somewhat debonair, but he had noticed that at family dinners the immemorial discussion as to whether the Third Street block would be sold to the railroads had given place to anxious talk of Western Public Utilities. At half-past six his mother telephoned for him to have his dinner, and with growing uneasiness he sat alone at the table, undistracted by *The Mississippi Bubble*, open beside his plate. She came in at seven, distraught and miserable, and dropping down at the table, gave him his first exact information about finance – she and her father and her brother Everett had lost something more than eighty thousand dollars. She was in a panic and she looked wildly around the dining-room as if money were slipping away even here, and she wanted to retrench at once.

'I've got to stop selling securities or we won't have anything,' she declared. 'This leaves us only three thousand a year – do you realise that, Basil? I don't see how I can possibly afford to send you to Yale.'

His heart tumbled into his stomach; the future, always glowing like a comfortable beacon ahead of him, flared up in glory and went out. His mother shivered, and then emphatically shook her head.

'You'll just have to make up your mind to go to the state university.'

'Gosh!' Basil said.

Sorry for his shocked, rigid face, she yet spoke somewhat sharply, as people will with a bitter refusal to convey.

'I feel terribly about it – your father wanted you to go to Yale. But everyone says that, with clothes and railroad fare, I can count on it costing two thousand a year. Your grandfather helped me to send you to St Regis School, but he always thought you ought to finish at the state university.'

After she went distractedly upstairs with a cup of tea, Basil sat thinking in the dark parlour. For the present the loss meant only one thing to him – he wasn't going to Yale after all. The sentence itself, divorced from its meaning, overwhelmed him, so many times had he announced casually, 'I'm going to Yale,' but gradually he realised how many friendly and familiar dreams had been swept away. Yale was the faraway East, that he had loved with a vast nostalgia since he had first read books about great cities. Beyond the dreary railroad stations of Chicago and the night fires of Pittsburgh, back in the old states, something went on that made his heart beat fast with excitement. He was attuned to the vast, breathless bustle of New York, to the metropolitan days and nights that were tense as singing wires. Nothing needed to be imagined there, for it was all the very stuff of romance – life was as vivid and satisfactory as in books and dreams.

But first, as a sort of gateway to that deeper, richer life, there was

Yale. The name evoked the memory of a heroic team backed up against its own impassable goal in the crisp November twilight, and later, of half a dozen immaculate noblemen with opera hats and canes standing at the Manhattan Hotel bar. And tangled up with its triumphs and rewards, its struggles and glories, the vision of the inevitable, incomparable girl.

Well, then, why not work his way through Yale? In a moment the idea had become a reality. He began walking rapidly up and down the room, declaring half aloud, 'Of course, that's the thing to do.' Rushing upstairs, he knocked at his mother's door and announced in the inspired voice of a prophet: 'Mother, I know what I'm going to do! I'm going to work my way through Yale.'

He sat down on her bed and she considered uncertainly. The men in her family had not been resourceful for several generations, and the idea startled her.

'It doesn't seem to me you're a boy who likes to work,' she said. 'Besides, boys who work their way through college have scholarships and prizes, and you've never been much of a student.'

He was annoyed. He was ready for Yale a year ahead of his age and her reproach seemed unfair.

'What would you work at?' she said.

'Take care of furnaces,' said Basil promptly. 'And shovel snow off sidewalks. I think they mostly do that – and tutor people. You could let me have as much money as it would take to go to the state university?'

'We'll have to think it over.'

'Well, don't you worry about anything,' he said emphatically, 'because my earning my way through Yale will really make up for the money you've lost, almost.'

'Why don't you start by finding something to do this summer?'

'I'll get a job tomorrow. Maybe I can pile up enough so you won't have to help me. Good-night, Mother.'

Up in his room he paused only to thunder grimly to the mirror that he was going to work his way through Yale, and going to his bookcase, he took down half a dozen dusty volumes of Horatio Alger, unopened for years. Then, much as a postwar young man might consult the George Washington Condensed Business Course, he sat at his desk and slowly began to turn the pages of *Bound to Rise*.

Two days later, after being insulted by the doorkeepers, office boys and telephone girls of the *Press*, the *Evening News*, the *Socialist Gazette* and a green scandal sheet called the *Courier*, and assured that no one wanted a reporter practically seventeen, after enduring every ignominy prepared for a young man in a free country trying to work his way through Yale, Basil Duke Lee, too 'stuck-up' to apply to the parents of his friends, got a position with the railroad, through Eddie Parmelee, who lived across the way.

At half-past six the following morning, carrying his lunch, and a new suit of overalls that had cost four dollars, he strode self-consciously into the Great Northern car shops. It was like entering a new school, except that no one showed any interest in him or asked him if he was going out for the team. He punched a time clock, which affected him strangely, and without even an admonition from the foreman to 'go in and win', was put to carrying boards for the top of a car.

Twelve o'clock arrived; nothing had happened. The sun was blazing hot and his hands and back were sore, but no real events had ruffled the dull surface of the morning. The president's little daughter had not come by, dragged by a runaway horse; not even a superintendent had walked through the yard and singled him out with an approving eye. Undismayed, he toiled on – you couldn't expect much the first morning.

He and Eddie Parmelee ate their lunches together. For several years Eddie had worked here in vacations; he was sending himself to the state university this fall. He shook his head doubtfully over the idea of Basil's earning his way through Yale.

'Here's what you ought to do,' he said. 'You borrow two thousand dollars from your mother and buy twenty shares in Ware Plow and Tractor. Then go to a bank and borrow two thousand more with those shares for collateral, and with that two thousand buy twenty more shares. Then you sit on your back for a year, and after that you won't have to think about earning your way through Yale.'

'I don't think mother would give me two thousand dollars.'

'Well, anyhow, that's what I'd do.'

If the morning had been uneventful, the afternoon was distinguished by an incident of some unpleasantness. Basil had risen a little, having been requested to mount to the top of a freight car and help nail the boards he had carried in the morning. He found that nailing nails into a board was more highly technical than nailing tacks into a wall, but he considered that he was progressing satisfactorily when an angry voice hailed him from below: 'Hey, you! Get up!'

He looked down. A foreman stood there, unpleasantly red in the face.

'Yes, you in the new suit. Get up!'

Basil looked about to see if someone was lying down, but the two sullen hunyaks seemed to be hard at work and it grew on him that he was indeed being addressed.

'I beg your pardon, sir,' he said.

'Get up on your knees or get out! What the hell do you think this is?'

He had been sitting down as he nailed, and apparently the foreman thought that he was loafing. After another look at the foreman, he suppressed the explanation that he felt steadier sitting down and decided to just let it go. There were probably no railroad shops at Yale; yet, he remembered with a pang the ominous name, New York, New Haven and Hartford.

The third morning, just as he had become aware that his overalls were not where he had hung them in the shop, it was announced that all men of less than six months' service were to be laid off. Basil received four dollars and lost his overalls. Learning that nails are driven from a kneeling position had cost him only car-fare.

In a large old-fashioned house in the old section of the city lived Basil's great-uncle, Benjamin Reilly, and there Basil presented himself that evening. It was a last resort – Benjamin Reilly and Basil's grandfather were brothers and they had not spoken for twenty years.

He was received in the living-room by the small, dumpy old man whose inscrutable face was hidden behind a white poodle beard. Behind him stood a woman of forty, his wife of six months, and her daughter, a girl of fifteen. Basil's branch of the family had not been invited to the wedding, and he had never seen these two additions before.

'I thought I'd come down and see you, Uncle Ben,' he said with some embarrassment.

There was a certain amount of silence.

'Your mother well?' asked the old man.

'Oh, yes, thank you.'

Mr Reilly waited. Mrs Reilly spoke to her daughter, who threw a curious glance at Basil and reluctantly left the room. Her mother made the old man sit down.

Out of sheer embarrassment Basil came to the point. He wanted a summer job in the Reilly Wholesale Drug Company.

His uncle fidgeted for a minute and then replied that there were no positions open.

'Oh.'

'It might be different if you wanted a permanent place, but you say you want to go to Yale.' He said this with some irony of his own, and glanced at his wife.

'Why, yes,' said Basil. 'That's really why I want the job.'

'Your mother can't afford to send you, eh?' The note of pleasure in his voice was unmistakable. 'Spent all her money?'

'Oh, no,' answered Basil quickly. 'She's going to help me.'

To his surprise, aid came from an unpromising quarter. Mrs Reilly suddenly bent and whispered in her husband's ear, whereupon the old man nodded and said aloud: 'I'll think about it, Basil. You go in there.'

And his wife repeated: 'We'll think about it. You go in the library with Rhoda while Mr Reilly looks up and sees.'

The door of the library closed behind him and he was alone with Rhoda, a square-chinned, decided girl with fleshy white arms and a white dress that reminded Basil domestically of the lacy pants that blew among the laundry in the yard. Puzzled by his uncle's change of front, he eyed her abstractedly for a moment.

'I guess you're my cousin,' said Rhoda, closing her book, which he saw was *The Little Colonel, Maid of Honour*.

'Yes,' he admitted.

'I heard about you from somebody.' The implication was that her information was not flattering.

'From who?'

'A girl named Elaine Washmer.'

'Elaine Washmer!' His tone dismissed the name scornfully. 'That girl!'

'She's my best friend.' He made no reply. 'She said you thought you were wonderful.'

Young people do not perceive at once that the giver of wounds is the enemy and the quoted tattle merely the arrow. His heart smouldered with wrath at Elaine Washmer.

'I don't know many kids here,' said the girl, in a less aggressive key. 'We've only been here six months. I never saw such a stuck-up bunch.'

'Oh, I don't think so,' he protested. 'Where did you live before?'

'Sioux City. All the kids have much more fun in Sioux City.'

Mrs Reilly opened the door and called Basil back into the living-room. The old man was again on his feet.

'Come down tomorrow morning and I'll find you something,' he said.

'And why don't you have dinner with us tomorrow night?' added Mrs Reilly, with a cordiality wherein an adult might have detected disingenuous purpose.

'Why, thank you very much.'

His heart, buoyant with gratitude, had scarcely carried him out the door before Mrs Reilly laughed shortly and called in her daughter.

'Now we'll see if you don't get around a little more,' she announced. 'When was it you said they had those dances?'

'Thursdays at the College Club and Saturdays at the Lake Club,' said Rhoda promptly.

'Well, if this young man wants to hold the position your father has given him, you'll go to them all the rest of the summer.'

Arbitrary groups formed by the hazards of money or geography may be sufficiently quarrelsome and dull, but for sheer unpleasantness the condition of young people who have been thrust together by a common unpopularity can be compared only with that of prisoners herded in a cell. In Basil's eyes the guests at the little dinner the following night were a collection of cripples. Lewis and Hector Crum, dullard cousins who were tolerable only to each other; Sidney Rosen, rich but awful; ugly Mary Haupt, Elaine Washmer and Betty Geer, who reminded Basil of a cruel parody they had once sung to the tune of 'Jungle Town':

Down below the hill
There lives a pill
That makes me ill,
And her name is Betty Geer.
We had better stop right here . . .
She's so fat,
She looks just like a cat,
And she's the queen of pills.

Moreover, they resented Basil, who was presumed to be 'stuck-up', and walking home afterwards, he felt dreary and vaguely exploited. Of course, he was grateful to Mrs Reilly for her kindness, yet he couldn't help wondering if a cleverer boy couldn't have got out of taking Rhoda to the Lake Club next Saturday night. The proposal had caught him unaware; but when he was similarly trapped the following week, and the week after that, he began to realise the situation. It was a part of his job, and he accepted it grimly, unable, nevertheless, to understand how such a bad dancer and so unsociable a person should want to go where she was obviously a burden. 'Why doesn't she just sit at home and read a book,' he thought disgustedly, 'or go away somewhere – or sew?'

It was one Saturday afternoon, while he watched a tennis tournament and felt the unwelcome duty of the evening creep up on him, that he found himself suddenly fascinated by a girl's face a few yards away. His heart leaped into his throat and the blood in his pulse beat with excitement; and then, when the crowd rose to go, he saw to his astonishment that he had been staring at a child ten years old. He looked away, oddly disappointed; after a moment he looked back again. The lovely, self-conscious face suggested a train of thought and sensation that he could not identify. As he passed on, forgoing a vague intention of discovering the child's identity, there was beauty suddenly all around him in the afternoon; he could hear its unmistakable whisper, its never-inadequate, never-failing promise of happiness. 'Tomorrow – one day soon now – this fall – maybe tonight.' Irresistibly compelled to express himself, he sat down and tried to write to a girl in New York. His words were stilted and the girl seemed cold and far away. The real image on his mind, the force that had propelled him into this state of yearning, was the face of the little girl seen that afternoon.

When he arrived with Rhoda Sinclair at the Lake Club that night, he immediately cast a quick look around to see what boys were present who were indebted to Rhoda or else within his own sphere of influence. This was just before cutting-in arrived, and ordinarily he was able to dispose of half a dozen dances in advance, but tonight an older crowd was in evidence and the situation was unpromising. However, as Rhoda emerged from the dressing-room he saw Bill Kampf and thankfully bore down upon him.

'Hello, old boy,' he said, exuding personal goodwill. 'How about dancing once with Rhoda tonight?'

'Can't,' Bill answered briskly. 'We've got people visiting us. Didn't you know?'

'Well, why couldn't we swap a dance anyhow?'

Bill looked at him in surprise.

'I thought you knew,' he exclaimed. 'Erminie's here. She's been talking about you all afternoon.'

'Erminie Bibble!'

'Yes. And her father and mother and her kid sister. Got here this morning.'

Now, indeed, the emotion of two hours before bubbled up in Basil's blood, but this time he knew why. It was the little sister of Erminie Gilbert Labouisse Bibble whose strangely familiar face had so attracted him. As his mind swung sharply back to a long afternoon on the Kampfs' veranda at the lake, ages ago, a year ago, a real voice rang in his ear, 'Basil!' and a sparkling little beauty of fifteen came up to him with a fine burst of hurry, taking his hand as though she was stepping into the circle of his arm.

'Basil, I'm so glad!' Her voice was husky with pleasure, though she was at the age when pleasure usually hides behind grins and mumbles. It was Basil who was awkward and embarrassed, despite the intention of his heart. He was a little relieved when Bill Kampf, more conscious of his lovely cousin than he had been a year ago, led her out on the floor.

'Who was that?' Rhoda demanded, as he returned in a daze. 'I never saw her around.'

'Just a girl.' He scarcely knew what he was saying.

'Well, I know that. What's her name?'

'Minnie Bibble, from New Orleans.'

'She certainly looks conceited. I never saw anybody so affected in my life.'

'Hush!' Basil protested involuntarily. 'Let's dance.'

It was a long hour before Basil was relieved by Hector Crum, and then several dances passed before he could get possession of Minnie, who was now the centre of a moving whirl. But she made it up to him by pressing his hand and drawing him out to a veranda which overhung the dark lake.

'It's about time,' she whispered. With a sort of instinct she found the darkest corner. 'I might have known you'd have another crush.'

'I haven't,' he insisted in horror. 'That's a sort of a cousin of mine.'

'I always knew you were fickle. But I didn't think you'd forget me so soon.'

She had wriggled up until she was touching him. Her eyes, floating into his, said, What does it matter? We're alone.

In a curious panic he jumped to his feet. He couldn't possibly kiss her like this – right at once. It was all so different and older than a year ago. He was too excited to do more than walk up and down and say, 'Gosh, I certainly am glad to see you,' supplementing this unoriginal statement with an artificial laugh.

Already mature in poise, she tried to soothe him: 'Basil, come and sit down!'

'I'll be all right,' he gasped, as if he had just fainted. 'I'm a little fussed, that's all.'

Again he contributed what, even to his pounding ears, sounded like a silly laugh.

'I'll be here three weeks. Won't it be fun?' And she added, with warm emphasis: 'Do you remember on Bill's veranda that afternoon?'

All he could find to answer was: 'I work now in the afternoon.'

'You can come out in the evenings, Basil. It's only half an hour in a car.'

'I haven't got a car.'

'I mean you can get your family's car.'

'It's an electric.'

She waited patiently. He was still romantic to her – handsome, incalculable, a little sad.

'I saw your sister,' he blurted out. Beginning with that, he might bridge this perverse and intolerable reverence she inspired. 'She certainly looks like you.'

'Does she?'

'It was wonderful,' he said. 'Wonderful! Let me tell you – '

'Yes, do.' She folded her hands expectantly in her lap.

'Well, this afternoon – '

The music had stopped and started several times. Now, in an intermission, there was the sound of determined footsteps on the veranda, and Basil looked up to find Rhoda and Hector Crum.

'I got to go home, Basil,' squeaked Hector in his changing voice. 'Here's Rhoda.'

Take Rhoda out to the dock and push her in the lake. But only Basil's mind said this; his body stood up politely.

'I didn't know where you were, Basil,' said Rhoda in an aggrieved tone. 'Why didn't you come back?'

'I was just coming.' His voice trembled a little as he turned to Minnie. 'Shall I find your partner for you?'

'Oh, don't bother,' said Minnie. She was not angry, but she was somewhat astonished. She could not be expected to guess that the young man walking away from her so submissively was at the moment employed in working his way through Yale.

From the first, Basil's grandfather, who had once been a regent at the state university, wanted him to give up the idea of Yale, and now his mother, picturing him hungry and ragged in a garret, adjoined her persuasions. The sum on which he could count from her was far below the necessary minimum, and although he stubbornly refused to consider defeat, he consented, 'just in case anything happened', to register at the university for the coming year.

In the administration building he ran into Eddie Parmelee, who introduced his companion, a small, enthusiastic Japanese.

'Well, well,' said Eddie. 'So you've given up Yale!'

'I given up Yale,' put in Mr Utsonomia, surprisingly. 'Oh, yes, long time I given up Yale.' He broke into enthusiastic laughter. 'Oh, sure. Oh, yes.'

'Mr Utsonomia's a Japanese,' explained Eddie, winking. 'He's a sub-freshman too.'

'Yes, I given up Harvard, Princeton too,' continued Mr Utsonomia. 'They give me choice back in my country. I choose here.'

'You did?' said Basil, almost indignantly.

'Sure, more strong here. More peasants come, with strength and odour of ground.'

Basil stared at him. 'You like that?' he asked incredulously.

Utsonomia nodded. 'Here I get to know real American peoples. Girls too. Yale got only boys.'

'But they haven't got college spirit here,' explained Basil patiently.

Utsonomia looked blankly at Eddie.

'Rah-rah!' elucidated Eddie, waving his arms. 'Rah-rah-rah! You know.'

'Besides, the girls here – ' began Basil, and stopped.

'You know girls here?' grinned Utsonomia.

'No, I don't know them,' said Basil firmly. 'But I know they're not like the girls that you'd meet down at the Yale proms. I don't think they even have proms here. I don't mean the girls aren't all right, but they're just not like the ones at Yale. They're just co-eds.'

'I hear you got a crush on Rhoda Sinclair,' said Eddie.

'Yes, I have!' said Basil ironically.

'They used to invite me to dinner sometimes last spring, but since you take her around to all the club dances – '

'Goodbye,' said Basil hastily. He exchanged a jerky bow for Mr Utsonomia's more formal dip, and departed.

From the moment of Minnie's arrival the question of Rhoda had begun to assume enormous proportions. At first he had been merely indifferent to her person and a little ashamed of her lacy, oddly reminiscent clothes, but now, as he saw how relentlessly his services were commandeered, he began to hate her. When she complained of a headache, his imagination would eagerly convert it into a long, lingering illness from which she would recover only after college opened in the fall. But the eight dollars a week which he received from his great-uncle would pay his fare to New Haven, and he knew that if he failed to hold this position his mother would refuse to let him go.

Not suspecting the truth, Minnie Bibble found the fact that he only danced with her once or twice at each hop, and was then strangely moody and silent, somehow intriguing. Temporarily, at least, she was fascinated by his indifference, and even a little unhappy. But her precociously emotional temperament would not long stand neglect, and it was agony for Basil to watch several rivals beginning to emerge. There were moments when it seemed too big a price to pay even for Yale.

All his hopes centred upon one event. That was a farewell party in her honour for which the Kampfs had engaged the College Club and to which Rhoda was not invited. Given the mood and the moment, he might speed her departure knowing that he had stamped himself indelibly on her heart.

Three days before the party he came home from work at six to find the Kampfs' car before his door and Minnie sitting alone on the front porch.

'Basil, I had to see you,' she said. 'You've been so funny and distant to me.'

Intoxicated by her presence on his familiar porch, he found no words to answer.

'I'm meeting the family in town for dinner and I've got an hour. Can't we go somewhere? I've been frightened to death your mother would come home and think it was fresh for me to call on you.' She spoke in a whisper, though there was no one close enough to hear. 'I wish we didn't have the old chauffeur. He listens.'

'Listens to what?' Basil asked, with a flash of jealousy.

'He just listens.'

'I'll tell you,' he proposed: 'We'll have him drop us by grampa's house and I'll borrow the electric.'

The hot wind blew the brown curls around her forehead as they glided along Crest Avenue.

That he contributed the car made him feel more triumphantly astride the moment. There was a place he had saved for such a time as this – a little pigtail of a road left from the excavations of Prospect Park, where Crest Avenue ran obliviously above them and the late sun glinted on the Mississippi flats a mile away.

The end of summer was in the afternoon; it had turned a corner, and what was left must be used while there was yet time.

Suddenly she was whispering in his arms, 'You're first, Basil – nobody but you.'

'You just admitted you were a flirt.'

'I know, but that was years ago. I used to like to be called fast when I was thirteen or fourteen, because I didn't care what people said; but about a year ago I began to see there was something better in life – honestly, Basil – and I've tried to act properly. But I'm afraid I'll never be an angel.'

The river flowed in a thin scarlet gleam between the public baths and the massed tracks upon the other side. Booming, whistling, faraway railroad sounds reached them from down there; the voices of children playing tennis in Prospect Park sailed frailly overhead.

'I really haven't got such a line as everybody thinks, Basil, for I mean a lot of what I say way down deep, and nobody believes me. You know how much alike we are, and in a boy it doesn't matter, but a girl has to control her feelings, and that's hard for me, because I'm emotional.'

'Haven't you kissed anybody since you've been in St Paul?'

'No.'

He saw she was lying, but it was a brave lie. They talked from their hearts – with the half truths and evasions peculiar to that organ, which has never been famed as an instrument of precision. They pieced together all the shreds of romance they knew and made garments for each other no less warm than their childish passion, no less wonderful than their sense of wonder.

He held her away suddenly, looked at her, made a strained sound of delight. There it was, in her face touched by sun – that promise – in the curve of her mouth, the tilted shadow of her nose on her cheek, the point of dull fire in her eyes – the promise that she could lead him into a world in which he would always be happy.

'Say I love you,' he whispered.

'I'm in love with you.'

'Oh, no; that's not the same.'

She hesitated. 'I've never said the other to anybody.'

'Please say it.'

She blushed the colour of the sunset.

'At my party,' she whispered. 'It'd be easier at night.'

When she dropped him in front of his house she spoke from the window of the car: 'This is my excuse for coming to see you. My uncle couldn't get the club Thursday, so we're having the party at the regular dance Saturday night.'

Basil walked thoughtfully into the house; Rhoda Sinclair was also giving a dinner at the College Club dance Saturday night.

It was put up to him frankly. Mrs Reilly listened to his tentative excuses in silence and then said: 'Rhoda invited you first for Saturday night, and she already has one girl too many. Of course, if you choose to simply turn your back on your engagement and go to another party, I don't know how Rhoda will feel, but I know how I should feel.'

And the next day his great-uncle, passing through the stock room, stopped and said: 'What's all this trouble about parties?'

Basil started to explain, but Mr Reilly cut him short. 'I don't see the use of hurting a young girl's feelings. You better think it over.'

Basil had thought it over; on Saturday afternoon he was still expected at both dinners and he had hit upon no solution at all.

Yale was only a month away now, but in four days Erminie Bibble would be gone, uncommitted, unsecured, grievously offended, lost for ever. Not yet delivered from adolescence, Basil's moments of foresight alternated with those when the future was measured by a day. The glory that was Yale faded beside the promise of that incomparable hour.

On the other side loomed up the gaunt spectre of the university, with phantoms flitting in and out its portals that presently disclosed themselves as peasants and girls. At five o'clock, in a burst of contempt for his weakness, he went to the phone and left word with a maid at the Kampfs' house that he was sick and couldn't come tonight. Nor would he sit with the dull leftovers of his generation – too sick for one party, he was too sick for the other. The Reillys could have no complaint as to that.

Rhoda answered the phone and Basil tried to reduce his voice to a weak murmur: 'Rhoda, I've been taken sick. I'm in bed now,' he murmured feebly, and then added: 'The phone's right next to the bed, you see; so I thought I'd call you up myself.'

'You mean to say you can't come?' Dismay and anger were in her voice.

'I'm sick in bed,' he repeated doggedly. 'I've got chills and a pain and a cold.'

'Well, can't you come anyhow?' she asked, with what to the invalid seemed a remarkable lack of consideration. 'You've just got to. Otherwise there'll be two extra girls.'

'I'll send someone to take my place,' he said desperately. His glance, roving wildly out the window, fell on a house over the way. 'I'll send Eddie Parmelee.'

Rhoda considered. Then she asked with quick suspicion: 'You're not going to that other party?'

'Oh, no; I told them I was sick too.'

Again Rhoda considered. Eddie Parmelee was mad at her.

'I'll fix it up,' Basil promised. 'I know he'll come. He hasn't got anything to do tonight.'

A few minutes later he dashed across the street. Eddie himself, tying a bow on his collar, came to the door. With certain reservations, Basil hastily outlined the situation. Would Eddie go in his place?

'Can't do it, old boy, even if I wanted to. Got a date with my real girl tonight.'

'Eddie, I'd make it worth your while,' he said recklessly. 'I'd pay you for your time – say, five dollars.'

Eddie considered, there was hesitation in his eyes, but he shook his head.

'It isn't worth it, Basil. You ought to see what I'm going out with tonight.'

'You could see her afterwards. They only want you – I mean me – because they've got more girls than men for dinner – and listen, Eddie, I'll make it ten dollars.'

Eddie clapped him on the shoulder.

'All right, old boy, I'll do it for an old friend. Where's the pay?'

More than a week's salary melted into Eddie's palm, but another sort of emptiness accompanied Basil back across the street – the emptiness of the coming night. In an hour or so the Kampfs' limousine would draw up at the College Club and – time and time again his imagination halted miserably before that single picture, unable to endure any more.

In despair he wandered about the dark house. His mother had let the maid go out and was at his grandfather's for dinner, and momentarily Basil considered finding some rake like Elwood Leaming and going down to Carling's Restaurant to drink whiskey, wines and beer. Perhaps on her way back to the lake after the dance, Minnie, passing by, would see his face among the wildest of the revellers and understand.

'I'm going to Maxim's,' he hummed to himself desperately; then he added impatiently: 'Oh, to heck with Maxim's!'

He sat in the parlour and watched a pale moon come up over the Lindsays' fence at McKubben Street. Some young people came by, heading for the trolley that went to Como Park. He pitied their horrible dreariness – they were not going to dance with Minnie at the College Club tonight.

Eight-thirty – she was there now. Nine – they were dancing between courses to 'Peg o' My Heart' or doing the Castle Walk that Andy Lockheart brought home from Yale.

At ten o'clock he heard his mother come in, and almost immediately the phone rang. For a moment he listened without interest to her voice; then abruptly he sat up in his chair.

'Why, yes; how do you do, Mrs Reilly . . . Oh, I see . . . Oh . . . Are you sure it isn't Basil you want to speak to? . . . Well, frankly, Mrs Reilly, I don't see that it's my affair.'

Basil got up and took a step towards the door; his mother's voice was growing thin and annoyed: 'I wasn't here at the time and I don't know who he promised to send.'

Eddie Parmelee hadn't gone after all – well, that was the end.

' . . . Of course not. It must be a mistake. I don't think Basil would possibly do that; I don't think he even knows any Japanese.'

Basil's brain reeled. For a moment he was about to dash across the street after Eddie Parmelee. Then he heard a definitely angry note come into his mother's voice: 'Very well, Mrs Reilly. I'll tell my son. But his going to Yale is scarcely a matter I care to discuss with you. In any case, he no longer needs anyone's assistance.'

He had lost his position and his mother was trying to put a proud face on it. But her voice continued, soaring a little: 'Uncle Ben might be interested to know that this afternoon we sold the Third Street block to the Union Depot Company for four hundred thousand dollars.'

Mr Utsonomia was enjoying himself. In his whole six months in America he had never felt so caught up in its inner life before. At first it had been a little hard to make plain to the lady just whose place it was he was taking, but Eddie Parmelee had assured him that such substitutions were an American custom, and he was spending the evening collecting as much data upon American customs as possible.

He did not dance, so he sat with two elderly ladies until both the ladies went home, early and apparently a little agitated, shortly after dinner. But Mr Utsonomia stayed on. He watched and he wandered. He was not lonesome; he had grown accustomed to being alone.

About eleven he sat on the veranda pretending to be blowing the smoke of a cigarette – which he hated – out over the city, but really listening to a conversation which was taking place just behind. It had been going on for half an hour, and it puzzled him, for apparently it was a proposal, and it was not refused. Yet, if his eyes did not deceive him, the contracting parties were of an age that Americans did not associate with such serious affairs. Another thing puzzled him even more: obviously, if one substituted for an absent guest, the absent guest should not be among those present, and he was almost sure that the young man who had just engaged himself for marriage was Mr Basil Lee. It would be bad manners to intrude now, but he would urbanely ask him about a solution of this puzzle when the state university opened in the fall.

The Rough Crossing

Saturday Evening Post (8 June 1929)

1

Once on the long, covered piers, you have come into a ghostly country that is no longer Here and not yet There. Especially at night. There is a hazy yellow vault full of shouting, echoing voices. There is the rumble of trucks and the clump of trunks, the strident chatter of a crane and the first salt smell of the sea. You hurry through, even though there's time. The past, the continent, is behind you; the future is that glowing mouth in the side of the ship; this dim turbulent alley is too confusedly the present.

Up the gangplank, and the vision of the world adjusts itself, narrows. One is a citizen of a commonwealth smaller than Andorra. One is no longer so sure of anything. Curiously unmoved the men at the purser's desk, cell-like the cabin, disdainful the eyes of voyagers and their friends, solemn the officer who stands on the deserted promenade deck thinking something of his own as he stares at the crowd below. A last odd idea that one didn't really have to come, then the loud, mournful whistles, and the thing – certainly not the boat, but rather a human idea, a frame of mind – pushes forth into the big dark night.

Adrian Smith, one of the celebrities on board – not a very great celebrity, but important enough to be bathed in flashlight by a photographer who had been given his name, but wasn't sure what his subject 'did' – Adrian Smith and his blonde wife, Eva, went up to the promenade deck, passed the melancholy ship's officer, and, finding a quiet eerie, put their elbows on the rail.

'We're going!' he cried presently, and they both laughed in ecstasy. 'We've escaped. They can't get us now.'

'Who?'

He waved his hand vaguely at the civic tiara.

'All those people out there. They'll come with their posses and their warrants and list of crimes we've committed, and ring the bell at our door on Park Avenue and ask for the Adrian Smiths, but what ho! the Adrian Smiths and their children and nurse are off for France.'

'You make me think we really have committed crimes.'

'They can't have you,' he said frowning. 'That's one thing they're after me about – they know I haven't got any right to a person like you, and they're furious. That's one reason I'm glad to get away.'

'Darling,' said Eva.

She was twenty-six – five years younger than he. She was something precious to everyone who knew her.

'I like this boat better than the *Majestic* or the *Aquitania*,' she remarked, unfaithful to the ships that had served their honeymoon.

'It's much smaller.'

'But it's very slick and it has all those little shops along the corridors. And I think the staterooms are bigger.'

'The people are very formal – did you notice? – as if they thought everyone else was a card sharp. And in about four days half of them will be calling the other half by their first names.'

Four of the people came by now – a quartet of young girls abreast, making a circuit of the deck. Their eight eyes swept momentarily towards Adrian and Eva, and then swept automatically back, save for one pair which lingered for an instant with a little start. They belonged to one of the girls in the middle, who was, indeed, the only passenger of the four. She was not more than eighteen – a dark little beauty with the fine crystal gloss over her that, in brunettes, takes the place of a blonde's bright glow.

'Now, who's that?' wondered Adrian. 'I've seen her before.'

'She's pretty,' said Eva.

'Yes.' He kept wondering, and Eva deferred momentarily to his distraction; then, smiling up at him, she drew him back into their privacy.

'Tell me more,' she said.

'About what?'

'About us – what a good time we'll have, and how we'll be much better and happier, and very close always.'

'How could we be any closer?' His arm pulled her to him.

'But I mean never even quarrel any more about silly things. You know, I made up my mind when you gave me my birthday present last week' – her fingers caressed the fine seed pearls at her throat – 'that I'd try never to say a mean thing to you again.'

'You never have, my precious.'

Yet even as he strained her against his side she knew that the moment of utter isolation had passed almost before it had begun. His antennae were already out, feeling over this new world.

'Most of the people look rather awful,' he said – 'little and swarthy and ugly. Americans didn't use to look like that.'

'They look dreary,' she agreed. 'Let's not get to know anybody, but just stay together.'

A gong was beating now, and stewards were shouting down the decks, 'Visitors ashore, please!' and voices rose to a strident chorus. For a while the gangplanks were thronged; then they were empty, and the jostling crowd behind the barrier waved and called unintelligible things, and kept up a grin of goodwill. As the stevedores began to work at the ropes a flat-faced, somewhat befuddled young man arrived in a great hurry and was assisted up the gangplank by a porter and a taxi driver. The ship having swallowed him as impassively as though he were a missionary for Beirut, a low, portentous vibration began. The pier with its faces commenced to slide by, and for a moment the boat was just a piece accidentally split off from it; then the faces became remote, voiceless, and the pier was one among many yellow blurs along the waterfront. Now the harbour flowed swiftly towards the sea.

On a northern parallel of latitude a hurricane was forming and moving south by southeast preceded by a strong west wind. On its course it was destined to swamp the *Peter I. Eudin* of Amsterdam, with a crew of sixty-six, to break a boom on the largest boat in the world, and to bring grief and want to the wives of several hundred seamen. This liner, leaving New York Sunday evening, would enter the zone of the storm Tuesday, and of the hurricane late Wednesday night.

2

Tuesday afternoon Adrian and Eva paid their first visit to the smoking-room. This was not in accord with their intentions – they had 'never wanted to see a cocktail again' after leaving America – but they had forgotten the staccato loneliness of ships, and all activity centred about the bar. So they went in for just a minute.

It was full. There were those who had been there since luncheon, and those who would be there until dinner, not to mention a faithful few who had been there since nine this morning. It was a prosperous assembly, taking its recreation at bridge, solitaire, detective stories, alcohol, argument and love. Up to this point you could have matched it in the club or casino life of any country, but over it all played a repressed nervous energy, a barely disguised impatience that extended to old and young alike. The cruise had begun, and they had enjoyed the beginning, but the show was not varied enough to last six days, and already they wanted it to be over.

At a table near them Adrian saw the pretty girl who had stared at him on the deck the first night. Again he was fascinated by her loveliness; there was no mist upon the brilliant gloss that gleamed through the smoky confusion of the room. He and Eva had decided from the passenger list that she was probably 'Miss Elizabeth D'Amido and maid', and he had heard her called Betsy as he walked past a deck-tennis game. Among the young people with her was the flat-nosed youth who had been 'poured on board' the night of their departure; yesterday he had walked the deck morosely, but he was apparently reviving. Miss D'Amido whispered something to him, and he looked over at the Smiths with curious eyes. Adrian was new enough at being a celebrity to turn self-consciously away.

'There's a little roll. Do you feel it?' Eva demanded.

'Perhaps we'd better split a pint of champagne.'

While he gave the order a short colloquy was taking place at the other table; presently a young man rose and came over to them.

'Isn't this Mr Adrian Smith?'

'Yes.'

'We wondered if we couldn't put you down for the deck-tennis tournament. We're going to have a deck-tennis tournament.'

'Why – ' Adrian hesitated.

'My name's Stacomb,' burst out the young man. 'We all know your – your plays or whatever it is, and all that – and we wondered if you wouldn't like to come over to our table.'

Somewhat overwhelmed, Adrian laughed; Mr Stacomb, glib, soft, slouching, waited, evidently under the impression that he had delivered himself of a graceful compliment.

Adrian, understanding that, too, replied: 'Thanks, but perhaps you'd better come over here.'

'We've got a bigger table.'

'But we're older and more – more settled.'

The young man laughed kindly, as if to say, 'That's all right.'

'Put me down,' said Adrian. 'How much do I owe you?'

'One buck. Call me Stac.'

'Why?' asked Adrian, startled.

'It's shorter.'

When he had gone they smiled broadly.

'Heavens,' Eva gasped, 'I believe they are coming over.'

They were. With a great draining of glasses, calling of waiters, shuffling of chairs, three boys and two girls moved to the Smiths' table. If there was any diffidence, it was confined to the hosts; for the new additions gathered around them eagerly, eyeing Adrian with respect – too much respect – as if to say: 'This was probably a mistake and won't be amusing, but maybe we'll get something out of it to help us in our after life, like at school.'

In a moment Miss D'Amido changed seats with one of the men and placed her radiant self at Adrian's side, looking at him with manifest admiration.

'I fell in love with you the minute I saw you,' she said audibly and without self-consciousness; 'so I'll take all the blame for butting in. I've seen your play four times.'

Adrian called a waiter to take their orders.

'You see,' continued Miss D'Amido, 'we're going into a storm, and you might be prostrated the rest of the trip, so I couldn't take any chances.'

He saw that there was no undertone or innuendo in what she said, nor the need of any. The words themselves were enough, and the deference with which she neglected the young men and bent her politeness on him was somehow very touching. A little glow went over him; he was having rather more than a pleasant time.

Eva was less entertained; but the flat-nosed young man, whose name was Butterworth, knew people that she did, and that seemed to make the affair less careless and casual. She did not like meeting new people unless they had 'something to contribute', and she was often bored by the great streams of them, of all types and conditions and classes, that passed through Adrian's life. She herself 'had everything' – which is to say that she was well endowed with talents and with charm – and the mere novelty of people did not seem a sufficient reason for eternally offering everything up to them.

Half an hour later when she rose to go and see the children, she was content that the episode was over. It was colder on deck, with a damp that was almost rain, and there was a perceptible motion. Opening the door of her stateroom she was surprised to find the cabin steward sitting languidly on her bed, his head slumped upon the upright pillow. He looked at her listlessly as she came in, but made no move to get up.

'When you've finished your nap you can fetch me a new pillowcase,' she said briskly.

Still the man didn't move. She perceived then that his face was green.

'You can't be seasick in here,' she announced firmly. 'You go and lie down in your own quarters.'

'It's me side,' he said faintly. He tried to rise, gave out a little rasping sound of pain and sank back again. Eva rang for the stewardess.

A steady pitch, toss, roll had begun in earnest and she felt no sympathy for the steward, but only wanted to get him out as quickly as possible. It was outrageous for a member of the crew to be seasick. When the stewardess came in Eva tried to explain this, but now her own head was whirring, and throwing herself on the bed, she covered her eyes.

'It's his fault,' she groaned when the man was assisted from the room. 'I was all right and it made me sick to look at him. I wish he'd die.'

In a few minutes Adrian came in.

'Oh, but I'm sick!' she cried.

'Why, you poor baby.' He leaned over and took her in his arms. 'Why didn't you tell me?'

'I was all right upstairs, but there was a steward – Oh, I'm too sick to talk.'

'You'd better have dinner in bed.'

'Dinner! Oh, my heavens!'

He waited solicitously, but she wanted to hear his voice, to have it drown out the complaining sound of the beams.

'Where've you been?'

'Helping to sign up people for the tournament.'

'Will they have it if it's like this? Because if they do I'll just lose for you.'

He didn't answer; opening her eyes, she saw that he was frowning.

'I didn't know you were going in the doubles,' he said.

'Why, that's the only fun.'

'I told the D'Amido girl I'd play with her.'

'Oh.'

'I didn't think. You know I'd much rather play with you.'

'Why didn't you, then?' she asked coolly.

'It never occurred to me.'

She remembered that on their honeymoon they had been in the finals and won a prize. Years passed. But Adrian never frowned in this regretful way unless he felt a little guilty. He stumbled about, getting his dinner clothes out of the trunk, and she shut her eyes.

When a particular violent lurch startled her awake again he was dressed and tying his tie. He looked healthy and fresh, and his eyes were bright.

'Well, how about it?' he enquired. 'Can you make it, or no?'

'No.'

'Can I do anything for you before I go?'

'Where are you going?'

'Meeting those kids in the bar. Can I do anything for you?'

'No.'

'Darling, I hate to leave you like this.'

'Don't be silly. I just want to sleep.'

That solicitous frown – when she knew he was crazy to be out and away from the close cabin. She was glad when the door closed. The thing to do was to sleep, sleep.

Up – down – sideways. Hey there, not so far! Pull her round the corner there! Now roll her, right – left – Crea-eak! Wrench! Swoop!

Some hours later Eva was dimly conscious of Adrian bending over her. She wanted him to put his arms around her and draw her up out of this dizzy lethargy, but by the time she was fully awake the cabin was empty. He had looked in and gone. When she awoke next the cabin was dark and he was in bed.

The morning was fresh and cool, and the sea was just enough calmer to make Eva think she could get up. They breakfasted in the cabin and with Adrian's help she accomplished an unsatisfactory makeshift toilet and they went up on the boat deck. The tennis tournament had already begun and was furnishing action for a dozen amateur movie cameras, but the majority of passengers were represented by lifeless bundles in deckchairs beside untasted trays.

Adrian and Miss D'Amido played their first match. She was deft and graceful; blatantly well. There was even more warmth behind her ivory skin than there had been the day before. The strolling first officer stopped and talked to her; half a dozen men whom she couldn't have known three days ago called her Betsy. She was already the pretty girl of the voyage, the cynosure of starved ship's eyes.

But after a while Eva preferred to watch the gulls in the wireless masts and the slow slide of the roll-top sky. Most of the passengers looked silly with their movie cameras that they had all rushed to get and now didn't know what to use for, but the sailors painting the lifeboat stanchions were quiet and beaten and sympathetic, and probably wished, as she did, that the voyage was over.

Butterworth sat down on the deck beside her chair.

'They're operating on one of the stewards this morning. Must be terrible in this sea.'

'Operating? What for?' she asked listlessly.

'Appendicitis. They have to operate now because we're going into worse weather. That's why they're having the ship's party tonight.'

'Oh, the poor man!' she cried, realising it must be her steward.

Adrian was showing off now by being very courteous and thoughtful in the game.

'Sorry. Did you hurt yourself? . . . No, it was my fault. . . You better put on your coat right away, pardner, or you'll catch cold.'

The match was over and they had won. Flushed and hearty, he came up to Eva's chair.

'How do you feel?'

'Terrible.'

'Winners are buying a drink in the bar,' he said apologetically.

'I'm coming, too,' Eva said, but an immediate dizziness made her sink back in her chair.

'You'd better stay here. I'll send you up something.'

She felt that his public manner had hardened towards her slightly.

'You'll come back?'

'Oh, right away.'

She was alone on the boat deck, save for a solitary ship's officer who slanted obliquely as he paced the bridge. When the cocktail arrived she forced herself to drink it, and felt better. Trying to distract her mind with pleasant things, she reached back to the sanguine talks that she and Adrian had had before sailing. There was the little villa in Brittany, the children learning French – that was all she could think of now – the little villa in Brittany, the children learning French – so she repeated the words over and over to herself until they became as meaningless as the wide white sky. The why of their being here had suddenly eluded her; she felt unmotivated, accidental, and she wanted Adrian to come back quick, all responsive and tender, to reassure her. It was in the hope that there was some secret of graceful living, some real compensation for the lost, careless confidence of twenty-one, that they were going to spend a year in France.

The day passed darkly, with fewer people around and a wet sky falling. Suddenly it was five o'clock, and they were all in the bar again, and Mr Butterworth was telling her about his past. She took a good deal of champagne, but she was seasick dimly through it, as if the illness was her soul trying to struggle up through some thickening encrustation of abnormal life.

'You're my idea of a Greek goddess, physically,' Butterworth was saying.

It was pleasant to be Mr Butterworth's idea of a Greek goddess physically, but where was Adrian? He and Miss D'Amido had gone out on a forward deck to feel the spray. Eva heard herself promising to get out her colours and paint the Eiffel Tower on Butterworth's shirt-front for the party tonight.

When Adrian and Betsy D'Amido, soaked with spray, opened the door with difficulty against the driving wind and came into the now-covered security of the promenade deck, they stopped and turned towards each other.

'Well?' she said. But he only stood with his back to the rail, looking at her, afraid to speak. She was silent, too, because she wanted him to be first; so for a moment nothing happened. Then she made a step towards him, and he took her in his arms and kissed her forehead.

'You're just sorry for me, that's all.' She began to cry a little. 'You're just being kind.'

'I feel terribly about it.' His voice was taut and trembling.

'Then kiss me.'

The deck was empty. He bent over her swiftly.

'No, really kiss me.'

He could not remember when anything had felt so young and fresh as her lips. The rain lay, like tears shed for him, upon the softly shining porcelain cheeks. She was all new and immaculate, and her eyes were wild.

'I love you,' she whispered. 'I can't help loving you, can I? When I first saw you – oh, not on the boat, but over a year ago – Grace Heally took me to a rehearsal and suddenly you jumped up in the second row and began telling them what to do. I wrote you a letter and tore it up.'

'We've got to go.'

She was weeping as they walked along the deck. Once more, imprudently, she held up her face to him at the door of her cabin. His blood was beating through him in wild tumult as he walked on to the bar.

He was thankful that Eva scarcely seemed to notice him or to know that he had been gone. After a moment he pretended an interest in what she was doing.

'What's that?'

'She's painting the Eiffel Tower on my shirt-front for tonight,' explained Butterworth.

'There,' Eva laid away her brush and wiped her hands.

'How's that?'

'A *chef-d'oeuvre.*'

Her eyes swept around the watching group, lingered casually upon Adrian.

'You're wet. Go and change.'

'You come too.'

'I want another champagne cocktail.'

'You've had enough. It's time to dress for the party.'

Unwilling she closed her paints and preceded him.

'Stacomb's got a table for nine,' he remarked as they walked along the corridor.

'The younger set,' she said with unnecessary bitterness. 'Oh, the younger set. And you just having the time of your life – with a child.'

They had a long discussion in the cabin, unpleasant on her part and evasive on his, which ended when the ship gave a sudden gigantic heave, and Eva, the edge worn off her champagne, felt ill again. There was nothing to do but to have a cocktail in the cabin, and after that they decided to go to the party – she believed him now, or she didn't care.

Adrian was ready first – he never wore fancy dress.

'I'll go on up. Don't be long.'

'Wait for me, please; it's rocking so.'

He sat down on a bed, concealing his impatience.

'You don't mind waiting, do you? I don't want to parade up there all alone.'

She was taking a tuck in an oriental costume rented from the barber.

'Ships make people feel crazy,' she said. 'I think they're awful.'

'Yes,' he muttered absently.

'When it gets very bad I pretend I'm in the top of a tree, rocking to and fro. But finally I get pretending everything, and finally I have to pretend I'm sane when I know I'm not.'

'If you get thinking that way you will go crazy.'

'Look, Adrian.' She held up the string of pearls before clasping them on. 'Aren't they lovely?'

In Adrian's impatience she seemed to move around the cabin like a figure in a slow-motion picture. After a moment he demanded: 'Are you going to be long? It's stifling in here.'

'You go on!' she fired up.

'I don't want – '

'Go on, please! You just make me nervous trying to hurry me.'

With a show of reluctance he left her. After a moment's hesitation he went down a flight to a deck below and knocked at a door.

'Betsy.'

'Just a minute.'

She came out in the corridor attired in a red pea-jacket and trousers borrowed from the elevator boy.

'Do elevator boys have fleas?' she demanded. 'I've got everything in the world on under this as a precaution.'

'I had to see you,' he said quickly.

'Careful,' she whispered. 'Mrs Worden, who's supposed to be chaperoning me, is across the way. She's sick.'

'I'm sick for you.'

They kissed suddenly, clung close together in the narrow corridor, swaying to and fro with the motion of the ship.

'Don't go away,' she murmured.

'I've got to. I've – '

Her youth seemed to flow into him, bearing him up into a delicate romantic ecstasy that transcended passion. He couldn't relinquish it; he had discovered something that he had thought was lost with his own youth for ever. As he walked along the passage he knew that he had stopped thinking, no longer dared to think.

He met Eva going into the bar.

'Where've you been?' she asked with a strained smile.

'To see about the table.'

She was lovely; her cool distinction conquered the trite costume and filled him with a resurgence of approval and pride. They sat down at a table.

The gale was rising hour by hour and the mere traversing of a passage had become a rough matter. In every stateroom trunks were lashed to the washstands, and the *Vestris* disaster was being reviewed in detail by nervous ladies, tossing, ill and wretched, upon their beds. In the smoking-room a stout gentleman had been hurled backwards and suffered a badly cut head; and now the lighter chairs and tables were stacked and roped against the wall.

The crowd who had donned fancy dress and were dining together had swollen to about sixteen. The only remaining qualification for membership was the ability to reach the smoking-room. They ranged from a Groton-Harvard lawyer to an ungrammatical broker they had nicknamed Gyp the Blood, but distinctions had disappeared; for the moment they were samurai, chosen from several hundred for their triumphant resistance to the storm.

The gala dinner, overhung sardonically with lanterns and streamers, was interrupted by great communal slides across the room, precipitate retirements and spilled wine, while the ship roared and complained that under the panoply of a palace it was a ship after all. Upstairs afterwards a dozen couples tried to dance, shuffling and galloping here and there in a crazy fandango, thrust around fantastically by a will alien to their own. In view of the condition of tortured hundreds below, there grew to be something indecent about it, like a revel in a house of mourning, and presently there was an egress of the ever-dwindling survivors towards the bar.

As the evening passed, Eva's feeling of unreality increased. Adrian had disappeared – presumably with Miss D'Amido – and her mind, distorted by illness and champagne, began to enlarge upon the fact; annoyance changed slowly to dark and brooding anger, grief to desperation. She had never tried to bind Adrian, never needed to – for they were serious people, with all sorts of mutual interests, and satisfied with each other – but this was a breach of the contract, this was cruel. How could he think that she didn't know?

It seemed several hours later that he leaned over her chair in the bar, where she was giving some woman an impassioned lecture upon babies, and said: 'Eva, we'd better turn in.'

Her lip curled. 'So that you can leave me there and then come back to your eighteen-year – '

'Be quiet.'

'I won't come to bed.'

'Very well. Good-night.'

More time passed and the people at the table changed. The stewards wanted to close up the room, and thinking of Adrian – her Adrian – off somewhere saying tender things to someone fresh and lovely, Eva began to cry.

'But he's gone to bed,' her last attendants assured her. 'We saw him go.'

She shook her head. She knew better. Adrian was lost. The long seven-year dream was broken. Probably she was punished for something she had done; as this thought occurred to her the shrieking timbers overhead began to mutter that she had guessed at last. This was for the selfishness to her mother, who hadn't wanted her to marry Adrian; for all the sins and omissions of her life. She stood up, saying she must go out and get some air.

The deck was dark and drenched with wind and rain. The ship pounded through valleys, fleeing from black mountains of water that roared towards it. Looking out at the night, Eva saw that there was no chance for them unless she could make atonement, propitiate the storm. It was Adrian's love that was demanded of her. Deliberately she unclasped her pearl necklace, lifted it to her lips – for she knew that with it went the freshest, fairest part of her life – and flung it out into the gale.

3

When Adrian awoke it was lunchtime, but he knew that some heavier sound than the bugle had called him up from his deep sleep. Then he realised that the trunk had broken loose from its lashings and was being thrown back and forth between a wardrobe and Eva's bed. With an exclamation he jumped up, but she was unharmed – still in costume and stretched out in deep sleep. When the steward had helped him secure the trunk, Eva opened a single eye.

'How are you?' he demanded, sitting on the side of her bed.

She closed the eye, opened it again.

'We're in a hurricane now,' he told her. 'The steward says it's the worst he's seen in twenty years.'

'My head,' she muttered. 'Hold my head.'

'How?'

'In front. My eyes are going out. I think I'm dying.'

'Nonsense. Do you want the doctor?'

She gave a funny little gasp that frightened him; he rang and sent the steward for the doctor.

The young doctor was pale and tired. There was a stubble of beard upon his face. He bowed curtly as he came in and, turning to Adrian, said with scant ceremony: 'What's the matter?'

'My wife doesn't feel well.'

'Well, what is it you want – a bromide?'

A little annoyed by his shortness, Adrian said: 'You'd better examine her and see what she needs.'

'She needs a bromide,' said the doctor. 'I've given orders that she is not to have any more to drink on this ship.'

'Why not?' demanded Adrian in astonishment.

'Don't you know what happened last night?'

'Why, no, I was asleep.'

'Mrs Smith wandered around the boat for an hour, not knowing what she was doing. A sailor was sent to follow her, and then the medical stewardess tried to get her to bed, and your wife insulted her.'

'Oh, my heavens!' cried Eva faintly.

'The nurse and I had both been up all night with Steward Carton, who died this morning.' He picked up his case. 'I'll send down a bromide for Mrs Smith. Goodbye.'

For a few minutes there was silence in the cabin. Then Adrian put his arm around her quickly.

'Never mind,' he said. 'We'll straighten it out.'

'I remember now.' Her voice was an awed whisper. 'My pearls. I threw them overboard.'

'Threw them overboard!'

'Then I began looking for you.'

'But I was here in bed.'

'I didn't believe it; I thought you were with that girl.'

'She collapsed during dinner. I was taking a nap down here.'

Frowning, he rang the bell and asked the steward for luncheon and a bottle of beer.

'Sorry, but we can't serve any beer to your cabin, sir.'

When he went out Adrian exploded: 'This is an outrage. You were simply crazy from that storm and they can't be so high-handed. I'll see the captain.'

'Isn't that awful?' Eva murmured. 'The poor man died.'

She turned over and began to sob into her pillow. There was a knock at the door.

'Can I come in?'

The assiduous Mr Butterworth, surprisingly healthy and immaculate, came into the crazily tipping cabin.

'Well, how's the mystic?' he demanded of Eva. 'Do you remember praying to the elements in the bar last night?'

'I don't want to remember anything about last night.'

They told him about the stewardess, and with the telling the situation lightened; they all laughed together.

'I'm going to get you some beer to have with your luncheon,' Butterworth said. 'You ought to get up on deck.'

'Don't go,' Eva said. 'You look so cheerful and nice.'

'Just for ten minutes.'

When he had gone, Adrian rang for two baths.

'The thing is to put on our best clothes and walk proudly three times around the deck,' he said.

'Yes.' After a moment she added abstractedly: 'I like that young man. He was awfully nice to me last night when you'd disappeared.'

The bath steward appeared with the information that bathing was too dangerous today. They were in the midst of the wildest hurricane in the North Atlantic in ten years; there were two broken arms this morning from attempts to take baths. An elderly lady had been thrown down a staircase and was not expected to live. Furthermore, they had received the SOS signal from several boats this morning.

'Will we go to help them?'

'They're all behind us, sir, so we have to leave them to the *Mauretania*. If we tried to turn in this sea the portholes would be smashed.'

This array of calamities minimised their own troubles. Having eaten a sort of luncheon and drunk the beer provided by Butterworth, they dressed and went on deck.

Despite the fact that it was only possible to progress step by step, holding on to rope or rail, more people were abroad than on the day before. Fear had driven them from their cabins, where the trunks bumped and the waves pounded the portholes, and they awaited momentarily the call to the boats. Indeed, as Adrian and Eva stood on the transverse deck above the second class, there was a bugle call, followed by a gathering of stewards and stewardesses on the deck below. But the boat was sound: it had outlasted one of its cargo – Steward James Carton was being buried at sea.

It was very British and sad. There were the rows of stiff, disciplined men and women standing in the driving rain, and there was a shape covered by the flag of the Empire that lived by the sea. The chief purser read the service, a hymn was sung, the body slid off into the hurricane. With Eva's burst of wild weeping for this humble end, some last string snapped within her. Now she really didn't care. She responded eagerly when Butterworth suggested that he get some champagne to their cabin. Her mood worried Adrian; she wasn't used to so much drinking and he wondered what he ought to do. At his suggestion that they sleep instead, she merely laughed, and the bromide the doctor had sent stood untouched on the washstand. Pretending to listen to the insipidities of several Mr Stacombs, he watched her; to his surprise and discomfort she seemed on intimate and even sentimental terms with Butterworth and he wondered if this was a form of revenge for his attention to Betsy D'Amido.

The cabin was full of smoke, the voices went on incessantly, the suspension of activity, the waiting for the storm's end, was getting on his nerves. They had been at sea only four days; it was like a year.

The two Mr Stacombs left finally, but Butterworth remained. Eva was urging him to go for another bottle of champagne.

'We've had enough,' objected Adrian. 'We ought to go to bed.'

'I won't go to bed!' she burst out. 'You must be crazy! You play around all you want, and then, when I find somebody I – I like, you want to put me to bed.'

'You're hysterical.'

'On the contrary, I've never been so sane.'

'I think you'd better leave us, Butterworth,' Adrian said. 'Eva doesn't know what she's saying.'

'He won't go, I won't let him go.' She clasped Butterworth's hand passionately. 'He's the only person that's been half decent to me.'

'You'd better go, Butterworth,' repeated Adrian.

The young man looked at him uncertainly.

'It seems to me you're being unjust to your wife,' he ventured.

'My wife isn't herself.'

'That's no reason for bullying her.'

Adrian lost his temper. 'You get out of here!' he cried.

The two men looked at each other for a moment in silence. Then Butterworth turned to Eva, said, 'I'll be back later,' and left the cabin.

'Eva, you've got to pull yourself together,' said Adrian when the door closed.

She didn't answer, looking at him from sullen, half-closed eyes.

'I'll order dinner here for us both and then we'll try to get some sleep.'

'I want to go up and send a wireless.'

'Who to?'

'Some Paris lawyer. I want a divorce.'

In spite of his annoyance, he laughed. 'Don't be silly.'

'Then I want to see the children.'

'Well, go and see them. I'll order dinner.'

He waited for her in the cabin twenty minutes. Then impatiently he opened the door across the corridor; the nurse told him that Mrs Smith had not been there.

With a sudden prescience of disaster he ran upstairs, glanced in the bar, the salons, even knocked at Butterworth's door. Then a quick round of the decks, feeling his way through the black spray and rain. A sailor stopped him at a network of ropes.

'Orders are no one goes by, sir. A wave has gone over the wireless room.'

'Have you seen a lady?'

'There was a young lady here – ' He stopped and glanced around. 'Hello, she's gone.'

'She went up the stairs!' Adrian said anxiously. 'Up to the wireless room!'

The sailor ran up to the boat deck; stumbling and slipping, Adrian followed. As he cleared the protected sides of the companionway, a tremendous body of water struck the boat a staggering blow and, as she keeled over to an angle of forty-five degrees, he was thrown in a helpless roll down the drenched deck, to bring up dizzy and bruised against a stanchion.

'Eva!' he called. His voice was soundless in the black storm. Against the faint light of the wireless-room window he saw the sailor making his way forward.

'Eva!'

The wind blew him like a sail up against a lifeboat. Then there was another shuddering crash, and high over his head, over the very boat, he saw a gigantic, glittering white wave, and in the split second that it balanced there he became conscious of Eva, standing beside a ventilator twenty feet away. Pushing out from the stanchion, he lunged desperately towards her, just as the wave broke with a smashing roar. For a moment the rushing water was five feet deep, sweeping with enormous force towards the side, and then a human body was washed against him, and frantically he clutched it and was swept with it back towards the rail. He felt his body bump against it, but desperately he held on to his burden; then, as the ship rocked slowly back, the two of them, still joined by his fierce grip, were rolled out exhausted on the wet planks. For a moment he knew no more.

4

Two days later, as the boat-train moved tranquilly south towards Paris, Adrian tried to persuade his children to look out of the window at the Norman countryside.

'It's beautiful,' he assured them. 'All the little farms like toys. Why, in heaven's name, won't you look?'

'I like the boat better,' said Estelle.

Her parents exchanged an infanticidal glance.

'The boat is still rocking for me,' Eva said with a shiver. 'Is it for you?'

'No. Somehow, it all seems a long way off. Even the passengers looked unfamiliar going through the customs.'

'Most of them hadn't appeared above ground before.'

He hesitated. 'By the way, I cashed Butterworth's cheque for him.'

'You're a fool. You'll never see the money again.'

'He must have needed it pretty badly or he would not have come to me.'

A pale and wan girl, passing along the corridor, recognised them and put her head through the doorway.

'How do you feel?'

'Awful.'

'Me, too,' agreed Miss D'Amido. 'I'm vainly hoping my fiancé will recognise me at the Gare du Nord. Do you know two waves went over the wireless room?'

'So we heard,' Adrian answered dryly.

She passed gracefully along the corridor and out of their life.

'The real truth is that none of it happened,' said Adrian after a moment. 'It was a nightmare – an incredibly awful nightmare.'

'Then, where are my pearls?'

'Darling, there are better pearls in Paris. I'll take the responsibility for those pearls. My real belief is that you saved the boat.'

'Adrian, let's never get to know anyone else, but just stay together always – just we two.'

He tucked her arm under his and they sat close. 'Who do you suppose those Adrian Smiths on the boat were?' he demanded. 'It certainly wasn't me.'

'Nor me.'

'It was two other people,' he said, nodding to himself. 'There are so many Smiths in this world.'

At Your Age

Saturday Evening Post (17 August 1929)

1

Tom Squires came into the drugstore to buy a toothbrush, a can of talcum, a gargle, Castile soap, Epsom salts and a box of cigars. Having lived alone for many years, he was methodical, and while waiting to be served he held the list in his hand. It was Christmas week and Minneapolis was under two feet of exhilarating, constantly refreshed snow; with his cane Tom knocked two clean crusts of it from his overshoes. Then, looking up, he saw the blonde girl.

She was a rare blonde, even in that Promised Land of Scandinavians, where pretty blondes are not rare. There was warm colour in her cheeks, lips and pink little hands that folded powders into papers; her hair, in long braids twisted about her head, was shining and alive. She seemed to Tom suddenly the cleanest person he knew of, and he caught his breath as he stepped forward and looked into her grey eyes.

'A can of talcum.'

'What kind?'

'Any kind . . . That's fine.'

She looked back at him apparently without self-consciousness, and, as the list melted away, his heart raced with it wildly.

'I am not old,' he wanted to say. 'At fifty I'm younger than most men of forty. Don't I interest you at all?'

But she only said, 'What kind of gargle?'

And he answered, 'What can you recommend? . . . That's fine.'

Almost painfully he took his eyes from her, went out and got into his coupé.

'If that young idiot only knew what an old imbecile like me could do for her,' he thought humorously – 'what worlds I could open out to her!'

As he drove away into the winter twilight he followed this train of thought to a totally unprecedented conclusion. Perhaps the time of day was the responsible stimulant, for the shop windows glowing into the cold, the tinkling bells of a delivery sleigh, the white gloss left by shovels on the sidewalks, the enormous distance of the stars, brought back the feel of other nights thirty years ago. For an instant the girls he had known then slipped like phantoms out of their dull matronly selves of today and fluttered past him with frosty, seductive laughter, until a pleasant shiver crawled up his spine.

'Youth! Youth! Youth!' he apostrophised with conscious lack of originality, and, as a somewhat ruthless and domineering man of no morals whatsoever, he considered going back to the drugstore to seek the blonde girl's address. It was not his sort of thing, so the half-formed intention passed; the idea remained.

'Youth, by heaven – youth!' he repeated under his breath. 'I want it near me, all around me, just once more before I'm too old to care.'

He was tall, lean and handsome, with the ruddy, bronzed face of a sportsman and a just faintly greying moustache. Once he had been among the city's best beaus, organiser of cotillions and charity balls, popular with men and women, and with several generations of them. After the war he had suddenly felt poor, gone into business, and in ten years accumulated nearly a million dollars. Tom Squires was not introspective, but he perceived now that the wheel of his life had revolved again, bringing up forgotten, yet familiar, dreams and yearnings. Entering his house, he turned suddenly to a pile of disregarded invitations to see whether or not he had been bidden to a dance tonight.

Throughout his dinner, which he ate alone at the Downtown Club, his eyes were half closed and on his face was a faint smile. He was practising so that he would be able to laugh at himself painlessly, if necessary.

'I don't even know what they talk about,' he admitted. 'They pet – prominent broker goes to petting party with débutante. What is a petting party? Do they serve refreshments? Will I have to learn to play a saxophone?'

These matters, lately as remote as China in a newsreel, came alive to him. They were serious questions. At ten o'clock he walked up the steps of the College Club to a private dance with the same sense of entering a new world as when he had gone into a training camp back in 1917. He spoke to a hostess of his generation and to her daughter, overwhelmingly of another, and sat down in a corner to acclimate himself.

He was not alone long. A silly young man named Leland Jaques, who lived across the street from Tom, remarked him kindly and came over to brighten his life. He was such an exceedingly fatuous young man that, for a moment, Tom was annoyed, but he perceived craftily that he might be of service.

'Hello, Mr Squires. How are you, sir?'

'Fine, thanks, Leland. Quite a dance.'

As one man of the world with another, Mr Jaques sat, or lay, down on the couch and lit – or so it seemed to Tom – three or four cigarettes at once.

'You should of been here last night, Mr Squires. Oh, boy, that was a party and a half! The Caulkins. Hap-past five!'

'Who's that girl who changes partners every minute?' Tom asked . . . 'No, the one in white passing the door.'

'That's Annie Lorry.'

'Arthur Lorry's daughter?'

'Yes.'

'She seems popular.'

'About the most popular girl in town – anyway, at a dance.'

'Not popular except at dances?'

'Oh, sure, but she hangs around with Randy Cambell all the time.'

'What Cambell?'

'D. B.'

There were new names in town in the last decade.

'It's a boy-and-girl affair.' Pleased with this phrase, Jaques tried to repeat it: 'One of those boy-and-girls affair – boys-and-girl affairs – ' He gave it up and lit several more cigarettes, crushing out the first series on Tom's lap.

'Does she drink?'

'Not especially. At least I never saw her passed out . . . That's Randy Cambell just cut in on her now.'

They were a nice couple. Her beauty sparkled bright against his strong, tall form, and they floated hoveringly, delicately, like two people in a nice, amusing dream. They came near and Tom admired the faint dust of powder over her freshness, the guarded sweetness of her smile, the fragility of her body calculated by nature to a millimetre to suggest a bud, yet guarantee a flower. Her innocent, passionate eyes were brown, perhaps; but almost violet in the silver light.

'Is she out this year?'

'Who?'

'Miss Lorry.'

'Yes.'

Although the girl's loveliness interested Tom, he was unable to picture himself as one of the attentive, grateful queue that pursued her around the room. Better meet her when the holidays were over and most of these young men were back in college 'where they belonged'. Tom Squires was old enough to wait.

He waited a fortnight while the city sank into the endless Northern midwinter, where grey skies were friendlier than metallic blue skies, and dusk, whose lights were a reassuring glimpse into the continuity of human cheer, was warmer than the afternoons of bloodless sunshine. The coat of snow lost its press and became soiled and shabby, and ruts froze in the street; some of the big houses on Crest Avenue began to close as their occupants went South. In those cold days Tom asked Annie and her parents to go as his guests to the last Bachelors' Ball.

The Lorrys were an old family in Minneapolis, grown a little harassed and poor since the war. Mrs Lorry, a contemporary of Tom's, was not surprised that he should send mother and daughter orchids and dine them luxuriously in his apartment on fresh caviare, quail and champagne. Annie saw him only dimly – he lacked vividness, as the old do for the young – but she perceived his interest in her and performed for him the traditional ritual of young beauty – smiles, polite, wide-eyed attention, a profile held obligingly in this light or in that. At the ball he danced with her twice, and, though she was teased about it, she was flattered that such a man of the world – he had become that instead of a mere old man – had singled her out. She accepted his invitation to the symphony the following week, with the idea that it would be uncouth to refuse.

There were several 'nice invitations' like that. Sitting beside him, she dozed in the warm shadow of Brahms and thought of Randy Cambell and other romantic nebulosities who might appear tomorrow. Feeling casually mellow one afternoon, she deliberately provoked Tom to kiss her on the way home, but she wanted to laugh when he took her hands and told her fervently he was falling in love.

'But how could you?' she protested. 'Really, you musn't say such crazy things. I won't go out with you any more, and then you'll be sorry.'

A few days later her mother spoke to her as Tom waited outside in his car: 'Who's that, Annie?'

'Mr Squires.'

'Shut the door a minute. You're seeing him quite a bit.'

'Why not?'

'Well, dear, he's fifty years old.'

'But, mother, there's hardly anybody else in town.'

'But you musn't get any silly ideas about him.'

'Don't worry. Actually, he bores me to extinction most of the time.' She came to a sudden decision: 'I'm not going to see him any more. I just couldn't get out of going with him this afternoon.'

And that night, as she stood by her door in the circle of Randy Cambell's arm, Tom and his single kiss had no existence for her.

'Oh, I do love you so,' Randy whispered. 'Kiss me once more.'

Their cool cheeks and warm lips met in the crisp darkness, and, watching the icy moon over his shoulder, Annie knew that she was his surely and, pulling his face down, kissed him again, trembling with emotion.

'When'll you marry me then?' he whispered.

'When can you – we afford it?'

'Couldn't you announce our engagement? If you knew the misery of having you out with somebody else and then making love to you.'

'Oh, Randy, you ask so much.'

'It's so awful to say good-night. Can't I come in for a minute?'

'Yes.'

Sitting close together in a trance before the flickering, lessening fire, they were oblivious that their common fate was being coolly weighed by a man of fifty who lay in a hot bath some blocks away.

2

Tom Squires had guessed from Annie's extremely kind and detached manner of the afternoon that he had failed to interest her. He had promised himself that in such an eventuality he would drop the matter, but now he found himself in no such humour. He did not want to marry her; he simply wanted to see her and be with her a little; and up to the moment of her sweetly casual, half passionate, yet wholly unemotional kiss, giving her up would have been easy, for he was past the romantic age; but since that kiss the thought of her made his heart move up a few inches in his chest and beat there steady and fast.

'But this is the time to get out,' he said to himself. 'My age; no possible right to force myself into her life.'

He rubbed himself dry, brushed his hair before the mirror, and, as he laid down the comb, said decisively: 'That is that.' And after reading for an hour he turned out the lamp with a snap and repeated aloud: 'That is that.'

In other words, that was not that at all, and the click of material things did not finish off Annie Lorry as a business decision might be settled by the tap of a pencil on the table.

'I'm going to carry this matter a little further,' he said to himself about half-past four; on that acknowledgement he turned over and found sleep.

In the morning she had receded somewhat, but by four o'clock in the afternoon she was all around him – the phone was for calling her, a woman's footfalls passing his office were her footfalls, the snow outside the window was blowing, perhaps, against her rosy face.

'There is always the little plan I thought of last night,' he said to himself. 'In ten years I'll be sixty, and then no youth, no beauty for me ever any more.'

In a sort of panic he took a sheet of notepaper and composed a carefully phrased letter to Annie's mother, asking permission to pay court to her daughter. He took it himself into the hall, but before the letter slide he tore it up and dropped the pieces in a cuspidor.

'I couldn't do such an underhand trick,' he told himself, 'at my age.' But this self-congratulation was premature, for he rewrote the letter and mailed it before he left his office that night.

Next day the reply he had counted on arrived – he could have guessed its very words in advance. It was a curt and indignant refusal. It ended:

I think it best that you and my daughter meet no more.
Very sincerely yours,
MABEL TOLLMAN LORRY

'And now,' Tom thought coolly, 'we'll see what the girl says to that.' He wrote a note to Annie. Her mother's letter had surprised him, it said, but perhaps it was best that they should meet no more, in view of her mother's attitude.

By return post came Annie's defiant answer to her mother's fiat: 'This isn't the Dark Ages. I'll see you whenever I like.' She named a rendezvous for the following afternoon. Her mother's short-sightedness brought about what he had failed to achieve directly; for where Annie had been on the point of dropping him, she was now determined to do nothing of the sort. And the secrecy engendered by disapproval at home simply contributed the missing excitement. As February hardened into deep, solemn, interminable winter, she met him frequently and on a new basis. Sometimes they drove over to St Paul to see a picture or to have dinner; sometimes they parked far out on a boulevard in his coupé, while the bitter sleet glazed the windshield to opacity and furred his lamps with ermine. Often he brought along something special to drink – enough to make her gay, but, carefully, never more; for mingled with his other emotions about her was something paternally concerned.

Laying his cards on the table, he told her that it was her mother who had unwittingly pushed her towards him, but Annie only laughed at his duplicity.

She was having a better time with him than with anyone else she had ever known. In place of the selfish exigency of a younger man, he showed her a never-failing consideration. What if his eyes were tired, his cheeks a little leathery and veined, if his will was masculine and strong. Moreover, his experience was a window looking out upon a wider, richer world; and with Randy Cambell next day she would feel less taken care of, less valued, less rare.

It was Tom now who was vaguely discontented. He had what he wanted – her youth at his side – and he felt that anything further would be a mistake. His liberty was precious to him and he could offer her only a dozen years before he would be old, but she had become something precious to him and he perceived that drifting wasn't fair. Then one day late in February the matter was decided out of hand.

They had ridden home from St Paul and dropped into the College Club for tea, breaking together through the drifts that masked the walk and rimmed the door. It was a revolving door; a young man came around in it, and stepping into his space, they smelt onions and whiskey. The door revolved again after them, and he was back within, facing them. It was Randy Cambell; his face was flushed, his eyes dull and hard.

'Hello, beautiful,' he said, approaching Annie.

'Don't come so close,' she protested lightly. 'You smell of onions.'

'You're particular all of a sudden.'

'Always. I'm always particular.' Annie made a slight movement back towards Tom.

'Not always,' said Randy unpleasantly. Then, with increased emphasis and a fractional glance at Tom: 'Not always.' With his remark he seemed to join the hostile world outside. 'And I'll just give you a tip,' he continued: 'Your mother's inside.'

The jealous ill-temper of another generation reached Tom only faintly, like the protest of a child, but at this impertinent warning he bristled with annoyance.

'Come on, Annie,' he said brusquely. 'We'll go in.'

With her glance uneasily averted from Randy, Annie followed Tom into the big room.

It was sparsely populated; three middle-aged women sat near the fire. Momentarily Annie drew back, then she walked towards them.

'Hello, mother . . . Mrs Trumble . . . Aunt Caroline.'

The two latter responded; Mrs Trumble even nodded faintly at Tom. But Annie's mother got to her feet without a word, her eyes frozen, her mouth drawn. For a moment she stood staring at her daughter; then she turned abruptly and left the room.

Tom and Annie found a table across the room.

'Wasn't she terrible?' said Annie, breathing aloud. He didn't answer.

'For three days she hasn't spoken to me.' Suddenly she broke out: 'Oh, people can be so small! I was going to sing the leading part in the Junior League show, and yesterday Cousin Mary Betts, the president, came to me and said I couldn't.'

'Why not?'

'Because a representative Junior League girl mustn't defy her mother. As if I were a naughty child!'

Tom stared at a row of cups on the mantelpiece – two or three of them bore his name. 'Perhaps she was right,' he said suddenly. 'When I begin to do harm to you it's time to stop.'

'What do you mean?'

At her shocked voice his heart poured a warm liquid forth into his body, but he answered quietly: 'You remember I told you I was going South? Well, I'm going tomorrow.'

There was an argument, but he had made up his mind. At the station next evening she wept and clung to him.

'Thank you for the happiest month I've had in years,' he said.

'But you'll come back, Tom.'

'I'll be two months in Mexico; then I'm going East for a few weeks.'

He tried to sound fortunate, but the frozen city he was leaving seemed to be in blossom. Her frozen breath was a flower on the air, and his heart sank as he realised that some young man was waiting outside to take her home in a car hung with blooms.

'Goodbye, Annie. Goodbye, sweet!'

Two days later he spent the morning in Houston with Hal Meigs, a classmate at Yale.

'You're in luck for such an old fella,' said Meigs at luncheon, 'because I'm going to introduce you to the cutest little travelling companion you ever saw, who's going all the way to Mexico City.'

The lady in question was frankly pleased to learn at the station that she was not returning alone. She and Tom dined together on the train and later played rummy for an hour; but when, at ten o'clock, standing in the door of the stateroom, she turned back to him suddenly with a certain look, frank and unmistakable, and stood there holding that look for a long moment, Tom Squires was suddenly in the grip of an emotion that was not the one in question. He wanted desperately to see Annie, call her for a second on the phone, and then fall asleep, knowing she was young and pure as a star, and safe in bed.

'Good-night,' he said, trying to keep any repulsion out of his voice.

'Oh! Good-night.'

Arriving in El Paso next day, he drove over the border to Juarez. It was bright and hot, and after leaving his bags at the station he went into a bar for an iced drink; as he sipped it a girl's voice addressed him thickly from the table behind: 'You'n American?'

He had noticed her slumped forward on her elbows as he came in; now, turning, he faced a young girl of about seventeen, obviously drunk, yet with gentility in her unsteady, sprawling voice.

The American bartender leaned confidentially forward. 'I don't know what to do about her,' he said. 'She come in about three o'clock with two young fellows – one of them her sweetie. They had a fight and the men went off, and this one's been here ever since.'

A spasm of distaste passed over Tom – the rules of his generation were outraged and defiled. That an American girl should be drunk and deserted in a tough foreign town – that such things happened, might happen to Annie. He looked at his watch, hesitated.

'Has she got a bill?' he asked.

'She owes for five gins. But suppose her boyfriends come back?'

'Tell them she's at the Roosevelt Hotel in El Paso.'

Approaching, he put his hand on her shoulder. She looked up.

'You look like Santa Claus,' she said vaguely. 'You couldn't possibly be Santa Claus, could you?'

'I'm going to take you to El Paso.'

'Well,' she considered, 'you look perfectly safe to me.'

She was so young – a drenched little rose. He could have wept for her wretched unconsciousness of the old facts, the old penalties of life. Jousting at nothing in an empty tilt yard with a shaking spear. The taxi moved too slowly through the suddenly poisonous night.

Having explained things to a reluctant night clerk, he went out and found a telegraph office.

'Have given up Mexican trip,' he wired. 'Leaving here tonight. Please meet train in the St Paul station at three o'clock and ride with me to Minneapolis, as I can't spare you for another minute. All my love.'

He could at least keep an eye on her, advise her, see what she did with her life. That silly mother of hers!

On the train, as the baked tropical lands and green fields fell away and the North swept near again with patches of snow, then fields of it, fierce winds in the vestibule and bleak, hibernating farms, he paced the corridors with intolerable restlessness. When they drew into the St Paul station he swung himself off like a young man and searched the platform eagerly, but his eyes failed to find her. He had counted on those few minutes between the cities; they had become a symbol of her fidelity to their friendship, and as the train started again he searched it desperately from smoker to observation car. But he could not find her, and now he knew that he was mad for her; at the thought that she had taken his advice and plunged into affairs with other men, he grew weak with fear.

Drawing into Minneapolis, his hands fumbled so that he must call the porter to fasten his baggage. Then there was an interminable wait in the corridor while the baggage was taken off and he was pressed up against a girl in a squirrel-trimmed coat.

'Tom!'

'Well, I'll be – '

Her arms went up around his neck. 'But, Tom,' she cried, 'I've been right here in this car since St Paul!'

His cane fell in the corridor, he drew her very tenderly close and their lips met like starved hearts.

3

The new intimacy of their definite engagement brought Tom a feeling of young happiness. He awoke on winter mornings with the sense of undeserved joy hovering in the room; meeting young men, he found himself matching the vigour of his mind and body against theirs. Suddenly his life had a purpose and a background; he felt rounded and complete. On grey March afternoons when she wandered familiarly in his apartment the warm sureties of his youth flooded back – ecstasy and poignancy, the mortal and the eternal posed in their immemorially tragic juxtaposition and, a little astounded, he found himself relishing the very terminology of young romance. But he was more thoughtful than a younger lover; and to Annie he seemed to 'know everything', to stand holding open the gates for her passage into the truly golden world.

'We'll go to Europe first,' he said.

'Oh, we'll go there a lot, won't we? Let's spend our winters in Italy and the spring in Paris.'

'But, little Annie, there's business.'

'Well, we'll stay away as much as we can anyhow. I hate Minneapolis.'

'Oh, no.' He was a little shocked. 'Minneapolis is all right.'

'When you're here it's all right.'

Mrs Lorry yielded at length to the inevitable. With ill grace she acknowledged the engagement, asking only that the marriage should not take place until fall.

'Such a long time,' Annie sighed.

'After all, I'm your mother. It's so little to ask.'

It was a long winter, even in a land of long winters. March was full of billowy drifts, and when it seemed at last as though the cold must be defeated, there was a series of blizzards, desperate as last stands. The people waited; their first energy to resist was spent, and man, like weather, simply hung on. There was less to do now and the general restlessness was expressed by surliness in daily contacts. Then, early in April, with a long sigh the ice cracked, the snow ran into the ground and the green, eager spring broke up through.

One day, riding along a slushy road in a fresh, damp breeze with a little starved, smothered grass in it, Annie began to cry. Sometimes she cried for nothing, but this time Tom suddenly stopped the car and put his arm around her.

'Why do you cry like that? Are you unhappy?'

'Oh, no, no!' she protested.

'But you cried yesterday the same way. And you wouldn't tell me why. You must always tell me.'

'Nothing, except the spring. It smells so good, and it always has so many sad thoughts and memories in it.'

'It's our spring, my sweetheart,' he said. 'Annie, don't let's wait. Let's be married in June.'

'I promised mother, but if you like we can announce our engagement in June.'

The spring came fast now. The sidewalks were damp, then dry, and the children roller-skated on them and boys played baseball in the soft, vacant lots. Tom got up elaborate picnics of Annie's contemporaries and encouraged her to play golf and tennis with them. Abruptly, with a final, triumphant lurch of nature, it was full summer.

On a lovely May evening Tom came up the Lorrys' walk and sat down beside Annie's mother on the porch.

'It's so pleasant,' he said, 'I thought Annie and I would walk instead of driving this evening. I want to show her the funny old house I was born in.'

'On Chambers Street, wasn't it? Annie'll be home in a few minutes. She went riding with some young people after dinner.'

'Yes, on Chambers Street.'

He looked at his watch presently, hoping Annie would come while it was still light enough to see. Quarter of nine. He frowned. She had kept him waiting the night before, kept him waiting an hour yesterday afternoon.

'If I was twenty-one,' he said to himself, 'I'd make scenes and we'd both be miserable.'

He and Mrs Lorry talked; the warmth of the night precipitated the vague evening lassitude of the fifties and softened them both, and for the first time since his attentions to Annie began, there was no unfriendliness between them. By and by long silences fell, broken only by the scratch of a match or the creak of her swinging settee. When Mr Lorry came home, Tom threw away his second cigar in surprise and looked at his watch; it was after ten.

'Annie's late,' Mrs Lorry said.

'I hope there's nothing wrong,' said Tom anxiously. 'Who is she with?'

'There were four when they started out. Randy Cambell and another couple – I didn't notice who. They were only going for a soda.'

'I hope there hasn't been any trouble. Perhaps – Do you think I ought to go and see?'

'Ten isn't late nowadays. You'll find – ' Remembering that Tom Squires was marrying Annie, not adopting her, she kept herself from adding: 'You'll get used to it.'

Her husband excused himself and went up to bed, and the conversation became more forced and desultory. When the church clock over the way struck eleven they both broke off and listened to the beats. Twenty minutes later, just as Tom impatiently crushed out his last cigar, an automobile drifted down the street and came to rest in front of the door.

For a minute no one moved on the porch or in the auto. Then

Annie, with a hat in her hand, got out and came quickly up the walk. Defying the tranquil night, the car snorted away.

'Oh, hello!' she cried. 'I'm so sorry! What time is it? Am I terribly late?'

Tom didn't answer. The street lamp threw wine colour upon her face and expressed with a shadow the heightened flush of her cheek. Her dress was crushed, her hair was in brief, expressive disarray. But it was the strange little break in her voice that made him afraid to speak, made him turn his eyes aside.

'What happened?' Mrs Lorry asked casually.

'Oh, a blow-out and something wrong with the engine – and we lost our way. Is it terribly late?'

And then, as she stood before them, her hat still in her hand, her breast rising and falling a little, her eyes wide and bright, Tom realised with a shock that he and her mother were people of the same age looking at a person of another. Try as he might, he could not separate himself from Mrs Lorry. When she excused herself he suppressed a frantic tendency to say, 'But why should you go now? After sitting here all evening?'

They were alone. Annie came up to him and pressed his hand. He had never been so conscious of her beauty; her damp hands were touched with dew.

'You were out with young Cambell,' he said.

'Yes. Oh, don't be mad. I feel – I feel so upset tonight.'

'Upset?'

She sat down, whimpering a little.

'I couldn't help it. Please don't be mad. He wanted so for me to take a ride with him and it was such a wonderful night, so I went just for an hour. And we began talking and I didn't realise the time. I felt so sorry for him.'

'How do you think I felt?' He scorned himself, but it was said now.

'Don't, Tom. I told you I was terribly upset. I want to go to bed.'

'I understand. Good-night, Annie.'

'Oh, please don't act that way, Tom. Can't you understand?'

But he could, and that was just the trouble. With the courteous bow of another generation, he walked down the steps and off into the obliterating moonlight. In a moment he was just a shadow passing the street lamps and then a faint footfall up the street.

4

All through that summer he often walked abroad in the evenings. He liked to stand for a minute in front of the house where he was born, and then in front of another house where he had been a little boy. On his customary routes there were other sharp landmarks of the 90s, converted habitats of gaieties that no longer existed – the shell of Jansen's Livery Stables and the old Nushka Rink, where every winter his father had curled on the well-kept ice.

'And it's a darn pity,' he would mutter. 'A darn pity.'

He had a tendency, too, to walk past the lights of a certain drugstore, because it seemed to him that it had contained the seed of another and nearer branch of the past. Once he went in, and enquiring casually about the blonde clerk, found that she had married and departed several months before. He obtained her name and on an impulse sent her a wedding present 'from a dumb admirer', for he felt he owed something to her for his happiness and pain. He had lost the battle against youth and spring, and with his grief paid the penalty for age's unforgivable sin – refusing to die. But he could not have walked down wasted into the darkness without being used up a little; what he had wanted, after all, was only to break his strong old heart. Conflict itself has a value beyond victory and defeat, and those three months – he had them for ever.

Two Wrongs

Saturday Evening Post (18 January 1930)

1

'Look at those shoes,' said Bill – 'twenty-eight dollars.'

Mr Brancusi looked. 'Purty.'

'Made to order.'

'I knew you were a great swell. You didn't get me up here to show me those shoes, did you?'

'I am not a great swell. Who said I was a great swell?' demanded Bill. 'Just because I've got more education than most people in show business.'

'And then, you know, you're a handsome young fellow,' said Brancusi dryly.

'Sure I am – compared to you anyhow. The girls think I must be an actor, till they find out . . . Got a cigarette? What's more, I look like a man – which is more than most of these pretty boys round Times Square do.'

'Good-looking. Gentleman. Good shoes. Shot with luck.'

'You're wrong there,' objected Bill. 'Brains. Three years – nine shows – four big hits – only one flop. Where do you see any luck in that?'

A little bored, Brancusi just gazed. What he would have seen – had he not made his eyes opaque and taken to thinking about something else – was a fresh-faced young Irishman exuding aggressiveness and self-confidence until the air of his office was thick with it. Presently, Brancusi knew, Bill would hear the sound of his own voice and be ashamed and retire into his other humour – the quietly superior, sensitive one, the patron of the arts, modelled on the intellectuals of the Theatre Guild. Bill McChesney had not quite decided between the two, such blends are seldom complete before thirty.

'Take Ames, take Hopkins, take Harris – take any of them,' Bill insisted. 'What have they got on me? What's the matter? Do you want a drink?' – seeing Brancusi's glance wander towards the cabinet on the opposite wall.

'I never drink in the morning. I just wondered who was it keeps on knocking. You ought to make it stop it. I get a nervous fidgets, kind of half crazy, with that kind of thing.'

Bill went quickly to the door and threw it open.

'Nobody,' he said . . . 'Hello! What do you want?'

'Oh, I'm so sorry,' a voice answered; 'I'm terribly sorry. I got so excited and I didn't realise I had this pencil in my hand.'

'What is it you want?'

'I want to see you, and the clerk said you were busy. I have a letter for you from Alan Rogers, the playwright – and I wanted to give it to you personally.'

'I'm busy,' said Bill. 'See Mr Cadorna.'

'I did, but he wasn't very encouraging, and Mr Rogers said – '

Brancusi, edging over restlessly, took a quick look at her. She was very young, with beautiful red hair, and more character in her face than her chatter would indicate; it did not occur to Mr Brancusi that this was due to her origin in Delaney, South Carolina.

'What shall I do?' she enquired, quietly laying her future in Bill's hands. 'I had a letter to Mr Rogers, and he just gave me this one to you.'

'Well, what do you want me to do – marry you?' exploded Bill.

'I'd like to get a part in one of your plays.'

'Then sit down and wait. I'm busy . . . Where's Miss Cohalan?' He rang a bell, looked once more, crossly, at the girl and closed the door of his office. But during the interruption his other mood had come over him, and he resumed his conversation with Brancusi in the key of one who was hand in glove with Reinhardt for the artistic future of the theatre.

By twelve-thirty he had forgotten everything except that he was going to be the greatest producer in the world and that he had an engagement to tell Sol Lincoln about it at lunch. Emerging from his office, he looked expectantly at Miss Cohalan.

'Mr Lincoln won't be able to meet you,' she said. 'He jus 'is minute called.'

'Just this minute,' repeated Bill, shocked. 'All right. Just cross him off that list for Thursday night.'

Miss Cohalan drew a line on a sheet of paper before her.

'Mr McChesney, now you haven't forgotten me, have you?'

He turned to the red-headed girl.

'No,' he said vaguely, and then to Miss Cohalan: 'That's all right; ask him for Thursday anyhow. To hell with him.'

He did not want to lunch alone. He did not like to do anything alone now, because contacts were too much fun when one had prominence and power.

'If you would just let me talk to you two minutes – ' she began.

'Afraid I can't now.' Suddenly he realised that she was the most beautiful person he had ever seen in his life.

He stared at her.

'Mr Rogers told me – '

'Come and have a spot of lunch with me,' he said, and then, with an air of great hurry, he gave Miss Cohalan some quick and contradictory instructions and held open the door.

They stood on Forty-Second Street and he breathed his pre-empted air – there is only enough air there for a few people at a time. It was November and the first exhilarating rush of the season was over, but he could look east and see the electric sign of one of his plays, and west and see another. Around the corner was the one he had put on with Brancusi – the last time he would produce anything except alone.

They went to the Bedford, where there was a to-do of waiters and captains as he came in.

'This is ver' tractive restaurant,' she said, impressed and on company behaviour.

'This is hams' paradise.' He nodded to several people. 'Hello, Jimmy – Bill . . . Hello there, Jack . . . That's Jack Dempsey . . . I don't eat here much. I usually eat up at the Harvard Club.'

'Oh, did you go to Harvard? I used to know – '

'Yes.' He hesitated; there were two versions about Harvard, and he decided suddenly on the true one. 'Yes, and they had me down for a hick there, but not any more. About a week ago I was out on Long Island at the Gouverneer Haights – very fashionable people – and a couple of Gold Coast boys that never knew I was alive up in Cambridge began pulling this "Hello, Bill, old boy" on me.'

He hesitated and suddenly decided to leave the story there.

'What do you want – a job?' he demanded. He remembered suddenly that she had holes in her stockings. Holes in stockings always moved him, softened him.

'Yes, or else I've got to go home,' she said. 'I want to be a dancer – you know, Russian ballet. But the lessons cost so much, so I've got to get a job. I thought it'd give me stage presence anyhow.'

'Hoofer, eh?'

'Oh, no, serious.'

'Well, Pavlova's a hoofer, isn't she?'

'Oh, no.' She was shocked at this profanity, but after a moment she continued: 'I took with Miss Campbell – Georgia Berriman Campbell – back home – maybe you know her. She took from New Wayburn, and she's really wonderful. She – '

'Yeah?' he said abstractedly. 'Well, it's a tough business – casting agencies bursting with people that can all do anything, till I give them a try. How old are you?'

'Eighteen.'

'I'm twenty-six. Came here four years ago without a cent.'

'My!'

'I could quit now and be comfortable the rest of my life.'

'My!'

'Going to take a year off next year – get married . . . Ever hear of Irene Rikker?'

'I should say! She's about my favourite of all.'

'We're engaged.'

'My!'

When they went out into Times Square after a while he said carelessly, 'What are you doing now?'

'Why, I'm trying to get a job.'

'I mean right this minute.'

'Why, nothing.'

'Do you want to come up to my apartment on Forty-Sixth Street and have some coffee?'

Their eyes met, and Emmy Pinkard made up her mind she could take care of herself.

It was a great bright studio apartment with a ten-foot divan, and after she had coffee and he a highball, his arm dropped round her shoulder.

'Why should I kiss you?' she demanded. 'I hardly know you, and besides, you're engaged to somebody else.'

'Oh, that! She doesn't care.'

'No, really!'

'You're a good girl.'

'Well, I'm certainly not an idiot.'

'All right, go on being a good girl.'

She stood up, but lingered a minute, very fresh and cool, and not upset at all.

'I suppose this means you won't give me a job?' she asked pleasantly.

He was already thinking about something else – about an interview and a rehearsal – but now he looked at her again and saw that she still had holes in her stockings. He telephoned: 'Joe, this is the Fresh Boy . . . You didn't think I knew you called me that, did you? . . . It's all right . . . Say, have you got those three girls for the party scene? Well, listen; save one for a Southern kid I'm sending around today.'

He looked at her jauntily, conscious of being such a good fellow.

'Well, I don't know how to thank you. And Mr Rogers,' she added audaciously. 'Goodbye, Mr McChesney.'

He disdained to answer.

2

During rehearsal he used to come around a great deal and stand watching with a wise expression, as if he knew everything in people's minds; but actually he was in a haze about his own good fortune and didn't see much and didn't for the moment care. He spent most of his weekends on Long Island with the fashionable people who had 'taken him up'. When Brancusi referred to him as the 'big social butterfly', he would answer, 'Well, what about it? Didn't I go to Harvard? You think they found me in a Grand Street apple cart, like you?' He was well liked among his new friends for his good looks and good nature, as well as his success.

His engagement to Irene Rikker was the most unsatisfactory thing in his life; they were tired of each other but unwilling to put an end to it. Just as, often, the two richest young people in a town are drawn together by the fact, so Bill McChesney and Irene Rikker, borne side by side on waves of triumph, could not spare each other's nice appreciation of what was due such success. Nevertheless, they indulged in fiercer and more frequent quarrels, and the end was approaching. It was embodied in one Frank Llewellen, a big, fine-looking actor playing opposite Irene. Seeing the situation at once, Bill became bitterly humorous about it; from the second week of rehearsals there was tension in the air.

Meanwhile Emmy Pinkard, with enough money for crackers and milk, and a friend who took her out to dinner, was being happy. Her friend, Easton Hughes from Delaney, was studying at Columbia to be a dentist. He sometimes brought along other lonesome young men studying to be dentists, and at the price, if it can be called that, of a few casual kisses in taxicabs, Emmy dined when hungry. One afternoon she introduced Easton to Bill McChesney at the stage door, and afterwards Bill made his facetious jealousy the basis of their relationship.

'I see that dental number has been slipping it over on me again. Well, don't let him give you any laughing gas is my advice.'

Though their encounters were few, they always looked at each other. When Bill looked at her he stared for an instant as if he had not seen her before, and then remembered suddenly that she was to be teased. When she looked at him she saw many things – a bright day outside, with great crowds of people hurrying through the streets; a very good new limousine that waited at the curb for two people with very good new clothes, who got in and went somewhere that was just like New York, only away, and more fun there. Many times she had wished she had kissed him, but just as many times she was glad she hadn't; since, as the weeks passed, he grew less romantic, tied up, like the rest of them, to the play's laborious evolution.

They were opening in Atlantic City. A sudden moodiness, apparent to everyone, came over Bill. He was short with the director and sarcastic with the actors. This, it was rumoured, was because Irene Rikker had come down with Frank Llewellen on a different train. Sitting beside the author on the night of the dress rehearsal, he was an almost sinister figure in the twilight of the auditorium; but he said nothing until the end of the second act, when, with Llewellen and Irene Rikker on the stage alone, he suddenly called: 'We'll go over that again – and cut out the mush!'

Llewellen came down to the footlights.

'What do you mean – cut out the mush?' he enquired. 'Those are the lines, aren't they?'

'You know what I mean – stick to business.'

'I don't know what you mean.'

Bill stood up. 'I mean all that damn whispering.'

'There wasn't any whispering. I simply asked –'

'That'll do – take it over.'

Llewellen turned away furiously and was about to proceed, when Bill added audibly: 'Even a ham has got to do his stuff.'

Llewellen whipped about. 'I don't have to stand that kind of talk, Mr McChesney.'

'Why not? You're a ham, aren't you? When did you get ashamed of being a ham? I'm putting on this play and I want you to stick to your stuff.' Bill got up and walked down the aisle. 'And when you don't do it, I'm going to call you just like anybody else.'

'Well, you watch out for your tone of voice –'

'What'll you do about it?'

Llewellen jumped down into the orchestra pit.

'I'm not taking anything from you!' he shouted.

Irene Rikker called to them from the stage, 'For heaven's sake, are you two crazy?' And then Llewellen swung at him, one short, mighty blow. Bill pitched back across a row of seats, fell through one, splintering it, and lay wedged there. There was a moment's wild confusion, then people holding Llewellen, then the author, with a white face, pulling Bill up, and the stage manager crying: 'Shall I kill him, chief? Shall I break his fat face?' and Llewellen panting and Irene Rikker frightened.

'Get back there!' Bill cried, holding a handkerchief to his face and teetering in the author's supporting arms. 'Everybody get back! Take that scene again, and no talk! Get back, Llewellen!'

Before they realised it they were all back on the stage, Irene pulling Llewellen's arm and talking to him fast. Someone put on the auditorium lights full and then dimmed them again hurriedly. When Emmy came out presently for her scene, she saw in a quick glance that Bill was sitting with a whole mask of handkerchiefs over his bleeding face. She hated Llewellen and was afraid that presently they would break up and go back to New York. But Bill had saved the show from his own folly, since for Llewellen to take the further initiative of quitting would hurt his professional standing. The act ended and the next one began without an interval. When it was over, Bill was gone.

Next night, during the performance, he sat on a chair in the wings in view of everyone coming on or off. His face was swollen and bruised, but he neglected to seem conscious of the fact and there were no comments. Once he went around in front, and when he returned, word leaked out that two of the New York agencies were making big buys. He had a hit – they all had a hit.

At the sight of him to whom Emmy felt they all owed so much, a great wave of gratitude swept over her. She went up and thanked him.

'I'm a good picker, redhead,' he agreed grimly.

'Thank you for picking me.'

And suddenly Emmy was moved to a rash remark.

'You've hurt your face so badly!' she exclaimed. 'Oh, I think it was so brave of you not to let everything go to pieces last night.'

He looked at her hard for a moment and then an ironic smile tried unsuccessfully to settle on his swollen face.

'Do you admire me, baby?'

'Yes.'

'Even when I fell in the seats, did you admire me?'

'You got control of everything so quick.'

'That's loyalty for you. You found something to admire in that fool mess.'

And her happiness bubbled up into, 'Anyhow, you behaved just wonderfully.' She looked so fresh and young that Bill, who had had a wretched day, wanted to rest his swollen cheek against her cheek.

He took both the bruise and the desire with him to New York next morning; the bruise faded, but the desire remained. And when they opened in the city, no sooner did he see other men begin to crowd around her beauty than she became this play for him, this success, the thing that he came to see when he came to the theatre. After a good run it closed just as he was drinking too much and needed someone on the grey days of reaction. They were married suddenly in Connecticut, early in June.

3

Two men sat in the Savoy Grill in London, waiting for the Fourth of July. It was already late in May.

'Is he a nice guy?' asked Hubbel.

'Very nice,' answered Brancusi; 'very nice, very handsome, very popular.' After a moment, he added: 'I want to get him to come home.'

'That's what I don't get about him,' said Hubbel. 'Show business over here is nothing compared to home. What does he want to stay here for?'

'He goes around with a lot of dukes and ladies.'

'Oh?'

'Last week when I met him he was with three ladies – Lady this, Lady that, Lady the other thing.'

'I thought he was married.'

'Married three years,' said Brancusi, 'got a fine child, going to have another.'

He broke off as McChesney came in, his very American face staring about boldly over the collar of a box-shouldered topcoat.

'Hello, Mac; meet my friend Mr Hubbel.'

'J'doo,' said Bill. He sat down, continuing to stare around the bar to see who was present. After a few minutes Hubbel left, and Bill asked: 'Who's that bird?'

'He's only been here a month. He ain't got a title yet. You been here six months, remember.'

Bill grinned.

'You think I'm high-hat, don't you? Well, I'm not kidding myself anyhow. I like it; it gets me. I'd like to be the Marquis of McChesney.'

'Maybe you can drink yourself into it,' suggested Brancusi.

'Shut your trap. Who said I was drinking? Is that what they say now? Look here; if you can tell me any American manager in the history of the theatre who's had the success that I've had in London in less than eight months, I'll go back to America with you tomorrow. If you'll just tell me – '

'It was with your old shows. You had two flops in New York.'

Bill stood up, his face hardening.

'Who do you think you are?' he demanded. 'Did you come over here to talk to me like that?'

'Don't get sore now, Bill. I just want you to come back. I'd say anything for that. Put over three seasons like you had in 1922 and 1923, and you're fixed for life.'

'New York makes me sick,' said Bill moodily. 'One minute you're a king; then you have two flops, they go around saying you're on the toboggan.'

Brancusi shook his head.

'That wasn't why they said it. It was because you had that quarrel with Aronstael, your best friend.'

'Friend hell!'

'Your best friend in business anyhow. Then – '

'I don't want to talk about it.' He looked at his watch. 'Look here; Emmy's feeling bad so I'm afraid I can't have dinner with you tonight. Come around to the office before you sail.'

Five minutes later, standing by the cigar counter, Brancusi saw Bill enter the Savoy again and descend the steps that led to the tea-room.

'Grown to be a great diplomat,' thought Brancusi; 'he just used to say when he had a date. Going with these dukes and ladies is polishing him up even more.'

Perhaps he was a little hurt, though it was not typical of him to be hurt. At any rate he made a decision, then and there, that McChesney was on the down grade; it was quite typical of him that at that point he erased him from his mind for ever.

There was no outward indication that Bill was on the down grade; a hit at the New Strand, a hit at the Prince of Wales, and the weekly grosses pouring in almost as well as they had two or three years before in New York. Certainly a man of action was justified in changing his base. And the man who, an hour later, turned into his Hyde Park house for dinner had all the vitality of the late twenties. Emmy, very tired and clumsy, lay on a couch in the upstairs sitting-room. He held her for a moment in his arms.

'Almost over now,' he said. 'You're beautiful.'

'Don't be ridiculous.'

'It's true. You're always beautiful. I don't know why. Perhaps because you've got character, and that's always in your face, even when you're like this.'

She was pleased; she ran her hand through his hair.

'Character is the greatest thing in the world,' he declared, 'and you've got more than anybody I know.'

'Did you see Brancusi?'

'I did, the little louse! I decided not to bring him home to dinner.'

'What was the matter?'

'Oh, just snooty – talking about my row with Aronstael, as if it was my fault.'

She hesitated, closed her mouth tight, and then said quietly, 'You got into that fight with Aronstael because you were drinking.'

He rose impatiently.

'Are you going to start – '

'No, Bill, but you're drinking too much now. You know you are.'

Aware that she was right, he evaded the matter and they went in to dinner. On the glow of a bottle of claret he decided he would go on the wagon tomorrow till after the baby was born.

'I always stop when I want, don't I? I always do what I say. You never saw me quit yet.'

'Never yet.'

They had coffee together, and afterwards he got up.

'Come back early,' said Emmy.

'Oh, sure . . . What's the matter, baby?'

'I'm just crying. Don't mind me. Oh, go on; don't just stand there like a big idiot.'

'But I'm worried, naturally. I don't like to see you cry.'

'Oh, I don't know where you go in the evenings; I don't know who you're with. And that Lady Sybil Combrinck who kept phoning. It's all right, I suppose, but I wake up in the night and I feel so alone, Bill. Because we've always been together, haven't we, until recently?'

'But we're together still . . . What's happened to you, Emmy?'

'I know – I'm just crazy. We'd never let each other down, would we? We never have – '

'Of course not.'

'Come back early, or when you can.'

He looked in for a minute at the Prince of Wales Theatre; then he went into the hotel next door and called a number.

'I'd like to speak to her ladyship. Mr McChesney calling.'

It was some time before Lady Sybil answered: 'This is rather a surprise. It's been several weeks since I've been lucky enough to hear from you.'

Her voice was flip as a whip and cold as automatic refrigeration, in the mode grown familiar since British ladies took to piecing themselves together out of literature. It had fascinated Bill for a while, but just for a while. He had kept his head.

'I haven't had a minute,' he explained easily. 'You're not sore, are you?'

'I should scarcely say "sore".'

'I was afraid you might be; you didn't send me an invitation to your party tonight. My idea was that after we talked it all over we agreed – '

'You talked a great deal,' she said; 'possibly a little too much.'

Suddenly, to Bill's astonishment, she hung up.

'Going British on me,' he thought. 'A little skit entitled *The Daughter of a Thousand Earls*.'

The snub roused him, the indifference revived his waning interest. Usually women forgave his changes of heart because of his obvious devotion to Emmy, and he was remembered by various ladies with a not unpleasant sigh. But he had detected no such sigh upon the phone.

'I'd like to clear up this mess,' he thought. Had he been wearing evening clothes, he might have dropped in at the dance and talked it over with her, still he didn't want to go home. Upon consideration it seemed important that the misunderstanding should be fixed up at once, and presently he began to entertain the idea of going as he was; Americans were excused unconventionalities of dress. In any case, it was not nearly time, and, in the company of several highballs, he considered the matter for an hour.

At midnight he walked up the steps of her Mayfair house. The coat-room attendants scrutinised his tweeds disapprovingly and a footman peered in vain for his name on the list of guests. Fortunately his friend Sir Humphrey Dunn arrived at the same time and convinced the footman it must be a mistake.

Inside, Bill immediately looked about for his hostess.

She was a very tall young woman, half American and all the more intensely English. In a sense, she had discovered Bill McChesney, vouched for his savage charms; his retirement was one of her most humiliating experiences since she had begun being bad.

She stood with her husband at the head of the receiving line – Bill had never seen them together before. He decided to choose a less formal moment for presenting himself.

As the receiving went on interminably, he became increasingly uncomfortable. He saw a few people he knew, but not many, and he was conscious that his clothes were attracting a certain attention; he was aware also that Lady Sybil saw him and could have relieved his embarrassment with a wave of her hand, but she made no sign. He was sorry he had come, but to withdraw now would be absurd, and going to a buffet table, he took a glass of champagne.

When he turned around she was alone at last, and he was about to approach her when the butler spoke to him: 'Pardon me, sir. Have you a card?'

'I'm a friend of Lady Sybil's,' said Bill impatiently. He turned away, but the butler followed.

'I'm sorry, sir, but I'll have to ask you to step aside with me and straighten this up.'

'There's no need. I'm just about to speak to Lady Sybil now.'

'My orders are different, sir,' said the butler firmly.

Then, before Bill realised what was happening, his arms were pressed quietly to his sides and he was propelled into a little ante-room back of the buffet.

There he faced a man in a pince-nez in whom he recognised the Combrincks' private secretary.

The secretary nodded to the butler, saying, 'This is the man'; whereupon Bill was released.

'Mr McChesney,' said the secretary, 'you have seen fit to force your way here without a card, and his lordship requests that you leave his house at once. Will you kindly give me the check for your coat?'

Then Bill understood, and the single word that he found applicable to Lady Sybil sprang to his lips; whereupon the secretary gave a sign to two footmen, and in a furious struggle Bill was carried through a pantry, where busy bus-boys stared at the scene, down a long hall and pushed out of a door into the night. The door closed; a moment later it was opened again to let his coat billow forth and his cane clatter down the steps.

As he stood there, overwhelmed, stricken aghast, a taxicab stopped beside him and the driver called: 'Feeling ill, gov'nor?'

'What?'

'I know where you can get a good pick-me-up, gov'nor. Never too late.' The door of the taxi opened on a nightmare. There was a cabaret that broke the closing hours; there was being with strangers he had picked up somewhere; then there were arguments, and trying to cash a cheque, and suddenly proclaiming over and over that he was William McChesney, the producer, and convincing no one of the fact, not even himself. It seemed important to see Lady Sybil right away and call her to account; but presently nothing was important at all. He was in a taxicab whose driver had just shaken him awake in front of his own home.

The telephone was ringing as he went in, but he walked stonily past the maid and only heard her voice when his foot was on the stair.

'Mr McChesney, it's the hospital calling again. Mrs McChesney's there and they've been phoning every hour.'

Still in a daze, he held the receiver up to his ear.

'We're calling from the Midland Hospital, for your wife. She was delivered of a stillborn child at nine this morning.'

'Wait a minute.' His voice was dry and cracking. 'I don't understand.'

After a while he understood that Emmy's child was dead and she wanted him. His knees sagged groggily as he walked down the street, looking for a taxi.

The room was dark; Emmy looked up and saw him from a rumpled bed.

'It's you!' she cried. 'I thought you were dead! Where did you go?'

He threw himself down on his knees beside the bed, but she turned away.

'Oh, you smell awful,' she said. 'It makes me sick.'

But she kept her hand in his hair, and he knelt there motionless for a long time.

'I'm done with you,' she muttered, 'but it was awful when I thought you were dead. Everybody's dead. I wish I was dead.'

A curtain parted with the wind, and as he rose to arrange it, she saw him in the full morning light, pale and terrible, with rumpled clothes and bruises on his face. This time she hated him instead of those who had hurt him. She could feel him slipping out of her heart, feel the space he left, and all at once he was gone, and she could even forgive him and be sorry for him. All this in a minute.

She had fallen down at the door of the hospital, trying to get out of the taxicab alone.

4

When Emmy was well, physically and mentally, her incessant idea was to learn to dance; the old dream inculcated by Miss Georgia Berriman Campbell of South Carolina persisted as a bright avenue leading back to first youth and days of hope in New York. To her, dancing meant that elaborate blend of tortuous attitudes and formal pirouettes that evolved out of Italy several hundred years ago and reached its apogee in Russia at the beginning of this century. She wanted to use herself on something she could believe in, and it seemed to her that the dance was woman's interpretation of music; instead of strong fingers, one had limbs with which to render Tchaikovsky and Stravinsky; and feet could be as eloquent in Chopiniana as voices in the *Ring*. At the bottom, it was something sandwiched in between the acrobats and the trained seals; at the top it was Pavlova and art.

Once they were settled in an apartment back in New York, she plunged into her work like a girl of sixteen – four hours a day at bar exercises, attitudes, *sauts*, arabesques and pirouettes. It became the realest part of her life, and her only worry was whether or not she was too old. At twenty-six she had ten years to make up, but she was a natural dancer with a fine body – and that lovely face.

Bill encouraged it; when she was ready he was going to build the first real American ballet around her. There were even times when he envied her her absorption; for affairs in his own line were more difficult since they had come home. For one thing, he had made many enemies in those early days of self-confidence; there were exaggerated stories of his drinking and of his being hard on actors and difficult to work with.

It was against him that he had always been unable to save money and must beg a backing for each play. Then, too, in a curious way, he was intelligent, as he was brave enough to prove in several uncommercial ventures, but he had no Theatre Guild behind him, and what money he lost was charged against him.

There were successes, too, but he worked harder for them, or it seemed so, for he had begun to pay a price for his irregular life. He always intended to take a rest or give up his incessant cigarettes, but there was so much competition now – new men coming up, with new reputations for infallibility – and besides, he wasn't used to regularity. He liked to do his work in those great spurts, inspired by black coffee, that seem so inevitable in show business, but which took so much out of a man after thirty. He had come to lean, in a way, on Emmy's fine health and vitality. They were always together, and if he felt a vague dissatisfaction that he had grown to need her more than she needed him, there was always the hope that things would break better for him next month, next season.

Coming home from ballet school one November evening, Emmy swung her little grey bag, pulled her hat far down over her still damp hair, and gave herself up to pleasant speculation. For a month she had been aware of people who had come to the studio especially to watch her – she was ready to dance. Once she had worked just as hard and for as long a time on something else – her relations with Bill – only to reach a climax of misery and despair, but here there was nothing to fail her except herself. Yet even now she felt a little rash in thinking: 'Now it's come. I'm going to be happy.'

She hurried, for something had come up today that she must talk over with Bill.

Finding him in the living-room, she called him to come back while she dressed. She began to talk without looking around: 'Listen what happened!' Her voice was loud, to compete with the water running in the tub. 'Paul Makova wants me to dance with him at the Metropolitan this season; only it's not sure, so it's a secret – even I'm not supposed to know.'

'That's great.'

'The only thing is whether it wouldn't be better for me to make a début abroad? Anyhow Donilof says I'm ready to appear. What do you think?'

'I don't know.'

'You don't sound very enthusiastic.'

'I've got something on my mind. I'll tell you about it later. Go on.'

'That's all, dear. If you still feel like going to Germany for a month, like you said, Donilof would arrange a début for me in Berlin, but I'd rather open here and dance with Paul Makova. Just imagine – ' She broke off, feeling suddenly through the thick skin of her elation how abstracted he was. 'Tell me what you've got on your mind.'

'I went to Dr Kearns this afternoon.'

'What did he say?' Her mind was still singing with her own happiness. Bill's intermittent attacks of hypochondria had long ceased to worry her.

'I told him about that blood this morning, and he said what he said last year – it was probably a little broken vein in my throat. But since

I'd been coughing and was worried, perhaps it was safer to take an X-ray and clear the matter up. Well, we cleared it up all right. My left lung is practically gone.'

'Bill!'

'Luckily there are no spots on the other.'

She waited, horribly afraid.

'It's come at a bad time for me,' he went on steadily, 'but it's got to be faced. He thinks I ought to go to the Adirondacks or to Denver for the winter, and his idea is Denver. That way it'll probably clear up in five or six months.'

'Of course we'll have to – ' she stopped suddenly.

'I wouldn't expect you to go – especially if you have this opportunity.'

'Of course I'll go,' she said quickly. 'Your health comes first. We've always gone everywhere together.'

'Oh, no.'

'Why, of course.' She made her voice strong and decisive. 'We've always been together. I couldn't stay here without you. When do you have to go?'

'As soon as possible. I went in to see Brancusi to find out if he wanted to take over the Richmond piece, but he didn't seem enthusiastic.' His face hardened. 'Of course there won't be anything else for the present, but I'll have enough, with what's owing – '

'Oh, if I was only making some money!' Emmy cried. 'You work so hard, and here I've been spending two hundred dollars a week for just my dancing lessons alone – more than I'll be able to earn for years.'

'Of course in six months I'll be as well as ever – he says.'

'Sure, dearest; we'll get you well. We'll start as soon as we can.'

She put an arm around him and kissed his cheek. 'I'm just an old parasite,' she said. 'I should have known my darling wasn't well.'

He reached automatically for a cigarette, and then stopped.

'I forgot – I've got to start cutting down smoking.' He rose to the occasion suddenly: 'No, baby, I've decided to go alone. You'd go crazy with boredom out there, and I'd just be thinking I was keeping you away from your dancing.'

'Don't think about that. The thing is to get you well.'

They discussed the matter hour after hour for the next week, each of them saying everything except the truth – that he wanted her to go with him and that she wanted passionately to stay in New York. She talked it over guardedly with Donilof, her ballet master, and found that he thought any postponement would be a terrible mistake. Seeing other girls in the ballet school making plans for the winter, she wanted to die rather than go, and Bill saw all the involuntary indications of her misery. For a while they talked of compromising on the Adirondacks, whither she would commute by aeroplane for the weekends, but he was running a little fever now and he was definitely ordered West.

Bill settled it all one gloomy Sunday night, with that rough, generous justice that had first made her admire him, that made him rather tragic in his adversity, as he had always been bearable in his overweening success: 'It's just up to me, baby. I got into this mess because I didn't have any self-control – you seem to have all of that in this family – and now it's only me that can get me out. You've worked hard at your stuff for three years and you deserve your chance – and if you came out there now you'd have it on me the rest of my life.' He grinned. 'And I couldn't stand that. Besides, it wouldn't be good for the kid.'

Eventually she gave in, ashamed of herself, miserable – and glad. For the world of her work, where she existed without Bill, was bigger to her now than the world in which they existed together. There was more room to be glad in one than to be sorry in the other.

Two days later, with his ticket bought for that afternoon at five, they passed the last hours together, talking of everything hopeful. She protested still, and sincerely; had he weakened for a moment she would have gone. But the shock had done something to him, and he showed more character under it than he had for years. Perhaps it would be good for him to work it out alone.

'In the spring!' they said.

Then in the station with little Billy, and Bill saying: 'I hate these graveside partings. You leave me here. I've got to make a phone call from the train before it goes.'

They had never spent more than a night apart in six years, save when Emmy was in the hospital; save for the time in England they had a good record of faithfulness and of tenderness towards each other, even though she had been alarmed and often unhappy at this insecure bravado from the first. After he went through the gate alone, Emmy was glad he had a phone call to make and tried to picture him making it.

She was a good woman; she had loved him with all her heart. When she went out into Thirty-Third Street, it was just as dead as dead for a while, and the apartment he paid for would be empty of him, and she was here, about to do something that would make her happy.

She stopped after a few blocks, thinking: 'Why, this is terrible – what I'm doing! I'm letting him down like the worst person I ever heard of. I'm leaving him flat and going off to dinner with Donilof and Paul Makova, whom I like for being beautiful and for having the same colour eyes and hair. Bill's on the train alone.'

She swung little Billy around suddenly as if to go back to the station. She could see him sitting in the train, with his face so pale and tired, and no Emmy.

'I can't let him down,' she cried to herself as wave after wave of sentiment washed over her. But only sentiment – hadn't he let her down – hadn't he done what he wanted in London?

'Oh, poor Bill!'

She stood irresolute, realising for one last honest moment how quickly she would forget this and find excuses for what she was doing. She had to think hard of London, and her conscience cleared. But with Bill all alone in the train it seemed terrible to think that way. Even now she could turn and go back to the station and tell him that she was coming, but still she waited, with life very strong in her, fighting for her. The sidewalk was narrow where she stood; presently a great wave of people, pouring out of the theatre, came flooding along it, and she and little Billy were swept along with the crowd.

In the train, Bill telephoned up to the last minute, postponed going back to his stateroom, because he knew it was almost certain that he would not find her there. After the train started he went back and, of course, there was nothing but his bags in the rack and some magazines on the seat.

He knew then that he had lost her. He saw the set-up without any illusions – this Paul Makova, and months of proximity, and loneliness – afterwards nothing would ever be the same. When he had thought about it all a long time, reading *Variety* and *Zit's* in between, it began to seem, each time he came back to it, as if Emmy somehow were dead.

'She was a fine girl – one of the best. She had character.' He realised perfectly that he had brought all this on himself and that there was some law of compensation involved. He saw, too, that by going away he had again become as good as she was; it was all evened up at last.

He felt beyond everything, even beyond his grief, an almost comfortable sensation of being in the hands of something bigger than himself; and grown a little tired and unconfident – two qualities he could never for a moment tolerate – it did not seem so terrible if he were going West for a definite finish. He was sure that Emmy would come at the end, no matter what she was doing or how good an engagement she had.

A Nice Quiet Place

Saturday Evening Post (31 May, 1930)

1

All that week she couldn't decide whether she was a lollipop or a roman candle – through her dreams, dreams that promised uninterrupted sleep through many vacation mornings, drove a series of long, incalculable murmurings in tune with the put-put-put of their cut-outs, 'I love you – I love you,' over and over. She wrote in the evening:

> DEAR RIDGE – When I think of not being able to come to the freshman dance with you this June, I could lie down and *die*, but mother is sort of narrow-minded in some ways, and she feels that sixteen is too young to go to a prom; and Lil Hammel's mother feels the same way. When I think of you dancing around with *some other girl* and hear you handing her a line, like you do to everybody, I could lie down and *scream.* Oh, I *know* – because a girl here at school met you after I left Hot Springs at Easter. Anyhow, if you start rushing some other kid when you come out to Ed Bement's house party this summer, I intend to *cut her throat*, or my own, or something desperate. And probably no one will even be sorry I'm dead. Ha-ha –

Summer, summer, summer – bland inland sun and friendly rain. Lake Forest, with its thousand enchanted verandas, the dancing on the outdoor platform at the club, and always the boys, centaurs, in new cars. Her mother came East to meet her, and as they walked together out of the Grand Central Station, the symphony of promise became so loud that Josephine's face was puckered and distorted, as with the pressure of strong sunshine.

'We've got the best plans,' her mother said.

'Oh, what? What, mother?'

'A real change. I'll tell you all about it when we get to the hotel.'

There was a sudden discord; a shadow fell upon Josephine's heart.

'What do you mean? Aren't we going to Lake Forest?'

'Some place much better' – her mother's voice was alarmingly cheerful. 'I'm saving it till we get to the hotel.'

Before Mrs Perry had left Chicago, she and Josephine's father had decided, from observations of their own and some revelations on the part of their elder daughter, Constance, that Josephine knew her way around Lake Forest all too well. The place had changed in the twenty years that it had been the summer rendezvous of fashionable Chicago; less circumscribed children of new families were resoundingly in evidence and, like most parents, Mrs Perry thought of her daughter as one easily led into mischief by others. The more impartial eyes of other members of the colony had long regarded Josephine herself as the principal agent of corruption. But, preventive or penalty, the appalling thing to Josephine was that the Perrys were going to a 'nice quiet place' this summer.

'Mother, I simply can't go to Island Farms. I simply – '

'Father feels – '

'Why don't you take me to a reform school if I'm so awful? Or to state's penitentiary? I simply can't go to a horrible old farm with a lot of country jakes and no fun and no friends except a lot of hicks.'

'But, dear, it's not like that at all. They just call it Island Farms. In fact, your aunt's place isn't a farm; it's really a nice little resort up in Michigan where lots of people spend the summer. Tennis and swimming and – and fishing.'

'Fishing?' repeated Josephine incredulously. 'Do you call *that* something to do?' She shook her head in mute incomprehension. 'I'll just be forgotten, that's all. When it's my year to come out nobody will know who I am. They'll just say, "Who in heck is this Josephine Perry? I never saw her around here." "Oh, she's just some hick from a horrible old farm up in Michigan. Let's not invite her." Just when everybody else is having a wonderful time – '

'Nobody'll forget you in one summer, dear.'

'Yes, they will. Everybody'll have new friends and know new dances, and I'll be up there in the backwoods, full of hayseed, forgetting everything I know. If it's so wonderful why isn't Constance coming?'

Lying awake in their drawing-room on the Twentieth Century, Josephine brooded upon the terrible injustice of it all. She knew that her mother was going on her account, and mostly because of the gossip of a few ugly and jealous girls. These ugly and jealous girls, her relentless enemies, were not entirely creatures of Josephine's imagination. There was something in the frank sensuousness of her beauty that plain women found absolutely intolerable; they stared at her in a frightened, guarded way.

It was only recently that gossip had begun to worry Josephine. Her own theory was that, though at thirteen or fourteen she had been 'speedy' – a convenient word that lacked the vulgar implication of 'fast' – she was now trying to do her best, and a difficult enough business it was, without the past being held against her; for the only thing she cared about in the world was being in love and being with the person she currently loved.

Towards midnight her mother spoke to her softly and found that she was asleep. Turning on the berth light, she looked for a moment at the flushed young face, smoothed now of all its disappointment by a faint, peculiar smile. She leaned over and kissed Josephine's brow, behind which, doubtless, were passing in review those tender and eagerly awaited orgies of which she was to be deprived this summer.

2

Into Chicago, resonant with shrill June clamour; out to Lake Forest, where her friends moved already in an aura of new boys, new tunes, parties and house parties yet to be. One concession was granted her – she was to come back from Island Farms in time for Ed Bement's house party – which is to say, for Ridgeway Saunders's visit, the first of September.

Then northward, leaving all gaiety behind, to the nice quiet place, implicit in its very station, which breathed no atmosphere of hectic arrivals or feverish partings: there was her aunt, her fifteen-year-old cousin, Dick, with the blank resentful stare of youth in spectacles, there were the dozen or so estates with tired people asleep inside them and the drab village three miles away. It was worse, even, than Josephine had imagined; to her the vicinity was literally unpopulated, for, as a representative of her generation, she stood alone. In despair, she buried herself in ceaseless correspondence with the outer world or, as a variant, played tennis with Dick and carried on a slow indifferent quarrel at his deliberately spiteful immaturity.

'Are you going to be this way always?' she demanded, breaking down at his stupidity one day. 'Can't you do anything about it? Does it hurt?'

'What way?' Dick shambled around the tennis net in the way that so offended her.

'Oh, such a pill! You ought to be sent away to some good school.'

'I am going to be.'

'Why, at your age most of the boys in Chicago have cars of their own.'

'Too many,' he responded.

'How do you mean?' Josephine flared up.

'I heard my aunt say there was too much of that there. That's why they made you come up here. You're too much for that sort of thing.'

Josephine flushed. 'Couldn't you *help* being such a pill, if you honestly tried?'

'I don't know,' admitted Dick. 'I don't even think that maybe I *am* one.'

'Oh, yes, you are. I can assure you of that.'

It occurred to her, not very hopefully, that under proper supervision something might be made of him. Perhaps she could teach him to dance or have him learn to drive his mother's car. She went to the extent of trying to smarten him up, to make him wash his hands bidiurnally and to soak his hair and cleave it down the middle. She suggested that he would be more beautiful without his spectacles, and he obediently bumped around without them for several afternoons. But when he developed a feverish headache one night and confessed to his mother why he had been 'so utterly insane', Josephine gave him up without a pang.

But she could have cared for almost anyone. She wanted to hear the mystical terminology of love, to feel the lift and pull inside herself that each one of a dozen affairs had given her. She had written, of course, to Ridgeway Saunders. He answered. She wrote again. He answered – but after two weeks. On the first of August, with one month gone and one to go, came a letter from Lillian Hammel, her best friend in Lake Forest.

> DEAREST JO – You said to write you every single thing, and I will, but some of it will be sort of a fatal blow to you – about Ridgeway Saunders. Ed Bement visited him in Philadelphia, and he says he is so crazy about a girl there that he wants to leave Yale and get married. Her name is Evangeline Ticknor and she was fired from Foxcroft last year for smoking; quite a speed and said to be beautiful and something like you, from what I hear. Ed said that Ridgeway was so crazy about her that he wouldn't even come out here in September unless Ed invited her, too; so Ed did. Probably a lot you care! You've probably had lots of crushes up there where you are, or aren't there any attractive boys –

Josephine walked slowly up and down her room. Her parents had what they wanted now; the plot against her was complete. For the first time in her life she had been thrown over, and by the most attractive, the most desirable boy she had ever known, cut out by a girl 'very much like herself'. Josephine wished passionately that she had been fired from school – then the family might have given up and let her alone.

She was not so much humiliated as full of angry despair, but for the sake of her pride, she had a letter to write immediately. Her eyes were bright with tears as she began:

> DEAREST LIL – I was not surprised when I heard that about R. S. I knew he was fickle and never gave him a second *thought* after school closed in June. As a matter of fact, you know how fickle I am myself, darling, and you can imagine that I haven't had time to let it worry *me.* Everybody has a right to do what they want, say I. Live and let live is my motto. I wish you could have been here this summer. More *wonderful* parties –

She paused, knowing that she should invent more circumstantial evidence of gaiety. Pen in air, she gazed out into the deep, still mass of northern trees. Inventing was delicate work, and having dealt always in realities, her imagination was ill-adapted to the task. Nevertheless, after several minutes a vague, synthetic figure began to take shape in her mind. She dipped the pen and wrote: 'One of the darlingest – ' hesitated and turned again for inspiration to the window.

Suddenly she started and bent forward, the tears drying in her eyes. Striding down the road, not fifty feet from her window, was the handsomest, the most fascinating boy she had ever seen in her life.

3

He was about nineteen and tall, with a blond viking head; the fresh colour in his slender, almost gaunt cheeks was baked warm and dry by the sun. She had a glimpse of his eyes – enough to know that they were 'sad' and of an extraordinary glistening blue. His model legs were in riding breeches, above which he wore a soft sweater jacket of blue chamois, and as he walked he swung a crop acrimoniously at the overhanging leaves.

For a moment the vision endured; then the path turned into a clump of trees and he was gone, save for the small crunch of his boots on the pine needles.

Josephine did not move. The dark green trees that had seemed so lacking in promise were suddenly like a magic wall that had opened and revealed a short cut to possible delight; the trees gave forth a great trembling rustle. For another instant she waited; then she threw herself at the unfinished letter:

– he usually wears the best-looking riding clothes. He has the *most* beautiful eyes. On top he usually wears a blue chamois thing that is simply *divine.*

4

When her mother came in, half an hour later, she found Josephine getting into her best afternoon dress with an expression that was at once animated and far away.

'I thought – ' she said. 'I don't suppose you'd want to come with me and pay a few calls?'

'I'd adore to,' said Josephine unexpectedly.

Her mother hesitated. 'I'm afraid it's been a rather stupid month for you. I didn't realise that there wouldn't be anyone your age. But something nice has happened that I can't tell you about yet, and perhaps I'll soon have some news for you.'

Josephine did not appear to hear.

'Who shall we call on?' she demanded eagerly. 'Let's just call on everybody, even if it takes until ten o'clock tonight. Let's start at the nearest house and just keep going until we've killed everybody off.'

'I don't know whether we can do that.'

'Come on.' Josephine was putting on her hat. 'Let's get going, mother.'

Perhaps, Mrs Perry thought, the summer was really making a difference in her daughter; perhaps it was developing in her a more gently social vein. At each house they visited she positively radiated animation, and displayed sincere disappointment when they found no one home. When her mother called it a day, the light in her eyes went out.

'We can try again tomorrow,' she said impatiently. 'We'll kill the rest of them off. We'll go back to those houses where there was no one home.'

It was almost seven – a nostalgic hour, for it had been the loveliest of all at Lake Forest a year ago. Bathed and positively shining, one had intruded then for a last minute into the departing day, and, sitting alone on the veranda, turned over the romantic prospects of the night, while lighted windows sprang out on the blurring shapes of houses, and cars flew past with people late home from tea.

But tonight the murmurous Indian twilight of the lake country had a promise of its own, and strolling out into the lane that passed the house, Josephine broke suddenly into a certain walk, rather an externalised state of mind, that had been hitherto reserved for more sophisticated localities. It implied, through a skimming lift of the feet, through an impatience of the moving hips, through an abstracted smile, lastly through a glance that fell twenty feet ahead, that this girl was about to cross some material threshold where she was eagerly awaited; that, in fact, she had already crossed it in her imagination and left her surroundings behind. It was just at that moment she heard a strong clear whistle in front of her and the sound as of a stick swishing through leaves:

'Hello,
Fris-co,
Hello!
How do you do, my dear?
I only wish that you were here.'

Her heart beat a familiar tattoo; she realised that they would pass each other just where a last rift of sunset came down through the pines.

'Hello,
Fris-co,
Hel-lo!'

There he was, a fine shape against the foreground. His gallant face, drawn in a single dashing line, his chamois vest, so blue – she was so near she could have touched it. Then she realised with a shock that he had passed without noticing her proximity by a single flicker of his unhappy eyes.

'The conceited pill!' she thought indignantly. 'Of all the conceited –'

She was silent during dinner; at the end she said to her aunt, with small preliminary: 'I passed the most conceited-looking young man today. I wonder who he could have been.'

'Maybe it was the nephew of old Dorrance,' offered Dick, 'or the fellow staying at old Dorrance's. Somebody said it was his nephew or some sort of relation.'

His mother said pointedly to Josephine: 'We don't see the Dorrances.

Mr Charles Dorrance considered that my husband was unjust to him about our boundary some years ago. Old Mr Dorrance was a very stubborn man indeed.'

Josephine wondered if that was why he had failed to respond this afternoon. It was a silly reason.

But next day, at the same place, at the same hour, he literally jumped at her soft 'Good-evening'; he stared at her with unmistakable signs of dismay. Then his hand went up as if to remove a hat, found none, and he bowed instead and went on by.

But Josephine turned swiftly and walked at his side, smiling.

'You might be more sociable. You really shouldn't be so exclusive, since we're the only two people in this place. I do think it's silly to let older people influence young people.'

He was walking so fast that she could scarcely keep up with him.

'Honestly, I'm a nice girl,' she persisted, still smiling. 'Quite a few people rush me at dances and I once had a blind man in love with me.'

They were almost at her aunt's gate, still walking furiously.

'Here's where I live,' she said.

'Then I'll say goodbye.'

'What *is* the matter?' she demanded. 'How *can* you be so rude?'

His lips formed the words, 'I'm sorry.'

'I suppose you've got to hurry home so you can stare at yourself at the mirror.'

She knew this was untrue. He wore his good looks in almost an apologetic way. But it reached him, for he came to a precipitate halt, immediately moving off a little.

'Excuse my rudeness,' he exploded. 'But I'm not used to girls.'

She was too winded to answer. But as her shaken composure gradually returned, she became aware of an odd weariness in his face.

'At least you might talk to me for a minute, if I don't come any nearer.'

After a moment's hesitation he hoisted himself tentatively on to a fence rail.

'If you're so frightened of females, isn't it time something was done about it?' she enquired.

'It's too late.'

'Never,' she said positively. 'Why, you're missing half of life. Don't you want to marry and have children and make some woman a fine wife – I mean, a fine husband?'

In answer he only shivered.

'I used to be terribly timid myself,' she lied kindly. 'But I saw that I was missing half of life.'

'It isn't a question of willpower. It's just that I'm a little crazy on the subject. A minute ago I had an instinct to throw a stone at you. I know it's terrible, so if you'll excuse me – '

He jumped down off the fence, but she cried quickly: 'Wait! Let's talk it all over.'

He lingered reluctantly.

'Why, in Chicago,' she said, 'any man as good-looking as you could have any girl he wanted. Everyone would simply pursue him.'

The idea seemed to distress him still further; his face grew so sad that impulsively she moved nearer, but he swung one leg over the fence.

'All right. We'll talk about something else,' she conceded. 'Isn't this the most dismal place you ever saw? I was supposed to be a speed in Lake Forest, so the family sentenced me to this, and I've had the most *kill*ing month, just sitting and twirling my thumbs. Then yesterday I looked out the window and saw you.'

'What do you mean you were a speed?' he enquired.

'Just sort of speedy – you know, sort of pash.'

He got up – this time with an air of finality.

'You really must excuse me. I know I'm an idiot on this woman question, but there's nothing to do about it.'

'Will you meet me here tomorrow?'

'Heavens, no!'

Josephine was suddenly angry; she had humbled herself enough for one afternoon. With a cold nod, she started homeward down the lane.

'Wait!'

Now that there was thirty feet between them, his timidity had left him. She was tempted to go back, resisted the impulse with difficulty.

'I'll be here tomorrow,' she said coolly.

Walking slowly home, she saw, by instinct rather than logic, that there was something here she failed to understand. In general, a lack of self-confidence was enough to disqualify any boy from her approval; it was the unforgivable sin, the white flag, the refusal of battle. Yet now that this young man was out of sight, she saw him as he had appeared the previous afternoon – unself-conscious, probably arrogant, utterly debonair. Again she wondered if the unpleasantness between the families could be responsible for his attitude.

In spite of their unsatisfactory conversation, she was happy. In the soft glow of the sunset it seemed certain that it would all come right tomorrow. Already the oppressive sense of being wasted had deserted her. The boy who had passed her window yesterday afternoon was capable of anything – love, drama, or even that desperate recklessness that she loved best of all.

Her mother was waiting on the veranda.

'I wanted to see you alone,' she said, 'because I thought Aunt Gladys would be offended if you looked too delighted. We're going back to Lake Forest tomorrow.'

'Mother!'

'Constance is announcing her engagement tomorrow and getting married in ten days. Malcolm Libby is in the State Department and he's ordered abroad. Isn't it wonderful? Your sister's opening up the Lake Forest house today.'

'It'll be marvellous.' After a moment Josephine repeated, with more conviction: 'Perfectly marvellous.'

Lake Forest – she could feel the fast-beating excitement of it already. Yet there was something missing, as if the note of an essential trumpet had become separated from the band. For five weeks she had passionately hated Island Farms, but glancing around her in the gathering dusk, she felt rather sorry for it, a little ashamed of her desertion.

Throughout dinner the odd feeling persisted. She would be deep in exciting thoughts that began, 'Won't it be fun to – ' then the imminent brilliance would fade and there would be a stillness inside her like the stillness of these Michigan nights. That was what was lacking in Lake Forest – a stillness for things to happen in, for people to walk into.

'We'll be terribly busy,' her mother said. 'Next week there'll be bridesmaids in the house, and parties, and the wedding itself. We should have left tonight.'

Josephine went up to her room immediately and sat looking out into the darkness. Too bad; a wasted summer after all. If yesterday had happened sooner she might have gone away with some sense of having lived after all. Too late. 'But there'll be lots of boys,' she told herself – Ridgeway Saunders.

She could hear their confident lines, and somehow they rang silly on her ears. Suddenly she realised that what she was regretting was not the lost past but the lost future, not what had not been but what would never be. She stood up, breathing quickly.

A few minutes later she left the house by a side door and crossed the lawn to the gardener's gate. She heard Dick call after her uncertainly, but she did not answer. It was dark and cool, and the feeling that the summer was rushing away from her. As if to overtake it, she walked faster, and in ten minutes turned in at the gate of the Dorrance house, set behind the jagged silhouettes of many trees. Someone on the veranda hailed her as she came near: 'Good-evening. I can't see who it is.'

'It's the girl who was so fresh this afternoon.'

She heard him catch his breath suddenly.

'May I sit here on the steps for a moment? See? Quite safe and far away. I came to say goodbye, because we're going home tomorrow.'

'Are you really?' She could not tell whether his tone showed concern or relief. 'It'll be very quiet.'

'I want to explain about this afternoon, because I don't want you to think I was just being fresh. Usually I like boys with more experience, but I just thought that since we were the only ones here, we might manage to have a good time, and there weren't any days to waste.'

'I see.' After a moment he asked, 'What will you do in Lake Forest? Be a – a speed?'

'I don't much care what I do. I've wasted the whole six weeks.'

She heard him laugh. 'I gather from your tone that someone is going to have to pay for it,' he said.

'I hope so,' she answered rather grimly. She felt tears rise in her eyes. Everything was wrong. Everything seemed to be fixed against her.

'Please let me come up there on the settee,' she asked suddenly.

There was a creak as it stopped swinging.

'Please don't. I hate to ask you, but really I'll have to go if you do. Let's talk about – Do you like horses?'

She got up swiftly, mounted the steps and walked towards the corner where he sat. 'No,' she said, 'I think that what I'd like would be to be liked by you.'

In the light of the moon just lifting over the woods his face was positively haggard. He jumped to his feet; then his hands were on her arms and he was drawing her slowly towards him.

'You simply want to be kissed,' he was saying through scarcely opened lips. 'I knew it the first time I saw that mouth of yours – that perfectly selfish, self-sufficient look that – '

Suddenly he dropped his arms and stepped away from her with a gesture of horror.

'Don't stop!' she cried. 'Do anything, tell me anything, even if it isn't complimentary. I don't care.'

But he had vaulted swiftly over the railing and, with his hands clasping the back of his head, was walking across the lawn. In a minute she overtook him and stood beseechingly in his path, her small bosom rising and falling.

'Why do you suppose I'm here?' he demanded suddenly. 'Do you think I'm alone?'

'What – '

'My wife is with me.'

Josephine shivered.

'Oh – oh – then why doesn't anybody know?'

'Because my wife is – my wife is coloured.'

If it had not been so dark Josephine would have seen that for an instant he was laughing silently and uncontrollably.

'Oh,' she repeated.

'I didn't know,' he continued.

In spite of a subconscious scepticism, an uncanny feeling stole over Josephine.

'What dealings could I have with a girl like you?'

She began to weep softly.

'Oh, I'm sorry. If I could only help you.'

'You can't help me.' He turned gruffly away.

'You want me to go.'

He nodded.

'All right. I'll go.'

Still sobbing, she half walked, half backed away from him, intimidated now, yet still hoping he would call to her. When she saw him for the last time from the gate, he was standing where she had left him, his fine thin face clear and handsome in the suddenly streaming light of an emergent moon.

She had gone a quarter of a mile down the road when she became conscious of running footsteps behind her. Before she could do more than start and turn anxiously, a figure sprang out at her. It was her cousin, Dick.

'Oh!' she cried. 'You frightened me!'

'I followed you here. You had no business going out at night like this.'

'What a sneaky thing!' she said contemptuously.

They walked along side by side.

'I heard you with that fellow. You had a crush on him, didn't you?'

'Will you be quiet! What does a horrible little pill like you know about anything?'

'I know a lot,' said Dick glumly. 'I know there's too much of that sort of thing at Lake Forest.'

She scorned to answer; they reached her aunt's gate in silence.

'I tell you one thing,' he said uncertainly. 'I'll bet you wouldn't want your mother to know about this.'

'You mean you're going to my mother?'

'Just hold your horses. I was going to say I wouldn't say anything about it – '

'I should hope not.'

' – on one condition.'

'Well?'

'The condition is – ' He fidgeted uncomfortably. 'You told me once that a lot of girls at Lake Forest had kissed boys and never thought anything about it.'

'Yes.' Suddenly she guessed what was coming, and an astonished laugh rose to her lips.

'Well, will you, then – kiss me?'

A vision of her mother arose – of a return to Lake Forest in chains. Deciding quickly, she bent towards him. Less than a minute later she was in her room, almost hysterical with tears and laughter. That, then, was the kiss with which destiny had seen fit to crown the summer.

5

Josephine's sensational return to Lake Forest that August marked a revision of opinion about her; it can be compared to the moment when the robber bandit evolved through sheer power into the feudal seignior.

To the three months of nervous energy conserved since Easter beneath the uniform of her school were added six weeks of resentment – added, that is, as the match might be said to be added to the powder. For Josephine exploded with an audible, visible bang; for weeks thereafter pieces of her were gathered up from Lake Forest's immaculate lawns.

It began quietly; it began with the long-awaited house party, on the first evening of which she was placed next to the unfaithful Ridgeway Saunders at dinner.

'I certainly felt pretty badly when you threw me over,' Josephine said indifferently – to rid him of any lingering idea that he had thrown her over. Once she had chilled him into wondering if, after all, he had come off best in the affair, she turned to the man on the other side. By the time the salad was served, Ridgeway was explaining himself to her. And his girl from the East, Miss Ticknor, was becoming increasingly aware of what an obnoxious person Josephine Perry was. She made the mistake of saying so to Ridgeway. Josephine made no such mistake; towards the end of dinner she merely asked him the innocent question as to who was his friend with the high button shoes.

By ten o'clock Josephine and Ridgeway were out in somebody's car – far out where the colony becomes a prairie. As minute by minute she grew wearier of his softness, his anguish increased. She let him kiss her, just to be sure; and it was a desperate young man who returned to his host's that night.

All next day his eyes followed her about miserably; Miss Ticknor was unexpectedly called East the following afternoon. This was pathetic, but certainly someone had to pay for Josephine's summer. That score settled, she returned her attention to her sister's wedding.

Immediately on her return she had demanded a trousseau in keeping with the splendour of a maid of honour, and under cover of the family rush had so managed to equip herself as to add a charming year to her age. Doubtless this contributed to the change of attitude towards her, for though her emotional maturity, cropping out of a schoolgirl dress, had seemed not quite proper, in more sophisticated clothes she was an incontestable little beauty; and as such she was accepted by at least the male half of the wedding party.

Constance was openly hostile. On the morning of the wedding itself, she unburdened herself to her mother.

'I do hope you'll take her in hand after I'm gone, mother. It's really unendurable the way she's behaving. None of the bridesmaids have had a good time.'

'Let's not worry,' Mrs Perry urged. 'After all, she's had a very quiet summer.'

'I'm not worrying about *her*,' said Constance indignantly.

The wedding party were lunching at the club, and Josephine found herself next to a jovial usher who had arrived inebriated and remained in that condition ever since. However, it was early enough in the day for him to be coherent.

'The belle of Chicago, the golden girl of the golden West. Oh, why didn't I come out here this summer?'

'I wasn't here. I was up in a place called Island Farms.'

'Ah!' he exclaimed. 'Ah-ha! That accounts for a lot of things – that accounts for the sudden pilgrimage of Sonny Dorrance.'

'Of who?'

'The famous Sonny Dorrance, the shame of Harvard, but the maiden's prayer. Now don't tell me you didn't exchange a few warm glances with Sonny Dorrance.'

'But isn't he,' she demanded faintly – 'isn't he supposed to be – married?'

He roared with laughter.

'Married – sure, married to a mulatto! You didn't fall for *that* old line. He always pulls it when he's reacting from some violent affair – that's to protect himself while he recovers. You see, his whole life has been cursed by that fatal beauty.'

In a few minutes she had the story. Apart from everything else, Sonny Dorrance was fabulously rich – women had pursued him since he was fifteen – married women, débutantes, chorus girls. It was legendary.

There actually had been plots to entangle him into marriage, to entangle him into anything. There was the girl who tried to kill herself, there was the one who tried to kill him. Then, this spring, there was the annulled marriage business that had cost him an election to Porcellian at Harvard, and was rumoured to have cost his father fifty thousand dollars.

'And now,' Josephine asked tensely, 'you say he doesn't like women?'

'Sonny? I tell you he's the most susceptible man in America. This last thing shook him, and so he keeps off admirers by telling them anything. But by this time next month he'll be involved again.'

As he talked, the dining-room faded out like a scene in a moving picture, and Josephine was back at Island Farms, staring out the window as a young man appeared between the pine trees.

'He was afraid of me,' she thought to herself, her heart tapping like a machine-gun. 'He thought I was like the others.'

Half an hour later she interrupted her mother in the midst of the wedding's last and most violent confusion.

'Mother, I want to go back to Island Farms for the rest of the summer,' she said at once.

Mrs Perry looked at her in a daze, and Josephine repeated her statement.

'Why, in less than a month you'll be starting back to school.'

'I want to go anyhow.'

'I simply can't understand you. In the first place, you haven't been invited, and in the second place, I think a little gaiety is good for you before you go back to school, and in the third place, I want you here with me.'

'Mother,' Josephine wailed, 'don't you understand? I want to go! You take me up there all summer when I don't want to go, and just when I *do* want to, you make me stay in this ghastly place. Let me tell you this isn't any place for a sixteen-year-old girl, if you knew everything.'

'What nonsense to be bothering me with just at this time!'

Josephine threw up her hands in despair; the tears were streaming down her cheeks.

'It's ruining me here!' she cried. 'Nobody thinks of anything but boys and dances from morning till night. They go out in their cars and kiss them from morning till night.'

'Well, I know my little girl doesn't do anything like that.'

Josephine hesitated, taken a little aback.

'Well, I will,' she announced. 'I'm weak. You told me I was. I always do what anybody tells me to do, and all these boys are just simply immoral, that's all. The first thing you know I'll be entirely ruined, and then you'll be sorry you didn't let me go to Island Farms. You'll be sorry – '

She was working herself into hysteria. Her distracted mother took her by the shoulders and forced her down into a chair.

'I've never heard such silly talk. If you weren't so old I'd spank you. If you keep this up you'll be punished.'

Suddenly dry-eyed, Josephine got up and stalked out of the room. Punished! They had been punishing her all summer, and now they refused to punish her, refused to send her away. Oh, she was tired of trying. If she could think of something really awful to do, so that they would send her away for ever –

Mr Malcolm Libby, the prospective bridegroom, happened upon her fifteen minutes later, in an obscure corner of the garden. He was pacing restlessly about, steadying himself for the rehearsal at four o'clock and for the ceremony two hours later.

'Why, hello!' he cried. 'Why, what's the matter? You've been crying.'

He sat down on the bench, full of sympathy for Constance's little sister.

'I'm not crying,' she sobbed. 'I'm just angry.'

'About Constance going away? Don't you think I'll take good care of her?'

Leaning over, he patted her hand. If he had seen the look that flashed suddenly across her face it would have alarmed him, for it was curiously like the expression associated with a prominent character in *Faust*.

When she spoke, her voice was calm, almost cool, and yet tenderly sad: 'No, that wasn't it. It was something else.'

'Tell me about it. Maybe I can help.'

'I was crying' – she hesitated delicately – 'I was crying because Constance has all the luck.'

Half an hour later when, with the rehearsal twenty minutes late, the frantic bride-to-be came searching through the garden and happened upon them suddenly, Malcolm Libby's arm was around Josephine, who seemed dissolved in uncontrollable grief, and on his face was a wildly harassed expression she had never seen there before. Constance gave a little gasping cry and sank down upon the pebbled path.

The next hour passed in an uproar. There was a doctor; there were shut doors; there was Mr Malcolm Libby in an agonised condition, the sweat pouring off his brow, explaining to Mrs Perry over and over that he could explain if he could only see Constance. There was Josephine, tight-lipped, in a room, being talked to coldly by various members of the family. There was the clamour of arriving guests; then frantic last-minute patching-up of things, with Constance and Malcolm in each other's arms and Josephine, unforgiven, being bundled into her dress.

Then a solemn silence fell and, moving to music, the maid of honour, her head demurely bowed, followed her sister up the two aisles of people that crowded the drawing-room. It was a lovely, sad wedding; the two sisters, light and dark, were a lovely contrast; there was as much interest in one as in the other. Josephine had become a great beauty and the prophets were busy; she stood for the radiant future, there at her sister's side.

The crush was so great at the reception that not until it was over was Josephine missed. And long before nine o'clock, before Mrs Perry had time to be uneasy, a note from the station had been handed in at the door:

> MY DEAREST MOTHER – Ed Bement brought me here in his car, and I am catching the train to Island Farms at seven. I have wired the housekeeper to meet me, so don't worry. I feel I have behaved *terribly* and am ashamed to *face* anyone, and I am punishing myself

as I deserve by going back to the *simple* life. It is, after all, better for a girl of sixteen, I feel, and when you think it over you will agree.

With dearest love.

JOSEPHINE

After all, thought Mrs Perry, perhaps it was just as well. Her husband was really angry, and she herself was exhausted and didn't feel up to another problem at the moment. Perhaps a nice quiet place was best.

Josephine: A Woman with a Past

Saturday Evening Post (6 September 1930)

1

Driving slowly through New Haven, two of the young girls became alert. Josephine and Lillian darted soft frank glances into strolling groups of three or four undergraduates, into larger groups on corners, which swung about as one man to stare at their receding heads. Believing that they recognised an acquaintance in a solitary loiterer, they waved wildly, whereupon the youth's mouth fell open, and as they turned the next corner he made a dazed dilatory gesture with his hand. They laughed. 'We'll send him a postcard when we get back to school tonight, to see if it really was him.'

Adele Craw, sitting on one of the little seats, kept on talking to Miss Chambers, the chaperone. Glancing sideways at her, Lillian winked at Josephine without batting an eye, but Josephine had gone into a reverie.

This was New Haven – city of her adolescent dreams, of glittering proms where she would move on air among men as intangible as the tunes they danced to. City sacred as Mecca, shining as Paris, hidden as Timbuktu. Twice a year the life-blood of Chicago, her home, flowed into it, and twice a year flowed back, bringing Christmas or bringing summer. Bingo, bingo, bingo, that's the lingo; love of mine, I pine for one of your glances; the darling boy on the left there; underneath the stars I wait.

Seeing it for the first time, she found herself surprisingly unmoved – the men they passed seemed young and rather bored with the possibilities of the day, glad of anything to stare at; seemed undynamic and purposeless against the background of bare elms, lakes of dirty snow and buildings crowded together under the February sky. A wisp of hope, a well-turned-out derby-crowned man, hurrying with stick and suitcase towards the station, caught her attention, but his reciprocal glance was too startled, too ingenuous. Josephine wondered at the extent of her own disillusionment.

She was exactly seventeen and she was blasé. Already she had been a sensation and a scandal; she had driven mature men to a state of disequilibrium; she had, it was said, killed her grandfather, but as he was over eighty at the time perhaps he just died. Here and there in the Middle West were discouraged little spots which upon inspection turned out to be the youths who had once looked full into her green and wistful eyes. But her love affair of last summer had ruined her faith in the all-sufficiency of men. She had grown bored with the waning September days – and it seemed as though it had happened once too often. Christmas with its provocative shortness, its travelling glee clubs, had brought no one new. There remained to her only a persistent, a physical hope; hope in her stomach that there was someone whom she would love more than he loved her.

They stopped at a sporting-goods store and Adele Craw, a pretty girl with clear honourable eyes and piano legs, purchased the sporting equipment which was the reason for their trip – they were the spring hockey committee for the school. Adele was in addition the president of the senior class and the school's ideal girl. She had lately seen a change for the better in Josephine Perry – rather as an honest citizen might guilelessly approve a speculator retired on his profits. On the other hand, Adele was simply incomprehensible to Josephine – admirable, without doubt, but a member of another species. Yet with the charming adaptability that she had hitherto reserved for men, Josephine was trying hard not to disillusion her, trying to be honestly interested in the small, neat, organised politics of the school.

Two men who had stood with their backs to them at another counter turned to leave the store, when they caught sight of Miss Chambers and Adele. Immediately they came forward. The one who spoke to Miss Chambers was thin and rigid of face. Josephine recognised him as Miss Brereton's nephew, a student at New Haven, who had spent several weekends with his aunt at the school. The other man Josephine had never seen before. He was tall and broad, with blond curly hair and an open expression in which strength of purpose and a nice consideration were pleasantly mingled. It was not the sort of face that generally appealed to Josephine. The eyes were obviously without a secret, with a sidewise gambol, without a desperate flicker to show that they had a life of their own apart from the mouth's speech. The mouth itself was large and masculine; its smile was an act of kindness and control. It was rather with curiosity as to the sort of man who would be attentive to Adele Craw that Josephine continued to look at him, for his voice that obviously couldn't lie greeted Adele as if this meeting was the pleasant surprise of his day.

In a moment Josephine and Lillian were called over and introduced.

'This is Mr Waterbury' – that was Miss Brereton's nephew – 'and Mr Dudley Knowleton.'

Glancing at Adele, Josephine saw on her face an expression of tranquil pride, even of possession. Mr Knowleton spoke politely, but it was obvious that though he looked at the younger girls he did not quite see them. But since they were friends of Adele's he made suitable remarks, eliciting the fact that they were both coming down to New Haven to their first prom the following week. Who were their hosts? Sophomores; he knew them slightly. Josephine thought that was unnecessarily superior. Why, they were the charter members of the Loving Brothers' Association – Ridgeway Saunders and George Davey – and on the glee-club trip the girls they picked out to rush in each city considered themselves a sort of élite, second only to the girls they asked to New Haven.

'And oh, I've got some bad news for you,' Knowleton said to Adele. 'You may be leading the prom. Jack Coe went to the infirmary with appendicitis, and against my better judgement I'm the provisional chairman.' He looked apologetic. 'Being one of those stone-age dancers, the two-step king, I don't see how I ever got on the committee at all.'

When the car was on its way back to Miss Brereton's school, Josephine and Lillian bombarded Adele with questions.

'He's an old friend from Cincinnati,' she explained demurely. 'He's captain of the baseball team and he was last man for Skull and Bones.'

'You're going to the prom with him?'

'Yes. You see, I've known him all my life.'

Was there a faint implication in this remark that only those who had known Adele all her life knew her at her true worth?

'Are you engaged?' Lillian demanded.

Adele laughed. 'Mercy, I don't think of such matters! It doesn't seem to be time for that sort of thing yet, does it?' ('Yes,' interpolated Josephine silently.) 'We're just good friends. I think there can be a perfectly healthy friendship between a man and a girl without a lot of – '

'Mush,' supplied Lillian helpfully.

'Well, yes, but I don't like that word. I was going to say without a lot of sentimental romantic things that ought to come later.'

'Bravo, Adele!' said Miss Chambers somewhat perfunctorily.

But Josephine's curiosity was unappeased.

'Doesn't he say he's in love with you, and all that sort of thing?'

'Mercy, no! Dud doesn't believe in such stuff any more than I do. He's got enough to do at New Haven, serving on the committees and the team.'

'Oh!' said Josephine.

She was oddly interested. That two people who were attracted to each other should never even say anything about it but be content to 'not believe in such stuff', was something new in her experience. She had known girls who had no beaux, others who seemed to have no emotions, and still others who lied about what they thought and did; but here was a girl who spoke of the attentions of the last man tapped for Skull and Bones as if they were two of the limestone gargoyles that Miss Chambers had pointed out on the just completed Harkness Hall. Yet Adele seemed happy – happier than Josephine, who had always believed that boys and girls were made for nothing but each other, and as soon as possible.

In the light of his popularity and achievements, Knowleton seemed more attractive. Josephine wondered if he would remember her and dance with her at the prom, or if that depended on how well he knew her escort, Ridgeway Saunders. She tried to remember whether she had smiled at him when he was looking at her. If she had really smiled he would remember her and dance with her. She was still trying to be sure of that over her two French irregular verbs and her ten stanzas of *The Ancient Mariner* that night; but she was still uncertain when she fell asleep.

2

Three gay young sophomores, the founders of the Loving Brothers' Association, took a house together for Josephine, Lillian and a girl from Farmington and their three mothers. For the girls it was a first prom, and they arrived at New Haven with all the nervousness of the condemned; but a Sheffield fraternity tea in the afternoon yielded up such a plethora of boys from home, and boys who had visited there and friends of those boys, and new boys with unknown possibilities but obvious eagerness, that they were glowing with self-confidence as they poured into the glittering crowd that thronged the armoury at ten.

It was impressive; for the first time Josephine was at a function run by men upon men's standards – an outward projection of the New Haven world from which women were excluded and which went on mysteriously behind the scenes. She perceived that their three escorts, who had once seemed the very embodiments of worldliness, were modest fry in this relentless microcosm of accomplishment and success. A man's world! Looking around her at the glee-club concert, Josephine had felt a grudging admiration for the good fellowship, the good feeling. She envied Adele Craw, barely glimpsed in the dressing-room, for the position she automatically occupied by being Dudley Knowleton's girl tonight. She envied her more stepping off under the draped bunting through a gateway of hydrangeas at the head of the grand march, very demure and faintly unpowdered in a plain white dress. She was temporarily the centre of all attention, and at the sight something that had long lain dormant in Josephine awakened – her sense of a problem, a scarcely defined possibility.

'Josephine,' Ridgeway Saunders began, 'you can't realise how happy I am now that it's come true. I've looked forward to this so long, and dreamed about it – '

She smiled up at him automatically, but her mind was elsewhere, and as the dance progressed the idea continued to obsess her. She was rushed from the beginning; to the men from the tea were added a dozen new faces, a dozen confident or timid voices, until, like all the more popular girls, she had her own queue trailing her about the room. Yet all this had happened to her before, and there was something missing. One might have ten men to Adele's two, but Josephine was abruptly aware that here a girl took on the importance of the man who had brought her.

She was discomforted by the unfairness of it. A girl earned her popularity by being beautiful and charming. The more beautiful and charming she was, the more she could afford to disregard public opinion. It seemed absurd that simply because Adele had managed to attach a baseball captain, who mightn't know anything about girls at all, or be able to judge their attractions, she should be thus elevated in spite of her thick ankles, her rather too pinkish face.

Josephine was dancing with Ed Bement from Chicago. He was her earliest beau, a flame of pigtail days in dancing school when one wore white cotton stockings, lace drawers with a waist attached and ruffled dresses with the inevitable sash.

'What's the matter with me?' she asked Ed, thinking aloud. 'For months I've felt as if I were a hundred years old, and I'm just seventeen and that party was only seven years ago.'

'You've been in love a lot since then,' Ed said.

'I haven't,' she protested indignantly. 'I've had a lot of silly stories started about me, without any foundation, usually by girls who were jealous.'

'Jealous of what?'

'Don't get fresh,' she said tartly. 'Dance me near Lillian.'

Dudley Knowleton had just cut in on Lillian. Josephine spoke to her friend; then waiting until their turns would bring them face to face over a space of seconds, she smiled at Knowleton. This time she made sure that smile intersected as well as met glance, that he passed beside the circumference of her fragrant charm. If this had been named like French perfume of a later day it might have been called 'Please'. He bowed and smiled back; a minute later he cut in on her.

It was in an eddy in a corner of the room and she danced slower so that he adapted himself, and for a moment they went around in a slow circle.

'You looked so sweet leading the march with Adele,' she told him. 'You seemed so serious and kind, as if the others were a lot of children. Adele looked sweet, too.' And she added on an inspiration, 'At school I've taken her for a model.'

'You have!' She saw him conceal his sharp surprise as he said, 'I'll have to tell her that.'

He was handsomer than she had thought, and behind his cordial good manners there was a sort of authority. Though he was correctly attentive to her, she saw his eyes search the room quickly to see if all went well; he spoke quietly, in passing, to the orchestra leader, who came down deferentially to the edge of his dais. Last man for Bones. Josephine knew what that meant – her father had been Bones. Ridgeway Saunders and the rest of the Loving Brothers' Association would certainly not be Bones. She wondered, if there had been a Bones for girls, whether she would be tapped – or Adele Craw with her ankles, symbol of solidity.

Come on o-ver here.
Want to have you near;
Get a wel-come heart-y.
Come on join the part-y.

'I wonder how many boys here have taken you for a model,' she said. 'If I were a boy you'd be exactly what I'd like to be. Except I'd be terribly bothered having girls falling in love with me all the time.'

'They don't,' he said simply. 'They never have.'

'Oh yes – but they hide it because they're so impressed with you, and they're afraid of Adele.'

'Adele wouldn't object.' And he added hastily, ' – if it ever happened. Adele doesn't believe in being serious about such things.'

'Are you engaged to her?'

He stiffened a little. 'I don't believe in being engaged till the right time comes.'

'Neither do I,' agreed Josephine readily. 'I'd rather have one good friend than a hundred people hanging around being mushy all the time.'

'Is that what that crowd does that keeps following you around tonight?'

'What crowd?' she asked innocently.

'The fifty per cent of the sophomore class that's rushing you.'

'A lot of parlour snakes,' she said ungratefully.

Josephine was radiantly happy now as she turned beautifully through the newly enchanted hall in the arms of the chairman of the prom committee. Even this extra time with him she owed to the awe which he inspired in her entourage; but a man cut in eventually and there was a sharp fall in her elation. The man was impressed that Dudley Knowleton had danced with her; he was more respectful, and his modulated admiration bored her. In a little while, she hoped, Dudley Knowleton would cut back, but as midnight passed, dragging on another hour with it, she wondered if after all it had only been a courtesy to a girl from Adele's school. Since then Adele had probably painted him a neat little landscape of Josephine's past. When finally he approached her she grew tense and watchful, a state which made her exteriorly pliant and tender and quiet. But instead of dancing he drew her into the edge of a row of boxes.

'Adele had an accident on the cloakroom steps. She turned her ankle a little and tore her stocking on a nail. She'd like to borrow a pair from you because you're staying near here and we're way out at the Lawn Club.'

'Of course.'

'I'll run over with you – I have a car outside.'

'But you're busy; you mustn't bother.'

'Of course I'll go with you.'

There was thaw in the air; a hint of thin and lucid spring hovered delicately around the elms and cornices of buildings whose bareness and coldness had so depressed her the week before. The night had a quality of asceticism, as if the essence of masculine struggle were seeping everywhere through the little city where men of three centuries had brought their energies and aspirations for winnowing. And Dudley Knowleton sitting beside her, dynamic and capable, was symbolic of it all. It seemed that she had never met a man before.

'Come in, please,' she said as he went up the steps of the house with her. 'They've made it very comfortable.'

There was an open fire burning in the dark parlour. When she came downstairs with the stockings she went in and stood beside him, very still for a moment, watching it with him. Then she looked up, still silent, looked down, looked at him again.

'Did you get the stockings?' he asked, moving a little.

'Yes,' she said breathlessly. 'Kiss me for being so quick.'

He laughed as if she had said something witty and moved towards the door. She was smiling and her disappointment was deeply hidden as they got into the car.

'It's been wonderful meeting you,' she told him. 'I can't tell you how many ideas I've gotten from what you said.'

'But I haven't any ideas.'

'You have. All that about not getting engaged till the proper time comes. I haven't had much opportunity to talk to a man like you. Otherwise my ideas would be different, I guess. I've just realised that I've been wrong about a lot of things. I used to want to be exciting. Now I want to help people.'

'Yes,' he agreed, 'that's very nice.'

He seemed about to say more when they arrived at the armoury. In their absence supper had begun; and crossing the great floor by his side, conscious of many eyes regarding them, Josephine wondered if people thought that they had been up to something.

'We're late,' said Knowleton when Adele went off to put on the stockings. 'The man you're with has probably given you up long ago. You'd better let me get you something here.'

'That would be too divine.'

Afterwards, back on the floor again, she moved in a sweet aura of abstraction. The followers of several departed belles merged with hers until now no girl on the floor was cut in on with such frequency. Even Miss Brereton's nephew, Ernest Waterbury, danced with her in stiff approval. Danced? With a tentative change of pace she simply swung from man to man in a sort of hands-right-and-left around the floor. She felt a sudden need to relax, and as if in answer to her mood a new man was presented, a tall, sleek Southerner with a persuasive note: 'You lovely creacha. I been strainin' my eyes watchin' your cameo face floatin' round. You stand out above all these othuz like an Amehken Beauty Rose over a lot of field daisies.'

Dancing with him a second time, Josephine hearkened to his pleadings.

'All right. Let's go outside.'

'It wasn't outdaws I was considering,' he explained as they left the floor. 'I happen to have a mortgage on a nook right hee in the building.'

'All right.'

Book Chaffee, of Alabama, led the way through the cloakroom, through a passage to an inconspicuous door.

'This is the private apartment of my friend Sergeant Boone, instructa of the battery. He wanted to be particularly sure it'd be used as a nook tonight and not a readin' room or anything like that.'

Opening the door he turned on a dim light; she came in and shut it behind her, and they faced each other.

'Mighty sweet,' he murmured. His tall face came down, his long arms wrapped around her tenderly, and very slowly so that their eyes met for quite a long time, he drew her up to him. Josephine kept thinking that she had never kissed a Southern boy before.

They started apart at the sudden sound of a key turning in the lock outside. Then there was a muffed snicker followed by retreating footsteps, and Book sprang for the door and wrenched at the handle just as Josephine noticed that this was not only Sergeant Boone's parlour; it was his bedroom as well.

'Who was it?' she demanded. 'Why did they lock us in?'

'Some funny boy. I'd like to get my hands on him.'

'Will he come back?'

Book sat down on the bed to think. 'I couldn't say. Don't even know who it was. But if somebody on the committee came along it wouldn't look too good, would it?'

Seeing her expression change, he came over and put his arm around her. 'Don't you worry, honey. We'll fix it.'

She returned his kiss, briefly but without distraction. Then she broke away and went into the next apartment, which was hung with boots, uniform coats and various military equipment.

'There's a window up here,' she said. It was high in the wall and had not been opened for a long time. Book mounted on a chair and forced it ajar.

'About ten feet down,' he reported, after a moment, 'but there's a big pile of snow just underneath. You might get a nasty fall and you'll sure soak your shoes and stockin's.'

'We've got to get out,' Josephine said sharply.

'We'd better wait and give this funny man a chance – '

'I won't wait. I want to get out. Look – throw out all the blankets from the bed and I'll jump on that: or you jump first and spread them over the pile of snow.'

After that it was merely exciting. Carefully Book Chaffee wiped the dust from the window to protect her dress; then they were struck silent by a footstep that approached – and passed the outer door. Book jumped, and she heard him kicking profanely as he waded out of the soft drift below. He spread the blankets. At the moment when Josephine swung her legs out of the window, there was the sound of voices outside the door and the key turned again in the lock. She landed softly, reaching for his hand, and convulsed with laughter they ran and skidded down the half-block towards the corner, and reaching the entrance to the armoury, they stood panting for a moment, breathing in the fresh night. Book was reluctant to go inside.

'Why don't you let me conduct you where you're stayin'? We can sit around and sort of recuperate.'

She hesitated, drawn towards him by the community of their late predicament; but something was calling her inside, as if the fulfilment of her elation awaited her there.

'No,' she decided.

As they went in she collided with a man in a great hurry, and looked up to recognise Dudley Knowleton.

'So sorry,' he said. 'Oh hello – '

'Won't you dance me over to my box?' she begged him impulsively. 'I've torn my dress.'

As they started off he said abstractedly: 'The fact is, a little mischief has come up and the buck has been passed to me. I was going along to see about it.'

Her heart raced wildly and she felt the need of being another sort of person immediately.

'I can't tell you how much it's meant meeting you. It would be wonderful to have one friend I could be serious with without being all mushy and sentimental. Would you mind if I wrote you a letter – I mean, would Adele mind?'

'Lord, no!' His smile had become utterly unfathomable to her. As they reached the box she thought of one more thing: 'Is it true that the baseball team is training at Hot Springs during Easter?'

'Yes. You going there?'

'Yes. Good-night, Mr Knowleton.'

But she was destined to see him once more. It was outside the men's coat room, where she waited among a crowd of other pale survivors and their paler mothers, whose wrinkles had doubled and tripled with the passing night. He was explaining something to Adele, and Josephine heard the phrase, 'The door was locked, and the window open – '

Suddenly it occurred to Josephine that, meeting her coming in damp and breathless, he must have guessed at the truth – and Adele would doubtless confirm his suspicion. Once again the spectre of her old enemy, the plain and jealous girl, arose before her. Shutting her mouth tight together she turned away.

But they had seen her, and Adele called to her in her cheerful ringing voice: 'Come say good-night. You were so sweet about the stockings. Here's a girl you won't find doing shoddy, silly things, Dudley.' Impulsively she leaned and kissed Josephine on the cheek. 'You'll see I'm right, Dudley – next year she'll be the most respected girl in school.'

3

As things go in the interminable days of early March, what happened next happened quickly. The annual senior dance at Miss Brereton's school came on a night soaked through with spring, and all the junior girls lay awake listening to the sighing tunes from the gymnasium. Between the numbers, when boys up from New Haven and Princeton wandered about the grounds, cloistered glances looked down from dark open windows upon the vague figures.

Not Josephine, though she lay awake like the others. Such vicarious diversions had no place in the sober patterns she was spinning now from day to day; yet she might as well have been in the forefront of those who called down to the men and threw notes and entered into conversations, for destiny had suddenly turned against her and was spinning a dark web of its own.

> Lit-tle lady, don't be depressed and blue,
> After all, we're both in the same can-noo –

Dudley Knowleton was over in the gymnasium fifty yards away, but proximity to a man did not thrill her as it would have done a year ago – not, at least, in the same way. Life, she saw now, was a serious matter, and in the modest darkness a line of a novel ceaselessly recurred to her: 'He is a man fit to be the father of my children.' What were the seductive graces, the fast lines of a hundred parlour snakes compared to such realities. One couldn't go on forever kissing comparative strangers behind half-closed doors.

Under her pillow now were two letters, answers to her letters. They spoke in a bold round hand of the beginning of baseball practice; they were glad Josephine felt as she did about things; and the writer certainly looked forward to seeing her at Easter. Of all the letters she had ever received they were the most difficult from which to squeeze a single drop of heart's blood – one couldn't even read the 'Yours' of the subscription as 'Your' – but Josephine knew them by heart. They were precious because he had taken the time to write them; they were eloquent in the very postage stamp because he used so few.

She was restless in her bed – the music had begun again in the gymnasium:

> Oh, my love, I've waited so long for you,
> Oh, my love, I'm singing this song for you –
> Oh-h-h –

From the next room there was light laughter, and then from below a male voice, and a long interchange of comic whispers. Josephine recognised Lillian's laugh and the voices of two other girls. She could imagine them as they lay across the window in their nightgowns, their heads just showing from the open window. 'Come right down,' one boy kept saying. 'Don't be formal – come, just as you are.'

There was a sudden silence, then a quick crunching of footsteps on gravel, a suppressed snicker and a scurry, and the sharp, protesting groan of several beds in the next room and the banging of a door down the hall. Trouble for somebody, maybe. A few minutes later Josephine's door half opened, she caught a glimpse of Miss Kwain against the dim corridor light, and then the door closed.

The next afternoon Josephine and four other girls, all of whom denied having breathed so much as a word into the night, were placed on probation. There was absolutely nothing to do about it. Miss Kwain had recognised their faces in the window and they were all from two rooms. It was an injustice, but it was nothing compared to what happened next. One week before Easter vacation the school motored off on a one-day trip to inspect a milk farm – all save the ones on probation. Miss Chambers, who sympathised with Josephine's misfortune, enlisted her services in entertaining Mr Ernest Waterbury, who was spending a weekend with his aunt. This was only vaguely better than nothing, for Mr Waterbury was a very dull, very priggish young man. He was so dull and so priggish that the following morning Josephine was expelled from school.

It happened like this: they had strolled in the grounds, they had sat down at a garden table and had tea. Ernest Waterbury had expressed a desire to see something in the chapel, just a few minutes before his aunt's car rolled up the drive. The chapel was reached by descending winding mock-medieval stairs; and, her shoes still wet from the garden, Josephine had slipped on the top step and fallen five feet directly into Mr Waterbury's unwilling arms, where she lay helpless, convulsed with irresistible laughter. It was in this position that Miss Brereton and the visiting trustee had found them.

'But I had nothing to do with it!' declared the ungallant Mr Waterbury. Flustered and outraged, he was packed back to New Haven, and Miss Brereton, connecting this with last week's sin, proceeded to lose her head. Josephine, humiliated and furious, lost hers, and Mr Perry, who happened to be in New York, arrived at the school the same night.

At his passionate indignation, Miss Brereton collapsed and retracted, but the damage was done, and Josephine packed her trunk. Unexpectedly, monstrously, just as it had begun to mean something, her school life was over.

For the moment all her feelings were directed against Miss Brereton, and the only tears she shed at leaving were of anger and resentment. Riding with her father up to New York, she saw that while at first he had instinctively and wholeheartedly taken her part, he felt also a certain annoyance with her misfortune.

'We'll all survive,' he said. 'Unfortunately, even that old idiot Miss Brereton will survive. She ought to be running a reform school.' He brooded for a moment. 'Anyhow, your mother arrives tomorrow and you and she go down to Hot Springs as you planned.'

'Hot Springs!' Josephine cried, in a choked voice. 'Oh, no!'

'Why not?' he demanded in surprise. 'It seems the best thing to do. Give it a chance to blow over before you go back to Chicago.'

'I'd rather go to Chicago,' said Josephine breathlessly. 'Daddy, I'd much rather go to Chicago.'

'That's absurd. Your mother's started East and the arrangements are all made. At Hot Springs you can get out and ride and play golf and forget that old she-devil – '

'Isn't there another place in the East we could go? There's people I know going to Hot Springs who'll know all about this, people that I don't want to meet – girls from school.'

'Now, Jo, you keep your chin up – this is one of those times. Sorry I said that about letting it blow over in Chicago; if we hadn't made other plans we'd go back and face every old shrew and gossip in town right away. When anybody slinks off in a corner they think you've been up to something bad. If anybody says anything to you, you tell them the truth – what I said to Miss Brereton. You tell them she said you could come back and I damn well wouldn't let you go back.'

'They won't believe it.'

There would be, at all events, four days of respite at Hot Springs before the vacations of the schools. Josephine passed this time taking golf lessons from a professional so newly arrived from Scotland that he surely knew nothing of her misadventure; she even went riding with a young man one afternoon, feeling almost at home with him after his admission that he had flunked out of Princeton in February – a confidence, however, which she did not reciprocate in kind. But in the evenings, despite the young man's importunity, she stayed with her mother, feeling nearer to her than she ever had before.

But one afternoon in the lobby Josephine saw by the desk two dozen good-looking young men waiting by a stack of hat cases and bags, and knew that what she dreaded was at hand. She ran upstairs and with an invented headache dined there that night, but after dinner she walked restlessly around their apartment. She was ashamed not only of her situation but of her reaction to it. She had never felt any pity for the unpopular girls who skulked in dressing-rooms because they could attract no partners on the floor, or for girls who were outsiders at Lake Forest, and now she was like them – hiding miserably out of life. Alarmed lest already the change was written in her face, she paused in front of the mirror, fascinated as ever by what she found there.

'The darn fools!' she said aloud. And as she said it her chin went up and the faint cloud about her eyes lifted. The phrases of the myriad love letters she had received passed before her eyes; behind her, after all, was the reassurance of a hundred lost and pleading faces, of innumerable tender and pleading voices. Her pride flooded back into her till she could see the warm blood rushing up into her cheeks.

There was a knock at the door – it was the Princeton boy.

'How about slipping downstairs?' he proposed. 'There's a dance. It's full of E-lies, the whole Yale baseball team. I'll pick up one of them and introduce you and you'll have a big time. How about it?'

'All right, but I don't want to meet anybody. You'll just have to dance with me all evening.'

'You know that suits me.'

She hurried into a new spring evening dress of the frailest fairy blue. In the excitement of seeing herself in it, it seemed as if she had shed the old skin of winter and emerged a shining chrysalis with no stain; and going downstairs her feet fell softly just off the beat of the music from below. It was a tune from a play she had seen a week ago in New York, a tune with a future – ready for gaieties as yet unthought of, lovers not yet met. Dancing off, she was certain that life had innumerable beginnings. She had hardly gone ten steps when she was cut in upon by Dudley Knowleton.

'Why, Josephine!' He had never used her first name before – he stood holding her hand. 'Why, I'm so glad to see you! I've been hoping and hoping you'd be here.'

She soared skyward on a rocket of surprise and delight. He was actually glad to see her – the expression on his face was obviously sincere. Could it be possible that he hadn't heard?

'Adele wrote me you might be here. She wasn't sure.'

Then he knew and didn't care; he liked her anyhow.

'I'm in sackcloth and ashes,' she said.

'Well, they're very becoming to you.'

'You know what happened – ' she ventured.

'I do. I wasn't going to say anything, but it's generally agreed that Waterbury behaved like a fool – and it's not going to be much help to him in the elections next month. Look – I want you to dance with some men who are just starving for a touch of beauty.'

Presently she was dancing with, it seemed to her, the entire team at once. Intermittently Dudley Knowleton cut back in, as well as the Princeton man, who was somewhat indignant at this unexpected competition. There were many girls from many schools in the room, but with an admirable team spirit, the Yale men displayed a sharp prejudice in Josephine's favour; already she was pointed out from the chairs along the wall.

But interiorly she was waiting for what was coming, for the moment when she would walk with Dudley Knowleton into the warm, Southern night. It came naturally, just at the end of a number, and they strolled along an avenue of early-blooming lilacs and turned a corner and another corner . . .

'You were glad to see me, weren't you?' Josephine said.

'Of course.'

'I was afraid at first. I was sorriest about what happened at school because of you. I'd been trying so hard to be different – because of you.'

'You mustn't think of that school business any more. Everybody that matters knows you got a bad deal. Forget it and start over.'

'Yes,' she agreed tranquilly. She was happy. The breeze and the scent of lilacs – that was she, lovely and intangible; the rustic bench where they sat and the trees – that was he, rugged and strong beside her, protecting her.

'I'd thought so much of meeting you here,' she said after a minute. 'You'd been so good for me, that I thought maybe in a different way I could be good for you – I mean I know ways of having a good time that you don't know. For instance, we've certainly got to go horseback riding by moonlight some night. That'll be fun.'

He didn't answer.

'I can really be very nice when I like somebody – that's really not often,' she interpolated hastily, 'not seriously. But I mean when I do feel seriously that a boy and I are really friends I don't believe in having a whole mob of other boys hanging around taking up time. I like to be with him all the time, all day and all evening, don't you?'

He stirred a little on the bench; he leaned forward with his elbows on his knees, looking at his strong hands.

Her gently modulated voice sank a note lower. 'When I like anyone I don't even like dancing. It's sweeter to be alone.'

Silence for a moment.

'Well, you know' – he hesitated, frowning – 'as a matter of fact, I'm mixed up in a lot of engagements made some time ago with some people.' He floundered about unhappily. 'In fact, I won't even be at the hotel after tomorrow. I'll be at the house of some people down the valley – a sort of house party. As a matter of fact, Adele's getting here tomorrow.'

Absorbed in her own thoughts, she hardly heard him at first, but at the name she caught her breath sharply.

'We're both to be at this house party while we're here, and I imagine it's more or less arranged what we're going to do. Of course, in the daytime I'll be here for baseball practice.'

'I see.' Her lips were quivering. 'You won't be – you'll be with Adele.'

'I think that – more or less – I will. She'll – want to see you, of course.'

Another silence while he twisted his big fingers and she helplessly imitated the gesture.

'You were just sorry for me,' she said. 'You like Adele – much better.'

'Adele and I understand each other. She's been more or less my ideal since we were children together.'

'And I'm not your kind of girl?' Josephine's voice trembled with a sort of fright. 'I suppose because I've kissed a lot of boys and got a reputation for speed and raised the deuce.'

'It isn't that.'

'Yes, it is,' she declared passionately. 'I'm just paying for things.' She stood up. 'You'd better take me back inside so I can dance with the kind of boys that like me.'

She walked quickly down the path, tears of misery streaming from her eyes. He overtook her by the steps, but she only shook her head and said, 'Excuse me for being so fresh. I'll grow up – I got what was coming to me – it's all right.'

A little later when she looked around the floor for him he had gone – and Josephine realised with a shock that for the first time in her life, she had tried for a man and failed. But, save in the very young, only love begets love, and from the moment Josephine had perceived that his interest in her was merely kindness she realised the wound was not in her heart but in her pride. She would forget him quickly, but she would never forget what she had learned from him. There were two kinds of men, those you played with and those you might marry. And as this passed through her mind, her restless eyes wandered casually over the group of stags, resting very lightly on Mr Gordon Tinsley, the current catch of Chicago, reputedly the richest young man in the Middle West. He had never paid any attention to young Josephine until tonight. Ten minutes ago he had asked her to go driving with him tomorrow.

But he did not attract her – and she decided to refuse. One mustn't run through people, and, for the sake of a romantic half-hour, trade a possibility that might develop – quite seriously – later, at the proper time. She did not know that this was the first mature thought that she had ever had in her life, but it was.

The orchestra were packing their instruments and the Princeton man was still at her ear, still imploring her to walk out with him into the night. Josephine knew without cogitation which sort of man he was – and the moon was bright even on the windows. So with a certain sense of relaxation she took his arm and they strolled out to the pleasant bower she had so lately quitted, and their faces turned towards each other, like little moons under the great white one which hovered high over the Blue Ridge; his arm dropped softly about her yielding shoulder.

'Well?' he whispered.

'Well.'

The Bridal Party

Saturday Evening Post (9 August 1930)

1

There was the usual insincere little note saying: 'I wanted you to be the first to know.' It was a double shock to Michael, announcing, as it did, both the engagement and the imminent marriage; which, moreover, was to be held, not in New York, decently and far away, but here in Paris under his very nose, if that could be said to extend over the Protestant Episcopal Church of the Holy Trinity, Avenue George-Cinq. The date was two weeks off, early in June.

At first Michael was afraid and his stomach felt hollow. When he left the hotel that morning, the *femme de chambre*, who was in love with his fine, sharp profile and his pleasant buoyancy, scented the hard abstraction that had settled over him. He walked in a daze to his bank, he bought a detective story at Smith's on the Rue de Rivoli, he sympathetically stared for a while at a faded panorama of the battlefields in a tourist-office window and cursed a Greek tout who followed him with a half-displayed packet of innocuous postcards warranted to be very dirty indeed.

But the fear stayed with him, and after a while he recognised it as the fear that now he would never be happy. He had met Caroline Dandy when she was seventeen, possessed her young heart all through her first season in New York, and then lost her, slowly, tragically, uselessly, because he had no money and could make no money; because, with all the energy and goodwill in the world, he could not find himself; because, loving him still, Caroline had lost faith and begun to see him as something pathetic, futile and shabby, outside the great, shining stream of life towards which she was inevitably drawn.

Since his only support was that she loved him, he leaned weakly on that; the support broke, but still he held on to it and was carried out to sea and washed up on the French coast with its broken pieces still in his hands. He carried them around with him in the form of photographs and packets of correspondence and a liking for a maudlin popular song called 'Among My Souvenirs'. He kept clear of other girls, as if Caroline would somehow know it and reciprocate with a faithful heart. Her note informed him that he had lost her for ever.

It was a fine morning. In front of the shops in the Rue de Castiglione, proprietors and patrons were on the sidewalk gazing upward, for the Graf Zeppelin, shining and glorious, symbol of escape and destruction – of escape, if necessary, through destruction – glided in the Paris sky. He heard a woman say in French that it would not her astonish if that commenced to let fall the bombs. Then he heard another voice, full of husky laughter, and the void in his stomach froze. Jerking about, he was face to face with Caroline Dandy and her fiancé.

'Why, Michael! Why, we were wondering where you were. I asked at the Guaranty Trust, and Morgan and Company, and finally sent a note to the National City – '

Why didn't they back away? Why didn't they back right up, walking backwards down the Rue de Castiglione, across the Rue de Rivoli, through the Tuileries Gardens, still walking backwards as fast as they could till they grew vague and faded out across the river?

'This is Hamilton Rutherford, my fiancé.'

'We've met before.'

'At Pat's, wasn't it?'

'And last spring in the Ritz Bar.'

'Michael, where have you been keeping yourself?'

'Around here.' This agony. Previews of Hamilton Rutherford flashed before his eyes – a quick series of pictures, sentences. He remembered hearing that he had bought a seat in 1920 for a hundred and twenty-five thousand of borrowed money, and just before the break sold it for more than half a million. Not handsome like Michael, but vitally attractive, confident, authoritative, just the right height over Caroline there – Michael had always been too short for Caroline when they danced.

Rutherford was saying: 'No, I'd like it very much if you'd come to the bachelor dinner. I'm taking the Ritz Bar from nine o'clock on. Then right after the wedding there'll be a reception and breakfast at the Hôtel George-Cinq.'

'And, Michael, George Packman is giving a party day after tomorrow at Chez Victor, and I want you to be sure and come. And also to tea Friday at Jebby West's; she'd want to have you if she knew where you were. What's your hotel, so we can send you an invitation? You see, the reason we decided to have it over here is because mother has been sick in a nursing home here and the whole clan is in Paris. Then Hamilton's mother's being here too – '

The entire clan; they had always hated him, except her mother; always discouraged his courtship. What a little counter he was in this game of families and money! Under his hat his brow sweated with the humiliation of the fact that for all his misery he was worth just exactly so many invitations. Frantically he began to mumble something about going away.

Then it happened – Caroline saw deep into him, and Michael knew that she saw. She saw through to his profound woundedness, and something quivered inside her, died out along the curve of her mouth and in her eyes. He had moved her. All the unforgettable impulses of first love had surged up once more; their hearts had in some way touched across two feet of Paris sunlight. She took her fiancé's arm suddenly, as if to steady herself with the feel of it.

They parted. Michael walked quickly for a minute; then he stopped, pretending to look in a window, and saw them farther up the street, walking fast into the Place Vendôme, people with much to do.

He had things to do also – he had to get his laundry.

'Nothing will ever be the same again,' he said to himself. 'She will never be happy in her marriage and I will never be happy at all any more.'

The two vivid years of his love for Caroline moved back around him like years in Einstein's physics. Intolerable memories arose – of rides in the Long Island moonlight; of a happy time at Lake Placid with her cheeks so cold there, but warm just underneath the surface; of a despairing afternoon in a little café on Forty-Eighth Street in the last sad months when their marriage had come to seem impossible.

'Come in,' he said aloud.

The concierge with a telegram; brusque because Mr Curly's clothes were a little shabby. Mr Curly gave few tips; Mr Curly was obviously a *petit client.*

Michael read the telegram.

'An answer?' the concierge asked.

'No,' said Michael, and then, on an impulse: 'Look.'

'Too bad – too bad,' said the concierge. 'Your grandfather is dead.'

'Not too bad,' said Michael. 'It means that I come into a quarter of a million dollars.'

Too late by a single month; after the first flush of the news his misery was deeper than ever. Lying awake in bed that night, he listened endlessly to the long caravan of a circus moving through the street from one Paris fair to another.

When the last van had rumbled out of hearing and the corners of the furniture were pastel blue with the dawn, he was still thinking of the look in Caroline's eyes that morning – the look that seemed to say: 'Oh, why couldn't you have done something about it? Why couldn't you have been stronger, made me marry you? Don't you see how sad I am?'

Michael's fists clenched.

'Well, I won't give up till the last moment,' he whispered. 'I've had all the bad luck so far, and maybe it's turned at last. One takes what one can get, up to the limit of one's strength, and if I can't have her, at least she'll go into this marriage with some of me in her heart.'

2

Accordingly he went to the party at Chez Victor two days later, upstairs and into the little salon off the bar where the party was to assemble for cocktails. He was early; the only other occupant was a tall lean man of fifty. They spoke.

'You waiting for George Packman's party?'

'Yes. My name's Michael Curly.'

'My name's — '

Michael failed to catch the name. They ordered a drink, and Michael supposed that the bride and groom were having a gay time.

'Too much so,' the other agreed, frowning. 'I don't see how they stand it. We all crossed on the boat together; five days of that crazy life and then two weeks of Paris. You' – he hesitated, smiling faintly – 'you'll excuse me for saying that your generation drinks too much.'

'Not Caroline.'

'No, not Caroline. She seems to take only a cocktail and a glass of champagne, and then she's had enough, thank God. But Hamilton drinks too much and all this crowd of young people drink too much. Do you live in Paris?'

'For the moment,' said Michael.

'I don't like Paris. My wife – that is to say, my ex-wife, Hamilton's mother – lives in Paris.'

'You're Hamilton Rutherford's father?'

'I have that honour. And I'm not denying that I'm proud of what he's done; it was just a general comment.'

'Of course.'

Michael glanced up nervously as four people came in. He felt suddenly that his dinner coat was old and shiny; he had ordered a new one that morning. The people who had come in were rich and at home in their richness with one another – a dark, lovely girl with a hysterical little laugh whom he had met before; two confident men whose jokes referred invariably to last night's scandal and tonight's potentialities, as if they had important roles in a play that extended indefinitely into the past and the future. When Caroline arrived, Michael had scarcely a moment of her, but it was enough to note that, like all the others, she was strained and tired. She was pale beneath her rouge; there were shadows under her eyes. With a mixture of relief and wounded vanity, he found himself placed far from her and at another table; he needed a moment to adjust himself to his surroundings. This was not like the immature set in which he and Caroline had moved; the men were more than thirty and had an air of sharing the best of this world's goods. Next to him was Jebby West, whom he knew; and, on the other side, a jovial man who immediately began to talk to Michael about a stunt for the bachelor dinner. They were going to hire a French girl to appear with an actual baby in her arms, crying: 'Hamilton, you can't desert me now!' The idea seemed stale and unamusing to Michael, but its originator shook with anticipatory laughter.

Farther up the table there was talk of the market – another drop today, the most appreciable since the crash; people were kidding Rutherford about it: 'Too bad, old man. You better not get married, after all.'

Michael asked the man on his left, 'Has he lost a lot?'

'Nobody knows. He's heavily involved, but he's one of the smartest young men in Wall Street. Anyhow, nobody ever tells you the truth.'

It was a champagne dinner from the start, and towards the end it reached a pleasant level of conviviality, but Michael saw that all these people were too weary to be exhilarated by any ordinary stimulant; for weeks they had drunk cocktails before meals like Americans, wines and brandies like Frenchmen, beer like Germans, whisky-and-soda like the English, and as they were no longer in their twenties, this preposterous *mélange*, that was like some gigantic cocktail in a nightmare, served only to make them temporarily less conscious of the mistakes of the night before. Which is to say that it was not really a gay party; what gaiety existed was displayed in the few who drank nothing at all.

But Michael was not tired, and the champagne stimulated him and made his misery less acute. He had been away from New York for more than eight months and most of the dance music was unfamiliar to him, but at the first bars of 'The Painted Doll', to which he and Caroline had moved through so much happiness and despair the previous summer, he crossed to Caroline's table and asked her to dance.

She was lovely, in a dress of thin ethereal blue, and the proximity of her crackly yellow hair, of her cool and tender grey eyes, turned his body clumsy and rigid; he stumbled with their first step on the floor. For a moment it seemed that there was nothing to say; he wanted to tell her about his inheritance, but the idea seemed abrupt, unprepared for.

'Michael, it's so nice to be dancing with you again.'

He smiled grimly.

'I'm so happy you came,' she continued. 'I was afraid maybe you'd be silly and stay away. Now we can be just good friends and natural together. Michael, I want you and Hamilton to like each other.'

The engagement was making her stupid; he had never heard her make such a series of obvious remarks before.

'I could kill him without a qualm,' he said pleasantly, 'but he looks like a good man. He's fine. What I want to know is, what happens to people like me who aren't able to forget?'

As he said this he could not prevent his mouth from dropping suddenly, and glancing up, Caroline saw, and her heart quivered violently, as it had the other morning.

'Do you mind so much, Michael?'

'Yes.'

For a second as he said this, in a voice that seemed to have come up from his shoes, they were not dancing; they were simply clinging together. Then she leaned away from him and twisted her mouth into a lovely smile.

'I didn't know what to do at first, Michael. I told Hamilton about you – that I'd cared for you an awful lot – but it didn't worry him, and he was right. Because I'm over you now – yes, I am. And you'll wake up some sunny morning and be over me just like that.'

He shook his head stubbornly.

'Oh, yes. We weren't for each other. I'm pretty flighty, and I need somebody like Hamilton to decide things. It was that more than the question of – of – '

'Of money?' Again he was on the point of telling her what had happened, but again something told him it was not the time.

'Then how do you account for what happened when we met the other day,' he demanded helplessly – 'what happened just now? When we just pour towards each other like we used to – as if we were one person, as if the same blood was flowing through both of us?'

'Oh, don't,' she begged him. 'You mustn't talk like that; everything's decided now. I love Hamilton with all my heart. It's just that I remember certain things in the past and I feel sorry for you – for us – for the way we were.'

Over her shoulder, Michael saw a man come towards them to cut in. In a panic he danced her away, but inevitably the man came on.

'I've got to see you alone, if only for a minute,' Michael said quickly. 'When can I?'

'I'll be at Jebby West's tea tomorrow,' she whispered as a hand fell politely upon Michael's shoulder.

But he did not talk to her at Jebby West's tea. Rutherford stood next to her, and each brought the other into all conversations. They left early. The next morning the wedding cards arrived in the first mail.

Then Michael, grown desperate with pacing up and down his room, determined on a bold stroke; he wrote to Hamilton Rutherford, asking him for a rendezvous the following afternoon. In a short telephone communication Rutherford agreed, but for a day later than Michael had asked. And the wedding was only six days away.

They were to meet in the bar of the Hôtel Jéna. Michael knew what he would say: 'See here, Rutherford, do you realise the responsibility you're taking in going through with this marriage? Do you realise the harvest of trouble and regret you're sowing in persuading a girl into something contrary to the instincts of her heart?' He would explain that the barrier between Caroline and himself had been an artificial one and was now removed, and demand that the matter be put up to Caroline frankly before it was too late.

Rutherford would be angry, conceivably there would be a scene, but Michael felt that he was fighting for his life now.

He found Rutherford in conversation with an older man, whom Michael had met at several of the wedding parties.

'I saw what happened to most of my friends,' Rutherford was saying, 'and I decided it wasn't going to happen to me. It isn't so difficult; if you take a girl with common sense, and tell her what's what, and do your stuff damn well, and play decently square with her, it's a marriage. If you stand for any nonsense at the beginning, it's one of these arrangements – within five years the man gets out, or else the girl gobbles him up and you have the usual mess.'

'Right!' agreed his companion enthusiastically. 'Hamilton, boy, you're right.'

Michael's blood boiled slowly.

'Doesn't it strike you,' he enquired coldly, 'that your attitude went out of fashion about a hundred years ago?'

'No, it didn't,' said Rutherford pleasantly, but impatiently. 'I'm as modern as anybody. I'd get married in an aeroplane next Saturday if it'd please my girl.'

'I don't mean that way of being modern. You can't take a sensitive woman – '

'Sensitive? Women aren't so darn sensitive. It's fellows like you who are sensitive; it's fellows like you they exploit – all your devotion and kindness and all that. They read a couple of books and see a few pictures because they haven't got anything else to do, and then they say they're finer in grain than you are, and to prove it they take the bit in their teeth and tear off for a fare-you-well – just about as sensitive as a fire horse.'

'Caroline happens to be sensitive,' said Michael in a clipped voice.

At this point the other man got up to go; when the dispute about the check had been settled and they were alone, Rutherford leaned back to Michael as if a question had been asked him.

'Caroline's more than sensitive,' he said. 'She's got sense.'

His combative eyes, meeting Michael's, flickered with a grey light. 'This all sounds pretty crude to you, Mr Curly, but it seems to me that the average man nowadays just asks to be made a monkey of by some woman who doesn't even get any fun out of reducing him to that level. There are darn few men who possess their wives any more, but I am going to be one of them.'

To Michael it seemed time to bring the talk back to the actual situation: 'Do you realise the responsibility you're taking?'

'I certainly do,' interrupted Rutherford. 'I'm not afraid of responsibility. I'll make the decisions – fairly, I hope, but anyhow they'll be final.'

'What if you didn't start right?' said Michael impetuously. 'What if your marriage isn't founded on mutual love?'

'I think I see what you mean,' Rutherford said, still pleasant. 'And since you've brought it up, let me say that if you and Caroline had married, it wouldn't have lasted three years. Do you know what your affair was founded on? On sorrow. You got sorry for each other. Sorrow's a lot of fun for most women and for some men, but it seems to me that a marriage ought to be based on hope.' He looked at his watch and stood up.

'I've got to meet Caroline. Remember, you're coming to the bachelor dinner day after tomorrow.'

Michael felt the moment slipping away. 'Then Caroline's personal feelings don't count with you?' he demanded fiercely.

'Caroline's tired and upset. But she has what she wants, and that's the main thing.'

'Are you referring to yourself?' demanded Michael incredulously.

'Yes.'

'May I ask how long she's wanted you?'

'About two years.' Before Michael could answer, he was gone.

During the next two days Michael floated in an abyss of helplessness. The idea haunted him that he had left something undone that would sever this knot drawn tighter under his eyes. He phoned Caroline, but she insisted that it was physically impossible for her to see him until the day before the wedding, for which day she granted him a tentative rendezvous. Then he went to the bachelor dinner, partly in fear of an evening alone at his hotel, partly from a feeling that by his presence at that function he was somehow nearer to Caroline, keeping her in sight.

The Ritz Bar had been prepared for the occasion by French and American banners and by a great canvas covering one wall, against which the guests were invited to concentrate their proclivities in breaking glasses.

At the first cocktail, taken at the bar, there were many slight spillings from many trembling hands, but later, with the champagne, there was a rising tide of laughter and occasional bursts of song.

Michael was surprised to find what a difference his new dinner coat, his new silk hat, his new, proud linen made in his estimate of himself; he felt less resentment towards all these people for being so rich and assured. For the first time since he had left college he felt rich and assured himself; he felt that he was part of all this, and even entered into the scheme of Johnson, the practical joker, for the appearance of the woman betrayed, now waiting tranquilly in the room across the hall.

'We don't want to go too heavy,' Johnson said, 'because I imagine Ham's had a pretty anxious day already. Did you see Fullman Oil's sixteen points off this morning?'

'Will that matter to him?' Michael asked, trying to keep the interest out of his voice.

'Naturally. He's in heavily; he's always in everything heavily. So far he's had luck; anyhow, up to a month ago.'

The glasses were filled and emptied faster now, and men were shouting at one another across the narrow table. Against the bar a group of ushers was being photographed, and the flashlight surged through the room in a stifling cloud.

'Now's the time,' Johnson said. 'You're to stand by the door, remember, and we're both to try and keep her from coming in – just till we get everybody's attention.'

He went on out into the corridor, and Michael waited obediently by the door. Several minutes passed. Then Johnson reappeared with a curious expression on his face.

'There's something funny about this.'

'Isn't the girl there?'

'She's there all right, but there's another woman there, too; and it's nobody we engaged either. She wants to see Hamilton Rutherford, and she looks as if she had something on her mind.'

They went out into the hall. Planted firmly in a chair near the door sat an American girl a little the worse for liquor, but with a determined expression on her face. She looked up at them with a jerk of her head.

'Well, j'tell him?' she demanded. 'The name is Marjorie Collins, and he'll know it. I've come a long way, and I want to see him now and quick, or there's going to be more trouble than you ever saw.' She rose unsteadily to her feet.

'You go in and tell Ham,' whispered Johnson to Michael. 'Maybe he'd better get out. I'll keep her here.'

Back at the table, Michael leaned close to Rutherford's ear and, with a certain grimness, whispered: 'A girl outside named Marjorie Collins says she wants to see you. She looks as if she wanted to make trouble.'

Hamilton Rutherford blinked and his mouth fell ajar; then slowly the lips came together in a straight line and he said in a crisp voice: 'Please keep her there. And send the head barman to me right away.'

Michael spoke to the barman, and then, without returning to the table, asked quietly for his coat and hat. Out in the hall again, he passed Johnson and the girl without speaking and went out into the Rue Cambon. Calling a cab, he gave the address of Caroline's hotel.

His place was beside her now. Not to bring bad news, but simply to be with her when her house of cards came falling around her head.

Rutherford had implied that he was soft – well, he was hard enough not to give up the girl he loved without taking advantage of every chance within the pale of honour. Should she turn away from Rutherford, she would find him there.

She was in; she was surprised when he called, but she was still dressed and would be down immediately. Presently she appeared in a dinner gown, holding two blue telegrams in her hand. They sat down in armchairs in the deserted lobby.

'But, Michael, is the dinner over?'

'I wanted to see you, so I came away.'

'I'm glad.' Her voice was friendly, but matter-of-fact. 'Because I'd just phoned your hotel that I had fittings and rehearsals all day tomorrow. Now we can have our talk after all.'

'You're tired,' he guessed. 'Perhaps I shouldn't have come.'

'No. I was waiting up for Hamilton. Telegrams that may be important. He said he might go on somewhere, and that may mean any hour, so I'm glad I have someone to talk to.'

Michael winced at the impersonality in the last phrase.

'Don't you care when he gets home?'

'Naturally,' she said, laughing, 'but I haven't got much say about it, have I?'

'Why not?'

'I couldn't start by telling him what he could and couldn't do.'

'Why not?'

'He wouldn't stand for it.'

'He seems to want merely a housekeeper,' said Michael ironically.

'Tell me about your plans, Michael,' she asked quickly.

'My plans? I can't see any future after the day after tomorrow. The only real plan I ever had was to love you.'

Their eyes brushed past each other's, and the look he knew so well was staring out at him from hers. Words flowed quickly from his heart: 'Let me tell you just once more how well I've loved you, never wavering for a moment, never thinking of another girl. And now when I think of all the years ahead without you, without any hope, I don't want to live, Caroline darling. I used to dream about our home, our children, about holding you in my arms and touching your face and hands and hair that used to belong to me, and now I just can't wake up.'

Caroline was crying softly. 'Poor Michael – poor Michael.' Her hand reached out and her fingers brushed the lapel of his dinner coat. 'I was so sorry for you the other night. You looked so thin, and as if you needed a new suit and somebody to take care of you.' She sniffled and looked more closely at his coat. 'Why, you've got a new suit! And a new silk hat! Why, Michael, how swell!' She laughed, suddenly cheerful through her tears. 'You must have come into money, Michael; I never saw you so well turned out.'

For a moment, at her reaction, he hated his new clothes.

'I have come into money,' he said. 'My grandfather left me about a quarter of a million dollars.'

'Why, Michael,' she cried, 'how perfectly swell! I can't tell you how glad I am. I've always thought you were the sort of person who ought to have money.'

'Yes, just too late to make a difference.'

The revolving door from the street groaned around and Hamilton Rutherford came into the lobby. His face was flushed, his eyes were restless and impatient.

'Hello, darling; hello, Mr Curly.' He bent and kissed Caroline. 'I broke away for a minute to find out if I had any telegrams. I see you've got them there.' Taking them from her, he remarked to Curly, 'That was an odd business there in the bar, wasn't it? Especially as I understand some of you had a joke fixed up in the same line.' He opened one of the telegrams, closed it and turned to Caroline with the divided expression of a man carrying two things in his head at once.

'A girl I haven't seen for two years turned up,' he said. 'It seemed to be some clumsy form of blackmail, for I haven't and never have had any sort of obligation towards her whatever.'

'What happened?'

'The head barman had a Sûreté Générale man there in ten minutes and it was settled in the hall. The French blackmail laws make ours look like a sweet wish, and I gather they threw a scare into her that she'll remember. But it seems wiser to tell you.'

'Are you implying that I mentioned the matter?' said Michael stiffly.

'No,' Rutherford said slowly. 'No, you were just going to be on hand. And since you're here, I'll tell you some news that will interest you even more.'

He handed Michael one telegram and opened the other.

'This is in code,' Michael said.

'So is this. But I've got to know all the words pretty well this last week. The two of them together mean that I'm due to start life all over.'

Michael saw Caroline's face grow a shade paler, but she sat quiet as a mouse.

'It was a mistake and I stuck to it too long,' continued Rutherford. 'So you see I don't have all the luck, Mr Curly. By the way, they tell me you've come into money.'

'Yes,' said Michael.

'There we are, then.' Rutherford turned to Caroline. 'You understand, darling, that I'm not joking or exaggerating. I've lost almost every cent I had and I'm starting life over.'

Two pairs of eyes were regarding her – Rutherford's noncommittal and unrequiring, Michael's hungry, tragic, pleading. In a minute she had raised herself from the chair and with a little cry thrown herself into Hamilton Rutherford's arms.

'Oh, darling,' she cried, 'what does it matter! It's better; I like it better, honestly I do! I want to start that way; I want to! Oh, please don't worry or be sad even for a minute!'

'All right, baby,' said Rutherford. His hand stroked her hair gently for a moment; then he took his arm from around her.

'I promised to join the party for an hour,' he said. 'So I'll say goodnight, and I want you to go to bed soon and get a good sleep. Goodnight, Mr Curly. I'm sorry to have let you in for all these financial matters.'

But Michael had already picked up his hat and cane. 'I'll go along with you,' he said.

3

It was such a fine morning. Michael's cutaway hadn't been delivered, so he felt rather uncomfortable passing before the cameras and moving-picture machines in front of the little church on the Avenue George-Cinq.

It was such a clean, new church that it seemed unforgivable not to be dressed properly, and Michael, white and shaky after a sleepless night, decided to stand in the rear. From there he looked at the back of Hamilton Rutherford, and the lacy, filmy back of Caroline, and the fat back of George Packman, which looked unsteady, as if it wanted to lean against the bride and groom.

The ceremony went on for a long time under the gay flags and pennons overhead, under the thick beams of June sunlight slanting down through the tall windows upon the well-dressed people.

As the procession, headed by the bride and groom, started down the aisle, Michael realised with alarm he was just where everyone would dispense with their parade stiffness, become informal and speak to him.

So it turned out. Rutherford and Caroline spoke first to him; Rutherford grim with the strain of being married, and Caroline lovelier than he had ever seen her, floating all softly down through the friends and relatives of her youth, down through the past and forward to the future by the sunlit door.

Michael managed to murmur, 'Beautiful, simply beautiful,' and then other people passed and spoke to him – old Mrs Dandy, straight from her sickbed and looking remarkably well, or carrying it off like the very fine old lady she was; and Rutherford's father and mother, ten years divorced, but walking side by side and looking made for each other and proud. Then all Caroline's sisters and their husbands and her little nephews in Eton suits, and then a long parade, all speaking to Michael because he was still standing paralysed just at that point where the procession broke.

He wondered what would happen now. Cards had been issued for a reception at the George-Cinq; an expensive enough place, heaven knew. Would Rutherford try to go through with that on top of those disastrous telegrams? Evidently, for the procession outside was streaming up there through the June morning, three by three and four by four. On the corner the long dresses of girls, five abreast, fluttered many-coloured in the wind. Girls had become gossamer again, perambulatory flora; such lovely fluttering dresses in the bright noon wind.

Michael needed a drink; he couldn't face that reception line without a drink. Diving into a side doorway of the hotel, he asked for the bar, whither a *chasseur* led him through half a kilometre of new American-looking passages.

But – how did it happen? – the bar was full. There were ten – fifteen men and two – four girls, all from the wedding, all needing a drink. There were cocktails and champagne in the bar; Rutherford's cocktails and champagne, as it turned out, for he had engaged the whole bar and the ballroom and the two great reception rooms and all the stairways leading up and down, and windows looking out over the whole square block of Paris. By and by Michael went and joined the long, slow drift of the receiving line. Through a flowery mist of, 'Such a lovely wedding,' 'My dear, you were simply lovely,' 'You're a lucky man, Rutherford,' he passed down the line. When Michael came to Caroline, she took a single step forward and kissed him on the lips, but he felt no contact in the kiss; it was unreal and he floated on away from it. Old Mrs Dandy, who had always liked him, held his hand for a minute and thanked him for the flowers he had sent when he heard she was ill.

'I'm so sorry not to have written; you know, we old ladies are grateful for – ' The flowers, the fact that she had not written, the wedding – Michael saw that they all had the same relative importance to her now; she had married off five other children and seen two of the marriages go to pieces, and this scene, so poignant, so confusing to Michael, appeared to her simply a familiar charade in which she had played her part before.

A buffet luncheon with champagne was already being served at small tables and there was an orchestra playing in the empty ballroom. Michael sat down with Jebby West; he was still a little embarrassed at not wearing a morning coat, but he perceived now that he was not alone in the omission and felt better. 'Wasn't Caroline divine?' Jebby West said. 'So entirely self-possessed. I asked her this morning if she wasn't a little nervous at stepping off like this. And she said, "Why should I be? I've been after him for two years, and now I'm just happy, that's all." '

'It must be true,' said Michael gloomily.

'What?'

'What you just said.'

He had been stabbed, but, rather to his distress, he did not feel the wound.

He asked Jebby to dance. Out on the floor, Rutherford's father and mother were dancing together.

'It makes me a little sad, that,' she said. 'Those two hadn't met for years; both of them were married again and she divorced again. She went to the station to meet him when he came over for Caroline's wedding, and invited him to stay at her house in the Avenue du Bois with a whole lot of other people, perfectly proper, but he was afraid his wife would hear about it and not like it, so he went to a hotel. Don't you think that's sort of sad?'

An hour or so later Michael realised suddenly that it was afternoon. In one corner of the ballroom an arrangement of screens like a moving-picture stage had been set up and photographers were taking official pictures of the bridal party. The bridal party, still as death and pale as wax under the bright lights, appeared, to the dancers circling the modulated semi-darkness of the ballroom, like those jovial or sinister groups that one comes upon in the Old Mill at an amusement park.

After the bridal party had been photographed, there was a group of the ushers; then the bridesmaids, the families, the children. Later, Caroline, active and excited, having long since abandoned the repose implicit in her flowing dress and great bouquet, came and plucked Michael off the floor.

'Now we'll have them take one of just old friends.' Her voice implied that this was the best, most intimate of all. 'Come here, Jebby, George – not you, Hamilton; this is just my friends – Sally – '

A little after that, what remained of formality disappeared and the hours flowed easily down the profuse stream of champagne. In the modern fashion, Hamilton Rutherford sat at the table with his arm about an old girl of his and assured his guests, which included not a few bewildered but enthusiastic Europeans, that the party was not nearly at an end; it was to reassemble at Zelli's after midnight. Michael saw Mrs Dandy, not quite over her illness, rise to go and become caught in polite group after group, and he spoke of it to one of her daughters, who thereupon forcibly abducted her mother and called her car. Michael felt very considerate and proud of himself after having done this, and drank much more champagne.

'It's amazing,' George Packman was telling him enthusiastically. 'This show will cost Ham about five thousand dollars, and I understand they'll be just about his last. But did he countermand a bottle of champagne or a flower? Not he! He happens to have it – that young man. Do you know that T. G. Vance offered him a salary of fifty thousand dollars a year ten minutes before the wedding this morning? In another year he'll be back with the millionaires.'

The conversation was interrupted by a plan to carry Rutherford out on communal shoulders – a plan which six of them put into effect, and then stood in the four-o'clock sunshine waving goodbye to the bride and groom. But there must have been a mistake somewhere, for five minutes later Michael saw both bride and groom descending the stairway to the reception, each with a glass of champagne held defiantly on high.

'This is our way of doing things,' he thought. 'Generous and fresh and free; a sort of Virginia-plantation hospitality, but at a different pace now, nervous as a ticker tape.'

Standing unself-consciously in the middle of the room to see which was the American ambassador, he realised with a start that he hadn't really thought of Caroline for hours. He looked about him with a sort of alarm, and then he saw her across the room, very bright and young, and radiantly happy. He saw Rutherford near her, looking at her as if he could never look long enough, and as Michael watched them they seemed to recede as he had wished them to do that day in the Rue de Castiglione – recede and fade off into joys and griefs of their own, into the years that would take the toll of Rutherford's fine pride and Caroline's young, moving beauty; fade far away, so that now he could scarcely see them, as if they were shrouded in something as misty as her white, billowing dress.

Michael was cured. The ceremonial function, with its pomp and its revelry, had stood for a sort of initiation into a life where even his regret could not follow them. All the bitterness melted out of him suddenly and the world reconstituted itself out of the youth and happiness that was all around him, profligate as the spring sunshine. He was trying to remember which one of the bridesmaids he had made a date to dine with tonight as he walked forward to bid Hamilton and Caroline Rutherford goodbye.

A Freeze-Out

Saturday Evening Post (19 December 1931)

1

Here and there in a sunless corner skulked a little snow under a veil of coal specks, but the men taking down storm windows were labouring in shirt sleeves and the turf was becoming firm underfoot.

In the streets, dresses dyed after fruit, leaf and flower emerged from beneath the shed sombre skins of animals; now only a few old men wore mousy caps pulled down over their ears. That was the day Forrest Winslow forgot the long fret of the past winter as one forgets inevitable afflictions, sickness and war, and turned with blind confidence towards the summer, thinking he already recognised in it all the summers of the past – the golfing, sailing, swimming summers.

For eight years Forrest had gone East to school and then to college; now he worked for his father in a large Minnesota city. He was handsome, popular and rather spoiled in a conservative way, and so the past year had been a comedown. The discrimination that had picked Scroll and Key at New Haven was applied to sorting furs; the hand that had signed the Junior Prom expense checks had since rocked in a sling for two months with mild *dermatitis venenata*. After work, Forrest found no surcease in the girls with whom he had grown up. On the contrary, the news of a stranger within the tribe stimulated him and during the transit of a popular visitor he displayed a convulsive activity. So far, nothing had happened; but here was summer.

On the day spring broke through and summer broke through – it is much the same thing in Minnesota – Forrest stopped his coupé in front of a music store and took his pleasant vanity inside. As he said to the clerk, 'I want some records,' a little bomb of excitement exploded in his larynx, causing an unfamiliar and almost painful vacuum in his upper diaphragm. The unexpected detonation was caused by the sight of a corn-coloured girl who was being waited on across the counter.

She was a stalk of ripe corn, but bound not as cereals are but as a rare first edition, with all the binder's art. She was lovely and expensive, and about nineteen, and he had never seen her before. She looked at him for just an unnecessary moment too long, with so much self-confidence that he felt his own rush out and away to join hers – '. . . from him that hath not shall be taken away even that which he hath.' Then her head swayed forward and she resumed her inspection of a catalogue.

Forrest looked at the list a friend had sent him from New York. Unfortunately, the first title was: 'When Voo-do-o-do Meets Boop-boop-a-doop, There'll Soon be a Hot-Cha-Cha'. Forrest read it with horror. He could scarcely believe a title could be so repulsive.

Meanwhile the girl was asking: 'Isn't there a record of Prokofiev's *Fils prodigue*?'

'I'll see, madam.' The saleswoman turned to Forrest.

' "When Voo – " ' Forrest began, and then repeated, ' "When Voo – " '

There was no use; he couldn't say it in front of that nymph of the harvest across the table.

'Never mind that one,' he said quickly. 'Give me "Huggable – " '

Again he broke off.

' "Huggable, Kissable You"?' suggested the clerk helpfully, and her assurance that it was very nice suggested a humiliating community of taste.

'I want Stravinsky's *Fire Bird*,' said the other customer, 'and this album of Chopin waltzes.'

Forrest ran his eye hastily down the rest of his list: 'Digga Diggity', 'Ever So Goosy','Unkey Doodle I Do'.

'Anybody would take me for a moron,' he thought. He crumpled up the list and fought for air – his own kind of air, the air of casual superiority.

'I'd like,' he said coldly, 'Beethoven's *Moonlight Sonata*.'

There was a record of it at home, but it didn't matter. It gave him the right to glance at the girl again and again. Life became interesting; she was the loveliest concoction; it would be easy to trace her. With the *Moonlight Sonata* wrapped face to face with 'Huggable, Kissable You', Forrest quitted the shop.

There was a new bookstore down the street, and here also he entered, as if books and records could fill the vacuum that spring was making in his heart. As he looked among the lifeless words of many titles together, he was wondering how soon he could find her, and what then.

'I'd like a hard-boiled detective story,' he said.

A weary young man shook his head with patient reproof; simultaneously, a spring draft from the door blew in with it the familiar glow of cereal hair.

'We don't carry detective stories or stuff like that,' said the young man in an unnecessarily loud voice. 'I imagine you'll find it at a department store.'

'I thought you carried books,' said Forrest feebly.

'Books, yes, but not that kind.' The young man turned to wait on his other customer.

As Forrest stalked out, passing within the radius of the girl's perfume, he heard her ask: 'Have you got anything of Louis Arragon's, either in French or in translation?'

'She's just showing off,' he thought angrily. 'They skip right from Peter Rabbit to Marcel Proust these days.'

Outside, parked just behind his own adequate coupé, he found an enormous silver-coloured roadster of English make and custom design. Disturbed, even upset, he drove homeward through the moist, golden afternoon.

The Winslows lived in an old, wide-verandaed house on Crest Avenue – Forrest's father and mother, his great-grandmother and his sister Eleanor. They were solid people as that phrase goes since the war. Old Mrs Forrest was entirely solid, with convictions based on a way of life that had worked for eighty-four years. She was a character in the city; she remembered the Sioux war and she had been in Stillwater the day the James brothers shot up the main street.

Her own children were dead and she looked on these remoter descendants from a distance, oblivious of the forces that had formed them. She understood that the Civil War and the opening up of the West were forces, while the free-silver movement and the World War had reached her only as news. But she knew that her father, killed at Cold Harbour, and her husband, the merchant, were larger in scale than her son or her grandson. People who tried to explain contemporary phenomena to her seemed, to her, to be talking against the evidence of their own senses. Yet she was not atrophied; last summer she had travelled over half of Europe with only a maid.

Forrest's father and mother were something else again. They had been in the susceptible middle thirties when the cocktail party and its concomitants arrived in 1921. They were divided people, leaning forward and backwards. Issues that presented no difficulty to Mrs

Forrest caused them painful heat and agitation. Such an issue arose before they had been five minutes at table that night.

'Do you know the Rikkers are coming back?' said Mrs Winslow. 'They've taken the Warner house.' She was a woman with many uncertainties, which she concealed from herself by expressing her opinions very slowly and thoughtfully, to convince her own ears. 'It's a wonder Dan Warner would rent them his house. I suppose Cathy thinks everybody will fall all over themselves.'

'What Cathy?' asked old Mrs Forrest.

'She was Cathy Chase. Her father was Reynold Chase. She and her husband are coming back here.'

'Oh, yes.'

'I scarcely knew her,' continued Mrs Winslow, 'but I know that when they were in Washington they were pointedly rude to everyone from Minnesota – went out of their way. Mary Cowan was spending a winter there, and she invited Cathy to lunch or tea at least half a dozen times. Cathy never appeared.'

'I could beat that record,' said Pierce Winslow. 'Mary Cowan could invite me a hundred times and I wouldn't go.'

'Anyhow,' pursued his wife slowly, 'in view of all the scandal, it's just asking for the cold shoulder to come out here.'

'They're asking for it, all right,' said Winslow. He was a Southerner, well liked in the city, where he had lived for thirty years. 'Walter Hannan came in my office this morning and wanted me to second Rikker for the Kennemore Club. I said: "Walter, I'd rather second Al Capone." What's more, Rikker'll get into the Kennemore Club over my dead body.'

'Walter had his nerve. What's Chauncey Rikker to you? It'll be hard to get anyone to second him.'

'Who are they?' Eleanor asked. 'Somebody awful?'

She was eighteen and a débutante. Her current appearances at home were so rare and brief that she viewed such table topics with as much detachment as her great-grandmother.

'Cathy was a girl here; she was younger then I was, but I remember that she was always considered fast. Her husband, Chauncey Rikker, came from some little town upstate.'

'What did they do that was so awful?'

'Rikker went bankrupt and left town,' said her father. 'There were a lot of ugly stories. Then he went to Washington and got mixed up in the alien-property scandal; and then he got in trouble in New York –

he was in the bucket-shop business – but he skipped out to Europe. After a few years the chief government witness died and he came back to America. They got him for a few months for contempt of court.' He expanded into eloquent irony: 'And now, with true patriotism, he comes back to his beautiful Minnesota, a product of its lovely woods, its rolling wheatfields – '

Forrest called him impatiently: 'Where do you get that, father? When did two Kentuckians ever win Nobel prizes in the same year? And how about an upstate boy named Lind – '

'Have the Rikkers any children?' Eleanor asked.

'I think Cathy has a daughter about your age, and a boy about sixteen.'

Forrest uttered a small, unnoticed exclamation. Was it possible? French books and Russian music – that girl this afternoon had lived abroad. And with the probability his resentment deepened – the daughter of a crook putting on all that dog! He sympathised passionately with his father's refusal to second Rikker for the Kennemore Club.

'Are they rich?' old Mrs Forrest suddenly demanded.

'They must be well off if they took Dan Warner's house.'

'Then they'll get in all right.'

'They won't get into the Kennemore Club,' said Pierce Winslow. 'I happen to come from a state with certain traditions.'

'I've seen the bottom rail get to be the top rail many times in this town,' said the old lady blandly.

'But this man's a criminal, grandma,' explained Forrest. 'Can't you see the difference? It isn't a social question. We used to argue at New Haven whether we'd shake hands with Al Capone if we met him – '

'Who is Al Capone?' asked Mrs Forrest.

'He's another criminal, in Chicago.'

'Does he want to join the Kennemore Club too?'

They laughed, but Forrest had decided that if Rikker came up for the Kennemore Club, his father's would not be the only black ball in the box.

Abruptly it became full summer. After the last April storm someone came along the street one night, blew up the trees like balloons, scattered bulbs and shrubs like confetti, opened a cage full of robins and, after a quick look around, signalled up the curtain upon a new backdrop of summer sky.

Tossing back a strayed baseball to some kids in a vacant lot, Forrest's fingers, on the stitched seams of the stained leather cover, sent a wave of ecstatic memories to his brain. One must hurry and get there – 'there' was now the fairway of the golf course, but his feeling was the same. Only when he teed off at the eighteenth that afternoon did he realise that it wasn't the same, that it would never be enough any more. The evening stretched large and empty before him, save for the set pieces of a dinner party and bed.

While he waited with his partner for a match to play off, Forrest glanced at the tenth tee, exactly opposite and two hundred yards away.

One of the two figures on the ladies' tee was addressing her ball; as he watched, she swung up confidently and cracked a long drive down the fairway.

'Must be Mrs Horrick,' said his friend. 'No other woman can drive like that.'

At that moment the sun glittered on the girl's hair and Forrest knew who it was; simultaneously, he remembered what he must do this afternoon. That night Chauncey Rikker's name was to come up before the membership committee on which his father sat, and before going home, Forrest was going to pass the clubhouse and leave a certain black slip in a little box. He had carefully considered all that; he loved the city where his people had lived honourable lives for five generations. His grandfather had been a founder of this club in the 90s when it went in for sailboat racing instead of golf, and when it took a fast horse three hours to trot out here from town. He agreed with his father that certain people were without the pale. Tightening his face, he drove his ball two hundred yards down the fairway, where it curved gently into the rough.

The eighteenth and tenth holes were parallel and faced in opposite directions. Between tees they were separated by a belt of trees forty feet wide. Though Forrest did not know it, Miss Rikker's hostess, Helen Hannan, had dubbed into this same obscurity, and as he went in search of his ball he heard female voices twenty feet away.

'You'll be a member after tonight,' he heard Helen Hannan say, 'and then you can get some real competition from Stella Horrick.'

'Maybe I won't be a member,' said a quick, clear voice. 'Then you'll have to come and play with me on the public links.'

'Alida, don't be absurd.'

'Why? I played on the public links in Buffalo all last spring. For the moment there wasn't anywhere else. It's like playing on some courses in Scotland.'

'But I'd feel so silly . . . Oh, gosh, let's let the ball go.'

'There's nobody behind us. As to feeling silly – if I cared about public opinion any more, I'd spend my time in my bedroom.' She laughed scornfully. 'A tabloid published a picture of me going to see father in prison. And I've seen people change their tables away from us on steamers, and once I was cut by all the American girls in a French school . . . Here's your ball.'

'Thanks . . . Oh, Alida, it seems terrible.'

'All the terrible part is over. I just said that so you wouldn't be too sorry for us if people didn't want us in this club. I wouldn't care; I've got a life of my own and my own standard of what trouble is. It wouldn't touch me at all.'

They passed out of the clearing and their voices disappeared into the open sky on the other side. Forrest abandoned the search for his lost ball and walked towards the caddie house.

'What a hell of a note,' he thought. 'To take it out on a girl that had nothing to do with it' – which was what he was doing this minute as he went up towards the club. 'No,' he said to himself abruptly, 'I can't do it. Whatever her father may have done, she happens to be a lady. Father can do what he feels he has to do, but I'm out.'

After lunch the next day, his father said rather diffidently: 'I see you didn't do anything about the Rikkers and the Kennemore Club.'

'No.'

'It's just as well,' said his father. 'As a matter of fact, they got by. The club has got rather mixed anyhow in the last five years – a good many queer people in it. And, after all, in a club you don't have to know anybody you don't want to. The other people on the committee felt the same way.'

'I see,' said Forrest dryly. 'Then you didn't argue against the Rikkers?'

'Well, no. The thing is I do a lot of business with Walter Hannan, and it happened yesterday I was obliged to ask him rather a difficult favour.'

'So you traded with him.' To both father and son, the word 'traded' sounded like traitor.

'Not exactly. The matter wasn't mentioned.'

'I understand,' Forrest said. But he did not understand, and some old childhood faith in his father died at that moment.

2

To snub anyone effectively one must have him within range. The admission of Chauncey Rikker to the Kennemore Club and, later, to the Downtown Club was followed by angry talk and threats of resignation that simulated the sound of conflict, but there was no indication of a will underneath. On the other hand, unpleasantness in crowds is easy, and Chauncey Rikker was a facile object for personal dislike; moreover, a recurrent echo of the bucket-shop scandal sounded from New York, and the matter was reviewed in the local newspapers, in case anyone had missed it. Only the liberal Hannan family stood by the Rikkers, and their attitude aroused considerable resentment, and their attempt to launch them with a series of small parties proved a failure. Had the Rikkers attempted to 'bring Alida out', it would have been for the inspection of a motley crowd indeed, but they didn't.

When, occasionally during the summer, Forrest encountered Alida Rikker, they crossed eyes in the curious way of children who don't know each other. For a while he was haunted by her curly yellow head, by the golden-brown defiance of her eyes; then he became interested in another girl. He wasn't in love with Jane Drake, though he thought he might marry her. She was 'the girl across the street'; he knew her qualities, good and bad, so that they didn't matter. She had an essential reality underneath, like a relative. It would please their families. Once, after several highballs and some casual necking, he almost answered seriously when she provoked him with, 'But you don't really care about me'; but he sat tight and next morning was relieved that he had. Perhaps in the dull days after Christmas – Meanwhile, at the Christmas dances among the Christmas girls he might find the ecstasy and misery, the infatuation that he wanted. By autumn he felt that his predestined girl was already packing her trunk in some Eastern or Southern city.

It was in his more restless mood that one November Sunday he went to a small tea. Even as he spoke to his hostess he felt Alida Rikker across the firelit room; her glowing beauty and her unexplored novelty pressed up against him, and there was a relief in being presented to her at last. He bowed and passed on, but there had been some sort of communication. Her look said that she knew the stand that his family had taken, that she didn't mind, and was even sorry to see him in such a silly position, for she knew that he admired her. His look said: 'Naturally, I'm sensitive to your beauty, but you see how it is; we've had to draw the line at the fact that your father is a dirty dog, and I can't withdraw from my present position.'

Suddenly, in a silence, she was talking, and his ears swayed away from his own conversation.

'. . . Helen had this odd pain for over a year and, of course, they suspected cancer. She went to have an X-ray; she undressed behind a screen, and the doctor looked at her through the machine, and then he said, "But I told you to take off all your clothes," and Helen said, "I have." The doctor looked again, and said, "Listen, my dear, I brought you into the world, so there's no use being modest with me. Take off everything." So Helen said, "I've got every stitch off; I swear." But the doctor said, "You have not. The X ray shows me a safety pin in your brassiere." Well, they finally found out that she'd been suspected of swallowing a safety pin when she was two years old.'

The story, floating in her clear, crisp voice upon the intimate air, disarmed Forrest. It had nothing to do with what had taken place in Washington or New York ten years before. Suddenly he wanted to go and sit near her, because she was the tongue of flame that made the firelight vivid. Leaving, he walked for an hour through feathery snow, wondering again why he couldn't know her, why it was his business to represent a standard.

'Well, maybe I'll have a lot of fun someday doing what I ought to do,' he thought ironically – 'when I'm fifty.'

The first Christmas dance was the charity ball at the armoury. It was a large, public affair; the rich sat in boxes. Everyone came who felt he belonged, and many out of curiosity, so the atmosphere was tense with a strange haughtiness and aloofness.

The Rikkers had a box. Forrest, coming in with Jane Drake, glanced at the man of evil reputation and at the beaten woman frozen with jewels who sat beside him. They were the city's villains, gaped at by the people of reserved and timid lives. Oblivious of the staring eyes, Alida and Helen Hannan held court for several young men from out of town. Without question, Alida was incomparably the most beautiful girl in the room.

Several people told Forrest the news – the Rikkers were giving a big dance after New Year's. There were written invitations, but these were being supplemented by oral ones. Rumour had it that one had merely to be presented to any Rikker in order to be bidden to the dance.

As Forrest passed through the hall, two friends stopped him and with a certain hilarity introduced him to a youth of seventeen, Mr Teddy Rikker.

'We're giving a dance,' said the young man immediately. 'January third. Be very happy if you could come.'

Forrest was afraid he had an engagement.

'Well, come if you change your mind.'

'Horrible kid, but shrewd,' said one of his friends later. 'We were feeding him people, and when we brought up a couple of saps, he looked at them and didn't say a word. Some refuse and a few accept and most of them stall, but he goes right on; he's got his father's crust.'

Into the highways and byways. Why didn't the girl stop it? He was sorry for her when he found Jane in a group of young women revelling in the story.

'I hear they asked Bodman, the undertaker, by mistake, and then took it back.'

'Mrs Carleton pretended she was deaf.'

'There's going to be a carload of champagne from Canada.'

'Of course, I won't go, but I'd love to, just to see what happens. There'll be a hundred men to every girl – and that'll be meat for her.'

The accumulated malice repelled him, and he was angry at Jane for being part of it. Turning away, his eyes fell on Alida's proud form swaying along a wall, watched the devotion of her partners with an unpleasant resentment. He did not know that he had been a little in love with her for many months. Just as two children can fall in love during a physical struggle over a ball, so their awareness of each other had grown to surprising proportions.

'She's pretty,' said Jane. 'She's not exactly overdressed, but considering everything, she dresses too elaborately.'

'I suppose she ought to wear sackcloth and ashes or half-mourning.'

'I was honoured with a written invitation, but, of course, I'm not going.'

'Why not?'

Jane looked at him in surprise. 'You're not going.'

'That's different. I would if I were you. You see, you don't care what her father did.'

'Of course, I care.'

'No, you don't. And all this small meanness just debases the whole thing. Why don't they let her alone? She's young and pretty and she's done nothing wrong.'

Later in the week he saw Alida at the Hannans' dance and noticed that many men danced with her. He saw her lips moving, heard her laughter, caught a word or so of what she said; irresistibly he found himself guiding partners around in her wake. He envied visitors to the city who didn't know who she was.

The night of the Rikkers' dance he went to a small dinner; before they sat down at table he realised that the others were all going on to the Rikkers'. They talked of it as a sort of comic adventure; insisted that he come too.

'Even if you weren't invited, it's all right,' they assured him. 'We were told we could bring anyone. It's just a free-for-all; it doesn't put you under any obligations. Norma Nash is going and she didn't invite Alida Rikker to her party. Besides, she's really very nice. My brother's quite crazy about her. Mother is worried sick, because he says he wants to marry her.'

Clasping his hand about a new highball, Forrest knew that if he drank it he would probably go. All his reasons for not going seemed old and tired, and, fatally, he had begun to seem absurd to himself. In vain he tried to remember the purpose he was serving, and found none. His father had weakened on the matter of the Kennemore Club. And now suddenly he found reasons for going – men could go where their women could not.

'All right,' he said.

The Rikkers' dance was in the ballroom of the Minnekada Hotel. The Rikkers' gold, ill-gotten, tainted, had taken the form of a forest of palms, vines and flowers. The two orchestras moaned in pergolas lit with fireflies, and many-coloured spotlights swept the floor, touching a buffet where dark bottles gleamed. The receiving line was still in action when Forrest's party came in, and Forrest grinned ironically at the prospect of taking Chauncey Rikker by the hand. But at the sight of Alida, her look that at last fell frankly on him, he forgot everything else.

'Your brother was kind enough to invite me,' he said.

'Oh, yes,' she was polite, but vague; not at all overwhelmed by his presence. As he waited to speak to her parents, he started, seeing his sister in a group of dancers. Then, one after another, he identified people he knew: it might have been any one of the Christmas dances; all the younger crowd were there. He discovered abruptly that he and Alida were alone; the receiving line had broken up. Alida glanced at him questioningly and with a certain amusement.

So he danced out on the floor with her, his head high, but slightly spinning. Of all things in the world, he had least expected to lead off the Chauncey Rikkers' ball.

3

Next morning his first realisation was that he had kissed her; his second was a feeling of profound shame for his conduct of the evening. Lord help him, he had been the life of the party; he had helped to run the cotillion. From the moment when he danced out on the floor, coolly meeting the surprised and interested glances of his friends, a mood of desperation had come over him. He rushed Alida Rikker, until a friend asked him what Jane was going to say. 'What business is it of Jane's?' he demanded impatiently. 'We're not engaged.' But he was impelled to approach his sister and ask her if he looked all right.

'Apparently,' Eleanor answered, 'but when in doubt, don't take any more.'

So he hadn't. Exteriorly he remained correct, but his libido was in a state of wild extroversion. He sat with Alida Rikker and told her he had loved her for months.

'Every night I thought of you just before you went to sleep,' his voice trembled with insincerity, 'I was afraid to meet you or speak to you. Sometimes I'd see you in the distance moving along like a golden chariot, and the world would be good to live in.'

After twenty minutes of this eloquence, Alida began to feel exceedingly attractive. She was tired and rather happy, and eventually she said: 'All right, you can kiss me if you want to, but it won't mean anything. I'm just not in that mood.'

But Forrest had moods enough for both; he kissed her as if they stood together at the altar. A little later he had thanked Mrs Rikker with deep emotion for the best time he had ever had in his life.

It was noon, and as he groped his way upright in bed, Eleanor came in in her dressing-gown.

'How are you?' she asked.

'Awful.'

'How about what you told me coming back in the car? Do you actually want to marry Alida Rikker?'

'Not this morning.'

'That's all right then. Now, look: the family are furious.'

'Why?' he asked with some redundancy.

'Both you and I being there. Father heard that you led the cotillion.

My explanation was that my dinner party went, and so I had to go; but then you went too!'

Forrest dressed and went down to Sunday dinner. Over the table hovered an atmosphere of patient, puzzled, unworldly disappointment. Finally Forrest launched into it: 'Well, we went to Al Capone's party and had a fine time.'

'So I've heard,' said Pierce Winslow dryly. Mrs Winslow said nothing.

'Everybody was there – the Kayes, the Schwanes, the Martins and the Blacks. From now on, the Rikkers are pillars of society. Every house is open to them.'

'Not this house,' said his mother. 'They won't come into this house.' And after a moment: 'Aren't you going to eat anything, Forrest?'

'No, thanks. I mean, yes, I am eating.' He looked cautiously at his plate. 'The girl is very nice. There isn't a girl in town with better manners or more stuff. If things were like they were before the war, I'd say – '

He couldn't think exactly what it was he would have said; all he knew was that he was now on an entirely different road from his parents.

'This city was scarcely more than a village before the war,' said old Mrs Forrest.

'Forrest means the World War, granny,' said Eleanor.

'Some things don't change,' said Pierce Winslow. Both he and Forrest thought of the Kennemore Club matter and, feeling guilty, the older man lost his temper: 'When people start going to parties given by a convicted criminal, there's something serious the matter with them.'

'We won't discuss it any more at table,' said Mrs Winslow hastily.

About four, Forrest called a number on the telephone in his room. He had known for some time that he was going to call a number.

'Is Miss Rikker at home? . . . Oh, hello. This is Forrest Winslow.'

'How are you?'

'Terrible. It was a good party.'

'Wasn't it?'

'Too good. What are you doing?'

'Entertaining two awful hangovers.'

'Will you entertain me too?'

'I certainly will. Come on over.'

The two young men could only groan and play sentimental music on the phonograph, but presently they departed; the fire leaped up, day went out behind the windows, and Forrest had rum in his tea.

'So we met at last,' he said.

'The delay was all yours.'

'Damn prejudice,' he said. 'This is a conservative city, and your father being in this trouble – '

'I can't discuss my father with you.'

'Excuse me. I only wanted to say that I've felt like a fool lately for not knowing you. For cheating myself out of the pleasure of knowing you for a silly prejudice,' he blundered on. 'So I decided to follow my own instincts.'

She stood up suddenly. 'Goodbye, Mr Winslow.'

'What? Why?'

'Because it's absurd for you to come here as if you were doing me a favour. And after accepting our hospitality, to remind me of my father's troubles is simply bad manners.'

He was on his feet, terribly upset. 'That isn't what I meant. I said I had felt that way, and I despised myself for it. Please don't be sore.'

'Then don't be condescending.' She sat back in her chair. Her mother came in, stayed only a moment, and threw Forrest a glance of resentment and suspicion as she left. But her passage through had brought them together, and they talked frankly for a long time.

'I ought to be upstairs dressing.'

'I ought to have gone an hour ago, and I can't.'

'Neither can I.'

With the admission, they had travelled far. At the door he kissed her unreluctant lips and walked home, throwing futile buckets of reason on the wild fire.

Less than two weeks later it happened. In a car parked in a blizzard he poured out his worship, and she lay on his chest, sighing, 'Oh, me too – me too.'

Already Forrest's family knew where he went in the evenings; there was a frightened coolness, and one morning his mother said: 'Son, you don't want to throw yourself away on some girl that isn't up to you. I thought you were interested in Jane Drake.'

'Don't bring that up. I'm not going to talk about it.'

But it was only a postponement. Meanwhile the days of this February were white and magical, the nights were starry and crystalline. The town lay under a cold glory; the smell of her furs was incense, her bright cheeks were flames upon a northern altar. An ecstatic pantheism for his land and its weather welled up in him. She had brought him finally back to it; he would live here always.

'I want you so much that nothing can stand in the way of that,' he said to Alida. 'But I owe my parents a debt that I can't explain to you. They did more than spend money on me; they tried to give me something more intangible – something that their parents had given them and that they thought was worth handing on. Evidently it didn't take with me, but I've got to make this as easy as possible for them.' He saw by her face that he had hurt her. 'Darling – '

'Oh, it frightens me when you talk like that,' she said. 'Are you going to reproach me later? It would be awful. You'll have to get it out of your head that you're doing anything wrong. My standards are as high as yours, and I can't start out with my father's sins on my shoulders.' She thought for a moment. 'You'll never be able to reconcile it all like a children's story. You've got to choose. Probably you'll have to hurt either your family or hurt me.'

A fortnight later the storm broke at the Winslow house. Pierce Winslow came home in a quiet rage and had a session behind closed doors with his wife. Afterwards she knocked at Forrest's door.

'Your father had a very embarrassing experience today. Chauncey Rikker came up to him in the Downtown Club and began talking about you as if you were on terms of some understanding with his daughter. Your father walked away, but we've got to know. Are you serious about Miss Rikker?'

'I want to marry her,' he said.

'Oh, Forrest!'

She talked for a long time, recapitulating, as if it were a matter of centuries, the eighty years that his family had been identified with the city; when she passed from this to the story of his father's health, Forrest interrupted: 'That's all so irrelevant, mother. If there was anything against Alida personally, what you say would have some weight, but there isn't.'

'She's overdressed; she runs around with everybody – '

'She isn't a bit different from Eleanor. She's absolutely a lady in every sense. I feel like a fool even discussing her like this. You're just afraid it'll connect you in some way with the Rikkers.'

'I'm not afraid of that,' said his mother, annoyed. 'Nothing would ever do that. But I'm afraid that it'll separate you from everything worth while, everybody that loves you. It isn't fair for you to upset our lives, let us in for disgraceful gossip – '

'I'm to give up the girl I love because you're afraid of a little gossip.'

The controversy was resumed next day, with Pierce Winslow debating. His argument was that he was born in old Kentucky, that he had always felt uneasy at having begotten a son upon a pioneer Minnesota family, and that this was what he might have expected. Forrest felt that his parents' attitude was trivial and disingenuous. Only when he was out of the house, acting against their wishes, did he feel any compunction. But always he felt that something precious was being frayed away – his youthful companionship with his father and his love and trust for his mother. Hour by hour he saw the past being irreparably spoiled, and save when he was with Alida, he was deeply unhappy.

One spring day when the situation had become unendurable, with half the family meals taken in silence, Forrest's great-grandmother stopped him on the stair landing and put her hand on his arm.

'Has this girl really a good character?' she asked, her fine, clear, old eyes resting on his.

'Of course she has, gramma.'

'Then marry her.'

'Why do you say that?' Forrest asked curiously.

'It would stop all this nonsense and we could have some peace. And I've been thinking I'd like to be a great-great-grandmother before I die.'

Her frank selfishness appealed to him more than the righteousness of the others. That night he and Alida decided to be married the first of June, and telephoned the announcement to the papers.

Now the storm broke in earnest. Crest Avenue rang with gossip – how Mrs Rikker had called on Mrs Winslow, who was not at home. How Forrest had gone to live in the University Club. How Chauncey Rikker and Pierce Winslow had had words in the Downtown Club.

It was true that Forrest had gone to the University Club. On a May night, with summer sounds already gathered on the window screens, he packed his trunk and his suitcases in the room where he had lived as a boy. His throat contracted and he smeared his face with his dusty hand as he took a row of golf cups off the mantelpiece, and he choked to himself: 'If they won't take Alida, then they're not my family any more.'

As he finished packing, his mother came in.

'You're not really leaving.' Her voice was stricken.

'I'm moving to the University Club.'

'That's so unnecessary. No one bothers you here. You do what you want.'

'I can't bring Alida here.'

'Father – '

'Hell with father!' he said wildly.

She sat down on the bed beside him. 'Stay here, Forrest. I promise not to argue with you any more. But stay here.'

'I can't.'

'I can't have you go!' she wailed. 'It seems as if we're driving you out, and we're not!'

'You mean it looks as though you were driving me out.'

'I don't mean that.'

'Yes, you do. And I want to say that I don't think you and father really care a hang about Chauncey Rikker's moral character.'

'That's not true, Forrest. I hate people that behave badly and break the laws. My own father would never have let Chauncey Rikker –'

'I'm not talking about your father. But neither you nor my father care a bit what Chauncey Rikker did. I bet you don't even know what it was.'

'Of course I know. He stole some money and went abroad, and when he came back they put him in prison.'

'They put him in prison for contempt of court.'

'Now you're defending him, Forrest.'

'I'm not! I hate his guts; undoubtedly he's a crook. But I tell you it was a shock to me to find that father didn't have any principles. He and his friends sit around the Downtown Club and pan Chauncey Rikker, but when it comes to keeping him out of a club, they develop weak spines.'

'That was a small thing.'

'No, it wasn't. None of the men of father's age have any principles. I don't know why. I'm willing to make an allowance for an honest conviction, but I'm not going to be booed by somebody that hasn't got any principles and simply pretends to have.'

His mother sat helplessly, knowing that what he said was true. She and her husband and all their friends had no principles. They were good or bad according to their natures; often they struck attitudes remembered from the past, but they were never sure as her father or her grandfather had been sure. Confusedly she supposed it was something about religion. But how could you get principles just by wishing for them?

The maid announced the arrival of a taxi.

'Send up Olsen for my baggage,' said Forrest; then to his mother, 'I'm not taking the coupé; I left the keys. I'm just taking my clothes. I suppose father will let me keep my job downtown.'

'Forrest, don't talk that way. Do you think your father would take your living away from you, no matter what you did?'

'Such things have happened.'

'You're hard and difficult,' she wept. 'Please stay here a little longer, and perhaps things will be better and father will get a little more reconciled. Oh, stay, stay! I'll talk to father again. I'll do my best to fix things.'

'Will you let me bring Alida here?'

'Not now. Don't ask me that. I couldn't bear – '

'All right,' he said grimly.

Olsen came in for the bags. Crying and holding on to his coat sleeve, his mother went with him to the front door.

'Won't you say goodbye to father?'

'Why? I'll see him tomorrow in the office.'

'Forrest, I was thinking, why don't you go to a hotel instead of the University Club?'

'Why, I thought I'd be more comfortable – ' Suddenly he realised that his presence would be less conspicuous at a hotel. Shutting up his bitterness inside him, he kissed his mother roughly and went to the cab.

Unexpectedly, it stopped by the corner lamp-post at a hail from the sidewalk, and the May twilight yielded up Alida, miserable and pale.

'What is it?' he demanded.

'I had to come,' she said. 'Stop the car. I've been thinking of you leaving your house on account of me, and how you loved your family – the way I'd like to love mine – and I thought how terrible it was to spoil all that. Listen, Forrest! Wait! I want you to go back. Yes, I do. We can wait. We haven't any right to cause all this pain. We're young. I'll go away for a while, and then we'll see.'

He pulled her towards him by her shoulders.

'You've got more principles than the whole bunch of them,' he said. 'Oh, my girl, you love me and, gosh, it's good that you do!'

4

It was to be a house wedding, Forrest and Alida having vetoed the Rikkers' idea that it was to be a sort of public revenge. Only a few intimate friends were invited.

During the week before the wedding, Forrest deduced from a series of irresolute and ambiguous telephone calls that his mother wanted to attend the ceremony, if possible. Sometimes he hoped passionately she would; at others it seemed unimportant.

The wedding was to be at seven. At five o'clock Pierce Winslow was walking up and down the two interconnecting sitting-rooms of his house.

'This evening,' he murmured, 'my only son is being married to the daughter of a swindler.'

He spoke aloud so that he could listen to the words, but they had been evoked so often in the past few months that their strength was gone and they died thinly upon the air.

He went to the foot of the stairs and called: 'Charlotte!' No answer. He called again, and then went into the dining-room, where the maid was setting the table.

'Is Mrs Winslow out?'

'I haven't seen her come in, Mr Winslow.'

Back in the sitting-room he resumed his walking; unconsciously he was walking like his father, the judge, dead thirty years ago; he was parading his dead father up and down the room.

'You can't bring that woman into this house to meet your mother. Bad blood is bad blood.'

The house seemed unusually quiet. He went upstairs and looked into his wife's room, but she was not there; old Mrs Forrest was slightly indisposed; Eleanor, he knew, was at the wedding.

He felt genuinely sorry for himself as he went downstairs again. He knew his role – the usual evening routine carried out in complete obliviousness of the wedding – but he needed support, people begging him to relent, or else deferring to his wounded sensibilities. This isolation was different; it was almost the first isolation he had ever felt, and like all men who are fundamentally of the group, of the herd, he was incapable of taking a strong stand with the inevitable loneliness that it implied. He could only gravitate towards those who did.

'What have I done to deserve this?' he demanded of the standing ash tray. 'What have I failed to do for my son that lay within my power?'

The maid came in. 'Mrs Winslow told Hilda she wouldn't be here for dinner, and Hilda didn't tell me.'

The shameful business was complete. His wife had weakened, leaving him absolutely alone. For a moment he expected to be furiously angry with her, but he wasn't; he had used up his anger exhibiting it to others. Nor did it make him feel more obstinate, more determined; it merely made him feel silly.

'That's it. I'll be the goat. Forrest will always hold it against me, and Chauncey Rikker will be laughing up his sleeve.'

He walked up and down furiously.

'So I'm left holding the bag. They'll say I'm an old grouch and drop me out of the picture entirely. They've licked me. I suppose I might as well be graceful about it.' He looked down in horror at the hat he held in his hand. 'I can't – I can't bring myself to do it, but I must. After all, he's my only son. I couldn't bear that he should hate me. He's determined to marry her, so I might as well put a good face on the matter.'

In sudden alarm he looked at his watch, but there was still time. After all, it was a large gesture he was making, sacrificing his principles in this manner. People would never know what it cost him.

An hour later, old Mrs Forrest woke up from her doze and rang for her maid.

'Where's Mrs Winslow?'

'She's not in for dinner. Everybody's out.'

The old lady remembered.

'Oh, yes, they've gone over to get married. Give me my glasses and the telephone book . . . Now, I wonder how you spell Capone.'

'Rikker, Mrs Forrest.'

In a few minutes she had the number. 'This is Mrs Hugh Forrest,' she said firmly. 'I want to speak to young Mrs Forrest Winslow . . . No, not to Miss Rikker; to Mrs Forrest Winslow.' As there was as yet no such person, this was impossible. 'Then I will call after the ceremony,' said the old lady.

When she called again, in an hour, the bride came to the phone.

'This is Forrest's great-grandmother. I called up to wish you every happiness and to ask you to come and see me when you get back from your trip if I'm still alive.'

'You're very sweet to call, Mrs Forrest.'

'Take good care of Forrest, and don't let him get to be a ninny like his father and mother. God bless you.'

'Thank you.'

'All right. Goodbye, Miss Capo – Goodbye, my dear.'

Having done her whole duty, Mrs Forrest hung up the receiver.

Family in the Wind

Saturday Evening Post (4 June 1932)

1

The two men drove up the hill towards the blood-red sun. The cotton fields bordering the road were thin and withered, and no breeze stirred in the pines.

'When I am totally sober,' the doctor was saying – 'I mean when I am totally sober – I don't see the same world that you do. I'm like a friend of mine who had one good eye and got glasses made to correct his bad eye; the result was that he kept seeing elliptical suns and falling off tilted curbs, until he had to throw the glasses away. Granted that I am thoroughly anaesthetised the greater part of the day – well, I only undertake work that I know I can do when I am in that condition.'

'Yeah,' agreed his brother Gene uncomfortably. The doctor was a little tight at the moment and Gene could find no opening for what he had to say. Like so many Southerners of the humbler classes, he had a deep-seated courtesy, characteristic of all violent and passionate lands – he could not change the subject until there was a moment's silence, and Forrest would not shut up.

'I'm very happy,' he continued, 'or very miserable. I chuckle or I weep alcoholically and, as I continue to slow up, life accommodatingly goes faster, so that the less there is of myself inside, the more diverting becomes the moving picture without. I have cut myself off from the respect of my fellow man, but I am aware of a compensatory cirrhosis of the emotions. And because my sensitivity, my pity, no longer has direction, but fixes itself on whatever is at hand, I have become an exceptionally good fellow – much more so than when I was a good doctor.'

As the road straightened after the next bend and Gene saw his house in the distance, he remembered his wife's face as she had made him promise, and he could wait no longer: 'Forrest, I got a thing –'

But at that moment the doctor brought his car to a sudden stop in front of a small house just beyond a grove of pines. On the front steps a girl of eight was playing with a grey cat.

'This is the sweetest little kid I ever saw,' the doctor said to Gene, and then to the child, in a grave voice: 'Helen, do you need any pills for kitty?'

The little girl laughed.

'Well, I don't know,' she said doubtfully. She was playing another game with the cat now and this came as rather an interruption.

'Because kitty telephoned me this morning,' the doctor continued, 'and said her mother was neglecting her and couldn't I get her a trained nurse from Montgomery.'

'She did not.' The little girl grabbed the cat close indignantly; the doctor took a nickel from his pocket and tossed it to the steps.

'I recommend a good dose of milk,' he said as he put the car into gear. 'Good-night, Helen.'

'Good-night, doctor.'

As they drove off, Gene tried again: 'Listen; stop,' he said. 'Stop here a little way down . . . Here.'

The doctor stopped the car and the brothers faced each other. They were alike as to robustness of figure and a certain asceticism of feature and they were both in their middle forties; they were unlike in that the doctor's glasses failed to conceal the veined, weeping eyes of a soak, and that he wore corrugated city wrinkles; Gene's wrinkles bounded fields, followed the lines of roof trees, of poles propping up sheds. His eyes were a fine, furry blue. But the sharpest contrast lay in the fact that Gene Janney was a country man while Dr Forrest Janney was obviously a man of education.

'Well?' the doctor asked.

'You know Pinky's at home,' Gene said, looking down the road.

'So I hear,' the doctor answered noncommittally.

'He got in a row in Birmingham and somebody shot him in the head.' Gene hesitated. 'We got Doc Behrer because we thought maybe you wouldn't – maybe you wouldn't – '

'I wouldn't,' agreed Dr Janney blandly.

'But look, Forrest; here's the thing,' Gene insisted. 'You know how it is – you often say Doc Behrer doesn't know nothing. Shucks, I never thought he was much either. He says the bullet's pressing on the – pressing on the brain, and he can't take it out without causin' a hemmering, and he says he doesn't know whether we could get him to Birmingham or Montgomery or not, he's so low. Doc wasn't no help. What we want – '

'No,' said his brother, shaking his head. 'No.'

'I just want you to look at him and tell us what to do,' Gene begged. 'He's unconscious, Forrest. He wouldn't know you; you'd hardly know him. Thing is his mother's about crazy.'

'She's in the grip of a purely animal instinct.' The doctor took from his hip a flask containing half water and half Alabama corn, and drank. 'You and I know that boy ought to been drowned the day he was born.'

Gene flinched. 'He's bad,' he admitted, 'but I don't know – You see him lying there – '

As the liquor spread over the doctor's insides he felt an instinct to do something, not to violate his prejudices but simply to make some gesture, to assert his own moribund but still struggling will to power.

'All right, I'll see him,' he said. 'I'll do nothing myself to help him, because he ought to be dead. And even his death wouldn't make up for what he did to Mary Decker.'

Gene Janney pursed his lips. 'Forrest, you sure about that?'

'Sure about it!' exclaimed the doctor. 'Of course I'm sure. She died of starvation; she hadn't had more than a couple cups of coffee in a week. And if you looked at her shoes, you could see she'd walked for miles.'

'Doc Behrer says – '

'What does he know? I performed the autopsy the day they found her on the Birmingham Highway. There was nothing the matter with her but starvation. That – that' – his voice shook with feeling – 'that Pinky got tired of her and turned her out, and she was trying to get home. It suits me fine that he was invalided home himself a couple of weeks later.'

As he talked, the doctor had plunged the car savagely into gear and let the clutch out with a jump; in a moment they drew up before Gene Janney's home.

It was a square frame house with a brick foundation and a well-kept lawn blocked off from the farm, a house rather superior to the buildings that composed the town of Bending and the surrounding agricultural area, yet not essentially different in type or in its interior economy. The last of the plantation houses in this section of Alabama had long disappeared, the proud pillars yielding to poverty, rot and rain.

Gene's wife, Rose, got up from her rocking-chair on the porch.

'Hello, doc.' She greeted him a little nervously and without meeting his eyes. 'You been a stranger here lately.'

The doctor met her eyes for several seconds. 'How do you do,

Rose,' he said. 'Hi, Edith . . . Hi, Eugene' – this to the little boy and girl who stood beside their mother; and then: 'Hi, Butch!' to the stocky youth of nineteen who came around the corner of the house hugging a round stone.

'Goin to have a sort of low wall along the front here – kind of neater,' Gene explained.

All of them had a lingering respect for the doctor. They felt reproachful towards him because they could no longer refer to him as their celebrated relative – 'one of the bess surgeons up in Montgomery, yes, suh' – but there was his learning and the position he had once occupied in the larger world, before he had committed professional suicide by taking to cynicism and drink. He had come home to Bending and bought a half interest in the local drugstore two years ago, keeping up his licence, but practising only when sorely needed.

'Rose,' said Gene, 'doc says he'll take a look at Pinky.'

Pinky Janney, his lips curved mean and white under a new beard, lay in bed in a darkened room. When the doctor removed the bandage from his head, his breath blew into a low groan, but his paunchy body did not move. After a few minutes, the doctor replaced the bandage and, with Gene and Rose, returned to the porch.

'Behrer wouldn't operate?' he asked.

'No.'

'Why didn't they operate in Birmingham?'

'I don't know.'

'H'm.' The doctor put on his hat. 'That bullet ought to come out, and soon. It's pressing against the carotid sheath. That's the – anyhow, you can't get him to Montgomery with that pulse.'

'What'll we do?' Gene's question carried a little tail of silence as he sucked his breath back.

'Get Behrer to think it over. Or else get somebody in Montgomery. There's about a twenty-five-per-cent chance that the operation would save him; without the operation he hasn't any chance at all.'

'Who'll we get in Montgomery?' asked Gene.

'Any good surgeon would do it. Even Behrer could do it if he had any nerve.'

Suddenly Rose Janney came close to him, her eyes straining and burning with an animal maternalism. She seized his coat where it hung open.

'Doc, you do it! You can do it. You know you were as good a surgeon as any of 'em once. Please, doc, you go on do it.'

He stepped back a little so that her hands fell from his coat, and held out his own hands in front of him.

'See how they tremble?' he said with elaborate irony. 'Look close and you'll see. I wouldn't dare operate.'

'You could do it all right,' said Gene hastily, 'with a drink to stiffen you up.'

The doctor shook his head and said, looking at Rose: 'No. You see, my decisions are not reliable, and if anything went wrong, it would seem to be my fault.' He was acting a little now – he chose his words carefully. 'I hear that when I found that Mary Decker died of starvation, my opinion was questioned on the ground that I was a drunkard.'

'I didn't say that,' lied Rose breathlessly.

'Certainly not. I just mention it to show how careful I've got to be.' He moved down the steps. 'Well, my advice is to see Behrer again, or, failing that, get somebody from the city. Good-night.'

But before he had reached the gate, Rose came tearing after him, her eyes white with fury.

'I did say you were a drunkard!' she cried. 'When you said Mary Decker died of starvation, you made it out as if it was Pinky's fault – you, swilling yourself full of corn all day! How can anybody tell whether you know what you're doing or not? Why did you think so much about Mary Decker, anyhow – a girl half your age? Everybody saw how she used to come in your drugstore and talk to you – '

Gene, who had followed, seized her arms. 'Shut up now, Rose . . . Drive along, Forrest.'

Forrest drove along, stopping at the next bend to drink from his flask. Across the fallow cotton fields he could see the house where Mary Decker had lived, and had it been six months before, he might have detoured to ask her why she hadn't come into the store that day for her free soda, or to delight her with a sample cosmetic left by a salesman that morning. He had not told Mary Decker how he felt about her; never intended to – she was seventeen, he was forty-five, and he no longer dealt in futures – but only after she ran away to Birmingham with Pinky Janney did he realise how much his love for her had counted in his lonely life.

His thoughts went back to his brother's house.

'Now, if I were a gentleman,' he thought, 'I wouldn't have done like that. And another person might have been sacrificed to that dirty dog, because if he died afterwards Rose would say I killed him.'

Yet he felt pretty bad as he put his car away; not that he could have acted differently, but just that it was all so ugly.

He had been home scarcely ten minutes when a car creaked to rest outside and Butch Janney came in. His mouth was set tight and his eyes were narrowed as though to permit of no escape to the temper that possessed him until it should be unleashed upon its proper objective.

'Hi, Butch.'

'I want to tell you, Uncle Forrest, you can't talk to my mother thataway. I'll kill you, you talk to my mother like that!'

'Now shut up, Butch, and sit down,' said the doctor sharply.

'She's already bout sick on account of Pinky, and you come over and talk to her like that.'

'Your mother did all the insulting that was done, Butch. I just took it.'

'She doesn't know what she's saying and you ought to understand that.'

The doctor thought a minute. 'Butch, what do you think of Pinky?'

Butch hesitated uncomfortably. 'Well, I can't say I ever thought so much of him' – his tone changed defiantly – 'but after all, he's my own brother – '

'Wait a minute, Butch. What do you think of the way he treated Mary Decker?'

But Butch had shaken himself free, and now he let go the artillery of his rage: 'That ant the point; the point is anybody that doesn't do right to my mother has me to answer to. It's only fair when you got all the education – '

'I got my education myself, Butch.'

'I don't care. We're going to try again to get Doc Behrer to operate or get us some fellow from the city. But if we can't, I'm coming and get you, and you're going to take that bullet out if I have to hold a gun to you while you do it.' He nodded, panting a little; then he turned and went out and drove away.

'Something tells me,' said the doctor to himself, 'that there's no more peace for me in Chilton County.' He called to his coloured boy to put supper on the table. Then he rolled himself a cigarette and went out on the back stoop.

The weather had changed. The sky was now overcast and the grass stirred restlessly and there was a sudden flurry of drops without a sequel. A minute ago it had been warm, but now the moisture on his forehead was suddenly cool, and he wiped it away with his handkerchief. There was a buzzing in his ears and he swallowed and shook his head. For a moment he thought he must be sick; then suddenly the buzzing detached itself from him, grew into a swelling sound, louder and ever nearer, that might have been the roar of an approaching train.

2

Butch Janney was halfway home when he saw it – a huge, black, approaching cloud whose lower edge bumped the ground. Even as he stared at it vaguely, it seemed to spread until it included the whole southern sky, and he saw pale electric fire in it and heard an increasing roar. He was in a strong wind now; blown débris, bits of broken branches, splinters, larger objects unidentifiable in the growing darkness, flew by him. Instinctively he got out of his car and, by now hardly able to stand against the wind, ran for a bank, or rather found himself thrown and pinned against a bank. Then for a minute, two minutes, he was in the black centre of pandemonium.

First there was the sound, and he was part of the sound, so engulfed in it and possessed by it that he had no existence apart from it. It was not a collection of sounds, it was just Sound itself; a great screeching bow drawn across the chords of the universe. The sound and force were inseparable. The sound as well as the force held him to what he felt was the bank like a man crucified. Somewhere in this first moment his face, pinned sideways, saw his automobile make a little jump, spin halfway around and then go bobbing off over a field in a series of great helpless leaps. Then began the bombardment, the sound dividing its sustained cannon note into the cracks of a gigantic machine-gun. He was only half-conscious as he felt himself become part of one of those cracks, felt himself lifted away from the bank to tear through space, through a blinding, lacerating mass of twigs and branches, and then, for an incalculable time, he knew nothing at all.

His body hurt him. He was lying between two branches in the top of a tree; the air was full of dust and rain, and he could hear nothing; it was a long time before he realised that the tree he was in had been blown down and that his involuntary perch among the pine needles was only five feet from the ground.

'Say, man!' he cried aloud, outraged. 'Say, man! Say, what a wind! Say, man!'

Made acute by pain and fear, he guessed that he had been standing on the tree's root and had been catapulted by the terrific wrench as the big pine was torn from the earth. Feeling over himself, he found that his left ear was caked full of dirt, as if someone had wanted to take an impression of the inside. His clothes were in rags, his coat had torn on the back seam, and he could feel where, as some stray gust tried to undress him, it had cut into him under the arms.

Reaching the ground, he set off in the direction of his father's house, but it was a new and unfamiliar landscape he traversed. The Thing – he did not know it was a tornado – had cut a path a quarter of a mile wide, and he was confused, as the dust slowly settled, by vistas he had never seen before. It was unreal that Bending church tower should be visible from here; there had been groves of trees between.

But where was here? For he should be close to the Baldwin house; only as he tripped over great piles of boards, like a carelessly kept lumber yard, did Butch realise that there was no more a Baldwin house, and then, looking around wildly, that there was no Necrawney house on the hill, no Peltzer house below it. There was not a light, not a sound, save the rain falling on the fallen trees.

He broke into a run. When he saw the bulk of his father's house in the distance, he gave a 'Hey!' of relief, but coming closer, he realised that something was missing. There were no outhouses and the built-on wing that held Pinky's room had been sheared completely away.

'Mother!' he called. 'Dad!' There was no answer; a dog bounded out of the yard and licked his hand . . .

. . . It was full dark twenty minutes later when Doc Janney stopped his car in front of his own drugstore in Bending. The electric lights had gone out, but there were men with lanterns in the street, and in a minute a small crowd had collected around him. He unlocked the door hurriedly.

'Somebody break open the old Wiggins Hospital.' He pointed across the street. 'I've got six badly injured in my car. I want some fellows to carry 'em in. Is Doc Behrer here?'

'Here he is,' offered eager voices out of the darkness as the doctor, case in hand, came through the crowd. The two men stood face to face by lantern light, forgetting that they disliked each other.

'God knows how many more there's going to be,' said Doc Janney. 'I'm getting dressing and disinfectant. There'll be a lot of fractures – ' He raised his voice, 'Somebody bring me a barrel!'

'I'll get started over there,' said Doc Behrer. 'There's about half a dozen more crawled in.'

'What's been done?' demanded Doc Janney of the men who followed him into the drugstore. 'Have they called Birmingham and Montgomery?'

'The telephone wires are down, but the telegraph got through.'

'Well, somebody get Dr Cohen from Wettala, and tell any people who have automobiles to go up the Willard Pike and cut across towards Corsica and all through those roads there. There's not a house left at the crossroads by the nigger store. I passed a lot of folks walking in, all of them hurt, but I didn't have room for anybody else.' As he talked he was throwing bandages, disinfectant and drugs into a blanket. 'I thought I had a lot more stuff than this in stock! And wait!' he called. 'Somebody drive out and look down in that hollow where the Wooleys live. Drive right across the fields – the road's blocked . . . Now, you with the cap – Ed Jenks, ain't it?'

'Yes, doc.'

'You see what I got here? You collect everything in the store that looks like this and bring it across the way, understand?'

'Yes, doc.'

As the doctor went out into the street, the victims were streaming into town – a woman on foot with a badly injured child, a buckboard full of groaning Negroes, frantic men gasping terrible stories. Everywhere confusion and hysteria mounted in the dimly illumined darkness. A mud-covered reporter from Birmingham drove up in a sidecar, the wheels crossing the fallen wires and brushwood that clogged the street, and there was the siren of a police car from Cooper, thirty miles away.

Already a crowd pressed around the doors of the hospital, closed these three months for lack of patients. The doctor squeezed past the *mêlée* of white faces and established himself in the nearest ward, grateful for the waiting row of old iron beds. Dr Behrer was already at work across the hall.

'Get me half a dozen lanterns,' he ordered.

'Dr Behrer wants idodine and adhesive.'

'All right, there it is . . . Here, you, Shinkey, stand by the door and keep everybody out except cases that can't walk. Somebody run over and see if there ain't some candles in the grocery store.'

The street outside was full of sound now – the cries of women, the contrary directions of volunteer gangs trying to clear the highway, the tense staccato of people rising to an emergency. A little before midnight arrived the first unit of the Red Cross. But the three doctors, presently joined by two others from nearby villages, had lost track of time long before that. The dead began to be brought in by ten o'clock; there were twenty, twenty-five, thirty, forty – the list grew. Having no more needs, these waited, as became simple husbandmen, in a garage behind, while the stream of injured – hundreds of them – flowed through the old hospital built to house only a score. The storm had dealt out fractures of the leg, collarbone, ribs and hip, lacerations of the back, elbows, ears, eyelids, nose; there were wounds from flying planks, and odd splinters in odd places, and a scalped man, who would recover to grow a new head of hair. Living or dead, Doc Janney knew every face, almost every name.

'Don't you fret now. Billy's all right. Hold still and let me tie this. People are drifting in every minute, but it's so consarned dark they can't find 'em – All right, Mrs Oakey. That's nothing. Ev here'll touch it with iodine . . . Now let's see this man.'

Two o'clock. The old doctor from Wettala gave out, but now there were fresh men from Montgomery to take his place. Upon the air of the room, heavy with disinfectant, floated the ceaseless babble of human speech reaching the doctor dimly through layer after layer of increasing fatigue: ' . . . Over and over – just rolled me over and over. Got hold of a bush and the bush came along too.'

'Jeff! Where's Jeff?'

' . . . I bet that pig sailed a hundred yards – '

' – just stopped the train in time. All the passengers got out and helped pull the poles – '

'Where's Jeff?'

'He says, "Let's get down the cellar," and I says, "We ain't got no cellar – " '

' – If there's no more stretchers, find some light doors.'

' . . . Five seconds? Say, it was more like five minutes!'

At some time he heard that Gene and Rose had been seen with their two youngest children. He had passed their house on the way in and, seeing it standing, hurried on. The Janney family had been lucky; the doctor's own house was outside the sweep of the storm.

Only as he saw the electric lights go on suddenly in the streets and glimpsed the crowd waiting for hot coffee in front of the Red Cross did the doctor realise how tired he was.

'You better go rest,' a young man was saying. 'I'll take this side of the room. I've got two nurses with me.'

'All right – all right. I'll finish this row.'

The injured were being evacuated to the cities by train as fast as their wounds were dressed, and their places taken by others. He had only two beds to go – in the first one he found Pinky Janney.

He put his stethoscope to the heart. It was beating feebly. That he, so weak, so nearly gone, had survived this storm at all was remarkable. How he had got there, who had found him and carried him, was a mystery in itself. The doctor went over the body; there were small contusions and lacerations, two broken fingers, the dirt-filled ears that marked every case – nothing else. For a moment the doctor hesitated, but even when he closed his eyes, the image of Mary Decker seemed to have receded, eluding him. Something purely professional that had nothing to do with human sensibilities had been set in motion inside him, and he was powerless to head it off. He held out his hands before him; they were trembling slightly.

'Hell's bells!' he muttered.

He went out of the room and around the corner of the hall, where he drew from his pocket the flask containing the last of the corn and water he had had in the afternoon. He emptied it. Returning to the ward, he disinfected two instruments and applied a local anaesthetic to a square section at the base of Pinky's skull where the wound had healed over the bullet. He called a nurse to his side and then, scalpel in hand, knelt on one knee beside his nephew's bed.

3

Two days later the doctor drove slowly around the mournful countryside. He had withdrawn from the emergency work after the first desperate night, feeling that his status as a pharmacist might embarrass his collaborators. But there was much to be done in bringing the damage to outlying sections under the aegis of the Red Cross, and he devoted himself to that.

The path of the demon was easy to follow. It had pursued an irregular course in its seven-league boots, cutting cross-country, through woods, or even urbanely keeping to roads until they curved, when it went off on its own again. Sometimes the trail could be traced by cotton fields, apparently in full bloom, but this cotton came from the insides of hundreds of quilts and mattresses redistributed in the fields by the storm.

At a lumber pile that had lately been a Negro cabin, he stopped a moment to listen to a dialogue between two reporters and two shy piccaninnies. The old grandmother, her head bandaged, sat among the ruins, gnawing some vague meat and moving her rocker ceaselessly.

'But where is the river you were blown across?' one of the reporters demanded.

'There.'

'Where?'

The piccaninnies looked to their grandmother for aid.

'Right there behind y'all,' spoke up the old woman.

The newspapermen looked disgustedly at a muddy stream four yards wide.

'That's no river.'

'That's a Menada River, we always calls it ever since I was a gull. Yes, suh, that's a Menada River. An' them two boys was blowed right across it an set down on the othah side just as pretty, 'thout any hurt at all. Chimney fell on me,' she concluded, feeling her head.

'Do you mean to say that's all it was?' demanded the younger reporter indignantly. 'That's the river they were blown across! And one hundred and twenty million people have been led to believe – '

'That's all right, boys,' interrupted Doc Janney. 'That's a right good river for these parts. And it'll get bigger as those little fellahs get older.'

He tossed a quarter to the old woman and drove on.

Passing a country church, he stopped and counted the new brown mounds that marred the graveyard. He was nearing the centre of the holocaust now. There was the Howden house where three had been killed; there remained a gaunt chimney, a rubbish heap and a scarecrow surviving ironically in the kitchen garden. In the ruins of the house across the way a rooster strutted on top of a piano, reigning vociferously over an estate of trunks, boots, cans, books, calendars, rugs, chairs and window frames, a twisted radio and a legless sewing machine. Everywhere there was bedding – blankets, mattresses, bent springs, shredded padding – he had not realised how much of people's lives was spent in bed. Here and there, cows and horses, often stained with disinfectant, were grazing again in the fields. At intervals there were Red Cross tents, and sitting by one of these, with the grey cat in her arms, the doctor came upon little Helen Kilrain. The usual lumber pile, like a child's building game knocked down in a fit of temper, told the story.

'Hello, dear,' he greeted her, his heart sinking. 'How did kitty like the tornado?'

'She didn't.'

'What did she do?'

'She meowed.'

'Oh.'

'She wanted to get away, but I hanged on to her and she scratched me – see?'

He glanced at the Red Cross tent. 'Who's taking care of you?'

'The lady from the Red Cross and Mrs Wells,' she answered. 'My father got hurt. He stood over me so it wouldn't fall on me, and I stood over kitty. He's in the hospital in Birmingham. When he comes back, I guess he'll build our house again.'

The doctor winced. He knew that her father would build no more houses; he had died that morning. She was alone, and she did not know she was alone. Around her stretched the dark universe, impersonal, inconscient. Her lovely little face looked up at him confidently as he asked: 'You got any kin anywhere, Helen?'

'I don't know.'

'You've got kitty, anyhow, haven't you?'

'It's just a cat,' she admitted calmly, but anguished by her own betrayal of her love, she hugged it closer.

'Taking care of a cat must be pretty hard.'

'Oh, no,' she said hurriedly. 'It isn't any trouble at all. It doesn't eat hardly anything.'

He put his hand in his pocket, and then changed his mind suddenly. 'Dear, I'm coming back and see you later – later today. You take good care of kitty now, won't you?'

'Oh, yes,' she answered lightly.

The doctor drove on. He stopped next at a house that had escaped damage. Walt Cupps, the owner, was cleaning a shotgun on his front porch.

'What's that, Walt? Going to shoot up the next tornado?'

'Ain't going to be a next tornado.'

'You can't tell. Just take a look at that sky now. It's getting mighty dark.'

Walt laughed and slapped his gun. 'Not for a hundred years, anyhow. This here is for looters. There's a lot of 'em around, and not all black either. Wish when you go to town that you'd tell 'em to scatter some militia out here.'

'I'll tell 'em now. You come out all right?'

'I did, thank God. With six of us in the house. It took off one hen, and probably it's still carrying it around somewhere.'

The doctor drove on towards town, overcome by a feeling of uneasiness he could not define.

'It's the weather,' he thought. 'It's the same kind of feel in the air there was last Saturday.'

For a month the doctor had felt an urge to go away permanently.

Once this countryside had seemed to promise peace. When the impetus that had lifted him temporarily out of tired old stock was exhausted, he had come back here to rest, to watch the earth put forth, and live on simple, pleasant terms with his neighbours. Peace! He knew that the present family quarrel would never heal, nothing would ever be the same; it would all be bitter for ever. And he had seen the placid countryside turned into a land of mourning. There was no peace here. Move on!

On the road he overtook Butch Janney walking to town.

'I was coming to see you,' said Butch, frowning. 'You operated on Pinky after all, didn't you?'

'Jump in . . . Yes, I did. How did you know?'

'Doc Behrer told us.' He shot a quick look at the doctor, who did not miss the quality of suspicion in it. 'They don't think he'll last out the day.'

'I'm sorry for your mother.'

Butch laughed unpleasantly. 'Yes, you are.'

'I said I'm sorry for your mother,' said the doctor sharply.

'I heard you.'

They drove for a moment in silence.

'Did you find your automobile?'

'Did I?' Butch laughed ruefully. 'I found something – I don't know whether you'd call it a car any more. And, you know, I could of had tornado insurance for twenty-five cents.' His voice trembled indignantly: 'Twenty-five cents – but who would ever of thought of getting tornado insurance?'

It was growing darker; there was a thin crackle of thunder far to the southward.

'Well, all I hope,' said Butch with narrowed glance, 'is that you hadn't been drinking anything when you operated on Pinky.'

'You know, Butch,' the doctor said slowly, 'that was a pretty dirty trick of mine to bring that tornado here.'

He had not expected the sarcasm to hit home, but he expected a retort – when suddenly he caught sight of Butch's face. It was fish-white, the mouth was open, the eyes fixed and staring, and from the throat came a mewling sound. Limply he raised one hand before him, and then the doctor saw.

Less than a mile away, an enormous, top-shaped black cloud filled the sky and bore towards them, dipping and swirling, and in front of it sailed already a heavy, singing wind.

'It's come back!' the doctor yelled.

Fifty yards ahead of them was the old iron bridge spanning Bilby Creek. He stepped hard on the accelerator and drove for it. The fields were full of running figures headed in the same direction. Reaching the bridge, he jumped out and yanked Butch's arm.

'Get out, you fool! Get out!'

A nerveless mass stumbled from the car; in a moment they were in a group of half a dozen, huddled in the triangular space that the bridge made with the shore.

'Is it coming here?'

'No, it's turning!'

'We had to leave grampa!'

'Oh, save me, save me! Jesus save me! Help me!'

'Jesus save my soul!'

There was a quick rush of wind outside, sending little tentacles under the bridge with a curious tension in them that made the doctor's skin crawl. Then immediately there was a vacuum, with no more wind, but a sudden thresh of rain. The doctor crawled to the edge of the bridge and put his head up cautiously.

'It's passed,' he said. 'We only felt the edge; the centre went way to the right of us.'

He could see it plainly; for a second he could even distinguish objects in it – shrubbery and small trees, planks and loose earth. Crawling farther out, he produced his watch and tried to time it, but the thick curtain of rain blotted it from sight.

Soaked to the skin, he crawled back underneath. Butch lay shivering in the farthest corner, and the doctor shook him.

'It went in the direction of your house!' the doctor cried. 'Pull yourself together! Who's there?'

'No one,' Butch groaned. 'They're all down with Pinky.'

The rain had changed to hail now; first small pellets, then larger ones, and larger, until the sound of their fall upon the iron bridge was an ear-splitting tattoo.

The spared wretches under the bridge were slowly recovering, and in the relief there were titters of hysterical laughter. After a certain point of strain, the nervous system makes its transitions without dignity or reason. Even the doctor felt the contagion.

'This is worse than a calamity,' he said dryly. 'It's getting to be a nuisance.'

4

There were to be no more tornadoes in Alabama that spring. The second one – it was popularly thought to be the first one come back; for to the people of Chilton County it had become a personified force, definite as a pagan god – took a dozen houses, Gene Janney's among them, and injured about thirty people. But this time – perhaps because everyone had developed some scheme of self-protection – there were no fatalities. It made its last dramatic bow by sailing down the main street of Bending, prostrating the telephone poles and crushing in the fronts of three shops, including Doc Janney's drugstore.

At the end of a week, houses were going up again, made of the old boards; and before the end of the long, lush Alabama summer the grass would be green on all the graves. But it will be years before the people of the country cease to reckon events as happening 'before the tornado' or 'after the tornado' – and for many families things will never be the same.

Dr Janney decided that this was as good a time to leave as any. He sold the remains of his drugstore, gutted alike by charity and catastrophe, and turned over his house to his brother until Gene could rebuild his own. He was going up to the city by train, for his car had been rammed against a tree and couldn't be counted on for much more than the trip to the station.

Several times on the way in he stopped by the roadside to say goodbye – once it was to Walter Cupps.

'So it hit you, after all,' he said, looking at the melancholy back house which alone marked the site.

'It's pretty bad,' Walter answered. 'But just think; they was six of us in or about the house and not one was injured. I'm content to give thanks to God for that.'

'You were lucky there, Walt,' the doctor agreed. 'Do you happen to have heard whether the Red Cross took little Helen Kilrain to Montgomery or to Birmingham?'

'To Montgomery. Say, I was there when she came into town with that cat, tryin' to get somebody to bandage up its paw. She must of walked miles through that rain and hail, but all that mattered to her was her kitty. Bad as I felt, I couldn't help laughin' at how spunky she was.'

The doctor was silent for a moment. 'Do you happen to recollect if she has any people left?'

'I don't, suh,' Walter replied, 'but I think as not.'

At his brother's place, the doctor made his last stop. They were all there, even the youngest, working among the ruins; already Butch had a shed erected to house the salvage of their goods. Save for this the most orderly thing surviving was the pattern of round white stones which was to have enclosed the garden.

The doctor took a hundred dollars in bills from his pocket and handed it to Gene.

'You can pay it back sometime, but don't strain yourself,' he said. 'It's money I got from the store.' He cut off Gene's thanks: 'Pack up my books carefully when I send for 'em.'

'You reckon to practice medicine up there, Forrest?'

'I'll maybe try it.'

The brothers held on to each other's hands for a moment; the two youngest children came up to say goodbye. Rose stood in the background in an old blue dress – she had no money to wear black for her eldest son.

'Goodbye, Rose,' said the doctor.

'Goodbye,' she responded, and then added in a dead voice, 'Good luck to you, Forrest.'

For a moment he was tempted to say something conciliatory, but he saw it was no use. He was up against the maternal instinct, the same force that had sent little Helen through the storm with her injured cat.

At the station he bought a one-way ticket to Montgomery. The village was drab under the sky of a retarded spring, and as the train pulled out, it was odd to think that six months ago it had seemed to him as good a place as any other.

He was alone in the white section of the day coach; presently he felt for a bottle on his hip and drew it forth. 'After all, a man of forty-five is entitled to more artificial courage when he starts over again.' He began thinking of Helen. 'She hasn't got any kin. I guess she's my little girl now.'

He patted the bottle, then looked down at it as if in surprise.

'Well, we'll have to put you aside for a while, old friend. Any cat that's worth all that trouble and care is going to need a lot of grade-B milk.'

He settled down in his seat, looking out the window. In his memory of that terrible week the winds still sailed about him, came in as draughts through the corridor of the car – winds of the world – cyclones, hurricanes, tornadoes – grey and black, expected or unforeseen, some from the sky, some from the caves of hell.

But he would not let them touch Helen again – if he could help it.

He dozed momentarily, but a haunting dream woke him: *'Daddy stood over me and I stood over kitty.'*

'All right, Helen,' he said aloud, for he often talked to himself, 'I guess the old brig can keep afloat a little longer – in any wind.'

What a Handsome Pair!

Saturday Evening Post (27 August 1932)

1

At four o'clock on a November afternoon in 1902, Teddy Van Beck got out of a hansom cab in front of a brownstone house on Murray Hill. He was a tall, round-shouldered young man with a beaked nose and soft brown eyes in a sensitive face. In his veins quarrelled the blood of colonial governors and celebrated robber barons; in him the synthesis had produced, for that time and place, something different and something new.

His cousin, Helen Van Beck, waited in the drawing-room. Her eyes were red from weeping, but she was young enough for it not to detract from her glossy beauty – a beauty that had reached the point where it seemed to contain in itself the secret of its own growth, as if it would go on increasing for ever.

She was nineteen and, contrary to the evidence, she was extremely happy.

Teddy put his arm around her and kissed her cheek, and found it changing into her ear as she turned her face away. He held her for a moment, his own enthusiasm chilling; then he said: 'You don't seem very glad to see me.'

Helen had a premonition that this was going to be one of the memorable scenes of her life, and with unconscious cruelty she set about extracting from it its full dramatic value. She sat in a corner of the couch, facing an easy-chair.

'Sit there,' she commanded, in what was then admired as a 'regal manner', and then, as Teddy straddled the piano stool: 'No, don't sit there. I can't talk to you if you're going to revolve around.'

'Sit on my lap,' he suggested.

'No.'

Playing a one-handed flourish on the piano, he said, 'I can listen better here.'

Helen gave up hopes of beginning on the sad and quiet note.

'This is a serious matter, Teddy. Don't think I've decided it without a lot of consideration. I've got to ask you – to ask you to release me from our understanding.'

'What?' Teddy's face paled with shock and dismay.

'I'll have to tell you from the beginning. I've realised for a long time that we have nothing in common. You're interested in your music, and I can't even play chopsticks.' Her voice was weary as if with suffering; her small teeth tugged at her lower lip.

'What of it?' he demanded, relieved. 'I'm musician enough for both. You wouldn't have to understand banking to marry a banker, would you?'

'This is different,' Helen answered. 'What would we do together? One important thing is that you don't like riding; you told me you were afraid of horses.'

'Of course I'm afraid of horses,' he said, and added reminiscently: 'They try to bite me.'

'It makes it so – '

'I've never met a horse – socially, that is – who didn't try to bite me. They used to do it when I put the bridle on; then, when I gave up putting the bridle on, they began reaching their heads around trying to get at my calves.'

The eyes of her father, who had given her a Shetland at three, glistened, cold and hard, from her own.

'You don't even like the people I like, let alone the horses,' she said.

'I can stand them. I've stood them all my life.'

'Well, it would be a silly way to start a marriage. I don't see any grounds for mutual – mutual – '

'Riding?'

'Oh, not that.' Helen hesitated, and then said in an unconvinced tone, 'Probably I'm not clever enough for you.'

'Don't talk such stuff!' He demanded some truth: 'Who's the man?'

It took her a moment to collect herself. She had always resented Teddy's tendency to treat women with less ceremony than was the custom of the day. Often he was an unfamiliar, almost frightening young man.

'There is someone,' she admitted. 'It's someone I've always known slightly, but about a month ago, when I went to Southampton, I was – thrown with him.'

'Thrown from a horse?'

'Please, Teddy,' she protested gravely. 'I'd been getting more unhappy about you and me, and whenever I was with him everything seemed all right.' A note of exaltation that she would not conceal came into Helen's voice. She rose and crossed the room, her straight, slim legs outlined by the shadows of her dress. 'We rode and swam and played tennis together – did the things we both liked to do.'

He stared into the vacant space she had created for him. 'Is that all that drew you to this fellow?'

'No, it was more than that. He was thrilling to me like nobody ever has been.' She laughed. 'I think what really started me thinking about it was one day we came in from riding and everybody said aloud what a nice pair we made.'

'Did you kiss him?'

She hesitated. 'Yes, once.'

He got up from the piano stool. 'I feel as if I had a cannon ball in my stomach,' he exclaimed.

The butler announced Mr Stuart Oldhorne.

'Is he the man?' Teddy demanded tensely.

She was suddenly upset and confused. 'He should have come later. Would you rather go without meeting him?'

But Stuart Oldhorne, made confident by his new sense of proprietorship, had followed the butler.

The two men regarded each other with a curious impotence of expression; there can be no communication between men in that position, for their relation is indirect and consists in how much each of them has possessed or will possess of the woman in question, so that their emotions pass through her divided self as through a bad telephone connection.

Stuart Oldhorne sat beside Helen, his polite eyes never leaving Teddy. He had the same glowing physical power as she. He had been a star athlete at Yale and a Rough Rider in Cuba, and was the best young horseman on Long Island. Women loved him not only for his points but for a real sweetness of temper.

'You've lived so much in Europe that I don't often see you,' he said to Teddy. Teddy didn't answer and Stuart Oldhorne turned to Helen: 'I'm early; I didn't realise – '

'You came at the right time,' said Teddy rather harshly. 'I stayed to play you my congratulations.'

To Helen's alarm, he turned and ran his fingers over the keyboard. Then he began.

What he was playing, neither Helen nor Stuart knew, but Teddy always remembered. He put his mind in order with a short résumé of the history of music, beginning with some chords from the *Messiah* and ending with Debussy's *La plus que lent*, which had an evocative quality for him, because he had first heard it the day his brother died. Then, pausing for an instant, he began to play more thoughtfully, and the lovers on the sofa could feel that they were alone – that he had left them and had no more traffic with them – and Helen's discomfort lessened. But the flight, the elusiveness of the music, piqued her, gave her a feeling of annoyance. If Teddy had played the current sentimental song from *Erminie*, and had played it with feeling, she would have understood and been moved, but he was plunging her suddenly into a world of mature emotions, whither her nature neithrer could nor wished to follow.

She shook herself slightly and said to Stuart: 'Did you buy the horse?'

'Yes, and at a bargain . . . Do you know I love you?'

'I'm glad,' she whispered.

The piano stopped suddenly. Teddy closed it and swung slowly around: 'Did you like my congratulations?'

'Very much,' they said together.

'It was pretty good,' he admitted. 'That last was only based on a little counterpoint. You see, the idea of it was that you make such a handsome pair.'

He laughed unnaturally; Helen followed him out into the hall.

'Goodbye, Teddy,' she said. 'We're going to be good friends, aren't we?'

'Aren't we?' he repeated. He winked without smiling, and with a clicking, despairing sound of his mouth, went out quickly.

For a moment Helen tried vainly to apply a measure to the situation, wondering how she had come off with him, realising reluctantly that she had never for an instant held the situation in her hands. She had a dim realisation that Teddy was larger in scale; then the very largeness frightened her and, with relief and a warm tide of emotion, she hurried into the drawing-room and the shelter of her lover's arms.

Their engagement ran through a halcyon summer. Stuart visited Helen's family at Tuxedo, and Helen visited his family in Wheatley Hills. Before breakfast, their horses' hoofs sedately scattered the dew in sentimental glades, or curtained them with dust as they raced on dirt roads. They bought a tandem bicycle and pedalled all over Long Island – which Mrs Cassius Ruthven, a contemporary Cato, considered 'rather fast' for a couple not yet married. They were seldom at rest, but when they were, they reminded people of His Move on a Gibson pillow.

Helen's taste for sport was advanced for her generation. She rode nearly as well as Stuart and gave him a decent game of tennis. He taught her some polo, and they were golf crazy when it was still considered a comic game. They liked to feel fit and cool together. They thought of themselves as a team, and it was often remarked how well mated they were. A chorus of pleasant envy followed in the wake of their effortless glamour.

They talked.

'It seems a pity you've got to go to the office,' she would say. 'I wish you did something we could do together, like taming lions.'

'I've always thought that at a pinch I could make a living breeding and racing horses,' said Stuart.

'I know you could, you darling.'

In August he bought a Thomas automobile and toured all the way to Chicago with three other men. It was an event of national interest and their pictures were in all the papers. Helen wanted to go, but it wouldn't have been proper, so they compromised by driving down Fifth Avenue on a sunny September morning, one with the fine day and the fashionable crowd, but distinguished by their unity, which made them each as strong as two.

'What do you suppose?' Helen demanded. 'Teddy sent me the oddest present – a cup rack.'

Stuart laughed. 'Obviously, he means that all we'll ever do is win cups.'

'I thought it was rather a slam,' Helen ruminated. 'I saw that he was invited to everything, but he didn't answer a single invitation. Would you mind very much stopping by his apartment now? I haven't seen him for months and I don't like to leave anything unpleasant in the past.'

He wouldn't go in with her. 'I'll sit and answer questions about the auto from passers-by.'

The door was opened by a woman in a cleaning cap, and Helen heard the sound of Teddy's piano from the room beyond. The woman seemed reluctant to admit her.

'He said don't interrupt him, but I suppose if you're his cousin – '

Teddy welcomed her, obviously startled and somewhat upset, but in a minute he was himself again.

'I won't marry you,' he assured her. 'You've had your chance.'

'All right,' she laughed.

'How are you?' He threw a pillow at her. 'You're beautiful! Are you happy with this – this centaur? Does he beat you with his riding crop?' He peered at her closely. 'You look a little duller than when I knew you. I used to whip you up to a nervous excitement that bore a resemblance to intelligence.'

'I'm happy, Teddy. I hope you are.'

'Sure, I'm happy; I'm working. I've got MacDowell on the run and I'm going to have a shebang at Carnegie Hall next September.' His eyes became malicious. 'What did you think of my girl?'

'Your girl?'

'The girl who opened the door for you.'

'Oh, I thought it was a maid.' She flushed and was silent.

He laughed. 'Hey, Betty!' he called. 'You were mistaken for the maid!'

'And that's the fault of my cleaning on Sunday,' answered a voice from the next room.

Teddy lowered his voice. 'Do you like her?' he demanded.

'Teddy!' She teetered on the arm of the sofa, wondering whether she should leave at once.

'What would you think if I married her?' he asked confidentially.

'Teddy!' She was outraged; it had needed but a glance to place the woman as common. 'You're joking. She's older than you . . . You wouldn't be such a fool as to throw away your future that way.'

He didn't answer.

'Is she musical?' Helen demanded. 'Does she help you with your work?'

'She doesn't know a note. Neither did you, but I've got enough music in me for twenty wives.'

Visualising herself as one of them, Helen rose stiffly.

'All I can ask you is to think how your mother would have felt – and those who care for you . . . Goodbye, Teddy.'

He walked out the door with her and down the stairs.

'As a matter of fact, we've been married for two months,' he said casually. 'She was a waitress in a place where I used to eat.'

Helen felt that she should be angry and aloof, but tears of hurt vanity were springing to her eyes.

'And do you love her?'

'I like her; she's a good person and good for me. Love is something else. I loved you, Helen, and that's all dead in me for the present.

Maybe it's coming out in my music. Someday I'll probably love other women – or maybe there'll never be anything but you. Goodbye, Helen.'

The declaration touched her. 'I hope you'll be happy, Teddy. Bring your wife to the wedding.'

He bowed noncommittally. When she had gone, he returned thoughtfully to his apartment.

'That was the cousin that I was in love with,' he said.

'And was it?' Betty's face, Irish and placid, brightened with interest. 'She's a pretty thing.'

'She wouldn't have been as good for me as a nice peasant like you.'

'Always thinking of yourself, Teddy Van Beck.'

He laughed. 'Sure I am, but you love me, anyhow?'

'That's a big wur-red.'

'All right. I'll remember that when you come begging around for a kiss. If my grandfather knew I married a bog trotter, he'd turn over in his grave. Now get out and let me finish my work.'

He sat at the piano, a pencil behind his ear. Already his face was resolved, composed, but his eyes grew more intense minute by minute, until there was a glaze in them, behind which they seemed to have joined his ears in counting and hearing. Presently there was no more indication in his face that anything had occurred to disturb the tranquillity of his Sunday morning.

2

Mrs Cassius Ruthven and a friend, veils flung back across their hats, sat in their auto on the edge of the field.

'A young woman playing polo in breeches.' Mrs Ruthven sighed. 'Amy Van Beck's daughter. I thought when Helen organised the Amazons she'd stop at divided skirts. But her husband apparently has no objections, for there he stands, egging her on. Of course, they always have liked the same things.'

'A pair of thoroughbreds, those two,' said the other woman complacently, meaning that she admitted them to be her equals. 'You'd never look at them and think that anything had gone wrong.'

She was referring to Stuart's mistake in the panic of 1907. His father had bequeathed him a precarious situation and Stuart had made an error of judgement. His honour was not questioned and his crowd stood by him loyally, but his usefulness in Wall Street was over and his small fortune was gone.

He stood in a group of men with whom he would presently play, noting things to tell Helen after the game – she wasn't turning with the play soon enough and several times she was unnecessarily ridden off at important moments. Her ponies were sluggish – the penalty for playing with borrowed mounts – but she was, nevertheless, the best player on the field, and in the last minute she made a save that brought applause.

'Good girl! Good girl!'

Stuart had been delegated with the unpleasant duty of chasing the women from the field. They had started an hour late and now a team from New Jersey was waiting to play; he sensed trouble as he cut across to join Helen and walked beside her towards the stables. She was splendid, with her flushed cheeks, her shining, triumphant eyes, her short, excited breath. He temporised for a minute.

'That was good – that last,' he said.

'Thanks. It almost broke my arm. Wasn't I pretty good all through?'

'You were the best out there.'

'I know it.'

He waited while she dismounted and handed the pony to a groom.

'Helen, I believe I've got a job.'

'What is it?'

'Don't jump on the idea till you think it over. Gus Myers wants me to manage his racing stables. Eight thousand a year.'

Helen considered. 'It's a nice salary; and I bet you could make yourself up a nice string from his ponies.'

'The principal thing is that I need the money; I'd have as much as you and things would be easier.'

'You'd have as much as me,' Helen repeated. She almost regretted that he would need no more help from her. 'But with Gus Myers, isn't there a string attached? Wouldn't he expect a boost up?'

'He probably would,' answered Stuart bluntly, 'and if I can help him socially, I will. As a matter of fact, he wants me at a stag dinner tonight.'

'All right, then,' Helen said absently.

Still hesitating to tell her her game was over, Stuart followed her glance towards the field, where a runabout had driven up and parked by the ropes.

'There's your old friend Teddy,' he remarked dryly – 'or rather, your new friend Teddy. He's taking a sudden interest in polo. Perhaps he thinks the horses aren't biting this summer.'

'You're not in a very good humour,' protested Helen. 'You know, if you say the word, I'll never see him again. All I want in the world is for you and I to be together.'

'I know,' he admitted regretfully. 'Selling horses and giving up clubs put a crimp in that. I know the women all fall for Teddy, now he's getting famous, but if he tries to fool around with you I'll break his piano over his head . . . Oh, another thing,' he began, seeing the men already riding on the field. 'About your last chukker – '

As best he could, he put the situation up to her. He was not prepared for the fury that swept over her.

'But it's an outrage! I got up the game and it's been posted on the bulletin board for three days.'

'You started an hour late.'

'And do you know why?' she demanded. 'Because your friend Joe Morgan insisted that Celie ride sidesaddle. He tore her habit off her three times, and she only got here by climbing out the kitchen window.'

'I can't do anything about it.'

'Why can't you? Weren't you once a governor of this club? How can women ever expect to be any good if they have to quit every time the men want the field? All the men want is for the women to come up to them in the evening and tell them what a beautiful game they played!'

Still raging and blaming Stuart, she crossed the field to Teddy's car. He got out and greeted her with concentrated intensity: 'I've reached the point where I can neither sleep nor eat from thinking of you. What point is that?'

There was something thrilling about him that she had never been conscious of in the old days; perhaps the stories of his philanderings had made him more romantic to her.

'Well, don't think of me as I am now,' she said. 'My face is getting rougher every day and my muscles lean out of an evening dress like a female impersonator. People are beginning to refer to me as handsome instead of pretty. Besides, I'm in a vile humour. It seems to me women are always just edged out of everything.'

Stuart's game was brutal that afternoon. In the first five minutes, he realised that Teddy's runabout was no longer there, and his long slugs began to tally from all angles. Afterwards, he bumped home across country at a gallop; his mood was not assuaged by a note handed him by the children's nurse:

Dear – Since your friends made it impossible for us to play, I wasn't going to sit there just dripping; so I had Teddy bring me home. And since you'll be out to dinner, I'm going into New York with him to the theatre. I'll either be out on the theatre train or spend the night at mother's.

Helen

Stuart went upstairs and changed into his dinner coat. He had no defence against the unfamiliar claws of jealousy that began a slow dissection of his insides. Often Helen had gone to plays or dances with other men, but this was different. He felt towards Teddy the faint contempt of the physical man for the artist, but the last six months had bruised his pride. He perceived the possibility that Helen might be seriously interested in someone else.

He was in a bad humour at Gus Myers' dinner – annoyed with his host for talking so freely about their business arrangement. When at last they rose from the table, he decided that it was no go and called Myers aside.

'Look here. I'm afraid this isn't a good idea, after all.'

'Why not?' His host looked at him in alarm. 'Are you going back on me? My dear fellow – '

'I think we'd better call it off.'

'And why, may I ask? Certainly I have the right to ask why.'

Stuart considered. 'All right, I'll tell you. When you made that little speech, you mentioned me as if you had somehow bought me, as if I was a sort of employee in your office. Now, in the sporting world that doesn't go; things are more – more democratic. I grew up with all these men here tonight, and they didn't like it any better than I did.'

'I see,' Mr Myers reflected carefully – 'I see.' Suddenly he clapped Stuart on the back. 'That is exactly the sort of thing I like to be told; it helps me. From now on I won't mention you as if you were in my – as if we had a business arrangement. Is that all right?'

After all, the salary was eight thousand dollars.

'Very well, then,' Stuart agreed. 'But you'll have to excuse me tonight. I'm catching a train to the city.'

'I'll put an automobile at your disposal.'

At ten o'clock he rang the bell of Teddy's apartment on Forty-Eighth Street.

'I'm looking for Mr Van Beck,' he said to the woman who answered the door. 'I know he's gone to the theatre, but I wonder if you can tell me – ' Suddenly he guessed who the woman was. 'I'm Stuart Oldhorne,' he explained. 'I married Mr Van Beck's cousin.'

'Oh, come in,' said Betty pleasantly. 'I know all about who you are.'

She was just this side of forty, stoutish and plain of face, but full of a keen, brisk vitality. In the living-room they sat down.

'You want to see Teddy?'

'He's with my wife and I want to join them after the theatre. I wonder if you know where they went?'

'Oh, so Teddy's with your wife.' There was a faint, pleasant brogue in her voice. 'Well, now, he didn't say exactly where he'd be tonight.'

'Then you don't know?'

'I don't – not for the life of me,' she admitted cheerfully. 'I'm sorry.'

He stood up, and Betty saw the thinly hidden anguish in his face. Suddenly she was really sorry.

'I did hear him say something about the theatre,' she said ruminatively. 'Now sit down and let me think what it was. He goes out so much and a play once a week is enough for me, so that one night mixes up with the others in my head. Didn't your wife say where to meet them?'

'No. I only decided to come in after they'd started. She said she'd catch the theatre train back to Long Island or go to her mother's.'

'That's it,' Betty said triumphantly, striking her hands together like cymbals. 'That's what he said when he called up – that he was putting a lady on the theatre train for Long Island, and would be home himself right afterwards. We've had a child sick and it's driven things from my mind.'

'I'm very sorry I bothered you under those conditions.'

'It's no bother. Sit down. It's only just after ten.'

Feeling easier, Stuart relaxed a little and accepted a cigar.

'No, if I tried to keep up with Teddy, I'd have white hair by now,' Betty said. 'Of course, I go to his concerts, but often I fall asleep – not that he ever knows it. So long as he doesn't take too much to drink and knows where his home is, I don't bother about where he wanders.' As Stuart's face grew serious again, she changed her tone: 'All and all, he's a good husband to me and we have a happy life together, without interfering with each other. How would he do working next to the nursery and groaning at every sound? And how would I do going to Mrs Ruthven's with him, and all of them talking about high society and high art?'

A phrase of Helen's came back to Stuart: 'Always together – I like for us to do everything together.'

'You have children, haven't you, Mr Oldhorne?'

'Yes. My boy's almost big enough to sit a horse.'

'Ah, yes; you're both great for horses.'

'My wife says that as soon as their legs are long enough to reach stirrups, she'll be interested in them again.' This didn't sound right to Stuart and he modified it: 'I mean she always has been interested in them, but she never let them monopolise her or come between us. We've always believed that marriage ought to be founded on companionship, on having the same interests. I mean, you're musical and you help your husband.'

Betty laughed. 'I wish Teddy could hear that. I can't read a note or carry a tune.'

'No?' He was confused. 'I'd somehow got the impression that you were musical.'

'You can't see why else he'd have married me?'

'Not at all. On the contrary.'

After a few minutes, he said good-night, somehow liking her. When he had gone, Betty's expression changed slowly to one of exasperation; she went to the telephone and called her husband's studio: 'There you are, Teddy. Now listen to me carefully. I know your cousin is with you and I want to talk with her . . . Now, don't lie. You put her on the phone. Her husband has been here, and if you don't let me talk to her, it might be a serious matter.'

She could hear an unintelligible colloquy, and then Helen's voice: 'Hello.'

'Good-evening, Mrs Oldhorne. Your husband came here, looking for you and Teddy. I told him I didn't know which play you were at, so you'd better be thinking which one. And I told him Teddy was leaving you at the station in time for the theatre train.'

'Oh, thank you very much. We – '

'Now, you meet your husband or there's trouble for you, or I'm no judge of men. And – wait a minute. Tell Teddy, if he's going to be up late, that Josie's sleeping light, and he's not to touch the piano when he gets home.'

Betty heard Teddy come in at eleven, and she came into the drawing-room smelling of camomile vapour. He greeted her absently; there was a look of suffering in his face and his eyes were bright and far away.

'You call yourself a great musician, Teddy Van Beck,' she said, 'but it seems to me you're much more interested in women.'

'Let me alone, Betty.'

'I do let you alone, but when the husbands start coming here, it's another matter.'

'This was different, Betty. This goes way back into the past.'

'It sounds like the present to me.'

'Don't make any mistake about Helen,' he said. 'She's a good woman.'

'Not through any fault of yours, I know.'

He sank his head wearily in his hands. 'I've tried to forget her. I've avoided her for six years. And then, when I met her a month ago, it all rushed over me. Try and understand, Bet. You're my best friend; you're the only person that ever loved me.'

'When you're good I love you,' she said.

'Don't worry. It's over. She loves her husband; she just came to New York with me because she's got some spite against him. She follows me a certain distance just like she always has, and then – Anyhow, I'm not going to see her any more. Now go to bed, Bet. I want to play for a while.'

He was on his feet when she stopped him.

'You're not to touch the piano tonight.'

'Oh, I forgot about Josie,' he said remorsefully. 'Well, I'll drink a bottle of beer and then I'll come to bed.'

He came close and put his arm around her.

'Dear Bet, nothing could ever interfere with us.'

'You're a bad boy, Teddy,' she said. 'I wouldn't ever be so bad to you.'

'How do you know, Bet? How do you know what you'd do?'

He smoothed down her plain brown hair, knowing for the thousandth time that she had none of the world's dark magic for him, and that he couldn't live without her for six consecutive hours. 'Dear Bet,' he whispered. 'Dear Bet.'

3

The Oldhornes were visiting. In the last four years, since Stuart had terminated his bondage to Gus Myers, they had become visiting people. The children visited Grandmother Van Beck during the winter and attended school in New York. Stuart and Helen visited friends in Asheville, Aiken and Palm Beach, and in the summer usually occupied a small cottage on someone's Long Island estate. 'My dear, it's just standing there empty. I wouldn't dream of accepting any rent. You'll be doing us a favour by occupying it.'

Usually, they were; they gave out a great deal of themselves in that eternal willingness and enthusiasm which makes a successful guest – it became their profession. Moving through a world that was growing rich with the war in Europe, Stuart had somewhere lost his way. Twice playing brilliant golf in the national amateur, he accepted a job as professional at a club which his father had helped to found. He was restless and unhappy.

This weekend they were visiting a pupil of his. As a consequence of a mixed foursome, the Oldhornes went upstairs to dress for dinner surcharged with the unpleasant accumulation of many unsatisfactory months. In the afternoon, Stuart had played with their hostess and Helen with another man – a situation which Stuart always dreaded, because it forced him into competition with Helen. He had actually tried to miss that putt on the eighteenth – to just miss it. But the ball dropped in the cup. Helen went through the superficial motions of a good loser, but she devoted herself pointedly to her partner for the rest of the afternoon.

Their expressions still counterfeited amusement as they entered their room.

When the door closed, Helen's pleasant expression faded and she walked towards the dressing-table as though her own reflection was the only decent company with which to forgather. Stuart watched her, frowning.

'I know why you're in a rotten humour,' he said; 'though I don't believe you know yourself.'

'I'm not in a rotten humour,' Helen responded in a clipped voice.

'You are; and I know the real reason – the one you don't know. It's because I holed that putt this afternoon.'

She turned slowly, incredulously, from the mirror.

'Oh, so I have a new fault! I've suddenly become, of all things, a poor sport!'

'It's not like you to be a poor sport,' he admitted, 'but otherwise why all this interest in other men, and why do you look at me as if I'm – well, slightly gamey?'

'I'm not aware of it.'

'I am.' He was aware, too, that there was always some man in their life now – some man of power and money who paid court to Helen and gave her the sense of solidity which he failed to provide. He had no cause to be jealous of any particular man, but the pressure of many was irritating. It annoyed him that on so slight a grievance, Helen should remind him by her actions that he no longer filled her entire life.

'If Anne can get any satisfaction out of winning, she's welcome to it,' said Helen suddenly.

'Isn't that rather petty? She isn't in your class; she won't qualify for the third flight in Boston.'

Feeling herself in the wrong, she changed her tone.

'Oh, that isn't it,' she broke out. 'I just keep wishing you and I could play together like we used to. And now you have to play with dubs, and get their wretched shots out of traps. Especially' – she hesitated – 'especially when you're so unnecessarily gallant.'

The faint contempt in her voice, the mock jealousy that covered a growing indifference was apparent to him. There had been a time when, if he danced with another woman, Helen's stricken eyes followed him around the room.

'My gallantry is simply a matter of business,' he answered. 'Lessons have brought in three hundred a month all summer. How could I go to see you play at Boston next week, except that I'm going to coach other women?'

'And you're going to see me win,' announced Helen. 'Do you know that?'

'Naturally, I want nothing more,' Stuart said automatically. But the unnecessary defiance in her voice repelled him, and he suddenly wondered if he really cared whether she won or not.

At the same moment, Helen's mood changed and for a moment she saw the true situation – that she could play in amateur tournaments and Stuart could not, that the new cups in the rack were all hers now, that he had given up the fiercely competitive sportsmanship that had been the breath of life to him in order to provide necessary money.

'Oh, I'm so sorry for you, Stuart!' There were tears in her eyes. 'It seems such a shame that you can't do the things you love, and I can. Perhaps I oughtn't to play this summer.'

'Nonsense,' he said. 'You can't sit home and twirl your thumbs.'

She caught at this: 'You wouldn't want me to. I can't help being good at sports; you taught me nearly all I know. But I wish I could help you.'

'Just try to remember I'm your best friend. Sometimes you act as if we were rivals.'

She hesitated, annoyed by the truth of his words and unwilling to concede an inch; but a wave of memories rushed over her, and she thought how brave he was in his eked-out, pieced-together life; she came and threw her arms around him.

'Darling, darling, things are going to be better. You'll see.'

Helen won the finals in the tournament at Boston the following week. Following around with the crowd, Stuart was very proud of her. He hoped that instead of feeding her egotism, the actual achievement would make things easier between them. He hated the conflict that had grown out of their wanting the same excellences, the same prizes from life.

Afterwards he pursued her progress towards the clubhouse, amused and a little jealous of the pack that fawned around her. He reached the club among the last, and a steward accosted him. 'Professionals are served in the lower grill, please,' the man said.

'That's all right. My name's Oldhorne.'

He started to walk by, but the man barred his way.

'Sorry, sir. I realise that Mrs Oldhorne's playing in the match, but my orders are to direct the professionals to the lower grill, and I understand you are a professional.'

'Why, look here – ' Stuart began, wildly angry, and stopped. A group of people were listening. 'All right; never mind,' he said gruffly, and turned away.

The memory of the experience rankled; it was the determining factor that drove him, some weeks later, to a momentous decision. For a long time he had been playing with the idea of joining the Canadian Air Force, for service in France. He knew that his absence would have little practical bearing on the lives of Helen and the children; happening on some friends who were also full of the restlessness of 1915, the matter was suddenly decided. But he had not counted on the effect upon Helen; her reaction was not so much one of grief or alarm, but as if she had been somehow outwitted.

'But you might have told me!' she wailed. 'You leave me dangling; you simply take yourself away without any warning.'

Once again Helen saw him as the bright and intolerably blinding hero, and her soul winced before him as it had when they first met. He was a warrior; for him, peace was only the interval between wars, and peace was destroying him. Here was the game of games beckoning him – Without throwing over the whole logic of their lives, there was nothing she could say.

'This is my sort of thing,' he said confidently, younger with his excitement. 'A few more years of this life and I'd go to pieces, take to drink. I've somehow lost your respect, and I've got to have that, even if I'm far away.'

She was proud of him again; she talked to everyone of his impending departure. Then, one September afternoon, she came home from the city, full of the old feeling of comradeship and bursting with news, to find him buried in an utter depression.

'Stuart,' she cried, 'I've got the – ' She broke off. 'What's the matter, darling? Is something the matter?'

He looked at her dully. 'They turned me down,' he said.

'What?'

'My left eye.' He laughed bitterly. 'Where that dub cracked me with the brassie. I'm nearly blind in it.'

'Isn't there anything you can do?'

'Nothing.'

'Stuart!' She stared at him aghast. 'Stuart, and I was going to tell you! I was saving it for a surprise. Elsa Prentice has organised a Red Cross unit to serve with the French, and I joined it because I thought it would be wonderful if we both went. We've been measured for uniforms and bought our outfits, and we're sailing the end of next week.'

4

Helen was a blurred figure among other blurred figures on a boat deck, dark against the threat of submarines. When the ship had slid out into the obscure future, Stuart walked eastward along Fifty-Seventh Street. His grief at the severance of many ties was a weight he carried in his body, and he walked slowly, as if adjusting himself to it. To balance this there was a curious sensation of lightness in his mind. For the first time in twelve years he was alone, and the feeling came over him that he was alone for good; knowing Helen and knowing war, he could guess at the experiences she would go through, and he could not form any picture of a renewed life together afterwards. He was discarded; she had proved the stronger at last. It seemed very strange and sad that his marriage should have such an ending.

He came to Carnegie Hall, dark after a concert, and his eye caught the name of Theodore Van Beck, large on the posted bills. As he stared at it, a green door opened in the side of the building and a group of people in evening dress came out. Stuart and Teddy were face to face before they recognised each other.

'Hello, there!' Teddy cried cordially. 'Did Helen sail?'

'Just now.'

'I met her on the street yesterday and she told me. I wanted you both to come to my concert. Well, she's quite a heroine, going off like that . . . Have you met my wife?'

Stuart and Betty smiled at each other.

'We've met.'

'And I didn't know it,' protested Teddy. 'Women need watching when they get towards their dotage . . . Look here, Stuart; we're having a few people up to the apartment. No heavy music or anything. Just supper and a few débutantes to tell me I was divine. It will do you good to come. I imagine you're missing Helen like the devil.'

'I don't think I – '

'Come along. They'll tell you you're divine too.'

Realising that the invitation was inspired by kindliness, Stuart accepted. It was the sort of gathering he had seldom attended, and he was surprised to meet so many people he knew. Teddy played the lion in a manner at once assertive and sceptical. Stuart listened as he enlarged to Mrs Cassius Ruthven on one of his favourite themes: 'People tried to make marriages cooperative and they've ended by becoming competitive. Impossible situation. Smart men will get to fight shy of ornamental women. A man ought to marry somebody who'll be grateful, like Betty here.'

'Now don't talk so much, Theodore Van Beck,' Betty interrupted. 'Since you're such a fine musician, you'd do well to express yourself with music instead of rash words.'

'I don't agree with your husband,' said Mrs Ruthven. 'English girls hunt with their men and play politics with them on absolutely equal terms, and it tends to draw them together.'

'It does not,' insisted Teddy. 'That's why English society is the most disorganised in the world. Betty and I are happy because we haven't any qualities in common at all.'

His exuberance grated on Stuart, and the success that flowed from him swung his mind back to the failure of his own life. He could not know that his life was not destined to be a failure. He could not read the fine story that three years later would be carved proud above his soldier's grave, or know that his restless body, which never spared itself in sport or danger, was destined to give him one last proud gallop at the end.

'They turned me down,' he was saying to Mrs Ruthven. 'I'll have to stick to Squadron A, unless we get drawn in.'

'So Helen's gone.' Mrs Ruthven looked at him, reminiscing. 'I'll never forget your wedding. You were both so handsome, so ideally suited to each other. Everybody spoke of it.'

Stuart remembered; for the moment it seemed that he had little else that it was fun to remember.

'Yes,' he agreed, nodding his head thoughtfully, 'I suppose we were a handsome pair.'

Afternoon of an Author

Esquire (August 1936)

1

When he woke up he felt better than he had for many weeks, a fact that became plain to him negatively – he did not feel ill. He leaned for a moment against the door frame between his bedroom and bath till he could be sure he was not dizzy. Not a bit, not even when he stooped for a slipper under the bed.

It was a bright April morning, he had no idea what time because his clock was long unwound, but as he went back through the apartment to the kitchen he saw that his daughter had breakfasted and departed and that the mail was in, so it was after nine.

'I think I'll go out today,' he said to the maid.

'Do you good – it's a lovely day.' She was from New Orleans, with the features and colouring of an Arab.

'I want two eggs like yesterday and toast, orange juice and tea.'

He lingered for a moment in his daughter's end of the apartment and read his mail. It was an annoying mail with nothing cheerful in it – mostly bills and advertisements with the diurnal Oklahoma schoolboy and his gaping autograph album. Sam Goldwyn might do a ballet picture with Spessiwitza and might not – it would all have to wait till Mr Goldwyn got back from Europe when he might have half a dozen new ideas. Paramount wanted a release on a poem that had appeared in one of the author's books, as they didn't know whether it was an original or quoted. Maybe they were going to get a title from it. Anyhow he had no more equity in that property – he had sold the silent rights many years ago and the sound rights last year.

'Never any luck with movies,' he said to himself. 'Stick to your last, boy.'

He looked out the window during breakfast at the students changing classes on the college campus across the way.

'Twenty years ago I was changing classes,' he said to the maid. She laughed her débutante's laugh.

'I'll need a cheque,' she said, 'if you're going out.'

'Oh, I'm not going out yet. I've got two or three hours' work. I meant late this afternoon.'

'Going for a drive?'

'I wouldn't drive that old junk – I'd sell it for fifty dollars. I'm going on the top of a bus.'

After breakfast he lay down for fifteen minutes. Then he went into the study and began to work.

The problem was a magazine story that had become so thin in the middle that it was about to blow away. The plot was like climbing endless stairs, he had no element of surprise in reserve, and the characters who started so bravely day-before-yesterday couldn't have qualified for a newspaper serial.

'Yes, I certainly need to get out,' he thought. 'I'd like to drive down the Shenandoah Valley, or go to Norfolk on the boat.'

But both of these ideas were impractical – they took time and energy and he had not much of either – what there was must be conserved for work. He went through the manuscript underlining good phrases in red crayon and after tucking these into a file slowly tore up the rest of the story and dropped it in the waste-basket. Then he walked the room and smoked, occasionally talking to himself.

'Wee-l, let's see –

'Nau-ow, the next thing – would be –

'Now let's see, now – '

After awhile he sat down thinking: 'I'm just stale – I shouldn't have touched a pencil for two days.'

He looked through the heading 'Story Ideas' in his notebook until the maid came to tell him his secretary was on the phone – part-time secretary since he had been ill.

'Not a thing,' he said. 'I just tore up everything I'd written. It wasn't worth a damn. I'm going out this afternoon.'

'Good for you. It's a fine day.'

'Better come up tomorrow afternoon – there's a lot of mail and bills.'

He shaved, and then as a precaution rested five minutes before he dressed. It was exciting to be going out – he hoped the elevator boys wouldn't say they were glad to see him up and he decided to go down the back elevator where they did not know him. He put on his best suit with the coat and trousers that didn't match. He had bought only two suits in six years but they were the very best suits – the coat alone of this one had cost a hundred and ten dollars. As he must have a destination – it wasn't good to go places without a destination – he put a tube of shampoo ointment in his pocket for his barber to use, and also a small phial of luminol.

'The perfect neurotic,' he said, regarding himself in the mirror. 'By-product of an idea, slag of a dream.'

2

He went into the kitchen and said goodbye to the maid as if he were going to Little America. Once in the war he had commandeered an engine on sheer bluff and had it driven from New York to Washington to keep from being AWOL. Now he stood carefully on the street corner waiting for the light to change, while young people hurried past him with a fine disregard for traffic. On the bus corner under the trees it was green and cool and he thought of Stonewall Jackson's last words: 'Let us cross over the river and rest under the shade of the trees.' Those Civil War leaders seemed to have realised very suddenly how tired they were – Lee shrivelling into another man, Grant with his desperate memoir-writing at the end.

The bus was all he expected – only one other man on the roof and the green branches ticking against each window through whole blocks. They would probably have to trim those branches and it seemed a pity. There was so much to look at – he tried to define the colour of one line of houses and could only think of an old opera cloak of his mother's that was full of tints and yet was of no tint – a mere reflector of light. Somewhere church bells were playing 'Venite Adoremus' and he wondered why, because Christmas was eight months off. He didn't like bells but it had been very moving when they played 'Maryland, My Maryland' at the governor's funeral.

On the college football field men were working with rollers and a title occurred to him: 'Turf-keeper' or else 'The Grass Grows', something about a man working on turf for years and bringing up his son to go to college and play football there. Then the son dying in youth and the man's going to work in the cemetery and putting turf over his son instead of under his feet. It would be the kind of piece that is often placed in anthologies, but not his sort of thing – it was sheer swollen antithesis, as formalised as a popular magazine story and easier to write. Many people, however, would consider it excellent because it was melancholy, had digging in it and was simple to understand.

The bus went past a pale Athenian railroad station brought to life by the blue-shirted red-caps out in front. The street narrowed as the business section began and there were suddenly brightly dressed girls, all very beautiful – he thought he had never seen such beautiful girls. There were men too but they all looked rather silly, like himself in the mirror, and there were old undecorative women, and presently, too, there were plain and unpleasant faces among the girls; but in general they were lovely, dressed in real colours all the way from six to thirty, no plans or struggles in their faces, only a state of sweet suspension, provocative and serene. He loved life terribly for a minute, not wanting to give it up at all. He thought perhaps he had made a mistake in coming out so soon.

He got off the bus, holding carefully to all the railings, and walked a block to the hotel barbershop. He passed a sporting-goods store and looked in the window unmoved except by a first baseman's glove which was already dark in the pocket. Next to that was a haberdasher's and here he stood for quite a while looking at the deep shade of shirts and the ones of checker and plaid. Ten years ago on the summer Riviera the author and some others had bought dark blue workmen's shirts, and probably that had started that style. The checkered shirts were nice looking, bright as uniforms, and he wished he were twenty and going to a beach club all dolled up like a Turner sunset or Guido Reni's dawn.

The barbershop was large, shining and scented – it had been several months since the author had come downtown on such a mission and he found that his familiar barber was laid up with arthritis; however, he explained to another man how to use the ointment, refused a newspaper and sat, rather happy and sensually content at the strong fingers on his scalp, while a pleasant mingled memory of all the barbershops he had ever known flowed through his mind.

Once he had written a story about a barber. Back in 1929 the proprietor of his favourite shop in the city where he was then living had made a fortune of $300,000 on tips from a local industrialist and was about to retire. The author had no stake in the market, in fact, was about to sail for Europe for a few years with such accumulation as he had, and that autumn hearing how the barber had lost all his fortune he was prompted to write a story, thoroughly disguised in every way yet hinging on the fact of a barber rising in the world and then tumbling; he heard, nevertheless, that the story had been identified in the city and caused some hard feelings.

The shampoo ended. When he came out into the hall an orchestra had started to play in the cocktail room across the way and he stood for a moment in the door listening. So long since he had danced, perhaps two evenings in five years, yet a review of his last book had mentioned him as being fond of nightclubs; the same review had also spoken of him as being indefatigable. Something in the sound of the word in his mind broke him momentarily and feeling tears of weakness behind his eyes he turned away. It was like in the beginning fifteen years ago when they said he had 'fatal facility', and he laboured like a slave over every sentence so as not to be like that.

'I'm getting bitter again,' he said to himself. 'That's no good, no good – I've got to go home.'

The bus was a long time coming but he didn't like taxis and he still hoped that something would occur to him on that upper deck, passing through the green leaves of the boulevard. When it came finally he had some trouble climbing the steps but it was worth it for the first thing he saw was a pair of high-school kids, a boy and a girl, sitting without any self-consciousness on the high pedestal of the Lafayette statue, their attention fast upon each other. Their isolation moved him and he knew he would get something out of it professionally, if only in contrast to the growing seclusion of his life and the increasing necessity of picking over an already well-picked past. He needed reforestation and he was well aware of it, and he hoped the soil would stand one more growth. It had never been the very best soil for he had had an early weakness for showing off instead of listening and observing.

Here was the apartment house – he glanced up at his own windows on the top floor before he went in.

'The residence of the successful writer,' he said to himself. 'I wonder what marvellous books he's tearing off up there. It must be great to have a gift like that – just sit down with pencil and paper. Work when you want – go where you please.'

His child wasn't home yet but the maid came out of the kitchen and said: 'Did you have a nice time?'

'Perfect,' he said. 'I went roller-skating and bowled and played around with Man Mountain Dean and finished up in a Turkish bath. Any telegrams?'

'Not a thing.'

'Bring me a glass of milk, will you?'

He went through the dining-room and turned into his study, struck blind for a moment with the glow of his two thousand books in the late sunshine. He was quite tired – he would lie down for ten minutes and then see if he could get started on an idea in the two hours before dinner.

Financing Finnegan

Esquire (January 1938)

1

Finnegan and I have the same literary agent to sell our writings for us – but though I'd often been in Mr Cannon's office just before and just after Finnegan's visits, I had never met him. Likewise we had the same publisher and often when I arrived there Finnegan had just departed. I gathered from a thoughtful sighing way in which they spoke of him –

'Ah – Finnegan – '

'Oh yes, Finnegan was here.'

– that the distinguished author's visit had been not uneventful. Certain remarks implied that he had taken something with him when he went – manuscripts, I supposed, one of those great successful novels of his. He had taken 'it' off for a final revision, a last draft, of which he was rumoured to make ten in order to achieve that facile flow, that ready wit, which distinguished his work. I discovered only gradually that most of Finnegan's visits had to do with money.

'I'm sorry you're leaving,' Mr Cannon would tell me, 'Finnegan will be here tomorrow.' Then after a thoughtful pause, 'I'll probably have to spend some time with him.'

I don't know what note in his voice reminded me of a talk with a nervous bank president when Dillinger was reported in the vicinity. His eyes looked out into the distance and he spoke as to himself: 'Of course he may be bringing a manuscript. He has a novel he's working on, you know. And a play too.'

He spoke as though he were talking about some interesting but remote events of the cinquecento; but his eyes became more hopeful as he added: 'Or maybe a short story.'

'He's very versatile, isn't he?' I said.

'Oh yes,' Mr Cannon perked up. 'He can do anything – anything when he puts his mind to it. There's never been such a talent.'

'I haven't seen much of his work lately.'

'Oh, but he's working hard. Some of the magazines have stories of his that they're holding.'

'Holding for what?'

'Oh, for a more appropriate time – an upswing. They like to think they have something of Finnegan's.'

His was indeed a name with ingots in it. His career had started brilliantly and if it had not kept up to its first exalted level, at least it started brilliantly all over again every few years. He was the perennial man of promise in American letters – what he could actually do with words was astounding, they glowed and coruscated – he wrote sentences, paragraphs, chapters that were masterpieces of fine weaving and spinning. It was only when I met some poor devil of a screenwriter who had been trying to make a logical story out of one of his books that I realised he had his enemies.

'It's all beautiful when you read it,' this man said disgustedly, 'but when you write it down plain it's like a week in the nut-house.'

From Mr Cannon's office I went over to my publishers on Fifth Avenue and there too I learned in no time that Finnegan was expected tomorrow.

Indeed he had thrown such a long shadow before him that the luncheon where I expected to discuss my own work was largely devoted to Finnegan. Again I had the feeling that my host, Mr George Jaggers, was talking not to me but to himself.

'Finnegan's a great writer,' he said.

'Undoubtedly.'

'And he's really quite all right, you know.'

As I hadn't questioned the fact I enquired whether there was any doubt about it.

'Oh no,' he said hurriedly. 'It's just that he's had such a run of hard luck lately – '

I shook my head sympathetically. 'I know. That diving into a half-empty pool was a tough break.'

'Oh, it wasn't half-empty. It was full of water. Full to the brim. You ought to hear Finnegan on the subject – he makes a side-splitting story of it. It seems he was in a run-down condition and just diving from the side of the pool, you know – ' Mr Jaggers pointed his knife and fork at the table, 'and he saw some young girls diving from the fifteen-foot board. He says he thought of his lost youth and went up to do the same and made a beautiful swan dive – but his shoulder broke while he was still in the air.' He looked at me rather anxiously. 'Haven't you heard of cases like that – a ball player throwing his arm out of joint?'

I couldn't think of any orthopaedic parallels at the moment.

'And then,' he continued dreamily, 'Finnegan had to write on the ceiling.'

'On the ceiling?'

'Practically. He didn't give up writing – he has plenty of guts, that fellow, though you may not believe it. He had some sort of arrangement built that was suspended from the ceiling and he lay on his back and wrote in the air.'

I had to grant that it was a courageous arrangement.

'Did it affect his work?' I enquired. 'Did you have to read his stories backward – like Chinese?'

'They were rather confused for a while,' he admitted, 'but he's all right now. I got several letters from him that sounded more like the old Finnegan – full of life and hope and plans for the future – '

The faraway look came into his face and I turned the discussion to affairs closer to my heart. Only when we were back in his office did the subject recur – and I blush as I write this because it includes confessing something I seldom do – reading another man's telegram. It happened because Mr Jaggers was intercepted in the hall and when I went into his office and sat down it was stretched out open before me:

> With fifty I could at least pay typist and ger haircut and pencils. Life has become impossible and I exist on dream of good news. Desperately, Finnegan.

I couldn't believe my eyes – fifty dollars, and I happened to know that Finnegan's price for short stories was somewhere around three thousand. George Jaggers found me still staring dazedly at the telegram. After he read it he stared at me with stricken eyes.

'I don't see how I can conscientiously do it,' he said.

I started and glanced around to make sure I was in the prosperous publishing office in New York. Then I understood – I had misread the telegram. Finnegan was asking for fifty thousand as an advance – a demand that would have staggered any publisher no matter who the writer was.

'Only last week,' said Mr Jaggers disconsolately, 'I sent him a hundred dollars. It puts my department in the red every season, so I don't dare tell my partners any more. I take it out of my own pocket – give up a suit and a pair of shoes.'

'You mean Finnegan's broke?'

'Broke!' He looked at me and laughed soundlessly – in fact I didn't exactly like the way that he laughed. My brother had a nervous – but that is afield from this story. After a minute he pulled himself together. 'You won't say anything about this, will you? The truth is Finnegan's been in a slump, he's had blow after blow in the past few years, but now he's snapping out of it and I know we'll get back every cent we've – ' He tried to think of a word but 'given him' slipped out. This time it was he who was eager to change the subject.

Don't let me give the impression that Finnegan's affairs absorbed me during a whole week in New York – it was inevitable, though, that being much in the offices of my agent and my publisher, I happened in on a lot. For instance, two days later, using the telephone in Mr Cannon's office, I was accidentally switched in on a conversation he was having with George Jaggers. It was only partly eavesdropping, you see, because I could only hear one end of the conversation and that isn't as bad as hearing it all.

'But I got the impression he was in good health . . . he did say something about his heart a few months ago but I understood it got well . . . yes, and he talked about some operation he wanted to have – I think he said it was cancer . . . Well, I felt like telling him I had a little operation up my sleeve too, that I'd have had by now if I could afford it . . . No, I didn't say it. He seemed in such good spirits that it would have been a shame to bring him down. He's starting a story today, he read me some of it on the phone . . .

' . . . I did give him twenty-five because he didn't have a cent in his pocket . . . oh, yes – I'm sure he'll be all right now. He sounds as if he means business.'

I understood it all now. The two men had entered into a silent conspiracy to cheer each other up about Finnegan. Their investment in him, in his future, had reached a sum so considerable that Finnegan belonged to them. They could not bear to hear a word against him – even from themselves.

2

I spoke my mind to Mr Cannon. 'If this Finnegan is a four-flusher you can't go on indefinitely giving him money. If he's through he's through and there's nothing to be done about it. It's absurd that you should put off an operation when Finnegan's out somewhere diving into half-empty swimming pools.'

'It was full,' said Mr Cannon patiently – 'full to the brim.'

'Well, full or empty the man sounds like a nuisance to me.'

'Look here,' said Cannon, 'I've got a talk to Hollywood due on the wire. Meanwhile you might glance over that.' He threw a manuscript into my lap. 'Maybe it'll help you understand. He brought it in yesterday.'

It was a short story. I began it in a mood of disgust but before I'd read five minutes I was completely immersed in it, utterly charmed, utterly convinced and wishing to God I could write like that. When Cannon finished his phone call I kept him waiting while I finished it and when I did there were tears in these hard old professional eyes. Any magazine in the country would have run it first in any issue.

But then nobody had ever denied that Finnegan could write.

3

Months passed before I went again to New York, and then, so far as the offices of my agent and my publisher were concerned, I descended upon a quieter, more stable world. There was at last time to talk about my own conscientious if uninspired literary pursuits, to visit Mr Cannon in the country and to kill summer evenings with George Jaggers where the vertical New York starlight falls like lingering lightning into restaurant gardens. Finnegan might have been at the North Pole – and as a matter of fact he was. He had quite a group with him, including three Bryn Mawr anthropologists, and it sounded as if he might collect a lot of material there. They were going to stay several months, and if the thing had somehow the ring of a promising little house party about it, that was probably due to my jealous, cynical disposition.

'We're all just delighted,' said Cannon. 'It's a godsend for him. He was fed up and he needed just this – this – '

'Ice and snow,' I supplied.

'Yes, ice and snow. The last thing he said was characteristic of him. Whatever he writes is going to be pure white – it's going to have a blinding glare about it.'

'I can imagine it will. But tell me – who's financing it? Last time I was here I gathered the man was insolvent.'

'Oh, he was really very decent about that. He owed me some money and I believe he owed George Jaggers a little too – ' He 'believed', the old hypocrite. He knew damn well – 'so before he left he made most of his life insurance over to us. That's in case he doesn't come back – those trips are dangerous of course.'

'I should think so,' I said – 'especially with three anthropologists.'

'So Jaggers and I are absolutely covered in case anything happens – it's as simple as that.'

'Did the life-insurance company finance the trip?'

He fidgeted perceptibly.

'Oh, no. In fact when they learned the reason for the assignments they were a little upset. George Jaggers and I felt that when he had a specific plan like this with a specific book at the end of it, we were justified in backing him a little further.'

'I don't see it,' I said flatly.

'You don't?' The old harassed look came back into his eyes. 'Well, I'll admit we hesitated. In principle I know it's wrong. I used to advance authors small sums from time to time, but lately I've made a rule against it – and kept it. It's only been waived once in the last two years and that was for a woman who was having a bad struggle – Margaret Trahill, do you know her? She was an old girl of Finnegan's, by the way.'

'Remember I don't even know Finnegan.'

'That's right. You must meet him when he comes back – if he does come back. You'd like him – he's utterly charming.'

Again I departed from New York, to imaginative North Poles of my own, while the year rolled through summer and fall. When the first snap of November was in the air, I thought of the Finnegan expedition with a sort of shiver and any envy of the man departed. He was probably earning any loot, literary or anthropological, he might bring back. Then, when I hadn't been back in New York three days, I read in the paper that he and some other members of his party had walked off into a snowstorm when the food supply gave out, and the Arctic had claimed another sacrifice.

I was sorry for him, but practical enough to be glad that Cannon and Jaggers were well protected. Of course, with Finnegan scarcely cold – if such a simile is not too harrowing – they did not talk about it but I gathered that the insurance companies had waived habeas corpus, or whatever it is in their lingo, and it seemed quite sure that they would collect.

His son, a fine looking young fellow, came into George Jaggers's office while I was there and from him I could guess at Finnegan's charm – a shy frankness together with an impression of a very quiet brave battle going on inside of him that he couldn't quite bring himself to talk about – but that showed as heat lightning in his work.

'The boy writes well too,' said George after he had gone. 'He's brought in some remarkable poems. He's not ready to step into his father's shoes, but there's a definite promise.'

'Can I see one of his things?'

'Certainly – here's one he left just as he went out.'

George took a paper from his desk, opened it and cleared his throat. Then he squinted and bent over a little in his chair.

'Dear Mr Jaggers,' he began, 'I didn't like to ask you this in person –' Jaggers stopped, his eyes reading ahead rapidly.

'How much does he want?' I enquired.

He sighed.

'He gave me the impression that this was some of his work,' he said in a pained voice.

'But it is,' I consoled him. 'Of course he isn't quite ready to step into his father's shoes.'

I was sorry afterwards to have said this, for after all Finnegan had paid his debts, and it was nice to be alive now that better times were back and books were no longer rated as unnecessary luxuries. Many authors I knew who had skimped along during the Depression were now making long-deferred trips or paying off mortgages or turning out the more finished kind of work that can only be done with a certain leisure and security. I had just got a thousand-dollar advance for a venture in Hollywood and was going to fly out with all the verve of the old days when there was chicken feed in every pot. Going in to say goodbye to Cannon and collect the money, it was nice to find he too was profiting – wanted me to go along and see a motor boat he was buying.

But some last-minute stuff came up to delay him and I grew impatient and decided to skip it. Getting no response to a knock on the door of his sanctum, I opened it anyhow.

The inner office seemed in some confusion. Mr Cannon was on several telephones at once and dictating something about an insurance company to a stenographer. One secretary was getting hurriedly into her hat and coat as upon an errand and another was counting bills from her purse.

'It'll be only a minute,' said Cannon, 'it's just a little office riot – you never saw us like this.'

'Is it Finnegan's insurance?' I couldn't help asking. 'Isn't it any good?'

'His insurance – oh, perfectly all right, perfectly. This is just a matter of trying to raise a few hundred in a hurry. The banks are closed and we're all contributing.'

'I've got that money you just gave me,' I said. 'I don't need all of it to get to the coast.' I peeled off a couple of hundred. 'Will this be enough?'

'That'll be fine – it just saves us. Never mind, Miss Carlsen. Mrs Mapes, you needn't go now.'

'I think I'll be running along,' I said.

'Just wait two minutes,' he urged. 'I've only got to take care of this wire. It's really splendid news. Bucks you up.'

It was a cablegram from Oslo, Norway – before I began to read I was full of a premonition.

> Am miraculously safe here but detained by authorities. Please wire passage money for four people and two hundred extra. I am bringing back plenty. Greetings from the dead. Finnegan.

'Yes, that's splendid,' I agreed. 'He'll have a story to tell now.'

'Won't he though,' said Cannon. 'Miss Carlsen, will you wire the parents of those girls – and you'd better inform Mr Jaggers.'

As we walked along the street a few minutes later, I saw that Mr Cannon, as if stunned by the wonder of this news, had fallen into a brown study, and I did not disturb him, for after all I did not know Finnegan and could not wholeheartedly share his joy. His mood of silence continued until we arrived at the door of the motor-boat show. Just under the sign he stopped and stared upward, as if aware for the first time where we were going.

'Oh, my,' he said, stepping back. 'There's no use going in here now. I thought we were going to get a drink.'

We did. Mr Cannon was still a little vague, a little under the spell of the vast surprise – he fumbled so long for the money to pay his round that I insisted it was on me.

I think he was in a daze during that whole time because, though he is a man of the most punctilious accuracy, the two hundred I handed him in his office has never shown to my credit in the statements he has sent me. I imagine, though, that someday I will surely get it because someday Finnegan will click again and I know that people will clamour to read what he writes. Recently I've taken it upon myself to investigate some of the stories about him and I've found that they're mostly as false as the half-empty pool. That pool was full to the brim.

So far there's only been a short story about the polar expedition, a love story. Perhaps it wasn't as big a subject as he expected. But the movies are interested in him – if they can get a good long look at him first – and I have every reason to think that he will come through. He'd better.

Design in Plaster

Esquire (November 1939)

'How long does the doctor think now?' Mary asked. With his good arm Martin threw back the top of the sheet, disclosing that the plaster armour had been cut away in front in the form of a square, so that his abdomen and the lower part of his diaphragm bulged a little from the aperture. His dislocated arm was still high over his head in an involuntary salute.

'This was a great advance,' he told her. 'But it took the heatwave to make Ottinger put in this window. I can't say much for the view but – have you seen the wire collection?'

'Yes, I've seen it,' his wife answered, trying to look amused.

It was laid out on the bureau like a set of surgeon's tools – wires bent to every length and shape so that the nurse could reach any point inside the plaster cast when perspiration made the itching unbearable.

Martin was ashamed at repeating himself.

'I apologise,' he said. 'After two months you get medical psychology. All this stuff is fascinating to me. In fact – ' he added, and with only faint irony, ' – it is in a way of becoming my life.'

Mary came over and sat beside the bed raising him, cast and all, into her slender arms. He was chief electrical engineer at the studio and his thirty-foot fall wasn't costing a penny in doctor's bills. But that – and the fact that the catastrophe had swung them together after a four months' separation, was its only bright spot.

'I feel so close,' she whispered. 'Even through this plaster.'

'Do you think that's a nice way to talk?'

'Yes.'

'So do I.'

Presently she stood up and rearranged her bright hair in the mirror. He had seen her do it half a thousand times but suddenly there was a quality of remoteness about it that made him sad.

'What are you doing tonight?' he asked.

Mary turned, almost with surprise.

'It seems strange to have you ask me.'

'Why? You almost always tell me. You're my contact with the world of glamour.'

'But you like to keep bargains. That was our arrangement when we began to live apart.'

'You're being very technical.'

'No – but that *was* the arrangement. As a matter of fact I'm not doing anything. Bieman asked me to go to a preview, but he bores me. And that French crowd called up.'

'Which member of it?'

She came closer and looked at him.

'Why, I believe you're jealous,' she said. 'The wife of course. Or *he* did, to be exact, but he was calling for his wife – she'd be there. I've never seen you like this before.'

Martin was wise enough to wink as if it meant nothing and let it die away, but Mary said an unfortunate last word.

'I thought you liked me to go with them.'

'That's it,' Martin tried to go slow, ' – with "them", but now it's "he".'

'They're all leaving Monday,' she said almost impatiently. 'I'll probably never see him again.'

Silence for a minute. Since his accident there were not an unlimited number of things to talk about, except when there was love between them. Or even pity – he was accepting even pity in the past fortnight. Especially their uncertain plans about the future were in need of being preceded by a mood of love.

'I'm going to get up for a minute,' he said suddenly. 'No, don't help me – don't call the nurse. I've got it figured out.'

The cast extended halfway to his knee on one side but with a snake-like motion he managed to get to the side of the bed – then rise with a gigantic heave. He tied on a dressing-gown, still without assistance, and went to the window. Young people were splashing and calling in the outdoor pool of the hotel.

'I'll go along,' said Mary. 'Can I bring you anything tomorrow? Or tonight if you feel lonely?'

'Not tonight. You know I'm always cross at night – and I don't like you making that long drive twice a day. Go along – be happy.'

'Shall I ring for the nurse?'

'I'll ring presently.'

He didn't though – he just stood. He knew that Mary was wearing out, that this resurgence of her love was wearing out. His accident was a very temporary dam of a stream that had begun to overflow months before.

When the pains began at six with their customary regularity the nurse gave him something with codein in it, shook him a cocktail and ordered dinner, one of those dinners it was a struggle to digest since he had been sealed up in his individual bomb-shelter. Then she was off duty four hours and he was alone. Alone with Mary and the Frenchman.

He didn't know the Frenchman except by name but Mary had said once: 'Joris is rather like you – only naturally not formed – rather immature.'

Since she said that, the company of Mary and Joris had grown increasingly unattractive in the long hours between seven and eleven. He had talked with them, driven around with them, gone to pictures and parties with them – sometimes with the half-comforting ghost of Joris's wife along. He had been near as they made love and even that was endurable as long as he could seem to hear and see them. It was when they became hushed and secret that his stomach winced inside the plaster cast. That was when he had pictures of the Frenchman going towards Mary and Mary waiting. Because he was not sure just how Joris felt about her or about the whole situation.

'I told him I loved you,' Mary said – and he believed her, 'I told him that I could never love anyone but you.'

Still he could not be sure how Mary felt as she waited in her apartment for Joris. He could not tell if, when she said good-night at her door, she turned away relieved, or whether she walked around her living-room a little and later, reading her book, dropped it in her lap and looked up at the ceiling. Or whether her phone rang once more for one more good-night.

Martin hadn't worried about any of these things in the first two months of their separation when he had been on his feet and well.

At half-past eight he took up the phone and called her; the line was busy and still busy at a quarter to nine. At nine it was out of order; at nine-fifteen it didn't answer and at a little before nine-thirty it was busy again. Martin got up, slowly drew on his trousers and with the help of a bellboy put on a shirt and coat.

'Don't you want me to come, Mr Harris?' asked the bellboy.

'No thanks. Tell the taxi I'll be right down.'

When the boy had gone he tripped on the slightly raised floor of the bathroom, swung about on one arm and cut his head against the washbowl. It was not so much, but he did a clumsy repair job with the adhesive and, feeling ridiculous at his image in the mirror, sat down and called Mary's number a last time – for no answer. Then he went out, not because he wanted to go to Mary's but because he had to go somewhere towards the flame, and he didn't know any other place to go.

At ten-thirty Mary, in her nightgown, was at the phone.

'Thanks for calling. But, Joris, if you want to know the truth I have a splitting headache. I'm turning in.'

'Mary, listen,' Joris insisted. 'It happens Marianne has a headache too and has turned in. This is the last night I'll have a chance to see you alone. Besides, you told me you'd *never* had a headache.'

Mary laughed.

'That's true – but I *am* tired.'

'I would promise to stay one half-hour – word of honour. I am only just around the corner.'

'No,' she said and a faint touch of annoyance gave firmness to the word. 'Tomorrow I'll have either lunch or dinner if you like, but now I'm going to bed.'

She stopped. She had heard a sound, a weight crunching against the outer door of her apartment. Then three odd, short bell rings.

'There's someone – call me in the morning,' she said. Hurriedly hanging up the phone she got into a dressing-gown.

By the door of her apartment she asked cautiously.

'Who's there?'

No answer – only a heavier sound – a human slipping to the floor.

'Who is it?'

She drew back and away from a frightening moan. There was a little shutter high in the door, like the peephole of a speakeasy, and feeling sure from the sound that whoever it was, wounded or drunk, was on the floor Mary reached up and peeped out. She could see only a hand covered with freshly ripening blood, and shut the trap hurriedly. After a shaken moment, she peered once more.

This time she recognised something – afterwards she could not have said what – a way the arm lay, a corner of the plaster cast – but it was enough to make her open the door quickly and duck down to Martin's side.

'Get doctor,' he whispered. 'Fell on the steps and broke.'

His eyes closed as she ran for the phone.

Doctor and ambulance came at the same time. What Martin had

done was simple enough, a little triumph of misfortune. On the first flight of stairs that he had gone up for eight weeks, he had stumbled, tried to save himself with the arm that was no good for anything, then spun down catching and ripping on the stair rail. After that a five-minute drag up to her door.

Mary wanted to exclaim, 'Why? Why?' but there was no one to hear. He came awake as the stretcher was put under him to carry him to the hospital, repair the new breakage with a new cast, start it over again. Seeing Mary he called quickly. 'Don't you come. I don't like anyone around when – when – Promise on your word of honour not to come?'

The orthopaedist said he would phone her in an hour. And five minutes later it was with the confused thought that he was already calling that Mary answered the phone.

'I can't talk, Joris,' she said. 'There was an awful accident – '

'Can I help?'

'It's gone now. It was my husband – '

Suddenly Mary knew she wanted to do anything but wait alone for word from the hospital.

'Come over then,' she said. 'You can take me up there if I'm needed.'

She sat in place by the phone until he came – jumped to her feet with an exclamation at his ring.

'Why? Why?' she sobbed at last. 'I offered to go and see him at his hotel.'

'Not drunk?'

'No, no – he almost never takes a drink. Will you wait right outside my door while I dress and get ready?'

The news came half an hour later that Martin's shoulder was set again, that he was sleeping under the ethylene gas and would sleep till morning. Joris Deglen was very gentle, swinging her feet up on the sofa, putting a pillow at her back and answering her incessant 'Why?' with a different response every time – Martin had been delirious; he was lonely; then at a certain moment telling the truth he had long guessed at: Martin was jealous.

'That was it,' Mary said bitterly. 'We were to be free – only I wasn't free. Only free to sneak about behind his back.'

She was free now though, free as air. And later, when he said he wouldn't go just yet, but would sit in the living-room reading until she quieted down, Mary went into her room with her head clear as morning. After she undressed for the second time that night she stayed for a few minutes before the mirror arranging her hair and keeping her mind free of all thoughts about Martin except that he was sleeping and at the moment felt no pain.

Then she opened her bedroom door and called down the corridor into the living-room: 'Do you want to come and tell me good-night?'

A Patriotic Short

Esquire (December 1940)

Pat Hobby, the writer and the man, had his great success in Hollywood during what Irving Cobb refers to as 'the mosaic-swimming-pool age – just before the era when they had to have a shinbone of St Sebastian for a clutch lever'.

Mr Cobb no doubt exaggerates, for when Pat had his pool in those fat days of silent pictures, it was entirely cement, unless you should count the cracks where the water stubbornly sought its own level through the mud.

'But it *was* a pool,' he assured himself one afternoon more than a decade later. Though he was now more than grateful for this small chore he had assigned him by producer Berners – one week at two-fifty – all the insolence of office could not take that memory away.

He had been called in to the studio to work upon a humble short. It was based on the career of General Fitzhugh Lee who fought for the Confederacy and later for the USA against Spain – so it would offend neither North nor South. And in the recent conference Pat had tried to co-operate.

'I was thinking – ' he suggested to Jack Berners ' – that it might be a good thing if we could give it a Jewish touch.'

'What do you mean?' demanded Jack Berners quickly.

'Well I thought – the way things are and all, it would be a sort of good thing to show that there were a number of Jews in it too.'

'In what?'

'In the Civil War.' Quickly he reviewed his meagre history. 'They were, weren't they?'

'Naturally,' said Berners, with some impatience, 'I suppose everybody was except the Quakers.'

'Well, my idea was that we could have this Fitzhugh Lee in love with a Jewish girl. He's going to be shot at curfew so she grabs a church bell – '

Jack Berners leaned forward earnestly.

'Say, Pat, you want this job, don't you? Well, I told you the story.

You got the first script. If you thought up this tripe to please me you're losing your grip.'

Was that a way to treat a man who had once owned a pool which had been talked about by –

That was how he happened to be thinking about his long lost swimming pool as he entered the shorts department. He was remembering a certain day over a decade ago in all its details: how he had arrived at the studio in his car driven by a Filipino in uniform; the deferential bow of the guard at the gate which had admitted car and all to the lot; his ascent to that long lost office which had a room for the secretary and was really a director's office . . .

His reverie was broken off by the voice of Ben Brown, head of the shorts department, who walked him into his own chambers.

'Jack Berners just phoned me,' he said. 'We don't want any new angles, Pat. We've got a good story. Fitzhugh Lee was a dashing cavalry commander. He was a nephew of Robert E. Lee and we want to show him at Appomattox, pretty bitter and all that. And then show how he became reconciled – we'll have to be careful because Virginia is swarming with Lees – and how he finally accepts a US commission from President McKinley – '

Pat's mind darted back again into the past. The President – that was the magic word that had gone around that morning many years ago. The President of the United States was going to make a visit to the lot. Everyone had been agog about it – it seemed to mark a new era in pictures because a President of the United States had never visited a studio before. The executives of the company were all dressed up – from a window of his long lost Beverly Hills house Pat had seen Mr Maranda, whose mansion was next door to him, bustle down his walk in a cutaway coat at nine o'clock, and had known that something was up. He thought maybe it was clergy but when he reached the lot he had found it was the President of the United States himself who was coming . . .

'Clean up the stuff about Spain,' Ben Brown was saying. 'The guy that wrote it was a Red and he's got all the Spanish officers with ants in their pants. Fix up that.'

In the office assigned him Pat looked at the script of *True to Two Flags*. The first scene showed General Fitzhugh Lee at the head of his cavalry receiving word that Petersburg had been evacuated. In the script Lee took the blow in pantomime, but Pat was getting two-fifty a week – so, casually and without effort, he wrote in one of his favourite lines: 'LEE (*to his officers*): "Well, what are you standing here gawking for? *Do* something!" Medium shot – Officers pepping up, slapping each other on back, etc. Dissolve to . . . '

To what? Pat's mind dissolved once more into the glamorous past. On that happy day in the twenties his phone had rung at about noon. It had been Mr Maranda.

'Pat, the President is lunching in the private dining-room. Doug Fairbanks can't come so there's a place empty and anyhow we think there ought to be one writer there.'

His memory of the luncheon was palpitant with glamour. The Great Man had asked some questions about pictures and had told a joke and Pat had laughed and laughed with the others – all of them solid men together – rich, happy and successful.

Afterwards the President was to go on some sets and see some scenes taken and still later he was going to Mr Maranda's house to meet some of the women stars at tea. Pat was not invited to that party but he went home early anyhow and from his veranda saw the cortège drive up, with Mr Maranda beside the President in the back seat. Ah he was proud of pictures then – of his position in them – of the President of the happy country where he was born . . .

Returning to reality Pat looked down at the script of *True to Two Flags* and wrote slowly and thoughtfully: 'Insert: A calendar – with the years plainly marked and the sheets blowing off in a cold wind, to show Fitzhugh Lee growing older and older.'

His labours had made him thirsty – not for water, but he knew better than to take anything else his first day on the job. He got up and went out into the hall and along the corridor to the water-cooler.

As he walked he slipped back into his reverie.

That had been a lovely California afternoon so Mr Maranda had taken his exalted guest and the coterie of stars into his garden, which adjoined Pat's garden. Pat had gone out his back door and followed a low privet hedge keeping out of sight – and then accidentally come face to face with the Presidential party.

The President had smiled and nodded. Mr Maranda smiled and nodded.

'You met Mr Hobby at lunch,' Mr Maranda said to the President. 'He's one of our writers.'

'Oh yes,' said the President, 'you write the pictures.'

'Yes I do,' said Pat.

The President glanced over into Pat's property.

'I suppose,' he said, 'that you get lots of inspiration sitting by the side of that fine pool.'

'Yes,' said Pat, 'yes, I do.'

. . . Pat filled his cup at the cooler. Down the hall there was a group approaching – Jack Berners, Ben Brown and several other executives and with them a girl to whom they were very attentive and deferential. He recognised her face – she was the girl of the year, the It girl, the Oomph girl, the Glamour Girl, the girl for whose services every studio was in violent competition.

Pat lingered over his drink. He had seen many phonies break in and break out again, but this girl was the real thing, someone to stir every pulse in the nation. He felt his own heart beat faster. Finally, as the procession drew near, he put down the cup, dabbed at his hair with his hand and took a step out into the corridor.

The girl looked at him – he looked at the girl. Then she took one arm of Jack Berners' and one of Ben Brown's and suddenly the party seemed to walk right through him – so that he had to take a step back against the wall.

An instant later Jack Berners turned around and said back to him, 'Hello, Pat.' And then some of the others threw half glances around but no one else spoke, so interested were they in the girl.

In his office, Pat looked at the scene where President McKinley offers a United States commission to Fitzhugh Lee. Suddenly he gritted his teeth and bore down on his pencil as he wrote: 'LEE: "Mr President, you can take your commission and go straight to hell." '

Then he bent down over his desk, his shoulders shaking as he thought of that happy day when he had had a swimming pool.

Three Hours Between Planes

Esquire (July 1941)

It was a wild chance but Donald was in the mood, healthy and bored, with a sense of tiresome duty done. He was now rewarding himself. Maybe.

When the plane landed he stepped out into a midwestern summer night and headed for the isolated pueblo airport, conventionalised as an old red 'railway depot'. He did not know whether she was alive, or living in this town, or what was her present name. With mounting excitement he looked through the phone book for her father, who might be dead too, somewhere in these twenty years.

No. Judge Harmon Holmes – Hillside 3194.

A woman's amused voice answered his enquiry for Miss Nancy Holmes.

'Nancy is Mrs Walter Gifford now. Who is this?'

But Donald hung up without answering. He had found out what he wanted to know and had only three hours. He did not remember any Walter Gifford and there was another suspended moment while he scanned the phone book. She might have married out of town.

No. Walter Gifford – Hillside 1191. Blood flowed back into his fingertips.

'Hello?'

'Hello. Is Mrs Gifford there – this is an old friend of hers.'

'This is Mrs Gifford.'

He remembered, or thought he remembered, the funny magic in the voice. 'This is Donald Plant. I haven't seen you since I was twelve years old.'

'Oh-h-h!' The note was utterly surprised, very polite, but he could distinguish in it neither joy nor certain recognition.

' – Donald!' added the voice. This time there was something more in it than struggling memory.

' . . . when did you come back to town?' Then cordially, 'Where *are* you?'

'I'm out at the airport – for just a few hours.'

'Well, come up and see me.'

'Sure you're not just going to bed?'

'Heavens, no!' she exclaimed. 'I was sitting here – having a highball by myself. Just tell your taxi man . . . '

On his way Donald analysed the conversation. His words 'at the airport' established that he had retained his position in the upper bourgeoisie. Nancy's aloneness might indicate that she had matured into an unattractive woman without friends. Her husband might be either away or in bed. And – because she was always ten years old in his dreams – the highball shocked him. But he adjusted himself with a smile – she was very close to thirty.

At the end of a curved drive he saw a dark-haired little beauty standing against the lighted door, a glass in her hand. Startled by her final materialisation, Donald got out of the cab, saying: 'Mrs Gifford?'

She turned on the porch light and stared at him, wide-eyed and tentative. A smile broke through the puzzled expression.

'Donald – it is you – we all change so. Oh, this is remarkable!'

As they walked inside, their voices jingled the words 'all these years', and Donald felt a sinking in his stomach. This derived in part from a vision of their last meeting – when she rode past him on a bicycle, cutting him dead – and in part from fear lest they have nothing to say. It was like a college reunion – but there the failure to find the past was disguised by the hurried boisterous occasion. Aghast, he realised that this might be a long and empty hour. He plunged in desperately.

'You always were a lovely person. But I'm a little shocked to find you as beautiful as you are.'

It worked. The immediate recognition of their changed state, the bold compliment, made them interesting strangers instead of fumbling childhood friends.

'Have a highball?' she asked. 'No? Please don't think I've become a secret drinker, but this was a blue night. I expected my husband but he wired he'd be two days longer. He's very nice, Donald, and very attractive. Rather your type and colouring.' She hesitated, ' – and I think he's interested in someone in New York – and I don't know.'

'After seeing you it sounds impossible,' he assured her. 'I was married for six years, and there was a time I tortured myself that way. Then one day I just put jealousy out of my life for ever. After my wife died I was very glad of that. It left a very rich memory – nothing marred or spoiled or hard to think over.'

She looked at him attentively, then sympathetically as he spoke.

'I'm very sorry,' she said. And after a proper moment, 'You've changed a lot. Turn your head. I remember father saying, "That boy has a brain." '

'You probably argued against it.'

'I was impressed. Up to then I thought everybody had a brain. That's why it sticks in my mind.'

'What else sticks in your mind?' he asked smiling.

Suddenly Nancy got up and walked quickly a little away.

'Ah, now,' she reproached him. 'That isn't fair! I suppose I was a naughty girl.'

'You were not,' he said stoutly. 'And I *will* have a drink now.'

As she poured it, her face still turned from him, he continued: 'Do you think you were the only little girl who was ever kissed?'

'Do you like the subject?' she demanded. Her momentary irritation melted and she said: 'What the hell! We *did* have fun. Like in the song.'

'On the sleigh-ride.'

'Yes – and somebody's picnic – Trudy James's. And at Frontenac that – those summers.'

It was the sleigh-ride he remembered most and kissing her cool cheeks in the straw in one corner while she laughed up at the cold white stars. The couple next to them had their backs turned and he kissed her little neck and her ears and never her lips.

'And the Macks' party where they played post office and I couldn't go because I had the mumps,' he said.

'I don't remember that.'

'Oh, you were there. And you were kissed and I was crazy with jealousy like I never have been since.'

'Funny I don't remember. Maybe I wanted to forget.'

'But why?' he asked in amusement. 'We were two perfectly innocent kids. Nancy, whenever I talked to my wife about the past, I told her you were the girl I loved almost as much as I loved her. But I think I really loved you just as much. When we moved out of town I carried you like a cannon ball in my insides.'

'Were you *that* much – stirred up?'

'My God, yes! I—' He suddenly realised that they were standing just two feet from each other, that he was talking as if he loved her in the present, that she was looking up at him with her lips half-parted and a clouded look in her eyes.

'Go on,' she said, 'I'm ashamed to say – I like it. I didn't know you were so upset *then*. I thought it was *me* who was upset.'

'You!' he exclaimed. 'Don't you remember throwing me over at the drugstore.' He laughed. 'You stuck out your tongue at me.'

'I don't remember at all. It seemed to me you did the throwing over.' Her hand fell lightly, almost consolingly on his arm. 'I've got a photograph book upstairs I haven't looked at for years. I'll dig it out.'

Donald sat for five minutes with two thoughts – first the hopeless impossibility of reconciling what different people remembered about the same event – and secondly that in a frightening way Nancy moved him as a woman as she had moved him as a child. Half an hour had developed an emotion that he had not known since the death of his wife – that he had never hoped to know again.

Side by side on a couch they opened the book between them. Nancy looked at him, smiling and very happy.

'Oh, this is *such* fun,' she said. 'Such fun that you're so nice, that you remember me so – beautifully. Let me tell you – I wish I'd known it then! After you'd gone I hated you.'

'What a pity,' he said gently.

'But not now,' she reassured him, and then impulsively, 'Kiss and make up – '

' . . . that isn't being a good wife,' she said after a minute. 'I really don't think I've kissed two men since I was married.'

He was excited – but most of all confused. Had he kissed Nancy? or a memory? or this lovely trembly stranger who looked away from him quickly and turned a page of the book?

'Wait!' he said. 'I don't think I could *see* a picture for a few seconds.'

'We won't do it again. I don't feel so very calm myself.'

Donald said one of those trivial things that cover so much ground. 'Wouldn't it be awful if we fell in love again?'

'Stop it!' She laughed, but very breathlessly. 'It's all over. It was a moment. A moment I'll have to forget.'

'Don't tell your husband.'

'Why not? Usually I tell him everything.'

'It'll hurt him. Don't ever tell a man such things.'

'All right, I won't.'

'Kiss me once more,' he said inconsistently, but Nancy had turned a page and was pointing eagerly at a picture.

'Here's you,' she cried. 'Right away!'

He looked. It was a little boy in shorts standing on a pier with a sailboat in the background.

'I remember – ' she laughed triumphantly, ' – the very day it was taken. Kitty took it and I stole it from her.'

For a moment Donald failed to recognise himself in the photo – then, bending closer – he failed utterly to recognise himself.

'That's not me,' he said.

'Oh yes. It was at Frontenac – the summer we – we used to go to the cave.'

'What cave? I was only three days in Frontenac.' Again he strained his eyes at the slightly yellowed picture. 'And that isn't me. That's Donald Bowers. We did look rather alike.'

Now she was staring at him – leaning back, seeming to lift away from him.

'But you're Donald Bowers!' she exclaimed; her voice rose a little. 'No, you're not. You're Donald *Plant*.'

'I told you on the phone.'

She was on her feet – her face faintly horrified.

'Plant! Bowers! I must be crazy. Or it was that drink? I was mixed up a little when I first saw you. Look here! What have I told you?'

He tried for a monkish calm as he turned a page of the book.

'Nothing at all,' he said. Pictures that did not include him formed and re-formed before his eyes – Frontenac – a cave – Donald Bowers – 'You threw *me* over!'

Nancy spoke from the other side of the room. 'You'll never tell this story,' she said. 'Stories have a way of getting around.'

'There isn't any story,' he hesitated. But he thought: So she was a bad little girl.

And now suddenly he was filled with wild raging jealousy of little Donald Bowers – he who had banished jealousy from his life for ever. In the five steps he took across the room he crushed out twenty years and the existence of Walter Gifford with his stride.

'Kiss me again, Nancy,' he said, sinking to one knee beside her chair, putting his hand upon her shoulder. But Nancy strained away.

'You said you had to catch a plane.'

'It's nothing. I can miss it. It's of no importance.'

'Please go,' she said in a cool voice. 'And please try to imagine how I feel.'

'But you act as if you don't remember me,' he cried, ' – as if you don't remember Donald *Plant*!'

'I do. I remember you too . . . But it was all so long ago.' Her voice grew hard again. 'The taxi number is Crestwood 8484.'

On his way to the airport Donald shook his head from side to side. He was completely himself now but he could not digest the experience. Only as the plane roared up into the dark sky and its passengers became a different entity from the corporate world below did he draw a parallel from the fact of its flight. For five blinding minutes he had lived like a madman in two worlds at once. He had been a boy of twelve and a man of thirty-two, indissolubly and helplessly commingled.

Donald had lost a good deal, too, in those hours between the planes – but since the second half of life is a long process of getting rid of things, that part of the experience probably didn't matter.